The Treasury of Allan Quatermain

The Treasury of Allan Quatermain Vol. I
by H. Rider Haggard

King Solomon's Mines
Allan Quatermain
Allan's Wife
Maiwa's Revenge
or The War of the Little Hand
Marie
Child of Storm

King Solomon's Mines

Dedication

This faithful but unpretending record of a remarkable adventure is hereby respectfully dedicated by the narrator,
Allan Quatermain,
to all the big and little boys who read it.

Table of Contents

Introduction

Now that this book is printed, and about to be given to the world, a sense of its shortcomings both in style and contents, weighs very heavily upon me. As regards the latter, I can only say that it does not pretend to be a full account of everything we did and saw. There are many things connected with our journey into Kukuanaland that I should have liked to dwell upon at length, which, as it is, have been scarcely alluded to. Amongst these are the curious legends which I collected about the chain armour that saved us from destruction in the great battle of Loo, and also about the "Silent Ones" or Colossi at the mouth of the stalactite cave. Again, if I had given way to my own impulses, I should have wished to go into the differences, some of which are to my mind very suggestive, between the Zulu and Kukuana dialects. Also a few pages might have been given up profitably to the consideration of the indigenous flora and fauna of Kukuanaland. Then there remains the most interesting subject—that, as it is, has only been touched on incidentally—of the magnificent system of military organisation in force in that country, which, in my opinion, is much superior to that inaugurated by Chaka in Zululand, inasmuch as it permits of even more rapid mobilisation, and does not necessitate the employment of the pernicious system of enforced celibacy. Lastly, I have scarcely spoken of the domestic and family customs of the Kukuanas, many of which are exceedingly quaint, or of their proficiency in the art of smelting and welding metals. This science they carry to considerable perfection, of which a good example is to be seen in their "tollas," or heavy throwing knives, the backs of these weapons being made of hammered iron, and the edges of beautiful steel welded with great skill on to the iron frames. The fact of the matter is, I thought, with Sir Henry Curtis and Captain Good, that the best plan would be to tell my story in a plain, straightforward manner, and to leave these matters to be dealt with subsequently in whatever way ultimately may appear to be desirable. In the meanwhile I shall, of course, be delighted to give all information in my power to anybody interested in such things.

And now it only remains for me to offer apologies for my blunt way of writing. I can but say in excuse of it that I am more accustomed to handle a rifle than a pen, and cannot make any pretence to the grand literary flights and flourishes which I see in novels—for sometimes I like to read a novel. I suppose they—the flights and flourishes—are desirable, and I regret not being able to supply them; but at the same time I cannot help thinking that simple things are always the most impressive, and that books are easier to understand when they are written in plain language, though perhaps I have no right to set up an opinion on such a matter. "A sharp spear," runs the Kukuana saying, "needs no polish"; and on the same principle I venture to hope that a true story, however strange it may be, does not require to be decked out in fine words.

Allan Quatermain

I Meet Sir Henry Curtis

It is a curious thing that at my age—fifty-five last birthday—I should find myself taking up a pen to try to write a history. I wonder what sort of a history it will be when I have finished it, if ever I come to the end of the trip! I have done a good many things in my life, which seems a long one to me, owing to my having begun work so young, perhaps. At an age when other boys are at school I was earning my living as a trader in the old Colony. I have been trading, hunting, fighting, or mining ever since. And yet it is only eight months ago that I made my pile. It is a big pile now that I have got it—I don't yet know how big—but I do not think I would go through the last fifteen or sixteen months again for it; no, not if I knew that I should come out safe at the end, pile and all. But then I am a timid man, and dislike violence; moreover, I am almost sick of adventure. I wonder why I am going to write this book: it is not in my line. I am not a literary man, though very devoted to the Old Testament and also to the "Ingoldsby Legends." Let me try to set down my reasons, just to see if I have any.

First reason: Because Sir Henry Curtis and Captain John Good asked me.

Second reason: Because I am laid up here at Durban with the pain in my left leg. Ever since that confounded lion got hold of me I have been liable to this trouble, and being rather bad just now, it makes me limp more than ever. There must be some poison in a lion's teeth, otherwise how is it that when your wounds are healed they break out again, generally, mark you, at the same time of year that you got your mauling? It is a hard thing when one has shot sixty-five lions or more, as I have in the course of my life, that the sixty-sixth should chew your leg like a quid of tobacco. It breaks the routine of the thing, and putting other considerations aside, I am an orderly man and don't like that. This is by the way.

Third reason: Because I want my boy Harry, who is over there at the hospital in London studying to become a doctor, to have something to amuse him and keep him out of mischief for a week or so. Hospital work must sometimes pall and grow rather dull, for even of cutting up dead bodies there may come satiety, and as this history will not be dull, whatever else it may be, it will put a little life into things for a day or two while Harry is reading of our adventures.

Fourth reason and last: Because I am going to tell the strangest story that I remember. It may seem a queer thing to say, especially considering that there is no woman in it—except Foulata. Stop, though! there is Gagaoola, if she was a woman, and not a fiend. But she was a hundred at least, and therefore not marriageable, so I don't count her. At any rate, I can safely say that there is not a *petticoat* in the whole history.

Well, I had better come to the yoke. It is a stiff place, and I feel as though I were bogged up to the axle. But, "*sutjes, sutjes*," as the Boers say—I am sure I don't know how they spell it—softly does it. A strong team will come through at last, that is, if they are not too poor. You can never do anything with poor oxen. Now to make a start.

I, Allan Quatermain, of Durban, Natal, Gentleman, make oath and say— That's how I headed my deposition before the magistrate about poor Khiva's and Ventvogel's sad deaths; but somehow it doesn't seem quite the right way to begin a book. And, besides, am I a gentleman? What is a gentleman? I don't quite know, and yet I have had to do with niggers —no, I will scratch out that word "niggers," for I do not like it. I've known natives who *are*, and so you will say, Harry, my boy, before you have done with this tale, and I have known mean whites with lots of money and fresh out from home, too, who *are not*.

At any rate, I was born a gentleman, though I have been nothing but a poor travelling trader and hunter all my life. Whether I have remained so I known not, you must judge of that. Heaven knows I've tried. I have killed many men in my time, yet I have never slain wantonly or stained my hand in innocent blood, but only in self-defence. The Almighty gave us our lives, and I suppose He meant us to defend them, at least I have always acted on that, and I hope it will not be brought up against me when my clock strikes. There, there, it is a cruel and a wicked world, and for a timid man I have been mixed up in a great deal of fighting. I cannot tell the rights of it, but at any rate I have never stolen, though once I cheated a Kafir out of a herd of cattle. But then he had done me a dirty turn, and it has troubled me ever since into the bargain.

Well, it is eighteen months or so ago since first I met Sir Henry Curtis and Captain Good. It was in this way. I had been up elephant hunting beyond Bamangwato, and had met with bad luck. Everything went wrong that trip, and to top up with I got the fever badly. So soon as I was well enough I trekked down to the Diamond Fields, sold such ivory as I had, together with my wagon and oxen, discharged my hunters, and took the post-cart to the Cape. After spending a week in Cape Town, finding that they overcharged me at the hotel, and having seen everything there was to see, including the botanical gardens, which seem to me likely to confer a great benefit on the country, and the new Houses of Parliament, which I expect will do nothing of the sort, I determined to go back to Natal by the *Dunkeld*, then lying at the docks waiting for the *Edinburgh Castle* due in from England. I took my berth and went aboard, and that afternoon the Natal passengers from the *Edinburgh Castle* transhipped, and we weighed and put to sea.

Among these passengers who came on board were two who excited my curiosity. One, a gentleman of about thirty, was perhaps the biggest- chested and longest-armed man I ever saw. He had yellow hair, a thick yellow beard, clear-cut features, and large grey eyes set deep in his head. I never saw a finer-looking man, and somehow he reminded me of an ancient Dane. Not that I know much of ancient Danes, though I knew a modern Dane who did me out of ten pounds; but I remember once seeing a picture of some of those gentry, who, I take it, were a kind of white Zulus. They were drinking out of big horns, and their long hair hung down their backs. As I looked at my friend standing there by the companion-ladder, I thought that if he only let his grow a little, put one of those chain shirts on to his great shoulders, and took hold of a battle-axe and a horn mug, he might have sat as a model for that picture. And by the way it is a curious thing, and just shows how the blood will out, I discovered afterwards that Sir Henry Curtis, for that was the big man's name, is of Danish blood. He also reminded me strongly of somebody else, but at the time I could not remember who it was.

The other man, who stood talking to Sir Henry, was stout and dark, and of quite a different cut. I suspected at once that he was a naval officer; I don't know why, but it is difficult to mistake a navy man. I have gone shooting trips with several of them in the course of my life, and they have always proved themselves the best and bravest and nicest fellows I ever met, though sadly given, some of them, to the use of profane language. I asked a page or two back, what is a gentleman? I'll answer the question now: A Royal Naval officer is, in a general sort of way, though of course there may be a black sheep among them here and there. I fancy it is just the wide seas and the breath of God's winds that wash their hearts and blow the bitterness out of their minds and make them what men ought to be.

Well, to return, I proved right again; I ascertained that the dark man *was* a naval officer, a lieutenant of thirty-one, who, after seventeen years' service, had been turned out of her Majesty's employ with the barren honour of a commander's rank, because it was impossible that he should be promoted. This is what people who serve the Queen have to expect: to be shot out into the cold world to find a living just when they are beginning really to understand their work, and to reach the prime of life. I suppose they don't mind it, but for my own part I had rather earn my bread as a hunter. One's halfpence are as scarce perhaps, but you do not get so many kicks.

The officer's name I found out—by referring to the passengers' lists —was Good—Captain John Good. He was broad, of medium height, dark, stout, and rather a curious man to look at. He was so very neat and so very clean-shaved, and he always wore an eye-glass in his right eye. It seemed to grow there, for it had no string, and he never took it out except to wipe it. At first I thought he used to sleep in it, but afterwards I found that this was a mistake. He put it in his trousers pocket when he went to bed, together with his false teeth, of which he had two beautiful sets that, my own being none of the best, have often caused me to break the tenth commandment. But I am anticipating.

Soon after we had got under way evening closed in, and brought with it very dirty weather. A keen breeze sprung up off land, and a kind of aggravated Scotch mist soon drove everybody from the deck. As for the *Dunkeld*, she is a flat-bottomed punt, and going up light as she was, she rolled very heavily. It almost seemed as though she would go right over, but she never did. It was quite impossible to walk about, so I stood near the engines where it was warm, and amused myself with watching the pendulum, which was fixed opposite to me, swinging slowly backwards and forwards as the vessel rolled, and marking the angle she touched at each lurch.

"That pendulum's wrong; it is not properly weighted," suddenly said a somewhat testy voice at my shoulder. Looking round I saw the naval officer whom I had noticed when the passengers came aboard.

"Indeed, now what makes you think so?" I asked.

"Think so. I don't think at all. Why there"—as she righted herself after a roll—"if the ship had really rolled to the degree that thing pointed to, then she would never have rolled again, that's all. But it is just like these merchant skippers, they are always so confoundedly careless."

Just then the dinner-bell rang, and I was not sorry, for it is a dreadful thing to have to listen to an officer of the Royal Navy when he gets on to that subject. I only know one worse thing, and that is to hear a merchant skipper express his candid opinion of officers of the Royal Navy.

Captain Good and I went down to dinner together, and there we found Sir Henry Curtis already seated. He and Captain Good were placed together, and I sat opposite to them. The captain and I soon fell into talk about shooting and what not; he asking me many questions, for he is very inquisitive about all sorts of things, and I answering them as well as I could. Presently he got on to elephants.

"Ah, sir," called out somebody who was sitting near me, "you've reached the right man for that; Hunter Quatermain should be able to tell you about elephants if anybody can."

Sir Henry, who had been sitting quite quiet listening to our talk, started visibly.

"Excuse me, sir," he said, leaning forward across the table, and speaking in a low deep voice, a very suitable voice, it seemed to me, to come out of those great lungs. "Excuse me, sir, but is your name Allan Quatermain?"

I said that it was.

The big man made no further remark, but I heard him mutter "fortunate" into his beard.

Presently dinner came to an end, and as we were leaving the saloon Sir Henry strolled up and asked me if I would come into his cabin to smoke a pipe. I accepted, and he led the way to the *Dunkeld* deck cabin, and a very good cabin it is. It had been two cabins, but when Sir Garnet Wolseley or one of those big swells went down the coast in the *Dunkeld*, they knocked away the partition and have never put it up again. There was a sofa in the cabin, and a little table in front of it. Sir Henry sent the steward for a bottle of whisky, and the three of us sat down and lit our pipes.

"Mr. Quatermain," said Sir Henry Curtis, when the man had brought the whisky and lit the lamp, "the year before last about this time, you were, I believe, at a place called Bamangwato, to the north of the Transvaal."

"I was," I answered, rather surprised that this gentleman should be so well acquainted with my movements, which were not, so far as I was aware, considered of general interest.

"You were trading there, were you not?" put in Captain Good, in his quick way.

"I was. I took up a wagon-load of goods, made a camp outside the settlement, and stopped till I had sold them."

Sir Henry was sitting opposite to me in a Madeira chair, his arms leaning on the table. He now looked up, fixing his large grey eyes full upon my face. There was a curious anxiety in them, I thought.

"Did you happen to meet a man called Neville there?"

"Oh, yes; he outspanned alongside of me for a fortnight to rest his oxen before going on to the interior. I had a letter from a lawyer a few months back, asking me if I knew what had become of him, which I answered to the best of my ability at the time."

"Yes," said Sir Henry, "your letter was forwarded to me. You said in it that the gentleman called Neville left Bamangwato at the beginning of May in a wagon with a driver, a voorlooper, and a Kafir hunter called Jim, announcing his intention of trekking if possible as far as Inyati, the extreme trading post in the Matabele country, where he would sell his wagon and proceed on foot. You also said that he did sell his wagon, for six months afterwards you saw the wagon in the possession of a Portuguese trader, who told you that he had bought it at Inyati from a white man whose name he had forgotten, and that he believed the white man with the native servant had started off for the interior on a shooting trip."

"Yes."

Then came a pause.

"Mr. Quatermain," said Sir Henry suddenly, "I suppose you know or can guess nothing more of the reasons of my—of Mr. Neville's journey to the northward, or as to what point that journey was directed?"

"I heard something," I answered, and stopped. The subject was one which I did not care to discuss.

Sir Henry and Captain Good looked at each other, and Captain Good nodded.

"Mr. Quatermain," went on the former, "I am going to tell you a story, and ask your advice, and perhaps your assistance. The agent who forwarded me your letter told me that I might rely on it implicitly, as you were," he said, "well known and universally respected in Natal, and especially noted for your discretion."

I bowed and drank some whisky and water to hide my confusion, for I am a modest man—and Sir Henry went on.

"Mr. Neville was my brother."

"Oh," I said, starting, for now I knew of whom Sir Henry had reminded me when first I saw him. His brother was a much smaller man and had a dark beard, but now that I thought of it, he possessed eyes of the same shade of grey and with the same keen look in them: the features too were not unlike.

"He was," went on Sir Henry, "my only and younger brother, and till five years ago I do not suppose that we were ever a month away from each other. But just about five years ago a misfortune befell us, as sometimes does happen in families. We quarrelled bitterly, and I behaved unjustly to my brother in my anger."

Here Captain Good nodded his head vigorously to himself. The ship gave a big roll just then, so that the looking-glass, which was fixed opposite us to starboard, was for a moment nearly over our heads, and as I was sitting with my hands in my pockets and staring upwards, I could see him nodding like anything.

"As I daresay you know," went on Sir Henry, "if a man dies intestate, and has no property but land, real property it is called in England, it all descends to his eldest son. It so happened that just at the time when we quarrelled our father died intestate. He had put off making his will until it was too late. The result was that my brother, who had not been brought up to any profession, was left without a penny. Of course it would have been my duty to provide for him, but at the time the quarrel between us was so bitter that I did not—to my shame I say it (and he sighed deeply)—offer to do anything. It was not that I grudged him justice, but I waited for him to make advances, and he made none. I am sorry to trouble you with all this, Mr. Quatermain, but I must to make things clear, eh, Good?"

"Quite so, quite so," said the captain. "Mr. Quatermain will, I am sure, keep this history to himself."

"Of course," said I, for I rather pride myself on my discretion, for which, as Sir Henry had heard, I have some repute.

"Well," went on Sir Henry, "my brother had a few hundred pounds to his account at the time. Without saying anything to me he drew out this paltry sum, and, having adopted the name of Neville, started off for South Africa in the wild hope of making a fortune. This I learned afterwards. Some three years passed, and I heard nothing of my brother, though I wrote several times. Doubtless the letters never reached him. But as time went on I grew more and more troubled about him. I found out, Mr. Quatermain, that blood is thicker than water."

"That's true," said I, thinking of my boy Harry.

"I found out, Mr. Quatermain, that I would have given half my fortune to know that my brother George, the only relation I possess, was safe and well, and that I should see him again."

"But you never did, Curtis," jerked out Captain Good, glancing at the big man's face.

"Well, Mr. Quatermain, as time went on I became more and more anxious to find out if my brother was alive or dead, and if alive to get him home again. I set enquiries on foot, and your letter was one of the results. So far as it went it was satisfactory, for it showed that till lately George was alive, but it did not go far enough. So, to cut a long story short, I made up my mind to come out and look for him myself, and Captain Good was so kind as to come with me."

"Yes," said the captain; "nothing else to do, you see. Turned out by my Lords of the Admiralty to starve on half pay. And now perhaps, sir, you will tell us what you know or have heard of the gentleman called Neville."

The Legend of Solomon's Mines

"What was it that you heard about my brother's journey at Bamangwato?" asked Sir Henry, as I paused to fill my pipe before replying to Captain Good.

"I heard this," I answered, "and I have never mentioned it to a soul till to-day. I heard that he was starting for Solomon's Mines."

"Solomon's Mines?" ejaculated both my hearers at once. "Where are they?"

"I don't know," I said; "I know where they are said to be. Once I saw the peaks of the mountains that border them, but there were a hundred and thirty miles of desert between me and them, and I am not aware that any white man ever got across it save one. But perhaps the best thing I can do is to tell you the legend of Solomon's Mines as I know it, you passing your word not to reveal anything I tell you without my permission. Do you agree to that? I have my reasons for asking."

Sir Henry nodded, and Captain Good replied, "Certainly, certainly."

"Well," I began, "as you may guess, generally speaking, elephant hunters are a rough set of men, who do not trouble themselves with much beyond the facts of life and the ways of Kafirs. But here and there you meet a man who takes the trouble to collect traditions from the natives, and tries to make out a little piece of the history of this dark land. It was such a man as this who first told me the legend of Solomon's Mines, now a matter of nearly thirty years ago. That was when I was on my first elephant hunt in the Matalebe country. His name was Evans, and he was killed the following year, poor fellow, by a wounded buffalo, and lies buried near the Zambesi Falls. I was telling Evans one night, I remember, of some wonderful workings I had found whilst hunting koodoo and eland in what is now the Lydenburg district of the Transvaal. I see they have come across these workings again lately in prospecting for gold, but I knew of them years ago. There is a great wide wagon road cut out of the solid rock, and leading to the mouth of the working or gallery. Inside the mouth of this gallery are stacks of gold quartz piled up ready for roasting, which shows that the workers, whoever they were, must have left in a hurry. Also, about twenty paces in, the gallery is built across, and a beautiful bit of masonry it is.

"'Ay,' said Evans, 'but I will spin you a queerer yarn than that'; and he went on to tell me how he had found in the far interior a ruined city, which he believed to be the Ophir of the Bible, and, by the way, other more learned men have said the same long since poor Evans's time. I was, I remember, listening open-eared to all these wonders, for I was young at the time, and this story of an ancient civilisation and of the treasures which those old Jewish or Phoenician adventurers used to extract from a country long since lapsed into the darkest barbarism took a great hold upon my imagination, when suddenly he said to me, 'Lad, did you ever hear of the Suliman Mountains up to the north-west of the Mushakulumbwe country?' I told him I never had. 'Ah, well,' he said, 'that is where Solomon really had his mines, his diamond mines, I mean.'

"How do you know that?' I asked.

"Know it! why, what is "Suliman" but a corruption of Solomon? Besides, an old Isanusi or witch doctoress up in the Manica country told me all about it. She said that the people who lived across those mountains were a "branch" of the Zulus, speaking a dialect of Zulu, but finer and bigger men even; that there lived among them great wizards, who had learnt their art from white men when "all the world was dark," and who had the secret of a wonderful mine of "bright stones.""

"Well, I laughed at this story at the time, though it interested me, for the Diamond Fields were not discovered then, but poor Evans went off and was killed, and for twenty years I never thought any more of the matter. However, just twenty years afterwards—and that is a long time, gentlemen; an elephant hunter does not often live for twenty years at his business—I heard something more definite about Suliman's Mountains and the country which lies beyond them. I was up beyond the Manica country, at a place called Sitanda's Kraal, and a miserable place it was, for a man could get nothing to eat, and there was but little game about. I had an attack of fever, and was in a bad way generally, when one day a Portugee arrived with a single companion—a half-breed. Now I know your low-class Delagoa Portugee well. There is no greater devil unhung in a general way, battening as he does upon human agony and flesh in the shape of slaves. But this was quite a different type of man to the mean fellows whom I had been accustomed to meet; indeed, in appearance he reminded me more of the polite doms I have read about, for he was tall and thin, with large dark eyes and curling grey mustachios. We talked together for a while, for he could speak broken English, and I understood a little Portugee, and he told me that his name was Jose Silvestre, and that he had a place near Delagoa Bay. When he went on next day with his half-breed companion, he said 'Good-bye,' taking off his hat quite in the old style.

"'Good-bye, senor,' he said; 'if ever we meet again I shall be the richest man in the world, and I will remember you.' I laughed a little —I was too weak to laugh much—and watched him strike out for the great desert to the west, wondering if he was mad, or what he thought he was going to find there.

"A week passed, and I got the better of my fever. One evening I was sitting on the ground in front of the little tent I had with me, chewing the last leg of a miserable fowl I had bought from a native for a bit of cloth worth twenty fowls, and staring at the hot red sun sinking down over the desert, when suddenly I saw a figure, apparently that of a European, for it wore a coat, on the slope of the rising ground opposite to me, about three hundred yards away. The figure crept along on its hands and knees, then it got up and staggered forward a few yards on its legs, only to fall and crawl again. Seeing that it must be somebody in distress, I sent one of my hunters to help him, and presently he arrived, and who do you suppose it turned out to be?'

"Jose Silvestre, of course," said Captain Good.

"Yes, Jose Silvestre, or rather his skeleton and a little skin. His face was a bright yellow with bilious fever, and his large dark eyes stood nearly out of his head, for all the flesh had gone. There was nothing but yellow parchment-like skin, white hair, and the gaunt bones sticking up beneath.

"Water! for the sake of Christ, water!' he moaned and I saw that his lips were cracked, and his tongue, which protruded between them, was swollen and blackish.

"I gave him water with a little milk in it, and he drank it in great gulps, two quarts or so, without stopping. I would not let him have any more. Then the fever took him again, and he fell down and began to rave about Suliman's Mountains, and the diamonds, and the desert. I carried him into the tent and did what I could for him, which was little enough; but I saw how it must end. About eleven o'clock he grew quieter, and I lay down for a little rest and went to sleep. At dawn I woke again, and in the half light saw Silvestre sitting up, a strange, gaunt form, and gazing out towards the desert. Presently the first ray of the sun shot right across the wide plain before us till it reached the faraway crest of one of the tallest of the Suliman Mountains more than a hundred miles away.

"'There it is!' cried the dying man in Portuguese, and pointing with his long, thin arm, 'but I shall never reach it, never. No one will ever reach it!'

"Suddenly, he paused, and seemed to take a resolution. 'Friend,' he said, turning towards me, 'are you there? My eyes grow dark.'

"'Yes,' I said; 'yes, lie down now, and rest.'

"'Ay,' he answered, 'I shall rest soon, I have time to rest—all eternity. Listen, I am dying! You have been good to me. I will give you the writing. Perhaps you will get there if you can live to pass the desert, which has killed my poor servant and me.'

"Then he groped in his shirt and brought out what I thought was a Boer tobacco pouch made of the skin of the Swart-vet-pens or sable antelope. It was fastened with a little strip of hide, what we call a rimpi, and this he tried to loose, but could not. He handed it to me. 'Untie it,' he said. I did so, and extracted a bit of torn yellow linen on which something was written in rusty letters. Inside this rag was a paper.

"Then he went on feebly, for he was growing weak: 'The paper has all that is on the linen. It took me years to read. Listen: my ancestor, a political refugee from Lisbon, and one of the first Portuguese who landed on these shores, wrote that when he was dying on those mountains which no white foot ever pressed before or since. His name was Jose da Silvestra, and he lived three hundred years ago. His slave, who waited for him on this side of the mountains, found him dead, and brought the writing home to Delagoa. It has been in the family ever since, but none have cared to read it, till at last I did. And I have lost my life over it, but another may succeed, and become the richest man in the world—the richest man in the world. Only give it to no one, senor; go yourself!'

"Then he began to wander again, and in an hour it was all over.

"God rest him! he died very quietly, and I buried him deep, with big boulders on his breast; so I do not think that the jackals can have dug him up. And then I came away."

"Ay, but the document?" said Sir Henry, in a tone of deep interest.

"Yes, the document; what was in it?" added the captain.

"Well, gentlemen, if you like I will tell you. I have never showed it to anybody yet except to a drunken old Portuguese trader who translated it for me, and had forgotten all about it by the next morning. The original rag is at my home in Durban, together with poor Dom Jose's translation, but I have the English rendering in my pocket- book, and a facsimile of the map, if it can be called a map. Here it is."

"I, Jose da Silvestra, who am now dying of hunger in the little cave here no snow is on the north side of the nipple of the southernmost of the two mountains I have named Sheba's Breasts, write this in the year 1590 with a cleft bone upon a remnant of my raiment, my blood being the ink. If my slave should find it when he comes, and should bring it to Delagoa, let my friend (name illegible) bring the matter to the knowledge of the king, that he may send an army which, if they live through the desert and the mountains, and can overcome the brave Kukuanes and their devilish arts, to which end many priests should be brought, will make him the richest king since Solomon. With my own eyes I have seen the countless diamonds stored in Solomon's treasure chamber behind the white Death; but through the treachery of Gagool the witch-finder I might bring nought away, scarcely my life. Let him who comes follow the map, and climb the snow of Sheba's left breast till he reaches the nipple, on the north side of which is the great road Solomon made, from whence three days' journey to the King's Palace. Let him kill Gagool. Pray for my soul. Farewell.

Jose da Silvestra." When I had finished reading the above, and shown the copy of the map, drawn by the dying hand of the old Dom with his blood for ink, there followed a silence of astonishment.

"Well," said Captain Good, "I have been round the world twice, and put in at most ports, but may I be hung for a mutineer if ever I heard a yarn like this out of a story book, or in it either, for the matter of that."

"It's a queer tale, Mr. Quatermain," said Sir Henry. "I suppose you are not hoaxing us? It is, I know, sometimes thought allowable to take in a greenhorn."

"If you think that, Sir Henry," I said, much put out, and pocketing my paper—for I do not like to be thought one of those silly fellows who consider it witty to tell lies, and who are for ever boasting to newcomers of extraordinary hunting adventures which never happened— "if you think that, why, there is an end to the matter," and I rose to go.

Sir Henry laid his large hand upon my shoulder. "Sit down, Mr. Quatermain," he said, "I beg your pardon; I see very well you do not wish to deceive us, but the story sounded so strange that I could hardly believe it."

"You shall see the original map and writing when we reach Durban," I answered, somewhat mollified, for really when I came to consider the question it was scarcely wonderful that he should doubt my good faith.

"But," I went on, "I have not told you about your brother. I knew the man Jim who was with him. He was a Bechuana by birth, a good hunter, and for a native a very clever man. That morning on which Mr. Neville was starting I saw Jim standing by my wagon and cutting up tobacco on the disselboom.

"'Jim,' said I, 'where are you off to this trip? It is elephants?'

"'No, Baas,' he answered, 'we are after something worth much more than ivory.'

"'And what might that be?' I said, for I was curious. 'Is it gold?'

"'No, Baas, something worth more than gold,' and he grinned.

"I asked no more questions, for I did not like to lower my dignity by seeming inquisitive, but I was puzzled. Presently Jim finished cutting his tobacco.

"'Baas,' said he.

"I took no notice.

"'Baas,' said he again.

"'Eh, boy, what is it?' I asked.

"'Baas, we are going after diamonds.'

"'Diamonds! why, then, you are steering in the wrong direction; you should head for the Fields.'

"'Baas, have you ever heard of Suliman's Berg?'—that is, Solomon's Mountains, Sir Henry.

"'Ay!'

"'Have you ever heard of the diamonds there?'

"'I have heard a foolish story, Jim.'

"'It is no story, Baas. Once I knew a woman who came from there, and reached Natal with her child, she told me:—she is dead now.'

"'Your master will feed the assvogels'—that is, vultures—'Jim, if he tries to reach Suliman's country, and so will you if they can get any pickings off your worthless old carcass,' said I.

"He grinned. 'Mayhap, Baas. Man must die; I'd rather like to try a new country myself; the elephants are getting worked out about here.'

"'Ah! my boy,' I said, 'you wait till the "pale old man" gets a grip of your yellow throat, and then we shall hear what sort of a tune you sing.'

"Half an hour after that I saw Neville's wagon move off. Presently Jim came back running. 'Good-bye, Baas,' he said. 'I didn't like to start without bidding you good-bye, for I daresay you are right, and that we shall never trek south again.'

"'Is your master really going to Suliman's Berg, Jim, or are you lying?'

"'No,' he answered, 'he is going. He told me he was bound to make his fortune somehow, or try to; so he might as well have a fling for the diamonds.'

"'Oh!' I said; 'wait a bit, Jim; will you take a note to your master, Jim, and promise not to give it to him till you reach Inyati?' which was some hundred miles off.

"'Yes, Baas.'

"So I took a scrap of paper, and wrote on it, 'Let him who comes . . . climb the snow of Sheba's left breast, till he reaches the nipple, on the north side of which is Solomon's great road.'

"'Now, Jim,' I said, 'when you give this to your master, tell him he had better follow the advice on it implicitly. You are not to give it to him now, because I don't want him back asking me questions which I won't answer. Now be off, you idle fellow, the wagon is nearly out of sight.'

"Jim took the note and went, and that is all I know about your brother, Sir Henry; but I am much afraid—"

"Mr. Quatermain," said Sir Henry, "I am going to look for my brother; I am going to trace him to Suliman's Mountains, and over them if necessary, till I find him, or until I know that he is dead. Will you come with me?"

I am, as I think I have said, a cautious man, indeed a timid one, and this suggestion frightened me. It seemed to me that to undertake such a journey would be to go to certain death, and putting other considerations aside, as I had a son to support, I could not afford to die just then.

"No, thank you, Sir Henry, I think I had rather not," I answered. "I am too old for wild-goose chases of that sort, and we should only end up like my poor friend Silvestre. I have a son dependent on me, so I cannot afford to risk my life foolishly."

Both Sir Henry and Captain Good looked very disappointed.

"Mr. Quatermain," said the former, "I am well off, and I am bent upon this business. You may put the remuneration for your services at whatever figure you like in reason, and it shall be paid over to you before we start. Moreover, I will arrange in the event of anything untoward happening to us or to you, that your son shall be suitably provided for. You will see from this offer how necessary I think your presence. Also if by chance we should reach this place, and find diamonds, they shall belong to you and Good equally. I do not want them. But of course that promise is worth nothing at all, though the same thing would apply to any ivory we might get. You may pretty well make your own terms with me, Mr. Quatermain; and of course I shall pay all expenses."

"Sir Henry," said I, "this is the most liberal proposal I ever had, and one not to be sneezed at by a poor hunter and trader. But the job is the biggest I have come across, and I must take time to think it over. I will give you my answer before we get to Durban."

"Very good," answered Sir Henry.

Then I said good-night and turned in, and dreamt about poor long-dead Silvestre and the diamonds.

Umbopa Enters Our Service

It takes from four to five days, according to the speed of the vessel and the state of the weather, to run up from the Cape to Durban. Sometimes, if the landing is bad at East London, where they have not yet made that wonderful harbour they talk so much of, and sink such a mint of money in, a ship is delayed for twenty-four hours before the cargo boats can get out to take off the goods. But on this occasion we had not to wait at all, for there were no breakers on the Bar to speak of, and the tugs came out at once with the long strings of ugly flat- bottomed boats behind them, into which the packages were bundled with a crash. It did not matter what they might be, over they went slap- bang; whether they contained china or woollen goods they met with the same treatment. I saw one case holding four dozen of champagne smashed all to bits, and there was the champagne fizzing and boiling about in the bottom of the dirty cargo boat. It was a wicked waste, and evidently so the Kafirs in the boat thought, for they found a couple of unbroken bottles, and knocking off the necks drank the contents. But they had not allowed for the expansion caused by the fizz in the wine, and, feeling themselves swelling, rolled about in the bottom of the boat, calling out that the good liquor was "tagati"—that is, bewitched. I spoke to them from the vessel, and told them it was the white man's strongest medicine, and that they were as good as dead men. Those Kafirs went to the shore in a very great fright, and I do not think that they will touch champagne again.

Well, all the time that we were steaming up to Natal I was thinking over Sir Henry Curtis's offer. We did not speak any more on the subject for a day or two, though I told them many hunting yarns, all true ones. There is no need to tell lies about hunting, for so many curious things happen within the knowledge of a man whose business it is to hunt; but this is by the way.

At last, one beautiful evening in January, which is our hottest month, we steamed past the coast of Natal, expecting to make Durban Point by sunset. It is a lovely coast all along from East London, with its red sandhills and wide sweeps of vivid green, dotted here and there with Kafir kraals, and bordered by a ribbon of white surf, which spouts up in pillars of foam where it hits the rocks. But just before you come to Durban there is a peculiar richness about the landscape. There are the sheer kloofs cut in the hills by the rushing rains of centuries, down which the rivers sparkle; there is the deepest green of the bush, growing as God planted it, and the other greens of the mealie gardens and the sugar patches, while now and again a white house, smiling out at the placid sea, puts a finish and gives an air of homeliness to the scene. For to my mind, however beautiful a view may be, it requires the presence of man to make it complete, but perhaps that is because I have lived so much in the wilderness, and therefore know the value of civilisation, though to be sure it drives away the game. The Garden of Eden, no doubt, looked fair before man was, but I always think that it must have been fairer when Eve adorned it.

To return, we had miscalculated a little, and the sun was well down before we dropped anchor off the Point, and heard the gun which told the good folks of Durban that the English Mail was in. It was too late to think of getting over the Bar that night, so we went comfortably to dinner, after seeing the Mails carried off in the life-boat.

When we came up again the moon was out, and shining so brightly over sea and shore that she almost paled the quick, large flashes from the lighthouse. From the shore floated sweet spicy odours that always remind me of hymns and missionaries, and in the windows of the houses on the Berea sparkled a hundred lights. From a large brig lying near also came the music of the sailors as they worked at getting the anchor up in order to be ready for the wind. Altogether it was a perfect night, such a night as you sometimes get in Southern Africa, and it threw a garment of peace over everybody as the moon threw a garment of silver over everything. Even the great bulldog, belonging to a sporting passenger, seemed to yield to its gentle influences, and forgetting his yearning to come to close quarters with the baboon in a cage on the foc'sle, snored happily at the door of the cabin, dreaming no doubt that he had finished him, and happy in his dream.

We three—that is, Sir Henry Curtis, Captain Good, and myself—went and sat by the wheel, and were quiet for a while.

"Well, Mr. Quatermain," said Sir Henry presently, "have you been thinking about my proposals?"

"Ay," echoed Captain Good, "what do you think of them, Mr. Quatermain? I hope that you are going to give us the pleasure of your company so far as Solomon's Mines, or wherever the gentleman you knew as Neville may have got to."

I rose and knocked out my pipe before I answered. I had not made up my mind, and wanted an additional moment to decide. Before the burning tobacco had fallen into the sea I had decided; just that little extra second did the trick. It is often the way when you have been bothering a long time over a thing.

"Yes, gentlemen," I said, sitting down again, "I will go, and by your leave I will tell you why, and on what conditions. First for the terms which I ask.

"1. You are to pay all expenses, and any ivory or other valuables we may get is to be divided between Captain Good and myself.

"2. That you give me £500 for my services on the trip before we start, I undertaking to serve you faithfully till you choose to abandon the enterprise, or till we succeed, or disaster overtakes us.

"3. That before we trek you execute a deed agreeing, in the event of my death or disablement, to pay my boy Harry, who is studying medicine over there in London, at Guy's Hospital, a sum of £200 a year for five years, by which time he ought to be able to earn a living for himself if he is worth his salt. That is all, I think, and I daresay you will say quite enough too."

"No," answered Sir Henry, "I accept them gladly. I am bent upon this project, and would pay more than that for your help, considering the peculiar and exclusive knowledge which you possess."

"Pity I did not ask it, then, but I won't go back on my word. And now that I have got my terms I will tell you my reasons for making up my mind to go. First of all, gentlemen, I have been observing you both for the last few days, and if you will not think me impertinent I may say that I like you, and believe that we shall come up well to the yoke together. That is something, let me tell you, when one has a long journey like this before one.

"And now as to the journey itself, I tell you flatly, Sir Henry and Captain Good, that I do not think it probable we can come out of it alive, that is, if we attempt to cross the Suliman Mountains. What was the fate of the old Dom da Silvestra three hundred years ago? What was the fate of his descendant twenty years ago? What has been your brother's fate? I tell you frankly, gentlemen, that as their fates were so I believe ours will be."

I paused to watch the effect of my words. Captain Good looked a little uncomfortable, but Sir Henry's face did not change. "We must take our chance," he said.

"You may perhaps wonder," I went on, "why, if I think this, I, who am, as I told you, a timid man, should undertake such a journey. It is for two reasons. First I am a fatalist, and believe that my time is appointed to come quite without reference to my own movements and will, and that if I am to go to Suliman's Mountains to be killed, I shall go there and shall be killed. God Almighty, no doubt, knows His mind about me, so I need not trouble on that point. Secondly, I am a poor man. For nearly forty years I have hunted and traded, but I have never made more than a living. Well, gentlemen, I don't know if you are aware that the average life of an elephant hunter from the time he takes to the trade is between four and five years. So you see I have lived through about seven generations of my class, and I should think that my time cannot be far off, anyway. Now, if anything were to happen to me in the ordinary course of business, by the time my debts are paid there would be nothing left to support my son Harry whilst he was getting in the way of earning a living, whereas now he will be set up for five years. There is the whole affair in a nutshell."

"Mr. Quatermain," said Sir Henry, who had been giving me his most serious attention, "your motives for undertaking an enterprise which you believe can only end in disaster reflect a great deal of credit on you. Whether or not you are right, of course time and the event alone can show. But whether you are right or wrong, I may as well tell you at once that I am going through with it to the end, sweet or bitter. If we are to be knocked on the head, all I have to say is, that I hope we get a little shooting first, eh, Good?"

"Yes, yes," put in the captain. "We have all three of us been accustomed to face danger, and to hold our lives in our hands in various ways, so it is no good turning back now. And now I vote we go down to the saloon and take an observation just for luck, you know." And we did—through the bottom of a tumbler.

Next day we went ashore, and I put up Sir Henry and Captain Good at the little shanty I have built on the Berea, and which I call my home. There are only three rooms and a kitchen in it, and it is constructed of green brick with a galvanised iron roof, but there is a good garden with the best loquot trees in it that I know, and some nice young mangoes, of which I hope great things. The curator of the botanical gardens gave them to me. It is looked after by an old hunter of mine named Jack, whose thigh was so badly broken by a buffalo cow in Sikukunis country that he will never hunt again. But he can potter about and garden, being a Griqua by birth. You will never persuade a Zulu to take much interest in gardening. It is a peaceful art, and peaceful arts are not in his line.

Sir Henry and Good slept in a tent pitched in my little grove of orange trees at the end of the garden, for there was no room for them in the house, and what with the smell of the bloom, and the sight of the green and golden fruit—in Durban you will see all three on the tree together—I daresay it is a pleasant place enough, for we have few mosquitos here on the Berea, unless there happens to come an unusually heavy rain.

Well, to get on—for if I do not, Harry, you will be tired of my story before ever we fetch up at Suliman's Mountains—having once made up my mind to go I set about making the necessary preparations. First I secured the deed from Sir Henry, providing for you, my boy, in case of accidents. There was some difficulty about its legal execution, as Sir Henry was a stranger here, and the property to be charged is over the water; but it was ultimately got over with the help of a lawyer, who charged £20 for the job—a price that I thought outrageous. Then I pocketed my cheque for £500.

Having paid this tribute to my bump of caution, I purchased a wagon and a span of oxen on Sir Henry's behalf, and beauties they were. It was a twenty-two-foot wagon with iron axles, very strong, very light, and built throughout of stink wood; not quite a new one, having been to the Diamond Fields and back, but, in my opinion, all the better for that, for I could see that the wood was well seasoned. If anything is going to give in a wagon, or if there is green wood in it, it will show out on the first trip. This particular vehicle was what we call a "half-tented" wagon, that is to say, only covered in over the after twelve feet, leaving all the front part free for the necessaries we had to carry with us. In this after part were a hide "cartle," or bed, on which two people could sleep, also racks for rifles, and many other little conveniences. I gave £125 for it, and think that it was cheap at the price.

Then I bought a beautiful team of twenty Zulu oxen, which I had kept my eye on for a year or two. Sixteen oxen is the usual number for a team, but I took four extra to allow for casualties. These Zulu cattle are small and light, not more than half the size of the Africander oxen, which are generally used for transport purposes; but they will live where the Africanders would starve, and with a moderate load can make five miles a day better going, being quicker and not so liable to become footsore. What is more, this lot were thoroughly "salted," that is, they had worked all over South Africa, and so had become proof, comparatively speaking, against red water, which so frequently destroys whole teams of oxen when they get on to strange "veldt" or grass country. As for "lung sick," which is a dreadful form of pneumonia, very prevalent in this country, they had all been inoculated against it. This is done by cutting a slit in the tail of an ox, and binding in a piece of the diseased lung of an animal which has died of the sickness. The result is that the ox sickens, takes the disease in a mild form, which causes its tail to drop off, as a rule about a foot from the root, and becomes proof against future attacks. It seems cruel to rob the animal of his tail, especially in a country where there are so many flies, but it is better to sacrifice the tail and keep the ox than to lose both tail and ox, for a tail without an ox is not much good, except to dust with. Still it does look odd to trek along behind twenty stumps, where there ought to be tails. It seems as though Nature made a trifling mistake, and stuck the stern ornaments of a lot of prize bull-dogs on to the rumps of the oxen.

Next came the question of provisioning and medicines, one which required the most careful consideration, for what we had to do was to avoid lumbering the wagon, and yet to take everything absolutely necessary. Fortunately, it turned out that Good is a bit of a doctor, having at some point in his previous career managed to pass through a course of medical and surgical instruction, which he has more or less kept up. He is not, of course, qualified, but he knows more about it than many a man who can write M.D. after his name, as we found out afterwards, and he had a splendid travelling medicine chest and a set of instruments. Whilst we were at Durban he cut off a Kafir's big toe in a way which it was a pleasure to see. But he was quite nonplussed when the Kafir, who had sat stolidly watching the operation, asked him to put on another, saying that a "white one" would do at a pinch.

There remained, when these questions were satisfactorily settled, two further important points for consideration, namely, that of arms and that of servants. As to the arms I cannot do better than put down a list of those which we finally decided on from among the ample store that Sir Henry had brought with him from England, and those which I owned. I copy it from my pocket-book, where I made the entry at the time.

"Three heavy breech-loading double-eight elephant guns, weighing about fifteen pounds each, to carry a charge of eleven drachms of black powder." Two of these were by a well-known London firm, most excellent makers, but I do not know by whom mine, which is not so highly finished, was made. I have used it on several trips, and shot a good many elephants with it, and it has always proved a most superior weapon, thoroughly to be relied on.

"Three double-500 Expresses, constructed to stand a charge of six drachms," sweet weapons, and admirable for medium-sized game, such as eland or sable antelope, or for men, especially in an open country and with the semi-hollow bullet.

"One double No. 12 central-fire Keeper's shot-gun, full choke both barrels." This gun proved of the greatest service to us afterwards in shooting game for the pot.

"Three Winchester repeating rifles (not carbines), spare guns.

"Three single-action Colt's revolvers, with the heavier, or American pattern of cartridge."

This was our total armament, and doubtless the reader will observe that the weapons of each class were of the same make and calibre, so that the cartridges were interchangeable, a very important point. I make no apology for detailing it at length, as every experienced hunter will know how vital a proper supply of guns and ammunition is to the success of an expedition.

Now as to the men who were to go with us. After much consultation we decided that their number should be limited to five, namely, a driver, a leader, and three servants.

The driver and leader I found without much difficulty, two Zulus, named respectively Goza and Tom; but to get the servants proved a more difficult matter. It was necessary that they should be thoroughly trustworthy and brave men, as in a business of this sort our lives might depend upon their conduct. At last I secured two, one a Hottentot named Ventvogel, or "windbird," and one a little Zulu named Khiva, who had the merit of speaking English perfectly. Ventvogel I had known before; he was one of the most perfect "spoorers," that is, game trackers, I ever had to do with, and tough as whipcord. He never seemed to tire. But he had one failing, so common with his race, drink. Put him within reach of a bottle of gin and you could not trust him. However, as we were going beyond the region of grog-shops this little weakness of his did not so much matter.

Having secured these two men I looked in vain for a third to suit my purpose, so we determined to start without one, trusting to luck to find a suitable man on our way up country. But, as it happened, on the evening before the day we had fixed for our departure the Zulu Khiva informed me that a Kafir was waiting to see me. Accordingly, when we had done dinner, for we were at table at the time, I told Khiva to bring him in. Presently a tall, handsome-looking man, somewhere about thirty years of age, and very light-coloured for a Zulu, entered, and lifting his knob-stick by way of salute, squatted himself down in the corner on his haunches, and sat silent. I did not take any notice of him for a while, for it is a great mistake to do so. If you rush into conversation at once, a Zulu is apt to think you a person of little dignity or consequence. I observed, however, that he was a "Keshla" or ringed man; that is, he wore on his head the black ring, made of a species of gum polished with fat and worked up in the hair, which is usually assumed by Zulus on attaining a certain age or dignity. Also it struck me that his face was familiar to me.

"Well," I said at last, "What is your name?"

"Umbopa," answered the man in a slow, deep voice.

"I have seen your face before."

"Yes; the Inkoosi, the chief, my father, saw my face at the place of the Little Hand"—that is, Isandhlwana—"on the day before the battle."

Then I remembered. I was one of Lord Chelmsford's guides in that unlucky Zulu War, and had the good fortune to leave the camp in charge of some wagons on the day before the battle. While I was waiting for the cattle to be inspanned I fell into conversation with this man, who held some small command among the native auxiliaries, and he had expressed to me his doubts as to the safety of the camp. At the time I told him to hold his tongue, and leave such matters to wiser heads; but afterwards I thought of his words.

"I remember," I said; "what is it you want?"

"It is this, 'Macumazahn.'" That is my Kafir name, and means the man who gets up in the middle of the night, or, in vulgar English, he who keeps his eyes open. "I hear that you go on a great expedition far into the North with the white chiefs from over the water. Is it a true word?"

"It is."

"I hear that you go even to the Lukanga River, a moon's journey beyond the Manica country. Is this so also, 'Macumazahn?'"

"Why do you ask whither we go? What is it to you?" I answered suspiciously, for the objects of our journey had been kept a dead secret.

"It is this, O white men, that if indeed you travel so far I would travel with you."

There was a certain assumption of dignity in the man's mode of speech, and especially in his use of the words "O white men," instead of "O Inkosis," or chiefs, which struck me.

"You forget yourself a little," I said. "Your words run out unawares. That is not the way to speak. What is your name, and where is your kraal? Tell us, that we may know with whom we have to deal."

"My name is Umbopa. I am of the Zulu people, yet not of them. The house of my tribe is in the far North; it was left behind when the Zulus came down here a 'thousand years ago,' long before Chaka reigned in Zululand. I have no kraal. I have wandered for many years. I came from the North as a child to Zululand. I was Cetewayo's man in the Nkomabakosi Regiment, serving there under the great Captain, Umslopogaasi of the Axe, who taught my hands to fight. Afterwards I ran away from Zululand and came to Natal because I wanted to see the white man's ways. Next I fought against Cetewayo in the war. Since then I have been working in Natal. Now I am tired, and would go North again. Here is not my place. I want no money, but I am a brave man, and am worth my place and meat. I have spoken."

I was rather puzzled by this man and his way of speech. It was evident to me from his manner that in the main he was telling the truth, but somehow he seemed different from the ordinary run of Zulus, and I rather mistrusted his offer to come without pay. Being in a difficulty, I translated his words to Sir Henry and Good, and asked them their opinion.

Sir Henry told me to ask him to stand up. Umbopa did so, at the same time slipping off the long military great coat which he wore, and revealing himself naked except for the moocha round his centre and a necklace of lions' claws. Certainly he was a magnificent-looking man; I never saw a finer native. Standing about six foot three high he was broad in proportion, and very shapely. In that light, too, his skin looked scarcely more than dark, except here and there where deep black scars marked old assegai wounds. Sir Henry walked up to him and looked into his proud, handsome face.

"They make a good pair, don't they?" said Good; "one as big as the other."

"I like your looks, Mr. Umbopa, and I will take you as my servant," said Sir Henry in English.

Umbopa evidently understood him, for he answered in Zulu, "It is well"; and then added, with a glance at the white man's great stature and breadth, "We are men, thou and I."

An Elephant Hunt

Now I do not propose to narrate at full length all the incidents of our long travel up to Sitanda's Kraal, near the junction of the Lukanga and Kalukwe Rivers. It was a journey of more than a thousand miles from Durban, the last three hundred or so of which we had to make on foot, owing to the frequent presence of the dreadful "tsetse" fly, whose bite is fatal to all animals except donkeys and men.

We left Durban at the end of January, and it was in the second week of May that we camped near Sitanda's Kraal. Our adventures on the way were many and various, but as they are of the sort which befall every African hunter—with one exception to be presently detailed—I shall not set them down here, lest I should render this history too wearisome.

At Inyati, the outlying trading station in the Matabele country, of which Lobengula (a great and cruel scoundrel) is king, with many regrets we parted from our comfortable wagon. Only twelve oxen remained to us out of the beautiful span of twenty which I had bought at Durban. One we lost from the bite of a cobra, three had perished from "poverty" and the want of water, one strayed, and the other three died from eating the poisonous herb called "tulip." Five more sickened from this cause, but we managed to cure them with doses of an infusion made by boiling down the tulip leaves. If administered in time this is a very effective antidote.

The wagon and the oxen we left in the immediate charge of Goza and Tom, our driver and leader, both trustworthy boys, requesting a worthy Scotch missionary who lived in this distant place to keep an eye on them. Then, accompanied by Umbopa, Khiva, Ventvogel, and half a dozen bearers whom we hired on the spot, we started off on foot upon our wild quest. I remember we were all a little silent on the occasion of this departure, and I think that each of us was wondering if we should ever see our wagon again; for my part I never expected to do so. For a while we tramped on in silence, till Umbopa, who was marching in front, broke into a Zulu chant about how some brave men, tired of life and the tameness of things, started off into a vast wilderness to find new things or die, and how, lo and behold! when they had travelled far into the wilderness they found that it was not a wilderness at all, but a beautiful place full of young wives and fat cattle, of game to hunt and enemies to kill.

Then we all laughed and took it for a good omen. Umbopa was a cheerful savage, in a dignified sort of way, when he was not suffering from one of his fits of brooding, and he had a wonderful knack of keeping up our spirits. We all grew very fond of him.

And now for the one adventure to which I am going to treat myself, for I do dearly love a hunting yarn.

About a fortnight's march from Inyati we came across a peculiarly beautiful bit of well-watered woodland country. The kloofs in the hills were covered with dense bush, "idoro" bush as the natives call it, and in some places, with the "wacht-een-beche," or "wait-a-little thorn," and there were great quantities of the lovely "machabell" tree, laden with refreshing yellow fruit having enormous stones. This tree is the elephant's favourite food, and there were not wanting signs that the great brutes had been about, for not only was their spoor frequent, but in many places the trees were broken down and even uprooted. The elephant is a destructive feeder.

One evening, after a long day's march, we came to a spot of great loveliness. At the foot of a bush-clad hill lay a dry river-bed, in which, however, were to be found pools of crystal water all trodden round with the hoof-prints of game. Facing this hill was a park-like plain, where grew clumps of flat-topped mimosa, varied with occasional glossy-leaved machabells, and all round stretched the sea of pathless, silent bush.

As we emerged into this river-bed path suddenly we started a troop of tall giraffes, who galloped, or rather sailed off, in their strange gait, their tails screwed up over their backs, and their hoofs rattling like castanets. They were about three hundred yards from us, and therefore practically out of shot, but Good, who was walking ahead, and who had an express loaded with solid ball in his hand, could not resist temptation. Lifting his gun, he let drive at the last, a young cow. By some extraordinary chance the ball struck it full on the back of the neck, shattering the spinal column, and that giraffe went rolling head over heels just like a rabbit. I never saw a more curious thing.

"Curse it!" said Good—for I am sorry to say he had a habit of using strong language when excited—contracted, no doubt, in the course of his nautical career; "curse it! I've killed him."

"*Ou*, Bougwan," ejaculated the Kafirs; "*ou! ou!*"

They called Good "Bougwan," or Glass Eye, because of his eye-glass.

"Oh, 'Bougwan!'" re-echoed Sir Henry and I, and from that day Good's reputation as a marvellous shot was established, at any rate among the Kafirs. Really he was a bad one, but whenever he missed we overlooked it for the sake of that giraffe.

Having set some of the "boys" to cut off the best of the giraffe's meat, we went to work to build a "scherm" near one of the pools and about a hundred yards to its right. This is done by cutting a quantity of thorn bushes and piling them in the shape of a circular hedge. Then the space enclosed is smoothed, and dry tambouki grass, if obtainable, is made into a bed in the centre, and a fire or fires lighted.

By the time the "scherm" was finished the moon peeped up, and our dinners of giraffe steaks and roasted marrow-bones were ready. How we enjoyed those marrow-bones, though it was rather a job to crack them! I know of no greater luxury than giraffe marrow, unless it is elephant's heart, and we had that on the morrow. We ate our simple meal by the light of the moon, pausing at times to thank Good for his wonderful shot; then we began to smoke and yarn, and a curious picture we must have made squatting there round the fire. I, with my short grizzled hair sticking up straight, and Sir Henry with his yellow locks, which were getting rather long, were rather a contrast, especially as I am thin, and short, and dark, weighing only nine stone and a half, and Sir Henry is tall, and broad, and fair, and weighs fifteen. But perhaps the most curious-looking of the three, taking all the circumstances of the case into consideration, was Captain John Good, R.N. There he sat upon a leather bag, looking just as though he had come in from a comfortable day's shooting in a civilised country, absolutely clean, tidy, and well dressed. He wore a shooting suit of brown tweed, with a hat to match, and neat gaiters. As usual, he was beautifully shaved, his eye-glass and his false teeth appeared to be in perfect order, and altogether he looked the neatest man I ever had to do with in the wilderness. He even sported a collar, of which he had a supply, made of white gutta-percha.

"You see, they weigh so little," he said to me innocently, when I expressed my astonishment at the fact; "and I always like to turn out like a gentleman." Ah! if he could have foreseen the future and the raiment prepared for him.

Well, there we three sat yarning away in the beautiful moonlight, and watching the Kafirs a few yards off sucking their intoxicating "daccha" from a pipe of which the mouthpiece was made of the horn of an eland, till one by one they rolled themselves up in their blankets and went to sleep by the fire, that is, all except Umbopa, who was a little apart, his chin resting on his hand, and thinking deeply. I noticed that he never mixed much with the other Kafirs.

Presently, from the depths of the bush behind us, came a loud "*woof, woof!*" "That's a lion," said I, and we all started up to listen. Hardly had we done so, when from the pool, about a hundred yards off, we heard the strident trumpeting of an elephant. "*Unkungunklovo! Indlovu!*" "Elephant! Elephant!" whispered the Kafirs, and a few minutes afterwards we saw a succession of vast shadowy forms moving slowly from the direction of the water towards the bush.

Up jumped Good, burning for slaughter, and thinking, perhaps, that it was as easy to kill elephant as he had found it to shoot giraffe, but I caught him by the arm and pulled him down.

"It's no good," I whispered, "let them go."

"It seems that we are in a paradise of game. I vote we stop here a day or two, and have a go at them," said Sir Henry, presently.

I was rather surprised, for hitherto Sir Henry had always been for pushing forward as fast as possible, more especially since we ascertained at Inyati that about two years ago an Englishman of the name of Neville *had* sold his wagon there, and gone on up country. But I suppose his hunter instincts got the better of him for a while.

Good jumped at the idea, for he was longing to have a shot at those elephants; and so, to speak the truth, did I, for it went against my conscience to let such a herd as that escape without a pull at them.

"All right, my hearties," said I. "I think we want a little recreation. And now let's turn in, for we ought to be off by dawn, and then perhaps we may catch them feeding before they move on."

The others agreed, and we proceeded to make our preparations. Good took off his clothes, shook them, put his eye-glass and his false teeth into his trousers pocket, and folding each article neatly, placed it out of the dew under a corner of his mackintosh sheet. Sir Henry and I contented ourselves with rougher arrangements, and soon were curled up in our blankets, and dropping off into the dreamless sleep that rewards the traveller.

Going, going, go—What was that?

Suddenly, from the direction of the water came sounds of violent scuffling, and next instant there broke upon our ears a succession of the most awful roars. There was no mistaking their origin; only a lion could make such a noise as that. We all jumped up and looked towards the water, in the direction of which we saw a confused mass, yellow and black in colour, staggering and struggling towards us. We seized our rifles, and slipping on our veldtschoons, that is shoes made of untanned hide, ran out of the scherm. By this time the mass had fallen, and was rolling over and over on the ground, and when we reached the spot it struggled no longer, but lay quite still.

Now we saw what it was. On the grass there lay a sable antelope bull—the most beautiful of all the African antelopes—quite dead, and transfixed by its great curved horns was a magnificent black-maned lion, also dead. Evidently what had happened was this: The sable antelope had come down to drink at the pool where the lion—no doubt the same which we had heard—was lying in wait. While the antelope drank, the lion had sprung upon him, only to be received upon the sharp curved horns and transfixed. Once before I saw a similar thing happen. Then the lion, unable to free himself, had torn and bitten at the back and neck of the bull, which, maddened with fear and pain, had rushed on until it dropped dead.

As soon as we had examined the beasts sufficiently we called the Kafirs, and between us managed to drag their carcases up to the scherm. After that we went in and lay down, to wake no more till dawn.

With the first light we were up and making ready for the fray. We took with us the three eight-bore rifles, a good supply of ammunition, and our large water-bottles, filled with weak cold tea, which I have always found the best stuff to shoot on. After swallowing a little breakfast we started, Umbopa, Khiva, and Ventvogel accompanying us. The other Kafirs we left with instructions to skin the lion and the sable antelope, and to cut up the latter.

We had no difficulty in finding the broad elephant trail, which Ventvogel, after examination, pronounced to have been made by between twenty and thirty elephants, most of them full-grown bulls. But the herd had moved on some way during the night, and it was nine o'clock, and already very hot, before, by the broken trees, bruised leaves and bark, and smoking droppings, we knew that we could not be far from them.

Presently we caught sight of the herd, which numbered, as Ventvogel had said, between twenty and thirty, standing in a hollow, having finished their morning meal, and flapping their great ears. It was a splendid sight, for they were only about two hundred yards from us. Taking a handful of dry grass, I threw it into the air to see how the wind was; for if once they winded us I knew they would be off before we could get a shot. Finding that, if anything, it blew from the elephants to us, we crept on stealthily, and thanks to the cover managed to get within forty yards or so of the great brutes. Just in front of us, and broadside on, stood three splendid bulls, one of them with enormous tusks. I whispered to the others that I would take the middle one; Sir Henry covering the elephant to the left, and Good the bull with the big tusks.

"Now," I whispered.

Boom! boom! boom! went the three heavy rifles, and down came Sir Henry's elephant dead as a hammer, shot right through the heart. Mine fell on to its knees and I thought that he was going to die, but in another moment he was up and off, tearing along straight past me. As he went I gave him the second barrel in the ribs, and this brought him down in good earnest. Hastily slipping in two fresh cartridges I ran close up to him, and a ball through the brain put an end to the poor brute's struggles. Then I turned to see how Good had fared with the big bull, which I had heard screaming with rage and pain as I gave mine its quietus. On reaching the captain I found him in a great state of excitement. It appeared that on receiving the bullet the bull had turned and come straight for his assailant, who had barely time to get out of his way, and then charged on blindly past him, in the direction of our encampment. Meanwhile the herd had crashed off in wild alarm in the other direction.

For awhile we debated whether to go after the wounded bull or to follow the herd, and finally deciding for the latter alternative, departed, thinking that we had seen the last of those big tusks. I have often wished since that we had. It was easy work to follow the elephants, for they had left a trail like a carriage road behind them, crushing down the thick bush in their furious flight as though it were tambouki grass.

But to come up with them was another matter, and we had struggled on under the broiling sun for over two hours before we found them. With the exception of one bull, they were standing together, and I could see, from their unquiet way and the manner in which they kept lifting their trunks to test the air, that they were on the look-out for mischief. The solitary bull stood fifty yards or so to this side of the herd, over which he was evidently keeping sentry, and about sixty yards from us. Thinking that he would see or wind us, and that it would probably start them off again if we tried to get nearer, especially as the ground was rather open, we all aimed at this bull, and at my whispered word, we fired. The three shots took effect, and down he went dead. Again the herd started, but unfortunately for them about a hundred yards further on was a nullah, or dried-out water track, with steep banks, a place very much resembling the one where the Prince Imperial was killed in Zululand. Into this the elephants plunged, and when we reached the edge we found them struggling in wild confusion to get up the other bank, filling the air with their screams, and trumpeting as they pushed one another aside in their selfish panic, just like so many human beings. Now was our opportunity, and firing away as quickly as we could load, we killed five of the poor beasts, and no doubt should have bagged the whole herd, had they not suddenly given up their attempts to climb the bank and rushed headlong down the nullah. We were too tired to follow them, and perhaps also a little sick of slaughter, eight elephants being a pretty good bag for one day.

So after we were rested a little, and the Kafirs had cut out the hearts of two of the dead elephants for supper, we started homewards, very well pleased with our day's work, having made up our minds to send the bearers on the morrow to chop away the tusks.

Shortly after we re-passed the spot where Good had wounded the patriarchal bull we came across a herd of eland, but did not shoot at them, as we had plenty of meat. They trotted past us, and then stopped behind a little patch of bush about a hundred yards away, wheeling round to look at us. As Good was anxious to get a near view of them, never having seen an eland close, he handed his rifle to Umbopa, and, followed by Khiva, strolled up to the patch of bush. We sat down and waited for him, not sorry of the excuse for a little rest.

The sun was just going down in its reddest glory, and Sir Henry and I were admiring the lovely scene, when suddenly we heard an elephant scream, and saw its huge and rushing form with uplifted trunk and tail silhouetted against the great fiery globe of the sun. Next second we saw something else, and that was Good and Khiva tearing back towards us with the wounded bull—for it was he—charging after them. For a moment we did not dare to fire—though at that distance it would have been of little use if we had done so—for fear of hitting one of them, and the next a dreadful thing happened—Good fell a victim to his passion for civilised dress. Had he consented to discard his trousers and gaiters like the rest of us, and to hunt in a flannel shirt and a pair of veldt-schoons, it would have been all right. But as it was, his trousers cumbered him in that desperate race, and presently, when he was about sixty yards from us, his boot, polished by the dry grass, slipped, and down he went on his face right in front of the elephant.

We gave a gasp, for we knew that he must die, and ran as hard as we could towards him. In three seconds it had ended, but not as we thought. Khiva, the Zulu boy, saw his master fall, and brave lad as he was, turned and flung his assegai straight into the elephant's face. It stuck in his trunk.

With a scream of pain, the brute seized the poor Zulu, hurled him to the earth, and placing one huge foot on to his body about the middle, twined its trunk round his upper part and *tore him in two.*

We rushed up mad with horror, and fired again and again, till presently the elephant fell upon the fragments of the Zulu.

As for Good, he rose and wrung his hands over the brave man who had given his life to save him, and, though I am an old hand, I felt a lump grow in my throat. Umbopa stood contemplating the huge dead elephant and the mangled remains of poor Khiva.

"Ah, well," he said presently, "he is dead, but he died like a man!"

Our March into the Desert

We had killed nine elephants, and it took us two days to cut out the tusks, and having brought them into camp, to bury them carefully in the sand under a large tree, which made a conspicuous mark for miles round. It was a wonderfully fine lot of ivory. I never saw a better, averaging as it did between forty and fifty pounds a tusk. The tusks of the great bull that killed poor Khiva scaled one hundred and seventy pounds the pair, so nearly as we could judge.

As for Khiva himself, we buried what remained of him in an ant-bear hole, together with an assegai to protect himself with on his journey to a better world. On the third day we marched again, hoping that we might live to return to dig up our buried ivory, and in due course, after a long and wearisome tramp, and many adventures which I have not space to detail, we reached Sitanda's Kraal, near the Lukanga River, the real starting-point of our expedition. Very well do I recollect our arrival at that place. To the right was a scattered native settlement with a few stone cattle kraals and some cultivated lands down by the water, where these savages grew their scanty supply of grain, and beyond it stretched great tracts of waving "veld" covered with tall grass, over which herds of the smaller game were wandering. To the left lay the vast desert. This spot appears to be the outpost of the fertile country, and it would be difficult to say to what natural causes such an abrupt change in the character of the soil is due. But so it is.

Just below our encampment flowed a little stream, on the farther side of which is a stony slope, the same down which, twenty years before, I had seen poor Silvestre creeping back after his attempt to reach Solomon's Mines, and beyond that slope begins the waterless desert, covered with a species of karoo shrub.

It was evening when we pitched our camp, and the great ball of the sun was sinking into the desert, sending glorious rays of many-coloured light flying all over its vast expanse. Leaving Good to superintend the arrangement of our little camp, I took Sir Henry with me, and walking to the top of the slope opposite, we gazed across the desert. The air was very clear, and far, far away I could distinguish the faint blue outlines, here and there capped with white, of the Suliman Berg.

"There," I said, "there is the wall round Solomon's Mines, but God knows if we shall ever climb it."

"My brother should be there, and if he is, I shall reach him somehow," said Sir Henry, in that tone of quiet confidence which marked the man.

"I hope so," I answered, and turned to go back to the camp, when I saw that we were not alone. Behind us, also gazing earnestly towards the far-off mountains, stood the great Kafir Umbopa.

The Zulu spoke when he saw that I had observed him, addressing Sir Henry, to whom he had attached himself.

"Is it to that land that thou wouldst journey, Incubu?" (a native word meaning, I believe, an elephant, and the name given to Sir Henry by the Kafirs), he said, pointing towards the mountain with his broad assegai.

I asked him sharply what he meant by addressing his master in that familiar way. It is very well for natives to have a name for one among themselves, but it is not decent that they should call a white man by their heathenish appellations to his face. The Zulu laughed a quiet little laugh which angered me.

"How dost thou know that I am not the equal of the Inkosi whom I serve?" he said. "He is of a royal house, no doubt; one can see it in his size and by his mien; so, mayhap, am I. At least, I am as great a man. Be my mouth, O Macumazahn, and say my words to the Inkoos Incubu, my master, for I would speak to him and to thee."

I was angry with the man, for I am not accustomed to be talked to in that way by Kafirs, but somehow he impressed me, and besides I was curious to know what he had to say. So I translated, expressing my opinion at the same time that he was an impudent fellow, and that his swagger was outrageous.

"Yes, Umbopa," answered Sir Henry, "I would journey there."

"The desert is wide and there is no water in it, the mountains are high and covered with snow, and man cannot say what lies beyond them behind the place where the sun sets; how shalt thou come thither, Incubu, and wherefore dost thou go?"

I translated again.

"Tell him," answered Sir Henry, "that I go because I believe that a man of my blood, my brother, has gone there before me, and I journey to seek him."

"That is so, Incubu; a Hottentot I met on the road told me that a white man went out into the desert two years ago towards those mountains with one servant, a hunter. They never came back."

"How do you know it was my brother?" asked Sir Henry.

"Nay, I know not. But the Hottentot, when I asked what the white man was like, said that he had thine eyes and a black beard. He said, too, that the name of the hunter with him was Jim; that he was a Bechuana hunter and wore clothes."

"There is no doubt about it," said I; "I knew Jim well."

Sir Henry nodded. "I was sure of it," he said. "If George set his mind upon a thing he generally did it. It was always so from his boyhood. If he meant to cross the Suliman Berg he has crossed it, unless some accident overtook him, and we must look for him on the other side."

Umbopa understood English, though he rarely spoke it.

"It is a far journey, Incubu," he put in, and I translated his remark.

"Yes," answered Sir Henry, "it is far. But there is no journey upon this earth that a man may not make if he sets his heart to it. There is nothing, Umbopa, that he cannot do, there are no mountains he may not climb, there are no deserts he cannot cross, save a mountain and a desert of which you are spared the knowledge, if love leads him and he holds his life in his hands counting it as nothing, ready to keep it or lose it as Heaven above may order."

I translated.

"Great words, my father," answered the Zulu—I always called him a Zulu, though he was not really one—"great swelling words fit to fill the mouth of a man. Thou art right, my father Incubu. Listen! what is life? It is a feather, it is the seed of the grass, blown hither and thither, sometimes multiplying itself and dying in the act, sometimes carried away into the heavens. But if that seed be good and heavy it may perchance travel a little way on the road it wills. It is well to try and journey one's road and to fight with the air. Man must die. At the worst he can but die a little sooner. I will go with thee across the desert and over the mountains, unless perchance I fall to the ground on the way, my father."

He paused awhile, and then went on with one of those strange bursts of rhetorical eloquence that Zulus sometimes indulge in, which to my mind, full though they are of vain repetitions, show that the race is by no means devoid of poetic instinct and of intellectual power.

"What is life? Tell me, O white men, who are wise, who know the secrets of the world, and of the world of stars, and the world that lies above and around the stars; who flash your words from afar without a voice; tell me, white men, the secret of our life—whither it goes and whence it comes!

"You cannot answer me; you know not. Listen, I will answer. Out of the dark we came, into the dark we go. Like a storm-driven bird at night we fly out of the Nowhere; for a moment our wings are seen in the light of the fire, and, lo! we are gone again into the Nowhere. Life is nothing. Life is all. It is the Hand with which we hold off Death. It is the glow-worm that shines in the night-time and is black in the morning; it is the white breath of the oxen in winter; it is the little shadow that runs across the grass and loses itself at sunset."

"You are a strange man," said Sir Henry, when he had ceased.

Umbopa laughed. "It seems to me that we are much alike, Incubu. Perhaps *I* seek a brother over the mountains."

I looked at him suspiciously. "What dost thou mean?" I asked; "what dost thou know of those mountains?"

"A little; a very little. There is a strange land yonder, a land of witchcraft and beautiful things; a land of brave people, and of trees, and streams, and snowy peaks, and of a great white road. I have heard of it. But what is the good of talking? It grows dark. Those who live to see will see."

Again I looked at him doubtfully. The man knew too much.

"You need not fear me, Macumazahn," he said, interpreting my look. "I dig no holes for you to fall in. I make no plots. If ever we cross those mountains behind the sun I will tell what I know. But Death sits upon them. Be wise and turn back. Go and hunt elephants, my masters. I have spoken."

And without another word he lifted his spear in salutation, and returned towards the camp, where shortly afterwards we found him cleaning a gun like any other Kafir.

"That is an odd man," said Sir Henry.

"Yes," answered I, "too odd by half. I don't like his little ways. He knows something, and will not speak out. But I suppose it is no use quarrelling with him. We are in for a curious trip, and a mysterious Zulu won't make much difference one way or another."

Next day we made our arrangements for starting. Of course it was impossible to drag our heavy elephant rifles and other kit with us across the desert, so, dismissing our bearers, we made an arrangement with an old native who had a kraal close by to take care of them till we returned. It went to my heart to leave such things as those sweet tools to the tender mercies of an old thief of a savage whose greedy eyes I could see gloating over them. But I took some precautions.

First of all I loaded all the rifles, placing them at full cock, and informed him that if he touched them they would go off. He tried the experiment instantly with my eight-bore, and it did go off, and blew a hole right through one of his oxen, which were just then being driven up to the kraal, to say nothing of knocking him head over heels with the recoil. He got up considerably startled, and not at all pleased at the loss of the ox, which he had the impudence to ask me to pay for, and nothing would induce him to touch the guns again.

"Put the live devils out of the way up there in the thatch," he said, "or they will murder us all."

Then I told him that, when we came back, if one of those things was missing I would kill him and his people by witchcraft; and if we died and he tried to steal the rifles I would come and haunt him and turn his cattle mad and his milk sour till life was a weariness, and would make the devils in the guns come out and talk to him in a way he did not like, and generally gave him a good idea of judgment to come. After that he promised to look after them as though they were his father's spirit. He was a very superstitious old Kafir and a great villain.

Having thus disposed of our superfluous gear we arranged the kit we five—Sir Henry, Good, myself, Umbopa, and the Hottentot Ventvogel—were to take with us on our journey. It was small enough, but do what we would we could not get its weight down under about forty pounds a man. This is what it consisted of:—

The three express rifles and two hundred rounds of ammunition.

The two Winchester repeating rifles (for Umbopa and Ventvogel), with two hundred rounds of cartridge.

Five Cochrane's water-bottles, each holding four pints.

Five blankets.

Twenty-five pounds' weight of biltong—i.e. sun-dried game flesh.

Ten pounds' weight of best mixed beads for gifts.

A selection of medicine, including an ounce of quinine, and one or two small surgical instruments.

Our knives, a few sundries, such as a compass, matches, a pocket filter, tobacco, a trowel, a bottle of brandy, and the clothes we stood in.

This was our total equipment, a small one indeed for such a venture, but we dared not attempt to carry more. Indeed, that load was a heavy one per man with which to travel across the burning desert, for in such places every additional ounce tells. But we could not see our way to reducing the weight. There was nothing taken but what was absolutely necessary.

With great difficulty, and by the promise of a present of a good hunting-knife each, I succeeded in persuading three wretched natives from the village to come with us for the first stage, twenty miles, and to carry a large gourd holding a gallon of water apiece. My object was to enable us to refill our water-bottles after the first night's march, for we determined to start in the cool of the evening. I gave out to these natives that we were going to shoot ostriches, with which the desert abounded. They jabbered and shrugged their shoulders, saying that we were mad and should perish of thirst, which I must say seemed probable; but being desirous of obtaining the knives, which were almost unknown treasures up there, they consented to come, having probably reflected that, after all, our subsequent extinction would be no affair of theirs.

All next day we rested and slept, and at sunset ate a hearty meal of fresh beef washed down with tea, the last, as Good remarked sadly, we were likely to drink for many a long day. Then, having made our final preparations, we lay down and waited for the moon to rise. At last, about nine o'clock, up she came in all her glory, flooding the wild country with light, and throwing a silver sheen on the expanse of rolling desert before us, which looked as solemn and quiet and as alien to man as the star-studded firmament above. We rose up, and in a few minutes were ready, and yet we hesitated a little, as human nature is prone to hesitate on the threshold of an irrevocable step. We three white men stood by ourselves. Umbopa, assegai in hand and a rifle across his shoulders, looked out fixedly across the desert a few paces ahead of us; while the hired natives, with the gourds of water, and Ventvogel, were gathered in a little knot behind.

"Gentlemen," said Sir Henry presently, in his deep voice, "we are going on about as strange a journey as men can make in this world. It is very doubtful if we can succeed in it. But we are three men who will stand together for good or for evil to the last. Now before we start let us for a moment pray to the Power who shapes the destinies of men, and who ages since has marked out our paths, that it may please Him to direct our steps in accordance with His will."

Taking off his hat, for the space of a minute or so, he covered his face with his hands, and Good and I did likewise.

I do not say that I am a first-rate praying man, few hunters are, and as for Sir Henry, I never heard him speak like that before, and only once since, though deep down in his heart I believe that he is very religious. Good too is pious, though apt to swear. Anyhow I do not remember, excepting on one single occasion, ever putting up a better prayer in my life than I did during that minute, and somehow I felt the happier for it. Our future was so completely unknown, and I think that the unknown and the awful always bring a man nearer to his Maker.

"And now," said Sir Henry, "*trek!*"

So we started.

We had nothing to guide ourselves by except the distant mountains and old Jose da Silvestre's chart, which, considering that it was drawn by a dying and half-distraught man on a fragment of linen three centuries ago, was not a very satisfactory sort of thing with work with. Still, our sole hope of success depended upon it, such as it was. If we failed in finding that pool of bad water which the old Dom marked as being situated in the middle of the desert, about sixty miles from our starting-point, and as far from the mountains, in all probability we must perish miserably of thirst. But to my mind the chances of our finding it in that great sea of sand and karoo scrub seemed almost infinitesimal. Even supposing that da Silvestra had marked the pool correctly, what was there to prevent its having been dried up by the sun generations ago, or trampled in by game, or filled with the drifting sand?

On we tramped silently as shades through the night and in the heavy sand. The karoo bushes caught our feet and retarded us, and the sand worked into our veldtschoons and Good's shooting-boots, so that every few miles we had to stop and empty them; but still the night kept fairly cool, though the atmosphere was thick and heavy, giving a sort of creamy feel to the air, and we made fair progress. It was very silent and lonely there in the desert, oppressively so indeed. Good felt this, and once began to whistle "The Girl I left behind me," but the notes sounded lugubrious in that vast place, and he gave it up.

Shortly afterwards a little incident occurred which, though it startled us at the time, gave rise to a laugh. Good was leading, as the holder of the compass, which, being a sailor, of course he understood thoroughly, and we were toiling along in single file behind him, when suddenly we heard the sound of an exclamation, and he vanished. Next second there arose all around us a most extraordinary hubbub, snorts, groans, and wild sounds of rushing feet. In the faint light, too, we could descry dim galloping forms half hidden by wreaths of sand. The natives threw down their loads and prepared to bolt, but remembering that there was nowhere to run to, they cast themselves upon the ground and howled out that it was ghosts. As for Sir Henry and myself, we stood amazed; nor was our amazement lessened when we perceived the form of Good careering off in the direction of the mountains, apparently mounted on the back of a horse and halloaing wildly. In another second he threw up his arms, and we heard him come to the earth with a thud.

Then I saw what had happened; we had stumbled upon a herd of sleeping quagga, on to the back of one of which Good actually had fallen, and the brute naturally enough got up and made off with him. Calling out to the others that it was all right, I ran towards Good, much afraid lest he should be hurt, but to my great relief I found him sitting in the sand, his eye-glass still fixed firmly in his eye, rather shaken and very much frightened, but not in any way injured.

After this we travelled on without any further misadventure till about one o'clock, when we called a halt, and having drunk a little water, not much, for water was precious, and rested for half an hour, we started again.

On, on we went, till at last the east began to blush like the cheek of a girl. Then there came faint rays of primrose light, that changed presently to golden bars, through which the dawn glided out across the desert. The stars grew pale and paler still, till at last they vanished; the golden moon waxed wan, and her mountain ridges stood out against her sickly face like the bones on the cheek of a dying man. Then came spear upon spear of light flashing far away across the boundless wilderness, piercing and firing the veils of mist, till the desert was draped in a tremulous golden glow, and it was day.

Still we did not halt, though by this time we should have been glad enough to do so, for we knew that when once the sun was fully up it would be almost impossible for us to travel. At length, about an hour later, we spied a little pile of boulders rising out of the plain, and to this we dragged ourselves. As luck would have it, here we found an overhanging slab of rock carpeted beneath with smooth sand, which afforded a most grateful shelter from the heat. Underneath this we crept, and each of us having drunk some water and eaten a bit of biltong, we lay down and soon were sound asleep.

It was three o'clock in the afternoon before we woke, to find our bearers preparing to return. They had seen enough of the desert already, and no number of knives would have tempted them to come a step farther. So we took a hearty drink, and having emptied our water- bottles, filled them up again from the gourds that they had brought with them, and then watched them depart on their twenty miles' tramp home.

At half-past four we also started. It was lonely and desolate work, for with the exception of a few ostriches there was not a single living creature to be seen on all the vast expanse of sandy plain. Evidently it was too dry for game, and with the exception of a deadly- looking cobra or two we saw no reptiles. One insect, however, we found abundant, and that was the common or house fly. There they came, "not as single spies, but in battalions," as I think the Old Testament says somewhere. He is an extraordinary insect is the house fly. Go where you will you find him, and so it must have been always. I have seen him enclosed in amber, which is, I was told, quite half a million years old, looking exactly like his descendant of to-day, and I have little doubt but that when the last man lies dying on the earth he will be buzzing round—if this event happens to occur in summer— watching for an opportunity to settle on his nose.

At sunset we halted, waiting for the moon to rise. At last she came up, beautiful and serene as ever, and, with one halt about two o'clock in the morning, we trudged on wearily through the night, till at last the welcome sun put a period to our labours. We drank a little and flung ourselves down on the sand, thoroughly tired out, and soon were all asleep. There was no need to set a watch, for we had nothing to fear from anybody or anything in that vast untenanted plain. Our only enemies were heat, thirst, and flies, but far rather would I have faced any danger from man or beast than that awful trinity. This time we were not so lucky as to find a sheltering rock to guard us from the glare of the sun, with the result that about seven o'clock we woke up experiencing the exact sensations one would attribute to a beefsteak on a gridiron. We were literally being baked through and through. The burning sun seemed to be sucking our very blood out of us. We sat up and gasped.

"Phew," said I, grabbing at the halo of flies which buzzed cheerfully round my head. The heat did not affect *them*.

"My word!" said Sir Henry.

"It is hot!" echoed Good.

It was hot, indeed, and there was not a bit of shelter to be found. Look where we would there was no rock or tree, nothing but an unending glare, rendered dazzling by the heated air that danced over the surface of the desert as it dances over a red-hot stove.

"What is to be done?" asked Sir Henry; "we can't stand this for long."

We looked at each other blankly.

"I have it," said Good, "we must dig a hole, get in it, and cover ourselves with the karoo bushes."

It did not seem a very promising suggestion, but at least it was better than nothing, so we set to work, and, with the trowel we had brought with us and the help of our hands, in about an hour we succeeded in delving out a patch of ground some ten feet long by twelve wide to the depth of two feet. Then we cut a quantity of low scrub with our hunting-knives, and creeping into the hole, pulled it over us all, with the exception of Ventvogel, on whom, being a Hottentot, the heat had no particular effect. This gave us some slight shelter from the burning rays of the sun, but the atmosphere in that amateur grave can be better imagined than described. The Black Hole of Calcutta must have been a fool to it; indeed, to this moment I do not know how we lived through the day. There we lay panting, and every now and again moistening our lips from our scanty supply of water. Had we followed our inclinations we should have finished all we possessed in the first two hours, but we were forced to exercise the most rigid care, for if our water failed us we knew that very soon we must perish miserably.

But everything has an end, if only you live long enough to see it, and somehow that miserable day wore on towards evening. About three o'clock in the afternoon we determined that we could bear it no longer. It would be better to die walking that to be killed slowly by heat and thirst in this dreadful hole. So taking each of us a little drink from our fast diminishing supply of water, now warmed to about the same temperature as a man's blood, we staggered forward.

We had then covered some fifty miles of wilderness. If the reader will refer to the rough copy and translation of old da Silvestra's map, he will see that the desert is marked as measuring forty leagues across, and the "pan bad water" is set down as being about in the middle of it. Now forty leagues is one hundred and twenty miles, consequently we ought at the most to be within twelve or fifteen miles of the water if any should really exist.

Through the afternoon we crept slowly and painfully along, scarcely doing more than a mile and a half in an hour. At sunset we rested again, waiting for the moon, and after drinking a little managed to get some sleep.

Before we lay down, Umbopa pointed out to us a slight and indistinct hillock on the flat surface of the plain about eight miles away. At the distance it looked like an ant-hill, and as I was dropping off to sleep I fell to wondering what it could be.

With the moon we marched again, feeling dreadfully exhausted, and suffering tortures from thirst and prickly heat. Nobody who has not felt it can know what we went through. We walked no longer, we staggered, now and again falling from exhaustion, and being obliged to call a halt every hour or so. We had scarcely energy left in us to speak. Up to this Good had chatted and joked, for he is a merry fellow; but now he had not a joke in him.

At last, about two o'clock, utterly worn out in body and mind, we came to the foot of the queer hill, or sand koppie, which at first sight resembled a gigantic ant-heap about a hundred feet high, and covering at the base nearly two acres of ground.

Here we halted, and driven to it by our desperate thirst, sucked down our last drops of water. We had but half a pint a head, and each of us could have drunk a gallon.

Then we lay down. Just as I was dropping off to sleep I heard Umbopa remark to himself in Zulu—

"If we cannot find water we shall all be dead before the moon rises to-morrow."

I shuddered, hot as it was. The near prospect of such an awful death is not pleasant, but even the thought of it could not keep me from sleeping.

Water! Water!

Two hours later, that is, about four o'clock, I woke up, for so soon as the first heavy demand of bodily fatigue had been satisfied, the torturing thirst from which I was suffering asserted itself. I could sleep no more. I had been dreaming that I was bathing in a running stream, with green banks and trees upon them, and I awoke to find myself in this arid wilderness, and to remember, as Umbopa had said, that if we did not find water this day we must perish miserably. No human creature could live long without water in that heat. I sat up and rubbed my grimy face with my dry and horny hands, as my lips and eyelids were stuck together, and it was only after some friction and with an effort that I was able to open them. It was not far from dawn, but there was none of the bright feel of dawn in the air, which was thick with a hot murkiness that I cannot describe. The others were still sleeping.

Presently it began to grow light enough to read, so I drew out a little pocket copy of the "Ingoldsby Legends" which I had brought with me, and read "The Jackdaw of Rheims." When I got to where

"A nice little boy held a golden ewer,
Embossed, and filled with water as pure
As any that flows between Rheims and Namur,"

literally I smacked my cracking lips, or rather tried to smack them. The mere thought of that pure water made me mad. If the Cardinal had been there with his bell, book, and candle, I would have whipped in and drunk his water up; yes, even if he had filled it already with the suds of soap "worthy of washing the hands of the Pope," and I knew that the whole consecrated curse of the Catholic Church should fall upon me for so doing. I almost think that I must have been a little light-headed with thirst, weariness and the want of food; for I fell to thinking how astonished the Cardinal and his nice little boy and the jackdaw would have looked to see a burnt up, brown-eyed, grizzly-haired little elephant hunter suddenly bound between them, put his dirty face into the basin, and swallow every drop of the precious water. The idea amused me so much that I laughed or rather cackled aloud, which woke the others, and they began to rub *their* dirty faces and drag *their* gummed-up lips and eyelids apart.

As soon as we were all well awake we began to discuss the situation, which was serious enough. Not a drop of water was left. We turned the bottles upside down, and licked their tops, but it was a failure; they were dry as a bone. Good, who had charge of the flask of brandy, got it out and looked at it longingly; but Sir Henry promptly took it away from him, for to drink raw spirit would only have been to precipitate the end.

"If we do not find water we shall die," he said.

"If we can trust to the old Dom's map there should be some about," I said; but nobody seemed to derive much satisfaction from this remark. It was so evident that no great faith could be put in the map. Now it was gradually growing light, and as we sat staring blankly at each other, I observed the Hottentot Ventvogel rise and begin to walk about with his eyes on the ground. Presently he stopped short, and uttering a guttural exclamation, pointed to the earth.

"What is it?" we exclaimed; and rising simultaneously we went to where he was standing staring at the sand.

"Well," I said, "it is fresh Springbok spoor; what of it?"

"Springbucks do not go far from water," he answered in Dutch.

"No," I answered, "I forgot; and thank God for it."

This little discovery put new life into us; for it is wonderful, when a man is in a desperate position, how he catches at the slightest hope, and feels almost happy. On a dark night a single star is better than nothing.

Meanwhile Ventvogel was lifting his snub nose, and sniffing the hot air for all the world like an old Impala ram who scents danger. Presently he spoke again.

"I *smell* water," he said.

Then we felt quite jubilant, for we knew what a wonderful instinct these wild-bred men possess.

Just at that moment the sun came up gloriously, and revealed so grand a sight to our astonished eyes that for a moment or two we even forgot our thirst.

There, not more than forty or fifty miles from us, glittering like silver in the early rays of the morning sun, soared Sheba's Breasts; and stretching away for hundreds of miles on either side of them ran the great Suliman Berg. Now that, sitting here, I attempt to describe the extraordinary grandeur and beauty of that sight, language seems to fail me. I am impotent even before its memory. Straight before us, rose two enormous mountains, the like of which are not, I believe, to be seen in Africa, if indeed there are any other such in the world, measuring each of them at least fifteen thousand feet in height, standing not more than a dozen miles apart, linked together by a precipitous cliff of rock, and towering in awful white solemnity straight into the sky. These mountains placed thus, like the pillars of a gigantic gateway, are shaped after the fashion of a woman's breasts, and at times the mists and shadows beneath them take the form of a recumbent woman, veiled mysteriously in sleep. Their bases swell gently from the plain, looking at that distance perfectly round and smooth; and upon the top of each is a vast hillock covered with snow, exactly corresponding to the nipple on the female breast. The stretch of cliff that connects them appears to be some thousands of feet in height, and perfectly precipitous, and on each flank of them, so far as the eye can reach, extent similar lines of cliff, broken only here and there by flat table-topped mountains, something like the world- famed one at Cape Town; a formation, by the way, that is very common in Africa.

To describe the comprehensive grandeur of that view is beyond my powers. There was something so inexpressibly solemn and overpowering about those huge volcanoes—for doubtless they are extinct volcanoes— that it quite awed us. For a while the morning lights played upon the snow and the brown and swelling masses beneath, and then, as though to veil the majestic sight from our curious eyes, strange vapours and clouds gathered and increased around the mountains, till presently we could only trace their pure and gigantic outlines, showing ghostlike through the fleecy envelope. Indeed, as we afterwards discovered, usually they were wrapped in this gauze-like mist, which doubtless accounted for our not having seen them more clearly before.

Sheba's Breasts had scarcely vanished into cloud-clad privacy, before our thirst—literally a burning question—reasserted itself.

It was all very well for Ventvogel to say that he smelt water, but we could see no signs of it, look which way we would. So far as the eye might reach there was nothing but arid sweltering sand and karoo scrub. We walked round the hillock and gazed about anxiously on the other side, but it was the same story, not a drop of water could be found; there was no indication of a pan, a pool, or a spring.

"You are a fool," I said angrily to Ventvogel; "there is no water."

But still he lifted his ugly snub nose sniffed.

"I smell it, Baas," he answered; "it is somewhere in the air."

"Yes," I said, "no doubt it is in the clouds, and about two months hence it will fall and wash our bones."

Sir Henry stroked his yellow beard thoughtfully. "Perhaps it is on the top of the hill," he suggested.

"Rot," said Good; "whoever heard of water being found at the top of a hill!"

"Let us go and look," I put in, and hopelessly enough we scrambled up the sandy sides of the hillock, Umbopa leading. Presently he stopped as though he was petrified.

"*Nanzia manzie!*" that is, "Here is water!" he cried with a loud voice.

We rushed up to him, and there, sure enough, in a deep cut or indentation on the very top of the sand koppie, was an undoubted pool of water. How it came to be in such a strange place we did not stop to inquire, nor did we hesitate at its black and unpleasant appearance. It was water, or a good imitation of it, and that was enough for us. We gave a bound and a rush, and in another second we were all down on our stomachs sucking up the uninviting fluid as though it were nectar fit for the gods. Heavens, how we did drink! Then when we had done drinking we tore off our clothes and sat down in the pool, absorbing the moisture through our parched skins. You, Harry, my boy, who have only to turn on a couple of taps to summon "hot" and "cold" from an unseen, vasty cistern, can have little idea of the luxury of that muddy wallow in brackish tepid water.

After a while we rose from it, refreshed indeed, and fell to on our "biltong," of which we had scarcely been able to touch a mouthful for twenty-four hours, and ate our fill. Then we smoked a pipe, and lay down by the side of that blessed pool, under the overhanging shadow of its bank, and slept till noon.

All that day we rested there by the water, thanking our stars that we had been lucky enough to find it, bad as it was, and not forgetting to render a due share of gratitude to the shade of the long-departed da Silvestra, who had set its position down so accurately on the tail of his shirt. The wonderful thing to us was that the pan should have lasted so long, and the only way in which I can account for this is on the supposition that it is fed by some spring deep down in the sand.

Having filled both ourselves and our water-bottles as full as possible, in far better spirits we started off again with the moon. That night we covered nearly five-and-twenty miles; but, needless to say, found no more water, though we were lucky enough the following day to get a little shade behind some ant-heaps. When the sun rose, and, for awhile, cleared away the mysterious mists, Suliman's Berg with the two majestic Breasts, now only about twenty miles off, seemed to be towering right above us, and looked grander than ever. At the approach of evening we marched again, and, to cut a long story short, by daylight next morning found ourselves upon the lowest slopes of Sheba's left breast, for which we had been steadily steering. By this time our water was exhausted once more, and we were suffering severely from thirst, nor indeed could we see any chance of relieving it till we reached the snow line far, far above us. After resting an hour or two, driven to it by our torturing thirst, we went on, toiling painfully in the burning heat up the lava slopes, for we found that the huge base of the mountain was composed entirely of lava beds belched from the bowels of the earth in some far past age.

By eleven o'clock we were utterly exhausted, and, generally speaking, in a very bad state indeed. The lava clinker, over which we must drag ourselves, though smooth compared with some clinker I have heard of, such as that on the Island of Ascension, for instance, was yet rough enough to make our feet very sore, and this, together with our other miseries, had pretty well finished us. A few hundred yards above us were some large lumps of lava, and towards these we steered with the intention of lying down beneath their shade. We reached them, and to our surprise, so far as we had a capacity for surprise left in us, on a little plateau or ridge close by we saw that the clinker was covered with a dense green growth. Evidently soil formed of decomposed lava had rested there, and in due course had become the receptacle of seeds deposited by birds. But we did not take much further interest in the green growth, for one cannot live on grass like Nebuchadnezzar. That requires a special dispensation of Providence and peculiar digestive organs.

So we sat down under the rocks and groaned, and for one I wished heartily that we had never started on this fool's errand. As we were sitting there I saw Umbopa get up and hobble towards the patch of green, and a few minutes afterwards, to my great astonishment, I perceived that usually very dignified individual dancing and shouting like a maniac, and waving something green. Off we all scrambled towards him as fast as our wearied limbs would carry us, hoping that he had found water.

"What is it, Umbopa, son of a fool?" I shouted in Zulu.

"It is food and water, Macumazahn," and again he waved the green thing.

Then I saw what he had found. It was a melon. We had hit upon a patch of wild melons, thousands of them, and dead ripe.

"Melons!" I yelled to Good, who was next me; and in another minute his false teeth were fixed in one of them.

I think we ate about six each before we had done, and poor fruit as they were, I doubt if I ever thought anything nicer.

But melons are not very nutritious, and when we had satisfied our thirst with their pulpy substance, and put a stock to cool by the simple process of cutting them in two and setting them end on in the hot sun to grow cold by evaporation, we began to feel exceedingly hungry. We had still some biltong left, but our stomachs turned from biltong, and besides, we were obliged to be very sparing of it, for we could not say when we should find more food. Just at this moment a lucky thing chanced. Looking across the desert I saw a flock of about ten large birds flying straight towards us.

"*Skit, Baas, skit!*" "Shoot, master, shoot!" whispered the Hottentot, throwing himself on his face, an example which we all followed.

Then I saw that the birds were a flock of *pauw* or bustards, and that they would pass within fifty yards of my head. Taking one of the repeating Winchesters, I waited till they were nearly over us, and then jumped to my feet. On seeing me the *pauw* bunched up together, as I expected that they would, and I fired two shots straight into the thick of them, and, as luck would have it, brought one down, a fine fellow, that weighed about twenty pounds. In half an hour we had a fire made of dry melon stalks, and he was toasting over it, and we made such a feed as we had not tasted for a week. We ate that *pauw*; nothing was left of him but his leg-bones and his beak, and we felt not a little the better afterwards.

That night we went on again with the moon, carrying as many melons as we could with us. As we ascended we found the air grew cooler and cooler, which was a great relief to us, and at dawn, so far as we could judge, we were not more than about a dozen miles from the snow line. Here we discovered more melons, and so had no longer any anxiety about water, for we knew that we should soon get plenty of snow. But the ascent had now become very precipitous, and we made but slow progress, not more than a mile an hour. Also that night we ate our last morsel of biltong. As yet, with the exception of the *pauw*, we had seen no living thing on the mountain, nor had we come across a single spring or stream of water, which struck us as very odd, considering the expanse of snow above us, which must, we thought, melt sometimes. But as we afterwards discovered, owing to a cause which it is quite beyond my power to explain, all the streams flowed down upon the north side of the mountains.

Now we began to grow very anxious about food. We had escaped death by thirst, but it seemed probable that it was only to die of hunger. The events of the next three miserable days are best described by copying the entries made at the time in my note-book.

"21st May.—Started 11 a.m., finding the atmosphere quite cold enough to travel by day, and carrying some water-melons with us. Struggled on all day, but found no more melons, having evidently passed out of their district. Saw no game of any sort. Halted for the night at sundown, having had no food for many hours. Suffered much during the night from cold.

"22nd.—Started at sunrise again, feeling very faint and weak. Only made about five miles all day; found some patches of snow, of which we ate, but nothing else. Camped at night under the edge of a great plateau. Cold bitter. Drank a little brandy each, and huddled ourselves together, each wrapped up in his blanket, to keep ourselves alive. Are now suffering frightfully from starvation and weariness. Thought that Ventvogel would have died during the night.

"23rd.—Struggled forward once more as soon as the sun was well up, and had thawed our limbs a little. We are now in a dreadful plight, and I fear that unless we get food this will be our last day's journey. But little brandy left. Good, Sir Henry, and Umbopa bear up wonderfully, but Ventvogel is in a very bad way. Like most Hottentots, he cannot stand cold. Pangs of hunger not so bad, but have a sort of numb feeling about the stomach. Others say the same. We are now on a level with the precipitous chain, or wall of lava, linking the two Breasts, and the view is glorious. Behind us the glowing desert rolls away to the horizon, and before us lie mile upon mile of smooth hard snow almost level, but swelling gently upwards, out of the centre of which the nipple of the mountain, that appears to be some miles in circumference, rises about four thousand feet into the sky. Not a living thing is to be seen. God help us; I fear that our time has come."

And now I will drop the journal, partly because it is not very interesting reading; also what follows requires telling rather more fully.

All that day—the 23rd May—we struggled slowly up the incline of snow, lying down from time to time to rest. A strange gaunt crew we must have looked, while, laden as we were, we dragged our weary feet over the dazzling plain, glaring round us with hungry eyes. Not that there was much use in glaring, for we could see nothing to eat. We did not accomplish more than seven miles that day. Just before sunset we found ourselves exactly under the nipple of Sheba's left Breast, which towered thousands of feet into the air, a vast smooth hillock of frozen snow. Weak as we were, we could not but appreciate the wonderful scene, made even more splendid by the flying rays of light from the setting sun, which here and there stained the snow blood-red, and crowned the great dome above us with a diadem of glory.

"I say," gasped Good, presently, "we ought to be somewhere near that cave the old gentleman wrote about."

"Yes," said I, "if there is a cave."

"Come, Quatermain," groaned Sir Henry, "don't talk like that; I have every faith in the Dom; remember the water! We shall find the place soon."

"If we don't find it before dark we are dead men, that is all about it," was my consolatory reply.

For the next ten minutes we trudged in silence, when suddenly Umbopa, who was marching along beside me, wrapped in his blanket, and with a leather belt strapped so tightly round his stomach, to "make his hunger small," as he said, that his waist looked like a girl's, caught me by the arm.

"Look!" he said, pointing towards the springing slope of the nipple.

I followed his glance, and some two hundred yards from us perceived what appeared to be a hole in the snow.

"It is the cave," said Umbopa.

We made the best of our way to the spot, and found sure enough that the hole was the mouth of a cavern, no doubt the same as that of which da Silvestra wrote. We were not too soon, for just as we reached shelter the sun went down with startling rapidity, leaving the world nearly dark, for in these latitudes there is but little twilight. So we crept into the cave, which did not appear to be very big, and huddling ourselves together for warmth, swallowed what remained of our brandy—barely a mouthful each—and tried to forget our miseries in sleep. But the cold was too intense to allow us to do so, for I am convinced that at this great altitude the thermometer cannot have marked less than fourteen or fifteen degrees below freezing point. What such a temperature meant to us, enervated as we were by hardship, want of food, and the great heat of the desert, the reader may imagine better than I can describe. Suffice it to say that it was something as near death from exposure as I have ever felt. There we sat hour after hour through the still and bitter night, feeling the frost wander round and nip us now in the finger, now in the foot, now in the face. In vain did we huddle up closer and closer; there was no warmth in our miserable starved carcases. Sometimes one of us would drop into an uneasy slumber for a few minutes, but we could not sleep much, and perhaps this was fortunate, for if we had I doubt if we should have ever woke again. Indeed, I believe that it was only by force of will that we kept ourselves alive at all.

Not very long before dawn I heard the Hottentot Ventvogel, whose teeth had been chattering all night like castanets, give a deep sigh. Then his teeth stopped chattering. I did not think anything of it at the time, concluding that he had gone to sleep. His back was resting against mine, and it seemed to grow colder and colder, till at last it felt like ice.

At length the air began to grow grey with light, then golden arrows sped across the snow, and at last the glorious sun peeped above the lava wall and looked in upon our half-frozen forms. Also it looked upon Ventvogel, sitting there amongst us, *stone dead*. No wonder his back felt cold, poor fellow. He had died when I heard him sigh, and was now frozen almost stiff. Shocked beyond measure, we dragged ourselves from the corpse—how strange is that horror we mortals have of the companionship of a dead body—and left it sitting there, its arms clasped about its knees.

By this time the sunlight was pouring its cold rays, for here they were cold, straight into the mouth of the cave. Suddenly I heard an exclamation of fear from someone, and turned my head.

And this is what I saw: Sitting at the end of the cavern—it was not more than twenty feet long—was another form, of which the head rested on its chest and the long arms hung down. I stared at it, and saw that this too was a *dead man*, and, what was more, a white man.

The others saw also, and the sight proved too much for our shattered nerves. One and all we scrambled out of the cave as fast as our half- frozen limbs would carry us.

Solomon's Road

Outside the cavern we halted, feeling rather foolish.

"I am going back," said Sir Henry.

"Why?" asked Good.

"Because it has struck me that—what we saw—may be my brother."

This was a new idea, and we re-entered the place to put it to the proof. After the bright light outside, our eyes, weak as they were with staring at the snow, could not pierce the gloom of the cave for a while. Presently, however, they grew accustomed to the semi-darkness, and we advanced towards the dead man.

Sir Henry knelt down and peered into his face.

"Thank God," he said, with a sigh of relief, "it is *not* my brother."

Then I drew near and looked. The body was that of a tall man in middle life with aquiline features, grizzled hair, and a long black moustache. The skin was perfectly yellow, and stretched tightly over the bones. Its clothing, with the exception of what seemed to be the remains of a woollen pair of hose, had been removed, leaving the skeleton-like frame naked. Round the neck of the corpse, which was frozen perfectly stiff, hung a yellow ivory crucifix.

"Who on earth can it be?" said I.

"Can't you guess?" asked Good.

I shook my head.

"Why, the old Dom, Jose da Silvestra, of course—who else?"

"Impossible," I gasped; "he died three hundred years ago."

"And what is there to prevent him from lasting for three thousand years in this atmosphere, I should like to know?" asked Good. "If only the temperature is sufficiently low, flesh and blood will keep fresh as New Zealand mutton for ever, and Heaven knows it is cold enough here. The sun never gets in here; no animal comes here to tear or destroy. No doubt his slave, of whom he speaks on the writing, took off his clothes and left him. He could not have buried him alone. Look!" he went on, stooping down to pick up a queerly-shaped bone scraped at the end into a sharp point, "here is the 'cleft bone' that Silvestra used to draw the map with."

We gazed for a moment astonished, forgetting our own miseries in this extraordinary and, as it seemed to us, semi-miraculous sight.

"Ay," said Sir Henry, "and this is where he got his ink from," and he pointed to a small wound on the Dom's left arm. "Did ever man see such a thing before?"

There was no longer any doubt about the matter, which for my own part I confess perfectly appalled me. There he sat, the dead man, whose directions, written some ten generations ago, had led us to this spot. Here in my own hand was the rude pen with which he had written them, and about his neck hung the crucifix that his dying lips had kissed. Gazing at him, my imagination could reconstruct the last scene of the drama, the traveller dying of cold and starvation, yet striving to convey to the world the great secret which he had discovered:—the awful loneliness of his death, of which the evidence sat before us. It even seemed to me that I could trace in his strongly-marked features a likeness to those of my poor friend Silvestre his descendant, who had died twenty years before in my arms, but perhaps that was fancy. At any rate, there he sat, a sad memento of the fate that so often overtakes those who would penetrate into the unknown; and there doubtless he will still sit, crowned with the dread majesty of death, for centuries yet unborn, to startle the eyes of wanderers like ourselves, if ever any such should come again to invade his loneliness. The thing overpowered us, already almost perished as we were with cold and hunger.

"Let us go," said Sir Henry in a low voice; "stay, we will give him a companion," and lifting up the dead body of the Hottentot Ventvogel, he placed it near to that of the old Dom. Then he stooped, and with a jerk broke the rotten string of the crucifix which hung round da Silvestra's neck, for his fingers were too cold to attempt to unfasten it. I believe that he has it still. I took the bone pen, and it is before me as I write—sometimes I use it to sign my name.

Then leaving these two, the proud white man of a past age, and the poor Hottentot, to keep their eternal vigil in the midst of the eternal snows, we crept out of the cave into the welcome sunshine and resumed our path, wondering in our hearts how many hours it would be before we were even as they are.

When we had walked about half a mile we came to the edge of the plateau, for the nipple of the mountain does not rise out of its exact centre, though from the desert side it had seemed to do so. What lay below us we could not see, for the landscape was wreathed in billows of morning fog. Presently, however, the higher layers of mist cleared a little, and revealed, at the end of a long slope of snow, a patch of green grass, some five hundred yards beneath us, through which a stream was running. Nor was this all. By the stream, basking in the bright sun, stood and lay a group of from ten to fifteen *large antelopes*—at that distance we could not see of what species.

The sight filled us with an unreasoning joy. If only we could get it, there was food in plenty. But the question was how to do so. The beasts were fully six hundred yards off, a very long shot, and one not to be depended on when our lives hung on the results.

Rapidly we discussed the advisability of trying to stalk the game, but in the end dismissed it reluctantly. To begin with, the wind was not favourable, and further, we must certainly be perceived, however careful we were, against the blinding background of snow, which we should be obliged to traverse.

"Well, we must have a try from where we are," said Sir Henry. "Which shall it be, Quatermain, the repeating rifles or the expresses?"

Here again was a question. The Winchester repeaters—of which we had two, Umbopa carrying poor Ventvogel's as well as his own—were sighted up to a thousand yards, whereas the expresses were only sighted to three hundred and fifty, beyond which distance shooting with them was more or less guess-work. On the other hand, if they did hit, the express bullets, being "expanding," were much more likely to bring the game down. It was a knotty point, but I made up my mind that we must risk it and use the expresses.

"Let each of us take the buck opposite to him. Aim well at the point of the shoulder and high up," said I; "and Umbopa, do you give the word, so that we may all fire together."

Then came a pause, each of us aiming his level best, as indeed a man is likely to do when he knows that life itself depends upon the shot.

"Fire," said Umbopa in Zulu, and at almost the same instant the three rifles rang out loudly; three clouds of smoke hung for a moment before us, and a hundred echoes went flying over the silent snow. Presently the smoke cleared, and revealed—oh, joy!—a great buck lying on its back and kicking furiously in its death agony. We gave a yell of triumph—we were saved—we should not starve. Weak as we were, we rushed down the intervening slope of snow, and in ten minutes from the time of shooting, that animal's heart and liver were lying before us. But now a new difficulty arose, we had no fuel, and therefore could make no fire to cook them. We gazed at each other in dismay.

"Starving men should not be fanciful," said Good; "we must eat raw meat."

There was no other way out of the dilemma, and our gnawing hunger made the proposition less distasteful than it would otherwise have been. So we took the heart and liver and buried them for a few minutes in a patch of snow to cool them. Then we washed them in the ice-cold water of the stream, and lastly ate them greedily. It sounds horrible enough, but honestly, I never tasted anything so good as that raw meat. In a quarter of an hour we were changed men. Our life and vigour came back to us, our feeble pulses grew strong again, and the blood went coursing through our veins. But mindful of the results of over- feeding on starved stomachs, we were careful not to eat too much, stopping whilst we were still hungry.

"Thank Heaven!" said Sir Henry; "that brute has saved our lives. What is it, Quatermain?"

I rose and went to look at the antelope, for I was not certain. It was about the size of a donkey, with large curved horns. I had never seen one like it before; the species was new to me. It was brown in colour, with faint red stripes, and grew a thick coat. I afterwards discovered that the natives of that wonderful country call these bucks "inco." They are very rare, and only found at a great altitude where no other game will live. This animal was fairly hit high up in the shoulder, though whose bullet brought it down we could not, of course, discover. I believe that Good, mindful of his marvellous shot at the giraffe, secretly set it down to his own prowess, and we did not contradict him.

We had been so busy satisfying our hunger that hitherto we had not found time to look about us. But now, having set Umbopa to cut off as much of the best meat as we were likely to be able to carry, we began to inspect our surroundings. The mist had cleared away, for it was eight o'clock, and the sun had sucked it up, so we were able to take in all the country before us at a glance. I know not how to describe the glorious panorama which unfolded itself to our gaze. I have never seen anything like it before, nor shall, I suppose, again.

Behind and over us towered Sheba's snowy Breasts, and below, some five thousand feet beneath where we stood, lay league on league of the most lovely champaign country. Here were dense patches of lofty forest, there a great river wound its silvery way. To the left stretched a vast expanse of rich, undulating veld or grass land, whereon we could just make out countless herds of game or cattle, at that distance we could not tell which. This expanse appeared to be ringed in by a wall of distant mountains. To the right the country was more or less mountainous; that is, solitary hills stood up from its level, with stretches of cultivated land between, amongst which we could see groups of dome-shaped huts. The landscape lay before us as a map, wherein rivers flashed like silver snakes, and Alp-like peaks crowned with wildly twisted snow wreaths rose in grandeur, whilst over all was the glad sunlight and the breath of Nature's happy life.

Two curious things struck us as we gazed. First, that the country before us must lie at least three thousand feet higher than the desert we had crossed, and secondly, that all the rivers flowed from south to north. As we had painful reason to know, there was no water upon the southern side of the vast range on which we stood, but on the northern face were many streams, most of which appeared to unite with the great river we could see winding away farther than our eyes could follow.

We sat down for a while and gazed in silence at this wonderful view. Presently Sir Henry spoke.

"Isn't there something on the map about Solomon's Great Road?" he said.

I nodded, for I was still gazing out over the far country.

"Well, look; there it is!" and he pointed a little to our right.

Good and I looked accordingly, and there, winding away towards the plain, was what appeared to be a wide turnpike road. We had not seen it at first because, on reaching the plain, it turned behind some broken country. We did not say anything, at least, not much; we were beginning to lose the sense of wonder. Somehow it did not seem particularly unnatural that we should find a sort of Roman road in this strange land. We accepted the fact, that was all.

"Well," said Good, "it must be quite near us if we cut off to the right. Hadn't we better be making a start?"

This was sound advice, and so soon as we had washed our faces and hands in the stream we acted on it. For a mile or more we made our way over boulders and across patches of snow, till suddenly, on reaching the top of the little rise, we found the road at our feet. It was a splendid road cut out of the solid rock, at least fifty feet wide, and apparently well kept; though the odd thing was that it seemed to begin there. We walked down and stood on it, but one single hundred paces behind us, in the direction of Sheba's Breasts, it vanished, the entire surface of the mountain being strewn with boulders interspersed with patches of snow.

"What do you make of this, Quatermain?" asked Sir Henry.

I shook my head, I could make nothing of the thing.

"I have it!" said Good; "the road no doubt ran right over the range and across the desert on the other side, but the sand there has covered it up, and above us it has been obliterated by some volcanic eruption of molten lava."

This seemed a good suggestion; at any rate, we accepted it, and proceeded down the mountain. It proved a very different business travelling along down hill on that magnificent pathway with full stomachs from what it was travelling uphill over the snow quite starved and almost frozen. Indeed, had it not been for melancholy recollections of poor Ventvogel's sad fate, and of that grim cave where he kept company with the old Dom, we should have felt positively cheerful, notwithstanding the sense of unknown dangers before us. Every mile we walked the atmosphere grew softer and balmier, and the country before us shone with a yet more luminous beauty. As for the road itself, I never saw such an engineering work, though Sir Henry said that the great road over the St. Gothard in Switzerland is very similar. No difficulty had been too great for the Old World engineer who laid it out. At one place we came to a ravine three hundred feet broad and at least a hundred feet deep. This vast gulf was actually filled in with huge blocks of dressed stone, having arches pierced through them at the bottom for a waterway, over which the road went on sublimely. At another place it was cut in zigzags out of the side of a precipice five hundred feet deep, and in a third it tunnelled through the base of an intervening ridge, a space of thirty yards or more.

Here we noticed that the sides of the tunnel were covered with quaint sculptures, mostly of mailed figures driving in chariots. One, which was exceedingly beautiful, represented a whole battle scene with a convoy of captives being marched off in the distance.

"Well," said Sir Henry, after inspecting this ancient work of art, "it is very well to call this Solomon's Road, but my humble opinion is that the Egyptians had been here before Solomon's people ever set a foot on it. If this isn't Egyptian or Phoenician handiwork, I must say that it is very like it."

By midday we had advanced sufficiently down the mountain to search the region where wood was to be met with. First we came to scattered bushes which grew more and more frequent, till at last we found the road winding through a vast grove of silver trees similar to those which are to be seen on the slopes of Table Mountain at Cape Town. I had never before met with them in all my wanderings, except at the Cape, and their appearance here astonished me greatly.

"Ah!" said Good, surveying these shining-leaved trees with evident enthusiasm, "here is lots of wood, let us stop and cook some dinner; I have about digested that raw heart."

Nobody objected to this, so leaving the road we made our way to a stream which was babbling away not far off, and soon had a goodly fire of dry boughs blazing. Cutting off some substantial hunks from the flesh of the *inco* which we had brought with us, we proceeded to toast them on the end of sharp sticks, as one sees the Kafirs do, and ate them with relish. After filling ourselves, we lit our pipes and gave ourselves up to enjoyment that, compared with the hardships we had recently undergone, seemed almost heavenly.

The brook, of which the banks were clothed with dense masses of a gigantic species of maidenhair fern interspersed with feathery tufts of wild asparagus, sung merrily at our side, the soft air murmured through the leaves of the silver trees, doves cooed around, and bright-winged birds flashed like living gems from bough to bough. It was a Paradise.

The magic of the place combined with an overwhelming sense of dangers left behind, and of the promised land reached at last, seemed to charm us into silence. Sir Henry and Umbopa sat conversing in a mixture of broken English and Kitchen Zulu in a low voice, but earnestly enough, and I lay, with my eyes half shut, upon that fragrant bed of fern and watched them.

Presently I missed Good, and I looked to see what had become of him. Soon I observed him sitting by the bank of the stream, in which he had been bathing. He had nothing on but his flannel shirt, and his natural habits of extreme neatness having reasserted themselves, he was actively employed in making a most elaborate toilet. He had washed his gutta-percha collar, had thoroughly shaken out his trousers, coat and waistcoat, and was now folding them up neatly till he was ready to put them on, shaking his head sadly as he scanned the numerous rents and tears in them, which naturally had resulted from our frightful journey. Then he took his boots, scrubbed them with a handful of fern, and finally rubbed them over with a piece of fat, which he had carefully saved from the *inco* meat, till they looked, comparatively speaking, respectable. Having inspected them judiciously through his eye-glass, he put the boots on and began a fresh operation. From a little bag that he carried he produced a pocket-comb in which was fixed a tiny looking-glass, and in this he surveyed himself. Apparently he was not satisfied, for he proceeded to do his hair with great care. Then came a pause whilst he again contemplated the effect; still it was not satisfactory. He felt his chin, on which the accumulated scrub of a ten days' beard was flourishing.

"Surely," thought I, "he is not going to try to shave." But so it was. Taking the piece of fat with which he had greased his boots, Good washed it thoroughly in the stream. Then diving again into the bag he brought out a little pocket razor with a guard to it, such as are bought by people who are afraid of cutting themselves, or by those about to undertake a sea voyage. Then he rubbed his face and chin vigorously with the fat and began. Evidently it proved a painful process, for he groaned very much over it, and I was convulsed with inward laughter as I watched him struggling with that stubbly beard. It seemed so very odd that a man should take the trouble to shave himself with a piece of fat in such a place and in our circumstances. At last he succeeded in getting the hair off the right side of his face and chin, when suddenly I, who was watching, became conscious of a flash of light that passed just by his head.

Good sprang up with a profane exclamation (if it had not been a safety razor he would certainly have cut his throat), and so did I, without the exclamation, and this was what I saw. Standing not more than twenty paces from where I was, and ten from Good, were a group of men. They were very tall and copper-coloured, and some of them wore great plumes of black feathers and short cloaks of leopard skins; this was all I noticed at the moment. In front of them stood a youth of about seventeen, his hand still raised and his body bent forward in the attitude of a Grecian statue of a spear-thrower. Evidently the flash of light had been caused by a weapon which he had hurled.

As I looked an old soldier-like man stepped forward out of the group, and catching the youth by the arm said something to him. Then they advanced upon us.

Sir Henry, Good, and Umbopa by this time had seized their rifles and lifted them threateningly. The party of natives still came on. It struck me that they could not know what rifles were, or they would not have treated them with such contempt.

"Put down your guns!" I hallooed to the others, seeing that our only chance of safety lay in conciliation. They obeyed, and walking to the front I addressed the elderly man who had checked the youth.

"Greeting," I said in Zulu, not knowing what language to use. To my surprise I was understood.

"Greeting," answered the old man, not, indeed, in the same tongue, but in a dialect so closely allied to it that neither Umbopa nor myself had any difficulty in understanding him. Indeed, as we afterwards found out, the language spoken by this people is an old-fashioned form of the Zulu tongue, bearing about the same relationship to it that the English of Chaucer does to the English of the nineteenth century.

"Whence come you?" he went on, "who are you? and why are the faces of three of you white, and the face of the fourth as the face of our mother's sons?" and he pointed to Umbopa. I looked at Umbopa as he said it, and it flashed across me that he was right. The face of Umbopa was like the faces of the men before me, and so was his great form like their forms. But I had not time to reflect on this coincidence.

"We are strangers, and come in peace," I answered, speaking very slowly, so that he might understand me, "and this man is our servant."

"You lie," he answered; "no strangers can cross the mountains where all things perish. But what do your lies matter?—if ye are strangers then ye must die, for no strangers may live in the land of the Kukuanas. It is the king's law. Prepare then to die, O strangers!"

I was slightly staggered at this, more especially as I saw the hands of some of the men steal down to their sides, where hung on each what looked to me like a large and heavy knife.

"What does that beggar say?" asked Good.

"He says we are going to be killed," I answered grimly.

"Oh, Lord!" groaned Good; and, as was his way when perplexed, he put his hand to his false teeth, dragging the top set down and allowing them to fly back to his jaw with a snap. It was a most fortunate move, for next second the dignified crowd of Kukuanas uttered a simultaneous yell of horror, and bolted back some yards.

"What's up?" said I.

"It's his teeth," whispered Sir Henry excitedly. "He moved them. Take them out, Good, take them out!"

He obeyed, slipping the set into the sleeve of his flannel shirt.

In another second curiosity had overcome fear, and the men advanced slowly. Apparently they had now forgotten their amiable intention of killing us.

"How is it, O strangers," asked the old man solemnly, "that this fat man (pointing to Good, who was clad in nothing but boots and a flannel shirt, and had only half finished his shaving), whose body is clothed, and whose legs are bare, who grows hair on one side of his sickly face and not on the other, and who wears one shining and transparent eye— how is it, I ask, that he has teeth which move of themselves, coming away from the jaws and returning of their own will?"

"Open your mouth," I said to Good, who promptly curled up his lips and grinned at the old gentleman like an angry dog, revealing to his astonished gaze two thin red lines of gum as utterly innocent of ivories as a new-born elephant. The audience gasped.

"Where are his teeth?" they shouted; "with our eyes we saw them."

Turning his head slowly and with a gesture of ineffable contempt, Good swept his hand across his mouth. Then he grinned again, and lo, there were two rows of lovely teeth.

Now the young man who had flung the knife threw himself down on the grass and gave vent to a prolonged howl of terror; and as for the old gentleman, his knees knocked together with fear.

"I see that ye are spirits," he said falteringly; "did ever man born of woman have hair on one side of his face and not on the other, or a round and transparent eye, or teeth which moved and melted away and grew again? Pardon us, O my lords."

Here was luck indeed, and, needless to say, I jumped at the chance.

"It is granted," I said with an imperial smile. "Nay, ye shall know the truth. We come from another world, though we are men such as ye; we come," I went on, "from the biggest star that shines at night."

"Oh! oh!" groaned the chorus of astonished aborigines.

"Yes," I went on, "we do, indeed"; and again I smiled benignly, as I uttered that amazing lie. "We come to stay with you a little while, and to bless you by our sojourn. Ye will see, O friends, that I have prepared myself for this visit by the learning of your language."

"It is so, it is so," said the chorus.

"Only, my lord," put in the old gentleman, "thou hast learnt it very badly."

I cast an indignant glance at him, and he quailed.

"Now friends," I continued, "ye might think that after so long a journey we should find it in our hearts to avenge such a reception, mayhap to strike cold in death the imperious hand that—that, in short —threw a knife at the head of him whose teeth come and go."

"Spare him, my lords," said the old man in supplication; "he is the king's son, and I am his uncle. If anything befalls him his blood will be required at my hands."

"Yes, that is certainly so," put in the young man with great emphasis.

"Ye may perhaps doubt our power to avenge," I went on, heedless of this by-play. "Stay, I will show you. Here, thou dog and slave (addressing Umbopa in a savage tone), give me the magic tube that speaks"; and I tipped a wink towards my express rifle.

Umbopa rose to the occasion, and with something as nearly resembling a grin as I have ever seen on his dignified face he handed me the gun.

"It is here, O Lord of Lords," he said with a deep obeisance.

Now just before I had asked for the rifle I had perceived a little *klipspringer* antelope standing on a mass of rock about seventy yards away, and determined to risk the shot.

"Ye see that buck," I said, pointing the animal out to the party before me. "Tell me, is it possible for man born of woman to kill it from here with a noise?"

"It is not possible, my lord," answered the old man.

"Yet shall I kill it," I said quietly.

The old man smiled. "That my lord cannot do," he answered.

I raised the rifle and covered the buck. It was a small animal, and one which a man might well be excused for missing, but I knew that it would not do to miss.

I drew a deep breath, and slowly pressed on the trigger. The buck stood still as a stone.

"Bang! thud!" The antelope sprang into the air and fell on the rock dead as a door nail.

A groan of simultaneous terror burst from the group before us.

"If you want meat," I remarked coolly, "go fetch that buck."

The old man made a sign, and one of his followers departed, and presently returned bearing the *klipspringer*. I noticed with satisfaction that I had hit it fairly behind the shoulder. They gathered round the poor creature's body, gazing at the bullet-hole in consternation.

"Ye see," I said, "I do not speak empty words."

There was no answer.

"If ye yet doubt our power," I went on, "let one of you go stand upon that rock that I may make him as this buck."

None of them seemed at all inclined to take the hint, till at last the king's son spoke.

"It is well said. Do thou, my uncle, go stand upon the rock. It is but a buck that the magic has killed. Surely it cannot kill a man."

The old gentleman did not take the suggestion in good part. Indeed, he seemed hurt.

"No! no!" he ejaculated hastily, "my old eyes have seen enough. These are wizards, indeed. Let us bring them to the king. Yet if any should wish a further proof, let *him* stand upon the rock, that the magic tube may speak with him."

There was a most general and hasty expression of dissent.

"Let not good magic be wasted on our poor bodies," said one; "we are satisfied. All the witchcraft of our people cannot show the like of this."

"It is so," remarked the old gentleman, in a tone of intense relief; "without any doubt it is so. Listen, children of the Stars, children of the shining Eye and the movable Teeth, who roar out in thunder, and slay from afar. I am Infadoos, son of Kafa, once king of the Kukuana people. This youth is Scragga."

"He nearly scragged me," murmured Good.

"Scragga, son of Twala, the great king—Twala, husband of a thousand wives, chief and lord paramount of the Kukuanas, keeper of the great Road, terror of his enemies, student of the Black Arts, leader of a hundred thousand warriors, Twala the One-eyed, the Black, the Terrible."

"So," said I superciliously, "lead us then to Twala. We do not talk with low people and underlings."

"It is well, my lords, we will lead you; but the way is long. We are hunting three days' journey from the place of the king. But let my lords have patience, and we will lead them."

"So be it," I said carelessly; "all time is before us, for we do not die. We are ready, lead on. But Infadoos, and thou Scragga, beware! Play us no monkey tricks, set for us no foxes' snares, for before your brains of mud have thought of them we shall know and avenge. The light of the transparent eye of him with the bare legs and the half-haired face shall destroy you, and go through your land; his vanishing teeth shall affix themselves fast in you and eat you up, you and your wives and children; the magic tubes shall argue with you loudly, and make you as sieves. Beware!"

This magnificent address did not fail of its effect; indeed, it might almost have been spared, so deeply were our friends already impressed with our powers.

The old man made a deep obeisance, and murmured the words, "*Koom Koom,*" which I afterwards discovered was their royal salute, corresponding to the *Bayete* of the Zulus, and turning, addressed his followers. These at once proceeded to lay hold of all our goods and chattels, in order to bear them for us, excepting only the guns, which they would on no account touch. They even seized Good's clothes, that, as the reader may remember, were neatly folded up beside him.

He saw and made a dive for them, and a loud altercation ensued.

"Let not my lord of the transparent Eye and the melting Teeth touch them," said the old man. "Surely his slave shall carry the things."

"But I want to put 'em on!" roared Good, in nervous English.

Umbopa translated.

"Nay, my lord," answered Infadoos, "would my lord cover up his beautiful white legs (although he is so dark Good has a singularly white skin) from the eyes of his servants? Have we offended my lord that he should do such a thing?"

Here I nearly exploded with laughing; and meanwhile one of the men started on with the garments.

"Damn it!" roared Good, "that black villain has got my trousers."

"Look here, Good," said Sir Henry; "you have appeared in this country in a certain character, and you must live up to it. It will never do for you to put on trousers again. Henceforth you must exist in a flannel shirt, a pair of boots, and an eye-glass."

"Yes," I said, "and with whiskers on one side of your face and not on the other. If you change any of these things the people will think that we are impostors. I am very sorry for you, but, seriously, you must. If once they begin to suspect us our lives will not be worth a brass farthing."

"Do you really think so?" said Good gloomily.

"I do, indeed. Your 'beautiful white legs' and your eye-glass are now *the* features of our party, and as Sir Henry says, you must live up to them. Be thankful that you have got your boots on, and that the air is warm."

Good sighed, and said no more, but it took him a fortnight to become accustomed to his new and scant attire.

We Enter Kukuanaland

All that afternoon we travelled along the magnificent roadway, which trended steadily in a north-westerly direction. Infadoos and Scragga walked with us, but their followers marched about one hundred paces ahead.

"Infadoos," I said at length, "who made this road?"

"It was made, my lord, of old time, none know how or when, not even the wise woman Gagool, who has lived for generations. We are not old enough to remember its making. None can fashion such roads now, but the king suffers no grass to grow upon it."

"And whose are the writings on the wall of the caves through which we have passed on the road?" I asked, referring to the Egyptian-like sculptures that we had seen.

"My lord, the hands that made the road wrote the wonderful writings. We know not who wrote them."

"When did the Kukuana people come into this country?"

"My lord, the race came down here like the breath of a storm ten thousand thousand moons ago, from the great lands which lie there beyond," and he pointed to the north. "They could travel no further because of the high mountains which ring in the land, so say the old voices of our fathers that have descended to us the children, and so says Gagool, the wise woman, the smeller out of witches," and again he pointed to the snow-clad peaks. "The country, too, was good, so they settled here and grew strong and powerful, and now our numbers are like the sea sand, and when Twala the king calls up his regiments their plumes cover the plain so far as the eye of man can reach."

"And if the land is walled in with mountains, who is there for the regiments to fight with?"

"Nay, my lord, the country is open there towards the north, and now and again warriors sweep down upon us in clouds from a land we know not, and we slay them. It is the third part of the life of a man since there was a war. Many thousands died in it, but we destroyed those who came to eat us up. So since then there has been no war."

"Your warriors must grow weary of resting on their spears, Infadoos."

"My lord, there was one war, just after we destroyed the people that came down upon us, but it was a civil war; dog ate dog."

"How was that?"

"My lord the king, my half-brother, had a brother born at the same birth, and of the same woman. It is not our custom, my lord, to suffer twins to live; the weaker must always die. But the mother of the king hid away the feebler child, which was born the last, for her heart yearned over it, and that child is Twala the king. I am his younger brother, born of another wife."

"Well?"

"My lord, Kafa, our father, died when we came to manhood, and my brother Imotu was made king in his place, and for a space reigned and had a son by his favourite wife. When the babe was three years old, just after the great war, during which no man could sow or reap, a famine came upon the land, and the people murmured because of the famine, and looked round like a starved lion for something to rend. Then it was that Gagool, the wise and terrible woman, who does not die, made a proclamation to the people, saying, 'The king Imotu is no king.' And at the time Imotu was sick with a wound, and lay in his kraal not able to move.

"Then Gagool went into a hut and led out Twala, my half-brother, and twin brother to the king, whom she had hidden among the caves and rocks since he was born, and stripping the 'moocha' (waist-cloth) off his loins, showed the people of the Kukuanas the mark of the sacred snake coiled round his middle, wherewith the eldest son of the king is marked at birth, and cried out loud, 'Behold your king whom I have saved for you even to this day!'

"Now the people being mad with hunger, and altogether bereft of reason and the knowledge of truth, cried out—'The king! The king!' but I knew that it was not so, for Imotu my brother was the elder of the twins, and our lawful king. Then just as the tumult was at its height Imotu the king, though he was very sick, crawled from his hut holding his wife by the hand, and followed by his little son Ignosi—that is, by interpretation, the Lightning.

"'What is this noise?' he asked. 'Why cry ye The king! The king!'

"Then Twala, his twin brother, born of the same woman, and in the same hour, ran to him, and taking him by the hair, stabbed him through the heart with his knife. And the people being fickle, and ever ready to worship the rising sun, clapped their hands and cried, 'Twala is king! Now we know that Twala is king!'"

"And what became of Imotu's wife and her son Ignosi? Did Twala kill them too?"

"Nay, my lord. When she saw that her lord was dead the queen seized the child with a cry and ran away. Two days afterward she came to a kraal very hungry, and none would give her milk or food, now that her lord the king was dead, for all men hate the unfortunate. But at nightfall a little child, a girl, crept out and brought her corn to eat, and she blessed the child, and went on towards the mountains with her boy before the sun rose again, and there she must have perished, for none have seen her since, nor the child Ignosi."

"Then if this child Ignosi had lived he would be the true king of the Kukuana people?"

"That is so, my lord; the sacred snake is round his middle. If he lives he is king; but, alas! he is long dead."

"See, my lord," and Infadoos pointed to a vast collection of huts surrounded by a fence, which was in its turn encircled by a great ditch, that lay on the plain beneath us. "That is the kraal where the wife of Imotu was last seen with the child Ignosi. It is there that we shall sleep to-night, if, indeed," he added doubtfully, "my lords sleep at all upon this earth."

"When we are among the Kukuanas, my good friend Infadoos, we do as the Kukuanas do," I said majestically, and turned round quickly to address Good, who was tramping along sullenly behind, his mind fully occupied with unsatisfactory attempts to prevent his flannel shirt from flapping in the evening breeze. To my astonishment I butted into Umbopa, who was walking along immediately behind me, and very evidently had been listening with the greatest interest to my conversation with Infadoos. The expression on his face was most curious, and gave me the idea of a man who was struggling with partial success to bring something long ago forgotten back into his mind.

All this while we had been pressing on at a good rate towards the undulating plain beneath us. The mountains we had crossed now loomed high above our heads, and Sheba's Breasts were veiled modestly in diaphanous wreaths of mist. As we went the country grew more and more lovely. The vegetation was luxuriant, without being tropical; the sun was bright and warm, but not burning; and a gracious breeze blew softly along the odorous slopes of the mountains. Indeed, this new land was little less than an earthly paradise; in beauty, in natural wealth, and in climate I have never seen its like. The Transvaal is a fine country, but it is nothing to Kukuanaland.

So soon as we started Infadoos had despatched a runner to warn the people of the kraal, which, by the way, was in his military command, of our arrival. This man had departed at an extraordinary speed, which Infadoos informed me he would keep up all the way, as running was an exercise much practised among his people.

The result of this message now became apparent. When we arrived within two miles of the kraal we could see that company after company of men were issuing from its gates and marching towards us.

Sir Henry laid his hand upon my arm, and remarked that it looked as though we were going to meet with a warm reception. Something in his tone attracted Infadoos' attention.

"Let not my lords be afraid," he said hastily, "for in my breast there dwells no guile. This regiment is one under my command, and comes out by my orders to greet you."

I nodded easily, though I was not quite easy in my mind.

About half a mile from the gates of this kraal is a long stretch of rising ground sloping gently upwards from the road, and here the companies formed. It was a splendid sight to see them, each company about three hundred strong, charging swiftly up the rise, with flashing spears and waving plumes, to take their appointed place. By the time we reached the slope twelve such companies, or in all three thousand six hundred men, had passed out and taken up their positions along the road.

Presently we came to the first company, and were able to gaze in astonishment on the most magnificent set of warriors that I have ever seen. They were all men of mature age, mostly veterans of about forty, and not one of them was under six feet in height, whilst many stood six feet three or four. They wore upon their heads heavy black plumes of Sakaboola feathers, like those which adorned our guides. About their waists and beneath the right knees were bound circlets of white ox tails, while in their left hands they carried round shields measuring about twenty inches across. These shields are very curious. The framework is made of an iron plate beaten out thin, over which is stretched milk-white ox-hide.

The weapons that each man bore were simple, but most effective, consisting of a short and very heavy two-edged spear with a wooden shaft, the blade being about six inches across at the widest part. These spears are not used for throwing but like the Zulu "*bangwan*," or stabbing assegai, are for close quarters only, when the wound inflicted by them is terrible. In addition to his *bangwan* every man carried three large and heavy knives, each knife weighing about two pounds. One knife was fixed in the ox-tail girdle, and the other two at the back of the round shield. These knives, which are called "*tollas*" by the Kukuanas, take the place of the throwing assegai of the Zulus. The Kukuana warriors can cast them with great accuracy to a distance of fifty yards, and it is their custom on charging to hurl a volley of them at the enemy as they come to close quarters.

Each company remained still as a collection of bronze statues till we were opposite to it, when at a signal given by its commanding officer, who, distinguished by a leopard skin cloak, stood some paces in front, every spear was raised into the air, and from three hundred throats sprang forth with a sudden roar the royal salute of "*Koom*." Then, so soon as we had passed, the company formed up behind us and followed us towards the kraal, till at last the whole regiment of the "Greys"—so called from their white shields—the crack corps of the Kukuana people, was marching in our rear with a tread that shook the ground.

At length, branching off from Solomon's Great Road, we came to the wide fosse surrounding the kraal, which is at least a mile round, and fenced with a strong palisade of piles formed of the trunks of trees. At the gateway this fosse is spanned by a primitive drawbridge, which was let down by the guard to allow us to pass in. The kraal is exceedingly well laid out. Through the centre runs a wide pathway intersected at right angles by other pathways so arranged as to cut the huts into square blocks, each block being the quarters of a company. The huts are dome-shaped, and built, like those of the Zulus, of a framework of wattle, beautifully thatched with grass; but, unlike the Zulu huts, they have doorways through which men could walk. Also they are much larger, and surrounded by a verandah about six feet wide, beautifully paved with powdered lime trodden hard.

All along each side of this wide pathway that pierces the kraal were ranged hundreds of women, brought out by curiosity to look at us. These women, for a native race, are exceedingly handsome. They are tall and graceful, and their figures are wonderfully fine. The hair, though short, is rather curly than woolly, the features are frequently aquiline, and the lips are not unpleasantly thick, as is the case among most African races. But what struck us most was their exceedingly quiet and dignified air. They were as well-bred in their way as the *habituees* of a fashionable drawing-room, and in this respect they differ from Zulu women and their cousins the Masai who inhabit the district beyond

Zanzibar. Their curiosity had brought them out to see us, but they allowed no rude expressions of astonishment or savage criticism to pass their lips as we trudged wearily in front of them. Not even when old Infadoos with a surreptitious motion of the hand pointed out the crowning wonder of poor Good's "beautiful white legs," did they suffer the feeling of intense admiration which evidently mastered their minds to find expression. They fixed their dark eyes upon this new and snowy loveliness, for, as I think I have said, Good's skin is exceedingly white, and that was all. But it was quite enough for Good, who is modest by nature.

When we reached the centre of the kraal, Infadoos halted at the door of a large hut, which was surrounded at a distance by a circle of smaller ones.

"Enter, Sons of the Stars," he said, in a magniloquent voice, "and deign to rest awhile in our humble habitations. A little food shall be brought to you, so that ye may have no need to draw your belts tight from hunger; some honey and some milk, and an ox or two, and a few sheep; not much, my lords, but still a little food."

"It is good," said I. "Infadoos; we are weary with travelling through realms of air; now let us rest."

Accordingly we entered the hut, which we found amply prepared for our comfort. Couches of tanned skins were spread for us to lie on, and water was placed for us to wash in.

Presently we heard a shouting outside, and stepping to the door, saw a line of damsels bearing milk and roasted mealies, and honey in a pot. Behind these were some youths driving a fat young ox. We received the gifts, and then one of the young men drew the knife from his girdle and dexterously cut the ox's throat. In ten minutes it was dead, skinned, and jointed. The best of the meat was then cut off for us, and the rest, in the name of our party, I presented to the warriors round us, who took it and distributed the "white lords' gift."

Umbopa set to work, with the assistance of an extremely prepossessing young woman, to boil our portion in a large earthenware pot over a fire which was built outside the hut, and when it was nearly ready we sent a message to Infadoos, and asked him and Scragga, the king's son, to join us.

Presently they came, and sitting down upon little stools, of which there were several about the hut, for the Kukuanas do not in general squat upon their haunches like the Zulus, they helped us to get through our dinner. The old gentleman was most affable and polite, but it struck me that the young one regarded us with doubt. Together with the rest of the party, he had been overawed by our white appearance and by our magic properties; but it seemed to me that, on discovering that we ate, drank, and slept like other mortals, his awe was beginning to wear off, and to be replaced by a sullen suspicion—which made me feel rather uncomfortable.

In the course of our meal Sir Henry suggested to me that it might be well to try to discover if our hosts knew anything of his brother's fate, or if they had ever seen or heard of him; but, on the whole, I thought that it would be wiser to say nothing of the matter at this time. It was difficult to explain a relative lost from "the Stars."

After supper we produced our pipes and lit them; a proceeding which filled Infadoos and Scragga with astonishment. The Kukuanas were evidently unacquainted with the divine delights of tobacco-smoke. The herb is grown among them extensively; but, like the Zulus, they use it for snuff only, and quite failed to identify it in its new form.

Presently I asked Infadoos when we were to proceed on our journey, and was delighted to learn that preparations had been made for us to leave on the following morning, messengers having already departed to inform Twala the king of our coming.

It appeared that Twala was at his principal place, known as Loo, making ready for the great annual feast which was to be held in the first week of June. At this gathering all the regiments, with the exception of certain detachments left behind for garrison purposes, are brought up and paraded before the king; and the great annual witch-hunt, of which more by-and-by, is held.

We were to start at dawn; and Infadoos, who was to accompany us, expected that we should reach Loo on the night of the second day, unless we were detained by accident or by swollen rivers.

When they had given us this information our visitors bade us good- night; and, having arranged to watch turn and turn about, three of us flung ourselves down and slept the sweet sleep of the weary, whilst the fourth sat up on the look-out for possible treachery.

Twala the King

It will not be necessary for me to detail at length the incidents of our journey to Loo. It took two full days' travelling along Solomon's Great Road, which pursued its even course right into the heart of Kukuanaland. Suffice it to say that as we went the country seemed to grow richer and richer, and the kraals, with their wide surrounding belts of cultivation, more and more numerous. They were all built upon the same principles as the first camp which we had reached, and were guarded by ample garrisons of troops. Indeed, in Kukuanaland, as among the Germans, the Zulus, and the Masai, every able-bodied man is a soldier, so that the whole force of the nation is available for its wars, offensive or defensive. As we travelled we were overtaken by thousands of warriors hurrying up to Loo to be present at the great annual review and festival, and more splendid troops I never saw.

At sunset on the second day, we stopped to rest awhile upon the summit of some heights over which the road ran, and there on a beautiful and fertile plain before us lay Loo itself. For a native town it is an enormous place, quite five miles round, I should say, with outlying kraals projecting from it, that serve on grand occasions as cantonments for the regiments, and a curious horseshoe-shaped hill, with which we were destined to become better acquainted, about two miles to the north. It is beautifully situated, and through the centre of the kraal, dividing it into two portions, runs a river, which appeared to be bridged in several places, the same indeed that we had seen from the slopes of Sheba's Breasts. Sixty or seventy miles away three great snow-capped mountains, placed at the points of a triangle, started out of the level plain. The conformation of these mountains is unlike that of Sheba's Breasts, being sheer and precipitous, instead of smooth and rounded.

Infadoos saw us looking at them, and volunteered a remark.

"The road ends there," he said, pointing to the mountains known among the Kukuanas as the "Three Witches."

"Why does it end?" I asked.

"Who knows?" he answered with a shrug; "the mountains are full of caves, and there is a great pit between them. It is there that the wise men of old time used to go to get whatever it was they came for to this country, and it is there now that our kings are buried in the Place of Death."

"What was it they came for?" I asked eagerly.

"Nay, I know not. My lords who have dropped from the Stars should know," he answered with a quick look. Evidently he knew more than he chose to say.

"Yes," I went on, "you are right, in the Stars we learn many things. I have heard, for instance, that the wise men of old came to these mountains to find bright stones, pretty playthings, and yellow iron."

"My lord is wise," he answered coldly; "I am but a child and cannot talk with my lord on such matters. My lord must speak with Gagool the old, at the king's place, who is wise even as my lord," and he went away.

So soon as he was gone I turned to the others, and pointed out the mountains. "There are Solomon's diamond mines," I said.

Umbopa was standing with them, apparently plunged in one of the fits of abstraction which were common to him, and caught my words.

"Yes, Macumazahn," he put in, in Zulu, "the diamonds are surely there, and you shall have them, since you white men are so fond of toys and money."

"How dost thou know that, Umbopa?" I asked sharply, for I did not like his mysterious ways.

He laughed. "I dreamed it in the night, white men," then he too turned on his heel and went.

"Now what," said Sir Henry, "is our black friend driving at? He knows more than he chooses to say, that is clear. By the way, Quatermain, has he heard anything of—of my brother?"

"Nothing; he has asked everyone he has become friendly with, but they all declare that no white man has ever been seen in the country before."

"Do you suppose that he got here at all?" suggested Good; "we have only reached the place by a miracle; is it likely he could have reached it without the map?"

"I don't know," said Sir Henry gloomily, "but somehow I think that I shall find him."

Slowly the sun sank, then suddenly darkness rushed down on the land like a tangible thing. There was no breathing-space between the day and night, no soft transformation scene, for in these latitudes twilight does not exist. The change from day to night is as quick and as absolute as the change from life to death. The sun sank and the world was wreathed in shadows. But not for long, for see in the west there is a glow, then come rays of silver light, and at last the full and glorious moon lights up the plain and shoots its gleaming arrows far and wide, filling the earth with a faint refulgence.

We stood and watched the lovely sight, whilst the stars grew pale before this chastened majesty, and felt our hearts lifted up in the presence of a beauty that I cannot describe. Mine has been a rough life, but there are a few things I am thankful to have lived for, and one of them is to have seen that moon shine over Kukuanaland.

Presently our meditations were broken in upon by our polite friend Infadoos.

"If my lords are rested we will journey on to Loo, where a hut is made ready for my lords to-night. The moon is now bright, so that we shall not fall by the way."

We assented, and in an hour's time were at the outskirts of the town, of which the extent, mapped out as it was by thousands of camp fires, appeared absolutely endless. Indeed, Good, who is always fond of a bad joke, christened it "Unlimited Loo." Soon we came to a moat with a drawbridge, where we were met by the rattling of arms and the hoarse challenge of a sentry. Infadoos gave some password that I could not catch, which was met with a salute, and we passed on through the central street of the great grass city. After nearly half an hour's tramp, past endless lines of huts, Infadoos halted at last by the gate of a little group of huts which surrounded a small courtyard of powdered limestone, and informed us that these were to be our "poor" quarters.

We entered, and found that a hut had been assigned to each of us. These huts were superior to any that we had yet seen, and in each was a most comfortable bed made of tanned skins, spread upon mattresses of aromatic grass. Food too was ready for us, and so soon as we had washed ourselves with water, which stood ready in earthenware jars, some young women of handsome appearance brought us roasted meats, and mealie cobs daintily served on wooden platters, and presented them to us with deep obeisances.

We ate and drank, and then, the beds having been all moved into one hut by our request, a precaution at which the amiable young ladies smiled, we flung ourselves down to sleep, thoroughly wearied with our long journey.

When we woke it was to find the sun high in the heavens, and the female attendants, who did not seem to be troubled by any false shame, already standing inside the hut, having been ordered to attend and help us to "make ready."

"Make ready, indeed," growled Good; "when one has only a flannel shirt and a pair of boots, that does not take long. I wish you would ask them for my trousers, Quatermain."

I asked accordingly, but was informed that these sacred relics had already been taken to the king, who would see us in the forenoon.

Somewhat to their astonishment and disappointment, having requested the young ladies to step outside, we proceeded to make the best toilet of which the circumstances admitted. Good even went the length of again shaving the right side of his face; the left, on which now appeared a very fair crop of whiskers, we impressed upon him he must on no account touch. As for ourselves, we were contented with a good wash and combing our hair. Sir Henry's yellow locks were now almost upon his shoulders, and he looked more like an ancient Dane than ever, while my grizzled scrub was fully an inch long, instead of half an inch, which in a general way I considered my maximum length.

By the time that we had eaten our breakfast, and smoked a pipe, a message was brought to us by no less a personage than Infadoos himself that Twala the king was ready to see us, if we would be pleased to come.

We remarked in reply that we should prefer to wait till the sun was a little higher, we were yet weary with our journey, etc., etc. It is always well, when dealing with uncivilised people, not to be in too great a hurry. They are apt to mistake politeness for awe or servility. So, although we were quite as anxious to see Twala as Twala could be to see us, we sat down and waited for an hour, employing the interval in preparing such presents as our slender stock of goods permitted—namely, the Winchester rifle which had been used by poor Ventvogel, and some beads. The rifle and ammunition we determined to present to his royal highness, and the beads were for his wives and courtiers.

We had already given a few to Infadoos and Scragga, and found that they were delighted with them, never having seen such things before. At length we declared that we were ready, and guided by Infadoos, started off to the audience, Umbopa carrying the rifle and beads.

After walking a few hundred yards we came to an enclosure, something like that surrounding the huts which had been allotted to us, only fifty times as big, for it could not have covered less than six or seven acres of ground. All round the outside fence stood a row of huts, which were the habitations of the king's wives. Exactly opposite the gateway, on the further side of the open space, was a very large hut, built by itself, in which his majesty resided. All the rest was open ground; that is to say, it would have been open had it not been filled by company after company of warriors, who were mustered there to the number of seven or eight thousand. These men stood still as statues as we advanced through them, and it would be impossible to give an adequate idea of the grandeur of the spectacle which they presented, with their waving plumes, their glancing spears, and iron- backed ox-hide shields.

The space in front of the large hut was empty, but before it were placed several stools. On three of these, at a sign from Infadoos, we seated ourselves, Umbopa standing behind us. As for Infadoos, he took up a position by the door of the hut. So we waited for ten minutes or more in the midst of a dead silence, but conscious that we were the object of the concentrated gaze of some eight thousand pairs of eyes. It was a somewhat trying ordeal, but we carried it off as best we could. At length the door of the hut opened, and a gigantic figure, with a splendid tiger-skin karross flung over its shoulders, stepped out, followed by the boy Scragga, and what appeared to us to be a withered-up monkey, wrapped in a fur cloak. The figure seated itself upon a stool, Scragga took his stand behind it, and the withered-up monkey crept on all fours into the shade of the hut and squatted down.

Still there was silence.

Then the gigantic figure slipped off the karross and stood up before us, a truly alarming spectacle. It was that of an enormous man with the most entirely repulsive countenance we had ever beheld. This man's lips were as thick as a Negro's, the nose was flat, he had but one gleaming black eye, for the other was represented by a hollow in the face, and his whole expression was cruel and sensual to a degree. From the large head rose a magnificent plume of white ostrich feathers, his body was clad in a shirt of shining chain armour, whilst round the waist and right knee were the usual garnishes of white ox-tail. In his right hand was a huge spear, about the neck a thick torque of gold, and bound on the forehead shone dully a single and enormous uncut diamond.

Still there was silence; but not for long. Presently the man, whom we rightly guessed to be the king, raised the great javelin in his hand. Instantly eight thousand spears were lifted in answer, and from eight thousand throats rang out the royal salute of "*Koom.*" Three times this was repeated, and each time the earth shook with the noise, that can only be compared to the deepest notes of thunder.

"Be humble, O people," piped out a thin voice which seemed to come from the monkey in the shade, "it is the king."

"*It is the king*," boomed out the eight thousand throats in answer. "*Be humble, O people, it is the king.*"

Then there was silence again—dead silence. Presently, however, it was broken. A soldier on our left dropped his shield, which fell with a clatter on to the limestone flooring.

Twala turned his one cold eye in the direction of the noise.

"Come hither, thou," he said, in a cold voice.

A fine young man stepped out of the ranks, and stood before him.

"It was thy shield that fell, thou awkward dog. Wilt thou make me a reproach in the eyes of these strangers from the Stars? What hast thou to say for thyself?"

We saw the poor fellow turn pale under his dusky skin.

"It was by chance, O Calf of the Black Cow," he murmured.

"Then it is a chance for which thou must pay. Thou hast made me foolish; prepare for death."

"I am the king's ox," was the low answer.

"Scragga," roared the king, "let me see how thou canst use thy spear. Kill me this blundering fool."

Scragga stepped forward with an ill-favoured grin, and lifted his spear. The poor victim covered his eyes with his hand and stood still. As for us, we were petrified with horror.

"Once, twice," he waved the spear, and then struck, ah! right home— the spear stood out a foot behind the soldier's back. He flung up his hands and dropped dead. From the multitude about us rose something like a murmur, it rolled round and round, and died away. The tragedy was finished; there lay the corpse, and we had not yet realised that it had been enacted. Sir Henry sprang up and swore a great oath, then, overpowered by the sense of silence, sat down again.

"The thrust was a good one," said the king; "take him away."

Four men stepped out of the ranks, and lifting the body of the murdered man, carried it thence.

"Cover up the blood-stains, cover them up," piped out the thin voice that proceeded from the monkey-like figure; "the king's word is spoken, the king's doom is done!"

Thereupon a girl came forward from behind the hut, bearing a jar filled with powdered lime, which she scattered over the red mark, blotting it from sight.

Sir Henry meanwhile was boiling with rage at what had happened; indeed, it was with difficulty that we could keep him still.

"Sit down, for heaven's sake," I whispered; "our lives depend on it."

He yielded and remained quiet.

Twala sat silent until the traces of the tragedy had been removed, then he addressed us.

"White people," he said, "who come hither, whence I know not, and why I know not, greeting."

"Greeting, Twala, King of the Kukuanas," I answered.

"White people, whence come ye, and what seek ye?"

"We come from the Stars, ask us not how. We come to see this land."

"Ye journey from far to see a little thing. And that man with you," pointing to Umbopa, "does he also come from the Stars?"

"Even so; there are people of thy colour in the heavens above; but ask not of matters too high for thee, Twala the king."

"Ye speak with a loud voice, people of the Stars," Twala answered in a tone which I scarcely liked. "Remember that the Stars are far off, and ye are here. How if I make you as him whom they bore away?"

I laughed out loud, though there was little laughter in my heart.

"O king," I said, "be careful, walk warily over hot stones, lest thou shouldst burn thy feet; hold the spear by the handle, lest thou should cut thy hands. Touch but one hair of our heads, and destruction shall come upon thee. What, have not these"—pointing to Infadoos and Scragga, who, young villain that he was, was employed in cleaning the blood of the soldier off his spear—"told thee what manner of men we are? Hast thou seen the like of us?" and I pointed to Good, feeling quite sure that he had never seen anybody before who looked in the least like *him* as he then appeared.

"It is true, I have not," said the king, surveying Good with interest.

"Have they not told thee how we strike with death from afar?" I went on.

"They have told me, but I believe them not. Let me see you kill. Kill me a man among those who stand yonder"—and he pointed to the opposite side of the kraal—"and I will believe."

"Nay," I answered; "we shed no blood of men except in just punishment; but if thou wilt see, bid thy servants drive in an ox through the kraal gates, and before he has run twenty paces I will strike him dead."

"Nay," laughed the king, "kill me a man and I will believe."

"Good, O king, so be it," I answered coolly; "do thou walk across the open space, and before thy feet reach the gate thou shalt be dead; or if thou wilt not, send thy son Scragga" (whom at that moment it would have given me much pleasure to shoot).

On hearing this suggestion Scragga uttered a sort of howl, and bolted into the hut.

Twala frowned majestically; the suggestion did not please him.

"Let a young ox be driven in," he said.

Two men at once departed, running swiftly.

"Now, Sir Henry," said I, "do you shoot. I want to show this ruffian that I am not the only magician of the party."

Sir Henry accordingly took his "express," and made ready.

"I hope I shall make a good shot," he groaned.

"You must," I answered. "If you miss with the first barrel, let him have the second. Sight for 150 yards, and wait till the beast turns broadside on."

Then came a pause, until presently we caught sight of an ox running straight for the kraal gate. It came on through the gate, then, catching sight of the vast concourse of people, stopped stupidly, turned round, and bellowed.

"Now's your time," I whispered.

Up went the rifle.

Bang! *thud*! and the ox was kicking on his back, shot in the ribs. The semi-hollow bullet had done its work well, and a sigh of astonishment went up from the assembled thousands.

I turned round coolly—

"Have I lied, O king?"

"Nay, white man, it is the truth," was the somewhat awed answer.

"Listen, Twala," I went on. "Thou hast seen. Now know we come in peace, not in war. See," and I held up the Winchester repeater; "here is a hollow staff that shall enable thee to kill even as we kill, only I lay this charm upon it, thou shalt kill no man with it. If thou liftest it against a man, it shall kill thee. Stay, I will show thee. Bid a soldier step forty paces and place the shaft of a spear in the ground so that the flat blade looks towards us."

In a few seconds it was done.

"Now, see, I will break yonder spear."

Taking a careful sight I fired. The bullet struck the flat of the spear, and shattered the blade into fragments.

Again the sigh of astonishment went up.

"Now, Twala, we give this magic tube to thee, and by-and-by I will show thee how to use it; but beware how thou turnest the magic of the Stars against a man of earth," and I handed him the rifle.

The king took it very gingerly, and laid it down at his feet. As he did so I observed the wizened monkey-like figure creeping from the shadow of the hut. It crept on all fours, but when it reached the place where the king sat it rose upon its feet, and throwing the furry covering from its face, revealed a most extraordinary and weird countenance. Apparently it was that of a woman of great age so shrunken that in size it seemed no larger than the face of a year-old child, although made up of a number of deep and yellow wrinkles. Set in these wrinkles was a sunken slit, that represented the mouth, beneath which the chin curved outwards to a point. There was no nose to speak of; indeed, the visage might have been taken for that of a sun-dried corpse had it not been for a pair of large black eyes, still full of fire and intelligence, which gleamed and played under the snow-white eyebrows, and the projecting parchment-coloured skull, like jewels in a charnel-house. As for the head itself, it was perfectly bare, and yellow in hue, while its wrinkled scalp moved and contracted like the hood of a cobra.

The figure to which this fearful countenance belonged, a countenance so fearful indeed that it caused a shiver of fear to pass through us as we gazed on it, stood still for a moment. Then suddenly it projected a skinny claw armed with nails nearly an inch long, and laying it on the shoulder of Twala the king, began to speak in a thin and piercing voice—

"Listen, O king! Listen, O warriors! Listen, O mountains and plains and rivers, home of the Kukuana race! Listen, O skies and sun, O rain and storm and mist! Listen, O men and women, O youths and maidens, and O ye babes unborn! Listen, all things that live and must die! Listen, all dead things that shall live again—again to die! Listen, the spirit of life is in me and I prophesy. I prophesy! I prophesy!"

The words died away in a faint wail, and dread seemed to seize upon the hearts of all who heard them, including our own. This old woman was very terrible.

"*Blood! blood! blood!* rivers of blood; blood everywhere. I see it, I smell it, I taste it—it is salt! it runs red upon the ground, it rains down from the skies.

"*Footsteps! footsteps! footsteps!* the tread of the white man coming from afar. It shakes the earth; the earth trembles before her master.

"Blood is good, the red blood is bright; there is no smell like the smell of new-shed blood. The lions shall lap it and roar, the vultures shall wash their wings in it and shriek with joy.

"I am old! I am old! I have seen much blood; *ha, ha!* but I shall see more ere I die, and be merry. How old am I, think ye? Your fathers knew me, and *their* fathers knew me, and *their* fathers' fathers' fathers. I have seen the white man and know his desires. I am old, but the mountains are older than I. Who made the great road, tell me? Who wrote the pictures on the rocks, tell me? Who reared up the three Silent Ones yonder, that gaze across the pit, tell me?" and she pointed towards the three precipitous mountains which we had noticed on the previous night.

"Ye know not, but I know. It was a white people who were before ye are, who shall be when ye are not, who shall eat you up and destroy you. *Yea!*yea! yea!

"And what came they for, the White Ones, the Terrible Ones, the skilled in magic and all learning, the strong, the unswerving? What is that bright stone upon thy forehead, O king? Whose hands made the iron garments upon thy breast, O king? Ye know not, but I know. I the Old One, I the Wise One, I the *Isanusi*, the witch doctress!"

Then she turned her bald vulture-head towards us.

"What seek ye, white men of the Stars—ah, yes, of the Stars? Do ye seek a lost one? Ye shall not find him here. He is not here. Never for ages upon ages has a white foot pressed this land; never except once, and I remember that he left it but to die. Ye come for bright stones; I know it—I know it; ye shall find them when the blood is dry; but shall ye return whence ye came, or shall ye stop with me? *Ha! ha! ha!*

"And thou, thou with the dark skin and the proud bearing," and she pointed her skinny finger at Umbopa, "who art *thou*, and what seekest *thou*? Not stones that shine, not yellow metal that gleams, these thou leavest to 'white men from the Stars.' Methinks I know thee; methinks I can smell the smell of the blood in thy heart. Strip off the girdle—"

Here the features of this extraordinary creature became convulsed, and she fell to the ground foaming in an epileptic fit, and was carried into the hut.

The king rose up trembling, and waved his hand. Instantly the regiments began to file off, and in ten minutes, save for ourselves, the king, and a few attendants, the great space was left empty.

"White people," he said, "it passes in my mind to kill you. Gagool has spoken strange words. What say ye?"

I laughed. "Be careful, O king, we are not easy to slay. Thou hast seen the fate of the ox; wouldst thou be as the ox is?"

The king frowned. "It is not well to threaten a king."

"We threaten not, we speak what is true. Try to kill us, O king, and learn."

The great savage put his hand to his forehead and thought.

"Go in peace," he said at length. "To-night is the great dance. Ye shall see it. Fear not that I shall set a snare for you. To-morrow I will think."

"It is well, O king," I answered unconcernedly, and then, accompanied by Infadoos, we rose and went back to our kraal.

The Witch-Hunt

On reaching our hut I motioned to Infadoos to enter with us.

"Now, Infadoos," I said, "we would speak with thee."

"Let my lords say on."

"It seems to us, Infadoos, that Twala the king is a cruel man."

"It is so, my lords. Alas! the land cries out because of his cruelties. To-night ye shall see. It is the great witch-hunt, and many will be smelt out as wizards and slain. No man's life is safe. If the king covets a man's cattle, or a man's wife, or if he fears a man that he should excite a rebellion against him, then Gagool, whom ye saw, or some of the witch-finding women whom she has taught, will smell that man out as a wizard, and he will be killed. Many must die before the moon grows pale to-night. It is ever so. Perhaps I too shall be killed. As yet I have been spared because I am skilled in war, and am beloved by the soldiers; but I know not how long I have to live. The land groans at the cruelties of Twala the king; it is wearied of him and his red ways."

"Then why is it, Infadoos, that the people do not cast him down?"

"Nay, my lords, he is the king, and if he were killed Scragga would reign in his place, and the heart of Scragga is blacker than the heart of Twala his father. If Scragga were king his yoke upon our neck would be heavier than the yoke of Twala. If Imotu had never been slain, or if Ignosi his son had lived, it might have been otherwise; but they are both dead."

"How knowest thou that Ignosi is dead?" said a voice behind us. We looked round astonished to see who spoke. It was Umbopa.

"What meanest thou, boy?" asked Infadoos; "who told thee to speak?"

"Listen, Infadoos," was the answer, "and I will tell thee a story. Years ago the king Imotu was killed in this country and his wife fled with the boy Ignosi. Is it not so?"

"It is so."

"It was said that the woman and her son died upon the mountains. Is it not so?"

"It is even so."

"Well, it came to pass that the mother and the boy Ignosi did not die. They crossed the mountains and were led by a tribe of wandering desert men across the sands beyond, till at last they came to water and grass and trees again."

"How knowest thou this?"

"Listen. They travelled on and on, many months' journey, till they reached a land where a people called the Amazulu, who also are of the Kukuana stock, live by war, and with them they tarried many years, till at length the mother died. Then the son Ignosi became a wanderer again, and journeyed into a land of wonders, where white people live, and for many more years he learned the wisdom of the white people."

"It is a pretty story," said Infadoos incredulously.

"For years he lived there working as a servant and a soldier, but holding in his heart all that his mother had told him of his own place, and casting about in his mind to find how he might journey thither to see his people and his father's house before he died. For long years he lived and waited, and at last the time came, as it ever comes to him who can wait for it, and he met some white men who would seek this unknown land, and joined himself to them. The white men started and travelled on and on, seeking for one who is lost. They crossed the burning desert, they crossed the snow-clad mountains, and at last reached the land of the Kukuanas, and there they found *thee*, O Infadoos."

"Surely thou art mad to talk thus," said the astonished old soldier.

"Thou thinkest so; see, I will show thee, O my uncle.

"*I am Ignosi, rightful king of the Kukuanas!*"

Then with a single movement Umbopa slipped off his "moocha" or girdle, and stood naked before us.

"Look," he said; "what is this?" and he pointed to the picture of a great snake tattooed in blue round his middle, its tail disappearing into its open mouth just above where the thighs are set into the body.

Infadoos looked, his eyes starting nearly out of his head. Then he fell upon his knees.

"*Koom! Koom!*" he ejaculated; "it is my brother's son; it is the king."

"Did I not tell thee so, my uncle? Rise; I am not yet the king, but with thy help, and with the help of these brave white men, who are my friends, I shall be. Yet the old witch Gagool was right, the land shall run with blood first, and hers shall run with it, if she has any and can die, for she killed my father with her words, and drove my mother forth. And now, Infadoos, choose thou. Wilt thou put thy hands between my hands and be my man? Wilt thou share the dangers that lie before me, and help me to overthrow this tyrant and murderer, or wilt thou not? Choose thou."

The old man put his hand to his head and thought. Then he rose, and advancing to where Umbopa, or rather Ignosi, stood, he knelt before him, and took his hand.

"Ignosi, rightful king of the Kukuanas, I put my hand between thy hands, and am thy man till death. When thou wast a babe I dandled thee upon my knees, now shall my old arm strike for thee and freedom."

"It is well, Infadoos; if I conquer, thou shalt be the greatest man in the kingdom after its king. If I fail, thou canst only die, and death is not far off from thee. Rise, my uncle."

"And ye, white men, will ye help me? What have I to offer you! The white stones! If I conquer and can find them, ye shall have as many as ye can carry hence. Will that suffice you?"

I translated this remark.

"Tell him," answered Sir Henry, "that he mistakes an Englishman. Wealth is good, and if it comes in our way we will take it; but a gentleman does not sell himself for wealth. Still, speaking for myself, I say this. I have always liked

Umbopa, and so far as lies in me I will stand by him in this business. It will be very pleasant to me to try to square matters with that cruel devil Twala. What do you say, Good, and you, Quatermain?"

"Well," said Good, "to adopt the language of hyperbole, in which all these people seem to indulge, you can tell him that a row is surely good, and warms the cockles of the heart, and that so far as I am concerned I'm his boy. My only stipulation is that he allows me to wear trousers."

I translated the substance of these answers.

"It is well, my friends," said Ignosi, late Umbopa; "and what sayest thou, Macumazahn, art thou also with me, old hunter, cleverer than a wounded buffalo?"

I thought awhile and scratched my head.

"Umbopa, or Ignosi," I said, "I don't like revolutions. I am a man of peace and a bit of a coward"—here Umbopa smiled—"but, on the other hand, I stick up for my friends, Ignosi. You have stuck to us and played the part of a man, and I will stick by you. But mind you, I am a trader, and have to make my living, so I accept your offer about those diamonds in case we should ever be in a position to avail ourselves of it. Another thing: we came, as you know, to look for Incubu's (Sir Henry's) lost brother. You must help us to find him."

"That I will do," answered Ignosi. "Stay, Infadoos, by the sign of the snake about my middle, tell me the truth. Has any white man to thy knowledge set his foot within the land?"

"None, O Ignosi."

"If any white man had been seen or heard of, wouldst thou have known?"

"I should certainly have known."

"Thou hearest, Incubu," said Ignosi to Sir Henry; "he has not been here."

"Well, well," said Sir Henry, with a sigh; "there it is; I suppose that he never got so far. Poor fellow, poor fellow! So it has all been for nothing. God's will be done."

"Now for business," I put in, anxious to escape from a painful subject. "It is very well to be a king by right divine, Ignosi, but how dost thou propose to become a king indeed?"

"Nay, I know not. Infadoos, hast thou a plan?"

"Ignosi, Son of the Lightning," answered his uncle, "to-night is the great dance and witch-hunt. Many shall be smelt out and perish, and in the hearts of many others there will be grief and anguish and fury against the king Twala. When the dance is over, then I will speak to some of the great chiefs, who in turn, if I can win them over, will speak to their regiments. I shall speak to the chiefs softly at first, and bring them to see that thou art indeed the king, and I think that by to-morrow's light thou shalt have twenty thousand spears at thy command. And now I must go and think, and hear, and make ready. After the dance is done, if I am yet alive, and we are all alive, I will meet thee here, and we can talk. At the best there must be war."

At this moment our conference was interrupted by the cry that messengers had come from the king. Advancing to the door of the hut we ordered that they should be admitted, and presently three men entered, each bearing a shining shirt of chain armour, and a magnificent battle-axe.

"The gifts of my lord the king to the white men from the Stars!" said a herald who came with them.

"We thank the king," I answered; "withdraw."

The men went, and we examined the armour with great interest. It was the most wonderful chain work that either of us had ever seen. A whole coat fell together so closely that it formed a mass of links scarcely too big to be covered with both hands.

"Do you make these things in this country, Infadoos?" I asked; "they are very beautiful."

"Nay, my lord, they came down to us from our forefathers. We know not who made them, and there are but few left. None but those of royal blood may be clad in them. They are magic coats through which no spear can pass, and those who wear them are well-nigh safe in the battle. The king is well pleased or much afraid, or he would not have sent these garments of steel. Clothe yourselves in them to-night, my lords."

The remainder of that day we spent quietly, resting and talking over the situation, which was sufficiently exciting. At last the sun went down, the thousand watch fires glowed out, and through the darkness we heard the tramp of many feet and the clashing of hundreds of spears, as the regiments passed to their appointed places to be ready for the great dance. Then the full moon shone out in splendour, and as we stood watching her rays, Infadoos arrived, clad in his war dress, and accompanied by a guard of twenty men to escort us to the dance. As he recommended, we had already donned the shirts of chain armour which the king had sent us, putting them on under our ordinary clothing, and finding to our surprise that they were neither very heavy nor uncomfortable. These steel shirts, which evidently had been made for men of a very large stature, hung somewhat loosely upon Good and myself, but Sir Henry's fitted his magnificent frame like a glove. Then strapping our revolvers round our waists, and taking in our hands the battle-axes which the king had sent with the armour, we started.

On arriving at the great kraal, where we had that morning been received by the king, we found that it was closely packed with some twenty thousand men arranged round it in regiments. These regiments were in turn divided into companies, and between each company ran a little path to allow space for the witch-finders to pass up and down. Anything more imposing than the sight that was presented by this vast and orderly concourse of armed men it is impossible to conceive. There they stood perfectly silent, and the moon poured her light upon the forest of their raised spears, upon their majestic forms, waving plumes, and the harmonious shading of their various-coloured shields. Wherever we looked were line upon line of dim faces surmounted by range upon range of shimmering spears.

"Surely," I said to Infadoos, "the whole army is here?"

"Nay, Macumazahn," he answered, "but a third of it. One third is present at this dance each year, another third is mustered outside in case there should be trouble when the killing begins, ten thousand more garrison the outposts round Loo, and the rest watch at the kraals in the country. Thou seest it is a great people."

"They are very silent," said Good; and indeed the intense stillness among such a vast concourse of living men was almost overpowering.

"What says Bougwan?" asked Infadoos.

I translated.

"Those over whom the shadow of Death is hovering are silent," he answered grimly.

"Will many be killed?"

"Very many."

"It seems," I said to the others, "that we are going to assist at a gladiatorial show arranged regardless of expense."

Sir Henry shivered, and Good said he wished that we could get out of it.

"Tell me," I asked Infadoos, "are we in danger?"

"I know not, my lords, I trust not; but do not seem afraid. If ye live through the night all may go well with you. The soldiers murmur against the king."

All this while we had been advancing steadily towards the centre of the open space, in the midst of which were placed some stools. As we proceeded we perceived another small party coming from the direction of the royal hut.

"It is the king Twala, Scragga his son, and Gagool the old; and see, with them are those who slay," said Infadoos, pointing to a little group of about a dozen gigantic and savage-looking men, armed with spears in one hand and heavy kerries in the other.

The king seated himself upon the centre stool, Gagool crouched at his feet, and the others stood behind him.

"Greeting, white lords," Twala cried, as we came up; "be seated, waste not precious time—the night is all too short for the deeds that must be done. Ye come in a good hour, and shall see a glorious show. Look round, white lords; look round," and he rolled his one wicked eye from regiment to regiment. "Can the Stars show you such a sight as this? See how they shake in their wickedness, all those who have evil in their hearts and fear the judgment of 'Heaven above.'"

"*Begin! begin!*" piped Gagool, in her thin piercing voice; "the hyaenas are hungry, they howl for food. *Begin! begin!*"

Then for a moment there was intense stillness, made horrible by a presage of what was to come.

The king lifted his spear, and suddenly twenty thousand feet were raised, as though they belonged to one man, and brought down with a stamp upon the earth. This was repeated three times, causing the solid ground to shake and tremble. Then from a far point of the circle a solitary voice began a wailing song, of which the refrain ran something as follows:—

"*What is the lot of man born of woman?*"

Back came the answer rolling out from every throat in that vast company—

"*Death!*"

Gradually, however, the song was taken up by company after company, till the whole armed multitude were singing it, and I could no longer follow the words, except in so far as they appeared to represent various phases of human passions, fears, and joys. Now it seemed to be a love song, now a majestic swelling war chant, and last of all a death dirge ending suddenly in one heart-breaking wail that went echoing and rolling away in a volume of blood-curdling sound.

Again silence fell upon the place, and again it was broken by the king lifting his hand. Instantly we heard a pattering of feet, and from out of the masses of warriors strange and awful figures appeared running towards us. As they drew near we saw that these were women, most of them aged, for their white hair, ornamented with small bladders taken from fish, streamed out behind them. Their faces were painted in stripes of white and yellow; down their backs hung snake-skins, and round their waists rattled circlets of human bones, while each held a small forked wand in her shrivelled hand. In all there were ten of them. When they arrived in front of us they halted, and one of them, pointing with her wand towards the crouching figure of Gagool, cried out—

"Mother, old mother, we are here."

"*Good! good! good!*" answered that aged Iniquity. "Are your eyes keen, *Isanusis* [witch doctresses], ye seers in dark places?"

"Mother, they are keen."

"*Good! good! good!* Are your ears open, *Isanusis*, ye who hear words that come not from the tongue?"

"Mother, they are open."

"*Good! good! good!* Are your senses awake, *Isanusis*—can ye smell blood, can ye purge the land of the wicked ones who compass evil against the king and against their neighbours? Are ye ready to do the justice of 'Heaven above,' ye whom I have taught, who have eaten of the bread of my wisdom, and drunk of the water of my magic?"

"Mother, we can."

"Then go! Tarry not, ye vultures; see, the slayers"—pointing to the ominous group of executioners behind—"make sharp their spears; the white men from afar are hungry to see. *Go!*"

With a wild yell Gagool's horrid ministers broke away in every direction, like fragments from a shell, the dry bones round their waists rattling as they ran, and headed for various points of the dense human circle. We could not watch them all, so we fixed our eyes upon the *Isanusi* nearest to us. When she came to within a few paces of the warriors she halted and began to dance wildly, turning round and round with an almost incredible rapidity, and shrieking out sentences such as "I smell him, the evil-doer!" "He is near, he who poisoned his mother!" "I hear the thoughts of him who thought evil of the king!"

Quicker and quicker she danced, till she lashed herself into such a frenzy of excitement that the foam flew in specks from her gnashing jaws, till her eyes seemed to start from her head, and her flesh to quiver visibly. Suddenly she stopped dead and stiffened all over, like a pointer dog when he scents game, and then with outstretched wand she began to creep stealthily towards the soldiers before her. It seemed to us that as she came their stoicism gave way, and that they shrank from her. As for ourselves, we followed her movements with a horrible fascination. Presently, still creeping and crouching like a dog, the *Isanusi* was before them. Then she halted and pointed, and again crept on a pace or two.

Suddenly the end came. With a shriek she sprang in and touched a tall warrior with her forked wand. Instantly two of his comrades, those standing immediately next to him, seized the doomed man, each by one arm, and advanced with him towards the king.

He did not resist, but we saw that he dragged his limbs as though they were paralysed, and that his fingers, from which the spear had fallen, were limp like those of a man newly dead.

As he came, two of the villainous executioners stepped forward to meet him. Presently they met, and the executioners turned round, looking towards the king as though for orders.

"*Kill!*" said the king.

"*Kill!*" squeaked Gagool.

"*Kill!*" re-echoed Scragga, with a hollow chuckle.

Almost before the words were uttered the horrible dead was done. One man had driven his spear into the victim's heart, and to make assurance double sure, the other had dashed out his brains with a great club.

"*One,*" counted Twala the king, just like a black Madame Defarge, as Good said, and the body was dragged a few paces away and stretched out.

Hardly was the thing done before another poor wretch was brought up, like an ox to the slaughter. This time we could see, from the leopard- skin cloak which he wore, that the man was a person of rank. Again the awful syllables were spoken, and the victim fell dead.

"*Two,*" counted the king.

And so the deadly game went on, till about a hundred bodies were stretched in rows behind us. I have heard of the gladiatorial shows of the Caesars, and of the Spanish bull-fights, but I take the liberty of doubting if either of them could be half so horrible as this Kukuana witch-hunt. Gladiatorial shows and Spanish bull-fights at any rate contributed to the public amusement, which certainly was not the case here. The most confirmed sensation-monger would fight shy of sensation if he knew that it was well on the cards that he would, in his own proper person, be the subject of the next "event."

Once we rose and tried to remonstrate, but were sternly repressed by Twala.

"Let the law take its course, white men. These dogs are magicians and evil-doers; it is well that they should die," was the only answer vouchsafed to us.

About half-past ten there was a pause. The witch-finders gathered themselves together, apparently exhausted with their bloody work, and we thought that the performance was done with. But it was not so, for presently, to our surprise, the ancient woman, Gagool, rose from her crouching position, and supporting herself with a stick, staggered off into the open space. It was an extraordinary sight to see this frightful vulture-headed old creature, bent nearly double with extreme age, gather strength by degrees, until at last she rushed about almost as actively as her ill-omened pupils. To and fro she ran, chanting to herself, till suddenly she made a dash at a tall man standing in front of one of the regiments, and touched him. As she did this a sort of groan went up from the regiment which evidently he commanded. But two of its officers seized him all the same, and brought him up for execution. We learned afterwards that he was a man of great wealth and importance, being indeed a cousin of the king.

He was slain, and Twala counted one hundred and three. Then Gagool again sprang to and fro, gradually drawing nearer and nearer to ourselves.

"Hang me if I don't believe she is going to try her games on us," ejaculated Good in horror.

"Nonsense!" said Sir Henry.

As for myself, when I saw that old fiend dancing nearer and nearer, my heart positively sank into my boots. I glanced behind us at the long rows of corpses, and shivered.

Nearer and nearer waltzed Gagool, looking for all the world like an animated crooked stick or comma, her horrid eyes gleaming and glowing with a most unholy lustre.

Nearer she came, and yet nearer, every creature in that vast assemblage watching her movements with intense anxiety. At last she stood still and pointed.

"Which is it to be?" asked Sir Henry to himself.

In a moment all doubts were at rest, for the old hag had rushed in and touched Umbopa, alias Ignosi, on the shoulder.

"I smell him out," she shrieked. "Kill him, kill him, he is full of evil; kill him, the stranger, before blood flows from him. Slay him, O king."

There was a pause, of which I instantly took advantage.

"O king," I called out, rising from my seat, "this man is the servant of thy guests, he is their dog; whosoever sheds the blood of our dog sheds our blood. By the sacred law of hospitality I claim protection for him."

"Gagool, mother of the witch-finders, has smelt him out; he must die, white men," was the sullen answer.

"Nay, he shall not die," I replied; "he who tries to touch him shall die indeed."

"Seize him!" roared Twala to the executioners; who stood round red to the eyes with the blood of their victims.

They advanced towards us, and then hesitated. As for Ignosi, he clutched his spear, and raised it as though determined to sell his life dearly.

"Stand back, ye dogs!" I shouted, "if ye would see to-morrow's light. Touch one hair of his head and your king dies," and I covered Twala with my revolver. Sir Henry and Good also drew their pistols, Sir Henry pointing his at the leading executioner, who was advancing to carry out the sentence, and Good taking a deliberate aim at Gagool.

Twala winced perceptibly as my barrel came in a line with his broad chest.

"Well," I said, "what is it to be, Twala?"

Then he spoke.

"Put away your magic tubes," he said; "ye have adjured me in the name of hospitality, and for that reason, but not from fear of what ye can do, I spare him. Go in peace."

"It is well," I answered unconcernedly; "we are weary of slaughter, and would sleep. Is the dance ended?"

"It is ended," Twala answered sulkily. "Let these dead dogs," pointing to the long rows of corpses, "be flung out to the hyaenas and the vultures," and he lifted his spear.

Instantly the regiments began to defile through the kraal gateway in perfect silence, a fatigue party only remaining behind to drag away the corpses of those who had been sacrificed.

Then we rose also, and making our salaam to his majesty, which he hardly deigned to acknowledge, we departed to our huts.

"Well," said Sir Henry, as we sat down, having first lit a lamp of the sort used by the Kukuanas, of which the wick is made from the fibre of a species of palm leaf, and the oil from clarified hippopotamus fat, "well, I feel uncommonly inclined to be sick."

"If I had any doubts about helping Umbopa to rebel against that infernal blackguard," put in Good, "they are gone now. It was as much as I could do to sit still while that slaughter was going on. I tried to keep my eyes shut, but they would open just at the wrong time. I wonder where Infadoos is. Umbopa, my friend, you ought to be grateful to us; your skin came near to having an air-hole made in it."

"I am grateful, Bougwan," was Umbopa's answer, when I had translated, "and I shall not forget. As for Infadoos, he will be here by-and-by. We must wait."

So we lit out pipes and waited.

We Give a Sign

For a long while—two hours, I should think—we sat there in silence, being too much overwhelmed by the recollection of the horrors we had seen to talk. At last, just as we were thinking of turning in—for the night drew nigh to dawn—we heard a sound of steps. Then came the challenge of a sentry posted at the kraal gate, which apparently was answered, though not in an audible tone, for the steps still advanced; and in another second Infadoos had entered the hut, followed by some half-dozen stately-looking chiefs.

"My lords," he said, "I have come according to my word. My lords and Ignosi, rightful king of the Kukuanas, I have brought with me these men," pointing to the row of chiefs, "who are great men among us, having each one of them the command of three thousand soldiers, that live but to do their bidding, under the king's. I have told them of what I have seen, and what my ears have heard. Now let them also behold the sacred snake around thee, and hear thy story, Ignosi, that they may say whether or no they will make cause with thee against Twala the king."

By way of answer Ignosi again stripped off his girdle, and exhibited the snake tattooed about him. Each chief in turn drew near and examined the sign by the dim light of the lamp, and without saying a word passed on to the other side.

Then Ignosi resumed his moocha, and addressing them, repeated the history he had detailed in the morning.

"Now ye have heard, chiefs," said Infadoos, when he had done, "what say ye: will ye stand by this man and help him to his father's throne, or will ye not? The land cries out against Twala, and the blood of the people flows like the waters in spring. Ye have seen to-night. Two other chiefs there were with whom I had it in my mind to speak, and where are they now? The hyaenas howl over their corpses. Soon shall ye be as they are if ye strike not. Choose then, my brothers."

The eldest of the six men, a short, thick-set warrior, with white hair, stepped forward a pace and answered—

"Thy words are true, Infadoos; the land cries out. My own brother is among those who died to-night; but this is a great matter, and the thing is hard to believe. How know we that if we lift our spears it may not be for a thief and a liar? It is a great matter, I say, of which none can see the end. For of this be sure, blood will flow in rivers before the deed is done; many will still cleave to the king, for men worship the sun that still shines bright in the heavens, rather than that which has not risen. These white men from the Stars, their magic is great, and Ignosi is under the cover of their wing. If he be indeed the rightful king, let them give us a sign, and let the people have a sign, that all may see. So shall men cleave to us, knowing of a truth that the white man's magic is with them."

"Ye have the sign of the snake," I answered.

"My lord, it is not enough. The snake may have been placed there since the man's childhood. Show us a sign, and it will suffice. But we will not move without a sign."

The others gave a decided assent, and I turned in perplexity to Sir Henry and Good, and explained the situation.

"I think that I have it," said Good exultingly; "ask them to give us a moment to think."

I did so, and the chiefs withdrew. So soon as they had gone Good went to the little box where he kept his medicines, unlocked it, and took out a note-book, in the fly-leaves of which was an almanack. "Now look here, you fellows, isn't to-morrow the 4th of June?" he said.

We had kept a careful note of the days, so were able to answer that it was.

"Very good; then here we have it—'4 June, total eclipse of the moon commences at 8.15 Greenwich time, visible in Teneriffe—*South Africa*, etc.' There's a sign for you. Tell them we will darken the moon to-morrow night."

The idea was a splendid one; indeed, the only weak spot about it was a fear lest Good's almanack might be incorrect. If we made a false prophecy on such a subject, our prestige would be gone for ever, and so would Ignosi's chance of the throne of the Kukuanas.

"Suppose that the almanack is wrong," suggested Sir Henry to Good, who was busily employed in working out something on a blank page of the book.

"I see no reason to suppose anything of the sort," was his answer. "Eclipses always come up to time; at least that is my experience of them, and it especially states that this one will be visible in South Africa. I have worked out the reckonings as well as I can, without knowing our exact position; and I make out that the eclipse should begin here about ten o'clock tomorrow night, and last till half-past twelve. For an hour and a half or so there should be almost total darkness."

"Well," said Sir Henry, "I suppose we had better risk it."

I acquiesced, though doubtfully, for eclipses are queer cattle to deal with—it might be a cloudy night, for instance, or our dates might be wrong—and sent Umbopa to summon the chiefs back. Presently they came, and I addressed them thus—

"Great men of the Kukuanas, and thou, Infadoos, listen. We love not to show our powers, for to do so is to interfere with the course of nature, and to plunge the world into fear and confusion. But since this matter is a great one, and as we are angered against the king because of the slaughter we have seen, and because of the act of the *Isanusi* Gagool, who would have put our friend Ignosi to death, we have determined to break a rule, and to give such a sign as all men may see. Come hither"; and I led them to the door of the hut and pointed to the red ball of the moon. "What see ye there?"

"We see the sinking moon," answered the spokesman of the party.

"It is so. Now tell me, can any mortal man put out that moon before her hour of setting, and bring the curtain of black night down upon the land?"

The chief laughed a little at the question. "No, my lord, that no man can do. The moon is stronger than man who looks on her, nor can she vary in her courses."

"Ye say so. Yet I tell you that to-morrow night, about two hours before midnight, we will cause the moon to be eaten up for a space of an hour and half an hour. Yes, deep darkness shall cover the earth, and it shall be for a sign that Ignosi is indeed king of the Kukuanas. If we do this thing, will ye be satisfied?"

"Yea, my lords," answered the old chief with a smile, which was reflected on the faces of his companions; "*if* ye do this thing, we will be satisfied indeed."

"It shall be done; we three, Incubu, Bougwan, and Macumazahn, have said it, and it shall be done. Dost thou hear, Infadoos?"

"I hear, my lord, but it is a wonderful thing that ye promise, to put out the moon, the mother of the world, when she is at her full."

"Yet shall we do it, Infadoos."

"It is well, my lords. To-day, two hours after sunset, Twala will send for my lords to witness the girls dance, and one hour after the dance begins the girl whom Twala thinks the fairest shall be killed by Scragga, the king's son, as a sacrifice to the Silent Ones, who sit and keep watch by the mountains yonder," and he pointed towards the three strange-looking peaks where Solomon's road was supposed to end. "Then let my lords darken the moon, and save the maiden's life, and the people will believe indeed."

"Ay," said the old chief, still smiling a little, "the people will believe indeed."

"Two miles from Loo," went on Infadoos, "there is a hill curved like a new moon, a stronghold, where my regiment, and three other regiments which these chiefs command, are stationed. This morning we will make a plan whereby two or three other regiments may be moved there also. Then, if in truth my lords can darken the moon, in the darkness I will take my lords by the hand and lead them out of Loo to this place, where they shall be safe, and thence we can make war upon Twala the king."

"It is good," said I. "Let leave us to sleep awhile and to make ready our magic."

Infadoos rose, and, having saluted us, departed with the chiefs.

"My friends," said Ignosi, so soon as they were gone, "can ye do this wonderful thing, or were ye speaking empty words to the captains?"

"We believe that we can do it, Umbopa—Ignosi, I mean."

"It is strange," he answered, "and had ye not been Englishmen I would not have believed it; but I have learned that English 'gentlemen' tell no lies. If we live through the matter, be sure that I will repay you."

"Ignosi," said Sir Henry, "promise me one thing."

"I will promise, Incubu, my friend, even before I hear it," answered the big man with a smile. "What is it?"

"This: that if ever you come to be king of this people you will do away with the smelling out of wizards such as we saw last night; and that the killing of men without trial shall no longer take place in the land."

Ignosi thought for a moment after I had translated this request, and then answered—

"The ways of black people are not as the ways of white men, Incubu, nor do we value life so highly. Yet I will promise. If it be in my power to hold them back, the witch-finders shall hunt no more, nor shall any man die the death without trial or judgment."

"That's a bargain, then," said Sir Henry; "and now let us get a little rest."

Thoroughly wearied out, we were soon sound asleep, and slept till Ignosi woke us about eleven o'clock. Then we rose, washed, and ate a hearty breakfast. After that we went outside the hut and walked about, amusing ourselves with examining the structure of the Kukuana huts and observing the customs of the women.

"I hope that eclipse will come off," said Sir Henry presently.

"If it does not it will soon be all up with us," I answered mournfully; "for so sure as we are living men some of those chiefs will tell the whole story to the king, and then there will be another sort of eclipse, and one that we shall certainly not like."

Returning to the hut we ate some dinner, and passed the rest of the day in receiving visits of ceremony and curiosity. At length the sun set, and we enjoyed a couple of hours of such quiet as our melancholy forebodings would allow to us. Finally, about half-past eight, a messenger came from Twala to bid us to the great annual "dance of girls" which was about to be celebrated.

Hastily we put on the chain shirts that the king had sent us, and taking our rifles and ammunition with us, so as to have them handy in case we had to fly, as suggested by Infadoos, we started boldly enough, though with inward fear and trembling. The great space in front of the king's kraal bore a very different appearance from that which it had presented on the previous evening. In place of the grim ranks of serried warriors were company after company of Kukuana girls, not over-dressed, so far as clothing went, but each crowned with a wreath of flowers, and holding a palm leaf in one hand and a white arum lily in the other. In the centre of the open moonlit space sat Twala the king, with old Gagool at his feet, attended by Infadoos, the boy Scragga, and twelve guards. There were also present about a score of chiefs, amongst whom I recognised most of our friends of the night before.

Twala greeted us with much apparent cordiality, though I saw him fix his one eye viciously on Umbopa.

"Welcome, white men from the Stars," he said; "this is another sight from that which your eyes gazed on by the light of last night's moon, but it is not so good a sight. Girls are pleasant, and were it not for such as these," and he pointed round him, "we should none of us be here this day; but men are better. Kisses and the tender words of women are sweet, but the sound of the clashing of the spears of warriors, and the smell of men's blood, are sweeter far! Would ye have wives from among our people, white men? If so, choose the fairest here, and ye shall have them, as many as ye will," and he paused for an answer.

As the prospect did not seem to be without attractions for Good, who, like most sailors, is of a susceptible nature,—being elderly and wise, foreseeing the endless complications that anything of the sort would involve, for women bring trouble so surely as the night follows the day, I put in a hasty answer—

"Thanks to thee, O king, but we white men wed only with white women like ourselves. Your maidens are fair, but they are not for us!"

The king laughed. "It is well. In our land there is a proverb which runs, 'Women's eyes are always bright, whatever the colour,' and another that says, 'Love her who is present, for be sure she who is absent is false to thee;' but perhaps these things are not so in the Stars. In a land where men are white all things are possible. So be it, white men; the girls will not go begging! Welcome again; and welcome, too, thou black one; if Gagool here had won her way, thou wouldst have been stiff and cold by now. It is lucky for thee that thou too camest from the Stars; ha! ha!"

"I can kill thee before thou killest me, O king," was Ignosi's calm answer, "and thou shalt be stiff before my limbs cease to bend."

Twala started. "Thou speakest boldly, boy," he replied angrily; "presume not too far."

"He may well be bold in whose lips are truth. The truth is a sharp spear which flies home and misses not. It is a message from 'the Stars,' O king."

Twala scowled, and his one eye gleamed fiercely, but he said nothing more.

"Let the dance begin," he cried, and then the flower-crowned girls sprang forward in companies, singing a sweet song and waving the delicate palms and white lilies. On they danced, looking faint and spiritual in the soft, sad light of the risen moon; now whirling round and round, now meeting in mimic warfare, swaying, eddying here and there, coming forward, falling back in an ordered confusion delightful to witness. At last they paused, and a beautiful young woman sprang out of the ranks and began to pirouette in front of us with a grace and vigour which would have put most ballet girls to shame. At length she retired exhausted, and another took her place, then another and another, but none of them, either in grace, skill, or personal attractions, came up to the first.

When the chosen girls had all danced, the king lifted his hand.

"Which deem ye the fairest, white men?" he asked.

"The first," said I unthinkingly. Next second I regretted it, for I remembered that Infadoos had told us that the fairest woman must be offered up as a sacrifice.

"Then is my mind as your minds, and my eyes as your eyes. She is the fairest! and a sorry thing it is for her, for she must die!"

"*Ay, must die*" piped out Gagool, casting a glance of her quick eyes in the direction of the poor girl, who, as yet ignorant of the awful fate in store for her, was standing some ten yards off in front of a company of maidens, engaged in nervously picking a flower from her wreath to pieces, petal by petal.

"Why, O king?" said I, restraining my indignation with difficulty; "the girl has danced well, and pleased us; she is fair too; it would be hard to reward her with death."

Twala laughed as he answered—

"It is our custom, and the figures who sit in stone yonder," and he pointed towards the three distant peaks, "must have their due. Did I fail to put the fairest girl to death to-day, misfortune would fall upon me and my house. Thus runs the prophecy of my people: 'If the king offer not a sacrifice of a fair girl, on the day of the dance of maidens, to the Old Ones who sit and watch on the mountains, then shall he fall, and his house.' Look ye, white men, my brother who reigned before me offered not the sacrifice, because of the tears of the woman, and he fell, and his house, and I reign in his stead. It is finished; she must die!" Then turning to the guards—"Bring her hither; Scragga, make sharp thy spear."

Two of the men stepped forward, and as they advanced, the girl, for the first time realising her impending fate, screamed aloud and turned to fly. But the strong hands caught her fast, and brought her, struggling and weeping, before us.

"What is thy name, girl?" piped Gagool. "What! wilt thou not answer? Shall the king's son do his work at once?"

At this hint, Scragga, looking more evil than ever, advanced a step and lifted his great spear, and at that moment I saw Good's hand creep to his revolver. The poor girl caught the faint glint of steel through her tears, and it sobered her anguish. She ceased struggling, and clasping her hands convulsively, stood shuddering from head to foot.

"See," cried Scragga in high glee, "she shrinks from the sight of my little plaything even before she has tasted it," and he tapped the broad blade of his spear.

"If ever I get the chance you shall pay for that, you young hound!" I heard Good mutter beneath his breath.

"Now that thou art quiet, give us thy name, my dear. Come, speak out, and fear not," said Gagool in mockery.

"Oh, mother," answered the girl, in trembling accents, "my name is Foulata, of the house of Suko. Oh, mother, why must I die? I have done no wrong!"

"Be comforted," went on the old woman in her hateful tone of mockery. "Thou must die, indeed, as a sacrifice to the Old Ones who sit yonder," and she pointed to the peaks; "but it is better to sleep in the night than to toil in the daytime; it is better to die than to live, and thou shalt die by the royal hand of the king's own son."

The girl Foulata wrung her hands in anguish, and cried out aloud, "Oh, cruel! and I so young! What have I done that I should never again see the sun rise out of the night, or the stars come following on his track in the evening, that I may no more gather the flowers when the dew is heavy, or listen to the laughing of the waters? Woe is me, that I shall never see my father's hut again, nor feel my mother's kiss, nor tend the lamb that is sick! Woe is me, that no lover shall put his arm around me and look into my eyes, nor shall men children be born of me! Oh, cruel, cruel!"

And again she wrung her hands and turned her tear-stained flower-crowned face to Heaven, looking so lovely in her despair—for she was indeed a beautiful woman—that assuredly the sight of her would have melted the hearts of any less cruel than were the three fiends before us. Prince Arthur's appeal to the ruffians who came to blind him was not more touching than that of this savage girl.

But it did not move Gagool or Gagool's master, though I saw signs of pity among the guards behind, and on the faces of the chiefs; and as for Good, he gave a fierce snort of indignation, and made a motion as though to go to her assistance. With all a woman's quickness, the doomed girl interpreted what was passing in his mind, and by a sudden movement flung herself before him, and clasped his "beautiful white legs" with her hands.

"Oh, white father from the Stars!" she cried, "throw over me the mantle of thy protection; let me creep into the shadow of thy strength, that I may be saved. Oh, keep me from these cruel men and from the mercies of Gagool!"

"All right, my hearty, I'll look after you," sang out Good in nervous Saxon. "Come, get up, there's a good girl," and he stooped and caught her hand.

Twala turned and motioned to his son, who advanced with his spear lifted.

"Now's your time," whispered Sir Henry to me; "what are you waiting for?"

"I am waiting for that eclipse," I answered; "I have had my eye on the moon for the last half-hour, and I never saw it look healthier."

"Well, you must risk it now, or the girl will be killed. Twala is losing patience."

Recognising the force of the argument, and having cast one more despairing look at the bright face of the moon, for never did the most ardent astronomer with a theory to prove await a celestial event with such anxiety, I stepped with all the dignity that I could command between the prostrate girl and the advancing spear of Scragga.

"King," I said, "it shall not be; we will not endure this thing; let the girl go in safety."

Twala rose from his seat in wrath and astonishment, and from the chiefs and serried ranks of maidens who had closed in slowly upon us in anticipation of the tragedy came a murmur of amazement.

"*Shall not be!* thou white dog, that yappest at the lion in his cave; *shall not be!* art thou mad? Be careful, lest this chicken's fate overtake thee, and those with thee. How canst thou save her or thyself? Who art thou that thou settest thyself between me and my will? Back, I say. Scragga, kill her! Ho, guards! seize these men."

At his cry armed men ran swiftly from behind the hut, where they had evidently been placed beforehand.

Sir Henry, Good, and Umbopa ranged themselves alongside of me, and lifted their rifles.

"Stop!" I shouted boldly, though at the moment my heart was in my boots. "Stop! we, the white men from the Stars, say that it shall not be. Come but one pace nearer, and we will put out the moon like a wind-blown lamp, as we who dwell in her House can do, and plunge the land in darkness. Dare to disobey, and ye shall taste of our magic."

My threat produced an effect; the men halted, and Scragga stood still before us, his spear lifted.

"Hear him! hear him!" piped Gagool; "hear the liar who says that he will put out the moon like a lamp. Let him do it, and the girl shall be speared. Yes, let him do it, or die by the girl, he and those with him."

I glanced up at the moon despairingly, and now to my intense joy and relief saw that we—or rather the almanack—had made no mistake. On the edge of the great orb lay a faint rim of shadow, while a smoky hue grew and gathered upon its bright surface. Never shall I forget that supreme, that superb moment of relief.

Then I lifted my hand solemnly towards the sky, an example which Sir Henry and Good followed, and quoted a line or two from the "Ingoldsby Legends" at it in the most impressive tones that I could command. Sir Henry followed suit with a verse out of the Old Testament, and something about Balbus building a wall, in Latin, whilst Good addressed the Queen of Night in a volume of the most classical bad language which he could think of.

Slowly the penumbra, the shadow of a shadow, crept on over the bright surface, and as it crept I heard deep gasps of fear rising from the multitude around.

"Look, O king!" I cried; "look, Gagool! Look, chiefs and people and women, and see if the white men from the Stars keep their word, or if they be but empty liars!

"The moon grows black before your eyes; soon there will be darkness— ay, darkness in the hour of the full moon. Ye have asked for a sign; it is given to you. Grow dark, O Moon! withdraw thy light, thou pure and holy One; bring the proud heart of usurping murderers to the dust, and eat up the world with shadows."

A groan of terror burst from the onlookers. Some stood petrified with dread, others threw themselves upon their knees and cried aloud. As for the king, he sat still and turned pale beneath his dusky skin. Only Gagool kept her courage.

"It will pass," she cried; "I have often seen the like before; no man can put out the moon; lose not heart; sit still—the shadow will pass."

"Wait, and ye shall see," I replied, hopping with excitement. "O Moon! Moon! Moon! wherefore art thou so cold and fickle?" This appropriate quotation was from the pages of a popular romance that I chanced to have read recently, though now I come to think of it, it was ungrateful of me to abuse the Lady of the Heavens, who was showing herself to be the truest of friends to us, however she may have behaved to the impassioned lover in the novel. Then I added: "Keep it up, Good, I can't remember any more poetry. Curse away, there's a good fellow."

Good responded nobly to this tax upon his inventive faculties. Never before had I the faintest conception of the breadth and depth and height of a naval officer's objurgatory powers. For ten minutes he went on in several languages without stopping, and he scarcely ever repeated himself.

Meanwhile the dark ring crept on, while all that great assembly fixed their eyes upon the sky and stared and stared in fascinated silence. Strange and unholy shadows encroached upon the moonlight, an ominous quiet filled the place. Everything grew still as death. Slowly and in the midst of this most solemn silence the minutes sped away, and while they sped the full moon passed deeper and deeper into the shadow of the earth, as the inky segment of its circle slid in awful majesty across the lunar craters. The great pale orb seemed to draw near and to grow in size. She turned a coppery hue, then that portion of her surface which was unobscured as yet grew grey and ashen, and at length, as totality approached, her mountains and her plains were to be seen glowing luridly through a crimson gloom.

On, yet on, crept the ring of darkness; it was now more than half across the blood-red orb. The air grew thick, and still more deeply tinged with dusky crimson. On, yet on, till we could scarcely see the fierce faces of the group before us. No sound rose now from the spectators, and at last Good stopped swearing.

"The moon is dying—the white wizards have killed the moon," yelled the prince Scragga at last. "We shall all perish in the dark," and animated by fear or fury, or by both, he lifted his spear and drove it with all his force at Sir Henry's breast. But he forgot the mail shirts that the king had given us, and which we wore beneath our clothing. The steel rebounded harmless, and before he could repeat the blow Curtis had snatched the spear from his hand and sent it straight through him.

Scragga dropped dead.

At the sight, and driven mad with fear of the gathering darkness, and of the unholy shadow which, as they believed, was swallowing the moon, the companies of girls broke up in wild confusion, and ran screeching for the gateways. Nor did the panic stop there. The king himself, followed by his guards, some of the chiefs, and Gagool, who hobbled away after them with marvellous alacrity, fled for the huts, so that in another minute we ourselves, the would-be victim Foulata, Infadoos, and most of the chiefs who had interviewed us on the previous night, were left alone upon the scene, together with the dead body of Scragga, Twala's son.

"Chiefs," I said, "we have given you the sign. If ye are satisfied, let us fly swiftly to the place of which ye spoke. The charm cannot now be stopped. It will work for an hour and the half of an hour. Let us cover ourselves in the darkness."

"Come," said Infadoos, turning to go, an example which was followed by the awed captains, ourselves, and the girl Foulata, whom Good took by the arm.

Before we reached the gate of the kraal the moon went out utterly, and from every quarter of the firmament the stars rushed forth into the inky sky.

Holding each other by the hand we stumbled on through the darkness.

Before the Battle

Luckily for us, Infadoos and the chiefs knew all the paths of the great town perfectly, so that we passed by side-ways unmolested, and notwithstanding the gloom we made fair progress.

For an hour or more we journeyed on, till at length the eclipse began to pass, and that edge of the moon which had disappeared the first became again visible. Suddenly, as we watched, there burst from it a silver streak of light, accompanied by a wondrous ruddy glow, which hung upon the blackness of the sky like a celestial lamp, and a wild and lovely sight it was. In another five minutes the stars began to fade, and there was sufficient light to see our whereabouts. We then discovered that we were clear of the town of Loo, and approaching a large flat-topped hill, measuring some two miles in circumference. This hill, which is of a formation common in South Africa, is not very high; indeed, its greatest elevation is scarcely more than 200 feet, but it is shaped like a horseshoe, and its sides are rather precipitous and strewn with boulders. On the grass table-land at its summit is ample camping-ground, which had been utilised as a military cantonment of no mean strength. Its ordinary garrison was one regiment of three thousand men, but as we toiled up the steep side of the mountain in the returning moonlight we perceived that there were several of such regiments encamped there.

Reaching the table-land at last, we found crowds of men roused from their sleep, shivering with fear and huddled up together in the utmost consternation at the natural phenomenon which they were witnessing. Passing through these without a word, we gained a hut in the centre of the ground, where we were astonished to find two men waiting, laden with our few goods and chattels, which of course we had been obliged to leave behind in our hasty flight.

"I sent for them," explained Infadoos; "and also for these," and he lifted up Good's long-lost trousers.

With an exclamation of rapturous delight Good sprang at them, and instantly proceeded to put them on.

"Surely my lord will not hide his beautiful white legs!" exclaimed Infadoos regretfully.

But Good persisted, and once only did the Kukuana people get the chance of seeing his beautiful legs again. Good is a very modest man. Henceforward they had to satisfy their aesthetic longings with his one whisker, his transparent eye, and his movable teeth.

Still gazing with fond remembrance at Good's trousers, Infadoos next informed us that he had commanded the regiments to muster so soon as the day broke, in order to explain to them fully the origin and circumstances of the rebellion which was decided on by the chiefs, and to introduce to them the rightful heir to the throne, Ignosi.

Accordingly, when the sun was up, the troops—in all some twenty thousand men, and the flower of the Kukuana army—were mustered on a large open space, to which we went. The men were drawn up in three sides of a dense square, and presented a magnificent spectacle. We took our station on the open side of the square, and were speedily surrounded by all the principal chiefs and officers.

These, after silence had been proclaimed, Infadoos proceeded to address. He narrated to them in vigorous and graceful language—for, like most Kukuanas of high rank, he was a born orator—the history of Ignosi's father, and of how he had been basely murdered by Twala the king, and his wife and child driven out to starve. Then he pointed out that the people suffered and groaned under Twala's cruel rule, instancing the proceedings of the previous night, when, under pretence of their being evil-doers, many of the noblest in the land had been dragged forth and wickedly done to death. Next he went on to say that the white lords from the Stars, looking down upon their country, had perceived its trouble, and determined, at great personal inconvenience, to alleviate its lot: That they had accordingly taken the real king of the Kukuanas, Ignosi, who was languishing in exile, by the hand, and led him over the mountains: That they had seen the wickedness of Twala's doings, and for a sign to the wavering, and to save the life of the girl Foulata, actually, by the exercise of their high magic, had put out the moon and slain the young fiend Scragga; and that they were prepared to stand by them, and assist them to overthrow Twala, and set up the rightful king, Ignosi, in his place.

He finished his discourse amidst a murmur of approbation. Then Ignosi stepped forward and began to speak. Having reiterated all that Infadoos his uncle had said, he concluded a powerful speech in these words:—

"O chiefs, captains, soldiers, and people, ye have heard my words. Now must ye make choice between me and him who sits upon my throne, the uncle who killed his brother, and hunted his brother's child forth to die in the cold and the night. That I am indeed the king these"— pointing to the chiefs—"can tell you, for they have seen the snake about my middle. If I were not the king, would these white men be on my side with all their magic? Tremble, chiefs, captains, soldiers, and people! Is not the darkness they have brought upon the land to confound Twala and cover our flight, darkness even in the hour of the full moon, yet before your eyes?"

"It is," answered the soldiers.

"I am the king; I say to you, I am the king," went on Ignosi, drawing up his great stature to its full, and lifting his broad-bladed battle- axe above his head. "If there be any man among you who says that it is not so, let him stand forth and I will fight him now, and his blood shall be a red token that I tell you true. Let him stand forth, I say;" and he shook the great axe till it flashed in the sunlight.

As nobody seemed inclined to respond to this heroic version of "Dilly, Dilly, come and be killed," our late henchman proceeded with his address.

"I am indeed the king, and should ye stand by my side in the battle, if I win the day ye shall go with me to victory and honour. I will give you oxen and wives, and ye shall take place of all the regiments; and if ye fall, I will fall with you.

"And behold, I give you this promise, that when I sit upon the seat of my fathers, bloodshed shall cease in the land. No longer shall ye cry for justice to find slaughter, no longer shall the witch-finder hunt you out so that ye may be slain without a cause. No man shall die save he who offends against the laws. The 'eating up' of your kraals shall cease; each one of you shall sleep secure in his own hut and fear naught, and justice shall walk blindfold throughout the land. Have ye chosen, chiefs, captains, soldiers, and people?"

"We have chosen, O king," came back the answer.

"It is well. Turn your heads and see how Twala's messengers go forth from the great town, east and west, and north and south, to gather a mighty army to slay me and you, and these my friends and protectors. To-morrow, or perchance the next day, he will come against us with all who are faithful to him. Then I shall see the man who is indeed my man, the man who fears not to die for his cause; and I tell you that he shall not be forgotten in the time of spoil. I have spoken, O chiefs, captains, soldiers, and people. Now go to your huts and make you ready for war."

There was a pause, till presently one of the chiefs lifted his hand, and out rolled the royal salute, "*Koom.*" It was a sign that the soldiers accepted Ignosi as their king. Then they marched off in battalions.

Half an hour afterwards we held a council of war, at which all the commanders of regiments were present. It was evident to us that before very long we should be attacked in overwhelming force. Indeed, from our point of vantage on the hill we could see troops mustering, and runners going forth from Loo in every direction, doubtless to summon soldiers to the king's assistance. We had on our side about twenty thousand men, composed of seven of the best regiments in the country. Twala, so Infadoos and the chiefs calculated, had at least thirty to thirty-five thousand on whom he could rely at present assembled in Loo, and they thought that by midday on the morrow he would be able to gather another five thousand or more to his aid. It was, of course, possible that some of his troops would desert and come over to us, but it was not a contingency which could be reckoned on. Meanwhile, it was clear that active preparations were being made by Twala to subdue us. Already strong bodies of armed men were patrolling round and round the foot of the hill, and there were other signs also of coming assault.

Infadoos and the chiefs, however, were of opinion that no attack would take place that day, which would be devoted to preparation and to the removal of every available means of the moral effect produced upon the minds of the soldiery by the supposed magical darkening of the moon. The onslaught would be on the morrow, they said, and they proved to be right.

Meanwhile, we set to work to strengthen the position in all ways possible. Almost every man was turned out, and in the course of the day, which seemed far too short, much was done. The paths up the hill —that was rather a sanatorium than a fortress, being used generally as the camping place of regiments suffering from recent service in unhealthy portions of the country—were carefully blocked with masses of stones, and every other approach was made as impregnable as time would allow. Piles of boulders were collected at various spots to be rolled down upon an advancing enemy, stations were appointed to the different regiments, and all preparation was made which our joint ingenuity could suggest.

Just before sundown, as we rested after our toil, we perceived a small company of men advancing towards us from the direction of Loo, one of whom bore a palm leaf in his hand for a sign that he came as a herald.

As he drew near, Ignosi, Infadoos, one or two chiefs and ourselves, went down to the foot of the mountain to meet him. He was a gallant-looking fellow, wearing the regulation leopard-skin cloak.

"Greeting!" he cried, as he came; "the king's greeting to those who make unholy war against the king; the lion's greeting to the jackals that snarl around his heels."

"Speak," I said.

"These are the king's words. Surrender to the king's mercy ere a worse thing befall you. Already the shoulder has been torn from the black bull, and the king drives him bleeding about the camp."

"What are Twala's terms?" I asked from curiosity.

"His terms are merciful, worthy of a great king. These are the words of Twala, the one-eyed, the mighty, the husband of a thousand wives, lord of the Kukuanas, keeper of the Great Road (Solomon's Road), beloved of the Strange Ones who sit in silence at the mountains yonder (the Three Witches), Calf of the Black Cow, Elephant whose tread shakes the earth, Terror of the evil-doer, Ostrich whose feet devour the desert, huge One, black One, wise One, king from generation to generation! these are the words of Twala: 'I will have mercy and be satisfied with a little blood. One in every ten shall die, the rest shall go free; but the white man Incubu, who slew Scragga my son, and the black man his servant, who pretends to my throne, and Infadoos my brother, who brews rebellion against me, these shall die by torture as an offering to the Silent Ones.' Such are the merciful words of Twala."

After consulting with the others a little, I answered him in a loud voice, so that the soldiers might hear, thus—

"Go back, thou dog, to Twala, who sent thee, and say that we, Ignosi, veritable king of the Kukuanas, Incubu, Bougwan, and Macumazahn, the wise ones from the Stars, who make dark the moon, Infadoos, of the royal house, and the chiefs, captains, and people here gathered, make answer and say, 'That we will not surrender; that before the sun has gone down twice, Twala's corpse shall stiffen at Twala's gate, and Ignosi, whose father Twala slew, shall reign in his stead.' Now go, ere we whip thee away, and beware how thou dost lift a hand against such as we are."

The herald laughed loudly. "Ye frighten not men with such swelling words," he cried out. "Show yourselves as bold to-morrow, O ye who darken the moon. Be bold, fight, and be merry, before the crows pick your bones till they are whiter than your faces. Farewell; perhaps we may meet in the fight; fly not to the Stars, but wait for me, I pray, white men." With this shaft of sarcasm he retired, and almost immediately the sun sank.

That night was a busy one, for weary as we were, so far as was possible by the moonlight all preparations for the morrow's fight were continued, and messengers were constantly coming and going from the place where we sat in council. At last, about an hour after midnight, everything that could be done was done, and the camp, save for the occasional challenge of a sentry, sank into silence. Sir Henry and I, accompanied by Ignosi and one of the chiefs, descended the hill and made a round of the pickets. As we went, suddenly, from all sorts of unexpected places, spears gleamed out in the moonlight, only to vanish again when we uttered the password. It was clear to us that none were sleeping at their posts. Then we returned, picking our way warily through thousands of sleeping warriors, many of whom were taking their last earthly rest.

The moonlight flickering along their spears, played upon their features and made them ghastly; the chilly night wind tossed their tall and hearse-like plumes. There they lay in wild confusion, with arms outstretched and twisted limbs; their stern, stalwart forms looking weird and unhuman in the moonlight.

"How many of these do you suppose will be alive at this time to-morrow?" asked Sir Henry.

I shook my head and looked again at the sleeping men, and to my tired and yet excited imagination it seemed as though Death had already touched them. My mind's eye singled out those who were sealed to slaughter, and there rushed in upon my heart a great sense of the mystery of human life, and an overwhelming sorrow at its futility and sadness. To-night these thousand slept their healthy sleep, to-morrow they, and many others with them, ourselves perhaps among them, would be stiffening in the cold; their wives would be widows, their children fatherless, and their place know them no more for ever. Only the old moon would shine on serenely, the night wind would stir the grasses, and the wide earth would take its rest, even as it did aeons before we were, and will do aeons after we have been forgotten.

Yet man dies not whilst the world, at once his mother and his monument, remains. His name is lost, indeed, but the breath he breathed still stirs the pine-tops on the mountains, the sound of the words he spoke yet echoes on through space; the thoughts his brain gave birth to we have inherited to-day; his passions are our cause of life; the joys and sorrows that he knew are our familiar friends—the end from which he fled aghast will surely overtake us also!

Truly the universe is full of ghosts, not sheeted churchyard spectres, but the inextinguishable elements of individual life, which having once been, can never *die*, though they blend and change, and change again for ever.

All sorts of reflections of this nature passed through my mind—for as I grow older I regret to say that a detestable habit of thinking seems to be getting a hold of me—while I stood and stared at those grim yet fantastic lines of warriors, sleeping, as their saying goes, "upon their spears."

"Curtis," I said, "I am in a condition of pitiable fear."

Sir Henry stroked his yellow beard and laughed, as he answered—

"I have heard you make that sort of remark before, Quatermain."

"Well, I mean it now. Do you know, I very much doubt if one of us will be alive to-morrow night. We shall be attacked in overwhelming force, and it is quite a chance if we can hold this place."

"We'll give a good account of some of them, at any rate. Look here, Quatermain, this business is nasty, and one with which, properly speaking, we ought not to be mixed up, but we are in for it, so we must make the best of our job. Speaking personally, I had rather be killed fighting than any other way, and now that there seems little chance of our finding my poor brother, it makes the idea easier to me. But fortune favours the brave, and we may succeed. Anyway, the battle will be awful, and having a reputation to keep up, we shall need to be in the thick of the thing."

He made this last remark in a mournful voice, but there was a gleam in his eye which belied its melancholy. I have an idea Sir Henry Curtis actually likes fighting.

After this we went to sleep for a couple of hours or so.

Just about dawn we were awakened by Infadoos, who came to say that great activity was to be observed in Loo, and that parties of the king's skirmishers were driving in our outposts.

We rose and dressed ourselves for the fray, each putting on his chain armour shirt, for which garments at the present juncture we felt exceedingly thankful. Sir Henry went the whole length about the matter, and dressed himself like a native warrior. "When you are in Kukuanaland, do as the Kukuanas do," he remarked, as he drew the shining steel over his broad breast, which it fitted like a glove. Nor did he stop there. At his request Infadoos had provided him with a complete set of native war uniform. Round his throat he fastened the leopard-skin cloak of a commanding officer, on his brows he bound the plume of black ostrich feathers worn only by generals of high rank, and about his middle a magnificent moocha of white ox-tails. A pair of sandals, a leglet of goat's hair, a heavy battle-axe with a rhinoceros-horn handle, a round iron shield covered with white ox- hide, and the regulation number of *tollas*, or throwing-knives, made up his equipment, to which, however, he added his revolver. The dress was, no doubt, a savage one, but I am bound to say that I seldom saw a finer sight than Sir Henry Curtis presented in this guise. It showed off his magnificent physique to the greatest advantage, and when Ignosi arrived presently, arrayed in a similar costume, I thought to myself that I had never before seen two such splendid men.

As for Good and myself, the armour did not suit us nearly so well. To begin with, Good insisted upon keeping on his new-found trousers, and a stout, short gentleman with an eye-glass, and one half of his face shaved, arrayed in a mail shirt, carefully tucked into a very seedy pair of corduroys, looks more remarkable than imposing. In my case, the chain shirt being too big for me, I put it on over all my clothes, which caused it to bulge in a somewhat ungainly fashion. I discarded my trousers, however, retaining only my veldtschoons, having determined to go into battle with bare legs, in order to be the lighter for running, in case it became necessary to retire quickly. The mail coat, a spear, a shield, that I did not know how to use, a couple of *tollas*, a revolver, and a huge plume, which I pinned into the top of my shooting hat, in order to give a bloodthirsty finish to my appearance, completed my modest equipment. In addition to all these articles, of course we had our rifles, but as ammunition was scarce, and as they would be useless in case of a charge, we arranged that they should be carried behind us by bearers.

When at length we had equipped ourselves, we swallowed some food hastily, and then started out to see how things were going on. At one point in the table-land of the mountain, there was a little koppie of brown stone, which served the double purpose of head-quarters and of a conning tower. Here we found Infadoos surrounded by his own regiment, the Greys, which was undoubtedly the finest in the Kukuana army, and the same that we had first seen at the outlying kraal. This regiment, now three thousand five hundred strong, was being held in reserve, and the men were lying down on the grass in companies, and watching the king's forces creep out of Loo in long ant-like columns. There seemed to be no end to the length of these columns—three in all, and each of them numbering, as we judged, at least eleven or twelve thousand men.

As soon as they were clear of the town the regiments formed up. Then one body marched off to the right, one to the left, and the third came on slowly towards us.

"Ah," said Infadoos, "they are going to attack us on three sides at once."

This seemed rather serious news, for our position on the top of the mountain, which measured a mile and a half in circumference, being an extended one, it was important to us to concentrate our comparatively small defending force as much as possible. But since it was impossible for us to dictate in what way we should be assailed, we had to make the best of it, and accordingly sent orders to the various regiments to prepare to receive the separate onslaughts.

The Attack

Slowly, and without the slightest appearance of haste or excitement, the three columns crept on. When within about five hundred yards of us, the main or centre column halted at the root of a tongue of open plain which ran up into the hill, to give time to the other divisions to circumvent our position, which was shaped more or less in the form of a horse-shoe, with its two points facing towards the town of Loo. The object of this manoeuvre was that the threefold assault should be delivered simultaneously.

"Oh, for a gatling!" groaned Good, as he contemplated the serried phalanxes beneath us. "I would clear that plain in twenty minutes."

"We have not got one, so it is no use yearning for it; but suppose you try a shot, Quatermain," said Sir Henry. "See how near you can go to that tall fellow who appears to be in command. Two to one you miss him, and an even sovereign, to be honestly paid if ever we get out of this, that you don't drop the bullet within five yards."

This piqued me, so, loading the express with solid ball, I waited till my friend walked some ten yards out from his force, in order to get a better view of our position, accompanied only by an orderly; then, lying down and resting the express on a rock, I covered him. The rifle, like all expresses, was only sighted to three hundred and fifty yards, so to allow for the drop in trajectory I took him half-way down the neck, which ought, I calculated, to find him in the chest. He stood quite still and gave me every opportunity, but whether it was the excitement or the wind, or the fact of the man being a long shot, I don't know, but this was what happened. Getting dead on, as I thought, a fine sight, I pressed, and when the puff of smoke had cleared away, to my disgust, I saw my man standing there unharmed, whilst his orderly, who was at least three paces to the left, was stretched upon the ground apparently dead. Turning swiftly, the officer I had aimed at began to run towards his men in evident alarm.

"Bravo, Quatermain!" sang out Good; "you've frightened him."

This made me very angry, for, if possible to avoid it, I hate to miss in public. When a man is master of only one art he likes to keep up his reputation in that art. Moved quite out of myself at my failure, I did a rash thing. Rapidly covering the general as he ran, I let drive with the second barrel. Instantly the poor man threw up his arms, and fell forward on to his face. This time I had made no mistake; and—I say it as a proof of how little we think of others when our own safety, pride, or reputation is in question—I was brute enough to feel delighted at the sight.

The regiments who had seen the feat cheered wildly at this exhibition of the white man's magic, which they took as an omen of success, while the force the general had belonged to—which, indeed, as we ascertained afterwards, he had commanded—fell back in confusion. Sir Henry and Good now took up their rifles and began to fire, the latter industriously "browning" the dense mass before him with another Winchester repeater, and I also had another shot or two, with the result, so far as we could judge, that we put some six or eight men *hors de combat* before they were out of range.

Just as we stopped firing there came an ominous roar from our far right, then a similar roar rose on our left. The two other divisions were engaging us.

At the sound, the mass of men before us opened out a little, and advanced towards the hill and up the spit of bare grass land at a slow trot, singing a deep-throated song as they ran. We kept up a steady fire from our rifles as they came, Ignosi joining in occasionally, and accounted for several men, but of course we produced no more effect upon that mighty rush of armed humanity than he who throws pebbles does on the breaking wave.

On they came, with a shout and the clashing of spears; now they were driving in the pickets we had placed among the rocks at the foot of the hill. After that the advance was a little slower, for though as yet we had offered no serious opposition, the attacking forces must climb up hill, and they came slowly to save their breath. Our first line of defence was about half-way down the side of the slope, our second fifty yards further back, while our third occupied the edge of the plateau.

On they stormed, shouting their war-cry, *"Twala! Twala! Chiele! Chiele!"* (Twala! Twala! Smite! Smite!) *"Ignosi! Ignosi! Chiele! Chiele!"* answered our people. They were quite close now, and the *tollas*, or throwing-knives, began to flash backwards and forwards, and now with an awful yell the battle closed in.

To and fro swayed the mass of struggling warriors, men falling fast as leaves in an autumn wind; but before long the superior weight of the attacking force began to tell, and our first line of defence was slowly pressed back till it merged into the second. Here the struggle was very fierce, but again our people were driven back and up, till at length, within twenty minutes of the commencement of the fight, our third line came into action.

But by this time the assailants were much exhausted, and besides had lost many men killed and wounded, and to break through that third impenetrable hedge of spears proved beyond their powers. For a while the seething lines of savages swung backwards and forwards, in the fierce ebb and flow of battle, and the issue was doubtful. Sir Henry watched the desperate struggle with a kindling eye, and then without a word he rushed off, followed by Good, and flung himself into the hottest of the fray. As for myself, I stopped where I was.

The soldiers caught sight of his tall form as he plunged into battle, and there rose a cry of—

"Nanzia Incubu! Nanzia Unkungunklovo!" (Here is the Elephant!) *"Chiele! Chiele!"*

From that moment the end was no longer in doubt. Inch by inch, fighting with splendid gallantry, the attacking force was pressed back down the hillside, till at last it retreated upon its reserves in something like confusion. At that instant, too, a messenger arrived to say that the left attack had been repulsed; and I was just beginning to congratulate myself, believing that the affair was over for the present, when, to our horror, we perceived our men who had been engaged in the right defence being driven towards us across the plain, followed by swarms of the enemy, who had evidently succeeded at this point.

Ignosi, who was standing by me, took in the situation at a glance, and issued a rapid order. Instantly the reserve regiment around us, the Greys, extended itself.

Again Ignosi gave a word of command, which was taken up and repeated by the captains, and in another second, to my intense disgust, I found myself involved in a furious onslaught upon the advancing foe. Getting as much as I could behind Ignosi's huge frame, I made the best of a bad job, and toddled along to be killed as though I liked it. In a minute or two—we were plunging through the flying groups of our men, who at once began to re-form behind us, and then I am sure I do not know what happened. All I can remember is a dreadful rolling noise of the meeting of shields, and the sudden apparition of a huge ruffian, whose eyes seemed literally to be starting out of his head, making straight at me with a bloody spear. But—I say it with pride—I rose— or rather sank—to the occasion. It was one before which most people would have collapsed once and for all. Seeing that if I stood where I was I must be killed, as the horrid apparition came I flung myself down in front of him so cleverly that, being unable to stop himself, he took a header right over my prostrate form. Before he could rise again, *I* had risen and settled the matter from behind with my revolver.

Shortly after this somebody knocked me down, and I remember no more of that charge.

When I came to I found myself back at the koppie, with Good bending over me holding some water in a gourd.

"How do you feel, old fellow?" he asked anxiously.

I got up and shook myself before replying.

"Pretty well, thank you," I answered.

"Thank Heaven! When I saw them carry you in, I felt quite sick; I thought you were done for."

"Not this time, my boy. I fancy I only got a rap on the head, which knocked me stupid. How has it ended?"

"They are repulsed at every point for a while. The loss is dreadfully heavy; we have quite two thousand killed and wounded, and they must have lost three. Looks, there's a sight!" and he pointed to long lines of men advancing by fours.

In the centre of every group of four, and being borne by it, was a kind of hide tray, of which a Kukuana force always carries a quantity, with a loop for a handle at each corner. On these trays—and their number seemed endless—lay wounded men, who as they arrived were hastily examined by the medicine men, of whom ten were attached to a regiment. If the wound was not of a fatal character the sufferer was taken away and attended to as carefully as circumstances would allow. But if, on the other hand, the injured man's condition proved hopeless, what followed was very dreadful, though doubtless it may have been the truest mercy. One of the doctors, under pretence of carrying out an examination, swiftly opened an artery with a sharp knife, and in a minute or two the sufferer expired painlessly. There were many cases that day in which this was done. In fact, it was done in the majority of cases when the wound was in the body, for the gash made by the entry of the enormously broad spears used by the Kukuanas generally rendered recovery impossible. In most instances the poor sufferers were already unconscious, and in others the fatal "nick" of the artery was inflicted so swiftly and painlessly that they did not seem to notice it. Still it was a ghastly sight, and one from which we were glad to escape; indeed, I never remember anything of the kind that affected me more than seeing those gallant soldiers thus put out of pain by the red-handed medicine men, except, indeed, on one occasion when, after an attack, I saw a force of Swazis burying their hopelessly wounded *alive*.

Hurrying from this dreadful scene to the further side of the koppie, we found Sir Henry, who still held a battle-axe in his hand, Ignosi, Infadoos, and one or two of the chiefs in deep consultation.

"Thank Heaven, here you are, Quatermain! I can't quite make out what Ignosi wants to do. It seems that though we have beaten off the attack, Twala is now receiving large reinforcements, and is showing a disposition to invest us, with the view of starving us out."

"That's awkward."

"Yes; especially as Infadoos says that the water supply has given out."

"My lord, that is so," said Infadoos; "the spring cannot supply the wants of so great a multitude, and it is failing rapidly. Before night we shall all be thirsty. Listen, Macumazahn. Thou art wise, and hast doubtless seen many wars in the lands from whence thou camest—that is if indeed they make wars in the Stars. Now tell us, what shall we do? Twala has brought up many fresh men to take the place of those who have fallen. Yet Twala has learnt his lesson; the hawk did not think to find the heron ready; but our beak has pierced his breast; he fears to strike at us again. We too are wounded, and he will wait for us to die; he will wind himself round us like a snake round a buck, and fight the fight of 'sit down.'"

"I hear thee," I said.

"So, Macumazahn, thou seest we have no water here, and but a little food, and we must choose between these three things—to languish like a starving lion in his den, or to strive to break away towards the north, or"—and here he rose and pointed towards the dense mass of our foes—"to launch ourselves straight at Twala's throat. Incubu, the great warrior—for to-day he fought like a buffalo in a net, and Twala's soldiers went down before his axe like young corn before the hail; with these eyes I saw it—Incubu says 'Charge'; but the Elephant is ever prone to charge. Now what says Macumazahn, the wily old fox, who has seen much, and loves to bite his enemy from behind? The last word is in Ignosi the king, for it is a king's right to speak of war; but let us hear thy voice, O Macumazahn, who watchest by night, and the voice too of him of the transparent eye."

"What sayest thou, Ignosi," I asked.

"Nay, my father," answered our quondam servant, who now, clad as he was in the full panoply of savage war, looked every inch a warrior king, "do thou speak, and let me, who am but a child in wisdom beside thee, hearken to thy words."

Thus adjured, after taking hasty counsel with Good and Sir Henry, I delivered my opinion briefly to the effect that, being trapped, our best chance, especially in view of the failure of our water supply, was to initiate an attack upon Twala's forces. Then I recommended that the attack should be delivered at once, "before our wounds grew stiff," and also before the sight of Twala's overpowering force caused the hearts of our soldiers "to wax small like fat before a fire." Otherwise, I pointed out, some of the captains might change their minds, and, making peace with Twala, desert to him, or even betray us into his hands.

This expression of opinion seemed, on the whole, to be favourably received; indeed, among the Kukuanas my utterances met with a respect which has never been accorded to them before or since. But the real decision as to our plans lay with Ignosi, who, since he had been recognised as rightful king, could exercise the almost unbounded rights of sovereignty, including, of course, the final decision on matters of generalship, and it was to him that all eyes were now turned.

At length, after a pause, during which he appeared to be thinking deeply, he spoke.

"Incubu, Macumazahn, and Bougwan, brave white men, and my friends; Infadoos, my uncle, and chiefs; my heart is fixed. I will strike at Twala this day, and set my fortunes on the blow, ay, and my life—my life and your lives also. Listen; thus will I strike. Ye see how the hill curves round like the half-moon, and how the plain runs like a green tongue towards us within the curve?"

"We see," I answered.

"Good; it is now mid-day, and the men eat and rest after the toil of battle. When the sun has turned and travelled a little way towards the darkness, let thy regiment, my uncle, advance with one other down to the green tongue, and it shall be that when Twala sees it he will hurl his force at it to crush it. But the spot is narrow, and the regiments can come against thee one at a time only; so may they be destroyed one by one, and the eyes of all Twala's army shall be fixed upon a struggle the like of which has not been seen by living man. And with thee, my uncle, shall go Incubu my friend, that when Twala sees his battle-axe flashing in the first rank of the Greys his heart may grow faint. And I will come with the second regiment, that which follows thee, so that if ye are destroyed, as it might happen, there may yet be a king left to fight for; and with me shall come Macumazahn the wise."

"It is well, O king," said Infadoos, apparently contemplating the certainty of the complete annihilation of his regiment with perfect calmness. Truly, these Kukuanas are a wonderful people. Death has no terrors for them when it is incurred in the course of duty.

"And whilst the eyes of the multitude of Twala's soldiers are thus fixed upon the fight," went on Ignosi, "behold, one-third of the men who are left alive to us (i.e. about 6,000) shall creep along the right horn of the hill and fall upon the left flank of Twala's force, and one-third shall creep along the left horn and fall upon Twala's right flank. And when I see that the horns are ready to toss Twala, then will I, with the men who remain to me, charge home in Twala's face, and if fortune goes with us the day will be ours, and before Night drives her black oxen from the mountains to the mountains we shall sit in peace at Loo. And now let us eat and make ready; and, Infadoos, do thou prepare, that the plan be carried out without fail; and stay, let my white father Bougwan go with the right horn, that his shining eye may give courage to the captains."

The arrangements for attack thus briefly indicated were set in motion with a rapidity that spoke well for the perfection of the Kukuana military system. Within little more than an hour rations had been served out and devoured, the divisions were formed, the scheme of onslaught was explained to the leaders, and the whole force, numbering about 18,000 men, was ready to move, with the exception of a guard left in charge of the wounded.

Presently Good came up to Sir Henry and myself.

"Good-bye, you fellows," he said; "I am off with the right wing according to orders; and so I have come to shake hands, in case we should not meet again, you know," he added significantly.

We shook hands in silence, and not without the exhibition of as much emotion as Anglo-Saxons are wont to show.

"It is a queer business," said Sir Henry, his deep voice shaking a little, "and I confess I never expect to see to-morrow's sun. So far as I can make out, the Greys, with whom I am to go, are to fight until they are wiped out in order to enable the wings to slip round unawares and outflank Twala. Well, so be it; at any rate, it will be a man's death. Good-bye, old fellow. God bless you! I hope you will pull through and live to collar the diamonds; but if you do, take my advice and don't have anything more to do with Pretenders!"

In another second Good had wrung us both by the hand and gone; and then Infadoos came up and led off Sir Henry to his place in the forefront of the Greys, whilst, with many misgivings, I departed with Ignosi to my station in the second attacking regiment.

The Last Stand of the Greys

In a few more minutes the regiments destined to carry out the flanking movements had tramped off in silence, keeping carefully to the lee of the rising ground in order to conceal their advance from the keen eyes of Twala's scouts.

Half an hour or more was allowed to elapse between the setting out of the horns or wings of the army before any stir was made by the Greys and their supporting regiment, known as the Buffaloes, which formed its chest, and were destined to bear the brunt of the battle.

Both of these regiments were almost perfectly fresh, and of full strength, the Greys having been in reserve in the morning, and having lost but a small number of men in sweeping back that part of the attack which had proved successful in breaking the line of defence, on the occasion when I charged with them and was stunned for my pains. As for the Buffaloes, they had formed the third line of defence on the left, and since the attacking force at that point had not succeeded in breaking through the second, they had scarcely come into action at all.

Infadoos, who was a wary old general, and knew the absolute importance of keeping up the spirits of his men on the eve of such a desperate encounter, employed the pause in addressing his own regiment, the Greys, in poetical language: explaining to them the honour that they were receiving in being put thus in the forefront of the battle, and in having the great white warrior from the Stars to fight with them in their ranks; and promising large rewards of cattle and promotion to all who survived in the event of Ignosi's arms being successful.

I looked down the long lines of waving black plumes and stern faces beneath them, and sighed to think that within one short hour most, if not all, of those magnificent veteran warriors, not a man of whom was under forty years of age, would be laid dead or dying in the dust. It could not be otherwise; they were being condemned, with that wise recklessness of human life which marks the great general, and often saves his forces and attains his ends, to certain slaughter, in order to give their cause and the remainder of the army a chance of success. They were foredoomed to die, and they knew the truth. It was to be their task to engage regiment after regiment of Twala's army on the narrow strip of green beneath us, till they were exterminated or till the wings found a favourable opportunity for their onslaught. And yet they never hesitated, nor could I detect a sign of fear upon the face of a single warrior. There they were—going to certain death, about to quit the blessed light of day for ever, and yet able to contemplate their doom without a tremor. Even at that moment I could not help contrasting their state of mind with my own, which was far from comfortable, and breathing a sigh of envy and admiration.

Never before had I seen such an absolute devotion to the idea of duty, and such a complete indifference to its bitter fruits.

"Behold your king!" ended old Infadoos, pointing to Ignosi; "go fight and fall for him, as is the duty of brave men, and cursed and shameful for ever be the name of him who shrinks from death for his king, or who turns his back to the foe. Behold your king, chiefs, captains, and soldiers! Now do your homage to the sacred Snake, and then follow on, that Incubu and I may show you a road to the heart of Twala's host."

There was a moment's pause, then suddenly a murmur arose from the serried phalanxes before us, a sound like the distant whisper of the sea, caused by the gentle tapping of the handles of six thousand spears against their holders' shields. Slowly it swelled, till its growing volume deepened and widened into a roar of rolling noise, that echoed like thunder against the mountains, and filled the air with heavy waves of sound. Then it decreased, and by faint degrees died away into nothing, and suddenly out crashed the royal salute.

Ignosi, I thought to myself, might well be a proud man that day, for no Roman emperor ever had such a salutation from gladiators "about to die."

Ignosi acknowledged this magnificent act of homage by lifting his battle-axe, and then the Greys filed off in a triple-line formation, each line containing about one thousand fighting men, exclusive of officers. When the last companies had advanced some five hundred yards, Ignosi put himself at the head of the Buffaloes, which regiment was drawn up in a similar three-fold formation, and gave the word to march, and off we went, I, needless to say, uttering the most heartfelt prayers that I might emerge from that entertainment with a whole skin. Many a queer position have I found myself in, but never before in one quite so unpleasant as the present, or one in which my chance of coming off safe was smaller.

By the time that we reached the edge of the plateau the Greys were already half-way down the slope ending in the tongue of grass land that ran up into the bend of the mountain, something as the frog of a horse's foot runs up into the shoe. The excitement in Twala's camp on the plain beyond was very great, and regiment after regiment was starting forward at a long swinging trot in order to reach the root of the tongue of land before the attacking force could emerge into the plain of Loo.

This tongue, which was some four hundred yards in depth, even at its root or widest part was not more than six hundred and fifty paces across, while at its tip it scarcely measured ninety. The Greys, who, in passing down the side of the hill and on to the tip of the tongue, had formed into a column, on reaching the spot where it broadened out again, reassumed their triple-line formation, and halted dead.

Then we—that is, the Buffaloes—moved down the tip of the tongue and took our stand in reserve, about one hundred yards behind the last line of the Greys, and on slightly higher ground. Meanwhile we had leisure to observe Twala's entire force, which evidently had been reinforced since the morning attack, and could not now, notwithstanding their losses, number less than forty thousand, moving swiftly up towards us. But as they drew near the root of the tongue they hesitated, having discovered that only one regiment could advance into the gorge at a time, and that there, some seventy yards from the mouth of it, unassailable except in front, on account of the high walls of boulder-strewn ground on each side, stood the famous regiment of Greys, the pride and glory of the Kukuana army, ready to hold the way against their power as the three Romans once held the bridge against thousands.

They hesitated, and finally stopped their advance; there was no eagerness to cross spears with these three grim ranks of warriors who stood so firm and ready. Presently, however, a tall general, wearing the customary head-dress of nodding ostrich plumes, appeared, attended by a group of chiefs and orderlies, being, I thought, none other than Twala himself. He gave an order, and the first regiment, raising a shout, charged up towards the Greys, who remained perfectly still and silent till the attacking troops were within forty yards, and a volley of *tollas*, or throwing-knives, came rattling among their ranks.

Then suddenly with a bound and a roar, they sprang forward with uplifted spears, and the regiment met in deadly strife. Next second the roll of the meeting shields came to our ears like the sound of thunder, and the plain seemed to be alive with flashes of light reflected from the shimmering spears. To and fro swung the surging mass of struggling, stabbing humanity, but not for long. Suddenly the attacking lines began to grow thinner, and then with a slow, long heave the Greys passed over them, just as a great wave heaves up its bulk and passes over a sunken ridge. It was done; that regiment was completely destroyed, but the Greys had but two lines left now; a third of their number were dead.

Closing up shoulder to shoulder, once more they halted in silence and awaited attack; and I was rejoiced to catch sight of Sir Henry's yellow beard as he moved to and fro arranging the ranks. So he was yet alive!

Meanwhile we moved on to the ground of the encounter, which was cumbered by about four thousand prostrate human beings, dead, dying, and wounded, and literally stained red with blood. Ignosi issued an order, which was rapidly passed down the ranks, to the effect that none of the enemy's wounded were to be killed, and so far as we could see this command was scrupulously carried out. It would have been a shocking sight, if we had found time to think of such things.

But now a second regiment, distinguished by white plumes, kilts, and shields, was moving to the attack of the two thousand remaining Greys, who stood waiting in the same ominous silence as before, till the foe was within forty yards or so, when they hurled themselves with irresistible force upon them. Again there came the awful roll of the meeting shields, and as we watched the tragedy repeated itself.

But this time the issue was left longer in doubt; indeed, it seemed for awhile almost impossible that the Greys should again prevail. The attacking regiment, which was formed of young men, fought with the utmost fury, and at first seemed by sheer weight to be driving the veterans back. The slaughter was truly awful, hundreds falling every minute; and from among the shouts of the warriors and the groans of the dying, set to the music of clashing spears, came a continuous hissing undertone of "*S'gee, s'gee,*" the note of triumph of each victor as he passed his assegai through and through the body of his fallen foe.

But perfect discipline and steady and unchanging valour can do wonders, and one veteran soldier is worth two young ones, as soon became apparent in the present case. For just when we thought that it was all over with the Greys, and were preparing to take their place so soon as they made room by being destroyed, I heard Sir Henry's deep voice ringing out through the din, and caught a glimpse of his circling battle-axe as he waved it high above his plumes. Then came a change; the Greys ceased to give; they stood still as a rock, against which the furious waves of spearmen broke again and again, only to recoil. Presently they began to move once more—forward this time; as they had no firearms there was no smoke, so we could see it all. Another minute and the onslaught grew fainter.

"Ah, these are *men*, indeed; they will conquer again," called out Ignosi, who was grinding his teeth with excitement at my side. "See, it is done!"

Suddenly, like puffs of smoke from the mouth of a cannon, the attacking regiment broke away in flying groups, their white head- dresses streaming behind them in the wind, and left their opponents victors, indeed, but, alas! no more a regiment. Of the gallant triple line, which forty minutes before had gone into action three thousand strong, there remained at most some six hundred blood-spattered men; the rest were under foot. And yet they cheered and waved their spears in triumph, and then, instead of falling back upon us as we expected, they ran forward, for a hundred yards or so, after the flying groups of foemen, took possession of a rising knoll of ground, and, resuming their triple formation, formed a threefold ring around its base. And there, thanks be to Heaven, standing on the top of the mound for a minute, I saw Sir Henry, apparently unharmed, and with him our old friend Infadoos. Then Twala's regiments rolled down upon the doomed band, and once more the battle closed in.

As those who read this history will probably long ago have gathered, I am, to be honest, a bit of a coward, and certainly in no way given to fighting, though somehow it has often been my lot to get into unpleasant positions, and to be obliged to shed man's blood. But I have always hated it, and kept my own blood as undiminished in quantity as possible, sometimes by a judicious use of my heels. At this moment, however, for the first time in my life, I felt my bosom burn with martial ardour. Warlike fragments from the "Ingoldsby Legends," together with numbers of sanguinary verses in the Old Testament, sprang up in my brain like mushrooms in the dark; my blood, which hitherto had been half-frozen with horror, went beating through my veins, and there came upon me a savage desire to kill and spare not. I glanced round at the serried ranks of warriors behind us, and somehow, all in an instant, I began to wonder if my face looked like theirs. There they stood, the hands twitching, the lips apart, the fierce features instinct with the hungry lust of battle, and in the eyes a look like the glare of a bloodhound when after long pursuit he sights his quarry.

Only Ignosi's heart, to judge from his comparative self-possession, seemed, to all appearances, to beat as calmly as ever beneath his leopard-skin cloak, though even *he* still ground his teeth. I could bear it no longer.

"Are we to stand here till we put out roots, Umbopa—Ignosi, I mean—while Twala swallows our brothers yonder?" I asked.

"Nay, Macumazahn," was the answer; "see, now is the ripe moment: let us pluck it."

As he spoke a fresh regiment rushed past the ring upon the little mound, and wheeling round, attacked it from the hither side.

Then, lifting his battle-axe, Ignosi gave the signal to advance, and, screaming the wild Kukuana war-cry, the Buffaloes charged home with a rush like the rush of the sea.

What followed immediately on this it is out of my power to tell. All I can remember is an irregular yet ordered advance, that seemed to shake the ground; a sudden change of front and forming up on the part of the regiment against which the charge was directed; then an awful shock, a dull roar of voices, and a continuous flashing of spears, seen through a red mist of blood.

When my mind cleared I found myself standing inside the remnant of the Greys near the top of the mound, and just behind no less a person than Sir Henry himself. How I got there I had at the moment no idea, but Sir Henry afterwards told me that I was borne up by the first furious charge of the Buffaloes almost to his feet, and then left, as they in turn were pressed back. Thereon he dashed out of the circle and dragged me into shelter.

As for the fight that followed, who can describe it? Again and again the multitudes surged against our momentarily lessening circle, and again and again we beat them back.

"The stubborn spearmen still made good
The dark impenetrable wood,
Each stepping where his comrade stood
The instant that he fell,"
As someone or other beautifully says.

It was a splendid thing to see those brave battalions come on time after time over the barriers of their dead, sometimes lifting corpses before them to receive our spear-thrusts, only to leave their own corpses to swell the rising piles. It was a gallant sight to see that old warrior, Infadoos, as cool as though he were on parade, shouting out orders, taunts, and even jests, to keep up the spirit of his few remaining men, and then, as each charge rolled on, stepping forward to wherever the fighting was thickest, to bear his share in its repulse. And yet more gallant was the vision of Sir Henry, whose ostrich plumes had been shorn off by a spear thrust, so that his long yellow hair streamed out in the breeze behind him. There he stood, the great Dane, for he was nothing else, his hands, his axe, and his armour all red with blood, and none could live before his stroke. Time after time I saw it sweeping down, as some great warrior ventured to give him battle, and as he struck he shouted "*O-hoy!*

O-hoy!' like his Berserkir forefathers, and the blow went crashing through shield and spear, through head-dress, hair, and skull, till at last none would of their own will come near the great white "*umtagati*," the wizard, who killed and failed not.

But suddenly there rose a cry of "*Twala, y' Twala,*" and out of the press sprang forward none other than the gigantic one-eyed king himself, also armed with battle-axe and shield, and clad in chain armour.

"Where art thou, Incubu, thou white man, who slewest Scragga my son— see if thou canst slay me!" he shouted, and at the same time hurled a *tolla* straight at Sir Henry, who fortunately saw it coming, and caught it on his shield, which it transfixed, remaining wedged in the iron plate behind the hide.

Then, with a cry, Twala sprang forward straight at him, and with his battle-axe struck him such a blow upon the shield that the mere force and shock of it brought Sir Henry, strong man as he is, down upon his knees.

But at this time the matter went no further, for that instant there rose from the regiments pressing round us something like a shout of dismay, and on looking up I saw the cause.

To the right and to the left the plain was alive with the plumes of charging warriors. The outflanking squadrons had come to our relief. The time could not have been better chosen. All Twala's army, as Ignosi predicted would be the case, had fixed their attention on the bloody struggle which was raging round the remnant of the Greys and that of the Buffaloes, who were now carrying on a battle of their own at a little distance, which two regiments had formed the chest of our army. It was not until our horns were about to close upon them that they had dreamed of their approach, for they believed these forces to be hidden in reserve upon the crest of the moon-shaped hill. And now, before they could even assume a proper formation for defence, the outflanking *Impis* had leapt, like greyhounds, on their flanks.

In five minutes the fate of the battle was decided. Taken on both flanks, and dismayed at the awful slaughter inflicted upon them by the Greys and Buffaloes, Twala's regiments broke into flight, and soon the whole plain between us and Loo was scattered with groups of running soldiers making good their retreat. As for the hosts that had so recently surrounded us and the Buffaloes, they melted away as though by magic, and presently we were left standing there like a rock from which the sea has retreated. But what a sight it was! Around us the dead and dying lay in heaped-up masses, and of the gallant Greys there remained but ninety-five men upon their feet. More than three thousand four hundred had fallen in this one regiment, most of them never to rise again.

"Men," said Infadoos calmly, as between the intervals of binding a wound on his arm he surveyed what remained to him of his corps, "ye have kept up the reputation of your regiment, and this day's fighting will be well spoken of by your children's children." Then he turned round and shook Sir Henry Curtis by the hand. "Thou art a great captain, Incubu," he said simply; "I have lived a long life among warriors, and have known many a brave one, yet have I never seen a man like unto thee."

At this moment the Buffaloes began to march past our position on the road to Loo, and as they went a message was brought to us from Ignosi requesting Infadoos, Sir Henry, and myself to join them. Accordingly, orders having been issued to the remaining ninety men of the Greys to employ themselves in collecting the wounded, we joined Ignosi, who informed us that he was pressing on to Loo to complete the victory by capturing Twala, if that should be possible. Before we had gone far, suddenly we discovered the figure of Good sitting on an ant-heap about one hundred paces from us. Close beside him was the body of a Kukuana.

"He must be wounded," said Sir Henry anxiously. As he made the remark, an untoward thing happened. The dead body of the Kukuana soldier, or rather what had appeared to be his dead body, suddenly sprang up, knocked Good head over heels off the ant-heap, and began to spear him. We rushed forward in terror, and as we drew near we saw the brawny warrior making dig after dig at the prostrate Good, who at each prod jerked all his limbs into the air. Seeing us coming, the Kukuana gave one final and most vicious dig, and with a shout of "Take that, wizard!" bolted away. Good did not move, and we concluded that our poor comrade was done for. Sadly we came towards him, and were astonished to find him pale and faint indeed, but with a serene smile upon his face, and his eyeglass still fixed in his eye.

"Capital armour this," he murmured, on catching sight of our faces bending over him. "How sold that beggar must have been," and then he fainted. On examination we discovered that he had been seriously wounded in the leg by a *tolla* in the course of the pursuit, but that the chain armour had prevented his last assailant's spear from doing anything more than bruise him badly. It was a merciful escape. As nothing could be done for him at the moment, he was placed on one of the wicker shields used for the wounded, and carried along with us.

On arriving before the nearest gate of Loo we found one of our regiments watching it in obedience to orders received from Ignosi. The other regiments were in the same way guarding the different exits to the town. The officer in command of this regiment saluted Ignosi as king, and informed him that Twala's army had taken refuge in the town, whither Twala himself had also escaped, but he thought that they were thoroughly demoralised, and would surrender. Thereupon Ignosi, after taking counsel with us, sent forward heralds to each gate ordering the defenders to open, and promising on his royal word life and forgiveness to every soldier who laid down his arms, but saying that if they did not do so before nightfall he would certainly burn the town and all within its gates. This message was not without its effect. Half an hour later, amid the shouts and cheers of the Buffaloes, the bridge was dropped across the fosse, and the gates upon the further side were flung open.

Taking due precautions against treachery, we marched on into the town. All along the roadways stood thousands of dejected warriors, their heads drooping, and their shields and spears at their feet, who, headed by their officers, saluted Ignosi as king as he passed. On we marched, straight to Twala's kraal. When we reached the great space, where a day or two previously we had seen the review and the witch hunt, we found it deserted. No, not quite deserted, for there, on the further side, in front of his hut, sat Twala himself, with but one attendant—Gagool.

It was a melancholy sight to see him seated, his battle-axe and shield by his side, his chin upon his mailed breast, with but one old crone for companion, and notwithstanding his crimes and misdeeds, a pang of compassion shot through me as I looked upon Twala thus "fallen from his high estate." Not a soldier of all his armies, not a courtier out of the hundreds who had cringed round him, not even a solitary wife, remained to share his fate or halve the bitterness of his fall. Poor savage! he was learning the lesson which Fate teaches to most of us who live long enough, that the eyes of mankind are blind to the discredited, and that he who is defenceless and fallen finds few friends and little mercy. Nor, indeed, in this case did he deserve any.

Filing through the kraal gate, we marched across the open space to where the ex-king sat. When within about fifty yards of him the regiment was halted, and accompanied only by a small guard we advanced towards him, Gagool reviling us bitterly as we came. As we drew near, Twala, for the first time, lifted his plumed head, and fixed his one eye, which seemed to flash with suppressed fury almost as brightly as the great diamond bound round his forehead, upon his successful rival—Ignosi.

"Hail, O king!" he said, with bitter mockery; "thou who hast eaten of my bread, and now by the aid of the white man's magic hast seduced my regiments and defeated mine army, hail! What fate hast thou in store for me, O king?"

"The fate thou gavest to my father, whose throne thou hast sat on these many years!" was the stern answer.

"It is good. I will show thee how to die, that thou mayest remember it against thine own time. See, the sun sinks in blood," and he pointed with his battle-axe towards the setting orb; "it is well that my sun should go down in its company. And now, O king! I am ready to die, but I crave the boon of the Kukuana royal House to die fighting. Thou canst refuse it, or even those cowards who fled to-day will hold thee shamed."

"It is granted. Choose—with whom wilt thou fight? Myself I cannot fight with thee, for the king fights not except in war."

Twala's sombre eye ran up and down our ranks, and I felt, as for a moment it rested on myself, that the position had developed a new horror. What if he chose to begin by fighting *me*? What chance should I have against a desperate savage six feet five high, and broad in proportion? I might as well commit suicide at once. Hastily I made up my mind to decline the combat, even if I were hooted out of Kukuanaland as a consequence. It is, I think, better to be hooted than to be quartered with a battle-axe.

Presently Twala spoke.

"Incubu, what sayest thou, shall we end what we began to-day, or shall I call thee coward, white—even to the liver?"

"Nay," interposed Ignosi hastily; "thou shalt not fight with Incubu."

"Not if he is afraid," said Twala.

Unfortunately Sir Henry understood this remark, and the blood flamed up into his cheeks.

"I will fight him," he said; "he shall see if I am afraid."

"For Heaven's sake," I entreated, "don't risk your life against that of a desperate man. Anybody who saw you to-day will know that you are brave enough."

"I will fight him," was the sullen answer. "No living man shall call me a coward. I am ready now!" and he stepped forward and lifted his axe.

I wrung my hands over this absurd piece of Quixotism; but if he was determined on this deed, of course I could not stop him.

"Fight not, my white brother," said Ignosi, laying his hand affectionately on Sir Henry's arm; "thou hast fought enough, and if aught befell thee at his hands it would cut my heart in twain."

"I will fight, Ignosi," was Sir Henry's answer.

"It is well, Incubu; thou art a brave man. It will be a good fray. Behold, Twala, the Elephant is ready for thee."

The ex-king laughed savagely, and stepping forward faced Curtis. For a moment they stood thus, and the light of the sinking sun caught their stalwart frames and clothed them both in fire. They were a well- matched pair.

Then they began to circle round each other, their battle-axes raised.

Suddenly Sir Henry sprang forward and struck a fearful blow at Twala, who stepped to one side. So heavy was the stroke that the striker half overbalanced himself, a circumstance of which his antagonist took a prompt advantage. Circling his massive battle-axe round his head, he brought it down with tremendous force. My heart jumped into my mouth; I thought that the affair was already finished. But no; with a quick upward movement of the left arm Sir Henry interposed his shield between himself and the axe, with the result that its outer edge was shorn away, the axe falling on his left shoulder, but not heavily enough to do any serious damage. In another moment Sir Henry got in a second blow, which was also received by Twala upon his shield.

Then followed blow upon blow, that were, in turn, either received upon the shields or avoided. The excitement grew intense; the regiment which was watching the encounter forgot its discipline, and, drawing near, shouted and groaned at every stroke. Just at this time, too, Good, who had been laid upon the ground by me, recovered from his faint, and, sitting up, perceived what was going on. In an instant he was up, and catching hold of my arm, hopped about from place to place on one leg, dragging me after him, and yelling encouragements to Sir Henry—

"Go it, old fellow!" he hallooed. "That was a good one! Give it him amidships," and so on.

Presently Sir Henry, having caught a fresh stroke upon his shield, hit out with all his force. The blow cut through Twala's shield and through the tough chain armour behind it, gashing him in the shoulder. With a yell of pain and fury Twala returned the blow with interest, and, such was his strength, shore right through the rhinoceros' horn handle of his antagonists battle-axe, strengthened as it was with bands of steel, wounding Curtis in the face.

A cry of dismay rose from the Buffaloes as our hero's broad axe-head fell to the ground; and Twala, again raising his weapon, flew at him with a shout. I shut my eyes. When I opened them again it was to see Sir Henry's shield lying on the ground, and Sir Henry himself with his great arms twined round Twala's middle. To and fro they swung, hugging each other like bears, straining with all their mighty muscles for dear life, and dearer honour. With a supreme effort Twala swung the Englishman clean off his feet, and down they came together, rolling over and over on the lime paving, Twala striking out at Curtis' head with the battle-axe, and Sir Henry trying to drive the *tolla* he had drawn from his belt through Twala's armour.

It was a mighty struggle, and an awful thing to see.

"Get his axe!" yelled Good; and perhaps our champion heard him.

At any rate, dropping the *tolla*, he snatched at the axe, which was fastened to Twala's wrist by a strip of buffalo hide, and still rolling over and over, they fought for it like wild cats, drawing their breath in heavy gasps. Suddenly the hide string burst, and then, with a great effort, Sir Henry freed himself, the weapon remaining in his hand. Another second and he was upon his feet, the red blood streaming from the wound in his face, and so was Twala. Drawing the heavy *tolla* from his belt, he reeled straight at Curtis and struck him in the breast. The stab came home true and strong, but whoever it was who made that chain armour, he understood his art, for it withstood the steel. Again Twala struck out with a savage yell, and again the sharp knife rebounded, and Sir Henry went staggering back. Once more Twala came on, and as he came our great Englishman gathered himself together, and swinging the big axe round his head with both hands, hit at him with all his force.

There was a shriek of excitement from a thousand throats, and, behold! Twala's head seemed to spring from his shoulders: then it fell and came rolling and bounding along the ground towards Ignosi, stopping just as his feet. For a second the corpse stood upright; then with a dull crash it came to the earth, and the gold torque from its neck rolled away across the pavement. As it did so Sir Henry, overpowered by faintness and loss of blood, fell heavily across the body of the dead king.

In a second he was lifted up, and eager hands were pouring water on his face. Another minute, and the grey eyes opened wide.

He was not dead.

Then I, just as the sun sank, stepping to where Twala's head lay in the dust, unloosed the diamond from the dead brows, and handed it to Ignosi.

"Take it," I said, "lawful king of the Kukuanas—king by birth and victory."

Ignosi bound the diadem upon his brows. Then advancing, he placed his foot upon the broad chest of his headless foe and broke out into a chant, or rather a paean of triumph, so beautiful, and yet so utterly savage, that I despair of being able to give an adequate version of his words. Once I heard a scholar with a fine voice read aloud from the Greek poet Homer, and I remember that the sound of the rolling lines seemed to make my blood stand still. Ignosi's chant, uttered as it was in a language as beautiful and sonorous as the old Greek, produced exactly the same effect on me, although I was exhausted with toil and many emotions.

"Now," he began, "now our rebellion is swallowed up in victory, and our evil-doing is justified by strength.

"In the morning the oppressors arose and stretched themselves; they bound on their harness and made them ready to war.

"They rose up and tossed their spears: the soldiers called to the captains, 'Come, lead us'—and the captains cried to the king, 'Direct thou the battle.'

"They laughed in their pride, twenty thousand men, and yet a twenty thousand.

"Their plumes covered the valleys as the plumes of a bird cover her nest; they shook their shields and shouted, yea, they shook their shields in the sunlight; they lusted for battle and were glad.

"They came up against me; their strong ones ran swiftly to slay me; they cried, 'Ha! ha! he is as one already dead.'

"Then breathed I on them, and my breath was as the breath of a wind, and lo! they were not.

"My lightnings pierced them; I licked up their strength with the lightning of my spears; I shook them to the ground with the thunder of my shoutings.

"They broke—they scattered—they were gone as the mists of the morning.

"They are food for the kites and the foxes, and the place of battle is fat with their blood.

"Where are the mighty ones who rose up in the morning?

"Where are the proud ones who tossed their spears and cried, 'He is as a man already dead'?

"They bow their heads, but not in sleep; they are stretched out, but not in sleep.

"They are forgotten; they have gone into the blackness; they dwell in the dead moons; yea, others shall lead away their wives, and their children shall remember them no more.

"And I—! the king—like an eagle I have found my eyrie.

"Behold! far have I flown in the night season, yet have I returned to my young at the daybreak.

"Shelter ye under the shadow of my wings, O people, and I will comfort you, and ye shall not be dismayed.

"Now is the good time, the time of spoil.

"Mine are the cattle on the mountains, mine are the virgins in the kraals.

"The winter is overpast with storms, the summer is come with flowers.

"Now Evil shall cover up her face, now Mercy and Gladness shall dwell in the land.

"Rejoice, rejoice, my people!

"Let all the stars rejoice in that this tyranny is trodden down, in that I am the king."

Ignosi ceased his song, and out of the gathering gloom came back the deep reply—

"Thou art the king!"

Thus was my prophecy to the herald fulfilled, and within the forty- eight hours Twala's headless corpse was stiffening at Twala's gate.

Good Falls Sick

After the fight was ended, Sir Henry and Good were carried into Twala's hut, where I joined them. They were both utterly exhausted by exertion and loss of blood, and, indeed, my own condition was little better. I am very wiry, and can stand more fatigue than most men, probably on account of my light weight and long training; but that night I was quite done up, and, as is always the case with me when exhausted, that old wound which the lion gave me began to pain. Also my head was aching violently from the blow I had received in the morning, when I was knocked senseless. Altogether, a more miserable trio than we were that evening it would have been difficult to discover; and our only comfort lay in the reflection that we were exceedingly fortunate to be there to feel miserable, instead of being stretched dead upon the plain, as so many thousands of brave men were that night, who had risen well and strong in the morning.

Somehow, with the assistance of the beautiful Foulata, who, since we had been the means of saving her life, had constituted herself our handmaiden, and especially Good's, we managed to get off the chain shirts, which had certainly saved the lives of two of us that day. As I expected, we found that the flesh underneath was terribly contused, for though the steel links had kept the weapons from entering, they had not prevented them from bruising. Both Sir Henry and Good were a mass of contusions, and I was by no means free. As a remedy Foulata brought us some pounded green leaves, with an aromatic odour, which, when applied as a plaster, gave us considerable relief.

But though the bruises were painful, they did not give us such anxiety as Sir Henry's and Good's wounds. Good had a hole right through the fleshy part of his "beautiful white leg," from which he had lost a great deal of blood; and Sir Henry, with other hurts, had a deep cut over the jaw, inflicted by Twala's battle-axe. Luckily Good is a very decent surgeon, and so soon as his small box of medicines was forthcoming, having thoroughly cleansed the wounds, he managed to stitch up first Sir Henry's and then his own pretty satisfactorily, considering the imperfect light given by the primitive Kukuana lamp in the hut. Afterwards he plentifully smeared the injured places with some antiseptic ointment, of which there was a pot in the little box, and we covered them with the remains of a pocket-handkerchief which we possessed.

Meanwhile Foulata had prepared us some strong broth, for we were too weary to eat. This we swallowed, and then threw ourselves down on the piles of magnificent karrosses, or fur rugs, which were scattered about the dead king's great hut. By a very strange instance of the irony of fate, it was on Twala's own couch, and wrapped in Twala's own particular karross, that Sir Henry, the man who had slain him, slept that night.

I say slept; but after that day's work, sleep was indeed difficult. To begin with, in very truth the air was full

"Of farewells to the dying And mournings for the dead."

From every direction came the sound of the wailing of women whose husbands, sons, and brothers had perished in the battle. No wonder that they wailed, for over twelve thousand men, or nearly a fifth of the Kukuana army, had been destroyed in that awful struggle. It was heart-rending to lie and listen to their cries for those who never would return; and it made me understand the full horror of the work done that day to further man's ambition. Towards midnight, however, the ceaseless crying of the women grew less frequent, till at length the silence was only broken at intervals of a few minutes by a long piercing howl that came from a hut in our immediate rear, which, as I afterwards discovered, proceeded from Gagool "keening" over the dead king Twala.

After that I got a little fitful sleep, only to wake from time to time with a start, thinking that I was once more an actor in the terrible events of the last twenty-four hours. Now I seemed to see that warrior whom my hand had sent to his last account charging at me on the mountain-top; now I was once more in that glorious ring of Greys, which made its immortal stand against all Twala's regiments upon the little mound; and now again I saw Twala's plumed and gory head roll past my feet with gnashing teeth and glaring eye.

At last, somehow or other, the night passed away; but when dawn broke I found that my companions had slept no better than myself. Good, indeed, was in a high fever, and very soon afterwards began to grow light-headed, and also, to my alarm, to spit blood, the result, no doubt, of some internal injury, inflicted during the desperate efforts made by the Kukuana warrior on the previous day to force his big spear through the chain armour. Sir Henry, however, seemed pretty fresh, notwithstanding his wound on the face, which made eating difficult and laughter an impossibility, though he was so sore and stiff that he could scarcely stir.

About eight o'clock we had a visit from Infadoos, who appeared but little the worse—tough old warrior that he was—for his exertions in the battle, although he informed us that he had been up all night. He was delighted to see us, but much grieved at Good's condition, and shook our hands cordially. I noticed, however, that he addressed Sir Henry with a kind of reverence, as though he were something more than man; and, indeed, as we afterwards found out, the great Englishman was looked on throughout Kukuanaland as a supernatural being. No man, the soldiers said, could have fought as he fought or, at the end of a day of such toil and bloodshed, could have slain Twala, who, in addition to being the king, was supposed to be the strongest warrior in the country, in single combat, shearing through his bull-neck at a stroke. Indeed, that stroke became proverbial in Kukuanaland, and any extraordinary blow or feat of strength was henceforth known as 'Incubu's blow."

Infadoos told us also that all Twala's regiments had submitted to Ignosi, and that like submissions were beginning to arrive from chiefs in the outlying country. Twala's death at the hands of Sir Henry had put an end to all further chance of disturbance; for Scragga had been his only legitimate son, so there was no rival claimant to the throne left alive.

I remarked that Ignosi had swum to power through blood. The old chief shrugged his shoulders. "Yes," he answered; "but the Kukuana people can only be kept cool by letting their blood flow sometimes. Many are killed, indeed, but the women are left, and others must soon grow up to take the places of the fallen. After this the land would be quiet for a while."

Afterwards, in the course of the morning, we had a short visit from Ignosi, on whose brows the royal diadem was now bound. As I contemplated him advancing with kingly dignity, an obsequious guard following his steps, I could not help recalling to my mind the tall Zulu who had presented himself to us at Durban some few months back, asking to be taken into our service, and reflecting on the strange revolutions of the wheel of fortune.

"Hail, O king!" I said, rising.

"Yes, Macumazahn. King at last, by the might of your three right hands," was the ready answer.

All was, he said, going well; and he hoped to arrange a great feast in two weeks' time in order to show himself to the people.

I asked him what he had settled to do with Gagool.

"She is the evil genius of the land," he answered, "and I shall kill her, and all the witch doctors with her! She has lived so long that none can remember when she was not very old, and she it is who has always trained the witch-hunters, and made the land wicked in the sight of the heavens above."

"Yet she knows much," I replied; "it is easier to destroy knowledge, Ignosi, than to gather it."

"That is so," he said thoughtfully. "She, and she only, knows the secret of the 'Three Witches,' yonder, whither the great road runs, where the kings are buried, and the Silent Ones sit."

"Yes, and the diamonds are. Forget not thy promise, Ignosi; thou must lead us to the mines, even if thou hast to spare Gagool alive to show the way."

"I will not forget, Macumazahn, and I will think on what thou sayest."

After Ignosi's visit I went to see Good, and found him quite delirious. The fever set up by his wound seemed to have taken a firm hold of his system, and to be complicated with an internal injury. For four or five days his condition was most critical; indeed, I believe firmly that had it not been for Foulata's indefatigable nursing he must have died.

Women are women, all the world over, whatever their colour. Yet somehow it seemed curious to watch this dusky beauty bending night and day over the fevered man's couch, and performing all the merciful errands of a sick-room swiftly, gently, and with as fine an instinct as that of a trained hospital nurse. For the first night or two I tried to help her, and so did Sir Henry as soon as his stiffness allowed him to move, but Foulata bore our interference with impatience, and finally insisted upon our leaving him to her, saying that our movements made him restless, which I think was true. Day and night she watched him and tended him, giving him his only medicine, a native cooling drink made of milk, in which was infused juice from the bulb of a species of tulip, and keeping the flies from settling on him. I can see the whole picture now as it appeared night after night by the light of our primitive lamp; Good tossing to and fro, his features emaciated, his eyes shining large and luminous, and jabbering nonsense by the yard; and seated on the ground by his side, her back resting against the wall of the hut, the soft-eyed, shapely Kukuana beauty, her face, weary as it was with her long vigil, animated by a look of infinite compassion—or was it something more than compassion?

For two days we thought that he must die, and crept about with heavy hearts.

Only Foulata would not believe it.

"He will live," she said.

For three hundred yards or more around Twala's chief hut, where the sufferer lay, there was silence; for by the king's order all who lived in the habitations behind it, except Sir Henry and myself, had been removed, lest any noise should come to the sick man's ears. One night, it was the fifth of Good's illness, as was my habit, I went across to see how he was doing before turning in for a few hours.

I entered the hut carefully. The lamp placed upon the floor showed the figure of Good tossing no more, but lying quite still.

So it had come at last! In the bitterness of my heart I gave something like a sob.

"Hush—h—h!" came from the patch of dark shadow behind Good's head.

Then, creeping closer, I saw that he was not dead, but sleeping soundly, with Foulata's taper fingers clasped tightly in his poor white hand. The crisis had passed, and he would live. He slept like that for eighteen hors; and I scarcely like to say it, for fear I should not be believed, but during the entire period did this devoted girl sit by him, fearing that if she moved and drew away her hand it would wake him. What she must have suffered from cramp and weariness, to say nothing of want of food, nobody will ever know; but it is the fact that, when at last he woke, she had to be carried away—her limbs were so stiff that she could not move them.

After the turn had once been taken, Good's recovery was rapid and complete. It was not till he was nearly well that Sir Henry told him of all he owed to Foulata; and when he came to the story of how she sat by his side for eighteen hours, fearing lest by moving she should wake him, the honest sailor's eyes filled with tears. He turned and went straight to the hut where Foulata was preparing the mid-day meal, for we were back in our old quarters now, taking me with him to interpret in case he could not make his meaning clear to her, though I am bound to say that she understood him marvellously as a rule, considering how extremely limited was his foreign vocabulary.

"Tell her," said Good, "that I owe her my life, and that I will never forget her kindness to my dying day."

I interpreted, and under her dark skin she actually seemed to blush.

Turning to him with one of those swift and graceful motions that in her always reminded me of the flight of a wild bird, Foulata answered softly, glancing at him with her large brown eyes—

"Nay, my lord; my lord forgets! Did he not save *my* life, and am I not my lord's handmaiden?"

It will be observed that the young lady appeared entirely to have forgotten the share which Sir Henry and myself had taken in her preservation from Twala's clutches. But that is the way of women! I remember my dear wife was just the same. Well, I retired from that little interview sad at heart. I did not like Miss Foulata's soft glances, for I knew the fatal amorous propensities of sailors in general, and of Good in particular.

There are two things in the world, as I have found out, which cannot be prevented: you cannot keep a Zulu from fighting, or a sailor from falling in love upon the slightest provocation!

It was a few days after this last occurrence that Ignosi held his great "indaba," or council, and was formally recognised as king by the "indunas," or head men, of Kukuanaland. The spectacle was a most imposing one, including as it did a grand review of troops. On this day the remaining fragments of the Greys were formally paraded, and in the face of the army thanked for their splendid conduct in the battle. To each man the king made a large present of cattle, promoting them one and all to the rank of officers in the new corps of Greys which was in process of formation. An order was also promulgated throughout the length and breadth of Kukuanaland that, whilst we honoured the country by our presence, we three were to be greeted with the royal salute, and to be treated with the same ceremony and respect that was by custom accorded to the king. Also the power of life and death was publicly conferred upon us. Ignosi, too, in the presence of his people, reaffirmed the promises which he had made, to the effect that no man's blood should be shed without trial, and that witch-hunting should cease in the land.

When the ceremony was over we waited upon Ignosi, and informed him that we were now anxious to investigate the mystery of the mines to which Solomon's Road ran, asking him if he had discovered anything about them.

"My friends," he answered, "I have discovered this. It is there that the three great figures sit, who here are called the 'Silent Ones,' and to whom Twala would have offered the girl Foulata as a sacrifice. It is there, too, in a great cave deep in the mountain, that the kings of the land are buried; there ye shall find Twala's body, sitting with those who went before him. There, also, is a deep pit, which, at some time, long-dead men dug out, mayhap for the stones ye speak of, such as I have heard men in Natal tell of at Kimberley. There, too, in the Place of Death is a secret chamber, known to none but the king and Gagool. But Twala, who knew it, is dead, and I know it not, nor know I what is in it. Yet there is a legend in the land that once, many generations gone, a white man crossed the mountains, and was led by a woman to the secret chamber and shown the wealth hidden in it. But before he could take it she betrayed him, and he was driven by the king of that day back to the mountains, and since then no man has entered the place."

"The story is surely true, Ignosi, for on the mountains we found the white man," I said.

"Yes, we found him. And now I have promised you that if ye can come to that chamber, and the stones are there—"

"The gem upon thy forehead proves that they are there," I put in, pointing to the great diamond I had taken from Twala's dead brows.

"Mayhap; if they are there," he said, "ye shall have as many as ye can take hence—if indeed ye would leave me, my brothers."

"First we must find the chamber," said I.

"There is but one who can show it to thee—Gagool."

"And if she will not?"

"Then she must die," said Ignosi sternly. "I have saved her alive but for this. Stay, she shall choose," and calling to a messenger he ordered Gagool to be brought before him.

In a few minutes she came, hurried along by two guards, whom she was cursing as she walked.

"Leave her," said the king to the guards.

So soon as their support was withdrawn, the withered old bundle—for she looked more like a bundle than anything else, out of which her two bright and wicked eyes gleamed like those of a snake—sank in a heap on to the floor.

"What will ye with me, Ignosi?" she piped. "Ye dare not touch me. If ye touch me I will slay you as ye sit. Beware of my magic."

"Thy magic could not save Twala, old she-wolf, and it cannot hurt me," was the answer. "Listen; I will this of thee, that thou reveal to us the chamber where are the shining stones."

"Ha! ha!" she piped, "none know its secret but I, and I will never tell thee. The white devils shall go hence empty-handed."

"Thou shalt tell me. I will make thee tell me."

"How, O king? Thou art great, but can thy power wring the truth from a woman?"

"It is difficult, yet will I do so."

"How, O king?"

"Nay, thus; if thou tellest not thou shalt slowly die."

"Die!" she shrieked in terror and fury; "ye dare not touch me—man, ye know not who I am. How old think ye am I? I knew your fathers, and your fathers' fathers' fathers. When the country was young I was here; when the country grows old I shall still be here. I cannot die unless I be killed by chance, for none dare slay me."

"Yet will I slay thee. See, Gagool, mother of evil, thou art so old that thou canst no longer love thy life. What can life be to such a hag as thou, who hast no shape, nor form, nor hair, nor teeth—hast naught, save wickedness and evil eyes? It will be mercy to make an end of thee, Gagool."

"Thou fool," shrieked the old fiend, "thou accursed fool, deemest thou that life is sweet only to the young? It is not so, and naught thou knowest of the heart of man to think it. To the young, indeed, death is sometimes welcome, for the young can feel. They love and suffer, and it wrings them to see their beloved pass to the land of shadows. But the old feel not, they love not, and, *ha! ha!* they laugh to see another go out into the dark; *ha! ha!* they laugh to see the evil that is done under the stars. All they love is life, the warm, warm sun, and the sweet, sweet air. They are afraid of the cold, afraid of the cold and the dark, *ha! ha! ha!*" and the old hag writhed in ghastly merriment on the ground.

"Cease thine evil talk and answer me," said Ignosi angrily. "Wilt thou show the place where the stones are, or wilt thou not? If thou wilt not thou diest, even now," and he seized a spear and held it over her.

"I will not show it; thou darest not kill me, darest not! He who slays me will be accursed for ever."

Slowly Ignosi brought down the spear till it pricked the prostrate heap of rags.

With a wild yell Gagool sprang to her feet, then fell again and rolled upon the floor.

"Nay, I will show thee. Only let me live, let me sit in the sun and have a bit of meat to suck, and I will show thee."

"It is well. I thought that I should find a way to reason with thee. To-morrow shalt thou go with Infadoos and my white brothers to the place, and beware how thou failest, for if thou showest it not, then thou shalt slowly die. I have spoken."

"I will not fail, Ignosi. I always keep my word—*ha! ha! ha!* Once before a woman showed the chamber to a white man, and behold! evil befell him," and here her wicked eyes glinted. "Her name was Gagool also. Perchance I was that woman."

"Thou liest," I said, "that was ten generations gone."

"Mayhap, mayhap; when one lives long one forgets. Perhaps it was my mother's mother who told me; surely her name was Gagool also. But mark, ye will find in the place where the bright things are a bag of hide full of stones. The man filled that bag, but he never took it away. Evil befell him, I say, evil befell him! Perhaps it was my mother's mother who told me. It will be a merry journey—we can see the bodies of those who died in the battle as we go. Their eyes will be gone by now, and their ribs will be hollow. *Ha! ha! ha!*"

The Place of Death

It was already dark on the third day after the scene described in the previous chapter when we camped in some huts at the foot of the "Three Witches," as the triangle of mountains is called to which Solomon's Great Road runs. Our party consisted of our three selves and Foulata, who waited on us—especially on Good—Infadoos, Gagool, who was borne along in a litter, inside which she could be heard muttering and cursing all day long, and a party of guards and attendants. The mountains, or rather the three peaks of the mountain, for the mass was evidently the result of a solitary upheaval, were, as I have said, in the form of a triangle, of which the base was towards us, one peak being on our right, one on our left, and one straight in front of us. Never shall I forget the sight afforded by those three towering peaks in the early sunlight of the following morning. High, high above us, up into the blue air, soared their twisted snow-wreaths. Beneath the snow-line the peaks were purple with heaths, and so were the wild moors that ran up the slopes towards them. Straight before us the white ribbon of Solomon's Great Road stretched away uphill to the foot of the centre peak, about five miles from us, and there stopped. It was its terminus.

I had better leave the feelings of intense excitement with which we set out on our march that morning to the imagination of those who read this history. At last we were drawing near to the wonderful mines that had been the cause of the miserable death of the old Portuguese Dom three centuries ago, of my poor friend, his ill-starred descendant, and also, as we feared, of George Curtis, Sir Henry's brother. Were we destined, after all that we had gone through, to fare any better? Evil befell them, as that old fiend Gagool said; would it also befall us? Somehow, as we were marching up that last stretch of beautiful road, I could not help feeling a little superstitious about the matter, and so I think did Good and Sir Henry.

For an hour and a half or more we tramped on up the heather-fringed way, going so fast in our excitement that the bearers of Gagool's hammock could scarcely keep pace with us, and its occupant piped out to us to stop.

"Walk more slowly, white men," she said, projecting her hideous shrivelled countenance between the grass curtains, and fixing her gleaming eyes upon us; "why will ye run to meet the evil that shall befall you, ye seekers after treasure?" and she laughed that horrible laugh which always sent a cold shiver down my back, and for a while quite took the enthusiasm out of us.

However, on we went, till we saw before us, and between ourselves and the peak, a vast circular hole with sloping sides, three hundred feet or more in depth, and quite half a mile round.

"Can't you guess what this is?" I said to Sir Henry and Good, who were staring in astonishment at the awful pit before us.

They shook their heads.

"Then it is clear that you have never seen the diamond diggings at Kimberley. You may depend on it that this is Solomon's Diamond Mine. Look there," I said, pointing to the strata of stiff blue clay which were yet to be seen among the grass and bushes that clothed the sides of the pit, "the formation is the same. I'll be bound that if we went down there we should find 'pipes' of soapy brecciated rock. Look, too," and I pointed to a series of worn flat slabs of stone that were placed on a gentle slope below the level of a watercourse which in some past age had been cut out of the solid rock; "if those are not tables once used to wash the 'stuff,' I'm a Dutchman."

At the edge of this vast hole, which was none other than the pit marked on the old Dom's map, the Great Road branched into two and circumvented it. In many places, by the way, this surrounding road was built entirely out of blocks of stone, apparently with the object of supporting the edges of the pit and preventing falls of reef. Along this path we pressed, driven by curiosity to see what were the three towering objects which we could discern from the hither side of the great gulf. As we drew near we perceived that they were Colossi of some sort or another, and rightly conjectured that before us sat the three "Silent Ones" that are held in such awe by the Kukuana people. But it was not until we were quite close to them that we recognised the full majesty of these "Silent Ones."

There, upon huge pedestals of dark rock, sculptured with rude emblems of the Phallic worship, separated from each other by a distance of forty paces, and looking down the road which crossed some sixty miles of plain to Loo, were three colossal seated forms—two male and one female—each measuring about thirty feet from the crown of its head to the pedestal.

The female form, which was nude, was of great though severe beauty, but unfortunately the features had been injured by centuries of exposure to the weather. Rising from either side of her head were the points of a crescent. The two male Colossi, on the contrary, were draped, and presented a terrifying cast of features, especially the one to our right, which had the face of a devil. That to our left was serene in countenance, but the calm upon it seemed dreadful. It was the calm of that inhuman cruelty, Sir Henry remarked, which the ancients attributed to beings potent for good, who could yet watch the sufferings of humanity, if not without rejoicing, at least without sorrow. These three statues form a most awe-inspiring trinity, as they sit there in their solitude, and gaze out across the plain for ever.

Contemplating these "Silent Ones," as the Kukuanas call them, an intense curiosity again seized us to know whose were the hands which had shaped them, who it was that had dug the pit and made the road. Whilst I was gazing and wondering, suddenly it occurred to me—being familiar with the Old Testament—that Solomon went astray after strange gods, the names of three of whom I remembered—"Ashtoreth, the goddess of the Zidonians, Chemosh, the god of the Moabites, and Milcom, the god of the children of Ammon"—and I suggested to my companions that the figures before us might represent these false and exploded divinities.

"Hum," said Sir Henry, who is a scholar, having taken a high degree in classics at college, "there may be something in that; Ashtoreth of the Hebrews was the Astarte of the Phoenicians, who were the great traders of Solomon's time. Astarte, who afterwards became the Aphrodite of the Greeks, was represented with horns like the half-moon, and there on the brow of the female figure are distinct horns. Perhaps these Colossi were designed by some Phoenician official who managed the mines. Who can say?"

"With these in troop
Came Ashtoreth, whom the Phoenicians called
Astarte, Queen of Heaven, with crescent horns;
To whose bright image nightly by the moon
Sidonian virgins paid their vows and songs."

Before we had finished examining these extraordinary relics of remote antiquity, Infadoos came up, and having saluted the "Silent Ones" by lifting his spear, asked us if we intended entering the "Place of Death" at once, or if we would wait till after we had taken food at mid-day. If we were ready to go at once, Gagool had announced her willingness to guide us. As it was not later than eleven o'clock— driven to it by a burning curiosity—we announced our intention of proceeding instantly, and I suggested that, in case we should be detained in the cave, we should take some food with us. Accordingly Gagool's litter was brought up, and that lady herself assisted out of it. Meanwhile Foulata, at my request, stored some "biltong," or dried game-flesh, together with a couple of gourds of water, in a reed basket with a hinged cover. Straight in front of us, at a distance of some fifty paces from the backs of the Colossi, rose a sheer wall of rock, eighty feet or more in height, that gradually sloped upwards till it formed the base of the lofty snow-wreathed peak, which soared into the air three thousand feet above us. As soon as she was clear of her hammock, Gagool cast one evil grin upon us, and then, leaning on a stick, hobbled off towards the face of this wall. We followed her till we came to a narrow portal solidly arched that looked like the opening of a gallery of a mine.

Here Gagool was waiting for us, still with that evil grin upon her horrid face.

"Now, white men from the Stars," she piped; "great warriors, Incubu, Bougwan, and Macumazahn the wise, are ye ready? Behold, I am here to do the bidding of my lord the king, and to show you the store of bright stones. *Ha! ha! ha!*"

"We are ready," I said.

"Good, good! Make strong your hearts to bear what ye shall see. Comest thou too, Infadoos, thou who didst betray thy master?"

Infadoos frowned as he answered—

"Nay, I come not; it is not for me to enter there. But thou, Gagool, curb thy tongue, and beware how thou dealest with my lords. At thy hands will I require them, and if a hair of them be hurt, Gagool, be'st thou fifty times a witch, thou shalt die. Hearest thou?"

"I hear Infadoos; I know thee, thou didst ever love big words; when thou wast a babe I remember thou didst threaten thine own mother. That was but the other day. But, fear not, fear not, I live only to do the bidding of the king. I have done the bidding of many kings, Infadoos, till in the end they did mine. *Ha! ha!* I go to look upon their faces once more, and Twala's also! Come on, come on, here is the lamp," and she drew a large gourd full of oil, and fitted with a rush wick, from under her fur cloak.

"Art thou coming, Foulata?" asked Good in his villainous Kitchen Kukuana, in which he had been improving himself under that young lady's tuition.

"I fear, my lord," the girl answered timidly.

"Then give me the basket."

"Nay, my lord, whither thou goest there I go also."

"The deuce you will!" thought I to myself; "that may be rather awkward if we ever get out of this."

Without further ado Gagool plunged into the passage, which was wide enough to admit of two walking abreast, and quite dark. We followed the sound of her voice as she piped to us to come on, in some fear and trembling, which was not allayed by the flutter of a sudden rush of wings.

"Hullo! what's that?" halloed Good; "somebody hit me in the face."

"Bats," said I; "on you go."

When, so far as we could judge, we had gone some fifty paces, we perceived that the passage was growing faintly light. Another minute, and we were in perhaps the most wonderful place that the eyes of living man have beheld.

Let the reader picture to himself the hall of the vastest cathedral he ever stood in, windowless indeed, but dimly lighted from above, presumably by shafts connected with the outer air and driven in the roof, which arched away a hundred feet above our heads, and he will get some idea of the size of the enormous cave in which we found ourselves, with the difference that this cathedral designed by nature was loftier and wider than any built by man. But its stupendous size was the least of the wonders of the place, for running in rows adown its length were gigantic pillars of what looked like ice, but were, in reality, huge stalactites. It is impossible for me to convey any idea of the overpowering beauty and grandeur of these pillars of white spar, some of which were not less than twenty feet in diameter at the base, and sprang up in lofty and yet delicate beauty sheer to the distant roof. Others again were in process of formation. On the rock floor there was in these cases what looked, Sir Henry said, exactly like a broken column in an old Grecian temple, whilst high above, depending from the roof, the point of a huge icicle could be dimly seen.

Even as we gazed we could hear the process going on, for presently with a tiny splash a drop of water would fall from the far-off icicle on to the column below. On some columns the drops only fell once in two or three minutes, and in these cases it would be an interesting calculation to discover how long, at that rate of dripping, it would take to form a pillar, say eighty feet by ten in diameter. That the process, in at least one instance, was incalculably slow, the following example will suffice to show. Cut on one of these pillars we discovered the crude likeness of a mummy, by the head of which sat what appeared to be the figure of an Egyptian god, doubtless the handiwork of some old-world labourer in the mine. This work of art was executed at the natural height at which an idle fellow, be he Phoenician workman or British cad, is in the habit of trying to immortalise himself at the expense of nature's masterpieces, namely, about five feet from the ground. Yet at the time that we saw it, which *must* have been nearly three thousand years after the date of the execution of the carving, the column was only eight feet high, and was still in process of formation, which gives a rate of growth of a foot to a thousand years, or an inch and a fraction to a century. This we knew because, as we were standing by it, we heard a drop of water fall.

Sometimes the stalagmites took strange forms, presumably where the dropping of the water had not always been on the same spot. Thus, one huge mass, which must have weighed a hundred tons or so, was in the shape of a pulpit, beautifully fretted over outside with a design that looked like lace. Others resembled strange beasts, and on the sides of the cave were fanlike ivory tracings, such as the frost leaves upon a pane.

Out of the vast main aisle there opened here and there smaller caves, exactly, Sir Henry said, as chapels open out of great cathedrals. Some were large, but one or two—and this is a wonderful instance of how nature carries out her handiwork by the same unvarying laws, utterly irrespective of size—were tiny. One little nook, for instance, was no larger than an unusually big doll's house, and yet it might have been a model for the whole place, for the water dropped, tiny icicles hung, and spar columns were forming in just the same way.

We had not, however, enough time to examine this beautiful cavern so thoroughly as we should have liked to do, since unfortunately, Gagool seemed to be indifferent as to stalactites, and only anxious to get her business over. This annoyed me the more, as I was particularly anxious to discover, if possible, by what system the light was admitted into the cave, and whether it was by the hand of man or by that of nature that this was done; also if the place had been used in any way in ancient times, as seemed probable. However, we consoled ourselves with the idea that we would investigate it thoroughly on our way back, and followed on at the heels of our uncanny guide.

On she led us, straight to the top of the vast and silent cave, where we found another doorway, not arched as the first was, but square at the top, something like the doorways of Egyptian temples.

"Are ye prepared to enter the Place of Death, white men?" asked Gagool, evidently with a view to making us feel uncomfortable.

"Lead on, Macduff," said Good solemnly, trying to look as though he was not at all alarmed, as indeed we all did except Foulata, who caught Good by the arm for protection.

"This is getting rather ghastly," said Sir Henry, peeping into the dark passageway. "Come on, Quatermain—*seniores priores*. We mustn't keep the old lady waiting!" and he politely made way for me to lead the van, for which inwardly I did not bless him.

Tap, tap, went old Gagool's stick down the passage, as she trotted along, chuckling hideously; and still overcome by some unaccountable presentiment of evil, I hung back.

"Come, get on, old fellow," said Good, "or we shall lose our fair guide."

Thus adjured, I started down the passage, and after about twenty paces found myself in a gloomy apartment some forty feet long, by thirty broad, and thirty high, which in some past age evidently had been hollowed, by hand-labour, out of the mountain. This apartment was not nearly so well lighted as the vast stalactite ante-cave, and at the first glance all I could discern was a massive stone table running down its length, with a colossal white figure at its head, and life- sized white figures all round it. Next I discovered a brown thing, seated on the table in the centre, and in another moment my eyes grew accustomed to the light, and I saw what all these things were, and was tailing out of the place as hard as my legs could carry me.

I am not a nervous man in a general way, and very little troubled with superstitions, of which I have lived to see the folly; but I am free to own that this sight quite upset me, and had it not been that Sir Henry caught me by the collar and held me, I do honestly believe that in another five minutes I should have been outside the stalactite cave, and that a promise of all the diamonds in Kimberley would not have induced me to enter it again. But he held me tight, so I stopped because I could not help myself. Next second, however, *his* eyes became accustomed to the light, and he let go of me, and began to mop the perspiration off his forehead. As for Good, he swore feebly, while Foulata threw her arms round his neck and shrieked.

Only Gagool chuckled loud and long.

It *was* a ghastly sight. There at the end of the long stone table, holding in his skeleton fingers a great white spear, sat *Death* himself, shaped in the form of a colossal human skeleton, fifteen feet or more in height. High above his head he held the spear, as though in the act to strike; one bony hand rested on the stone table before him, in the position a man assumes on rising from his seat, whilst his frame was bent forward so that the vertebrae of the neck and the grinning, gleaming skull projected towards us, and fixed its hollow eye-places upon us, the jaws a little open, as though it were about to speak.

"Great heavens!" said I faintly, at last, "what can it be?"

"And what are *those things*?" asked Good, pointing to the white company round the table.

"And what on earth is *that thing*?" said Sir Henry, pointing to the brown creature seated on the table.

"*Hee! hee! hee!*" laughed Gagool. "To those who enter the Hall of the Dead, evil comes. *Hee! hee! hee! ha! ha!*"

"Come, Incubu, brave in battle, come and see him thou slewest;" and the old creature caught Curtis' coat in her skinny fingers, and led him away towards the table. We followed.

Presently she stopped and pointed at the brown object seated on the table. Sir Henry looked, and started back with an exclamation; and no wonder, for there, quite naked, the head which Curtis' battle-axe had shorn from the body resting on its knees, was the gaunt corpse of Twala, the last king of the Kukuanas. Yes, there, the head perched upon the knees, it sat in all its ugliness, the vertebrae projecting a full inch above the level of the shrunken flesh of the neck, for all the world like a black double of Hamilton Tighe. Over the surface of the corpse there was gathered a thin glassy film, that made its appearance yet more appalling, for which we were, at the moment, quite unable to account, till presently we observed that from the roof of the chamber the water fell steadily, *drip! drop! drip!* on to the neck of the corpse, whence it ran down over the entire surface, and finally escaped into the rock through a tiny hole in the table. Then I guessed what the film was—*Twala's body was being transformed into a stalactite.*

A look at the white forms seated on the stone bench which ran round that ghastly board confirmed this view. They were human bodies indeed, or rather they had been human; now they were *stalactites.* This was the way in which the Kukuana people had from time immemorial preserved their royal dead. They petrified them. What the exact system might be, if there was any, beyond the placing of them for a long period of years under the drip, I never discovered, but there they sat, iced over and preserved for ever by the siliceous fluid.

Anything more awe-inspiring than the spectacle of this long line of departed royalties (there were twenty-seven of them, the last being Ignosi's father), wrapped, each of them, in a shroud of ice-like spar, through which the features could be dimly discovered, and seated round that inhospitable board, with Death himself for a host, it is impossible to imagine. That the practice of thus preserving their kings must have been an ancient one is evident from the number, which, allowing for an average reign of fifteen years, supposing that every king who reigned was placed here—an improbable thing, as some are sure to have perished in battle far from home—would fix the date of its commencement at four and a quarter centuries back.

But the colossal Death, who sits at the head of the board, is far older than that, and, unless I am much mistaken, owes his origin to the same artist who designed the three Colossi. He is hewn out of a single stalactite, and, looked at as a work of art, is most admirably conceived and executed. Good, who understands such things, declared that, so far as he could see, the anatomical design of the skeleton is perfect down to the smallest bones.

My own idea is, that this terrific object was a freak of fancy on the part of some old-world sculptor, and that its presence had suggested to the Kukuanas the idea of placing their royal dead under its awful presidency. Or perhaps it was set there to frighten away any marauders who might have designs upon the treasure chamber beyond. I cannot say. All I can do is to describe it as it is, and the reader must form his own conclusion.

Such, at any rate, was the White Death and such were the White Dead!

Solomon's Treasure Chamber

While we were engaged in recovering from our fright, and in examining the grisly wonders of the Place of Death, Gagool had been differently occupied. Somehow or other—for she was marvellously active when she chose—she had scrambled on to the great table, and made her way to where our departed friend Twala was placed, under the drip, to see, suggested Good, how he was "pickling," or for some dark purpose of her own. Then, after bending down to kiss his icy lips as though in affectionate greeting, she hobbled back, stopping now and again to address the remark, the tenor of which I could not catch, to one or other of the shrouded forms, just as you or I might welcome an old acquaintance. Having gone through this mysterious and horrible ceremony, she squatted herself down on the table immediately under the White Death, and began, so far as I could make out, to offer up prayers. The spectacle of this wicked creature pouring out supplications, evil ones no doubt, to the arch enemy of mankind, was so uncanny that it caused us to hasten our inspection.

"Now, Gagool," said I, in a low voice—somehow one did not dare to speak above a whisper in that place—"lead us to the chamber."

The old witch promptly scrambled down from the table.

"My lords are not afraid?" she said, leering up into my face.

"Lead on."

"Good, my lords;" and she hobbled round to the back of the great Death. "Here is the chamber; let my lords light the lamp, and enter," and she placed the gourd full of oil upon the floor, and leaned herself against the side of the cave. I took out a match, of which we had still a few in a box, and lit a rush wick, and then looked for the doorway, but there was nothing before us except the solid rock. Gagool grinned. "The way is there, my lords. *Ha! ha! ha!*"

"Do not jest with us," I said sternly.

"I jest not, my lords. See!" and she pointed at the rock.

As she did so, on holding up the lamp we perceived that a mass of stone was rising slowly from the floor and vanishing into the rock above, where doubtless there is a cavity prepared to receive it. The mass was of the width of a good-sized door, about ten feet high and not less than five feet thick. It must have weighed at least twenty or thirty tons, and was clearly moved upon some simple balance principle of counter-weights, probably the same as that by which the opening and shutting of an ordinary modern window is arranged. How the principle was set in motion, of course none of us saw; Gagool was careful to avoid this; but I have little doubt that there was some very simple lever, which was moved ever so little by pressure at a secret spot, thereby throwing additional weight on to the hidden counter-balances, and causing the monolith to be lifted from the ground.

Very slowly and gently the great stone raised itself, till at last it had vanished altogether, and a dark hole presented itself to us in the place which the door had filled.

Our excitement was so intense, as we saw the way to Solomon's treasure chamber thrown open at last, that I for one began to tremble and shake. Would it prove a hoax after all, I wondered, or was old Da Silvestra right? Were there vast hoards of wealth hidden in that dark place, hoards which would make us the richest men in the whole world? We should know in a minute or two.

"Enter, white men from the Stars," said Gagool, advancing into the doorway; "but first hear your servant, Gagool the old. The bright stones that ye will see were dug out of the pit over which the Silent Ones are set, and stored here, I know not by whom, for that was done longer ago than even I remember. But once has this place been entered since the time that those who hid the stones departed in haste, leaving them behind. The report of the treasure went down indeed among the people who lived in the country from age to age, but none knew where the chamber was, nor the secret of the door. But it happened that a white man reached this country from over the mountains— perchance he too came 'from the Stars'—and was well received by the king of that day. He it is who sits yonder," and she pointed to the fifth king at the table of the Dead. "And it came to pass that he and a woman of the country who was with him journeyed to this place, and that by chance the woman learnt the secret of the door—a thousand years might ye search, but ye should never find that secret. Then the white man entered with the woman, and found the stones, and filled with stones the skin of a small goat, which the woman had with her to hold food. And as he was going from the chamber he took up one more stone, a large one, and held it in his hand."

Here she paused.

"Well," I asked, breathless with interest as we all were, "what happened to Da Silvestra?"

The old hag started at the mention of the name.

"How knowest thou the dead man's name?" she asked sharply; and then, without waiting for an answer, went on—

"None can tell what happened; but it came about that the white man was frightened, for he flung down the goat-skin, with the stones, and fled out with only the one stone in his hand, and that the king took, and it is the stone which thou, Macumazahn, didst take from Twala's brow."

"Have none entered here since?" I asked, peering again down the dark passage.

"None, my lords. Only the secret of the door has been kept, and every king has opened it, though he has not entered. There is a saying, that those who enter there will die within a moon, even as the white man died in the cave upon the mountain, where ye found him, Macumazahn, and therefore the kings do not enter. *Ha! ha!* mine are true words."

Our eyes met as she said it, and I turned sick and cold. How did the old hag know all these things?

"Enter, my lords. If I speak truth, the goat-skin with the stones will lie upon the floor; and if there is truth as to whether it is death to enter here, that ye will learn afterwards. *Ha! ha! ha!*" and she hobbled through the doorway, bearing the light with her; but I confess that once more I hesitated about following.

"Oh, confound it all!" said Good; "here goes. I am not going to be frightened by that old devil," and followed by Foulata, who, however, evidently did not at all like the business, for she was shivering with fear, he plunged into the passage after Gagool—an example which we quickly followed.

A few yards down the passage, in the narrow way hewn out of the living rock, Gagool had paused, and was waiting for us.

"See, my lords," she said, holding the light before her, "those who stored the treasure here fled in haste, and bethought them to guard against any who should find the secret of the door, but had not the time," and she pointed to large square blocks of stone, which, to the height of two courses (about two feet three), had been placed across the passage with a view to walling it up. Along the side of the passage were similar blocks ready for use, and, most curious of all, a heap of mortar and a couple of trowels, which tools, so far as we had time to examine them, appeared to be of a similar shape and make to those used by workmen to this day.

Here Foulata, who had been in a state of great fear and agitation throughout, said that she felt faint and could go no farther, but would wait there. Accordingly we set her down on the unfinished wall, placing the basket of provisions by her side, and left her to recover.

Following the passage for about fifteen paces farther, we came suddenly to an elaborately painted wooden door. It was standing wide open. Whoever was last there had either not found the time to shut it, or had forgotten to do so.

Across the threshold of this door lay a skin bag, formed of a goat- skin, that appeared to be full of pebbles.

"*Hee! hee!* white men," sniggered Gagool, as the light from the lamp fell upon it. "What did I tell you, that the white man who came here fled in haste, and dropped the woman's bag—behold it! Look within also and ye will find a water-gourd amongst the stones."

Good stooped down and lifted it. It was heavy and jingled.

"By Jove! I believe it's full of diamonds," he said, in an awed whisper; and, indeed, the idea of a small goat-skin full of diamonds is enough to awe anybody.

"Go on," said Sir Henry impatiently. "Here, old lady, give me the lamp," and taking it from Gagool's hand, he stepped through the doorway and held it high above his head.

We pressed in after him, forgetful for the moment of the bag of diamonds, and found ourselves in King Solomon's treasure chamber.

At first, all that the somewhat faint light given by the lamp revealed was a room hewn out of the living rock, and apparently not more than ten feet square. Next there came into sight, stored one on the other to the arch of the roof, a splendid collection of elephant-tusks. How many of them there were we did not know, for of course we could not see to what depth they went back, but there could not have been less than the ends of four or five hundred tusks of the first quality visible to our eyes. There, alone, was enough ivory to make a man wealthy for life. Perhaps, I thought, it was from this very store that Solomon drew the raw material for his "great throne of ivory," of which "there was not the like made in any kingdom."

On the opposite side of the chamber were about a score of wooden boxes, something like Martini-Henry ammunition boxes, only rather larger, and painted red.

"There are the diamonds," cried I; "bring the light."

Sir Henry did so, holding it close to the top box, of which the lid, rendered rotten by time even in that dry place, appeared to have been smashed in, probably by Da Silvestra himself. Pushing my hand through the hole in the lid I drew it out full, not of diamonds, but of gold pieces, of a shape that none of us had seen before, and with what looked like Hebrew characters stamped upon them.

"Ah!" I said, replacing the coin, "we shan't go back empty-handed, anyhow. There must be a couple of thousand pieces in each box, and there are eighteen boxes. I suppose this was the money to pay the workmen and merchants."

"Well," put in Good, "I think that is the lot; I don't see any diamonds, unless the old Portuguese put them all into his bag."

"Let my lords look yonder where it is darkest, if they would find the stones," said Gagool, interpreting our looks. "There my lords will find a nook, and three stone chests in the nook, two sealed and one open."

Before translating this to Sir Henry, who carried the light, I could not resist asking how she knew these things, if no one had entered the place since the white man, generations ago.

"Ah, Macumazahn, the watcher by night," was the mocking answer, "ye who dwell in the stars, do ye not know that some live long, and that some have eyes which can see through rock? *Ha! ha! ha!*"

"Look in that corner, Curtis," I said, indicating the spot Gagool had pointed out.

"Hullo, you fellows," he cried, "here's a recess. Great heavens! see here."

We hurried up to where he was standing in a nook, shaped something like a small bow window. Against the wall of this recess were placed three stone chests, each about two feet square. Two were fitted with stone lids, the lid of the third rested against the side of the chest, which was open.

"*See!*" he repeated hoarsely, holding the lamp over the open chest. We looked, and for a moment could make nothing out, on account of a silvery sheen which dazzled us. When our eyes grew used to it we saw that the chest was three-parts full of uncut diamonds, most of them of considerable size. Stooping, I picked some up. Yes, there was no doubt of it, there was the unmistakable soapy feel about them.

I fairly gasped as I dropped them.

"We are the richest men in the whole world," I said. "Monte Christo was a fool to us."

"We shall flood the market with diamonds," said Good.

"Got to get them there first," suggested Sir Henry.

We stood still with pale faces and stared at each other, the lantern in the middle and the glimmering gems below, as though we were conspirators about to commit a crime, instead of being, as we thought, the most fortunate men on earth.

"*Hee! hee! hee!*" cackled old Gagool behind us, as she flitted about like a vampire bat. "There are the bright stones ye love, white men, as many as ye will; take them, run them through your fingers, *eat* of them, *hee! hee! drink* of them, *ha! ha!*"

At that moment there was something so ridiculous to my mind at the idea of eating and drinking diamonds, that I began to laugh outrageously, an example which the others followed, without knowing why. There we stood and shrieked with laughter over the gems that were ours, which had been found for *us* thousands of years ago by the patient delvers in the great hole yonder, and stored for *us* by Solomon's long-dead overseer, whose name, perchance, was written in the characters stamped on the faded wax that yet adhered to the lids of the chest. Solomon never got them, nor David, or Da Silvestra, nor anybody else. *We* had got them: there before us were millions of pounds' worth of diamonds, and thousands of pounds' worth of gold and ivory only waiting to be taken away.

Suddenly the fit passed off, and we stopped laughing.

"Open the other chests, white men," croaked Gagool, "there are surely more therein. Take your fill, white lords! *Ha! ha!* take your fill."

Thus adjured, we set to work to pull up the stone lids on the other two, first—not without a feeling of sacrilege—breaking the seals that fastened them.

Hoorah! they were full too, full to the brim; at least, the second one was; no wretched burglarious Da Silvestra had been filling goat-skins out of that. As for the third chest, it was only about a fourth full, but the stones were all picked ones; none less than twenty carats, and some of them as large as pigeon-eggs. A good many of these bigger ones, however, we could see by holding them up to the light, were a little yellow, "off coloured," as they call it at Kimberley.

What we did *not* see, however, was the look of fearful malevolence that old Gagool favoured us with as she crept, crept like a snake, out of the treasure chamber and down the passage towards the door of solid rock.

Hark! Cry upon cry comes ringing up the vaulted path. It is Foulata's voice!

"*Oh, Bougwan! help! help! the stone falls!*"

"Leave go, girl! Then—"

"*Help! help! she has stabbed me!*"

By now we are running down the passage, and this is what the light from the lamp shows us. The door of the rock is closing down slowly; it is not three feet from the floor. Near it struggle Foulata and Gagool. The red blood of the former runs to her knee, but still the brave girl holds the old witch, who fights like a wild cat. Ah! she is free! Foulata falls, and Gagool throws herself on the ground, to twist like a snake through the crack of the closing stone. She is under—ah! god! too late! too late! The stone nips her, and she yells in agony. Down, down it comes, all the thirty tons of it, slowly pressing her old body against the rock below. Shriek upon shriek, such as we have never heard, then a long sickening *crunch*, and the door was shut just as, rushing down the passage, we hurled ourselves against it.

It was all done in four seconds.

Then we turned to Foulata. The poor girl was stabbed in the body, and I saw that she could not live long.

"Ah! Bougwan, I die!" gasped the beautiful creature. "She crept out—Gagool; I did not see her, I was faint—and the door began to fall; then she came back, and was looking up the path—I saw her come in through the slowly falling door, and caught her and held her, and she stabbed me, and *I die*, Bougwan!"

"Poor girl! poor girl!" Good cried in his distress; and then, as he could do nothing else, he fell to kissing her.

"Bougwan," she said, after a pause, "is Macumazahn there? It grows so dark, I cannot see."

"Here I am, Foulata."

"Macumazahn, be my tongue for a moment, I pray thee, for Bougwan cannot understand me, and before I go into the darkness I would speak to him a word."

"Say on, Foulata, I will render it."

"Say to my lord, Bougwan, that—I love him, and that I am glad to die because I know that he cannot cumber his life with such as I am, for the sun may not mate with the darkness, nor the white with the black.

"Say that, since I saw him, at times I have felt as though there were a bird in my bosom, which would one day fly hence and sing elsewhere. Even now, though I cannot lift my hand, and my brain grows cold, I do not feel as though my heart were dying; it is so full of love that it could live ten thousand years, and yet be young. Say that if I live again, mayhap I shall see him in the Stars, and that—I will search them all, though perchance there I should still be black and he would —still be white. Say—nay, Macumazahn, say no more, save that I love —Oh, hold me closer, Bougwan, I cannot feel thine arms—*oh! oh!*"

"She is dead—she is dead!" muttered Good, rising in grief, the tears running down his honest face.

"You need not let that trouble you, old fellow," said Sir Henry.

"Eh!" exclaimed Good; "what do you mean?"

"I mean that you will soon be in a position to join her. *Man, don't you see that we are buried alive?*"

Until Sir Henry uttered these words I do not think that the full horror of what had happened had come home to us, preoccupied as we were with the sight of poor Foulata's end. But now we understood. The ponderous mass of rock had closed, probably for ever, for the only brain which knew its secret was crushed to powder beneath its weight. This was a door that none could hope to force with anything short of dynamite in large quantities. And we were on the wrong side!

For a few minutes we stood horrified, there over the corpse of Foulata. All the manhood seemed to have gone out of us. The first shock of this idea of the slow and miserable end that awaited us was overpowering. We saw it all now; that fiend Gagool had planned this snare for us from the first.

It would have been just the jest that her evil mind would have rejoiced in, the idea of the three white men, whom, for some reason of her own, she had always hated, slowly perishing of thirst and hunger in the company of the treasure they had coveted. Now I saw the point of that sneer of hers about eating and drinking the diamonds. Probably somebody had tried to serve the poor old Dom in the same way, when he abandoned the skin full of jewels.

"This will never do," said Sir Henry hoarsely; "the lamp will soon go out. Let us see if we can't find the spring that works the rock."

We sprang forward with desperate energy, and, standing in a bloody ooze, began to feel up and down the door and the sides of the passage. But no knob or spring could we discover.

"Depend on it," I said, "it does not work from the inside; if it did Gagool would not have risked trying to crawl underneath the stone. It was the knowledge of this that made her try to escape at all hazards, curse her."

"At all events," said Sir Henry, with a hard little laugh, "retribution was swift; hers was almost as awful an end as ours is likely to be. We can do nothing with the door; let us go back to the treasure room."

We turned and went, and as we passed it I perceived by the unfinished wall across the passage the basket of food which poor Foulata had carried. I took it up, and brought it with me to the accursed treasure chamber that was to be our grave. Then we returned and reverently bore in Foulata's corpse, laying it on the floor by the boxes of coin.

Next we seated ourselves, leaning our backs against the three stone chests which contained the priceless treasure.

"Let us divide the food," said Sir Henry, "so as to make it last as long as possible." Accordingly we did so. It would, we reckoned, make four infinitesimally small meals for each of us, enough, say, to support life for a couple of days. Besides the "biltong," or dried game-flesh, there were two gourds of water, each of which held not more than a quart.

"Now," said Sir Henry grimly, "let us eat and drink, for to-morrow we die."

We each ate a small portion of the "biltong," and drank a sip of water. Needless to say, we had but little appetite, though we were sadly in need of food, and felt better after swallowing it. Then we got up and made a systematic examination of the walls of our prison- house, in the faint hope of finding some means of exit, sounding them and the floor carefully.

There was none. It was not probable that there would be any to a treasure chamber.

The lamp began to burn dim. The fat was nearly exhausted.

"Quatermain," said Sir Henry, "what is the time—your watch goes?"

I drew it out, and looked at it. It was six o'clock; we had entered the cave at eleven.

"Infadoos will miss us," I suggested. "If we do not return to-night he will search for us in the morning, Curtis."

"He may search in vain. He does not know the secret of the door, nor even where it is. No living person knew it yesterday, except Gagool. To-day no one knows it. Even if he found the door he could not break it down. All the Kukuana army could not break through five feet of living rock. My friends, I see nothing for it but to bow ourselves to the will of the Almighty. The search for treasure has brought many to a bad end; we shall go to swell their number."

The lamp grew dimmer yet.

Presently it flared up and showed the whole scene in strong relief, the great mass of white tusks, the boxes of gold, the corpse of the poor Foulata stretched before them, the goat-skin full of treasure, the dim glimmer of the diamonds, and the wild, wan faces of us three white men seated there awaiting death by starvation.

Then the flame sank and expired.

We Abandon Hope

I can give no adequate description of the horrors of the night which followed. Mercifully they were to some extent mitigated by sleep, for even in such a position as ours wearied nature will sometimes assert itself. But I, at any rate, found it impossible to sleep much. Putting aside the terrifying thought of our impending doom—for the bravest man on earth might well quail from such a fate as awaited us, and I never made any pretensions to be brave—the *silence* itself was too great to allow of it. Reader, you may have lain awake at night and thought the quiet oppressive, but I say with confidence that you can have no idea what a vivid, tangible thing is perfect stillness. On the surface of the earth there is always some sound or motion, and though it may in itself be imperceptible, yet it deadens the sharp edge of absolute silence. But here there was none. We were buried in the bowels of a huge snow-clad peak. Thousands of feet above us the fresh air rushed over the white snow, but no sound of it reached us. We were separated by a long tunnel and five feet of rock even from the awful chamber of the Dead; and the dead make no noise. Did we not know it who lay by poor Foulata's side? The crashing of all the artillery of earth and heaven could not have come to our ears in our living tomb. We were cut off from every echo of the world—we were as men already in the grave.

Then the irony of the situation forced itself upon me. There around us lay treasures enough to pay off a moderate national debt, or to build a fleet of ironclads, and yet we would have bartered them all gladly for the faintest chance of escape. Soon, doubtless, we should be rejoiced to exchange them for a bit of food or a cup of water, and, after that, even for the privilege of a speedy close to our sufferings. Truly wealth, which men spend their lives in acquiring, is a valueless thing at the last.

And so the night wore on.

"Good," said Sir Henry's voice at last, and it sounded awful in the intense stillness, "how many matches have you in the box?"

"Eight, Curtis."

"Strike one and let us see the time."

He did so, and in contrast to the dense darkness the flame nearly blinded us. It was five o'clock by my watch. The beautiful dawn was now blushing on the snow-wreaths far over our heads, and the breeze would be stirring the night mists in the hollows.

"We had better eat something and keep up our strength," I suggested.

"What is the good of eating?" answered Good; "the sooner we die and get it over the better."

"While there is life there is hope," said Sir Henry.

Accordingly we ate and sipped some water, and another period of time elapsed. Then Sir Henry suggested that it might be well to get as near the door as possible and halloa, on the faint chance of somebody catching a sound outside. Accordingly Good, who, from long practice at sea, has a fine piercing note, groped his way down the passage and set to work. I must say that he made a most diabolical noise. I never heard such yells; but it might have been a mosquito buzzing for all the effect they produced.

After a while he gave it up and came back very thirsty, and had to drink. Then we stopped yelling, as it encroached on the supply of water.

So we sat down once more against the chests of useless diamonds in that dreadful inaction which was one of the hardest circumstances of our fate; and I am bound to say that, for my part, I gave way in despair. Laying my head against Sir Henry's broad shoulder I burst into tears; and I think that I heard Good gulping away on the other side, and swearing hoarsely at himself for doing so.

Ah, how good and brave that great man was! Had we been two frightened children, and he our nurse, he could not have treated us more tenderly. Forgetting his own share of miseries, he did all he could to soothe our broken nerves, telling stories of men who had been in somewhat similar circumstances, and miraculously escaped; and when these failed to cheer us, pointing out how, after all, it was only anticipating an end which must come to us all, that it would soon be over, and that death from exhaustion was a merciful one (which is not true). Then, in a diffident sort of way, as once before I had heard him do, he suggested that we should throw ourselves on the mercy of a higher Power, which for my part I did with great vigour.

His is a beautiful character, very quiet, but very strong.

And so somehow the day went as the night had gone, if, indeed, one can use these terms where all was densest night, and when I lit a match to see the time it was seven o'clock.

Once more we ate and drank, and as we did so an idea occurred to me.

"How is it," said I, "that the air in this place keeps fresh? It is thick and heavy, but it is perfectly fresh."

"Great heavens!" said Good, starting up, "I never thought of that. It can't come through the stone door, for it's air-tight, if ever a door was. It must come from somewhere. It there were no current of air in the place we should have been stifled or poisoned when we first came in. Let us have a look."

It was wonderful what a change this mere spark of hope wrought in us. In a moment we were all three groping about on our hands and knees, feeling for the slightest indication of a draught. Presently my ardour received a check. I put my hand on something cold. It was dead Foulata's face.

For an hour or more we went on feeling about, till at last Sir Henry and I gave it up in despair, having been considerably hurt by constantly knocking our heads against tusks, chests, and the sides of the chamber. But Good still persevered, saying, with an approach to cheerfulness, that it was better than doing nothing.

"I say, you fellows," he said presently, in a constrained sort of voice, "come here."

Needless to say we scrambled towards him quickly enough.

"Quatermain, put your hand here where mine is. Now, do you feel anything?"

"I *think* I feel air coming up."

"Now listen." He rose and stamped upon the place, and a flame of hope shot up in our hearts. *It rang hollow.*

With trembling hands I lit a match. I had only three left, and we saw that we were in the angle of the far corner of the chamber, a fact that accounted for our not having noticed the hollow sound of the place during our former exhaustive examination. As the match burnt we scrutinised the spot. There was a join in the solid rock floor, and, great heavens! there, let in level with the rock, was a stone ring. We said no word, we were too excited, and our hearts beat too wildly with hope to allow us to speak. Good had a knife, at the back of which was one of those hooks that are made to extract stones from horses' hoofs. He opened it, and scratched round the ring with it. Finally he worked it under, and levered away gently for fear of breaking the hook. The ring began to move. Being of stone it had not rusted fast in all the centuries it had lain there, as would have been the case had it been of iron. Presently it was upright. Then he thrust his hands into it and tugged with all his force, but nothing budged.

"Let me try," I said impatiently, for the situation of the stone, right in the angle of the corner, was such that it was impossible for two to pull at once. I took hold and strained away, but no results.

Then Sir Henry tried and failed.

Taking the hook again, Good scratched all round the crack where we felt the air coming up.

"Now, Curtis," he said, "tackle on, and put your back into it; you are as strong as two. Stop," and he took off a stout black silk handkerchief, which, true to his habits of neatness, he still wore, and ran it through the ring. "Quatermain, get Curtis round the middle and pull for dear life when I give the word. *Now.*"

Sir Henry put out all his enormous strength, and Good and I did the same, with such power as nature had given us.

"Heave! heave! it's giving," gasped Sir Henry; and I heard the muscles of his great back cracking. Suddenly there was a grating sound, then a rush of air, and we were all on our backs on the floor with a heavy flag-stone upon the top of us. Sir Henry's strength had done it, and never did muscular power stand a man in better stead.

"Light a match, Quatermain," he said, so soon as we had picked ourselves up and got our breath; "carefully, now."

I did so, and there before us, Heaven be praised! was the *first step of a stone stair.*

"Now what is to be done?" asked Good.

"Follow the stair, of course, and trust to Providence."

"Stop!" said Sir Henry; "Quatermain, get the bit of biltong and the water that are left; we may want them."

I went, creeping back to our place by the chests for that purpose, and as I was coming away an idea struck me. We had not thought much of the diamonds for the last twenty-four hours or so; indeed, the very idea of diamonds was nauseous, seeing what they had entailed upon us; but, reflected I, I may as well pocket some in case we ever should get out of this ghastly hole. So I just put my fist into the first chest and filled all the available pockets of my old shooting-coat and trousers, topping up—this was a happy thought—with a few handfuls of big ones from the third chest. Also, by an afterthought, I stuffed Foulata's basket, which, except for one water-gourd and a little biltong, was empty now, with great quantities of the stones.

"I say, you fellows," I sang out, "won't you take some diamonds with you? I've filled my pockets and the basket."

"Oh, come on, Quatermain! and hang the diamonds!" said Sir Henry. "I hope that I may never see another."

As for Good, he made no answer. He was, I think, taking his last farewell of all that was left of the poor girl who had loved him so well. And curious as it may seem to you, my reader, sitting at home at ease and reflecting on the vast, indeed the immeasurable, wealth which we were thus abandoning, I can assure you that if you had passed some twenty-eight hours with next to nothing to eat and drink in that place, you would not have cared to cumber yourself with diamonds whilst plunging down into the unknown bowels of the earth, in the wild hope of escape from an agonising death. If from the habits of a lifetime, it had not become a sort of second nature with me never to leave anything worth having behind if there was the slightest chance of my being able to carry it away, I am sure that I should not have bothered to fill my pockets and that basket.

"Come on, Quatermain," repeated Sir Henry, who was already standing on the first step of the stone stair. "Steady, I will go first."

"Mind where you put your feet, there may be some awful hole underneath," I answered.

"Much more likely to be another room," said Sir Henry, while he descended slowly, counting the steps as he went.

When he got to "fifteen" he stopped. "Here's the bottom," he said. "Thank goodness! I think it's a passage. Follow me down."

Good went next, and I came last, carrying the basket, and on reaching the bottom lit one of the two remaining matches. By its light we could just see that we were standing in a narrow tunnel, which ran right and left at right angles to the staircase we had descended. Before we could make out any more, the match burnt my fingers and went out. Then arose the delicate question of which way to go. Of course, it was impossible to know what the tunnel was, or where it led to, and yet to turn one way might lead us to safety, and the other to destruction. We were utterly perplexed, till suddenly it struck Good that when I had lit the match the draught of the passage blew the flame to the left.

"Let us go against the draught," he said; "air draws inwards, not outwards."

We took this suggestion, and feeling along the wall with our hands, whilst trying the ground before us at every step, we departed from that accursed treasure chamber on our terrible quest for life. If ever it should be entered again by living man, which I do not think probable, he will find tokens of our visit in the open chests of jewels, the empty lamp, and the white bones of poor Foulata.

When we had groped our way for about a quarter of an hour along the passage, suddenly it took a sharp turn, or else was bisected by another, which we followed, only in course of time to be led into a third. And so it went on for some hours. We seemed to be in a stone labyrinth that led nowhere. What all these passages are, of course I cannot say, but we thought that they must be the ancient workings of a mine, of which the various shafts and adits travelled hither and thither as the ore led them. This is the only way in which we could account for such a multitude of galleries.

At length we halted, thoroughly worn out with fatigue and with that hope deferred which maketh the heart sick, and ate up our poor remaining piece of biltong and drank our last sup of water, for our throats were like lime-kilns. It seemed to us that we had escaped Death in the darkness of the treasure chamber only to meet him in the darkness of the tunnels.

As we stood, once more utterly depressed, I thought that I caught a sound, to which I called the attention of the others. It was very faint and very far off, but it *was* a sound, a faint, murmuring sound, for the others heard it too, and no words can describe the blessedness of it after all those hours of utter, awful stillness.

"By heaven! it's running water," said Good. "Come on."

Off we started again in the direction from which the faint murmur seemed to come, groping our way as before along the rocky walls. I remember that I laid down the basket full of diamonds, wishing to be rid of its weight, but on second thoughts took it up again. One might as well die rich as poor, I reflected. As we went the sound became more and more audible, till at last it seemed quite loud in the quiet. On, yet on; now we could distinctly make out the unmistakable swirl of rushing water. And yet how could there be running water in the bowels of the earth? Now we were quite near it, and Good, who was leading, swore that he could smell it.

"Go gently, Good," said Sir Henry, "we must be close." *Splash!* and a cry from Good.

He had fallen in.

"Good! Good! where are you?" we shouted, in terrified distress. To our intense relief an answer came back in a choky voice.

"All right; I've got hold of a rock. Strike a light to show me where you are."

Hastily I lit the last remaining match. Its faint gleam discovered to us a dark mass of water running at our feet. How wide it was we could not see, but there, some way out, was the dark form of our companion hanging on to a projecting rock.

"Stand clear to catch me," sung out Good. "I must swim for it."

Then we heard a splash, and a great struggle. Another minute and he had grabbed at and caught Sir Henry's outstretched hand, and we had pulled him up high and dry into the tunnel.

"My word!" he said, between his gasps, "that was touch and go. If I hadn't managed to catch that rock, and known how to swim, I should have been done. It runs like a mill-race, and I could feel no bottom."

We dared not follow the banks of the subterranean river for fear lest we should fall into it again in the darkness. So after Good had rested a while, and we had drunk our fill of the water, which was sweet and fresh, and washed our faces, that needed it sadly, as well as we could, we started from the banks of this African Styx, and began to retrace our steps along the tunnel, Good dripping unpleasantly in front of us. At length we came to another gallery leading to our right.

"We may as well take it," said Sir Henry wearily; "all roads are alike here; we can only go on till we drop."

Slowly, for a long, long while, we stumbled, utterly exhausted, along this new tunnel, Sir Henry now leading the way. Again I thought of abandoning that basket, but did not.

Suddenly he stopped, and we bumped up against him.

"Look!" he whispered, "is my brain going, or is that light?"

We stared with all our eyes, and there, yes, there, far ahead of us, was a faint, glimmering spot, no larger than a cottage window pane. It was so faint that I doubt if any eyes, except those which, like ours, had for days seen nothing but blackness, could have perceived it at all.

With a gasp of hope we pushed on. In five minutes there was no longer any doubt; it *was* a patch of faint light. A minute more and a breath of real live air was fanning us. On we struggled. All at once the tunnel narrowed. Sir Henry went on his knees. Smaller yet it grew, till it was only the size of a large fox's earth—it was *earth* now, mind you; the rock had ceased.

A squeeze, a struggle, and Sir Henry was out, and so was Good, and so was I, dragging Foulata's basket after me; and there above us were the blessed stars, and in our nostrils was the sweet air. Then suddenly something gave, and we were all rolling over and over and over through grass and bushes and soft, wet soil.

The basket caught in something and I stopped. Sitting up I hallooed lustily. An answering shout came from below, where Sir Henry's wild career had been checked by some level ground. I scrambled to him, and found him unhurt, though breathless. Then we looked for Good. A little way off we discovered him also, hammed in a forked root. He was a good deal knocked about, but soon came to himself.

We sat down together, there on the grass, and the revulsion of feeling was so great that really I think we cried with joy. We had escaped from that awful dungeon, which was so near to becoming our grave. Surely some merciful Power guided our footsteps to the jackal hole, for that is what it must have been, at the termination of the tunnel. And see, yonder on the mountains the dawn we had never thought to look upon again was blushing rosy red.

Presently the grey light stole down the slopes, and we saw that we were at the bottom, or rather, nearly at the bottom, of the vast pit in front of the entrance to the cave. Now we could make out the dim forms of the three Colossi who sat upon its verge. Doubtless those awful passages, along which we had wandered the livelong night, had been originally in some way connected with the great diamond mine. As for the subterranean river in the bowels of the mountain, Heaven only knows what it is, or whence it flows, or whither it goes. I, for one, have no anxiety to trace its course.

Lighter it grew, and lighter yet. We could see each other now, and such a spectacle as we presented I have never set eyes on before or since. Gaunt-cheeked, hollow-eyed wretches, smeared all over with dust and mud, bruised, bleeding, the long fear of imminent death yet written on our countenances, we were, indeed, a sight to frighten the daylight. And yet it is a solemn fact that Good's eye-glass was still fixed in Good's eye. I doubt whether he had ever taken it out at all. Neither the darkness, nor the plunge in the subterranean river, nor the roll down the slope, had been able to separate Good and his eye- glass.

Presently we rose, fearing that our limbs would stiffen if we stopped there longer, and commenced with slow and painful steps to struggle up the sloping sides of the great pit. For an hour or more we toiled steadfastly up the blue clay, dragging ourselves on by the help of the roots and grasses with which it was clothed. But now I had no more thought of leaving the basket; indeed, nothing but death should have parted us.

At last it was done, and we stood by the great road, on that side of the pit which is opposite to the Colossi.

At the side of the road, a hundred yards off, a fire was burning in front of some huts, and round the fire were figures. We staggered towards them, supporting one another, and halting every few paces. Presently one of the figures rose, saw us and fell on to the ground, crying out for fear.

"Infadoos, Infadoos! it is we, thy friends."

He rose; he ran to us, staring wildly, and still shaking with fear.

"Oh, my lords, my lords, it is indeed you come back from the dead!— come back from the dead!"

And the old warrior flung himself down before us, and clasping Sir Henry's knees, he wept aloud for joy.

Ignosi's Farewell

Ten days from that eventful morning found us once more in our old quarters at Loo; and, strange to say, but little the worse for our terrible experience, except that my stubbly hair came out of the treasure cave about three shades greyer than it went in, and that Good never was quite the same after Foulata's death, which seemed to move him very greatly. I am bound to say, looking at the thing from the point of view of an oldish man of the world, that I consider her removal was a fortunate occurrence, since, otherwise, complications would have been sure to ensue. The poor creature was no ordinary native girl, but a person of great, I had almost said stately, beauty, and of considerable refinement of mind. But no amount of beauty or refinement could have made an entanglement between Good and herself a desirable occurrence; for, as she herself put it, "Can the sun mate with the darkness, or the white with the black?"

I need hardly state that we never again penetrated into Solomon's treasure chamber. After we had recovered from our fatigues, a process which took us forty-eight hours, we descended into the great pit in the hope of finding the hole by which we had crept out of the mountain, but with no success. To begin with, rain had fallen, and obliterated our spoor; and what is more, the sides of the vast pit were full of ant-bear and other holes. It was impossible to say to which of these we owed our salvation. Also, on the day before we started back to Loo, we made a further examination of the wonders of the stalactite cave, and, drawn by a kind of restless feeling, even penetrated once more into the Chamber of the Dead. Passing beneath the spear of the White Death we gazed, with sensations which it would be quite impossible for me to describe, at the mass of rock that had shut us off from escape, thinking the while of priceless treasures beyond, of the mysterious old hag whose flattened fragments lay crushed beneath it, and of the fair girl of whose tomb it was the portal. I say gazed at the "rock," for, examine as we could, we could find no traces of the join of the sliding door; nor, indeed, could we hit upon the secret, now utterly lost, that worked it, though we tried for an hour or more. It is certainly a marvellous bit of mechanism, characteristic, in its massive and yet inscrutable simplicity, of the age which produced it; and I doubt if the world has such another to show.

At last we gave it up in disgust; though, if the mass had suddenly risen before our eyes, I doubt if we should have screwed up courage to step over Gagool's mangled remains, and once more enter the treasure chamber, even in the sure and certain hope of unlimited diamonds. And yet I could have cried at the idea of leaving all that treasure, the biggest treasure probably that in the world's history has ever been accumulated in one spot. But there was no help for it. Only dynamite could force its way through five feet of solid rock.

So we left it. Perhaps, in some remote unborn century, a more fortunate explorer may hit upon the "Open Sesame," and flood the world with gems. But, myself, I doubt it. Somehow, I seem to feel that the tens of millions of pounds' worth of jewels which lie in the three stone coffers will never shine round the neck of an earthly beauty. They and Foulata's bones will keep cold company till the end of all things.

With a sigh of disappointment we made our way back, and next day started for Loo. And yet it was really very ungrateful of us to be disappointed; for, as the reader will remember, by a lucky thought, I had taken the precaution to fill the wide pockets of my old shooting coat and trousers with gems before we left our prison-house, also Foulata's basket, which held twice as many more, notwithstanding that the water bottle had occupied some of its space. A good many of these fell out in the course of our roll down the side of the pit, including several of the big ones, which I had crammed in on the top in my coat pockets. But, comparatively speaking, an enormous quantity still remained, including ninety-three large stones ranging from over two hundred to seventy carats in weight. My old shooting coat and the basket still held sufficient treasure to make us all, if not millionaires as the term is understood in America, at least exceedingly wealthy men, and yet to keep enough stones each to make the three finest sets of gems in Europe. So we had not done so badly.

On arriving at Loo we were most cordially received by Ignosi, whom we found well, and busily engaged in consolidating his power, and reorganising the regiments which had suffered most in the great struggle with Twala.

He listened with intense interest to our wonderful story; but when we told him of old Gagool's frightful end he grew thoughtful.

"Come hither," he called, to a very old Induna or councillor, who was sitting with others in a circle round the king, but out of ear-shot. The ancient man rose, approached, saluted, and seated himself.

"Thou art aged," said Ignosi.

"Ay, my lord the king! Thy father's father and I were born on the same day."

"Tell me, when thou wast little, didst thou know Gagaoola the witch doctress?"

"Ay, my lord the king!"

"How was she then—young, like thee?"

"Not so, my lord the king! She was even as she is now and as she was in the days of my great grandfather before me; old and dried, very ugly, and full of wickedness."

"She is no more; she is dead."

"So, O king! then is an ancient curse taken from the land."

"Go!"

"*Koom!* I go, Black Puppy, who tore out the old dog's throat. *Koom!*"

"Ye see, my brothers," said Ignosi, "this was a strange woman, and I rejoice that she is dead. She would have let you die in the dark place, and mayhap afterwards she had found a way to slay me, as she found a way to slay my father, and set up Twala, whom her black heart loved, in his place. Now go on with the tale; surely there never was its like!"

After I had narrated all the story of our escape, as we had agreed between ourselves that I should, I took the opportunity to address Ignosi as to our departure from Kukuanaland.

"And now, Ignosi," I said, "the time has come for us to bid thee farewell, and start to see our own land once more. Behold, Ignosi, thou camest with us a servant, and now we leave thee a mighty king. If thou art grateful to us, remember to do even as thou didst promise: to rule justly, to respect the law, and to put none to death without a cause. So shalt thou prosper. To-morrow, at break of day, Ignosi, thou wilt give us an escort who shall lead us across the mountains. Is it not so, O king?"

Ignosi covered his face with his hands for a while before answering.

"My heart is sore," he said at last; "your words split my heart in twain. What have I done to you, Incubu, Macumazahn, and Bougwan, that ye should leave me desolate? Ye who stood by me in rebellion and in battle, will ye leave me in the day of peace and victory? What will ye —wives? Choose from among the maidens! A place to live in? Behold, the land is yours as far as ye can see. The white man's houses? Ye shall teach my people how to build them. Cattle for beef and milk? Every married man shall bring you an ox or a cow. Wild game to hunt? Does not the elephant walk through my forests, and the river-horse sleep in the reeds? Would ye make war? My Impis wait your word. If there is anything more which I can give, that will I give you."

"Nay, Ignosi, we want none of these things," I answered; "we would seek our own place."

"Now do I learn," said Ignosi bitterly, and with flashing eyes, "that ye love the bright stones more than me, your friend. Ye have the stones; now ye would go to Natal and across the moving black water and sell them, and be rich, as it is the desire of a white man's heart to be. Cursed for your sake be the white stones, and cursed he who seeks them. Death shall it be to him who sets foot in the place of Death to find them. I have spoken. White men, ye can go."

I laid my hand upon his arm. "Ignosi," I said, "tell us, when thou didst wander in Zululand, and among the white people of Natal, did not thine heart turn to the land thy mother told thee of, thy native place, where thou didst see the light, and play when thou wast little, the land where thy place was?"

"It was even so, Macumazahn."

"In like manner, Ignosi, do our hearts turn to our land and to our own place."

Then came a silence. When Ignosi broke it, it was in a different voice.

"I do perceive that now as ever thy words are wise and full of reason, Macumazahn; that which flies in the air loves not to run along the ground; the white man loves not to live on the level of the black or to house among his kraals. Well, ye must go, and leave my heart sore, because ye will be as dead to me, since from where ye are no tidings can come to me.

"But listen, and let all your brothers know my words. No other white man shall cross the mountains, even if any man live to come so far. I will see no traders with their guns and gin. My people shall fight with the spear, and drink water, like their forefathers before them. I will have no praying-men to put a fear of death into men's hearts, to stir them up against the law of the king, and make a path for the white folk who follow to run on. If a white man comes to my gates I will send him back; if a hundred come I will push them back; if armies come, I will make war on them with all my strength, and they shall not prevail against me. None shall ever seek for the shining stones: no, not an army, for if they come I will send a regiment and fill up the pit, and break down the white columns in the caves and choke them with rocks, so that none can reach even to that door of which ye speak, and whereof the way to move it is lost. But for you three, Incubu, Macumazahn, and Bougwan, the path is always open; for, behold, ye are dearer to me than aught that breathes.

"And ye would go. Infadoos, my uncle, and my Induna, shall take you by the hand and guide you with a regiment. There is, as I have learned, another way across the mountains that he shall show you. Farewell, my brothers, brave white men. See me no more, for I have no heart to bear it. Behold! I make a decree, and it shall be published from the mountains to the mountains; your names, Incubu, Macumazahn, and Bougwan, shall be "*hlonipa*" even as the names of dead kings, and he who speaks them shall die. So shall your memory be preserved in the land for ever.

"Go now, ere my eyes rain tears like a woman's. At times as ye look back down the path of life, or when ye are old and gather yourselves together to crouch before the fire, because for you the sun has no more heat, ye will think of how we stood shoulder to shoulder, in that great battle which thy wise words planned, Macumazahn; of how thou wast the point of the horn that galled Twala's flank, Bougwan; whilst thou stood in the ring of the Greys, Incubu, and men went down before thine axe like corn before a sickle; ay, and of how thou didst break that wild bull Twala's strength, and bring his pride to dust. Fare ye well for ever, Incubu, Macumazahn, and Bougwan, my lords and my friends."

Ignosi rose and looked earnestly at us for a few seconds. Then he threw the corner of his karross over his head, so as to cover his face from us.

We went in silence.

Next day at dawn we left Loo, escorted by our old friend Infadoos, who was heart-broken at our departure, and by the regiment of Buffaloes. Early as was the hour, all the main street of the town was lined with multitudes of people, who gave us the royal salute as we passed at the head of the regiment, while the women blessed us for having rid the land of Twala, throwing flowers before us as we went. It was really very affecting, and not the sort of thing one is accustomed to meet with from natives.

One ludicrous incident occurred, however, which I rather welcomed, as it gave us something to laugh at.

Just before we reached the confines of the town, a pretty young girl, with some lovely lilies in her hand, ran forward and presented them to Good—somehow they all seemed to like Good; I think his eye-glass and solitary whisker gave him a fictitious value—and then said that she had a boon to ask.

"Speak on," he answered.

"Let my lord show his servant his beautiful white legs, that his servant may look upon them, and remember them all her days, and tell of them to her children; his servant has travelled four days' journey to see them, for the fame of them has gone throughout the land."

"I'll be hanged if I do!" exclaimed Good excitedly.

"Come, come, my dear fellow," said Sir Henry, "you can't refuse to oblige a lady."

"I won't," replied Good obstinately; "it is positively indecent."

However, in the end he consented to draw up his trousers to the knee, amidst notes of rapturous admiration from all the women present, especially the gratified young lady, and in this guise he had to walk till we got clear of the town.

Good's legs, I fear, will never be so greatly admired again. Of his melting teeth, and even of his "transparent eye," the Kukuanas wearied more or less, but of his legs never.

As we travelled, Infadoos told us that there was another pass over the mountains to the north of the one followed by Solomon's Great Road, or rather that there was a place where it was possible to climb down the wall of cliff which separates Kukuanaland from the desert, and is broken by the towering shapes of Sheba's Breasts. It appeared, also, that rather more than two years previously a party of Kukuana hunters had descended this path into the desert in search of ostriches, whose plumes are much prized among them for war head-dresses, and that in the course of their hunt they had been led far from the mountains and were much troubled by thirst. Seeing trees on the horizon, however, they walked towards them, and discovered a large and fertile oasis some miles in extent, and plentifully watered. It was by way of this oasis that Infadoos suggested we should return, and the idea seemed to us a good one, for it appeared that we should thus escape the rigours of the mountain pass. Also some of the hunters were in attendance to guide us to the oasis, from which, they stated, they could perceive other fertile spots far away in the desert.

Travelling easily, on the night of the fourth day's journey we found ourselves once more on the crest of the mountains that separate Kukuanaland from the desert, which rolled away in sandy billows at our feet, and about twenty-five miles to the north of Sheba's Breasts.

At dawn on the following day, we were led to the edge of a very precipitous chasm, by which we were to descend the precipice, and gain the plain two thousand and more feet below.

Here we bade farewell to that true friend and sturdy old warrior, Infadoos, who solemnly wished all good upon us, and nearly wept with grief. "Never, my lords," he said, "shall mine old eyes see the like of you again. Ah! the way that Incubu cut his men down in the battle! Ah! for the sight of that stroke with which he swept off my brother Twala's head! It was beautiful—beautiful! I may never hope to see such another, except perchance in happy dreams."

We were very sorry to part from him; indeed, Good was so moved that he gave him as a souvenir—what do you think?—an *eye-glass*; afterwards we discovered that it was a spare one. Infadoos was delighted, foreseeing that the possession of such an article would increase his prestige enormously, and after several vain attempts he actually succeeded in screwing it into his own eye. Anything more incongruous than the old warrior looked with an eye-glass I never saw. Eye-glasses do not go well with leopard-skin cloaks and black ostrich plumes.

Then, after seeing that our guides were well laden with water and provisions, and having received a thundering farewell salute from the Buffaloes, we wrung Infadoos by the hand, and began our downward climb. A very arduous business it proved to be, but somehow that evening we found ourselves at the bottom without accident.

"Do you know," said Sir Henry that night, as we sat by our fire and gazed up at the beetling cliffs above us, "I think that there are worse places than Kukuanaland in the world, and that I have known unhappier times than the last month or two, though I have never spent such queer ones. Eh! you fellows?"

"I almost wish I were back," said Good, with a sigh.

As for myself, I reflected that all's well that ends well; but in the course of a long life of shaves, I never had such shaves as those which I had recently experienced. The thought of that battle makes me feel cold all over, and as for our experience in the treasure chamber—!

Next morning we started on a toilsome trudge across the desert, having with us a good supply of water carried by our five guides, and camped that night in the open, marching again at dawn on the morrow.

By noon of the third day's journey we could see the trees of the oasis of which the guides spoke, and within an hour of sundown we were walking once more upon grass and listening to the sound of running water.

Found

And now I come to perhaps the strangest adventure that happened to us in all this strange business, and one which shows how wonderfully things are brought about.

I was walking along quietly, some way in front of the other two, down the banks of the stream which runs from the oasis till it is swallowed up in the hungry desert sands, when suddenly I stopped and rubbed my eyes, as well I might. There, not twenty yards in front of me, placed in a charming situation, under the shade of a species of fig-tree, and facing to the stream, was a cosy hut, built more or less on the Kafir principle with grass and withes, but having a full-length door instead of a bee-hole.

"What the dickens," said I to myself, "can a hut be doing here?" Even as I said it the door of the hut opened, and there limped out of it a *white man* clothed in skins, and with an enormous black beard. I thought that I must have got a touch of the sun. It was impossible. No hunter ever came to such a place as this. Certainly no hunter would ever settle in it. I stared and stared, and so did the other man, and just at that juncture Sir Henry and Good walked up.

"Look here, you fellows," I said, "is that a white man, or am I mad?"

Sir Henry looked, and Good looked, and then all of a sudden the lame white man with a black beard uttered a great cry, and began hobbling towards us. When he was close he fell down in a sort of faint.

With a spring Sir Henry was by his side.

"Great Powers!" he cried, "*it is my brother George!*"

At the sound of this disturbance, another figure, also clad in skins, emerged from the hut, a gun in his hand, and ran towards us. On seeing me he too gave a cry.

"Macumazahn," he halloed, "don't you know me, Baas? I'm Jim the hunter. I lost the note you gave me to give to the Baas, and we have been here nearly two years." And the fellow fell at my feet, and rolled over and over, weeping for joy.

"You careless scoundrel!" I said; "you ought to be well *sjambocked*" —that is, hided.

Meanwhile the man with the black beard had recovered and risen, and he and Sir Henry were pump-handling away at each other, apparently without a word to say. But whatever they had quarrelled about in the past—I suspect it was a lady, though I never asked—it was evidently forgotten now.

"My dear old fellow," burst out Sir Henry at last, "I thought you were dead. I have been over Solomon's Mountains to find you. I had given up all hope of ever seeing you again, and now I come across you perched in the desert, like an old *assvogel*."

"I tried to cross Solomon's Mountains nearly two years ago," was the answer, spoken in the hesitating voice of a man who has had little recent opportunity of using his tongue, "but when I reached here a boulder fell on my leg and crushed it, and I have been able to go neither forward nor back."

Then I came up. "How do you do, Mr. Neville?" I said; "do you remember me?"

"Why," he said, "isn't it Hunter Quatermain, eh, and Good too? Hold on a minute, you fellows, I am getting dizzy again. It is all so very strange, and, when a man has ceased to hope, so very happy!"

That evening, over the camp fire, George Curtis told us his story, which, in its way, was almost as eventful as our own, and, put shortly, amounted to this. A little less than two years before, he had started from Sitanda's Kraal, to try to reach Suliman's Berg. As for the note I had sent him by Jim, that worthy lost it, and he had never heard of it till to-day. But, acting upon information he had received from the natives, he headed not for Sheba's Breasts, but for the ladder-like descent of the mountains down which we had just come, which is clearly a better route than that marked out in old Dom Silvestra's plan. In the desert he and Jim had suffered great hardships, but finally they reached this oasis, where a terrible accident befell George Curtis. On the day of their arrival he was sitting by the stream, and Jim was extracting the honey from the nest of a stingless bee which is to be found in the desert, on the top of a bank immediately above him. In so doing he loosened a great boulder of rock, which fell upon George Curtis's right leg, crushing it frightfully. From that day he had been so lame that he found it impossible to go either forward or back, and had preferred to take the chances of dying in the oasis to the certainty of perishing in the desert.

As for food, however, they got on pretty well, for they had a good supply of ammunition, and the oasis was frequented, especially at night, by large quantities of game, which came thither for water. These they shot, or trapped in pitfalls, using the flesh for food, and, after their clothes wore out, the hides for clothing.

"And so," George Curtis ended, "we have lived for nearly two years, like a second Robinson Crusoe and his man Friday, hoping against hope that some natives might come here to help us away, but none have come. Only last night we settled that Jim should leave me, and try to reach Sitanda's Kraal to get assistance. He was to go to-morrow, but I had little hope of ever seeing him back again. And now *you*, of all people in the world, *you*, who, as I fancied, had long ago forgotten all about me, and were living comfortably in old England, turn up in a promiscuous way and find me where you least expected. It is the most wonderful thing that I have ever heard of, and the most merciful too."

Then Sir Henry set to work, and told him the main facts of our adventures, sitting till late into the night to do it.

"By Jove!" said George Curtis, when I showed him some of the diamonds: "well, at least you have got something for your pains, besides my worthless self."

Sir Henry laughed. "They belong to Quatermain and Good. It was a part of the bargain that they should divide any spoils there might be."

This remark set me thinking, and having spoken to Good, I told Sir Henry that it was our joint wish that he should take a third portion of the diamonds, or, if he would not, that his share should be handed to his brother, who had suffered even more than ourselves on the chance of getting them. Finally, we prevailed upon him to consent to this arrangement, but George Curtis did not know of it until some time afterwards.

Here, at this point, I think that I shall end my history. Our journey across the desert back to Sitanda's Kraal was most arduous, especially as we had to support George Curtis, whose right leg was very weak indeed, and continually threw out splinters of bone. But we did accomplish it somehow, and to give its details would only be to reproduce much of what happened to us on the former occasion.

Six months from the date of our re-arrival at Sitanda's, where we found our guns and other goods quite safe, though the old rascal in charge was much disgusted at our surviving to claim them, saw us all once more safe and sound at my little place on the Berea, near Durban, where I am now writing. Thence I bid farewell to all who have accompanied me through the strangest trip I ever made in the course of a long and varied experience.

P.S.—Just as I had written the last word, a Kafir came up my avenue of orange trees, carrying a letter in a cleft stick, which he had brought from the post. It turned out to be from Sir Henry, and as it speaks for itself I give it in full.

October 1, 1884.
Brayley Hall, Yorkshire.

My Dear Quatermain,

I send you a line a few mails back to say that the three of us, George, Good, and myself, fetched up all right in England. We got off the boat at Southampton, and went up to town. You should have seen what a swell Good turned out the very next day, beautifully shaved, frock coat fitting like a glove, brand new eye-glass, etc., etc. I went and walked in the park with him, where I met some people I know, and at once told them the story of his "beautiful white legs."

He is furious, especially as some ill-natured person has printed it in a Society paper.

To come to business, Good and I took the diamonds to Streeter's to be valued, as we arranged, and really I am afraid to tell you what they put them at, it seems so enormous. They say that of course it is more or less guess-work, as such stones have never to their knowledge been put on the market in anything like such quantities. It appears that (with the exception of one or two of the largest) they are of the finest water, and equal in every way to the best Brazilian stones. I asked them if they would buy them, but they said that it was beyond their power to do so, and recommended us to sell by degrees, over a period of years indeed, for fear lest we should flood the market. They offer, however, a hundred and eighty thousand for a very small portion of them.

You must come home, Quatermain, and see about these things, especially if you insist upon making the magnificent present of the third share, which does *not* belong to me, to my brother George. As for Good, he is *no good*. His time is too much occupied in shaving, and other matters connected with the vain adorning of the body. But I think he is still down on his luck about Foulata. He told me that since he had been home he hadn't seen a woman to touch her, either as regards her figure or the sweetness of her expression.

I want you to come home, my dear old comrade, and to buy a house near here. You have done your day's work, and have lots of money now, and there is a place for sale quite close which would suit you admirably. Do come; the sooner the better; you can finish writing the story of our adventures on board ship. We have refused to tell the tale till it is written by you, for fear lest we shall not be believed. If you start on receipt of this you will reach here by Christmas, and I book you to stay with me for that. Good is coming, and George; and so, by the way, is your boy Harry (there's a bribe for you). I have had him down for a week's shooting, and like him. He is a cool young hand; he shot me in the leg, cut out the pellets, and then remarked upon the advantages of having a medical student with every shooting party!

Good-bye, old boy; I can't say any more, but I know that you will come, if it is only to oblige

Your sincere friend,
Henry Curtis.

P.S.—The tusks of the great bull that killed poor Khiva have now been put up in the hall here, over the pair of buffalo horns you gave me, and look magnificent; and the axe with which I chopped off Twala's head is fixed above my writing-table. I wish that we could have managed to bring away the coats of chain armour. Don't lose poor Foulata's basket in which you brought away the diamonds.
H.C.

To-day is Tuesday. There is a steamer going on Friday, and I really think that I must take Quatermain at his word, and sail by her for England, if it is only to see you, Harry, my boy, and to look after the printing of this history, which is a task that I do not like to trust to anybody else.
Allan Quatermain.

Allan Quatermain

Table of Contents

Introduction

December 23

'I have just buried my boy, my poor handsome boy of whom I was so proud, and my heart is broken. It is very hard having only one son to lose him thus, but God's will be done. Who am I that I should complain? The great wheel of Fate rolls on like a Juggernaut, and crushes us all in turn, some soon, some late — it does not matter when, in the end, it crushes us all. We do not prostrate ourselves before it like the poor Indians; we fly hither and thither — we cry for mercy; but it is of no use, the black Fate thunders on and in its season reduces us to powder.

'Poor Harry to go so soon! just when his life was opening to him. He was doing so well at the hospital, he had passed his last examination with honours, and I was proud of them, much prouder than he was, I think. And then he must needs go to that smallpox hospital. He wrote to me that he was not afraid of smallpox and wanted to gain the experience; and now the disease has killed him, and I, old and grey and withered, am left to mourn over him, without a chick or child to comfort me. I might have saved him, too — I have money enough for both of us, and much more than enough — King Solomon's Mines provided me with that; but I said, "No, let the boy earn his living, let him labour that he may enjoy rest." But the rest has come to him before the labour. Oh, my boy, my boy!

'I am like the man in the Bible who laid up much goods and builded barns — goods for my boy and barns for him to store them in; and now his soul has been required of him, and I am left desolate. I would that it had been my soul and not my boy's!

'We buried him this afternoon under the shadow of the grey and ancient tower of the church of this village where my house is. It was a dreary December afternoon, and the sky was heavy with snow, but not much was falling. The coffin was put down by the grave, and a few big flakes lit upon it. They looked very white upon the black cloth! There was a little hitch about getting the coffin down into the grave — the necessary ropes had been forgotten: so we drew back from it, and waited in silence watching the big flakes fall gently one by one like heavenly benedictions, and melt in tears on Harry's pall. But that was not all. A robin redbreast came as bold as could be and lit upon the coffin and began to sing. And then I am afraid that I broke down, and so did Sir Henry Curtis, strong man though he is; and as for Captain Good, I saw him turn away too; even in my own distress I could not help noticing it.'

The above, signed 'Allan Quatermain', is an extract from my diary written two years and more ago. I copy it down here because it seems to me that it is the fittest beginning to the history that I am about to write, if it please God to spare me to finish it. If not, well it does not matter. That extract was penned seven thousand miles or so from the spot where I now lie painfully and slowly writing this, with a pretty girl standing by my side fanning the flies from my august countenance. Harry is there and I am here, and yet somehow I cannot help feeling that I am not far off Harry.

When I was in England I used to live in a very fine house — at least I call it a fine house, speaking comparatively, and judging from the standard of the houses I have been accustomed to all my life in Africa — not five hundred yards from the old church where Harry is asleep, and thither I went after the funeral and ate some food; for it is no good starving even if one has just buried all one's earthly hopes. But I could not eat much, and soon I took to walking, or rather limping — being permanently lame from the bite of a lion — up and down, up and down the oak-panelled vestibule; for there is a vestibule in my house in England. On all the four walls of this vestibule were placed pairs of horns — about a hundred pairs altogether, all of which I had shot myself. They are beautiful specimens, as I never keep any horns which are not in every way perfect, unless it may be now and again on account of the associations connected with them. In the centre of the room, however, over the wide fireplace, there was a clear space left on which I had fixed up all my rifles. Some of them I have had for forty years, old muzzle-loaders that nobody would look at nowadays. One was an elephant gun with strips of rimpi, or green hide, lashed round the stock and locks, such as used to be owned by the Dutchmen — a 'roer' they call it. That gun, the Boer I bought it from many years ago told me, had been used by his father at the battle of the Blood River, just after Dingaan swept into Natal and slaughtered six hundred men, women, and children, so that the Boers named the place where they died 'Weenen', or the 'Place of Weeping'; and so it is called to this day, and always will be called. And many an elephant have I shot with that old gun. She always took a handful of black powder and a three-ounce ball, and kicked like the very deuce.

Well, up and down I walked, staring at the guns and the horns which the guns had brought low; and as I did so there rose up in me a great craving: — I would go away from this place where I lived idly and at ease, back again to the wild land where I had spent my life, where I met my dear wife and poor Harry was born, and so many things, good, bad, and indifferent, had happened to me. The thirst for the wilderness was on me; I could tolerate this place no more; I would go and die as I had lived, among the wild game and the savages. Yes, as I walked, I began to long to see the moonlight gleaming silvery white over the wide veldt and mysterious sea of bush, and watch the lines of game travelling down the ridges to the water. The ruling passion is strong in death, they say, and my heart was dead that night. But, independently of my trouble, no man who has for forty years lived the life I have, can with impunity go coop himself in this prim English country, with its trim hedgerows and cultivated fields, its stiff formal manners, and its well-dressed crowds. He begins to long — ah, how he longs! — for the keen breath of the desert air; he dreams of the sight of Zulu impis breaking on their foes like surf upon the rocks, and his heart rises up in rebellion against the strict limits of the civilized life.

Ah! this civilization, what does it all come to? For forty years and more I lived among savages, and studied them and their ways; and now for several years I have lived here in England, and have in my own stupid manner done my best to learn the ways of the children of light; and what have I found? A great gulf fixed? No, only a very little one, that a plain man's thought may spring across. I say that as the savage is, so is the white man, only the latter is more inventive, and possesses the faculty of combination; save and except also that the savage, as I have known him, is to a large extent free from the greed of money, which eats like a cancer into the heart of the white man. It is a depressing conclusion, but in all essentials the savage and the child of civilization are identical. I dare say that the highly civilized lady reading this will smile at an old fool of a hunter's simplicity when she thinks of her black bead-bedecked sister; and so will the superfine cultured idler scientifically eating a dinner at his club, the cost of which would keep a starving family for a week. And yet, my dear young lady, what are those pretty things round your own neck? — they have a strong family resemblance, especially when you wear that *very* low dress, to the savage woman's beads. Your habit of turning round and round to the sound of horns and tom-toms, your fondness for pigments and powders, the way in which you love to subjugate yourself to the rich warrior who has captured you in marriage, and the quickness with which your taste in feathered head-dresses varies — all these things suggest touches of kinship; and you remember that in the fundamental principles of your nature you are quite identical. As for you, sir, who also laugh, let some man come and strike you in the face whilst you are enjoying that marvellous-looking dish, and we shall soon see how much of the savage there is in *you*.

There, I might go on for ever, but what is the good? Civilization is only savagery silver-gilt. A vainglory is it, and like a northern light, comes but to fade and leave the sky more dark. Out of the soil of barbarism it has grown like a tree, and, as I believe, into the soil like a tree it will once more, sooner or later, fall again, as the Egyptian civilization fell, as the Hellenic civilization fell, and as the Roman civilization and many others of which the world has now lost count, fell also. Do not let me, however, be understood as decrying our modern institutions, representing as they do the gathered experience of humanity applied for the good of all. Of course they have great advantages — hospitals for instance; but then, remember, we breed the sickly people who fill them. In a savage land they do not exist. Besides, the question will arise: How many of these blessings are due to Christianity as distinct from civilization? And so the balance sways and the story runs — here a gain, there a loss, and Nature's great average struck across the two, whereof the sum total forms one of the factors in that mighty equation in which the result will equal the unknown quantity of her purpose.

I make no apology for this digression, especially as this is an introduction which all young people and those who never like to think (and it is a bad habit) will naturally skip. It seems to me very desirable that we should sometimes try to understand the limitations of our nature, so that we may not be carried away by the pride of knowledge. Man's cleverness is almost indefinite, and stretches like an elastic band, but human nature is like an iron ring. You can go round and round it, you can polish it highly, you can even flatten it a little on one side, whereby you will make it bulge out the other, but you will *never*, while the world endures and man is man, increase its total circumference. It is the one fixed unchangeable thing — fixed as the stars, more enduring than the mountains, as unalterable as the way of the Eternal. Human nature is God's kaleidoscope, and the little bits of coloured glass which represent our passions, hopes, fears, joys, aspirations towards good and evil and what not, are turned in His mighty hand as surely and as certainly as it turns the stars, and continually fall into new patterns and combinations. But the composing elements remain the same, nor will there be one more bit of coloured glass nor one less for ever and ever.

This being so, supposing for the sake of argument we divide ourselves into twenty parts, nineteen savage and one civilized, we must look to the nineteen savage portions of our nature, if we would really understand ourselves, and not to the twentieth, which, though so insignificant in reality, is spread all over the other nineteen, making them appear quite different from what they really are, as the blacking does a boot, or the veneer a table. It is on the nineteen rough serviceable savage portions that we fall back on emergencies, not on the polished but unsubstantial twentieth. Civilization should wipe away our tears, and yet we weep and cannot be comforted. Warfare is abhorrent to her, and yet we strike out for hearth and home, for honour and fair fame, and can glory in the blow. And so on, through everything.

So, when the heart is stricken, and the head is humbled in the dust, civilization fails us utterly. Back, back, we creep, and lay us like little children on the great breast of Nature, she that perchance may soothe us and make us forget, or at least rid remembrance of its sting. Who has not in his great grief felt a longing to look upon the outward features of the universal Mother; to lie on the mountains and watch the clouds drive across the sky and hear the rollers break in thunder on the shore, to let his poor struggling life mingle for a while in her life; to feel the slow beat of her eternal heart, and to forget his woes, and let his identity be swallowed in the vast imperceptibly moving energy of her of whom we are, from whom we came, and with whom we shall again be mingled, who gave us birth, and will in a day to come give us our burial also.

And so in my trouble, as I walked up and down the oak-panelled vestibule of my house there in Yorkshire, I longed once more to throw myself into the arms of Nature. Not the Nature which you know, the Nature that waves in well-kept woods and smiles out in corn-fields, but Nature as she was in the age when creation was complete, undefiled as yet by any human sinks of sweltering humanity. I would go again where the wild game was, back to the land whereof none know the history, back to the savages, whom I love, although some of them are almost as merciless as Political Economy. There, perhaps, I should be able to learn to think of poor Harry lying in the churchyard, without feeling as though my heart would break in two.

And now there is an end of this egotistical talk, and there shall be no more of it. But if you whose eyes may perchance one day fall upon my written thoughts have got so far as this, I ask you to persevere, since what I have to tell you is not without its interest, and it has never been told before, nor will again.

The Consul's Yarn

A week had passed since the funeral of my poor boy Harry, and one evening I was in my room walking up and down and thinking, when there was a ring at the outer door. Going down the steps I opened it myself, and in came my old friends Sir Henry Curtis and Captain John Good, RN. They entered the vestibule and sat themselves down before the wide hearth, where, I remember, a particularly good fire of logs was burning.

'It is very kind of you to come round,' I said by way of making a remark; 'it must have been heavy walking in the snow.'

They said nothing, but Sir Henry slowly filled his pipe and lit it with a burning ember. As he leant forward to do so the fire got hold of a gassy bit of pine and flared up brightly, throwing the whole scene into strong relief, and I thought, What a splendid-looking man he is! Calm, powerful face, clear-cut features, large grey eyes, yellow beard and hair — altogether a magnificent specimen of the higher type of humanity. Nor did his form belie his face. I have never seen wider shoulders or a deeper chest. Indeed, Sir Henry's girth is so great that, though he is six feet two high, he does not strike one as a tall man. As I looked at him I could not help thinking what a curious contrast my little dried-up self presented to his grand face and form. Imagine to yourself a small, withered, yellow-faced man of sixty-three, with thin hands, large brown eyes, a head of grizzled hair cut short and standing up like a half-worn scrubbing-brush — total weight in my clothes, nine stone six — and you will get a very fair idea of Allan Quatermain, commonly called Hunter Quatermain, or by the natives 'Macumazahn' — Anglic/CHAR: e grave/, he who keeps a bright look-out at night, or, in vulgar English, a sharp fellow who is not to be taken in.

Then there was Good, who is not like either of us, being short, dark, stout — *very* stout — with twinkling black eyes, in one of which an eyeglass is everlastingly fixed. I say stout, but it is a mild term; I regret to state that of late years Good has been running to fat in a most disgraceful way. Sir Henry tells him that it comes from idleness and over-feeding, and Good does not like it at all, though he cannot deny it.

We sat for a while, and then I got a match and lit the lamp that stood ready on the table, for the half-light began to grow dreary, as it is apt to do when one has a short week ago buried the hope of one's life. Next, I opened a cupboard in the wainscoting and got a bottle of whisky and some tumblers and water. I always like to do these things for myself: it is irritating to me to have somebody continually at my elbow, as though I were an eighteen-month-old baby. All this while Curtis and Good had been silent, feeling, I suppose, that they had nothing to say that could do me any good, and content to give me the comfort of their presence and unspoken sympathy; for it was only their second visit since the funeral. And it is, by the way, from the *presence* of others that we really derive support in our dark hours of grief, and not from their talk, which often only serves to irritate us. Before a bad storm the game always herd together, but they cease their calling.

They sat and smoked and drank whisky and water, and I stood by the fire also smoking and looking at them.

At last I spoke. 'Old friends,' I said, 'how long is it since we got back from Kukuanaland?'

'Three years,' said Good. 'Why do you ask?'

'I ask because I think that I have had a long enough spell of civilization. I am going back to the veldt.'

Sir Henry laid his head back in his arm-chair and laughed one of his deep laughs. 'How very odd,' he said, 'eh, Good?'

Good beamed at me mysteriously through his eyeglass and murmured, 'Yes, odd — very odd.'

'I don't quite understand,' said I, looking from one to the other, for I dislike mysteries.

'Don't you, old fellow?' said Sir Henry; 'then I will explain. As Good and I were walking up here we had a talk.'

'If Good was there you probably did,' I put in sarcastically, for Good is a great hand at talking. 'And what may it have been about?'

'What do you think?' asked Sir Henry.

I shook my head. It was not likely that I should know what Good might be talking about. He talks about so many things.

'Well, it was about a little plan that I have formed — namely, that if you were willing we should pack up our traps and go off to Africa on another expedition.'

I fairly jumped at his words. 'You don't say so!' I said.

'Yes I do, though, and so does Good; don't you, Good?'

'Rather,' said that gentleman.

'Listen, old fellow,' went on Sir Henry, with considerable animation of manner. 'I'm tired of it too, dead-tired of doing nothing more except play the squire in a country that is sick of squires. For a year or more I have been getting as restless as an old elephant who scents danger. I am always dreaming of Kukuanaland and Gagool and King Solomon's Mines. I can assure you I have become the victim of an almost unaccountable craving. I am sick of shooting pheasants and partridges, and want to have a go at some large game again. There, you know the feeling — when one has once tasted brandy and water, milk becomes insipid to the palate. That year we spent together up in Kukuanaland seems to me worth all the other years of my life put together. I dare say that I am a fool for my pains, but I can't help it; I long to go, and, what is more, I mean to go.' He paused, and then went on again. 'And, after all, why should I not go? I have no wife or parent, no chick or child to keep me. If anything happens to me the baronetcy will go to my brother George and his boy, as it would ultimately do in any case. I am of no importance to any one.'

'Ah!' I said, 'I thought you would come to that sooner or later. And now, Good, what is your reason for wanting to trek; have you got one?'

'I have,' said Good, solemnly. 'I never do anything without a reason; and it isn't a lady — at least, if it is, it's several.'

I looked at him again. Good is so overpoweringly frivolous. 'What is it?' I said.

'Well, if you really want to know, though I'd rather not speak of a delicate and strictly personal matter, I'll tell you: I'm getting too fat.'

'Shut up, Good!' said Sir Henry. 'And now, Quatermain, tell us, where do you propose going to?'

I lit my pipe, which had gone out, before answering.

'Have you people ever heard of Mt Kenia?' I asked.

'Don't know the place,' said Good.

'Did you ever hear of the Island of Lamu?' I asked again.

'No. Stop, though — isn't it a place about 300 miles north of Zanzibar?'

'Yes. Now listen. What I have to propose is this. That we go to Lamu and thence make our way about 250 miles inland to Mt Kenia; from Mt Kenia on inland to Mt Lekakisera, another 200 miles, or thereabouts, beyond which no white man has to the best of my belief ever been; and then, if we get so far, right on into the unknown interior. What do you say to that, my hearties?'

'It's a big order,' said Sir Henry, reflectively.

'You are right,' I answered, 'it is; but I take it that we are all three of us in search of a big order. We want a change of scene, and we are likely to get one — a thorough change. All my life I have longed to visit those parts, and I mean to do it before I die. My poor boy's death has broken the last link between me and civilization, and I'm off to my native wilds. And now I'll tell you another thing, and that is, that for years and years I have heard rumours of a great white race which is supposed to have its home somewhere up in this direction, and I have a mind to see if there is any truth in them. If you fellows like to come, well and good; if not, I'll go alone.'

'I'm your man, though I don't believe in your white race,' said Sir Henry Curtis, rising and placing his arm upon my shoulder.

'Ditto,' remarked Good. 'I'll go into training at once. By all means let's go to Mt Kenia and the other place with an unpronounceable name, and look for a white race that does not exist. It's all one to me.'

'When do you propose to start?' asked Sir Henry.

'This day month,' I answered, 'by the British India steamboat; and don't you be so certain that things have no existence because you do not happen to have heard of them. Remember King Solomon's mines!'

Some fourteen weeks or so had passed since the date of this conversation, and this history goes on its way in very different surroundings.

After much deliberation and inquiry we came to the conclusion that our best starting-point for Mt Kenia would be from the neighbourhood of the mouth of the Tana River, and not from Mombassa, a place over 100 miles nearer Zanzibar. This conclusion we arrived at from information given to us by a German trader whom we met upon the steamer at Aden. I think that he was the dirtiest German I ever knew; but he was a good fellow, and gave us a great deal of valuable information. 'Lamu,' said he, 'you goes to Lamu — oh ze beautiful place!' and he turned up his fat face and beamed with mild rapture. 'One year and a half I live there and never change my shirt — never at all.'

And so it came to pass that on arriving at the island we disembarked with all our goods and chattels, and, not knowing where to go, marched boldly up to the house of Her Majesty's Consul, where we were most hospitably received.

Lamu is a very curious place, but the things which stand out most clearly in my memory in connection with it are its exceeding dirtiness and its smells. These last are simply awful. Just below the Consulate is the beach, or rather a mud bank that is called a beach. It is left quite bare at low tide, and serves as a repository for all the filth, offal, and refuse of the town. Here it is, too, that the women come to bury coconuts in the mud, leaving them there till the outer husk is quite rotten, when they dig them up again and use the fibres to make mats with, and for various other purposes. As this process has been going on for generations, the condition of the shore can be better imagined than described. I have smelt many evil odours in the course of my life, but the concentrated essence of stench which arose from that beach at Lamu as we sat in the moonlit night — not under, but *on* our friend the Consul's hospitable roof — and sniffed it, makes the remembrance of them very poor and faint. No wonder people get fever at Lamu. And yet the place was not without a certain quaintness and charm of its own, though possibly — indeed probably — it was one which would quickly pall.

'Well, where are you gentlemen steering for?' asked our friend the hospitable Consul, as we smoked our pipes after dinner.

'We propose to go to Mt Kenia and then on to Mt Lekakisera,' answered Sir Henry. 'Quatermain has got hold of some yarn about there being a white race up in the unknown territories beyond.'

The Consul looked interested, and answered that he had heard something of that, too.

'What have you heard?' I asked.

'Oh, not much. All I know about it is that a year or so ago I got a letter from Mackenzie, the Scotch missionary, whose station, "The Highlands", is placed at the highest navigable point of the Tana River, in which he said something about it.'

'Have you the letter?' I asked.

'No, I destroyed it; but I remember that he said that a man had arrived at his station who declared that two months' journey beyond Mt Lekakisera, which no white man has yet visited — at least, so far as I know — he found a lake called Laga, and that then he went off to the north-east, a month's journey, over desert and thorn veldt and great mountains, till he came to a country where the people are white and live in stone houses. Here he was hospitably entertained for a while, till at last the priests of the country set it about that he was a devil, and the people drove him away, and he journeyed for eight months and reached Mackenzie's place, as I heard, dying. That's all I know; and if you ask me, I believe that it is a lie; but if you want to find out more about it, you had better go up the Tana to Mackenzie's place and ask him for information.'

Sir Henry and I looked at each other. Here was something tangible.

'I think that we will go to Mr Mackenzie's,' I said.

'Well,' answered the Consul, 'that is your best way, but I warn you that you are likely to have a rough journey, for I hear that the Masai are about, and, as you know, they are not pleasant customers. Your best plan will be to choose a few picked men for personal servants and hunters, and to hire bearers from village to village. It will give you an infinity of trouble, but perhaps on the whole it will prove a cheaper and more advantageous course than engaging a caravan, and you will be less liable to desertion.'

Fortunately there were at Lamu at this time a party of Wakwafi Askari (soldiers). The Wakwafi, who are a cross between the Masai and the Wataveta, are a fine manly race, possessing many of the good qualities of the Zulu, and a great capacity for civilization. They are also great hunters. As it happened, these particular men had recently been on a long trip with an Englishman named Jutson, who had started from Mombasa, a port about 150 miles below Lamu, and journeyed right round Kilimanjaro, one of the highest known mountains in Africa. Poor fellow, he had died of fever when on his return journey, and within a day's march of Mombasa. It does seem hard that he should have gone off thus when within a few hours of safety, and after having survived so many perils, but so it was. His hunters buried him, and then came on to Lamu in a dhow. Our friend the Consul suggested to us that we had better try and hire these men, and accordingly on the following morning we started to interview the party, accompanied by an interpreter.

In due course we found them in a mud hut on the outskirts of the town. Three of the men were sitting outside the hut, and fine frank-looking fellows they were, having a more or less civilized appearance. To them we cautiously opened the object of our visit, at first with very scant success. They declared that they could not entertain any such idea, that they were worn and weary with long travelling, and that their hearts were sore at the loss of their master. They meant to go back to their homes and rest awhile. This did not sound very promising, so by way of effecting a diversion I asked where the remainder of them were. I was told there were six, and I saw but three. One of the men said they slept in the hut, and were yet resting after their labours — 'sleep weighed down their eyelids, and sorrow made their hearts as lead: it was best to sleep, for with sleep came forgetfulness. But the men should be awakened.'

Presently they came out of the hut, yawning — the first two men being evidently of the same race and style as those already before us; but the appearance of the third and last nearly made me jump out of my skin. He was a very tall, broad man, quite six foot three, I should say, but gaunt, with lean, wiry-looking limbs. My first glance at him told me that he was no Wakwafi: he was a pure bred Zulu. He came out with his thin aristocratic-looking hand placed before his face to hide a yawn, so I could only see that he was a 'Keshla' or ringed man, and that he had a great three-cornered hole in his forehead. In another second he removed his hand, revealing a powerful-looking Zulu face, with a humorous mouth, a short woolly beard, tinged with grey, and a pair of brown eyes keen as a hawk's. I knew my man at once, although I had not seen him for twelve years. 'How do you do, Umslopogaas?' I said quietly in Zulu.

The tall man (who among his own people was commonly known as the 'Woodpecker', and also as the 'Slaughterer') started, and almost let the long-handled battleaxe he held in his hand fall in his astonishment. Next second he had recognized me, and was saluting me in an outburst of sonorous language which made his companions the Wakwafi stare.

'Koos' (chief), he began, 'Koos-y-Pagete! Koos-y-umcool! (Chief from of old — mighty chief) Koos! Baba! (father) Macumazahn, old hunter, slayer of elephants, eater up of lions, clever one! watchful one! brave one! quick one! whose shot never misses, who strikes straight home, who grasps a hand and holds it to the death (i.e. is a true friend) Koos! Baba! Wise is the voice of our people that says, "Mountain never meets with mountain, but at daybreak or at even man shall meet again with man." Behold! a messenger came up from Natal, "Macumazahn is dead!" cried he. "The land knows Macumazahn no more." That is years ago. And now, behold, now in this strange place of stinks I find Macumazahn, my friend. There is no room for doubt. The brush of the old jackal has gone a little grey; but is not his eye as keen, and are not his teeth as sharp? Ha! ha! Macumazahn, mindest thou how thou didst plant the ball in the eye of the charging buffalo — mindest thou —'

I had let him run on thus because I saw that his enthusiasm was producing a marked effect upon the minds of the five Wakwafi, who appeared to understand something of his talk; but now I thought it time to put a stop to it, for there is nothing that I hate so much as this Zulu system of extravagant praising — 'bongering' as they call it. 'Silence!' I said. 'Has all thy noisy talk been stopped up since last I saw thee that it breaks out thus, and sweeps us away? What doest thou here with these men — thou whom I left a chief in Zululand? How is it that thou art far from thine own place, and gathered together with strangers?'

Umslopogaas leant himself upon the head of his long battleaxe (which was nothing else but a pole-axe, with a beautiful handle of rhinoceros horn), and his grim face grew sad.

'My Father,' he answered, 'I have a word to tell thee, but I cannot speak it before these low people (umfagozana),' and he glanced at the Wakwafi Askari; 'it is for thine own ear. My Father, this will I say,' and here his face grew stern again, 'a woman betrayed me to the death, and covered my name with shame — ay, my own wife, a round-faced girl, betrayed me; but I escaped from death; ay, I broke from the very hands of those who came to slay me. I struck but three blows with this mine axe Inkosikaas — surely my Father will remember it — one to the right, one to the left, and one in front, and yet I left three men dead. And then I fled, and, as my Father knows, even now that I am old my feet are as the feet of the Sassaby, and there breathes not the man who, by running, can touch me again when once I have bounded from his side. On I sped, and after me came the messengers of death, and their voice was as the voice of dogs that hunt. From my own kraal I flew, and, as I passed, she who had betrayed me was drawing water from the spring. I fleeted by her like the shadow of Death, and as I went I smote with mine axe, and lo! her head fell: it fell into the water pan. Then I fled north. Day after day I journeyed on; for three moons I journeyed, resting not, stopping not, but running on towards forgetfulness, till I met the party of the white hunter who is now dead, and am come hither with his servants. And nought have I brought with me. I who was high-born, ay, of the blood of Chaka, the great king — a chief, and a captain of the regiment of the Nkomabakosi — am a wanderer in strange places, a man without a kraal. Nought have I brought save this mine axe; of all my belongings this remains alone. They have divided my cattle; they have taken my wives; and my children know my face no more. Yet with this axe' — and he swung the formidable weapon round his head, making the air hiss as he clove it — 'will I cut another path to fortune. I have spoken.'

I shook my head at him. 'Umslopogaas,' I said, 'I know thee from of old. Ever ambitious, ever plotting to be great, I fear me that thou hast overreached thyself at last. Years ago, when thou wouldst have plotted against Cetywayo, son of Panda, I warned thee, and thou didst listen. But now, when I was not by thee to stay thy hand, thou hast dug a pit for thine own feet to fall in. Is it not so? But what is done is done. Who can make the dead tree green, or gaze again upon last year's light? Who can recall the spoken word, or bring back the spirit of the fallen? That which Time swallows comes not up again. Let it be forgotten!

'And now, behold, Umslopogaas, I know thee for a great warrior and a brave man, faithful to the death. Even in Zululand, where all the men are brave, they called thee the "Slaughterer", and at night told stories round the fire of thy strength and deeds. Hear me now. Thou seest this great man, my friend' — and I pointed to Sir Henry; 'he also is a warrior as great as thou, and, strong as thou art, he could throw thee over his shoulder. Incubu is his name. And thou seest this one also; him with the round stomach, the shining eye, and the pleasant face. Bougwan (glass eye) is his name, and a good man is he and a true, being of a curious tribe who pass their life upon the water, and live in floating kraals.

'Now, we three whom thou seest would travel inland, past Dongo Egere, the great white mountain (Mt Kenia), and far into the unknown beyond. We know not what we shall find there; we go to hunt and seek adventures, and new places, being tired of sitting still, with the same old things around us. Wilt thou come with us? To thee shall be given command of all our servants; but what shall befall thee, that I know not. Once before we three journeyed thus, in search of adventure, and we took with us a man such as thou — one Umbopa; and, behold, we left him the king of a great country, with twenty Impis (regiments), each of 3,000 plumed warriors, waiting on his word. How it shall go with thee, I know not; mayhap death awaits thee and us. Wilt thou throw thyself to Fortune and come, or fearest thou, Umslopogaas?'

The great man smiled. 'Thou art not altogether right, Macumazahn,' he said; 'I have plotted in my time, but it was not ambition that led me to my fall; but, shame on me that I should have to say it, a fair woman's face. Let it pass.

So we are going to see something like the old times again, Macumazahn, when we fought and hunted in Zululand? Ay, I will come. Come life, come death, what care I, so that the blows fall fast and the blood runs red? I grow old, I grow old, and I have not fought enough! And yet am I a warrior among warriors; see my scars' — and he pointed to countless cicatrices, stabs and cuts, that marked the skin of his chest and legs and arms. 'See the hole in my head; the brains gushed out therefrom, yet did I slay him who smote, and live. Knowest thou how many men I have slain, in fair hand-to-hand combat, Macumazahn? See, here is the tale of them' — and he pointed to long rows of notches cut in the rhinoceros-horn handle of his axe. 'Number them, Macumazahn — one hundred and three — and I have never counted but those whom I have ripped open , nor have I reckoned those whom another man had struck.'

'Be silent,' I said, for I saw that he was getting the blood-fever on him; 'be silent; well art thou called the "Slaughterer". We would not hear of thy deeds of blood. Remember, if thou comest with us, we fight not save in self-defence. Listen, we need servants. These men,' and I pointed to the Wakwafi, who had retired a little way during our 'indaba' (talk), 'say they will not come.'

'Will not come!' shouted Umslopogaas; 'where is the dog who says he will not come when my Father orders? Here, thou' — and with a single bound he sprang upon the Wakwafi with whom I had first spoken, and, seizing him by the arm, dragged him towards us. 'Thou dog!' he said, giving the terrified man a shake, 'didst thou say that thou wouldst not go with my Father? Say it once more and I will choke thee' — and his long fingers closed round his throat as he said it — 'thee, and those with thee. Hast thou forgotten how I served thy brother?'

'Nay, we will come with the white man,' gasped the man.

'White man!' went on Umslopogaas, in simulated fury, which a very little provocation would have made real enough; 'of whom speakest thou, insolent dog?'

'Nay, we will go with the great chief.'

'So!' said Umslopogaas, in a quiet voice, as he suddenly released his hold, so that the man fell backward. 'I thought you would.'

'That man Umslopogaas seems to have a curious moral ascendency over his companions,' Good afterwards remarked thoughtfully.

The Black Hand

In due course we left Lamu, and ten days afterwards we found ourselves at a spot called Charra, on the Tana River, having gone through many adventures which need not be recorded here. Amongst other things we visited a ruined city, of which there are many on this coast, and which must once, to judge from their extent and the numerous remains of mosques and stone houses, have been very populous places. These ruined cities are immeasurably ancient, having, I believe, been places of wealth and importance as far back as the Old Testament times, when they were centres of trade with India and elsewhere. But their glory has departed now — the slave trade has finished them — and where wealthy merchants from all parts of the then civilized world stood and bargained in the crowded market-places, the lion holds his court at night, and instead of the chattering of slaves and the eager voices of the bidders, his awful note goes echoing down the ruined corridors. At this particular place we discovered on a mound, covered up with rank growth and rubbish, two of the most beautiful stone doorways that it is possible to conceive. The carving on them was simply exquisite, and I only regret that we had no means of getting them away. No doubt they had once been the entrances to a palace, of which, however, no traces were now to be seen, though probably its ruins lay under the rising mound.

Gone! quite gone! the way that everything must go. Like the nobles and the ladies who lived within their gates, these cities have had their day, and now they are as Babylon and Nineveh, and as London and Paris will one day be. Nothing may endure. That is the inexorable law. Men and women, empires and cities, thrones, principalities, and powers, mountains, rivers, and unfathomed seas, worlds, spaces, and universes, all have their day, and all must go. In this ruined and forgotten place the moralist may behold a symbol of the universal destiny. For this system of ours allows no room for standing still — nothing can loiter on the road and check the progress of things upwards towards Life, or the rush of things downwards towards Death. The stern policeman Fate moves us and them on, on, uphill and downhill and across the level; there is no resting-place for the weary feet, till at last the abyss swallows us, and from the shores of the Transitory we are hurled into the sea of the Eternal.

At Charra we had a violent quarrel with the headman of the bearers we had hired to go as far as this, and who now wished to extort large extra payment from us. In the result he threatened to set the Masai — about whom more anon — on to us. That night he, with all our hired bearers, ran away, stealing most of the goods which had been entrusted to them to carry. Luckily, however, they had not happened to steal our rifles, ammunition, and personal effects; not because of any delicacy of feeling on their part, but owing to the fact that they chanced to be in the charge of the five Wakwafis. After that, it was clear to us that we had had enough of caravans and of bearers. Indeed, we had not much left for a caravan to carry. And yet, how were we to get on?

It was Good who solved the question. 'Here is water,' he said, pointing to the Tana River; 'and yesterday I saw a party of natives hunting hippopotami in canoes. I understand that Mr Mackenzie's mission station is on the Tana River. Why not get into canoes and paddle up to it?'

This brilliant suggestion was, needless to say, received with acclamation; and I instantly set to work to buy suitable canoes from the surrounding natives. I succeeded after a delay of three days in obtaining two large ones, each hollowed out of a single log of some light wood, and capable of holding six people and baggage. For these two canoes we had to pay nearly all our remaining cloth, and also many other articles.

On the day following our purchase of the two canoes we effected a start. In the first canoe were Good, Sir Henry, and three of our Wakwafi followers; in the second myself, Umslopogaas, and the other two Wakwafis. As our course lay upstream, we had to keep four paddles at work in each canoe, which meant that the whole lot of us, except Good, had to row away like galley-slaves; and very exhausting work it was. I say, except Good, for, of course, the moment that Good got into a boat his foot was on his native heath, and he took command of the party. And certainly he worked us. On shore Good is a gentle, mild-mannered man, and given to jocosity; but, as we found to our cost, Good in a boat was a perfect demon. To begin with, he knew all about it, and we didn't. On all nautical subjects, from the torpedo fittings of a man-of-war down to the best way of handling the paddle of an African canoe, he was a perfect mine of information, which, to say the least of it, we were not. Also his ideas of discipline were of the sternest, and, in short, he came the royal naval officer over us pretty considerably, and paid us out amply for all the chaff we were wont to treat him to on land; but, on the other hand, I am bound to say that he managed the boats admirably.

After the first day Good succeeded, with the help of some cloth and a couple of poles, in rigging up a sail in each canoe, which lightened our labours not a little. But the current ran very strong against us, and at the best we were not able to make more than twenty miles a day. Our plan was to start at dawn, and paddle along till about half-past ten, by which time the sun got too hot to allow of further exertion. Then we moored our canoes to the bank, and ate our frugal meal; after which we ate or otherwise amused ourselves till about three o'clock, when we again started, and rowed till within an hour of sundown, when we called a halt for the night. On landing in the evening, Good would at once set to work, with the help of the Askari, to build a little 'scherm', or small enclosure, fenced with thorn bushes, and to light a fire. I, with Sir Henry and Umslopogaas, would go out to shoot something for the pot. Generally this was an easy task, for all sorts of game abounded on the banks of the Tana. One night Sir Henry shot a young cow-giraffe, of which the marrow-bones were excellent; on another I got a couple of waterbuck right and left; and once, to his own intense satisfaction, Umslopogaas (who, like most Zulus, was a vile shot with a rifle) managed to kill a fine fat eland with a Martini I had lent him.

Sometimes we varied our food by shooting some guinea-fowl, or bush-bustard (paau) — both of which were numerous — with a shot-gun, or by catching a supply of beautiful yellow fish, with which the waters of the Tana swarmed, and which form, I believe, one of the chief food-supplies of the crocodiles.

Three days after our start an ominous incident occurred. We were just drawing in to the bank to make our camp as usual for the night, when we caught sight of a figure standing on a little knoll not forty yards away, and intensely watching our approach. One glance was sufficient — although I was personally unacquainted with the tribe — to tell me that he was a Masai Elmoran, or young warrior. Indeed, had I had any doubts, they would have quickly been dispelled by the terrified ejaculation of '*Masai!*' that burst simultaneously from the lips of our Wakwafi followers, who are, as I think I have said, themselves bastard Masai.

And what a figure he presented as he stood there in his savage war-gear! Accustomed as I have been to savages all my life, I do not think that I have ever before seen anything quite so ferocious or awe-inspiring. To begin with, the man was enormously tall, quite as tall as Umslopogaas, I should say, and beautifully, though somewhat slightly, shaped; but with the face of a devil. In his right hand he held a spear about five and a half feet long, the blade being two and a half feet in length, by nearly three inches in width, and having an iron spike at the end of the handle that measured more than a foot. On his left arm was a large and well-made elliptical shield of buffalo hide, on which were painted strange heraldic-looking devices. On his shoulders was a huge cape of hawk's feathers, and round his neck was a 'naibere', or strip of cotton, about seventeen feet long, by one and a half broad, with a stripe of colour running down the middle of it. The tanned goatskin robe, which formed his ordinary attire in times of peace, was tied lightly round his waist, so as to serve the purposes of a belt, and through it were stuck, on the right and left sides respectively, his short pear-shaped sime, or sword, which is made of a single piece of steel, and carried in a wooden sheath, and an enormous knobkerrie. But perhaps the most remarkable feature of his attire consisted of a headdress of ostrich-feathers, which was fixed on the chin, and passed in front of the ears to the forehead, and, being shaped like an ellipse, completely framed the face, so that the diabolical countenance appeared to project from a sort of feather fire-screen. Round the ankles he wore black fringes of hair, and, projecting from the upper portion of the calves, to which they were attached, were long spurs like spikes, from which flowed down tufts of the beautiful black and waving hair of the Colobus monkey. Such was the elaborate array of the Masai Elmoran who stood watching the approach of our two canoes, but it is one which, to be appreciated, must be seen; only those who see it do not often live to describe it. Of course I could not make out all these details of his full dress on the occasion of this my first introduction, being, indeed, amply taken up with the consideration of the general effect, but I had plenty of subsequent opportunities of becoming acquainted with the items that went to make it up.

Whilst we were hesitating what to do, the Masai warrior drew himself up in a dignified fashion, shook his huge spear at us, and, turning, vanished on the further side of the slope.

'Hulloa!' holloaed Sir Henry from the other boat; 'our friend the caravan leader has been as good as his word, and set the Masai after us. Do you think it will be safe to go ashore?'

I did not think it would be at all safe; but, on the other hand, we had no means of cooking in the canoes, and nothing that we could eat raw, so it was difficult to know what to do. At last Umslopogaas simplified matters by volunteering to go and reconnoitre, which he did, creeping off into the bush like a snake, while we hung off in the stream waiting for him. In half an hour he returned, and told us that there was not a Masai to be seen anywhere about, but that he had discovered a spot where they had recently been encamped, and that from various indications he judged that they must have moved on an hour or so before; the man we saw having, no doubt, been left to report upon our movements.

Thereupon we landed; and, having posted a sentry, proceeded to cook and eat our evening meal. This done, we took the situation into our serious consideration. Of course, it was possible that the apparition of the Masai warrior had nothing to do with us, that he was merely one of a band bent upon some marauding and murdering expedition against another tribe. But when we recalled the threat of the caravan leader, and reflected on the ominous way in which the warrior had shaken his spear at us, this did not appear very probable. On the contrary, what did seem probable was that the party was after us and awaiting a favourable opportunity to attack us. This being so, there were two things that we could do — one of which was to go on, and the other to go back. The latter idea was, however, rejected at once, it being obvious that we should encounter as many dangers in retreat as in advance; and, besides, we had made up our minds to journey onwards at any price. Under these circumstances, however, we did not consider it safe to sleep ashore, so we got into our canoes, and, paddling out into the middle of the stream, which was not very wide here, managed to anchor them by means of big stones fastened to ropes made of coconut-fibre, of which there were several fathoms in each canoe.

Here the mosquitoes nearly ate us up alive, and this, combined with anxiety as to our position, effectually prevented me from sleeping as the others were doing, notwithstanding the attacks of the aforesaid Tana mosquitoes. And so I lay awake, smoking and reflecting on many things, but, being of a practical turn of mind, chiefly on how we were to give those Masai villains the slip. It was a beautiful moonlight night, and, notwithstanding the mosquitoes, and the great risk we were running from fever from sleeping in such a spot, and forgetting that I had the cramp very badly in my right leg from squatting in a constrained position in the canoe, and that the Wakwafi who was sleeping beside me smelt horribly, I really began to enjoy myself. The moonbeams played upon the surface of the running water that speeded unceasingly past us towards the sea, like men's lives towards the grave, till it glittered like a wide sheet of silver, that is in the open where the trees threw no shadows. Near the banks, however, it was very dark, and the night wind sighed sadly in the reeds. To our left, on the further side of the river, was a little sandy bay which was clear of trees, and here I could make out the forms of numerous antelopes advancing to the water, till suddenly there came an ominous roar, whereupon they all made off hurriedly. Then after a pause I caught sight of the massive form of His Majesty the Lion, coming down to drink his fill after meat. Presently he moved on, then came a crashing of the reeds about fifty yards above us, and a few minutes later a huge black mass rose out of the water, about twenty yards from me, and snorted. It was the head of a hippopotamus. Down it went without a sound, only to rise again within five yards of where I sat. This was decidedly too near to be comfortable, more especially as the hippopotamus was evidently animated by intense curiosity to know what on earth our canoes were. He opened his great mouth, to yawn, I suppose, and gave me an excellent view of his ivories; and I could not help reflecting how easily he could crunch up our frail canoe with a single bite. Indeed, I had half a mind to give him a ball from my eight-bore, but on reflection determined to let him alone unless he actually charged the boat. Presently he sank again as noiselessly as before, and I saw no more of him. Just then, on looking towards the bank on our right, I fancied that I caught sight of a dark figure flitting between the tree trunks. I have very keen sight, and I was almost sure that I saw something, but whether it was bird, beast, or man I could not say. At the moment, however, a dark cloud passed over the moon, and I saw no more of it. Just then, too, although all the other sounds of the forest had ceased, a species of horned owl with which I was well acquainted began to hoot with great persistency. After that, save for the rustling of trees and reeds when the wind caught them, there was complete silence.

But somehow, in the most unaccountable way, I had suddenly become nervous. There was no particular reason why I should be, beyond the ordinary reasons which surround the Central African traveller, and yet I undoubtedly was. If there is one thing more than another of which I have the most complete and entire scorn and disbelief, it is of presentiments, and yet here I was all of a sudden filled with and possessed by a most undoubted presentiment of approaching evil. I would not give way to it, however, although I felt the cold perspiration stand out upon my forehead. I would not arouse the others. Worse and worse I grew, my pulse fluttered like a dying man's, my nerves thrilled with the horrible sense of impotent terror which anybody who is subject to nightmare will be familiar with, but still my will triumphed over my fears, and I lay quiet (for I was half sitting, half lying, in the bow of the canoe), only turning my face so as to command a view of Umslopogaas and the two Wakwafi who were sleeping alongside of and beyond me.

In the distance I heard a hippopotamus splash faintly, then the owl hooted again in a kind of unnatural screaming note, and the wind began to moan plaintively through the trees, making a heart-chilling music. Above was the black bosom of the cloud, and beneath me swept the black flood of the water, and I felt as though I and Death were utterly alone between them. It was very desolate.

Suddenly my blood seemed to freeze in my veins, and my heart to stand still. Was it fancy, or were we moving? I turned my eyes to look for the other canoe which should be alongside of us. I could not see it, but instead I saw a lean and clutching black hand lifting itself above the gunwale of the little boat. Surely it was a nightmare! At the same instant a dim but devilish-looking face appeared to rise out of the water, and then came a lurch of the canoe, the quick flash of a knife, and an awful yell from the Wakwafi who was sleeping by my side (the same poor fellow whose odour had been annoying me), and something warm spurted into my face. In an instant the spell was broken; I knew that it was no nightmare, but that we were attacked by swimming Masai. Snatching at the first weapon that came to hand, which happened to be Umslopogaas' battleaxe, I struck with all my force in the direction in which I had seen the flash of the knife. The blow fell upon a man's arm, and, catching it against the thick wooden gunwale of the canoe, completely severed it from the body just above the wrist. As for its owner, he uttered no sound or cry. Like a ghost he came, and like a ghost he went, leaving behind him a bloody hand still gripping a great knife, or rather a short sword, that was buried in the heart of our poor servant.

Instantly there arose a hubbub and confusion, and I fancied, rightly or wrongly, that I made out several dark heads gliding away towards the right-hand bank, whither we were rapidly drifting, for the rope by which we were moored had been severed with a knife. As soon as I had realized this fact, I also realized that the scheme had been to cut the boat loose so that it should drift on to the right bank (as it would have done with the natural swing of the current), where no doubt a party of Masai were waiting to dig their shovel-headed spears into us. Seizing one paddle myself, I told Umslopogaas to take another (for the remaining Askari was too frightened and bewildered to be of any use), and together we rowed vigorously out towards the middle of the stream; and not an instant too soon, for in another minute we should have been aground, and then there would have been an end of us.

As soon as we were well out, we set to work to paddle the canoe upstream again to where the other was moored; and very hard and dangerous work it was in the dark, and with nothing but the notes of Good's stentorian shouts, which he kept firing off at intervals like a fog-horn, to guide us. But at last we fetched up, and were thankful to find that they had not been molested at all. No doubt the owner of the same hand that severed our rope should have severed theirs also, but was led away from his purpose by an irresistible inclination to murder when he got the chance, which, while it cost us a man and him his hand, undoubtedly saved all the rest of us from massacre. Had it not been for that ghastly apparition over the side of the boat — an apparition that I shall never forget till my dying hour — the canoe would undoubtedly have drifted ashore before I realized what had happened, and this history would never have been written by me.

The Mission Station

We made the remains of our rope fast to the other canoe, and sat waiting for the dawn and congratulating ourselves upon our merciful escape, which really seemed to result more from the special favour of Providence than from our own care or prowess. At last it came, and I have not often been more grateful to see the light, though so far as my canoe was concerned it revealed a ghastly sight. There in the bottom of the little boat lay the unfortunate Askari, the sime, or sword, in his bosom, and the severed hand gripping the handle. I could not bear the sight, so hauling up the stone which had served as an anchor to the other canoe, we made it fast to the murdered man and dropped him overboard, and down he went to the bottom, leaving nothing but a train of bubbles behind him. Alas! when our time comes, most of us like him leave nothing but bubbles behind, to show that we have been, and the bubbles soon burst. The hand of his murderer we threw into the stream, where it slowly sank. The sword, of which the handle was ivory, inlaid with gold (evidently Arab work), I kept and used as a hunting-knife, and very useful it proved.

Then, a man having been transferred to my canoe, we once more started on in very low spirits and not feeling at all comfortable as to the future, but fondly hoping to arrive at the 'Highlands' station by night. To make matters worse, within an hour of sunrise it came on to rain in torrents, wetting us to the skin, and even necessitating the occasional baling of the canoes, and as the rain beat down the wind we could not use the sails, and had to get along as best as we could with our paddles.

At eleven o'clock we halted on an open piece of ground on the left bank of the river, and, the rain abating a little, managed to make a fire and catch and broil some fish. We did not dare to wander about to search for game. At two o'clock we got off again, taking a supply of broiled fish with us, and shortly afterwards the rain came on harder than ever. Also the river began to get exceedingly difficult to navigate on account of the numerous rocks, reaches of shallow water, and the increased force of the current; so that it soon became clear to us that we should not reach the Rev. Mackenzie's hospitable roof that night — a prospect that did not tend to enliven us. Toil as we would, we could not make more than an average of a mile an hour, and at five o'clock in the afternoon (by which time we were all utterly worn out) we reckoned that we were still quite ten miles below the station. This being so, we set to work to make the best arrangements we could for the night. After our recent experience, we simply did not dare to land, more especially as the banks of the Tana were clothed with dense bush that would have given cover to five thousand Masai, and at first I thought that we were going to have another night of it in the canoes. Fortunately, however, we espied a little rocky islet, not more than fifteen miles or so square, situated nearly in the middle of the river.

For this we paddled, and, making fast the canoes, landed and made ourselves as comfortable as circumstances would permit, which was very uncomfortable indeed. As for the weather, it continued to be simply vile, the rain coming down in sheets till we were chilled to the marrow, and utterly preventing us from lighting a fire. There was, however, one consoling circumstance about this rain; our Askari declared that nothing would induce the Masai to make an attack in it, as they intensely disliked moving about in the wet, perhaps, as Good suggested, because they hate the idea of washing. We ate some insipid and sodden cold fish — that is, with the exception of Umslopogaas, who, like most Zulus, cannot bear fish — and took a pull of brandy, of which we fortunately had a few bottles left, and then began what, with one exception — when we same three white men nearly perished of cold on the snow of Sheba's Breast in the course of our journey to Kukuanaland — was, I think, the most trying night I ever experienced. It seemed absolutely endless, and once or twice I feared that two of the Askari would have died of the wet, cold, and exposure. Indeed, had it not been for timely doses of brandy I am sure that they would have died, for no African people can stand much exposure, which first paralyses and then kills them. I could see that even that iron old warrior Umslopogaas felt it keenly; though, in strange contrast to the Wakwafis, who groaned and bemoaned their fate unceasingly, he never uttered a single complaint. To make matters worse, about one in the morning we again heard the owl's ominous hooting, and had at once to prepare ourselves for another attack; though, if it had been attempted, I do not think that we could have offered a very effective resistance. But either the owl was a real one this time, or else the Masai were themselves too miserable to think of offensive operations, which, indeed, they rarely, if ever, undertake in bush veldt. At any rate, we saw nothing of them.

At last the dawn came gliding across the water, wrapped in wreaths of ghostly mist, and, with the daylight, the rain ceased; and then, out came the glorious sun, sucking up the mists and warming the chill air. Benumbed, and utterly exhausted, we dragged ourselves to our feet, and went and stood in the bright rays, and were thankful for them. I can quite understand how it is that primitive people become sun worshippers, especially if their conditions of life render them liable to exposure.

In half an hour more we were once again making fair progress with the help of a good wind. Our spirits had returned with the sunshine, and we were ready to laugh at difficulties and dangers that had been almost crushing on the previous day.

And so we went on cheerily till about eleven o'clock. Just as we were thinking of halting as usual, to rest and try to shoot something to eat, a sudden bend in the river brought us in sight of a substantial-looking European house with a veranda round it, splendidly situated upon a hill, and surrounded by a high stone wall with a ditch on the outer side. Right against and overshadowing the house was an enormous pine, the tope of which we had seen through a glass for the last two days, but of course without knowing that it marked the site of the mission station. I was the first to see the house, and could not restrain myself from giving a hearty cheer, in which the others, including the natives, joined lustily. There was no thought of halting now. On we laboured, for, unfortunately, though the house seemed quite near, it was still a long way off by river, until at last, by one o'clock, we found ourselves at the bottom of the slope on which the building stood. Running the canoes to the bank, we disembarked, and were just hauling them up on to the shore, when we perceived three figures, dressed in ordinary English-looking clothes, hurrying down through a grove of trees to meet us.

'A gentleman, a lady, and a little girl,' ejaculated Good, after surveying the trio through his eyeglass, 'walking in a civilized fashion, through a civilized garden, to meet us in this place. Hang me, if this isn't the most curious thing we have seen yet!'

Good was right: it certainly did seem odd and out of place — more like a scene out of a dream or an Italian opera than a real tangible fact; and the sense of unreality was not lessened when we heard ourselves addressed in good broad Scotch, which, however, I cannot reproduce.

'How do you do, sirs,' said Mr Mackenzie, a grey-haired, angular man, with a kindly face and red cheeks; 'I hope I see you very well. My natives told me an hour ago they spied two canoes with white men in them coming up the river; so we have just come down to meet you.'

'And it is very glad that we are to see a white face again, let me tell you,' put in the lady — a charming and refined-looking person.

We took off our hats in acknowledgment, and proceeded to introduce ourselves.

'And now,' said Mr Mackenzie, 'you must all be hungry and weary; so come on, gentlemen, come on, and right glad we are to see you. The last white who visited us was Alphonse — you will see Alphonse presently — and that was a year ago.'

Meanwhile we had been walking up the slope of the hill, the lower portion of which was fenced off, sometimes with quince fences and sometimes with rough stone walls, into Kaffir gardens, just now full of crops of mealies, pumpkins, potatoes, etc. In the corners of these gardens were groups of neat mushroom-shaped huts, occupied by Mr Mackenzie's mission natives, whose women and children came pouring out to meet us as we walked. Through the centre of the gardens ran the roadway up which we were walking. It was bordered on each side by a line of orange trees, which, although they had only been planted ten years, had in the lovely climate of the uplands below Mt Kenia, the base of which is about 5,000 feet above the coastline level, already grown to imposing proportions, and were positively laden with golden fruit. After a stiffish climb of a quarter of a mile or so — for the hillside was steep — we came to a splendid quince fence, also covered with fruit, which enclosed, Mr Mackenzie told us, a space of about four acres of ground that contained his private garden, house, church, and outbuildings, and, indeed, the whole hilltop. And what a garden it was! I have always loved a good garden, and I could have thrown up my hands for joy when I saw Mr Mackenzie's. First there were rows upon rows of standard European fruit-trees, all grafted; for on top of this hill the climate was so temperate that nearly all the English vegetables, trees, and flowers flourished luxuriantly, even including several varieties of the apple, which, generally, runs to wood in a warm climate and obstinately refuses to fruit. Then there were strawberries and tomatoes (such tomatoes!), and melons and cucumbers, and, indeed, every sort of vegetable and fruit.

'Well, you have something like a garden!' I said, overpowered with admiration not untouched by envy.

'Yes,' answered the missionary, 'it is a very good garden, and has well repaid my labour; but it is the climate that I have to thank. If you stick a peach-stone into the ground it will bear fruit the fourth year, and a rose-cutting will bloom in a year. It is a lovely clime.'

Just then we came to a ditch about ten feet wide, and full of water, on the other side of which was a loopholed stone wall eight feet high, and with sharp flints plentifully set in mortar on the coping.

'There,' said Mr Mackenzie, pointing to the ditch and wall, 'this is my magnum opus; at least, this and the church, which is the other side of the house. It took me and twenty natives two years to dig the ditch and build the wall, but I never felt safe till it was done; and now I can defy all the savages in Africa, for the spring that fills the ditch is inside the wall, and bubbles out at the top of the hill winter and summer alike, and I always keep a store of four months' provision in the house.'

Crossing over a plank and through a very narrow opening in the wall, we entered into what Mrs Mackenzie called *her* domain — namely, the flower garden, the beauty of which is really beyond my power to describe. I do not think I ever saw such roses, gardenias, or camellias (all reared from seeds or cuttings sent from England); and there was also a patch given up to a collection of bulbous roots mostly collected by Miss Flossie, Mr Mackenzie's little daughter, from the surrounding country, some of which were surpassingly beautiful. In the middle of this garden, and exactly opposite the veranda, a beautiful fountain of clear water bubbled up from the ground, and fell into a stone-work basin which had been carefully built to receive it, whence the overflow found its way by means of a drain to the moat round the outer wall, this moat in its turn serving as a reservoir, whence an unfailing supply of water was available to irrigate all the gardens below. The house itself, a massively built single-storied building, was roofed with slabs of stone, and had a handsome veranda in front. It was built on three sides of a square, the fourth side being taken up by the kitchens, which stood separate from the house — a very good plan in a hot country. In the centre of this square thus formed was, perhaps, the most remarkable object that we had yet seen in this charming place, and that was a single tree of the conifer tribe, varieties of which grow freely on the highlands of this part of Africa. This splendid tree, which Mr Mackenzie informed us was a landmark for fifty miles round, and which we had ourselves seen for the last forty miles of our journey, must have been nearly three hundred feet in height, the trunk measuring about sixteen feet in diameter at a yard from the ground. For some seventy feet it rose a beautiful tapering brown pillar without a single branch, but at that height splendid dark green boughs, which, looked at from below, had the appearance of gigantic fern-leaves, sprang out horizontally from the trunk, projecting right over the house and flower-garden, to both of which they furnished a grateful proportion of shade, without — being so high up — offering any impediment to the passage of light and air.

'What a beautiful tree!' exclaimed Sir Henry.

'Yes, you are right; it is a beautiful tree. There is not another like it in all the country round, that I know of,' answered Mr Mackenzie. 'I call it my watch tower. As you see, I have a rope ladder fixed to the lowest bough; and if I want to see anything that is going on within fifteen miles or so, all I have to do is to run up it with a spyglass. But you must be hungry, and I am sure the dinner is cooked. Come in, my friends; it is but a rough place, but well enough for these savage parts; and I can tell you what, we have got — a French cook.' And he led the way on to the veranda.

As I was following him, and wondering what on earth he could mean by this, there suddenly appeared, through the door that opened on to the veranda from the house, a dapper little man, dressed in a neat blue cotton suit, with shoes made of tanned hide, and remarkable for a bustling air and most enormous black mustachios, shaped into an upward curve, and coming to a point for all the world like a pair of buffalo-horns.

'Madame bids me for to say that dinnar is sarved. Messieurs, my compliments;' then suddenly perceiving Umslopogaas, who was loitering along after us and playing with his battleaxe, he threw up his hands in astonishment. 'Ah, mais quel homme!' he ejaculated in French, 'quel sauvage affreux! Take but note of his huge choppare and the great pit in his head.'

'Ay,' said Mr Mackenzie; 'what are you talking about, Alphonse?'

'Talking about!' replied the little Frenchman, his eyes still fixed upon Umslopogaas, whose general appearance seemed to fascinate him; 'why I talk of him' — and he rudely pointed — 'of ce monsieur noir.'

At this everybody began to laugh, and Umslopogaas, perceiving that he was the object of remark, frowned ferociously, for he had a most lordly dislike of anything like a personal liberty.

'Parbleu!' said Alphonse, 'he is angered — he makes the grimace. I like not his air. I vanish.' And he did with considerable rapidity.

Mr Mackenzie joined heartily in the shout of laughter which we indulged in. 'He is a queer character — Alphonse,' he said. 'By and by I will tell you his history; in the meanwhile let us try his cooking.'

'Might I ask,' said Sir Henry, after we had eaten a most excellent dinner, 'how you came to have a French cook in these wilds?'

'Oh,' answered Mrs Mackenzie, 'he arrived here of his own accord about a year ago, and asked to be taken into our service. He had got into some trouble in France, and fled to Zanzibar, where he found an application had been made by the French Government for his extradition. Whereupon he rushed off up-country, and fell in, when nearly starved, with our caravan of men, who were bringing us our annual supply of goods, and was brought on here. You should get him to tell you the story.'

When dinner was over we lit our pipes, and Sir Henry proceeded to give our host a description of our journey up here, over which he looked very grave.

'It is evident to me,' he said, 'that those rascally Masai are following you, and I am very thankful that you have reached this house in safety. I do not think that they will dare to attack you here. It is unfortunate, though, that nearly all my men have gone down to the coast with ivory and goods. There are two hundred of them in the caravan, and the consequence is that I have not more than twenty men available for defensive purposes in case they should attack us. But, still, I will just give a few orders;' and, calling a black man who was loitering about outside in the garden, he went to the window, and addressed him in a Swahili dialect. The man listened, and then saluted and departed.

'I am sure I devoutly hope that we shall bring no such calamity upon you,' said I, anxiously, when he had taken his seat again. 'Rather than bring those bloodthirsty villains about your ears, we will move on and take our chance.'

'You will do nothing of the sort. If the Masai come, they come, and there is an end on it; and I think we can give them a pretty warm greeting. I would not show any man the door for all the Masai in the world.'

'That reminds me,' I said, 'the Consul at Lamu told me that he had had a letter from you, in which you said that a man had arrived here who reported that he had come across a white people in the interior. Do you think that there was any truth in his story? I ask, because I have once or twice in my life heard rumours from natives who have come down from the far north of the existence of such a race.'

Mr Mackenzie, by way of answer, went out of the room and returned, bringing with him a most curious sword. It was long, and all the blade, which was very thick and heavy, was to within a quarter of an inch of the cutting edge worked into an ornamental pattern exactly as we work soft wood with a fret-saw, the steel, however, being invariably pierced in such a way as not to interfere with the strength of the sword. This in itself was sufficiently curious, but what was still more so was that all the edges of the hollow spaces cut through the substance of the blade were most beautifully inlaid with gold, which was in some way that I cannot understand welded on to the steel.

'There,' said Mr Mackenzie, 'did you ever see a sword like that?'

We all examined it and shook our heads.

'Well, I have got it to show you, because this is what the man who said he had seen the white people brought with him, and because it does more or less give an air of truth to what I should otherwise have set down as a lie. Look here; I will tell you all that I know about the matter, which is not much. One afternoon, just before sunset, I was sitting on the veranda, when a poor, miserable, starved-looking man came limping up and squatted down before me. I asked him where he came from and what he wanted, and thereon he plunged into a long rambling narrative about how he belonged to a tribe far in the north, and how his tribe was destroyed by another tribe, and he with a few other survivors driven still further north past a lake named Laga. Thence, it appears, he made his way to another lake that lay up in the mountains, "a lake without a bottom" he called it, and here his wife and brother died of an infectious sickness — probably smallpox — whereon the people drove him out of their villages into the wilderness, where he wandered miserably over mountains for ten days, after which he got into dense thorn forest, and was one day found there by some *white men* who were hunting, and who took him to a place where all the people were white and lived in stone houses. Here he remained a week shut up in a house, till one night a man with a white beard, whom he understood to be a "medicine-man", came and inspected him, after which he was led off and taken through the thorn forest to the confines of the wilderness, and given food and this sword (at least so he said), and turned loose.'

'Well,' said Sir Henry, who had been listening with breathless interest, 'and what did he do then?'

'Oh! he seems, according to his account, to have gone through sufferings and hardships innumerable, and to have lived for weeks on roots and berries, and such things as he could catch and kill. But somehow he did live, and at last by slow degrees made his way south and reached this place. What the details of his journey were I never learnt, for I told him to return on the morrow, bidding one of my headmen look after him for the night. The headman took him away, but the poor man had the itch so badly that the headman's wife would not have him in the hut for fear of catching it, so he was given a blanket and told to sleep outside. As it happened, we had a lion hanging about here just then, and most unhappily he winded this unfortunate wanderer, and, springing on him, bit his head almost off without the people in the hut knowing anything about it, and there was an end of him and his story about the white people; and whether or no there is any truth in it is more than I can tell you. What do you think, Mr Quatermain?'

I shook my head, and answered, 'I don't know. There are so many queer things hidden away in the heart of this great continent that I should be sorry to assert that there was no truth in it. Anyhow, we mean to try and find out. We intend to journey to Lekakisera, and thence, if we live to get so far, to this Lake Laga; and, if there are any white people beyond, we will do our best to find them.'

'You are very venturesome people,' said Mr Mackenzie, with a smile, and the subject dropped.

Alphonse and His Annette

After dinner we thoroughly inspected all the outbuildings and grounds of the station, which I consider the most successful as well as the most beautiful place of the sort that I have seen in Africa. We then returned to the veranda, where we found Umslopogaas taking advantage of this favourable opportunity to clean all the rifles thoroughly. This was the only *work* that he ever did or was asked to do, for as a Zulu chief it was beneath his dignity to work with his hands; but such as it was he did it very well. It was a curious sight to see the great Zulu sitting there upon the floor, his battleaxe resting against the wall behind him, whilst his long aristocratic-looking hands were busily employed, delicately and with the utmost care, cleaning the mechanism of the breech-loaders. He had a name for each gun. One — a double four-bore belonging to Sir Henry — was the Thunderer; another, my 500 Express, which had a peculiarly sharp report, was 'the little one who spoke like a whip'; the Winchester repeaters were 'the women, who talked so fast that you could not tell one word from another'; the six Martinis were 'the common people'; and so on with them all. It was very curious to hear him addressing each gun as he cleaned it, as though it were an individual, and in a vein of the quaintest humour. He did the same with his battle-axe, which he seemed to look upon as an intimate friend, and to which he would at times talk by the hour, going over all his old adventures with it — and dreadful enough some of them were. By a piece of grim humour, he had named this axe 'Inkosi-kaas', which is the Zulu word for chieftainess. For a long while I could not make out why he gave it such a name, and at last I asked him, when he informed me that the axe was very evidently feminine, because of her womanly habit of prying very deep into things, and that she was clearly a chieftainess because all men fell down before her, struck dumb at the sight of her beauty and power. In the same way he would consult 'Inkosi-kaas' if in any dilemma; and when I asked him why he did so, he informed me it was because she must needs be wise, having 'looked into so many people's brains'.

I took up the axe and closely examined this formidable weapon. It was, as I have said, of the nature of a pole-axe. The haft, made out of an enormous rhinoceros horn, was three feet three inches long, about an inch and a quarter thick, and with a knob at the end as large as a Maltese orange, left there to prevent the hand from slipping. This horn haft, though so massive, was as flexible as cane, and practically unbreakable; but, to make assurance doubly sure, it was whipped round at intervals of a few inches with copper wire — all the parts where the hands grip being thus treated. Just above where the haft entered the head were scored a number of little nicks, each nick representing a man killed in battle with the weapon. The axe itself was made of the most beautiful steel, and apparently of European manufacture, though Umslopogaas did not know where it came from, having taken it from the hand of a chief he had killed in battle many years before. It was not very heavy, the head weighing two and a half pounds, as nearly as I could judge. The cutting part was slightly concave in shape — not convex, as it generally the case with savage battleaxes — and sharp as a razor, measuring five and three-quarter inches across the widest part. From the back of the axe sprang a stout spike four inches long, for the last two of which it was hollow, and shaped like a leather punch, with an opening for anything forced into the hollow at the punch end to be pushed out above — in fact, in this respect it exactly resembled a butcher's pole-axe. It was with this punch end, as we afterwards discovered, that Umslopogaas usually struck when fighting, driving a neat round hole in his adversary's skull, and only using the broad cutting edge for a circular sweep, or sometimes in a melee. I think he considered the punch a neater and more sportsmanlike tool, and it was from his habit of pecking at his enemy with it that he got his name of 'Woodpecker'. Certainly in his hands it was a terribly efficient one.

Such was Umslopogaas' axe, Inkosi-kaas, the most remarkable and fatal hand-to-hand weapon that I ever saw, and one which he cherished as much as his own life. It scarcely ever left his hand except when he was eating, and then he always sat with it under his leg.

Just as I returned his axe to Umslopogaas, Miss Flossie came up and took me off to see her collection of flowers, African liliums, and blooming shrubs, some of which are very beautiful, many of the varieties being quite unknown to me and also, I believe, to botanical science. I asked her if she had ever seen or heard of the 'Goya' lily, which Central African explorers have told me they have occasionally met with and whose wonderful loveliness has filled them with astonishment. This lily, which the natives say blooms only once in ten years, flourishes in the most arid soil. Compared to the size of the bloom, the bulb is small, generally weighing about four pounds. As for the flower itself (which I afterwards saw under circumstances likely to impress its appearance fixedly in my mind), I know not how to describe its beauty and splendour, or the indescribable sweetness of its perfume. The flower — for it has only one bloom — rises from the crown of the bulb on a thick fleshy and flat-sided stem, the specimen that I saw measured fourteen inches in diameter, and is somewhat trumpet-shaped like the bloom of an ordinary 'longiflorum' set vertically. First there is the green sheath, which in its early stage is not unlike that of a water-lily, but which as the bloom opens splits into four portions and curls back gracefully towards the stem. Then comes the bloom itself, a single dazzling arch of white enclosing another cup of richest velvety crimson, from the heart of which rises a golden-coloured pistil. I have never seen anything to equal this bloom in beauty or fragrance, and as I believe it is but little known, I take the liberty to describe it at length. Looking at it for the first time I well remember that I realized how even in a flower there dwells something of the majesty of its Maker. To my great delight Miss Flossie told me that she knew the flower well and had tried to grow it in her garden, but without success, adding, however, that as it should be in bloom at this time of the year she thought that she could procure me a specimen.

After that I fell to asking her if she was not lonely up here among all these savage people and without any companions of her own age.

'Lonely?' she said. 'Oh, indeed no! I am as happy as the day is long, and besides I have my own companions. Why, I should hate to be buried in a crowd of white girls all just like myself so that nobody could tell the difference! Here,' she said, giving her head a little toss, 'I am I; and every native for miles around knows the "Water-lily", — for that is what they call me — and is ready to do what I want, but in the books that I have read about little girls in England it is not like that. Everybody thinks them a trouble, and they have to do what their schoolmistress likes. Oh! it would break my heart to be put in a cage like that and not to be free — free as the air.'

'Would you not like to learn?' I asked.

'So I do learn. Father teaches me Latin and French and arithmetic.'

'And are you never afraid among all these wild men?'

'Afraid? Oh no! they never interfere with me. I think they believe that I am "Ngai" (of the Divinity) because I am so white and have fair hair. And look here,' and diving her little hand into the bodice of her dress she produced a double-barrelled nickel-plated Derringer, 'I always carry that loaded, and if anybody tried to touch me I should shoot him. Once I shot a leopard that jumped upon my donkey as I was riding along. It frightened me very much, but I shot it in the ear and it fell dead, and I have its skin upon my bed. Look there!' she went on in an altered voice, touching me on the arm and pointing to some far-away object, 'I said just now that I had companions; there is one of them.'

I looked, and for the first time there burst upon my sight the glory of Mount Kenia. Hitherto the mountain had always been hidden in mist, but now its radiant beauty was unveiled for many thousand feet, although the base was still wrapped in vapour so that the lofty peak or pillar, towering nearly twenty thousand feet into the sky, appeared to be a fairy vision, hanging between earth and heaven, and based upon the clouds. The solemn majesty and beauty of this white peak are together beyond the power of my poor pen to describe. There it rose straight and sheer — a glittering white glory, its crest piercing the very blue of heaven. As I gazed at it with that little girl I felt my whole heart lifted up with an indescribable emotion, and for a moment great and wonderful thoughts seemed to break upon my mind, even as the arrows of the setting sun were breaking upon Kenia's snows. Mr Mackenzie's natives call the mountain the 'Finger of God', and to me it did seem eloquent of immortal peace and of the pure high calm that surely lies above this fevered world. Somewhere I had heard a line of poetry,

A thing of beauty is a joy for ever, and now it came into my mind, and for the first time I thoroughly understood what it meant. Base, indeed, would be the man who could look upon that mighty snow-wreathed pile — that white old tombstone of the years — and not feel his own utter insignificance, and, by whatever name he calls Him, worship God in his heart. Such sights are like visions of the spirit; they throw wide the windows of the chamber of our small selfishness and let in a breath of that air that rushes round the rolling spheres, and for a while illumine our darkness with a far-off gleam of the white light which beats upon the Throne.

Yes, such things of beauty are indeed a joy for ever, and I can well understand what little Flossie meant when she talked of Kenia as her companion. As Umslopogaas, savage old Zulu that he was, said when I pointed out to him the peak hanging in the glittering air: 'A man might look thereon for a thousand years and yet be hungry to see.' But he gave rather another colour to his poetical idea when he added in a sort of chant, and with a touch of that weird imagination for which the man was remarkable, that when he was dead he should like his spirit to sit upon that snow-clad peak for ever, and to rush down the steep white sides in the breath of the whirlwind, or on the flash of the lightning, and 'slay, and slay, and slay'.

'Slay what, you old bloodhound?' I asked.

This rather puzzled him, but at length he answered —

'The other shadows.'

'So thou wouldst continue thy murdering even after death?' I said.

'I murder not,' he answered hotly; 'I kill in fair fight. Man is born to kill. He who kills not when his blood is hot is a woman, and no man. The people who kill not are slaves. I say I kill in fair fight; and when I am "in the shadow", as you white men say, I hope to go on killing in fair fight. May my shadow be accursed and chilled to the bone for ever if it should fall to murdering like a bushman with his poisoned arrows!' And he stalked away with much dignity, and left me laughing.

Just then the spies whom our host had sent out in the morning to find out if there were any traces of our Masai friends about, returned, and reported that the country had been scoured for fifteen miles round without a single Elmoran being seen, and that they believed that those gentry had given up the pursuit and returned whence they came. Mr Mackenzie gave a sigh of relief when he heard this, and so indeed did we, for we had had quite enough of the Masai to last us for some time. Indeed, the general opinion was that, finding we had reached the mission station in safety, they had, knowing its strength, given up the pursuit of us as a bad job. How ill-judged that view was the sequel will show.

After the spies had gone, and Mrs Mackenzie and Flossie had retired for the night, Alphonse, the little Frenchman, came out, and Sir Henry, who is a very good French scholar, got him to tell us how he came to visit Central Africa, which he did in a most extraordinary lingo, that for the most part I shall not attempt to reproduce.

'My grandfather,' he began, 'was a soldier of the Guard, and served under Napoleon. He was in the retreat from Moscow, and lived for ten days on his own leggings and a pair he stole from a comrade. He used to get drunk — he died drunk, and I remember playing at drums on his coffin. My father —'

Here we suggested that he might skip his ancestry and come to the point.

'Bien, messieurs!' replied this comical little man, with a polite bow. 'I did only wish to demonstrate that the military principle is not hereditary. My grandfather was a splendid man, six feet two high, broad in proportion, a swallower of fire and gaiters. Also he was remarkable for his moustache. To me there remains the moustache and — nothing more.

'I am, messieurs, a cook, and I was born at Marseilles. In that dear town I spent my happy youth. For years and years I washed the dishes at the Hotel Continental. Ah, those were golden days!' and he sighed. 'I am a Frenchman. Need I say, messieurs, that I admire beauty? Nay, I adore the fair. Messieurs, we admire all the roses in a garden, but we pluck one. I plucked one, and alas, messieurs, it pricked my finger. She was a chambermaid, her name Annette, her figure ravishing, her face an angel's, her heart — alas, messieurs, that I should have to own it! — black and slippery as a patent leather boot. I loved to desperation, I adored her to despair. She transported me — in every sense; she inspired me. Never have I cooked as I cooked (for I had been promoted at the hotel) when Annette, my adored Annette, smiled on me. Never' — and here his manly voice broke into a sob — 'never shall I cook so well again.' Here he melted into tears.

'Come, cheer up!' said Sir Henry in French, smacking him smartly on the back. 'There's no knowing what may happen, you know. To judge from your dinner today, I should say you were in a fair way to recovery.'

Alphonse stopped weeping, and began to rub his back. 'Monsieur,' he said, 'doubtless means to console, but his hand is heavy. To continue: we loved, and were happy in each other's love. The birds in their little nest could not be happier than Alphonse and his Annette. Then came the blow — sapristi! — when I think of it. Messieurs will forgive me if I wipe away a tear. Mine was an evil number; I was drawn for the conscription. Fortune would be avenged on me for having won the heart of Annette.

'The evil moment came; I had to go. I tried to run away, but I was caught by brutal soldiers, and they banged me with the butt-end of muskets till my mustachios curled with pain. I had a cousin a linen-draper, well-to-do, but very ugly. He had drawn a good number, and sympathized when they thumped me. "To thee, my cousin," I said, "to thee, in whose veins flows the blue blood of our heroic grandparent, to thee I consign Annette. Watch over her whilst I hunt for glory in the bloody field."

'"Make your mind easy," said he; "I will." As the sequel shows, he did!

'I went. I lived in barracks on black soup. I am a refined man and a poet by nature, and I suffered tortures from the coarse horror of my surroundings. There was a drill sergeant, and he had a cane. Ah, that cane, how it curled! Alas, never can I forget it!

'One morning came the news; my battalion was ordered to Tonquin. The drill sergeant and the other coarse monsters rejoiced. I — I made enquiries about Tonquin. They were not satisfactory. In Tonquin are savage Chinese who rip you open. My artistic tastes — for I am also an artist — recoiled from the idea of being ripped open. The great man makes up his mind quickly. I made up my mind. I determined not to be ripped open. I deserted.

'I reached Marseilles disguised as an old man. I went to the house of my cousin — he in whom runs my grandfather's heroic blood — and there sat

Annette. It was the season of cherries. They took a double stalk. At each end was a cherry. My cousin put one into his mouth, Annette put the other in hers. Then they drew the stalks in till their eyes met — and alas, alas that I should have to say it! — they kissed. The game was a pretty one, but it filled me with fury. The heroic blood of my grandfather boiled up in me. I rushed into the kitchen. I struck my cousin with the old man's crutch. He fell — I had slain him. Alas, I believe that I did slay him. Annette screamed. The gendarmes came. I fled. I reached the harbour. I hid aboard a vessel. The vessel put to sea. The captain found me and beat me. He took an opportunity. He posted a letter from a foreign port to the police. He did not put me ashore because I cooked so well. I cooked for him all the way to Zanzibar. When I asked for payment he kicked me. The blood of my heroic grandfather boiled within me, and I shook my fist in his face and vowed to have my revenge. He kicked me again. At Zanzibar there was a telegram. I cursed the man who invented telegraphs. Now I curse him again. I was to be arrested for desertion, for murder, and que sais-je? I escaped from the prison. I fled, I starved. I met the men of Monsieur le Cure. They brought me here. I am full of woe. But I return not to France. Better to risk my life in these horrible places than to know the Bagne.'

He paused, and we nearly choked with laughter, having to turn our faces away.

'Ah! you weep, messieurs,' he said. 'No wonder — it is a sad story.'

'Perhaps,' said Sir Henry, 'the heroic blood of your grandparent will triumph after all; perhaps you will still be great. At any rate we shall see. And now I vote we go to bed. I am dead tired, and we had not much sleep on that confounded rock last night.'

And so we did, and very strange the tidy rooms and clean white sheets seemed to us after our recent experiences.

Umslopogaas Makes a Promise

Next morning at breakfast I missed Flossie and asked where she was.

'Well,' said her mother, 'when I got up this morning I found a note put outside my door in which — But here it is, you can read it for yourself,' and she gave me the slip of paper on which the following was written: —

'Dearest M—, — It is just dawn, and I am off to the hills to get Mr Q— a bloom of the lily he wants, so don't expect me till you see me. I have taken the white donkey; and nurse and a couple of boys are coming with me — also something to eat, as I may be away all day, for I am determined to get the lily if I have to go twenty miles for it. — Flossie.'

'I hope she will be all right,' I said, a little anxiously; 'I never meant her to trouble after the flower.'

'Ah, Flossie can look after herself,' said her mother; 'she often goes off in this way like a true child of the wilderness.' But Mr Mackenzie, who came in just then and saw the note for the first time, looked rather grave, though he said nothing.

After breakfast was over I took him aside and asked him whether it would not be possible to send after the girl and get her back, having in view the possibility of there still being some Masai hanging about, at whose hands she might come to harm.

'I fear it would be of no use,' he answered. 'She may be fifteen miles off by now, and it is impossible to say what path she has taken. There are the hills;' and he pointed to a long range of rising ground stretching almost parallel with the course followed by the river Tana, but gradually sloping down to a dense bush-clad plain about five miles short of the house.

Here I suggested that we might get up the great tree over the house and search the country round with a spyglass; and this, after Mr Mackenzie had given some orders to his people to try and follow Flossie's spoor, we did.

The ascent of the mighty tree was rather an alarming performance, even with a sound rope-ladder fixed at both ends to climb up, at least to a landsman; but Good came up like a lamplighter.

On reaching the height at which the first fern-shaped boughs sprang from the bole, we stepped without any difficulty upon a platform made of boards, nailed from one bough to another, and large enough to accommodate a dozen people. As for the view, it was simply glorious. In every direction the bush rolled away in great billows for miles and miles, as far as the glass would show, only here and there broken by the brighter green of patches of cultivation, or by the glittering surface of lakes. To the northwest, Kenia reared his mighty head, and we could trace the Tana river curling like a silver snake almost from his feet, and far away beyond us towards the ocean. It is a glorious country, and only wants the hand of civilized man to make it a most productive one.

But look as we would, we could see no signs of Flossie and her donkey, so at last we had to come down disappointed. On reaching the veranda I found Umslopogaas sitting there, slowly and lightly sharpening his axe with a small whetstone he always carried with him.

'What doest thou, Umslopogaas?' I asked.

'I smell blood,' was the answer; and I could get no more out of him.

After dinner we again went up the tree and searched the surrounding country with a spyglass, but without result. When we came down Umslopogaas was still sharpening Inkosi-kaas, although she already had an edge like a razor. Standing in front of him, and regarding him with a mixture of fear and fascination, was Alphonse. And certainly he did seem an alarming object — sitting there, Zulu fashion, on his haunches, a wild look upon his intensely savage and yet intellectual face, sharpening, sharpening, sharpening at the murderous-looking axe.

'Oh, the monster, the horrible man!' said the little French cook, lifting his hands in amazement. 'See but the hole in his head; the skin beats on it up and down like a baby's! Who would nurse such a baby?' and he burst out laughing at the idea.

For a moment Umslopogaas looked up from his sharpening, and a sort of evil light played in his dark eyes.

'What does the little "buffalo-heifer" [so named by Umslopogaas, on account of his mustachios and feminine characteristics] say? Let him be careful, or I will cut his horns. Beware, little man monkey, beware!'

Unfortunately Alphonse, who was getting over his fear of him, went on laughing at 'ce drole d'un monsieur noir'. I was about to warn him to desist, when suddenly the huge Zulu bounded off the veranda on to the open space where Alphonse was standing, his features alive with a sort of malicious enthusiasm, and began swinging the axe round and round over the Frenchman's head.

'Stand still,' I shouted; 'do not move as you value your life — he will not hurt you;' but I doubt if Alphonse heard me, being, fortunately for himself, almost petrified with horror.

Then followed the most extraordinary display of sword, or rather of axemanship, that I ever saw. First of all the axe went flying round and round over the top of Alphonse's head, with an angry whirl and such extraordinary swiftness that it looked like a continuous band of steel, ever getting nearer and yet nearer to that unhappy individual's skull, till at last it grazed it as it flew. Then suddenly the motion was changed, and it seemed to literally flow up and down his body and limbs, never more than an eighth of an inch from them, and yet never striking them. It was a wonderful sight to see the little man fixed there, having apparently realized that to move would be to run the risk of sudden death, while his black tormentor towered over him, and wrapped him round with the quick flashes of the axe. For a minute or more this went on, till suddenly I saw the moving brightness travel down the side of Alphonse's face, and then outwards and stop. As it did so a tuft of something black fell to the ground; it was the tip of one of the little Frenchman's curling mustachios.

Umslopogaas leant upon the handle of Inkosi-kaas, and broke into a long, low laugh; and Alphonse, overcome with fear, sank into a sitting posture on the ground, while we stood astonished at this exhibition of almost superhuman skill and mastery of a weapon. 'Inkosi-kaas is sharp enough,' he shouted; 'the blow that clipped the "buffalo-heifer's" horn would have split a man from the crown to the chin. Few could have struck it but I; none could have struck it and not taken off the shoulder too. Look, thou little heifer! Am I a good man to laugh at, thinkest thou? For a space hast thou stood within a hair's-breadth of death. Laugh not again, lest the hair's-breadth be wanting. I have spoken.'

'What meanest thou by such mad tricks?' I asked of Umslopogaas, indignantly. 'Surely thou art mad. Twenty times didst thou go near to slaying the man.'

'And yet, Macumazahn, I slew not. Thrice as Inkosi-kaas flew the spirit entered into me to end him, and send her crashing through his skull; but I did not. Nay, it was but a jest; but tell the "heifer" that it is not well to mock at such as I. Now I go to make a shield, for I smell blood, Macumazahn — of a truth I smell blood. Before the battle hast thou not seen the vulture grow of a sudden in the sky? They smell the blood, Macumazahn, and my scent is more keen than theirs. There is a dry ox-hide down yonder; I go to make a shield.'

'That is an uncomfortable retainer of yours,' said Mr Mackenzie, who had witnessed this extraordinary scene. 'He has frightened Alphonse out of his wits; look!' and he pointed to the Frenchman, who, with a scared white face and trembling limbs, was making his way into the house. 'I don't think that he will ever laugh at "le monsieur noir" again.'

'Yes,' answered I, 'it is ill jesting with such as he. When he is roused he is like a fiend, and yet he has a kind heart in his own fierce way. I remember years ago seeing him nurse a sick child for a week. He is a strange character, but true as steel, and a strong stick to rest on in danger.'

'He says he smells blood,' said Mr Mackenzie. 'I only trust he is not right. I am getting very fearful about my little girl. She must have gone far, or she would be home by now. It is half-past three o'clock.'

I pointed out that she had taken food with her, and very likely would not in the ordinary course of events return till nightfall; but I myself felt very anxious, and fear that my anxiety betrayed itself.

Shortly after this, the people whom Mr Mackenzie had sent out to search for Flossie returned, stating that they had followed the spoor of the donkey for a couple of miles and had then lost it on some stony ground, nor could they discover it again. They had, however, scoured the country far and wide, but without success.

After this the afternoon wore drearily on, and towards evening, there still being no signs of Flossie, our anxiety grew very keen. As for the poor mother, she was quite prostrated by her fears, and no wonder, but the father kept his head wonderfully well. Everything that could be done was done: people were sent out in all directions, shots were fired, and a continuous outlook kept from the great tree, but without avail.

And then it grew dark, and still no sign of fair-haired little Flossie.

At eight o'clock we had supper. It was but a sorrowful meal, and Mrs Mackenzie did not appear at it. We three also were very silent, for in addition to our natural anxiety as to the fate of the child, we were weighed down by the sense that we had brought this trouble on the head of our kind host. When supper was nearly at an end I made an excuse to leave the table. I wanted to get outside and think the situation over. I went on to the veranda and, having lit my pipe, sat down on a seat about a dozen feet from the right-hand end of the structure, which was, as the reader may remember, exactly opposite one of the narrow doors of the protecting wall that enclosed the house and flower garden. I had been sitting there perhaps six or seven minutes when I thought I heard the door move. I looked in that direction and I listened, but, being unable to make out anything, concluded that I must have been mistaken. It was a darkish night, the moon not having yet risen.

Another minute passed, when suddenly something round fell with a soft but heavy thud upon the stone flooring of the veranda, and came bounding and rolling along past me. For a moment I did not rise, but sat wondering what it could be. Finally, I concluded it must have been an animal. Just then, however, another idea struck me, and I got up quick enough. The thing lay quite still a few feet beyond me. I put down my hand towards it and it did not move: clearly it was not an animal. My hand touched it. It was soft and warm and heavy. Hurriedly I lifted it and held it up against the faint starlight.

It was a newly severed human head!

I am an old hand and not easily upset, but I own that that ghastly sight made me feel sick. How had the thing come there? Whose was it? I put it down and ran to the little doorway. I could see nothing, hear nobody. I was about to go out into the darkness beyond, but remembering that to do so was to expose myself to the risk of being stabbed, I drew back, shut the door, and bolted it. Then I returned to the veranda, and in as careless a voice as I could command called Curtis. I fear, however, that my tones must have betrayed me, for not only Sir Henry but also Good and Mackenzie rose from the table and came hurrying out.

'What is it?' said the clergyman, anxiously.

Then I had to tell them.

Mr Mackenzie turned pale as death under his red skin. We were standing opposite the hall door, and there was a light in it so that I could see. He snatched the head up by the hair and held it against the light.

'It is the head of one of the men who accompanied Flossie,' he said with a gasp. 'Thank God it is not hers!'

We all stood and stared at each other aghast. What was to be done?

Just then there was a knocking at the door that I had bolted, and a voice cried, 'Open, my father, open!'

The door was unlocked, and in sped a terrified man. He was one of the spies who had been sent out.

'My father,' he cried, 'the Masai are on us! A great body of them have passed round the hill and are moving towards the old stone kraal down by the little stream. My father, make strong thy heart! In the midst of them I saw the white ass, and on it sat the Water-lily [Flossie]. An Elmoran [young warrior] led the ass, and by its side walked the nurse weeping. The men who went with her in the morning I saw not.'

'Was the child alive?' asked Mr Mackenzie, hoarsely.

'She was white as the snow, but well, my father. They passed quite close to me, and looking up from where I lay hid I saw her face against the sky.'

'God help her and us!' groaned the clergyman.

'How many are there of them?' I asked.

'More than two hundred — two hundred and half a hundred.'

Once more we looked one on the other. What was to be done? Just then there rose a loud insistent cry outside the wall.

'Open the door, white man; open the door! A herald — a herald to speak with thee.' Thus cried the voice.

Umslopogaas ran to the wall, and, reaching with his long arms to the coping, lifted his head above it and gazed over.

'I see but one man,' he said. 'He is armed, and carries a basket in his hand.'

'Open the door,' I said. 'Umslopogaas, take thine axe and stand thereby. Let one man pass. If another follows, slay.'

The door was unbarred. In the shadow of the wall stood Umslopogaas, his axe raised above his head to strike. Just then the moon came out. There was a moment's pause, and then in stalked a Masai Elmoran, clad in the full war panoply that I have already described, but bearing a large basket in his hand. The moonlight shone bright upon his great spear as he walked. He was physically a splendid man, apparently about thirty-five years of age. Indeed, none of the Masai that I saw were under six feet high, though mostly quite young. When he got opposite to us he halted, put down the basket, and stuck the spike of his spear into the ground, so that it stood upright.

'Let us talk,' he said. 'The first messenger we sent to you could not talk;' and he pointed to the head which lay upon the paving of the stoep — a ghastly sight in the moonlight; 'but I have words to speak if ye have ears to hear. Also I bring presents;' and he pointed to the basket and laughed with an air of swaggering insolence that is perfectly indescribable, and yet which one could not but admire, seeing that he was surrounded by enemies.

'Say on,' said Mr Mackenzie.

'I am the "Lygonani" [war captain] of a party of the Masai of the Guasa Amboni. I and my men followed these three white men,' and he pointed to Sir Henry, Good, and myself, 'but they were too clever for us, and escaped hither. We have a quarrel with them, and are going to kill them.'

'Are you, my friend?' said I to myself.

'In following these men we this morning caught two black men, one black woman, a white donkey, and a white girl. One of the black men we killed — there is his head upon the pavement; the other ran away. The black woman, the little white girl, and the white ass we took and brought with us. In proof thereof have I brought this basket that she carried. Is it not thy daughter's basket?'

Mr Mackenzie nodded, and the warrior went on.

'Good! With thee and thy daughter we have no quarrel, nor do we wish to harm thee, save as to thy cattle, which we have already gathered, two hundred and forty head — a beast for every man's father.'

Here Mr Mackenzie gave a groan, as he greatly valued this herd of cattle, which he bred with much care and trouble.

'So, save for the cattle, thou mayst go free; more especially,' he added frankly, glancing at the wall, 'as this place would be a difficult one to take. But as to these men it is otherwise; we have followed them for nights and days, and must kill them. Were we to return to our kraal without having done so, all the girls would make a mock of us. So, however troublesome it may be, they must die.

'Now I have a proposition for thee. We would not harm the little girl; she is too fair to harm, and has besides a brave spirit. Give us one of these three men — a life for a life — and we will let her go, and throw in the black woman with her also. This is a fair offer, white man. We ask but for one, not for the three; we must take another opportunity to kill the other two. I do not even pick my man, though I should prefer the big one,' pointing to Sir Henry; 'he looks strong, and would die more slowly.'

'And if I say I will not yield the man?' said Mr Mackenzie.

'Nay, say not so, white man,' answered the Masai, 'for then thy daughter dies at dawn, and the woman with her says thou hast no other child. Were she older I would take her for a servant; but as she is so young I will slay her with my own hand — ay, with this very spear. Thou canst come and see, an' thou wilt. I give thee a safe conduct;' and the fiend laughed aloud as his brutal jest.

Meanwhile I had been thinking rapidly, as one does in emergencies, and had come to the conclusion that I would exchange myself against Flossie. I scarcely like to mention the matter for fear it should be misunderstood. Pray do not let any one be misled into thinking that there was anything heroic about this, or any such nonsense. It was merely a matter of common sense and common justice. My life was an old and worthless one, hers was young and valuable. Her death would pretty well kill her father and mother also, whilst nobody would be much the worse for mine; indeed, several charitable institutions would have cause to rejoice thereat. It was indirectly through me that the dear little girl was in her present position. Lastly, a man was better fitted to meet death in such a peculiarly awful form than a sweet young girl. Not, however, that I meant to let these gentry torture me to death — I am far too much of a coward to allow that, being naturally a timid man; my plan was to see the girl safely exchanged and then to shoot myself, trusting that the Almighty would take the peculiar circumstances of the case into consideration and pardon the act. All this and more went through my mind in very few seconds.

'All right, Mackenzie,' I said, 'you can tell the man that I will exchange myself against Flossie, only I stipulate that she shall be safely in this house before they kill me.'

'Eh?' said Sir Henry and Good simultaneously. 'That you don't.'

'No, no,' said Mr Mackenzie. 'I will have no man's blood upon my hands. If it please God that my daughter should die this awful death, His will be done. You are a brave man (which I am not by any means) and a noble man, Quatermain, but you shall not go.'

'If nothing else turns up I shall go,' I said decidedly.

'This is an important matter,' said Mackenzie, addressing the Lygonani, 'and we must think it over. You shall have our answer at dawn.'

'Very well, white man,' answered the savage indifferently; 'only remember if thy answer is late thy little white bud will never grow into a flower, that is all, for I shall cut it with this,' and he touched the spear. 'I should have thought that thou wouldst play a trick and attack us at night, but I know from the woman with the girl that your men are down at the coast, and that thou hast but twenty men here. It is not wise, white man,' he added with a laugh, 'to keep so small a garrison for your "boma" [kraal]. Well, good night, and good night to you also, other white men, whose eyelids I shall soon close once and for all. At dawn thou wilt bring me word. If not, remember it shall be as I have said.' Then turning to Umslopogaas, who had all the while been standing behind him and shepherding him as it were, 'Open the door for me, fellow, quick now.'

This was too much for the old chief's patience. For the last ten minutes his lips had been, figuratively speaking, positively watering over the Masai Lygonani, and this he could not stand. Placing his long hand on the Elmoran's shoulder he gripped it and gave him such a twist as brought him face to face with himself. Then, thrusting his fierce countenance to within a few inches of the Masai's evil feather-framed features, he said in a low growling voice: —

'Seest thou me?'

'Ay, fellow, I see thee.'

'And seest thou this?' and he held Inkosi-kaas before his eyes.

'Ay, fellow, I see the toy; what of it?'

'Thou Masai dog, thou boasting windbag, thou capturer of little girls, with this "toy" will I hew thee limb from limb. Well for thee that thou art a herald, or even now would I strew thy members about the grass.'

The Masai shook his great spear and laughed loud and long as he answered, 'I would that thou stoodst against me man to man, and we would see,' and again he turned to go still laughing.

'Thou shalt stand against me man to man, be not afraid,' replied Umslopogaas, still in the same ominous voice. 'Thou shalt stand face to face with Umslopogaas, of the blood of Chaka, of the people of the Amazulu, a captain in the regiment of the Nkomabakosi, as many have done before, and bow thyself to Inkosi-kaas, as many have done before. Ay, laugh on, laugh on! tomorrow night shall the jackals laugh as they crunch thy ribs.'

When the Lygonani had gone, one of us thought of opening the basket he had brought as a proof that Flossie was really their prisoner. On lifting the lid it was found to contain a most lovely specimen of both bulb and flower of the Goya lily, which I have already described, in full bloom and quite uninjured, and what was more a note in Flossie's childish hand written in pencil upon a greasy piece of paper that had been used to wrap up some food in: —

'Dearest Father and Mother,' ran the note, 'The Masai caught us when we were coming home with the lily. I tried to escape but could not. They killed Tom: the other man ran away. They have not hurt nurse and me, but say that they mean to exchange us against one of Mr Quatermain's party. *I will have nothing of the sort.* Do not let anybody give his life for me. Try and attack them at night; they are going to feast on three bullocks they have stolen and killed. I have my pistol, and if no help comes by dawn I will shoot myself. They shall not kill me. If so, remember me always, dearest father and mother. I am very frightened, but I trust in God. I dare not write any more as they are beginning to notice. Goodbye. — Flossie.'

Scrawled across the outside of this was 'Love to Mr Quatermain. They are going to take the basket, so he will get the lily.'

When I read those words, written by that brave little girl in an hour of danger sufficiently near and horrible to have turned the brain of a strong man, I own I wept, and once more in my heart I vowed that she should not die while my life could be given to save her.

Then eagerly, quickly, almost fiercely, we fell to discussing the situation. Again I said that I would go, and again Mackenzie negatived it, and Curtis and Good, like the true men that they are, vowed that, if I did, they would go with me, and die back to back with me.

'It is,' I said at last, 'absolutely necessary that an effort of some sort should be made before the morning.'

'Then let us attack them with what force we can muster, and take our chance,' said Sir Henry.

'Ay, ay,' growled Umslopogaas, in Zulu; 'spoken like a man, Incubu. What is there to be afraid of? Two hundred and fifty Masai, forsooth! How many are we? The chief there [Mr Mackenzie] has twenty men, and thou, Macumazahn, hast five men, and there are also five white men — that is, thirty men in all — enough, enough. Listen now, Macumazahn, thou who art very clever and old in war. What says the maid? These men eat and make merry; let it be their funeral feast. What said the dog whom I hope to hew down at daybreak? That he feared no attack because we were so few. Knowest thou the old kraal where the men have camped? I saw it this morning; it is thus:' and he drew an oval on the floor; 'here is the big entrance, filled up with thorn bushes, and opening on to a steep rise. Why, Incubu, thou and I with axes will hold it against an hundred men striving to break out! Look, now; thus shall the battle go. Just as the light begins to glint upon the oxen's horns — not before, or it will be too dark, and not later, or they will be awakening and perceive us — let Bougwan creep round with ten men to the top end of the kraal, where the narrow entrance is. Let them silently slay the sentry there so that he makes no sound, and stand ready. Then, Incubu, let thee and me and one of the Askari — the one with the broad chest — he is a brave man — creep to the wide entrance that is filled with thorn bushes, and there also slay the sentry, and armed with battleaxes take our stand also one on each side of the pathway, and one a few paces beyond to deal with such as pass the twain at the gate. It is there that the rush will come. That will leave sixteen men. Let these men be divided into two parties, with one of which shalt thou go, Macumazahn, and with one the "praying man" [Mr Mackenzie], and, all armed with rifles, let them make their way one to the right side of the kraal and one to the left; and when thou, Macumazahn, lowest like an ox, all shall open fire with the guns upon the sleeping men, being very careful not to hit the little maid. Then shall Bougwan at the far end and his ten men raise the war-cry, and, springing over the wall, put the Masai there to the sword. And it shall happen that, being yet heavy with food and sleep, and bewildered by the firing of the guns, the falling of men, and the spears of Bougwan, the soldiers shall rise and rush like wild game towards the thorn-stopped entrance, and there the bullets from either side shall plough through them, and there shall Incubu and the Askari and I wait for those who break across. Such is my plan, Macumazahn; if thou hast a better, name it.'

When he had done, I explained to the others such portions of his scheme as they had failed to understand, and they all joined with me in expressing the greatest admiration of the acute and skilful programme devised by the old Zulu, who was indeed, in his own savage fashion, the finest general I ever knew. After some discussion we determined to accept the scheme, as it stood, it being the only one possible under the circumstances, and giving the best chance of success that such a forlorn hope would admit of — which, however, considering the enormous odds and the character of our foe, was not very great.

'Ah, old lion!' I said to Umslopogaas, 'thou knowest how to lie in wait as well as how to bite, where to seize as well as where to hang on.'

'Ay, ay, Macumazahn,' he answered. 'For thirty years have I been a warrior, and have seen many things. It will be a good fight. I smell blood — I tell thee, I smell blood.'

The Night Wears on

As may be imagined, at the very first sign of a Masai the entire population of the Mission Station had sought refuge inside the stout stone wall, and were now to be seen — men, women, and countless children — huddled up together in little groups, and all talking at once in awed tones of the awfulness of Masai manners and customs, and of the fate that they had to expect if those bloodthirsty savages succeeded in getting over the stone wall.

Immediately after we had settled upon the outline of our plan of action as suggested by Umslopogaas, Mr Mackenzie sent for four sharp boys of from twelve to fifteen years of age, and despatched them to various points where they could keep an outlook upon the Masai camp, with others to report from time to time what was going on. Other lads and even women were stationed at intervals along the wall in order to guard against the possibility of surprise.

After this the twenty men who formed his whole available fighting force were summoned by our host into the square formed by the house, and there, standing by the bole of the great conifer, he earnestly addressed them and our four Askari. Indeed, it formed a very impressive scene — one not likely to be forgotten by anybody who witnessed it. Immediately by the tree stood the angular form of Mr Mackenzie, one arm outstretched as he talked, and the other resting against the giant bole, his hat off, and his plain but kindly face clearly betraying the anguish of his mind. Next to him was his poor wife, who, seated on a chair, had her face hidden in her hand. On the other side of her was Alphonse, looking exceedingly uncomfortable, and behind him stood the three of us, with Umslopogaas' grim and towering form in the background, resting, as usual, on his axe. In front stood and squatted the group of armed men — some with rifles in their hands, and others with spears and shields — following with eager attention every word that fell from the speaker's lips. The white light of the moon peering in beneath the lofty boughs threw a strange wild glamour over the scene, whilst the melancholy soughing of the night wind passing through the millions of pine needles overhead added a sadness of its own to what was already a sufficiently tragic occasion.

'Men,' said Mr Mackenzie, after he had put all the circumstances of the case fully and clearly before them, and explained to them the proposed plan of our forlorn hope — 'men, for years I have been a good friend to you, protecting you, teaching you, guarding you and yours from harm, and ye have prospered with me. Ye have seen my child — the Water-lily, as ye call her — grow year by year, from tenderest infancy to tender childhood, and from childhood on towards maidenhood. She has been your children's playmate, she has helped to tend you when sick, and ye have loved her.'

'We have,' said a deep voice, 'and we will die to save her.'

'I thank you from my heart — I thank you. Sure am I that now, in this hour of darkest trouble; now that her young life is like to be cut off by cruel and savage men — who of a truth "know not what they do" — ye will strive your best to save her, and to save me and her mother from broken hearts. Think, too, of your own wives and children. If she dies, her death will be followed by an attack upon us here, and at the best, even if we hold our own, your houses and gardens will be destroyed, and your goods and cattle swept away. I am, as ye well know, a man of peace. Never in all these years have I lifted my hand to shed man's blood; but now I say strike, strike, in the name of God, Who bade us protect our lives and homes. Swear to me,' he went on with added fervour — 'swear to me that whilst a man of you remains alive ye will strive your uttermost with me and with these brave white men to save the child from a bloody and cruel death.'

'Say no more, my father,' said the same deep voice, that belonged to a stalwart elder of the Mission; 'we swear it. May we and ours die the death of dogs, and our bones be thrown to the jackals and the kites, if we break the oath! It is a fearful thing to do, my father, so few to strike at so many, yet will we do it or die in the doing. We swear!'

'Ay, thus say we all,' chimed in the others.

'Thus say we all,' said I.

'It is well,' went on Mr Mackenzie. 'Ye are true men and not broken reeds to lean on. And now, friends — white and black together — let us kneel and offer up our humble supplication to the Throne of Power, praying that He in the hollow of Whose hand lie all our lives, Who giveth life and giveth death, may be pleased to make strong our arms that we may prevail in what awaits us at the morning's light.'

And he knelt down, an example that we all followed except Umslopogaas, who still stood in the background, grimly leaning on Inkosi-kaas. The fierce old Zulu had no gods and worshipped nought, unless it were his battleaxe.

'Oh God of gods!' began the clergyman, his deep voice, tremulous with emotion, echoing up in the silence even to the leafy roof; 'Protector of the oppressed, Refuge of those in danger, Guardian of the helpless, hear Thou our prayer! Almighty Father, to Thee we come in supplication. Hear Thou our prayer! Behold, one child hast Thou given us — an innocent child, nurtured in Thy knowledge — and now she lies beneath the shadow of the sword, in danger of a fearful death at the hands of savage men. Be with her now, oh God, and comfort her! Save her, oh Heavenly Father! Oh God of battle, Who teacheth our hands to war and our fingers to fight, in Whose strength are hid the destinies of men, be Thou with us in the hour of strife. When we go forth into the shadow of death, make Thou us strong to conquer. Breathe Thou upon our foes and scatter them; turn Thou their strength to water, and bring their high-blown pride to nought; compass us about with Thy protection; throw over us the shield of Thy power; forget us not now in the hour of our sore distress; help us now that the cruel man would dash our little ones against the stones! Hear Thou our prayer! And for those of us who, kneeling now on earth in health before Thee, shall at the sunrise adore Thy Presence on the Throne, hear our prayer! Make them clean, oh God; wash away their offences in the blood of the Lamb; and when their spirits pass, oh receive Thou them into the haven of the just. Go forth, oh Father, go forth with us into the battle, as with the Israelites of old. Oh God of battle, hear Thou our prayer!'

He ceased, and after a moment's silence we all rose, and then began our preparations in good earnest. As Umslopogaas said, it was time to stop 'talking' and get to business. The men who were to form each little party were carefully selected, and still more carefully and minutely instructed as to what was to be done. After much consideration it was agreed that the ten men led by Good, whose duty it was to stampede the camp, were not to carry firearms; that is, with the exception of Good himself, who had a revolver as well as a short sword — the Masai 'sime' which I had taken from the body of our poor servant who was murdered in the canoe. We feared that if they had firearms the result of three cross-fires carried on at once would be that some of our own people would be shot; besides, it appeared to all of us that the work they had to do would best be carried out with cold steel — especially to Umslopogaas, who was, indeed, a great advocate of cold steel. We had with us four Winchester repeating rifles, besides half a dozen Martinis. I armed myself with one of the repeaters — my own; an excellent weapon for this kind of work, where great rapidity of fire is desirable, and fitted with ordinary flap-sights instead of the cumbersome sliding mechanism which they generally have. Mr Mackenzie took another, and the two remaining ones were given to two of his men who understood the use of them and were noted shots. The Martinis and some rifles of Mr Mackenzie's were served out, together with a plentiful supply of ammunition, to the other natives who were to form the two parties whose duty it was to be to open fire from separate sides of the kraal on the sleeping Masai, and who were fortunately all more or less accustomed to the use of a gun.

As for Umslopogaas, we know how he was armed — with an axe. It may be remembered that he, Sir Henry, and the strongest of the Askari were to hold the thorn-stopped entrance to the kraal against the anticipated rush of men striving to escape. Of course, for such a purpose as this guns were useless. Therefore Sir Henry and the Askari proceeded to arm themselves in like fashion. It so happened that Mr Mackenzie had in his little store a selection of the very best and English-made hammer-backed axe-heads. Sir Henry selected one of these weighing about two and a half pounds and very broad in the blade, and the Askari took another a size smaller. After Umslopogaas had put an extra edge on these two axe-heads, we fixed them to three feet six helves, of which Mr Mackenzie fortunately had some in stock, made of a light but exceedingly tough native wood, something like English ash, only more springy. When two suitable helves had been selected with great care and the ends of the hafts notched to prevent the hand from slipping, the axe-heads were fixed on them as firmly as possible, and the weapons immersed in a bucket of water for half an hour. The result of this was to swell the wood in the socket in such a fashion that nothing short of burning would get it out again. When this important matter had been attended to by Umslopogaas, I went into my room and proceeded to open a little tin-lined deal case, which contained — what do you think? — nothing more or less than four mail shirts.

It had happened to us three on a previous journey that we had made in another part of Africa to owe our lives to iron shirts of native make, and remembering this, I had suggested before we started on our present hazardous expedition that we should have some made to fit us. There was a little difficulty about this, as armour-making is pretty well an extinct art, but they can do most things in the way of steel work in Birmingham if they are put to it and you will pay the price, and the end of it was that they turned us out the loveliest steel shirts it is possible to see. The workmanship was exceedingly fine, the web being composed of thousands upon thousands of stout but tiny rings of the best steel made. These shirts, or rather steel-sleeved and high-necked jerseys, were lined with ventilated wash leather, were not bright, but browned like the barrel of a gun; and mine weighed exactly seven pounds and fitted me so well that I found I could wear it for days next to my skin without being chafed. Sir Henry had two, one of the ordinary make, viz. a jersey with little dependent flaps meant to afford some protection to the upper part of the thighs, and another of his own design fashioned on the pattern of the garments advertised as 'combinations' and weighing twelve pounds. This combination shirt, of which the seat was made of wash-leather, protected the whole body down to the knees, but was rather more cumbersome, inasmuch as it had to be laced up at the back and, of course, involved some extra weight. With these shirts were what looked like four brown cloth travelling caps with ear pieces. Each of these caps was, however, quilted with steel links so as to afford a most valuable protection for the head.

It seems almost laughable to talk of steel shirts in these days of bullets, against which they are of course quite useless; but where one has to do with savages, armed with cutting weapons such as assegais or battleaxes, they afford the most valuable protection, being, if well made, quite invulnerable to them. I have often thought that if only the English Government had in our savage wars, and more especially in the Zulu war, thought fit to serve out light steel shirts, there would be many a man alive today who, as it is, is dead and forgotten.

To return: on the present occasion we blessed our foresight in bringing these shirts, and also our good luck, in that they had not been stolen by our rascally bearers when they ran away with our goods. As Curtis had two, and after considerable deliberation, had made up his mind to wear his combination one himself — the extra three or four pounds' weight being a matter of no account to so strong a man, and the protection afforded to the thighs being a very important matter to a fighting man not armed with a shield of any kind — I suggested that he should lend the other to Umslopogaas, who was to share the danger and the glory of his post. He readily consented, and called the Zulu, who came bearing Sir Henry's axe, which he had now fixed up to his satisfaction, with him. When we showed him the steel shirt, and explained to him that we wanted him to wear it, he at first declined, saying that he had fought in his own skin for thirty years, and that he was not going to begin now to fight in an iron one. Thereupon I took a heavy spear, and, spreading the shirt upon the floor, drove the spear down upon it with all my strength, the weapon rebounding without leaving a mark upon the tempered steel. This exhibition half converted him; and when I pointed out to him how necessary it was that he should not let any old-fashioned prejudices he might possess stand in the way of a precaution which might preserve a valuable life at a time when men were scarce, and also that if he wore this shirt he might dispense with a shield, and so have both hands free, he yielded at once, and proceeded to invest his frame with the 'iron skin'. And indeed, although made for Sir Henry, it fitted the great Zulu like a skin. The two men were almost of a height; and, though Curtis looked the bigger man, I am inclined to think that the difference was more imaginary than real, the fact being that, although he was plumper and rounder, he was not really bigger, except in the arm. Umslopogaas had, comparatively speaking, thin arms, but they were as strong as wire ropes. At any rate, when they both stood, axe in hand, invested in the brown mail, which clung to their mighty forms like a web garment, showing the swell of every muscle and the curve of every line, they formed a pair that any ten men might shrink from meeting.

It was now nearly one o'clock in the morning, and the spies reported that, after having drunk the blood of the oxen and eaten enormous quantities of meat, the Masai were going to sleep round their watchfires; but that sentries had been posted at each opening of the kraal. Flossie, they added, was sitting not far from the wall in the centre of the western side of the kraal, and by her were the nurse and the white donkey, which was tethered to a peg. Her feet were bound with a rope, and warriors were lying about all round her.

As there was absolutely nothing further that could be done then we all took some supper, and went to lie down for a couple of hours. I could not help admiring the way in which old Umslopogaas flung himself upon the floor, and, unmindful of what was hanging over him, instantly sank into a deep sleep. I do not know how it was with the others, but I could not do as much. Indeed, as is usual with me on these occasions, I am sorry to say that I felt rather frightened; and, now that some of the enthusiasm had gone out of me, and I began to calmly contemplate what we had undertaken to do, truth compels me to add that I did not like it. We were but thirty men all told, a good many of whom were no doubt quite unused to fighting, and we were going to engage two hundred and fifty of the fiercest, bravest, and most formidable savages in Africa, who, to make matters worse, were protected by a stone wall. It was, indeed, a mad undertaking, and what made it even madder was the exceeding improbability of our being able to take up our positions without attracting the notice of the sentries. Of course if we once did that — and any slight accident, such as the chance discharge of a gun, might do it — we were done for, for the whole camp would be up in a second, and our only hope lay in surprise.

The bed whereon I lay indulging in these uncomfortable reflections was near an open window that looked on to the veranda, through which came an extraordinary sound of groaning and weeping. For a time I could not make out what it was, but at last I got up and, putting my head out of the window, stared about. Presently I saw a dim figure kneeling on the end of the veranda and beating his breast — in which I recognized Alphonse. Not being able to understand his French talk or what on earth he was at, I called to him and asked him what he was doing.

'Ah, monsieur,' he sighed, 'I do make prayer for the souls of those whom I shall slay tonight.'

'Indeed,' I said, 'then I wish that you would do it a little more quietly.'

Alphonse retreated, and I heard no more of his groans. And so the time passed, till at length Mr Mackenzie called me in a whisper through the window, for of course everything had now to be done in the most absolute silence. 'Three o'clock,' he said: 'we must begin to move at half-past.'

I told him to come in, and presently he entered, and I am bound to say that if it had not been that just then I had not got a laugh anywhere about me, I should have exploded at the sight he presented armed for battle. To begin with, he had on a clergyman's black swallow-tail and a kind of broad-rimmed black felt hat, both of which he had donned on account, he said, of their dark colour. In his hand was the Winchester repeating rifle we had lent him; and stuck in an elastic cricketing belt, like those worn by English boys, were, first, a huge buckhorn-handled carving knife with a guard to it, and next a long-barrelled Colt's revolver.

'Ah, my friend,' he said, seeing me staring at his belt, 'you are looking at my "carver". I thought it might come in handy if we came to close quarters; it is excellent steel, and many is the pig I have killed with it.'

By this time everybody was up and dressing. I put on a light Norfolk jacket over my mail shirt in order to have a pocket handy to hold my cartridges, and buckled on my revolver. Good did the same, but Sir Henry put on nothing except his mail shirt, steel-lined cap, and a pair of 'veldt-schoons' or soft hide shoes, his legs being bare from the knees down. His revolver he strapped on round his middle outside the armoured shirt.

Meanwhile Umslopogaas was mustering the men in the square under the big tree and going the rounds to see that each was properly armed, etc. At the last moment we made one change. Finding that two of the men who were to have gone with the firing parties knew little or nothing of guns, but were good spearsmen, we took away their rifles, supplied them with shields and long spears of the Masai pattern, and took them off to join Curtis, Umslopogaas, and the Askari in holding the wide opening; it having become clear to us that three men, however brave and strong, were too few for the work.

A Slaughter Grim and Great

Then there was a pause, and we stood there in the chilly silent darkness waiting till the moment came to start. It was, perhaps, the most trying time of all — that slow, slow quarter of an hour. The minutes seemed to drag along with leaden feet, and the quiet, the solemn hush, that brooded over all — big, as it were, with a coming fate, was most oppressive to the spirits. I once remember having to get up before dawn to see a man hanged, and I then went through a very similar set of sensations, only in the present instance my feelings were animated by that more vivid and personal element which naturally appertains rather to the person to be operated on than to the most sympathetic spectator. The solemn faces of the men, well aware that the short passage of an hour would mean for some, and perhaps all of them, the last great passage to the unknown or oblivion; the bated whispers in which they spoke; even Sir Henry's continuous and thoughtful examination of his woodcutter's axe and the fidgety way in which Good kept polishing his eyeglass, all told the same tale of nerves stretched pretty nigh to breaking-point. Only Umslopogaas, leaning as usual upon Inkosi-kaas and taking an occasional pinch of snuff, was to all appearance perfectly and completely unmoved. Nothing could touch his iron nerves.

The moon went down. For a long while she had been getting nearer and nearer to the horizon. Now she finally sank and left the world in darkness save for a faint grey tinge in the eastern sky that palely heralded the dawn.

Mr Mackenzie stood, watch in hand, his wife clinging to his arm and striving to stifle her sobs.

'Twenty minutes to four,' he said, 'it ought to be light enough to attack at twenty minutes past four. Captain Good had better be moving, he will want three or four minutes' start.'

Good gave one final polish to his eyeglass, nodded to us in a jocular sort of way — which I could not help feeling it must have cost him something to muster up — and, ever polite, took off his steel-lined cap to Mrs Mackenzie and started for his position at the head of the kraal, to reach which he had to make a detour by some paths known to the natives.

Just then one of the boys came in and reported that everybody in the Masai camp, with the exception of the two sentries who were walking up and down in front of the respective entrances, appeared to be fast asleep. Then the rest of us took the road. First came the guide, then Sir Henry, Umslopogaas, the Wakwafi Askari, and Mr Mackenzie's two mission natives armed with long spears and shields. I followed immediately after with Alphonse and five natives all armed with guns, and Mr Mackenzie brought up the rear with the six remaining natives.

The cattle kraal where the Masai were camped lay at the foot of the hill on which the house stood, or, roughly speaking, about eight hundred yards from the Mission buildings. The first five hundred yards of this distance we traversed quietly indeed, but at a good pace; after that we crept forward as silently as a leopard on his prey, gliding like ghosts from bush to bush and stone to stone. When I had gone a little way I chanced to look behind me, and saw the redoubtable Alphonse staggering along with white face and trembling knees, and his rifle, which was at full cock, pointed directly at the small of my back. Having halted and carefully put the rifle at 'safety', we started again, and all went well till we were within one hundred yards or so of the kraal, when his teeth began to chatter in the most aggressive way.

'If you don't stop that I will kill you,' I whispered savagely; for the idea of having all our lives sacrificed to a tooth-chattering cook was too much for me. I began to fear that he would betray us, and heartily wished we had left him behind.

'But, monsieur, I cannot help it,' he answered, 'it is the cold.'

Here was a dilemma, but fortunately I devised a plan. In the pocket of the coat I had on was a small piece of dirty rag that I had used some time before to clean a gun with. 'Put this in your mouth,' I whispered again, giving him the rag; 'and if I hear another sound you are a dead man.' I knew that that would stifle the clatter of his teeth. I must have looked as if I meant what I said, for he instantly obeyed me, and continued his journey in silence.

Then we crept on again.

At last we were within fifty yards of the kraal. Between us and it was an open space of sloping grass with only one mimosa bush and a couple of tussocks of a sort of thistle for cover. We were still hidden in fairly thick bush. It was beginning to grow light. The stars had paled and a sickly gleam played about the east and was reflected on the earth. We could see the outline of the kraal clearly enough, and could also make out the faint glimmer of the dying embers of the Masai camp-fires. We halted and watched, for the sentry we knew was posted at the opening. Presently he appeared, a fine tall fellow, walking idly up and down within five paces of the thorn-stopped entrance. We had hoped to catch him napping, but it was not to be. He seemed particularly wide awake. If we could not kill that man, and kill him silently, we were lost. There we crouched and watched him. Presently Umslopogaas, who was a few paces ahead of me, turned and made a sign, and next second I saw him go down on his stomach like a snake, and, taking an opportunity when the sentry's head was turned, begin to work his way through the grass without a sound.

The unconscious sentry commenced to hum a little tune, and Umslopogaas crept on. He reached the shelter of the mimosa bush unperceived and there waited. Still the sentry walked up and down. Presently he turned and looked over the wall into the camp. Instantly the human snake who was stalking him glided on ten yards and got behind one of the tussocks of the thistle-like plant, reaching it as the Elmoran turned again. As he did so his eye fell upon this patch of thistles, and it seemed to strike him that it did not look quite right. He advanced a pace towards it — halted, yawned, stooped down, picked up a little pebble and threw it at it. It hit Umslopogaas upon the head, luckily not upon the armour shirt. Had it done so the clink would have betrayed us. Luckily, too, the shirt was browned and not bright steel, which would certainly have been detected. Apparently satisfied that there was nothing wrong, he then gave over his investigations and contented himself with leaning on his spear and standing gazing idly at the tuft. For at least three minutes did he stand thus, plunged apparently in a gentle reverie, and there we lay in the last extremity of anxiety, expecting every moment that we should be discovered or that some untoward accident would happen. I could hear Alphonse's teeth going like anything on the oiled rag, and turning my head round made an awful face at him. But I am bound to state that my own heart was at much the same game as the Frenchman's castanets, while the perspiration was pouring from my body, causing the wash-leather-lined shirt to stick to me unpleasantly, and altogether I was in the pitiable state known by schoolboys as a 'blue fright'.

At last the ordeal came to an end. The sentry glanced at the east, and appeared to note with satisfaction that his period of duty was coming to an end — as indeed it was, once and for all — for he rubbed his hands and began to walk again briskly to warm himself.

The moment his back was turned the long black snake glided on again, and reached the other thistle tuft, which was within a couple of paces of his return beat.

Back came the sentry and strolled right past the tuft, utterly unconscious of the presence that was crouching behind it. Had he looked down he could scarcely have failed to see, but he did not do so.

He passed, and then his hidden enemy erected himself, and with outstretched hand followed in his tracks.

A moment more, and, just as the Elmoran was about to turn, the great Zulu made a spring, and in the growing light we could see his long lean hands close round the Masai's throat. Then followed a convulsive twining of the two dark bodies, and in another second I saw the Masai's head bent back, and heard a sharp crack, something like that of a dry twig snapping, and he fell down upon the ground, his limbs moving spasmodically.

Umslopogaas had put out all his iron strength and broken the warrior's neck.

For a moment he knelt upon his victim, still gripping his throat till he was sure that there was nothing more to fear from him, and then he rose and beckoned to us to advance, which we did on all fours, like a colony of huge apes. On reaching the kraal we saw that the Masai had still further choked this entrance, which was about ten feet wide — no doubt in order to guard against attack — by dragging four or five tops of mimosa trees up to it. So much the better for us, I reflected; the more obstruction there was the slower would they be able to come through. Here we separated; Mackenzie and his party creeping up under the shadow of the wall to the left, while Sir Henry and Umslopogaas took their stations one on each side of the thorn fence, the two spearmen and the Askari lying down in front of it. I and my men crept on up the right side of the kraal, which was about fifty paces long.

When I was two-thirds up I halted, and placed my men at distances of four paces from one another, keeping Alphonse close to me, however. Then I peeped for the first time over the wall. It was getting fairly light now, and the first thing I saw was the white donkey, exactly opposite to me, and close by it I could make out the pale face of little Flossie, who was sitting as the lad had described, some ten paces from the wall. Round her lay many warriors, sleeping. At distances all over the surface of the kraal were the remains of fires, round each of which slept some five-and-twenty Masai, for the most part gorged with food. Now and then a man would raise himself, yawn, and look at the east, which was turning primrose; but none got up. I determined to wait another five minutes, both to allow the light to increase, so that we could make better shooting, and to give Good and his party — of whom we could see or hear nothing — every opportunity to make ready.

The quiet dawn began to throw her ever-widening mantle over plain and forest and river — mighty Kenia, wrapped in the silence of eternal snows, looked out across the earth — till presently a beam from the unrisen sun lit upon his heaven-kissing crest and purpled it with blood; the sky above grew blue, and tender as a mother's smile; a bird began to pipe his morning song, and a little breeze passing through the bush shook down the dewdrops in millions to refresh the waking world. Everywhere was peace and the happiness of arising strength, everywhere save in the heart of cruel man!

Suddenly, just as I was nerving myself for the signal, having already selected my man on whom I meant to open fire — a great fellow sprawling on the ground within three feet of little Flossie — Alphonse's teeth began to chatter again like the hoofs of a galloping giraffe, making a great noise in the silence. The rag had dropped out in the agitation of his mind. Instantly a Masai within three paces of us woke, and, sitting up, gazed about him, looking for the cause of the sound. Moved beyond myself, I brought the butt-end of my rifle down on to the pit of the Frenchman's stomach. This stopped his chattering; but, as he doubled up, he managed to let off his gun in such a manner that the bullet passed within an inch of my head.

There was no need for a signal now. From both sides of the kraal broke out a waving line of fire, in which I myself joined, managing with a snap shot to knock over my Masai by Flossie, just as he was jumping up. Then from the top end of the kraal there rang an awful yell, in which I rejoiced to recognize Good's piercing notes rising clear and shrill above the din, and in another second followed such a scene as I have never seen before nor shall again. With an universal howl of terror and fury the brawny crowd of savages within the kraal sprang to their feet, many of them to fall again beneath our well-directed hail of lead before they had moved a yard. For a moment they stood undecided, and then hearing the cries and curses that rose unceasingly from the top end of the kraal, and bewildered by the storm of bullets, they as by one impulse rushed down towards the thorn-stopped entrance. As they went we kept pouring our fire with terrible effect into the thickening mob as fast as we could load. I had emptied my repeater of the ten shots it contained and was just beginning to slip in some more when I bethought me of little Flossie. Looking up, I saw that the white donkey was lying kicking, having been knocked over either by one of our bullets or a Masai spear-thrust. There were no living Masai near, but the black nurse was on her feet and with a spear cutting the rope that bound Flossie's feet. Next second she ran to the wall of the kraal and began to climb over it, an example which the little girl followed. But Flossie was evidently very stiff and cramped, and could only go slowly, and as she went two Masai flying down the kraal caught sight of her and rushed towards her to kill her. The first fellow came up just as the poor little girl, after a desperate effort to climb the wall, fell back into the kraal. Up flashed the great spear, and as it did so a bullet from my rifle found its home in the holder's ribs, and over he went like a shot rabbit. But behind him was the other man, and, alas, I had only that one cartridge in the magazine! Flossie had scrambled to her feet and was facing the second man, who was advancing with raised spear. I turned my head aside and felt sick as death. I could not bear to see him stab her. Glancing up again, to my surprise I saw the Masai's spear lying on the ground, while the man himself was staggering about with both hands to his head. Suddenly I saw a puff of smoke proceeding apparently from Flossie, and the man fell down headlong. Then I remembered the Derringer pistol she carried, and saw that she had fired both barrels of it at him, thereby saving her life. In another instant she had made an effort, and assisted by the nurse, who was lying on the top, had scrambled over the wall, and I knew that she was, comparatively speaking, safe.

All this takes time to tell, but I do not suppose that it took more than fifteen seconds to enact. I soon got the magazine of the repeater filled again with cartridges, and once more opened fire, not on the seething black mass which was gathering at the end of the kraal, but on fugitives who bethought them to climb the wall. I picked off several of these men, moving down towards the end of the kraal as I did so, and arriving at the corner, or rather the bend of the oval, in time to see, and by means of my rifle to assist in, the mighty struggle that took place there.

By this time some two hundred Masai — allowing that we had up to the present accounted for fifty — had gathered together in front of the thorn-stopped entrance, driven thither by the spears of Good's men, whom they doubtless supposed were a large force instead of being but ten strong. For some reason it never occurred to them to try and rush the wall, which they could have scrambled over with comparative ease; they all made for the fence, which was really a strongly interwoven fortification. With a bound the first warrior went at it, and even before he touched the ground on the other side I saw Sir Henry's great axe swing up and fall with awful force upon his feather head-piece, and he sank into the middle of the thorns. Then with a yell and a crash they began to break through as they might, and ever as they came the great axe swung and Inkosi-kaas flashed and they fell dead one by one, each man thus helping to build up a barrier against his fellows. Those who escaped the axes of the pair fell at the hands of the Askari and the two Mission Kaffirs, and those who passed scatheless from them were brought low by my own and Mackenzie's fire.

Faster and more furious grew the fighting. Single Masai would spring upon the dead bodies of their comrades, and engage one or other of the axemen with their long spears; but, thanks chiefly to the mail shirts, the result was always the same. Presently there was a great swing of the axe, a crashing sound, and another dead Masai. That is, if the man was engaged with Sir Henry. If it was Umslopogaas that he fought with the result indeed would be the same, but it would be differently attained. It was but rarely that the Zulu used the crashing double-handed stroke; on the contrary, he did little more than tap continually at his adversary's head, pecking at it with the pole-axe end of the axe as a woodpecker pecks at rotten wood. Presently a peck would go home, and his enemy would drop down with a neat little circular hole in his forehead or skull, exactly similar to that which a cheese-scoop makes in a cheese. He never used the broad blade of the axe except when hard pressed, or when striking at a shield. He told me afterwards that he did not consider it sportsmanlike.

Good and his men were quite close by now, and our people had to cease firing into the mass for fear of killing some of them (as it was, one of them was slain in this way). Mad and desperate with fear, the Masai by a frantic effort burst through the thorn fence and piled-up dead, and, sweeping Curtis, Umslopogaas, and the other three before them, into the open. And now it was that we began to lose men fast. Down went our poor Askari who was armed with the axe, a great spear standing out a foot behind his back; and before long the two spearsmen who had stood with him went down too, dying fighting like tigers; and others of our party shared their fate. For a moment I feared the fight was lost — certainly it trembled in the balance. I shouted to my men to cast down their rifles, and to take spears and throw themselves into the melee. They obeyed, their blood being now thoroughly up, and Mr Mackenzie's people followed their example.

This move had a momentary good result, but still the fight hung in the balance.

Our people fought magnificently, hurling themselves upon the dark mass of Elmoran, hewing, thrusting, slaying, and being slain. And ever above the din rose Good's awful yell of encouragement as he plunged to wherever the fight was thickest; and ever, with an almost machine-like regularity, the two axes rose and fell, carrying death and disablement at every stroke. But I could see that the strain was beginning to tell upon Sir Henry, who was bleeding from several flesh wounds: his breath was coming in gasps, and the veins stood out on his forehead like blue and knotted cords. Even Umslopogaas, man of iron that he was, was hard pressed. I noticed that he had given up 'woodpecking', and was now using the broad blade of Inkosi-kaas, 'browning' his enemy wherever he could hit him, instead of drilling scientific holes in his head. I myself did not go into the melee, but hovered outside like the swift 'back' in a football scrimmage, putting a bullet through a Masai whenever I got a chance. I was more use so. I fired forty-nine cartridges that morning, and I did not miss many shots.

Presently, do as we would, the beam of the balance began to rise against us. We had not more than fifteen or sixteen effectives left now, and the Masai had at least fifty. Of course if they had kept their heads, and shaken themselves together, they could soon have made an end of the matter; but that is just what they did not do, not having yet recovered from their start, and some of them having actually fled from their sleeping-places without their weapons. Still by now many individuals were fighting with their normal courage and discretion, and this alone was sufficient to defeat us. To make matters worse just then, when Mackenzie's rifle was empty, a brawny savage armed with a 'sime', or sword, made a rush for him. The clergyman flung down his gun, and drawing his huge carver from his elastic belt (his revolver had dropped out in the fight), they closed in desperate struggle. Presently, locked in a close embrace, missionary and Masai rolled on the ground behind the wall, and for some time I, being amply occupied with my own affairs, and in keeping my skin from being pricked, remained in ignorance of his fate or how the duel had ended.

To and fro surged the fight, slowly turning round like the vortex of a human whirlpool, and the matter began to look very bad for us. Just then, however, a fortunate thing happened. Umslopogaas, either by accident or design, broke out of the ring and engaged a warrior at some few paces from it. As he did so, another man ran up and struck him with all his force between his shoulders with his great spear, which, falling on the tough steel shirt, failed to pierce it and rebounded. For a moment the man stared aghast — protective armour being unknown among these tribes — and then he yelled out at the top of his voice —

'They are devils — bewitched, bewitched!' And seized by a sudden panic, he threw down his spear, and began to fly. I cut short his career with a bullet, and Umslopogaas brained his man, and then the panic spread to the others.

'Bewitched, bewitched!' they cried, and tried to escape in every direction, utterly demoralized and broken-spirited, for the most part even throwing down their shields and spears.

On the last scene of that dreadful fight I need not dwell. It was a slaughter great and grim, in which no quarter was asked or given. One incident, however, is worth detailing. Just as I was hoping that it was all done with, suddenly from under a heap of slain where he had been hiding, an unwounded warrior sprang up, and, clearing the piles of dying dead like an antelope, sped like the wind up the kraal towards the spot where I was standing at the moment. But he was not alone, for Umslopogaas came gliding on his tracks with the peculiar swallow-like motion for which he was noted, and as they neared me I recognized in the Masai the herald of the previous night. Finding that, run as he would, his pursuer was gaining on him, the man halted and turned round to give battle. Umslopogaas also pulled up.

'Ah, ah,' he cried, in mockery, to the Elmoran, 'it is thou whom I talked with last night — the Lygonani! the Herald! the capturer of little girls — he who would kill a little girl! And thou didst hope to stand man to man and face to face with Umslopogaas, an Induna of the tribe of the Maquilisini, of the people of the Amazulu? Behold, thy prayer is granted! And I didst swear to hew thee limb from limb, thou insolent dog. Behold, I will do it even now!'

The Masai ground his teeth with fury, and charged at the Zulu with his spear. As he came, Umslopogaas deftly stepped aside, and swinging Inkosi-kaas high above his head with both hands, brought the broad blade down with such fearful force from behind upon the Masai's shoulder just where the neck is set into the frame, that its razor edge shore right through bone and flesh and muscle, almost severing the head and one arm from the body.

'*Ou!*' ejaculated Umslopogaas, contemplating the corpse of his foe; 'I have kept my word. It was a good stroke.'

Alphonse Explains

And so the fight was ended. On returning from the shocking scene it suddenly struck me that I had seen nothing of Alphonse since the moment, some twenty minutes before — for though this fight has taken a long while to describe, it did not take long in reality — when I had been forced to hit him in the wind with the result of nearly getting myself shot. Fearing that the poor little man had perished in the battle, I began to hunt among the dead for his body, but, not being able either to see or hear anything of it, I concluded that he must have survived, and walked down the side of the kraal where we had first taken our stand, calling him by name. Now some fifteen paces back from the kraal wall stood a very ancient tree of the banyan species. So ancient was it that all the inside had in the course of ages decayed away, leaving nothing but a shell of bark.

'Alphonse,' I called, as I walked down the wall. 'Alphonse!'

'Oui, monsieur,' answered a voice. 'Here am I.'

I looked round but could see nobody. 'Where?' I cried.

'Here am I, monsieur, in the tree.'

I looked, and there, peering out of a hole in the trunk of the banyan about five feet from the ground, I saw a pale face and a pair of large mustachios, one clipped short and the other as lamentably out of curl as the tail of a newly whipped pug. Then, for the first time, I realized what I had suspected before — namely, that Alphonse was an arrant coward. I walked up to him. 'Come out of that hole,' I said.

'Is it finished, monsieur?' he asked anxiously; 'quite finished? Ah, the horrors I have undergone, and the prayers I have uttered!'

'Come out, you little wretch,' I said, for I did not feel amiable; 'it is all over.'

'So, monsieur, then my prayers have prevailed? I emerge,' and he did.

As we were walking down together to join the others, who were gathered in a group by the wide entrance to the kraal, which now resembled a veritable charnel-house, a Masai, who had escaped so far and been hiding under a bush, suddenly sprang up and charged furiously at us. Off went Alphonse with a howl of terror, and after him flew the Masai, bent upon doing some execution before he died. He soon overtook the poor little Frenchman, and would have finished him then and there had I not, just as Alphonse made a last agonized double in the vain hope of avoiding the yard of steel that was flashing in his immediate rear, managed to plant a bullet between the Elmoran's broad shoulders, which brought matters to a satisfactory conclusion so far as the Frenchman was concerned. But just then he tripped and fell flat, and the body of the Masai fell right on the top of him, moving convulsively in the death struggle. Thereupon there arose such a series of piercing howls that I concluded that before he died the savage must have managed to stab poor Alphonse. I ran up in a hurry and pulled the Masai off, and there beneath him lay Alphonse covered with blood and jerking himself about like a galvanized frog. Poor fellow! thought I, he is done for, and kneeling down by him I began to search for his wound as well as his struggles would allow.

'Oh, the hole in my back!' he yelled. 'I am murdered. I am dead. Oh, Annette!'

I searched again, but could see no wound. Then the truth dawned on me — the man was frightened, not hurt.

'Get up!' I shouted, 'Get up. Aren't you ashamed of yourself? You are not touched.'

Thereupon he rose, not a penny the worse. 'But, monsieur, I thought I was,' he said apologetically; 'I did not know that I had conquered.' Then, giving the body of the Masai a kick, he ejaculated triumphantly, 'Ah, dog of a black savage, thou art dead; what victory!'

Thoroughly disgusted, I left Alphonse to look after himself, which he did by following me like a shadow, and proceeded to join the others by the large entrance. The first thing that I saw was Mackenzie, seated on a stone with a handkerchief twisted round his thigh, from which he was bleeding freely, having, indeed, received a spear-thrust that passed right through it, and still holding in his hand his favourite carving knife now bent nearly double, from which I gathered that he had been successful in his rough and tumble with the Elmoran.

'Ah, Quatermain!' he sang out in a trembling, excited voice, 'so we have conquered; but it is a sorry sight, a sorry sight;' and then breaking into broad Scotch and glancing at the bent knife in his hand, 'It fashes me sair to have bent my best carver on the breastbone of a savage,' and he laughed hysterically. Poor fellow, what between his wound and the killing excitement he had undergone his nerves were much shaken, and no wonder! It is hard upon a man of peace and kindly heart to be called upon to join in such a gruesome business. But there, fate puts us sometimes into very comical positions!

At the kraal entrance the scene was a strange one. The slaughter was over by now, and the wounded men had been put out of their pain, for no quarter had been given. The bush-closed entrance was trampled flat, and in place of bushes it was filled with the bodies of dead men. Dead men, everywhere dead men — they lay about in knots, they were flung by ones and twos in every position upon the open spaces, for all the world like the people on the grass in one of the London parks on a particularly hot Sunday in August. In front of this entrance, on a space which had been cleared of dead and of the shields and spears which were scattered in all directions as they had fallen or been thrown from the hands of their owners, stood and lay the survivors of the awful struggle, and at their feet were four wounded men. We had gone into the fight thirty strong, and of the thirty but fifteen remained alive, and five of them (including Mr Mackenzie) were wounded, two mortally. Of those who held the entrance, Curtis and the Zulu alone remained. Good had lost five men killed, I had lost two killed, and Mackenzie no less than five out of the six with him. As for the survivors they were, with the exception of myself who had never come to close quarters, red from head to foot — Sir Henry's armour might have been painted that colour — and utterly exhausted, except Umslopogaas, who, as he grimly stood on a little mound above a heap of dead, leaning as usual upon his axe, did not seem particularly distressed, although the skin over the hole in his head palpitated violently.

'Ah, Macumazahn!' he said to me as I limped up, feeling very sick, 'I told thee that it would be a good fight, and it has. Never have I seen a better, or one more bravely fought. As for this iron shirt, surely it is "tagati" [bewitched]; nothing could pierce it. Had it not been for the garment I should have been *there*,' and he nodded towards the great pile of dead men beneath him.

'I give it thee; thou art a brave man,' said Sir Henry, briefly.

'Koos!' answered the Zulu, deeply pleased both at the gift and the compliment. 'Thou, too, Incubu, didst bear thyself as a man, but I must give thee some lessons with the axe; thou dost waste thy strength.'

Just then Mackenzie asked about Flossie, and we were all greatly relieved when one of the men said he had seen her flying towards the house with the nurse. Then bearing such of the wounded as could be moved at the moment with us, we slowly made our way towards the Mission-house, spent with toil and bloodshed, but with the glorious sense of victory against overwhelming odds glowing in our hearts. We had saved the life of the little maid, and taught the Masai of those parts a lesson that they will not forget for ten years — but at what a cost!

Painfully we made our way up the hill which, just a little more than an hour before, we had descended under such different circumstances. At the gate of the wall stood Mrs Mackenzie waiting for us. When her eyes fell upon us, however, she shrieked out, and covered her face with her hands, crying, 'Horrible, horrible!' Nor were her fears allayed when she discovered her worthy husband being borne upon an improvized stretcher; but her doubts as to the nature of his injury were soon set at rest. Then when in a few brief words I had told her the upshot of the struggle (of which Flossie, who had arrived in safety, had been able to explain something) she came up to me and solemnly kissed me on the forehead.

'God bless you all, Mr Quatermain; you have saved my child's life,' she said simply.

Then we went in and got our clothes off and doctored our wounds; I am glad to say I had none, and Sir Henry's and Good's were, thanks to those invaluable chain shirts, of a comparatively harmless nature, and to be dealt with by means of a few stitches and sticking- plaster. Mackenzie's, however, were serious, though fortunately the spear had not severed any large artery. After that we had a bath, and what a luxury it was! And having clad ourselves in ordinary clothes, proceeded to the dining-room, where breakfast was set as usual. It was curious sitting down there, drinking tea and eating toast in an ordinary nineteenth-century sort of way just as though we had not employed the early hours in a regular primitive hand-to-hand Middle-Ages kind of struggle. As Good said, the whole thing seemed more as though one had had a bad nightmare just before being called, than as a deed done. When we were finishing our breakfast the door opened, and in came little Flossie, very pale and tottery, but quite unhurt. She kissed us all and thanked us. I congratulated her on the presence of mind she had shown in shooting the Masai with her Derringer pistol, and thereby saving her own life.

'Oh, don't talk of it!' she said, beginning to cry hysterically; 'I shall never forget his face as he went turning round and round, never — I can see it now.'

I advised her to go to bed and get some sleep, which she did, and awoke in the evening quite recovered, so far as her strength was concerned. It struck me as an odd thing that a girl who could find the nerve to shoot a huge black ruffian rushing to kill her with a spear should have been so affected at the thought of it afterwards; but it is, after all, characteristic of the sex. Poor Flossie! I fear that her nerves will not get over that night in the Masai camp for many a long year. She told me afterwards that it was the suspense that was so awful, having to sit there hour after hour through the livelong night utterly ignorant as to whether or not any attempt was to be made to rescue her. She said that on the whole she did not expect it, knowing how few of us, and how many of the Masai — who, by the way, came continually to stare at her, most of them never having seen a white person before, and handled her arms and hair with their filthy paws. She said also that she had made up her mind that if she saw no signs of succour by the time the first rays of the rising sun reached the kraal she would kill herself with the pistol, for the nurse had heard the Lygonani say that they were to be tortured to death as soon as the sun was up if one of the white men did not come in their place. It was an awful resolution to have to take, but she meant to act on it, and I have little doubt but what she would have done so. Although she was at an age when in England girls are in the schoolroom and come down to dessert, this 'child of the wilderness' had more courage, discretion, and power of mind than many a woman of mature age nurtured in idleness and luxury, with minds carefully drilled and educated out of any originality or self-resource that nature may have endowed them with.

When breakfast was over we all turned in and had a good sleep, only getting up in time for dinner; after which meal we once more adjourned, together with all the available population — men, women, youths, and girls — to the scene of the morning's slaughter, our object being to bury our own dead and get rid of the Masai by flinging them into the Tana River, which ran within fifty yards of the kraal. On reaching the spot we disturbed thousands upon thousands of vultures and a sort of brown bush eagle, which had been flocking to the feast from miles and miles away. Often have I watched these great and repulsive birds, and marvelled at the extraordinary speed with which they arrive on a scene of slaughter. A buck falls to your rifle, and within a minute high in the blue ether appears a speck that gradually grows into a vulture, then another, and another. I have heard many theories advanced to account for the wonderful power of perception nature has given these birds. My own, founded on a good deal of observation, is that the vultures, gifted as they are with powers of sight greater than those given by the most powerful glass, quarter out the heavens among themselves, and hanging in mid-air at a vast height — probably from two to three miles above the earth — keep watch, each of them, over an enormous stretch of country. Presently one of them spies food, and instantly begins to sink towards it. Thereon his next neighbour in the airy heights sailing leisurely through the blue gulf, at a distance perhaps of some miles, follows his example, knowing that food has been sighted. Down he goes, and all the vultures within sight of him follow after, and so do all those in sight of them. In this way the vultures for twenty miles round can be summoned to the feast in a few minutes.

We buried our dead in solemn silence, Good being selected to read the Burial Service over them (in the absence of Mr Mackenzie, confined to bed), as he was generally allowed to possess the best voice and most impressive manner. It was melancholy in the extreme, but, as Good said, it might have been worse, for we might have had 'to bury ourselves'. I pointed out that this would have been a difficult feat, but I knew what he meant.

Next we set to work to load an ox-wagon which had been brought round from the Mission with the dead bodies of the Masai, having first collected the spears, shields, and other arms. We loaded the wagon five times, about fifty bodies to the load, and emptied it into the Tana. From this it was evident that very few of the Masai could have escaped. The crocodiles must have been well fed that night. One of the last bodies we picked up was that of the sentry at the upper end. I asked Good how he managed to kill him, and he told me that he had crept up much as Umslopogaas had done, and stabbed him with his sword. He groaned a good deal, but fortunately nobody heard him. As Good said, it was a horrible thing to have to do, and most unpleasantly like cold-blooded murder.

And so with the last body that floated away down the current of the Tana ended the incident of our attack on the Masai camp. The spears and shields and other arms we took up to the Mission, where they filled an outhouse. One incident, however, I must not forget to mention. As we were returning from performing the obsequies of our Masai friends we passed the hollow tree where Alphonse had secreted himself in the morning. It so happened that the little man himself was with us assisting in our unpleasant task with a far better will than he had shown where live Masai were concerned. Indeed, for each body that he handled he found an appropriate sarcasm. Alphonse throwing Masai into the Tana was a very different creature from Alphonse flying for dear life from the spear of a live Masai. He was quite merry and gay, he clapped his hands and warbled snatches of French songs as the grim dead warriors went 'splash' into the running waters to carry a message of death and defiance to their kindred a hundred miles below. In short, thinking that he wanted taking down a peg, I suggested holding a court-martial on him for his conduct in the morning.

Accordingly we brought him to the tree where he had hidden, and proceeded to sit in judgment on him, Sir Henry explaining to him in the very best French the unheard-of cowardice and enormity of his conduct, more especially in letting the oiled rag out of his mouth, whereby he nearly aroused the Masai camp with teeth-chattering and brought about the failure of our plans: ending up with a request for an explanation.

But if we expected to find Alphonse at a loss and put him to open shame we were destined to be disappointed. He bowed and scraped and smiled, and acknowledged that his conduct might at first blush appear strange, but really it was not, inasmuch as his teeth were not chattering from fear — oh, dear no! oh, certainly not! he marvelled how the 'messieurs' could think of such a thing — but from the chill air of the morning. As for the rag, if monsieur could have but tasted its evil flavour, being compounded indeed of a mixture of stale paraffin oil, grease, and gunpowder, monsieur himself would have spat it out. But he did nothing of the sort; he determined to keep it there till, alas! his stomach 'revolted', and the rag was ejected in an access of involuntary sickness.

'And what have you to say about getting into the hollow tree?' asked Sir Henry, keeping his countenance with difficulty.

'But, monsieur, the explanation is easy; oh, most easy! it was thus: I stood there by the kraal wall, and the little grey monsieur hit me in the stomach so that my rifle exploded, and the battle began. I watched whilst recovering myself from monsieur's cruel blow; then, messieurs, I felt the heroic blood of my grandfather boil up in my veins. The sight made me mad. I ground my teeth! Fire flashed from my eyes! I shouted "En avant!" and longed to slay. Before my eyes there rose a vision of my heroic grandfather! In short, I was mad! I was a warrior indeed! But then in my heart I heard a small voice: "Alphonse," said the voice, "restrain thyself, Alphonse! Give not way to this evil passion! These men, though black, are brothers! And thou wouldst slay them? Cruel Alphonse!" The voice was right. I knew it; I was about to perpetrate the most horrible cruelties: to wound! to massacre! to tear limb from limb! And how restrain myself? I looked round; I saw the tree, I perceived the hole. "Entomb thyself," said the voice, "and hold on tight! Thou wilt thus overcome temptation by main force!" It was bitter, just when the blood of my heroic grandfather boiled most fiercely; but I obeyed! I dragged my unwilling feet along; I entombed myself! Through the hole I watched the battle! I shouted curses and defiance on the foe! I noted them fall with satisfaction! Why not? I had not robbed them of their lives. Their gore was not upon my head. The blood of my heroic —'

'Oh, get along with you, you little cur!' broke out Sir Henry, with a shout of laughter, and giving Alphonse a good kick which sent him flying off with a rueful face.

In the evening I had an interview with Mr Mackenzie, who was suffering a good deal from his wounds, which Good, who was a skilful though unqualified doctor, was treating him for. He told me that this occurrence had taught him a lesson, and that, if he recovered safely, he meant to hand over the Mission to a younger man, who was already on his road to join him in his work, and return to England.

'You see, Quatermain,' he said, 'I made up my mind to it, this very morning, when we were creeping down those benighted savages. "If we live through this and rescue Flossie alive," I said to myself, "I will go home to

England; I have had enough of savages." Well, I did not think that we should live through it at the time; but thanks be to God and you four, we have lived through it, and I mean to stick to my resolution, lest a worse thing befall us. Another such time would kill my poor wife. And besides, Quatermain, between you and me, I am well off; it is thirty thousand pounds I am worth today, and every farthing of it made by honest trade and savings in the bank at Zanzibar, for living here costs me next to nothing. So though it will be hard to leave this place, which I have made to blossom like a rose in the wilderness, and harder still to leave the people I have taught, I shall go.'

'I congratulate you on your decision,' answered I, 'for two reasons. The first is, that you owe a duty to your wife and daughter, and more especially to the latter, who should receive some education and mix with girls of her own race, otherwise she will grow up wild, shunning her kind. The other is, that as sure as I am standing here, sooner or later the Masai will try to avenge the slaughter inflicted on them today. Two or three men are sure to have escaped the confusion who will carry the story back to their people, and the result will be that a great expedition will one day be sent against you. It might be delayed for a year, but sooner or later it will come. Therefore, if only for that reason, I should go. When once they have learnt that you are no longer here they may perhaps leave the place alone.'

'You are quite right,' answered the clergyman. 'I will turn my back upon this place in a month. But it will be a wrench, it will be a wrench.'

Into the Unknown

A week had passed, and we all sat at supper one night in the Mission dining-room, feeling very much depressed in spirits, for the reason that we were going to say goodbye to our kind friends, the Mackenzies, and depart upon our way at dawn on the morrow. Nothing more had been seen or heard of the Masai, and save for a spear or two which had been overlooked and was rusting in the grass, and a few empty cartridges where we had stood outside the wall, it would have been difficult to tell that the old cattle kraal at the foot of the slope had been the scene of so desperate a struggle. Mackenzie was, thanks chiefly to his being so temperate a man, rapidly recovering from his wound, and could get about on a pair of crutches; and as for the other wounded men, one had died of gangrene, and the rest were in a fair way to recovery. Mr Mackenzie's caravan of men had also returned from the coast, so that the station was now amply garrisoned.

Under these circumstances we concluded, warm and pressing as were the invitations for us to stay, that it was time to move on, first to Mount Kenia, and thence into the unknown in search of the mysterious white race which we had set our hearts on discovering. This time we were going to progress by means of the humble but useful donkey, of which we had collected no less than a dozen, to carry our goods and chattels, and, if necessary, ourselves. We had now but two Wakwafis left for servants, and found it quite impossible to get other natives to venture with us into the unknown parts we proposed to explore — and small blame to them. After all, as Mr Mackenzie said, it was odd that three men, each of whom possessed many of those things that are supposed to make life worth living — health, sufficient means, and position, etc. — should from their own pleasure start out upon a wild-goose chase, from which the chances were they never would return. But then that is what Englishmen are, adventurers to the backbone; and all our magnificent muster-roll of colonies, each of which will in time become a great nation, testify to the extraordinary value of the spirit of adventure which at first sight looks like a mild form of lunacy. 'Adventurer' — he that goes out to meet whatever may come. Well, that is what we all do in the world one way or another, and, speaking for myself, I am proud of the title, because it implies a brave heart and a trust in Providence. Besides, when many and many a noted Croesus, at whose feet the people worship, and many and many a time-serving and word-coining politician are forgotten, the names of those grand-hearted old adventurers who have made England what she is, will be remembered and taught with love and pride to little children whose unshaped spirits yet slumber in the womb of centuries to be. Not that we three can expect to be numbered with such as these, yet have we done something — enough, perhaps, to throw a garment over the nakedness of our folly.

That evening, whilst we were sitting on the veranda, smoking a pipe before turning in, who should come up to us but Alphonse, and, with a magnificent bow, announce his wish for an interview. Being requested to 'fire away', he explained at some length that he was anxious to attach himself to our party — a statement that astonished me not a little, knowing what a coward the little man was. The reason, however, soon appeared. Mr Mackenzie was going down to the coast, and thence on to England. Now, if he went down country, Alphonse was persuaded that he would be seized, extradited, sent to France, and to penal servitude. This was the idea that haunted him, as King Charles's head haunted Mr Dick, and he brooded over it till his imagination exaggerated the danger ten times. As a matter of fact, the probability is that his offence against the laws of his country had long ago been forgotten, and that he would have been allowed to pass unmolested anywhere except in France; but he could not be got to see this. Constitutional coward as the little man was, he infinitely preferred to face the certain hardships and great risks and dangers of such an expedition as ours, than to expose himself, notwithstanding his intense longing for his native land, to the possible scrutiny of a police officer — which is after all only another exemplification of the truth that, to the majority of men, a far-off foreseen danger, however shadowy, is much more terrible than the most serious present emergency. After listening to what he had to say, we consulted among ourselves, and finally agreed, with Mr Mackenzie's knowledge and consent, to accept his offer. To begin with, we were very short-handed, and Alphonse was a quick, active fellow, who could turn his hand to anything, and cook — ah, he *could* cook! I believe that he would have made a palatable dish of those gaiters of his heroic grandfather which he was so fond of talking about. Then he was a good-tempered little man, and merry as a monkey, whilst his pompous, vainglorious talk was a source of infinite amusement to us; and what is more, he never bore malice. Of course, his being so pronounced a coward was a great drawback to him, but now that we knew his weakness we could more or less guard against it. So, after warning him of the undoubted risks he was exposing himself to, we told him that we would accept his offer on condition that he would promise implicit obedience to our orders. We also promised to give him wages at the rate of ten pounds a month should he ever return to a civilized country to receive them. To all of this he agreed with alacrity, and retired to write a letter to his Annette, which Mr Mackenzie promised to post when he got down country. He read it to us afterwards, Sir Henry translating, and a wonderful composition it was. I am sure the depth of his devotion and the narration of his sufferings in a barbarous country, 'far, far from thee, Annette, for whose adored sake I endure such sorrow,' ought to have touched the feelings of the stoniest-hearted chambermaid.

Well, the morrow came, and by seven o'clock the donkeys were all loaded, and the time of parting was at hand. It was a melancholy business, especially saying goodbye to dear little Flossie. She and I were great friends, and often used to have talks together — but her nerves had never got over the shock of that awful night when she lay in the power of those bloodthirsty Masai. 'Oh,

Mr Quatermain,' she cried, throwing her arms round my neck and bursting into tears, 'I can't bear to say goodbye to you. I wonder when we shall meet again?'

'I don't know, my dear little girl,' I said, 'I am at one end of life and you are at the other. I have but a short time before me at best, and most things lie in the past, but I hope that for you there are many long and happy years, and everything lies in the future. By-and-by you will grow into a beautiful woman, Flossie, and all this wild life will be like a far-off dream to you; but I hope, even if we never do meet again, that you will think of your old friend and remember what I say to you now. Always try to be good, my dear, and to do what is right, rather than what happens to be pleasant, for in the end, whatever sneering people may say, what is good and what is happy are the same. Be unselfish, and whenever you can, give a helping hand to others — for the world is full of suffering, my dear, and to alleviate it is the noblest end that we can set before us. If you do that you will become a sweet and God-fearing woman, and make many people's lives a little brighter, and then you will not have lived, as so many of your sex do, in vain. And now I have given you a lot of old-fashioned advice, and so I am going to give you something to sweeten it with. You see this little piece of paper. It is what is called a cheque. When we are gone give it to your father with this note — not before, mind. You will marry one day, my dear little Flossie, and it is to buy you a wedding present which you are to wear, and your daughter after you, if you have one, in remembrance of Hunter Quatermain.'

Poor little Flossie cried very much, and gave me a lock of her bright hair in return, which I still have. The cheque I gave her was for a thousand pounds (which being now well off, and having no calls upon me except those of charity, I could well afford), and in the note I directed her father to invest it for her in Government security, and when she married or came of age to buy her the best diamond necklace he could get for the money and accumulated interest. I chose diamonds because I think that now that King Solomon's Mines are lost to the world, their price will never be much lower than it is at present, so that if in after-life she should ever be in pecuniary difficulties, she will be able to turn them into money.

Well, at last we got off, after much hand-shaking, hat-waving, and also farewell saluting from the natives, Alphonse weeping copiously (for he has a warm heart) at parting with his master and mistress; and I was not sorry for it at all, for I hate those goodbyes. Perhaps the most affecting thing of all was to witness Umslopogaas' distress at parting with Flossie, for whom the grim old warrior had conceived a strong affection. He used to say that she was as sweet to see as the only star on a dark night, and was never tired of loudly congratulating himself on having killed the Lygonani who had threatened to murder her. And that was the last we saw of the pleasant Mission-house — a true oasis in the desert — and of European civilization. But I often think of the Mackenzies, and wonder how they got down country, and if they are now safe and well in England, and will ever see these words. Dear little Flossie! I wonder how she fares there where there are no black folk to do her imperious bidding, and no sky-piercing snow-clad Kenia for her to look at when she gets up in the morning. And so goodbye to Flossie.

After leaving the Mission-house we made our way, comparatively unmolested, past the base of Mount Kenia, which the Masai call 'Donyo Egere', or the 'speckled mountain', on account of the black patches of rock that appear upon its mighty spire, where the sides are too precipitous to allow of the snow lying on them; then on past the lonely lake Baringo, where one of our two remaining Askari, having unfortunately trodden on a puff-adder, died of snake-bite, in spite of all our efforts to save him. Thence we proceeded a distance of about a hundred and fifty miles to another magnificent snow-clad mountain called Lekakisera, which has never, to the best of my belief, been visited before by a European, but which I cannot now stop to describe. There we rested a fortnight, and then started out into the trackless and uninhabited forest of a vast district called Elgumi. In this forest alone there are more elephants than I ever met with or heard of before. The mighty mammals literally swarm there entirely unmolested by man, and only kept down by the natural law that prevents any animals increasing beyond the capacity of the country they inhabit to support them. Needless to say, however, we did not shoot many of them, first because we could not afford to waste ammunition, of which our stock was getting perilously low, a donkey loaded with it having been swept away in fording a flooded river; and secondly, because we could not carry away the ivory, and did not wish to kill for the mere sake of slaughter. So we let the great beasts be, only shooting one or two in self-protection. In this district, the elephants, being unacquainted with the hunter and his tender mercies, would allow one to walk up to within twenty yards of them in the open, while they stood, with their great ears cocked for all the world like puzzled and gigantic puppy-dogs, and stared at that new and extraordinary phenomenon — man. Occasionally, when the inspection did not prove satisfactory, the staring ended in a trumpet and a charge, but this did not often happen. When it did we had to use our rifles. Nor were elephants the only wild beasts in the great Elgumi forest. All sorts of large game abounded, including lions — confound them! I have always hated the sight of a lion since one bit my leg and lamed me for life. As a consequence, another thing that abounded was the dreadful tsetse fly, whose bite is death to domestic animals. Donkeys have, together with men, hitherto been supposed to enjoy a peculiar immunity from its attacks; but all I have to say, whether it was on account of their poor condition, or because the tsetse in those parts is more poisonous than usual, I do not know, but ours succumbed to its onslaught. Fortunately, however, that was not till two months or so after the bites had been inflicted, when suddenly, after a two days' cold rain, they all died, and on removing the skins of several of them I found the long yellow streaks upon the flesh which are characteristic of death from bites from the tsetse, marking the spot where the insect had inserted his proboscis. On emerging from the great Elgumi forest, we, still steering northwards, in accordance with the information Mr Mackenzie had collected from the unfortunate wanderer who reached him only to die so tragically, struck the base in due course of the large lake, called Laga by the natives, which is about fifty miles long by twenty broad, and of which, it may be remembered, he made mention. Thence we pushed on nearly a month's journey over great rolling uplands, something like those in the Transvaal, but diversified by patches of bush country.

All this time we were continually ascending at the rate of about one hundred feet every ten miles. Indeed the country was on a slope which appeared to terminate at a mass of snow-tipped mountains, for which we were steering, and where we learnt the second lake of which the wanderer had spoken as the lake without a bottom was situated. At length we arrived there, and, having ascertained that there *was* a large lake on top of the mountains, ascended three thousand feet more till we came to a precipitous cliff or edge, to find a great sheet of water some twenty miles square lying fifteen hundred feet below us, and evidently occupying an extinct volcanic crater or craters of vast extent. Perceiving villages on the border of this lake, we descended with great difficulty through forests of pine trees, which now clothed the precipitous sides of the crater, and were well received by the people, a simple, unwarlike folk, who had never seen or even heard of a white man before, and treated us with great reverence and kindness, supplying us with as much food and milk as we could eat and drink. This wonderful and beautiful lake lay, according to our aneroid, at a height of no less than 11,450 feet above sea-level, and its climate was quite cold, and not at all unlike that of England. Indeed, for the first three days of our stay there we saw little or nothing of the scenery on account of an unmistakable Scotch mist which prevailed. It was this rain that set the tsetse poison working in our remaining donkeys, so that they all died.

This disaster left us in a very awkward position, as we had now no means of transport whatever, though on the other hand we had not much to carry. Ammunition, too, was very short, amounting to but one hundred and fifty rounds of rifle cartridges and some fifty shot-gun cartridges. How to get on we did not know; indeed it seemed to us that we had about reached the end of our tether. Even if we had been inclined to abandon the object of our search, which, shadow as it was, was by no means the case, it was ridiculous to think of forcing our way back some seven hundred miles to the coast in our present plight; so we came to the conclusion that the only thing to be done was to stop where we were — the natives being so well disposed and food plentiful — for the present, and abide events, and try to collect information as to the countries beyond.

Accordingly, having purchased a capital log canoe, large enough to hold us all and our baggage, from the headman of the village we were staying in, presenting him with three empty cold-drawn brass cartridges by way of payment, with which he was perfectly delighted, we set out to make a tour of the lake in order to find the most favourable place to make a camp. As we did not know if we should return to this village, we put all our gear into the canoe, and also a quarter of cooked water-buck, which when young is delicious eating, and off we set, natives having already gone before us in light canoes to warn the inhabitants of the other villages of our approach.

As we were puddling leisurely along Good remarked upon the extraordinary deep blue colour of the water, and said that he understood from the natives, who were great fishermen — fish, indeed, being their principal food — that the lake was supposed to be wonderfully deep, and to have a hole at the bottom through which the water escaped and put out some great fire that was raging below.

I pointed out to him that what he had heard was probably a legend arising from a tradition among the people which dated back to the time when one of the extinct parasitic volcanic cones was in activity. We saw several round the borders of the lake which had no doubt been working at a period long subsequent to the volcanic death of the central crater which now formed the bed of the lake itself. When it finally became extinct the people would imagine that the water from the lake had run down and put out the big fire below, more especially as, though it was constantly fed by streams running from the snow-tipped peaks about, there was no visible exit to it.

The farther shore of the lake we found, on approaching it, to consist of a vast perpendicular wall of rock, which held the water without any intermediate sloping bank, as elsewhere. Accordingly we paddled parallel with this precipice, at a distance of about a hundred paces from it, shaping our course for the end of the lake, where we knew that there was a large village.

As we went we began to pass a considerable accumulation of floating rushes, weed, boughs of trees, and other rubbish, brought, Good supposed, to this spot by some current, which he was much puzzled to account for. Whilst we were speculating about this, Sir Henry pointed out a flock of large white swans, which were feeding on the drift some little way ahead of us. Now I had already noticed swans flying about this lake, and, having never come across them before in Africa, was exceedingly anxious to obtain a specimen. I had questioned the natives about them, and learnt that they came from over the mountain, always arriving at certain periods of the year in the early morning, when it was very easy to catch them, on account of their exhausted condition. I also asked them what country they came from, when they shrugged their shoulders, and said that on the top of the great black precipice was stony inhospitable land, and beyond that were mountains with snow, and full of wild beasts, where no people lived, and beyond the mountains were hundreds of miles of dense thorn forest, so thick that even the elephants could not get through it, much less men. Next I asked them if they had ever heard of white people like ourselves living on the farther side of the mountains and the thorn forest, whereat they laughed. But afterwards a very old woman came and told me that when she was a little girl her grandfather had told her that in his youth *his* grandfather had crossed the desert and the mountains, and pierced the thorn forest, and seen a white people who lived in stone kraals beyond. Of course, as this took the tale back some two hundred and fifty years, the information was very indefinite; but still there it was again, and on thinking it over I grew firmly convinced that there was some truth in all these rumours, and equally firmly determined to solve the mystery. Little did I guess in what an almost miraculous way my desire was to be gratified.

Well, we set to work to stalk the swans, which kept drawing, as they fed, nearer and nearer to the precipice, and at last we pushed the canoe under shelter of a patch of drift within forty yards of them. Sir Henry had the shot-gun, loaded with No. 1, and, waiting for a chance, got two in a line, and, firing at their necks, killed them both. Up rose the rest, thirty or more of them, with a mighty splashing; and, as they did so, he gave them the other barrel. Down came one fellow with a broken wing, and I saw the leg of another drop and a few feathers start out of his back; but he went on quite strong. Up went the swans, circling ever higher till at last they were mere specks level with the top of the frowning precipice, when I saw them form into a triangle and head off for the unknown north-east. Meanwhile we had picked up our two dead ones, and beautiful birds they were, weighing not less than about thirty pounds each, and were chasing the winged one, which had scrambled over a mass of driftweed into a pool of clear water beyond. Finding a difficulty in forcing the canoe through the rubbish, I told our only remaining Wakwafi servant, whom I knew to be an excellent swimmer, to jump over, dive under the drift, and catch him, knowing that as there were no crocodiles in this lake he could come to no harm. Entering into the fun of the thing, the man obeyed, and soon was dodging about after the winged swan in fine style, getting gradually nearer to the rock wall, against which the water washed as he did so.

Presently he gave up swimming after the swan, and began to cry out that he was being carried away; and, indeed, we saw that, though he was swimming with all his strength towards us, he was being drawn slowly to the precipice. With a few desperate strokes of our paddles we pushed the canoe through the crust of drift and rowed towards the man as hard as we could, but, fast as we went, he was drawn faster to the rock. Suddenly I saw that before us, just rising eighteen inches or so above the surface of the lake, was what looked like the top of the arch of a submerged cave or railway tunnel. Evidently, from the watermark on the rock several feet above it, it was generally entirely submerged; but there had been a dry season, and the cold had prevented the snow from melting as freely as usual; so the lake was low and the arch showed. Towards this arch our poor servant was being sucked with frightful rapidity. He was not more than ten fathoms from it, and we were about twenty when I saw it, and with little help from us the canoe flew along after him. He struggled bravely, and I thought that we should have saved him, when suddenly I perceived an expression of despair come upon his face, and there before our eyes he was sucked down into the cruel swirling blue depths, and vanished. At the same moment I felt our canoe seized as with a mighty hand, and propelled with resistless force towards the rock.

We realized our danger now and rowed, or rather paddled, furiously in our attempt to get out of the vortex. In vain; in another second we were flying straight for the arch like an arrow, and I thought that we were lost. Luckily I retained sufficient presence of mind to shout out, instantly setting the example by throwing myself into the bottom of the canoe, 'Down on your faces — down!' and the others had the sense to take the hint. In another instant there was a grinding noise, and the boat was pushed down till the water began to trickle over the sides, and I thought that we were gone. But no, suddenly the grinding ceased, and we could again feel the canoe flying along. I turned my head a little — I dared not lift it — and looked up. By the feeble light that yet reached the canoe, I could make out that a dense arch of rock hung just over our heads, and that was all. In another minute I could not even see as much as that, for the faint light had merged into shadow, and the shadows had been swallowed up in darkness, utter and complete.

For an hour or so we lay there, not daring to lift our heads for fear lest the brains should be dashed out of them, and scarcely able to speak even, on account of the noise of the rushing water which drowned our voices. Not, indeed, that we had much inclination to speak, seeing that we were overwhelmed by the awfulness of our position and the imminent fear of instant death, either by being dashed against the sides of the cavern, or on a rock, or being sucked down in the raging waters, or perhaps asphyxiated by want of air. All of these and many other modes of death presented themselves to my imagination as I lay at the bottom of the canoe, listening to the swirl of the hurrying waters which ran whither we knew not. One only other sound could I hear, and that was Alphonse's intermittent howl of terror coming from the centre of the canoe, and even that seemed faint and unnatural. Indeed, the whole thing overpowered my brain, and I began to believe that I was the victim of some ghastly spirit-shaking nightmare.

The Rose of Fire

On we flew, drawn by the mighty current, till at last I noticed that the sound of the water was not half so deafening as it had been, and concluded that this must be because there was more room for the echoes to disperse in. I could now hear Alphonse's howls much more distinctly; they were made up of the oddest mixture of invocations to the Supreme Power and the name of his beloved Annette that it is possible to conceive; and, in short, though their evident earnestness saved them from profanity, were, to say the least, very remarkable. Taking up a paddle I managed to drive it into his ribs, whereon he, thinking that the end had come, howled louder than ever. Then I slowly and cautiously raised myself on my knees and stretched my hand upwards, but could touch no roof. Next I took the paddle and lifted it above my head as high as I could, but with the same result. I also thrust it out laterally to the right and left, but could touch nothing except water. Then I bethought me that there was in the boat, amongst our other remaining possessions, a bull's-eye lantern and a tin of oil. I groped about and found it, and having a match on me carefully lit it, and as soon as the flame had got a hold of the wick I turned it on down the boat. As it happened, the first thing the light lit on was the white and scared face of Alphonse, who, thinking that it was all over at last, and that he was witnessing a preliminary celestial phenomenon, gave a terrific yell and was with difficulty reassured with the paddle. As for the other three, Good was lying on the flat of his back, his eyeglass still fixed in his eye, and gazing blankly into the upper darkness. Sir Henry had his head resting on the thwarts of the canoe, and with his hand was trying to test the speed of the water. But when the beam of light fell upon old Umslopogaas I could really have laughed. I think I have said that we had put a roast quarter of water-buck into the canoe. Well, it so happened that when we all prostrated ourselves to avoid being swept out of the boat and into the water by the rock roof, Umslopogaas's head had come down uncommonly near this roast buck, and so soon as he had recovered a little from the first shock of our position it occurred to him that he was hungry. Thereupon he coolly cut off a chop with Inkosi-kaas, and was now employed in eating it with every appearance of satisfaction. As he afterwards explained, he thought that he was going 'on a long journey', and preferred to start on a full stomach. It reminded me of the people who are going to be hanged, and who are generally reported in the English daily papers to have made 'an excellent breakfast'.

As soon as the others saw that I had managed to light the lamp, we bundled Alphonse into the farther end of the canoe with a threat which calmed him down wonderfully, that if he would insist upon making the darkness hideous with his cries we would put him out of suspense by sending him to join the Wakwafi and wait for Annette in another sphere, and began to discuss the situation as well as we could. First, however, at Good's suggestion, we bound two paddles mast-fashion in the bows so that they might give us warning against any sudden lowering of the roof of the cave or waterway. It was clear to us that we were in an underground river or, as Alphonse defined it, 'main drain', which carried off the superfluous waters of the lake. Such rivers are well known to exist in many parts of the world, but it has not often been the evil fortune of explorers to travel by them. That the river was wide we could clearly see, for the light from the bull's-eye lantern failed to reach from shore to shore, although occasionally, when the current swept us either to one side or the other, we could distinguish the rock wall of the tunnel, which, as far as we could make out, appeared to arch about twenty-five feet above our heads. As for the current itself, it ran, Good estimated, at least eight knots, and, fortunately for us, was, as is usual, fiercest in the middle of the stream. Still, our first act was to arrange that one of us, with the lantern and a pole there was in the canoe, should always be in the bows ready, if possible, to prevent us from being stove in against the side of the cave or any projecting rock. Umslopogaas, having already dined, took the first turn. This was absolutely, with one exception, all that we could do towards preserving our safety. The exception was that another of us took up a position in the stern with a paddle by means of which it was possible to steer the canoe more or less and to keep her from the sides of the cave. These matters attended to, we made a somewhat sparing meal off the cold buck's meat (for we did not know how long it might have to last us), and then feeling in rather better spirits I gave my opinion that, serious as it undoubtedly was, I did not consider our position altogether without hope, unless, indeed, the natives were right, and the river plunged straight down into the bowels of the earth. If not, it was clear that it must emerge somewhere, probably on the other side of the mountains, and in that case all we had to think of was to keep ourselves alive till we got there, wherever 'there' might be. But, of course, as Good lugubriously pointed out, on the other hand we might fall victims to a hundred unsuspected horrors — or the river might go on winding away inside the earth till it dried up, in which case our fate would indeed be an awful one.

'Well, let us hope for the best and prepare ourselves for the worst,' said Sir Henry, who is always cheerful and even spirited — a very tower of strength in the time of trouble. 'We have come out of so many queer scrapes together, that somehow I almost fancy we shall come out of this,' he added.

This was excellent advice, and we proceeded to take it each in our separate way — that is, except Alphonse, who had by now sunk into a sort of terrified stupor. Good was at the helm and Umslopogaas in the bows, so there was nothing left for Sir Henry and myself to do except to lie down in the canoe and think. It certainly was a curious, and indeed almost a weird, position to be placed in — rushing along, as we were, through the bowels of the earth, borne on the bosom of a Stygian river, something after the fashion of souls being ferried by Charon, as Curtis said. And how dark it was! The feeble ray from our little lamp did but serve to show the darkness. There in the bows sat old Umslopogaas, like Pleasure in the poem, watchful and untiring, the pole ready to his hand, and behind in the shadow I could just make out the form of Good peering forward at the ray of light in order to make out how to steer with the paddle that he held and now and again dipped into the water.

'Well, well,' thought I, 'you have come in search of adventures, Allan my boy, and you have certainly got them. At your time of life, too! You ought to be ashamed of yourself; but somehow you are not, and, awful as it all is, perhaps you will pull through after all; and if you don't, why, you cannot help it, you see! And when all's said and done an underground river will make a very appropriate burying-place.'

At first, however, I am bound to say that the strain upon the nerves was very great. It is trying to the coolest and most experienced person not to know from one hour to another if he has five minutes more to live, but there is nothing in this world that one cannot get accustomed to, and in time we began to get accustomed even to that. And, after all, our anxiety, though no doubt natural, was, strictly speaking, illogical, seeing that we never know what is going to happen to us the next minute, even when we sit in a well-drained house with two policemen patrolling under the window — nor how long we have to live. It is all arranged for us, my sons, so what is the use of bothering?

It was nearly midday when we made our dive into darkness, and we had set our watch (Good and Umslopogaas) at two, having agreed that it should be of a duration of five hours. At seven o'clock, accordingly, Sir Henry and I went on, Sir Henry at the bow and I at the stern, and the other two lay down and went to sleep. For three hours all went well, Sir Henry only finding it necessary once to push us off from the side; and I that but little steering was required to keep us straight, as the violent current did all that was needed, though occasionally the canoe showed a tendency which had to be guarded against to veer and travel broadside on. What struck me as the most curious thing about this wonderful river was: how did the air keep fresh? It was muggy and thick, no doubt, but still not sufficiently so to render it bad or even remarkably unpleasant. The only explanation that I can suggest is that the water of the lake had sufficient air in it to keep the atmosphere of the tunnel from absolute stagnation, this air being given out as it proceeded on its headlong way. Of course I only give the solution of the mystery for what it is worth, which perhaps is not much.

When I had been for three hours or so at the helm, I began to notice a decided change in the temperature, which was getting warmer. At first I took no notice of it, but when, at the expiration of another half-hour, I found that it was getting hotter and hotter, I called to Sir Henry and asked him if he noticed it, or if it was only my imagination. 'Noticed it!' he answered; 'I should think so. I am in a sort of Turkish bath.' Just about then the others woke up gasping, and were obliged to begin to discard their clothes. Here Umslopogaas had the advantage, for he did not wear any to speak of, except a moocha.

Hotter it grew, and hotter yet, till at last we could scarcely breathe, and the perspiration poured out of us. Half an hour more, and though we were all now stark naked, we could hardly bear it. The place was like an antechamber of the infernal regions proper. I dipped my hand into the water and drew it out almost with a cry; it was nearly boiling. We consulted a little thermometer we had — the mercury stood at 123 degrees. From the surface of the water rose a dense cloud of steam. Alphonse groaned out that we were already in purgatory, which indeed we were, though not in the sense that he meant it. Sir Henry suggested that we must be passing near the seat of some underground volcanic fire, and I am inclined to think, especially in the light of what subsequently occurred, that he was right. Our sufferings for some time after this really pass my powers of description. We no longer perspired, for all the perspiration had been sweated out of us. We simply lay in the bottom of the boat, which we were now physically incapable of directing, feeling like hot embers, and I fancy undergoing very much the same sensations that the poor fish do when they are dying on land — namely, that of slow suffocation. Our skins began to crack, and the blood to throb in our heads like the beating of a steam-engine.

This had been going on for some time, when suddenly the river turned a little, and I heard Sir Henry call out from the bows in a hoarse, startled voice, and, looking up, saw a most wonderful and awful thing. About half a mile ahead of us, and a little to the left of the centre of the stream — which we could now see was about ninety feet broad — a huge pillar-like jet of almost white flame rose from the surface of the water and sprang fifty feet into the air, when it struck the roof and spread out some forty feet in diameter, falling back in curved sheets of fire shaped like the petals of a full-blown rose. Indeed this awful gas jet resembled nothing so much as a great flaming flower rising out of the black water. Below was the straight stalk, a foot or more thick, and above the dreadful bloom. And as for the fearfulness of it and its fierce and awesome beauty, who can describe it? Certainly I cannot. Although we were now some five hundred yards away, it, notwithstanding the steam, lit up the whole cavern as clear as day, and we could see that the roof was here about forty feet above us, and washed perfectly smooth with water. The rock was black, and here and there I could make out long shining lines of ore running through it like great veins, but of what metal they were I know not.

On we rushed towards this pillar of fire, which gleamed fiercer than any furnace ever lit by man.

'Keep the boat to the right, Quatermain — to the right,' shouted Sir Henry, and a minute afterwards I saw him fall forward senseless. Alphonse had already gone. Good was the next to go. There they lay as though dead; only Umslopogaas and I kept our senses. We were within fifty yards of it now, and I saw the Zulu's head fall forward on his hands. He had gone too, and I was alone. I could not breathe; the fierce heat dried me up. For yards and yards round the great rose of fire the rock-roof was red-hot. The wood of the boat was almost burning. I saw the feathers on one of the dead swans begin to twist and shrivel up; but I would not give in. I knew that if I did we should pass within three or four yards of the gas jet and perish miserably. I set the paddle so as to turn the canoe as far from it as possible, and held on grimly.

My eyes seemed to be bursting from my head, and through my closed lids I could see the fierce light. We were nearly opposite now; it roared like all the fires of hell, and the water boiled furiously around it. Five seconds more. We were past; I heard the roar behind me.

Then I too fell senseless. The next thing that I recollect is feeling a breath of air upon my face. My eyes opened with great difficulty. I looked up. Far, far above me there was light, though around me was great gloom. Then I remembered and looked. The canoe still floated down the river, and in the bottom of it lay the naked forms of my companions. 'Were they dead?' I wondered. 'Was I left alone in this awful place?' I knew not. Next I became conscious of a burning thirst. I put my hand over the edge of the boat into the water and drew it up again with a cry. No wonder: nearly all the skin was burnt off the back of it. The water, however, was cold, or nearly so, and I drank pints and splashed myself all over. My body seemed to suck up the fluid as one may see a brick wall suck up rain after a drought; but where I was burnt the touch of it caused intense pain. Then I bethought myself of the others, and, dragging myself towards them with difficulty, I sprinkled them with water, and to my joy they began to recover — Umslopogaas first, then the others. Next they drank, absorbing water like so many sponges. Then, feeling chilly — a queer contrast to our recent sensations — we began as best we could to get into our clothes. As we did so Good pointed to the port side of the canoe: it was all blistered with heat, and in places actually charred. Had it been built like our civilized boats, Good said that the planks would certainly have warped and let in enough water to sink us; but fortunately it was dug out of the soft, willowy wood of a single great tree, and had sides nearly three inches and a bottom four inches thick. What that awful flame was we never discovered, but I suppose that there was at this spot a crack or hole in the bed of the river through which a vast volume of gas forced its way from its volcanic home in the bowels of the earth towards the upper air. How it first became ignited is, of course, impossible to say — probably, I should think, from some spontaneous explosion of mephitic gases.

As soon as we had got some things together and shaken ourselves together a little, we set to work to make out where we were now. I have said that there was light above, and on examination we found that it came from the sky. Our river that was, Sir Henry said, a literal realization of the wild vision of the poet, was no longer underground, but was running on its darksome way, not now through 'caverns measureless to man', but between two frightful cliffs which cannot have been less than two thousand feet high. So high were they, indeed, that though the sky was above us, where we were was dense gloom — not darkness indeed, but the gloom of a room closely shuttered in the daytime. Up on either side rose the great straight cliffs, grim and forbidding, till the eye grew dizzy with trying to measure their sheer height. The little space of sky that marked where they ended lay like a thread of blue upon their soaring blackness, which was unrelieved by any tree or creeper. Here and there, however, grew ghostly patches of a long grey lichen, hanging motionless to the rock as the white beard to the chin of a dead man. It seemed as though only the dregs or heavier part of the light had sunk to the bottom of this awful place. No bright-winged sunbeam could fall so low: they died far, far above our heads.

By the river's edge was a little shore formed of round fragments of rock washed into this shape by the constant action of water, and giving the place the appearance of being strewn with thousands of fossil cannon balls. Evidently when the water of the underground river is high there is no beach at all, or very little, between the border of the stream and the precipitous cliffs; but now there was a space of seven or eight yards. And here, on this beach, we determined to land, in order to rest ourselves a little after all that we had gone through and to stretch our limbs. It was a dreadful place, but it would give an hour's respite from the terrors of the river, and also allow of our repacking and arranging the canoe. Accordingly we selected what looked like a favourable spot, and with some little difficulty managed to beach the canoe and scramble out on to the round, inhospitable pebbles.

'My word,' called out Good, who was on shore the first, 'what an awful place! It's enough to give one a fit.' And he laughed.

Instantly a thundering voice took up his words, magnifying them a hundred times. *'Give one a fit — Ho! ho! ho!'* — *'A fit, Ho! ho! ho!'* answered another voice in wild accents from far up the cliff — *a fit! a fit! a fit!* chimed in voice after voice — each flinging the words to and fro with shouts of awful laughter to the invisible lips of the other till the whole place echoed with the words and with shrieks of fiendish merriment, which at last ceased as suddenly as they had begun.

'Oh, mon Dieu!' yelled Alphonse, startled quite out of such self-command as he possessed.

'Mon Dieu! Mon Dieu! Mon Dieu!' the Titanic echoes thundered, shrieked, and wailed in every conceivable tone.

'Ah,' said Umslopogaas calmly, 'I clearly perceive that devils live here. Well, the place looks like it.'

I tried to explain to him that the cause of all the hubbub was a very remarkable and interesting echo, but he would not believe it.

'Ah,' he said, 'I know an echo when I hear one. There was one lived opposite my kraal in Zululand, and the Intombis [maidens] used to talk with it. But if what we hear is a full-grown echo, mine at home can only have been a baby. No, no — they are devils up there. But I don't think much of them, though,' he added, taking a pinch of snuff. 'They can copy what one says, but they don't seem to be able to talk on their own account, and they dare not show their faces,' and he relapsed into silence, and apparently paid no further attention to such contemptible fiends.

After this we found it necessary to keep our conversation down to a whisper — for it was really unbearable to have every word one uttered tossed to and fro like a tennis-ball, as precipice called to precipice.

But even our whispers ran up the rocks in mysterious murmurs till at last they died away in long-drawn sighs of sound. Echoes are delightful and romantic things, but we had more than enough of them in that dreadful gulf.

As soon as we had settled ourselves a little on the round stones, we went on to wash and dress our burns as well as we could. As we had but a little oil for the lantern, we could not spare any for this purpose, so we skinned one of the swans, and used the fat off its breast, which proved an excellent substitute. Then we repacked the canoe, and finally began to take some food, of which I need scarcely say we were in need, for our insensibility had endured for many hours, and it was, as our watches showed, midday. Accordingly we seated ourselves in a circle, and were soon engaged in discussing our cold meat with such appetite as we could muster, which, in my case at any rate, was not much, as I felt sick and faint after my sufferings of the previous night, and had besides a racking headache. It was a curious meal. The gloom was so intense that we could scarcely see the way to cut our food and convey it to our mouths. Still we got on pretty well, till I happened to look behind me — my attention being attracted by a noise of something crawling over the stones, and perceived sitting upon a rock in my immediate rear a huge species of black freshwater crab, only it was five times the size of any crab I ever saw. This hideous and loathsome-looking animal had projecting eyes that seemed to glare at one, very long and flexible antennae or feelers, and gigantic claws. Nor was I especially favoured with its company. From every quarter dozens of these horrid brutes were creeping up, drawn, I suppose, by the smell of the food, from between the round stones and out of holes in the precipice. Some were already quite close to us. I stared quite fascinated by the unusual sight, and as I did so I saw one of the beasts stretch out its huge claw and give the unsuspecting Good such a nip behind that he jumped up with a howl, and set the 'wild echoes flying' in sober earnest. Just then, too, another, a very large one, got hold of Alphonse's leg, and declined to part with it, and, as may be imagined, a considerable scene ensued. Umslopogaas took his axe and cracked the shell of one with the flat of it, whereon it set up a horrid screaming which the echoes multiplied a thousandfold, and began to foam at the mouth, a proceeding that drew hundreds more of its friends out of unsuspected holes and corners. Those on the spot perceiving that the animal was hurt fell upon it like creditors on a bankrupt, and literally rent it limb from limb with their huge pincers and devoured it, using their claws to convey the fragments to their mouths. Seizing whatever weapons were handy, such as stones or paddles, we commenced a war upon the monsters — whose numbers were increasing by leaps and bounds, and whose stench was overpowering. So fast as we cracked their armour others seized the injured ones and devoured them, foaming at the mouth, and screaming as they did so. Nor did the brutes stop at that. When they could they nipped hold of us — and awful nips they were — or tried to steal the meat. One enormous fellow got hold of the swan we had skinned and began to drag it off. Instantly a score of others flung themselves upon the prey, and then began a ghastly and disgusting scene. How the monsters foamed and screamed, and rent the flesh, and each other! It was a sickening and unnatural sight, and one that will haunt all who saw it till their dying day — enacted as it was in the deep, oppressive gloom, and set to the unceasing music of the many-toned nerve-shaking echoes. Strange as it may seem to say so, there was something so shockingly human about these fiendish creatures — it was as though all the most evil passions and desires of man had got into the shell of a magnified crab and gone mad. They were so dreadfully courageous and intelligent, and they looked as if they *understood*. The whole scene might have furnished material for another canto of Dante's 'Inferno', as Curtis said.

'I say, you fellows, let's get out of this or we shall all go off our heads,' sung out Good; and we were not slow to take the hint. Pushing the canoe, around which the animals were now crawling by hundreds and making vain attempts to climb, off the rocks, we bundled into it and got out into mid-stream, leaving behind us the fragments of our meal and the screaming, foaming, stinking mass of monsters in full possession of the ground.

'Those are the devils of the place,' said Umslopogaas with the air of one who has solved a problem, and upon my word I felt almost inclined to agree with him.

Umslopogaas' remarks were like his axe — very much to the point.

'What's to be done next?' said Sir Henry blankly.

'Drift, I suppose,' I answered, and we drifted accordingly. All the afternoon and well into the evening we floated on in the gloom beneath the far-off line of blue sky, scarcely knowing when day ended and night began, for down in that vast gulf the difference was not marked, till at length Good pointed out a star hanging right above us, which, having nothing better to do, we observed with great interest. Suddenly it vanished, the darkness became intense, and a familiar murmuring sound filled the air. 'Underground again,' I said with a groan, holding up the lamp. Yes, there was no doubt about it. I could just make out the roof. The chasm had come to an end and the tunnel had recommenced. And then there began another long, long night of danger and horror. To describe all its incidents would be too wearisome, so I will simply say that about midnight we struck on a flat projecting rock in mid-stream and were as nearly as possible overturned and drowned. However, at last we got off, and went upon the uneven tenor of our way. And so the hours passed till it was nearly three o'clock. Sir Henry, Good, and Alphonse were asleep, utterly worn out; Umslopogaas was at the bow with the pole, and I was steering, when I perceived that the rate at which we were travelling had perceptibly increased. Then, suddenly, I heard Umslopogaas make an exclamation, and next second came a sound as of parting branches, and I became aware that the canoe was being forced through hanging bushes or creepers. Another minute, and the breath of sweet open air fanned my face, and I felt that we had emerged from the tunnel and were floating upon clear water. I say felt, for I could see nothing, the darkness being absolutely pitchy, as it often is just before the dawn. But even this could scarcely damp my joy. We were out of that dreadful river, and wherever we might have got to this at least was something to be thankful for. And so I sat down and inhaled the sweet night air and waited for the dawn with such patience as I could command.

The Frowning City

For an hour or more I sat waiting (Umslopogaas having meanwhile gone to sleep also) till at length the east turned grey, and huge misty shapes moved over the surface of the water like ghosts of long-forgotten dawns. They were the vapours rising from their watery bed to greet the sun. Then the grey turned to primrose, and the primrose grew to red. Next, glorious bars of light sprang up across the eastern sky, and through them the radiant messengers of the dawn came speeding upon their arrowy way, scattering the ghostly vapours and awaking the mountains with a kiss, as they flew from range to range and longitude to longitude. Another moment, and the golden gates were open and the sun himself came forth as a bridegroom from his chamber, with pomp and glory and a flashing as of ten million spears, and embraced the night and covered her with brightness, and it was day.

But as yet I could see nothing save the beautiful blue sky above, for over the water was a thick layer of mist exactly as though the whole surface had been covered with billows of cotton wool. By degrees, however, the sun sucked up the mists, and then I saw that we were afloat upon a glorious sheet of blue water of which I could not make out the shore. Some eight or ten miles behind us, however, there stretched as far as the eye could reach a range of precipitous hills that formed a retaining wall of the lake, and I have no doubt but that it was through some entrance in these hills that the subterranean river found its way into the open water. Indeed, I afterwards ascertained this to be the fact, and it will be some indication of the extraordinary strength and directness of the current of the mysterious river that the canoe, even at this distance, was still answering to it. Presently, too, I, or rather Umslopogaas, who woke up just then, discovered another indication, and a very unpleasant one it was. Perceiving some whitish object upon the water, Umslopogaas called my attention to it, and with a few strokes of the paddle brought the canoe to the spot, whereupon we discovered that the object was the body of a man floating face downwards. This was bad enough, but imagine my horror when Umslopogaas having turned him on to his back with the paddle, we recognized in the sunken features the lineaments of — whom do you suppose? None other than our poor servant who had been sucked down two days before in the waters of the subterranean river. It quite frightened me. I thought that we had left him behind for ever, and behold! borne by the current, he had made the awful journey with us, and with us had reached the end. His appearance also was dreadful, for he bore traces of having touched the pillar of fire — one arm being completely shrivelled up and all his hair being burnt off. The features were, as I have said, sunken, and yet they preserved upon them that awful look of despair that I had seen upon his living face as the poor fellow was sucked down. Really the sight unnerved me, weary and shaken as I felt with all that we had gone through, and I was heartily glad when suddenly and without any warning the body began to sink just as though it had had a mission, which having been accomplished, it retired; the real reason no doubt being that turning it on its back allowed a free passage to the gas. Down it went to the transparent depths — fathom after fathom we could trace its course till at last a long line of bright air-bubbles, swiftly chasing each other to the surface, alone remained where it had passed. At length these, too, were gone, and that was an end of our poor servant. Umslopogaas thoughtfully watched the body vanish.

'What did he follow us for?' he asked. ''Tis an ill omen for thee and me, Macumazahn.' And he laughed.

I turned on him angrily, for I dislike these unpleasant suggestions. If people have such ideas, they ought in common decency to keep them to themselves. I detest individuals who make on the subject of their disagreeable presentiments, or who, when they dream that they saw one hanged as a common felon, or some such horror, will insist upon telling one all about it at breakfast, even if they have to get up early to do it.

Just then, however, the others woke up and began to rejoice exceedingly at finding that we were out of that dreadful river and once more beneath the blue sky. Then followed a babel of talk and suggestions as to what we were to do next, the upshot of all of which was that, as we were excessively hungry, and had nothing whatsoever left to eat except a few scraps of biltong (dried game-flesh), having abandoned all that remained of our provisions to those horrible freshwater crabs, we determined to make for the shore. But a new difficulty arose. We did not know where the shore was, and, with the exception of the cliffs through which the subterranean river made its entry, could see nothing but a wide expanse of sparkling blue water. Observing, however, that the long flights of aquatic birds kept flying from our left, we concluded that they were advancing from their feeding-grounds on shore to pass the day in the lake, and accordingly headed the boat towards the quarter whence they came, and began to paddle. Before long, however, a stiffish breeze sprang up, blowing directly in the direction we wanted, so we improvised a sail with a blanket and the pole, which took us along merrily. This done, we devoured the remnants of our biltong, washed down with the sweet lake water, and then lit our pipes and awaited whatever might turn up.

When we had been sailing for an hour, Good, who was searching the horizon with the spy-glass, suddenly announced joyfully that he saw land, and pointed out that, from the change in the colour of the water, he thought we must be approaching the mouth of a river. In another minute we perceived a great golden dome, not unlike that of St Paul's, piercing the morning mists, and while we were wondering what in the world it could be, Good reported another and still more important discovery, namely, that a small sailing-boat was advancing towards us. This bit of news, which we were very shortly able to verify with our own eyes, threw us into a considerable flutter. That the natives of this unknown lake should understand the art of sailing seemed to suggest that they possessed some degree of civilization. In a few more minutes it became evident that the occupant or occupants of the advancing boat had made us out. For a moment or two she hung in the wind as though in doubt, and then came tacking towards us with great swiftness. In ten more minutes she was within a hundred yards, and we saw that she was a neat little boat — not a canoe 'dug out', but built more or less in the European fashion with planks, and carrying a singularly large sail for her size. But our attention was soon diverted from the boat to her crew, which consisted of a man and a woman, *nearly as white as ourselves.*

We stared at each other in amazement, thinking that we must be mistaken; but no, there was no doubt about it. They were not fair, but the two people in the boat were decidedly of a white as distinguished from a black race, as white, for instance, as Spaniards or Italians. It was a patent fact. So it was true, after all; and, mysteriously led by a Power beyond our own, we had discovered this wonderful people. I could have shouted for joy when I thought of the glory and the wonder of the thing; and as it was, we all shook hands and congratulated each other on the unexpected success of our wild search. All my life had I heard rumours of a white race that existed in the highlands of this vast continent, and longed to put them to the proof, and now here I saw it with my own eyes, and was dumbfounded. Truly, as Sir Henry said, the old Roman was right when he wrote 'Ex Africa semper aliquid novi', which he tells me means that out of Africa there always comes some new thing.

The man in the boat was of a good but not particularly fine physique, and possessed straight black hair, regular aquiline features, and an intelligent face. He was dressed in a brown cloth garment, something like a flannel shirt without the sleeves, and in an unmistakable kilt of the same material. The legs and feet were bare. Round the right arm and left leg he wore thick rings of yellow metal that I judged to be gold. The woman had a sweet face, wild and shy, with large eyes and curling brown hair. Her dress was made of the same material as the man's, and consisted, as we afterwards discovered, first of a linen under-garment that hung down to her knee, and then of a single long strip of cloth, about four feet wide by fifteen long, which was wound round the body in graceful folds and finally flung over the left shoulder so that the end, which was dyed blue or purple or some other colour, according to the social standing of the wearer, hung down in front, the right arm and breast being, however, left quite bare. A more becoming dress, especially when, as in the present case, the wearer was young and pretty, it is quite impossible to conceive. Good (who has an eye for such things) was greatly struck with it, and so indeed was I. It was so simple and yet so effective.

Meanwhile, if we had been astonished at the appearance of the man and woman, it was clear that they were far more astonished at us. As for the man, he appeared to be overcome with fear and wonder, and for a while hovered round our canoe, but would not approach. At last, however, he came within hailing distance, and called to us in a language that sounded soft and pleasing enough, but of which we could not understand one word. So we hailed back in English, French, Latin, Greek, German, Zulu, Dutch, Sisutu, Kukuana, and a few other native dialects that I am acquainted with, but our visitor did not understand any of these tongues; indeed, they appeared to bewilder him. As for the lady, she was busily employed in taking stock of us, and Good was returning the compliment by staring at her hard through his eyeglass, a proceeding that she seemed rather to enjoy than otherwise. At length, the man, being unable to make anything of us, suddenly turned his boat round and began to head off for the shore, his little boat skimming away before the wind like a swallow. As she passed across our bows the man turned to attend to the large sail, and Good promptly took the opportunity to kiss his hand to the young lady. I was horrified at this proceeding, both on general grounds and because I feared that she might take offence, but to my delight she did not, for, first glancing round and seeing that her husband, or brother, or whoever he was, was engaged, she promptly kissed hers back.

'Ah!' said I. 'It seems that we have at last found a language that the people of this country understand.'

'In which case,' said Sir Henry, 'Good will prove an invaluable interpreter.'

I frowned, for I do not approve of Good's frivolities, and he knows it, and I turned the conversation to more serious subjects. 'It is very clear to me,' I said, 'that the man will be back before long with a host of his fellows, so we had best make up our minds as to how we are going to receive them.'

'The question is how will they receive us?' said Sir Henry.

As for Good he made no remark, but began to extract a small square tin case that had accompanied us in all our wanderings from under a pile of baggage. Now we had often remonstrated with Good about this tin case, inasmuch as it had been an awkward thing to carry, and he had never given any very explicit account as to its contents; but he had insisted on keeping it, saying mysteriously that it might come in very useful one day.

'What on earth are you going to do, Good?' asked Sir Henry.

'Do — why dress, of course! You don't expect me to appear in a new country in these things, do you?' and he pointed to his soiled and worn garments, which were however, like all Good's things, very tidy, and with every tear neatly mended.

We said no more, but watched his proceedings with breathless interest. His first step was to get Alphonse, who was thoroughly competent in such matters, to trim his hair and beard in the most approved fashion. I think that if he had had some hot water and a cake of soap at hand he would have shaved off the latter; but he had not. This done, he suggested that we should lower the sail of the canoe and all take a bath, which we did, greatly to the horror and astonishment of Alphonse, who lifted his hands and ejaculated that these English were indeed a wonderful people. Umslopogaas, who, though he was, like most high-bred Zulus, scrupulously cleanly in his person, did not see the fun of swimming about in a lake, also regarded the proceeding with mild amusement. We got back into the canoe much refreshed by the cold water, and sat to dry in the sun, whilst Good undid his tin box, and produced first a beautiful clean white shirt, just as it had left a London steam laundry, and then some garments wrapped first in brown, then in white, and finally in silver paper. We watched this undoing with the tenderest interest and much speculation. One by one Good removed the dull husks that hid their splendours, carefully folding and replacing each piece of paper as he did so; and there at last lay, in all the majesty of its golden epaulettes, lace, and buttons, a Commander of the Royal Navy's full-dress uniform — dress sword, cocked hat, shiny patent leather boots and all. We literally gasped.

'*What!*' we said, '*what!* Are you going to put those things on?'

'Certainly,' he answered composedly; 'you see so much depends upon a first impression, especially,' he added, 'as I observe that there are ladies about. One at least of us ought to be decently dressed.'

We said no more; we were simply dumbfounded, especially when we considered the artful way in which Good had concealed the contents of that box for all these months. Only one suggestion did we make — namely, that he should wear his mail shirt next his skin. He replied that he feared it would spoil the set of his coat, now carefully spread in the sun to take the creases out, but finally consented to this precautionary measure. The most amusing part of the affair, however, was to see old Umslopogaas's astonishment and Alphonse's delight at Good's transformation. When at last he stood up in all his glory, even down to the medals on his breast, and contemplated himself in the still waters of the lake, after the fashion of the young gentleman in ancient history, whose name I cannot remember, but who fell in love with his own shadow, the old Zulu could no longer restrain his feelings.

'Oh, Bougwan!' he said. 'Oh, Bougwan! I always thought thee an ugly little man, and fat — fat as the cows at calving time; and now thou art like a blue jay when he spreads his tail out. Surely, Bougwan, it hurts my eyes to look at thee.'

Good did not much like this allusion to his fat, which, to tell the truth, was not very well deserved, for hard exercise had brought him down three inches; but on the whole he was pleased at Umslopogaas's admiration. As for Alphonse, he was quite delighted.

'Ah! but Monsieur has the beautiful air — the air of the warrior. It is the ladies who will say so when we come to get ashore. Monsieur is complete; he puts me in mind of my heroic grand —'

Here we stopped Alphonse.

As we gazed upon the beauties thus revealed by Good, a spirit of emulation filled our breasts, and we set to work to get ourselves up as well as we could. The most, however, that we were able to do was to array ourselves in our spare suits of shooting clothes, of which we each had several, all the fine clothes in the world could never make it otherwise than scrubby and insignificant; but Sir Henry looked what he is, a magnificent man in his nearly new tweed suit, gaiters, and boots. Alphonse also got himself up to kill, giving an extra turn to his enormous moustaches. Even old Umslopogaas, who was not in a general way given to the vain adorning of his body, took some oil out of the lantern and a bit of tow, and polished up his head-ring with it till it shone like Good's patent leather boots. Then he put on the mail shirt Sir Henry had given him and his 'moocha', and, having cleaned up Inkosi-kaas a little, stood forth complete.

All this while, having hoisted the sail again as soon as we had finished bathing, we had been progressing steadily for the land, or, rather, for the mouth of a great river. Presently — in all about an hour and a half after the little boat had left us — we saw emerging from the river or harbour a large number of boats, ranging up to ten or twelve tons burden. One of these was propelled by twenty-four oars, and most of the rest sailed. Looking through the glass we soon made out that the row-boat was an official vessel, her crew being all dressed in a sort of uniform, whilst on the half-deck forward stood an old man of venerable appearance, and with a flowing white beard, and a sword strapped to his side, who was evidently the commander of the craft. The other boats were apparently occupied by people brought out by curiosity, and were rowing or sailing towards us as quickly as they could.

'Now for it,' said I. 'What is the betting? Are they going to be friendly or to put an end to us?'

Nobody could answer this question, and, not liking the warlike appearance of the old gentleman and his sword, we felt a little anxious.

Just then Good spied a school of hippopotami on the water about two hundred yards off us, and suggested that it would not be a bad plan to impress the natives with a sense of our power by shooting some of them if possible. This, unluckily enough, struck us as a good idea, and accordingly we at once got out our eight-bore rifles, for which we still had a few cartridges left, and prepared for action. There were four of the animals, a big bull, a cow, and two young ones, one three parts grown. We got up to them without difficulty, the great animals contenting themselves with sinking down into the water and rising again a few yards farther on; indeed, their excessive tameness struck me as being peculiar. When the advancing boats were about five hundred yards away, Sir Henry opened the ball by firing at the three parts grown young one. The heavy bullet struck it fair between the eyes, and, crashing through the skull, killed it, and it sank, leaving a long train of blood behind it. At the same moment I fired at the cow, and Good at the old bull. My shot took effect, but not fatally, and down went the hippopotamus with a prodigious splashing, only to rise again presently blowing and grunting furiously, dyeing all the water round her crimson, when I killed her with the left barrel. Good, who is an execrable shot, missed the head of the bull altogether, the bullet merely cutting the side of his face as it passed. On glancing up, after I had fired my second shot, I perceived that the people we had fallen among were evidently ignorant of the nature of firearms, for the consternation caused by our shots and their effect upon the animals was prodigious. Some of the parties in the boats began to cry out in fear; others turned and made off as hard as they could; and even the old gentleman with the sword looked greatly puzzled and alarmed, and halted his big row-boat. We had, however, but little time for observation, for just then the old bull, rendered furious by the wound he had received, rose fair within forty yards of us, glaring savagely. We all fired, and hit him in various places, and down he went, badly wounded. Curiosity now began to overcome the fear of the onlookers, and some of them sailed on up close to us, amongst these being the man and woman whom we had first seen a couple of hours or so before, who drew up almost alongside. Just then the great brute rose again within ten yards of their base, and instantly with a roar of fury made at it open-mouthed. The woman shrieked, and the man tried to give the boat way, but without success. In another second I saw the huge red jaws and gleaming ivories close with a crunch on the frail craft, taking an enormous mouthful out of its side and capsizing it. Down went the boat, leaving its occupants struggling in the water. Next moment, before we could do anything towards saving them, the huge and furious creature was up again and making open-mouthed at the poor girl, who was struggling in the water. Lifting my rifle just as the grinding jaws were about to close on her, I fired over her head right down the hippopotamus's throat. Over he went, and commenced turning round and round, snorting, and blowing red streams of blood through his nostrils. Before he could recover himself, however, I let him have the other barrel in the side of the throat, and that finished him. He never moved or struggled again, but instantly sank. Our next effort was directed towards saving the girl, the man having swum off towards another boat; and in this we were fortunately successful, pulling her into the canoe (amidst the shouts of the spectators) considerably exhausted and frightened, but otherwise unhurt.

Meanwhile the boats had gathered together at a distance, and we could see that the occupants, who were evidently much frightened, were consulting what to do. Without giving them time for further consideration, which we thought might result unfavourably to ourselves, we instantly took our paddles and advanced towards them, Good standing in the bow and taking off his cocked hat politely in every direction, his amiable features suffused by a bland but intelligent smile. Most of the craft retreated as we advanced, but a few held their ground, while the big row-boat came on to meet us. Presently we were alongside, and I could see that our appearance — and especially Good's and Umslopogaas's — filled the venerable-looking commander with astonishment, not unmixed with awe. He was dressed after the same fashion as the man we first met, except that his shirt was not made of brown cloth, but of pure white linen hemmed with purple. The kilt, however, was identical, and so were the thick rings of gold around the arm and beneath the left knee. The rowers wore only a kilt, their bodies being naked to the waist. Good took off his hat to the old gentleman with an extra flourish, and inquired after his health in the purest English, to which he replied by laying the first two fingers of his right hand horizontally across his lips and holding them there for a moment, which we took as his method of salutation. Then he also addressed some remarks to us in the same soft accents that had distinguished our first interviewer, which we were forced to indicate we did not understand by shaking our heads and shrugging our shoulders. This last Alphonse, being to the manner born, did to perfection, and in so polite a way that nobody could take any offence. Then we came a standstill, till I, being exceedingly hungry, thought I might as well call attention to the fact, and did so first by opening my mouth and pointing down it, and then rubbing my stomach. These signals the old gentleman clearly understood, for he nodded his head vigorously, and pointed towards the harbour; and at the same time one of the men on his boat threw us a line and motioned to us to make it fast, which we did. The row-boat then took us in tow, and went with great rapidity towards the mouth of the river, accompanied by all the other boats. In about twenty minutes more we reached the entrance to the harbour, which was crowded with boats full of people who had come out to see us. We observed that all the occupants were more or less of the same type, though some were fairer than others. Indeed, we noticed certain ladies whose skin was of a most dazzling whiteness; and the darkest shade of colour which we saw was about that of a rather swarthy Spaniard. Presently the wide river gave a sweep, and when it did so an exclamation of astonishment and delight burst from our lips as we caught our first view of the place that we afterwards knew as Milosis, or the Frowning City (from mi, which means city, and losis, a frown).

At a distance of some five hundred yards from the river's bank rose a sheer precipice of granite, two hundred feet or so in height, which had no doubt once formed the bank itself — the intermediate space of land now utilized as docks and roadways having been gained by draining, and deepening and embanking the stream.

On the brow of this precipice stood a great building of the same granite that formed the cliff, built on three sides of a square, the fourth side being open, save for a kind of battlement pierced at its base by a little door. This imposing place we afterwards discovered was the palace of the queen, or rather of the queens. At the back of the palace the town sloped gently upwards to a flashing building of white marble, crowned by the golden dome which we had already observed. The city was, with the exception of this one building, entirely built of red granite, and laid out in regular blocks with splendid roadways between. So far as we could see also the houses were all one-storied and detached, with gardens round them, which gave some relief to the eye wearied with the vista of red granite. At the back of the palace a road of extraordinary width stretched away up the hill for a distance of a mile and a half or so, and appeared to terminate at an open space surrounding the gleaming building that crowned the hill. But right in front of us was the wonder and glory of Milosis — the great staircase of the palace, the magnificence of which took our breath away. Let the reader imagine, if he can, a splendid stairway, sixty-five feet from balustrade to balustrade, consisting of two vast flights, each of one hundred and twenty-five steps of eight inches in height by three feet broad, connected by a flat resting-place sixty feet in length, and running from the palace wall on the edge of the precipice down to meet a waterway or canal cut to its foot from the river. This marvellous staircase was supported upon a single enormous granite arch, of which the resting-place between the two flights formed the crown; that is, the connecting open space lay upon it. From this archway sprang a subsidiary flying arch, or rather something that resembled a flying arch in shape, such as none of us had seen in any other country, and of which the beauty and wonder surpassed all that we had ever imagined. Three hundred feet from point to point, and no less than five hundred and fifty round the curve, that half-arc soared touching the bridge it supported for a space of fifty feet only, one end resting on and built into the parent archway, and the other embedded in the solid granite of the side of the precipice.

This staircase with its supports was, indeed, a work of which any living man might have been proud, both on account of its magnitude and its surpassing beauty. Four times, as we afterwards learnt, did the work, which was commenced in remote antiquity, fail, and was then abandoned for three centuries when half-finished, till at last there rose a youthful engineer named Rademas, who said that he would complete it successfully, and staked his life upon it. If he failed he was to be hurled from the precipice he had undertaken to scale; if he succeeded, he was to be rewarded by the hand of the king's daughter. Five years was given to him to complete the work, and an unlimited supply of labour and material. Three times did his arch fall, till at last, seeing failure to be inevitable, he determined to commit suicide on the morrow of the third collapse. That night, however, a beautiful woman came to him in a dream and touched his forehead, and of a sudden he saw a vision of the completed work, and saw too through the masonry and how the difficulties connected with the flying arch that had hitherto baffled his genius were to be overcome. Then he awoke and once more commenced the work, but on a different plan, and behold! he achieved it, and on the last day of the five years he led the princess his bride up the stair and into the palace. And in due course he became king by right of his wife, and founded the present Zu-Vendi dynasty, which is to this day called the 'House of the Stairway', thus proving once more how energy and talent are the natural stepping-stones to grandeur. And to commemorate his triumph he fashioned a statue of himself dreaming, and of the fair woman who touched him on the forehead, and placed it in the great hall of the palace, and there it stands to this day.

Such was the great stair of Milosis, and such the city beyond. No wonder they named it the 'Frowning City', for certainly those mighty works in solid granite did seem to frown down upon our littleness in their sombre splendour. This was so even in the sunshine, but when the storm-clouds gathered on her imperial brow Milosis looked more like a supernatural dwelling-place, or some imagining of a poet's brain, than what she is — a mortal city, carven by the patient genius of generations out of the red silence of the mountain side.

The Sister Queens

The big rowing-boat glided on up the cutting that ran almost to the foot of the vast stairway, and then halted at a flight of steps leading to the landing-place. Here the old gentleman disembarked, and invited us to do so likewise, which, having no alternative, and being nearly starved, we did without hesitation — taking our rifles with us, however. As each of us landed, our guide again laid his fingers on his lips and bowed deeply, at the same time ordering back the crowds which had assembled to gaze on us. The last to leave the canoe was the girl we had picked out of the water, for whom her companion was waiting. Before she went away she kissed my hand, I suppose as a token of gratitude for having saved her from the fury of the hippopotamus; and it seemed to me that she had by this time quite got over any fear she might have had of us, and was by no means anxious to return in such a hurry to her lawful owners. At any rate, she was going to kiss Good's hand as well as mine, when the young man interfered and led her off. As soon as we were on shore, a number of the men who had rowed the big boat took possession of our few goods and chattels, and started with them up the splendid staircase, our guide indicating to us by means of motions that the things were perfectly safe. This done, he turned to the right and led the way to a small house, which was, as I afterwards discovered, an inn. Entering into a good-sized room, we saw that a wooden table was already furnished with food, presumably in preparation for us. Here our guide motioned us to be seated on a bench that ran the length of the table. We did not require a second invitation, but at once fell to ravenously on the viands before us, which were served on wooden platters, and consisted of cold goat's-flesh, wrapped up in some kind of leaf that gave it a delicious flavour, green vegetables resembling lettuces, brown bread, and red wine poured from a skin into horn mugs. This wine was peculiarly soft and good, having something of the flavour of Burgundy. Twenty minutes after we sat down at that hospitable board we rose from it, feeling like new men. After all that we had gone through we needed two things, food and rest, and the food of itself was a great blessing to us. Two girls of the same charming cast of face as the first whom we had seen waited on us while we ate, and very nicely they did it. They were also dressed in the same fashion namely, in a white linen petticoat coming to the knee, and with the toga-like garment of brown cloth, leaving bare the right arm and breast. I afterwards found out that this was the national dress, and regulated by an iron custom, though of course subject to variations. Thus, if the petticoat was pure white, it signified that the wearer was unmarried; if white, with a straight purple stripe round the edge, that she was married and a first or legal wife; if with a black stripe, that she was a widow. In the same way the toga, or 'kaf', as they call it, was of different shades of colour, from pure white to the deepest brown, according to the rank of the wearer, and embroidered at the end in various ways. This also applies to the 'shirts' or tunics worn by the men, which varied in material and colour; but the kilts were always the same except as regards quality. One thing, however, every man and woman in the country wore as the national insignia, and that was the thick band of gold round the right arm above the elbow, and the left leg beneath the knee. People of high rank also wore a torque of gold round the neck, and I observed that our guide had one on.

So soon as we had finished our meal our venerable conductor, who had been standing all the while, regarding us with inquiring eyes, and our guns with something as like fear as his pride would allow him to show, bowed towards Good, whom he evidently took for the leader of the party on account of the splendour of his apparel, and once more led the way through the door and to the foot of the great staircase. Here we paused for a moment to admire two colossal lions, each hewn from a single block of pure black marble, and standing rampant on the terminations of the wide balustrades of the staircase. These lions are magnificently executed, and it is said were sculptured by Rademas, the great prince who designed the staircase, and who was without doubt, to judge from the many beautiful examples of his art that we saw afterwards, one of the finest sculptors who ever lived, either in this or any other country. Then we climbed almost with a feeling of awe up that splendid stair, a work executed for all time and that will, I do not doubt, be admired thousands of years hence by generations unborn unless an earthquake should throw it down. Even Umslopogaas, who as a general rule made it a point of honour not to show astonishment, which he considered undignified, was fairly startled out of himself, and asked if the 'bridge had been built by men or devils', which was his vague way of alluding to any supernatural power. But Alphonse did not care about it. Its solid grandeur jarred upon the frivolous little Frenchman, who said that it was all 'tres magnifique, mais triste — ah, triste!' and went on to suggest that it would be improved if the balustrades were *gilt*.

On we went up the first flight of one hundred and twenty steps, across the broad platform joining it to the second flight, where we paused to admire the glorious view of one of the most beautiful stretches of country that the world can show, edged by the blue waters of the lake. Then we passed on up the stair till at last we reached the top, where we found a large standing space to which there were three entrances, all of small size. Two of these opened on to rather narrow galleries or roadways cut in the face of the precipice that ran round the palace walls and led to the principal thoroughfares of the city, and were used by the inhabitants passing up and down from the docks. These were defended by gates of bronze, and also, as we afterwards learnt, it was possible to let down a portion of the roadways themselves by withdrawing certain bolts, and thus render it quite impracticable for an enemy to pass. The third entrance consisted of a flight of ten curved black marble steps leading to a doorway cut in the palace wall. This wall was in itself a work of art, being built of huge blocks of granite to the height of forty feet, and so fashioned that its face was concave, whereby it was rendered practically impossible for it to be scaled. To this doorway our guide led us. The door, which was massive, and made of wood protected by an outer gate of bronze, was closed; but on our approach it was thrown wide, and we were met by the challenge of a sentry, who was armed with a heavy triangular-bladed spear, not unlike a bayonet in shape, and a cutting sword, and protected by breast and back plates of skilfully prepared hippopotamus hide, and a small round shield fashioned of the same tough material. The sword instantly attracted our attention; it was practically identical with the one in the possession of Mr Mackenzie which he had obtained from the ill-starred wanderer. There was no mistaking the gold-lined fretwork cut in the thickness of the blade. So the man had told the truth after all. Our guide instantly gave a password, which the soldier acknowledged by letting the iron shaft of his spear fall with a ringing sound upon the pavement, and we passed on through the massive wall into the courtyard of the palace. This was about forty yards square, and laid out in flower-beds full of lovely shrubs and plants, many of which were quite new to me. Through the centre of this garden ran a broad walk formed of powdered shells brought from the lake in the place of gravel. Following this we came to another doorway with a round heavy arch, which is hung with thick curtains, for there are no doors in the palace itself. Then came another short passage, and we were in the great hall of the palace, and once more stood astonished at the simple and yet overpowering grandeur of the place.

The hall is, as we afterwards learnt, one hundred and fifty feet long by eighty wide, and has a magnificent arched roof of carved wood. Down the entire length of the building there are on either side, and at a distance of twenty feet from the wall, slender shafts of black marble springing sheer to the roof, beautifully fluted, and with carved capitals. At one end of this great place which these pillars support is the group of which I have already spoken as executed by the King Rademas to commemorate his building of the staircase; and really, when we had time to admire it, its loveliness almost struck us dumb. The group, of which the figures are in white, and the rest is black marble, is about half as large again as life, and represents a young man of noble countenance and form sleeping heavily upon a couch. One arm is carelessly thrown over the side of this couch, and his head reposes upon the other, its curling locks partially hiding it. Bending over him, her hand resting on his forehead, is a draped female form of such white loveliness as to make the beholder's breath stand still. And as for the calm glory that shines upon her perfect face — well, I can never hope to describe it. But there it rests like the shadow of an angel's smile; and power, love, and divinity all have their part in it. Her eyes are fixed upon the sleeping youth, and perhaps the most extraordinary thing about this beautiful work is the success with which the artist has succeeded in depicting on the sleeper's worn and weary face the sudden rising of a new and spiritual thought as the spell begins to work within his mind. You can see that an inspiration is breaking in upon the darkness of the man's soul as the dawn breaks in upon the darkness of night. It is a glorious piece of statuary, and none but a genius could have conceived it. Between each of the black marble columns is some such group of figures, some allegorical, and some representing the persons and wives of deceased monarchs or great men; but none of them, in our opinion, comes up the one I have described, although several are from the hand of the sculptor and engineer, King Rademas.

In the exact centre of the hall was a solid mass of black marble about the size of a baby's arm-chair, which it rather resembled in appearance. This, as we afterwards learnt, was the sacred stone of this remarkable people, and on it their monarchs laid their hand after the ceremony of coronation, and swore by the sun to safeguard the interests of the empire, and to maintain its customs, traditions, and laws. This stone was evidently exceedingly ancient (as indeed all stones are), and was scored down its sides with long marks or lines, which Sir Henry said proved it to have been a fragment that at some remote period in its history had been ground in the iron jaws of glaciers. There was a curious prophecy about this block of marble, which was reported among the people to have fallen from the sun, to the effect that when it was shattered into fragments a king of alien race should rule over the land. As the stone, however, looked remarkably solid, the native princes seemed to have a fair chance of keeping their own for many a long year.

At the end of the hall is a dais spread with rich carpets, on which two thrones are set side by side. These thrones are shaped like great chairs, and made of solid gold. The seats are richly cushioned, but the backs are left bare, and on each is carved the emblem of the sun, shooting out his fiery rays in all directions. The footstools are golden lions couchant, with yellow topazes set in them for eyes. There are no other gems about them.

The place is lighted by numerous but narrow windows, placed high up, cut on the principle of the loopholes to be seen in ancient castles, but innocent of glass, which was evidently unknown here.

Such is a brief description of this splendid hall in which we now found ourselves, compiled of course from our subsequent knowledge of it. On this occasion we had but little time for observation, for when we entered we perceived that a large number of men were gathered together in front of the two thrones, which were unoccupied. The principal among them were seated on carved wooden chairs ranged to the right and the left of the thrones, but not in front of them, and were dressed in white tunics, with various embroideries and different coloured edgings, and armed with the usual pierced and gold-inlaid swords. To judge from the dignity of their appearance, they seemed one and all to be individuals of very great importance. Behind each of these great men stood a small knot of followers and attendants.

Seated by themselves, in a little group to the left of the throne, were six men of a different stamp. Instead of wearing the ordinary kilt, they were clothed in long robes of pure white linen, with the same symbol of the sun that is to be seen on the back of the chairs, emblazoned in gold thread upon the breast. This garment was girt up at the waist with a simple golden curb-like chain, from which hung long elliptic plates of the same metal, fashioned in shiny scales like those of a fish, that, as their wearers moved, jingled and reflected the light. They were all men of mature age and of a severe and impressive cast of features, which was rendered still more imposing by the long beards they wore.

The personality of one individual among them, however, impressed us at once. He seemed to stand out among his fellows and refuse to be overlooked. He was very old — eighty at least — and extremely tall, with a long snow-white beard that hung nearly to his waist. His features were aquiline and deeply cut, and his eyes were grey and cold-looking. The heads of the others were bare, but this man wore a round cap entirely covered with gold embroidery, from which we judged that he was a person of great importance; and indeed we afterwards discovered that he was Agon, the High Priest of the country. As we approached, all these men, including the priests, rose and bowed to us with the greatest courtesy, at the same time placing the two fingers across the lips in salutation. Then soft-footed attendants advanced from between the pillars, bearing seats, which were placed in a line in front of the thrones. We three sat down, Alphonse and Umslopogaas standing behind us. Scarcely had we done so when there came a blare of trumpets from some passage to the right, and a similar blare from the left. Next a man with a long white wand of ivory appeared just in front of the right-hand throne, and cried out something in a loud voice, ending with the word *Nyleptha*, repeated three times; and another man, similarly attired, called out a similar sentence before the other throne, but ending with the word *Sorais*, also repeated thrice. Then came the tramp of armed men from each side entrance, and in filed about a score of picked and magnificently accoutred guards, who formed up on each side of the thrones, and let their heavy iron-handled spears fall simultaneously with a clash upon the black marble flooring. Another double blare of trumpets, and in from either side, each attended by six maidens, swept the two Queens of Zu-Vendis, everybody in the hall rising to greet them as they came.

I have seen beautiful women in my day, and am no longer thrown into transports at the sight of a pretty face; but language fails me when I try to give some idea of the blaze of loveliness that then broke upon us in the persons of these sister Queens. Both were young — perhaps five-and-twenty years of age — both were tall and exquisitely formed; but there the likeness stopped. One, Nyleptha, was a woman of dazzling fairness; her right arm and breast bare, after the custom of her people, showed like snow even against her white and gold-embroidered 'kaf', or toga. And as for her sweet face, all I can say is, that it was one that few men could look on and forget. Her hair, a veritable crown of gold, clustered in short ringlets over her shapely head, half hiding the ivory brow, beneath which eyes of deep and glorious grey flashed out in tender majesty. I cannot attempt to describe her other features, only the mouth was most sweet, and curved like Cupid's bow, and over the whole countenance there shone an indescribable look of loving-kindness, lit up by a shadow of delicate humour that lay upon her face like a touch of silver on a rosy cloud.

She wore no jewels, but on her neck, arm, and knee were the usual torques of gold, in this instance fashioned like a snake; and her dress was of pure white linen of excessive fineness, plentifully embroidered with gold and with the familiar symbols of the sun.

Her twin sister, Sorais, was of a different and darker type of beauty. Her hair was wavy like Nyleptha's but coal-black, and fell in masses on her shoulders; her complexion was olive, her eyes large, dark, and lustrous; the lips were full, and I thought rather cruel. Somehow her face, quiet and even cold as it is, gave an idea of passion in repose, and caused one to wonder involuntarily what its aspect would be if anything occurred to break the calm. It reminded me of the deep sea, that even on the bluest days never loses its visible stamp of power, and in its murmuring sleep is yet instinct with the spirit of the storm. Her figure, like her sister's, was almost perfect in its curves and outlines, but a trifle more rounded, and her dress was absolutely the same.

As this lovely pair swept onwards to their respective thrones, amid the deep attentive silence of the Court, I was bound to confess to myself that they did indeed fulfil my idea of royalty. Royal they were in every way — in form, in grace, and queenly dignity, and in the barbaric splendour of their attendant pomp. But methought that they needed no guards or gold to proclaim their power and bind the loyalty of wayward men. A glance from those bright eyes or a smile from those sweet lips, and while the red blood runs in the veins of youth women such as these will never lack subjects ready to do their biddings to the death.

But after all they were women first and queens afterwards, and therefore not devoid of curiosity. As they passed to their seats I saw both of them glance swiftly in our direction. I saw, too, that their eyes passed by me, seeing nothing to charm them in the person of an insignificant and grizzled old man. Then they looked with evident astonishment on the grim form of old Umslopogaas, who raised his axe in salutation. Attracted next by the splendour of Good's apparel, for a second their glance rested on him like a humming moth upon a flower, then off it darted to where Sir Henry Curtis stood, the sunlight from a window playing upon his yellow hair and peaked beard, and marking the outlines of his massive frame against the twilight of the somewhat gloomy hall. He raised his eyes, and they met the fair Nyleptha's full, and thus for the first time the goodliest man and woman that it has ever been my lot to see looked one upon another. And why it was I know not, but I saw the swift blood run up Nyleptha's skin as the pink lights run up the morning sky. Red grew her fair bosom and shapely arm, red the swanlike neck; the rounded cheeks blushed red as the petals of a rose, and then the crimson flood sank back to whence it came and left her pale and trembling.

I glanced at Sir Henry. He, too, had coloured up to the eyes.

'Oh, my word!' thought I to myself, 'the ladies have come on the stage, and now we may look to the plot to develop itself.' And I sighed and shook my head, knowing that the beauty of a woman is like the beauty of the lightning — a destructive thing and a cause of desolation. By the time that I had finished my reflections both the Queens were on the thrones, for all this had happened in about six seconds. Once more the unseen trumpets blared out, and then the Court seated itself, and Queen Sorais motioned to us to do likewise.

Next from among the crowd whither he had withdrawn stepped forward our guide, the old gentleman who had towed us ashore, holding by the hand the girl whom we had seen first and afterwards rescued from the hippopotamus. Having made obeisance he proceeded to address the Queens, evidently describing to them the way and place where we had been found. It was most amusing to watch the astonishment, not unmixed with fear, reflected upon their faces as they listened to his tale. Clearly they could not understand how we had reached the lake and been found floating on it, and were inclined to attribute our presence to supernatural causes. Then the narrative proceeded, as I judged from the frequent appeals that our guide made to the girl, to the point where we had shot the hippopotami, and we at once perceived that there was something very wrong about those hippopotami, for the history was frequently interrupted by indignant exclamations from the little group of white-robed priests and even from the courtiers, while the two Queens listened with an amazed expression, especially when our guide pointed to the rifles in our hands as being the means of destruction. And here, to make matters clear, I may as well explain at once that the inhabitants of Zu-Vendis are sun-worshippers, and that for some reason or another the hippopotamus is sacred among them. Not that they do not kill it, because at a certain season of the year they slaughter thousands — which are specially preserved in large lakes up the country — and use their hides for armour for soldiers; but this does not prevent them from considering these animals as sacred to the sun. Now, as ill luck would have it, the particular hippopotami we had shot were a family of tame animals that were kept in the mouth of the port and daily fed by priests whose special duty it was to attend to them. When we shot them I thought that the brutes were suspiciously tame, and this was, as we afterwards ascertained, the cause of it. Thus it came about that in attempting to show off we had committed sacrilege of a most aggravated nature.

When our guide had finished his tale, the old man with the long beard and round cap, whose appearance I have already described, and who was, as I have said, the High Priest of the country, and known by the name of Agon, rose and commenced an impassioned harangue. I did not like the look of his cold grey eye as he fixed it on us. I should have liked it still less had I known that in the name of the outraged majesty of his god he was demanding that the whole lot of us should be offered up as a sacrifice by means of being burnt alive.

After he had finished speaking the Queen Sorais addressed him in a soft and musical voice, and appeared, to judge from his gestures of dissent, to be putting the other side of the question before him. Then Nyleptha spoke in liquid accents. Little did we know that she was pleading for our lives. Finally, she turned and addressed a tall, soldierlike man of middle age with a black beard and a long plain sword, whose name, as we afterwards learnt, was Nasta, and who was the greatest lord in the country; apparently appealing to him for support. Now when Sir Henry had caught her eye and she had blushed so rosy red, I had seen that the incident had not escaped this man's notice, and, what is more, that it was eminently disagreeable to him, for he bit his lip and his hand tightened on his sword-hilt. Afterwards we learnt that he was an aspirant for the hand of this Queen in marriage, which accounted for it. This being so, Nyleptha could not have appealed to a worse person, for, speaking in slow, heavy tones, he appeared to confirm all that the High Priest Agon had said. As he spoke, Sorais put her elbow on her knee, and, resting her chin on her hand, looked at him with a suppressed smile upon her lips, as though she saw through the man, and was determined to be his match; but Nyleptha grew very angry, her cheek flushed, her eyes flashed, and she did indeed look lovely. Finally she turned to Agon and seemed to give some sort of qualified assent, for he bowed at her words; and as she spoke she moved her hands as though to emphasize what she said; while all the time Sorais kept her chin on her hand and smiled. Then suddenly Nyleptha made a sign, the trumpets blew again, and everybody rose to leave the hall save ourselves and the guards, whom she motioned to stay.

When they were all gone she bent forward and, smiling sweetly, partially by signs and partially by exclamations made it clear to us that she was very anxious to know where we came from. The difficulty was how to explain, but at last an idea struck me. I had my large pocket-book in my pocket and a pencil. Taking it out, I made a little sketch of a lake, and then as best I could I drew the underground river and the lake at the other end. When I had done this I advanced to the steps of the throne and gave it to her. She understood it at once and clapped her hands with delight, and then descending from the throne took it to her sister Sorais, who also evidently understood. Next she took the pencil from me, and after examining it with curiosity proceeded to make a series of delightful little sketches, the first representing herself holding out both hands in welcome, and a man uncommonly like Sir Henry taking them. Next she drew a lovely little picture of a hippopotamus rolling about dying in the water, and of an individual, in whom we had no difficulty in recognizing Agon the High Priest, holding up his hands in horror on the bank. Then followed a most alarming picture of a dreadful fiery furnace and of the same figure, Agon, poking us into it with a forked stick. This picture perfectly horrified me, but I was a little reassured when she nodded sweetly and proceeded to make a fourth drawing — a man again uncommonly like Sir Henry, and of two women, in whom I recognized Sorais and herself, each with one arm around him, and holding a sword in protection over him. To all of these Sorais, who I saw was employed in carefully taking us all in — especially Curtis — signified her approval by nodding.

At last Nyleptha drew a final sketch of a rising sun, indicating that she must go, and that we should meet on the following morning; whereat Sir Henry looked so disappointed that she saw it, and, I suppose by way of consolation, extended her hand to him to kiss, which he did with pious fervour. At the same time Sorais, off whom Good had never taken his eyeglass during the whole indaba [interview], rewarded him by giving him her hand to kiss, though, while she did so, her eyes were fixed upon Sir Henry. I am glad to say that I was not implicated in these proceedings; neither of them gave *me* her hand to kiss.

Then Nyleptha turned and addressed the man who appeared to be in command of the bodyguard, apparently from her manner and his frequent obeisances, giving him very stringent and careful orders; after which, with a somewhat coquettish nod and smile, she left the hall, followed by Sorais and most of the guards.

When the Queens had gone, the officer whom Nyleptha had addressed came forward and with many tokens of deep respect led us from the hall through various passages to a sumptuous set of apartments opening out of a large central room lighted with brazen swinging lamps (for it was now dusk) and richly carpeted and strewn with couches. On a table in the centre of the room was set a profusion of food and fruit, and, what is more, flowers. There was a delicious wine also in ancient-looking sealed earthenware flagons, and beautifully chased golden and ivory cups to drink it from. Servants, male and female, also were there to minister to us, and whilst we ate, from some recess outside the apartment

'The silver lute did speak between The trumpet's lordly blowing;'

and altogether we found ourselves in a sort of earthly paradise which was only disturbed by the vision of that disgusting High Priest who intended to commit us to the flames. But so very weary were we with our labours that we could scarcely keep ourselves awake through the sumptuous meal, and as soon as it was over we indicated that we desired to sleep. As a further precaution against surprise we left Umslopogaas with his axe to sleep in the main chamber near the curtained doorways leading to the apartments which we occupied respectively, Good and I in the one, and Sir Henry and Alphonse in the other. Then throwing off our clothes, with the exception of the mail shirts, which we considered it safer to keep on, we flung ourselves down upon the low and luxurious couches, and drew the silk-embroidered coverlids over us.

In two minutes I was just dropping off when I was aroused by Good's voice.

'I say, Quatermain,' he said, 'did you ever see such eyes?'

'Eyes!' I said, crossly; 'what eyes?'

'Why, the Queen's, of course! Sorais, I mean — at least I think that is her name.'

'Oh, I don't know,' I yawned; 'I didn't notice them much: I suppose they are good eyes,' and again I dropped off.

Five minutes or so elapsed, and I was once more awakened.

'I say, Quatermain,' said the voice.

'Well,' I answered testily, 'what is it now?'

'Did you notice her ankle? The shape —'

This was more than I could stand. By my bed stood the veldtschoons I had been wearing. Moved quite beyond myself, I took them up and threw them straight at Good's head — and hit it.

Afterwards I slept the sleep of the just, and a very heavy sleep it must be. As for Good, I don't know if he went to sleep or if he continued to pass Sorais' beauties in mental review, and, what is more, I don't care.

About the Zu-Vendi People

And now the curtain is down for a few hours, and the actors in this novel drama are plunged in dewy sleep. Perhaps we should except Nyleptha, whom the reader may, if poetically inclined, imagine lying in her bed of state encompassed by her maidens, tiring women, guards, and all the other people and appurtenances that surround a throne, and yet not able to slumber for thinking of the strangers who had visited a country where no such strangers had ever come before, and wondering, as she lay awake, who they were and what their past has been, and if she was ugly compared to the women of their native place. I, however, not being poetically inclined, will take advantage of the lull to give some account of the people among whom we found ourselves, compiled, needless to state, from information which we subsequently collected.

The name of this country, to begin at the beginning, is Zu-Vendis, from Zu, 'yellow', and Vendis, 'place or country'. Why it is called the Yellow Country I have never been able to ascertain accurately, nor do the inhabitants themselves know. Three reasons are, however, given, each of which would suffice to account for it. The first is that the name owes its origin to the great quantity of gold that is found in the land. Indeed, in this respect Zu-Vendis is a veritable Eldorado, the precious metal being extraordinarily plentiful. At present it is collected from purely alluvial diggings, which we subsequently inspected, and which are situated within a day's journey from Milosis, being mostly found in pockets and in nuggets weighing from an ounce up to six or seven pounds in weight. But other diggings of a similar nature are known to exist, and I have besides seen great veins of gold-bearing quartz. In Zu-Vendis gold is a much commoner metal than silver, and thus it has curiously enough come to pass that silver is the legal tender of the country.

The second reason given is, that at certain times of the year the native grasses of the country, which are very sweet and good, turn as yellow as ripe corn; and the third arises from a tradition that the people were originally yellow skinned, but grew white after living for many generations upon these high lands. Zu-Vendis is a country about the size of France, is, roughly speaking, oval in shape; and on every side cut off from the surrounding territory by illimitable forests of impenetrable thorn, beyond which are said to be hundreds of miles of morasses, deserts, and great mountains. It is, in short, a huge, high tableland rising up in the centre of the dark continent, much as in southern Africa flat-topped mountains rise from the level of the surrounding veldt. Milosis itself lies, according to my aneroid, at a level of about nine thousand feet above the sea, but most of the land is even higher, the greatest elevation of the open country being, I believe, about eleven thousand feet. As a consequence the climate is, comparatively speaking, a cold one, being very similar to that of southern England, only brighter and not so rainy. The land is, however, exceedingly fertile, and grows all cereals and temperate fruits and timber to perfection; and in the lower-lying parts even produces a hardy variety of sugar-cane. Coal is found in great abundance, and in many places crops out from the surface; and so is pure marble, both black and white. The same may be said of almost every metal except silver, which is scarce, and only to be obtained from a range of mountains in the north.

Zu-Vendis comprises in her boundaries a great variety of scenery, including two ranges of snow-clad mountains, one on the western boundary beyond the impenetrable belt of thorn forest, and the other piercing the country from north to south, and passing at a distance of about eighty miles from Milosis, from which town its higher peaks are distinctly visible. This range forms the chief watershed of the land. There are also three large lakes — the biggest, namely that whereon we emerged, and which is named Milosis after the city, covering some two hundred square miles of country — and numerous small ones, some of them salt.

The population of this favoured land is, comparatively speaking, dense, numbering at a rough estimate from ten to twelve millions. It is almost purely agricultural in its habits, and divided into great classes as in civilized countries. There is a territorial nobility, a considerable middle class, formed principally of merchants, officers of the army, etc.; but the great bulk of the people are well-to-do peasants who live upon the lands of the lords, from whom they hold under a species of feudal tenure. The best bred people in the country are, as I think I have said, pure whites with a somewhat southern cast of countenance; but the common herd are much darker, though they do not show any negro or other African characteristics. As to their descent I can give no certain information. Their written records, which extend back for about a thousand years, give no hint of it. One very ancient chronicler does indeed, in alluding to some old tradition that existed in his day, talk of it as having probably originally 'come down with the people from the coast', but that may mean little or nothing. In short, the origin of the Zu-Vendi is lost in the mists of time. Whence they came or of what race they are no man knows. Their architecture and some of their sculptures suggest an Egyptian or possibly an Assyrian origin; but it is well known that their present remarkable style of building has only sprung up within the last eight hundred years, and they certainly retain no traces of Egyptian theology or customs. Again, their appearance and some of their habits are rather Jewish; but here again it seems hardly conceivable that they should have utterly lost all traces of the Jewish religion. Still, for aught I know, they may be one of the lost ten tribes whom people are so fond of discovering all over the world, or they may not. I do not know, and so can only describe them as I find them, and leave wiser heads than mine to make what they can out of it, if indeed this account should ever be read at all, which is exceedingly doubtful.

And now after I have said all this, I am, after all, going to hazard a theory of my own, though it is only a very little one, as the young lady said in mitigation of her baby. This theory is founded on a legend which I have heard among the Arabs on the east coast, which is to the effect that 'more than two thousand years ago' there were troubles in the country which was known as

Babylonia, and that thereon a vast horde of Persians came down to Bushire, where they took ship and were driven by the north-east monsoon to the east coast of Africa, where, according to the legend, 'the sun and fire worshippers' fell into conflict with the belt of Arab settlers who even then were settled on the east coast, and finally broke their way through them, and, vanishing into the interior, were no more seen. Now, I ask, is it not at least possible that the Zu-Vendi people are the descendants of these 'sun and fire worshippers' who broke through the Arabs and vanished? As a matter of fact, there is a good deal in their characters and customs that tallies with the somewhat vague ideas that I have of Persians. Of course we have no books of reference here, but Sir Henry says that if his memory does not fail him, there was a tremendous revolt in Babylon about 500 BC, whereon a vast multitude were expelled from the city. Anyhow, it is a well-established fact that there have been many separate emigrations of Persians from the Persian Gulf to the east coast of Africa up to as lately as seven hundred years ago. There are Persian tombs at Kilwa, on the east coast, still in good repair, which bear dates showing them to be just seven hundred years old.

In addition to being an agricultural people, the Zu-Vendi are, oddly enough, excessively warlike, and as they cannot from the exigencies of their position make war upon other nations, they fight among each other like the famed Kilkenny cats, with the happy result that the population never outgrows the power of the country to support it. This habit of theirs is largely fostered by the political condition of the country. The monarchy is nominally an absolute one, save in so far as it is tempered by the power of the priests and the informal council of the great lords; but, as in many other institutions, the king's writ does not run unquestioned throughout the length and breadth of the land. In short, the whole system is a purely feudal one (though absolute serfdom or slavery is unknown), all the great lords holding nominally from the throne, but a number of them being practically independent, having the power of life and death, waging war against and making peace with their neighbours as the whim or their interests lead them, and even on occasion rising in open rebellion against their royal master or mistress, and, safely shut up in their castles and fenced cities, as far from the seat of government, successfully defying them for years.

Zu-Vendis has had its king-makers as well as England, a fact that will be well appreciated when I state that eight different dynasties have sat upon the throne in the last one thousand years, every one of which took its rise from some noble family that succeeded in grasping the purple after a sanguinary struggle. At the date of our arrival in the country things were a little better than they had been for some centuries, the last king, the father of Nyleptha and Sorais, having been an exceptionally able and vigorous ruler, and, as a consequence, he kept down the power of the priests and nobles. On his death, two years before we reached Zu-Vendis, the twin sisters, his children, were, following an ancient precedent, called to the throne, since an attempt to exclude either would instantly have provoked a sanguinary civil war; but it was generally felt in the country that this measure was a most unsatisfactory one, and could hardly be expected to be permanent. Indeed, as it was, the various intrigues that were set on foot by ambitious nobles to obtain the hand of one or other of the queens in marriage had disquieted the country, and the general opinion was that there would be bloodshed before long.

I will now pass on to the question of the Zu-Vendi religion, which is nothing more or less than sun-worship of a pronounced and highly developed character. Around this sun-worship is grouped the entire social system of the Zu-Vendi. It sends its roots through every institution and custom of the land. From the cradle to the grave the Zu-Vendi follows the sun in every sense of the saying. As an infant he is solemnly held up in its light and dedicated to 'the symbol of good, the expression of power, and the hope of Eternity', the ceremony answering to our baptism. Whilst still a tiny child, his parents point out the glorious orb as the presence of a visible and beneficent god, and he worships it at its up-rising and down-setting. Then when still quite small, he goes, holding fast to the pendent end of his mother's 'kaf' (toga), up to the temple of the Sun of the nearest city, and there, when at midday the bright beams strike down upon the golden central altar and beat back the fire that burns thereon, he hears the white-robed priests raise their solemn chant of praise and sees the people fall down to adore, and then, amidst the blowing of the golden trumpets, watches the sacrifice thrown into the fiery furnace beneath the altar. Here he comes again to be declared 'a man' by the priests, and consecrated to war and to good works; here before the solemn altar he leads his bride; and here too, if differences shall unhappily arise, he divorces her.

And so on, down life's long pathway till the last mile is travelled, and he comes again armed indeed, and with dignity, but no longer a man. Here they bear him dead and lay his bier upon the falling brazen doors before the eastern altar, and when the last ray from the setting sun falls upon his white face the bolts are drawn and he vanishes into the raging furnace beneath and is ended.

The priests of the Sun do not marry, but are recruited as young men specially devoted to the work by their parents and supported by the State. The nomination to the higher offices of the priesthood lies with the Crown, but once appointed the nominees cannot be dispossessed, and it is scarcely too much to say that they really rule the land. To begin with, they are a united body sworn to obedience and secrecy, so that an order issued by the High Priest at Milosis will be instantly and unhesitatingly acted upon by the resident priest of a little country town three or four hundred miles off. They are the judges of the land, criminal and civil, an appeal lying only to the lord paramount of the district, and from him to the king; and they have, of course, practically unlimited jurisdiction over religious and moral offences, together with a right of excommunication, which, as in the faiths of more highly civilized lands, is a very effective weapon. Indeed, their rights and powers are almost unlimited, but I may as well state here that the priests of the Sun are wise in their generation, and do not push things too far. It is but very seldom that they go to extremes against anybody, being more inclined to exercise the prerogative of mercy than run the risk of exasperating the powerful and vigorous-minded people on whose neck they have set their yoke, lest it should rise and break it off altogether.

Another source of the power of the priests is their practical monopoly of learning, and their very considerable astronomical knowledge, which enables them to keep a hold on the popular mind by predicting eclipses and even comets. In Zu-Vendis only a few of the upper classes can read and write, but nearly all the priests have this knowledge, and are therefore looked upon as learned men.

The law of the country is, on the whole, mild and just, but differs in several respects from our civilized law. For instance, the law of England is much more severe upon offences against property than against the person, as becomes a people whose ruling passion is money. A man may half kick his wife to death or inflict horrible sufferings upon his children at a much cheaper rate of punishment than he can compound for the theft of a pair of old boots. In Zu-Vendis this is not so, for there they rightly or wrongly look upon the person as of more consequence than goods and chattels, and not, as in England, as a sort of necessary appendage to the latter. For murder the punishment is death, for treason death, for defrauding the orphan and the widow, for sacrilege, and for attempting to quit the country (which is looked on as a sacrilege) death. In each case the method of execution is the same, and a rather awful one. The culprit is thrown alive into the fiery furnace beneath one of the altars to the Sun. For all other offences, including the offence of idleness, the punishment is forced labour upon the vast national buildings which are always going on in some part of the country, with or without periodical floggings, according to the crime.

The social system of the Zu-Vendi allows considerable liberty to the individual, provided he does not offend against the laws and customs of the country. They are polygamous in theory, though most of them have only one wife on account of the expense. By law a man is bound to provide a separate establishment for each wife. The first wife also is the legal wife, and her children are said to be 'of the house of the Father'. The children of the other wives are of the houses of their respective mothers. This does not, however, imply any slur upon either mother or children. Again, a first wife can, on entering into the married state, make a bargain that her husband shall marry no other wife. This, however, is very rarely done, as the women are the great upholders of polygamy, which not only provides for their surplus numbers but gives greater importance to the first wife, who is thus practically the head of several households. Marriage is looked upon as primarily a civil contract, and, subject to certain conditions and to a proper provision for children, is dissoluble at the will of both contracting parties, the divorce, or 'unloosing', being formally and ceremoniously accomplished by going through certain portions of the marriage ceremony backwards.

The Zu-Vendi are on the whole a very kindly, pleasant, and light-hearted people. They are not great traders and care little about money, only working to earn enough to support themselves in that class of life in which they were born. They are exceedingly conservative, and look with disfavour upon changes. Their legal tender is silver, cut into little squares of different weights; gold is the baser coin, and is about of the same value as our silver. It is, however, much prized for its beauty, and largely used for ornaments and decorative purposes. Most of the trade, however, is carried on by means of sale and barter, payment being made in kind. Agriculture is the great business of the country, and is really well understood and carried out, most of the available acreage being under cultivation. Great attention is also given to the breeding of cattle and horses, the latter being unsurpassed by any I have ever seen either in Europe or Africa.

The land belongs theoretically to the Crown, and under the Crown to the great lords, who again divide it among smaller lords, and so on down to the little peasant farmer who works his forty 'reestu' (acres) on a system of half-profits with his immediate lord. In fact the whole system is, as I have said, distinctly feudal, and it interested us much to meet with such an old friend far in the unknown heart of Africa.

The taxes are very heavy. The State takes a third of a man's total earnings, and the priesthood about five per cent on the remainder. But on the other hand, if a man through any cause falls into bona fide misfortune the State supports him in the position of life to which he belongs. If he is idle, however, he is sent to work on the Government undertakings, and the State looks after his wives and children. The State also makes all the roads and builds all town houses, about which great care is shown, letting them out to families at a small rent. It also keeps up a standing army of about twenty thousand men, and provides watchmen, etc. In return for their five per cent the priests attend to the service of the temples, carry out all religious ceremonies, and keep schools, where they teach whatever they think desirable, which is not very much. Some of the temples also possess private property, but priests as individuals cannot hold property.

And now comes a question which I find some difficulty in answering. Are the Zu-Vendi a civilized or barbarous people? Sometimes I think the one, sometimes the other. In some branches of art they have attained the very highest proficiency. Take for instance their buildings and their statuary. I do not think that the latter can be equalled either in beauty or imaginative power anywhere in the world, and as for the former it may have been rivalled in ancient Egypt, but I am sure that it has never been since. But, on the other hand, they are totally ignorant of many other arts. Till Sir Henry, who happened to know something about it, showed them how to do it by mixing silica and lime, they could not make a piece of glass, and their crockery is rather primitive. A water-clock is their nearest approach to a watch; indeed, ours delighted them exceedingly. They know nothing about steam, electricity, or gunpowder, and mercifully for themselves nothing about printing or the penny post. Thus they are spared many evils, for of a truth our age has learnt the wisdom of the old-world saying, 'He who increaseth knowledge, increaseth sorrow.'

As regards their religion, it is a natural one for imaginative people who know no better, and might therefore be expected to turn to the sun and worship him as the all-Father, but it cannot justly be called elevating or spiritual. It is true that they do sometimes speak of the sun as the 'garment of the Spirit', but it is a vague term, and what they really adore is the fiery orb himself. They also call him the 'hope of eternity', but here again the meaning is vague, and I doubt if the phrase conveys any very clear impression to their minds. Some of them do indeed believe in a future life for the good — I know Nyleptha does firmly — but it is a private faith arising from the promptings of the spirit, not an essential of their creed. So on the whole I cannot say that I consider this sun-worship as a religion indicative of a civilized people, however magnificent and imposing its ritual, or however moral and high-sounding the maxims of its priests, many of whom, I am sure, have their own opinions on the whole subject; though of course they have nothing but praise for a system which provides them with so many of the good things of this world.

There are now only two more matters to which I need allude — namely, the language and the system of calligraphy. As for the former, it is soft-sounding, and very rich and flexible. Sir Henry says that it sounds something like modern Greek, but of course it has no connection with it. It is easy to acquire, being simple in its construction, and a peculiar quality about it is its euphony, and the way in which the sound of the words adapts itself to the meaning to be expressed. Long before we mastered the language, we could frequently make out what was meant by the ring of the sentence. It is on this account that the language lends itself so well to poetical declamation, of which these remarkable people are very fond. The Zu-Vendi alphabet seems, Sir henry says, to be derived, like every other known system of letters, from a Phoenician source, and therefore more remotely still from the ancient Egyptian hieratic writing. Whether this is a fact I cannot say, not being learned in such matters. All I know about it is that their alphabet consists of twenty-two characters, of which a few, notably B, E, and O, are not very unlike our own. The whole affair is, however, clumsy and puzzling. But as the people of Zu-Vendi are not given to the writing of novels, or of anything except business documents and records of the briefest character, it answers their purpose well enough.

The Flower Temple

It was half-past eight by my watch when I woke on the morning following our arrival at Milosis, having slept almost exactly twelve hours, and I must say that I did indeed feel better. Ah, what a blessed thing is sleep! and what a difference twelve hours of it or so makes to us after days and nights of toil and danger. It is like going to bed one man and getting up another.

I sat up upon my silken couch — never had I slept upon such a bed before — and the first thing that I saw was Good's eyeglass fixed on me from the recesses of his silken couch. There was nothing else of him to be seen except his eyeglass, but I knew from the look of it that he was awake, and waiting till I woke up to begin.

'I say, Quatermain,' he commenced sure enough, 'did you observe her skin? It is as smooth as the back of an ivory hairbrush.'

'Now look here, Good,' I remonstrated, when there came a sound at the curtain, which, on being drawn, admitted a functionary, who signified by signs that he was there to lead us to the bath. We gladly consented, and were conducted to a delightful marble chamber, with a pool of running crystal water in the centre of it, into which we gaily plunged. When we had bathed, we returned to our apartment and dressed, and then went into the central room where we had supped on the previous evening, to find a morning meal already prepared for us, and a capital meal it was, though I should be puzzled to describe the dishes. After breakfast we lounged round and admired the tapestries and carpets and some pieces of statuary that were placed about, wondering the while what was going to happen next. Indeed, by this time our minds were in such a state of complete bewilderment that we were, as a matter of fact, ready for anything that might arrive. As for our sense of astonishment, it was pretty well obliterated. Whilst we were still thus engaged, our friend the captain of the guard presented himself, and with many obeisances signified that we were to follow him, which we did, not without doubts and heart-searchings — for we guessed that the time had come when we should have to settle the bill for those confounded hippopotami with our cold-eyed friend Agon, the High Priest. However, there was no help for it, and personally I took great comfort in the promise of the protection of the sister Queens, knowing that if ladies have a will they can generally find a way; so off we started as though we liked it. A minute's walk through a passage and an outer court brought us to the great double gates of the palace that open on to the wide highway which runs uphill through the heart of Milosis to the Temple of the Sun a mile away, and thence down the slope on the farther side of the temple to the outer wall of the city.

These gates are very large and massive, and an extraordinarily beautiful work in metal. Between them — for one set is placed at the entrance to an interior, and one at that of the exterior wall — is a fosse, forty-five feet in width. This fosse is filled with water and spanned by a drawbridge, which when lifted makes the palace nearly impregnable to anything except siege guns. As we came, one half of the wide gates were flung open, and we passed over the drawbridge and presently stood gazing up one of the most imposing, if not the most imposing, roadways in the world. It is a hundred feet from curb to curb, and on either side, not cramped and crowded together, as is our European fashion, but each standing in its own grounds, and built equidistant from and in similar style to the rest, are a series of splendid, single-storied mansions, all of red granite. These are the town houses of the nobles of the Court, and stretch away in unbroken lines for a mile or more till the eye is arrested by the glorious vision of the Temple of the Sun that crowns the hill and heads the roadway.

As we stood gazing at this splendid sight, of which more anon, there suddenly dashed up to the gateway four chariots, each drawn by two white horses. These chariots are two-wheeled, and made of wood. They are fitted with a stout pole, the weight of which is supported by leathern girths that form a portion of the harness. The wheels are made with four spokes only, are tired with iron, and quite innocent of springs. In the front of the chariot, and immediately over the pole, is a small seat for the driver, railed round to prevent him from being jolted off. Inside the machine itself are three low seats, one at each side, and one with the back to the horses, opposite to which is the door. The whole vehicle is lightly and yet strongly made, and, owing to the grace of the curves, though primitive, not half so ugly as might be expected.

But if the chariots left something to be desired, the horses did not. They were simply splendid, not very large but strongly built, and well ribbed up, with small heads, remarkably large and round hoofs, and a great look of speed and blood. I have often wondered whence this breed, which presents many distinct characteristics, came, but like that of its owners, it history is obscure. Like the people the horses have always been there. The first and last of these chariots were occupied by guards, but the centre two were empty, except for the driver, and to these we were conducted. Alphonse and I got into the first, and Sir Henry, Good, and Umslopogaas into the one behind, and then suddenly off we went. And we did go! Among the Zu-Vendi it is not usual to trot horses either riding or driving, especially when the journey to be made is a short one — they go at full gallop. As soon as we were seated the driver called out, the horses sprang forward, and we were whirled away at a speed sufficient to take one's breath, and which, till I got accustomed to it, kept me in momentary fear of an upset. As for the wretched Alphonse, he clung with a despairing face to the side of what he called this 'devil of a fiacre', thinking that every moment was his last. Presently it occurred to him to ask where we were going, and I told him that, as far as I could ascertain, we were going to be sacrificed by burning. You should have seen his face as he grasped the side of the vehicle and cried out in his terror.

But the wild-looking charioteer only leant forward over his flying steeds and shouted; and the air, as it went singing past, bore away the sound of Alphonse's lamentations.

And now before us, in all its marvellous splendour and dazzling loveliness, shone out the Temple of the Sun — the peculiar pride of the Zu-Vendi, to whom it was what Solomon's, or rather Herod's, Temple was to the Jews. The wealth, and skill, and labour of generations had been given to the building of this wonderful place, which had been only finally completed within the last fifty years. Nothing was spared that the country could produce, and the result was indeed worthy of the effort, not so much on account of its size — for there are larger fanes in the world — as because of its perfect proportions, the richness and beauty of its materials, and the wonderful workmanship. The building (that stands by itself on a space of some eight acres of garden ground on the hilltop, around which are the dwelling-places of the priests) is built in the shape of a sunflower, with a dome-covered central hall, from which radiate twelve petal-shaped courts, each dedicated to one of the twelve months, and serving as the repositories of statues reared in memory of the illustrious dead. The width of the circle beneath the dome is three hundred feet, the height of the dome is four hundred feet, and the length of the rays is one hundred and fifty feet, and the height of their roofs three hundred feet, so that they run into the central dome exactly as the petals of the sunflower run into the great raised heart. Thus the exact measurement from the centre of the central altar to the extreme point of any one of the rounded rays would be three hundred feet (the width of the circle itself), or a total of six hundred feet from the rounded extremity of one ray or petal to the extremity of the opposite one.

The building itself is of pure and polished white marble, which shows out in marvellous contrast to the red granite of the frowning city, on whose brow it glistens indeed like an imperial diadem upon the forehead of a dusky queen. The outer surface of the dome and of the twelve petal courts is covered entirely with thin sheets of beaten gold; and from the extreme point of the roof of each of these petals a glorious golden form with a trumpet in its hand and widespread wings is figured in the very act of soaring into space. I really must leave whoever reads this to imagine the surpassing beauty of these golden roofs flashing when the sun strikes — flashing like a thousand fires aflame on a mountain of polished marble — so fiercely that the reflection can be clearly seen from the great peaks of the range a hundred miles away.

It is a marvellous sight — this golden flower upborne upon the cool white marble walls, and I doubt if the world can show such another. What makes the whole effect even more gorgeous is that a belt of a hundred and fifty feet around the marble wall of the temple is planted with an indigenous species of sunflower, which were at the time when we first saw them a sheet of golden bloom.

The main entrance to this wonderful place is between the two northernmost of the rays or petal courts, and is protected first by the usual bronze gates, and then by doors made of solid marble, beautifully carved with allegorical subjects and overlaid with gold. When these are passed there is only the thickness of the wall, which is, however, twenty-five feet (for the Zu-Vendi build for all time), and another slight wall also of white marble, introduced in order to avoid causing a visible gap in the inner skin of the wall, and you stand in the circular hall under the great dome. Advancing to the central altar you look upon as beautiful a sight as the imagination of man can conceive. You are in the middle of the holy place, and above you the great white marble dome (for the inner skin, like the outer, is of polished marble throughout) arches away in graceful curves something like that of St Paul's in London, only at a slighter angle, and from the funnel-like opening at the exact apex a bright beam of light pours down upon the golden altar. At the east and the west are other altars, and other beams of light stab the sacred twilight to the heart. In every direction, 'white, mystic, wonderful', open out the ray-like courts, each pierced through by a single arrow of light that serves to illumine its lofty silence and dimly to reveal the monuments of the dead.

Overcome at so awe-inspiring a sight, the vast loveliness of which thrills the nerves like a glance from beauty's eyes, you turn to the central golden altar, in the midst of which, though you cannot see it now, there burns a pale but steady flame crowned with curls of faint blue smoke. It is of marble overlaid with pure gold, in shape round like the sun, four feet in height, and thirty-six in circumference. Here also, hinged to the foundations of the altar, are twelve petals of beaten gold. All night and, except at one hour, all day also, these petals are closed over the altar itself exactly as the petals of a water-lily close over the yellow crown in stormy weather; but when the sun at midday pierces through the funnel in the dome and lights upon the golden flower, the petals open and reveal the hidden mystery, only to close again when the ray has passed.

Nor is this all. Standing in semicircles at equal distances from each other on the north and south of the sacred place are ten golden angels, or female winged forms, exquisitely shaped and draped. These figures, which are slightly larger than life-size, stand with bent heads in an attitude of adoration, their faces shadowed by their wings, and are most imposing and of exceeding beauty.

There is but one thing further which calls for description in this altar, which is, that to the east the flooring in front of it is not of pure white marble, as elsewhere throughout the building, but of solid brass, and this is also the case in front of the other two altars.

The eastern and western altars, which are semicircular in shape, and placed against the wall of the building, are much less imposing, and are not enfolded in golden petals. They are, however, also of gold, the sacred fire burns on each, and a golden-winged figure stands on either side of them. Two great golden rays run up the wall behind them, but where the third or middle one should be is an opening in the wall, wide on the outside, but narrow within, like a loophole turned inwards. Through the eastern loophole stream the first beams of the rising sun, and strike right across the circle, touching the folded petals of the great gold flower as they pass till they impinge upon the western altar. In the same way at night the last rays of the sinking sun rest for a while on the eastern altar before they die away into darkness. It is the promise of the dawn to the evening and the evening to the dawn.

With the exception of those three altars and the winged figures about them, the whole space beneath the vast white dome is utterly empty and devoid of ornamentation — a circumstance that to my fancy adds greatly to its splendour.

Such is a brief description of this wonderful and lovely building, to the glories of which, to my mind so much enhanced by their complete simplicity, I only wish I had the power to do justice. But I cannot, so it is useless talking more about it. But when I compare this great work of genius to some of the tawdry buildings and tinsel ornamentation produced in these latter days by European ecclesiastical architects, I feel that even highly civilized art might learn something from the Zu-Vendi masterpieces. I can only say that the exclamation which sprang to my lips as soon as my eyes first became accustomed to the dim light of that glorious building, and its white and curving beauties, perfect and thrilling as those of a naked goddess, grew upon me one by one, was, 'Well! a dog would feel religious here.' It is vulgarly put, but perhaps it conveys my meaning more clearly than any polished utterance.

At the temple gates our party was received by a guard of soldiers, who appeared to be under the orders of a priest; and by them we were conducted into one of the ray or 'petal' courts, as the priests call them, and there left for at least half-an-hour. Here we conferred together, and realizing that we stood in great danger of our lives, determined, if any attempt should be made upon us, to sell them as dearly as we could — Umslopogaas announcing his fixed intention of committing sacrilege on the person of Agon, the High Priest, by splitting his head with Inkosi-kaas. From where we stood we could perceive that an immense multitude were pouring into the temple, evidently in expectation of some unusual event, and I could not help fearing that we had to do with it. And here I may explain that every day, when the sunlight falls upon the central altar, and the trumpets sound, a burnt sacrifice is offered to the Sun, consisting generally of the carcase of a sheep or ox, or sometimes of fruit or corn. This event comes off about midday; of course, not always exactly at that hour, but as Zu-Vendis is situated not far from the Line, although — being so high above the sea it is very temperate — midday and the falling of the sunlight on the altar were generally simultaneous. Today the sacrifice was to take place at about eight minutes past twelve.

Just at twelve o'clock a priest appeared, and made a sign, and the officer of the guard signified to us that we were expected to advance, which we did with the best grace that we could muster, all except Alphonse, whose irrepressible teeth instantly began to chatter. In a few seconds we were out of the court and looking at a vast sea of human faces stretching away to the farthest limits of the great circle, all straining to catch a glimpse of the mysterious strangers who had committed sacrilege; the first strangers, mind you, who, to the knowledge of the multitude, had ever set foot in Zu-Vendis since such time that the memory of man runneth not to the contrary.

As we appeared there was a murmur through the vast crowd that went echoing away up the great dome, and we saw a visible blush of excitement grow on the thousands of faces, like a pink light on a stretch of pale cloud, and a very curious effect it was. On we passed down a lane cut through the heart of the human mass, till presently we stood upon the brazen patch of flooring to the east of the central altar, and immediately facing it. For some thirty feet around the golden-winged figures the space was roped off, and the multitudes stood outside the ropes. Within were a circle of white-robed gold-cinctured priests holding long golden trumpets in their hands, and immediately in front of us was our friend Agon, the High Priest, with his curious cap upon his head. His was the only covered head in that vast assemblage. We took our stand upon the brazen space, little knowing what was prepared for us beneath, but I noticed a curious hissing sound proceeding apparently from the floor for which I could not account. Then came a pause, and I looked around to see if there was any sign of the two Queens, Nyleptha and Sorais, but they were not there. To the right of us, however, was a bare space that I guessed was reserved for them.

We waited, and presently a far-off trumpet blew, apparently high up in the dome. Then came another murmur from the multitude, and up a long lane, leading to the open space to our right, we saw the two Queens walking side by side. Behind them were some nobles of the Court, among whom I recognized the great lord Nasta, and behind them again a body of about fifty guards. These last I was very glad to see. Presently they had all arrived and taken their stand, the two Queens in the front, the nobles to the right and left, and the guards in a double semicircle behind them.

Then came another silence, and Nyleptha looked up and caught my eye; it seemed to me that there was meaning in her glance, and I watched it narrowly. From my eye it travelled down to the brazen flooring, on the outer edge of which we stood. Then followed a slight and almost imperceptible sidelong movement of the head. I did not understand it, and it was repeated. Then I guessed that she meant us to move back off the brazen floor. One more glance and I was sure of it — there was danger in standing on the floor. Sir Henry was placed on one side of me, Umslopogaas on the other. Keeping my eyes fixed straight before me, I whispered to them, first in Zulu and then in English, to draw slowly back inch by inch till half their feet were resting on the marble flooring where the brass ceased. Sir Henry whispered on to Good and Alphonse, and slowly, very very slowly, we shifted backwards; so slowly that nobody, except Nyleptha and Sorais, who saw everything seemed to notice the movement. Then I glanced again at Nyleptha, and saw that, by an almost imperceptible nod, she indicated approval. All the while Agon's eyes were fixed upon the altar before him apparently in an ecstasy of contemplation, and mine were fixed upon the small of his back in another sort of ecstasy. Suddenly he flung up his long arm, and in a solemn and resounding voice commenced a chant, of which for convenience' sake I append a rough, a *very* rough, translation here, though, of course, I did not then comprehend its meaning. It was an invocation to the Sun, and ran somewhat as follows: —

There is silence upon the face of the Earth and the waters thereof! Yea, the silence doth brood on the waters like a nesting bird; The silence sleepeth also upon the bosom of the profound darkness, Only high up in the great spaces star doth speak unto star, The Earth is faint with longing and wet with the tears of her desire; The star-girdled night doth embrace her, but she is not comforted. She lies enshrouded in mists like a corpse in the grave-clothes, And stretches her pale hands to the East.

Lo! away in the farthest East there is the shadow of a light; The Earth seeth and lifts herself. She looks out from beneath the hollow of her hand. Then thy great angels fly forth from the Holy Place, oh Sun, They shoot their fiery swords into the darkness and shrivel it up. They climb the heavens and cast down the pale stars from their thrones; Yea, they hurl the changeful stars back into the womb of the night; They cause the moon to become wan as the face of a dying man, And behold! Thy glory comes, oh Sun!

Oh, Thou beautiful one, Thou drapest thyself in fire. The wide heavens are thy pathway: thou rollest o'er them as a chariot. The Earth is thy bride. Thou dost embrace her and she brings forth children; Yea, Thou favourest her, and she yields her increase. Thou art the All Father and the giver of life, oh Sun. The young children stretch out their hands and grow in thy brightness; The old men creep forth and seeing remember their strength. Only the dead forget Thee, oh Sun!

When Thou art wroth then Thou dost hide Thy face; Thou drawest around Thee a thick curtain of shadows. Then the Earth grows cold and the Heavens are dismayed; They tremble, and the sound thereof is the sound of thunder: They weep, and their tears are outpoured in the rain; They sigh, and the wild winds are the voice of their sighing. The flowers die, the fruitful fields languish and turn pale; The old men and the little children go unto their appointed place When Thou withdrawest thy light, oh Sun!

Say, what art Thou, oh Thou matchless Splendour — Who set Thee on high, oh Thou flaming Terror? When didst Thou begin, and when is the day of Thy ending? Thou art the raiment of the living Spirit. None did place Thee on high, for Thou was the Beginning. Thou shalt not be ended when thy children are forgotten; Nay, Thou shalt never end, for thy hours are eternal. Thou sittest on high within thy golden house and measurest out the centuries. Oh Father of Life! oh dark-dispelling Sun!

He ceased this solemn chant, which, though it seems a poor enough thing after going through my mill, is really beautiful and impressive in the original; and then, after a moment's pause, he glanced up towards the funnel-sloped opening in the dome and added —

Oh Sun, descend upon thine Altar!

As he spoke a wonderful and a beautiful thing happened. Down from on high flashed a splendid living ray of light, cleaving the twilight like a sword of fire. Full upon the closed petals it fell and ran shimmering down their golden sides, and then the glorious flower opened as though beneath the bright influence. Slowly it opened, and as the great petals fell wide and revealed the golden altar on which the fire ever burns, the priests blew a blast upon the trumpets, and from all the people there rose a shout of praise that beat against the domed roof and came echoing down the marble walls. And now the flower altar was open, and the sunlight fell full upon the tongue of sacred flame and beat it down, so that it wavered, sank, and vanished into the hollow recesses whence it rose. As it vanished, the mellow notes of the trumpets rolled out once more. Again the old priest flung up his hands and called aloud —

We sacrifice to thee, oh Sun!

Once more I caught Nyleptha's eye; it was fixed upon the brazen flooring.

'Look out,' I said, aloud; and as I said it, I saw Agon bend forward and touch something on the altar. As he did so, the great white sea of faces around us turned red and then white again, and a deep breath went up like a universal sigh. Nyleptha leant forward, and with an involuntary movement covered her eyes with her hand. Sorais turned and whispered to the officer of the royal bodyguard, and then with a rending sound the whole of the brazen flooring slid from before our feet, and there in its place was suddenly revealed a smooth marble shaft terminating in a most awful raging furnace beneath the altar, big enough and hot enough to heat the iron stern-post of a man-of-war.

With a cry of terror we sprang backwards, all except the wretched Alphonse, who was paralysed with fear, and would have fallen into the fiery furnace which had been prepared for us, had not Sir Henry caught him in his strong hand as he was vanishing and dragged him back.

Instantly there arose the most fearful hubbub, and we four got back to back, Alphonse dodging frantically round our little circle in his attempts to take shelter under our legs. We all had our revolvers on — for though we had been politely disarmed of our guns on leaving the palace, of course these people did not know what a revolver was. Umslopogaas, too, had his axe, of which no effort had been made to deprive him, and now he whirled it round his head and sent his piercing Zulu war-shout echoing up the marble walls in fine defiant fashion. Next second, the priests, baffled of their prey, had drawn swords from beneath their white robes and were leaping on us like hounds upon a stag at bay. I saw that, dangerous as action might be, we must act or be lost, so as the first man came bounding along — and a great tall fellow he was — I sent a heavy revolver ball through him, and down he fell at the mouth of the shaft, and slid, shrieking frantically, into the fiery gulf that had been prepared for us.

Whether it was his cries, or the, to them, awful sound and effect of the pistol shot, or what, I know not, but the other priests halted, paralysed and dismayed, and before they could come on again Sorais had called out something, and we, together with the two Queens and most of the courtiers, were being surrounded with a wall of armed men. In a moment it was done, and still the priests hesitated, and the people hung in the balance like a herd of startled buck as it were, making no sign one way or the other.

The last yell of the burning priest had died away, the fire had finished him, and a great silence fell upon the place.

Then the High Priest Agon turned, and his face was as the face of a devil. 'Let the sacrifice be sacrificed,' he cried to the Queens. 'Has not sacrilege enough been done by these strangers, and would ye, as Queens, throw the cloak of your majesty over evildoers? Are not the creatures sacred to the Sun dead? And is not a priest of the Sun also dead, but now slain by the magic of these strangers, who come as the winds out of heaven, whence we know not, and who are what we know not? Beware, oh Queens, how ye tamper with the great majesty of the God, even before His high altar! There is a Power that is more than your power; there is a Justice that is higher than your justice. Beware how ye lift an impious hand against it! Let the sacrifice be sacrificed, oh Queens.'

Then Sorais made answer in her deep quiet tones, that always seemed to me to have a suspicion of mockery about them, however serious the theme: 'Oh, Agon, thou hast spoken according to thy desire, and thou hast spoken truth. But it is thou who wouldst lift an impious hand against the justice of thy God. Bethink thee the midday sacrifice is accomplished; the Sun hath claimed his priest as a sacrifice.'

This was a novel idea, and the people applauded it.

'Bethink thee what are these men? They are strangers found floating on the bosom of a lake. Who brought them here? How came they here? How know you that they also are not servants of the Sun? Is this the hospitality that ye would have our nation show to those whom chance brings to them, to throw them to the flames? Shame on you! Shame on you! What is hospitality? To receive the stranger and show him favour. To bind up his wounds, and find a pillow for his head, and food for him to eat. But thy pillow is the fiery furnace, and thy food the hot savour of the flame. Shame on thee, I say!'

She paused a little to watch the effect of her speech upon the multitude, and seeing that it was favourable, changed her tone from one of remonstrance to one of command.

'Ho! place there,' she cried; 'place, I say; make way for the Queens, and those whom the Queens cover with their "kaf" (mantle).'

'And if I refuse, oh Queen?' said Agon between his teeth.

'Then will I cut a path with my guards,' was the proud answer; 'ay, even in the presence of thy sanctuary, and through the bodies of thy priests.'

Agon turned livid with baffled fury. He glanced at the people as though meditating an appeal to them, but saw clearly that their sympathies were all the other way. The Zu-Vendi are a very curious and sociable people, and great as was their sense of the enormity that we had committed in shooting the sacred hippopotami, they did not like the idea of the only real live strangers they had seen or heard of being consigned to a fiery furnace, thereby putting an end for ever to their chance of extracting knowledge and information from, and gossiping about us. Agon saw this and hesitated, and then for the first time Nyleptha spoke in her soft sweet voice.

'Bethink thee, Agon,' she said, 'as my sister Queen has said, these men may also be servants of the Sun. For themselves they cannot speak, for their tongues are tied. Let the matter be adjourned till such time as they have learnt our language. Who can be condemned without a hearing? When these men can plead for themselves, then it will be time to put them to the proof.'

Here was a clever loophole of escape, and the vindictive old priest took it, little as he liked it.

'So be it, oh Queens,' he said. 'Let the men go in peace, and when they have learnt our tongue then let them speak. And I, even I, will make humble supplication at the altar lest pestilence fall on the land by cause of the sacrilege.'

These words were received with a murmur of applause, and in another minute we were marching out of the temple surrounded by the royal guards.

But it was not till long afterwards that we learnt the exact substance of what had passed, and how hardly our lives had been wrung out of the cruel grip of the Zu-Vendi priesthood, in the face of which even the Queens were practically powerless. Had it not been for their strenuous efforts to protect us we should have been slain even before we set foot in the Temple of the Sun. The attempt to drop us bodily into the fiery pit as an offering was a last artifice to attain this end when several others quite unsuspected by us had already failed.

Sorais' Song

After our escape from Agon and his pious crew we returned to our quarters in the palace and had a very good time. The two Queens, the nobles and the people vied with each other in doing us honour and showering gifts upon us. As for that painful little incident of the hippopotami it sank into oblivion, where we were quite content to leave it. Every day deputations and individuals waited on us to examine our guns and clothing, our chain shirts, and our instruments, especially our watches, with which they were much delighted. In short, we became quite the rage, so much so that some of the fashionable young swells among the Zu-Vendi began to copy the cut of some of our clothes, notably Sir Henry's shooting jacket. One day, indeed, a deputation waited on us and, as usual, Good donned his full-dress uniform for the occasion. This deputation seemed somehow to be a different class to those who generally came to visit us. They were little insignificant men of an excessively polite, not to say servile, demeanour; and their attention appeared to be chiefly taken up with observing the details of Good's full-dress uniform, of which they took copious notes and measurements. Good was much flattered at the time, not suspecting that he had to deal with the six leading tailors of Milosis. A fortnight afterwards, however, when on attending court as usual he had the pleasure of seeing some seven or eight Zu-Vendi 'mashers' arrayed in all the glory of a very fair imitation of his full-dress uniform, he changed his mind. I shall never forget his face of astonishment and disgust. It was after this, chiefly to avoid remark, and also because our clothes were wearing out and had to be saved up, that we resolved to adopt the native dress; and a very comfortable one we found it, though I am bound to say that I looked sufficiently ridiculous in it, and as for Alphonse! Only Umslopogaas would have none of these things; when his moocha was worn out the fierce old Zulu made him a new one, and went about unconcerned, as grim and naked as his own battleaxe.

Meanwhile we pursued our study of the language steadily and made very good progress. On the morning following our adventure in the temple, three grave and reverend signiors presented themselves armed with manuscript books, ink-horns and feather pens, and indicated that they had been sent to teach us. So, with the exception of Umslopogaas, we all buckled to with a will, doing four hours a day. As for Umslopogaas, he would have none of that either. He did not wish to learn that 'woman's talk', not he; and when one of the teachers advanced on him with a book and an ink-horn and waved them before him in a mild persuasive way, much as a churchwarden invitingly shakes the offertory bag under the nose of a rich but niggardly parishioner, he sprang up with a fierce oath and flashed Inkosi-kaas before the eyes of our learned friend, and there was an end of the attempt to teach *him* Zu-Vendi.

Thus we spent our mornings in useful occupation which grew more and more interesting as we proceeded, and the afternoons were given up to recreation. Sometimes we made trips, notably one to the gold mines and another to the marble quarries both of which I wish I had space and time to describe; and sometimes we went out hunting buck with dogs trained for that purpose, and a very exciting sport it is, as the country is full of agricultural enclosures and our horses were magnificent. This is not to be wondered at, seeing that the royal stables were at our command, in addition to which we had four splendid saddle horses given to us by Nyleptha.

Sometimes, again, we went hawking, a pastime that is in great favour among the Zu-Vendi, who generally fly their birds at a species of partridge which is remarkable for the swiftness and strength of its flight. When attacked by the hawk this bird appears to lose its head, and, instead of seeking cover, flies high into the sky, thus offering wonderful sport. I have seen one of these partridges soar up almost out of sight when followed by the hawk. Still better sport is offered by a variety of solitary snipe as big as a small woodcock, which is plentiful in this country, and which is flown at with a very small, agile, and highly-trained hawk with an almost red tail. The zigzagging of the great snipe and the lightning rapidity of the flight and movements of the red-tailed hawk make the pastime a delightful one. Another variety of the same amusement is the hunting of a very small species of antelope with trained eagles; and it certainly is a marvellous sight to see the great bird soar and soar till he is nothing but a black speck in the sunlight, and then suddenly come dashing down like a cannon-ball upon some cowering buck that is hidden in a patch of grass from everything but that piercing eye. Still finer is the spectacle when the eagle takes the buck running.

On other days we would pay visits to the country seats at some of the great lords' beautiful fortified places, and the villages clustering beneath their walls. Here we saw vineyards and corn-fields and well-kept park-like grounds, with such timber in them as filled me with delight, for I do love a good tree. There it stands so strong and sturdy, and yet so beautiful, a very type of the best sort of man. How proudly it lifts its bare head to the winter storms, and with what a full heart it rejoices when the spring has come again! How grand its voice is, too, when it talks with the wind: a thousand aeolian harps cannot equal the beauty of the sighing of a great tree in leaf. All day it points to the sunshine and all night to the stars, and thus passionless, and yet full of life, it endures through the centuries, come storm, come shine, drawing its sustenance from the cool bosom of its mother earth, and as the slow years roll by, learning the great mysteries of growth and of decay. And so on and on through generations, outliving individuals, customs, dynasties — all save the landscape it adorns and human nature — till the appointed day when the wind wins the long battle and rejoices over a reclaimed space, or decay puts the last stroke to his fungus-fingered work.

Ah, one should always think twice before one cuts down a tree!

In the evenings it was customary for Sir Henry, Good, and myself to dine, or rather sup, with their Majesties — not every night, indeed, but about three or four times a week, whenever they had not much company, or the affairs of state would allow of it. And I am bound to say that those little suppers were quite the most charming things of their sort that I ever had to do with. How true is the saying that the very highest in rank are always the most simple and kindly. It is from your half-and-half sort of people that you get pomposity and vulgarity, the difference between the two being very much what one sees every day in England between the old, out-at-elbows, broken-down county family, and the overbearing, purse-proud people who come and 'take the place'. I really think that Nyleptha's greatest charm is her sweet simplicity, and her kindly genuine interest even in little things. She is the simplest woman I ever knew, and where her passions are not involved, one of the sweetest; but she can look queenly enough when she likes, and be as fierce as any savage too.

For instance, never shall I forget that scene when I for the first time was sure that she was really in love with Curtis. It came about in this way — all through Good's weakness for ladies' society. When we had been employed for some three months in learning Zu-Vendi, it struck Master Good that he was getting rather tired of the old gentlemen who did us the honour to lead us in the way that we should go, so he proceeded, without saying a word to anybody else, to inform them that it was a peculiar fact, but that we could not make any real progress in the deeper intricacies of a foreign language unless we were taught by ladies — young ladies, he was careful to explain. In his own country, he pointed out, it was habitual to choose the very best-looking and most charming girls who could be found to instruct any strangers who happened to come that way, etc.

All of this the old gentlemen swallowed open-mouthed. There was, they admitted, reason in what he said, since the contemplation of the beautiful, as their philosophy taught, induced a certain porosity of mind similar to that produced upon the physical body by the healthful influences of sun and air. Consequently it was probable that we might absorb the Zu-Vendi tongue a little faster if suitable teachers could be found. Another thing was that, as the female sex was naturally loquacious, good practice would be gained in the viva voce department of our studies.

To all of this Good gravely assented, and the learned gentlemen departed, assuring him that their orders were to fall in with our wishes in every way, and that, if possible, our views should be met.

Imagine, therefore the surprise and disgust of myself, and I trust and believe Sir Henry, when, on entering the room where we were accustomed to carry on our studies the following morning, we found, instead of our usual venerable tutors, three of the best-looking young women whom Milosis could produce — and that is saying a good deal — who blushed and smiled and curtseyed, and gave us to understand that they were there to carry on our instruction. Then Good, as we gazed at one another in bewilderment, thought fit to explain, saying that it had slipped his memory before — but the old gentlemen had told him, on the previous evening, that it was absolutely necessary that our further education should be carried on by the other sex. I was overwhelmed, and appealed to Sir Henry for advice in such a crisis.

'Well,' he said, 'you see the ladies are here, ain't they? If we sent them away, don't you think it might hurt their feelings, eh? One doesn't like to be rough, you see; and they look regular *blues*, don't they, eh?'

By this time Good had already begun his lessons with the handsomest of the three, and so with a sigh I yielded. That day everything went very well: the young ladies were certainly very clever, and they only smiled when we blundered. I never saw Good so attentive to his books before, and even Sir Henry appeared to tackle Zu-Vendi with a renewed zest. 'Ah,' thought I, 'will it always be thus?'

Next day we were much more lively, our work was pleasingly interspersed with questions about our native country, what the ladies were like there, etc., all of which we answered as best as we could in Zu-Vendi, and I heard Good assuring his teacher that her loveliness was to the beauties of Europe as the sun to the moon, to which she replied with a little toss of the head, that she was a plain teaching woman and nothing else, and that it was not kind 'to deceive a poor girl so'. Then we had a little singing that was really charming, so natural and unaffected. The Zu-Vendi love-songs are most touching. On the third day we were all quite intimate. Good narrated some of his previous love affairs to his fair teacher, and so moved was she that her sighs mingled with his own. I discoursed with mine, a merry blue-eyed girl, upon Zu-Vendian art, and never saw that she was waiting for an opportunity to drop a specimen of the cockroach tribe down my back, whilst in the corner Sir Henry and his governess appeared, so far as I could judge, to be going through a lesson framed on the great educational principles laid down by Wackford Squeers Esq., though in a very modified or rather spiritualized form. The lady softly repeated the Zu-Vendi word for 'hand', and he took hers; 'eyes', and he gazed deep into her brown orbs; 'lips', and — but just at that moment *my* young lady dropped the cockroach down my back and ran away laughing. Now if there is one thing I loathe more than another it is cockroaches, and moved quite beyond myself, and yet laughing at her impudence, I took up the cushion she had been sitting on and threw it after her. Imagine then my shame — my horror, and my distress — when the door opened, and, attended by two guards only, in walked *Nyleptha*. The cushion could not be recalled (it missed the girl and hit one of the guards on the head), but I instantly and ineffectually tried to look as though I had not thrown it. Good ceased his sighing, and began to murder Zu-Vendi at the top of his voice, and Sir Henry whistled and looked silly. As for the poor girls, they were utterly dumbfounded.

And Nyleptha! she drew herself up till her frame seemed to tower even above that of the tall guards, and her face went first red, and then pale as death.

'Guards,' she said in a quiet choked voice, and pointing at the fair but unconscious disciple of Wackford Squeers, 'slay me that woman.'

The men hesitated, as well they might.

'Will ye do my bidding,' she said again in the same voice, 'or will ye not?'

Then they advanced upon the girl with uplifted spears. By this time Sir Henry had recovered himself, and saw that the comedy was likely to turn into a tragedy.

'Stand back,' he said in a voice of thunder, at the same time getting in front of the terrified girl. 'Shame on thee, Nyleptha — shame! Thou shalt not kill her.'

'Doubtless thou hast good reason to try to protect her. Thou couldst hardly do less in honour,' answered the infuriated Queen; 'but she shall die — she shall die,' and she stamped her little foot.

'It is well,' he answered; 'then will I die with her. I am thy servant, oh Queen; do with me even as thou wilt.' And he bowed towards her, and fixed his clear eyes contemptuously on her face.

'I could wish to slay thee too,' she answered; 'for thou dost make a mock of me;' and then feeling that she was mastered, and I suppose not knowing what else to do, she burst into such a storm of tears and looked so royally lovely in her passionate distress, that, old as I am, I must say I envied Curtis his task of supporting her. It was rather odd to see him holding her in his arms considering what had just passed — a thought that seemed to occur to herself, for presently she wrenched herself free and went, leaving us all much disturbed.

Presently, however, one of the guards returned with a message to the girls that they were, on pain of death, to leave the city and return to their homes in the country, and that no further harm would come to them; and accordingly they went, one of them remarking philosophically that it could not be helped, and that it was a satisfaction to know that they had taught us a little serviceable Zu-Vendi. Mine was an exceedingly nice girl, and, overlooking the cockroach, I made her a present of my favourite lucky sixpence with a hole in it when she went away. After that our former masters resumed their course of instruction, needless to say to my great relief.

That night, when in fear and trembling we attended the royal supper table, we found that Nyleptha was laid up with a bad headache. That headache lasted for three whole days; but on the fourth she was present at supper as usual, and with the most gracious and sweet smile gave Sir Henry her hand to lead her to the table. No allusion was made to the little affair described above beyond her saying, with a charming air of innocence, that when she came to see us at our studies the other day she had been seized with a giddiness from which she had only now recovered. She supposed, she added with a touch of the humour that was common to her, that it was the sight of people working so hard which had affected her.

In reply Sir Henry said, dryly, that he had thought she did not look quite herself on that day, whereat she flashed one of those quick glances of hers at him, which if he had the feelings of a man must have gone through him like a knife, and the subject dropped entirely. Indeed, after supper was over Nyleptha condescended to put us through an examination to see what we had learnt, and to express herself well satisfied with the results. Indeed, she proceeded to give us, especially Sir Henry, a lesson on her own account, and very interesting we found it.

And all the while that we talked, or rather tried to talk, and laughed, Sorais would sit there in her carven ivory chair, and look at us and read us all like a book, only from time to time saying a few words, and smiling that quick ominous smile of hers which was more like a flash of summer lightning on a dark cloud than anything else. And as near to her as he dared would sit Good, worshipping through his eyeglass, for he really was getting seriously devoted to this sombre beauty, of whom, speaking personally, I felt terribly afraid. I watched her keenly, and soon I found out that for all her apparent impassibility she was at heart bitterly jealous of Nyleptha. Another thing I found out, and the discovery filled me with dismay, and that was, that she *also* was growing devoted to Sir Henry Curtis. Of course I could not be sure; it is not easy to read so cold and haughty a woman; but I noticed one or two little things, and, as elephant hunters know, dried grass shows which way the wind has set.

And so another three months passed over us, by which time we had all attained to a very considerable mastery of the Zu-Vendi language, which is an easy one to learn. And as the time went on we became great favourites with the people, and even with the courtiers, gaining an enormous reputation for cleverness, because, as I think I have said, Sir Henry was able to show them how to make glass, which was a national want, and also, by the help of a twenty-year almanac that we had with us, to predict various heavenly combinations which were quite unsuspected by the native astronomers. We even succeeded in demonstrating the principle of the steam-engine to a gathering of the learned men, who were filled with amazement; and several other things of the same sort we did. And so it came about that the people made up their minds that we must on no account be allowed to go out of the country (which indeed was an apparent impossibility even if we had wished it), and we were advanced to great honour and made officers to the bodyguards of the sister Queens while permanent quarters were assigned to us in the palace, and our opinion was asked upon questions of national policy.

But blue as the sky seemed, there was a cloud, and a big one, on the horizon. We had indeed heard no more of those confounded hippopotami, but it is not on that account to be supposed that our sacrilege was forgotten, or the enmity of the great and powerful priesthood headed by Agon appeased. On the contrary, it was burning the more fiercely because it was necessarily suppressed, and what had perhaps begun in bigotry was ending in downright direct hatred born of jealousy. Hitherto, the priests had been the wise men of the land, and were on this account, as well as from superstitious causes, looked on with peculiar veneration. But our arrival, with our outlandish wisdom and our strange inventions and hints of unimagined things, dealt a serious blow to this state of affairs, and, among the educated Zu-Vendi, went far towards destroying the priestly prestige. A still worse affront to them, however, was the favour with which we were regarded, and the trust that was reposed in us. All these things tended to make us excessively obnoxious to the great sacerdotal clan, the most powerful because the most united faction in the kingdom.

Another source of imminent danger to us was the rising envy of some of the great lords headed by Nasta, whose antagonism to us had at best been but thinly veiled, and which now threatened to break out into open flame. Nasta had for some years been a candidate for Nyleptha's hand in marriage, and when we appeared on the scene I fancy, from all I could gather, that though there were still many obstacles in his path, success was by no means out of his reach. But now all this had changed; the coy Nyleptha smiled no more in his direction, and he was not slow to guess the cause. Infuriated and alarmed, he turned his attention to Sorais, only to find that he might as well try to woo a mountain side. With a bitter jest or two about his fickleness, that door was closed on him for ever. So Nasta bethought himself of the thirty thousand wild swordsmen who would pour down at his bidding through the northern mountain passes, and no doubt vowed to adorn the gates of Milosis with our heads.

But first he determined, as I learned, to make one more attempt and to demand the hand of Nyleptha in the open Court after the formal annual ceremony of the signing of the laws that had been proclaimed by the Queens during the year.

Of this astounding fact Nyleptha heard with simulated nonchalance, and with a little trembling of the voice herself informed us of it as we sat at supper on the night preceding the great ceremony of the law-giving.

Sir Henry bit his lip, and do what he could to prevent it plainly showed his agitation.

'And what answer will the Queen be pleased to give to the great Lord?' asked I, in a jesting manner.

'Answer, Macumazahn' (for we had elected to pass by our Zulu names in Zu-Vendis), she said, with a pretty shrug of her ivory shoulder. 'Nay, I know not; what is a poor woman to do, when the wooer has thirty thousand swords wherewith to urge his love?' And from under her long lashes she glanced at Curtis.

Just then we rose from the table to adjourn into another room. 'Quatermain, a word, quick,' said Sir Henry to me. 'Listen. I have never spoken about it, but surely you have guessed: I love Nyleptha. What am I to do?'

Fortunately, I had more or less already taken the question into consideration, and was therefore able to give such answer as seemed the wisest to me.

'You must speak to Nyleptha tonight,' I said. 'Now is your time, now or never. Listen. In the sitting-chamber get near to her, and whisper to her to meet you at midnight by the Rademas statue at the end of the great hall. I will keep watch for you there. Now or never, Curtis.'

We passed on into the other room. Nyleptha was sitting, her hands before her, and a sad anxious look upon her lovely face. A little way off was Sorais talking to Good in her slow measured tones.

The time went on; in another quarter of an hour I knew that, according to their habit, the Queens would retire. As yet, Sir Henry had had no chance of saying a word in private: indeed, though we saw much of the royal sisters, it was by no means easy to see them alone. I racked my brains, and at last an idea came to me.

'Will the Queen be pleased,' I said, bowing low before Sorais, 'to sing to her servants? Our hearts are heavy this night; sing to us, oh Lady of the Night' (Sorais' favourite name among the people).

'My songs, Macumazahn, are not such as to lighten the heavy heart, yet will I sing if it pleases thee,' she answered; and she rose and went a few paces to a table whereon lay an instrument not unlike a zither, and struck a few wandering chords.

Then suddenly, like the notes of some deep-throated bird, her rounded voice rang out in song so wildly sweet, and yet with so eerie and sad a refrain, that it made the very blood stand still. Up, up soared the golden notes, that seemed to melt far away, and then to grow again and travel on, laden with all the sorrow of the world and all the despair of the lost. It was a marvellous song, but I had not time to listen to it properly. However, I got the words of it afterwards, and here is a translation of its burden, so far as it admits of being translated at all.

Sorais' Song

As a desolate bird that through darkness its lost way is winging,
As a hand that is helplessly raised when Death's sickle is swinging,
So is life! ay, the life that lends passion and breath to my singing.

As the nightingale's song that is full of a sweetness unspoken,   As a
spirit unbarring the gates of the skies for a token,
So is love! ay, the love that shall fall when his pinion is broken.

As the tramp of the legions when trumpets their challenge are sending,
As the shout of the Storm-god when lightnings the black sky are rending,
So is power! ay, the power that shall lie in the dust at its ending.

So short is our life; yet with space for all things to forsake us,   A
bitter delusion, a dream from which nought can awake us,
Till Death's dogging footsteps at morn or at eve shall o'ertake us.

Refrain

Oh, the world is fair at the dawning — dawning — dawning,
But the red sun sinks in blood — the red sun sinks in blood.

I only wish that I could write down the music too.

'Now, Curtis, now,' I whispered, when she began the second verse, and turned my back.

'Nyleptha,' he said — for my nerves were so much on the stretch that I could hear every word, low as it was spoken, even through Sorais' divine notes — 'Nyleptha, I must speak with thee this night, upon my life I must. Say me not nay; oh, say me not nay!'

'How can I speak with thee?' she answered, looking fixedly before her; 'Queens are not like other people. I am surrounded and watched.'

'Listen, Nyleptha, thus. I will be before the statue of Rademas in the great hall at midnight. I have the countersign and can pass in. Macumazahn will be there to keep guard, and with him the Zulu. Oh come, my Queen, deny me not.'

'It is not seemly,' she murmured, 'and tomorrow —'

Just then the music began to die in the last wail of the refrain, and Sorais slowly turned her round.

'I will be there,' said Nyleptha, hurriedly; 'on thy life see that thou fail me not.'

Before the Statue

It was night — dead night — and the silence lay on the Frowning City like a cloud.

Secretly, as evildoers, Sir Henry Curtis, Umslopogaas, and myself threaded our way through the passages towards a by-entrance to the great Throne Chamber. Once we were met by the fierce rattling challenge of the sentry. I gave the countersign, and the man grounded his spear and let us pass. Also we were officers of the Queens' bodyguard, and in that capacity had a right to come and go unquestioned.

We gained the hall in safety. So empty and so still was it, that even when we had passed the sound of our footsteps yet echoed up the lofty walls, vibrating faintly and still more faintly against the carven roof, like ghosts of the footsteps of dead men haunting the place that once they trod.

It was an eerie spot, and it oppressed me. The moon was full, and threw great pencils and patches of light through the high windowless openings in the walls, that lay pure and beautiful upon the blackness of the marble floor, like white flowers on a coffin. One of these silver arrows fell upon the statue of the sleeping Rademas, and of the angel form bent over him, illumining it, and a small circle round it, with a soft clear light, reminding me of that with which Catholics illumine the altars of their cathedrals.

Here by the statue we took our stand, and waited. Sir Henry and I close together, Umslopogaas some paces off in the darkness, so that I could only just make out his towering outline leaning on the outline of an axe.

So long did we wait that I almost fell asleep resting against the cold marble, but was suddenly aroused by hearing Curtis give a quick catching breath. Then from far away there came a little sound as though the statues that lined the walls were whispering to each other some message of the ages.

It was the faint sweep of a lady's dress. Nearer it grew, and nearer yet. We could see a figure steal from patch to patch of moonlight, and even hear the soft fall of sandalled feet. Another second and I saw the black silhouette of the old Zulu raise its arm in mute salute, and Nyleptha was before us.

Oh, how beautiful she looked as she paused a moment just within the circle of the moonlight! Her hand was pressed upon her heart, and her white bosom heaved beneath it. Round her head a broidered scarf was loosely thrown, partially shadowing the perfect face, and thus rendering it even more lovely; for beauty, dependent as it is to a certain extent upon the imagination, is never so beautiful as when it is half hid. There she stood radiant but half doubting, stately and yet so sweet. It was but a moment, but I then and there fell in love with her myself, and have remained so to this hour; for, indeed, she looked more like an angel out of heaven than a loving, passionate, mortal woman. Low we bowed before her, and then she spoke.

'I have come,' she whispered, 'but it was at great risk. Ye know not how I am watched. The priests watch me. Sorais watches me with those great eyes of hers. My very guards are spies upon me. Nasta watches me too. Oh, let him be careful!' and she stamped her foot. 'Let him be careful; I am a woman, and therefore hard to drive. Ay, and I am a Queen, too, and can still avenge. Let him be careful, I say, lest in place of giving him my hand I take his head,' and she ended the outburst with a little sob, and then smiled up at us bewitchingly and laughed.

'Thou didst bid me come hither, my Lord Incubu' (Curtis had taught her to call him so). 'Doubtless it is about business of the State, for I know that thou art ever full of great ideas and plans for my welfare and my people's. So even as a Queen should I have come, though I greatly fear the dark alone,' and again she laughed and gave him a glance from her grey eyes.

At this point I thought it wise to move a little, since secrets 'of the State' should not be made public property; but she would not let me go far, peremptorily stopping me within five yards or so, saying that she feared surprise. So it came to pass that, however unwillingly, I heard all that passed.

'Thou knowest, Nyleptha,' said Sir Henry, 'that it was for none of these things that I asked thee to meet me at this lonely place. Nyleptha, waste not the time in pleasantry, but listen to me, for — I love thee.'

As he said the words I saw her face break up, as it were, and change. The coquetry went out of it, and in its place there shone a great light of love which seemed to glorify it, and make it like that of the marble angel overhead. I could not help thinking that it must have been a touch of prophetic instinct which made the long dead Rademas limn, in the features of the angel of his inspiring vision, so strange a likeness of his own descendant. Sir Henry, also, must have observed and been struck by the likeness, for, catching the look upon Nyleptha's face, he glanced quickly from it to the moonlit statue, and then back again at his beloved.

'Thou sayest thou dost love me,' she said in a low voice, 'and thy voice rings true, but how am I to know that thou dost speak the truth?'

'Though,' she went on with proud humility, and in the stately third person which is so largely used by the Zu-Vendi, 'I be as nothing in the eyes of my lord,' and she curtseyed towards him, 'who comes from among a wonderful people, to whom my people are but children, yet here am I a queen and a leader of men, and if I would go to battle a hundred thousand spears shall sparkle in my train like stars glimmering down the path of the bent moon. And although my beauty be a little thing in the eyes of my lord,' and she lifted her broidered skirt and curtseyed again, 'yet here among my own people am I held right fair, and ever since I was a woman the great lords of my kingdom have made quarrel concerning me, as though forsooth,' she added with a flash of passion, 'I were a deer to be pulled down by the hungriest wolf, or a horse to be sold to the highest bidder. Let my lord pardon me if I weary my lord, but it hath pleased my lord to say that he loves me, Nyleptha, a Queen of the Zu-Vendi, and therefore would I say that though my love and my hand be not much to my lord, yet to me are they all.'

'Oh!' she cried, with a sudden and thrilling change of voice, and modifying her dignified mode of address. 'Oh, how can I know that thou lovest but me? How can I know that thou wilt not weary of me and seek thine own place again, leaving me desolate? Who is there to tell me but that thou lovest some other woman, some fair woman unknown to me, but who yet draws breath beneath this same moon that shines on me tonight? Tell me *how* am I to know?' And she clasped her hands and stretched them out towards him and looked appealingly into his face.

'Nyleptha,' answered Sir Henry, adopting the Zu-Vendi way of speech; 'I have told thee that I love thee; how am I to tell thee how much I love thee? Is there then a measure for love? Yet will I try. I say not that I have never looked upon another woman with favour, but this I say that I love thee with all my life and with all my strength; that I love thee now and shall love thee till I grow cold in death, ay, and as I believe beyond my death, and on and on for ever: I say that thy voice is music to my ear, and thy touch as water to a thirsty land, that when thou art there the world is beautiful, and when I see thee not it is as though the light was dead. Oh, Nyleptha, I will never leave thee; here and now for thy dear sake I will forget my people and my father's house, yea, I renounce them all. By thy side will I live, Nyleptha, and at thy side will I die.'

He paused and gazed at her earnestly, but she hung her head like a lily, and said never a word.

'Look!' he went on, pointing to the statue on which the moonlight played so brightly. 'Thou seest that angel woman who rests her hand upon the forehead of the sleeping man, and thou seest how at her touch his soul flames up and shines out through his flesh, even as a lamp at the touch of the fire, so is it with me and thee, Nyleptha. Thou hast awakened my soul and called it forth, and now, Nyleptha, it is not mine, not mine, but *thine* and thine only. There is no more for me to say; in thy hands is my life.' And he leaned back against the pedestal of the statue, looking very pale, and his eyes shining, but proud and handsome as a god.

Slowly, slowly she raised her head, and fixed her wonderful eyes, all alight with the greatness of her passion, full upon his face, as though to read his very soul. Then at last she spoke, low indeed, but clearly as a silver bell.

'Of a truth, weak woman that I am, I do believe thee. Ill will be the day for thee and for me also if it be my fate to learn that I have believed a lie. And now hearken to me, oh man, who hath wandered here from far to steal my heart and make me all thine own. I put my hand upon thy hand thus, and thus I, whose lips have never kissed before, do kiss thee on the brow; and now by my hand and by that first and holy kiss, ay, by my people's weal and by my throne that like enough I shall lose for thee — by the name of my high House, by the sacred Stone and by the eternal majesty of the Sun, I swear that for thee will I live and die. And I swear that I will love thee and thee only till death, ay, and beyond, if as thou sayest there be a beyond, and that thy will shall be my will, and thy ways my ways.

'Oh see, see, my lord! thou knowest not how humble is she who loves; I, who am a Queen, I kneel before thee, even at thy feet I do my homage;' and the lovely impassioned creature flung herself down on her knees on the cold marble before him. And after that I really do not know, for I could stand it no longer, and cleared off to refresh myself with a little of old Umslopogaas' society, leaving them to settle it their own way, and a very long time they were about it.

I found the old warrior leaning on Inkosi-kaas as usual, and surveying the scene in the patch of moonlight with a grim smile of amusement.

'Ah, Macumazahn,' he said, 'I suppose it is because I am getting old, but I don't think that I shall ever learn to understand the ways of you white people. Look there now, I pray thee, they are a pretty pair of doves, but what is all the fuss about, Macumazahn? He wants a wife, and she wants a husband, then why does he not pay his cows down like a man and have done with it? It would save a deal of trouble, and we should have had our night's sleep. But there they go, talk, talk, talk, and kiss, kiss, kiss, like mad things. Eugh!'

Some three-quarters of an hour afterwards the 'pair of doves' came strolling towards us, Curtis looking slightly silly, and Nyleptha remarking calmly that the moonlight made very pretty effects on the marble. Then, for she was in a most gracious mood, she took my hand and said that I was 'her Lord's' dear friend, and therefore most dear to her — not a word for my own sake, you see. Next she lifted Umslopogaas' axe, and examined it curiously, saying significantly as she did so that he might soon have cause to use it in defence of her.

After that she nodded prettily to us all, and casting a tender glance at her lover, glided off into the darkness like a beautiful vision.

When we got back to our quarters, which we did without accident, Curtis asked me jocularly what I was thinking about.

'I am wondering,' I answered, 'on what principle it is arranged that some people should find beautiful queens to fall in love with them, while others find nobody at all, or worse than nobody; and I am also wondering how many brave men's lives this night's work will cost.' It was rather nasty of me, perhaps, but somehow all the feelings do not evaporate with age, and I could not help being a little jealous of my old friend's luck. Vanity, my sons; vanity of vanities!

On the following morning, Good was informed of the happy occurrence, and positively rippled with smiles that, originating somewhere about the mouth, slowly travelled up his face like the rings in a duckpond, till they flowed over the brim of his eyeglass and went where sweet smiles go. The fact of the matter, however, was that not only was Good rejoiced about the thing on its own merits but also for personal reasons. He adored Sorais quite as earnestly as Sir Henry adored Nyleptha, and his adoration had not altogether prospered. Indeed, it had seemed to him and to me also that the dark Cleopatra-like queen favoured Curtis in her own curious inscrutable way much more than Good. Therefore it was a relief to him to learn that his unconscious rival was permanently and satisfactorily attached in another direction. His face fell a little, however, when he was told that the whole thing was to be kept as secret as the dead, above all from Sorais for the present, inasmuch as the political convulsion which would follow such an announcement at the moment would be altogether too great to face and would very possibly, if prematurely made, shake Nyleptha from her throne.

That morning we again attended in the Throne Hall, and I could not help smiling to myself when I compared the visit to our last, and reflecting that, if walls could speak, they would have strange tales to tell.

What actresses women are! There, high upon her golden throne, draped in her blazoned 'kaf' or robe of state, sat the fair Nyleptha, and when Sir Henry came in a little late, dressed in the full uniform of an officer of her guard and humbly bent himself before her, she merely acknowledged his salute with a careless nod and turned her head coldly aside. It was a very large Court, for not only did the signing of the laws attract many outside of those whose duty it was to attend, but also the rumour that Nasta was going to publicly ask the hand of Nyleptha in marriage had gone abroad, with the result that the great hall was crowded to its utmost capacity. There were our friends the priests in force, headed by Agon, who regarded us with a vindictive eye; and a most imposing band they were, with their long white embroidered robes girt with a golden chain from which hung the fish-like scales. There, too, were a number of the lords, each with a band of brilliantly attired attendants, and prominent among them was Nasta, stroking his black beard meditatively and looking unusually pleasant. It was a splendid and impressive sight, especially when the officer after having read out each law handed them to the Queens to sign, whereon the trumpets blared out and the Queens' guard grounded their spears with a crash in salute. This reading and signing of the laws took a long time, but at length it came to an end, the last one reciting that 'whereas distinguished strangers, etc.', and proceeding to confer on the three of us the rank of 'lords', together with certain military commands and large estates bestowed by the Queen. When it was read the trumpets blared and the spears clashed down as usual, but I saw some of the lords turn and whisper to each other, while Nasta ground his teeth. They did not like the favour that was shown to us, which under all the circumstances was not perhaps unnatural.

Then there came a pause, and Nasta stepped forward and bowing humbly, though with no humility in his eye, craved a boon at the hands of the Queen Nyleptha.

Nyleptha turned a little pale, but bowed graciously, and prayed the 'well-beloved lord' to speak on, whereon in a few straightforward soldier-like words he asked her hand in marriage.

Then, before she could find words to answer, the High Priest Agon took up the tale, and in a speech of real eloquence and power pointed out the many advantages of the proposed alliance; how it would consolidate the kingdom, for Nasta's dominions, of which he was virtually king, were to Zu-Vendis much what Scotland used to be to England; how it would gratify the wild mountaineers and be popular among the soldiery, for Nasta was a famous general; how it would set her dynasty firmly on the throne, and would gain the blessing and approval of the 'Sun', i.e. of the office of the High Priest, and so on. Many of his arguments were undoubtedly valid, and there was, looking at it from a political point of view, everything to be said for the marriage. But unfortunately it is difficult to play the game of politics with the persons of young and lovely queens as though they were ivory effigies of themselves on a chessboard. Nyleptha's face, while Agon spouted away, was a perfect study; she smiled indeed, but beneath the smile it set like a stone, and her eyes began to flash ominously.

At last he stopped, and she prepared herself to answer. Before she did so, however, Sorais leant towards her and said in a voice sufficiently loud for me to catch what she said, 'Bethink thee well, my sister, ere thou dost speak, for methinks that our thrones may hang upon thy words.'

Nyleptha made no answer, and with a shrug and a smile Sorais leant back again and listened.

'Of a truth a great honour has been done to me,' she said, 'that my poor hand should not only have been asked in marriage, but that Agon here should be so swift to pronounce the blessing of the Sun upon my union. Methinks that in another minute he would have wed us fast ere the bride had said her say. Nasta, I thank thee, and I will bethink me of thy words, but now as yet I have no mind for marriage, that is a cup of which none know the taste until they begin to drink it. Again I thank thee, Nasta,' and she made as though she would rise.

The great lord's face turned almost as black as his beard with fury, for he knew that the words amounted to a final refusal of his suit.

'Thanks be to the Queen for her gracious words,' he said, restraining himself with difficulty and looking anything but grateful, 'my heart shall surely treasure them. And now I crave another boon, namely, the royal leave to withdraw myself to my own poor cities in the north till such time as the Queen shall say my suit nay or yea. Mayhap,' he added, with a sneer, 'the Queen will be pleased to visit me there, and to bring with her these stranger lords,' and he scowled darkly towards us. ''Tis but a poor country and a rough, but we are a hardy race of mountaineers, and there shall be gathered thirty thousand swordsmen to shout a welcome to her.'

This speech, which was almost a declaration of rebellion, was received in complete silence, but Nyleptha flushed up and answered it with spirit.

'Oh, surely, Nasta, I will come, and the strange lords in my train, and for every man of thy mountaineers who calls thee Prince, will I bring two from the lowlands who call me Queen, and we will see which is the staunchest breed. Till then farewell.'

The trumpets blared out, the Queens rose, and the great assembly broke up in murmuring confusion, and for myself I went home with a heavy heart foreseeing civil war.

After this there was quiet for a few weeks. Curtis and the Queen did not often meet, and exercised the utmost caution not to allow the true relation in which they stood to each other to leak out; but do what they would, rumours as hard to trace as a buzzing fly in a dark room, and yet quite as audible, began to hum round and round, and at last to settle on her throne.

The Storm Breaks

And now it was that the trouble which at first had been but a cloud as large as a man's hand began to loom very black and big upon our horizon, namely, Sorais' preference for Sir Henry. I saw the storm drawing nearer and nearer; and so, poor fellow, did he. The affection of so lovely and highly-placed a woman was not a thing that could in a general way be considered a calamity by any man, but, situated as Curtis was, it was a grievous burden to bear.

To begin with, Nyleptha, though altogether charming, was, it must be admitted, of a rather jealous disposition, and was sometimes apt to visit on her lover's head her indignation at the marks of what Alphonse would have called the 'distinguished consideration' with which her royal sister favoured him. Then the enforced secrecy of his relation to Nyleptha prevented Curtis from taking some opportunity of putting a stop, or trying to put a stop, to this false condition of affairs, by telling Sorais, in a casual but confidential way, that he was going to marry her sister. A third sting in Sir Henry's honey was that he knew that Good was honestly and sincerely attached to the ominous-looking but most attractive Lady of the Night. Indeed, poor Bougwan was wasting himself to a shadow of his fat and jolly self about her, his face getting so thin that his eyeglass would scarcely stick in it; while she, with a sort of careless coquetry, just gave him encouragement enough to keep him going, thinking, no doubt, that he might be useful as a stalking-horse. I tried to give him a hint, in as delicate a way as I could, but he flew into a huff and would not listen to me, so I was determined to let ill along, for fear of making it worse. Poor Good, he really was very ludicrous in his distress, and went in for all sorts of absurdities, under the belief that he was advancing his suit. One of them was the writing — with the assistance of one of the grave and revered signiors who instructed us, and who, whatever may have been the measure of his erudition, did not understand how to scan a line — of a most interminable Zu-Vendi love-song, of which the continually recurring refrain was something about 'I will kiss thee; oh yes, I will kiss thee!' Now among the Zu-Vendi it is a common and most harmless thing for young men to serenade ladies at night, as I believe they do in the southern countries of Europe, and sing all sorts of nonsensical songs to them. The young men may or may not be serious; but no offence is meant and none is taken, even by ladies of the highest rank, who accept the whole thing as an English girl would a gracefully-turned compliment.

Availing himself of this custom, Good bethought him that would serenade Sorais, whose private apartments, together with those of her maidens, were exactly opposite our own, on the further side of a narrow courtyard which divided one section of the great palace from another. Accordingly, having armed himself with a native zither, on which, being an adept with the light guitar, he had easily learned to strum, he proceeded at midnight — the fashionable hour for this sort of caterwauling — to make night hideous with his amorous yells. I was fast asleep when they began, but they soon woke me up — for Good possesses a tremendous voice and has no notion of time — and I ran to my window-place to see what was the matter. And there, standing in the full moonlight in the courtyard, I perceived Good, adorned with an enormous ostrich feather head-dress and a flowing silken cloak, which it is the right thing to wear upon these occasions, and shouting out the abominable song which he and the old gentleman had evolved, to a jerky, jingling accompaniment. From the direction of the quarters of the maids of honour came a succession of faint sniggerings; but the apartments of Sorais herself — whom I devoutly pitied if she happened to be there — were silent as the grave. There was absolutely no end to that awful song, with its eternal 'I will kiss thee!' and at last neither I nor Sir Henry, whom I had summoned to enjoy the sight, could stand it any longer; so, remembering the dear old story, I put my head to the window opening, and shouted, 'For Heaven's sake, Good, don't go on talking about it, but *kiss* her and let's all go to sleep!' That choked him off, and we had no more serenading.

The whole thing formed a laughable incident in a tragic business. How deeply thankful we ought to be that even the most serious matters have generally a silver lining about them in the shape of a joke, if only people could see it. The sense of humour is a very valuable possession in life, and ought to be cultivated in the Board schools — especially in Scotland.

Well, the more Sir Henry held off the more Sorais came on, as is not uncommon in such cases, till at last things got very queer indeed. Evidently she was, by some strange perversity of mind, quite blinded to the true state of the case; and I, for one, greatly dreaded the moment of her awakening. Sorais was a dangerous woman to be mixed up with, either with or without one's consent. At last the evil moment came, as I saw it must come. One fine day, Good having gone out hawking, Sir Henry and I were sitting quietly talking over the situation, especially with reference to Sorais, when a Court messenger arrived with a written note, which we with some difficulty deciphered, and which was to the effect that 'the Queen Sorais commanded the attendance of the Lord Incubu in her private apartments, whither he would be conducted by the bearer'.

'Oh my word!' groaned Sir Henry. 'Can't you go instead, old fellow?'

'Not if I know it,' I said with vigour. 'I had rather face a wounded elephant with a shot-gun. Take care of your own business, my boy. If you will be so fascinating you must take the consequences. I would not be in your place for an empire.'

'You remind me of when I was going to be flogged at school and the other boys came to console me,' he said gloomily. 'What right has this Queen to command my attendance, I should like to know? I won't go.'

'But you must; you are one of her officers and bound to obey her, and she knows it. And after all it will soon be over.'

'That's just what they used to say,' he said again. 'I only hope she won't put a knife into me. I believe that she is quite capable of it.' And off he started very faintheartedly, and no wonder.

I sat and waited, and at the end of about forty-five minutes he returned, looking a good deal worse than when he went.

'Give me something to drink,' he said hoarsely.

I got him a cup of wine, and asked what was the matter.

'What is the matter? Why if ever there was trouble there's trouble now. You know when I left you? Well, I was shown straight into Sorais' private chamber, and a wonderful place it is; and there she sat, quite alone, upon a silken couch at the end of the room, playing gently upon that zither of hers. I stood before her, and for a while she took no notice of me, but kept on playing and singing a little, and very sweet music it was. At last she looked up and smiled.

"'So thou art come," she said. "I thought perchance thou hadst gone about the Queen Nyleptha's business. Thou art ever on her business, and I doubt not a good servant and a true."

'To this I merely bowed, and said I was there to receive the Queen's word.

"'Ah yes, I would talk with thee, but be thou seated. It wearies me to look so high," and she made room for me beside her on the couch, placing herself with her back against the end, so as to have a view of my face.

"'It is not meet," I said, "that I should make myself equal with the Queen."

"'I said be seated," was her answer, so I sat down, and she began to look at me with those dark eyes of hers. There she sat like an incarnate spirit of beauty, hardly talking at all, and when she did, very low, but all the while looking at me. There was a white flower in her black hair, and I tried to keep my eyes on it and count the petals, but it was of no use. At last, whether it was her gaze, or the perfume in her hair, or what I do not know, but I almost felt as though I was being mesmerized. At last she roused herself.

"'Incubu," she said, "lovest thou power?"

'I replied that I supposed all men loved power of one sort or another.

"'Thou shalt have it," she said. "Lovest thou wealth?"

'I said I liked wealth for what it brought.

"'Thou shalt have it," she said. "And lovest thou beauty?"

'To this I replied that I was very fond of statuary and architecture, or something silly of that sort, at which she frowned, and there was a pause. By this time my nerves were on such a stretch that I was shaking like a leaf. I knew that something awful was going to happen, but she held me under a kind of spell, and I could not help myself.

"'Incubu," she said at length, "wouldst thou be a king? Listen, wouldst thou be a king? Behold, stranger, I am minded to make thee king of all Zu-Vendis, ay and husband of Sorais of the Night. Nay, peace and hear me. To no man among my people had I thus opened out my secret heart, but thou art an outlander and therefore I speak without shame, knowing all I have to offer and how hard it had been thee to ask. See, a crown lies at thy feet, my lord Incubu, and with that fortune a woman whom some have wished to woo. Now mayst thou answer, oh my chosen, and soft shall thy words fall upon mine ears."

°"Oh Sorais," I said, "I pray thee speak not thus" — you see I had not time to pick and choose my words — "for this thing cannot be. I am betrothed to thy sister Nyleptha, oh Sorais, and I love her and her alone."

'Next moment it struck me that I had said an awful thing, and I looked up to see the results. When I spoke, Sorais' face was hidden in her hands, and as my words reached her she slowly raised it, and I shrank back dismayed. It was ashy white, and her eyes were flaming. She rose to her feet and seemed to be choking, but the awful thing was that she was so quiet about it all. Once she looked at a side table, on which lay a dagger, and from it to me, as though she thought of killing me; but she did not take it up. At last she spoke one word, and one only —

°"*Go*"

'And I went, and glad enough I was to get out of it, and here I am. Give me another cup of wine, there's a good fellow, and tell me, what is to be done?'

I shook my head, for the affair was indeed serious. As one of the poets says,

'Hell hath no fury like a woman scorned',

more especially if the woman is a queen and a Sorais, and indeed I feared the very worst, including imminent danger to ourselves.

'Nyleptha had better be told of this at once,' I said, 'and perhaps I had better tell her; she might receive your account with suspicion.'

'Who is captain of her guard tonight?' I went on.

'Good.'

'Very well then, there will be no chance of her being got at. Don't look surprised. I don't think that her sister would stick at that. I suppose one must tell Good of what has happened.'

'Oh, I don't know,' said Sir Henry. 'It would hurt his feelings, poor fellow! You see, he takes a lively personal interest in Sorais.'

'That's true; and after all, perhaps there is no need to tell him. He will find out the truth soon enough. Now, you mark my words, Sorais will throw in her lot with Nasta, who is sulking up in the North there, and there will be such a war as has not been known in Zu-Vendis for centuries. Look there!' and I pointed to two Court messengers, who were speeding away from the door of Sorais' private apartments. 'Now follow me,' and I ran up a stairway into an outlook tower that rose from the roof of our quarters, taking the spyglass with me, and looked out over the palace wall. The first thing we saw was one of the messengers speeding towards the Temple, bearing, without any doubt, the Queen's word to the High Priest Agon, but for the other I searched in vain. Presently, however, I spied a horseman riding furiously through the northern gate of the city, and in him I recognized the other messenger.

'Ah!' I said, 'Sorais is a woman of spirit. She is acting at once, and will strike quick and hard. You have insulted her, my boy, and the blood will flow in rivers before the stain is washed away, and yours with it, if she can get hold of you. Well, I'm off to Nyleptha. Just you stop where you are, old fellow, and try to get your nerves straight again. You'll need them all, I can tell you, unless I have observed human nature in the rough for fifty years for nothing.' And off I went accordingly.

I gained audience of the Queen without trouble. She was expecting Curtis, and was not best pleased to see my mahogany-coloured face instead.

'Is there aught wrong with my Lord, Macumazahn, that he waits not upon me? Say, is he sick?'

I said that he was well enough, and then, without further ado, I plunged into my story and told it from beginning to end. Oh, what a rage she flew into! It was a sight to see her, she looked so lovely.

'How darest thou come to me with such a tale?' she cried. 'It is a lie to say that my Lord was making love to Sorais, my sister.'

'Pardon me, oh Queen,' I answered, 'I said that Sorais was making love to thy lord.'

'Spin me no spiders' webs of words. Is not the thing the same thing? The one giveth, the other taketh; but the gift passes, and what matters it which is the most guilty? Sorais! oh, I hate her — Sorais is a queen and my sister. She had not stooped so low had he not shown the way. Oh, truly hath the poet said that man is like a snake, whom to touch is poison, and whom none can hold.'

'The remark, oh Queen, is excellent, but methinks thou hast misread the poet. Nyleptha,' I went on, 'thou knowest well that thy words are empty foolishness, and that this is no time for folly.'

'How darest thou?' she broke in, stamping her foot. 'Hast my false lord sent thee to me to insult me also? Who art thou, stranger, that thou shouldst speak to me, the Queen, after this sort? How darest thou?'

'Yea, I dare. Listen. The moments which thou dost waste in idle anger may well cost thee thy crown and all of us our lives. Already Sorais' horsemen go forth and call to arms. In three days' time Nasta will rouse himself in his fastnesses like a lion in the evening, and his growling will be heard throughout the North. The "Lady of the Night" (Sorais) hath a sweet voice, and she will not sing in vain. Her banner will be borne from range to range and valley to valley, and warriors will spring up in its track like dust beneath a whirlwind; half the army will echo her war-cry; and in every town and hamlet of this wide land the priests will call out against the foreigner and will preach her cause as holy. I have spoken, oh Queen!'

Nyleptha was quite calm now; her jealous anger had passed; and putting off the character of a lovely headstrong lady, with a rapidity and completeness that distinguished her, she put on that of a queen and a woman of business. The transformation was sudden but entire.

'Thy words are very wise, Macumazahn. Forgive me my folly. Ah, what a Queen I should be if only I had no heart! To be heartless — that is to conquer all. Passion is like the lightning, it is beautiful, and it links the earth to heaven, but alas it blinds!

'And thou thinkest that my sister Sorais would levy war upon me. So be it. She shall not prevail against me. I, too, have my friends and my retainers. There are many, I say, who will shout "Nyleptha!" when my pennon runs up on peak and pinnacle, and the light of my beacon fires leaps tonight from crag to crag, bearing the message of my war. I will break her strength and scatter her armies. Eternal night shall be the portion of Sorais of the Night. Give me that parchment and the ink. So. Now summon the officer in the ante-room. He is a trusty man.'

I did as I was bid! and the man, a veteran and quiet-looking gentleman of the guard, named Kara, entered, bowing low.

'Take this parchment,' said Nyleptha; 'it is thy warrant; and guard every place of in and outgoing in the apartments of my sister Sorais, the "Lady of the Night", and a Queen of the Zu-Vendi. Let none come in and none go out, or thy life shall pay the cost.'

The man looked startled, but he merely said, 'The Queen's word be done,' and departed. Then Nyleptha sent a messenger to Sir Henry, and presently he arrived looking uncommonly uncomfortable. I thought that another outburst was about to follow, but wonderful are the ways of woman; she said not a word about Sorais and his supposed inconstancy, greeting him with a friendly nod, and stating simply that she required his advice upon high matters. All the same there was a look in her eye, and a sort of suppressed energy in her manner towards him, that makes me think that she had not forgotten the affair, but was keeping it for a private occasion.

Just after Curtis arrived the officer returned, and reported that Sorais was *gone*. The bird had flown to the Temple, stating that she was going, as was sometimes the custom among Zu-Vendi ladies of rank, to spend the night in meditation before the altar. We looked at each other significantly. The blow had fallen very soon.

Then we set to work.

Generals who could be trusted were summoned from their quarters, and as much of the State affairs as was thought desirable was told to each, strict injunctions being given to them to get all their available force together. The same was done with such of the more powerful lords as Nyleptha knew she could rely on, several of whom left that very day for distant parts of the country to gather up their tribesmen and retainers. Sealed orders were dispatched to the rulers of far-off cities, and some twenty messengers were sent off before nightfall with instructions to ride early and late till they reached the distant chiefs to whom their letters were addressed: also many spies were set to work. All the afternoon and evening we laboured, assisted by some confidential scribes, Nyleptha showing an energy and resource of mind that astonished me, and it was eight o'clock before we got back to our quarters. Here we heard from Alphonse, who was deeply aggrieved because our non-return had spoilt his dinner (for he had turned cook again now), that Good had come back from his hawking and gone on duty. As instructions had already been given to the officer of the outer guard to double the sentries at the gate, and as we had no reason to fear any immediate danger, we did not think it worth while to hunt him up and tell him anything of what had passed, which at best was, under the peculiar circumstances of the case, one of those tasks that one prefers to postpone, so after swallowing our food we turned in to get some much-needed rest. Before we did so, however, it occurred to Curtis to tell old Umslopogaas to keep a look-out in the neighbourhood of Nyleptha's private apartments. Umslopogaas was now well known about the place, and by the Queen's order allowed to pass whither he would by the guards, a permission of which he often availed himself by roaming about the palace during the still hours in a nocturnal fashion that he favoured, and which is by no means uncommon amongst black men generally. His presence in the corridors would not, therefore, be likely to excite remark. Without any comment the Zulu took up his axe and departed, and we also departed to bed.

I seemed to have been asleep but a few minutes when I was awakened by a peculiar sensation of uneasiness. I felt that somebody was in the room and looking at me, and instantly sat up, to see to my surprise that it was already dawn, and that there, standing at the foot of my couch and looking peculiarly grim and gaunt in the grey light, was Umslopogaas himself.

'How long hast thou been there?' I asked testily, for it is not pleasant to be aroused in such a fashion.

'Mayhap the half of an hour, Macumazahn. I have a word for thee.'

'Speak on,' I said, now wide enough awake.

'As I was bid I went last night to the place of the White Queen and hid myself behind a pillar in the second anteroom, beyond which is the sleeping-place of the Queen. Bougwan (Good) was in the first anteroom alone, and outside the curtain of that room was a sentry, but I had a mind to see if I could pass in unseen, and I did, gliding behind them both. There I waited for many hours, when suddenly I perceived a dark figure coming secretly towards me. It was the figure of a woman, and in her hand she held a dagger. Behind that figure crept another unseen by the woman. It was Bougwan following in her tracks. His shoes were off, and for so fat a man he followed very well. The woman passed me, and the starlight shone upon her face.'

'Who was it?' I asked impatiently.

'The face was the face of the "Lady of the Night", and of a truth she is well named.

'I waited, and Bougwan passed me also. Then I followed. So we went slowly and without a sound up the long chamber. First the woman, then Bougwan, and then I; and the woman saw not Bougwan, and Bougwan saw not me. At last the "Lady of the Night" came to the curtains that shut off the sleeping place of the White Queen, and put out her left hand to part them. She passed through, and so did Bougwan, and so did I. At the far end of the room is the bed of the Queen, and on it she lay very fast asleep. I could hear her breathe, and see one white arm lying on the coverlid like a streak of snow on the dry grass. The "Lady of the Night" doubled herself thus, and with the long knife lifted crept towards the bed. So straight did she gaze thereat that she never thought to look behind her. When she was quite close Bougwan touched her on the arm, and she caught her breath and turned, and I saw the knife flash, and heard it strike. Well was it for Bougwan that he had the skin of iron on him, or he had been pierced. Then for the first time he saw who the woman was, and without a word he fell back astonished, and unable to speak. She, too, was astonished, and spoke not, but suddenly she laid her finger on her lip, thus, and walked towards and through the curtain, and with her went Bougwan. So close did she pass to me that her dress touched me, and I was nigh to slaying her as she went. In the first outer room she spoke to Bougwan in a whisper and, clasping her hands thus, she pleaded with him, but what she said I know not. And so they passed on to the second outer room, she pleading and he shaking his head, and saying, "Nay, nay, nay". And it seemed to me that he was about to call the guard, when she stopped talking and looked at him with great eyes, and I saw that he was bewitched by her beauty. Then she stretched out her hand and he kissed it, whereon I gathered myself together to advance and take her, seeing that now had Bougwan become a woman, and no longer knew the good from the evil, when behold! she was gone.'

'Gone!' I ejaculated.

'Ay, gone, and there stood Bougwan staring at the wall like one asleep, and presently he went too, and I waited a while and came away also.'

'Art thou sure, Umslopogaas,' said I, 'that thou hast not been a dreamer this night?'

In reply he opened his left hand, and produced about three inches of a blade of a dagger of the finest steel. 'If I be, Macumazahn, behold what the dream left with me. The knife broke upon Bougwan's bosom and as I passed I picked this up in the sleeping-place of the White Queen.'

War! Red War!

Telling Umslopogaas to wait, I tumbled into my clothes and went off with him to Sir Henry's room, where the Zulu repeated his story word for word. It was a sight to watch Curtis' face as he heard it.

'Great Heavens!' he said: 'here have I been sleeping away while Nyleptha was nearly murdered — and all through me, too. What a fiend that Sorais must be! It would have served her well if Umslopogaas had cut her down in the act.'

'Ay,' said the Zulu. 'Fear not; I should have slain her ere she struck. I was but waiting the moment.'

I said nothing, but I could not help thinking that many a thousand doomed lives would have been saved if he had meted out to Sorais the fate she meant for her sister. And, as the issue proved, I was right.

After he had told his tale Umslopogaas went off unconcernedly to get his morning meal, and Sir Henry and I fell to talking.

At first he was very bitter against Good, who, he said, was no longer to be trusted, having designedly allowed Sorais to escape by some secret stair when it was his duty to have handed her over to justice. Indeed, he spoke in the most unmeasured terms on the matter. I let him run on awhile, reflecting to myself how easy we find it to be hard on the weaknesses of others, and how tender we are to our own.

'Really, my dear fellow,' I said at length, 'one would never think, to hear you talk, that you were the man who had an interview with this same lady yesterday, and found it rather difficult to resist her fascinations, notwithstanding your ties to one of the loveliest and most loving women in the world. Now suppose it was Nyleptha who had tried to murder Sorais, and *you* had caught her, and she had pleaded with you, would you have been so very eager to hand her over to an open shame, and to death by fire? Just look at the matter through Good's eyeglass for a minute before you denounce an old friend as a scoundrel.'

He listened to this jobation submissively, and then frankly acknowledged that he had spoken hardly. It is one of the best points in Sir Henry's character that he is always ready to admit it when he is in the wrong.

But, though I spoke up thus for Good, I was not blind to the fact that, however natural his behaviour might be, it was obvious that he was being involved in a very awkward and disgraceful complication. A foul and wicked murder had been attempted, and he had let the murderess escape, and thereby, among other things, allowed her to gain a complete ascendency over himself. In fact, he was in a fair way to become her tool — and no more dreadful fate can befall a man than to become the tool of an unscrupulous woman, or indeed of any woman. There is but one end to it: when he is broken, or has served her purpose, he is thrown away — turned out on the world to hunt for his lost self-respect. Whilst I was pondering thus, and wondering what was to be done — for the whole subject was a thorny one — I suddenly heard a great clamour in the courtyard outside, and distinguished the voice of Umslopogaas and Alphonse, the former cursing furiously, and the latter yelling in terror.

Hurrying out to see what was the matter, I was met by a ludicrous sight. The little Frenchman was running up the courtyard at an extraordinary speed, and after him sped Umslopogaas like a great greyhound. Just as I came out he caught him, and, lifting him right off his legs, carried him some paces to a beautiful but very dense flowering shrub which bore a flower not unlike the gardenia, but was covered with short thorns. Next, despite his howls and struggles, he with one mighty thrust plunged poor Alphonse head first into the bush, so that nothing but the calves of his legs and heels remained in evidence. Then, satisfied with what he had done, the Zulu folded his arms and stood grimly contemplating the Frenchman's kicks, and listening to his yells, which were awful.

'What art thou doing?' I said, running up. 'Wouldst thou kill the man? Pull him out of the bush!'

With a savage grunt he obeyed, seizing the wretched Alphonse by the ankle, and with a jerk that must have nearly dislocated it, tearing him out of the heart of the shrub. Never did I see such a sight as he presented, his clothes half torn off his back, and bleeding as he was in every direction from the sharp thorns. There he lay and yelled and rolled, and there was no getting anything out of him.

At last, however, he got up and, ensconcing himself behind me, cursed old Umslopogaas by every saint in the calendar, vowing by the blood of his heroic grandfather that he would poison him, and 'have his revenge'.

At last I got to the truth of the matter. It appeared that Alphonse habitually cooked Umslopogaas's porridge, which the latter ate for breakfast in the corner of the courtyard, just as he would have done at home in Zululand, from a gourd, and with a wooden spoon. Now Umslopogaas had, like many Zulus, a great horror of fish, which he considered a species of water-snake; so Alphonse, who was as fond of playing tricks as a monkey, and who was also a consummate cook, determined to make him eat some. Accordingly he grated up a quantity of white fish very finely, and mixed it with the Zulu's porridge, who swallowed it nearly all down in ignorance of what he was eating. But, unfortunately for Alphonse, he could not restrain his joy at this sight, and came capering and peering round, till at last Umslopogaas, who was very clever in his way, suspected something, and, after a careful examination of the remains of his porridge, discovered 'the buffalo heifer's trick', and, in revenge, served him as I have said. Indeed, the little man was fortunate not to get a broken neck for his pains; for, as one would have thought, he might have learnt from the episode of his display of axemanship that 'le Monsieur noir' was an ill person to play practical jokes upon.

This incident was unimportant enough in itself, but I narrate it because it led to serious consequences. As soon as he had stanched the bleeding from his scratches and washed himself, Alphonse went off still cursing, to recover his temper, a process which I knew from experience would take a very long time. When he had gone I gave Umslopogaas a jobation and told him that I was ashamed of his behaviour.

'Ah, well, Macumazahn,' he said, 'you must be gentle with me, for here is not my place. I am weary of it, weary to death of eating and drinking, of sleeping and giving in marriage. I love not this soft life in stone houses that takes the heart out of a man, and turns his strength to water and his flesh to fat. I love not the white robes and the delicate women, the blowing of trumpets and the flying of hawks. When we fought the Masai at the kraal yonder, ah, then life was worth the living, but here is never a blow struck in anger, and I begin to think I shall go the way of my fathers and lift Inkosi-kaas no more,' and he held up the axe and gazed at it in sorrow.

'Ah,' I said, 'that is thy complaint, is it? Thou hast the blood-sickness, hast thou? And the Woodpecker wants a tree. And at thy age, too. Shame on thee! Umslopogaas.'

'Ay, Macumazahn, mine is a red trade, yet is it better and more honest than some. Better is it to slay a man in fair fight than to suck out his heart's blood in buying and selling and usury after your white fashion. Many a man have I slain, yet is there never a one that I should fear to look in the face again, ay, many are there who once were friends, and whom I should be right glad to snuff with. But there! there! thou hast thy ways, and I mine: each to his own people and his own place. The high-veldt ox will die in the fat bush country, and so is it with me, Macumazahn. I am rough, I know it, and when my blood is warm I know not what to do, but yet wilt thou be sorry when the night swallows me and I am utterly lost in blackness, for in thy heart thou lovest me, my father, Macumazahn the fox, though I be nought but a broken-down Zulu war-dog — a chief for whom there is no room in his own kraal, an outcast and a wanderer in strange places: ay, I love thee, Macumazahn, for we have grown grey together, and there is that between us that cannot be seen, and yet is too strong for breaking;' and he took his snuff-box, which was made of an old brass cartridge, from the slit in his ear where he always carried it, and handed it to me for me to help myself.

I took the pinch of snuff with some emotion. It was quite true, I was much attached to the bloodthirsty old ruffian. I do not know what was the charm of his character, but it had a charm; perhaps it was its fierce honesty and directness; perhaps one admired his almost superhuman skill and strength, or it may have been simply that he was so absolutely unique. Frankly, with all my experience of savages, I never knew a man quite like him, he was so wise and yet such a child with it all; and though it seems laughable to say so, like the hero of the Yankee parody, he 'had a tender heart'. Anyway, I was very fond of him, though I should never have thought of telling him so.

'Ay, old wolf,' I said, 'thine is a strange love. Thou wouldst split me to the chin if I stood in thy path tomorrow.'

'Thou speakest truth, Macumazahn, that would I if it came in the way of duty, but I should love thee all the same when the blow had gone fairly home.

Is there any chance of some fighting here, Macumazahn?' he went on in an insinuating voice. 'Methought that what I saw last night did show that the two great Queens were vexed one with another. Else had the "Lady of the Night" not brought that dagger with her.'

I agreed with him that it showed that more or less pique and irritation existed between the ladies, and told him how things stood, and that they were quarrelling over Incubu.

'Ah, is it so?' he exclaimed, springing up in delight; 'then will there be war as surely as the rivers rise in the rains — war to the end. Women love the last blow as well as the last word, and when they fight for love they are pitiless as a wounded buffalo. See thou, Macumazahn, a woman will swim through blood to her desire, and think nought of it. With these eyes have I seen it once, and twice also. Ah, Macumazahn, we shall see this fine place of houses burning yet, and hear the battle cries come ringing up the street. After all, I have not wandered for nothing. Can this folk fight, think ye?'

Just then Sir Henry joined us, and Good arrived, too, from another direction, looking very pale and hollow-eyed. The moment Umslopogaas saw the latter he stopped his bloodthirsty talk and greeted him.

'Ah, Bougwan,' he cried, 'greeting to thee, Inkoos! Thou art surely weary. Didst thou hunt too much yesterday?' Then, without waiting for an answer, he went on —

'Listen, Bougwan, and I will tell thee a story; it is about a woman, therefore wilt thou hear it, is it not so?

'There was a man and he had a brother, and there was a woman who loved the man's brother and was beloved of the man. But the man's brother had a favourite wife and loved not the woman, and he made a mock of her. Then the woman, being very cunning and fierce-hearted for revenge, took counsel with herself and said to the man, "I love thee, and if thou wilt make war upon thy brother I will marry thee." And he knew it was a lie, yet because of his great love of the woman, who was very fair, did he listen to her words and made war. And when many people had been killed his brother sent to him, saying, "Why slayest thou me? What hurt have I done unto thee? From my youth up have I not loved thee? When thou wast little did I not nurture thee, and have we not gone down to war together and divided the cattle, girl by girl, ox by ox, and cow by cow? Why slayest thou me, my brother, son of my own mother?"

'Then the man's heart was heavy, and he knew that his path was evil, and he put aside the tempting of the woman and ceased to make war on his brother, and lived at peace in the same kraal with him. And after a time the woman came to him and said, "I have lost the past, I will be thy wife." And in his heart he knew that it was a lie and that she thought the evil thing, yet because of his love did he take her to wife.

'And the very night that they were wed, when the man was plunged into a deep sleep, did the woman arise and take his axe from his hand and creep into the hut of his brother and slay him in his rest. Then did she slink back like a gorged lioness and place the thong of the red axe back upon his wrist and go her ways.

'And at the dawning the people came shouting, "Lousta is slain in the night," and they came unto the hut of the man, and there he lay asleep and by him was the red axe. Then did they remember the war and say, "Lo! he hath of a surety slain his brother," and they would have taken and killed him, but he rose and fled swiftly, and as he fleeted by he slew the woman.

'But death could not wipe out the evil she had done, and on him rested the weight of all her sin. Therefore is he an outcast and his name a scorn among his own people; for on him, and him only, resteth the burden of her who betrayed. And, therefore, does he wander afar, without a kraal and without an ox or a wife, and therefore will he die afar like a stricken buck and his name be accursed from generation to generation, in that the people say that he slew his brother, Lousta, by treachery in the night-time.'

The old Zulu paused, and I saw that he was deeply agitated by his own story. Presently he lifted his head, which he had bowed to his breast, and went on:

'I was the man, Bougwan. Ou! I was that man, and now hark thou! Even as I am so wilt thou be — a tool, a plaything, an ox of burden to carry the evil deeds of another. Listen! When thou didst creep after the "Lady of the Night" I was hard upon thy track. When she struck thee with the knife in the sleeping place of the White Queen I was there also; when thou didst let her slip away like a snake in the stones I saw thee, and I knew that she had bewitched thee and that a true man had abandoned the truth, and he who aforetime loved a straight path had taken a crooked way. Forgive me, my father, if my words are sharp, but out of a full heart are they spoken. See her no more, so shalt thou go down with honour to the grave. Else because of the beauty of a woman that weareth as a garment of fur shalt thou be even as I am, and perchance with more cause. I have said.'

Throughout this long and eloquent address Good had been perfectly silent, but when the tale began to shape itself so aptly to his own case, he coloured up, and when he learnt that what had passed between him and Sorais had been overseen he was evidently much distressed. And now, when at last he spoke, it was in a tone of humility quite foreign to him.

'I must say,' he said, with a bitter little laugh, 'that I scarcely thought that I should live to be taught my duty by a Zulu; but it just shows what we can come to. I wonder if you fellows can understand how humiliated I feel, and the bitterest part of it is that I deserve it all. Of course I should have handed Sorais over to the guard, but I could not, and that is a fact. I let her go and I promised to say nothing, more is the shame to me. She told me that if I would side with her she would marry me and make me king of this country, but thank goodness I did find the heart to say that even to marry her I could not desert my friends. And now you can do what you like, I deserve it all. All I have to say is that I hope that you may never love a woman with all your heart and then be so sorely tempted of her,' and he turned to go.

'Look here, old fellow,' said Sir Henry, 'just stop a minute. I have a little tale to tell you too.' And he went on to narrate what had taken place on the previous day between Sorais and himself.

This was a finishing stroke to poor Good. It is not pleasant to any man to learn that he has been made a tool of, but when the circumstances are as peculiarly atrocious as in the present case, it is about as bitter a pill as anybody can be called on to swallow.

'Do you know,' he said, 'I think that between you, you fellows have about worked a cure,' and he turned and walked away, and I for one felt very sorry for him. Ah, if the moths would always carefully avoid the candle, how few burnt wings there would be!

That day was a Court day, when the Queens sat in the great hall and received petitions, discussed laws, money grants, and so forth, and thither we adjourned shortly afterwards. On our way we were joined by Good, who was looking exceedingly depressed.

When we got into the hall Nyleptha was already on her throne and proceeding with business as usual, surrounded by councillors, courtiers, lawyers, priests, and an unusually strong guard. It was, however, easy to see from the air of excitement and expectation on the faces of everybody present that nobody was paying much attention to ordinary affairs, the fact being that the knowledge that civil war was imminent had now got abroad. We saluted Nyleptha and took our accustomed places, and for a little while things went on as usual, when suddenly the trumpets began to call outside the palace, and from the great crowd that was gathered there in anticipation of some unusual event there rose a roar of '*Sorais! Sorais!*'

Then came the roll of many chariot wheels, and presently the great curtains at the end of the hall were drawn wide and through them entered the 'Lady of the Night' herself. Nor did she come alone. Preceding her was Agon, the High Priest, arrayed in his most gorgeous vestments, and on either side were other priests. The reason for their presence was obvious — coming with them it would have been sacrilege to attempt to detain her. Behind her were a number of the great lords, and behind them a small body of picked guards. A glance at Sorais herself was enough to show that her mission was of no peaceful kind, for in place of her gold embroidered 'kaf' she wore a shining tunic formed of golden scales, and on her head a little golden helmet. In her hand, too, she bore a toy spear, beautifully made and fashioned of solid silver. Up the hall she came, looking like a lioness in her conscious pride and beauty, and as she came the spectators fell back bowing and made a path for her. By the sacred stone she halted, and laying her hand on it, she cried out with a loud voice to Nyleptha on the throne, 'Hail, oh Queen!'

'All hail, my royal sister!' answered Nyleptha. 'Draw thou near. Fear not, I give thee safe conduct.'

Sorais answered with a haughty look, and swept on up the hall till she stood right before the thrones.

'A boon, oh Queen!' she cried again.

'Speak on, my sister; what is there that I can give thee who hath half our kingdom?'

'Thou canst tell me a true word — me and the people of Zu-Vendis. Art thou, or art thou not, about to take this foreign wolf,' and she pointed to Sir Henry with her toy spear, 'to be a husband to thee, and share thy bed and throne?'

Curtis winced at this, and turning towards Sorais, said to her in a low voice, 'Methinks that yesterday thou hadst other names than wolf to call me by, oh Queen!' and I saw her bite her lips as, like a danger flag, the blood flamed red upon her face. As for Nyleptha, who is nothing if not original, she, seeing that the thing was out, and that there was nothing further to be gained by concealment, answered the question in a novel and effectual manner, inspired thereto, as I firmly believe, by coquetry and a desire to triumph over her rival.

Up she rose and, descending from the throne, swept in all the glory of her royal grace on to where her lover stood. There she stopped and untwined the golden snake that was wound around her arm. Then she bade him kneel, and he dropped on one knee on the marble before her, and next, taking the golden snake with both her hands, she bent the pure soft metal round his neck, and when it was fast, deliberately kissed him on the brow and called him her 'dear lord'.

'Thou seest,' she said, when the excited murmur of the spectators had died away, addressing her sister as Sir Henry rose to his feet, 'I have put my collar round the "wolf's" neck, and behold! he shall be my watchdog, and that is my answer to thee, Queen Sorais, my sister, and to those with thee. Fear not,' she went on, smiling sweetly on her lover, and pointing to the golden snake she had twined round his massive throat, 'if my yoke be heavy, yet is it of pure gold, and it shall not gall thee.'

Then, turning to the audience, she continued in a clear proud tone, 'Ay, Lady of the Night, Lords, Priests, and People here gathered together, by this sign do I take the foreigner to husband, even here in the face of you all. What, am I a Queen, and yet not free to choose the man whom I will love? Then should I be lower than the meanest girl in all my provinces. Nay, he hath won my heart, and with it goes my hand, and throne, and all I have — ay, had he been a beggar instead of a great lord fairer and stronger than any here, and having more wisdom and knowledge of strange things, I had given him all, how much more so being what he is!' And she took his hand and gazed proudly on him, and holding it, stood there boldly facing the people. And such was her sweetness and the power and dignity of her person, and so beautiful she looked standing hand in hand there at her lover's side, so sure of him and of herself, and so ready to risk all things and endure all things for him, that most of those who saw the sight, which I am sure no one of them will ever forget, caught the fire from her eyes and the happy colour from her blushing face, and cheered her like wild things. It was a bold stroke for her to make, and it appealed to the imagination; but human nature in Zu-Vendis, as elsewhere, loves that which is bold and not afraid to break a rule, and is moreover peculiarly susceptible to appeals to its poetical side.

And so the people cheered till the roof rang; but Sorais of the Night stood there with downcast eyes, for she could not bear to see her sister's triumph, which robbed her of the man whom she had hoped to win, and in the awfulness of her jealous anger she trembled and turned white like an aspen in the wind. I think I have said somewhere of her that she reminded me of the sea on a calm day, having the same aspect of sleeping power about her. Well, it was all awake now, and like the face of the furious ocean it awed and yet fascinated me. A really handsome woman in a royal rage is always a beautiful sight, but such beauty and such a rage I never saw combined before, and I can only say that the effect produced was well worthy of the two.

She lifted her white face, the teeth set, and there were purple rings beneath her glowing eyes. Thrice she tried to speak and thrice she failed, but at last her voice came. Raising her silver spear, she shook it, and the light gleamed from it and from the golden scales of her cuirass.

'And thinkest thou, Nyleptha,' she said in notes which pealed through the great hall like a clarion, 'thinkest thou that I, Sorais, a Queen of the Zu-Vendi, will brook that this base outlander shall sit upon my father's throne and rear up half-breeds to fill the place of the great House of the Stairway? Never! never! while there is life in my bosom and a man to follow me and a spear to strike with. Who is on my side? Who?

'Now hand thou over this foreign wolf and those who came hither to prey with him to the doom of fire, for have they not committed the deadly sin against the sun? or, Nyleptha, I give thee War — red War! Ay, I say to thee that the path of thy passion shall be marked out by the blazing of thy towns and watered with the blood of those who cleave to thee. On thy head rest the burden of the deed, and in thy ears ring the groans of the dying and the cries of the widows and those who are left fatherless for ever and for ever.

'I tell thee I will tear thee, Nyleptha, the White Queen, from thy throne, and that thou shalt be hurled — ay, hurled even from the topmost stair of the great way to the foot thereof, in that thou hast covered the name of the House of him who built it with black shame. And I tell ye strangers — all save Bougwan, whom because thou didst do me a service I will save alive if thou wilt leave these men and follow me' (here poor Good shook his head vigorously and ejaculated 'Can't be done' in English) — 'that I will wrap you in sheets of gold and hang you yet alive in chains from the four golden trumpets of the four angels that fly east and west and north and south from the giddiest pinnacles of the Temple, so that ye may be a token and a warning to the land. And as for thee, Incubu, thou shalt die in yet another fashion that I will not tell thee now.'

She ceased, panting for breath, for her passion shook her like a storm, and a murmur, partly of horror and partly of admiration, ran through the hall. Then Nyleptha answered calmly and with dignity:

'Ill would it become my place and dignity, oh sister, so to speak as thou hast spoken and so to threat as thou hast threatened. Yet if thou wilt make war, then will I strive to bear up against thee, for if my hand seem soft, yet shalt thou find it of iron when it grips thine armies by the throat. Sorais, I fear thee not. I weep for that which thou wilt bring upon our people and on thyself, but for myself I say — I fear thee not. Yet thou, who but yesterday didst strive to win my lover and my lord from me, whom today thou dost call a "foreign wolf", to be *thy* lover and *thy* lord' (here there was an immense sensation in the hall), 'thou who but last night, as I have learnt but since thou didst enter here, didst creep like a snake into my sleeping-place — ay, even by a secret way, and wouldst have foully murdered me, thy sister, as I lay asleep —'

'It is false, it is false!' rang out Agon's and a score of other voices.

'It is *not* false,' said I, producing the broken point of the dagger and holding it up. 'Where is the haft from which this flew, oh Sorais?'

'It is not false,' cried Good, determined at last to act like a loyal man. 'I took the Lady of the Night by the White Queen's bed, and on my breast the dagger broke.'

'Who is on my side?' cried Sorais, shaking her silver spear, for she saw that public sympathy was turning against her. 'What, Bougwan, thou comest not?' she said, addressing Good, who was standing close to her, in a low, concentrated voice. 'Thou pale-souled fool, for a reward thou shalt eat out thy heart with love of me and not be satisfied, and thou mightest have been my husband and a king! At least I hold *thee* in chains that cannot be broken.'

'War! War! War!' she cried. 'Here, with my hand upon the sacred stone that shall endure, so runs the prophecy, till the Zu-Vendi set their necks beneath an alien yoke, I declare war to the end. Who follows Sorais of the Night to victory and honour?'

Instantly the whole concourse began to break up in indescribable confusion. Many present hastened to throw in their lot with the 'Lady of the Night', but some came from her following to us. Amongst the former was an under officer of Nyleptha's own guard, who suddenly turned and made a run for the doorway through which Sorais' people were already passing. Umslopogaas, who was present and had taken the whole scene in, seeing with admirable presence of mind that if this soldier got away others would follow his example, seized the man, who drew his sword and struck at him. Thereon the Zulu sprang back with a wild shout, and, avoiding the sword cuts, began to peck at his foe with his terrible axe, till in a few seconds the man's fate overtook him and he fell with a clash heavily and quite dead upon the marble floor.

This was the first blood spilt in the war.

'Shut the gates,' I shouted, thinking that we might perhaps catch Sorais so, and not being troubled with the idea of committing sacrilege. But the order came too late, her guards were already passing through them, and in another minute the streets echoed with the furious galloping of horses and the rolling of her chariots.

So, drawing half the people after her, Sorais was soon passing like a whirlwind through the Frowning City on her road to her headquarters at

M'Arstuna, a fortress situated a hundred and thirty miles to the north of Milosis.

And after that the city was alive with the endless tramp of regiments and preparations for the gathering war, and old Umslopogaas once more began to sit in the sunshine and go through a show of sharpening Inkosi-kaas's razor edge.

A Strange Wedding

One person, however, did not succeed in getting out in time before the gates were shut, and that was the High Priest Agon, who, as we had every reason to believe, was Sorais' great ally, and the heart and soul of her party. This cunning and ferocious old man had not forgiven us for those hippopotami, or rather that was what he said. What he meant was that he would never brook the introduction of our wider ways of thought and foreign learning and influence while there was a possibility of stamping us out. Also he knew that we possessed a different system of religion, and no doubt was in daily terror of our attempting to introduce it into Zu-Vendis. One day he asked me if we had any religion in our country, and I told him that so far as I could remember we had ninety-five different ones. You might have knocked him down with a feather, and really it is difficult not to pity a high priest of a well-established cult who is haunted by the possible approach of one or all of ninety-five new religions.

When we knew that Agon was caught, Nyleptha, Sir Henry, and I discussed what was to be done with him. I was for closely incarcerating him, but Nyleptha shook her head, saying that it would produce a disastrous effect throughout the country. 'Ah!' she added, with a stamp of her foot, 'if I win and am once really Queen, I will break the power of those priests, with their rites and revels and dark secret ways.' I only wished that old Agon could have heard her, it would have frightened him.

'Well,' said Sir Henry, 'if we are not to imprison him, I suppose that we may as well let him go. He is of no use here.'

Nyleptha looked at him in a curious sort of way, and said in a dry little voice, 'Thinkest thou so, my lord?'

'Eh?' said Curtis. 'No, I do not see what is the use of keeping him.'

She said nothing, but continued looking at him in a way that was as shy as it was sweet.

Then at last he understood.

'Forgive me, Nyleptha,' he said, rather tremulously. 'Dost thou mean that thou wilt marry me, even now?'

'Nay, I know not; let my lord say,' was her rapid answer; 'but if my lord wills, the priest is there and the altar is there' — pointing to the entrance to a private chapel — 'and am I not ready to do the will of my lord? Listen, oh my lord! In eight days or less thou must leave me and go down to war, for thou shalt lead my armies, and in war — men sometimes fall, and so I would for a little space have had thee all my own, if only for memory's sake;' and the tears overflowed her lovely eyes and rolled down her face like heavy drops of dew down the red heart of a rose.

'Mayhap, too,' she went on, 'I shall lose my crown, and with my crown my life and thine also. Sorais is very strong and very bitter, and if she prevails she will not spare. Who can read the future? Happiness is the world's White Bird, that alights seldom, and flies fast and far till one day he is lost in the clouds. Therefore should we hold him fast if by any chance he rests for a little space upon our hand. It is not wise to neglect the present for the future, for who knows what the future will be, Incubu? Let us pluck our flowers while the dew is on them, for when the sun is up they wither and on the morrow will others bloom that we shall never see.' And she lifted her sweet face to him and smiled into his eyes, and once more I felt a curious pang of jealousy and turned and went away. They never took much notice of whether I was there or not, thinking, I suppose, that I was an old fool, and that it did not matter one way or the other, and really I believe that they were right.

So I went back to our quarters and ruminated over things in general, and watched old Umslopogaas whetting his axe outside the window as a vulture whets his beak beside a dying ox.

And in about an hour's time Sir Henry came tearing over, looking very radiant and wildly excited, and found Good and myself and even Umslopogaas, and asked us if we should like to assist at a real wedding. Of course we said yes, and off we went to the chapel, where we found Agon looking as sulky as any High Priest possibly could, and no wonder. It appeared that he and Nyleptha had a slight difference of opinion about the coming ceremony. He had flatly refused to celebrate it, or to allow any of his priests to do so, whereupon Nyleptha became very angry and told him that she, as Queen, was head of the Church, and meant to be obeyed. Indeed, she played the part of a Zu-Vendi Henry the Eighth to perfection, and insisted that, if she wanted to be married, she would be married, and that he should marry her.

He still refused to go through the ceremony, so she clinched her argument thus —

'Well, I cannot execute a High Priest, because there is an absurd prejudice against it, and I cannot imprison him because all his subordinates would raise a crying that would bring the stars down on Zu-Vendis and crush it; but I *can* leave him to contemplate the altar of the Sun without anything to eat, because that is his natural vocation, and if thou wilt not marry me, O Agon! thou shalt be placed before the altar yonder with nought but a little water till such time as thou hast reconsidered the matter.'

Now, as it happened, Agon had been hurried away that morning without his breakfast, and was already exceedingly hungry, so he presently modified his views and consented to marry them, saying at the same time that he washed his hands of all responsibility in the matter.

So it chanced that presently, attended only by two of her favourite maidens, came the Queen Nyleptha, with happy blushing face and downcast eyes, dressed in pure white, without embroidery of any sort, as seems to be the fashion on these occasions in most countries of the world. She did not wear a single ornament, even her gold circlets were removed, and I thought that if possible she looked more lovely than ever without them, as really superbly beautiful women do.

She came, curtseyed low to Sir Henry, and then took his hand and led him up before the altar, and after a little pause, in a slow, clear voice uttered the following words, which are customary in Zu-Vendis if the bride desires and the man consents: —

'Thou dost swear by the Sun that thou wilt take no other woman to wife unless I lay my hand upon her and bid her come?'

'I swear it,' answered Sir Henry; adding in English, 'One is quite enough for me.'

Then Agon, who had been sulking in a corner near the altar, came forward and gabbled off something into his beard at such a rate that I could not follow it, but it appeared to be an invocation to the Sun to bless the union and make it fruitful. I observed that Nyleptha listened very closely to every word, and afterwards discovered that she was afraid lest Agon should play her a trick, and by going through the invocations backwards divorce them instead of marry them. At the end of the invocations they were asked, as in our service, if they took each other for husband and wife, and on their assenting they kissed each other before the altar, and the service was over, so far as their rites were concerned. But it seemed to me that there was yet something wanting, and so I produced a Prayer-Book, which has, together which the 'Ingoldsby Legends', that I often read when I lie awake at night, accompanied me in all my later wanderings. I gave it to my poor boy Harry years ago, and after his death I found it among his things and took it back again.

'Curtis,' I said, 'I am not a clergyman, and I do not know if what I am going to propose is allowable — I know it is not legal — but if you and the Queen have no objection I should like to read the English marriage service over you. It is a solemn step which you are taking, and I think that you ought, so far as circumstances will allow, to give it the sanction of your own religion.'

'I have thought of that,' he said, 'and I wish you would. I do not feel half married yet.'

Nyleptha raised no objection, fully understanding that her husband wished to celebrate the marriage according to the rites prevailing in his own country, and so I set to work and read the service, from 'Dearly beloved' to 'amazement', as well as I could; and when I came to 'I, Henry, take thee, Nyleptha,' I translated, and also 'I, Nyleptha, take thee, Henry,' which she repeated after me very well. Then Sir Henry took a plain gold ring from his little finger and placed it on hers, and so on to the end. The ring had been Curtis' mother's wedding-ring, and I could not help thinking how astonished the dear old Yorkshire lady would have been if she could have foreseen that her wedding-ring was to serve a similar purpose for Nyleptha, a Queen of the Zu-Vendi.

As for Agon, he was with difficulty kept calm while this second ceremony was going on, for he at once understood that it was religious in its nature, and doubtless bethought him of the ninety-five new faiths which loomed so ominously in his eyes. Indeed, he at once set me down as a rival High Priest, and hated me accordingly. However, in the end off he went, positively bristling with indignation, and I knew that we might look out for danger from his direction.

And off went Good and I, and old Umslopogaas also, leaving the happy pair to themselves, and very low we all felt. Marriages are supposed to be cheerful things, but my experience is that they are very much the reverse to everybody, except perhaps the two people chiefly interested. They mean the breaking-up of so many old ties as well as the undertaking of so many new ones, and there is always something sad about the passing away of the old order. Now to take this case for instance: Sir Henry Curtis is the best and kindest fellow and friend in the world, but he has never been quite the same since that little scene in the chapel. It is always Nyleptha this and Nyleptha that — Nyleptha, in short, from morning till night in one way or another, either expressed or understood. And as for the old friends — well, of course they have taken the place that old friends ought to take, and which ladies are as a rule very careful to see they do take when a man marries, and that is, the second place. Yes, he would be angry if anybody said so, but it is a fact for all that. He is not quite the same, and Nyleptha is very sweet and very charming, but I think that she likes him to understand that she has married *him*, and not Quatermain, Good, and Co. But there! what is the use of grumbling? It is all very right and proper, as any married lady would have no difficulty in explaining, and I am a selfish, jealous old man, though I hope I never show it.

So Good and I went and ate in silence and then indulged in an extra fine flagon of old Zu-Vendian to keep our spirits up, and presently one of our attendants came and told a story that gave us something to think about.

It may, perhaps, be remembered that, after his quarrel with Umslopogaas, Alphonse had gone off in an exceedingly ill temper to sulk over his scratches. Well, it appears that he walked right past the Temple to the Sun, down the wide road on the further side of the slope it crowns, and thence on into the beautiful park, or pleasure gardens, which are laid out just beyond the outer wall. After wandering about there for a little he started to return, but was met near the outer gate by Sorais' train of chariots, which were galloping furiously along the great northern road. When she caught sight of Alphonse, Sorais halted her train and called to him. On approaching he was instantly seized and dragged into one of the chariots and carried off, 'crying out loudly', as our informant said, and as from my general knowledge of him I can well believe.

At first I was much puzzled to know what object Sorais could have had in carrying off the poor little Frenchman. She could hardly stoop so low as to try to wreak her fury on one whom she knew was only a servant. At last, however, an idea occurred to me. We three were, as I think I have said, much revered by the people of Zu-Vendis at large, both because we were the first strangers they had ever seen, and because we were supposed to be the possessors of almost supernatural wisdom. Indeed, though Sorais' cry against the 'foreign wolves' — or, to translate it more accurately, 'foreign hyenas' — was sure to go down very well with the nobles and the priests, it was not as we learnt, likely to be particularly effectual amongst the bulk of the population. The Zu-Vendi people, like the Athenians of old, are ever seeking for some new thing, and just because we were so new our presence was on the whole acceptable to them. Again, Sir Henry's magnificent personal appearance made a deep impression upon a race who possess a greater love of beauty than any other I have ever been acquainted with. Beauty may be prized in other countries, but in Zu-Vendis it is almost worshipped, as indeed the national love of statuary shows. The people said openly in the market-places that there was not a man in the country to touch Curtis in personal appearance, as with the exception of Sorais there was no woman who could compete with Nyleptha, and that therefore it was meet that they should marry; and that he had been sent by the Sun as a husband for their Queen. Now, from all this it will be seen that the outcry against us was to a considerable extent fictitious, and nobody knew it better than Sorais herself. Consequently it struck me that it might have occurred to her that down in the country and among the country people, it would be better to place the reason of her conflict with her sister upon other and more general grounds than Nyleptha's marriage with the stranger. It would be easy in a land where there had been so many civil wars to rake out some old cry that would stir up the recollection of buried feuds, and, indeed, she soon found an effectual one. This being so, it was of great importance to her to have one of the strangers with her whom she could show to the common people as a great Outlander, who had been so struck by the justice of her cause that he had elected to leave his companions and follow her standard.

This, no doubt, was the cause of her anxiety to get a hold of Good, whom she would have used till he ceased to be of service and then cast off. But Good having drawn back she grasped at the opportunity of securing Alphonse, who was not unlike him in personal appearance though smaller, no doubt with the object of showing him off in the cities and country as the great Bougwan himself. I told Good that I thought that that was her plan, and his face was a sight to see — he was so horrified at the idea.

'What,' he said, 'dress up that little wretch to represent me? Why, I shall have to get out of the country! My reputation will be ruined for ever.'

I consoled him as well as I could, but it is not pleasant to be personated all over a strange country by an arrant little coward, and I can quite sympathize with his vexation.

Well, that night Good and I messed as I have said in solitary grandeur, feeling very much as though we had just returned from burying a friend instead of marrying one, and next morning the work began in good earnest. The messages and orders which had been despatched by Nyleptha two days before now began to take effect, and multitudes of armed men came pouring into the city. We saw, as may be imagined, but very little of Nyleptha and not too much of Curtis during those next few days, but Good and I sat daily with the council of generals and loyal lords, drawing up plans of action, arranging commissariat matters, the distribution of commands, and a hundred and one other things. Men came in freely, and all the day long the great roads leading to Milosis were spotted with the banners of lords arriving from their distant placcs to rally round Nyleptha.

After the first few days it became clear that we should be able to take the field with about forty thousand infantry and twenty thousand cavalry, a very respectable force considering how short was the time we had to collect it, and that about half the regular army had elected to follow Sorais.

But if our force was large, Sorais' was, according to the reports brought in day by day by our spies, much larger. She had taken up her headquarters at a very strong town called M'Arstuna, situated, as I have said, to the north of Milosis, and all the countryside was flocking to her standard. Nasta had poured down from his highlands and was on his way to join her with no less than twenty-five thousand of his mountaineers, the most terrible soldiers to face in all Zu-Vendis. Another mighty lord, named Belusha, who lived in the great horse-breeding district, had come in with twelve thousand cavalry, and so on. Indeed, what between one thing and another, it seemed certain that she would gather a fully armed host of nearly one hundred thousand men.

And then came news that Sorais was proposing to break up her camp and march on the Frowning City itself, desolating the country as she came. Thereon arose the question whether it would be best to meet her at Milosis or to go out and give her battle. When our opinion was asked upon the subject, Good and I unhesitatingly gave it in favour of an advance. If we were to shut ourselves up in the city and wait to be attacked, it seemed to us that our inaction would be set down to fear. It is so important, especially on an occasion of this sort, when a very little will suffice to turn men's opinions one way or the other, to be up and doing something. Ardour for a cause will soon evaporate if the cause does not move but sits down to conquer. Therefore we cast our vote for moving out and giving battle in the open, instead of waiting till we were drawn from our walls like a badger from a hole.

Sir Henry's opinion coincided with ours, and so, needless to say, did that of Nyleptha, who, like a flint, was always ready to flash out fire. A great map of the country was brought and spread out before her. About thirty miles this side of M'Arstuna, where Sorais lay, and ninety odd miles from Milosis, the road ran over a neck of land some two and a half miles in width, and flanked on either side by forest-clad hills which, without being lofty, would, if the road were blocked, be quite impracticable for a great baggage-laden army to cross. She looked earnestly at the map, and then, with a quickness of perception that in some women amounts almost to an instinct, she laid her finger upon this neck of rising ground, and turning to her husband, said, with a proud air of confidence and a toss of the golden head —

'Here shalt thou meet Sorais' armies. I know the spot, here shalt thou meet them, and drive them before thee like dust before the storm.'

But Curtis looked grave and said nothing.

The Battle of the Pass

It was on the third morning after this incident of the map that Sir Henry and I started. With the exception of a small guard, all the great host had moved on the night before, leaving the Frowning City very silent and empty. Indeed, it was found impossible to leave any garrison with the exception of a personal guard for Nyleptha, and about a thousand men who from sickness or one cause or another were unable to proceed with the army; but as Milosis was practically impregnable, and as our enemy was in front of and not behind us, this did not so much matter.

Good and Umslopogaas had gone on with the army, but Nyleptha accompanied Sir Henry and myself to the city gates, riding a magnificent white horse called Daylight, which was supposed to be the fleetest and most enduring animal in Zu-Vendis. Her face bore traces of recent weeping, but there were no tears in her eyes now, indeed she was bearing up bravely against what must have been a bitter trial to her. At the gate she reined in her horse and bade us farewell. On the previous day she had reviewed and addressed the officers of the great army, speaking to them such high, eloquent words, and expressing so complete a confidence in their valour and in their ultimate victory, that she quite carried their hearts away, and as she rode from rank to rank they cheered her till the ground shook. And now today the same mood seemed to be on her.

'Fare thee well, Macumazahn!' she said. 'Remember, I trust to thy wits, which are as a needle to a spear-handle compared to those of my people, to save us from Sorais. I know that thou wilt do thy duty.'

I bowed and explained to her my horror of fighting, and my fear lest I should lose my head, at which she laughed gently and turned to Curtis.

'Fare thee well, my lord!' she said. 'Come back with victory, and as a king, or on thy soldiers' spears.'

Sir Henry said nothing, but turned his horse to go; perhaps he had a bit of a lump in his throat. One gets over it afterwards, but these sort of partings are trying when one has only been married a week.

'Here,' added Nyleptha, 'will I greet thee when ye return in triumph. And now, my lords, once more, farewell!'

Then we rode on, but when we had gone a hundred and fifty yards or so, we turned and perceived her still sitting on her horse at the same spot, and looking out after us beneath her hand, and that was the last we saw of her. About a mile farther on, however, we heard galloping behind us, and looking round, saw a mounted soldier coming towards us, leading Nyleptha's matchless steed — Daylight.

'The Queen sends the white stallion as a farewell gift to her Lord Incubu, and bids me tell my lord that he is the fleetest and most enduring horse in all the land,' said the soldier, bending to his saddle-bow before us.

At first Sir Henry did not want to take the horse, saying that he was too good for such rough work, but I persuaded him to do so, thinking that Nyleptha would be hurt if he did not. Little did I guess at the time what service that noble horse would render in our sorest need. It is curious to look back and realize upon what trivial and apparently coincidental circumstances great events frequently turn as easily and naturally as a door on its hinges.

Well, we took the horse, and a beauty he was, it was a perfect pleasure to see him move, and Curtis having sent back his greetings and thanks, we proceeded on our journey.

By midday we overtook the rear-guard of the great army of which Sir Henry then formally took over the command. It was a heavy responsibility, and it oppressed him very much, but the Queen's injunctions on the point were such as did not admit of being trifled with. He was beginning to find out that greatness has its responsibilities as well as its glories.

Then we marched on without meeting with any opposition, almost indeed without seeing anybody, for the populations of the towns and villages along our route had for the most part fled, fearing lest they should be caught between the two rival armies and ground to powder like grain between the upper and the nether stones.

On the evening of the fourth day, for the progress of so great a multitude was necessarily slow, we camped two miles this side of the neck or ridge I have spoken of, and our outposts brought us word that Sorais with all her power was rolling down upon us, and had pitched her camp that night ten miles the farther side of the neck.

Accordingly before dawn we sent forward fifteen hundred cavalry to seize the position. Scarcely had they occupied it, however, before they were attacked by about as many of Sorais' horsemen, and a very smart little cavalry fight ensued, with a loss to us of about thirty men killed. On the advance of our supports, however, Sorais' force drew off, carrying their dead and wounded with them.

The main body of the army reached the neck about dinner-time, and I must say that Nyleptha's judgment had not failed her, it was an admirable place to give battle in, especially to a superior force.

The road ran down a mile or more, through ground too broken to admit of the handling of any considerable force, till it reached the crest of a great green wave of land, that rolled down a gentle slope to the banks of a little stream, and then rolled away again up a still gentler slope to the plain beyond, the distance from the crest of the land-wave down to the stream being a little over half a mile, and from the stream up to the plain beyond a trifle less. The length of this wave of land at its highest point, which corresponded exactly with the width of the neck of the land between the wooded hills, was about two miles and a quarter, and it was protected on either side by dense, rocky, bush-clad ground, that afforded a most valuable cover to the flanks of the army and rendered it almost impossible for them to be turned.

It was on the hither slope of this neck of land that Curtis encamped his army in the same formation that he had, after consultation with the various generals, Good, and myself, determined that they should occupy in the great pitched battle which now appeared to be imminent.

Our force of sixty thousand men was, roughly speaking, divided as follows. In the centre was a dense body of twenty thousand foot-soldiers, armed with spears, swords, and hippopotamus-hide shields, breast and back plates. These formed the chest of the army, and were supported by five thousand foot, and three thousand horse in reserve. On either side of this chest were stationed seven thousand horse arranged in deep, majestic squadrons; and beyond and on either side but slightly in front of them again were two bodies, each numbering about seven thousand five hundred spearmen, forming the right and left wings of the army, and each supported by a contingent of some fifteen hundred cavalry. This makes in all sixty thousand men.

Curtis commanded in chief, I was in command of the seven thousand horse between the chest and right wing, which was commanded by Good, and the other battalions and squadrons were entrusted to Zu-Vendis generals.

Scarcely had we taken up our positions before Sorais' vast army began to swarm on the opposite slope about a mile in front of us, till the whole place seemed alive with the multitude of her spearpoints, and the ground shook with the tramp of her battalions. It was evident that the spies had not exaggerated; we were outnumbered by at least a third. At first we expected that Sorais was going to attack us at once, as the clouds of cavalry which hung upon her flanks executed some threatening demonstrations, but she thought better of it, and there was no fight that day. As for the formation of her great forces I cannot now describe it with accuracy, and it would only serve to bewilder if I did, but I may say, generally, that in its leading features it resembled our own, only her reserve was much greater.

Opposite our right wing, and forming Sorais' left wing, was a great army of dark, wild-looking men, armed with sword and shield only, which, I was informed, was composed of Nasta's twenty-five thousand savage hillsmen.

'My word, Good,' said I, when I saw them, 'you will catch it tomorrow when those gentlemen charge!' whereat Good not unnaturally looked rather anxious.

All day we watched and waited, but nothing happened, and at last night fell, and a thousand watch-fires twinkled brightly on the slopes, to wane and die one by one like the stars they resembled. As the hours wore on, the silence gradually gathered more deeply over the opposing hosts.

It was a very wearying night, for in addition to the endless things that had to be attended to, there was our gnawing suspense to reckon with. The fray which tomorrow would witness would be so vast, and the slaughter so awful, that stout indeed must the heart have been that was not overwhelmed at the prospect. And when I thought of all that hung upon it, I own I felt ill, and it made me very sad to reflect that these mighty forces were gathered for destruction, simply to gratify the jealous anger of a woman. This was the hidden power which was to send those dense masses of cavalry, flashing like human thunderbolts across the plain, and to roll together the fierce battalions as clouds when hurricane meets hurricane. It was a dreadful thought, and set one wondering about the responsibilities of the great ones of the earth. Deep into the night we sat, with pale faces and heavy hearts, and took counsel, whilst the sentries tramped up and down, down and up, and the armed and plumed generals came and went, grim and shadow-like.

And so the time wore away, till everything was ready for the coming slaughter; and I lay down and thought, and tried to get a little rest, but could not sleep for fear of the morrow — for who could say what the morrow would bring forth? Misery and death, this was certain; beyond that we knew not, and I confess I was very much afraid. But as I realized then, it is useless to question that eternal Sphinx, the future. From day to day she reads aloud the riddles of the yesterday, of which the puzzled wordlings of all ages have not answered one, nor ever will, guess they never so wildly or cry they never so loud.

And so at length I gave up wondering, being forced humbly to leave the issue in the balancing hands of Providence and the morrow.

And at last up came the red sun, and the huge camps awoke with a clash, and a roar, and gathered themselves together for battle. It was a beautiful and awe-inspiring scene, and old Umslopogaas, leaning on his axe, contemplated it with grim delight.

'Never have I seen the like, Macumazahn, never,' he said. 'The battles of my people are as the play of children to what this will be. Thinkest thou that they will fight it out?'

'Ay,' I answered sadly, 'to the death. Content thyself, "Woodpecker", for once shalt thou peck thy fill.'

Time went on, and still there was no sign of an attack. A force of cavalry crossed the brook, indeed, and rode slowly along our front, evidently taking stock of our position and numbers. With this we did not attempt to interfere, as our decision was to stand strictly on the defensive, and not to waste a single man. The men breakfasted and stood to their arms, and the hours wore on. About midday, when the men were eating their dinner, for we thought they would fight better on full stomachs, a shout of '*Sorais, Sorais*' arose like thunder from the enemy's extreme right, and taking the glass, I was able to clearly distinguish the 'Lady of the Night' herself, surrounded by a glittering staff, and riding slowly down the lines of her battalions. And as she went, that mighty, thundering shout rolled along before her like the rolling of ten thousand chariots, or the roaring of the ocean when the gale turns suddenly and carries the noise of it to the listener's ears, till the earth shook, and the air was full of the majesty of sound.

Guessing that this was a prelude to the beginning of the battle, we remained still and made ready.

We had not long to wait. Suddenly, like flame from a cannon's mouth, out shot two great tongue-like forces of cavalry, and came charging down the slope towards the little stream, slowly at first, but gathering speed as they came. Before they got to the stream, orders reached me from Sir Henry, who evidently feared that the shock of such a charge, if allowed to fall unbroken upon our infantry, would be too much for them, to send five thousand sabres to meet the force opposite to me, at the moment when it began to mount the stiffest of the rise about four hundred yards from our lines. This I did, remaining behind myself with the rest of my men.

Off went the five thousand horsemen, drawn up in a wedge-like form, and I must say that the general in command handled them very ably. Starting at a hand gallop, for the first three hundred yards he rode straight at the tip of the tongue-shaped mass of cavalry which, numbering, so far as I could judge, about eight thousand sabres, was advancing to charge us. Then he suddenly swerved to the right and put on the pace, and I saw the great wedge curl round, and before the foe could check himself and turn to meet it, strike him about halfway down his length, with a crashing rending sound, like that of the breaking-up of vast sheets of ice. In sank the great wedge, into his heart, and as it cut its way hundreds of horsemen were thrown up on either side of it, just as the earth is thrown up by a ploughshare, or more like still, as the foaming water curls over beneath the bows of a rushing ship. In, yet in, vainly does the tongue twist its ends round in agony, like an injured snake, and strive to protect its centre; still farther in, by Heaven! right through, and so, amid cheer after cheer from our watching thousands, back again upon the severed ends, beating them down, driving them as a gale drives spray, till at last, amidst the rushing of hundreds of riderless horses, the flashing of swords, and the victorious clamour of their pursuers, the great force crumples up like an empty glove, then turns and gallops pell-mell for safety back to its own lines.

I do not think it reached them more than two-thirds as strong as it went out ten minutes before. The lines which were now advancing to the attack, opened and swallowed them up, and my force returned, having only suffered a loss of about five hundred men — not much, I thought, considering the fierceness of the struggle. I could also see that the opposing bodies of cavalry on our left wing were drawing back, but how the fight went with them I do not quite know. It is as much as I can do to describe what took place immediately around me.

By this time the dense masses of the enemy's left, composed almost entirely of Nasta's swordsmen, were across the little stream, and with alternate yells of 'Nasta' and 'Sorais', with dancing banners and gleaming swords, were swarming up towards us like ants.

Again I received orders to try and check this movement, and also the main advance against the chest of our army, by means of cavalry charges, and this I did to the best of my ability, by continually sending squadrons of about a thousand sabres out against them. These squadrons did the enemy much damage, and it was a glorious sight to see them flash down the hillside, and bury themselves like a living knife in the heart of the foe. But, also, we lost many men, for after the experience of a couple of these charges, which had drawn a sort of bloody St Andrew's cross of dead and dying through the centre of Nasta's host, our foes no longer attempted to offer an unyielding front to their irresistible weight, but opened out to let the rush go through, throwing themselves on the ground and hamstringing hundreds of horses as they passed.

And so, notwithstanding all that we could do, the enemy drew nearer, till at last he hurled himself upon Good's force of seven thousand five hundred regulars, who were drawn up to receive them in three strong squares. About the same time, too, an awful and heartshaking roar told me that the main battle had closed in on the centre and extreme left. I raised myself in my stirrups and looked down to my left; so far as the eye could see there was a long dazzling shimmer of steel as the sun glanced upon falling sword and thrusting spear.

To and fro swung the contending lines in that dread struggle, now giving way, now gaining a little in the mad yet ordered confusion of attack and defence. But it was as much as I could do to keep count of what was happening to our own wing; and, as for the moment the cavalry had fallen back under cover of Good's three squares, I had a fair view of this.

Nasta's wild swordsmen were now breaking in red waves against the sullen rock-like squares. Time after time did they yell out their war-cries, and hurl themselves furiously against the long triple ridges of spear points, only to be rolled back as billows are when they meet the cliff.

And so for four long hours the battle raged almost without a pause, and at the end of that time, if we had gained nothing we had lost nothing. Two attempts to turn our left flank by forcing a way through the wood by which it was protected had been defeated; and as yet Nasta's swordsmen had, notwithstanding their desperate efforts, entirely failed to break Good's three squares, though they had thinned their numbers by quite a third.

As for the chest of the army where Sir Henry was with his staff and Umslopogaas, it had suffered dreadfully, but it had held its own with honour, and the same may be said of our left battle.

At last the attacks slackened, and Sorais' army drew back, having, I began to think, had enough of it. On this point, however, I was soon undeceived, for splitting up her cavalry into comparatively small squadrons, she charged us furiously with them, all along the line, and then once more sullenly rolled her tens of thousands of sword and spearmen down upon our weakened squares and squadrons; Sorais herself directing the movement, as fearless as a lioness heading the main attack. On they came like an avalanche — I saw her golden helm gleaming in the van — our counter charges of cavalry entirely failing to check their forward sweep. Now they had struck us, and our centre bent in like a bow beneath the weight of their rush — it parted, and had not the ten thousand men in reserve charged down to its support it must have been utterly destroyed. As for Good's three squares, they were swept backwards like boats upon an incoming tide, and the foremost one was burst into and lost half its remaining men. But the effort was too fierce and terrible to last. Suddenly the battle came, as it were, to a turning-point, and for a minute or two stood still.

Then it began to move towards Sorais' camp. Just then, too, Nasta's fierce and almost invincible highlanders, either because they were disheartened by their losses or by way of a ruse, fell back, and the remains of Good's gallant squares, leaving the positions they had held for so many hours, cheered wildly, and rashly followed them down the slope, whereon the swarms of swordsmen turned to envelop them, and once more flung themselves upon them with a yell. Taken thus on every side, what remained of the first square was quickly destroyed, and I perceived that the second, in which I could see Good himself mounted on a large horse, was on the point of annihilation. A few more minutes and it was broken, its streaming colours sank, and I lost sight of Good in the confused and hideous slaughter that ensued.

Presently, however, a cream-coloured horse with a snow-white mane and tail burst from the ruins of the square and came rushing past me riderless and with wide streaming reins, and in it I recognized the charger that Good had been riding. Then I hesitated no longer, but taking with me half my effective cavalry force, which now amounted to between four and five thousand men, I commended myself to God, and, without waiting for orders, I charged straight down upon Nasta's swordsmen. Seeing me coming, and being warned by the thunder of my horses' hoofs, the majority of them faced round, and gave us a right warm welcome. Not an inch would they yield; in vain did we hack and trample them down as we ploughed a broad red furrow through their thousands; they seemed to re-arise by hundreds, driving their terrible sharp swords into our horses, or severing their hamstrings, and then hacking the troopers who came to the ground with them almost into pieces. My horse was speedily killed under me, but luckily I had a fresh one, my own favourite, a coal-black mare Nyleptha had given me, being held in reserve behind, and on this I afterwards mounted. Meanwhile I had to get along as best I could, for I was pretty well lost sight of by my men in the mad confusion of the moment. My voice, of course, could not be heard in the midst of the clanging of steel and the shrieks of rage and agony. Presently I found myself mixed up with the remnants of the square, which had formed round its leader Good, and was fighting desperately for existence. I stumbled against somebody, and glancing down, caught sight of Good's eyeglass. He had been beaten to his knee. Over him was a great fellow swinging a heavy sword. Somehow I managed to run the man through with the sime I had taken from the Masai whose hand I had cut off; but as I did so, he dealt me a frightful blow on the left side and breast with the sword, and though my chain shirt saved my life, I felt that I was badly hurt. For a minute I fell on to my hands and knees among the dead and dying, and turned sick and faint. When I came to again I saw that Nasta's spearmen, or rather those of them who remained, were retreating back across the stream, and that Good was there by me smiling sweetly.

'Near go that,' he shouted; 'but all's well that ends well.'

I assented, but I could not help feeling that it had not ended well for me. I was sorely hurt.

Just then we saw the smaller bodies of cavalry stationed on our extreme right and left, and which were now reinforced by the three thousand sabres which we had held in reserve, flash out like arrows from their posts and fall upon the disordered flanks of Sorais' forces, and that charge decided the issue of the battle. In another minute or two the enemy was in slow and sullen retreat across the little stream, where they once more re-formed. Then came another lull, during which I managed to get a second horse, and received my orders to advance from Sir Henry, and then with one fierce deep-throated roar, with a waving of banners and a wide flashing of steel, the remains of our army took the offensive and began to sweep down, slowly indeed, but irresistibly from the positions they had so gallantly held all day.

At last it was our turn to attack.

On we moved, over the piled-up masses of dead and dying, and were approaching the stream, when suddenly I perceived an extraordinary sight. Galloping wildly towards us, his arms tightly clasped around his horse's neck, against which his blanched cheek was tightly pressed, was a man arrayed in the full costume of a Zu-Vendi general, but in whom, as he came nearer, I recognized none other than our lost Alphonse. It was impossible even then to mistake those curling mustachios. In a minute he was tearing through our ranks and narrowly escaped being cut down, till at last somebody caught his horse's bridle, and he was brought to me just as a momentary halt occurred in our advance to allow what remained of our shattered squares to form into line.

'Ah, monsieur,' he gasped out in a voice that was nearly inarticulate with fright, 'grace to the sky, it is you! Ah, what I have endured! But you win, monsieur, you win; they fly, the laches. But listen, monsieur — I forget, it is no good; the Queen is to be murdered tomorrow at the first light in the palace of Milosis; her guards will leave their posts, and the priests are going to kill her. Ah yes! they little thought it, but I was ensconced beneath a banner, and I heard it all.'

'What?' I said, horror-struck; 'what do you mean?'

'What I say, monsieur; that devil of a Nasta he went last night to settle the affair with the Archbishop [Agon]. The guard will leave open the little gate leading from the great stair and go away, and Nasta and Agon's priests will come in and kill her. Themselves they would not kill her.'

'Come with me,' I said, and, shouting to the staff-officer next to me to take over the command, I snatched his bridle and galloped as hard as I could for the spot, between a quarter and half a mile off, where I saw the royal pennon flying, and where I knew that I should find Curtis if he were still alive. On we tore, our horses clearing heaps of dead and dying men, and splashing through pools of blood, on past the long broken lines of spearmen to where, mounted on the white stallion Nyleptha had sent to him as a parting gift, I saw Sir Henry's form towering above the generals who surrounded him.

Just as we reached him the advance began again. A bloody cloth was bound around his head, but I saw that his eye was as bright and keen as ever. Beside him was old Umslopogaas, his axe red with blood, but looking quite fresh and uninjured.

'What's wrong, Quatermain?' he shouted.

'Everything. There is a plot to murder the Queen tomorrow at dawn. Alphonse here, who has just escaped from Sorais, has overheard it all,' and I rapidly repeated to him what the Frenchman had told me.

Curtis' face turned deadly pale and his jaw dropped.

'At dawn,' he gasped, 'and it is now sunset; it dawns before four and we are nearly a hundred miles off — nine hours at the outside. What is to be done?'

An idea entered into my head. 'Is that horse of yours fresh?' I said.

'Yes, I have only just got on to him — when my last was killed, and he has been fed.'

'So is mine. Get off him, and let Umslopogaas mount; he can ride well. We will be at Milosis before dawn, or if we are not — well, we cannot help it. No, no; it is impossible for you to leave now. You would be seen, and it would turn the fate of the battle. It is not half won yet. The soldiers would think you were making a bolt of it. Quick now.'

In a moment he was down, and at my bidding Umslopogaas sprang into the empty saddle.

'Now farewell,' I said. 'Send a thousand horsemen with remounts after us in an hour if possible. Stay, despatch a general to the left wing to take over the command and explain my absence.'

'You will do your best to save her, Quatermain?' he said in a broken voice.

'Ay, that I will. Go on; you are being left behind.'

He cast one glance at us, and accompanied by his staff galloped off to join the advance, which by this time was fording the little brook that now ran red with the blood of the fallen.

As for Umslopogaas and myself, we left that dreadful field as arrows leave a bow, and in a few minutes had passed right out of the sight of slaughter, the smell of blood, and the turmoil and shouting, which only came to our ears as a faint, far-off roaring like the sound of distant breakers.

Away! Away!

At the top of the rise we halted for a second to breathe our horses; and, turning, glanced at the battle beneath us, which, illumined as it was by the fierce rays of the sinking sun staining the whole scene red, looked from where we were more like some wild titanic picture than an actual hand-to-hand combat. The distinguishing scenic effect from that distance was the countless distinct flashes of light reflected from the swords and spears, otherwise the panorama was not so grand as might have been expected. The great green lap of sward in which the struggle was being fought out, the bold round outline of the hills behind, and the wide sweep of the plain beyond, seemed to dwarf it; and what was tremendous enough when one was in it, grew insignificant when viewed from the distance. But is it not thus with all the affairs and doings of our race about which we blow the loud trumpet and make such a fuss and worry? How utterly antlike, and morally and physically insignificant, must they seem to the calm eyes that watch them from the arching depths above!

'We win the day, Macumazahn,' said old Umslopogaas, taking in the whole situation with a glance of his practised eye. 'Look, the Lady of the Night's forces give on every side, there is no stiffness left in them, they bend like hot iron, they are fighting with but half a heart. But alas! the battle will in a manner be drawn, for the darkness gathers, and the regiments will not be able to follow and slay!' — and he shook his head sadly. 'But,' he added, 'I do not think that they will fight again. We have fed them with too strong a meat. Ah! it is well to have lived! At last I have seen a fight worth seeing.'

By this time we were on our way again, and as we went side by side I told him what our mission was, and how that, if it failed, all the lives that had been lost that day would have been lost in vain.

'Ah!' he said, 'nigh on a hundred miles and no horses but these, and to be there before the dawn! Well — away! away! man can but try, Macumazahn; and mayhap we shall be there in time to split that old "witch-finder's" [Agon's] skull for him. Once he wanted to burn us, the old "rain-maker", did he? And now he would set a snare for my mother [Nyleptha], would he? Good! So sure as my name is the name of the Woodpecker, so surely, be my mother alive or dead, will I split him to the beard. Ay, by T'Chaka's head I swear it!' and he shook Inkosi-kaas as he galloped. By now the darkness was closing in, but fortunately there would be a moon later, and the road was good.

On we sped through the twilight, the two splendid horses we bestrode had got their wind by this, and were sweeping along with a wide steady stride that neither failed nor varied for mile upon mile. Down the side of slopes we galloped, across wide vales that stretched to the foot of far-off hills. Nearer and nearer grew the blue hills; now we were travelling up their steeps, and now we were over and passing towards others that sprang up like visions in the far, faint distance beyond.

On, never pausing or drawing rein, through the perfect quiet of the night, that was set like a song to the falling music of our horses' hoofs; on, past deserted villages, where only some forgotten starving dog howled a melancholy welcome; on, past lonely moated dwellings; on, through the white patchy moonlight, that lay coldly upon the wide bosom of the earth, as though there was no warmth in it; on, knee to knee, for hour after hour!

We spake not, but bent us forward on the necks of those two glorious horses, and listened to their deep, long-drawn breaths as they filled their great lungs, and to the regular unfaltering ring of their round hoofs. Grim and black indeed did old Umslopogaas look beside me, mounted upon the great white horse, like Death in the Revelation of St John, as now and again lifting his fierce set face he gazed out along the road, and pointed with his axe towards some distant rise or house.

And so on, still on, without break or pause for hour after hour.

At last I felt that even the splendid animal that I rode was beginning to give out. I looked at my watch; it was nearly midnight, and we were considerably more than half way. On the top of a rise was a little spring, which I remembered because I had slept by it a few nights before, and here I motioned to Umslopogaas to pull up, having determined to give the horses and ourselves ten minutes to breathe in. He did so, and we dismounted — that is to say, Umslopogaas did, and then helped me off, for what with fatigue, stiffness, and the pain of my wound, I could not do so for myself; and then the gallant horses stood panting there, resting first one leg and then another, while the sweat fell drip, drip, from them, and the steam rose and hung in pale clouds in the still night air.

Leaving Umslopogaas to hold the horses, I hobbled to the spring and drank deep of its sweet waters. I had had nothing but a single mouthful of wine since midday, when the battle began, and I was parched up, though my fatigue was too great to allow me to feel hungry. Then, having laved my fevered head and hands, I returned, and the Zulu went and drank. Next we allowed the horses to take a couple of mouthfuls each — no more; and oh, what a struggle we had to get the poor beasts away from the water! There were yet two minutes, and I employed it in hobbling up and down to try and relieve my stiffness, and in inspecting the condition of the horses. My mare, gallant animal though she was, was evidently much distressed; she hung her head, and her eye looked sick and dull; but Daylight, Nyleptha's glorious horse — who, if he is served aright, should, like the steeds who saved great Rameses in his need, feed for the rest of his days out of a golden manger — was still comparatively speaking fresh, notwithstanding the fact that he had had by far the heavier weight to carry. He was 'tucked up', indeed, and his legs were weary, but his eye was bright and clear, and he held his shapely head up and gazed out into the darkness round him in a way that seemed to say that whoever failed *he* was good for those five-and-forty miles that yet lay between us and Milosis. Then Umslopogaas helped me into the saddle and — vigorous old savage that he was! — vaulted into his own without touching a stirrup, and we were off once more, slowly at first, till the horses got into their stride, and then more swiftly. So we passed over another ten miles, and then came a long, weary rise of some six or seven miles, and three times did my poor black mare nearly come to the ground with me. But on the top she seemed to gather herself together, and rattled down the slope with long, convulsive strides, breathing in gasps. We did that three or four miles more swiftly than any since we had started on our wild ride, but I felt it to be a last effort, and I was right. Suddenly my poor horse took the bit between her teeth and bolted furiously along a stretch of level ground for some three or four hundred yards, and then, with two or three jerky strides, pulled herself up and fell with a crash right on to her head, I rolling myself free as she did so. As I struggled to my feet the brave beast raised her head and looked at me with piteous bloodshot eyes, and then her head dropped with a groan and she was dead. Her heart was broken.

Umslopogaas pulled up beside the carcase, and I looked at him in dismay. There were still more than twenty miles to do by dawn, and how were we to do it with one horse? It seemed hopeless, but I had forgotten the old Zulu's extraordinary running powers.

Without a single word he sprang from the saddle and began to hoist me into it.

'What wilt thou do?' I asked.

'Run,' he answered, seizing my stirrup-leather.

Then off we went again, almost as fast as before; and oh, the relief it was to me to get that change of horses! Anybody who has ever ridden against time will know what it meant.

Daylight sped along at a long stretching hand-gallop, giving the gaunt Zulu a lift at every stride. It was a wonderful thing to see old Umslopogaas run mile after mile, his lips slightly parted and his nostrils agape like the horse's. Every five miles or so we stopped for a few minutes to let him get his breath, and then flew on again.

'Canst thou go farther,' I said at the third of these stoppages, 'or shall I leave thee to follow me?'

He pointed with his axe to a dim mass before us. It was the Temple of the Sun, now not more than five miles away.

'I reach it or I die,' he gasped.

Oh, that last five miles! The skin was rubbed from the inside of my legs, and every movement of my horse gave me anguish. Nor was that all. I was exhausted with toil, want of food and sleep, and also suffering very much from the blow I had received on my left side; it seemed as though a piece of bone or something was slowly piercing into my lung. Poor Daylight, too, was pretty nearly finished, and no wonder. But there was a smell of dawn in the air, and we might not stay; better that all three of us should die upon the road than that we should linger while there was life in us. The air was thick and heavy, as it sometimes is before the dawn breaks, and — another infallible sign in certain parts of Zu-Vendis that sunrise is at hand — hundreds of little spiders pendant on the end of long tough webs were floating about in it. These early-rising creatures, or rather their webs, caught upon the horse's and our own forms by scores, and, as we had neither the time nor the energy to brush them off, we rushed along covered with hundreds of long grey threads that streamed out a yard or more behind us — and a very strange appearance they must have given us.

And now before us are the huge brazen gates of the outer wall of the Frowning City, and a new and horrible doubt strikes me: What if they will not let us in?

'*Open! open!*' I shout imperiously, at the same time giving the royal password. '*Open! open!* a messenger, a messenger with tidings of the war!'

'What news?' cried the guard. 'And who art thou that ridest so madly, and who is that whose tongue lolls out' — and it actually did — 'and who runs by thee like a dog by a chariot?'

'It is the Lord Macumazahn, and with him is his dog, his black dog. *Open! open!* I bring tidings.'

The great gates ran back on their rollers, and the drawbridge fell with a rattling crash, and we dashed on through the one and over the other.

'What news, my lord, what news?' cried the guard.

'Incubu rolls Sorais back, as the wind a cloud,' I answered, and was gone.

One more effort, gallant horse, and yet more gallant man!

So, fall not now, Daylight, and hold thy life in thee for fifteen short minutes more, old Zulu war-dog, and ye shall both live for ever in the annals of the land.

On, clattering through the sleeping streets. We are passing the Flower Temple now — one mile more, only one little mile — hold on, keep your life in thee, see the houses run past of themselves. Up, good horse, up, there — but fifty yards now. Ah! you see your stables and stagger on gallantly.

'Thank God, the palace at last!' and see, the first arrows of the dawn are striking on the Temple's golden dome. But shall I get in here, or is the deed done and the way barred?

Once more I give the password and shout '*Open! open!*'"

No answer, and my heart grows very faint.

Again I call, and this time a single voice replies, and to my joy I recognize it as belonging to Kara, a fellow-officer of Nyleptha's guards, a man I know to be as honest as the light — indeed, the same whom Nyleptha had sent to arrest Sorais on the day she fled to the temple.

'Is it thou, Kara?' I cry; 'I am Macumazahn. Bid the guard let down the bridge and throw wide the gate. Quick, quick!'

Then followed a space that seemed to me endless, but at length the bridge fell and one half of the gate opened and we got into the courtyard, where at last poor Daylight fell down beneath me, as I thought, dead. Except Kara, there was nobody to be seen, and his look was wild, and his garments were all torn. He had opened the gate and let down the bridge alone, and was now getting them up and shut again (as, owing to a very ingenious arrangement of cranks and levers, one man could easily do, and indeed generally did do).

'Where are the guard?' I gasped, fearing his answer as I never feared anything before.

'I know not,' he answered; 'two hours ago, as I slept, was I seized and bound by the watch under me, and but now, this very moment, have I freed myself with my teeth. I fear, I greatly fear, that we are betrayed.'

His words gave me fresh energy. Catching him by the arm, I staggered, followed by Umslopogaas, who reeled after us like a drunken man, through the courtyards, up the great hall, which was silent as the grave, towards the Queen's sleeping-place.

We reached the first ante-room — no guards; the second, still no guards. Oh, surely the thing was done! we were too late after all, too late! The silence and solitude of those great chambers was dreadful, and weighed me down like an evil dream. On, right into Nyleptha's chamber we rushed and staggered, sick at heart, fearing the very worst; we saw there was a light in it, ay, and a figure bearing the light. Oh, thank God, it is the White Queen herself, the Queen unharmed! There she stands in her night gear, roused, by the clatter of our coming, from her bed, the heaviness of sleep yet in her eyes, and a red blush of fear and shame mantling her lovely breast and cheek.

'Who is it?' she cries. 'What means this? Oh, Macumazahn, is it thou? Why lookest thou so wildly? Thou comest as one bearing evil tidings — and my lord — oh, tell me not my lord is dead — not dead!' she wailed, wringing her white hands.

'I left Incubu wounded, but leading the advance against Sorais last night at sundown; therefore let thy heart have rest. Sorais is beaten back all along her lines, and thy arms prevail.'

'I knew it,' she cried in triumph. 'I knew that he would win; and they called him Outlander, and shook their wise heads when I gave him the command! Last night at sundown, sayest thou, and it is not yet dawn? Surely —'

'Throw a cloak around thee, Nyleptha,' I broke in, 'and give us wine to drink; ay, and call thy maidens quick if thou wouldst save thyself alive. Nay, stay not.'

Thus adjured she ran and called through the curtains towards some room beyond, and then hastily put on her sandals and a thick cloak, by which time a dozen or so of half-dressed women were pouring into the room.

'Follow us and be silent,' I said to them as they gazed with wondering eyes, clinging one to another. So we went into the first ante-room.

'Now,' I said, 'give us wine to drink and food, if ye have it, for we are near to death.'

The room was used as a mess-room for the officers of the guards, and from a cupboard some flagons of wine and some cold flesh were brought forth, and Umslopogaas and I drank, and felt life flow back into our veins as the good red wine went down.

'Hark to me, Nyleptha,' I said, as I put down the empty tankard. 'Hast thou here among these thy waiting-ladies any two of discretion?'

'Ay,' she said, 'surely.'

'Then bid them go out by the side entrance to any citizens whom thou canst bethink thee of as men loyal to thee, and pray them come armed, with all honest folk that they can gather, to rescue thee from death. Nay, question not; do as I say, and quickly. Kara here will let out the maids.'

She turned, and selecting two of the crowd of damsels, repeated the words I had uttered, giving them besides a list of the names of the men to whom each should run.

'Go swiftly and secretly; go for your very lives,' I added.

In another moment they had left with Kara, whom I told to rejoin us at the door leading from the great courtyard on to the stairway as soon as he had made fast behind the girls. Thither, too, Umslopogaas and I made our way, followed by the Queen and her women. As we went we tore off mouthfuls of food, and between them I told her what I knew of the danger which encompassed her, and how we found Kara, and how all the guards and men-servants were gone, and she was alone with her women in that great place; and she told me, too, that a rumour had spread through the town that our army had been utterly destroyed, and that Sorais was marching in triumph on Milosis, and how in consequence thereof all men had fallen away from her.

Though all this takes some time to tell, we had not been but six or seven minutes in the palace; and notwithstanding that the golden roof of the temple being very lofty was ablaze with the rays of the rising sun, it was not yet dawn, nor would be for another ten minutes. We were in the courtyard now, and here my wound pained me so that I had to take Nyleptha's arm, while Umslopogaas rolled along after us, eating as he went.

Now we were across it, and had reached the narrow doorway through the palace wall that opened on to the mighty stair.

I looked through and stood aghast, as well I might. The door was gone, and so were the outer gates of bronze — entirely gone. They had been taken from their hinges, and as we afterwards found, hurled from the stairway to the ground two hundred feet beneath. There in front of us was the semicircular standing-space, about twice the size of a large oval dining-table, and the ten curved black marble steps leading on to the main stair — and that was all.

How Umslopogaas Held the Stair

We looked at one another.

'Thou seest,' I said, 'they have taken away the door. Is there aught with which we may fill the place? Speak quickly for they will be on us ere the daylight.' I spoke thus, because I knew that we must hold this place or none, as there were no inner doors in the palace, the rooms being separated one from another by curtains. I also knew that if we could by any means defend this doorway the murderers could get in nowhere else; for the palace is absolutely impregnable, that is, since the secret door by which Sorais had entered on that memorable night of attempted murder had, by Nyleptha's order, been closed up with masonry.

'I have it,' said Nyleptha, who, as usual with her, rose to the emergency in a wonderful way. 'On the farther side of the courtyard are blocks of cut marble — the workmen brought them there for the bed of the new statue of Incubu, my lord; let us block the door with them.'

I jumped at the idea; and having despatched one of the remaining maidens down the great stair to see if she could obtain assistance from the docks below, where her father, who was a great merchant employing many men, had his dwelling-place, and set another to watch through the doorway, we made our way back across the courtyard to where the hewn marble lay; and here we met Kara returning from despatching the first two messengers. There were the marble blocks, sure enough, broad, massive lumps, some six inches thick, and weighing about eighty pounds each, and there, too, were a couple of implements like small stretchers, that the workmen used to carry them on. Without delay we got some of the blocks on to the stretchers, and four of the girls carried them to the doorway.

'Listen, Macumazahn,' said Umslopogaas, 'if those low fellows come, it is I who will hold the stair against them till the door is built up. Nay, nay, it will be a man's death: gainsay me not, old friend. It has been a good day, let it now be good night. See, I throw myself down to rest on the marble there; when their footsteps are nigh, wake thou me, not before, for I need my strength,' and without a word he went outside and flung himself down on the marble, and was instantly asleep.

At this time, I too was overcome, and was forced to sit down by the doorway, and content myself with directing operations. The girls brought the block, while Kara and Nyleptha built them up across the six-foot-wide doorway, a triple row of them, for less would be useless. But the marble had to be brought forty yards and then there were forty yards to run back, and though the girls laboured gloriously, even staggering along alone, each with a block in her arms, it was slow work, dreadfully slow.

The light was growing now, and presently, in the silence, we heard a commotion at the far-bottom of the stair, and the faint clinking of armed men.

As yet the wall was only two feet high, and we had been eight minutes at the building of it. So they had come. Alphonse had heard aright.

The clanking sound came nearer, and in the ghostly grey of the dawning we could make out long files of men, some fifty or so in all, slowly creeping up the stair. They were now at the half-way standing place that rested on the great flying arch; and here, perceiving that something was going on above, they, to our great gain, halted for three or four minutes and consulted, then slowly and cautiously advanced again.

We had been nearly a quarter of an hour at the work now, and it was almost three feet high.

Then I woke Umslopogaas. The great man rose, stretched himself, and swung Inkosi-kaas round his head.

'It is well,' he said. 'I feel as a young man once more. My strength has come back to me, ay, even as a lamp flares up before it dies. Fear not, I shall fight a good fight; the wine and the sleep have put a new heart into me.

'Macumazahn, I have dreamed a dream. I dreamed that thou and I stood together on a star, and looked down on the world, and thou wast as a spirit, Macumazahn, for light flamed through thy flesh, but I could not see what was the fashion of mine own face. The hour has come for us, old hunter. So be it: we have had our time, but I would that in it I had seen some more such fights as yesterday's.

'Let them bury me after the fashion of my people, Macumazahn, and set my eyes towards Zululand;' and he took my hand and shook it, and then turned to face the advancing foe.

Just then, to my astonishment, the Zu-Vendi officer Kara clambered over our improvised wall in his quiet, determined sort of way, and took his stand by the Zulu, unsheathing his sword as he did so.

'What, comest thou too?' laughed out the old warrior. 'Welcome — a welcome to thee, brave heart! Ow! for the man who can die like a man; ow! for the death grip and the ringing of steel. Ow! we are ready. We wet our beaks like eagles, our spears flash in the sun; we shake our assegais, and are hungry to fight. Who comes to give greeting to the Chieftainess [Inkosi-kaas]? Who would taste her kiss, whereof the fruit is death? I, the Woodpecker, I, the Slaughterer, I the Swiftfooted! I, Umslopogaas, of the tribe of the Maquilisini, of the people of Amazulu, a captain of the regiment of the Nkomabakosi: I, Umslopogaas, the son of Indabazimbi, the son of Arpi the son of Mosilikaatze, I of the royal blood of T'Chaka, I of the King's House, I the Ringed Man, I the Induna, I call to them as a buck calls, I challenge them, I await them. Ow! it is thou, it is thou!'

As he spake, or rather chanted, his wild war-song, the armed men, among whom in the growing light I recognized both Nasta and Agon, came streaming up the stair with a rush, and one big fellow, armed with a heavy spear, dashed up the ten semicircular steps ahead of his comrades and struck at the great Zulu with the spear. Umslopogaas moved his body but not his legs, so that the blow missed him, and next instant Inkosi-kaas crashed through headpiece, hair and skull, and the man's corpse was rattling down the steps. As he dropped, his round hippopotamus-hide shield fell from his hand on to the marble, and the Zulu stooped down and seized it, still chanting as he did so.

In another second the sturdy Kara had also slain a man, and then began a scene the like of which has not been known to me.

Up rushed the assailants, one, two, three at a time, and as fast as they came, the axe crashed and the sword swung, and down they rolled again, dead or dying. And ever as the fight thickened, the old Zulu's eye seemed to get quicker and his arm stronger. He shouted out his war-cries and the names of chiefs whom he had slain, and the blows of his awful axe rained straight and true, shearing through everything they fell on. There was none of the scientific method he was so fond of about this last immortal fight of his; he had no time for it, but struck with his full strength, and at every stroke a man sank in his tracks, and went rattling down the marble steps.

They hacked and hewed at him with swords and spears, wounding him in a dozen places till he streamed red with blood; but the shield protected his head and the chain-shirt his vitals, and for minute after minute, aided by the gallant Zu-Vendi, he still held the stair.

At last Kara's sword broke, and he grappled with a foe, and they rolled down together, and he was cut to pieces, dying like the brave man that he was.

Umslopogaas was alone now, but he never blenched or turned. Shouting out some wild Zulu battle-cry, he beat down a foe, ay, and another, and another, till at last they drew back from the slippery blood-stained steps, and stared at him with amazement, thinking that he was no mortal man.

The wall of marble block was four feet six high now, and hope rose in my teeth as I leaned there against it a miserable helpless log, and ground my teeth, and watched that glorious struggle. I could do no more for I had lost my revolver in the battle.

And old Umslopogaas, he leaned too on his good axe, and, faint as he was with wounds, he mocked them, he called them 'women' — the grand old warrior, standing there one against so many! And for a breathing space none would come against him, notwithstanding Nasta's exhortations, till at last old Agon, who, to do him justice, was a brave man, mad with baffled rage, and seeing that the wall would soon be built and his plans defeated, shook the great spear he held, and rushed up the dripping steps.

'Ah, ah!' shouted the Zulu, as he recognized the priest's flowing white beard, 'it is thou, old "witch-finder"! Come on! I await thee, white "medicine man"; come on! come on! I have sworn to slay thee, and I ever keep my faith.'

On he came, taking him at his word, and drave the big spear with such force at Umslopogaas that it sunk right through the tough shield and pierced him in the neck. The Zulu cast down the transfixed shield, and that moment was Agon's last, for before he could free his spear and strike again, with a shout of 'There's for thee, Rain-maker!' Umslopogaas gripped Inkosi-kaas with both hands and whirled on high and drave her right on to his venerable head, so that Agon rolled down dead among the corpses of his fellow-murderers, and there was an end to him and his plots altogether. And even as he fell, a great cry rose from the foot of the stair, and looking out through the portion of the doorway that was yet unclosed, we saw armed men rushing up to the rescue, and called an answer to their shouts. Then the would-be murderers who yet remained on the stairway, and amongst whom I saw several priests, turned to fly, but, having nowhere to go, were butchered as they fled. Only one man stayed, and he was the great lord Nasta, Nyleptha's suitor, and the father of the plot. For a moment the black-bearded Nasta stood with bowed face leaning on his long sword as though in despair, and then, with a dreadful shout, he too rushed up at the Zulu, and, swinging the glittering sword around his head, dealt him such a mighty blow beneath his guard, that the keen steel of the heavy blade bit right through the chain armour and deep into Umslopogaas' side, for a moment paralysing him and causing him to drop his axe.

Raising the sword again, Nasta sprang forward to make an end of him, but little he knew his foe. With a shake and a yell of fury, the Zulu gathered himself together and sprang straight at Nasta's throat, as I have sometimes seen a wounded lion spring. He struck him full as his foot was on the topmost stair, and his long arms closing round him like iron bands, down they rolled together struggling furiously. Nasta was a strong man and a desperate, but he could not match the strongest man in Zululand, sore wounded though he was, whose strength was as the strength of a bull. In a minute the end came. I saw old Umslopogaas stagger to his feet — ay, and saw him by a single gigantic effort swing up the struggling Nasta and with a shout of triumph hurl him straight over the parapet of the bridge, to be crushed to powder on the rocks two hundred feet below.

The succour which had been summoned by the girl who had passed down the stair before the assassins passed up was at hand, and the loud shouts which reached us from the outer gates told us that the town was also aroused, and the men awakened by the women were calling to be admitted. Some of Nyleptha's brave ladies, who in their night-shifts and with their long hair streaming down their backs, just as they had been aroused from rest, went off to admit them at the side entrance, whilst others, assisted by the rescuing party outside, pushed and pulled down the marble blocks they had placed there with so much labour.

Soon the wall was down again, and through the doorway, followed by a crowd of rescuers, staggered old Umslopogaas, an awful and, in a way, a glorious figure. The man was a mass of wounds, and a glance at his wild eye told me that he was dying. The 'keshla' gum-ring upon his head was severed in two places by sword-cuts, one just over the curious hole in his skull, and the blood poured down his face from the gashes. Also on the right side of his neck was a stab from a spear, inflicted by Agon; there was a deep cut on his left arm just below where the mail shirt-sleeve stopped, and on the right side of his body the armour was severed by a gash six inches long, where Nasta's mighty sword had bitten through it and deep into its wearer's vitals.

On, axe in hand, he staggered, that dreadful-looking, splendid savage, and the ladies forgot to turn faint at the scene of blood, and cheered him, as well they might, but he never stayed or heeded. With outstretched arms and tottering gait he pursued his way, followed by us all along the broad shell-strewn walk that ran through the courtyard, past the spot where the blocks of marble lay, through the round arched doorway and the thick curtains that hung within it, down the short passage and into the great hall, which was now filling with hastily-armed men, who poured through the side entrance. Straight up the hall he went, leaving behind him a track of blood on the marble pavement, till at last he reached the sacred stone, which stood in the centre of it, and here his strength seemed to fail him, for he stopped and leaned upon his axe. Then suddenly he lifted up his voice and cried aloud —

'I die, I die — but it was a kingly fray. Where are they who came up the great stair? I see them not. Art thou there, Macumazahn, or art thou gone before to wait for me in the dark whither I go? The blood blinds me — the place turns round — I hear the voice of waters.'

Next, as though a new thought had struck him, he lifted the red axe and kissed the blade.

'Farewell, Inkosi-kaas,' he cried. 'Nay, nay, we will go together; we cannot part, thou and I. We have lived too long one with another, thou and I.

'One more stroke, only one! A good stroke! a straight stroke! a strong stroke!' and, drawing himself to his full height, with a wild heart-shaking shout, he with both hands began to whirl the axe round his head till it looked like a circle of flaming steel. Then, suddenly, with awful force he brought it down straight on to the crown of the mass of sacred stone. A shower of sparks flew up, and such was the almost superhuman strength of the blow, that the massive marble split with a rending sound into a score of pieces, whilst of Inkosi-kaas there remained but some fragments of steel and a fibrous rope of shattered horn that had been the handle. Down with a crash on to the pavement fell the fragments of the holy stone, and down with a crash on to them, still grasping the knob of Inkosi-kaas, fell the brave old Zulu — *dead*.

And thus the hero died.

A gasp of wonder and astonishment rose from all those who witnessed the extraordinary sight, and then somebody cried, '*The prophecy! the prophecy!* He has shattered the sacred stone!' and at once a murmuring arose.

'Ay,' said Nyleptha, with that quick wit which distinguishes her. 'Ay, my people, he has shattered the stone, and behold the prophecy is fulfilled, for a stranger king rules in Zu-Vendis. Incubu, my lord, hath beat Sorais back, and I fear her no more, and to him who hath saved the Crown it shall surely be. And this man,' she said, turning to me and laying her hand upon my shoulder, 'wot ye that, though wounded in the fight of yesterday, he rode with that old warrior who lies there, one hundred miles 'twixt sun set and rise to save me from the plots of cruel men. Ay, and he has saved me, by a very little, and therefore because of the deeds that they have done — deeds of glory such as our history cannot show the like — therefore I say that the name of Macumazahn and the name of dead Umslopogaas, ay, and the name of Kara, my servant, who aided him to hold the stair, shall be blazoned in letters of gold above my throne, and shall be glorious for ever while the land endures. I, the Queen, have said it.'

This spirited speech was met with loud cheering, and I said that after all we had only done our duty, as it is the fashion of both Englishmen and Zulus to do, and there was nothing to make an outcry about; at which they cheered still more, and then I was supported across the outer courtyard to my old quarters, in order that I might be put to bed. As I went, my eyes lit upon the brave horse Daylight that lay there, his white head outstretched on the pavement, exactly as he had fallen on entering the yard; and I bade those who supported me take me near him, that I might look on the good beast once more before he was dragged away. And as I looked, to my astonishment he opened his eyes and, lifting his head a little, whinnied faintly. I could have shouted for joy to find that he was not dead, only unfortunately I had not a shout left in me; but as it was, grooms were sent for and he was lifted up and wine poured down his throat, and in a fortnight he was as well and strong as ever, and is the pride and joy of all the people of Milosis, who, whenever they see him, point him out to the little children as the 'horse which saved the White Queen's life'.

Then I went on and got off to bed, and was washed and had my mail shirt removed. They hurt me a great deal in getting it off, and no wonder, for on my left breast and side was a black bruise the size of a saucer.

The next thing that I remember was the tramp of horsemen outside the palace wall, some ten hours later. I raised myself and asked what was the news, and they told me that a large body of cavalry sent by Curtis to assist the Queen had arrived from the scene of the battle, which they had left two hours after sundown. When they left, the wreck of Sorais' army was in full retreat upon M'Arstuna, followed by all our effective cavalry. Sir Henry was encamping the remains of his worn-out forces on the site (such is the fortune of war) that Sorais had occupied the night before, and proposed marching to M'Arstuna on the morrow. Having heard this, I felt that I could die with a light heart, and then everything became a blank.

When next I awoke the first thing I saw was the round disc of a sympathetic eyeglass, behind which was Good.

'How are you getting on, old chap?' said a voice from the neighbourhood of the eyeglass.

'What are you doing here?' I asked faintly. 'You ought to be at M'Arstuna — have you run away, or what?'

'M'Arstuna,' he replied cheerfully. 'Ah, M'Arstuna fell last week — you've been unconscious for a fortnight, you see — with all the honours of war, you know — trumpets blowing, flags flying, just as though they had had the best of it; but for all that, weren't they glad to go. Israel made for his tents, I can tell you — never saw such a sight in my life.'

'And Sorais?' I asked.

'Sorais — oh, Sorais is a prisoner; they gave her up, the scoundrels,' he added, with a change of tone — 'sacrificed the Queen to save their skins, you see. She is being brought up here, and I don't know what will happen to her, poor soul!' and he sighed.

'Where is Curtis?' I asked.

'He is with Nyleptha. She rode out to meet us today, and there was a grand to-do, I can tell you. He is coming to see you tomorrow; the doctors (for there is a medical "faculty" in Zu-Vendis as elsewhere) thought that he had better not come today.'

I said nothing, but somehow I thought to myself that notwithstanding the doctors he might have given me a look; but there, when a man is newly married and has just gained a great victory, he is apt to listen to the advice of doctors, and quite right too.

Just then I heard a familiar voice informing me that 'Monsieur must now couch himself,' and looking up perceived Alphonse's enormous black mustachios curling away in the distance.

'So you are here?' I said.

'Mais oui, Monsieur; the war is now finished, my military instincts are satisfied, and I return to nurse Monsieur.'

I laughed, or rather tried to; but whatever may have been Alphonse's failings as a warrior (and I fear that he did not come up to the level of his heroic grandfather in this particular, showing thereby how true is the saying that it is a bad thing to be overshadowed by some great ancestral name), a better or kinder nurse never lived. Poor Alphonse! I hope he will always think of me as kindly as I think of him.

On the morrow I saw Curtis and Nyleptha with him, and he told me the whole history of what had happened since Umslopogaas and I galloped wildly away from the battle to save the life of the Queen. It seemed to me that he had managed the thing exceedingly well, and showed great ability as a general. Of course, however, our loss had been dreadfully heavy — indeed, I am afraid to say how many perished in the desperate battle I have described, but I know that the slaughter has appreciably affected the male population of the country. He was very pleased to see me, dear fellow that he is, and thanked me with tears in his eyes for the little that I had been able to do. I saw him, however, start violently when his eyes fell upon my face.

As for Nyleptha, she was positively radiant now that 'her dear lord' had come back with no other injury than an ugly scar on his forehead. I do not believe that she allowed all the fearful slaughter that had taken place to weigh ever so little in the balance against this one fact, or even to greatly diminish her joy; and I cannot blame her for it, seeing that it is the nature of loving woman to look at all things through the spectacles of her love, and little does she reck of the misery of the many if the happiness of the *one* be assured. That is human nature, which the Positivists tell us is just perfection; so no doubt it is all right.

'And what art thou going to do with Sorais?' I asked her.

Instantly her bright brow darkened to a frown.

'Sorais,' she said, with a little stamp of the foot; 'ah, but Sorais!'

Sir Henry hastened to turn the subject.

'You will soon be about and all right again now, old fellow,' he said.

I shook my head and laughed.

'Don't deceive yourselves,' I said. 'I may be about for a little, but I shall never be all right again. I am a dying man, Curtis. I may die slow, but die I must. Do you know I have been spitting blood all the morning? I tell you there is something working away into my lung; I can feel it. There, don't look distressed; I have had my day, and am ready to go. Give me the mirror, will you? I want to look at myself.'

He made some excuse, but I saw through it and insisted, and at last he handed me one of the discs of polished silver set in a wooden frame like a hand-screen, which serve as looking-glasses in Zu-Vendis. I looked and put it down.

'Ah,' I said quietly, 'I thought so; and you talk of my getting all right!' I did not like to let them see how shocked I really was at my own appearance. My grizzled stubby hair was turned snow-white, and my yellow face was shrunk like an aged woman's and had two deep purple rings painted beneath the eyes.

Here Nyleptha began to cry, and Sir Henry again turned the subject, telling me that the artists had taken a cast of the dead body of old Umslopogaas, and that a great statue in black marble was to be erected of him in the act of splitting the sacred stone, which was to be matched by another statue in white marble of myself and the horse Daylight as he appeared when, at the termination of that wild ride, he sank beneath me in the courtyard of the palace. I have since seen these statues, which at the time of writing this, six months after the battle, are nearly finished; and very beautiful they are, especially that of Umslopogaas, which is exactly like him. As for that of myself, it is good, but they have idealized my ugly face a little, which is perhaps as well, seeing that thousands of people will probably look at it in the centuries to come, and it is not pleasant to look at ugly things.

Then they told me that Umslopogaas' last wish had been carried out, and that, instead of being cremated, as I shall be, after the usual custom here, he had been tied up, Zulu fashion, with his knees beneath his chin, and, having been wrapped in a thin sheet of beaten gold, entombed in a hole hollowed out of the masonry of the semicircular space at the top of the stair he defended so splendidly, which faces, as far as we can judge, almost exactly towards Zululand. There he sits, and will sit for ever, for they embalmed him with spices, and put him in an air-tight stone coffer, keeping his grim watch beneath the spot he held alone against a multitude; and the people say that at night his ghost rises and stands shaking the phantom of Inkosi-kaas at phantom foes. Certainly they fear during the dark hours to pass the place where the hero is buried.

Oddly enough, too, a new legend or prophecy has arisen in the land in that unaccountable way in which such things to arise among barbarous and semi-civilized people, blowing, like the wind, no man knows whence. According to this saying, so long as the old Zulu sits there, looking down the stairway he defended when alive, so long will the New House of the Stairway, springing from the union of the Englishman and Nyleptha, endure and flourish; but when he is taken from thence, or when, ages after, his bones at last crumble into dust, the House will fall, and the Stairway shall fall, and the Nation of the Zu-Vendi shall cease to be a Nation.

I Have Spoken

It was a week after Nyleptha's visit, when I had begun to get about a little in the middle of the day, that a message came to me from Sir Henry to say that Sorais would be brought before them in the Queen's first antechamber at midday, and requesting my attendance if possible. Accordingly, greatly drawn by curiosity to see this unhappy woman once more, I made shift, with the help of that kind little fellow Alphonse, who is a perfect treasure to me, and that of another waiting-man, to reach the antechamber. I got there, indeed, before anybody else, except a few of the great Court officials who had been bidden to be present, but I had scarcely seated myself before Sorais was brought in by a party of guards, looking as beautiful and defiant as ever, but with a worn expression on her proud face. She was, as usual, dressed in her royal 'kaf', emblazoned with the emblem of the Sun, and in her right hand she still held the toy spear of silver. A pang of admiration and pity went through me as I looked at her, and struggling to my feet I bowed deeply, at the same time expressing my sorrow that I was not able, owing to my condition, to remain standing before her.

She coloured a little and then laughed bitterly. 'Thou dost forget, Macumazahn,' she said, 'I am no more a Queen, save in blood; I am an outcast and a prisoner, one whom all men should scorn, and none show deference to.'

'At least,' I replied, 'thou art still a lady, and therefore one to whom deference is due. Also, thou art in an evil case, and therefore it is doubly due.'

'Ah!' she answered, with a little laugh, 'thou dost forget that I would have wrapped thee in a sheet of gold and hung thee to the angel's trumpet at the topmost pinnacle of the Temple.'

'No,' I answered, 'I assure thee that I forgot it not; indeed, I often thought of it when it seemed to me that the battle of the Pass was turning against us; but the trumpet is there, and I am still here, though perchance not for long, so why talk of it now?'

'Ah!' she went on, 'the battle! the battle! Oh, would that I were once more a Queen, if only for one little hour, and I would take such a vengeance on those accursed jackals who deserted me in my need; that it should only be spoken of in whispers; those woman, those pigeon-hearted half-breeds who suffered themselves to be overcome!' and she choked in her wrath.

'Ay, and that little coward beside thee,' she went on, pointing at Alphonse with the silver spear, whereat he looked very uncomfortable; 'he escaped and betrayed my plans. I tried to make a general of him, telling the soldiers it was Bougwan, and to scourge valour into him' (here Alphonse shivered at some unhappy recollection), 'but it was of no avail. He hid beneath a banner in my tent and thus overheard my plans. I would that I had slain him, but, alas! I held my hand.

'And thou, Macumazahn, I have heard of what thou didst; thou art brave, and hast a loyal heart. And the black one too, ah, he was a *man*. I would fain have seen him hurl Nasta from the stairway.'

'Thou art a strange woman, Sorais,' I said; 'I pray thee now plead with the Queen Nyleptha, that perchance she may show mercy unto thee.'

She laughed out loud. 'I plead for mercy!' she said and at that moment the Queen entered, accompanied by Sir Henry and Good, and took her seat with an impassive face. As for poor Good, he looked intensely ill at ease.

'Greeting, Sorais!' said Nyleptha, after a short pause. 'Thou hast rent the kingdom like a rag, thou hast put thousands of my people to the sword, thou hast twice basely plotted to destroy my life by murder, thou hast sworn to slay my lord and his companions and to hurl me from the Stairway. What hast thou to say why thou shouldst not die? Speak, O Sorais!'

'Methinks my sister the Queen hath forgotten the chief count of the indictment,' answered Sorais in her slow musical tones. 'It runs thus: "Thou didst strive to win the love of my lord Incubu." It is for this crime that my sister will slay me, not because I levied war. It is perchance happy for thee, Nyleptha, that I fixed my mind upon his love too late.

'Listen,' she went on, raising her voice. 'I have nought to say save that I would I had won instead of lost. Do thou with me even as thou wilt, O Queen, and let my lord the King there' (pointing to Sir Henry) — 'for now will he be King — carry out the sentence, as it is meet he should, for as he is the beginning of the evil, let him also be the end.' And she drew herself up and shot one angry glance at him from her deep fringed eyes, and then began to toy with her spear.

Sir Henry bent towards Nyleptha and whispered something that I could not catch, and then the Queen spoke.

'Sorais, ever have I been a good sister to thee. When our father died, and there was much talk in the land as to whether thou shouldst sit upon the throne with me, I being the elder, I gave my voice for thee and said, "Nay, let her sit. She is twin with me; we were born at a birth; wherefore should the one be preferred before the other?" And so has it ever been 'twixt thee and me, my sister. But now thou knowest in what sort thou hast repaid me, but I have prevailed, and thy life is forfeit, Sorais. And yet art thou my sister, born at a birth with me, and we played together when we were little and loved each other much, and at night we slept in the same cot with our arms each around the other's neck, and therefore even now does my heart go out to thee, Sorais.

'But not for that would I spare thy life, for thy offence has been too heavy; it doth drag down the wide wings of my mercy even to the ground. Also, while thou dost live the land will never be at peace.

'Yet shalt thou not die, Sorais, because my dear lord here hath begged thy life of me as a boon; therefore as a boon and as a marriage gift give I it to him, to do with even as he wills, knowing that, though thou dost love him, he loves thee not, Sorais, for all thy beauty. Nay, though thou art lovely as the night in all her stars, O Lady of the Night, yet it is me his wife whom he loves, and not thee, and therefore do I give thy life to him.'

Sorais flushed up to her eyes and said nothing, and I do not think that I ever saw a man look more miserable than did Sir Henry at that moment. Somehow, Nyleptha's way of putting the thing, though true and forcible enough, was not altogether pleasant.

'I understand,' stammered Curtis, looking at Good, 'I understood that he were attached — eh — attached to — to the Queen Sorais. I am — eh — not aware what the — in short, the state of your feelings may be just now; but if they happened to be that way inclined, it has struck me that — in short, it might put a satisfactory end to an unpleasant business. The lady also has ample private estates, where I am sure she would be at liberty to live unmolested as far as we are concerned, eh, Nyleptha? Of course, I only suggest.'

'So far as I am concerned,' said Good, colouring up, 'I am quite willing to forget the past; and if the Lady of the Night thinks me worth the taking I will marry her tomorrow, or when she likes, and try to make her a good husband.'

All eyes were now turned to Sorais, who stood with that same slow smile upon her beautiful face which I had noticed the first time that I ever saw her. She paused a little while, and cleared her throat, and then thrice she curtseyed low, once to Nyleptha, once to Curtis, and once to Good, and began to speak in measured tones.

'I thank thee, most gracious Queen and royal sister, for the loving-kindness thou hast shown me from my youth up, and especially in that thou hast been pleased to give my person and my fate as a gift to the Lord Incubu — the King that is to be. May prosperity, peace and plenty deck the life-path of one so merciful and so tender, even as flowers do. Long mayst thou reign, O great and glorious Queen, and hold thy husband's love in both thy hands, and many be the sons and daughters of thy beauty. And I thank thee, my Lord Incubu — the King that is to be — I thank thee a thousand times in that thou hast been pleased to accept that gracious gift, and to pass it on to thy comrade in arms and in adventure, the Lord Bougwan. Surely the act is worthy of thy greatness, my Lord Incubu. And now, lastly, I thank thee also, my Lord Bougwan, who in thy turn hast deigned to accept me and my poor beauty. I thank thee a thousand times, and I will add that thou art a good and honest man, and I put my hand upon my heart and swear that I would that I could say thee "yea". And now that I have rendered thanks to all in turn' — and again she smiled — 'I will add one short word.

'Little can you understand of me, Queen Nyleptha and my lords, if ye know not that for me there is no middle path; that I scorn your pity and hate you for it; that I cast off your forgiveness as though it were a serpent's sting; and that standing here, betrayed, deserted, insulted, and alone, I yet triumph over you, mock you, and defy you, one and all, and *thus* I answer you.' And then, of a sudden, before anybody guessed what she intended to do, she drove the little silver spear she carried in her hand into her side with such a strong and steady aim that the keen point projected through her back, and she fell prone upon the pavement.

Nyleptha shrieked, and poor Good almost fainted at the sight, while the rest of us rushed towards her. But Sorais of the Night lifted herself upon her hand, and for a moment fixed her glorious eyes intently on Curtis' face, as though there were some message in the glance, then dropped her head and sighed, and with a sob her dark but splendid spirit passed.

Well, they gave her a royal funeral, and there was an end of her.

It was a month after the last act of the Sorais tragedy that a great ceremony was held in the Flower Temple, and Curtis was formally declared King-Consort of Zu-Vendis. I was too ill to go myself; and indeed, I hate all that sort of thing, with the crowds and the trumpet-blowing and banner-waving; but Good, who was there (in his full-dress uniform), came back much impressed, and told me that Nyleptha had looked lovely, and Curtis had borne himself in a right royal fashion, and had been received with acclamations that left no doubt as to his popularity. Also he told me that when the horse Daylight was led along in the procession, the populace had shouted '*Macumazahn, Macumazahn!*' till they were hoarse, and would only be appeased when he, Good, rose in his chariot and told them that I was too ill to be present.

Afterwards, too, Sir Henry, or rather the King, came to see me, looking very tired, and vowing that he had never been so bored in his life; but I dare say that that was a slight exaggeration. It is not in human nature that a man should be altogether bored on such an extraordinary occasion; and, indeed, as I pointed out to him, it was a marvellous thing that a man, who but little more than one short year before had entered a great country as an unknown wanderer, should today be married to its beautiful and beloved Queen, and lifted, amidst public rejoicings, to its throne. I even went the length to exhort him in the future not to be carried away by the pride and pomp of absolute power, but always to strive to remember that he was first a Christian gentleman, and next a public servant, called by Providence to a great and almost unprecedented trust. These remarks, which he might fairly have resented, he was so good as to receive with patience, and even to thank me for making them.

It was immediately after this ceremony that I caused myself to be moved to the house where I am now writing. It is a very pleasant country seat, situated about two miles from the Frowning City, on to which it looks. That was five months ago, during the whole of which time I have, being confined to a kind of couch, employed my leisure in compiling this history of our wanderings from my journal and from our joint memories. It is probable that it will never be read, but it does not much matter whether it is or not; at any rate, it has served to while away many hours of suffering, for I have suffered a deal of pain lately. Thank God, however, there will not be much more of it.

It is a week since I wrote the above, and now I take up my pen for the last time, for I know that the end is at hand. My brain is still clear and I can manage to write, though with difficulty. The pain in my lung, which has been very bad during the last week, has suddenly quite left me, and been succeeded by a feeling of numbness of which I cannot mistake the meaning. And just as the pain has gone, so with it all fear of that end has departed, and I feel only as though I were going to sink into the arms of an unutterable rest. Happily, contentedly, and with the same sense of security with which an infant lays itself to sleep in its mother's arms, do I lay myself down in the arms of the Angel Death. All the tremors, all the heart-shaking fears which have haunted me through a life that seems long as I looked back upon it, have left me now; the storms have passed, and the Star of our Eternal Hope shines clear and steady on the horizon that seems so far from man, and yet is so very near to me tonight.

And so this is the end of it — a brief space of troubling, a few restless, fevered, anguished years, and then the arms of that great Angel Death. Many times have I been near to them, and now it is my turn at last, and it is well. Twenty-four hours more and the world will be gone from me, and with it all its hopes and all its fears. The air will close in over the space that my form filled and my place know me no more; for the dull breath of the world's forgetfulness will first dim the brightness of my memory, and then blot it out for ever, and of a truth I shall be dead. So is it with us all. How many millions have lain as I lie, and thought these thoughts and been forgotten! — thousands upon thousands of years ago they thought them, those dying men of the dim past; and thousands on thousands of years hence will their descendants think them and be in their turn forgotten. 'As the breath of the oxen in winter, as the quick star that runs along the sky, as a little shadow that loses itself at sunset,' as I once heard a Zulu called Ignosi put it, such is the order of our life, the order that passeth away.

Well, it is not a good world — nobody can say that it is, save those who wilfully blind themselves to facts. How can a world be good in which Money is the moving power, and Self-interest the guiding star? The wonder is not that it is so bad, but that there should be any good left in it.

Still, now that my life is over, I am glad to have lived, glad to have known the dear breath of woman's love, and that true friendship which can even surpass the love of woman, glad to have heard the laughter of little children, to have seen the sun and the moon and the stars, to have felt the kiss of the salt sea on my face, and watched the wild game trek down to the water in the moonlight. But I should not wish to live again!

Everything is changing to me. The darkness draws near, and the light departs. And yet it seems to me that through that darkness I can already see the shining welcome of many a long-lost face. Harry is there, and others; one above all, to my mind the sweetest and most perfect woman that ever gladdened this grey earth. But of her I have already written elsewhere, and at length, so why speak of her now? Why speak of her after this long silence, now that she is again so near to me, now that I go where she has gone?

The sinking sun is turning the golden roof of the great Temple to a fiery flame, and my fingers tire.

So to all who have known me, or known of me, to all who can think one kindly thought of the old hunter, I stretch out my hand from the far-off shore and bid a long farewell.

And now into the hands of Almighty God, who sent it, do I commit my spirit.

'*I have spoken,*' as the Zulus say.

By Another Hand

A year has elapsed since our most dear friend Allan Quatermain wrote the words '*I have spoken*' at the end of his record of our adventures. Nor should I have ventured to make any additions to the record had it not happened that by a most strange accident a chance has arisen of its being conveyed to England. The chance is but a faint one, it is true; but, as it is not probable that another will arise in our lifetimes, Good and myself think that we may as well avail ourselves of it, such as it is. During the last six months several Frontier Commissions have been at work on the various boundaries of Zu-Vendis, with a view of discovering whether there exists any possible means of ingress or egress from the country, with the result that a channel of communication with the outer world hitherto overlooked has been discovered. This channel, apparently the only one (for I have discovered that it was by it that the native who ultimately reached Mr Mackenzie's mission station, and whose arrival in the country, together with the fact of his expulsion — for he *did* arrive about three years before ourselves — was for reasons of their own kept a dead secret by the priests to whom he was brought), is about to be effectually closed. But before this is done, a messenger is to be despatched bearing with him this manuscript, and also one or two letters from Good to his friends, and from myself to my brother George, whom it deeply grieves me to think I shall never see again, informing them, as our next heirs, that they are welcome to our effects in England, if the Court of Probate will allow them to take them, inasmuch as we have made up our minds never to return to Europe. Indeed, it would be impossible for us to leave Zu-Vendis even if we wished to do so.

The messenger who is to go — and I wish him joy of his journey — is Alphonse. For a long while he has been wearied to death of Zu-Vendis and its inhabitants. 'Oh, oui, c'est beau,' he says, with an expressive shrug; 'mais je m'ennuie; ce n'est pas chic.' Again, he complains dreadfully of the absence of cafes and theatres, and moans continually for his lost Annette, of whom he says he dreams three times a week. But I fancy his secret cause of disgust at the country, putting aside the homesickness to which every Frenchman is subject, is that the people here laugh at him so dreadfully about his conduct on the occasion of the great battle of the Pass about eighteen months ago, when he hid beneath a banner in Sorais's tent in order to avoid being sent forth to fight, which he says would have gone against his conscience. Even the little boys call out at him in the streets, thereby offending his pride and making his life unbearable. At any rate, he has determined to brave the horrors of a journey of almost unprecedented difficulty and danger, and also to run the risk of falling into the hands of the French police to answer for a certain little indiscretion of his own some years old (though I do not consider that a very serious matter), rather than remain in ce triste pays. Poor Alphonse! we shall be very sorry to part with him; but I sincerely trust, for his own sake and also for the sake of this history, which is, I think, worth giving to the world, that he may arrive in safety. If he does, and can carry the treasure we have provided him with in the shape of bars of solid gold, he will be, comparatively speaking, a rich man for life, and well able to marry his Annette, if she is still in the land of the living and willing to marry her Alphonse.

Anyhow, on the chance, I may as well add a word or two to dear old Quatermain's narrative.

He died at dawn on the day following that on which he wrote the last words of the last chapter. Nyleptha, Good and myself were present, and a most touching and yet in its way beautiful scene it was. An hour before the daybreak it became apparent to us that he was sinking, and our distress was very keen. Indeed, Good melted into tears at the idea — a fact that called forth a last gentle flicker of humour from our dying friend, for even at that hour he could be humorous. Good's emotion had, by loosening the muscles, naturally caused his eyeglass to fall from its accustomed place, and Quatermain, who always observed everything, observed this also.

'At last,' he gasped, with an attempt at a smile, 'I have seen Good without his eyeglass.'

After that he said no more till the day broke, when he asked to be lifted up to watch the rising of the sun for the last time.

'In a very few minutes,' he said, after gazing earnestly at it, 'I shall have passed through those golden gates.'

Ten minutes afterwards he raised himself and looked us fixedly in the face.

'I am going a stranger journey than any we have ever taken together. Think of me sometimes,' he murmured. 'God bless you all. I shall wait for you.' And with a sigh he fell back dead.

And so passed away a character that I consider went as near perfection as any it has ever been my lot to encounter.

Tender, constant, humorous, and possessing of many of the qualities that go to make a poet, he was yet almost unrivalled as a man of action and a citizen of the world. I never knew any one so competent to form an accurate judgment of men and their motives. 'I have studied human nature all my life,' he would say, 'and I ought to know something about it,' and he certainly did. He had but two faults — one was his excessive modesty, and the other a slight tendency which he had to be jealous of anybody on whom he concentrated his affections. As regards the first of these points, anybody who reads what he has written will be able to form his own opinion; but I will add one last instance of it.

As the reader will doubtless remember, it is a favourite trick of his to talk of himself as a timid man, whereas really, though very cautious, he possessed a most intrepid spirit, and, what is more, never lost his head. Well, in the great battle of the Pass, where he got the wound that finally killed him, one would imagine from the account which he gives of the occurrence that it was a chance blow that fell on him in the scrimmage. As a matter of fact, however, he was wounded in a most gallant and successful attempt to save Good's life, at the risk and, as it ultimately turned out, at the cost of his own. Good was down on the ground, and one of Nasta's highlanders was about to dispatch him, when Quatermain threw himself on to his prostrate form and received the blow on his own body, and then, rising, killed the soldier.

As regards his jealousy, a single instance which I give in justice to myself and Nyleptha will suffice. The reader will, perhaps, recollect that in one or two places he speaks as though Nyleptha monopolized me, and he was left by both of us rather out in the cold. Now Nyleptha is not perfect, any more than any other woman is, and she may be a little exigeante at times, but as regards Quatermain the whole thing is pure imagination. Thus when he complains about my not coming to see him when he is ill, the fact was that, in spite of my entreaties, the doctors positively forbade it. Those little remarks of his pained me very much when I read them, for I loved Quatermain as dearly as though he were my own father, and should never have dreamed of allowing my marriage to interfere with that affection. But let it pass; it is, after all, but one little weakness, which makes no great show among so many and such lovable virtues.

Well, he died, and Good read the Burial Service over him in the presence of Nyleptha and myself; and then his remains were, in deference to the popular clamour, accorded a great public funeral, or rather cremation. I could not help thinking, however, as I marched in that long and splendid procession up to the Temple, how he would have hated the whole thing could he have been there to see it, for he had a horror of ostentation.

And so, a few minutes before sunset, on the third night after his death, they laid him on the brazen flooring before the altar, and waited for the last ray of the setting sun to fall upon his face. Presently it came, and struck him like a golden arrow, crowning the pale brows with glory, and then the trumpets blew, and the flooring revolved, and all that remained of our beloved friend fell into the furnace below.

We shall never see his like again if we live a hundred years. He was the ablest man, the truest gentleman, the firmest friend, the finest sportsman, and, I believe, the best shot in all Africa.

And so ended the very remarkable and adventurous life of Hunter Quatermain.

Since then things have gone very well with us. Good has been, and still is, busily employed in the construction of a navy on Lake Milosis and another of the large lakes, by means of which we hope to be able to increase trade and commerce, and also to overcome some very troublesome and warlike sections of the population who live upon their borders. Poor fellow! he is beginning to get over the sad death of that misguided but most attractive woman, Sorais, but it is a sad blow to him, for he was really deeply attached to her. I hope, however, that he will in time make a suitable marriage and get that unhappy business out of his head. Nyleptha has one or two young ladies in view, especially a daughter of Nasta's (who was a widower), a very fine imperial-looking girl, but with too much of her father's intriguing, and yet haughty, spirit to suit my taste.

As for myself, I should scarcely know where to begin if I set to work to describe my doings, so I had best leave them undescribed, and content myself with saying that, on the whole, I am getting on very well in my curious position of King-Consort — better, indeed, than I had any right to expect. But, of course, it is not all plain sailing, and I find the responsibilities very heavy. Still, I hope to be able to do some good in my time, and I intend to devote myself to two great ends — namely, to the consolidation of the various clans which together make up the Zu-Vendi people, under one strong central government, and to the sapping of the power of the priesthood. The first of these reforms will, if it can be carried out, put an end to the disastrous civil wars that have for centuries devastated this country; and the second, besides removing a source of political danger, will pave the road for the introduction of true religion in the place of this senseless Sun worship. I yet hope to see the shadow of the Cross of Christ lying on the golden dome of the Flower Temple; or, if I do not, that my successors may.

There is one more thing that I intend to devote myself to, and that is the total exclusion of all foreigners from Zu-Vendis. Not, indeed, that any more are ever likely to get here, but if they do, I warn them fairly that they will be shown the shortest way out of the country. I do not say this from any sense of inhospitality, but because I am convinced of the sacred duty that rests upon me of preserving to this, on the whole, upright and generous-hearted people the blessings of comparative barbarism. Where would all my brave army be if some enterprising rascal were to attack us with field-guns and Martini-Henrys? I cannot see that gunpowder, telegraphs, steam, daily newspapers, universal suffrage, etc., etc., have made mankind one whit the happier than they used to be, and I am certain that they have brought many evils in their train. I have no fancy for handing over this beautiful country to be torn and fought for by speculators, tourists, politicians and teachers, whose voice is as the voice of Babel, just as those horrible creatures in the valley of the underground river tore and fought for the body of the wild swan; nor will I endow it with the greed, drunkenness, new diseases, gunpowder, and general demoralization which chiefly mark the progress of civilization amongst unsophisticated peoples. If in due course it pleases Providence to throw Zu-Vendis open to the world, that is another matter; but of myself I will not take the responsibility, and I may add that Good entirely approves of my decision. Farewell.

Henry Curtis

December 15, 18—.

PS — I quite forgot to say that about nine months ago Nyleptha (who is very well and, in my eyes at any rate, more beautiful than ever) presented me with a son and heir. He is a regular curly-haired, blue-eyed young Englishman in looks, and, though he is destined, if he lives, to inherit the throne of Zu-Vendis, I hope I may be able to bring him up to become what an English gentleman should be, and generally is — which is to my mind even a prouder and a finer thing than being born heir apparent to the great House of the Stairway, and, indeed, the highest rank that a man can reach upon this earth.

H. C.

Note by George Curtis, Esq.

The MS of this history, addressed to me in the handwriting of my dear brother Henry Curtis, whom we had given up for dead, and bearing the Aden postmark, reached me in safety on December 20, 18—, or a little more than two years after it left his hands in the far centre of Africa, and I hasten to give the astonishing story it contains to the world. Speaking for myself, I have read it with very mixed feelings; for though it is a great relief to know that he and Good are alive and strangely prosperous, I cannot but feel that for me and for all their friends they might as well be dead, since we can never hope to see them more.

They have cut themselves off from old England and from their homes and their relations for ever, and perhaps, under the circumstances, they were right and wise to do so.

How the MS came to be posted I have been quite unable to discover; but I presume, from the fact of its being posted at all, that the little Frenchman, Alphonse, accomplished his hazardous journey in safety. I have, however, advertised for him and caused various inquiries to be made in Marseilles and elsewhere with a view of discovering his whereabouts, but so far without the slightest success. Possibly he is dead, and the packet was posted by another hand; or possibly he is now happily wedded to his Annette, but still fears the vengeance of the law, and prefers to remain incognito. I cannot say, I have not yet abandoned my hopes of finding him, but I am bound to say that they grow fainter day by day, and one great obstacle to my search is that nowhere in the whole history does Mr Quatermain mention his surname. He is always spoken of as 'Alphonse', and there are so many Alphonses. The letters which my brother Henry says he is sending with the packet of manuscript have never arrived, so I presume that they are lost or destroyed.

George Curtis

Allan's Wife

Table of Contents

Dedication

My Dear Macumazahn,

It was your native name which I borrowed at the christening of that Allen who has become as well known to me as any other friend I have. It is therefore fitting that I should dedicate to you this, his last tale—the story of his wife, and the history of some further adventures which befell him.

They will remind you of many an African yarn—that with the baboons may recall an experience of your own which I did not share. And perhaps they will do more than this. Perhaps they will bring back to you some of the long past romance of days that are lost to us. The country of which Allan Quatermain tells his tale is now, for the most part, as well known and explored as are the fields of Norfolk. Where we shot and trekked and galloped, scarcely seeing the face of civilized man, there the gold-seeker builds his cities. The shadow of the flag of Britain has, for a while, ceased to fall on the Transvaal plains; the game has gone; the misty charm of the morning has become the glare of day. All is changed. The blue gums that we planted in the garden of the "Palatial" must be large trees by now, and the "Palatial" itself has passed from us. Jess sat in it waiting for her love after we were gone. There she nursed him back to life. But Jess is dead, and strangers own it, or perhaps it is a ruin.

For us too, Macumazahn, as for the land we loved, the mystery and promise of the morning are outworn; the mid-day sun burns overhead, and at times the way is weary. Few of those we knew are left. Some are victims to battle and murder, their bones strew the veldt; death has taken some in a more gentle fashion; others are hidden from us, we know not where. We might well fear to return to that land lest we also should see ghosts. But though we walk apart to-day, the past yet looks upon us with its unalterable eyes. Still we can remember many a boyish enterprise and adventure, lightly undertaken, which now would strike us as hazardous indeed. Still we can recall the long familiar line of the Pretoria Horse, the face of war and panic, the weariness of midnight patrols; aye, and hear the roar of guns echoed from the Shameful Hill.

To you then, Macumazahn, in perpetual memory of those eventful years of youth which we passed together in the African towns and on the African veldt, I dedicate these pages, subscribing myself now as always,

Your sincere friend,

Indanda

To Arthur H. D. Cochrane, Esq.

Early Days

It may be remembered that in the last pages of his diary, written just before his death, Allan Quatermain makes allusion to his long dead wife, stating that he has written of her fully elsewhere.

When his death was known, his papers were handed to myself as his literary executor. Among them I found two manuscripts, of which the following is one. The other is simply a record of events wherein Mr. Quatermain was not personally concerned—a Zulu novel, the story of which was told to him by the hero many years after the tragedy had occurred. But with this we have nothing to do at present.

I have often thought (Mr. Quatermain's manuscript begins) that I would set down on paper the events connected with my marriage, and the loss of my most dear wife. Many years have now passed since that event, and to some extent time has softened the old grief, though Heaven knows it is still keen enough. On two or three occasions I have even begun the record. Once I gave it up because the writing of it depressed me beyond bearing, once because I was suddenly called away upon a journey, and the third time because a Kaffir boy found my manuscript convenient for lighting the kitchen fire.

But now that I am at leisure here in England, I will make a fourth attempt. If I succeed, the story may serve to interest some one in after years when I am dead and gone; before that I should not wish it to be published. It is a wild tale enough, and suggests some curious reflections.

I am the son of a missionary. My father was originally curate in charge of a small parish in Oxfordshire. He had already been some ten years married to my dear mother when he went there, and he had four children, of whom I was the youngest. I remember faintly the place where we lived. It was an ancient long grey house, facing the road. There was a very large tree of some sort in the garden. It was hollow, and we children used to play about inside of it, and knock knots of wood from the rough bark. We all slept in a kind of attic, and my mother always came and kissed us when we were in bed. I used to wake up and see her bending over me, a candle in her hand. There was a curious kind of pole projecting from the wall over my bed. Once I was dreadfully frightened because my eldest brother made me hang to it by my hands. That is all I remember about our old home. It has been pulled down long ago, or I would journey there to see it.

A little further down the road was a large house with big iron gates to it, and on the top of the gate pillars sat two stone lions, which were so hideous that I was afraid of them. Perhaps this sentiment was prophetic. One could see the house by peeping through the bars of the gates. It was a gloomy-looking place, with a tall yew hedge round it; but in the summer-time some flowers grew about the sun-dial in the grass plat. This house was called the Hall, and Squire Carson lived there. One Christmas—it must have been the Christmas before my father emigrated, or I should not remember it—we children went to a Christmas-tree festivity at the Hall. There was a great party there, and footmen wearing red waistcoats stood at the door. In the dining-room, which was panelled with black oak, was the Christmas-tree. Squire Carson stood in front of it. He was a tall, dark man, very quiet in his manners, and he wore a bunch of seals on his waistcoat. We used to think him old, but as a matter of fact he was then not more than forty. He had been, as I afterwards learned, a great traveller in his youth, and some six or seven years before this date he married a lady who was half a Spaniard—a papist, my father called her. I can remember her well. She was small and very pretty, with a rounded figure, large black eyes, and glittering teeth. She spoke English with a curious accent. I suppose that I must have been a funny child to look at, and I know that my hair stood up on my head then as it does now, for I still have a sketch of myself that my mother made of me, in which this peculiarity is strongly marked. On this occasion of the Christmas-tree I remember that Mrs. Carson turned to a tall, foreign-looking gentleman who stood beside her, and, tapping him affectionately on the shoulder with her gold eye-glasses, said—

"Look, cousin, look at that droll little boy with the big brown eyes; his hair is like a...what you call him ...scrubbing-brush. Oh, what a droll little boy!"

The tall gentleman pulled at his moustache, and, taking Mrs. Carson's hand in his, began to smooth my hair down with it till I heard her whisper—

"Leave go my hand, cousin. Thomas is looking like—like the thunderstorm."

Thomas was the name of Mr. Carson, her husband.

After that I hid myself as well as I could behind a chair, for I was shy, and watched little Stella Carson, who was the squire's only child, giving the children presents off the tree. She was dressed as Father Christmas, with some soft white stuff round her lovely little face, and she had large dark eyes, which I thought more beautiful than anything I had ever seen. At last it came to my turn to receive a present—oddly enough, considered in the light of future events, it was a large monkey. Stella reached it down from one of the lower boughs of the tree and handed it to me, saying—

"Dat is my Christmas present to you, little Allan Quatermain."

As she did so her sleeve, which was covered with cotton wool, spangled over with something that shone, touched one of the tapers and caught fire—how I do not know—and the flame ran up her arm towards her throat. She stood quite still. I suppose that she was paralysed with fear; and the ladies who were near screamed very loud, but did nothing. Then some impulse seized me—perhaps instinct would be a better word to use, considering my age. I threw myself upon the child, and, beating at the fire with my hands, mercifully succeeded in extinguishing it before it really got hold. My wrists were so badly scorched that they had to be wrapped up in wool for a long time afterwards, but with the exception of a single burn upon her throat, little Stella Carson was not much hurt.

This is all that I remember about the Christmas-tree at the Hall. What happened afterwards is lost to me, but to this day in my sleep I sometimes see little Stella's sweet face and the stare of terror in her dark eyes as the fire ran up her arm. This, however, is not wonderful, for I had, humanly speaking, saved the life of her who was destined to be my wife.

The next event which I can recall clearly is that my mother and three brothers all fell ill of fever, owing, as I afterwards learned, to the poisoning of our well by some evil-minded person, who threw a dead sheep into it.

It must have been while they were ill that Squire Carson came one day to the vicarage. The weather was still cold, for there was a fire in the study, and I sat before the fire writing letters on a piece of paper with a pencil, while my father walked up and down the room talking to himself. Afterwards I knew that he was praying for the lives of his wife and children. Presently a servant came to the door and said that some one wanted to see him.

"It is the squire, sir," said the maid, "and he says he particularly wishes to see you."

"Very well," answered my father, wearily, and presently Squire Carson came in. His face was white and haggard, and his eyes shone so fiercely that I was afraid of him.

"Forgive me for intruding on you at such a time, Quatermain," he said, in a hoarse voice, "but to-morrow I leave this place for ever, and I wish to speak to you before I go—indeed, I must speak to you."

"Shall I send Allan away?" said my father, pointing to me.

"No; let him bide. He will not understand." Nor, indeed, did I at the time, but I remembered every word, and in after years their meaning grew on me.

"First tell me," he went on, "how are they?" and he pointed upwards with his thumb.

"My wife and two of the boys are beyond hope," my father answered, with a groan. "I do not know how it will go with the third. The Lord's will be done!"

"The Lord's will be done," the squire echoed, solemnly. "And now, Quatermain, listen—my wife's gone."

"Gone!" my father answered. "Who with?"

"With that foreign cousin of hers. It seems from a letter she left me that she always cared for him, not for me. She married me because she thought me a rich English milord. Now she has run through my property, or most of it, and gone. I don't know where. Luckily, she did not care to encumber her new career with the child; Stella is left to me."

"That is what comes of marrying a papist, Carson," said my father. That was his fault; he was as good and charitable a man as ever lived, but he was bigoted. "What are you going to do—follow her?"

He laughed bitterly in answer.

"Follow her!" he said; "why should I follow her— If I met her I might kill her or him, or both of them, because of the disgrace they have brought upon my child's name. No, I never want to look upon her face again. I trusted her, I tell you, and she has betrayed me. Let her go and find her fate. But I am going too. I am weary of my life."

"Surely, Carson, surely," said my father, "you do not mean—"

"No, no; not that. Death comes soon enough. But I will leave this civilized world which is a lie. We will go right away into the wilds, I and my child, and hide our shame. Where? I don't know where. Anywhere, so long as there are no white faces, no smooth educated tongues—"

"You are mad, Carson," my father answered. "How will you live? How can you educate Stella? Be a man and wear it down."

"I will be a man, and I will wear it down, but not here, Quatermain. Education! Was not she—that woman who was my wife—was not she highly educated?—the cleverest woman in the country forsooth. Too clever for me, Quatermain—too clever by half! No, no, Stella shall be brought up in a different school; if it be possible, she shall forget her very name. Good-bye, old friend, good-bye for ever. Do not try to find me out, henceforth I shall be like one dead to you, to you and all I knew," and he was gone.

"Mad," said my father, with a heavy sigh. "His trouble has turned his brain. But he will think better of it."

At that moment the nurse came hurrying in and whispered something in his ear. My father's face turned deadly pale. He clutched at the table to support himself, then staggered from the room. My mother was dying!

It was some days afterwards, I do not know exactly how long, that my father took me by the hand and led me upstairs into the big room which had been my mother's bedroom. There she lay, dead in her coffin, with flowers in her hand. Along the wall of the room were arranged three little white beds, and on each of the beds lay one of my brothers. They all looked as though they were asleep, and they all had flowers in their hands. My father told me to kiss them, because I should not see them any more, and I did so, though I was very frightened. I did not know why. Then he took me in his arms and kissed me.

"The Lord hath given," he said, "and the Lord hath taken away; blessed be the name of the Lord."

I cried very much, and he took me downstairs, and after that I have only a confused memory of men dressed in black carrying heavy burdens towards the grey churchyard!

Next comes a vision of a great ship and wide tossing waters. My father could no longer bear to live in England after the loss that had fallen on him, and made up his mind to emigrate to South Africa. We must have been poor at the time—indeed, I believe that a large portion of our income went from my father on my mother's death. At any rate we travelled with the steerage passengers, and the intense discomfort of the journey with the rough ways of our fellow emigrants still remain upon my mind. At last it came to an end, and we reached Africa, which I was not to leave again for many, many years.

In those days civilization had not made any great progress in Southern Africa. My father went up the country and became a missionary among the Kaffirs, near to where the town of Cradock now stands, and here I grew to manhood. There were a few Boer farmers in the neighbourhood, and gradually a little settlement of whites gathered round our mission station—a drunken Scotch blacksmith and wheelwright was about the most interesting character, who, when he was sober, could quote the Scottish poet Burns and the

Ingoldsby Legends, then recently published, literally by the page. It was from that I contracted a fondness for the latter amusing writings, which has never left me. Burns I never cared for so much, probably because of the Scottish dialect which repelled me. What little education I got was from my father, but I never had much leaning towards books, nor he much time to teach them to me. On the other hand, I was always a keen observer of the ways of men and nature. By the time that I was twenty I could speak Dutch and three or four Kaffir dialects perfectly, and I doubt if there was anybody in South Africa who understood native ways of thought and action more completely than I did. Also I was really a very good shot and horseman, and I think—as, indeed, my subsequent career proves to have been the case—a great deal tougher than the majority of men. Though I was then, as now, light and small, nothing seemed to tire me. I could bear any amount of exposure and privation, and I never met the native who was my master in feats of endurance. Of course, all that is different now, I am speaking of my early manhood.

It may be wondered that I did not run absolutely wild in such surroundings, but I was held back from this by my father's society. He was one of the gentlest and most refined men that I ever met; even the most savage Kaffir loved him, and his influence was a very good one for me. He used to call himself one of the world's failures. Would that there were more such failures. Every morning when his work was done he would take his prayer-book and, sitting on the little stoep or verandah of our station, would read the evening psalms to himself. Sometimes there was not light enough for this, but it made no difference, he knew them all by heart. When he had finished he would look out across the cultivated lands where the mission Kaffirs had their huts.

But I knew it was not these he saw, but rather the grey English church, and the graves ranged side by side before the yew near the wicket gate.

It was there on the stoep that he died. He had not been well, and one evening I was talking to him, and his mind went back to Oxfordshire and my mother. He spoke of her a good deal, saying that she had never been out of his mind for a single day during all these years, and that he rejoiced to think he was drawing near that land wither she had gone. Then he asked me if I remembered the night when Squire Carson came into the study at the vicarage, and told him that his wife had run away, and that he was going to change his name and bury himself in some remote land.

I answered that I remembered it perfectly.

"I wonder where he went to," said my father, "and if he and his daughter Stella are still alive. Well, well! I shall never meet them again. But life is a strange thing, Allan, and you may. If you ever do, give them my kind love."

After that I left him. We had been suffering more than usual from the depredations of the Kaffir thieves, who stole our sheep at night, and, as I had done before, and not without success, I determined to watch the kraal and see if I could catch them. Indeed, it was from this habit of mine of watching at night that I first got my native name of Macumazahn, which may be roughly translated as "he who sleeps with one eye open." So I took my rifle and rose to go. But he called me to him and kissed me on the forehead, saying, "God bless you, Allan! I hope that you will think of your old father sometimes, and that you will lead a good and happy life."

I remember that I did not much like his tone at the time, but set it down to an attack of low spirits, to which he grew very subject as the years went on. I went down to the kraal and watched till within an hour of sunrise; then, as no thieves appeared, returned to the station. As I came near I was astonished to see a figure sitting in my father's chair. At first I thought it must be a drunken Kaffir, then that my father had fallen asleep there.

And so he had,—for he was dead!

The Fire-Fight

When I had buried my father, and seen a successor installed in his place—for the station was the property of the Society—I set to work to carry out a plan which I had long cherished, but been unable to execute because it would have involved separation from my father. Put shortly, it was to undertake a trading journey of exploration right through the countries now known as the Free State and the Transvaal, and as much further North as I could go. It was an adventurous scheme, for though the emigrant Boers had begun to occupy positions in these territories, they were still to all practical purposes unexplored. But I was now alone in the world, and it mattered little what became of me; so, driven on by the overmastering love of adventure, which, old as I am, will perhaps still be the cause of my death, I determined to undertake the journey.

Accordingly I sold such stock and goods as we had upon the station, reserving only the two best waggons and two spans of oxen. The proceeds I invested in such goods as were then in fashion, for trading purposes, and in guns and ammunition. The guns would have moved any modern explorer to merriment; but such as they were I managed to do a good deal of execution with them. One of them was a single-barrelled, smooth bore, fitted for percussion caps—a roer we called it—which threw a three-ounce ball, and was charged with a handful of coarse black powder. Many is the elephant that I killed with that roer, although it generally knocked me backwards when I fired it, which I only did under compulsion. The best of the lot, perhaps, was a double-barrelled No. 12 shot-gun, but it had flint locks. Also there were some old tower muskets, which might or might not throw straight at seventy yards. I took six Kaffirs with me, and three good horses, which were supposed to be salted—that is, proof against the sickness. Among the Kaffirs was an old fellow named Indaba-zimbi, which, being translated, means "tongue of iron." I suppose he got this name from his strident voice and exhaustless eloquence. This man was a great character in his way. He had been a noted witch-doctor among a neighbouring tribe, and came to the station under the following circumstances, which, as he plays a considerable part in this history, are perhaps worth recording.

Two years before my father's death I had occasion to search the country round for some lost oxen. After a long and useless quest it occurred to me that I had better go to the place where the oxen were bred by a Kaffir chief, whose name I forget, but whose kraal was about fifty miles from our station. There I journeyed, and found the oxen safe at home. The chief entertained me handsomely, and on the following morning I went to pay my respects to him before leaving, and was somewhat surprised to find a collection of some hundreds of men and women sitting round him anxiously watching the sky in which the thunder-clouds were banking up in a very ominous way.

"You had better wait, white man," said the chief, "and see the rain-doctors fight the lightning."

I inquired what he meant, and learned that this man, Indaba-zimbi, had for some years occupied the position of wizard-in-chief to the tribe, although he was not a member of it, having been born in the country now known as Zululand. But a son of the chief's, a man of about thirty, had lately set up as a rival in supernatural powers. This irritated Indaba-zimbi beyond measure, and a quarrel ensued between the two witch-doctors that resulted in a challenge to trial by lightning being given and accepted. These were the conditions. The rivals must await the coming of a serious thunderstorm, no ordinary tempest would serve their turn. Then, carrying assegais in their hands, they must take their stand within fifty paces of each other upon a certain patch of ground where the big thunderbolts were observed to strike continually, and by the exercise of their occult powers and invocations to the lightning, must strive to avert death from themselves and bring it on their rival. The terms of this singular match had been arranged a month previously, but no storm worthy of the occasion had arisen. Now the local weather-prophets believed it to be brewing.

I inquired what would happen if neither of the men were struck, and was told that they must then wait for another storm. If they escaped the second time, however, they would be held to be equal in power, and be jointly consulted by the tribe upon occasions of importance.

The prospect of being a spectator of so unusual a sight overcame my desire to be gone, and I accepted the chief's invitation to see it out. Before mid-day I regretted it, for though the western heavens grew darker and darker, and the still air heralded the coming of the storm, yet it did not come. By four o'clock, however, it became obvious that it must burst soon—at sunset, the old chief said, and in the company of the whole assembly I moved down to the place of combat. The kraal was built on the top of a hill, and below it the land sloped gently to the banks of a river about half a mile away. On the hither side of the bank was the piece of land that was, the natives said, "loved of the lightning." Here the magicians took up their stand, while the spectators grouped themselves on the hillside about two hundred yards away—which was, I thought, rather too near to be pleasant. When we had sat there for a while my curiosity overcame me, and I asked leave of the chief to go down and inspect the arena. He said I might do so at my own risk. I told him that the fire from above would not hurt white men, and went to find that the spot was a bed of iron ore, thinly covered with grass, which of course accounted for its attracting the lightning from the storms as they travelled along the line of the river. At each end of this iron-stone area were placed the combatants, Indaba-zimbi facing the east, and his rival the west, and before each there burned a little fire made of some scented root. Moreover they were dressed in all the paraphernalia of their craft, snakeskins, fish-bladders, and I know not what beside, while round their necks hung circlets of baboons' teeth and bones from human hands. First I went to the western end where the chief's son stood. He was pointing with his assegai towards the advancing storm, and invoking it in a voice of great excitement.

"Come, fire, and lick up Indaba-zimbi!

"Hear me, Storm Devil, and lick Indaba-zimbi with your red tongue!

"Spit on him with your rain!

"Whirl him away in your breath!

"Make him as nothing—melt the marrow in his bones!

"Run into his heart and burn away the lies!

"Show all the people who is the true Witch Finder!

"Let me not be put to shame in the eyes of this white man!"

Thus he spoke, or rather chanted, and all the while rubbed his broad chest—for he was a very fine man—with some filthy compound of medicine or *mouti*.

After a while, getting tired of his song, I walked across the iron-stone, to where Indaba-zimbi sat by his fire. He was not chanting at all, but his performance was much more impressive. It consisted in staring at the eastern sky, which was perfectly clear of cloud, and every now and again beckoning at it with his finger, then turning round to point with the assegai towards his rival. For a while I looked at him in silence. He was a curious wizened man, apparently over fifty years of age, with thin hands that looked as tough as wire. His nose was much sharper than is usual among these races, and he had a queer habit of holding his head sideways like a bird when he spoke, which, in addition to the humour that lurked in his eye, gave him a most comical appearance. Another strange thing about him was that he had a single white lock of hair among his black wool. At last I spoke to him:

"Indaba-zimbi, my friend," I said, "you may be a good witch-doctor, but you are certainly a fool. It is no good beckoning at the blue sky while your enemy is getting a start with the storm."

"You may be clever, but don't think you know everything, white man," the old fellow answered, in a high, cracked voice, and with something like a grin.

"They call you Iron-tongue," I went on; "you had better use it, or the Storm Devil won't hear you."

"The fire from above runs down iron," he answered, "so I keep my tongue quiet. Oh, yes, let him curse away, I'll put him out presently. Look now, white man."

I looked, and in the eastern sky there grew a cloud. At first it was small, though very black, but it gathered with extraordinary rapidity.

This was odd enough, but as I had seen the same thing happen before it did not particularly astonish me. It is by no means unusual in Africa for two thunderstorms to come up at the same time from different points of the compass.

"You had better get on, Indaba-zimbi," I said, "the big storm is coming along fast, and will soon eat up that baby of yours," and I pointed to the west.

"Babies sometimes grow to giants, white man," said Indaba-zimbi, beckoning away vigorously. "Look now at my cloud-child."

I looked; the eastern storm was spreading itself from earth to sky, and in shape resembled an enormous man. There was its head, its shoulders, and its legs; yes, it was like a huge giant travelling across the heavens. The light of the setting sun escaping from beneath the lower edge of the western storm shot across the intervening space in a sheet of splendour, and, lighting upon the advancing figure of cloud, wrapped its middle in hues of glory too wonderful to be described; but beneath and above this glowing belt his feet and head were black as jet. Presently, as I watched, an awful flash of light shot from the head of the cloud, circled it about as though with a crown of living fire, and vanished.

"Aha," chuckled old Indaba-zimbi, "my little boy is putting on his man's ring," and he tapped the gum ring on his own head, which natives assume when they reach a certain age and dignity. "Now, white man, unless you are a bigger wizard than either of us you had better clear off, for the fire-fight is about to begin."

I thought this sound advice.

"Good luck go with you, my black uncle," I said. "I hope you don't feel the iniquities of a mis-spent life weighing on you at the last."

"You look after yourself, and think of your own sins, young man," he answered, with a grim smile, and taking a pinch of snuff, while at that very moment a flash of lightning, I don't know from which storm, struck the ground within thirty paces of me. That was enough for me, I took to my heels, and as I went I heard old Indaba-zimbi's dry chuckle of amusement.

I climbed the hill till I came to where the chief was sitting with his indunas, or headmen, and sat down near to him. I looked at the man's face and saw that he was intensely anxious for his son's safety, and by no means confident of the young man's powers to resist the magic of Indaba-zimbi. He was talking in a low voice to the induna next to him. I affected to take no notice and to be concentrating my attention on the novel scene before me; but in those days I had very quick ears, and caught the drift of the conversation.

"Hearken!" the chief was saying, "if the magic of Indaba-zimbi prevails against my son I will endure him no more. Of this I am sure, that when he has slain my son he will slay me, me also, and make himself chief in my place. I fear Indaba-zimbi. *Ou!*"

"Black One," answered the induna, "wizards die as dogs die, and, once dead, dogs bark no more."

"And once dead," said the chiefs, "wizards work no more spells," and he bent and whispered in the induna's ear, looking at the assegai in his hand as he whispered.

"Good, my father, good!" said the induna, presently. "It shall be done to-night, if the lightning does not do it first."

"A bad look-out for old Indaba-zimbi," I said to myself. "They mean to kill him." Then I thought no more of the matter for a while, the scene before me was too tremendous.

The two storms were rapidly rushing together. Between them was a gulf of blue sky, and from time to time flashes of blinding light passed across this gulf, leaping from cloud to cloud. I remember that they reminded me of the story of the heathen god Jove and his thunderbolts. The storm that was shaped like a giant and ringed with the glory of the sinking sun made an excellent Jove, and I am sure that the bolts which leapt from it could not have been surpassed even in mythological times. Oddly enough, as yet the flashes were not followed by thunder. A deadly stillness lay upon the place, the cattle stood silently on the hillside, even the natives were awed to silence. Dark shadows crept along the bosom of the hills, the river to the right and left was hidden in wreaths of cloud, but before us and beyond the combatants it shone like a line of silver beneath the narrowing space of open sky. Now the western tempest was scrawled all over with lines of intolerable light, while the inky head of the cloud-giant to the east was continually suffused with a white and deadly glow that came and went in pulses, as though a blood of flame was being pumped into it from the heart of the storm.

The silence deepened and deepened, the shadows grew blacker and blacker, then suddenly all nature began to moan beneath the breath of an icy wind. On sped the wind; the smooth surface of the river was ruffled by it into little waves, the tall grass bowed low before it, and in its wake came the hissing sound of furious rain.

Ah! the storms had met. From each there burst an awful blaze of dazzling flame, and now the hill on which we sat rocked at the noise of the following thunder. The light went out of the sky, darkness fell suddenly on the land, but not for long. Presently the whole landscape grew vivid in the flashes, it appeared and disappeared, now everything was visible for miles, now even the men at my side vanished in the blackness. The thunder rolled and cracked and pealed like the trump of doom, whirlwinds tore round, lifting dust and even stones high into the air, and in a low, continuous undertone rose the hiss of the rushing rain.

I put my hand before my eyes to shield them from the terrible glare, and looked beneath it towards the lists of iron-stone. As flash followed flash, from time to time I caught sight of the two wizards. They were slowly advancing towards one another, each pointing at his foe with the assegai in his hand. I could see their every movement, and it seemed to me that the chain lightning was striking the iron-stone all round them.

Suddenly the thunder and lightning ceased for a minute, everything grew black, and, except for the rain, silent.

"It is over one way or the other, chief," I called out into the darkness.

"Wait, white man, wait!" answered the chief, in a voice thick with anxiety and fear.

Hardly were the words out of his mouth when the heavens were lit up again till they literally seemed to flame. There were the men, not ten paces apart. A great flash fell between them, I saw them stagger beneath the shock. Indaba-zimbi recovered himself first—at any rate when the next flash came he was standing bolt upright, pointing with his assegai towards his enemy. The chief's son was still on his legs, but he was staggering like a drunken man, and the assegai had fallen from his hand.

Darkness! then again a flash, more fearful, if possible, than any that had gone before. To me it seemed to come from the east, right over the head of Indaba-zimbi. At that instant I saw the chief's son wrapped, as it were, in the heart of it. Then the thunder pealed, the rain burst over us like a torrent, and I saw no more.

The worst of the storm was done, but for a while the darkness was so dense that we could not move, nor, indeed, was I inclined to leave the safety of the hillside where the lightning was never known to strike, and venture down to the iron-stone. Occasionally there still came flashes, but, search as we would, we could see no trace of either of the wizards. For my part, I believed that they were both dead. Now the clouds slowly rolled away down the course of the river, and with them went the rain; and now the stars shone in their wake.

"Let us go and see," said the old chief, rising and shaking the water from his hair. "The fire-fight is ended, let us go and see who has conquered."

I rose and followed him, dripping as though I had swum a hundred yards with my clothes on, and after me came all the people of the kraal.

We reached the spot; even in that light I could see where the iron-stone had been split and fused by the thunderbolts. While I was staring about me, I suddenly heard the chief, who was on my right, give a low moan, and saw the people cluster round him. I went up and looked. There, on the ground, lay the body of his son. It was a dreadful sight. The hair was burnt off his head, the copper rings upon his arms were fused, the assegai handle which lay near was literally shivered into threads, and, when I took hold of his arm, it seemed to me that every bone of it was broken.

The men with the chief stood gazing silently, while the women wailed.

"Great is the magic of Indaba-zimbi!" said a man, at length. The chief turned and struck him a heavy blow with the kerrie in his hand.

"Great or not, thou dog, he shall die," he cried, "and so shalt thou if thou singest his praises so loudly."

I said nothing, but thinking it probable that Indaba-zimbi had shared the fate of his enemy, I went to look. But I could see nothing of him, and at length, being thoroughly chilled with the wet, started back to my waggon to change my clothes. On reaching it, I was rather surprised to see a strange Kaffir seated on the driving-box wrapped up in a blanket.

"Hullo! come out of that," I said.

The figure on the box slowly unrolled the blanket, and with great deliberation took a pinch of snuff.

"It was a good fire-fight, white man, was it not—" said Indaba-zimbi, in his high, cracked voice. "But he never had a chance against me, poor boy. He knew nothing about it. See, white man, what becomes of presumption in the young. It is sad, very sad, but I made the flashes fly, didn't I?"

"You old humbug," I said, "unless you are careful you will soon learn what comes of presumption in the old, for your chief is after you with an assegai, and it will take all your magic to dodge that."

"Now you don't say so," said Indaba-zimbi, clambering off the waggon with rapidity; "and all because of this wretched upstart. There's gratitude for you, white man. I expose him, and they want to kill me. Well, thank you for the hint. We shall meet again before long," and he was gone like a shot, and not too soon, for just then some of the chief's men came up to the waggon.

On the following morning I started homewards. The first face I saw on arriving at the station was that of Indaba-zimbi.

"How do you do, Macumazahn?" he said, holding his head on one side and nodding his white lock. "I hear you are Christians here, and I want to try a new religion. Mine must be a bad one seeing that my people wanted to kill me for exposing an impostor."

Northwards

I make no apology to myself, or to anybody who may happen to read this narrative in future, for having set out the manner of my meeting with Indaba-zimbi: first, because it was curious, and secondly, because he takes some hand in the subsequent events. If that old man was a humbug, he was a very clever one. What amount of truth there was in his pretensions to supernatural powers it is not for me to determine, though I may have my own opinion on the subject. But there was no mistake as to the extraordinary influence he exercised over his fellow-natives. Also he quite got round my poor father. At first the old gentleman declined to have him at the station, for he had a great horror of these Kaffir wizards or witch-finders. But Indaba-zimbi persuaded him that he was anxious to investigate the truths of Christianity, and challenged him to a discussion. The argument lasted two years—to the time of my father's death, indeed. At the conclusion of each stage Indaba-zimbi would remark, in the words of the Roman Governor, "Almost, praying white man, thou persuadest me to become a Christian," but he never quite became one—indeed, I do not think he ever meant to. It was to him that my father addressed his "Letters to a Native Doubter." This work, which, unfortunately, remains in manuscript, is full of wise saws and learned instances. It ought to be published together with a *précis* of the doubter's answers, which were verbal.

So the talk went on. If my father had lived I believe it would be going on now, for both the disputants were quite inexhaustible. Meanwhile Indaba-zimbi was allowed to live on the station on condition that he practised no witchcraft, which my father firmly believed to be a wile of the devil. He said that he would not, but for all that there was never an ox lost, or a sudden death, but he was consulted by those interested.

When he had been with us a year, a deputation came to him from the tribe he had left, asking him to return. Things had not gone well with them since he went away, they said, and now the chief, his enemy, was dead. Old Indaba-zimbi listened to them till they had done, and, as he listened, raked sand into a little heap with his toes. Then he spoke, pointing to the little heap, "There is your tribe to-day," he said. Then he lifted his heel and stamped the heap flat. "There is your tribe before three moons are gone. Nothing is left of it. You drove me away: I will have no more to do with you; but when you are being killed think of my words."

The messengers went. Three months afterwards I heard that the whole community had been wiped out by an Impi of raiding Pondos.

When I was at length ready to start upon my expedition, I went to old Indaba-zimbi to say good-bye to him, and was rather surprised to find him engaged in rolling up medicine, assegais, and other sundries in his blankets.

"Good-bye, Indaba-zimbi," I said, "I am going to trek north."

"Yes, Macumazahn," he answered, with his head on one side; "and so am I—I want to see that country. We will go together."

"Will we!" I said; "wait till you are asked, you old humbug."

"You had better ask me, then, Macumazahn, for if you don't you will never come back alive. Now that the old chief (my father) is gone to where the storms come from," and he nodded to the sky, "I feel myself getting into bad habits again. So last night I just threw up the bones and worked out about your journey, and I can tell you this, that if you don't take me you will die, and, what is more, you will lose one who is dearer to you than life in a strange fashion. So just because you gave me that hint a couple of years ago, I made up my mind to come with you."

"Don't talk stuff to me," I said.

"Ah, very well, Macumazahn, very well; but what happened to my own people six months ago, and what did I tell the messengers would happen? They drove me away, and they are gone. If you drive me away you will soon be gone too," and he nodded his white lock at me and smiled. Now I was not more superstitious than other people, but somehow old Indaba-zimbi impressed me. Also I knew his extraordinary influence over every class of native, and bethought me that he might be useful in that way.

"All right," I said: "I appoint you witch-finder to the expedition without pay."

"First serve, then ask for wages," he answered. "I am glad to see that you have enough imagination not to be altogether a fool, like most white men, Macumazahn. Yes, yes, it is want of imagination that makes people fools; they won't believe what they can't understand. You can't understand my prophecies any more than the fool at the kraal could understand that I was his master with the lightning. Well, it is time to trek, but if I were you, Macumazahn, I should take one waggon, not two."

"Why?" I said.

"Because you will lose your waggons, and it is better to lose one than two."

"Oh, nonsense!" I said.

"All right, Macumazahn, live and learn." And without another word he walked to the foremost waggon, put his bundle into it, and climbed on to the front seat.

So having bid an affectionate adieu to my white friends, including the old Scotchman who got drunk in honour of the event, and quoted Burns till the tears ran down his face, at length I started, and travelled slowly northwards. For the first three weeks nothing very particular befell me. Such Kaffirs as we came in contact with were friendly, and game literally swarmed. Nobody living in those parts of South Africa nowadays can have the remotest idea of what the veldt was like even thirty years ago.

Often and often I have crept shivering on to my waggon-box just as the sun rose and looked out. At first one would see nothing but a vast field of white mist suffused towards the east by a tremulous golden glow, through which the tops of stony koppies stood up like gigantic beacons. From the dense mist would come strange sounds—snorts, gruntings, bellows, and the thunder of countless hoofs. Presently this great curtain would grow thinner, then it would melt, as the smoke from a pipe melts into the air, and for miles on miles the wide rolling country interspersed with bush opened to the view. But it was not tenantless as it is now, for as far as the eye could reach it would be literally black with game. Here to the right might be a herd of vilderbeeste that could not number less than two thousand. Some were grazing, some gambolled, whisking their white tails into the air, while all round the old bulls stood upon hillocks sniffing suspiciously at the breeze. There, in front, a hundred yards away, though to the unpractised eye they looked much closer, because of the dazzling clearness of the atmosphere, was a great herd of springbok trekking along in single file. Ah, they have come to the waggon-track and do not like the look of it. What will they do?—go back? Not a bit of it. It is nearly thirty feet wide, but that is nothing to a springbok. See, the first of them bounds into the air like a ball. How beautifully the sunshine gleams upon his golden hide! He has cleared it, and the others come after him in numberless succession, all except the fawns, who cannot jump so far, and have to scamper over the doubtful path with a terrified *bah*. What is that yonder, moving above the tops of the mimosa, in the little dell at the foot of the koppie? Giraffes, by George! three of them; there will be marrow-bones for supper to-night. Hark! the ground shakes behind us, and over the brow of the rise rush a vast herd of blesbock. On they come at full gallop, their long heads held low, they look like so many bearded goats. I thought so—behind them is a pack of wild dogs, their fur draggled, their tongues lolling. They are in full cry; the giraffes hear them and are away, rolling round the koppie like a ship in a heavy sea. No marrow-bones after all. See! the foremost dogs are close on a buck. He has galloped far and is outworn. One springs at his flank and misses him. The buck gives a kind of groan, looks wildly round and sees the waggon. He seems to hesitate a moment, then in his despair rushes up to it, and falls exhausted among the oxen. The dogs pull up some thirty paces away, panting and snarling. Now, boy, the gun—no, not the rifle, the shot-gun loaded with loopers.

Bang! bang! there, my friends, two of you will never hunt buck again. No, don't touch the buck, for he has come to us for shelter, and he shall have it.

Ah, how beautiful is nature before man comes to spoil it!

Such a sight as this have I seen many a hundred times, and I hope to see it again before I die.

The first real adventure that befell me on this particular journey was with elephants, which I will relate because of its curious termination. Just before we crossed the Orange River we came to a stretch of forest-land some twenty miles broad. The night we entered this forest we camped in a lovely open glade. A few yards ahead tambouki grass was growing to the height of a man, or rather it had been; now, with the exception of a few stalks here and there, it was crushed quite flat. It was already dusk when we camped; but after the moon got up I walked from the fire to see how this had happened. One glance was enough for me; a great herd of elephants had evidently passed over the tall grass not many hours before. The sight of their spoor rejoiced me exceedingly, for though I had seen wild elephants, at that time I had never shot one. Moreover, the sight of elephant spoor to the African hunter is what "colour in the pan" is to the prospector of gold. It is by the ivory that he lives, and to shoot it or trade it is his chief aim in life. My resolution was soon taken. I would camp the waggons for a while in the forest, and start on horseback after the elephants.

I communicated my decision to Indaba-zimbi and the other Kaffirs. The latter were not loth, for your Kaffir loves hunting, which means plenty of meat and congenial occupation, but Indaba-zimbi would express no opinion. I saw him retire to a little fire that he had lit for himself, and go through some mysterious performances with bones and clay mixed with ashes, which were watched with the greatest interest by the other Kaffirs. At length he rose, and, coming forward, informed me that it was all right, and that I did well to go and hunt the elephants, as I should get plenty of ivory; but he advised me to go on foot. I said I should do nothing of the sort, but meant to ride. I am wiser now; this was the first and last time that I ever attempted to hunt elephants on horseback.

Accordingly we started at dawn, I, Indaba-zimbi, and three men; the rest I left with the waggons. I was on horseback, and so was my driver, a good rider and a skilful shot for a Kaffir, but Indaba-zimbi and the others walked. From dawn till mid-day we followed the trail of the herd, which was as plain as a high road. Then we off-saddled to let the horses rest and feed, and about three o'clock started on again. Another hour or so passed, and still there was no sign of elephants. Evidently the herd had travelled fast and far, and I began to think that we should have to give it up, when suddenly I caught sight of a brown mass moving through the thorn-trees on the side of a slope about a quarter of a mile away. My heart seemed to jump into my mouth. Where is the hunter who has not felt like this at the sight of his first elephant?

I called a halt, and then the wind being right, we set to work to stalk the bull. Very quietly I rode down the hither side of the slope till we came to the bottom, which was densely covered with bush. Here I saw the elephants had been feeding, for broken branches and upturned trees lay all about. I did not take much notice, however, for all my thoughts were fixed upon the bull I was stalking, when suddenly my horse gave a violent start that nearly threw me from the saddle, and there came a mighty rush and upheaval of something in front of me. I looked: there was the hinder part of a second bull elephant not four yards off. I could just catch sight of its outstretched ears projecting on either side. I had disturbed it sleeping, and it was running away.

Obviously the best thing to do would have been to let it run, but I was young in those days and foolish, and in the excitement of the moment I lifted my "roer" or elephant gun and fired at the great brute over my horse's head. The recoil of the heavy gun nearly knocked me off the horse. I recovered myself, however, and, as I did so, saw the bull lurch forward, for the impact of a three-ounce bullet in the flank will quicken the movement even of an elephant. By this time I had realized the folly of the shot, and devoutly hoped that the bull would take no further notice of it. But he took a different view of the matter. Pulling himself up in a series of plunges, he spun round and came for me with outstretched ears and uplifted trunk, screaming terribly. I was quite defenceless, for my gun was empty, and my first thought was of escape. I dug my heels into the sides of my horse, but he would not move an inch. The poor animal was paralyzed with terror, and he simply stood still, his fore-legs outstretched, and quivering all over like a leaf.

On rushed the elephant, awful to see; I made one more vain effort to stir the horse. Now the trunk of the great bull swung aloft above my head. A thought flashed through my brain. Quick as light I rolled from the saddle. By the side of the horse lay a fallen tree, as thick through as a man's body. The tree was lifted a little off the ground by the broken boughs which took its weight, and with a single movement, so active is one in such necessities, I flung myself beneath it. As I did so, I heard the trunk of the elephant descend with a mighty thud on the back of my poor horse, and the next instant I was almost in darkness, for the horse, whose back was broken, fell over across the tree under which I lay ensconced. But he did not stop there long. In ten seconds more the bull had wound his trunk about my dead nag's neck, and, with a mighty effort, hurled him clear of the tree. I wriggled backwards as far as I could towards the roots of the tree, for I knew what he was after. Presently I saw the red tip of the bull's trunk stretching itself towards me. If he could manage to hook it round any part of me I was lost. But in the position I occupied, that was just what he could not do, although he knelt down to facilitate his operations. On came the snapping tip like a great open-mouthed snake; it closed upon my hat, which vanished. Again it was thrust down, and a scream of rage was bellowed through it within four inches of my head. Now it seemed to elongate itself. Oh, heavens! now it had me by the hair, which, luckily for myself, was not very long. Then it was my turn to scream, for next instant half a square inch of hair was dragged from my scalp by the roots. I was being plucked alive, as I have seen cruel Kaffir kitchen boys pluck a fowl.

The elephant, however, disappointed with these moderate results, changed his tactics. He wound his trunk round the fallen tree and lifted. The tree stirred, but fortunately the broken branches embedded in the spongy soil, and some roots, which still held, prevented it from being turned over, though he lifted it so much that, had it occurred to him, he could now easily have drawn me out with his trunk. Again he hoisted with all his mighty strength, and I saw that the tree was coming, and roared aloud for help. Some shots were fired close by in answer, but if they hit the bull, their only effect was to stir his energies to more active life. In another few seconds my shelter would be torn away, and I should be done for. A cold perspiration burst out over me as I realized that I was lost. Then of a sudden I remembered that I had a pistol in my belt, which I often used for despatching wounded game. It was loaded and capped. By this time the tree was lifted so much that I could easily get my hand down to my middle and draw the pistol from its case. I drew and cocked it. Now the tree was coming over, and there, within three feet of my head, was the great brown trunk of the elephant. I placed the muzzle of the pistol within an inch of it and fired. The result was instantaneous. Down sunk the tree again, giving one of my legs a considerable squeeze, and next instant I heard a crashing sound. The elephant had bolted.

By this time, what between fright and struggling, I was pretty well tired. I cannot remember how I got from under the fallen tree, or indeed anything, until I found myself sitting on the ground drinking some peach brandy from a flask, and old Indaba-zimbi opposite to me nodding his white lock sagely, while he fired off moral reflections on the narrowness of my escape, and my unwisdom in not having taken his advice to go on foot. That reminded me of my horse—I got up and went to look at it. It was quite dead, the blow of the elephant's trunk had fallen on the saddle, breaking the framework, and rendering it useless. I reflected that in another two seconds it would have fallen on *me*. Then I called to Indaba-zimbi and asked which way the elephants had gone.

"There!" he said, pointing down the gully, "and we had better go after them, Macumazahn. We have had the bad luck, now for the good."

There was philosophy in this, though, to tell the truth, I did not feel particularly sharp set on elephants at the moment. I seemed to have had enough of them. However, it would never do to show the white feather before the boys, so I assented with much outward readiness, and we started, I on the second horse, and the others on foot. When we had travelled for the best part of an hour down the valley, all of a sudden we came upon the whole herd, which numbered a little more than eighty. Just in front of them the bush was so thick that they seemed to hesitate about entering it, and the sides of the valley were so rocky and steep at this point that they could not climb them.

They saw us at the same moment as we saw them, and inwardly I was filled with fears lest they should take it into their heads to charge back up the gully. But they did not; trumpeting aloud, they rushed at the thick bush which went down before them like corn before a sickle. I do not think that in all my experiences I ever heard anything to equal the sound they made as they crashed through and over the shrubs and trees. Before them was a dense forest belt from a hundred to a hundred and fifty feet in width. As they rushed on, it fell, so that behind them was nothing but a level roadway strewed with fallen trunks, crushed branches, and here and there a tree, too strong even for them, left stranded amid the wreck. On they went, and, notwithstanding the nature of the ground over which they had to travel, they kept their distance ahead of us. This sort of thing continued for a mile or more, and then I saw that in front of the elephants the valley opened into a space covered with reeds and grass—it might have been five or six acres in extent—beyond which the valley ran on again.

The herd reached the edge of this expanse, and for a moment pulled up, hesitating—evidently they mistrusted it. My men yelled aloud, as only Kaffirs can, and that settled them. Headed by the wounded bull, whose martial ardour, like my own, was somewhat cooled, they spread out and dashed into the treacherous swamp—for such it was, though just then there was no water to be seen. For a few yards all went well with them, though they clearly found it heavy going; then suddenly the great bull sank up to his belly in the stiff peaty soil, and remained fixed. The others, mad with fear, took no heed of his struggles and trumpetings, but plunged on to meet the same fate. In five minutes the whole herd of them were hopelessly bogged, and the more they struggled to escape, the deeper they sunk. There was one exception, indeed, a cow managed to win back to firm shore, and, lifting her trunk, prepared to charge us as we came up. But at that moment she heard the scream of her calf, and rushed back to its assistance, only to be bogged with the others.

Such a scene I never saw before or since. The swamp was spotted all over with the large forms of the elephants, and the air rang with their screams of rage and terror as they waved their trunks wildly to and fro. Now and then a monster would make a great effort and drag his mass from its peaty bed, only to stick fast again at the next step. It was a most pitiable sight, though one that gladdened the hearts of my men. Even the best natives have little compassion for the sufferings of animals.

Well, the rest was easy. The marsh that would not bear the elephants carried our weight well enough. Before midnight all were dead, for we shot them by moonlight. I would gladly have spared the young ones and some of the cows, but to do so would only have meant leaving them to perish of hunger; it was kinder to kill them at once. The wounded bull I slew with my own hand, and I cannot say that I felt much compunction in so doing. He knew me again, and made a desperate effort to get at me, but I am glad to say that the peat held him fast.

The pan presented a curious sight when the sun rose next morning. Owing to the support given by the soil, few of the dead elephants had fallen: there they stood as though they were asleep.

I sent back for the waggons, and when they arrived on the morrow, formed a camp, about a mile away from the pan. Then began the work of cutting out the elephants' tusks; it took over a week, and for obvious reasons was a disgusting task. Indeed, had it not been for the help of some wandering bushmen, who took their pay in elephant meat, I do not think we could ever have managed it.

At last it was done. The ivory was far too cumbersome for us to carry, so we buried it, having first got rid of our bushmen allies. My boys wanted me to go back to the Cape with it and sell it, but I was too much bent on my journey to do this. The tusks lay buried for five years. Then I came and dug them up; they were but little harmed. Ultimately I sold the ivory for something over twelve hundred pounds—not bad pay for one day's shooting.

This was how I began my career as an elephant hunter. I have shot many hundreds of them since, but have never again attempted to do so on horseback.

The Zulu Impi

After burying the elephant tusks, and having taken careful notes of the bearings and peculiarities of the country so that I might be able to find the spot again, we proceeded on our journey. For a month or more I trekked along the line which now divides the Orange Free State from Griqualand West, and the Transvaal from Bechuanaland. The only difficulties met with were such as are still common to African travellers—occasional want of water and troubles about crossing sluits and rivers. I remember that I outspanned on the spot where Kimberley now stands, and had to press on again in a hurry because there was no water. I little dreamed then that I should live to see Kimberley a great city producing millions of pounds worth of diamonds annually, and old Indaba-zimbi's magic cannot have been worth so much after all, or he would have told me.

I found the country almost entirely depopulated. Not very long before Mosilikatze the Lion, Chaka's General had swept across it in his progress towards what is now Matabeleland. His footsteps were evident enough. Time upon time I trekked up to what had evidently been the sites of Kaffir kraals. Now the kraals were ashes and piles of tumbled stones, and strewn about among the rank grass were the bones of hundreds of men, women, and children, all of whom had kissed the Zulu assegai. I remember that in one of these desolate places I found the skull of a child in which a ground-lark had built its nest. It was the twittering of the young birds inside that first called my attention to it. Shortly after this we met with our second great adventure, a much more serious and tragic one than the first.

We were trekking parallel with the Kolong river when a herd of blesbock crossed the track. I fired at one of them and hit it behind. It galloped about a hundred yards with the rest of the herd, then lay down. As we were in want of meat, not having met with any game for a few days past, I jumped on to my horse, and, telling Indaba-zimbi that I would overtake the waggons or meet them on the further side of a rise about an hour's trek away, I started after the wounded buck. As soon as I came within a hundred yards of it, however, it jumped up and ran away as fast as though it were untouched, only to lie down again at a distance. I followed, thinking that strength would soon fail it. This happened three times. On the third occasion it vanished behind a ridge, and, though by now I was out of both temper and patience, I thought I might as well ride to the crest and see if I could get a shot at it on the further side.

I reached the ridge, which was strewn with stones, looked over it, and saw—a Zulu Impi!

I rubbed my eyes and looked again. Yes, there was no doubt of it. They were halted about a thousand yards away, by the water; some were lying down, some were cooking at fires, others were stalking about with spears and shields in their hands; there might have been two thousand or more of them in all. While I was wondering—and that with no little uneasiness—what on earth they could be doing there, suddenly I heard a wild cry to the right and left of me. I glanced first one way, then the other. From either side a great Zulu was bearing down on me, their broad stabbing assegais aloft, and black shields in their left hands. The man to the right was about fifteen yards away, he to the left was not more than ten. On they came, their fierce eyes almost starting out of their heads, and I felt, with a cold thrill of fear, that in another three seconds those broad "bangwans" might be buried in my vitals. On such occasions we act, I suppose, more from instinct than from anything else—there is no time for thought. At any rate, I dropped the reins and, raising my gun, fired point blank at the left-hand man. The bullet struck him in the middle of his shield, pierced it, and passed through him, and over he rolled upon the veldt. I swung round in the saddle; most happily my horse was accustomed to standing still when I fired from his back, also he was so surprised that he did not know which way to shy. The other savage was almost on me; his outstretched shield reached the muzzle of my gun as I pulled the trigger of the left barrel. It exploded, the warrior sprung high into the air, and fell against my horse dead, his spear passing just in front of my face.

Without waiting to reload, or even to look if the main body of the Zulus had seen the death of their two scouts, I turned my horse and drove my heels into his sides. As soon as I was down the slope of the rise I pulled a little to the right in order to intercept the waggons before the Zulus saw them. I had not gone three hundred yards in this new direction when, to my utter astonishment, I struck a trail marked with waggon-wheels and the hoofs of oxen. Of waggons there must have been at least eight, and several hundred cattle. Moreover, they had passed within twelve hours; I could tell that by the spoor. Then I understood; the Impi was following the track of the waggons, which, in all probability, belonged to a party of emigrant Boers.

The spoor of the waggons ran in the direction I wished to go, so I followed it. About a mile further on I came to the crest of a rise, and there, about five furlongs away, I saw the waggons drawn up in a rough laager upon the banks of the river. There, too, were my own waggons trekking down the slope towards them.

In another five minutes I was there. The Boers—for Boers they were—were standing about outside the little laager watching the approach of my two waggons. I called to them, and they turned and saw me. The very first man my eyes fell on was a Boer named Hans Botha, whom I had known well years ago in the Cape. He was not a bad specimen of his class, but a very restless person, with a great objection to authority, or, as he expressed it, "a love of freedom." He had joined a party of the emigrant Boers some years before, but, as I learned presently, had quarrelled with its leader, and was now trekking away into the wilderness to found a little colony of his own. Poor fellow! It was his last trek.

"How do you do, Meinheer Botha?" I said to him in Dutch.

The man looked at me, looked again, then, startled out of his Dutch stolidity, cried to his wife, who was seated on the box of the waggon?

"Come here, Frau, come. Here is Allan Quatermain, the Englishman, the son of the 'Predicant.' How goes it, Heer Quatermain, and what is the news down in the Cape yonder?"

"I don't know what the news is in the Cape, Hans," I answered, solemnly; "but the news here is that there is a Zulu Impi upon your spoor and within two miles of the waggons. That I know, for I have just shot two of their sentries," and I showed him my empty gun.

For a moment there was a silence of astonishment, and I saw the bronzed faces of the men turn pale beneath their tan, while one or two of the women gave a little scream, and the children crept to their sides.

"Almighty!" cried Hans, "that must be the Umtetwa Regiment that Dingaan sent against the Basutus, but who could not come at them because of the marshes, and so were afraid to return to Zululand, and struck north to join Mosilikatze."

"Laager up, Carles! Laager up for your lives, and one of you jump on a horse and drive in the cattle."

At this moment my own waggons came up. Indaba-zimbi was sitting on the box of the first, wrapped in a blanket. I called him and told him the news.

"Ill tidings, Macumazahn," he said; "there will be dead Boers about to-morrow morning, but they will not attack till dawn, then they will wipe out the laager *so!*" and he passed his hand before his mouth.

"Stop that croaking, you white-headed crow," I said, though I knew his words were true. What chance had a laager of ten waggons all told against at least two thousand of the bravest savages in the world?

"Macumazahn, will you take my advice this time?" Indaba-zimbi said, presently.

"What is it?" I asked.

"This. Leave your waggons here, jump on that horse, and let us two run for it as hard as we can go. The Zulus won't follow us, they will be looking after the Boers."

"I won't leave the other white men," I said; "it would be the act of a coward. If I die, I die."

"Very well, Macumazahn, then stay and be killed," he answered, taking a pinch of snuff. "Come, let us see about the waggons," and we walked towards the laager.

Here everything was in confusion. However, I got hold of Hans Botha and put it to him if it would not be best to desert the waggons and make a run for it.

"How can we do it?" he answered; "two of the women are too fat to go a mile, one is sick in childbed, and we have only six horses among us. Besides, if we did we should starve in the desert. No, Heer Allan, we must fight it out with the savages, and God help us!"

"God help us, indeed. Think of the children, Hans!"

"I can't bear to think," he answered, in a broken voice, looking at his own little girl, a sweet, curly-haired, blue-eyed child of six, named Tota, whom I had often nursed as a baby. "Oh, Heer Allan, your father, the Predicant, always warned me against trekking north, and I never would listen to him because I thought him a cursed Englishman; now I see my folly. Heer Allan, if you can, try to save my child from those black devils; if you live longer than I do, or if you can't save her, kill her," and he clasped my hand.

"It hasn't come to that yet, Hans," I said.

Then we set to work on the laager. The waggons, of which, including my two, there were ten, were drawn into the form of a square, and the disselboom of each securely lashed with reims to the underworks of that in front of it. The wheels also were locked, and the space between the ground and the bed-planks of the waggons was stuffed with branches of the "wait-a-bit" thorn that fortunately grew near in considerable quantities. In this way a barrier was formed of no mean strength as against a foe unprovided with firearms, places being left for the men to fire from. In a little over an hour everything was done that could be done, and a discussion arose as to the disposal of the cattle, which had been driven up close to the camp. Some of the Boers were anxious to get them into the laager, small as it was, or at least as many of them as it would hold. I argued strongly against this, pointing out that the brutes would probably be seized with panic as soon as the firing began, and trample the defenders of the laager under foot. As an alternative plan I suggested that some of the native servants should drive the herd along the valley of the river till they reached a friendly tribe or some other place of safety. Of course, if the Zulus saw them they would be taken, but the nature of the ground was favourable, and it was possible that they might escape if they started at once. The proposition was promptly agreed to, and, what is more, it was settled that one Dutchman and such of the women and children as could travel should go with them. In half an hour's time twelve of them started with the natives, the Boer in charge, and the cattle. Three of my own men went with the latter, the three others and Indaba-zimbi stopped with me in the laager.

The parting was a heart-breaking scene, upon which I do not care to dwell. The women wept, the men groaned, and the children looked on with scared white faces. At length they were gone, and I for one was thankful of it. There remained in the laager seventeen white men, four natives, the two Boer fraus who were too stout to travel, the woman in childbed and her baby, and Hans Bother's little daughter Tota, whom he could not make up his mind to part with. Happily her mother was already dead. And here I may state that ten of the women and children, together with about half of the cattle, escaped. The Zulu Impi never saw them, and on the third day of travel they came to the fortified place of a Griqua chief, who sheltered them on receiving half the cattle in payment. Thence by slow degrees they journeyed down to the Cape Colony, reaching a civilized region within a little more than a year from the date of the attack on the laager.

The afternoon was now drawing towards evening, but still there were no signs of the Impi. A wild hope struck us that they might have gone on about their business. Ever since Indaba-zimbi had heard that the regiment was supposed to belong to the Umtetwa tribe, he had, I noticed, been plunged in deep thought. Presently he came to me and volunteered to go out and spy upon their movements. At first Hans Botha was against this idea, saying that he was a "verdomde swartzel"—an accursed black creature—and would betray us. I pointed out that there was nothing to betray. The Zulus must know where the waggons were, but it was important for us to gain information of their movements. So it was agreed that Indaba-zimbi should go. I told him this. He nodded his white lock, said "All right, Macumazahn," and started. I noticed with some surprise, however, that before he did so he went to the waggon and fetched his "mouti," or medicine, which, together with his other magical apparatus, he always carried in a skin bag. I asked him why he did this. He answered that it was to make himself invulnerable against the spears of the Zulus. I did not in the least believe his explanation, for in my heart I was sure that he meant to take the opportunity to make a bolt of it, leaving me to my fate. I did not, however, interfere to prevent this, for I had an affection for the old fellow, and sincerely hoped that he might escape the doom which overshadowed us.

So Indaba-zimbi sauntered off, and as I looked at his retreating form I thought I should never see it again. But I was mistaken, and little knew that he was risking his life, not for the Boers whom he hated one and all, but for me whom in his queer way he loved.

When he had gone we completed our preparations for defence, strengthening the waggons and the thorns beneath with earth and stones. Then at sunset we ate and drank as heartily as we could under the circumstances, and when we had done, Hans Botha, as head of the party, offered up prayer to God for our preservation. It was a touching sight to see the burly Dutchman, his hat off, his broad face lit up by the last rays of the setting sun, praying aloud in homely, simple language to Him who alone could save us from the spears of a cruel foe. I remember that the last sentence of his prayer was, "Almighty, if we must be killed, save the women and children and my little girl Tota from the accursed Zulus, and do not let us be tortured."

I echoed the request very earnestly in my own heart, that I know, for in common with the others I was dreadfully afraid, and it must be admitted not without reason.

Then the darkness came on, and we took up our appointed places each with a rifle in his hands and peered out into the gloom in silence. Occasionally one of the Boers would light his pipe with a brand from the smouldering fire, and the glow of it would shine for a few moments on his pale, anxious face.

Behind me one of the stout "fraus" lay upon the ground. Even the terror of our position could not keep her heavy eyes from their accustomed sleep, and she snored loudly. On the further side of her, just by the fire, lay little Tota, wrapped in a kaross. She was asleep also, her thumb in her mouth, and from time to time her father would come to look at her.

So the hours wore on while we waited for the Zulus. But from my intimate knowledge of the habits of natives I had little fear that they would attack us at night, though, had they done so, they could have compassed our destruction with but small loss to themselves. It is not the habit of this people, they like to fight in the light of day—at dawn for preference.

About eleven o'clock, just as I was nodding a little at my post, I heard a low whistle outside the laager. Instantly I was wide awake, and all along the line I heard the clicking of locks as the Boers cocked their guns.

"Macumazahn," said a voice, the voice of Indaba-zimbi, "are you there?"

"Yes," I answered.

"Then hold a light so that I can see how to climb into the laager," he said.

"Yah! yah! hold a light," put in one of the Boers. "I don't trust that black schepsel of yours, Heer Quatermain; he may have some of his countrymen with him." Accordingly a lantern was produced and held towards the voice. There was Indaba-zimbi alone. We let him into the laager and asked him the news.

"This is the news, white men," he said. "I waited till dark, and creeping up to the place where the Zulus are encamped, hid myself behind a stone and listened. They are a great regiment of Umtetwas as Baas Botha yonder thought. They struck the spoor of the waggons three days ago and followed it. To-night they sleep upon their spears, to-morrow at daybreak they will attack the laager and kill everybody. They are very bitter against the Boers, because of the battle at Blood River and the other fights, and that is why they followed the waggons instead of going straight north after Mosilikatze."

A kind of groan went up from the group of listening Dutchmen.

"I tell you what it is, Heeren," I said, "instead of waiting to be butchered here like buck in a pitfall, let us go out now and fall upon the Impi while it sleeps."

This proposition excited some discussion, but in the end only one man could be found to vote for it. Boers as a rule lack that dash which makes great soldiers; such forlorn hopes are not in their line, and rather than embark upon them they prefer to take their chance in a laager, however poor that chance may be. For my own part I firmly believe that had my advice been taken we should have routed the Zulus. Seventeen desperate white men, armed with guns, would have produced no small effect upon a camp of sleeping savages. But it was not taken, so it is no use talking about it.

After that we went back to our posts, and slowly the weary night wore on towards the dawn. Only those who have watched under similar circumstances while they waited the advent of almost certain and cruel death, can know the torturing suspense of those heavy hours. But they went somehow, and at last in the far east the sky began to lighten, while the cold breath of dawn stirred the tilts of the waggons and chilled me to the bone. The fat Dutchwoman behind me woke with a yawn, then, remembering all, moaned aloud, while her teeth chattered with cold and fear. Hans Botha went to his waggon and got a bottle of peach brandy, from which he poured into a tin pannikin, giving us each a stiff dram, and making attempts to be cheerful as he did so. But his affected jocularity only seemed to depress his comrades the more. Certainly it depressed me.

Now the light was growing, and we could see some way into the mist which still hung densely over the river, and now—ah! there it was. From the other side of the hill, a thousand yards or more from the laager, came a faint humming sound. It grew and grew till it gathered to a chant—the awful war chant of the Zulus. Soon I could catch the words. They were simple enough:

"We shall slay, we shall slay! Is it not so, my brothers? Our spears shall blush blood-red. Is it not so, my brothers? For we are the sucklings of Chaka, blood is our milk, my brothers. Awake, children of the Umtetwa, awake! The vulture wheels, the jackal sniffs the air; Awake, children of the Umtetwa—cry aloud, ye ringed men: There is the foe, we shall slay them. Is it not so, my brothers? *S'gee! S'gee! S'gee!*"

Such is a rough translation of that hateful chant which to this very day I often seem to hear. It does not look particularly imposing on paper, but if, while he waited to be killed, the reader could have heard it as it rolled through the still air from the throats of nearly three thousand warriors singing all to time, he would have found it impressive enough.

Now the shields began to appear over the brow of the rise. They came by companies, each company about ninety strong. Altogether there were thirty-one companies. I counted them. When all were over they formed themselves into a triple line, then trotted down the slope towards us. At a distance of a hundred and fifty yards or just out of the shot of such guns as we had in those days, they halted and began singing again?

"Yonder is the kraal of the white man—a little kraal, my brothers;
We shall eat it up, we shall trample it flat, my brothers.
But where are the white man's cattle—where are his oxen, my brothers?"

This question seemed to puzzle them a good deal, for they sang the song again and again. At last a herald came forward, a great man with ivory rings about his arm, and, putting his hands to his mouth, called out to us asking where our cattle were.

Hans Botha climbed on to the top of a waggon and roared out that they might answer that question themselves.

Then the herald called again, saying that he saw the cattle had been sent away.

"We shall go and find the cattle," he said, "then we shall come and kill you, because without cattle you must stop where you are, but if we wait to kill you before we get the cattle, they may have trekked too far for us to follow. And if you try to run away we shall easily catch you white men!"

This struck me as a very odd speech, for the Zulus generally attack an enemy first and take his cattle afterwards; still, there was a certain amount of plausibility about it. While I was still wondering what it all might mean, the Zulus began to run past us in companies towards the river. Suddenly a shout announced that they had found the spoor of the cattle, and the whole Impi of them started down it at a run till they vanished over a rise about a quarter of a mile away.

We waited for half an hour or more, but nothing could we see of them.

"Now I wonder if the devils have really gone," said Hans Botha to me. "It is very strange."

"I will go and see," said Indaba-zimbi, "if you will come with me, Macumazahn. We can creep to the top of the ridge and look over."

At first I hesitated, but curiosity overcame me. I was young in those days and weary with suspense.

"Very well," I said, "we will go."

So we started. I had my elephant gun and ammunition. Indaba-zimbi had his medicine bag and an assegai. We crept to the top of the rise like sportsmen stalking a buck. The slope on the other side was strewn with rocks, among which grew bushes and tall grass.

"They must have gone down the Donga," I said to Indaba-zimbi, "I can't see one of them."

As I spoke there came a roar of men all round me. From every rock, from every tuft of grass rose a Zulu warrior. Before I could turn, before I could lift a gun, I was seized and thrown.

"Hold him! Hold the White Spirit fast!" cried a voice. "Hold him, or he will slip away like a snake. Don't hurt him, but hold him fast. Let Indaba-zimbi walk by his side."

I turned on Indaba-zimbi. "You black devil, you have betrayed me!" I cried.

"Wait and see, Macumazahn," he answered, coolly. "Now the fight is going to begin."

The End of the Laager

I gasped with wonder and rage. What did that scoundrel Indaba-zimbi mean? Why had I been drawn out of the laager and seized, and why, being seized, was I not instantly killed? They called me the "White Spirit." Could it be that they were keeping me to make me into medicine? I had heard of such things being done by Zulus and kindred tribes, and my blood ran cold at the thought. What an end! To be pounded up, made medicine of, and eaten!

However, I had little time for further reflection, for now the whole Impi was pouring back from the donga and river-banks where it had hidden while their ruse was carried out, and once more formed up on the side of the slope. I was taken to the crest of the slope and placed in the centre of the reserve line in the especial charge of a huge Zulu named Bombyane, the same man who had come forward as a herald. This brute seemed to regard me with an affectionate curiosity. Now and again he poked me in the ribs with the handle of his assegai, as though to assure himself that I was solid, and several times he asked me to be so good as to prophesy how many Zulus would be killed before the "Amaboona," as they called the Boers, were "eaten up."

At first I took no notice of him beyond scowling, but presently, goaded into anger, I prophesied that he would be dead in an hour!

He only laughed aloud. "Oh! White Spirit," he said, "is it so? Well, I've walked a long way from Zululand, and shall be glad of a rest."

And he got it shortly, as will be seen.

Now the Zulus began to sing again—

"We have caught the White Spirit, my brother! my brother!

Iron-Tongue whispered of him, he smelt him out, my brother.

Now the Maboona are ours—they are already dead, my brother."

So that treacherous villain Indaba-zimbi had betrayed me. Suddenly the chief of the Impi, a grey-haired man named Sususa, held up his assegai, and instantly there was silence. Then he spoke to some indunas who stood near him. Instantly they ran to the right and left down the first line, saying a word to the captain of each company as they passed him. Presently they were at the respective ends of the line, and simultaneously held up their spears. As they did so, with an awful roar of "Bulala Amaboona"—"Slay the Boers," the entire line, numbering nearly a thousand men, bounded forward like a buck startled from its form, and rushed down upon the little laager. It was a splendid sight to see them, their assegais glittering in the sunlight as they rose and fell above their black shields, their war-plumes bending back upon the wind, and their fierce faces set intently on the foe, while the solid earth shook beneath the thunder of their rushing feet. I thought of my poor friends the Dutchmen, and trembled. What chance had they against so many?

Now the Zulus, running in the shape of a bow so as to wrap the laager round on three sides, were within seventy yards, and now from every waggon broke tongues of fire. Over rolled a number of the Umtetwa, but the rest cared little. Forward they sped straight to the laager, striving to force a way in. But the Boers plied them with volley after volley, and, packed as the Zulus were, the elephant guns loaded with slugs and small shot did frightful execution. Only one man even got on to a waggon, and as he did so I saw a Boer woman strike him on the head with an axe. He fell down, and slowly, amid howls of derision from the two lines on the hill-side, the Zulus drew back.

"Let us go, father!" shouted the soldiers on the slope, among whom I was, to their chief, who had come up. "You have sent out the little girls to fight, and they are frightened. Let us show them the way."

"No, no!" the chief Sususa answered, laughing. "Wait a minute and the little girls will grow to women, and women are good enough to fight against Boers!"

The attacking Zulus heard the mockery of their fellows, and rushed forward again with a roar. But the Boers in the laager had found time to load, and they met with a warm reception. Reserving their fire till the Zulus were packed like sheep in a kraal, they loosed into them with the roers, and the warriors fell in little heaps. But I saw that the blood of the Umtetwas was up; they did not mean to be beaten back this time, and the end was near. See! six men had leapt on to a waggon, slain the man behind it, and sprung into the laager. They were killed there, but others followed, and then I turned my head. But I could not shut my ears to the cries of rage and death, and the terrible *S'gee! S'gee!* of the savages as they did their work of murder. Once only I looked up and saw poor Hans Botha standing on a waggon smiting down men with the butt of his rifle. The assegais shot up towards him like tongues of steel, and when I looked again he was gone.

I turned sick with fear and rage. But alas! what could I do? They were all dead now, and probably my own turn was coming, only my death with not be so swift.

The fight was ended, and the two lines on the slope broke their order, and moved down to the laager. Presently we were there, and a dreadful sight it was. Many of the attacking Zulus were dead—quite fifty I should say, and at least a hundred and fifty were wounded, some of them mortally. The chief Sususa gave an order, the dead men were picked up and piled in a heap, while those who were slightly hurt walked off to find some one to tie up their wounds. But the more serious cases met with a different treatment. The chief or one of his indunas considered each case, and if it was in any way bad, the man was taken up and thrown into the river which ran near. None of them offered any objection, though one poor fellow swam to shore again. He did not stop there long, however, for they pushed him back and drowned him by force.

The strangest case of all was that of the chief's own brother. He had been captain of the line, and his ankle was smashed by a bullet. Sususa came up to him, and, having examined the wound, rated him soundly for failing in the first onslaught.

The poor fellow made the excuse that it was not his fault, as the Boers had hit him in the first rush. His brother admitted the truth of this, and talked to him amicably.

"Well," he said at length, offering him a pinch of snuff, "you cannot walk again."

"No, chief," said the wounded man, looking at his ankle.

"And to-morrow we must walk far," went on Sususa.

"Yes, chief."

"Say, then, will you sit here on the veldt, or—" and he nodded towards the river.

The man dropped his head on his breast for a minute as though in thought. Presently he lifted it and looked Sususa straight in the face.

"My ankle pains me, my brother," he said; "I think I will go back to Zululand, for there is the only kraal I wish to see again, even if I creep about it like a snake."

"It is well, my brother," said the chief. "Rest softly," and having shaken hands with him, he gave an order to one of the indunas, and turned away.

Then men came, and, supporting the wounded man, led him down to the banks of the stream. Here, at his request, they tied a heavy stone round his neck, and then threw him into a deep pool. I saw the whole sad scene, and the victim never even winced. It was impossible not to admire the extraordinary courage of the man, or to avoid being struck with the cold-blooded cruelty of his brother the chief. And yet the act was necessary from his point of view. The man must either die swiftly, or be left to perish of starvation, for no Zulu force will encumber itself with wounded men. Years of merciless warfare had so hardened these people that they looked on death as nothing, and were, to do them justice, as willing to meet it themselves as to inflict it on others. When this very Impi had been sent out by the Zulu King Dingaan, it consisted of some nine thousand men. Now it numbered less than three; all the rest were dead. They, too, would probably soon be dead. What did it matter? They lived by war to die in blood. It was their natural end. "Kill till you are killed." That is the motto of the Zulu soldier. It has the merit of simplicity.

Meanwhile the warriors were looting the waggons, including my own, having first thrown all the dead Boers into a heap. I looked at the heap; all of them were there, including the two stout fraus, poor things. But I missed one body, that of Hans Botha's daughter, little Tota. A wild hope came into my heart that she might have escaped; but no, it was not possible. I could only pray that she was already at rest.

Just then the great Zulu, Bombyane, who had left my side to indulge in the congenial occupation of looting, came out of a waggon crying that he had got the "little white one." I looked; he was carrying the child Tota, gripping her frock in one of his huge black hands. He stalked up to where we were, and held the child before the chief. "Is it dead, father?" he said, with a laugh.

Now, as I could well see, the child was not dead, but had been hidden away, and fainted with fear.

The chief glanced at it carelessly, and said—

"Find out with your kerrie."

Acting on this hint the black devil held up the child, and was about to kill it with his knobstick. This was more than I could bear. I sprang at him and struck him with all my force in the face, little caring if I was speared or not. He dropped Tota on the ground.

"Ou!" he said, putting his hand to his nose, "the White Spirit has a hard fist. Come, Spirit, I will fight you for the child."

The soldiers cheered and laughed. "Yes! yes!" they said, "let Bombyane fight the White Spirit for the child. Let them fight with assegais."

For a moment I hesitated. What chance had I against this black giant? But I had promised poor Hans to save the child if I could, and what did it matter? As well die now as later. However, I had wit enough left to make a favour of it, and intimated to the chief through Indaba-zimbi that I was quite willing to condescend to kill Bombyane, on condition that if I did so the child's life should be given to me. Indaba-zimbi interpreted my words, but I noticed that he would not look on me as he spoke, but covered his face with his hands and spoke of me as "the ghost" or the "son of the spirit." For some reason that I have never quite understood, the chief consented to the duel. I fancy it was because he believed me to be more than mortal, and was anxious to see the last of Bombyane.

"Let them fight," he said. "Give them assegais and no shields; the child shall be to him who conquers."

"Yes! yes!" cried the soldiers. "Let them fight. Don't be afraid, Bombyane; if he is a spirit, he's a very small one."

"I never was frightened of man or beast, and I am not going to run away from a White Ghost," answered the redoubtable Bombyane, as he examined the blade of his great bangwan or stabbing assegai.

Then they made a ring round us, gave me a similar assegai, and set us some ten paces apart. I kept my face as calm as I could, and tried to show no signs of fear, though in my heart I was terribly afraid. Humanly speaking, my doom was on me. The giant warrior before me had used the assegai from a child—I had no experience of the weapon. Moreover, though I was quick and active, he must have been at least twice as strong as I am. However, there was no help for it, so, setting my teeth, I grasped the great spear, breathed a prayer, and waited.

The giant stood awhile looking at me, and, as he stood, Indaba-zimbi walked across the ring behind me, muttering as he passed, "Keep cool, Macumazahn, and wait for him. I will make it all right."

As I had not the slightest intention of commencing the fray, I thought this good advice, though how Indaba-zimbi could "make it all right" I failed to see.

Heavens! how long that half-minute seemed! It happened many years ago, but the whole scene rises up before my eyes as I write. There behind us was the blood-stained laager, and near it lay the piles of dead; round us was rank upon rank of plumed savages, standing in silence to wait the issue of the duel, and in the centre stood the grey-haired chief and general, Sususa, in all his war finery, a cloak of leopard skin upon his shoulders. At his feet lay the senseless form of little Tota, to my left squatted Indaba-zimbi, nodding his white lock and muttering something—probably spells; while in front was my giant antagonist, his spear aloft and his plumes wavering in the gentle wind. Then over all, over grassy slope, river, and koppie, over the waggons of the laager, the piles of dead, the dense masses of the living, the swooning child, over all shone the bright impartial sun, looking down like the indifferent eye of Heaven upon the loveliness of nature and the cruelty of man. Down by the river grew thorn-trees, and from them floated the sweet scent of the mimosa flower, and came the sound of cooing turtle-doves. I never smell the one or hear the other without the scene flashing into my mind again, complete in its every detail.

Suddenly, without a sound, Bombyane shook his assegai and rushed straight at me. I saw his huge form come; like a man in a dream, I saw the broad spear flash on high; now he was on me! Then, prompted to it by some providential impulse—or had the spells of Indaba-zimbi anything to do with the matter?—I dropped to my knee, and quick as light stretched out my spear. He drove at me: the blade passed over my head. I felt a weight on my assegai; it was wrenched from my hand; his great limbs knocked against me. I glanced round. Bombyane was staggering along with head thrown back and outstretched arms from which his spear had fallen. His spear had fallen, but the blade of mine stood out between his shoulders—I had transfixed him. He stopped, swung slowly round as though to look at me: then with a sigh the giant sank down—*dead*.

For a moment there was silence; then a great cry rose—a cry of "Bombyane is dead. The White Spirit has slain Bombyane. Kill the wizard, kill the ghost who has slain Bombyane by witchcraft."

Instantly I was surrounded by fierce faces, and spears flashed before my eyes. I folded my arms and stood calmly waiting the end. In a moment it would have come, for the warriors were mad at seeing their champion overthrown thus easily. But presently through the tumult I heard the high, cracked voice of Indaba-zimbi.

"Stand back, you fools!" it cried; "can a spirit then be killed—"

"Spear him! spear him!" they roared in fury. "Let us see if he is a spirit. How did a spirit slay Bombyane with an assegai? Spear him, rain-maker, and we shall see."

"Stand back," cried Indaba-zimbi again, "and I will show you if he can be killed. I will kill him myself, and call him back to life again before your eyes."

"Macumazahn, trust me," he whispered in my ear in the Sisutu tongue, which the Zulus did not understand. "Trust me; kneel on the grass before me, and when I strike at you with the spear, roll over like one dead; then, when you hear my voice again, get up. Trust me—it is your only hope."

Having no choice I nodded my head in assent, though I had not the faintest idea of what he was about to do. The tumult lessened somewhat, and once more the warriors drew back.

"Great White Spirit—Spirit of victory," said Indaba-zimbi, addressing me aloud, and covering his eyes with his hand, "hear me and forgive me. These children are blind with folly, and think thee mortal because thou hast dealt death upon a mortal who dared to stand against thee. Deign to kneel down before me and let me pierce thy heart with this spear, then when I call upon thee, arise unhurt."

I knelt down, not because I wished to, but because I must. I had not overmuch faith in Indaba-zimbi, and thought it probable that he was in truth about to make an end of me. But really I was so worn out with fears, and the horrors of the night and day had so shaken my nerves, that I did not greatly care what befell me. When I had been kneeling thus for about half a minute Indaba-zimbi spoke.

"People of the Umtetwa, children of T'Chaka," he said, "draw back a little way, lest an evil fall on you, for now the air is thick with ghosts."

They drew back a space, leaving us in a circle about twelve yards in diameter.

"Look on him who kneels before you," went on Indaba-zimbi, "and listen to my words, to the words of the witch-finder, the words of the rain-maker, Indaba-zimbi, whose fame is known to you. He seems to be a young man, does he not? I tell you, children of the Umtetwa, he is no man. He is the Spirit who gives victory to the white men, he it is who gave them assegais that thunder and taught them how to slay. Why were the Impis of Dingaan rolled back at the Blood River? Because *he* was there. Why did the Amaboona slay the people of Mosilikatze by the thousand? Because *he* was there. And so I say to you that, had I not drawn him from the laager by my magic but three hours ago, you would have been conquered—yes, you would have been blown away like the dust before the wind; you would have been burnt up like the dry grass in the winter when the fire is awake among it. Ay, because he had but been there many of your bravest were slain in overcoming a few—a pinch of men who could be counted on the fingers. But because I loved you, because your chief Sususa is my half-brother—for had we not one father?—I came to you, I warned you. Then you prayed me and I drew the Spirit forth. But you were not satisfied when the victory was yours, when the Spirit, of all you had taken asked but one little thing—a white child to take away and sacrifice to himself, to make the medicine of his magic of—"

Here I could hardly restrain myself from interrupting, but thought better of it.

"You said him nay; you said, 'Let him fight with our bravest man, let him fight with Bombyane the giant for the child.' And he deigned to slay Bombyane as you have seen, and now you say, 'Slay him; he is no spirit.' Now I will show you if he is a spirit, for I will slay him before your eyes, and call him to life again. But you have brought this upon yourselves. Had you believed, had you offered no insult to the Spirit, he would have stayed with you, and you should have become unconquerable. Now he will arise and leave you, and woe be on you if you try to stay him.

"Now all men," he went on, "look for a space upon this assegai that I hold up," and he lifted the bangwan of the deceased Bombyane high above his head so that all the multitude could see it. Every eye was fixed upon the broad bright spear. For a while he held it still, then he moved it round and round in a circle, muttering as he did so, and still their gaze followed it. For my part, I watched his movements with the greatest anxiety. That assegai had already been nearer my person than I found at all pleasant, and I had no desire to make a further acquaintance with it. Nor, indeed, was I sure that Indaba-zimbi was not really going to kill me. I could not understand his proceedings at all, and at the best I did not relish playing the *corpus vile* to his magical experiments.

"*Look! look! look!*" he screamed.

Then suddenly the great spear flashed down towards my breast. I felt nothing, but, to my sight, it seemed as though it had passed through me.

"See!" roared the Zulus. "Indaba-zimbi has speared him; the red assegai stands out behind his back."

"Roll over, Macumazahn," Indaba-zimbi hissed in my ear, "roll over and pretend to die—quick! quick!"

I lost no time in following these strange instructions, but falling on to my side, threw my arms wide, kicked my legs about, and died as artistically as I could. Presently I gave a stage shiver and lay still.

"See!" said the Zulus, "he is dead, the Spirit is dead. Look at the blood upon the assegai!"

"Stand back! stand back!" cried Indaba-zimbi, "or the ghost will haunt you. Yes, he is dead, and now I will call him back to life again. Look!" and putting down his hand, he plucked the spear from wherever it was fixed, and held it aloft. "The spear is red, is it not? Watch, men, watch! *it grows white!*"

"Yes, it grows white," they said. "Ou! it grows white."

"It grows white because the blood returns to whence it came," said Indaba-zimbi. "Now, great Spirit, hear me. Thou art dead, the breath has gone out of thy mouth. Yet hear me and arise. Awake, White Spirit, awake and show thy power. Awake! arise unhurt!"

I began to respond cheerfully to this imposing invocation.

"Not so fast, Macumazahn," whispered Indaba-zimbi.

I took the hint, and first held up my arm, then lifted my head and let it fall again.

"He lives! by the head of T'Chaka he lives!" roared the soldiers, stricken with mortal fear.

Then slowly and with the greatest dignity I gradually arose, stretched my arms, yawned like one awaking from heavy sleep, turned and looked upon them unconcernedly. While I did so, I noticed that old Indaba-zimbi was almost fainting from exhaustion. Beads of perspiration stood upon his brow, his limbs trembled, and his breast heaved.

As for the Zulus, they waited for no more. With a howl of terror the whole regiment turned and fled across the rise, so that presently we were left alone with the dead, and the swooning child.

"How on earth did you do that, Indaba-zimbi?" I asked in amaze.

"Do not ask me, Macumazahn," he gasped. "You white men are very clever, but you don't quite know everything. There are men in the world who can make people believe they see things which they do not see. Let us be going while we may, for when those Umtetwas have got over their fright, they will come back to loot the waggons, and then perhaps *they* will begin asking questions that I can't answer."

And here I may as well state that I never got any further information on this matter from old Indaba-zimbi. But I have my theory, and here it is for whatever it may be worth. I believe that Indaba-zimbi *mesmerized* the whole crowd of onlookers, myself included, making them believe that they saw the assegai in my heart, and the blood upon the blade. The reader may smile and say, "Impossible;" but I would ask him how the Indian jugglers do their tricks unless it is by mesmerism. The spectators *seem* to see the boy go under the basket and there pierced with daggers, they *seem* to see women in a trance supported in mid-air upon the point of a single sword. In themselves these things are not possible, they violate the laws of nature, as those laws are known to us, and therefore must surely be illusion. And so through the glamour thrown upon them by Indaba-zimbi's will, that Zulu Impi seemed to see me transfixed with an assegai which never touched me. At least, that is my theory; if any one has a better, let him adopt it. The explanation lies between illusion and magic of a most imposing character, and I prefer to accept the first alternative.

Stella

I was not slow to take Indaba-zimbi's hint. About a hundred and fifty yards to the left of the laager was a little dell where I had hidden my horse, together with one belonging to the Boers, and my saddle and bridle. Thither we went, I carrying the swooning Tota in my arms. To our joy we found the horses safe, for the Zulus had not seen them. Now, of course, they were our only means of locomotion, for the oxen had been sent away, and even had they been there we could not have found time to inspan them. I laid Tota down, caught my horse, undid his knee halter, and saddled up. As I was doing so a thought struck me, and I told Indaba-zimbi to run to the laager and see if he could find my double-barrelled gun and some powder and shot, for I had only my elephant "roer" and a few charges of powder and ball with me.

He went, and while he was away, poor little Tota came to herself and began to cry, till she saw my face.

"Ah, I have had such a bad dream," she said, in Dutch: "I dreamed that the black Kaffirs were going to kill me. Where is my papa?"

I winced at the question. "Your papa has gone on a journey, dear," I said, "and left me to look after you. We shall find him one day. You don't mind going with Heer Allan, do you?"

"No," she said, a little doubtfully, and began to cry again. Presently she remembered that she was thirsty, and asked for water. I led her to the river and she drank. "Why is my hand red, Here Allan?" she asked, pointing to the smear of Bombyane's blood-stained fingers.

At this moment I felt very glad that I had killed Bombyane.

"It is only paint, dear," I said; "see, we will wash it and your face."

As I was doing this, Indaba-zimbi returned. The guns were all gone; he said the Zulus had taken them and the powder. But he had found some things and brought them in a sack. There was a thick blanket, about twenty pounds weight of biltong or sun-dried meat, a few double-handfuls of biscuits, two water-bottles, a tin pannikin, some matches and sundries.

"And now, Macumazahn," he said, "we had best be going, for those Umtetwas are coming back. I saw one of them on the brow of the rise."

That was enough for me. I lifted little Tota on to the bow of my saddle, climbed into it, and rode off, holding her in front of me. Indaba-zimbi slipped a reim into the mouth of the best of the Boer horses, threw of the sack of sundries on to its back and mounted also, holding the elephant gun in his hand. We went eight or nine hundred yards in silence till we were quite out of range of sight from the waggons, which were in a hollow. Then I pulled up, with such a feeling of thankfulness in my heart as cannot be told in words; for now I knew that, mounted as we were, those black demons could never catch us. But where were we to steer for? I put the question to Indaba-zimbi, asking him if he thought that we had better try and follow the oxen which we had sent away with the Kaffirs and women on the preceding night. He shook his head.

"The Umtetwas will go after the oxen presently," he answered, "and we have seen enough of them."

"Quite enough," I answered, with enthusiasm; "I never want to see another; but where are we to go? Here we are alone with one gun and a little girl in the vast and lonely veldt. Which way shall we turn?"

"Our faces were towards the north before we met the Zulus," answered Indaba-zimbi; "let us still keep them to the north. Ride on, Macumazahn; to-night when we off-saddle I will look into the matter."

So all that long afternoon we rode on, following the course of the river. From the nature of the ground we could only go slowly, but before sunset I had the satisfaction of knowing that there must be at least twenty-five miles between us and those accursed Zulus. Little Tota slept most of the way, the motion of the horse was easy, and she was worn out.

At last the sunset came, and we off-saddled in a dell by the river. There was not much to eat, but I soaked some biscuit in water for Tota, and Indaba-zimbi and I made a scanty meal of biltong. When we had done I took off Tota's frock, wrapped her up in a blanket near the fire we had made, and lit a pipe. I sat there by the side of the sleeping orphaned child, and from my heart thanked Providence for saving her life and mine from the slaughter of that day. What a horrible experience it had been! It seemed like a nightmare to look back upon. And yet it was sober fact, one among those many tragedies which dotted the paths of the emigrant Boers with the bones of men, women, and children. These horrors are almost forgotten now; people living in Natal now, for instance, can scarcely realize that some forty years ago six hundred white people, many of them women and children, were thus massacred by the Impis of Dingaan. But it was so, and the name of the district, *Weenen*, or the Place of Weeping, will commemorate them for ever.

Then I fell to reflecting on the extraordinary adroitness old Indaba-zimbi had shown in saving my life. It appeared that he himself had lived among the Umtetwa Zulus in his earlier manhood, and was a noted rain-doctor and witch-finder. But when T'Chaka, Dingaan's brother, ordered a general massacre of the witch-finders, he alone had saved his life by his skill in magic, and ultimately fled south for reasons too long to set out here. When he heard, therefore, that the regiment was an Umtetwa regiment, which, leaving their wives and children, had broken away from Zululand to escape the cruelties of Dingaan; under pretence of spying on them, he took the bold course of going straight up to the chief, Sususa, and addressing him as his brother, which he was. The chief knew him at once, and so did the soldiers, for his fame was still great among them. Then he told them his cock and bull story about my being a white spirit, whose presence in the laager would render it invincible, and with the object of saving my life in the slaughter which he knew must ensue, agreed to charm me out of the laager and deliver me into their keeping. How the plan worked has already been told; it was a risky one; still, but for it my troubles would have been done with these many days.

So I lay and thought with a heart full of gratitude, and as I did so saw old Indaba-zimbi sitting by the fire and going through some mysterious performances with bones which he produced from his bag, and ashes mixed with water. I spoke to him and asked what he was about. He replied that he was tracing out the route that we should follow. I felt inclined to answer "bosh!" but remembering the very remarkable instances which he had given of his prowess in occult matters I held my tongue, and taking little Tota into my arms, worn out with toil and danger and emotion, I went to sleep.

I awoke just as the dawn was beginning to flame across the sky in sheets of primrose and of gold, or rather it was little Tota who woke me by kissing me as she lay between sleep and waking, and calling me "papa." It wrung my heart to hear her, poor orphaned child. I got up, washed and dressed her as best I could, and we breakfasted as we had supped, on biltong and biscuit. Tota asked for milk, but I had none to give her. Then we caught the horses, and I saddled mine.

"Well, Indaba-zimbi," I said, "now what path do your bones point to?"

"Straight north," he said. "The journey will be hard, but in about four days we shall come to the kraal of a white man, an Englishman, not a Boer. His kraal is in a beautiful place, and there is a great peak behind it where there are many baboons."

I looked at him. "This is all nonsense, Indaba-zimbi," I said. "Whoever heard of an Englishman building a house in these wilds, and how do you know anything about it? I think that we had better strike east towards Port Natal."

"As you like, Macumazahn," he answered, "but it will take us three months' journey to get to Port Natal, if we ever get there, and the child will die on the road. Say, Macumazahn, have my words come true heretofore, or have they not? Did I not tell you not to hunt the elephants on horseback? Did I not tell you to take one waggon with you instead of two, as it is better to lose one than two?"

"You told me all these things," I answered.

"And so I tell you now to ride north, Macumazahn, for there you will find great happiness—yes, and great sorrow. But no man should run away from happiness because of the sorrow. As you will, as you will!"

Again I looked at him. In his divinations I did not believe, yet I came to the conclusion that he was speaking what he knew to be the truth. It struck me as possible that he might have heard of some white man living like a hermit in the wilds, but preferring to keep up his prophetic character would not say so.

"Very well, Indaba-zimbi," I said, "let us ride north."

Shortly after we started, the river we had followed hitherto turned off in a westerly direction, so we left it. All that day we rode across rolling uplands, and about an hour before sunset halted at a little stream which ran down from a range of hills in front of us. By this time I was heartily tired of the biltong, so taking my elephant rifle—for I had nothing else—I left Tota with Indaba-zimbi, and started to try if I could shoot something. Oddly enough we had seen no game all the day, nor did we see any on the subsequent days. For some mysterious reason they had temporarily left the district. I crossed the little streamlet in order to enter the belt of thorns which grew upon the hill-side beyond, for there I hoped to find buck. As I did so I was rather disturbed to see the spoor of two lions in the soft sandy edge of a pool. Breathing a hope that they might not still be in the neighbourhood, I went on into the belt of scattered thorns. For a long while I hunted about without seeing anything, except one duiker buck, which bounded off with a crash from the other side of a stone without giving me a chance. At length, just as it grew dusk, I spied a Petie buck, a graceful little creature, scarcely bigger than a large hare, standing on a stone, about forty yards from me. Under ordinary circumstances I should never have dreamed of firing at such a thing, especially with an elephant gun, but we were hungry. So I sat down with my back against a rock, and aimed steadily at its head. I did this because if I struck it in the body the three-ounce ball would have knocked it to bits. At last I pulled the trigger, the gun went off with the report of a small cannon, and the buck disappeared. I ran to the spot with more anxiety than I should have felt in an ordinary way over a koodoo or an eland. To my delight there the little creature lay—the huge bullet had decapitated it. Considering all the circumstances I do not think I have often made a better shot than this, but if any one doubts, let him try his hand at a rabbit's head fifty yards away with an elephant gun and a three-ounce ball.

I picked up the Petie in triumph, and returned to the camp. There we skinned him and toasted his flesh over the fire. He just made a good meal for us, though we kept the hind legs for breakfast.

There was no moon this night, and so it chanced that when I suddenly remembered about the lion spoor, and suggested that we had better tie up the horses quite close to us, we could not find them, though we knew they were grazing within fifty yards. This being so we could only make up the fire and take our chance. Shortly afterwards I went to sleep with little Tota in my arms. Suddenly I was awakened by hearing that peculiarly painful sound, the scream of a horse, quite close to the fire, which was still burning brightly. Next second there came a noise of galloping hoofs, and before I could even rise my poor horse appeared in the ring of firelight. As in a flash of lightning I saw his staring eyes and wide-stretched nostrils, and the broken reim with which he had been knee-haltered, flying in the air. Also I saw something else, for on his back was a great dark form with glowing eyes, and from the form came a growling sound. It was a lion.

The horse dashed on. He galloped right through the fire, for which he had run in his terror, fortunately, however, without treading on us, and vanished into the night. We heard his hoofs for a hundred yards or more, then there was silence, broken now and again by distant growls. As may be imagined, we did not sleep any more that night, but waited anxiously till the dawn broke, two hours later.

As soon as there was sufficient light we rose, and, leaving Tota still asleep, crept cautiously in the direction in which the horse had vanished. When we had gone fifty yards or so, we made out its remains lying on the veldt, and caught sight of two great cat-like forms slinking away in the grey light.

To go any further was useless; we knew all about it now, so we turned to look for the other horse. But our cup of misfortune was not yet full; the horse was nowhere to be found. Terrified by the sight and smell of the lions, it had with a desperate effort also burst the reim with which it had been knee-haltered, and galloped far away. I sat down, feeling as though I could cry like a woman. For now we were left alone in these vast solitudes without a horse to carry us, and with a child who was not old enough to walk for more than a little way at a time.

Well, it was no use giving in, so with a few words we went back to our camp, where I found Tota crying because she had woke to find herself alone. Then we ate a little food and prepared to start. First we divided such articles as we must take with us into two equal parts, rejecting everything that we could possibly do without. Then, by an afterthought, we filled our water-bottles, though at the time I was rather against doing so, because of the extra weight. But Indaba-zimbi overruled me in the matter, fortunately for all three of us. I settled to look after Tota for the first march, and to give the elephant gun to Indaba-zimbi. At length all was ready, and we set out on foot. By the help of occasional lifts over rough places, Tota managed to walk up the slope of the hill-side where I had shot the Petie buck. At length we reached it, and, looking at the country beyond, I gave an exclamation of dismay. To say that it was desert would be saying too much; it was more like the Karroo in the Cape—a vast sandy waste, studded here and there with low shrubs and scattered rocks. But it was a great expanse of desolate land, stretching further than the eye could reach, and bordered far away by a line of purple hills, in the centre of which a great solitary peak soared high into the air.

"Indaba-zimbi," I said, "we can never cross this if we take six days."

"As you will, Macumazahn," he answered; "but I tell you that there—" and he pointed to the peak—"there the white man lives. Turn which way you like, but if you turn you will perish."

I reflected for a moment, Our case was, humanly speaking, almost hopeless. It mattered little which way we went. We were alone, almost without food, with no means of transport, and a child to carry. As well perish in the sandy waste as on the rolling veldt or among the trees of the hill-side. Providence alone could save us, and we must trust to Providence.

"Come on," I said, lifting Tota on to my back, for she was already tired. "All roads lead to rest."

How am I to describe the misery of the next four days? How am I to tell how we stumbled on through that awful desert, almost without food, and quite without water, for there were no streams, and we saw no springs? We soon found how the case was, and saved almost all the water in our bottles for the child. To look back on it is like a nightmare. I can scarcely bear to dwell on it. Day after day, by turns carrying the child through the heavy sand; night after night lying down in the scrub, chewing the leaves, and licking such dew as there was from the scanty grass! Not a spring, not a pool, not a head of game!

It was the third night; we were nearly mad with thirst. Tota was in a comatose condition. Indaba-zimbi still had a little water in his bottle—perhaps a wine-glassful. With it we moistened our lips and blackened tongues. Then we gave the rest to the child. It revived her. She awoke from her swoon to sink into sleep.

See, the dawn was breaking. The hills were not more than eight miles or so away now, and they were green. There must be water there.

"Come," I said.

Indaba-zimbi lifted Tota into the kind of sling that we had made out of the blanket in which to carry her on our backs, and we staggered on for an hour through the sand. She awoke crying for water, and alas! we had none to give her; our tongues were hanging from our lips, we could scarcely speak.

We rested awhile, and Tota mercifully swooned away again. Then Indaba-zimbi took her. Though he was so thin the old man's strength was wonderful.

Another hour; the slope of the great peak could not be more than two miles away now. A couple of hundred yards off grew a large baobab tree. Could we reach its shade? We had done half the distance when Indaba-zimbi fell from exhaustion. We were now so weak that neither of us could lift the child on to our backs. He rose again, and we each took one of her hands and dragged her along the road. Fifty yards—they seemed to be fifty miles. Ah, the tree was reached at last; compared with the heat outside, the shade of its dense foliage seemed like the dusk and cool of a vault. I remember thinking that it was a good place to die in. Then I remember no more.

I woke with a feeling as though the blessed rain were falling on my face and head. Slowly, and with great difficulty, I opened my eyes, then shut them again, having seen a vision. For a space I lay thus, while the rain continued to fall; I saw now that I must be asleep, or off my head with thirst and fever. If I were not off my head how came I to imagine that a lovely dark-eyed girl was bending over me sprinkling water on my face? A white girl, too, not a Kaffir woman. However, the dream went on.

"Hendrika," said a voice in English, the sweetest voice that I had ever heard; somehow it reminded me of wind whispering in the trees at night. "Hendrika, I fear he dies; there is a flask of brandy in my saddle-bag; get it."

"Ah! ah!" grunted a harsh voice in answer; "let him die, Miss Stella. He will bring you bad luck—let him die, I say." I felt a movement of air above me as though the woman of my vision turned swiftly, and once again I opened my eyes. She had risen, this dream woman. Now I saw that she was tall and graceful as a reed. She was angry, too; her dark eyes flashed, and she pointed with her hand at a female who stood before her, dressed in nondescript kind of clothes such as might be worn by either a man or a woman. The woman was young, of white blood, very short, with bowed legs and enormous shoulders. In face she was not bad-looking, but the brow receded, the chin and ears were prominent—in short, she reminded me of nothing so much as a very handsome monkey. She might have been the missing link.

The lady was pointing at her with her hand. "How dare you?" she said. "Are you going to disobey me again? Have you forgotten what I told you, Babyan?"

"Ah! ah!" grunted the woman, who seemed literally to curl and shrivel up beneath her anger. "Don't be angry with me, Miss Stella, because I can't bear it. I only said it because it was true. I will fetch the brandy."

Then, dream or no dream, I determined to speak.

"Not brandy," I gasped in English as well as my swollen tongue would allow; "give me water."

"Ah, he lives!" cried the beautiful girl, "and he talks English. See, sir, here is water in your own bottle; you were quite close to a spring, it is on the other side of the tree."

I struggled to a sitting position, lifted the bottle to my lips, and drank from it. Oh! that drink of cool, pure water! never had I tasted anything so delicious. With the first gulp I felt life flow back into me. But wisely enough she would not let me have much. "No more! no more!" she said, and dragged the bottle from me almost by force.

"The child," I said—"is the child dead?"

"I do not know yet," she answered. "We have only just found you, and I tried to revive you first."

I turned and crept to where Tota lay by the side of Indaba-zimbi. It was impossible to say if they were dead or swooning. The lady sprinkled Tota's face with the water, which I watched greedily, for my thirst was still awful, while the woman Hendrika did the same office for Indaba-zimbi. Presently, to my vast delight, Tota opened her eyes and tried to cry, but could not, poor little thing, because her tongue and lips were so swollen. But the lady got some water into her mouth, and, as in my case, the effect was magical. We allowed her to drink about a quarter of a pint, and no more, though she cried bitterly for it. Just then old Indaba-zimbi came to with a groan. He opened his eyes, glanced round, and took in the situation.

"What did I tell you, Macumazahn?" he gasped, and seizing the bottle, he took a long pull at it.

Meanwhile I sat with my back against the trunk of the great tree and tried to realize the situation. Looking to my left I saw too good horses—one bare-backed, and one with a rudely made lady's saddle on it. By the side of the horses were two dogs, of a stout greyhound breed, that sat watching us, and near the dogs lay a dead Oribé buck, which they had evidently been coursing.

"Hendrika," said the lady presently, "they must not eat meat just yet. Go look up the tree and see if there is any ripe fruit on it."

The woman ran swiftly into the plain and obeyed. Presently she returned. "I see some ripe fruit," she said, "but it is high, quite at the top."

"Fetch it," said the lady.

"Easier said than done," I thought to myself; but I was much mistaken. Suddenly the woman bounded at least three feet into the air and caught one of the spreading boughs in her large flat hands; then came a swing that would have filled an acrobat with envy—and she was on it.

"Now there is an end," I thought again, for the next bough was beyond her reach. But again I was mistaken. She stood up on the bough, gripping it with her bare feet, and once more sprang at the one above, caught it and swung herself into it.

I suppose that the lady saw my expression of astonishment. "Do not wonder, sir," she said, "Hendrika is not like other people. She will not fall."

I made no answer, but watched the progress of this extraordinary person with the most breathless interest. On she went, swinging herself from bough to bough, and running along them like a monkey. At last she reached the top, and began to swarm up a thin branch towards the ripe fruit. When she was near enough she shook the branch violently. There was a crack—a crash—it broke. I shut my eyes, expecting to see her crushed on the ground before me.

"Don't be afraid," said the lady again, laughing gently. "Look, she is quite safe."

I looked, and so she was. She had caught a bough as she fell, clung to it, and was now calmly dropping to another. Old Indaba-zimbi had also watched this performance with interest, but it did not seem to astonish him over-much. "Baboon-woman?" he said, as though such people were common, and then turned his attention to soothing Tota, who was moaning for more water. Meanwhile Hendrika came down the tree with extraordinary rapidity, and swinging by one hand from a bough, dropped about eight feet to the ground.

In another two minutes we were all three sucking the pulpy fruit. In an ordinary way we should have found it tasteless enough: as it was I thought it the most delicious thing I had ever tasted. After three days spent without food or water, in the desert, one is not particular. While we were still eating the fruit, the lady of my vision set her companion to work to partially flay the oribé which her dogs had killed, and busied herself in making a fire of fallen boughs. As soon as it burned brightly she took strips of the oribé flesh, toasted them, and gave them to us on leaves. We ate, and now were allowed a little more water. After that she took Tota to the spring and washed her, which she sadly needed, poor child! Next came our turn to wash, and oh, the joy of it!

I came back to the tree, walking painfully, indeed, but a changed man. There sat the beautiful girl with Tota on her knees. She was lulling her to sleep, and held up her finger to me enjoining silence. At last the child went off into a sound natural slumber—an example that I should have been glad to follow had it not been for my burning curiosity. Then I spoke.

"May I ask what your name is?" I said.

"Stella," she answered.

"Stella what?" I said.

"Stella nothing," she answered, in some pique; "Stella is my name; it is short and easy to remember at any rate. My father's name is Thomas, and we live up there," and she pointed round the base of the great peak. I looked at her astonished. "Have you lived there long?" I asked.

"Ever since I was seven years old. We came there in a waggon. Before that we came from England—from Oxfordshire; I can show you the place on a big map. It is called Garsingham."

Again I thought I must be dreaming. "Do you know, Miss Stella," I said, "it is very strange—so strange that it almost seems as though it could not be true—but I also came from Garsingham in Oxfordshire many years ago."

She started up. "Are you an English gentleman?" she said. "Ah, I have always longed to see an English gentleman. I have never seen but one Englishman since we lived here, and he certainly was not a gentleman—no white people at all, indeed, except a few wandering Boers. We live among black people and baboons—only I have read about English people—lots of books—poetry and novels. But tell me what is your name? Macumazahn the black man called you, but you must have a white name, too."

"My name is Allan Quatermain," I said.

Her face turned quite white, her rosy lips parted, and she looked at me wildly with her beautiful dark eyes.

"It is wonderful," she said, "but I have often heard that name. My father has told me how a little boy called Allan Quatermain once saved my life by putting out my dress when it was on fire—see!"—and she pointed to a faint red mark upon her neck—"here is the scar of the burn."

"I remember it," I said. "You were dressed up as Father Christmas. It was I who put out the fire; my wrists were burnt in doing so."

Then for a space we sat silent, looking at each other, while Stella slowly fanned herself with her wide felt hat, in which some white ostrich plumes were fixed.

"This is God's doing," she said at last. "You saved my life when I was a child; now I have saved yours and the little girl's. Is she your own daughter?" she added, quickly.

"No," I answered; "I will tell you the tale presently."

"Yes," she said, "you shall tell me as we go home. It is time to be starting home, it will take us three hours to get there. Hendrika, Hendrika, bring the horses here!"

The Baboon-Woman

Hendrika obeyed, leading the horses to the side of the tree.

"Now, Mr. Allan," said Stella, "you must ride on my horse, and the old black man must ride on the other. I will walk, and Hendrika will carry the child. Oh, do not be afraid, she is very strong, she could carry you or me."

Hendrika grunted assent. I am sorry that I cannot express her method of speech by any more polite term. Sometimes she grunted like a monkey, sometimes she clicked like a Bushman, and sometimes she did both together, when she became quite unintelligible.

I expostulated against this proposed arrangement, saying that we could walk, which was a fib, for I do not think that I could have done a mile; but Stella would not listen, she would not even let me carry my elephant gun, but took it herself. So we mounted with some difficulty, and Hendrika took up the sleeping Tota in her long, sinewy arms.

"See that the 'Baboon-woman' does not run away into the mountains with the little white one," said Indaba-zimbi to me in Kaffir, as he climbed slowly on to the horse.

Unfortunately Hendrika understood his speech. Her face twisted and grew livid with fury. She put down Tota and literally sprang at Indaba-zimbi as a monkey springs. But weary and worn as he was, the old gentleman was too quick for her. With an exclamation of genuine fright he threw himself from the horse on the further side, with the somewhat ludicrous result that all in a moment Hendrika was occupying the seat which he had vacated. Just then Stella realized the position.

"Come down, you savage, come down!" she said, stamping her foot.

The extraordinary creature flung herself from the horse and literally grovelled on the ground before her mistress and burst into tears.

"Pardon, Miss Stella," she clicked and grunted in villainous English, "but he called me 'Babyan-frau' (Baboon-woman)."

"Tell your servant that he must not use such words to Hendrika, Mr. Allan," Stella said to me. "If he does," she added, in a whisper, "Hendrika will certainly kill him."

I explained this to Indaba-zimbi, who, being considerably frightened, deigned to apologize. But from that hour there was hate and war between these two.

Harmony having been thus restored, we started, the dogs following us. A small strip of desert intervened between us and the slope of the peak—perhaps it was two miles wide. We crossed it and reached rich grass lands, for here a considerable stream gathered from the hills; but it did not flow across the barren lands, it passed to the east along the foot of the hills. This stream we had to cross by a ford. Hendrika walked boldly through it, holding Tota in her arms. Stella leapt across from stone to stone like a roebuck;

I thought to myself that she was the most graceful creature that I had ever seen. After this the track passed around a pleasantly-wooded shoulder of the peak, which was, I found, known as Babyan Kap, or Baboon Head. Of course we could only go at a foot pace, so our progress was slow. Stella walked for some way in silence, then she spoke.

"Tell me, Mr. Allan," she said, "how it was that I came to find you dying in the desert?"

So I began and told her all. It took an hour or more to do so, and she listened intently, now and again asking a question.

"It is all very wonderful," she said when I had done, "very wonderful indeed. Do you know I went out this morning with Hendrika and the dogs for a ride, meaning to get back home by mid-day, for my father is ill, and I do not like to leave him for long. But just as I was going to turn, when we were about where we are now—yes, that was the very bush—an oribé got up, and the dogs chased it. I followed them for the gallop, and when we came to the river, instead of turning to the left as bucks generally do, the oribé swam the stream and took to the Bad Lands beyond. I followed it, and within a hundred yards of the big tree the dogs killed it. Hendrika wanted to turn back at once, but I said that we would rest under the shade of the tree, for I knew that there was a spring of water near. Well, we went; and there I saw you all lying like dead; but Hendrika, who is very clever in some ways, said no—and you know the rest. Yes, it is very wonderful."

"It is indeed," I said. "Now tell me, Miss Stella, who is Hendrika?"

She looked round before answering to see that the woman was not near.

"Hers is a strange story, Mr. Allan. I will tell you. You must know that all these mountains and the country beyond are full of baboons. When I was a girl of about ten I used to wander a great deal alone in the hills and valleys, and watch the baboons as they played among the rocks. There was one family of baboons that I watched especially—they used to live in a kloof about a mile from the house. The old man baboon was very large, and one of the females had a grey face. But the reason why I watched them so much was because I saw that they had with them a creature that looked like a girl, for her skin was quite white, and, what was more, that she was protected from the weather when it happened to be cold by a fur belt of some sort, which was tied round her throat. The old baboons seemed to be especially fond of her, and would sit with their arms round her neck. For nearly a whole summer I watched this particular white-skinned baboon till at last my curiosity quite overmastered me. I noticed that, though she climbed about the cliffs with the other monkeys, at a certain hour a little before sundown they used to put her with one or two other much smaller ones into a little cave, while the family went off somewhere to get food, to the mealie fields, I suppose. Then I got an idea that I would catch this white baboon and bring it home. But of course I could not do this by myself, so I took a Hottentot—a very clever man when he was not drunk—who lived on the stead, into my confidence. He was called Hendrik, and was very fond of me; but for a long while he would not listen to my plan, because he said that the babyans would kill us. At last I bribed him with a knife that had four blades, and one afternoon we started, Hendrik carrying a stout sack made of hide, with a rope running through it so that the mouth could be drawn tight.

"Well, we got to the place, and, hiding ourselves carefully in the trees at the foot of the kloof, watched the baboons playing about and grunting to each other, till at length, according to custom, they took the white one and three other little babies and put them in the cave. Then the old man came out, looked carefully round, called to his family, and went off with them over the brow of the kloof. Now very slowly and cautiously we crept up over the rocks till we came to the mouth of the cave and looked in. All the four little baboons were fast asleep, with their backs towards us, and their arms round each other's necks, the white one being in the middle. Nothing could have been better for our plans. Hendrik, who by this time had quite entered into the spirit of the thing, crept along the cave like a snake, and suddenly dropped the mouth of the hide bag over the head of the white baboon. The poor little thing woke up and gave a violent jump which caused it to vanish right into the bag. Then Hendrik pulled the string tight, and together we knotted it so that it was impossible for our captive to escape. Meanwhile the other baby baboons had rushed from the cave screaming, and when we got outside they were nowhere to be seen.

"'Come on, Missie,' said Hendrik; 'the babyans will soon be back.' He had shouldered the sack, inside of which the white baboon was kicking violently, and screaming like a child. It was dreadful to hear its shrieks.

"We scrambled down the sides of the kloof and ran for home as fast as we could manage. When we were near the waterfall, and within about three hundred yards of the garden wall, we heard a voice behind us, and there, leaping from rock to rock, and running over the grass, was the whole family of baboons headed by the old man.

"'Run, Missie, run!' gasped Hendrik, and I did, like the wind, leaving him far behind. I dashed into the garden, where some Kaffirs were working, crying, 'The babyans! the babyans!' Luckily the men had their sticks and spears by them and ran out just in time to save Hendrik, who was almost overtaken. The baboons made a good fight for it, however, and it was not till the old man was killed with an assegai that they ran away.

"Well, there is a stone hut in the kraal at the stead where my father sometimes shuts up natives who have misbehaved. It is very strong, and has a barred window. To this hut Hendrik carried the sack, and, having untied the mouth, put it down on the floor, and ran from the place, shutting the door behind him. In another moment the poor little thing was out and dashing round the stone hut as though it were mad. It sprung at the bars of the window, clung there, and beat its head against them till the blood came. Then it fell to the floor, and sat upon it crying like a child, and rocking itself backwards and forwards. It was so sad to see it that I began to cry too.

"Just then my father came in and asked what all the fuss was about. I told him that we had caught a young white baboon, and he was angry, and said that it must be let go. But when he looked at it through the bars of the window he nearly fell down with astonishment.

"Why!' he said, 'this is not a baboon, it is a white child that the baboons have stolen and brought up!'

"Now, Mr. Allan, whether my father is right or wrong, you can judge for yourself. You see Hendrika—we named her that after Hendrik, who caught her—she is a woman, not a monkey, and yet she has many of the ways of monkeys, and looks like one too. You saw how she can climb, for instance, and you hear how she talks. Also she is very savage, and when she is angry or jealous she seems to go mad, though she is as clever as anybody. I think that she must have been stolen by the baboons when she was quite tiny and nurtured by them, and that is why she is so like them.

"But to go on. My father said that it was our duty to keep Hendrika at any cost. The worst of it was, that for three days she would eat nothing, and I thought that she would die, for all the while she sat and wailed. On the third day, however, I went to the bars of the window place, and held out a cup of milk and some fruit to her. She looked at it for a long while, then crept up moaning, took the milk from my hand, drank it greedily, and afterwards ate the fruit. From that time forward she took food readily enough, but only if I would feed her.

"But I must tell you of the dreadful end of Hendrik. From the day that we captured Hendrika the whole place began to swarm with baboons which were evidently employed in watching the kraals. One day Hendrik went out towards the hills alone to gather some medicine. He did not come back again, so the next day search was made. By a big rock which I can show you, they found his scattered and broken bones, the fragments of his assegai, and four dead baboons. They had set upon him and torn him to pieces.

"My father was very much frightened at this, but still he would not let Hendrika go, because he said that she was human, and that it was our duty to reclaim her. And so we did—to a certain extent, at least. After the murder of Hendrik, the baboons vanished from the neighbourhood, and have only returned quite recently, so at length we ventured to let Hendrika out. By this time she had grown very fond of me; still, on the first opportunity she ran away. But in the evening she returned again. She had been seeking the baboons, and could not find them. Shortly afterwards she began to speak—I taught her—and from that time she has loved me so that she will not leave me. I think it would kill her if I went away from her. She watches me all day, and at night sleeps on the floor of my hut. Once, too, she saved my life when I was swept down the river in flood; but she is jealous, and hates everybody else. Look, how she is glaring at you now because I am talking to you!"

I looked. Hendrika was tramping along with the child in her arms and staring at me in a most sinister fashion out of the corners of her eyes.

While I was reflecting on the Baboon-woman's strange story, and thinking that she was an exceedingly awkward customer, the path took a sudden turn.

"Look!" said Stella, "there is our home. Is it not beautiful?"

It was beautiful indeed. Here on the western side of the great peak a bay had been formed in the mountain, which might have measured eight hundred or a thousand yards across by three-quarters of a mile in depth. At the back of this indentation the sheer cliff rose to the height of several hundred feet, and behind it and above it the great Babyan Peak towered up towards the heavens. The space of ground, embraced thus in the arms of the mountain, as it were, was laid out, as though by the cunning hand of man, in three terraces that rose one above the other. To the right and left of the topmost terrace were chasms in the cliff, and down each chasm fell a waterfall, from no great height, indeed, but of considerable volume. These two streams flowed away on either side of the enclosed space, one towards the north, and the other, the course of which we had been following, round the base of the mountain. At each terrace they made a cascade, so that the traveller approaching had a view of eight waterfalls at once. Along the edge of the stream to our left were placed Kaffir kraals, built in orderly groups with verandahs, after the Basutu fashion, and a very large part of the entire space of land was under cultivation. All of this I noted at once, as well as the extraordinary richness and depth of the soil, which for many ages past had been washed down from the mountain heights. Then following the line of an excellent waggon road, on which we now found ourselves, that wound up from terrace to terrace, my eye lit upon the crowning wonder of the scene. For in the centre of the topmost platform or terrace, which may have enclosed eight or ten acres of ground, and almost surrounded by groves of orange trees, gleamed buildings of which I had never seen the like. There were three groups of them, one in the middle, and one on either side, and a little to the rear, but, as I afterwards discovered, the plan of all was the same. In the centre was an edifice constructed like an ordinary Zulu hut—that is to say, in the shape of a beehive, only it was five times the size of any hut I ever saw, and built of blocks of hewn white marble, fitted together with extraordinary knowledge of the principles and properties of arch building, and with so much accuracy and finish that it was often difficult to find the joints of the massive blocks. From this centre hut ran three covered passages, leading to other buildings of an exactly similar character, only smaller, and each whole block was enclosed by a marble wall about four feet in height.

Of course we were as yet too far off to see all these details, but the general outline I saw at once, and it astonished me considerably. Even old Indaba-zimbi, whom the Baboon-woman had been unable to move, deigned to show wonder.

"Ou!" he said; "this is a place of marvels. Who ever saw kraals built of white stone?"

Stella watched our faces with an expression of intense amusement, but said nothing.

"Did your father build those kraals?" I gasped, at length.

"My father! no, of course not," she answered. "How would it have been possible for one white man to do so, or to have made this road? He found them as you see."

"Who built them, then?" I said again.

"I do not know. My father thinks that they are very ancient, for the people who live here now do not know how to lay one stone upon another, and these huts are so wonderfully constructed that, though they must have stood for ages, not a stone of them had fallen. But I can show you the quarry where the marble was cut; it is close by and behind it is the entrance to an ancient mine, which my father thinks was a silver mine. Perhaps the people who worked the mine built the marble huts. The world is old, and no doubt plenty of people have lived in it and been forgotten."

Then we rode on in silence. I have seen many beautiful sights in Africa, and in such matters, as in others, comparisons are odious and worthless, but I do not think that I ever saw a lovelier scene. It was no one thing—it was the combination of the mighty peak looking forth on to the everlasting plains, the great cliffs, the waterfalls that sparkled in rainbow hues, the rivers girdling the rich cultivated lands, the gold-specked green of the orange trees, the flashing domes of the marble huts, and a thousand other things. Then over all brooded the peace of evening, and the infinite glory of the sunset that filled heaven with changing hues of splendour, that wrapped the mountain and cliffs in cloaks of purple and of gold, and lay upon the quiet face of the water like the smile of a god.

Perhaps also the contrast, and the memory of those three awful days and nights in the hopeless desert, enhanced the charm, and perhaps the beauty of the girl who walked beside me completed it. For of this I am sure, that of all sweet and lovely things that I looked on then, she was the sweetest and the loveliest.

Ah, it did not take me long to find my fate. How long will it be before I find her once again?

The Marble Kraals

At length the last platform, or terrace, was reached, and we pulled up outside the wall surrounding the central group of marble huts—for so I must call them, for want of a better name. Our approach had been observed by a crowd of natives, whose race I have never been able to determine accurately; they belonged to the Basutu and peaceful section of the Bantu peoples rather than to the Zulu and warlike. Several of these ran up to take the horses, gazing on us with astonishment, not unmixed with awe. We dismounted—speaking for myself, not without difficulty—indeed, had it not been for Stella's support I should have fallen.

"Now you must come and see my father," she said. "I wonder what he will think of it, it is all so strange. Hendrika, take the child to my hut and give her milk, then put her into my bed; I will come presently."

Hendrika went off with a somewhat ugly grin to do her mistress's bidding, and Stella led the way through the narrow gateway in the marble wall, which may have enclosed nearly half an "erf," or three-quarters of an acre of ground in all. It was beautifully planted as a garden, many European vegetables and flowers were growing in it, besides others with which I was not acquainted. Presently we came to the centre hut, and it was then that I noticed the extraordinary beauty and finish of the marble masonry. In the hut, and facing the gateway, was a modern door, rather rudely fashioned of Buckenhout, a beautiful reddish wood that has the appearance of having been sedulously pricked with a pin. Stella opened it, and we entered. The interior of the hut was the size of a large and lofty room, the walls being formed of plain polished marble. It was lighted somewhat dimly, but quite effectively, by peculiar openings in the roof, from which the rain was excluded by overhanging eaves. The marble floor was strewn with native mats and skins of animals. Bookcases filled with books were placed against the walls, there was a table in the centre, chairs seated with rimpi or strips of hide stood about, and beyond the table was a couch on which a man was lying reading.

"Is that you, Stella?" said a voice, that even after so many years seemed familiar to me. "Where have you been, my dear? I began to think that you had lost yourself again."

"No, father, dear, I have not lost myself, but I have found somebody else."

At that moment I stepped forward so that the light fell on me. The old gentleman on the couch rose with some difficulty and bowed with much courtesy. He was a fine-looking old man, with deep-set dark eyes, a pale face that bore many traces of physical and mental suffering, and a long white beard.

"Be welcome, sir," he said. "It is long since we have seen a white face in these wilds, and yours, if I am not mistaken, is that of an Englishman. There has been but one Englishman here for twelve years, and he, I grieve to say, was an outcast flying from justice," and he bowed again and stretched out his hand.

I looked at him, and then of a sudden his name flashed back into my mind. I took his hand.

"How do you do, Mr. Carson?" I said.

He started as though he had been stung.

"Who told you that name?" he cried. "It is a dead name. Stella, is it you? I forbade you to let it pass your lips."

"I did not speak it, father. I have never spoken it," she answered.

"Sir," I broke in, "if you will allow me I will show you how I came to know your name. Do you remember many years ago coming into the study of a clergyman in Oxfordshire and telling him that you were going to leave England for ever?"

He bowed his head.

"And do you remember a little boy who sat upon the hearthrug writing with a pencil?"

"I do," he said.

"Sir, I was that boy, and my name is Allan Quatermain. Those children who lay sick are all dead, their mother is dead, and my father, your old friend, is dead also. Like you he emigrated, and last year he died in the Cape. But that is not all the story. After many adventures, I, one Kaffir, and a little girl, lay senseless and dying in the Bad Lands, where we had wandered for days without water, and there we should have perished, but your daughter, Miss—"

"Call her Stella," he broke in, hastily. "I cannot bear to hear that name. I have forsworn it."

"Miss Stella found us by chance and saved our lives."

"By chance, did you say, Allan Quatermain?" he answered. "There is little chance in all this; such chances spring from another will than ours. Welcome, Allan, son of my old friend. Here we live as it were in a hermitage, with Nature as our only friend, but such as we have is yours, and for as long as you will take it. But you must be starving; talk no more now. Stella, it is time to eat. To-morrow we will talk."

To tell the truth I can recall very little of the events of that evening. A kind of dizzy weariness overmastered me. I remember sitting at a table next to Stella, and eating heartily, and then I remember nothing more.

I awoke to find myself lying on a comfortable bed in a hut built and fashioned on the same model as the centre one. While I was wondering what time it was, a native came bringing some clean clothes on his arm, and, luxury of luxuries, produced a bath hollowed from wood. I rose, feeling a very different man, my strength had come back again to me; I dressed, and following a covered passage found myself in the centre hut. Here the table was set for breakfast with all manner of good things, such as I had not seen for many a month, which I contemplated with healthy satisfaction. Presently I looked up, and there before me was a more delightful sight, for standing in one of the doorways which led to the sleeping huts was Stella, leading little Tota by the hand.

She was very simply dressed in a loose blue gown, with a wide collar, and girdled in at the waist by a little leather belt. In the bosom of her robe was a bunch of orange blooms, and her rippling hair was tied in a single knot behind her shapely head. She greeted me with a smile, asking how I had slept, and then held Tota up for me to kiss. Under her loving care the child had been quite transformed. She was neatly dressed in a garment of the same blue stuff that Stella wore, her fair hair was brushed; indeed, had it not been for the sun blisters on her face and hands, one would scarcely have believed that this was the same child whom Indaba-zimbi and I had dragged for hour after hour through the burning, waterless desert.

"We must breakfast alone, Mr. Allan," she said; "my father is so upset by your arrival that he will not get up yet. Oh, you cannot tell how thankful I am that you have come. I have been so anxious about him of late. He grows weaker and weaker; it seems to me as though the strength were ebbing away from him. Now he scarcely leaves the kraal, I have to manage everything about the farm; he does nothing but read and think."

Just then Hendrika entered, bearing a jug of coffee in one hand and of milk in the other, which she set down upon the table, casting a look of little love at me as she did so.

"Be careful, Hendrika; you are spilling the coffee," said Stella. "Don't you wonder how we come to have coffee here, Mr. Allan— I will tell you—we grow it. That was my idea. Oh, I have lots of things to show you. You don't know what we have managed to do in the time that we have been here. You see we have plenty of labour, for the people about look upon my father as their chief."

"Yes," I said, "but how do you get all these luxuries of civilization?" and I pointed to the books, the crockery, and the knives and forks.

"Very simply. Most of the books my father brought with him when we first trekked into the wilds; there was nearly a waggon load of them. But every few years we have sent an expedition of three waggons right down to Port Natal. The waggons are loaded with ivory and other goods, and come back with all kinds of things that been sent out from England for us. So you see, although we live in this wild place, we are not altogether cut off. We can send runners to Natal and back in three months, and the waggons get there and back in a year. The last lot arrived quite safe about three months ago. Our servants are very faithful, and some of them speak Dutch well."

"Have you ever been with the waggons?" I asked.

"Since I was a child I have never been more than thirty miles from Babyan's Peak," she answered. "Do you know, Mr. Allan, that you are, with one exception, the first Englishman that I have known out of a book. I suppose that I must seem very wild and savage to you, but I have had one advantage—a good education. My father has taught me everything, and perhaps I know some things that you don't. I can read French and German, for instance. I think that my father's first idea was to let me run wild altogether, but he gave it up."

"And don't you wish to go into the world?" I asked.

"Sometimes," she said, "when I get lonely. But perhaps my father is right—perhaps it would frighten and bewilder me. At any rate he would never return to civilization; it is his idea, you know, although I am sure I do not know where he got it from, nor why he cannot bear that our name should be spoken. In short, Mr. Quatermain, we do not make our lives, we must take them as we find them. Have you done your breakfast? Let us go out, and I will show you our home."

I rose and went to my sleeping-place to fetch my hat. When I returned, Mr. Carson—for after all that was his name, though he would never allow it to be spoken—had come into the hut. He felt better now, he said, and would accompany us on our walk if Stella would give him an arm.

So we started, and after us came Hendrika with Tota and old Indaba-zimbi whom I found sitting outside as fresh as paint. Nothing could tire that old man.

The view from the platform was almost as beautiful as that from the lower ground looking up to the peak. The marble kraals, as I have said, faced west, consequently all the upper terrace lay in the shadow of the great peak till nearly eleven o'clock in the morning—a great advantage in that warm latitude. First we walked through the garden, which was beautifully cultivated, and one of the most productive that I ever saw. There were three or four natives working in it, and they all saluted my host as "Baba," or father. Then we visited the other two groups of marble huts. One of these was used for stables and outbuildings, the other as storehouses, the centre hut having been, however, turned into a chapel. Mr. Carson was not ordained, but he earnestly tried to convert the natives, most of whom were refugees who had come to him for shelter, and he had practised the more elementary rites of the church for so long that I think he began to believe that he really was a clergyman. For instance, he always married those of his people who would consent to a monogamous existence, and baptized their children.

When we had examined those wonderful remains of antiquity, the marble huts, and admired the orange trees, the vines and fruits which thrive like weeds in this marvellous soil and climate, we descended to the next platform, and saw the farming operations in full swing. I think that it was the best farm I have ever seen in Africa. There was ample water for purposes of irrigation, the grass lands below gave pasturage for hundreds of head of cattle and horses, and, for natives, the people were most industrious. Moreover, the whole place was managed by Mr. Carson on the co-operative system; he only took a tithe of the produce—indeed, in this land of teeming plenty, what was he to do with more? Consequently the tribesmen, who, by the way, called themselves the "Children of Thomas," were able to accumulate considerable wealth. All their disputes were referred to their "father," and he also was judge of offences and crimes. Some were punished by imprisonment, whipping, and loss of goods, other and graver transgressions by expulsion from the community, a fiat which to one of these favoured natives must have seemed as heavy as the decree that drove Adam from the Garden of Eden.

Old Mr. Carson leaned upon his daughter's arm and contemplated the scene with pride.

"I have done all this, Allan Quatermain," he said. "When renouncing civilization, I wandered here by chance; seeking a home in the remotest places of the world, I found this lonely spot a wilderness. Nothing was to be seen except the site, the domes of the marble huts, and the waterfalls. I took possession of the huts. I cleared the path of garden land and planted the orange grove. I had only six natives then, but by degrees others joined me, now my tribe is a thousand strong. Here we live in profound peace and plenty. I have all I need, and I seek no more. Heaven has prospered me so far—may it do so to the end, which for me draws nigh. And now I am tired and will go back. If you wish to see the old quarry and the mouth of the ancient mines, Stella will show them to you. No, my love, you need not trouble to come, I can manage. Look! some of the headmen are waiting to see me."

So he went; but still followed by Hendrika and Indaba-zimbi, we turned, and, walking along the bank of one of the rivers, passed up behind the marble kraals, and came to the quarry, whence the material of which they were built had been cut in some remote age. The pit opened up a very thick seam of the whitest and most beautiful marble. I know another like it in Natal. But by whom it had been worked I cannot say; not by natives, that is certain, though the builders of these kraals had condescended to borrow the shape of native huts for their model. By the way, the only relic of those builders that I ever saw was a highly finished bronze pick-axe which Stella had found one day in the quarry.

After we had examined this quarry we climbed the slope of the hill till we came to the mouth of the ancient mines which were situated in a gorge. I believe them to have been silver mines. The gorge was long and narrow, and the moment we entered it there rose from every side a sound of groaning and barking that was almost enough to deafen us. I knew what it was at once: the whole place was filled with baboons, which clambered down the rocks towards us from every direction, and in a manner that struck me as being unnaturally fearless. Stella turned a little pale and clung to my arm.

"It is very silly of me," she whispered. "I am not at all nervous, but ever since they killed Hendrik I cannot bear the sight of those animals. I always think that there is something human about them."

Meanwhile the baboons drew nearer, talking to each other as they came. Tota began to cry, and clung to Stella. Stella clung to me, while I and Indaba-zimbi put as bold a front on the matter as we could. Only Hendrika stood looking at the brutes with an unconcerned smile on her monkey face. When the great apes were quite near, she suddenly called aloud. Instantly they stopped their hideous clamour as though at a word of command. Then Hendrika addressed them: I can only describe it so. That is to say, she began to make a noise such as baboons do when they converse with each other. I have known Hottentots and Bushmen who said that they could talk with the baboons and understand their language, but I confess I never heard it done before or since.

From the mouth of Hendrika came a succession of grunts, groans, squeals, clicks, and every other abominable noise that can be conceived, conveying to my mind a general idea of expostulation. At any rate the baboons listened. One of them grunted back some answer, and then the whole mob drew off to the rocks.

I stood astonished, and without a word we turned back to the kraal, for Hendrika was too close to allow me to speak. When we reached the dining hut Stella went in, followed by Hendrika. But Indaba-zimbi plucked me by the sleeve, and I stopped outside.

"Macumazahn," he said. "Baboon-woman—devil-woman. Be careful, Macumazahn. She loves that Star (the natives aptly enough called Stella the Star), and is jealous. Be careful, Macumazahn, or the Star will set!"

"Let Us Go In, Allan!"

It is very difficult for me to describe the period of time which elapsed between my arrival at Babyan's Peak and my marriage with Stella. When I look back on it, it seems sweet as with the odour of flowers, and dim as with the happy dusk of summer eves, while through the sweetness comes the sound of Stella's voice, and through the gloom shines the starlight of her eyes. I think that we loved each other from the first, though for a while we said no word of love. Day by day I went about the place with her, accompanied by little Tota and Hendrika only, while she attended to the thousand and one matters which her father's ever-growing weakness had laid upon her; or rather, as time drew on, I attended to the business, and she accompanied me. All day through we were together. Then after supper, when the night had fallen, we would walk together in the garden and come at length to hear her father read aloud sometimes from the works of a poet, sometimes from history. Or, if he did not feel well, Stella would read, and when this was done, Mr. Carson would celebrate a short form of prayer, and we would separate till the morning once more brought our happy hour of meeting.

So the weeks went by, and with every week I grew to know my darling better. Often, I wonder now, if my fond fancy deceives me, or if indeed there are women as sweet and dear as she. Was it solitude that had given such depth and gentleness to her? Was it the long years of communing with Nature that had endowed her with such peculiar grace, the grace we find in opening flowers and budding trees? Had she caught that murmuring voice from the sound of the streams which fall continually about her rocky home? was it the tenderness of the evening sky beneath which she loved to walk, that lay like a shadow on her face, and the light of the evening stars that shone in her quiet eyes? At the least to me she was the realization of that dream which haunts the sleep of sin-stained men; so my memory paints her, so I hope to find her when at last the sleep has rolled away and the fevered dreams are done.

At last there came a day—the most blessed of my life, when we told our love. We had been together all the morning, but after dinner Mr. Carson was so unwell that Stella stopped in with him. At supper we met again, and after supper, when she had put little Tota, to whom she had grown much attached, to bed, we went out, leaving Mr. Carson dozing on the couch.

The night was warm and lovely, and without speaking we walked up the garden to the orange grove and sat down upon a rock. There was a little breeze which shook the petals of the orange blooms over us in showers, and bore their delicate fragrance far and wide. Silence reigned around, broken only by the sound of the falling waterfalls that now died to a faint murmur, and now, as the wavering breeze turned, boomed loudly in our ears. The moon was not yet visible, but already the dark clouds which floated through the sky above us—for there had been rain—showed a glow of silver, telling us that she shone brightly behind the peak. Stella began to talk in her low, gentle voice, speaking to me of her life in the wilderness, how she had grown to love it, how her mind had gone on from idea to idea, and how she pictured the great rushing world that she had never seen as it was reflected to her from the books which she had read. It was a curious vision of life that she had: things were out of proportion to it; it was more like a dream than a reality—a mirage than the actual face of things. The idea of great cities, and especially of London, had a kind of fascination for her: she could scarcely realize the rush, the roar and hurry, the hard crowds of men and women, strangers to each other, feverishly seeking for wealth and pleasure beneath a murky sky, and treading one another down in the fury of their competition.

"What is it all for?" she asked earnestly. "What do they seek? Having so few years to live, why do they waste them thus?"

I told her that in the majority of instances it was actual hard necessity that drove them on, but she could barely understand me. Living as she had done, in the midst of the teeming plenty of a fruitful earth, she did not seem to be able to grasp the fact that there were millions who from day to day know not how to stay their hunger.

"I never want to go there," she went on; "I should be bewildered and frightened to death. It is not natural to live like that. God put Adam and Eve in a garden, and that is how he meant their children to live—in peace, and looking always on beautiful things. This is my idea of perfect life. I want no other."

"I thought you once told me that you found it lonely," I said.

"So I did," she answered, innocently, "but that was before you came. Now I am not lonely any more, and it is perfect—perfect as the night."

Just then the full moon rose above the elbow of the peak, and her rays stole far and wide down the misty valley, gleaming on the water, brooding on the plain, searching out the hidden places of the rocks, wrapping the fair form of nature as in a silver bridal veil through which her beauty shone mysteriously.

Stella looked down the terraced valley; she turned and looked up at the scarred face of the golden moon, and then she looked at me. The beauty of the night was about her face, the scent of the night was on her hair, the mystery of the night shone in her shadowed eyes. She looked at me, I looked on her, and all our hearts' love blossomed within us. We spoke no word—we had no words to speak, but slowly we drew near, till lips were pressed to lips as we kissed our eternal troth.

It was she who broke that holy silence, speaking in a changed voice, in soft deep notes that thrilled me like the lowest chords of a smitten harp.

"Ah, now I understand," she said, "now I know why we are lonely, and how we can lose our loneliness. Now I know what it is that stirs us in the beauty of the sky, in the sound of water and in the scent of flowers. It is Love who speaks in everything, though till we hear his voice we understand nothing. But when we hear, then the riddle is answered and the gates of our heart are opened, and, Allan, we see the way that wends through death to heaven, and is lost in the glory of which our love is but a shadow.

"Let us go in, Allan. Let us go before the spell breaks, so that whatever overtakes us, sorrow, death, or separation, we may always have this perfect memory to save us. Come, dearest, let us go!"

I rose like a man in a dream, still holding her by the hand. But as I rose my eye fell upon something that gleamed white among the foliage of the orange bush at my side. I said nothing, but looked. The breeze stirred the orange leaves, the moonlight struck for a moment full upon the white object.

It was the face of Hendrika, the Babyan-woman, as Indaba-zimbi had called her, and on it was a glare of hate that made me shudder.

I said nothing; the face vanished, and just then I heard a baboon bark in the rocks behind.

Then we went down the garden, and Stella passed into the centre hut. I saw Hendrika standing in the shadow near the door, and went up to her.

"Hendrika," I said, "why were you watching Miss Stella and myself in the garden?"

She drew her lips up till her teeth gleamed in the moonlight.

"Have I not watched her these many years, Macumazahn? Shall I cease to watch because a wandering white man comes to steal her? Why were you kissing her in the garden, Macumazahn— How dare you kiss her who is a star?"

"I kissed her because I love her, and because she loves me," I answered. "What has that to do with you, Hendrika?"

"Because you love her," she hissed in answer; "and do I not love her also, who saved me from the babyans? I am a woman as she is, and you are a man, and they say in the kraals that men love women better than women love women. But it is a lie, though this is true, that if a woman loves a man she forgets all other love. Have I not seen it? I gather her flowers—beautiful flowers; I climb the rocks where you would never dare to go to find them; you pluck a piece of orange bloom in the garden and give it to her. What does she do?—she takes the orange bloom, she puts it in her breast, and lets my flowers die. I call to her—she does not hear me—she is thinking. You whisper to some one far away, and she hears and smiles. She used to kiss me sometimes; now she kisses that white brat you brought, because you brought it. Oh, I see it all—all; I have seen it from the first; you are stealing her from us, stealing her to yourself, and those who loved her before you came are forgotten. Be careful, Macumazahn, be careful, lest I am revenged upon you. You, you hate me; you think me half a monkey; that servant of yours calls me Baboon-woman. Well, I have lived with baboons, and they are clever—yes, they can play tricks and know things that you don't, and I am cleverer than they, for I have learnt the wisdom of white people also, and I say to you, Walk softly, Macumazahn, or you will fall into a pit," and with one more look of malice she was gone.

I stood for a moment reflecting. I was afraid of this strange creature who seemed to combine the cunning of the great apes that had reared her with the passions and skill of human kind. I foreboded evil at her hands. And yet there was something almost touching in the fierceness of her jealousy. It is generally supposed that this passion only exists in strength when the object loved is of another sex from the lover, but I confess that, both in this instance and in some others which I have met with, this has not been my experience. I have known men, and especially uncivilized men, who were as jealous of the affection of their friend or master as any lover could be of that of his mistress; and who has not seen cases of the same thing where parents and their children are concerned? But the lower one gets in the scale of humanity, the more readily this passion thrives; indeed, it may be said to come to its intensest perfection in brutes. Women are more jealous than men, small-hearted men are more jealous than those of larger mind and wider sympathy, and animals are the most jealous of all. Now Hendrika was in some ways not far removed from animal, which may perhaps account for the ferocity of her jealousy of her mistress's affection.

Shaking off my presentiments of evil, I entered the centre hut. Mr. Carson was resting on the sofa, and by him knelt Stella holding his hand, and her head resting on his breast. I saw at once that she had been telling him of what had come about between us; nor was I sorry, for it is a task that a would-be son-in-law is generally glad to do by deputy.

"Come here, Allan Quatermain," he said, almost sternly, and my heart gave a jump, for I feared lest he might be about to require me to go about my business. But I came.

"Stella tells me," he went on, "that you two have entered into a marriage engagement. She tells me also that she loves you, and that you say that you love her."

"I do indeed, sir," I broke in; "I love her truly; if ever a woman was loved in this world, I love her."

"I thank Heaven for it," said the old man. "Listen, my children. Many years ago a great shame and sorrow fell upon me, so great a sorrow that, as I sometimes think, it affected my brain. At any rate, I determined to do what most men would have considered the act of a madman, to go far away into the wilderness with my only child, there to live remote from civilization and its evils. I did so; I found this place, and here we have lived for many years, happily enough, and perhaps not without doing good in our generation, but still in a way unnatural to our race and status. At first I thought I would let my daughter grow up in a state of complete ignorance, that she should be Nature's child. But as time went on, I saw the folly and the wickedness of my plan. I had no right to degrade her to the level of the savages around me, for if the fruit of the tree of knowledge is a bitter fruit, still it teaches good from evil. So I educated her as well as I was able, till in the end I knew that in mind, as in body, she was in no way inferior to her sisters, the children of the civilized world. She grew up and entered into womanhood, and then it came into my mind that I was doing her a bitter wrong, that I was separating her from her kind and keeping her in a wilderness where she could find neither mate nor companion. But though I knew this, I could not yet make up my mind to return to active life; I had grown to love this place. I dreaded to return into the world I had abjured. Again and again I put my resolutions aside. Then at the commencement of this year I fell ill. For a while I waited, hoping that I might get better, but at last I realized that I should never get better, that the hand of Death was upon me."

"Ah, no, father, not that!" Stella said, with a cry.

"Yes, love, that, and it is true. Now you will be able to forget our separation in the happiness of a new meeting," and he glanced at me and smiled. "Well, when this knowledge came home to me, I determined to abandon this place and trek for the coast, though I well knew that the journey would kill me. I should never live to reach it. But Stella would, and it would be better than leaving her here alone with savages in the wilderness. On the very day that I had made up my mind to take this step Stella found you dying in the Bad Lands, Allan Quatermain, and brought you here. She brought you, of all men in the world, you, whose father had been my dear friend, and who once with your baby hands had saved her life from fire, that she might live to save yours from thirst. At the time I said little, but I saw the hand of Providence in this, and I determined to wait and see what came about between you. At the worst, if nothing came about, I soon learned that I could trust you to see her safely to the coast after I was gone. But many days ago I knew how it stood between you, and now things are determined as I prayed they might be. God bless you both, my children; may you be happy in your love; may it endure till death and beyond it. God bless you both!" and he stretched out his hand towards me.

I took it, and Stella kissed him.

Presently he spoke again—

"It is my intention," he said, "if you two consent, to marry you next Sunday. I wish to do so soon, for I do not know how much longer will be allowed to me. I believe that such a ceremony, solemnly celebrated and entered into before witnesses, will, under the circumstances, be perfectly legal; but of course you will repeat it with every formality the first moment it lies in your power so to do. And now, there is one more thing: when I left England my fortunes were in a shattered condition; in the course of years they have recovered themselves, the accumulated rents, as I heard but recently, when the waggons last returned from Port Natal, have sufficed to pay off all charges, and there is a considerable balance over. Consequently you will not marry on nothing, for of course you, Stella, are my heiress, and I wish to make a stipulation. It is this. That so soon as my death occurs you should leave this place and take the first opportunity of returning to England. I do not ask you to live there always; it might prove too much for people reared in the wilds, as both of you have been; but I do ask you to make it your permanent home. Do you consent and promise this?"

"I do," I answered.

"And so do I," said Stella.

"Very well," he answered; "and now I am tired out. Again God bless you both, and good-night."

Hendrika Plots Evil

On the following morning I had a conversation with Indaba-zimbi. First of all I told him that I was going to marry Stella.

"Oh!" he said, "I thought so, Macumazahn. Did I not tell you that you would find happiness on this journey? Most men must be content to watch the Star from a long way off, to you it is given to wear her on your heart. But remember, Macumazahn, remember that stars set."

"Can you not stop your croaking even for a day?" I answered, angrily, for his words sent a thrill of fear through me.

"A true prophet must tell the ill as well as the good, Macumazahn. I only speak what is on my mind. But what of it? What is life but loss, loss upon loss, till life itself be lost? But in death we may find all the things that we have lost. So your father taught, Macumazahn, and there was wisdom in his gentleness. Ou! I do not believe in death; it is change, that is all, Macumazahn. Look now, the rain falls, the drops of rain that were one water in the clouds fall side by side. They sink into the ground; presently the sun will come out, the earth will be dry, the drops will be gone. A fool looks and says the drops are dead, they will never be one again, they will never again fall side by side. But I am a rain-maker, and I know the ways of rain. It is not true. The drops will drain by many paths into the river, and will be one water there. They will go up to the clouds again in the mists of morning, and there will again be as they have been. We are the drops of rain, Macumazahn. When we fall that is our life. When we sink into the ground that is death, and when we are drawn up again to the sky, what is that, Macumazahn? No! no! when we find we lose, and when we seem to lose, then we shall really find. I am not a Christian, Macumazahn, but I am old, and have watched and seen things that perhaps Christians do not see. There, I have spoken. Be happy with your star, and if it sets, wait, Macumazahn, wait till it rises again. It will not be long; one day you will go to sleep, then your eyes will open on another sky, and there your star will be shining, Macumazahn."

I made no answer at the time. I could not bear to talk of such a thing. But often and often in the after years I have thought of Indaba-zimbi and his beautiful simile and gathered comfort from it. He was a strange man, this old rain-making savage, and there was more wisdom in him than in many learned atheists—those spiritual destroyers who, in the name of progress and humanity, would divorce hope from life, and leave us wandering in a lonesome, self-consecrated hell.

"Indaba-zimbi," I said, changing the subject, "I have something to say," and I told him of the threats of Hendrika.

He listened with an unmoved face, nodding his white lock at intervals as the narrative went on. But I saw that he was disturbed by it.

"Macumazahn," he said at length, "I have told you that this is an evil woman. She was nourished on baboon milk, and the baboon nature is in her veins. Such creatures should be killed, not kept. She will make you mischief if she can. But I will watch her, Macumazahn. Look, the Star is waiting for you; go, or she will hate me as Hendrika hates you."

So I went, nothing loth, for attractive as was the wisdom of Indaba-zimbi, I found a deeper meaning in Stella's simplest word. All the rest of that day I passed in her company, and the greater part of the two following days. At last came Saturday night, the eve of our marriage. It rained that night, so we did not go out, but spent the evening in the hut. We sat hand in hand, saying little, but Mr. Carson talked a good deal, telling us tales of his youth, and of countries that he had visited. Then he read aloud from the Bible, and bade us goodnight. I also kissed Stella and went to bed. I reached my hut by the covered way, and before I undressed opened the door to see what the night was like. It was very dark, and rain was still falling, but as the light streamed out into the gloom I fancied that I caught sight of a dusky form gliding away. The thought of Hendrika flashed into my mind; could she be skulking about outside there— Now I had said nothing of Hendrika and her threats either to Mr. Carson or Stella, because I did not wish to alarm them. Also I knew that Stella was attached to this strange person, and I did not wish to shake her confidence in her unless it was absolutely necessary. For a minute or two I stood hesitating, then, reflecting that if it was Hendrika, there she should stop, I went in and put up the stout wooden bar that was used to secure the door. For the last few nights old Indaba-zimbi had made a habit of sleeping in the covered passage, which was the only other possible way of access. As I came to bed I had stepped over him rolled up in his blanket, and to all appearances fast asleep. So it being evident that I had nothing to fear, I promptly dismissed the matter from my mind, which, as may be imagined, was indeed fully occupied with other thoughts.

I got into bed, and for awhile lay awake thinking of the great happiness in store for me, and of the providential course of events that had brought it within my reach. A few weeks since and I was wandering in the desert a dying man, bearing a dying child, and with scarcely a possession left in the world except a store of buried ivory that I never expected to see again. And now I was about to wed one of the sweetest and loveliest women on the whole earth—a woman whom I loved more than I could have thought possible, and who loved me back again. Also, as though that were not good fortune enough, I was to acquire with her very considerable possessions, quite sufficiently large to enable us to follow any plan of life we found agreeable. As I lay and reflected on all this I grew afraid of my good fortune. Old Indaba-zimbi's melancholy prophecies came into my mind. Hitherto he had always prophesied truly. What if these should be true also? I turned cold as I thought of it, and prayed to the Power above to preserve us both to live and love together. Never was prayer more needed. While its words were still upon my lips I dropped asleep and dreamed a most dreadful dream.

I dreamed that Stella and I were standing together to be married. She was dressed in white, and radiant with beauty, but it was a wild, spiritual beauty which frightened me. Her eyes shone like stars, a pale flame played about her features, and the wind that blew did not stir her hair. Nor was this all, for her white robes were death wrappings, and the altar at which we stood was formed of the piled-up earth from an open grave that yawned between us. So we stood waiting for one to wed us, but no one came. Presently from the open grave sprang the form of Hendrika. In her hand was a knife, with which she stabbed at me, but pierced the heart of Stella, who, without a cry, fell backwards into the grave, still looking at me as she fell. Then Hendrika leaped after her into the grave. I heard her feet strike heavily.

"*Awake, Macumazahn! awake!*" cried the voice of Indaba-zimbi.

I awoke and bounded from the bed, a cold perspiration pouring from me. In the darkness on the other side of the hut I heard sounds of furious struggling. Luckily I kept my head. Just by me was a chair on which were matches and a rush taper. I struck a match and held it to the taper. Now in the growing light I could see two forms rolling one over the other on the floor, and from between them came the flash of steel. The fat melted and the light burnt up. It was Indaba-zimbi and the woman Hendrika who were struggling, and, what is more, the woman was getting the better of the man, strong as he was. I rushed towards them. Now she was uppermost, now she had wrenched herself from his fierce grip, and now the great knife she had in her hand flashed up.

But I was behind her, and, placing my hands beneath her arms, jerked with all my strength. She fell backwards, and, in her effort to save herself, most fortunately dropped the knife. Then we flung ourselves upon her. Heavens! the strength of that she-devil! Nobody who has not experienced it could believe it. She fought and scratched and bit, and at one time nearly mastered the two of us. As it was she did break loose. She rushed at the bed, sprung on it, and bounded thence straight up at the roof of the hut. I never saw such a jump, and could not conceive what she meant to do. In the roof were the peculiar holes which I have described. They were designed to admit light, and covered with overhanging eaves. She sprung straight and true like a monkey, and, catching the edge of the hole with her hands, strove to draw herself through it. But here her strength, exhausted with the long struggle, failed her. For a moment she swung, then dropped to the ground and fell senseless.

"Ou!" gasped Indaba-zimbi. "Let us tie the devil up before she comes to life again."

I thought this a good counsel, so we took a reim that lay in the corner of the room, and lashed her hands and feet in such a fashion that even she could scarcely escape. Then we carried her into the passage, and Indaba-zimbi sat over her, the knife in his hand, for I did not wish to raise an alarm at that hour of the night.

"Do you know how I caught her, Macumazahn?" he said. "For several nights I have slept here with one eye open, for I thought she had made a plan. To-night I kept wide awake, though I pretended to be asleep. An hour after you got into the blankets the moon rose, and I saw a beam of light come into the hut through the hole in the roof. Presently I saw the beam of light vanish. At first I thought that a cloud was passing over the moon, but I listened and heard a noise as though some one was squeezing himself through a narrow space. Presently he was through, and hanging by his hands. Then the light came in again, and in the middle of it I saw the Babyan-frau swinging from the roof, and about to drop into the hut. She clung by both hands, and in her mouth was a great knife. She dropped, and I ran forward to seize her as she dropped, and gripped her round the middle. But she heard me come, and, seizing the knife, struck at me in the dark and missed me. Then we struggled, and you know the rest. You were very nearly dead to-night, Macumazahn."

"Very nearly indeed," I answered, still panting, and arranging the rags of my night-dress round me as best I might. Then the memory of my horrid dream flashed into my mind. Doubtless it had been conjured up by the sound of Hendrika dropping to the floor—in my dream it had been a grave that she dropped into. All of it, then, had been experienced in that second of time. Well, dreams are swift; perhaps Time itself is nothing but a dream, and events that seem far apart really occur simultaneously.

We passed the rest of the night watching Hendrika. Presently she came to herself and struggled furiously to break the reim. But the untanned buffalo hide was too strong even for her, and, moreover, Indaba-zimbi unceremoniously sat upon her to keep her quiet. At last she gave it up.

In due course the day broke—my marriage day. Leaving Indaba-zimbi to watch my would-be murderess, I went and fetched some natives from the stables, and with their aid bore Hendrika to the prison hut—that same hut in which she had been confined when she had been brought a baboon-child from the rocks. Here we shut her up, and, leaving Indaba-zimbi to watch outside, I returned to my sleeping-place and dressed in the best garments that the Babyan Kraals could furnish. But when I looked at the reflection of my face, I was horrified. It was covered with scratches inflicted by the nails of Hendrika. I doctored them up as best I could, then went out for a walk to calm my nerves, which, what between the events of the past night, and of those pending that day, were not a little disturbed.

When I returned it was breakfast time. I went into the dining hut, and there Stella was waiting to greet me, dressed in simple white and with orange flowers on her breast. She came forward to me shyly enough; then, seeing the condition of my face, started back.

"Why, Allan! what have you been doing to yourself?" she asked.

As I was about to answer, her father came in leaning on his stick, and, catching sight of me, instantly asked the same question.

Then I told them everything, both of Hendrika's threats and of her fierce attempt to carry them into execution. But I did not tell my horrid dream.

Stella's face grew white as the flowers on her breast, but that of her father became very stern.

"You should have spoken of this before, Allan," he said. "I now see that I did wrong to attempt to civilize this wicked and revengeful creature, who, if she is human, has all the evil passions of the brutes that reared her. Well, I will make an end of it this very day."

"Oh, father," said Stella, "don't have her killed. It is all dreadful enough, but that would be more dreadful still. I have been very fond of her, and, bad as she is, she has loved me. Do not have her killed on my marriage day."

"No," her father answered, "she shall not be killed, for though she deserves to die, I will not have her blood upon our hands. She is a brute, and has followed the nature of brutes. She shall go back whence she came."

No more was said on the matter at the time, but when breakfast—which was rather a farce—was done, Mr. Carson sent for his headman and gave him certain orders.

We were to be married after the service which Mr. Carson held every Sunday morning in the large marble hut set apart for that purpose. The service began at ten o'clock, but long before that hour all the natives on the place came up in troops, singing as they came, to be present at the wedding of the "Star." It was a pretty sight to see them, the men dressed in all their finery, and carrying shields and sticks in their hands, and the women and children bearing green branches of trees, ferns, and flowers. At length, about half-past nine, Stella rose, pressed my hand, and left me to my reflections. A few minutes to ten she reappeared again with her father, dressed in a white veil, a wreath of orange flowers on her dark curling hair, a bouquet of orange flowers in her hand. To me she seemed like a dream of loveliness. With her came little Tota in a high state of glee and excitement. She was Stella's only bridesmaid. Then we all passed out towards the church hut. The bare space in front of it was filled with hundreds of natives, who set up a song as we came. But we went on into the hut, which was crowded with such of the natives as usually worshipped there. Here Mr. Carson, as usual, read the service, though he was obliged to sit down in order to do so. When it was done—and to me it seemed interminable—Mr. Carson whispered that he meant to marry us outside the hut in sight of all the people. So we went out and took our stand under the shade of a large tree that grew near the hut facing the bare space where the natives were gathered.

Mr. Carson held up his hand to enjoin silence. Then, speaking in the native dialect, he told them that he was about to make us man and wife after the Christian fashion and in the sight of all men. This done, he proceeded to read the marriage service over us, and very solemnly and beautifully he did it. We said the words, I placed the ring—it was her father's signet ring, for we had no other—upon Stella's finger, and it was done.

Then Mr. Carson spoke. "Allan and Stella," he said, "I believe that the ceremony which has been performed makes you man and wife in the sight of God and man, for all that is necessary to make a marriage binding is, that it should be celebrated according to the custom of the country where the parties to it reside. It is according to the custom that has been in force here for fifteen years or more that you have been married in the face of all the people, and in token of it you will both sign the register that I have kept of such marriages, among those of my people who have adopted the Christian Faith. Still, in case there should be any legal flaw I again demand the solemn promise of you both that on the first opportunity you will cause this marriage to be re-celebrated in some civilized land. Do you promise?"

"We do," we answered.

Then the book was brought out and we signed our names. At first my wife signed hers "Stella" only, but her father bade her write it Stella Carson for the first and last time in her life. Then several of the indunas, or headmen, including old Indaba-zimbi, put their marks in witness. Indaba-zimbi drew his mark in the shape of a little star, in humorous allusion to Stella's native name. That register is before me now as I write. That, with a lock of my darling's hair which lies between its leaves, is my dearest possession. There are all the names and marks as they were written many years ago beneath the shadow of the tree at Babyan Kraals in the wilderness, but alas! and alas! where are those who wrote them?

"My people," said Mr. Carson, when the signing was done, and we had kissed each other before them all—"My people, Macumazahn and the Star, my daughter, are now man and wife, to live in one kraal, to eat of one bowl, to share one fortune till they reach the grave. Hear now, my people, you know this woman," and turning he pointed to Hendrika, who, unseen by us, had been led out of the prison hut.

"Yes, yes, we know her," said a little ring of headmen, who formed the primitive court of justice, and after the fashion of natives had squatted themselves in a circle on the ground in front of us. "We know her, she is the white Babyan-woman, she is Hendrika, the body servant of the Star."

"You know her," said Mr. Carson, "but you do not know her altogether. Stand forward, Indaba-zimbi, and tell the people what came about last night in the hut of Macumazahn."

Accordingly old Indaba-zimbi came forward, and, squatting down, told his moving tale with much descriptive force and many gestures, finishing up by producing the great knife from which his watchfulness had saved me.

Then I was called upon, and in a few brief words substantiated his story: indeed my face did that in the sight of all men.

Then Mr. Carson turned to Hendrika, who stood in sullen silence, her eyes fixed upon the ground, and asked her if she had anything to say.

She looked up boldly and answered—

"Macumazahn has robbed me of the love of my mistress. I would have robbed him of his life, which is a little thing compared to that which I have lost at his hands. I have failed, and I am sorry for it, for had I killed him and left no trace the Star would have forgotten him and shone on me again."

"Never," murmured Stella in my ear; but Mr. Carson turned white with wrath.

"My people," he said, "you hear the words of this woman. You hear how she pays me back, me and my daughter whom she swears she loves. She says that she would have murdered a man who has done her no evil, the man who is the husband of her mistress. We saved her from the babyans, we tamed her, we fed her, we taught her, and this is how she pays us back. Say, my people, what reward should be given to her?"

"Death," said the circle of indunas, pointing their thumbs downwards, and all the multitude beyond echoed the word "Death."

"Death," repeated the head induna, adding, "If you save her, my father, we will slay her with our own hands. She is a Babyan-woman, a devil-woman; ah, yes, we have heard of such before; let her be slain before she works more evil."

Then it was that Stella stepped forward and begged for Hendrika's life in moving terms. She pleaded the savagery of the woman's nature, her long service, and the affection that she had always shown towards herself. She said that I, whose life had been attempted, forgave her, and she, my wife, who had nearly been left a widow before she was made a bride, forgave her; let them forgive her also, let her be sent away, not slain, let not her marriage day be stained with blood.

Now her father listened readily enough, for he had no intention of killing Hendrika—indeed, he had already promised not to do so. But the people were in a different humour, they looked upon Hendrika as a devil, and would have torn her to pieces there and then, could they have had their way. Nor were matters mended by Indaba-zimbi, who had already gained a great reputation for wisdom and magic in the place. Suddenly the old man rose and made quite an impassioned speech, urging them to kill Hendrika at once or mischief would come of it.

At last matters got very bad, for two of the Indunas came forward to drag her off to execution, and it was not until Stella burst into tears that the sight of her grief, backed by Mr. Carson's orders and my own remonstrances, carried the day.

All this while Hendrika had been standing quite unmoved. At last the tumult ceased, and the leading induna called to her to go, promising that if ever she showed her face near the kraals again she should be stabbed like a jackal. Then Hendrika spoke to Stella in a low voice and in English—

"Better let them kill me, mistress, better for all. Without you to love I shall go mad and become a babyan again."

Stella did not answer, and they loosed her. She stepped forward and looked at the natives with a stare of hate. Then she turned and walked past me, and as she passed whispered a native phrase in my ear, that, being literally translated, means, "Till another moon," but which has the same significance as the French "au revoir."

It frightened me, for I knew she meant that she had not done with me, and saw that our mercy was misplaced. Seeing my face change she ran swiftly from me, and as she passed Indaba-zimbi, with a sudden movement snatched her great knife from his hand. When she had gone about twenty paces she halted, looked long and earnestly on Stella, gave one loud cry of anguish, and fled. A few minutes later we saw her far away, bounding up the face of an almost perpendicular cliff—a cliff that nobody except herself and the baboons could possibly climb.

"Look," said Indaba-zimbi in my ear—"Look, Macumazahn, there goes the Babyan-frau. But, Macumazahn, *she will come back again*. Ah, why will you not listen to my words. Have they not always been true words, Macumazahn?" and he shrugged his shoulders and turned away.

For a while I was much disturbed, but at any rate Hendrika was gone for the present, and Stella, my dear and lovely wife, was there at my side, and in her smiles I forgot my fears.

For the rest of that day, why should I write of it?—there are things too happy and too sacred to be written of.

At last I had, if only for a little while, found that rest, that perfect joy which we seek so continually and so rarely clasp.

Gone!

I wonder if many married couples are quite as happy as we found ourselves. Cynics, a growing class, declare that few illusions can survive a honeymoon. Well, I do not know about it, for I only married once, and can but speak from my limited experience. But certainly our illusion, or rather the great truth of which it is the shadow, did survive, as to this day it survives in my heart across all the years of utter separation, and across the unanswering gulf of gloom.

But complete happiness is not allowed in this world even for an hour. As our marriage day had been shadowed by the scene which has been described, so our married life was shadowed by its own sorrow.

Three days after our wedding Mr. Carson had a stroke. It had been long impending, now it fell. We came into the centre hut to dinner and found him lying speechless on the couch. At first I thought that he was dying, but this was not so. On the contrary, within four days he recovered his speech and some power of movement. But he never recovered his memory, though he still knew Stella, and sometimes myself. Curiously enough he remembered little Tota best of all three, though occasionally he thought that she was his own daughter in her childhood, and would ask her where her mother was. This state of affairs lasted for some seven months. The old man gradually grew weaker, but he did not die. Of course his condition quite precluded the idea of our leaving Babyan Kraals till all was over. This was the more distressing to me because I had a nervous presentiment that Stella was incurring danger by staying there, and also because the state of her health rendered it desirable that we should reach a civilized region as soon as possible. However, it could not be helped.

At length the end came very suddenly. We were sitting one evening by Mr. Carson's bedside in his hut, when to our astonishment he sat up and spoke in a strong, full voice.

"I hear you," he said. "Yes, yes, I forgive you. Poor woman! you too have suffered," and he fell back dead.

I have little doubt that he was addressing his lost wife, some vision of whom had flashed across his dying sense. Stella, of course, was overwhelmed with grief at her loss. Till I came her father had been her sole companion, and therefore, as may be imagined, the tie between them was much closer than is usual even in the case of father and daughter. So deeply did she mourn that I began to fear for the effect upon her health. Nor were we the only ones to grieve; all the natives on the settlement called Mr. Carson "father," and as a father they lamented him. The air resounded with the wailing of women, and the men went about with bowed heads, saying that "the sun had set in the heavens, now only the Star (Stella) remained." Indaba-zimbi alone did not mourn. He said that it was best that the Inkoos should die, for what was life worth when one lay like a log?—moreover, that it would have been well for all if he had died sooner.

On the following day we buried him in the little graveyard near the waterfall. It was a sad business, and Stella cried very much, in spite of all I could do to comfort her.

That night as I sat outside the hut smoking—for the weather was hot, and Stella was lying down inside—old Indaba-zimbi came up, saluted, and squatted at my feet.

"What is it, Indaba-zimbi?" I said.

"This, Macumazahn. When are you going to trek towards the coast?"

"I don't know," I answered. "The Star is not fit to travel now, we must wait awhile."

"No, Macumazahn, you must not wait, you must go, and the Star must take her chance. She is strong. It is nothing. All will be well."

"Why do you say so— why must we go?"

"For this reason, Macumazahn," and he looked cautiously round and spoke low. "The baboons have come back in thousands. All the mountain is full of them."

"I did not know that they had gone," I said.

"Yes," he answered, "they went after the marriage, all but one or two; now they are back, all the baboons in the world, I think. I saw a whole cliff back with them."

"Is that all?" I said, for I saw that he had something behind. "I am not afraid of a pack of baboons."

"No, Macumazahn, it is not all. The Babyan-frau, Hendrika, is with them."

Now nothing had been heard or seen of Hendrika since her expulsion, and though at first she and her threats had haunted me somewhat, by degrees she to a great extent had passed out of my mind, which was fully preoccupied with Stella and my father-in-law's illness. I started violently. "How do you know this?" I asked.

"I know it because I saw her, Macumazahn. She is disguised, she is dressed up in baboon skins, and her face is stained dark. But though she was a long way off, I knew her by her size, and I saw the white flesh of her arm when the skins slipped aside. She has come back, Macumazahn, with all the baboons in the world, and she has come back to do evil. Now do you understand why you should trek?"

"Yes," I said, "though I don't see how she and the baboons can harm us, I think that it will be better to go. If necessary we can camp the waggons somewhere for a while on the journey. Hearken, Indaba-zimbi: say nothing of this to the Star; I will not have her frightened. And hearken again. Speak to the headmen, and see that watchers are set all round the huts and gardens, and kept there night and day. To-morrow we will get the waggons ready, and next day we will trek."

He nodded his white lock and went to do my bidding, leaving me not a little disturbed—unreasonably so, indeed. It was a strange story. That this woman had the power of conversing with baboons I knew. That was not so very wonderful, seeing that the Bushmen claim to be able to do the same thing, and she had been nurtured by them. But that she had been able to muster them, and by the strength of her human will and intelligence muster them in order to forward her ends of revenge, seemed to me so incredible that after reflection my fears grew light. Still I determined to trek. After all, a journey in an ox waggon would not be such a very terrible thing to a strong woman accustomed to roughing it, whatever her state of health. And when all was said and done I did not like this tale of the presence of Hendrika with countless hosts of baboons.

So I went in to Stella, and without saying a word to her of the baboon story, told her I had been thinking matters over, and had come to the conclusion that it was our duty to follow her father's instructions to the letter, and leave Babyan Kraals at once. Into all our talk I need not enter, but the end of it was that she agreed with me, and declared that she could quite well manage the journey, saying, moreover, that now that her dear father was dead she would be glad to get away.

Nothing happened to disturb us that night, and on the following morning I was up early making preparations. The despair of the people when they learned that we were going to leave them was something quite pitiable. I could only console them by declaring that we were but on a journey, and would return the following year.

"They had lived in the shadow of their father, who was dead," they declared; "ever since they were little they had lived in his shadow. He had received them when they were outcasts and wanderers without a mat to lie on, or a blanket to cover them, and they had grown fat in his shadow. Then he had died, and the Star, their father's daughter, had married me, Macumazahn, and they had believed that I should take their father's place, and let them live in my shadow. What should they do when there was no one to protect them? The tribes were kept from attacking them by fear of the white man. If we went they would be eaten up," and so on. Alas! there was but too much foundation for their fears.

I returned to the huts at mid-day to get some dinner. Stella said that she was going to pack during the afternoon, so I did not think it necessary to caution her about going out alone, as I did not wish to allude to the subject of Hendrika and the baboons unless I was obliged to. I told her, however, that I would come back to help her as soon as I could get away. Then I went down to the native kraals to sort out such cattle as had belonged to Mr. Carson from those which belonged to the Kaffirs, for I proposed to take them with us. It was a large herd, and the business took an incalculable time. At length, a little before sundown, I gave it up, and leaving Indaba-zimbi to finish the job, got on my horse and rode homewards.

Arriving, I gave the horse to one of the stable boys, and went into the central hut. There was no sign of Stella, though the things she had been packing lay about the floor. I passed first into our sleeping hut, thence one by one into all the others, but still saw no sign of her. Then I went out, and calling to a Kaffir in the garden asked him if he had seen his mistress.

He answered "yes." He had seen her carrying flowers and walking towards the graveyard, holding the little white girl—my daughter—as he called her, by the hand, when the sun stood "there," and he pointed to a spot on the horizon where it would have been about an hour and a half before. "The two dogs were with them," he added. I turned and ran towards the graveyard, which was about a quarter of a mile from the huts. Of course there was no reason to be anxious—evidently she had gone to lay the flowers on her father's grave. And yet I was anxious.

When I got near the graveyard I met one of the natives, who, by my orders, had been set round the kraals to watch the place, and noticed that he was rubbing his eyes and yawning. Clearly he had been asleep. I asked him if he had seen his mistress, and he answered that he had not, which under the circumstances was not wonderful. Without stopping to reproach him, I ordered the man to follow me, and went on to the graveyard. There, on Mr. Carson's grave, lay the drooping flowers which Stella had been carrying, and there in the fresh mould was the spoor of Tota's veldschoon, or hide slipper. But where were they?

I ran from the graveyard and called aloud at the top of my voice, but no answer came. Meanwhile the native was more profitably engaged in tracing their spoor. He followed it for about a hundred yards till he came to a clump of mimosa bush that was situated between the stream and the ancient marble quarries just over the waterfall, and at the mouth of the ravine. Here he stopped, and I heard him give a startled cry. I rushed to the spot, passed through the trees, and saw this. The little open space in the centre of the glade had been the scene of a struggle. There, in the soft earth, were the marks of three pairs of human feet—two shod, one naked—Stella's, Tota's, and *Hendrika's*. Nor was this all. There, close by, lay the fragments of the two dogs—they were nothing more—and one baboon, not yet quite dead, which had been bitten in the throat by the dogs. All round was the spoor of numberless baboons. The full horror of what had happened flashed into my mind.

My wife and Tota had been carried off by the baboons. As yet they had not been killed, for if so their remains would have been found with those of the dogs. They had been carried off. The brutes, acting under the direction of that woman-monkey, Hendrika, had dragged them away to some secret den, there to keep them till they died—or kill them!

For a moment I literally staggered beneath the terror of the shock. Then I roused myself from my despair. I bade the native run and alarm the people at the kraals, telling them to come armed, and bring me guns and ammunition. He went like the wind, and I turned to follow the spoor. For a few yards it was plain enough—Stella had been dragged along. I could see where her heels had struck the ground; the child had, I presumed, been carried—at least there were no marks of her feet. At the water's edge the spoor vanished. The water was shallow, and they had gone along in it, or at least Hendrika and her victim had, in order to obliterate the trail. I could see where a moss-grown stone had been freshly turned over in the water-bed. I ran along the bank some way up the ravine, in the vain hope of catching a sight of them. Presently I heard a bark in the cliffs above me; it was answered by another, and then I saw that scores of baboons were hidden about among the rocks on either side, and were softly swinging themselves down to bar the path. To go on unarmed as I was would be useless. I should only be torn to pieces as the dogs had been. So I turned and fled back towards the huts. As I drew near I could see that my messenger had roused the settlement, for natives with spears and kerries in their hands were running up towards the kraals. When I reached the hut I met old Indaba-zimbi, who wore a very serious face.

"So the evil has fallen, Macumazahn," he said.

"It has fallen," I answered.

"Keep a good heart, Macumazahn," he said again. "She is not dead, nor is the little maid, and before they die we shall find them. Remember this, Hendrika loves her. She will not harm her, or allow the babyans to harm her. She will try to hide her away from you, that is all."

"Pray God that we may find her," I groaned. "The light is going fast."

"The moon rises in three hours," he answered; "we will search by moonlight. It is useless to start now; see, the sun sinks. Let us get the men together, eat, and make things ready. *Hamba gachla.* Hasten slowly, Macumazahn."

As there was no help, I took his advice. I could eat no food, but I packed some up to take with us, and made ready ropes, and a rough kind of litter. If we found them they would scarcely be able to walk. Ah! if we found them! How slowly the time passed! It seemed hours before the moon rose. But at last it did rise.

Then we started. In all we were about a hundred men, but we only mustered five guns between us, my elephant roer and four that had belonged to Mr. Carson.

The Magic of Indaba-Zimbi

We gained the spot by the stream where Stella had been taken. The natives looked at the torn fragments of the dogs, and at the marks of violence, and I heard them swearing to each other, that whether the Star lived or died they would not rest till they had exterminated every baboon on Babyan's Peak. I echoed the oath, and, as shall be seen, we kept it.

We started on along the stream, following the spoor of the baboons as we best could. But the stream left no spoor, and the hard, rocky banks very little. Still we wandered on. All night we wandered through the lonely moonlit valleys, startling the silence into a thousand echoes with our cries. But no answer came to them. In vain our eyes searched the sides of precipices formed of water-riven rocks fantastically piled one upon another; in vain we searched through endless dells and fern-clad crannies. There was nothing to be found. How could we expect to find two human beings hidden away in the recesses of this vast stretch of mountain ground, which no man yet had ever fully explored. They were lost, and in all human probability lost for ever.

To and fro we wandered hopelessly, till at last dawn found us footsore and weary nearly at the spot whence we had started. We sat down waiting for the sun to rise, and the men ate of such food as they had brought with them, and sent to the kraals for more.

I sat upon a stone with a breaking heart. I cannot describe my feelings. Let the reader put himself in my position and perhaps he may get some idea of them. Near me was old Indaba-zimbi, who sat staring straight before him as though he were looking into space, and taking note of what went on there. An idea struck me. This man had some occult power. Several times during our adventures he had prophesied, and in every case his prophecies had proved true. He it was who, when we escaped from the Zulu Impi, had told me to steer north, because there we should find the place of a white man who lived under the shadow of a great peak that was full of baboons. Perhaps he could help in this extremity—at any rate it was worth trying.

"Indaba-zimbi," I said, "you say that you can send your spirit through the doors of space and see what we cannot see. At the least I know that you can do strange things. Can you not help me now? If you can, and will save her, I will give you half the cattle that we have here."

"I never said anything of the sort, Macumazahn," he answered. "I do things, I do not talk about them. Neither do I seek reward for what I do like a common witch-doctor. It is well that you have asked me to use my wisdom, Macumazahn, for I should not have used it again without being asked—no, not even for the sake of the Star and yourself, whom I love, for if so my Spirit would have been angry. In the other matters I had a part, for my life was concerned as well as yours; but in this matter I have no part, and therefore I might not use my wisdom unless you thought well to call upon my Spirit.

However, it would have been no good to ask me before, for I have only just found the herb I want," and he produced a handful of the leaves of a plant that was unfamiliar to me. It had prickly leaves, shaped very much like those of the common English nettle.

"Now, Macumazahn," he went on, "bid the men leave us alone, and then follow me presently to the little glade down there by the water."

I did so. When I reached the glade I found Indaba-zimbi kindling a small fire under the shadow of a tree by the edge of the water.

"Sit there, Macumazahn," he said, pointing to a stone near the fire, "and do not be surprised or frightened at anything you see. If you move or call out we shall learn nothing."

I sat down and watched. When the fire was alight and burning brightly, the old fellow stripped himself stark naked, and, going to the foot of the pool, dipped himself in the water. Then he came back shivering with the cold, and, leaning over the little fire, thrust leaves of the plant I have mentioned into his mouth and began to chew them, muttering as he chewed. Most of the remaining leaves he threw on to the fire. A dense smoke rose from them, but he held his head in this smoke and drew it down his lungs till I saw that he was exhibiting every sign of suffocation. The veins in his throat and chest swelled, he gasped loudly, and his eyes, from which tears were streaming, seemed as though they were going to start from his head. Presently he fell over on his side, and lay senseless. I was terribly alarmed, and my first impulse was to run to his assistance, but fortunately I remembered his caution, and sat quiet.

Indaba-zimbi lay on the ground like a person quite dead. His limbs had all the utter relaxation of death. But as I watched I saw them begin to stiffen, exactly as though *rigor mortis* had set in. Then, to my astonishment, I perceived them once more relax, and this time there appeared upon his chest the stain of decomposition. It spread and spread; in three minutes the man, to all appearance, was a livid corpse.

I sat amazed watching this uncanny sight, and wondering if any further natural process was about to be enacted. Perhaps Indaba-zimbi was going to fall to dust before my eyes. As I watched I observed that the discoloration was beginning to fade. First it vanished from the extremities, then from the larger limbs, and lastly from the trunk. Then in turn came the third stage of relaxation, the second stage of stiffness or *rigor*, and the first stage of after-death collapse. When all these had rapidly succeeded each other, Indaba-zimbi quietly woke up.

I was too astonished to speak; I simply looked at him with my mouth open.

"Well, Macumazahn," he said, putting his head on one side like a bird, and nodding his white lock in a comical fashion, "it is all right; I have seen her."

"Seen who?" I said.

"The Star, your wife, and the little maid. They are much frightened, but unharmed. The Babyan-frau watches them. She is mad, but the baboons obey her, and do not hurt them. The Star was sleeping from weariness, so I whispered in her ear and told her not to be frightened, for you would soon rescue her, and that meanwhile she must seem to be pleased to have Hendrika near her."

"You whispered in her ear?" I said. "How could you whisper in her ear?"

"Bah! Macumazahn. How could I seem to die and go rotten before your eyes? You don't know, do you? Well, I will tell you one thing. I had to die to pass the doors of space, as you call them. I had to draw all the healthy strength and life from my body in order to gather power to speak with the Star. It was a dangerous business, Macumazahn, for if I had let things go a little further they must have stopped so, and there would have been an end of Indaba-zimbi. Ah, you white men, you know so much that you think you know everything. But you don't! You are always staring at the clouds and can't see the things that lie at your feet. You hardly believe me now, do you, Macumazahn? Well, I will show you. Have you anything on you that the Star has touched or worn?"

I thought for a moment, and said that I had a lock of her hair in my pocket-book. He told me to give it him. I did so. Going to the fire, he lit the lock of hair in the flame, and let it burn to ashes, which he caught in his left hand. These ashes he mixed up in a paste with the juice of one of the leaves of the plant I have spoken of.

"Now, Macumazahn, shut your eyes," he said.

I did so, and he rubbed his paste on to my eyelids. At first it burnt me, then my head swam strangely. Presently this effect passed off, and my brain was perfectly clear again, but I could not feel the ground with my feet. Indaba-zimbi led me to the side of the stream. Beneath us was a pool of beautifully clear water.

"Look into the pool, Macumazahn," said Indaba-zimbi, and his voice sounded hollow and far away in my ears.

I looked. The water grew dark; it cleared, and in it was a picture. I saw a cave with a fire burning in it. Against the wall of the cave rested Stella. Her dress was torn almost off her, she looked dreadfully pale and weary, and her eyelids were red as though with weeping. But she slept, and I could almost think that I saw her lips shape my name in her sleep. Close to her, her head upon Stella's breast, was little Tota; she had a skin thrown over her to keep out the night cold. The child was awake, and appeared to be moaning with fear. By the fire, and in such a position that the light fell full upon her face, and engaged in cooking something in a rough pot shaped from wood, sat the Baboon-woman, Hendrika. She was clothed in baboon skins, and her face had been rubbed with some dark stain, which was, however, wearing off it. In the intervals of her cooking she would turn on Stella her wild eyes, in which glared visible madness, with an expression of tenderness that amounted to worship. Then she would stare at the child and gnash her teeth as though with hate. Clearly she was jealous of it. Round the entrance arch of the cave peeped and peered the heads of many baboons. Presently Hendrika made a sign to one of them; apparently she did not speak, or rather grunt, in order not to wake Stella. The brute hopped forward, and she gave it a second rude wooden pot which was lying by her. It took it and went. The last thing that I saw, as the vision slowly vanished from the pool, was the dim shadow of the baboon returning with the pot full of water.

Presently everything had gone. I ceased to feel strange. There beneath me was the pool, and at my side stood Indaba-zimbi, smiling.

"You have seen things," he said.

"I have," I answered, and made no further remark on the matter. What was there to say? "Do you know the path to the cave?" I added.

He nodded his head. "I did not follow it all just now, because it winds," he said. "But I know it. We shall want the ropes."

"Then let us be starting; the men have eaten."

He nodded his head again, and going to the men I told them to make ready, adding that Indaba-zimbi knew the way. They said that was all right, if Indaba-zimbi had "smelt her out," they should soon find the Star. So we started cheerfully enough, and my spirits were so much improved that I was able to eat a boiled mealie cob or two as we walked.

We went up the valley, following the course of the stream for about a mile; then Indaba-zimbi made a sudden turn to the right, along another kloof, of which there were countless numbers in the base of the great hill.

On we went through kloof after kloof. Indaba-zimbi, who led us, was never at a loss, he turned up gulleys and struck across necks of hills with the certainty of a hound on a hot scent. At length, after about three hours' march, we came to a big silent valley on the northern slope of the great peak. On one side of this valley was a series of stony koppies, on the other rose a sheer wall of rock. We marched along the wall for a distance of some two miles. Then suddenly Indaba-zimbi halted.

"There is the place," he said, pointing to an opening in the cliff. This opening was about forty feet from the ground, and ellipse-shaped. It cannot have been more than twenty feet high by ten wide, and was partially hidden by ferns and bushes that grew about it in the surface of the cliff. Keen as my eyes were, I doubt if I should ever have noticed it, for there were many such cracks and crannies in the rocky face of the great mountain.

We drew near and looked carefully at the place. The first thing I noticed was that the rock, which was not quite perpendicular, had been worn by the continual passage of baboons; the second, that something white was hanging on a bush near the top of the ascent.

It was a pocket-handkerchief.

Now there was no more doubt about the matter. With a beating heart I began the ascent. For the first twenty feet it was comparatively easy, for the rock shelved; the next ten feet was very difficult, but still possible to an active man, and I achieved it, followed by Indaba-zimbi. But the last twelve or fifteen feet could only be scaled by throwing a rope over the trunk of a stunted tree, which grew at the bottom of the opening. This we accomplished with some trouble, and the rest was easy. A foot or two above my head the handkerchief fluttered in the wind. Hanging to the rope, I grasped it. It was my wife's. As I did so I noticed the face of a baboon peering at me over the edge of the cleft, the first baboon we had seen that morning. The brute gave a bark and vanished.

Thrusting the handkerchief into my breast, I set my feet against the cliff and scrambled up as hard as I could go. I knew that we had no time to lose, for the baboon would quickly alarm the others. I gained the cleft. It was a mere arched passage cut by water, ending in a gulley, which led to a wide open space of some sort. I looked through the passage and saw that the gulley was black with baboons. On they came by the hundred. I unslung my elephant gun from my shoulders and waited, calling to the men below to come up with all possible speed. The brutes streamed on down the gloomy gulf towards me, barking, grunting, and showing their huge teeth. I waited till they were within fifteen yards. Then I fired the elephant gun, which was loaded with slugs, right into the thick of them. In that narrow place the report echoed like a cannon shot, but its sound was quickly swallowed in the volley of piercing human-sounding groans and screams that followed. The charge of heavy slugs had ploughed through the host of baboons, of which at least a dozen lay dead or dying in the passage. For a moment they hesitated, then they came on again with a hideous clamour. Fortunately by this time Indaba-zimbi, who also had a gun, was standing by my side, otherwise I should have been torn to pieces before I could re-load. He fired both barrels into them, and again checked the rush. But they came on again, and notwithstanding the appearance of two other natives with guns, which they let off with more or less success, we should have been overwhelmed by the great and ferocious apes had I not by this time succeeded in re-loading the elephant gun. When they were right on us, I fired, with even more deadly effect than before, for at that distance every slug told on their long line. The howls and screams of pain and rage were now something inconceivable. One might have thought that we were doing battle with a host of demons; indeed in that light—for the overhanging arch of rock made it very dark—the gnashing snouts and sombre glowing eyes of the apes looked like those of devils as they are represented by monkish fancy. But the last shot was too much for them; they withdrew, dragging some of their wounded with them, and thus gave us time to get our men up the cliff. In a few minutes all were there, and we advanced down the passage, which presently opened into a rocky gulley with shelving sides. This gulley had a water-way at the bottom of it; it was about a hundred yards long, and the slopes on either side were topped by precipitous cliffs. I looked at these slopes; they literally swarmed with baboons, grunting, barking, screaming, and beating their breasts with their long arms, in fury. I looked up the water-way; along it, accompanied by a mob, or, as it were, a guard of baboons, ran Hendrika, her long hair flying, madness written on her face, and in her arms was the senseless form of little Tota.

She saw us, and a foam of rage burst from her lips. She screamed aloud. To me the sound was a mere inarticulate cry, but the baboons clearly understood it, for they began to roll rocks down on to us. One boulder leaped past me and struck down a Kaffir behind; another fell from the roof of the arch on to a man's head and killed him. Indaba-zimbi lifted his gun to shoot Hendrika; I knocked it up, so that the shot went over her, crying that he would kill the child. Then I shouted to the men to open out and form a line from side to side of the shelving gulley. Furious at the loss of their two comrades, they obeyed me, and keeping in the water-way myself, together with Indaba-zimbi and the other guns, I gave the word to charge.

Then the real battle began. It is difficult to say who fought the most fiercely, the natives or the baboons. The Kaffirs charged along the slopes, and as they came, encouraged by the screams of Hendrika, who rushed to and fro holding the wretched Tota before her as a shield, the apes bounded at them in fury. Scores were killed by the assegais, and many more fell beneath our gun-shots; but still they came on. Nor did we go scathless. Occasionally a man would slip, or be pulled over in the grip of a baboon. Then the others would fling themselves upon him like dogs on a rat, and worry him to death. We lost five men in this way, and I myself received a bite through the fleshy part of the left arm, but fortunately a native near me assegaied the animal before I was pulled down.

At length, and all of a sudden, the baboons gave up. A panic seemed to seize them. Notwithstanding the cries of Hendrika they thought no more of fight, but only of escape; some even did not attempt to get away from the assegais of the Kaffirs, they simply hid their horrible faces in their paws, and, moaning piteously, waited to be slain.

Hendrika saw that the battle was lost. Dropping the child from her arms, she rushed straight at us, a very picture of horrible insanity. I lifted my gun, but could not bear to shoot. After all she was but a mad thing, half ape, half woman. So I sprang to one side, and she landed full on Indaba-zimbi, knocking him down. But she did not stay to do any more. Wailing terribly, she rushed down the gulley and through the arch, followed by a few of the surviving baboons, and vanished from our sight.

What Happened to Stella

The fight was over. In all we had lost seven men killed, and several more severely bitten, while but few had escaped without some tokens whereby he might remember what a baboon's teeth and claws are like. How many of the brutes we killed I never knew, because we did not count, but it was a vast number. I should think that the stock must have been low about Babyan's Peak for many years afterwards. From that day to this, however, I have always avoided baboons, feeling more afraid of them than any beast that lives.

The path was clear, and we rushed forward along the water-course. But first we picked up little Tota. The child was not in a swoon, as I had thought, but paralyzed by terror, so that she could scarcely speak. Otherwise she was unhurt, though it took her many a week to recover her nerve. Had she been older, and had she not remembered Hendrika, I doubt if she would have recovered it. She knew me again, and flung her little arms about my neck, clinging to me so closely that I did not dare to give her to any one else to carry lest I should add to her terrors. So I went on with her in my arms. The fears that pierced my heart may well be imagined. Should I find Stella living or dead? Should I find her at all? Well, we should soon know now. We stumbled on up the stony watercourse; notwithstanding the weight of Tota I led the way, for suspense lent me wings. Now we were through, and an extraordinary scene lay before us. We were in a great natural amphitheatre, only it was three times the size of any amphitheatre ever shaped by man, and the walls were formed of precipitous cliffs, ranging from one to two hundred feet in height. For the rest, the space thus enclosed was level, studded with park-like trees, brilliant with flowers, and having a stream running through the centre of it, that, as I afterwards discovered, welled up from the ground at the head of the open space.

We spread ourselves out in a line, searching everywhere, for Tota was too overcome to be able to tell us where Stella was hidden away. For nearly half an hour we searched and searched, scanning the walls of rock for any possible openings to a cave. In vain, we could find none. I applied to old Indaba-zimbi, but his foresight was at fault here. All he could say was that this was the place, and that the "Star" was hidden somewhere in a cave, but where the cave was he could not tell. At last we came to the top of the amphitheatre. There before us was a wall of rock, of which the lower parts were here and there clothed in grasses, lichens, and creepers. I walked along it, calling at the top of my voice.

Presently my heart stood still, for I thought I heard a faint answer. I drew nearer to the place from which the sound seemed to come, and again called. Yes, there was an answer in my wife's voice. It seemed to come from the rock. I went up to it and searched among the creepers, but still could find no opening.

"Move the stone," cried Stella's voice, "the cave is shut with a stone."

I took a spear and prodded at the cliff whence the sound came. Suddenly the spear sunk in through a mass of lichen. I swept the lichen aside, revealing a boulder that had been rolled into the mouth of an opening in the rock, which it fitted so accurately that, covered as it was by the overhanging lichen, it might well have escaped the keenest eye. We dragged the boulder out; it was two men's work to do it. Beyond was a narrow, water-worn passage, which I followed with a beating heart. Presently the passage opened into a small cave, shaped like a pickle bottle, and coming to a neck at the top end. We passed through and found ourselves in a second, much larger cave, that I at once recognized as the one of which Indaba-zimbi had shown me a vision in the water. Light reached it from above—how I know not—and by it I could see a form half-sitting, half lying on some skins at the top end of the cave. I rushed to it. It was Stella! Stella bound with strips of hide, bruised, torn, but still Stella, and alive.

She saw me, she gave one cry, then, as I caught her in my arms, she fainted. It was happy indeed that she did not faint before, for had it not been for the sound of her voice I do not believe we should ever have found that cunningly hidden cave, unless, indeed, Indaba-zimbi's magic (on which be blessings) had come to our assistance.

We bore her to the open air, laid her beneath the shade of a tree, and cut the bonds loose from her ankles. As we went I glanced at the cave. It was exactly as I had seen it in the vision. There burnt the fire, there were the rude wooden vessels, one of them still half full of the water which I had seen the baboon bring. I felt awed as I looked, and marvelled at the power wielded by a savage who could not even read and write.

Now I could see Stella clearly. Her face was scratched, and haggard with fear and weeping, her clothes were almost torn off her, and her beautiful hair was loose and tangled. I sent for water, and we sprinkled her face. Then I forced a little of the brandy which we distilled from peaches at the kraals between her lips, and she opened her eyes, and throwing her arms about me clung to me as little Tota had done, sobbing, "Thank God! thank God!"

After a while she grew quieter, and I made her and Tota eat some food from the store that we had brought with us. I too ate and was thankful, for with the exception of the mealie cobs I had tasted nothing for nearly four-and-twenty hours. Then she washed her face and hands, and tidied her rags of dress as well as she was able. As she did so by degrees I drew her story from her.

It seemed that on the previous afternoon, being wearied with packing, she went out to visit her father's grave, taking Tota with her, and was followed there by the two dogs. She wished to lay some flowers on the grave and take farewell of the dust it covered, for as we had expected to trek early on the morrow she did not know if she would find a later opportunity. They passed up the garden, and gathering some flowers from the orange trees and elsewhere, went on to the little graveyard. Here she laid them on the grave as we had found them, and then sitting down, fell into a deep and sad reverie, such as the occasion would naturally induce. While she sat thus, Tota, who was a lively child and active as a kitten, strayed away without Stella observing it. With her went the dogs, who also had grown tired of inaction; a while passed, and suddenly she heard the dogs barking furiously about a hundred and fifty yards away. Then she heard Tota scream, and the dogs also yelling with fear and pain. She rose and ran as swiftly as she could towards the spot whence the sound came. Presently she was there. Before her in the glade, holding the screaming Tota in her arms, was a figure in which, notwithstanding the rough disguise of baboon skins and colouring matter, she had no difficulty in recognizing Hendrika, and all about her were numbers of baboons, rolling over and over in two hideous heaps, of which the centres were the unfortunate dogs now in process of being rent to fragments.

"Hendrika," Stella cried, "what does this mean? What are you doing with Tota and those brutes?"

The woman heard her and looked up. Then Stella saw that she was mad; madness stared from her eyes. She dropped the child, which instantly flew to Stella for protection. Stella clasped it, only to be herself clasped by Hendrika. She struggled fiercely, but it was of no use—the Babyan-frau had the strength of ten. She lifted her and Tota as though they were nothing, and ran off with them, following the bed of the stream in order to avoid leaving a spoor. Only the baboons who came with her, minus the one the dogs had killed, would not take to the water, but kept pace with them on the bank.

Stella said that the night which followed was more like a hideous nightmare than a reality. She was never able to tell me all that occurred in it. She had a vague recollection of being borne over rocks and along kloofs, while around her echoed the horrible grunts and clicks of the baboons. She spoke to Hendrika in English and Kaffir, imploring her to let them go; but the woman, if I may call her so, seemed in her madness to have entirely forgotten these tongues. When Stella spoke she would kiss her and stroke her hair, but she did not seem to understand what it was she said. On the other hand, she could, and did, talk to the baboons, that seemed to obey her implicitly. Moreover, she would not allow them to touch either Stella or the child in her arms. Once one of them tried to do so, and she seized a dead stick and struck it so heavily on the head that it fell senseless. Thrice Stella made an attempt to escape, for sometimes even Hendrika's giant strength waned and she had to set them down. But on each occasion she caught them, and it was in these struggles that Stella's clothes were so torn. At length before daylight they reached the cliff, and with the first break of light the ascent began. Hendrika dragged them up the first stages, but when they came to the precipitous place she tied the strips of hide, of which she had a supply wound round her waist, beneath Stella's arms. Steep as the place was the baboons ascended it easily enough, springing from a knock of rock to the trunk of the tree that grew on the edge of the crevasse. Hendrika followed them, holding the end of the hide reim in her teeth, one of the baboons hanging down from the tree to assist her ascent. It was while she was ascending that Stella bethought of letting fall her handkerchief in the faint hope that some searcher might see it.

By this time Hendrika was on the tree, and grunting out orders to the baboons which clustered about Stella below. Suddenly these seized her and little Tota who was in her arms, and lifted her from the ground. Then Hendrika above, aided by other baboons, put out all her great strength and pulled the two of them up the rock. Twice Stella swung heavily against the cliff. After the second blow she felt her senses going, and was consumed with terror lest she should drop Tota. But she managed to cling to her, and together they reached the cleft.

"From that time," Stella went on, "I remember no more till I woke to find myself in a gloomy cave resting on a bed of skins. My legs were bound, and Hendrika sat near me watching me, while round the edge of the cave peered the heads of those horrible baboons. Tota was still in my arms, and half dead from terror; her moans were pitiful to hear. I spoke to Hendrika, imploring her to release us; but either she has lost all understanding of human speech, or she pretends to have done so. All she would do was to caress me, and even kiss my hands and dress with extravagant signs of affection. As she did so, Tota shrunk closer to me. This Hendrika saw and glared so savagely at the child that I feared lest she was going to kill her. I diverted her attention by making signs that I wanted water, and this she gave me in a wooden bowl. As you saw, the cave was evidently Hendrika's dwelling-place. There are stores of fruit in it and some strips of dried flesh. She gave me some of the fruit and Tota a little, and I made Tota eat some. You can never know what I went through, Allan. I saw now that Hendrika was quite mad, and but little removed from the brutes to which she is akin, and over which she has such unholy power. The only trace of humanity left about her was her affection for me. Evidently her idea was to keep me here with her, to keep me away from you, and to carry out this idea she was capable of the exercise of every artifice and cunning. In this way she was sane enough, but in every other way she was mad. Moreover, she had not forgotten her horrible jealousy. Already I saw her glaring at Tota, and knew that the child's murder was only a matter of time. Probably within a few hours she would be killed before my eyes. Of escape, even if I had the strength, there was absolutely no chance, and little enough of our ever being found. No, we should be kept here guarded by a mad thing, half ape, half woman, till we perished miserably. Then I thought of you, dear, and of all that you must be suffering, and my heart nearly broke. I could only pray to God that I might either be rescued or die swiftly.

"As I prayed I dropped into a kind of doze from utter weariness, and then I had the strangest dream. I dreamed that Indaba-zimbi stood over me nodding his white lock, and spoke to me in Kaffir, telling me not to be frightened, for you would soon be with me, and that meanwhile I must humour Hendrika, pretending to be pleased to have her near me. The dream was so vivid that I actually seemed to see and hear him, as I see and hear him now."

Here I looked up and glanced at old Indaba-zimbi, who was sitting near. But it was not till afterwards that I told Stella of how her vision was brought about.

"At any rate," she went on, "when I awoke I determined to act on my dream. I took Hendrika's hand, and pressed it. She actually laughed in a wild kind of way with happiness, and laid her head upon my knee. Then I made signs that I wanted food, and she threw wood on the fire, which I forgot to tell you was burning in the cave, and began to make some of the broth that she used to cook very well, and she did not seem to have forgotten all about it. At any rate the broth was not bad, though neither Tota nor I could drink much of it. Fright and weariness had taken away our appetites.

"After the meal was done—and I prolonged it as much as possible—I saw Hendrika was beginning to get jealous of Tota again. She glared at her and then at the big knife which was tied round her own body. I knew the knife again, it was the one with which she had tried to murder you, dear. At last she went so far as to draw the knife. I was paralyzed with fear, then suddenly I remembered that when she was our servant, and used to get out of temper and sulk, I could always calm her by singing to her. So I began to sing hymns. Instantly she forgot her jealousy and put the knife back into its sheath. She knew the sound of the singing, and sat listening to it with a rapt face; the baboons, too, crowded in at the entrance of the cave to listen. I must have sung for an hour or more, all the hymns that I could remember. It was so very strange and dreadful sitting there singing to mad Hendrika and those hideous man-like apes that shut their eyes and nodded their great heads as I sang. It was a horrible nightmare; but I believe that the baboons are almost as human as the Bushmen.

"Well, this went on for a long time till my voice was getting exhausted. Then suddenly I heard the baboons outside raise a loud noise, as they do when they are angry. Then, dear, I heard the boom of your elephant gun, and I think it was the sweetest sound that ever came to my ears. Hendrika heard it too. She sprang up, stood for a moment, then, to my horror, swept Tota into her arms and rushed down the cave. Of course I could not stir to follow her, for my feet were tied. Next instant I heard the sound of a rock being moved, and presently the lessening of the light in the cave told me that I was shut in. Now the sound even of the elephant gun only reached me very faintly, and presently I could hear nothing more, straining my ears as I would.

"At last I heard a faint shouting that reached me through the wall of rock. I answered as loud as I could. You know the rest; and oh, my dear husband, thank God! thank God!" and she fell weeping into my arms.

Fifteen Years After

Both Stella and Tota were too weary to be moved, so we camped that night in the baboons' home, but were troubled by no baboons. Stella would not sleep in the cave; she said the place terrified her, so I made her up a kind of bed under a thorn-tree. As this rock-bound valley was one of the hottest places I ever was in, I thought that this would not matter; but when at sunrise on the following morning I saw a veil of miasmatic mist hanging over the surface of the ground, I changed my opinion. However, neither Stella nor Tota seemed the worse, so as soon as was practical we started homewards. I had already on the previous day sent some of the men back to the kraals to fetch a ladder, and when we reached the cliff we found them waiting for us beneath. With the help of the ladder the descent was easy. Stella simply got out of her rough litter at the top of the cliff, for we found it necessary to carry her, climbed down the ladder, and got into it again at the bottom.

Well, we reached the kraals safely enough, seeing nothing more of Hendrika, and, were this a story, doubtless I should end it here with—"and lived happily ever after." But alas! it is not so. How am I to write it?

My dearest wife's vital energy seemed completely to fail her now that the danger was past, and within twelve hours of our return I saw that her state was such as to necessitate the abandonment of any idea of leaving Babyan Kraals at present. The bodily exertion, the anguish of mind, and the terror which she had endured during that dreadful night, combined with her delicate state of health, had completely broken her down. To make matters worse, also, she was taken with an attack of fever, contracted no doubt in the unhealthy atmosphere of that accursed valley. In time she shook the fever off, but it left her dreadfully weak, and quite unfit to face the trial before her.

I think she knew that she was going to die; she always spoke of my future, never of *our* future. It is impossible for me to tell how sweet she was; how gentle, how patient and resigned. Nor, indeed, do I wish to tell it, it is too sad. But this I will say, I believe that if ever a woman drew near to perfection while yet living on the earth, Stella Quatermain did so.

The fatal hour drew on. My boy Harry was born, and his mother lived to kiss and bless him. Then she sank. We did what we could, but we had little skill, and might not hold her back from death. All through one weary night I watched her with a breaking heart.

The dawn came, the sun rose in the east. His rays falling on the peak behind were reflected in glory upon the bosom of the western sky. Stella awoke from her swoon and saw the light. She whispered to me to open the door of the hut. I did so, and she fixed her dying eyes on the splendour of the morning sky. She looked on me and smiled as an angel might smile. Then with a last effort she lifted her hand, and, pointing to the radiant heavens, whispered:

"There, Allan, there!"

It was done, and I was broken-hearted, and broken-hearted I must wander to the end. Those who have endured my loss will know my sorrow; it cannot be written. In such peace and at such an hour may I also die!

Yes, it is a sad story, but wander where we will about the world we can never go beyond the sound of the passing bell. For me, as for my father before me, and for the millions who have been and who shall be, there is but one word of comfort. "The Lord hath given, and the Lord hath taken away." Let us, then, bow our heads in hope, and add with a humble heart, "Blessed be the name of the Lord."

I buried her by her father's side, and the weeping of the people who had loved her went up to heaven. Even Indaba-zimbi wept, but I could weep no more.

On the second night from her burial I could not sleep. I rose, dressed myself, and went out into the night. The moon was shining brightly, and by its rays I shaped my course towards the graveyard. I drew near silently, and as I came I thought that I heard a sound of moaning on the further side of the wall. I looked over it. Crouched by Stella's grave, and tearing at its sods with her hands, as though she would unearth that which lay within, was *Hendrika*. Her face was wild and haggard, her form was so emaciated that when the pelts she wore slipped aside, the shoulder-blades seemed to project almost through her skin. Suddenly she looked up and saw me. Laughing a dreadful maniac laugh, she put her hand to her girdle and drew her great knife from it. I thought that she was about to attack me, and prepared to defend myself as I best could, for I was unarmed. But she made no effort to do so. Lifting the knife on high, for a moment she held it glittering in the moonlight, then plunged it into her own breast, and fell headlong to the ground.

I sprang over the wall and ran to her. She was not yet dead. Presently she opened her eyes, and I saw that the madness had gone out of them.

"Macumazahn," she said, speaking in English and in an thick difficult voice like one who half forgot and half remembered—"Macumazahn, I remember now. I have been mad. Is she really dead, Macumazahn?"

"Yes," I said, "she is dead, and you killed her."

"I killed her!" the dying woman faltered, "and I loved her. Yes, yes, I know now. I became a brute again and dragged her to the brutes, and now once more I am a woman, and she is dead, and I killed her—because I loved her so. I killed her who saved me from the brutes. I am not dead yet, Macumazahn. Take me and torture me to death, slowly, very slowly. It was jealousy of you that drove me mad, and I have killed her, and now she never can forgive me."

"Ask forgiveness from above," I said, for Hendrika had been a Christian, and the torment of her remorse touched me.

"I ask no forgiveness," she said. "May God torture me for ever, because I killed her; may I become a brute for ever till she comes to find me and forgives me! I only want her forgiveness." And wailing in an anguish of the heart so strong that her bodily suffering seemed to be forgotten, Hendrika, the Baboon-woman, died.

I went back to the kraals, and, waking Indaba-zimbi, told him what had happened, asking him to send some one to watch the body, as I proposed to give it burial. But next morning it was gone, and I found that the natives, hearing of the event, had taken the corpse and thrown it to the vultures with every mark of hate. Such, then, was the end of Hendrika.

A week after Hendrika's death I left Babyan Kraals. The place was hateful to me now; it was a haunted place. I sent for old Indaba-zimbi and told him that I was going. He answered that it was well. "The place has served your turn," he said; "here you have won that joy which it was fated you should win, and have suffered those things that it was fated you should suffer. Yes, and though you know it not now, the joy and the suffering, like the sunshine and the storm, are the same thing, and will rest at last in the same heaven, the heaven from which they came. Now go, Macumazahn."

I asked him if he was coming with me.

"No," he answered, "our paths lie apart henceforth, Macumazahn. We met together for certain ends. Those ends are fulfilled. Now each one goes his own way. You have still many years before you, Macumazahn; my years are few. When we shake hands here it will be for the last time. Perhaps we may meet again, but it will not be in this world. Henceforth we have each of us a friend the less."

"Heavy words," I said.

"True words," he answered.

Well, I have little heart to write the rest of it. I went, leaving Indaba-zimbi in charge of the place, and making him a present of such cattle and goods as I did not want.

Tota, I of course took with me. Fortunately by this time she had almost recovered the shock to her nerves. The baby Harry, as he was afterwards named, was a fine healthy child, and I was lucky in getting a respectable native woman, whose husband had been killed in the fight with the baboons, to accompany me as his nurse.

Slowly, and followed for a distance by all the people, I trekked away from Babyan Kraals. My route towards Natal was along the edge of the Bad Lands, and my first night's outspan was beneath that very tree where Stella, my lost wife, had found us as we lay dying of thirst.

I did not sleep much that night. And yet I was glad that I had not died in the desert about eleven months before. I felt then, as from year to year I have continued to feel while I wander through the lonely wilderness of life, that I had been preserved to an end. I had won my darling's love, and for a little while we had been happy together. Our happiness was too perfect to endure. She is lost to me now, but she is lost to be found again.

Here on the following morning I bade farewell to Indaba-zimbi.

"Good-bye, Macumazahn," he said, nodding his white lock at me. "Good-bye for a while. I am not a Christian; your father could not make me that. But he was a wise man, and when he said that those who loved each other shall meet again, he did not lie. And I too am a wise man in my way, Macumazahn, and I say it is true that we shall meet again. All my prophecies to you have come true, Macumazahn, and this one shall come true also. I tell you that you shall return to Babyan Kraals and shall not find me. I tell you that you shall journey to a further land than Babyan Kraals and shall find me. Farewell!" and he took a pinch of snuff, turned, and went.

Of my journey down to Natal there is little to tell. I met with many adventures, but they were of an every-day kind, and in the end arrived safely at Port Durban, which I now visited for the first time. Both Tota and my baby boy bore the journey well. And here I may as well chronicle the destiny of Tota. For a year she remained under my charge. Then she was adopted by a lady, the wife of an English colonel, who was stationed at the Cape. She was taken by her adopted parents to England, where she grew up a very charming and pretty girl, and ultimately married a clergyman in Norfolk. But I never saw her again, though we often wrote to each other.

Before I returned to the country of my birth, she too had been gathered to the land of shadows, leaving three children behind her. Ah me! all this took place so long ago, when I was young who now am old.

Perhaps it may interest the reader to know the fate of Mr. Carson's property, which should of course have gone to his grandson Harry. I wrote to England to claim the estate on his behalf, but the lawyer to whom the matter was submitted said that my marriage to Stella, not having been celebrated by an ordained priest, was not legal according to English law, and therefore Harry could not inherit. Foolishly enough I acquiesced in this, and the property passed to a cousin of my father-in-law's; but since I have come to live in England I have been informed that this opinion is open to great suspicion, and that there is every probability that the courts would have declared the marriage perfectly binding as having been solemnly entered into in accordance with the custom of the place where it was contracted. But I am now so rich that it is not worth while to move in the matter. The cousin is dead, his son is in possession, so let him keep it.

Once, and once only, did I revisit Babyan Kraals. Some fifteen years after my darling's death, when I was a man in middle life, I undertook an expedition to the Zambesi, and one night outspanned at the mouth of the well-known valley beneath the shadow of the great peak. I mounted my horse, and, quite alone, rode up the valley, noticing with a strange prescience of evil that the road was overgrown, and, save for the music of the waterfalls, the place silent as death. The kraals that used to be to the left of the road by the river had vanished. I rode towards their site; the mealie fields were choked with weeds, the paths were dumb with grass. Presently I reached the place. There, overgrown with grass, were the burnt ashes of the kraals, and there among the ashes, gleaming in the moonlight, lay the white bones of men. Now it was clear to me. The settlement had been fallen on by some powerful foe, and its inhabitants put to the assegai. The forebodings of the natives had come true; Babyan Kraals were peopled by memories alone.

I passed on up the terraces. There shone the roofs of the marble huts. They would not burn, and were too strong to be easily pulled down. I entered one of them—it had been our sleeping hut—and lit a candle which I had with me.

The huts had been sacked; leaves of books and broken mouldering fragments of the familiar furniture lay about. Then I remembered that there was a secret place hollowed in the floor and concealed by a stone, where Stella used to hide her little treasures. I went to the stone and dragged it up. There was something within wrapped in rotting native cloth. I undid it. It was the dress my wife had been married in. In the centre of the dress were the withered wreath and flowers she had worn, and with them a little paper packet. I opened it; it contained a lock of my own hair!

I remembered then that I had searched for this dress when I came away and could not find it, for I had forgotten the secret recess in the floor.

Taking the dress with me, I left the hut for the last time. Leaving my horse tied to a tree, I walked to the graveyard, through the ruined garden. There it was a mass of weeds, but over my darling's grave grew a self-sown orange bush, of which the scented petals fell in showers on to the mound beneath. As I drew near, there was a crash and a rush. A great baboon leapt from the centre of the graveyard and vanished into the trees. I could almost believe that it was the wraith of Hendrika doomed to keep an eternal watch over the bones of the woman her jealous rage had done to death.

I tarried there a while, filled with such thoughts as may not be written. Then, leaving my dead wife to her long sleep where the waters fall in melancholy music beneath the shadow of the everlasting mountain, I turned and sought that spot where first we had told our love. Now the orange grove was nothing but a tangled thicket; many of the trees were dead, choked with creepers, but some still flourished. There stood the one beneath which we had lingered, there was the rock that had been our seat, and there on the rock sat the wraith of *Stella*, the Stella whom I had wed! Ay! there she sat, and on her upturned face was that same spiritual look which I saw upon it in the hour when we first had kissed. The moonlight shone in her dark eyes, the breeze wavered in her curling hair, her breast rose and fell, a gentle smile played about her parted lips. I stood transfixed with awe and joy, gazing on that lost loveliness which once was mine. I could not speak, and she spoke no word; she did not even seem to see me. Now her eyes fell. For a moment they met mine, and their message entered into me.

Then she was gone. She was gone; nothing was left but the tremulous moonlight falling where she had been, the melancholy music of the waters, the shadow of the everlasting mountain, and, in my heart, the sorrow and the hope.

Maiwa's Revenge
or The War of the Little Hand

Table of Contents

Preface

It may be well to state that the incident of the "Thing that bites" recorded in this tale is not an effort of the imagination. On the contrary, it is "plagiarized." Mandara, a well-known chief on the east coast of Africa, has such an article, *and uses it*. In the same way the wicked conduct attributed to Wambe is not without a precedent. T'Chaka, the Zulu Napoleon, never allowed a child of his to live. Indeed he went further, for on discovering that his mother, Unandi, was bringing up one of his sons in secret, like Nero he killed her, and with his own hand.

Gobo Strikes

One day—it was about a week after Allan Quatermain told me his story of the "Three Lions," and of the moving death of Jim-Jim—he and I were walking home together on the termination of a day's shooting. He owned about two thousand acres of shooting round the place he had bought in Yorkshire, over a hundred of which were wood. It was the second year of his occupation of the estate, and already he had reared a very fair head of pheasants, for he was an all-round sportsman, and as fond of shooting with a shot-gun as with an eight-bore rifle. We were three guns that day, Sir Henry Curtis, Old Quatermain, and myself; but Sir Henry was obliged to leave in the middle of the afternoon in order to meet his agent, and inspect an outlying farm where a new shed was wanted. However, he was coming back to dinner, and going to bring Captain Good with him, for Brayley Hall was not more than two miles from the Grange.

We had met with very fair sport, considering that we were only going through outlying cover for cocks. I think that we had killed twenty- seven, a woodcock and a leash of partridges which we secured out of a driven covey. On our way home there lay a long narrow spinney, which was a very favourite "lie" for woodcocks, and generally held a pheasant or two as well.

"Well, what do you say?" said old Quatermain, "shall we beat through this for a finish?"

I assented, and he called to the keeper who was following with a little knot of beaters, and told him to beat the spinney.

"Very well, sir," answered the man, "but it's getting wonderful dark, and the wind's rising a gale. It will take you all your time to hit a woodcock if the spinney holds one."

"You show us the woodcocks, Jeffries," answered Quatermain quickly, for he never liked being crossed in anything to do with sport, "and we will look after shooting them."

The man turned and went rather sulkily. I heard him say to the under-keeper, "He's pretty good, the master is, I'm not saying he isn't, but if he kills a woodcock in this light and wind, I'm a Dutchman."

I think that Quatermain heard him too, though he said nothing. The wind was rising every minute, and by the time the beat begun it blew big guns. I stood at the right-hand corner of the spinney, which curved round somewhat, and Quatermain stood at the left, about forty paces from me. Presently an old cock pheasant came rocketing over me, looking as though the feathers were being blown out of his tail. I missed him clean with the first barrel, and was never more pleased with myself in my life than when I doubled him up with the second, for the shot was not an easy one. In the faint light I could see Quatermain nodding his head in approval, when through the groaning of the trees I heard the shouts of the beaters, "Cock forward, cock to the right." Then came a whole volley of shouts, "Woodcock to the right," "Cock to the left," "Cock over."

I looked up, and presently caught sight of one of the woodcocks coming down the wind upon me like a flash. In that dim light I could not follow all his movements as he zigzagged through the naked tree-tops; indeed I could see him when his wings flitted up. Now he was passing me—*bang*, and a flick of the wing, I had missed him; *bang* again. Surely he was down; no, there he went to my left.

"Cock to you," I shouted, stepping forward so as to get Quatermain between me and the faint angry light of the dying day, for I wanted to see if he would "wipe my eye." I knew him to be a wonderful shot, but I thought that cock would puzzle him.

I saw him raise his gun ever so little and bend forward, and at that moment out flashed two woodcocks into the open, the one I had missed to his right, and the other to his left.

At the same time a fresh shout arose of, "Woodcock over," and looking down the spinney I saw a third bird high up in the air, being blown along like a brown and whirling leaf straight over Quatermain's head. And then followed the prettiest little bit of shooting that I ever saw. The bird to the right was flying low, not ten yards from the line of a hedgerow, and Quatermain took him first because he would become invisible the soonest of any. Indeed, nobody who had not his hawk's eyes could have seen to shoot at all. But he saw the bird well enough to kill it dead as a stone. Then turning sharply, he pulled on the second bird at about forty-five yards, and over he went. By this time the third woodcock was nearly over him, and flying very high, straight down the wind, a hundred feet up or more, I should say. I saw him glance at it as he opened his gun, threw out the right cartridge and slipped in another, turning round as he did so. By this time the cock was nearly fifty yards away from him, and travelling like a flash. Lifting his gun he fired after it, and, wonderful as the shot was, killed it dead. A tearing gust of wind caught the dead bird, and blew it away like a leaf torn from an oak, so that it fell a hundred and thirty yards off or more.

"I say, Quatermain," I said to him when the beaters were up, "do you often do this sort of thing?"

"Well," he answered, with a dry smile, "the last time I had to load three shots as quickly as that was at rather larger game. It was at elephants. I killed them all three as dead as I killed those woodcocks; but it very nearly went the other way, I can tell you; I mean that they very nearly killed me."

Just at that moment the keeper came up, "Did you happen to get one of them there cocks, sir?" he said, with the air of a man who did not in the least expect an answer in the affirmative.

"Well, yes, Jeffries," answered Quatermain; "you will find one of them by the hedge, and another about fifty yards out by the plough there to the left—"

The keeper had turned to go, looking a little astonished, when Quatermain called him back.

"Stop a bit, Jeffries," he said. "You see that pollard about one hundred and forty yards off? Well, there should be another woodcock down in a line with it, about sixty paces out in the field."

"Well, if that bean't the very smartest bit of shooting," murmured Jeffries, and departed.

After that we went home, and in due course Sir Henry Curtis and Captain Good arrived for dinner, the latter arrayed in the tightest and most ornamental dress-suit I ever saw. I remember that the waistcoat was adorned with five pink coral buttons.

It was a very pleasant dinner. Old Quatermain was in an excellent humour; induced, I think, by the recollection of his triumph over the doubting Jeffries. Good, too, was full of anecdotes. He told us a most miraculous story of how he once went shooting ibex in Kashmir. These ibex, according to Good, he stalked early and late for four entire days. At last on the morning of the fifth day he succeeded in getting within range of the flock, which consisted of a magnificent old ram with horns so long that I am afraid to mention their measure, and five or six females. Good crawled upon his stomach, painfully taking shelter behind rocks, till he was within two hundred yards; then he drew a fine bead upon the old ram. At this moment, however, a diversion occurred. Some wandering native of the hills appeared upon a distant mountain top. The females turned, and rushing over a rock vanished from Good's ken. But the old ram took a bolder course. In front of him stretched a mighty crevasse at least thirty feet in width. He went at it with a bound. Whilst he was in mid-air Good fired, and killed him dead. The ram turned a complete somersault in space, and fell in such fashion that his horns hooked themselves upon a big projection of the opposite cliffs. There he hung, till Good, after a long and painful détour, gracefully dropped a lasso over him and fished him up.

This moving tale of wild adventure was received with undeserved incredulity.

"Well," said Good, "if you fellows won't believe my story when I tell it—a perfectly true story mind—perhaps one of you will give us a better; I'm not particular if it is true or not." And he lapsed into a dignified silence.

"Now, Quatermain," I said, "don't let Good beat you, let us hear how you killed those elephants you were talking about this evening just after you shot the woodcocks."

"Well," said Quatermain, dryly, and with something like a twinkle in his brown eyes, "it is very hard fortune for a man to have to follow on Good's "spoor." Indeed if it were not for that running giraffe which, as you will remember, Curtis, we saw Good bowl over with a Martini rifle at three hundred yards, I should almost have said that this was an impossible tale."

Here Good looked up with an air of indignant innocence.

"However," he went on, rising and lighting his pipe, "if you fellows like, I will spin you a yarn. I was telling one of you the other night about those three lions and how the lioness finished my unfortunate 'voorlooper,' Jim-Jim, the boy whom we buried in the bread-bag.

"Well, after this little experience I thought that I would settle down a bit, so I entered upon a venture with a man who, being of a speculative mind, had conceived the idea of running a store at Pretoria upon strictly cash principles. The arrangement was that I should find the capital and he the experience. Our partnership was not of a long duration. The Boers refused to pay cash, and at the end of four months my partner had the capital and I had the experience. After this I came to the conclusion that store-keeping was not in my line, and having four hundred pounds left, I sent my boy Harry to a school in Natal, and buying an outfit with what remained of the money, started upon a big trip.

"This time I determined to go further afield than I had ever been before; so I took a passage for a few pounds in a trading brig that ran between Durban and Delagoa Bay. From Delagoa Bay I marched inland accompanied by twenty porters, with the idea of striking up north, towards the Limpopo, and keeping parallel to the coast, but at a distance of about one hundred and fifty miles from it. For the first twenty days of our journey we suffered a good deal from fever, that is, my men did, for I think that I am fever proof. Also I was hard put to it to keep the camp in meat, for although the country proved to be very sparsely populated, there was but little game about. Indeed, during all that time I hardly killed anything larger than a waterbuck, and, as you know, waterbuck's flesh is not very appetising food. On the twentieth day, however, we came to the banks of a largish river, the Gonooroo it was called. This I crossed, and then struck inland towards a great range of mountains, the blue crests of which we could see lying on the distant heavens like a shadow, a continuation, as I believe, of the Drakensberg range that skirts the coast of Natal. From this main range a great spur shoots out some fifty miles or so towards the coast, ending abruptly in one tremendous peak. This spur I discovered separated the territories of two chiefs named Nala and Wambe, Wambe's territory being to the north, and Nala's to the south. Nala ruled a tribe of bastard Zulus called the Butiana, and Wambe a much larger tribe, called the Matuku, which presents marked Bantu characteristics. For instance, they have doors and verandahs to their huts, work skins perfectly, and wear a waistcloth and not a moocha. At this time the Butiana were more or less subject to the Matuku, having been surprised by them some twenty years before and mercilessly slaughtered down. The tribe was now recovering itself, however, and as you may imagine, it did not love the Matuku.

"Well, I heard as I went along that elephants were very plentiful in the dense forests which lie upon the slopes and at the foot of the mountains that border Wambe's territory. Also I heard a very ill report of that worthy himself, who lived in a kraal upon the side of the mountain, which was so strongly fortified as to be practically impregnable. It was said that he was the most cruel chief in this part of Africa, and that he had murdered in cold blood an entire party of English gentlemen, who, some seven years before, had gone into his country to hunt elephants. They took an old friend of mine with them as guide, John Every by name, and often had I mourned over his untimely death. All the same, Wambe or no Wambe, I determined to hunt elephants in his country. I never was afraid of natives, and I was not going to show the white feather now. I am a bit of a fatalist, as you fellows know, so I came to the conclusion that if it was fated that Wambe should send me to join my old friend John Every, I should have to go, and there was an end of it. Meanwhile, I meant to hunt elephants with a peaceful heart.

"On the third day from the date of our sighting the great peak, we found ourselves beneath its shadow. Still following the course of the river which wound through the forests at the base of the peak, we entered the territory of the redoubtable Wambe. This, however, was not accomplished without a certain difference of opinion between my bearers and myself, for when we reached the spot where Wambe's boundary was supposed to run, the bearers sat down and emphatically refused to go a step further. I sat down too, and argued with them, putting my fatalistic views before them as well as I was able. But I could not persuade them to look at the matter in the same light. 'At present,' they said, 'their skins were whole; if they went into Wambe's country without his leave they would soon be like a water- eaten leaf. It was very well for me to say that this would be Fate. Fate no doubt might be walking about in Wambe's country, but while they stopped outside they would not meet him.'

"'Well,' I said to Gobo, my head man, 'and what do you mean to do?'

"'We mean to go back to the coast, Macumazahn,' he answered insolently.

"'Do you?' I replied, for my bile was stirred. 'At any rate, Mr. Gobo, you and one or two others will never get there; see here, my friend,' and I took a repeating rifle and sat myself comfortably down, resting my back against a tree—'I have just breakfasted, and I had as soon spend the day here as anywhere else. Now if you or any of those men walk one step back from here, and towards the coast, I shall fire at you; and you know that I don't miss.'

"The man fingered the spear he was carrying—luckily all my guns were stacked against the tree—and then turned as though to walk away, the others keeping their eyes fixed upon him all the while. I rose and covered him with the rifle, and though he kept up a brave appearance of unconcern, I saw that he was glancing nervously at me all the time. When he had gone about twenty yards I spoke very quietly—

"'Now, Gobo,' I said, 'come back, or I shall fire.'

"Of course this was taking a very high hand; I had no real right to kill Gobo or anybody else because they objected to run the risk of death by entering the territory of a hostile chief. But I felt that if I wished to keep up any authority it was absolutely necessary that I should push matters to the last extremity short of actually shooting him. So I sat there, looking fierce as a lion, and keeping the sight of my rifle in a dead line for Gobo's ribs. Then Gobo, feeling that the situation was getting strained, gave in.

"'Don't shoot, Boss,' he shouted, throwing up his hand, 'I will come with you.'

"'I thought you would,' I answered quietly; 'you see Fate walks about outside Wambe's country as well as in it.'

"After that I had no more trouble, for Gobo was the ringleader, and when he collapsed the others collapsed also. Harmony being thus restored, we crossed the line, and on the following morning I began shooting in good earnest.

A Morning's Sport

"Moving some five or six miles round the base of the great peak of which I have spoken, we came the same day to one of the fairest bits of African country that I have seen outside of Kukuanaland. At this spot the mountain spur that runs out at right angles to the great range, which stretches its cloud-clad length north and south as far as the eye can reach, sweeps inwards with a vast and splendid curve. This curve measures some five-and-thirty miles from point to point, and across its moon-like segment the river flashed, a silver line of light. On the further side of the river is a measureless sea of swelling ground, a natural park covered with great patches of bush— some of them being many square miles in extent. These are separated one from another by glades of grass land, broken here and there with clumps of timber trees; and in some instances by curious isolated koppies, and even by single crags of granite that start up into the air as though they were monuments carved by man, and not tombstones set by nature over the grave of ages gone. On the west this beautiful plain is bordered by the lonely mountain, from the edge of which it rolls down toward the fever coast; but how far it runs to the north I cannot say—eight days' journey, according to the natives, when it is lost in an untravelled morass.

"On the hither side of the river the scenery is different. Along the edge of its banks, where the land is flat, are green patches of swamp. Then comes a wide belt of beautiful grass land covered thickly with game, and sloping up very gently to the borders of the forest, which, beginning at about a thousand feet above the level of the plain, clothes the mountain-side almost to its crest. In this forest grow great trees, most of them of the yellow-wood species. Some of these trees are so lofty, that a bird in their top branches would be out of range of an ordinary shot gun. Another peculiar thing about them is, that they are for the most part covered with a dense growth of the Orchilla moss; and from this moss the natives manufacture a most excellent deep purple dye, with which they stain tanned hides and also cloth, when they happen to get any of the latter. I do not think that I ever saw anything more remarkable than the appearance of one of these mighty trees festooned from top to bottom with trailing wreaths of this sad-hued moss, in which the wind whispers gently as it stirs them. At a distance it looks like the gray locks of a Titan crowned with bright green leaves, and here and there starred with the rich bloom of orchids.

"The night of that day on which I had my little difference of opinion with Gobo, we camped by the edge of this great forest, and on the following morning at daylight I started out shooting. As we were short of meat I determined to kill a buffalo, of which there were plenty about, before looking for traces of elephants. Not more than half a mile from camp we came across a trail broad as a cart-road, evidently made by a great herd of buffaloes which had passed up at dawn from their feeding ground in the marshes, to spend the day in the cool air of the uplands. This trail I followed boldly; for such wind as there was blew straight down the mountain-side, that is, from the direction in which the buffaloes had gone, to me. About a mile further on the forest began to be dense, and the nature of the trail showed me that I must be close to my game. Another two hundred yards and the bush was so thick that, had it not been for the trail, we could scarcely have passed through it. As it was, Gobo, who carried my eight-bore rifle (for I had the .570-express in my hand), and the other two men whom I had taken with me, showed the very strongest dislike to going any further, pointing out that there was 'no room to run away.' I told them that they need not come unless they liked, but that I was certainly going on; and then, growing ashamed, they came.

"Another fifty yards, and the trail opened into a little glade. I knelt down and peeped and peered, but no buffalo could I see. Evidently the herd had broken up here—I knew that from the spoor—and penetrated the opposite bush in little troops. I crossed the glade, and choosing one line of spoor, followed it for some sixty yards, when it became clear to me that I was surrounded by buffaloes; and yet so dense was the cover that I could not see any. A few yards to my left I could hear one rubbing its horns against a tree, while from my right came an occasional low and throaty grunt which told me that I was uncomfortably near an old bull. I crept on towards him with my heart in my mouth, as gently as though I were walking upon eggs for a bet, lifting every little bit of wood in my path, and placing it behind me lest it should crack and warn the game. After me in single file came my three retainers, and I don't know which of them looked the most frightened. Presently Gobo touched my leg; I glanced round, and saw him pointing slantwise towards the left. I lifted my head a little and peeped over a mass of creepers; beyond the creepers was a dense bush of sharp-pointed aloes, of that kind of which the leaves project laterally, and on the other side of the aloes, not fifteen paces from us, I made out the horns, neck, and the ridge of the back of a tremendous old bull. I took my eight-bore, and getting on to my knee prepared to shoot him through the neck, taking my chance of cutting his spine. I had already covered him as well as the aloe leaves would allow, when he gave a kind of sigh and lay down.

"I looked round in dismay. What was to be done now? I could not see to shoot him lying down, even if my bullet would have pierced the intervening aloes—which was doubtful—and if I stood up he would either run away or charge me. I reflected, and came to the conclusion that the only thing to do was to lie down also; for I did not fancy wandering after other buffaloes in that dense bush. If a buffalo lies down, it is clear that he must get up again some time, so it was only a case of patience—'fighting the fight of sit down,' as the Zulus say.

"Accordingly I sat down and lighted a pipe, thinking that the smell of it might reach the buffalo and make him get up. But the wind was the wrong way, and it did not; so when it was done I lit another. Afterwards I had cause to regret that pipe.

"Well, we squatted like this for between half and three quarters of an hour, till at length I began to grow heartily sick of the performance. It was about as dull a business as the last hour of a comic opera. I could hear buffaloes snorting and moving all round, and see the red- beaked tic birds flying up off their backs, making a kind of hiss as they did so, something like that of the English missel-thrush, but I could not see a single buffalo. As for my old bull, I think he must have slept the sleep of the just, for he never even stirred.

"Just as I was making up my mind that something must be done to save the situation, my attention was attracted by a curious grinding noise. At first I thought that it must be a buffalo chewing the cud, but was obliged to abandon the idea because the noise was too loud. I shifted myself round and stared through the cracks in the bush, in the direction whence the sound seemed to come, and once I thought that I saw something gray moving about fifty yards off, but could not make certain. Although the grinding noise still continued I could see nothing more, so I gave up thinking about it, and once again turned my attention to the buffalo. Presently, however, something happened. Suddenly from about forty yards away there came a tremendous snorting sound, more like that made by an engine getting a heavy train under weigh than anything else in the world.

"By Jove,' I thought, turning round in the direction from which the grinding sound had come, 'that must be a rhinoceros, and he has got our wind.' For, as you fellows know, there is no mistaking the sound made by a rhinoceros when he gets wind of you.

"Another second, and I heard a most tremendous crashing noise. Before I could think what to do, before I could even get up, the bush behind me seemed to burst asunder, and there appeared not eight yards from us, the great horn and wicked twinkling eye of a charging rhinoceros. He had winded us or my pipe, I do not know which, and, after the fashion of these brutes, had charged up the scent. I could not rise, I could not even get the gun up, I had no time. All that I was able to do was to roll over as far out of the monster's path as the bush would allow. Another second and he was over me, his great bulk towering above me like a mountain, and, upon my word, I could not get his smell out of my nostrils for a week. Circumstances impressed it on my memory, at least I suppose so. His hot breath blew upon my face, one of his front feet just missed my head, and his hind one actually trod upon the loose part of my trousers and pinched a little bit of my skin. I saw him pass over me lying as I was upon my back, and next second I saw something else. My men were a little behind me, and therefore straight in the path of the rhinoceros. One of them flung himself backwards into the bush, and thus avoided him. The second with a wild yell sprung to his feet, and bounded like an india-rubber ball right into the aloe bush, landing well among the spikes. But the third, it was my friend Gobo, could not by any means get away. He managed to gain his feet, and that was all. The rhinoceros was charging with his head low; his horn passed between Gobo's legs, and feeling something on his nose, he jerked it up. Away went Gobo, high into the air. He turned a complete somersault at the apex of the curve, and as he did so, I caught sight of his face. It was gray with terror, and his mouth was wide open. Down he came, right on to the great brute's back, and that broke his fall. Luckily for him the rhinoceros never turned, but crashed straight through the aloe bush, only missing the man who had jumped into it by about a yard.

"Then followed a complication. The sleeping buffalo on the further side of the bush, hearing the noise, sprang to his feet, and for a second, not knowing what to do, stood still. At that instant the huge rhinoceros blundered right on to him, and getting his horn beneath his stomach gave him such a fearful dig that the buffalo was turned over on to his back, while his assailant went a most amazing cropper over his carcase. In another moment, however, the rhinoceros was up, and wheeling round to the left, crashed through the bush down-hill and towards the open country.

"Instantly the whole place became alive with alarming sounds. In every direction troops of snorting buffaloes charged through the forest, wild with fright, while the injured bull on the further side of the bush began to bellow like a mad thing. I lay quite still for a moment, devoutly praying that none of the flying buffaloes would come my way. Then when the danger lessened I got on to my feet, shook myself, and looked round. One of my boys, he who had thrown himself backward into the bush, was already half way up a tree—if heaven had been at the top of it he could not have climbed quicker. Gobo was lying close to me, groaning vigorously, but, as I suspected, quite unhurt; while from the aloe bush into which No. 3 had bounded like a tennis ball, issued a succession of the most piercing yells.

"I looked, and saw that this unfortunate fellow was in a very tight place. A great spike of aloe had run through the back of his skin waist-belt, though without piercing his flesh, in such a fashion that it was impossible for him to move, while within six feet of him the injured buffalo bull, thinking, no doubt, that he was the aggressor, bellowed and ramped to get at him, tearing the thick aloes with his great horns. That no time was to be lost, if I wished to save the man's life, was very clear. So seizing my eight-bore, which was fortunately uninjured, I took a pace to the left, for the rhinoceros had enlarged the hole in the bush, and aimed at the point of the buffalo's shoulder, since on account of my position I could not get a fair side shot for the heart. As I did so I saw that the rhinoceros had given the bull a tremendous wound in the stomach, and that the shock of the encounter had put his left hind-leg out of joint at the hip. I fired, and the bullet striking the shoulder broke it, and knocked the buffalo down. I knew that he could not get up any more, because he was now injured fore and aft, so notwithstanding his terrific bellows I scrambled round to where he was. There he lay glaring furiously and tearing up the soil with his horns. Stepping up to within two yards of him I aimed at the vertebra of his neck and fired. The bullet struck true, and with a thud he dropped his head upon the ground, groaned, and died.

"This little matter having been attended to with the assistance of Gobo, who had now found his feet, I went on to extricate our unfortunate companion from the aloe bush. This we found a thorny task, but at last he was dragged forth uninjured, though in a very pious and prayerful frame of mind. His 'spirit had certainly looked that way,' he said, or he would now have been dead. As I never like to interfere with true piety, I did not venture to suggest that his spirit had deigned to make use of my eight-bore in his interest.

"Having despatched this boy back to the camp to tell the bearers to come and cut the buffalo up, I bethought me that I owed that rhinoceros a grudge which I should love to repay. So without saying a word of what was in my mind to Gobo, who was now more than ever convinced that Fate walked about loose in Wambe's country, I just followed on the brute's spoor. He had crashed through the bush till he reached the little glade. Then moderating his pace somewhat, he had followed the glade down its entire length, and once more turned to the right through the forest, shaping his course for the open land that lies between the edge of the bush and the river. Having followed him for a mile or so further, I found myself quite on the open. I took out my glasses and searched the plain. About a mile ahead was something brown—as I thought, the rhinoceros. I advanced another quarter of a mile, and looked once more —it was not the rhinoceros, but a big ant- heap. This was puzzling, but I did not like to give it up, because I knew from his spoor that he must be somewhere ahead. But as the wind was blowing straight from me towards the line that he had followed, and as a rhinoceros can smell you for about a mile, it would not, I felt, be safe to follow his trail any further; so I made a détour of a mile and more, till I was nearly opposite the ant-heap, and then once more searched the plain. It was no good, I could see nothing of him, and was about to give it up and start after some oryx I saw on the skyline, when suddenly at a distance of about three hundred yards from the ant-heap, and on its further side, I saw my rhino stand up in a patch of grass.

"'Heavens!' I thought to myself, 'he's off again;' but no, after standing staring for a minute or two he once more lay down.

"Now I found myself in a quandary. As you know, a rhinoceros is a very short-sighted brute, indeed his sight is as bad as his scent is good. Of this fact he is perfectly aware, but he always makes the most of his natural gifts. For instance, when he lies down he invariably does so with his head down wind. Thus, if any enemy crosses his wind he will still be able to escape, or attack him; and if, on the other hand, the danger approaches up wind he will at least have a chance of seeing it. Otherwise, by walking delicately, one might actually kick him up like a partridge, if only the advance was made up wind.

"Well, the point was, how on earth should I get within shot of this rhinoceros? After much deliberation I determined to try a side approach, thinking that in this way I might get a shoulder shot. Accordingly we started in a crouching attitude, I first, Gobo holding on to my coat tails, and the other boy on to Gobo's moocha. I always adopt this plan when stalking big game, for if you follow any other system the bearers will get out of line. We arrived within three hundred yards safely enough, and then the real difficulties began. The grass had been so closely eaten off by game that there was scarcely any cover. Consequently it was necessary to go on to our hands and knees, which in my case involved laying down the eight-bore at every step and then lifting it up again. However, I wriggled along somehow, and if it had not been for Gobo and his friend no doubt everything would have gone well. But as you have, I dare say, observed, a native out stalking is always of that mind which is supposed to actuate an ostrich—so long as his head is hidden he seems to think that nothing else can be seen. So it was in this instance, Gobo and the other boy crept along on their hands and toes with their heads well down, but, though unfortunately I did not notice it till too late, bearing the fundamental portions of their frames high in the air. Now all animals are quite as suspicious of this end of mankind as they are of his face, and of that fact I soon had a proof. Just when we had got within about two hundred yards, and I was congratulating myself that I had not had this long crawl with the sun beating on the back of my neck like a furnace for nothing, I heard the hissing note of the rhinoceros birds, and up flew four or five of them from the brute's back, where they had been comfortably employed in catching tics. Now this performance on the part of the birds is to a rhinoceros what the word 'cave' is to a schoolboy—it puts him on the *qui vive* at once. Before the birds were well in the air I saw the grass stir.

"'Down you go,' I whispered to the boys, and as I did so the rhinoceros got up and glared suspiciously around. But he could see nothing, indeed if we had been standing up I doubt if he would have seen us at that distance; so he merely gave two or three sniffs and then lay down, his head still down wind, the birds once more settling on his back.

"But it was clear to me that he was sleeping with one eye open, being generally in a suspicious and unchristian frame of mind, and that it was useless to proceed further on this stalk, so we quietly withdrew to consider the position and study the ground. The results were not satisfactory. There was absolutely no cover about except the ant-heap, which was some three hundred yards from the rhinoceros upon his up- wind side. I knew that if I tried to stalk him in front I should fail, and so I should if I attempted to do so from the further side—he or the birds would see me; so I came to a conclusion: I would go to the ant-heap, which would give him my wind, and instead of stalking him I would let him stalk me. It was a bold step, and one which I should never advise a hunter to take, but somehow I felt as though rhino and I must play the hand out.

"I explained my intentions to the men, who both held up their arms in horror. Their fears for my safety were a little mitigated, however, when I told them that I did not expect them to come with me.

"Gobo breathed a prayer that I might not meet Fate walking about, and the other one sincerely trusted that my spirit might look my way when the rhinoceros charged, and then they both departed to a place of safety.

"Taking my eight-bore, and half-a-dozen spare cartridges in my pocket, I made a détour, and reaching the ant-heap in safety lay down. For a moment the wind had dropped, but presently a gentle puff of air passed over me, and blew on towards the rhinoceros. By the way, I wonder what it is that smells so strong about a man? Is it his body or his breath? I have never been able to make out, but I saw it stated the other day, that in the duck decoys the man who is working the ducks holds a little piece of burning turf before his mouth, and that if he does this they cannot smell him, which looks as though it were the breath. Well, whatever it was about me that attracted his attention, the rhinoceros soon smelt me, for within half a minute after the puff of wind had passed me he was on his legs, and turning round to get his head up wind. There he stood for a few seconds and sniffed, and then he began to move, first of all at a trot, then, as the scent grew stronger, at a furious gallop. On he came, snorting like a runaway engine, with his tail stuck straight up in the air; if he had seen me lie down there he could not have made a better line. It was rather nervous work, I can tell you, lying there waiting for his onslaught, for he looked like a mountain of flesh. I determined, however, not to fire till I could plainly see his eye, for I think that rule always gives one the right distance for big game; so I rested my rifle on the ant-heap and waited for him, kneeling. At last, when he was about forty yards away, I saw that the time had come, and aiming straight for the middle of the chest I pulled.

"*Thud* went the heavy bullet, and with a tremendous snort over rolled the rhinoceros beneath its shock, just like a shot rabbit. But if I had thought that he was done for I was mistaken, for in another second he was up again, and coming at me as hard as ever, only with his head held low. I waited till he was within ten yards, in the hope that he would expose his chest, but he would do nothing of the sort; so I just had to fire at his head with the left barrel, and take my chance. Well, as luck would have it, of course the animal put its horn in the way of the bullet, which cut clean through it about three inches above the root and then glanced off into space.

"After that things got rather serious. My gun was empty and the rhinoceros was rapidly arriving, so rapidly indeed that I came to the conclusion that I had better make way for him. Accordingly I jumped to my feet and ran to the right as hard as I could go. As I did so he arrived full tilt, knocked my friendly ant-heap flat, and for the third time that day went a most magnificent cropper. This gave me a few seconds' start, and I ran down wind—my word, I did run! Unfortunately, however, my modest retreat was observed, and the rhinoceros, as soon as he had found his legs again, set to work to run after me. Now no man on earth can run so fast as an irritated rhinoceros can gallop, and I knew that he must soon catch me up. But having some slight experience of this sort of thing, luckily for myself, I kept my head, and as I fled I managed to open my rifle, get the old cartridges out, and put in two fresh ones. To do this I was obliged to steady my pace a little, and by the time that I had snapped the rifle to I heard the beast snorting and thundering away within a few paces of my back. I stopped, and as I did so rapidly cocked the rifle and slued round upon my heel. By this time the brute was within six or seven yards of me, but luckily his head was up. I lifted the rifle and fired at him. It was a snap shot, but the bullet struck him in the chest within three inches of the first, and found its way into his lungs. It did not stop him, however, so all I could do was to bound to one side, which I did with surprising activity, and as he brushed past me to fire the other barrel into his side. That did for him.

The ball passed in behind the shoulder and right through his heart. He fell over on to his side, gave one more awful squeal—a dozen pigs could not have made such a noise—and promptly died, keeping his wicked eyes wide open all the time.

"As for me, I blew my nose, and going up to the rhinoceros sat on his head, and reflected that I had done a capital morning's shooting.

The First Round

"After this, as it was now midday, and I had killed enough meat, we marched back triumphantly to camp, where I proceeded to concoct a stew of buffalo beef and compressed vegetables. When this was ready we ate the stew, and then I took a nap. About four o'clock, however, Gobo woke me up, and told me that the head man of one of Wambe's kraals had arrived to see me. I ordered him to be brought up, and presently he came, a little, wizened, talkative old man, with a waistcloth round his middle, and a greasy, frayed kaross made of the skins of rock rabbits over his shoulders.

"I told him to sit down, and then abused him roundly. 'What did he mean,' I asked, 'by disturbing me in this rude way? How did he dare to cause a person of my quality and evident importance to be awakened in order to interview his entirely contemptible self?'

"I spoke thus because I knew that it would produce an impression on him. Nobody, except a really great man, he would argue, would dare to speak to him in that fashion. Most savages are desperate bullies at heart, and look on insolence as a sign of power.

"The old man instantly collapsed. He was utterly overcome, he said; his heart was split in two, and well realized the extent of his misbehaviour. But the occasion was very urgent. He heard that a mighty hunter was in the neighbourhood, a beautiful white man, how beautiful he could not have imagined had he not seen (this to me!), and he came to beg his assistance. The truth was, that three bull elephants such as no man ever saw had for years been the terror of their kraal, which was but a small place—a cattle kraal of the great chief Wambe's, where they lived to keep the cattle. And now of late these elephants had done them much damage; but last night they had destroyed a whole patch of mealie land, and he feared that if they came back they would all starve next season for want of food. Would the mighty white man then be pleased to come and kill the elephants? It would be easy for him to do—oh, most easy! It was only necessary that he should hide himself in a tree, for there was a full moon, and then when the elephants appeared he would speak to them with the gun, and they would fall down dead, and there would be an end of their troubling.

"Of course I hummed and hawed, and made a great favour of consenting to his proposal, though really I was delighted to have such a chance. One of the conditions that I made was that a messenger should at once be despatched to Wambe, whose kraal was two days' journey from where I was, telling him that I proposed to come and pay my respects to him in a few days, and to ask his formal permission to shoot in his country. Also I intimated that I was prepared to present him with 'hongo,' that is, blackmail, and that I hoped to do a little trade with him in ivory, of which I heard he had a great quantity.

"This message the old gentleman promised to despatch at once, though there was something about his manner which showed me that he was doubtful as to how it would be received. After that we struck our camp and moved on to the kraal, which we reached about an hour before sunset. This kraal was a collection of huts surrounded by a slight thorn-fence, perhaps there were ten of them in all. It was situated in a kloof of the mountain down which a rivulet flowed. The kloof was densely wooded, but for some distance above the kraal it was free from bush, and here on the rich deep ground brought down by the rivulet were the cultivated lands, in extent somewhere about twenty or twenty- five acres. On the kraal side of these lands stood a single hut, that served for a mealie store, which at the moment was used as a dwelling- place by an old woman, the first wife of our friend the head man.

"It appears that this lady, having had some difference of opinion with her husband about the extent of authority allowed to a younger and more amiable wife, had refused to dwell in the kraal any more, and, by way of marking her displeasure, had taken up her abode among the mealies. As the issue will show, she was, it happened, cutting off her nose to spite her face.

"Close by this hut grew a large baobab tree. A glance at the mealie grounds showed me that the old head man had not exaggerated the mischief done by the elephants to his crops, which were now getting ripe. Nearly half of the entire patch was destroyed. The great brutes had eaten all they could, and the rest they had trampled down. I went up to their spoor and started back in amazement—never had I seen such a spoor before. It was simply enormous, more especially that of one old bull, that carried, so said the natives, but a single tusk. One might have used any of the footprints for a hip-bath.

"Having taken stock of the position, my next step was to make arrangements for the fray. The three bulls, according to the natives, had been spoored into the dense patch of bush above the kloof. Now it seemed to me very probable that they would return to-night to feed on the remainder of the ripening mealies. If so, there was a bright moon, and it struck me that by the exercise of a little ingenuity I might bag one or more of them without exposing myself to any risk, which, having the highest respect for the aggressive powers of bull elephants, was a great consideration to me.

"This then was my plan. To the right of the huts as you look up the kloof, and commanding the mealie lands, stands the baobab tree that I have mentioned. Into that baobab tree I made up my mind to go. Then if the elephants appeared I should get a shot at them. I announced my intentions to the head man of the kraal, who was delighted. 'Now,' he said, 'his people might sleep in peace, for while the mighty white hunter sat aloft like a spirit watching over the welfare of his kraal what was there to fear?'

"I told him that he was an ungrateful brute to think of sleeping in peace while, perched like a wounded vulture on a tree, I watched for his welfare in wakeful sorrow; and once more he collapsed, and owned that my words were 'sharp but just.'

"However, as I have said, confidence was completely restored; and that evening everybody in the kraal, including the superannuated victim of jealousy in the little hut where the mealie cobs were stored, went to bed with a sense of sweet security from elephants and all other animals that prowl by night.

"For my part, I pitched my camp below the kraal; and then, having procured a beam of wood from the head man—rather a rotten one, by the way—I set it across two boughs that ran out laterally from the baobab tree, at a height of about twenty-five feet from the ground, in such fashion that I and another man could sit upon it with our legs hanging down, and rest our backs against the bole of the tree. This done I went back to the camp and ate my supper. About nine o'clock, half-an- hour before the moon-rise, I summoned Gobo, who, thinking that he had seen about enough of the delights of big game hunting for that day, did not altogether relish the job; and, despite his remonstrances, gave him my eight-bore to carry, I having the .570-express. Then we set out for the tree. It was very dark, but we found it without difficulty, though climbing it was a more complicated matter. However, at last we got up and sat down, like two little boys on a form that is too high for them, and waited. I did not dare to smoke, because I remembered the rhinoceros, and feared that the elephants might wind the tobacco if they should come my way, and this made the business more wearisome, so I fell to thinking and wondering at the completeness of the silence.

"At last the moon came up, and with it a moaning wind, at the breath of which the silence began to whisper mysteriously. Lonely enough in the newborn light looked the wide expanse of mountain, plain, and forest, more like some vision of a dream, some reflection from a fair world of peace beyond our ken, than the mere face of garish earth made soft with sleep. Indeed, had it not been for the fact that I was beginning to find the log on which I sat very hard, I should have grown quite sentimental over the beautiful sight; but I will defy anybody to become sentimental when seated in the damp, on a very rough beam of wood, and half-way up a tree. So I merely made a mental note that it was a particularly lovely night, and turned my attention to the prospect of elephants. But no elephants came, and after waiting for another hour or so, I think that what between weariness and disgust, I must have dropped into a gentle doze. Presently I awoke with a start. Gobo, who was perched close to me, but as far off as the beam would allow—for neither white man nor black like the aroma which each vows is the peculiar and disagreeable property of the other—was faintly, very faintly clicking his forefinger against his thumb. I knew by this signal, a very favourite one among native hunters and gun-bearers, that he must have seen or heard something. I looked at his face, and saw that he was staring excitedly towards the dim edge of the bush beyond the deep green line of mealies. I stared too, and listened. Presently I heard a soft large sound as though a giant were gently stretching out his hands and pressing back the ears of standing corn. Then came a pause, and then, out into the open majestically stalked the largest elephant I ever saw or ever shall see. Heavens! what a monster he was; and how the moonlight gleamed upon his one splendid tusk—for the other was missing—as he stood among the mealies gently moving his enormous ears to and fro, and testing the wind with his trunk. While I was still marvelling at his girth, and speculating upon the weight of that huge tusk, which I swore should be my tusk before very long, out stepped a second bull and stood beside him. He was not quite so tall, but he seemed to me to be almost thicker-set than the first; and even in that light I could see that both his tusks were perfect. Another pause, and the third emerged. He was shorter than either of the others, but higher in the shoulder than No. 2; and when I tell you, as I afterwards learnt from actual measurement, that the smallest of these mighty bulls measured twelve feet one and a half inches at the shoulder, it will give you some idea of their size. The three formed into line and stood still for a minute, the one-tusked bull gently caressing the elephant on the left with his trunk.

"Then they began to feed, walking forward and slightly to the right as they gathered great bunches of the sweet mealies and thrust them into their mouths. All this time they were more than a hundred and twenty yards away from me (this I knew, because I had paced the distances from the tree to various points), much too far to allow of my attempting a shot at them in that uncertain light. They fed in a semicircle, gradually drawing round towards the hut near my tree, in which the corn was stored and the old woman slept.

"This went on for between an hour and an hour and a half, till, what between excitement and hope, that maketh the heart sick, I grew so weary that I was actually contemplating a descent from the tree and a moonlight stalk. Such an act in ground so open would have been that of a stark staring lunatic, and that I should even have been contemplating it will show you the condition of my mind. But everything comes to him who knows how to wait, and sometimes too to him who doesn't, and so at last those elephants, or rather one of them, came to me.

"After they had fed their fill, which was a very large one, the noble three stood once more in line some seventy yards to the left of the hut, and on the edge of the cultivated lands, or in all about eighty- five yards from where I was perched. Then at last the one with a single tusk made a peculiar rattling noise in his trunk, just as though he were blowing his nose, and without more ado began to walk deliberately toward the hut where the old woman slept. I made my rifle ready and glanced up at the moon, only to discover that a new complication was looming in the immediate future. I have said that a wind rose with the moon. Well, the wind brought rain-clouds along its track. Several light ones had already lessened the light for a little while, though without obscuring it, and now two more were coming up rapidly, both of them very black and dense. The first cloud was small and long, and the one behind big and broad. I remember noticing that the pair of them bore a most comical resemblance to a dray drawn by a very long raw-boned horse. As luck would have it, just as the elephant arrived within twenty-five yards or so of me, the head of the horse- cloud floated over the face of the moon, rendering it impossible for me to fire. In the faint twilight which remained, however, I could just make out the gray mass of the great brute still advancing towards the hut. Then the light went altogether and I had to trust to my ears. I heard him fumbling with his trunk, apparently at the roof of the hut; next came a sound as of straw being drawn out, and then for a little while there was complete silence.

"The cloud began to pass; I could see the outline of the elephant; he was standing with his head quite over the top of the hut. But I could not see his trunk, and no wonder, for it was *inside the hut*. He had thrust it through the roof, and, attracted no doubt by the smell of the mealies, was groping about with it inside. It was growing light now, and I got my rifle ready, when suddenly there was a most awful yell, and I saw the trunk reappear, and in its mighty fold the old woman who had been sleeping in the hut. Out she came through the hole like a periwinkle on the point of a pin, still wrapped up in her blanket, and with her skinny arms and legs stretched to the four points of the compass, and as she did so, gave that most alarming screech. I really don't know who was the most frightened, she, or I, or the elephant. At any rate the last was considerably startled; he had been fishing for mealies—the old woman was a mere accident, and one that greatly discomposed his nerves. He gave a sort of trumpet, and threw her away from him right into the crown of a low mimosa tree, where she stuck shrieking like a metropolitan engine. The old bull lifted his tail, and flapping his great ears prepared for flight. I put up my eight-bore, and aiming hastily at the point of his shoulder (for he was broadside on), I fired. The report rang out like thunder, making a thousand echoes in the quiet hills. I saw him go down all of a heap as though he were stone dead. Then, alas! whether it was the kick of the heavy rifle, or the excited bump of that idiot Gobo, or both together, or merely an unhappy coincidence, I do not know, but the rotten beam broke and I went down too, landing flat at the foot of the tree upon a certain humble portion of the human frame. The shock was so severe that I felt as though all my teeth were flying through the roof of my mouth, but although I sat slightly stunned for a few seconds, luckily for me I fell light, and was not in any way injured.

"Meanwhile the elephant began to scream with fear and fury, and, attracted by his cries, the other two charged up. I felt for my rifle; it was not there. Then I remembered that I had rested it on a fork of the bough in order to fire, and doubtless there it remained. My position was now very unpleasant. I did not dare to try and climb the tree again, which, shaken as I was, would have been a task of some difficulty, because the elephants would certainly see me, and Gobo, who had clung to a bough, was still aloft with the other rifle. I could not run because there was no shelter near. Under these circumstances I did the only thing feasible, clambered round the trunk as softly as possible, and keeping one eye on the elephants, whispered to Gobo to bring down the rifle, and awaited the development of the situation. I knew that if the elephants did not see me—which, luckily, they were too enraged to do—they would not smell me, for I was up-wind. Gobo, however, either did not, or, preferring the safety of the tree, would not hear me. He said the former, but I believed the latter, for I knew that he was not enough of a sportsman to really enjoy shooting elephants by moonlight in the open. So there I was behind my tree, dismayed, unarmed, but highly interested, for I was witnessing a remarkable performance.

"When the two other bulls arrived the wounded elephant on the ground ceased to scream, but began to make a low moaning noise, and to gently touch the wound near his shoulder, from which the blood was literally spouting. The other two seemed to understand; at any rate, they did this. Kneeling down on either side, they placed their trunks and tusks underneath him, and, aided by his own efforts, with one great lift got him on to his feet. Then leaning against him on either side to support him, they marched off at a walk in the direction of the village. It was a pitiful sight, and even then it made me feel a brute.

"Presently, from a walk, as the wounded elephant gathered himself together a little, they broke into a trot, and after that I could follow them no longer with my eyes, for the second black cloud came up over the moon and put her out, as an extinguisher puts out a dip. I say with my eyes, but my ears gave me a very fair notion of what was going on. When the cloud came up the three terrified animals were heading directly for the kraal, probably because the way was open and the path easy. I fancy that they grew confused in the darkness, for when they came to the kraal fence they did not turn aside, but crashed straight through it. Then there were 'times,' as the Irish servant- girl says in the American book. Having taken the fence, they thought that they might as well take the kraal also, so they just ran over it. One hive-shaped hut was turned quite over on to its top, and when I arrived upon the scene the people who had been sleeping there were bumbling about inside like bees disturbed at night, while two more were crushed flat, and a third had all its side torn out. Oddly enough, however, nobody was hurt, though several people had a narrow escape of being trodden to death.

"On arrival I found the old head man in a state painfully like that favoured by Greek art, dancing about in front of his ruined abodes as vigorously as though he had just been stung by a scorpion.

"I asked him what ailed him, and he burst out into a flood of abuse. He called me a Wizard, a Sham, a Fraud, a Bringer of bad luck! I had promised to kill the elephants, and I had so arranged things that the elephants had nearly killed him, etc.

"This, still smarting, or rather aching, as I was from that most terrific bump, was too much for my feelings, so I just made a rush at my friend, and getting him by the ear, I banged his head against the doorway of his own hut, which was all that was left of it.

"'You wicked old scoundrel,' I said, 'you dare to complain about your own trifling inconveniences, when you gave me a rotten beam to sit on, and thereby delivered me to the fury of the elephant' (*bump! bump! bump!*), 'when your own wife' (*bump!*) 'has just been dragged out of her hut' (*bump!*) 'like a snail from its shell, and thrown by the Earth-shaker into a tree' (*bump! bump!*).

"'Mercy, my father, mercy!' gasped the old fellow. 'Truly I have done amiss—my heart tells me so.'

"'I should hope it did, you old villain' (*bump!*).

"'Mercy, great white man! I thought the log was sound. But what says the unequalled chief—is the old woman, my wife, indeed dead? Ah, if she is dead all may yet prove to have been for the very best;' and he clasped his hands and looked up piously to heaven, in which the moon was once more shining brightly.

"I let go his ear and burst out laughing, the whole scene and his devout aspirations for the decease of the partner of his joys, or rather woes, were so intensely ridiculous.

"'No, you old iniquity,' I answered; 'I left her in the top of a thorn-tree, screaming like a thousand bluejays. The elephant put her there.'

"'Alas! alas!' he said, 'surely the back of the ox is shaped to the burden. Doubtless, my father, she will come down when she is tired;' and without troubling himself further about the matter, he began to blow at the smouldering embers of the fire.

"And, as a matter of fact, she did appear a few minutes later, considerably scratched and startled, but none the worse.

"After that I made my way to my little camp, which, fortunately, the elephants had not walked over, and wrapping myself up in a blanket, was soon fast asleep.

"And so ended my first round with those three elephants.

The Last Round

"On the morrow I woke up full of painful recollections, and not without a certain feeling of gratitude to the Powers above that I was there to wake up. Yesterday had been a tempestuous day; indeed, what between buffalo, rhinoceros, and elephant, it had been very tempestuous. Having realized this fact, I next bethought me of those magnificent tusks, and instantly, early as it was, broke the tenth commandment. I coveted my neighbours tusks, if an elephant could be said to be my neighbour *de jure*, as certainly, so recently as the previous night, he had been *de facto*—a much closer neighbour than I cared for, indeed. Now when you covet your neighbour's goods, the best thing, if not the most moral thing, to do is to enter his house as a strong man armed, and take them. I was not a strong man, but having recovered my eight-bore I was armed, and so was the other strong man—the elephant with the tusks. Consequently I prepared for a struggle to the death. In other words, I summoned my faithful retainers, and told them that I was now going to follow those elephants to the edge of the world, if necessary. They showed a certain bashfulness about the business, but they did not gainsay me, because they dared not. Ever since I had prepared with all due solemnity to execute the rebellious Gobo they had conceived a great respect for me.

"So I went up to bid adieu to the old head man, whom I found alternately contemplating the ruins of his kraal and, with the able assistance of his last wife, thrashing the jealous lady who had slept in the mealie hut, because she was, as he declared, the fount of all his sorrows.

"Leaving them to work a way through their domestic differences, I levied a supply of vegetable food from the kraal in consideration of services rendered, and left them with my blessing. I do not know how they settled matters, because I have not seen them since.

"Then I started on the spoor of the three bulls. For a couple of miles or so below the kraal—as far, indeed, as the belt of swamp that borders the river—the ground is at this spot rather stony, and clothed with scattered bushes. Rain had fallen towards the daybreak, and this fact, together with the nature of the soil, made spooring a very difficult business. The wounded bull had indeed bled freely, but the rain had washed the blood off the leaves and grass, and the ground being so rough and hard did not take the footmarks so clearly as was convenient. However, we got along, though slowly, partly by the spoor, and partly by carefully lifting leaves and blades of grass, and finding blood underneath them, for the blood gushing from a wounded animal often falls upon their inner surfaces, and then, of course, unless the rain is very heavy, it is not washed away. It took us something over an hour and a half to reach the edge of the marsh, but once there our task became much easier, for the soft soil showed plentiful evidences of the great brutes' passage. Threading our way through the swampy land, we came at last to a ford of the river, and here we could see where the poor wounded animal had lain down in the mud and water in the hope of easing himself of his pain, and could see also how his two faithful companions had assisted him to rise again. We crossed the ford, and took up the spoor on the further side, and followed it into the marsh-like land beyond. No rain had fallen on this side of the river, and the blood-marks were consequently much more frequent.

"All that day we followed the three bulls, now across open plains, and now through patches of bush. They seemed to have travelled on almost without stopping, and I noticed that as they went the wounded bull recovered his strength a little. This I could see from his spoor, which had become firmer, and also from the fact that the other two had ceased to support him. At last evening closed in, and having travelled some eighteen miles, we camped, thoroughly tired out.

"Before dawn on the following day we were up, and the first break of light found us once more on the spoor. About half-past five o'clock we reached the place where the elephants had fed and slept. The two unwounded bulls had taken their fill, as the condition of the neighbouring bushes showed, but the wounded one had eaten nothing. He had spent the night leaning against a good-sized tree, which his weight had pushed out of the perpendicular. They had not long left this place, and could not be very far ahead, especially as the wounded bull was now again so stiff after his night's rest that for the first few miles the other two had been obliged to support him. But elephants go very quick, even when they seem to be travelling slowly, for shrub and creepers that almost stop a man's progress are no hindrance to them. The three had now turned to the left, and were travelling back again in a semicircular line toward the mountains, probably with the idea of working round to their old feeding grounds on the further side of the river.

"There was nothing for it but to follow their lead, and accordingly we followed with industry. Through all that long hot day did we tramp, passing quantities of every sort of game, and even coming across the spoor of other elephants. But, in spite of my men's entreaties, I would not turn aside after these. I would have those mighty tusks or none.

"By evening we were quite close to our game, probably within a quarter of a mile, but the bush was dense, and we could see nothing of them, so once more we must camp, thoroughly disgusted with our luck. That night, just after the moon rose, while I was sitting smoking my pipe with my back against a tree, I heard an elephant trumpet, as though something had startled it, and not three hundred yards away. I was very tired, but my curiosity overcame my weariness, so, without saying a word to any of the men, all of whom were asleep, I took my eight- bore and a few spare cartridges, and steered toward the sound. The game path which we had been following all day ran straight on in the direction from which the elephant had trumpeted. It was narrow, but well trodden, and the light struck down upon it in a straight white line. I crept along it cautiously for some two hundred yards, when it opened suddenly into a most beautiful glade some hundred yards or more in width, wherein tall grass grew and flat-topped trees stood singly. With the caution born of long experience I watched for a few moments before I entered the glade, and then I saw why the elephant had trumpeted. There in the middle of the glade stood a large maned lion. He stood quite still, making a soft purring noise, and waving his tail to and fro. Presently the grass about forty yards on the hither side of him gave a wide ripple, and a lioness sprang out of it like a flash, and bounded noiselessly up to the lion. Reaching him, the great cat halted suddenly, and rubbed her head against his shoulder. Then they both began to purr loudly, so loudly that I believe that in the stillness one might have heard them two hundred yards or more away.

"After a time, while I was still hesitating what to do, either they got a whiff of my wind, or they wearied of standing still, and determined to start in search of game. At any rate, as though moved by a common impulse, they bounded suddenly away, leap by leap, and vanished in the depths of the forest to the left. I waited for a little while longer to see if there were any more yellow skins about, and seeing none, came to the conclusion that the lions must have frightened the elephants away, and that I had taken my stroll for nothing. But just as I was turning back I thought that I heard a bough break upon the further side of the glade, and, rash as the act was, I followed the sound. I crossed the glade as silently as my own shadow. On its further side the path went on. Albeit with many fears, I went on too. The jungle growth was so thick here that it almost met overhead, leaving so small a passage for the light that I could scarcely see to grope my way along. Presently, however, it widened, and then opened into a second glade slightly smaller than the first, and there, on the further side of it, about eighty yards from me, stood the three enormous elephants.

"They stood thus:—Immediately opposite and facing me was the wounded one-tusked bull. He was leaning his bulk against a dead thorn-tree, the only one in the place, and looked very sick indeed. Near him stood the second bull as though keeping a watch over him. The third elephant was a good deal nearer to me and broadside on. While I was still staring at them, this elephant suddenly walked off and vanished down a path in the bush to the right.

"There are now two things to be done—either I could go back to the camp and advance upon the elephants at dawn, or I could attack them at once. The first was, of course, by far the wiser and safer course. To engage one elephant by moonlight and single-handed is a sufficiently rash proceeding; to tackle three was little short of lunacy. But, on the other hand, I knew that they would be on the march again before daylight, and there might come another day of weary trudging before I could catch them up, or they might escape me altogether.

"'No,' I thought to myself, 'faint heart never won fair tusk. I'll risk it, and have a slap at them. But how?' I could not advance across the open, for they would see me; clearly the only thing to do was to creep round in the shadow of the bush and try to come upon them so. So I started. Seven or eight minutes of careful stalking brought me to the mouth of the path down which the third elephant had walked. The other two were now about fifty yards from me, and the nature of the wall of bush was such that I could not see how to get nearer to them without being discovered. I hesitated, and peeped down the path which the elephant had followed. About five yards in, it took a turn round a shrub. I thought that I would just have a look behind it, and advanced, expecting that I should be able to catch a sight of the elephant's tail. As it happened, however, I met his trunk coming round the corner. It is very disconcerting to see an elephant's trunk when you expect to see his tail, and for a moment I stood paralyzed almost under the vast brute's head, for he was not five yards from me. He too halted, threw up his trunk and trumpeted preparatory to a charge. I was in for it now, for I could not escape either to the right or left, on account of the bush, and I did not dare turn my back. So I did the only thing that I could do—raised the rifle and fired at the black mass of his chest. It was too dark for me to pick a shot; I could only brown him, as it were.

"The shot rung out like thunder on the quiet air, and the elephant answered it with a scream, then dropped his trunk and stood for a second or two as still as though he had been cut in stone. I confess that I lost my head; I ought to have fired my second barrel, but I did not. Instead of doing so, I rapidly opened my rifle, pulled out the old cartridge from the right barrel and replaced it. But before I could snap the breech to, the bull was at me. I saw his great trunk fly up like a brown beam, and I waited no longer. Turning, I fled for dear life, and after me thundered the elephant. Right into the open glade I ran, and then, thank Heaven, just as he was coming up with me the bullet took effect on him. He had been shot right through the heart, or lungs, and down he fell with a crash, stone dead.

"But in escaping from Scylla I had run into the jaws of Charybdis. I heard the elephant fall, and glanced round. Straight in front of me, and not fifteen paces away, were the other two bulls. They were staring about, and at that moment they caught sight of me. Then they came, the pair of them—came like thunderbolts, and from different angles. I had only time to snap my rifle to, lift it, and fire, almost at haphazard, at the head of the nearest, the unwounded bull.

"Now, as you know, in the case of the African elephant, whose skull is convex, and not concave like that of the Indian, this is always a most risky and very frequently a perfectly useless shot. The bullet loses itself in the masses of bone, that is all. But there is one little vital place, and should the bullet happen to strike there, it will follow the channel of the nostrils—at least I suppose it is that of the nostrils—and reach the brain. And this was what happened in the present case—the ball struck the fatal spot in the region of the eye and travelled to the brain. Down came the great bull all of a heap, and rolled on to his side as dead as a stone. I swung round at that instant to face the third, the monster bull with one tusk that I had wounded two days before. He was already almost over me, and in the dim moonlight seemed to tower above me like a house. I lifted the rifle and pulled at his neck. It would not go off! Then, in a flash, as it were, I remembered that it was on the half-cock. The lock of this barrel was a little weak, and a few days before, in firing at a cow eland, the left barrel had jarred off at the shock of the discharge of the right, knocking me backwards with the recoil; so after that I had kept it on the half-cock till I actually wanted to fire it.

"I gave one desperate bound to the right, and, my lame leg notwithstanding, I believe that few men could have made a better jump. At any rate, it was none too soon, for as I jumped I felt the wind made by the tremendous downward stroke of the monster's trunk. Then I ran for it.

"I ran like a buck, still keeping hold of my gun, however. My idea, so far as I could be said to have any fixed idea, was to bolt down the pathway up which I had come, like a rabbit down a burrow, trusting that he would lose sight of me in the uncertain light. I sped across the glade. Fortunately the bull, being wounded, could not go full speed; but wounded or no, he could go quite as fast as I could. I was unable to gain an inch, and away we went, with just about three feet between our separate extremities. We were at the other side now, and a glance served to show me that I had miscalculated and overshot the opening. To reach it now was hopeless; I should have blundered straight into the elephant. So I did the only thing I could do: I swerved like a course hare, and started off round the edge of the glade, seeking for some opening into which I could plunge. This gave me a moment's start, for the bull could not turn as quickly as I could, and I made the most of it. But no opening could I see; the bush was like a wall. We were speeding round the edge of the glade, and the elephant was coming up again. Now he was within about six feet, and now, as he trumpeted or rather screamed, I could feel the fierce hot blast of his breath strike upon my head. Heavens! how it frightened me!

"We were three parts round the glade now, and about fifty yards ahead was the single large dead thorn-tree against which the bull had been leaning. I spurted for it; it was my last chance of safety. But spurt as I would, it seemed hours before I got there. Putting out my right hand, I swung round the tree, thus bringing myself face to face with the elephant. I had not time to lift the rifle to fire, I had barely time to cock it, and run sideways and backward, when he was on to me. Crash! he came, striking the tree full with his forehead. It snapped like a carrot about forty inches from the ground. Fortunately I was clear of the trunk, but one of the dead branches struck me on the chest as it went down and swept me to the ground. I fell upon my back, and the elephant blundered past me as I lay. More by instinct than anything else I lifted the rifle with one hand and pulled the trigger. It exploded, and, as I discovered afterwards, the bullet struck him in the ribs. But the recoil of the heavy rifle held thus was very severe; it bent my arm up, and sent the butt with a thud against the top of my shoulder and the side of my neck, for the moment quite paralyzing me, and causing the weapon to jump from my grasp. Meanwhile the bull was rushing on. He travelled for some twenty paces, and then suddenly he stopped. Faintly I reflected that he was coming back to finish me, but even the prospect of imminent and dreadful death could not rouse me into action. I was utterly spent; I could not move.

"Idly, almost indifferently, I watched his movements. For a moment he stood still, next he trumpeted till the welkin rang, and then very slowly, and with great dignity, he knelt down. At this point I swooned away.

"When I came to myself again I saw from the moon that I must have been insensible for quite two hours. I was drenched with dew, and shivering all over. At first I could not think where I was, when, on lifting my head, I saw the outline of the one-tusked bull still kneeling some five-and-twenty paces from me. Then I remembered. Slowly I raised myself, and was instantly taken with a violent sickness, the result of over-exertion, after which I very nearly fainted a second time. Presently I grew better, and considered the position. Two of the elephants were, as I knew, dead; but how about No. 3? There he knelt in majesty in the lonely moonlight. The question was, was he resting, or dead? I rose on my hands and knees, loaded my rifle, and painfully crept a few paces nearer. I could see his eye now, for the moonlight fell full upon it—it was open, and rather prominent. I crouched and watched; the eyelid did not move, nor did the great brown body, or the trunk, or the ear, or the tail—nothing moved. Then I knew that he must be dead.

"I crept up to him, still keeping the rifle well forward, and gave him a thump, reflecting as I did so how very near I had been to being thumped instead of thumping. He never stirred; certainly he was dead, though to this day I do not know if it was my random shot that killed him, or if he died from concussion of the brain consequent upon the tremendous shock of his contact with the tree. Anyhow, there he was. Cold and beautiful he lay, or rather knelt, as the poet nearly puts it. Indeed, I do not think that I have ever seen a sight more imposing in its way than that of the mighty beast crouched in majestic death, and shone upon by the lonely moon.

"While I stood admiring the scene, and heartily congratulating myself upon my escape, once more I began to feel sick. Accordingly, without waiting to examine the other two bulls, I staggered back to the camp, which in due course I reached in safety. Everybody in it was asleep. I did not wake them, but having swallowed a mouthful of brandy I threw off my coat and shoes, rolled myself up in a blanket, and was soon fast asleep.

"When I woke it was already light, and at first I thought that, like Joseph, I had dreamed a dream. At that moment, however, I turned my head, and quickly knew that it was no dream, for my neck and face were so stiff from the blow of the butt-end of the rifle that it was agony to move them. I collapsed for a minute or two. Gobo and another man, wrapped up like a couple of monks in their blankets, thinking that I was still asleep, were crouched over a little fire they had made, for the morning was damp and chilly, and holding sweet converse.

"Gobo said that he was getting tired of running after elephants which they never caught. Macumazahn (that is, myself) was without doubt a man of parts, and of some skill in shooting, but also he was a fool. None but a fool would run so fast and far after elephants which it was impossible to catch, when they kept cutting the spoor of fresh ones. He certainly was a fool, but he must not be allowed to continue in his folly; and he, Gobo, had determined to put a stop to it. He should refuse to accompany him any further on so mad a hunt.

"'Yes,' the other answered, 'the poor man certainly was sick in his head, and it was quite time that they checked his folly while they still had a patch of skin left upon their feet. Moreover, he for his part certainly did not like this country of Wambe's, which really was full of ghosts. Only the last night he had heard the spooks at work— they were out shooting, at least it sounded as though they were. It was very queer, but perhaps their lunatic of a master——'

"'Gobo, you scoundrel!' I shouted out at this juncture, sitting bolt upright on the blankets, 'stop idling there and make me some coffee.'

"Up sprang Gobo and his friend, and in half a moment were respectfully skipping about in a manner that contrasted well with the lordly contempt of their previous conversation. But all the time they were in earnest in what they said about hunting the elephants any further, for before I had finished my coffee they came to me in a body, and said that if I wanted to follow those elephants I must follow them myself, for they would not go.

"I argued with them, and affected to be much put out. The elephants were close at hand, I said; I was sure of it; I had heard them trumpet in the night.

"'Yes,' answered the men mysteriously, 'they too had heard things in the night, things not nice to hear; they had heard the spooks out shooting, and no longer would they remain in a country so vilely haunted.'

"'It was nonsense,' I replied. 'If ghosts went out shooting, surely they would use air-guns and not black powder, and one would not hear an air-gun. Well, if they were cowards, and would not come, of course I could not force them to, but I would make a bargain with them. They should follow those elephants for one half-hour more, then if we failed to come upon them I would abandon the pursuit, and we would go straight to Wambe, chief of the Matuku, and give him hongo.'

"To this compromise the men agreed readily. Accordingly about half-an-hour later we struck our camp and started, and notwithstanding my aches and bruises, I do not think that I ever felt in better spirits in my life. It is something to wake up in the morning and remember that in the dead of the night, single-handed, one has given battle to and overthrown three of the largest elephants in Africa, slaying them with three bullets. Such a feat to my knowledge had never been done before, and on that particular morning I felt a very 'tall man of my hands' indeed. The only thing I feared was, that should I ever come to tell the story nobody would believe it, for when a strange tale is told by a hunter, people are apt to think it is necessarily a lie, instead of being only probably so.

"Well, we passed on till, having crossed the first glade where I had seen the lions, we reached the neck of bush that separated it from the second glade, where the dead elephants were. And here I began to take elaborate precautions, amongst others ordering Gobo to keep some yards ahead and look out sharp, as I thought that the elephants might be about. He obeyed my instructions with a superior smile, and pushed ahead. Presently I saw him pull up as though he had been shot, and begin to snap his fingers faintly.

"'What is it?' I whispered.

"'The elephant, the great elephant with one tusk kneeling down.'

"I crept up beside him. There knelt the bull as I had left him last night, and there too lay the other bulls.

"'Do these elephants sleep?' I whispered to the astonished Gobo.

"'Yes, Macumazahn, they sleep.'

"'Nay, Gobo, they are dead.'

"'Dead? How can they be dead? Who killed them?'

"'What do people call me, Gobo?'

"'They call you Macumazahn.'

"'And what does Macumazahn mean?'

"'It means the man who keeps his eyes open, the man who gets up in the night.'

"'Yes, Gobo, and I am that man. Look, you idle, lazy cowards; while you slept last night I rose, and alone I hunted those great elephants, and slew them by the moonlight. To each of them I gave one bullet and only one, and it fell dead. Look,' and I advanced into the glade, 'here is my spoor, and here is the spoor of the great bull charging after me, and there is the tree that I took refuge behind; see, the elephant shattered it in his charge. Oh, you cowards, you who would give up the chase while the blood spoor steamed beneath your nostrils, see what I did single-handed while you slept, and be ashamed.'

"'*Ou!*' said the men, '*Ou!* Koos! Koos y umcool!' (Chief, great Chief!) And then they held their tongues, and going up to the three dead beasts, gazed upon them in silence.

"But after that those men looked upon me with awe as being almost more than mortal. No mere man, they said, could have slain those three elephants alone in the night-time. I never had any further trouble with them. I believe that if I had told them to jump over a precipice and that they would take no harm, they would have believed me.

"Well, I went up and examined the bulls. Such tusks as they had I never saw and never shall see again. It took us all day to cut them out; and when they reached Delagoa Bay, as they did ultimately, though not in my keeping, the single tusk of the big bull scaled one hundred and sixty pounds, and the four other tusks averaged ninety-nine and a half pounds—a most wonderful, indeed an almost unprecedented, lot of ivory. Unfortunately I was forced to saw the big tusk in two, otherwise we could not have carried it."

"Oh, Quatermain, you barbarian!" I broke in here, "the idea of spoiling such a tusk! Why, I would have kept it whole if I had been obliged to drag it myself."

"Oh yes, young man," he answered, "it is all very well for you to talk like that, but if you had found yourself in the position which it was my privilege to occupy a few hours afterwards, it is my belief that you would have thrown the tusks away altogether and taken to your heels."

"Oh," said Good, "so that isn't the end of the yarn? A very good yarn, Quatermain, by the way—I couldn't have made up a better one myself."

The old gentleman looked at Good severely, for it irritated him to be chaffed about his stories.

"I don't know what you mean, Good. I don't see that there is any comparison between a true story of adventure and the preposterous tales which you invent about ibex hanging by their horns. No, it is not the end of the story; the most exciting part is to come. But I have talked enough for to-night; and if you go on in that way, Good, it will be some time before I begin again."

"Sorry I spoke, I'm sure," said Good, humbly. "Let's have a split to show that there is no ill-feeling." And they did.

The Message of Maiwa

On the following evening we once more dined together, and Quatermain, after some pressure, was persuaded to continue his story—for Good's remark still rankled in his breast.

"At last," he went on, "a few minutes before sunset, the task was finished. We had laboured at it all day, stopping only once for dinner, for it is no easy matter to hew out five such tusks as those which now lay before me in a white and gleaming line. It was a dinner worth eating, too, I can tell you, for we dined off the heart of the great one-tusked bull, which was so big that the man whom I sent inside the elephant to look for his heart was forced to remove it in two pieces. We cut it into slices and fried it with fat, and I never tasted heart to equal it, for the meat seemed to melt in one's mouth. By the way, I examined the jaw of the elephant; it never grew but one tusk; the other had not been broken off, nor was it present in a rudimentary form.

"Well, there lay the five beauties, or rather four of them, for Gobo and another man were engaged in sawing the grand one in two. At last with many sighs I ordered them to do this, but not until by practical experiment I had proved that it was impossible to carry it in any other way. One hundred and sixty pounds of solid ivory, or rather more in its green state, is too great a weight for two men to bear for long across a broken country. I sat watching the job and smoking the pipe of contentment, when suddenly the bush opened, and a very handsome and dignified native girl, apparently about twenty years of age, stood before me, carrying a basket of green mealies upon her head.

"Although I was rather surprised to see a native girl in such a wild spot, and, so far as I knew, a long way from any kraal, the matter did not attract my particular notice; I merely called to one of the men, and told him to bargain with the woman for the mealies, and ask her if there were any more to be bought in the neighbourhood. Then I turned my head and continued to superintend the cutting of the tusk. Presently a shadow fell upon me. I looked up, and saw that the girl was standing before me, the basket of mealies still on her head.

"'Marême, Marême,' she said, gently clapping her hands together. The word Marême among these Matuku (though she was no Matuku) answers to the Zulu 'Koos,' and the clapping of hands is a form of salutation very common among the tribes of the Basutu race.

"'What is it, girl?' I asked her in Sisutu. 'Are those mealies for sale?'

"'No, great white hunter,' she answered in Zulu, 'I bring them as a gift.'

"'Good,' I replied; 'set them down.'

"'A gift for a gift, white man.'

"'Ah,' I grumbled, 'the old story—nothing for nothing in this wicked world. What do you want—beads?'

"She nodded, and I was about to tell one of the men to go and fetch some from one of the packs, when she checked me.

"'A gift from the giver's own hand is twice a gift,' she said, and I thought that she spoke meaningly.

"'You mean that you want me to give them to you myself?'

"'Surely.'

"I rose to go with her. 'How is it that, being of the Matuku, you speak in the Zulu tongue?' I asked suspiciously.

"'I am not of the Matuku,' she answered as soon as we were out of hearing of the men. 'I am of the people of Nala, whose tribe is the Butiana tribe, and who lives there,' and she pointed over the mountain. 'Also I am one of the wives of Wambe,' and her eyes flashed as she said the name.

"'And how did you come here?'

"'On my feet,' she answered laconically.

"We reached the packs, and undoing one of them, I extracted a handful of beads. 'Now,' I said, 'a gift for a gift. Hand over the mealies.'

"She took the beads without even looking at them, which struck me as curious, and setting the basket of mealies on the ground, emptied it.

"At the bottom of the basket were some curiously-shaped green leaves, rather like the leaves of the gutta-percha tree in shape, only somewhat thicker and of a more fleshy substance. As though by hazard, the girl picked one of these leaves out of the basket and smelt it. Then she handed it to me. I took the leaf, and supposing that she wished me to smell it also, was about to oblige her by doing so, when my eye fell upon some curious red scratches on the green surface of the leaf.

"'Ah,' said the girl (whose name, by the way, was Maiwa), speaking beneath her breath, 'read the signs, white man.'

"Without answering her I continued to stare at the leaf. It had been scratched or rather written upon with a sharp tool, such as a nail, and wherever this instrument had touched it, the acid juice oozing through the outer skin had turned a rusty blood colour. Presently I found the beginning of the scrawl, and read this in English, and covering the surface of the leaf and of two others that were in the basket.

"'I hear that a white man is hunting in the Matuku country. This is   to warn him to fly over the mountain to Nala. Wambe sends an impi   at daybreak to eat him up, because he has hunted before bringing   hongo. For God's sake, whoever you are, try to help me. I have   been the slave of this devil Wambe for nearly seven years, and am   beaten and tortured continually. He murdered all the rest of us,   but kept me because I could work iron. Maiwa, his wife, takes   this; she is flying to Nala her father because Wambe killed her   child. Try to get Nala to attack Wambe; Maiwa can guide them over   the mountain. You won't come for nothing, for the stockade of   Wambe's private kraal is made of elephants' tusks. For God's sake,   don't desert me, or I shall kill myself. I can bear this no   longer.

"'John Every.'

"Great heavens!' I gasped. 'Every!—why, it must be my old friend.' The girl, or rather the woman Maiwa, pointed to the other side of the leaf, where there was more writing. It ran thus—'I have just heard that the white man is called Macumazahn. If so, it must be my friend Quatermain. Pray Heaven it is, for I know he won't desert an old chum in such a fix as I am. It isn't that I'm afraid of dying, I don't care if I die, but I want to get a chance at Wambe first.'

"No, old boy,' thought I to myself, 'it isn't likely that I am going to leave you there while there is a chance of getting you out. I have played fox before now—there's still a double or two left in me. I must make a plan, that's all. And then there's that stockade of tusks. I am not going to leave that either.' Then I spoke to the woman.

"You are called Maiwa?'

"It is so.'

"You are the daughter of Nala and the wife of Wambe?'

"It is so.'

"You fly from Wambe to Nala?'

"I do.'

"Why do you fly? Stay, I would give an order,'—and calling to Gobo, I ordered him to get the men ready for instant departure. The woman, who, as I have said, was quite young and very handsome, put her hand into a little pouch made of antelope hide which she wore fastened round the waist, and to my horror drew from it the withered hand of a child, which evidently had been carefully dried in the smoke.

"I fly for this cause,' she answered, holding the poor little hand towards me. 'See now, I bore a child. Wambe was its father, and for eighteen months the child lived and I loved it. But Wambe loves not his children; he kills them all. He fears lest they should grow up to slay one so wicked, and he would have killed this child also, but I begged its life. One day, some soldiers passing the hut saw the child and saluted him, calling him the "chief who soon shall be." Wambe heard, and was mad. He smote the babe, and it wept. Then he said that it should weep for good cause. Among the things that he had stolen from the white men whom he slew is a trap that will hold lions. So strong is the trap that four men must stand on it, two on either side, before it can be opened."'

Here old Quatermain broke off suddenly.

"Look here, you fellows," he said, "I can't bear to go on with this part of the story, because I never could stand either seeing or talking of the sufferings of children. You can guess what that devil did, and what the poor mother was forced to witness. Would you believe it, she told me the tale without a tremor, in the most matter-of-fact way. Only I noticed that her eyelid quivered all the time.

"Well,' I said, as unconcernedly as though I had been talking of the death of a lamb, though inwardly I was sick with horror and boiling with rage, 'and what do you mean to do about the matter, Maiwa, wife of Wambe?'

"I mean to do this, white man,' she answered, drawing herself up to her full height, and speaking in tones as hard as steel and cold as ice—'I mean to work, and work, and work, to bring this to pass, and to bring that to pass, until at length it comes to pass that with these living eyes I behold Wambe dying the death that he gave to his child and my child.'

"Well said,' I answered.

"Ay, well said, Macumazahn, well said, and not easily forgotten. Who could forget, oh, who could forget? See where this dead hand rests against my side; so once it rested when alive. And now, though it is dead, now every night it creeps from its nest and strokes my hair and clasps my fingers in its tiny palm. Every night it does this, fearing lest I should forget. Oh, my child! my child! ten days ago I held thee to my breast, and now this alone remains of thee,' and she kissed the dead hand and shivered, but never a tear did she weep.

"See now,' she went on, 'the white man, the prisoner at Wambe's kraal, he was kind to me. He loved the child that is dead, yes, he wept when its father slew it, and at the risk of his life told Wambe, my husband—ah, yes, my husband!—that which he is! He too it was who made a plan. He said to me, "Go, Maiwa, after the custom of thy people, go purify thyself in the bush alone, having touched a dead one. Say to Wambe thou goest to purify thyself alone for fifteen days, according to the custom of thy people. Then fly to thy father, Nala, and stir him up to war against Wambe for the sake of the child that is dead." This then he said, and his words seemed good to me, and that same night ere I left to purify myself came news that a white man hunted in the country, and Wambe, being mad with drink, grew very wrath, and gave orders that an impi should be gathered to slay the white man and his people and seize his goods. Then did the "Smiter of Iron" (Every) write the message on the green leaves, and bid me seek thee out, and show forth the matter, that thou mightest save thyself by flight; and behold, this thing have I done, Macumazahn, the hunter, the Slayer of Elephants.'

"Ah,' I said, 'I thank you. And how many men be there in the impi of Wambe?'

"A hundred of men and half a hundred.'

"And where is the impi?'

"There to the north. It follows on thy spoor. I saw it pass yesterday, but myself I guessed that thou wouldst be nigher to the mountain, and came this way, and found thee. To-morrow at the daybreak the slayers will be here.'

"Very possibly,' I thought to myself; 'but they won't find Macumazahn. I have half a mind to put some strychnine into the carcases of those elephants for their especial benefit though.' I knew that they would stop to eat the elephants, as indeed they did, to our great gain, but I abandoned the idea of poisoning them, because I was rather short of strychnine."

"Or because you did not like to play the trick, Quatermain?" I suggested with a laugh.

"I said because I had not enough strychnine. It would take a great deal of strychnine to poison three elephants effectually," answered the old gentleman testily.

I said nothing further, but I smiled, knowing that old Allan could never have resorted to such an artifice, however severe his strait. But that was his way; he always made himself out to be a most unmerciful person.

"Well," he went on, "at that moment Gobo came up and announced that we were ready to march. 'I am glad that you are ready,' I said, 'because if you don't march, and march quick, you will never march again, that is all. Wambe has an impi out to kill us, and it will be here presently.'

"Gobo turned positively green, and his knees knocked together. 'Ah, what did I say?' he exclaimed. 'Fate walks about loose in Wambe's country.'

"'Very good; now all you have to do is to walk a little quicker than he does. No, no, you don't leave those elephant tusks behind—I am not going to part with them I can tell you.'

"Gobo said no more, but hastily directed the men to take up their loads, and then asked which way we were to run.

"'Ah,' I said to Maiwa, 'which way?'

"'There,' she answered, pointing towards the great mountain spur which towered up into the sky some forty miles away, separating the territories of Nala and Wambe—'there, below that small peak, is one place where men may pass, and one only. Also it can easily be blocked from above. If men pass not there, then they must go round the great peak of the mountain, two days' journey and half a day.'

"'And how far is the peak from us?'

"'All to-night shall you walk and all to-morrow, and if you walk fast, at sunset you shall stand on the peak.'

"I whistled, for that meant a five-and-forty miles trudge without sleep. Then I called to the men to take each of them as much cooked elephant's meat as he could carry conveniently. I did the same myself, and forced the woman Maiwa to eat some as we went. This I did with difficulty, for at that time she seemed neither to sleep nor eat nor rest, so fiercely was she set on vengeance.

"Then we started, Maiwa guiding us. After going for a half-hour over gradually rising ground, we found ourselves on the further edge of a great bush-clad depression something like the bottom of a lake. This depression, through which we had been travelling, was covered with bush to a very great extent, indeed almost altogether so, except where it was pitted with glades such as that wherein I had shot the elephants.

"At the top of this slope Maiwa halted, and putting her hand over her eyes looked back. Presently she touched me on the arm and pointed across the sea of forest towards a comparatively vacant space of country some six or seven miles away. I looked, and suddenly I saw something flash in the red rays of the setting sun. A pause, and then another quick flash.

"'What is it?' I asked.

"'It is the spears of Wambe's impi, and they travel fast,' she answered coolly.

"I suppose that my face showed how little I liked the news, for she went on—

"'Fear not; they will stay to feast upon the elephants, and while they feast we shall journey. We may yet escape.'

"After that we turned and pushed on again, till at length it grew so dark that we had to wait for the rising of the moon, which lost us time, though it gave us rest. Fortunately none of the men had seen that ominous flashing of the spears; if they had, I doubt if even I could have kept control of them. As it was, they travelled faster than I had ever known loaded natives to go before, so thorough-paced was their desire to see the last of Wambe's country. I, however, took the precaution to march last of all, fearing lest they should throw away their loads to lighten themselves, or, worse still, the tusks; for these kind of fellows would be capable of throwing anything away if their own skins were at stake. If the pious Æneas, whose story you were reading to me the other night, had been a mongrel Delagoa Bay native, Anchises would have had a poor chance of getting out of Troy, that is, if he was known to have made a satisfactory will.

"At moonrise we set out again, and with short occasional halts travelled till dawn, when we were forced to rest and eat. Starting once more, about half-past five, we crossed the river at noon. Then began the long toilsome ascent through thick bush, the same in which I shot the bull buffalo, only some twenty miles to the west of that spot, and not more than twenty-five miles on the hither side of Wambe's kraal. There were six or seven miles of this dense bush, and hard work it was to get through it. Next came a belt of scattered forest which was easier to pass, though, in revenge, the ground was steeper. This was about two miles wide, and we passed it by about four in the afternoon. Above this scattered bush lay a long steep slope of boulder-strewn ground, which ran up to the foot of the little peak some three miles away. As we emerged, footsore and weary, on to this inhospitable plain, some of the men looking round caught sight of the spears of Wambe's impi advancing rapidly not more than a mile behind us.

"At first there was a panic, and the bearers tried to throw off their loads and run, but I harangued them, calling out to them that certainly I would shoot the first man who did so and that if they would but trust in me I would bring them through the mess. Now, ever since I had killed those three elephants single-handed, I had gained great influence over these men, and they listened to me. So off we went as hard as ever we could go—the members of the Alpine Club would not have been in it with us. We made the boulders burn, as a Frenchman would say.

"When we had done about a mile the spears began to emerge from the belt of scattered bush, and the whoop of their bearers as they viewed us broke upon our ears. Quick as our pace had been before, it grew much quicker now, for terror lent wings to my gallant crew. But they were sorely tired, and the loads were heavy, so that run, or rather climb, as we would, Wambe's soldiers, a scrubby-looking lot of men armed with big spears and small shields, but without plumes, climbed considerably faster. The last mile of that pleasing chase was like a fox hunt, we being the fox, and always in view. What astonished me was the extraordinary endurance and activity shown by Maiwa. She never even flagged. I think that girl's muscles must have been made of iron, or perhaps it was the strength of her will that supported her. At any rate she reached the foot of the peak second, poor Gobo, who was an excellent hand at running away, being first.

"Presently I came up panting, and glanced at the ascent. Before us was a wall of rock about one hundred and fifty feet in height, upon which the strata were laid so as to form a series of projections sufficiently resembling steps to make the ascent easy, comparatively speaking, except at one spot, where it was necessary to climb over a projecting angle of cliff and bear a little to the left. It was not a really difficult place, but what made it awkward was, that immediately beneath this projection gaped a deep fissure or donga, on the brink of which we now stood, originally dug out, no doubt, by the rush of water from the peak and cliff. This gulf beneath would be trying to the nerves of a weak-headed climber at the critical point, and so it proved in the result. The projecting angle once passed, the remainder of the ascent was very simple. At the summit, however, the brow of the cliff hung over and was pierced by a single narrow path cut through it by water, in such fashion that a single boulder rolled into it at the top would make the cliff quite impassable to men without ropes.

"At this moment Wambe's soldiers were about a thousand yards from us, so it was evident that we had no time to lose. I at once ordered the men to commence the ascent, the girl Maiwa, who was familiar with the pass, going first to show them the way. Accordingly they began to mount with alacrity, pushing and lifting their loads in front of them. When the first of them, led by Maiwa, reached the projecting angle, they put down their loads upon a ledge of rock and clambered over. Once there, by lying on their stomachs upon a boulder, they could reach the loads which were held to them by the men beneath, and in this way drag them over the awkward place, whence they were carried easily to the top.

"But all of this took time, and meanwhile the soldiers were coming up fast, screaming and brandishing their big spears. They were now within about four hundred yards, and several loads, together with all the tusks, had yet to be got over the rock. I was still standing at the bottom of the cliff, shouting directions to the men above, but it occurred to me that it would soon be time to move. Before doing so, however, I thought that it might be well to try and produce a moral effect upon the advancing enemy. In my hand I held a Winchester repeating carbine, but the distance was too great for me to use it with effect, so I turned to Gobo, who was shivering with terror at my side, and handing him the carbine, took my express from him.

"The enemy was now about three hundred and fifty yards away, and the express was only sighted to three hundred. Still I knew that it could be trusted for the extra fifty yards. Running in front of Wambe's soldiers were two men—captains, I suppose—one of them very tall. I put up the three hundred yard flap, and sitting down with my back against the rock, I drew a long breath to steady myself, and covered the tall man, giving him a full sight. Feeling that I was on him, I pulled, and before the sound of the striking bullet could reach my ears, I saw the man throw up his arms and pitch forward on to his head. His companion stopped dead, giving me a fair chance. I rapidly covered him, and fired the left barrel. He turned round once, and then sank down in a heap. This caused the enemy to hesitate—they had never seen men killed at such a distance before, and thought that there was something uncanny about the performance. Taking advantage of the lull, I gave the express back to Gobo, and slinging the Winchester repeater over my back I began to climb the cliff.

"When we reached the projecting angle all the loads were over, but the tusks still had to be passed up, and owing to their weight and the smoothness of their surface, this was a very difficult task. Of course I ought to have abandoned the tusks; often and often have I since reproached myself for not doing so. Indeed, I think that my obstinacy about them was downright sinful, but I was always obstinate about such things, and I could not bear the idea of leaving those splendid tusks which had cost me so much pains and danger to come by. Well, it nearly cost me my life also, and did cost poor Gobo his, as will be seen shortly, to say nothing of the loss inflicted by my rifle on the enemy. When I reached the projection I found that the men, with their usual stupidity, were trying to hand up the tusks point first. Now the result of this was that those above had nothing to grip except the round polished surface of the ivory, and in the position in which they were, this did not give them sufficient hold to enable them to lift the weight. I told them to reverse the tusks and push them up, so that the rough and hollow ends came to the hands of the men above. This they did, and the first two were dragged up in safety.

"At this point, looking behind me, I saw the Matukus streaming up the slope in a rough extended order, and not more than a hundred yards away. Cocking the Winchester I turned and opened fire on them. I don't quite know how many I missed, but I do know that I never shot better in my life. I had to keep shifting myself from one enemy to the other, firing almost without getting a sight, that is, by the eye alone, after the fashion of the experts who break glass balls. But quick as the work was, men fell thick, and by the time that I had emptied the carbine of its twelve cartridges, for the moment the advance was checked. I rapidly pushed in some more cartridges, and hardly had I done so when the enemy, seeing that we were about to escape them altogether, came on once more with a tremendous yell. By this time the two halves of the single tusk of the great bull alone remained to be passed up. I fired and fired as effectively as before, but notwithstanding all that I could do, some men escaped my hail of bullets and began to ascend the cliff. Presently my rifle was again empty. I slung it over my back, and, drawing my revolver, turned to run for it, the attackers being now quite close. As I did so, a spear struck the cliff close to my head.

"The last half of the tusk was now vanishing over the rock, and I sung out to Gobo and the other man who had been pushing it up to vanish after it. Gobo, poor fellow, required no second invitation; indeed, his haste was his undoing. He went at the projecting rock with a bound. The end of the tusk was still hanging over, and instead of grasping the rock he caught at it. It twisted in his hand—he slipped —he fell; with one wild shriek he vanished into the abyss beneath, his falling body brushing me as it passed. For a moment we stood aghast, and presently the dull thud of his fall smote heavily upon our ears. Poor fellow, he had met the Fate which, as he declared, walked about loose in Wambe's country. Then with an oath the remaining man sprung at the rock and clambered over it in safety. Aghast at the awfulness of what had happened, I stood still, till I saw the great blade of a Matuku spear pass up between my feet. That brought me to my senses, and I began to clamber up the rock like a cat. I was half way round it. Already I had clasped the hand of that brave girl Maiwa, who came down to help me, the men having scrambled forward with the ivory, when I felt some one seize my ankle.

"Pull, Maiwa, pull,' I gasped, and she certainly did pull. Maiwa was a very muscular woman, and never before did I appreciate the advantages of the physical development of females so keenly. She tugged at my left arm, the savage below tugged at my right leg, till I began to realize that something must give way ere long. Luckily I retained my presence of mind, like the man who threw his mother-in-law out of the window, and carried the mattress down-stairs, when a fire broke out in his house. My right hand was still free, and in it I held my revolver, which was secured to my wrist by a leather thong. The pistol was cocked, and I simply pointed it downwards and fired. The result was instantaneous—and so far as I am concerned, most satisfactory. The bullet hit the man beneath me somewhere, I am sure I don't know where; at any rate, he let go of my leg and plunged headlong into the gulf beneath to join Gobo. In another moment I was on the top of the rock, and going up the remaining steps like a lamplighter. A single other soldier appeared in pursuit, but one of my boys at the top fired my elephant gun at him. I don't know if he hit him or only frightened him; at any rate, he vanished whence he came. I do know, however, that he very nearly hit *me*, for I felt the wind of the bullet.

"Another thirty seconds, and I and the woman Maiwa were at the top of the cliff panting, but safe.

"My men, being directed thereto by Maiwa, had most fortunately rolled up some big boulders which lay about, and with these we soon managed to block the passage through the overhanging ridge of rock in such fashion that the soldiers below could not possibly climb over it. Indeed, so far as I could see, they did not even try to do so—their heart was turned to fat, as the Zulus say.

"Then having rested a few moments we took up the loads, including the tusks of ivory that had cost us so dear, and in silence marched on for a couple of miles or more, till we reached a patch of dense bush. And here, being utterly exhausted, we camped for the night, taking the precaution, however, of setting a guard to watch against any attempt at surprise.

The Plan of Campaign

"Notwithstanding all that we had gone through, perhaps indeed on account of it, for I was thoroughly worn out, I slept that night as soundly as poor Gobo, round whose crushed body the hyænas would now be prowling. Rising refreshed at dawn we went on our way towards Nala's kraal, which we reached at nightfall. It is built on open ground after the Zulu fashion, in a ring fence and with beehive huts. The cattle kraal is behind and a little to the left. Indeed, both from their habits and their talk it was easy to see that these Butiana belong to that section of the Bantu people which, since T'Chaka's time, has been known as the Zulu race. We did not see the chief Nala that night. His daughter Maiwa went on to his private huts as soon as we arrived, and very shortly afterwards one of his head men came to us bringing a sheep and some mealies and milk with him. 'The chief sent us greeting,' he said, 'and would see us on the morrow.' Meanwhile he was ordered to bring us to a place of resting, where we and our goods should be safe and undisturbed. Accordingly he led the way to some very good huts just outside Nala's private enclosure, and here we slept comfortably.

"On the morrow about eight o'clock the head man came again, and said that Nala requested that I would visit him. I followed him into the private enclosure and was introduced to the chief, a fine-looking man of about fifty, with very delicately-shaped hands and feet, and a rather nervous mouth. The chief was seated on a tanned ox-hide outside his hut. By his side stood his daughter Maiwa, and squatted on their haunches round him were some twenty head men or Indunas, whose number was continually added to by fresh arrivals. These men saluted me as I entered, and the chief rose and took my hand, ordering a stool to be brought for me to sit on. When this was done, with much eloquence and native courtesy he thanked me for protecting his daughter in the painful and dangerous circumstances in which she found herself placed, and also complimented me very highly upon what he was pleased to call the bravery with which I had defended the pass in the rocks. I answered in appropriate terms, saying that it was to Maiwa herself that thanks were due, for had it not been for her warning and knowledge of the country we should not have been here to-day; while as to the defence of the pass, I was fighting for my life, and that put heart into me.

"These courtesies concluded, Nala called upon his daughter Maiwa to tell her tale to the head men, and this she did most simply and effectively. She reminded them that she had gone as an unwilling bride to Wambe—that no cattle had been paid for her, because Wambe had threatened war if she was not sent as a free gift. Since she had entered the kraal of Wambe her days had been days of heaviness and her nights nights of weeping. She had been beaten, she had been neglected and made to do the work of a low-born wife—she, a chief's daughter. She had borne a child, and this was the story of the child.

Then amidst a dead silence she told them the awful tale which she had already narrated to me. When she had finished, her hearers gave a loud ejaculation. '*Ou!*' they said, '*Ou!* Maiwa, daughter of Nala!'

"Ay,' she went on with flashing eyes, 'ay, it is true; my mouth is as full of truth as a flower of honey, and for tears my eyes are like the dew upon the grass at dawn. It is true I saw the child die—here is the proof of it, councillors,' and she drew forth the little dead hand and held it before them.

"*Ou!*' they said again, '*Ou!* it is the dead hand!'

"Yes,' she continued, 'it is the dead hand of my dead child, and I bear it with me that I may never forget, never for one short hour, that I live that I may see Wambe die, and be avenged. Will you bear it, my father, that your daughter and your daughter's child should be so treated by a Matuku? Will ye bear it, men of my own people?'

"No,' said an old Induna, rising, 'it is not to be borne. Enough have we suffered at the hands of these Matuku dogs and their loud-tongued chief; let us put it to the issue.'

"It is not to be borne indeed,' said Nala; 'but how can we make head against so great a people?'

"Ask of him—ask of Macumazahn, the wise white man,' said Maiwa, pointing at me.

"How can we overcome Wambe, Macumazahn the hunter?'

"How does the jackal overreach the lion, Nala?'

"By cleverness, Macumazahn.'

"So shall you overcome Wambe, Nala.'

"At this moment an interruption occurred. A man entered and said that messengers had arrived from Wambe.

"What is their message?' asked Nala.

"They come to ask that thy daughter Maiwa be sent back, and with her the white hunter.'

"How shall I make answer to this, Macumazahn?' said Nala, when the man had withdrawn.

"Thus shalt thou answer,' I said after reflection; 'say that the woman shall be sent and I with her, and then bid the messengers be gone. Stay, I will hide myself here in the hut that the men may not see me,' and I did.

"Shortly afterwards, through a crack in the hut, I saw the messengers arrive, and they were great truculent-looking fellows. There were four of them, and evidently they had travelled night and day. They entered with a swagger and squatted down before Nala.

"Your business?' said Nala, frowning.

"We come from Wambe, bearing the orders of Wambe to Nala his servant,' answered the spokesman of the party.

"Speak,' said Nala, with a curious twitch of his nervous-looking mouth.

"These are the words of Wambe: "Send back the woman, my wife, who has run away from my kraal, and send with her the white man who has dared to hunt in my country without my leave, and to slay my soldiers." These are the words of Wambe.'

"'And if I say I will not send them?' asked Nala.

"'Then on behalf of Wambe we declare war upon you. Wambe will eat you up. He will wipe you out; your kraals shall be stamped flat—so,' and with an expressive gesture he drew his hand across his mouth to show how complete would be the annihilation of that chief who dared to defy Wambe.

"'These are heavy words,' said Nala. 'Let me take counsel before I answer.'

"Then followed a little piece of acting that was really very creditable to the untutored savage mind. The heralds withdrew, but not out of sight, and Nala went through the show of earnestly consulting his Indunas. The girl Maiwa too flung herself at his feet, and appeared to weep and implore his protection, while he wrung his hands as though in doubt and tribulation of mind. At length he summoned the messengers to draw near, and addressed them, while Maiwa sobbed very realistically at his side.

"'Wambe is a great chief,' said Nala, 'and this woman is his wife, whom he has a right to claim. She must return to him, but her feet are sore with walking, she cannot come now. In eight days from this day she shall be delivered at the kraal of Wambe; I will send her with a party of my men. As for the white hunter and his men, I have nought to do with them, and cannot answer for their misdeeds. They have wandered hither unbidden by me, and I will deliver them back whence they came, that Wambe may judge them according to his law; they shall be sent with the girl. For you, go your ways. Food shall be given you without the kraal, and a present for Wambe in atonement of the ill-doing of my daughter. I have spoken.'

"At first the heralds seemed inclined to insist upon Maiwa's accompanying them then and there, but on being shown the swollen condition of her feet, ultimately they gave up the point and departed.

"When they were well out of the way I emerged from the hut, and we went on to discuss the situation and make our plans. First of all, as I was careful to explain to Nala, I was not going to give him my experience and services for nothing. I heard that Wambe had a stockade round his kraal made of elephant tusks. These tusks, in the event of our succeeding in the enterprise, I should claim as my perquisite, with the proviso that Nala should furnish me with men to carry them down to the coast.

"To this modest request Nala and the head men gave an unqualified and hearty assent, the more hearty perhaps because they never expected to get the ivory.

"The next thing I stipulated was, that if we conquered, the white man John Every should be handed over to me, together with any goods which he might claim. His cruel captivity was, I need hardly say, the only reason that induced me to join in so hair-brained an expedition, but I was careful from motives of policy to keep this fact in the background. Nala accepted this condition. My third stipulation was that no women or children should be killed. This being also agreed to, wc wcnt on to consider ways and means. Wambe, it appeared, was a very powerful petty chief, that is, he could put at least six thousand fighting men into the field, and always had from three to four thousand collected about his kraal, which was supposed to be impregnable. Nala, on the contrary, at such short notice could not collect more than from twelve to thirteen hundred men, though, being of the Zulu stock, they were of much better stuff for fighting purposes than Wambe's Matukus.

"These odds, though large, under the circumstances were not overwhelming. The real obstacle to our chance of success was the difficulty of delivering a crushing assault against Wambe's strong place. This was, it appeared, fortified all round with schanses or stone walls, and contained numerous caves and koppies in the hill-side and at the foot of the mountain which no force had ever been able to capture. It is said that in the time of the Zulu monarch Dingaan, a great impi of that king's having penetrated to this district, had delivered an assault upon the kraal then owned by a forefather of Wambe's, and been beaten back with the loss of more than a thousand men.

"Having thought the question over, I interrogated Maiwa closely as to the fortifications and the topographical peculiarities of the spot, and not without results. I discovered that the kraal was indeed impregnable to a front attack, but that it was very slightly defended to the rear, which ran up a slope of the mountain, indeed only by two lines of stone walls. The reason of this was that the mountain is quite impassable except by one secret path supposed to be known only to the chief and his councillors, and this being so, it had not been considered necessary to fortify it.

"'Well,' I said, when she had done, 'and now as to this secret path of thine—knowest thou aught of it?'

"'Ay,' she answered, 'I am no fool, Macumazahn. Knowledge learned is power earned. I won the secret of that path.'

"'And canst thou guide an impi thereon so that it shall fall upon the town from behind?'

"'Yes, I can do this, if only Wambe's people know not that the impi comes, for if they know, then they can block the way.'

"'So then here is my plan. Listen, Nala, and say if it be good, or if thou hast a better, show it forth. Let messengers go out and summon all thy impi, that it be gathered here on the third day from now. This being done, let the impi, led by Maiwa, march on the morrow of the fourth day, and crossing the mountains let it travel along on the other side of the mountains till it come to the place on the further side of which is the kraal of Wambe; that shall be some three days' journey in all. Then on the night of the third day's journey, let Maiwa lead the impi in silence up the secret path, so that it comes to the crest of the mountain that is above the strong place, and here let it hide among the rocks.

"'Meanwhile on the sixth day from now let one of thy Indunas, Nala, bring with him two hundred men that have guns, and lead me and my men as prisoners, and take also a girl from among the Butiana people, who by form and face is like unto Maiwa, and bind her hands, and pass by the road on which we came and through the cutting in the cliff on to the kraal of Wambe. But the men shall take no shields or plumes with them, only their guns and one short spear, and when they meet the people of Wambe they shall say that they come to give up the woman and the white man and his party to Wambe, and to make atonement to Wambe. So shall they pass in peace. And travelling thus, on the evening of the seventh day we shall come to the gates of the place of Wambe, and nigh the gates there is, so says Maiwa, a koppie very strong and full of rocks and caves, but having no soldiers on it except in time of war, or at the worst but a few such as can easily be overpowered.

"'This being done, at the dawn of day the impi on the mountain behind the town must light a fire and put wet grass on it, so that the smoke goes up. Then at the sight of the smoke we in the koppie will begin to shoot into the town of Wambe, and all the soldiers will run to kill us. But we will hold our own, and while we fight the impi shall charge down the mountain side and climb the schanses, and put those who defend them to the assegai, and then falling upon the town shall surprise it, and drive the soldiers of Wambe as a wind blows the dead husks of corn. This is my plan. I have spoken.'

"'*Ou!*' said Nala, 'it is good, it is very good. The white man is cleverer than a jackal. Yes, so shall it be; and may the snake of the Butiana people stand up upon its tail and prosper the war, for so shall we be rid of Wambe and the tyrannies of Wambe.'

"After that the girl Maiwa stood up, and once more producing the dreadful little dried hand, made her father and several of his head councillors swear by it and upon it that they would carry out the war of vengeance to the bitter end. It was a very curious sight to see. And by the way, the fight that ensued was thereafter known among the tribes of that district as the War of the Little Hand.

"The next two days were busy ones for us. Messengers were sent out, and every available man of the Butiana tribe was ordered up to 'a great dance.' The country was small, and by the evening of the second day, some twelve hundred and fifty men were assembled with their assegais and shields, and a fine hardy troop they were. At dawn of the following day, the fourth from the departure of the heralds, the main impi, having been doctored in the usual fashion, started under the command of Nala himself, who, knowing that his life and chieftainship hung upon the issue of the struggle, wisely determined to be present to direct it. With them went Maiwa, who was to guide them up the secret path. Of course we were obliged to give them two days' start, as they had more than a hundred miles of rough country to pass, including the crossing of the great mountain range which ran north and south, for it was necessary that the impi should make a wide détour in order to escape detection.

"At length, however, at dawn on the sixth day, I took the road, accompanied by my most unwilling bearers, who did not at all like the idea of thus putting their heads into the lion's mouth. Indeed, it was only the fear of Nala's spears, together with a vague confidence in myself, that induced them to accept the adventure. With me also were about two hundred Butianas, all armed with guns of various kinds, for many of these people had guns, though they were not very proficient in the use of them. But they carried no shields and wore no head-dress or armlets; indeed, every warlike appearance was carefully avoided. With our party went also a sister of Maiwa's, though by a different mother, who strongly resembled her in face and form, and whose mission it was to impersonate the runaway wife.

"That evening we camped upon the top of the cliff up which we had so barely escaped, and next morning at the first breaking of the light we rolled away the stones with which we had blocked the passage some days before, and descended to the hill-side beneath. Here the bodies, or rather the skeletons of the men who had fallen before my rifle, still lay about. The Matuku soldiers had left their comrades to be buried by the vultures. I descended the gully into which poor Gobo had fallen, and searched for his body, but in vain, although I found the spot where he and the other man had struck, together with the bones of the latter, which I recognized by the waist-cloth. Either some beast of prey had carried Gobo off, or the Matuku people had disposed of his remains, and also of my express rifle which he carried. At any rate, I never saw or heard any more of him.

"Once in Wambe's country, we adopted a very circumspect method of proceeding. About fifty men marched ahead in loose order to guard against surprise, while as many more followed behind. The remaining hundred were gathered in a bunch between, and in the centre of these men I marched, together with the girl who was personating Maiwa, and all my bearers. We were disarmed, and some of my men were tied together to show that we were prisoners, while the girl had a blanket thrown over her head, and moved along with an air of great dejection. We headed straight for Wambe's place, which was at a distance of about twenty-five miles from the mountain-pass.

"When we had gone some five miles we met a party of about fifty of Wambe's soldiers, who were evidently on the look-out for us. They stopped us, and their captain asked where we were going. The head man of our party answered that he was conveying Maiwa, Wambe's runaway wife, together with the white hunter and his men, to be given up to Wambe in accordance with his command. The captain then wanted to know why we were so many, to which our spokesman replied that I and my men were very desperate fellows, and that it was feared that if we were sent with a smaller escort we should escape, and bring disgrace and the wrath of Wambe upon their tribe. Thereon this gentleman, the Matuku captain, began to amuse himself at my expense, and mock me, saying that Wambe would make me pay for the soldiers whom I had killed. He would put me into the 'Thing that bites,' in other words, the lion trap, and leave me there to die like a jackal caught by the leg. I made no answer to this, though my wrath was great, but pretended to look frightened. Indeed there was not much pretence about it, I was frightened. I could not conceal from myself that ours was a most hazardous enterprise, and that it was very possible that I might make acquaintance with that lion trap before I was many days older. However, it seemed quite impossible to desert poor Every in his misfortune, so I had to go on, and trust to Providence, as I have so often been obliged to do before and since.

"And now a fresh difficulty arose. Wambe's soldiers insisted upon accompanying us, and what is more, did all they could to urge us forward, as they were naturally anxious to get to the chief's place before evening. But we, on the other hand, had excellent reasons for not arriving till night was closing in, since we relied upon the gloom to cover our advance upon the koppie which commanded the town. Finally, they became so importunate that we were obliged to refuse flatly to move faster, alleging as a reason that the girl was tired. They did not accept this excuse in good part, and at one time I thought that we should have come to blows, for there is no love lost between Butianas and Matukus. At last, however, either from motives of policy, or because they were so evidently outnumbered, they gave in and suffered us to go our own pace. I earnestly wished that they would have added to the obligation by going theirs, but this they declined absolutely to do. On the contrary, they accompanied us every foot of the way, keeping up a running fire of allusions to the 'Thing that bites' that jarred upon my nerves and discomposed my temper.

"About half-past four in the afternoon we came to a neck or ridge of stony ground, whence we could see Wambe's town plainly lying some six or seven miles away, and three thousand feet beneath us. The town is built in a valley, with the exception of Wambe's own kraal, that is situated at the mouth of some caves upon the slope of the opposing mountains, over which I hoped to see our impi's spears flashing in the morrow's light. Even from where we stood, it was easy to see how strongly the place was fortified with schanses and stone walls, and how difficult of approach. Indeed, unless taken by surprise, it seemed to me quite impregnable to a force operating without cannon, and even cannon would not make much impression on rocks and stony koppies filled with caves.

"Then came the descent of the pass, and an arduous business it was, for the path—if it may be called a path—is almost entirely composed of huge water-worn boulders, from the one to the other of which we must jump like so many grasshoppers. It took us two hours to climb down, and, travelling through that burning sun, when at last we did reach the bottom, I for one was nearly played out. Shortly afterwards, just as it was growing dark, we came to the first line of fortifications, which consisted of a triple stone wall pierced by a gateway, so narrow that a man could hardly squeeze through it. We passed this without question, being accompanied by Wambe's soldiers. Then, came a belt of land three hundred paces or more in width, very rocky and broken, and having no huts upon it. Here in hollows in this belt the cattle were kraaled in case of danger. On the further side were more fortifications and another small gateway shaped like a V, and just beyond and through it I saw the koppie we had planned to seize looming up against the line of mountains behind.

"As we went I whispered my suggestions to our captain, with the result that at the second gateway he halted the cavalcade, and addressing the captain of Wambe's soldiers, said that we would wait here till we received Wambe's word to enter the town. The other man said that this was well, only he must hand over the prisoners to be taken up to the chief's kraal, for Wambe, was 'hungry to begin upon them,' and his 'heart desired to see the white man at rest before he closed his eyes in sleep,' and as for his wife, 'surely he would welcome her.' Our leader replied that he could not do this thing, because his orders were to deliver the prisoners to Wambe at Wambe's own kraal, and they might not be broken. How could he be responsible for the safety of the prisoners if he let them out of his hand? No, they would wait there till Wambe's word was brought.

"To this, after some demur, the other man consented, and went away, remarking that he would soon be back. As he passed me he called out with a sneer, pointing as he did so to the fading red in the western sky—'Look your last upon the light, White Man, for the "Thing that bites" lives in the dark.'

"Next day it so happened that I shot this man, and, do you know, I think that he is about the only human being who has come to harm at my hands for whom I do not feel sincere sorrow and, in a degree, remorse.

The Attack

"Just where we halted ran a little stream of water. I looked at it, and an idea struck me: probably there would be no water on the koppie. I suggested this to our captain, and, acting on the hint, he directed all the men to drink what they could, and also to fill the seven or eight cooking pots which we carried with us with water. Then came the crucial moment. How were we to get possession of the koppie? When the captain asked me, I said that I thought that we had better march up and take it, and this accordingly we went on to do. When we came to the narrow gateway we were, as I expected stopped by two soldiers who stood on guard there and asked our business. The captain answered that we had changed our minds, and would follow on to Wambe's kraal. The soldiers said no, we must now wait.

"To this we replied by pushing them to one side and marching in single file through the gateway, which was not distant more than a hundred yards from the koppie. While we were getting through, the men we had pushed away ran towards the town calling for assistance, a call that was promptly responded to, for in another minute we saw scores of armed men running hard in our direction. So we ran too, for the koppie. As soon as they understood what we were after, which they did not at first, owing to the dimness of the light, they did their best to get there before us. But we had the start of them, and with the exception of one unfortunate man who stumbled and fell, we were well on to the koppie before they arrived. This man they captured, and when fighting began on the following morning, and he refused to give any information, they killed him. Luckily they had no time to torture him, or they would certainly have done so, for these Matuku people are very fond of torturing their enemies.

"When we reached the koppie, the base of which covers about half an acre of ground, the soldiers who had been trying to cut us off halted, for they knew the strength of the position. This gave us a few minutes before the light had quite vanished to reconnoitre the place. We found that it was unoccupied, fortified with a regular labyrinth of stone walls, and contained three large caves and some smaller ones. The next business was to post the soldiers to such advantage as time would allow. My own men I was careful to place quite at the top. They were perfectly useless from terror, and I feared that they might try to escape and give information of our plans to Wambe. So I watched them like the apple of my eye, telling them that should they dare to stir they would be shot.

"Then it grew quite dark, and presently out of the darkness I heard a voice—it was that of the leader of the soldiers who had escorted us— calling us to come down. We replied that it was too dark to move, we should hit our feet against the stones. He insisted upon our descending, and we flatly refused, saying that if any attempt was made to dislodge us we would fire. After that, as they had no real intention of attacking us in the dark, the men withdrew, but we saw from the fires which were lit around that they were keeping a strict watch upon our position.

"That night was a wearing one, for we never quite knew how the situation was going to develop. Fortunately we had some cooked food with us, so we did not starve. It was lucky, however, that we drunk our fill before coming up, for, as I had anticipated, there was not a drop of water on the koppie.

"At length the night wore away, and with the first tinge of light I began to go my rounds, and stumbling along the stony paths, to make things as ready as I could for the attack, which I felt sure would be delivered before we were two hours older. The men were cramped and cold, and consequently low-spirited, but I exhorted them to the best of my ability, bidding them remember the race from which they sprang, and not to show the white feather before a crowd of Matuku dogs. At length it began to grow light, and presently I saw long columns of men advancing towards the koppie. They halted under cover at a distance of about a hundred and fifty yards, and just as the dawn broke a herald came forward and called to us. Our captain stood up upon a rock and answered him.

"'These are the words of Wambe,' the herald said. 'Come forth from the koppie, and give over the evil-doers, and go in peace, or stay in the koppie and be slain.'

"'It is too early to come out as yet,' answered our man in fine diplomatic style. 'When the sun sucks up the mist then we will come out. Our limbs are stiff with cold.'

"'Come forth even now,' said the herald.

"'Not if I know it, my boy,' said I to myself; but the captain replied that he would come out when he thought proper, and not before.

"'Then make ready to die,' said the herald, for all the world like the villain of a transpontine piece, and majestically stalked back to the soldiers.

"I made my final arrangements, and looked anxiously at the mountain crest a couple of miles or so away, from which the mist was now beginning to lift, but no column of smoke could I see. I whistled, for if the attacking force had been delayed or made any mistake, our position was likely to grow rather warm. We had barely enough water to wet the mouths of the men, and when once it was finished we could not hold the place for long in that burning heat.

"At length, just as the sun rose in glory over the heights behind us, the Matuku soldiers, of whom about fifteen hundred were now assembled, set up a queer whistling noise, which ended in a chant. Then some shots were fired, for the Matuku had a few guns, but without effect, though one bullet passed just by a man's head.

"'Now they are going to begin,' I thought to myself, and I was not far wrong, for in another minute the body of men divided into three companies, each about five hundred strong, and, heralded by a running fire, charged at us on three sides. Our men were now all well under cover, and the fire did us no harm. I mounted on a rock so as to command a view of as much of the koppie and plain as possible, and yelled to our men to reserve their fire till I gave the word, and then to shoot low and load as quickly as possible. I knew that, like all natives, they were sure to be execrable shots, and that they were armed with weapons made out of old gas-pipes, so the only chance of doing execution was to let the enemy get right on to us.

"On they came with a rush; they were within eighty yards now, and as they drew near the point of attack, I observed that they closed their ranks, which was so much the better for us.

"'Shall we not fire, my father?' sung out the captain.

"'No, confound you!' I answered.

"'Sixty yards—fifty—forty—thirty. Fire, you scoundrels!' I yelled, setting the example by letting off both barrels of my elephant gun into the thickest part of the company opposite to me.

"Instantly the place rang out with the discharge of two hundred and odd guns, while the air was torn by the passage of every sort of missile, from iron pot legs down to slugs and pebbles coated with lead. The result was very prompt. The Matukus were so near that we could not miss them, and at thirty yards a lead-coated stone out of a gas-pipe is as effective as a Martini rifle, or more so. Over rolled the attacking soldiers by the dozen, while the survivors, fairly frightened, took to their heels. We plied them with shot till they were out of range—I made it very warm for them with the elephant gun, by the way—and then we loaded up in quite a cheerful frame of mind, for we had not lost a man, whereas I could count more than fifty dead and wounded Matukus. The only thing that damped my ardour was that, stare as I would, I could see no column of smoke upon the mountain crest.

"Half an hour elapsed before any further steps were taken against us. Then the attacking force adopted different tactics. Seeing that it was very risky to try to rush us in dense masses, they opened out into skirmishing order and ran across the open space in lots of five and six. As it happened, right at the foot of the koppie the ground broke away a little in such fashion that it was almost impossible for us to search it effectually with our fire. On the hither side of this dip Wambe's soldiers were now congregating in considerable numbers. Of course we did them as much damage as we could while they were running across, but this sort of work requires good shots, and that was just what we had not got. Another thing was, that so many of our men would insist upon letting off the things they called guns at every little knot of the enemy that ran across. Thus, the first few lots were indeed practically swept away, but after that, as it took a long while to load the gas-pipes and old flint muskets, those who followed got across in comparative safety. For my own part, I fired away with the elephant gun and repeating carbine till they grew almost too hot to hold, but my individual efforts could do nothing to stop such a rush, or perceptibly to lessen the number of our enemies.

"At length there were at least a thousand men crowded into the dip of ground within a few yards of us, whence those of them who had guns kept up a continued fusillade upon the koppie. They killed two of my bearers in this way, and wounded a third, for being at the top of the koppie these men were most exposed to the fire from the dip at its base. Seeing that the situation was growing most serious, at length, by the dint of threats and entreaties, I persuaded the majority of our people to cease firing useless shots, to reload, and prepare for the rush. Scarcely had I done so when the enemy came for us with a roar. I am bound to say that I should never have believed that Matukus had it in them to make such a determined charge. A large party rushed round the base of the koppie, and attacked us in flank, while the others swarmed wherever they could get a foothold, so that we were taken on every side.

"*Fire!* I cried, and we did with terrible effect. Many of their men fell, but though we checked we could not stop them. They closed up and rushed the first fortification, killing a good number of its defenders. It was almost all cold steel work now, for we had no time to reload, and that suited the Butiana habits of fighting well enough, for the stabbing assegai is a weapon which they understand. Those of our people who escaped from the first line of walls took refuge in the second, where I stood myself, encouraging them, and there the fight raged fiercely. Occasionally parties of the enemy would force a passage, only to perish on the hither side beneath the Butiana spears. But still they kept it up, and I saw that, fight as we would, we were doomed. We were altogether outnumbered, and to make matters worse, fresh bodies of soldiers were pouring across the plain to the assistance of our assailants. So I made up my mind to direct a retreat into the caves, and there expire in a manner as heroic as circumstances would allow; and while mentally lamenting my hard fate and reflecting on my sins I fought away like a fiend. It was then, I remember, that I shot my friend the captain of our escort of the previous day. He had caught sight of me, and making a vicious dig at my stomach with a spear (which I successfully dodged), shouted out, or rather began to shout out, one of his unpleasant allusions to the 'Thing that——' He never got as far as 'bites,' because I shot him after 'that.'

"Well, the game was about up. Already I saw one man throw down his spear in token of surrender—which act of cowardice cost him his life, by the way—when suddenly a shout arose.

"'Look at the mountain,' they cried; 'there is an impi on the mountain side.'

"'I glanced up, and there sure enough, about half-way down the mountain, nearing the first fortification, the long-plumed double line of Nala's warriors was rushing down to battle, the bright light of the morning glancing on their spears. Afterwards we discovered that the reason of their delay was that they had been stopped by a river in flood, and could not reach the mountain crest by dawn. When they did reach it, however, they saw instantly that the fight was already going on, was 'in flower,' as they put it, and so advanced at once without waiting to light signal-fires.

"Meanwhile they had been observed from the town, and parties of soldiers were charging up the steep side of the hill, to occupy the schanses, and the second line of fortifications behind them. The first line they did not now attempt to reach or defend; Nala pressed them too close. But they got to the schanses or pits protected with stone walls, and constructed to hold from a dozen to twenty men, and soon began to open fire from them, and from isolated rocks. I turned my eyes to the gates of the town, which were placed to the north and south. Already they were crowded with hundreds of fugitive women and children flying to the rocks and caves for shelter from the foe.

"As for ourselves, the appearance of Nala's impi produced a wonderful change for the better in our position. The soldiers attacking us turned, realizing that the town was being assailed from the rear, and clambering down the koppie streamed off to protect their homes against this new enemy. In five minutes there was not a man left except those who would move no more, or were too sorely wounded to escape. I felt inclined to ejaculate '*Saved!*' like the gentleman in the play, but did not because the occasion was too serious. What I did do was to muster all the men and reckon up our losses. They amounted to fifty- one killed and wounded, sixteen men having been killed outright. Then I sent men with the cooking-pots to the stream of water, and we drank. This done I set my bearers, being the most useless part of the community, from a fighting point of view, to the task of attending the injured, and turned to watch the fray.

"By this time Nala's impi had climbed the first line of fortifications without opposition, and was advancing in a long line upon the schanses or pits which were scattered about between it and the second line, singing a war chant as it came. Presently puffs of smoke began to start from the schanses, and with my glasses I could see several of our men falling over. Then as they came opposite a schanse that portion of the long line of warriors would thicken up and charge it with a wild rush. I could see them leap on to the walls and vanish into the depths beneath, some of their number falling backward on each occasion, shot or stabbed to death.

"Next would come another act in the tragedy. Out from the hither side of the schanse would pour such of its defenders as were left alive, perhaps three or four and perhaps a dozen, running for dear life, with the war dogs on their tracks. One by one they would be caught, then up flashed the great spear and down fell the pursued—dead. I saw ten of our men leap into one large schanse, but though I watched for some time nobody came out. Afterwards we inspected the place and found these men all dead, together with twenty-three Matukus. Neither side would give in, and they had fought it out to the bitter end.

"At last they neared the second line of fortifications, behind which the whole remaining Matuku force, numbering some two thousand men, was rapidly assembling. One little pause to get their breath, and Nala's men came at it with a rush and a long wild shout of '*Bulala Matuku*' (kill the Matuku) that went right through me, thrilling every nerve. Then came an answering shout, and the sounds of heavy firing, and presently I saw our men retreating, somewhat fewer in numbers than they had advanced. Their welcome had been a warm one for the Matuku fight splendidly behind walls. This decided me that it was necessary to create a diversion; if we did not do so it seemed very probable that we should be worsted after all. I called to the captain of our little force, and rapidly put the position before him.

"Seeing the urgency of the occasion, he agreed with me that we must risk it, and in two minutes more, with the exception of my own men, whom I left to guard the wounded, we were trotting across the open space and through the deserted town towards the spot where the struggle was taking place, some seven hundred yards away. In six or eight minutes we reached a group of huts—it was a head man's kraal, that was situated about a hundred and twenty yards behind the fortified wall, and took possession of it unobserved. The enemy was too much engaged with the foe in front of him to notice us, and besides, the broken ground rose in a hog-back shape between. There we waited a minute or two and recovered our breath, while I gave my directions. So soon as we heard the Butiana impi begin to charge again, we were to run out in a line to the brow of the hogback and pour our fire into the mass of defenders behind the wall. Then the guns were to be thrown down and we must charge with the assegai. We had no shields, but that could not be helped; there would be no time to reload the guns, and it was absolutely necessary that the enemy should be disconcerted at the moment when the main attack was delivered.

"The men, who were as plucky a set of fellows as ever I saw, and whose blood was now thoroughly up, consented to this scheme, though I could see that they thought it rather a large order, as indeed I did myself. But I knew that if the impi was driven back a second time the game would be played, and for me at any rate it would be a case of the 'Thing that bites,' and this sure and certain knowledge filled my breast with valour.

"We had not long to wait. Presently we heard the Butiana war-song swelling loud and long; they had commenced their attack. I made a sign, and the hundred and fifty men, headed by myself, poured out of the kraal, and getting into a rough line ran up the fifty or sixty yards of slope that intervened between ourselves and the crest of the hog-backed ridge. In thirty seconds we were there, and immediately beyond us was the main body of the Matuku host waiting the onslaught of the enemy with guns and spears. Even now they did not see us, so intent were they upon the coming attack. I signed to my men to take careful aim, and suddenly called out to them to fire, which they did with a will, dropping thirty or forty Matukus.

"*Charge!* I shouted, again throwing down my smoking rifle and drawing my revolver, an example which they followed, snatching up their spears from the ground where they had placed them while they fired. The men set up a savage whoop, and we started. I saw the Matuku soldiers wheel around in hundreds, utterly taken aback at this new development of the situation. And looking over them, before we had gone twenty yards I saw something else. For of a sudden, as though they had risen from the earth, there appeared above the wall hundreds of great spears, followed by hundreds of savage faces shadowed with drooping plumes. With a yell they sprang upon the wall shaking their broad shields, and with a yell they bounded from it straight into our astonished foes.

"*Crash!* we were in them now, and fighting like demons. *Crash!* from the other side. Nala's impi was at its work, and still the spears and plumes appeared for a moment against the brown background of the mountain, and then sprang down and rushed like a storm upon the foe. The great mob of men turned this way and turned that way, astonished, bewildered, overborne by doubt and terror.

"Meanwhile the slayers stayed not their hands, and on every side spears flashed, and the fierce shout of triumph went up to heaven. There too on the wall stood Maiwa, a white garment streaming from her shoulders, an assegai in her hand, her breast heaving, her eyes flashing. Above all the din of battle I could catch the tones of her clear voice as she urged the soldiers on to victory. But victory was not yet. Wambe's soldiers gathered themselves together, and bore our men back by the sheer weight of numbers. They began to give, then once more they rallied, and the fight hung doubtfully.

"'Slay, you war-whelps,' cried Maiwa from the wall. 'Are you afraid, you women, you chicken-hearted women! Strike home, or die like dogs! What—you give way! Follow me, children of Nala.' And with one long cry she leapt from the wall as leaps a stricken antelope, and holding the spear poised rushed right into the thickest of the fray. The warriors saw her, and raised such a shout that it echoed like thunder against the mountains. They massed together, and following the flutter of her white robe crashed into the dense heart of the foe. Down went the Matuku before them like trees before a whirlwind. Nothing could stand in the face of such a rush as that. It was as the rush of a torrent bursting its banks. All along their line swept the wild desperate charge; and there, straight in the forefront of the battle, still waved the white robe of Maiwa.

"Then they broke, and, stricken with utter panic, Wambe's soldiers streamed away a scattered crowd of fugitives, while after them thundered the footfall of the victors.

"The fight was over, we had won the day; and for my part I sat down upon a stone and wiped my forehead, thanking Providence that I had lived to see the end of it. Twenty minutes later Nala's warriors began to return panting. 'Wambe's soldiers had taken to the bush and the caves,' they said, 'where they had not thought it safe to follow them,' adding significantly, that many had stopped on the way.

"I was utterly dazed, and now that the fight was over my energy seemed to have left me, and I did not pay much attention, till presently I was aroused by somebody calling me by my name. I looked up, and saw that it was the chief Nala himself, who was bleeding from a flesh wound in his arm. By his side stood Maiwa panting, but unhurt, and wearing on her face a proud and terrifying air.

"'They are gone, Macumazahn,' said the chief; 'there is little to fear from them, their heart is broken. But where is Wambe the chief?—and where is the white man thou camest to save?'

"'I know not,' I answered.

"Close to where we stood lay a Matuku, a young man who had been shot through the fleshy part of the calf. It was a trifling wound, but it prevented him from running away.

"Say, thou dog,' said Nala, stalking up to him and shaking his red spear in his face, 'say, where is Wambe? Speak, or I slay thee. Was he with the soldiers?'

"Nay, lord, I know not,' groaned the terrified man, 'he fought not with us; Wambe has no stomach for fighting. Perchance he is in his kraal yonder, or in the cave behind the kraal,' and he pointed to a small enclosure on the hillside, about four hundred yards to the right of where we were.

"Let us go and see,' said Nala, summoning his soldiers.

Maiwa Is Avenged

"The impi formed up; alas, an hour before it had been stronger by a third than it was now. Then Nala detached two hundred men to collect and attend to the injured, and at my suggestion issued a stringent order that none of the enemy's wounded, and above all no women or children, were to be killed, as is the savage custom among African natives. On the contrary, they were to be allowed to send word to their women that they might come in to nurse them and fear nothing, for Nala made war upon Wambe the tyrant, and not on the Matuku tribe.

"Then we started with some four hundred men for the chief's kraal. Very soon we were there. It was, as I have said, placed against the mountain side, but within the fortified lines, and did not at all cover more than an acre and a half of ground. Outside was a tiny reed fence, within which, neatly arranged in a semi-circular line, stood the huts of the chief's principal wives. Maiwa of course knew every inch of the kraal, for she had lived in it, and led us straight to the entrance. We peeped through the gateway—not a soul was to be seen. There were the huts and there was the clear open space floored with a concrete of lime, on which the sun beat fiercely, but nobody could we see or hear.

"'The jackal has gone to earth,' said Maiwa; 'he will be in the cave behind his hut,' and she pointed with her spear towards another small and semi-circular enclosure, over which a large hut was visible, that had the cliff itself for a background. I stared at this fence; by George! it was true, it was entirely made of tusks of ivory planted in the ground with their points bending outwards. The smallest ones, though none were small, were placed nearest to the cliff on either side, but they gradually increased in size till they culminated in two enormous tusks, which, set up so that their points met, something in the shape of an inverted V, formed the gateway to the hut. I was dumbfoundered with delight; and indeed, where is the elephant-hunter who would not be, if he suddenly saw five or six hundred picked tusks set up in a row, and only waiting for him to take them away? Of course the stuff was what is known as 'black' ivory; that is, the exterior of the tusks had become black from years or perhaps centuries of exposure to wind and weather, but I was certain that it would be none the worse for that. Forgetting the danger of the deed, in my excitement I actually ran right across the open space, and drawing my knife scratched vigorously at one of the great tusks to see how deep the damage might be. As I thought, it was nothing; there beneath the black covering gleamed the pure white ivory. I could have capered for joy, for I fear that I am very mercenary at heart, when suddenly I heard the faint echo of a cry for assistance. 'Help!' screamed a voice in the Sisutu dialect from somewhere behind the hut; 'help! they are murdering me.'

"*I knew the voice*; it was John Every's. Oh, what a selfish brute was I! For the moment that miserable ivory had driven the recollection of him out of my head, and now—perhaps it was too late.

"Nala, Maiwa, and the soldiers had now come up. They too heard the voice and interpreted its tone, though they had not caught the words.

"'This way,' cried Maiwa, and we started at a run, passing round the hut of Wambe. Behind was the narrow entrance to a cave. We rushed through it heedless of the danger of the ambush, and this is what we saw, though very confusedly at first, owing to the gloom.

"'In the centre of the cave, and with either end secured to the floor by strong stakes, stood a huge double-springed lion trap edged with sharp and grinning teeth. It was set, and beyond the trap, indeed almost over it, a terrible struggle was in progress. A naked or almost naked white man, with a great beard hanging down over his breast, in spite of his furious struggles, was being slowly forced and dragged towards the trap by six or eight women. Only one man was present, a fat, cruel-looking man with small eyes and a hanging lip. It was the chief Wambe, and he stood by the trap ready to force the victim down upon it so soon as the women had dragged him into the necessary position.

"At this instant they caught sight of us, and there came a moment's pause, and then, before I knew what she was going to do, Maiwa lifted the assegai she still held, and whirled it at Wambe's head. I saw the flash of light speed towards him, and so did he, for he stepped backward to avoid it—stepped backward right into the trap. He yelled with pain as the iron teeth of the 'Thing that bites' sprang up with a rattling sound like living fangs and fastened into him—such a yell I have not often heard. Now at last he tasted of the torture which he had inflicted upon so many, and though I trust I am a Christian, I cannot say that I felt sorry for him.

"The assegai sped on and struck one of the women who had hold of the unfortunate Every, piercing through her arm. This made her leave go, an example that the other women quickly followed, so that Every fell to the ground, where he lay gasping.

"'Kill the witches,' roared Nala, in a voice of thunder, pointing to the group of women.

"'Nay,' gasped Every, 'spare them. He made them do it,' and he pointed to the human fiend in the trap. Then Maiwa waved her hand to us to fall back, for the moment of her vengeance was come. We did so, and she strode up to her lord, and flinging the white robe from her stood before him, her fierce beautiful face fixed like stone.

"'Who am I?' she cried in so terrible a voice that he ceased his yells. 'Am I that woman who was given to thee for wife, and whose child thou slewest? Or am I an avenging spirit come to see thee die?

"'What is this?' she went on, drawing the withered baby-hand from the pouch at her side.

"Is it the hand of a babe? and how came that hand to be thus alone? What cut it off from the babe? and where is the babe? Is it a hand? or is it the vision of a hand that shall presently tear thy throat?

"Where are thy soldiers, Wambe? Do they sleep and eat and go forth to do thy bidding? or are they perchance dead and scattered like the winter leaves?'

"He groaned and rolled his eyes while the fierce-faced woman went on.

"Art thou still a chief, Wambe? or does another take thy place and power, and say, Lord, what doest thou there? and what is that slave's leglet upon thy knee?

"Is it a dream, Wambe, great lord and chief? or'—and she lifted her clenched hands and shook them in his face—'hath a woman's vengeance found thee out and a woman's wit o'ermatched thy tyrannous strength? and art thou about to slowly die in torments horrible to think on, oh, thou accursed murderer of little children?'

"And with one wild scream she dashed the dead hand of the child straight into his face, and then fell senseless on the floor. As for the demon in the trap, he shrank back so far as its iron bounds would allow, his yellow eyes starting out of his head with pain and terror, and then once more began to yell.

"The scene was more than I could bear.

"'Nala,' I said, 'this must stop. That man is a fiend, but he must not be left to die there. See thou to it.'

"'Nay,' answered Nala, 'let him taste of the food wherewith he hath fed so many; leave him till death shall find him.'

"'That I will not,' I answered. 'Let his end be swift; see thou to it.'

"'As thou wilt, Macumazahn,' answered the chief, with a shrug of the shoulders; 'first let the white man and Maiwa be brought forth.'

"So the soldiers came forward and carried Every and the woman into the open air. As the former was borne past his tormentor, the fallen chief, so cowardly was his wicked heart, actually prayed him to intercede for him, and save him from a fate which, but for our providential appearance, would have been Every's own.

"So we went away, and in another moment one of the biggest villains on the earth troubled it no more. Once in the fresh air Every recovered quickly. I looked at him, and horror and sorrow pierced me through to see such a sight. His face was the face of a man of sixty, though he was not yet forty, and his poor body was cut to pieces with stripes and scars, and other marks of the torments which Wambe had for years amused himself with inflicting on him.

"As soon as he recovered himself a little he struggled on to his knees, burst into a paroxysm of weeping, and clasping my legs with his emaciated arms, would have actually kissed my feet.

"'What are you about, old fellow?' I said, for I am not accustomed to that sort of thing, and it made me feel uncomfortable.

"'Oh, God bless you?' he moaned, 'God bless you! If only you knew what I have gone through; and to think that you should have come to help me, and at the risk of your own life! Well, you were always a true friend—yes, yes, a true friend.'

"Bosh,' I answered testily; 'I'm a trader, and I came after that ivory,' and I pointed to the stockade of tusks. 'Did you ever hear of an elephant-hunter who would not have risked his immortal soul for them, and much more his carcase?'

"But he took no notice of my explanations, and went on God blessing me as hard as ever, till at last I bethought me that a nip of brandy, of which I had a flask full, might steady his nerves a bit. I gave it him, and was not disappointed in the result, for he brisked up wonderfully. Then I hunted about in Wambe's hut, and found a kaross to put over his poor bruised shoulders, and he was quite a man again.

"'Now,' I said, 'why did the late lamented Wambe want to put you in that trap?'

"'Because as soon as they heard that the fight was going against them, and that Maiwa was charging at the head of Nala's impi, one of the women told Wambe that she had seen me write something on some leaves and give them to Maiwa before she went away to purify herself. Then of course he guessed that I had to do with your seizing the koppie and holding it while the impi rushed the place from the mountain, so he determined to torture me to death before help could come. Oh, heavens! what a mercy it is to hear English again.'

"How long have you been a prisoner here, Every?' I asked.

"'Six years and a bit, Quatermain; I have lost count of the odd months lately. I came up here with Major Aldey and three other gentlemen and forty bearers. That devil Wambe ambushed us, and murdered the lot to get their guns. They weren't much use to him when he got them, being breech-loaders, for the fools fired away all the ammunition in a month or two. However, they are all in good order, and hanging up in the hut there. They didn't kill me because one of them saw me mending a gun just before they attacked us, so they kept me as a kind of armourer. Twice I tried to make a bolt of it, but was caught each time. Last time Wambe had me flogged very nearly to death—you can see the scars upon my back. Indeed I should have died if it hadn't been for the girl Maiwa, who nursed me by stealth. He got that accursed lion trap among our things also, and I suppose he has tortured between one and two hundred people to death in it. It was his favourite amusement, and he would go every day and sit and watch his victim till he died. Sometimes he would give him food and water to keep him alive longer, telling him or her that he would let him go if he lived till a certain day. But he never did let them go. They all died there, and I could show you their bones behind that rock.'

"'The devil!' I said, grinding my teeth. 'I wish I hadn't interfered; I wish I had left him to the same fate.'

"'Well, he got a taste of it any way,' said Every; 'I'm glad he got a taste. There's justice in it, and now he's gone to hell, and I hope there is another one ready for him there. By Jove! I should like to have the setting of it.'

"And so he talked on, and I sat and listened to him, wondering how he had kept his reason for so many years. But he didn't talk as I have told it, in plain English. He spoke very slowly, and as though he had got something in his mouth, continually using native words because the English ones had slipped his memory.

"At last Nala came up and told us that food was made ready, and thankful enough we were to get it, I can tell you. After we had eaten we held a consultation. Quite a thousand of Wambe's soldiers were put *hors de combat*, but at least two thousand remained hidden in the bush and rocks, and these men, together with those in the outlying kraals, were a source of possible danger. The question arose, therefore, what was to be done—were they to be followed or left alone? I waited till everybody had spoken, some giving one opinion and some another, and then being appealed to I gave mine. It was to the effect that Nala should take a leaf out of the great Zulu T'Chaka's book, and incorporate the tribe, not destroy it. We had a good many women among the prisoners. Let them, I suggested, be sent to the hiding-places of the soldiers and make an offer. If the men would come and lay down their arms and declare allegiance to Nala, they and their town and cattle should be spared. Wambe's cattle alone would be seized as the prize of war. Moreover, Wambe having left no children, his wife Maiwa should be declared chieftainess of the tribe, under Nala. If they did not accept this offer by the morning of the second day it should be taken as a declaration that they wished to continue the war. Their town should be burned, their cattle, which our men were already collecting and driving in in great numbers, would be taken, and they should be hunted down.

"This advice was at once declared to be wise, and acted on. The women were despatched, and I saw from their faces that they never expected to get such terms, and did not think that their mission would be in vain. Nevertheless, we spent that afternoon in preparations against possible surprise, and also in collecting all the wounded of both parties into a hospital, which we extemporized out of some huts, and there attending to them as best we could.

"That evening Every had the first pipe of tobacco that he had tasted for six years. Poor fellow, he nearly cried with joy over it. The night passed without any sign of attack, and on the following morning we began to see the effect of our message, for women, children, and a few men came in in little knots, and took possession of their huts. It was of course rather difficult to prevent our men from looting, and generally going on as natives, and for the matter of that white men too, are in the habit of doing after a victory. But one man who after warning was caught maltreating a woman was brought out and killed by Nala's order, and though there was a little grumbling, that put a stop to further trouble.

"On the second morning the head men and numbers of their followers came in in groups, and about midday a deputation of the former presented themselves before us without their weapons. They were conquered, they said, and Wambe was dead, so they came to hear the words of the great lion who had eaten them up, and of the crafty white man, the jackal, who had dug a hole for them to fall in, and of Maiwa, Lady of War, who had led the charge and turned the fate of the battle.

"So we let them hear the words, and when we had done an old man rose and said, that in the name of the people he accepted the yoke that was laid upon their shoulders, and that the more gladly because even the rule of a woman could not be worse than the rule of Wambe. Moreover, they knew Maiwa, the Lady of War, and feared her not, though she was a witch and terrible to see in battle.

"Then Nala asked his daughter if she was willing to become chieftainess of the tribe under him.

"Maiwa, who had been very silent since her revenge was accomplished, answered yes, that she was, and that her rule should be good and gentle to those who were good and gentle to her, but the froward and rebellious she would smite with a rod of iron; which from my knowledge of her character I thought exceedingly probable.

"The head man replied that that was a good saying, and they did not complain at it, and so the meeting ended.

"Next day we spent in preparations for departure. Mine consisted chiefly in superintending the digging up of the stockade of ivory tusks, which I did with the greatest satisfaction. There were some five hundred of them altogether. I made inquiries about it from Every, who told me that the stockade had been there so long that nobody seemed to know exactly who had collected the tusks originally. There was, however, a kind of superstitious feeling about them which had always prevented the chiefs from trying to sell this great mass of ivory. Every and I examined it carefully, and found that although it was so old its quality was really as good as ever, and there was very little soft ivory in the lot. At first I was rather afraid lest, now that my services had been rendered, Nala should hesitate to part with so much valuable property, but this was not the case. When I spoke to him on the subject he merely said, 'Take it, Macumazahn, take it; you have earned it well,' and, to speak the truth, though I say it who shouldn't, I think I had. So we pressed several hundred Matuku bearers into our service, and next day marched off with the lot.

"Before we went I took a formal farewell of Maiwa, whom we left with a bodyguard of three hundred men to assist her in settling the country. She gave me her hand to kiss in a queenly sort of way, and then said,

"Macumazahn, you are a brave man, and have been a friend to me in my need. If ever you want help or shelter, remember that Maiwa has a good memory for friend and foe. All I have is yours.

"And so I thanked her and went. She was certainly a very remarkable woman. A year or two ago I heard that her father Nala was dead, and that she had succeeded to the chieftainship of both tribes, which she ruled with great justice and firmness.

"I can assure you that we ascended the pass leading to Wambe's town with feelings very different from those with which we had descended it a few days before. But if I was grateful for the issue of events, you can easily imagine what poor Every's feelings were. When we got to the top of the pass, before the whole impi he actually flopped down upon his knees and thanked Heaven for his escape, the tears running down his face. But then, as I have said, his nerves were shaken—though now that his beard was trimmed and he had some sort of clothes on his back, and hope in his heart, he looked a very different man from the poor wretch whom we had rescued from death by torture.

"Well, we separated from Nala at the little stairway or pass over the mountain—Every and I and the ivory going down the river which I had come up a few weeks before, and the chief returning to his own kraal on the further side of the mountain. He gave us an escort of a hundred and fifty men, however, with instructions to accompany us for six days' journey, and to keep the Matuku bearers in order and then return. I knew that in six days we should be able to reach a district where porters were plentiful, and whence we could easily get the ivory conveyed to Delagoa Bay."

"And did you land it up safe?" I asked.

"Well no," said Quatermain, "we lost about a third of it in crossing a river. A flood came down suddenly just as the men were crossing and many of them had to throw down their tusks to save their lives. We had no means of dragging it up, and so we were obliged to leave it, which was very sad. However, we sold what remained for nearly seven thousand pounds, so we did not do so badly. I don't mean that I got seven thousand pounds out of it, because, you see, I insisted upon Every taking a half share. Poor fellow, he had earned it, if ever a man did. He set up a store in the old colony on the proceeds and did uncommonly well."

"And what did you do with the lion trap?" asked Sir Henry.

"Oh, I brought that away with me also, and when I reached Durban I put it in my house. But really I could not bear to sit opposite to it at nights as I smoked. Visions of that poor woman and the hand of her dead child would rise up in my mind, and also of all the horrors of which it had been the instrument. I began to dream at last that it held me by the leg. This was too much for my nerves, so I just packed it up and shipped it to its maker in England, whose name was stamped upon the steel, sending him a letter at the same time to tell him to what purpose the infernal machine had been put. I believe that he gave it to some museum or other."

"And what became of the tusks of the three bulls which you shot! You must have left them at Nala's kraal, I suppose."

The old gentleman's face fell at this question.

"Ah," he said, "that is a very sad story. Nala promised to send them with my goods to my agent at Delagoa, and so he did. But the men who brought them were unarmed, and, as it happened, they fell in with a slave caravan under the command of a half-bred Portuguese, who seized the tusks, and what is worse, swore that he had shot them. I paid him out afterwards, however," he added with a smile of satisfaction, "but it did not give me back my tusks, which no doubt have been turned into hair brushes long ago;" and he sighed.

"Well," said Good, "that is a capital yarn of yours, Quatermain, but—"

"But what?" he asked sharply, foreseeing a draw.

"But I don't think that it was so good as mine about the ibex—it hasn't the same *finish*."

Mr. Quatermain made no reply. Good was beneath it.

"Do you know, gentlemen," he said, "it is half-past two in the morning, and if we are going to shoot the big wood to-morrow we ought to leave here at nine-thirty sharp."

"Oh, if you shoot for a hundred years you will never beat the record of those three woodcocks," I said.

"Or of those three elephants," added Sir Henry.

And then we all went to bed, and I dreamed that I had married Maiwa, and was much afraid of that attractive but determined lady.

Marie
An Episode in the Life of the Late Allan Quatermain

Dedication

Ditchingham, 1912.

My dear Sir Henry,—

Nearly thirty-seven years have gone by, more than a generation, since first we saw the shores of Southern Africa rising from the sea. Since then how much has happened: the Annexation of the Transvaal, the Zulu War, the first Boer War, the discovery of the Rand, the taking of Rhodesia, the second Boer War, and many other matters which in these quick-moving times are now reckoned as ancient history.

Alas! I fear that were we to re-visit that country we should find but few faces which we knew. Yet of one thing we may be glad. Those historical events, in some of which you, as the ruler of Natal, played a great part, and I, as it chanced, a smaller one, so far as we can foresee, have at length brought a period of peace to Southern Africa. To-day the flag of England flies from the Zambesi to the Cape. Beneath its shadow may all ancient feuds and blood jealousies be forgotten. May the natives prosper also and be justly ruled, for after all in the beginning the land was theirs. Such, I know, are your hopes, as they are mine.

It is, however, with an earlier Africa that this story deals. In 1836, hate and suspicion ran high between the Home Government and its Dutch subjects. Owing to the freeing of the slaves and mutual misunderstandings, the Cape Colony was then in tumult, almost in rebellion, and the Boers, by thousands, sought new homes in the unknown, savage-peopled North. Of this blood-stained time I have tried to tell; of the Great Trek and its tragedies, such as the massacre of the true-hearted Retief and his companions at the hands of the Zulu king, Dingaan.

But you have read the tale and know its substance. What, then, remains for me to say? Only that in memory of long-past days I dedicate it to you whose image ever springs to mind when I strive to picture an English gentleman as he should be. Your kindness I never shall forget; in memory of it, I offer you this book.

Ever sincerely yours,

H. RIDER HAGGARD.

To Sir Henry Bulwer, G.C.M.G.

Preface

The Author hopes that the reader may find some historical interest in the tale set out in these pages of the massacre of the Boer general, Retief, and his companions at the hands of the Zulu king, Dingaan. Save for some added circumstances, he believes it to be accurate in its details.

The same may be said of the account given of the hideous sufferings of the trek-Boers who wandered into the fever veld, there to perish in the neighbourhood of Delagoa Bay. Of these sufferings, especially those that were endured by Triechard and his companions, a few brief contemporary records still exist, buried in scarce works of reference. It may be mentioned, also, that it was a common belief among the Boers of that generation that the cruel death of Retief and his companions, and other misfortunes which befell them, were due to the treacherous plottings of an Englishman, or of Englishmen, with the despot, Dingaan.

Editor's Note

The following extract explains how the manuscript of "Marie," and with it some others, one of which is named "Child of Storm," came into the hands of the Editor.

It is from a letter, dated January 17th, 1909, and written by Mr. George Curtis, the brother of Sir Henry Curtis, Bart., who, it will be remembered, was one of the late Mr. Allan Quatermain's friends and companions in adventure when he discovered King Solomon's Mines, and who afterwards disappeared with him in Central Africa.

This extract runs as follows:—

"You may recall that our mutual and dear friend, old Allan Quatermain, left me the sole executor of his will, which he signed before he set out with my brother Henry for Zuvendis, where he was killed. The Court, however, not being satisfied that there was any legal proof of his death, invested the capital funds in trustee securities, and by my advice let his place in Yorkshire to a tenant who has remained in occupation of it during the last two decades. Now that tenant is dead, and at the earnest prayer of the Charities which benefit under Quatermain's will, and of myself—for in my uncertain state of health I have for long been most anxious to wind up this executorship—about eight months ago the Court at last consented to the distribution of this large fund in accordance with the terms of the will.

"This, of course, involved the sale of the real property, and before it was put up to auction I went over the house in company of the solicitor appointed by the Court. On the top landing, in the room Quatermain used to occupy, we found a sealed cupboard that I opened. It proved to be full of various articles which evidently he had prized because of their associations with his earthy life. These I need not enumerate here, especially as I have reserved them as his residuary legatee and, in the event of my death, they will pass to you under my will.

"Among these relics, however, I found a stout box, made of some red foreign wood, that contained various documents and letters and a bundle of manuscripts. Under the tape which fastened these manuscripts together, as you will see, is a scrap of paper on which is written, in blue pencil, a direction signed 'Allan Quatermain,' that in the event of anything happening to him, these MSS. are to be sent to you (for whom, as you know, he had a high regard), and that at your sole discretion you are to burn or publish them as you may see fit.

"So, after all these years, as we both remain alive, I carry out our old friend's instructions and send you his bequest, which I trust may prove of interest and value. I have read the MS. called 'Marie,' and certainly am of the opinion that it ought to be published, for I think it a strange and moving tale of a great love—full, moreover, of forgotten history.

"That named 'Child of Storm' also seems very interesting as a study of savage life, and the others may be the same; but my eyes are troubling me so much that I have not been able to decipher them. I hope, however, that I may be spared long enough to see them in print.

"Poor old Allan Quatermain. It is as though he had suddenly reappeared from the dead! So at least I thought as I perused these stories of a period of his life of which I do not remember his speaking to me.

"And now my responsibility in this matter is finished and yours begins. Do what you like about the manuscripts."

"George Curtis."

As may be imagined, I, the Editor, was considerably astonished when I received this letter and the accompanying bundle of closely-written MSS. To me also it was as though my old friend had risen from the grave and once more stood before me, telling some history of his stormy and tragic past in that quiet, measured voice that I have never been able to forget.

The first manuscript I read was that entitled "Marie." It deals with Mr. Quatermain's strange experiences when as a very young man he accompanied the ill-fated Pieter Retief and the Boer Commission on an embassy to the Zulu despot, Dingaan. This, it will be remembered, ended in their massacre, Quatermain himself and his Hottentot servant Hans being the sole survivors of the slaughter. Also it deals with another matter more personal to himself, namely, his courtship of and marriage to his first wife, Marie Marais.

Of this Marie I never heard him speak, save once. I remember that on a certain occasion—it was that of a garden fete for a local charity—I was standing by Quatermain when someone introduced to him a young girl who was staying in the neighborhood and had distinguished herself by singing very prettily at the fete. Her surname I forget, but her Christian name was Marie. He started when he heard it, and asked if she were French. The young lady answered No, but only of French extraction through her grandmother, who also was called Marie.

"Indeed?" he said. "Once I knew a maiden not unlike you who was also of French extraction and called Marie. May you prove more fortunate in life than she was, though better or nobler you can never be," and he bowed to her in his simple, courtly fashion, then turned away. Afterwards, when we were alone, I asked him who was this Marie of whom he had spoken to the young lady. He paused a little, then answered:

"She was my first wife, but I beg you not to speak of her to me or to anyone else, for I cannot bear to hear her name. Perhaps you will learn all about her one day." Then, to my grief and astonishment, he broke into something like a sob and abruptly left the room.

After reading the record of this Marie I can well understand why he was so moved. I print it practically as it left his hands.

There are other MSS. also, one of which, headed "Child of Storm," relates the moving history of a beautiful and, I fear I must add, wicked Zulu girl named Mameena who did much evil in her day and went unrepentant from the world.

Another, amongst other things, tells the secret story of the causes of the defeat of Cetewayo and his armies by the English in 1879, which happened not long before Quatermain met Sir Henry Curtis and Captain Good.

These three narratives are, indeed, more or less connected with each other. At least, a certain aged dwarf, called Zikali, a witch-doctor and an terrible man, has to do with all of them, although in the first, "Marie," he is only vaguely mentioned in connection with the massacre of Retief, whereof he was doubtless the primary instigator. As "Marie" comes first in chronological order, and was placed on the top of the pile by its author, I publish it first. With the others I hope to deal later on, as I may find time and opportunity.

But the future must take care of itself. We cannot control it, and its events are not in our hand. Meanwhile, I hope that those who in their youth have read of King Solomon's Mines and Zuvendis, and perhaps some others who are younger, may find as much of interest in these new chapters of the autobiography of Allan Quatermain as I have done myself.

Table of Contents

Allan Learns French

Although in my old age I, Allan Quatermain, have taken to writing—after a fashion—never yet have I set down a single word of the tale of my first love and of the adventures that are grouped around her beautiful and tragic history. I suppose this is because it has always seemed to me too holy and far-off a matter—as holy and far-off as is that heaven which holds the splendid spirit of Marie Marais. But now, in my age, that which was far-off draws near again; and at night, in the depths between the stars, sometimes I seem to see the opening doors through which I must pass, and leaning earthwards across their threshold, with outstretched arms and dark and dewy eyes, a shadow long forgotten by all save me—the shadow of Marie Marais.

An old man's dream, doubtless, no more. Still, I will try to set down that history which ended in so great a sacrifice, and one so worthy of record, though I hope that no human eye will read it until I also am forgotten, or, at any rate, have grown dim in the gathering mists of oblivion. And I am glad that I have waited to make this attempt, for it seems to me that only of late have I come to understand and appreciate at its true value the character of her of whom I tell, and the passionate affection which was her bounteous offering to one so utterly unworthy as myself. What have I done, I wonder, that to me should have been decreed the love of two such women as Marie and that of Stella, also now long dead, to whom alone in the world I told all her tale? I remember I feared lest she should take it ill, but this was not so. Indeed, during our brief married days, she thought and talked much of Marie, and some of her last words to me were that she was going to seek her, and that they would wait for me together in the land of love, pure and immortal.

So with Stella's death all that side of life came to an end for me, since during the long years which stretch between then and now I have never said another tender word to woman. I admit, however, that once, long afterwards, a certain little witch of a Zulu did say tender words to me, and for an hour or so almost turned my head, an art in which she had great skill. This I say because I wish to be quite honest, although it—I mean my head, for there was no heart involved in the matter—came straight again at once. Her name was Mameena, and I have set down her remarkable story elsewhere.

To return. As I have already written in another book, I passed my youth with my old father, a Church of England clergyman, in what is now the Cradock district of the Cape Colony.

Then it was a wild place enough, with a very small white population. Among our few neighbours was a Boer farmer of the name of Henri Marais, who lived about fifteen miles from our station, on a fine farm called Maraisfontein. I say he was a Boer, but, as may be guessed from both his Christian and surname, his origin was Huguenot, his forefather, who was also named Henri Marais—though I think the Marais was spelt rather differently then—having been one of the first of that faith who emigrated to South Africa to escape the cruelties of Louis XIV. at the time of the revocation of the Edict of Nantes.

Unlike most Boers of similar descent, these particular Marais—for, of course, there are many other families so called—never forgot their origin. Indeed, from father to son, they kept up some knowledge of the French tongue, and among themselves often spoke it after a fashion. At any rate, it was the habit of Henri Marais, who was excessively religious, to read his chapter of the Bible (which it is, or was, the custom of the Boers to spell out every morning, should their learning allow them to do so), not in the "taal" or patois Dutch, but in good old French. I have the very book from which he used to read now, for, curiously enough, in after years, when all these events had long been gathered to the past, I chanced to buy it among a parcel of other works at the weekly auction of odds and ends on the market square of Maritzburg. I remember that when I opened the great tome, bound over the original leather boards in buckskin, and discovered to whom it had belonged, I burst into tears. There was no doubt about it, for, as was customary in old days, this Bible had sundry fly-leaves sewn up with it for the purpose of the recording of events important to its owner.

The first entries were made by the original Henri Marais, and record how he and his compatriots were driven from France, his father having lost his life in the religious persecutions. After this comes a long list of births, marriages and deaths continued from generation to generation, and amongst them a few notes telling of such matters as the change of the dwelling-places of the family, always in French. Towards the end of the list appears the entry of the birth of the Henri Marais whom I knew, alas! too well, and of his only sister. Then is written his marriage to Marie Labuschagne, also, be it noted, of the Huguenot stock. In the next year follows the birth of Marie Marais, my Marie, and, after a long interval, for no other children were born, the death of her mother. Immediately below appears the following curious passage:

"Le 3 Janvier, 1836. Je quitte ce pays voulant me sauver du maudit gouvernement Britannique comme mes ancetres se sont sauves de ce diable—Louis XIV.

"A bas les rois et les ministres tyrannique! Vive la liberte!"

Which indicates very clearly the character and the opinions of Henri Marais, and the feeling among the trek-Boers at that time.

Thus the record closes and the story of the Marais ends—that is, so far as the writings in the Bible go, for that branch of the family is now extinct.

Their last chapter I will tell in due course.

There was nothing remarkable about my introduction to Marie Marais. I did not rescue her from any attack of a wild beast or pull her out of a raging river in a fashion suited to romance. Indeed, we interchanged our young ideas across a small and extremely massive table, which, in fact, had once done duty as a block for the chopping up of meat. To this hour I can see the hundreds of lines running criss-cross upon its surface, especially those opposite to where I used to sit.

One day, several years after my father had emigrated to the Cape, the Heer Marais arrived at our house in search, I think, of some lost oxen. He was a thin, bearded man with rather wild, dark eyes set close together, and a quick nervous manner, not in the least like that of a Dutch Boer—or so I recall him. My father received him courteously and asked him to stop to dine, which he did.

They talked together in French, a tongue that my father knew well, although he had not used it for years; Dutch he could not, or, rather, would not, speak if he could help it, and Mr. Marais preferred not to talk English. To meet someone who could converse in French delighted him, and although his version of the language was that of two centuries before and my father's was largely derived from reading, they got on very well together, if not too fast.

At length, after a pause, Mr. Marais, pointing to myself, a small and stubbly-haired youth with a sharp nose, asked my father whether he would like me to be instructed in the French tongue. The answer was that nothing would please him better.

"Although," he added severely, "to judge by my own experience where Latin and Greek are concerned, I doubt his capacity to learn anything."

So an arrangement was made that I should go over for two days in each week to Maraisfontein, sleeping there on the intervening night, and acquire a knowledge of the French tongue from a tutor whom Mr. Marais had hired to instruct his daughter in that language and other subjects. I remember that my father agreed to pay a certain proportion of this tutor's salary, a plan which suited the thrifty Boer very well indeed.

Thither, accordingly, I went in due course, nothing loth, for on the veld between our station and Maraisfontein many pauw and koran—that is, big and small bustards—were to be found, to say nothing of occasional buck, and I was allowed to carry a gun, which even in those days I could use fairly well. So to Maraisfontein I rode on the appointed day, attended by a Hottentot after-rider, a certain Hans, of whom I shall have a good deal to tell. I enjoyed very goof sport on the road, arriving at the stead laden with one pauw, two koran, and a little klipspringer buck which I had been lucky enough to shoot as it bounded out of some rocks in front of me.

There was a peach orchard planted round Maraisfontein, which just then was a mass of lovely pink blossom, and as I rode through it slowly, not being sure of my way to the house, a lanky child appeared in front of me, clad in a frock which exactly matched the colour of the peach bloom. I can see her now, her dark hair hanging down her back, and her big, shy eyes staring at me from the shadow of the Dutch "kappie" which she wore. Indeed, she seemed to be all eyes, like a "dikkop" or thick-headed plover; at any rate, I noted little else about her.

I pulled up my pony and stared at her, feeling very shy and not knowing what to say. For a while she stared back at me, being afflicted, presumably, with the same complaint, then spoke with an effort, in a voice that was very soft and pleasant.

"Are you the little Allan Quatermain who is coming to learn French with me?" she asked in Dutch.

"Of course," I answered in the same tongue, which I knew well; "but why do you call me little, missie? I am taller than you," I added indignantly, for when I was young my lack of height was always a sore point with me.

"I think not," she replied. "But get off that horse, and we will measure here against this wall."

So I dismounted, and, having assured herself that I had no heels to my boots (I was wearing the kind of raw-hide slippers that the Boers call "veld-shoon"), she took the writing slate which she was carrying—it had no frame, I remember, being, in fact, but a piece of the material used for roofing—and, pressing it down tight on my stubbly hair, which stuck up then as now, made a deep mark in the soft sandstone of the wall with the hard pointed pencil.

"There," she said, "that is justly done. Now, little Allan, it is your turn to measure me."

So I measured her, and, behold! she was the taller by a whole half-inch.

"You are standing on tiptoe," I said in my vexation.

"Little Allan," she replied, "to stand on tiptoe would be to lie before the good Lord, and when you come to know me better you will learn that, though I have a dreadful temper and many other sins, I do not lie."

I suppose that I looked snubbed and mortified, for she went on in her grave, grown-up way: "Why are you angry because God made me taller than you? especially as I am whole months older, for my father told me so. Come, let us write our names against these marks, so that in a year or two you may see how you outgrow me." Then with the slate pencil she scratched "Marie" against her mark very deeply, so that it might last, she said; after which I wrote "Allan" against mine.

Alas! Within the last dozen years chance took me past Maraisfontein once more. The house had long been rebuilt, but this particular wall yet stood. I rode to it and looked, and there faintly could still be seen the name Marie, against the little line, and by it the mark that I had made. My own name and with it subsequent measurements were gone, for in the intervening forty years or so the sandstone had flaked away in places. Only her autograph remained, and when I saw it I think that I felt even worse than I did on finding whose was the old Bible that I had bought upon the market square at Maritzburg.

I know that I rode away hurriedly without even stopping to inquire into whose hands the farm had passed. Through the peach orchard I rode, where the trees—perhaps the same, perhaps others—were once more in bloom, for the season of the year was that when Marie and I first met, nor did I draw rein for half a score of miles.

But here I may state that Marie always stayed just half an inch the taller in body, and how much taller in mind and spirit I cannot tell.

When we had finished our measuring match Marie turned to lead me to the house, and, pretending to observe for the first time the beautiful bustard and the two koran hanging from my saddle, also the klipspringer buck that Hans the Hottentot carried behind him on his horse, asked:

"Did you shoot all these, Allan Quatermain?"

"Yes," I answered proudly; "I killed them in four shots, and the pauw and koran were flying, not sitting, which is more than you could have done, although you are taller, Miss Marie."

"I do not know," she answered reflectively. "I can shoot very well with a rifle, for my father has taught me, but I never would shoot at living things unless I must because I was hungry, for I think that to kill is cruel. But, of course, it is different with men," she added hastily, "and no doubt you will be a great hunter one day, Allan Quatermain, since you can already aim so well."

"I hope so," I answered, blushing at the compliment, "for I love hunting, and when there are so many wild things it does not matter if we kill a few. I shot these for you and your father to eat."

"Come, then, and give them to him. He will thank you," and she led the way through the gate in the sandstone wall into the yard, where the outbuildings stood in which the riding horses and the best of the breeding cattle were kept at night, and so past the end of the long, one-storied house, that was stone-built and whitewashed, to the stoep or veranda in front of it.

On the broad stoep, which commanded a pleasant view over rolling, park-like country, where mimosa and other trees grew in clumps, two men were seated, drinking strong coffee, although it was not yet ten o'clock in the morning.

Hearing the sound of the horses, one of these, Mynheer Marais, whom I already knew, rose from his hide-strung chair. He was, as I think I have said, not in the least like one of the phlegmatic Boers, either in person or in temperament, but, rather, a typical Frenchman, although no member of his race had set foot in France for a hundred and fifty years. At least so I discovered afterwards, for, of course, in those days I knew nothing of Frenchmen.

His companion was also French, Leblanc by name, but of a very different stamp. In person he was short and stout. His large head was bald except for a fringe of curling, iron-grey hair which grew round it just above the ears and fell upon his shoulders, giving him the appearance of a tonsured but dishevelled priest. His eyes were blue and watery, his mouth was rather weak, and his cheeks were pale, full and flabby. When the Heer Marais rose, I, being an observant youth, noted that Monsieur

Leblanc took the opportunity to stretch out a rather shaky hand and fill up his coffee cup out of a black bottle, which from the smell I judged to contain peach brandy.

In fact, it may as well be said at once that the poor man was a drunkard, which explains how he, with all his high education and great ability, came to hold the humble post of tutor on a remote Boer farm. Years before, when under the influence of drink, he had committed some crime in France—I don't know what it was, and never inquired—and fled to the Cape to avoid prosecution. Here he obtained a professorship at one of the colleges, but after a while appeared in the lecture-room quite drunk and lost his employment. The same thing happened in other towns, till at last he drifted to distant Maraisfontein, where his employer tolerated his weakness for the sake of the intellectual companionship for which something in his own nature seemed to crave. Also, he looked upon him as a compatriot in distress, and a great bond of union between them was their mutual and virulent hatred of England and the English, which in the case of Monsieur Leblanc, who in his youth had fought at Waterloo and been acquainted with the great Emperor, was not altogether unnatural.

Henri Marais's case was different, but of that I shall have more to say later.

"Ah, Marie," said her father, speaking in Dutch, "so you have found him at last," and he nodded towards me, adding: "You should be flattered, little man. Look you, this missie has been sitting for two hours in the sun waiting for you, although I told her you would not arrive much before ten o'clock, as your father the predicant said you would breakfast before you started. Well, it is natural, for she is lonely here, and you are of an age, although of a different race"; and his face darkened as he spoke the words.

"Father," answered Marie, whose blushes I could see even in the shadow of her cap, "I was not sitting in the sun, but under the shade of a peach tree. Also, I was working out the sums that Monsieur Leblanc set me on my slate. See, here they are," and she held up the slate, which was covered with figures, somewhat smudged, it is true, by the rubbing of my stiff hair and of her cap.

Then Monsieur Leblanc broke in, speaking in French, of which, as it chanced I understood the sense, for my father had grounded me in that tongue, and I am naturally quick at modern languages. At any rate, I made out that he was asking if I was the little "cochon d'anglais," or English pig, whom for his sins he had to teach. He added that he judged I must be, as my hair stuck up on my head—I had taken off my hat out of politeness—as it naturally would do on a pig's back.

This was too much for me, so, before either of the others could speak, I answered in Dutch, for rage made me eloquent and bold:

"Yes, I am he; but, mynheer, if you are to be my master, I hope you will not call the English pigs any more to me."

"Indeed, gamin" (that is, little scamp), "and pray, what will happen if I am so bold as to repeat that truth?"

"I think, mynheer," I replied, growing white with rage at this new insult, "the same that has happened to yonder buck," and I pointed to the klipspringer behind Hans's saddle. "I mean that I shall shoot you."

"Peste! Au moins il a du courage, cet enfant" (At least the child is plucky), exclaimed Monsieur Leblanc, astonished. From that moment, I may add, he respected me, and never again insulted my country to my face.

Then Marais broke out, speaking in Dutch that I might understand:

"It is you who should be called pig, Leblanc, not this boy, for, early as it is, you have been drinking. Look! the brandy bottle is half empty. Is that the example you set to the young? Speak so again and I turn you out to starve on the veld. Allan Quatermain, although, as you may have heard, I do not like the English, I beg your pardon. I hope you will forgive the words this sot spoke, thinking that you did not understand," and he took off his hat and bowed to me quite in a grand manner, as his ancestors might have done to a king of France.

Leblanc's face fell. Then he rose and walked away rather unsteadily; as I learned afterwards, to plunge his head in a tub of cold water and swallow a pint of new milk, which were his favourite antidotes after too much strong drink. At any rate, when he appeared again, half an hour later, to begin out lesson, he was quite sober, and extremely polite.

When he had gone, my childish anger being appeased, I presented the Heer Marais with my father's compliments, also with the buck and the birds, whereof the latter seemed to please him more than the former. Then my saddle-bags were taken to my room, a little cupboard of a place next to that occupied by Monsieur Leblanc, and Hans was sent to turn the horses out with the others belonging to the farm, having first knee-haltered them tightly, so that they should not run away home.

This done, the Heer Marais showed me the room in which we were to have our lessons, one of the "sitkammer", or sitting chambers, whereof, unlike most Boer stead, this house boasted two. I remember that the floor was made of "daga", that is, ant-heap earth mixed with cow-dung, into which thousands of peach-stones had been thrown while it was still soft, in order to resist footwear—a rude but fairly efficient expedient, and one not unpleasing to the eye. For the rest, there was one window opening on to the veranda, which, in that bright climate, admitted a shaded but sufficient light, especially as it always stood open; the ceiling was of unplastered reeds; a large bookcase stood in the corner containing many French works, most of them the property of Monsieur Leblanc, and in the centre of the room was the strong, rough table made of native yellow-wood, that once had served as a butcher's block. I recollect also a coloured print of the great Napoleon commanding at some battle in which he was victorious, seated upon a white horse and waving a field-marshal's baton over piles of dead and wounded; and near the window, hanging to the reeds of the ceiling, the nest of a pair of red-tailed swallows, pretty creatures that, notwithstanding the mess they made, afforded to Marie and me endless amusement in the intervals of our work.

When, on that day, I shuffled shyly into this homely place, and, thinking myself alone there, fell to examining it, suddenly I was brought to a standstill by a curious choking sound which seemed to proceed from the shadows behind the bookcase. Wondering as to its cause, I advanced cautiously to discover a pink-clad shape standing in the corner like a naughty child, with her head resting against the wall, and sobbing slowly.

"Marie Marais, why do you cry?" I asked.

She turned, tossing back the locks of long, black hair which hung about her face, and answered:

"Allan Quatermain, I cry because of the shame which has been put upon you and upon our house by that drunken Frenchman."

"What of that?" I asked. "He only called me a pig, but I think I have shown him that even a pig has tusks."

"Yes," she replied, "but it was not you he meant; it was all the English, whom he hates; and the worst of it is that my father is of his mind. He, too, hates the English, and, oh! I am sure that trouble will come of his hatred, trouble and death to many."

"Well, if so, we have nothing to do with it, have we?" I replied with the cheerfulness of extreme youth.

"What makes you so sure?" she said solemnly. "Hush! here comes Monsieur Leblanc."

The Attack on Maraisfontein

I do not propose to set out the history of the years which I spent in acquiring a knowledge of French and various other subjects, under the tuition of the learned but prejudiced Monsieur Leblanc. Indeed, there is "none to tell, sir." When Monsieur Leblanc was sober, he was a most excellent and well-informed tutor, although one apt to digress into many side issues, which in themselves were not uninstructive. When tipsy, he grew excited and harangued us, generally upon politics and religion, or rather its reverse, for he was an advanced freethinker, although this was a side to his character which, however intoxicated he might be, he always managed to conceal from the Heer Marais. I may add that a certain childish code of honour prevented us from betraying his views on this and sundry other matters. When absolutely drunk, which, on an average, was not more than once a month, he simply slept, and we did what we pleased—a fact which our childish code of honour also prevented us from betraying.

But, on the whole, we got on very well together, for, after the incident of our first meeting, Monsieur Leblanc was always polite to me. Marie he adored, as did every one about the place, from her father down to the meanest slave. Need I add that I adored her more than all of them put together, first with the love that some children have for each other, and afterwards, as we became adult, with that wider love by which it is at once transcended and made complete. Strange would it have been if this were not so, seeing that we spent nearly half of every week practically alone together, and that, from the first, Marie, whose nature was as open as the clear noon, never concealed her affection for me. True, it was a very discreet affection, almost sisterly, or even motherly, in its outward and visible aspects, as though she could never forget that extra half-inch of height or month or two of age.

Moreover, from a child she was a woman, as an Irishman might say, for circumstances and character had shaped her thus. Not much more than a year before we met, her mother, whose only child she was, and whom she loved with all her strong and passionate heart, died after a lingering illness, leaving her in charge of her father and his house. I think it was this heavy bereavement in early youth which coloured her nature with a grey tinge of sadness and made her seem so much older than her years.

So the time went on, I worshipping Marie in my secret thought, but saying nothing about it, and Marie talking of and acting towards me as though I were her dear younger brother. Nobody, not even her father or mine, or Monsieur Leblanc, took the slightest notice of this queer relationship, or seemed to dream that it might lead to ultimate complications which, in fact, would have been very distasteful to them all for reasons that I will explain.

Needless to say, in due course, as they were bound to do, those complications arose, and under pressure of great physical and moral excitement the truth came out. It happened thus.

Every reader of the history of the Cape Colony has heard of the great Kaffir War of 1835. That war took place for the most part in the districts of Albany and Somerset, so that we inhabitants of Cradock, on the whole, suffered little. Therefore, with the natural optimism and carelessness of danger of dwellers in wild places, we began to think ourselves fairly safe from attack. Indeed, so we should have been, had it not been for a foolish action on the part of Monsieur Leblanc.

It seems that on a certain Sunday, a day that I always spent at home with my father, Monsieur Leblanc rode out alone to some hills about five miles distant from Maraisfontein. He had often been cautioned that this was an unsafe thing to do, but the truth is that the foolish man thought he had found a rich copper mine in these hills, and was anxious that no one should share his secret. Therefore, on Sundays, when there were no lessons, and the Heer Marais was in the habit of celebrating family prayers, which Leblanc disliked, it was customary for him to ride to these hills and there collect geological specimens and locate the strike of his copper vein. On this particular Sabbath, which was very hot, after he had done whatever he intended to do, he dismounted from his horse, a tame old beast. Leaving it loose, he partook of the meal he had brought with him, which seems to have included a bottle of peach brandy that induced slumber.

Waking up towards evening, he found that his horse had gone, and at once jumped to the conclusion that it had been stolen by Kaffirs, although in truth the animal had but strolled over a ridge in search of grass. Running hither and thither to seek it, he presently crossed this ridge and met the horse, apparently being led away by two of the Red Kaffirs, who, as was usual, were armed with assegais. As a matter of fact these men had found the beast, and, knowing well to whom it belonged, were seeking its owner, whom, earlier in the day, they had seen upon the hills, in order to restore it to him. This, however, never occurred to the mind of Monsieur Leblanc, excited as it was by the fumes of the peach brandy.

Lifting the double-barrelled gun he carried, he fired at the first Kaffir, a young man who chanced to be the eldest son and heir of the chief of the tribe, and, as the range was very close, shot him dead. Thereon his companion, leaving go of the horse, ran for his life. At him Leblanc fired also, wounding him slightly in the thigh, but no more, so that he escaped to tell the tale of what he and every other native for miles round considered a wanton and premeditated murder. The deed done, the fiery old Frenchman mounted his nag and rode quietly home. On the road, however, as the peach brandy evaporated from his brain, doubts entered it, with the result that he determined to say nothing of his adventure to Henri Marais, who he knew was particularly anxious to avoid any cause of quarrel with the Kaffirs.

So he kept his own counsel and went to bed. Before he was up next morning the Heer Marais, suspecting neither trouble nor danger, had ridden off to a farm thirty miles or more away to pay its owner for some cattle which he had recently bought, leaving his home and his daughter quite unprotected, except by Leblanc and the few native servants, who were really slaves, that lived about the place.

Now on the Monday night I went to bed as usual, and slept, as I have always done through life, like a top, till about four in the morning, when I was awakened by someone tapping at the glass of my window. Slipping from the bed, I felt for my pistol, as it was quite dark, crept to the window, opened it, and keeping my head below the level of the sill, fearing lest its appearance should be greeted with an assegai, asked who was there.

"Me, baas," said the voice of Hans, our Hottentot servant, who, it will be remembered, had accompanied me as after-rider when first I went to Maraisfontein. "I have bad news. Listen. The baas knows that I have been out searching for the red cow which was lost. Well, I found her, and was sleeping by her side under a tree on the veld when, about two hours ago, a woman whom I know came up to my camp fire and woke me. I asked her what she was doing at that hour of the night, and she answered that she had come to tell me something. She said that some young men of the tribe of the chief Quabie, who lives in the hills yonder, had been visiting at their kraal, and that a few hours before a messenger had arrived from the chief saying that they must return at once, as this morning at dawn he and all his men were going to attack Maraisfontein and kill everyone in it and take the cattle!"

"Good God!" I ejaculated. "Why?"

"Because, young baas," drawled the Hottentot from the other side of the window, "because someone from Maraisfontein—I think it was the Vulture" (the natives gave this name to Leblanc on account of his bald head and hooked nose)—"shot Quabie's son on Sunday when he was holding his horse."

"Good God!" I said again, "the old fool must have been drunk. When did you say the attack was to be—at dawn?" and I glanced at the stars, adding, "Why, that will be within less than an hour, and the Baas Marais is away."

"Yes," croaked Hans; "and Missie Marie—think of what the Red Kaffirs will do with Missie Marie when their blood is up."

I thrust my fist through the window and struck the Hottentot's toad-like face on which the starlight gleamed faintly.

"Dog!" I said, "saddle my mare and the roan horse and get your gun. In two minutes I come. Be swift or I kill you."

"I go," he answered, and shot out into the night like a frightened snake.

Then I began to dress, shouting as I dressed, till my father and the Kaffirs ran into the room. As I threw on my things I told them all.

"Send out messengers," I said, "to Marais—he is at Botha's farm—and to all the neighbours. Send, for your lives; gather up the friendly Kaffirs and ride like hell for Maraisfontein. Don't talk to me, father; don't talk! Go and do what I tell you. Stay! Give me two guns, fill the saddle-bags with powder tins and loopers, and tie them to my mare. Oh! be quick, be quick!"

Now at length they understood, and flew this way and that with candles and lanterns. Two minutes later—it could scarcely have been more—I was in front of the stables just as Hans led out the bay mare, a famous beast that for two years I had saved all my money to buy. Someone strapped on the saddle-bags while I tested the girths; someone else appeared with the stout roan stallion that I knew would follow the mare to the death. There was not time to saddle him, so Hans clambered on to his back like a monkey, holding two guns under his arm, for I carried but one and my double-barrelled pistol.

"Send off the messengers," I shouted to my father. "If you would see me again send them swiftly, and follow with every man you can raise."

Then we were away with fifteen miles to do and five-and-thirty minutes before the dawn.

"Softly up the slope," I said to Hans, "till the beasts get their wind, and then ride as you never rode before."

Those first two miles of rising ground! I thought we should never come to the end of them, and yet I dared not let the mare out lest she should bucket herself. Happily she and her companion, the stallion—a most enduring horse, though not so very swift—had stood idle for the last thirty hours, and, of course, had not eaten or drunk since sunset. Therefore being in fine fettle, they were keen for the business; also we were light weights.

I held in the mare as she spurted up the rise, and the horse kept his pace to hers. We reached its crest, and before us lay the great level plain, eleven miles of it, and then two miles down hill to Maraisfontein.

"Now," I said to Hans, shaking loose the reins, "keep up if you can!"

Away sped the mare till the keen air of the night sung past my ears, and behind her strained the good roan horse with the Hottentot monkey on its back. Oh! what a ride was that!

Further I have gone for a like cause, but never at such speed, for I knew the strength of the beasts and how long it would last them. Half an hour of it they might endure; more, and at this pace they must founder or die.

And yet such was the agony of my fear, that it seemed to me as though I only crept along the ground like a tortoise.

The roan was left behind, the sound of his foot-beats died away, and I was alone with the night and my fear. Mile added itself to mile, for now and again the starlight showed me a stone or the skeleton of some dead beast that I knew. Once I dashed into a herd of trekking game so suddenly, that a springbok, unable to stop itself, leapt right over me. Once the mare put her foot in an ant-bear hole and nearly fell, but recovered herself—thanks be to God, unharmed—and I worked myself back into the saddle whence I had been almost shaken. If I had fallen; oh! if I had fallen!

We were near the end of the flat, and she began to fail. I had over-pressed her; the pace was too tremendous. Her speed lessened to an ordinary fast gallop as she faced the gentle rise that led to the brow. And now, behind me, once more I heard the sound of the hoofs of the roan. The tireless beast was coming up. By the time we reached the edge of the plateau he was quite near, not fifty yards behind, for I heard him whinny faintly.

Then began the descent. The morning star was setting, the east grew grey with light. Oh! could we get there before the dawn? Could we get there before the dawn? That is what my horse's hoofs beat out to me.

Now I could see the mass of the trees about the stead. And now I dashed into something, though until I was through it, I did not know that it was a line of men, for the faint light gleamed upon the spear of one of them who had been overthrown!

So it was no lie! The Kaffirs were there! As I thought it, a fresh horror filled my heart; perhaps their murdering work was already done and they were departing.

The minute of suspense—or was it but seconds?—seemed an eternity. But it ended at last. Now I was at the door in the high wall that enclosed the outbuildings at the back of the house, and there, by an inspiration, pulled up the mare—glad enough she was to stop, poor thing—for it occurred to me that if I rode to the front I should very probably be assegaied and of no further use. I tried the door, which was made of stout stinkwood planks. By design, or accident, it had been left unbolted. As I thrust it open Hans arrived with a rush, clinging to the roan with his face hidden in its mane. The beast pulled up by the side of the mare which it had been pursuing, and in the faint light I saw that an assegai was fixed in its flank.

Five seconds later we were in the yard and locking and barring the door behind us. Then, snatching the saddle-bags of ammunition from the horses, we left them standing there, and I ran for the back entrance of the house, bidding Hans rouse the natives, who slept in the outbuildings, and follow with them. If any one of them showed signs of treachery he was to shoot him at once. I remember that as I went I tore the spear out of the stallion's flank and brought it away with me.

Now I was hammering upon the back door of the house, which I could not open. After a pause that seemed long, a window was thrown wide, and a voice—it was Marie's—asked in frightened tones who was there.

"I, Allan Quatermain," I answered. "Open at once, Marie. You are in great danger; the Red Kaffirs are going to attack the house."

She flew to the door in her nightdress, and at length I was in the place.

"Thank God! you are still safe," I gasped. "Put on your clothes while I call Leblanc. No, stay, do you call him; I must wait here for Hans and your slaves."

Away she sped without a word, and presently Hans arrived, bringing with him eight frightened men, who as yet scarcely knew whether they slept or woke.

"Is that all?" I asked. "Then bar the door and follow me to the 'sitkammer', where the baas keeps his guns."

Just as we reached it, Leblanc entered, clad in his shirt and trousers, and was followed presently by Marie with a candle.

"What is it?" he asked.

I took the candle from Marie's hand, and set it on the floor close to the wall, lest it should prove a target for an assegai or a bullet. Even in those days the Kaffirs had a few firearms, for the most part captured or stolen from white men. Then in a few words I told them all.

"And when did you learn all this?" asked Leblanc in French.

"At the Mission Station a little more than half an hour ago," I answered, looking at my watch.

"At the station a little more than half an hour ago! Peste! it is not possible. You dream or are drunken," he cried excitedly.

"All right, monsieur, we will argue afterwards," I answered. "Meanwhile the Kaffirs are here, for I rode through them; and if you want to save your life, stop talking and act. Marie, how many guns are there?"

"Four," she answered, "of my father's; two 'roers' and two smaller ones."

"And how many of these men"—and I pointed to the Kaffirs—"can shoot?"

"Three well and one badly, Allan."

"Good," I said. "Let them load the guns with 'loopers'"—that is, slugs, not bullets—"and let the rest stand in the passage with their assegais, in case the Quabies should try to force the back door."

Now, in this house there were in all but six windows, one to each sitting-room, one to each of the larger bedrooms, these four opening on to the veranda, and one at either end of the house, to give light and air to the two small bedrooms, which were approached through the larger bedrooms. At the back, fortunately, there were no windows, for the stead was but one room deep with passage running from the front to the back door, a distance of little over fifteen feet.

As soon as the guns were loaded I divided up the men, a man with a gun at each window. The right-hand sitting-room window I took myself with two guns, Marie coming with me to load, which, like all girls in that wild country, she could do well enough. So we arranged ourselves in a rough-and-ready fashion, and while we were doing it felt quite cheerful—that is, all except Monsieur Leblanc, who, I noticed, seemed very much disturbed.

I do not for one moment mean to suggest that he was afraid, as he might well have been, for he was an extremely brave and even rash man; but I think the knowledge that his drunken act had brought this terrible danger upon us all weighed on his mind. Also there may have been more; some subtle fore-knowledge of the approaching end to a life that, when all allowances were made, could scarcely be called well spent. At any rate he fidgeted at his window-place cursing beneath his breath, and soon, as I saw out of the corner of my eye, began to have recourse to his favourite bottle of peach brandy, which he fetched out of a cupboard.

The slaves, too, were gloomy, as all natives are when suddenly awakened in the night; but as the light grew they became more cheerful. It is a poor Kaffir that does not love fighting, especially when he has a gun and a white man or two to lead him.

Now that we had made such little preparations as we could, which, by the way, I supplemented by causing some furniture to be piled up against the front and back doors, there came a pause, which, speaking for my own part—being, after all, only a lad at the time—I found very trying to the nerves. There I stood at my window with the two guns, one a double-barrel and one a single "roer", or elephant gun, that took a tremendous charge, but both, be it remembered, flint locks; for, although percussion caps had been introduced, we were a little behind the times in Cradock. There, too, crouched on the ground beside me, holding the ammunition ready for re-loading, her long, black hair flowing about her shoulders, was Marie Marais, now a well-grown young woman. In the intense silence she whispered to me:

"Why did you come here, Allan? You were safe yonder, and now you will probably be killed."

"To try to save you," I answered simply. "What would you have had me do?"

"To try to save me? Oh! that is good of you, but you should have thought of yourself."

"Then I should still have thought of you, Marie."

"Why, Allan?"

"Because you are myself and more than myself. If anything happened to you, what would my life be to me?"

"I don't quite understand, Allan," she replied, staring down at the floor. "Tell me, what do you mean?"

"Mean, you silly girl," I said; "what can I mean, except that I love you, which I thought you knew long ago."

"Oh!" she said; "_now_ I understand." Then she raised herself upon her knees, and held up her face to me to kiss, adding, "There, that's my answer, the first and perhaps the last. Thank you, Allan dear; I am glad to have heard that, for you see one or both of us may die soon."

As she spoke the words, an assegai flashed through the window-place, passing just between our heads. So we gave over love-making and turned our attention to war.

Now the light was beginning to grow, flowing out of the pearly eastern sky; but no attack had yet been delivered, although that one was imminent that spear fixed in the plaster of the wall behind us showed clearly. Perhaps the Kaffirs had been frightened by the galloping of horses through their line in the dark, not knowing how many of them there might have been. Or perhaps they were waiting to see better where to deliver their onset. These were the ideas that occurred to me, but both were wrong.

They were staying their hands until the mist lifted a little from the hollow below the stead where the cattle kraals were situated, for while the fog remained they could not see to get the beasts out. These they wished to make sure of and drive away before the fight began, lest during its progress something should happen to rob them of their booty.

Presently, from these kraals, where the Heer Marais's horned beasts and sheep were penned at night, about one hundred and fifty of the former and some two thousand of the latter, to say nothing of the horses, for he was a large and prosperous farmer, there arose a sound of bellowing, neighing, and baaing, and with it that of the shouting of men.

"They are driving off the stock," said Marie. "Oh! my poor father, he is ruined; it will break his heart."

"Bad enough," I answered, "but there are things that might be worse. Hark!"

As I spoke there came a sound of stamping feet and of a wild war chant. Then in the edge of the mist that hung above the hollow where the cattle kraals were, figures appeared, moving swiftly to and fro, looking ghostly and unreal. The Kaffirs were marshalling their men for the attack. A minute more and it had begun. On up the slope they came in long, wavering lines, several hundreds of them, whistling and screaming, shaking their spears, their war-plumes and hair trappings blown back by the breeze, the lust of slaughter in their rolling eyes. Two or three of them had guns, which they fired as they ran, but where the bullets went I do not know, over the house probably.

I called out to Leblanc and the Kaffirs not to shoot till I did, for I knew that they were poor marksmen and that much depended upon our first volley being effective. Then as the captain of this attack came within thirty yards of the stoep—for now the light, growing swiftly, was strong enough to enable me to distinguish him by his apparel and the rifle which he held—I loosed at him with the "roer" and shot him dead. Indeed the heavy bullet passing through his body mortally wounded another of the Quabies behind. These were the first men that I ever killed in war.

As they fell, Leblanc and the rest of our people fired also, the slugs from their guns doing great execution at that range, which was just long enough to allow them to scatter. When the smoke cleared a little I saw that nearly a dozen men were down, and that the rest, dismayed by this reception, had halted. If they had come on then, while we were loading, doubtless they might have rushed the place; but, being unused to the terrible effects of firearms, they paused, amazed. A number of them, twenty or thirty perhaps, clustered about the bodies of the fallen Kaffirs, and, seizing my second gun, I fired both barrels at these with such fearful effect that the whole regiment took to their heels and fled, leaving their dead and wounded on the ground. As they ran our servants cheered, but I called to them to be silent and load swiftly, knowing well that the enemy would soon return.

For a time, however, nothing happened, although we could hear them talking somewhere near the cattle kraal, about a hundred and fifty yards away. Marie took advantage of this pause, I remember, to fetch food and distribute it among us. I, for one, was glad enough to get it.

Now the sun was up, a sight for which I thanked Heaven, for, at any rate, we could no longer be surprised. Also, with the daylight, some of my fear passed away, since darkness always makes danger twice as terrible to man and beast. Whilst we were still eating and fortifying the window-places as best we could, so as to make them difficult to enter, a single Kaffir appeared, waving above his head a stick to which was tied a white ox-tail as a sign of truce. I ordered that no one should fire, and when the man, who was a bold fellow, had reached the spot where the dead captain lay, called to him, asking his business, for I could speak his language well.

He answered that he had come with a message from Quabie. This was the message: that Quabie's eldest son had been cruelly murdered by the fat white man called "Vulture" who lived with the Heer Marais, and that he, Quabie, would have blood for blood. Still, he did not wish to kill the young white chieftainess (that was Marie) or the others in the house, with whom he had no quarrel. Therefore if we would give up the fat white man that he might make him "die slowly," Quabie would be content with his life and with the cattle that he had already taken by way of a fine, and leave us and the house unmolested.

Now, when Leblanc understood the nature of this offer he went perfectly mad with mingled fear and rage, and began to shout and swear in French.

"Be silent," I said; "we do not mean to surrender you, although you have brought all this trouble on us. Your chance of life is as good as ours. Are you not ashamed to act so before these black people?"

When at last he grew more or less quiet I called to the messenger that we white folk were not in the habit of abandoning each other, and that we would live or die together. Still, I bade him tell Quabie that if we did die, the vengeance taken on him and all his people would be to wipe them out till not one of them was left, and therefore that he would do well not to cause any of our blood to flow. Also, I added, that we had thirty men in the house (which, of course, was a lie) and plenty of ammunition and food, so that if he chose to continue the attack it would be the worse for him and his tribe.

On hearing this the herald shouted back that we should every one of us be dead before noon if he had his way. Still, he would report my words faithfully to Quabie and bring his answer.

Then he turned and began to walk off. Just as he did so a shot was fired from the house, and the man pitched forward to the ground, then rose again and staggered back towards his people, with his right shoulder shattered and his arm swinging.

"Who did that?" I asked through the smoke, which prevented me from seeing.

"I, parbleu!" shouted Leblanc. "Sapristi! that black devil wanted to torture me, Leblanc, the friend of the great Napoleon. Well, at least I have tortured him whom I meant to kill."

"Yes, you fool," I answered; "and we, too, shall be tortured because of your wickedness. You have shot a messenger carrying a flag of truce, and that the Quabies will never forgive. Oh! I tell you that you have hit us as well as him, who had it not been for you might have been spared."

These words I said quite quietly and in Dutch, so that our Kaffirs might understand them, though really I was boiling with wrath.

But Leblanc did not answer quietly.

"Who are you," he shouted, "you wretched little Englishman, who dare to lecture me, Leblanc, the friend of the great Napoleon?"

Now I drew my pistol and walked up to the man.

"Be quiet, you drunken sot," I said, for I guessed that he had drunk more of the brandy in the darkness. "If you are not quiet and do not obey me, who am in command here, either I will blow your brains out, or I will give you to these men," and I pointed to Hans and the Kaffirs, who had gathered round him, muttering ominously. "Do you know what they will do with you? They will throw you out of the house, and leave you to settle your quarrel with Quabie alone."

Leblanc looked first at the pistol, and next at the faces of the natives, and saw something in one or other of them, or in both, that caused him to change his note.

"Pardon, monsieur," he said; "I was excited. I knew not what I said. If you are young you are brave and clever, and I will obey you," and he went to his station and began to re-load his gun. As he did so a great shout of fury rose from the cattle kraal. The wounded herald had reached the Quabies and was telling them of the treachery of the white people.

The Rescue

The second Quabie advance did not begin till about half-past seven. Even savages love their lives and appreciate the fact that wounds hurt very much, and these were no exception to the rule. Their first rush had taught them a bitter lesson, of which the fruit was evident in the crippled or dying men who rolled to and fro baked in the hot sun within a few yards of the stoep, not to speak of those who would never stir again. Now, the space around the house being quite open and bare of cover, it was obvious that it could not be stormed without further heavy losses. In order to avoid such losses a civilised people would have advanced by means of trenches, but of these the Quabies knew nothing; moreover, digging tools were lacking to them.

So it came about that they hit upon another, and in the circumstances a not inefficient expedient. The cattle kraal was built of rough, unmortared stones. Those stones they took, each man carrying two or three, which, rushing forward, they piled up into scattered rough defences of about eighteen inches or two feet high. These defences were instantly occupied by as many warriors as could take shelter behind them, lying one on top of the other. Of course, those savages who carried the first stones were exposed to our fire, with the result that many of them fell, but there were always plenty more behind. As they were being built at a dozen different points, and we had but seven guns, before we could reload, a particular schanz, of which perhaps the first builders had fallen, would be raised so high that our slugs could no longer hurt those who lay behind it. Also, our supply of ammunition was limited, and the constant expenditure wasted it so much that at length only about six charges per man remained. At last, indeed, I was obliged to order the firing to cease, so that we might reserve ourselves for the great rush which could not now be much delayed.

Finding that they were no longer harassed by our bullets, the Quabies advanced more rapidly, directing their attack upon the south end of the house, where there was but one window, and thus avoiding the fire that might be poured upon them from the various openings under the veranda. At first I wondered why they selected this end, till Marie reminded me that this part of the dwelling was thatched with reeds, whereas the rest of the building, which had been erected more recently, was slated.

Their object was to fire the roof. So soon as their last wall was near enough (that is, about half-past ten of the clock) they began to throw into the thatch assegais to which were attached bunches of burning grass. Many of these went out, but at length, as we gathered from their shouts, one caught. Within ten minutes this part of the house was burning.

Now our state became desperate. We retreated across the central passage, fearing lest the blazing rafters should fall upon our natives, who were losing heart and would no longer stay beneath them. But the Quabies, more bold, clambered in through the south window, and attacked us in the doorway of the larger sitting-room.

Here the final fight began. As they rushed at us we shot, till they went down in heaps. Almost at our last charge they gave back, and just then the roof fell upon them.

Oh, what a terrible scene was that! The dense clouds of smoke, the screams of the trapped and burning men, the turmoil, the agony!

The front door was burst in by a flank onslaught.

Leblanc and a slave who was near him were seized by black, claw-like hands and dragged out. What became of the Frenchman I do not know, for the natives hauled him away, but I fear his end must have been dreadful, as he was taken alive. The servant I saw them assegai, so at least he died at once. I fired my last shot, killing a fellow who was flourishing a battle-axe, then dashed the butt of the gun into the face of the man behind him, felling him, and, seizing Marie by the hand, dragged her back into the northernmost room—that in which I was accustomed to sleep—and shut and barred the door.

"Allan," she gasped, "Allan dear, it is finished. I cannot fall into the hands of those men. Kill me, Allan."

"All right," I answered, "I will. I have my pistol. One barrel for you and one for me."

"No, no! Perhaps you might escape after all; but, you see, I am a woman, and dare not risk it. Come now, I am ready," and she knelt down, opening her arms to receive the embrace of death, and looked up at me with her lovely, pitiful eyes.

"It doesn't do to kill one's love and live on oneself," I answered hoarsely. "We have got to go together," and I cocked both barrels of the pistol.

The Hottentot, Hans, who was in the place with us, saw and understood.

"It is right, it is best!" he said; and turning, he hid his eyes with his hand.

"Wait a little, Allan," she exclaimed; "it will be time when the door is down, and perhaps God may still help us."

"He may," I answered doubtfully; "but I would not count on it. Nothing can save us now unless the others come to rescue us, and that's too much to hope for."

Then a thought struck me, and I added with a dreadful laugh: "I wonder where we shall be in five minutes."

"Oh! together, dear; together for always in some new and beautiful world, for you do love me, don't you, as I love you? Maybe that's better than living on here where we should be sure to have troubles and perhaps be separated at last."

I nodded my head, for though I loved life, I loved Marie more, and I felt that we were making a good end after a brave fight. They were battering at the door now, but, thank Heaven, Marais had made strong doors, and it held a while.

The wood began to give at last, an assegai appeared through a shattered plank, but Hans stabbed along the line of it with the spear he held, that which I had snatched from the flank of the horse, and it was dropped with a scream. Black hands were thrust through the hole, and the Hottentot hacked and cut at them with the spear. But others came, more than he could pierce, and the whole door-frame began to be dragged outwards.

"Now, Marie, be ready," I gasped, lifting the pistol.

"Oh, Christ receive me!" she answered faintly. "It won't hurt much, will it, Allan?"

"You will never feel anything," I whispered; as with the cold sweat pouring from me I placed the muzzle within an inch of her forehead and began to press the trigger. My God! yes, I actually began to press the trigger softly and steadily, for I wished to make no mistake.

It was at this very moment, above the dreadful turmoil of the roaring flames, the yells of the savages and the shrieks and groans of wounded and dying men, that I heard the sweetest sound which ever fell upon my ears—the sound of shots being fired, many shots, and quite close by.

"Great Heaven!" I screamed; "the Boers are here to save us. Marie, I will hold the door while I can. If I fall, scramble through the window—you can do it from the chest beneath—drop to the ground, and run towards the firing. There's a chance for you yet, a good chance."

"And you, you," she moaned. "I would rather die with you."

"Do what I bid you," I answered savagely, and bounded forward towards the rocking door.

It was falling outward, it fell, and on the top of it appeared two great savages waving broad spears. I lifted the pistol, and the bullet that had been meant for Marie's brain scattered that of the first of them, and the bullet which had been meant for my heart pierced that of the second. They both went down dead, there in the doorway.

I snatched up one of their spears and glanced behind me. Marie was climbing on to the chest; I could just see her through the thickening smoke. Another Quabie rushed on. Hans and I received him on the points of our assegais, but so fierce was his charge that they went through him as though he were nothing, and being but light, both of us were thrown backwards to the ground. I scrambled to my feet again, defenceless now, for the spear was broken in the Kaffir, and awaited the end. Looking back once more I saw that Marie had either failed to get through the window or abandoned the attempt. At any rate she was standing near the chest supporting herself by her right hand. In my despair I seized the blade end of the broken assegai and dragged it from the body of the Kaffir, thinking that it would serve to kill her, then turned to do the deed.

But even as I turned I heard a voice that I knew well shout: "Do you live, Marie?" and in the doorway appeared no savage, but Henri Marais.

Slowly I backed before him, for I could not speak, and the last dreadful effort of my will seemed to thrust me towards Marie. I reached her and threw my hand that still held the gory blade round her neck. Then as darkness came over me I heard her cry:

"Don't shoot, father. It is Allan, Allan who has saved my life!"

After that I remember no more. Nor did she for a while, for we both fell to the ground senseless.

When my senses returned to me I found myself lying on the floor of the wagon-house in the back yard. Glancing from my half-opened eyes, for I was still speechless, I saw Marie, white as a sheet, her hair all falling about her dishevelled dress. She was seated on one of those boxes that we put on the front of wagons to drive from, "voorkissies" they are called, and as her eyes were watching me I knew that she lived. By her stood a tall and dark young man whom I had never seen before. He was holding her hand and looking at her anxiously, and even then I felt angry with him. Also I saw other things; for instance, my old father leaning down and looking at _me_ anxiously, and outside in the yard, for there were no doors to the wagon-house, a number of men with guns in their hands, some of whom I knew and others who were strangers. In the shadow, too, against the wall, stood my blood mare with her head hanging down and trembling all over. Not far from her the roan lay upon the ground, its flank quite red.

I tried to rise and could not, then feeling pain in my left thigh, looked and saw that it was red also. As a matter of fact an assegai had gone half through it and hit upon the bone. Although I never felt it at the time, this wound was dealt to me by that great Quabie whom Hans and I had received upon our spears, doubtless as he fell. Hans, by the way, was there also, an awful and yet a ludicrous spectacle, for the Quabie had fallen right on the top of him and lain so with results that may, be imagined. There he sat upon the ground, looking upwards, gasping with his fish-like mouth. Each gasp, I remember, fashioned itself into the word "Allemachte!" that is "Almighty," a favourite Dutch expression.

Marie was the first to perceive that I had come to life again. Shaking herself free from the clasp of the young man, she staggered towards me and fell upon her knees at my side, muttering words that I could not catch, for they choked in her throat. Then Hans took in the situation, and wriggling his unpleasant self to my other side, lifted my hand and kissed it. Next my father spoke, saying:

"Praise be to God, he lives! Allan, my son, I am proud of you; you have done your duty as an Englishman should."

"Had to save my own skin if I could, thank you, father," I muttered.

"Why as an Englishman more than any other sort of man, Mynheer Predicant?" asked the tall stranger, speaking in Dutch, although he evidently understood our language.

"The point is one that I will not argue now, sir," answered my father, drawing himself up. "But if what I hear is true, there was a Frenchman in that house who did not do his duty; and if you belong to the same nation, I apologise to you."

"Thank you, sir; as it happens, I do, half. The rest of me is Portuguese, not English, thank God."

"God is thanked for many things that must surprise Him," replied my father in a suave voice.

At that moment this rather disagreeable conversation, which even then both angered and amused me faintly, came to an end, for the Heer Marais entered the place.

As might have been expected in so excitable a man, he was in a terrible state of agitation. Thankfulness at the escape of his only, beloved child, rage with the Kaffirs who had tried to kill her, and extreme distress at the loss of most of his property—all these conflicting emotions boiled together in his breast like antagonistic elements in a crucible.

The resulting fumes were parti-coloured and overpowering. He rushed up to me, blessed and thanked me (for he had learnt something of the story of the defence), called me a young hero and so forth, hoping that God would reward me. Here I may remark that _he_ never did, poor man. Then he began to rave at Leblanc, who had brought all this dreadful disaster upon his house, saying that it was a judgement on himself for having sheltered an atheist and a drunkard for so many years, just because he was French and a man of intellect. Someone, my father as a matter of fact, who with all his prejudices possessed a great sense of justice, reminded him that the poor Frenchman had expiated, or perchance was now expiating any crimes that he might have committed.

This turned the stream of his invective on to the Quabie Kaffirs, who had burned part of his house and stolen nearly all his stock, making him from a rich man into a poor one in a single hour. He shouted for vengeance on the "black devils," and called on all there to help him to recover his beasts and kill the thieves. Most of those present—they were about thirty in all, not counting the Kaffir and Hottentot after-riders—answered that they were willing to attack the Quabies. Being residents in the district, they felt, and, indeed, said, that his case to-day might and probably would be their case to-morrow. Therefore they were prepared to ride at once.

Then it was that my father intervened.

"Heeren," he said, "it seems to me that before you seek vengeance, which, as the Book tells us, is the Lord's, it would be well, especially for the Heer Marais, to return thanks for what has been saved to him. I mean his daughter, who might now very easily have been dead or worse."

He added that goods came or went according to the chances of fortune, but a beloved human life, once lost, could not be restored. This precious life had been preserved to him, he would not say by man—here he glanced at me—but by the Ruler of the world acting through man. Perhaps those present did not quite understand what he (my father) had learned from Hans the Hottentot, that I, his son, had been about to blow out the brains of Marie Marais and my own when the sound of the shots of those who had been gathered through the warning which I left before I rode from the Mission Station, had stayed my hand. He called upon the said Hans and Marie herself to tell them the story, since I was too weak to do so.

Thus adjured, the little Hottentot, smothered as he was in blood, stood up. In the simple, dramatic style characteristic of his race, he narrated all that had happened since he met the woman on the veld but little over twelve hours before, till the arrival of the rescue party. Never have I seen a tale followed with deeper interest, and when at last Hans pointed to me lying on the ground and said, "There is he who did these things which it might be thought no man could do—he, but a boy," even from those phlegmatic Dutchmen there came a general cheer. But, lifting myself upon my hands, I called out:

"Whatever I did, this poor Hottentot did also, and had it not been for him I could not have done anything—for him and the two good horses."

Then they cheered again, and Marie, rising, said:

"Yes, father; to these two I owe my life."

After this, my father offered his prayer of thanksgiving in very bad Dutch—for, having begun to learn it late in life, he never could really master that language—and the stalwart Boers, kneeling round him, said "Amen." As the reader may imagine, the scene, with all its details, which I will not repeat, was both remarkable and impressive.

What followed this prayer I do not very well remember, for I became faint from exhaustion and the loss of blood. I believe, however, that the fire having been extinguished, they removed the dead and wounded from the unburnt portion of the house and carried me into the little room where Marie and I had gone through that dreadful scene when I went within an ace of killing her. After this the Boers and Marais's Kaffirs, or rather slaves, whom he had collected from where they lived away from the house, to the number of thirty or forty, started to follow the defeated Quabie, leaving about ten of their number as a guard. Here I may mention that of the seven or eight men who slept in the outbuildings and had fought with us, two were killed in the fight and two wounded. The remainder, one way or another, managed to escape unhurt, so that in all this fearful struggle, in which we inflicted so terrible a punishment upon the Kaffirs, we lost only three slain, including the Frenchman, Leblanc.

As to the events of the next three days I know only what I have been told, for practically during all that time I was off my head from loss of blood, complicated with fever brought on by the fearful excitement and exertion I had undergone. All I can recall is a vision of Marie bending over me and making me take food of some sort—milk or soup, I suppose—for it seems I would touch it from no other hand. Also I had visions of the tall shape of my white-haired father, who, like most missionaries, understood something of surgery and medicine, attending to the bandages on my thigh. Afterwards he told me that the spear had actually cut the walls of the big artery, but, by good fortune, without going through them. Another fortieth of an inch and I should have bled to death in ten minutes!

On this third day my mind was brought back from its wanderings by the sound of a great noise about the house, above which I heard the voice of Marais storming and shouting, and that of my father trying to calm him. Presently Marie entered the room, drawing-to behind her a Kaffir karoos, which served as a curtain, for the door, it will be remembered, had been torn out. Seeing that I was awake and reasonable, she flew to my side with a little cry of joy, and, kneeling down, kissed me on the forehead.

"You have been very ill, Allan, but I know you will recover now. While we are alone, which," she added slowly and with meaning, "I dare say we shall not be much in future, I want to thank you from my heart for all that you did to save me. Had it not been for you, oh! had it not been for you"—and she glanced at the blood stains on the earthen floor, put her hands before her eyes and shuddered.

"Nonsense, Marie," I answered, taking her hand feebly enough, for I was very weak. "Anyone else would have done as much, even if they did not love you as I do. Let us thank God that it was not in vain. But what is all that noise? Have the Quabies come back?"

She shook her head.

"No; the Boers have come back from hunting them."

"And did they catch them and recover the cattle?"

"Not so. They only found some wounded men, whom they shot, and the body of Monsieur Leblanc with his head cut off, taken away with other bits of him for medicine, they say to make the warriors brave. Quabie has burnt his kraal and fled with all his people to join the other Kaffirs in the Big Mountains. Not a cow or a sheep did they find, except a few that had fallen exhausted, and those had their throats cut. My father wanted to follow them and attack the Red Kaffirs in the mountains, but the others would not go. They said there are thousands of them, and that it would be a mad war, from which not one of them would return alive. He is wild with grief and rage, for, Allan dear, we are almost ruined, especially as the British Government are freeing the slaves and only going to give us a very small price, not a third of their value. But, hark! he is calling me, and you must not talk much or excite yourself, lest you should be ill again. Now you have to sleep and eat and get strong. Afterwards, dear, you may talk"; and, bending down once more, she blessed and kissed me, then rose and glided away.

Hernando Pereira

Several more days passed before I was allowed out of that little war-stained room of which I grew to hate the very sight. I entreated my father to take me into the air, but he would not, saying that he feared lest any movement should cause the bleeding to begin again or even the cut artery to burst. Moreover, the wound was not hearing very well, the spear that caused it having been dirty or perhaps used to skin dead animals, which caused some dread of gangrene, that in those days generally meant death. As it chanced, although I was treated only with cold water, for antiseptics were then unknown, my young and healthy blood triumphed and no gangrene appeared.

What made those days even duller was that during them I saw very little of Marie, who now only entered the place in the company of her father. Once I managed to ask her why she did not come oftener and alone. Her face grew troubled as she whispered back, "Because it is not allowed, Allan," and then without another word left the place.

Why, I wondered to myself, was it not allowed, and an answer sprang up in my mind. Doubtless it was because of that tall young man who had argued with my father in the wagon-house. Marie had never spoken to me of him, but from the Hottentot Hans and my father I managed to collect a good deal of information concerning him and his business.

It appeared that he was the only child of Henri Marais's sister, who married a Portuguese from Delagoa Bay of the name of Pereira, who had come to the Cape Colony to trade many years before and settled there. Both he and his wife were dead, and their son, Hernando, Marie's cousin, had inherited all their very considerable wealth.

Indeed, now I remembered having heard this Hernando, or Hernan, as the Boers called him for short, spoken of in past years by the Heer Marais as the heir to great riches, since his father had made a large fortune by trading in wine and spirits under some Government monopoly which he held. Often he had been invited to visit Maraisfontein, but his parents, who doted on him and lived in one of the settled districts not far from Cape Town, would never allow him to travel so far from them into these wild regions.

Since their death, however, things had changed. It appeared that on the decease of old Pereira the Governor of the Colony had withdrawn the wine and spirit monopoly, which he said was a job and a scandal, an act that made Hernando Pereira very angry, although he needed no more money, and had caused him to throw himself heart and soul into the schemes of the disaffected Boers. Indeed, he was now engaged as one of the organisers of the Great Trek which was in contemplation. In fact, it had already begun, into the partially explored land beyond the borders of the Colony, where the Dutch farmers proposed to set up dominions of their own.

That was the story of Hernando Pereira, who was to be—nay, who had already become—my rival for the hand of the sweet and beautiful Marie Marais.

One night when my father and I were alone in the little room where he slept with me, and he had finished reading his evening portion of Scripture aloud, I plucked up my courage to tell him that I loved Marie and wished to marry her, and that we had plighted our troth during the attack of the Kaffirs on the stead.

"Love and war indeed!" he said, looking at me gravely, but showing no sign of surprise, for it appeared that he was already acquainted with our secret. This was not wonderful, for he informed me afterwards that during my delirium I had done nothing except rave of Marie in the most endearing terms. Also Marie herself, when I was at my worst, had burst into tears before him and told him straight out that she loved me.

"Love and war indeed!" he repeated, adding kindly, "My poor boy, I fear that you have fallen into great trouble."

"Why, father?" I asked. "Is it wrong that we should love each other?"

"Not wrong, but, in the circumstances, quite natural—I should have foreseen that it was sure to happen. No, not wrong, but most unfortunate. To begin with, I do not wish to see you marry a foreigner and become mixed up with these disloyal Boers. I hoped that one day, a good many years hence, for you are only a boy, Allan, you would find an English wife, and I still hope it."

"Never!" I ejaculated.

"Never is a long word, Allan, and I dare say that what you are so sure is impossible will happen after all," words that made me angry enough at the time, though in after years I often thought of them.

"But," he went on, "putting my own wishes, perhaps prejudices, aside, I think your suit hopeless. Although Henri Marais likes you well enough and is grateful to you just now because you have saved the daughter whom he loves, you must remember that he hates us English bitterly. I believe that he would almost as soon see his girl marry a half-caste as an Englishman, and especially a poor Englishman, as you are, and unless you can make money, must remain. I have little to leave you, Allan."

"I might make money, father, out of ivory, for instance. You know I am a good shot."

"Allan, I do not think you will ever make much money, it is not in your blood; or, if you do, you will not keep it. We are an old race, and I know our record, up to the time of Henry VIII. at any rate. Not one of us was ever commercially successful. Let us suppose, however, that you should prove yourself the exception to the rule, it can't be done at once, can it? Fortunes don't grow in a night, like mushrooms."

"No, I suppose not, father. Still, one might have some luck."

"Possibly. But meanwhile you have to fight against a man who has the luck, or rather the money in his pocket."

"What do you mean?" I asked, sitting up.

"I mean Hernando Pereira, Allan, Marais's nephew, who they say is one of the richest men in the Colony. I know that he wishes to marry Marie."

"How do you know it, father?"

"Because Marais told me so this afternoon, probably with a purpose. He was struck with her beauty when he first saw her after your escape, which he had not done since she was a child, and as he stopped to guard the house while the rest went after the Quabies—well, you can guess. Such things go quickly with these Southern men."

I hid my face in the pillow, biting my lips to keep back the groan that was ready to burst from them, for I felt the hopelessness of the situation. How could I compete with this rich and fortunate man, who naturally would be favoured of my betrothed's father? Then on the blackness of my despair rose a star of hope. I could not, but perchance Marie might. She was very strong-natured and very faithful. She was not to be bought, and I doubted whether she could be frightened.

"Father," I said, "I may never marry Marie, but I don't think that Hernando Pereira ever will either."

"Why not, my boy?"

"Because she loves me, father, and she is not one to change. I believe that she would rather die."

"Then she must be a very unusual sort of woman. Still, it may be so; the future will tell to those who live to see it. I can only pray and trust that whatever happens will be for the best for both of you. She is a sweet girl and I like her well, although she may be Boer—or French. And now, Allan, we have talked enough, and you had better go to sleep. You must not excite yourself, you know, or it may set up new inflammation in the wound."

"Go to sleep. Must not excite yourself." I kept muttering those words for hours, serving them up in my mind with a spice of bitter thought. At last torpor, or weakness, overcame me, and I fell into a kind of net of bad dreams which, thank Heaven! I have now forgotten. Yet when certain events happened subsequently I always thought, and indeed still think, that these or something like them, had been a part of those evil dreams.

On the morning following this conversation I was at length allowed to be carried to the stoep, where they laid me down, wrapped in a very dirty blanket, upon a rimpi-strung bench or primitive sofa. When I had satisfied my first delight at seeing the sun and breathing the fresh air, I began to study my surroundings. In front of the house, or what remained of it, so arranged that the last of them at either end we made fast to the extremities of the stoep, was arranged an arc of wagons, placed as they are in a laager and protected underneath by earth thrown up in a mound and by boughs of the mimosa thorn. Evidently these wagons, in which the guard of Boers and armed natives who still remained on the place slept at night, were set thus as a defence against a possible attack by the Quabies or other Kaffirs.

During the daytime, however, the centre wagon was drawn a little on one side to leave a kind of gate. Through this opening I saw that a long wall, also semicircular, had been built outside of them, enclosing a space large enough to contain at night all the cattle and horses that were left to the Heer Marais, together with those of his friends, who evidently did not wish to see their oxen vanish into the depths of the mountains. In the middle of this extemporised kraal was a long, low mound, which, as I learned afterwards, contained the dead who fell in the attack on the house. The two slaves who had been killed in the defence were buried in the little garden that Marie had made, and the headless body of Leblanc in a small walled place to the right of the stead, where lay some of its former owners and one or two relatives of the Heer Marais, including his wife.

Whilst I was noting these things Marie appeared at the end of the veranda, having come round the burnt part of the house, followed by Hernan Pereira. Catching sight of me, she ran to the side of my couch with outstretched arms as though she intended to embrace me. Then seeming to remember, stopped suddenly at my side, coloured to her hair, and said in an embarrassed voice:

"Oh, Heer Allan"—she had never called me Heer in her life before—"I am so glad to find you out! How have you been getting on?"

"Pretty well, I thank you," I answered, biting my lips, "as you would have learnt, Marie, had you come to see me."

Next moment I was sorry for the words, for I saw her eyes fill with tears and her breast shake with something like a sob. However, it was Pereira and not Marie who answered, for at the moment I believe she could not speak.

"My good boy," he said in a pompous, patronising way and in English, which he knew perfectly, "I think that my cousin has had plenty to do caring for all these people during the last few days without running to look at the cut in your leg. However, I am glad to hear from your worthy father that it is almost well and that you will soon be able to play games again, like others of your age."

Now it was my turn to be unable to speak and to feel my eyes fill with tears, tears of rage, for remember that I was still very feeble. But Marie spoke for me.

"Yes, Cousin Hernan," she said in a cold voice, "thank God the Heer Allan Quatermain will soon be able to play games again, such bloody games as the defence of Maraisfontein with eight men against all the Quabie horde. Then Heaven help those who stand in front of his rifle," and she glanced at the mound that covered the dead Kaffirs, many of whom, as a matter of fact, I had killed.

"Oh! no offence, no offence, Marie," said Pereira in his smooth, rich voice. "I did not want to laugh at your young friend, who doubtless is as brave as they say all Englishmen are, and who fought well when he was lucky enough to have the chance of protecting you, my dear cousin. But after all, you know, he is not the only one who can hold a gun straight, as you seem to think, which I shall be happy to prove to him in a friendly fashion when he is stronger."

Here he stepped forward a pace and looked down at me, then added with a laugh, "Allemachte! I fear that won't be just at present. Why, the lad looks as though one might blow him away like a feather."

Still I said nothing, only glanced up at this tall and splendid man standing above me in his fine clothes, for he was richly dressed as the fashion of the time went, with his high colouring, broad shoulders, and face full of health and vigour. Mentally I compared him with myself, as I was after my fever and loss of blood, a poor, white-faced rat of a lad, with stubbly brown hair on my head and only a little down on my chin, with arms like sticks, and a dirty blanket for raiment. How could I compare with him in any way? What chance had I against this opulent bully who hated me and all my race, and in whose hands, even if I were well, I should be nothing but a child?

And yet, and yet as I lay there humiliated and a mock, an answer came into my mind, and I felt that whatever might be the case with my outward form; in spirit, in courage, in determination and in ability, in all, in short, that really makes a man, I was more than Pereira's equal. Yes, and that by the help of these qualities, poor as I was and frail as I seemed to be, I would beat him at the last and keep for myself what I had won, the prize of Marie's love.

Such were the thoughts which passed through me, and I think that something of the tenor of them communicated itself to Marie, who often could read my heart before my lips spoke. At any rate, her demeanour changed. She drew herself up. Her fine nostrils expanded and a proud look came into her dark eyes, as she nodded her head and murmured in a voice so low that I think I alone caught her words:

"Yes, yes, have no fear."

Pereira was speaking again (he had turned aside to strike the steel of his tinder-box, and was now blowing the spark to a glow before lighting his big pipe).

"By the way, Heer Allan," he said, "that is a very good mare of yours. She seems to have done the distance between the Mission Station and Maraisfontein in wonderful time, as, for the matter of that, the roan did too. I have taken a fancy to her, after a gallop on her back yesterday just to give her some exercise, and although I don't know that she is quite up to my weight, I'll buy her."

"The mare is not for sale, Heer Pereira," I said, speaking for the first time, "and I do not remember giving anyone leave to exercise her."

"No, your father did, or was it that ugly little beast of a Hottentot? I forget which. As for her not being for sale—why, in this world everything is for sale, at a price. I'll give you—let me see—oh, what does the money matter when one has plenty? I'll give you a hundred English pounds for that mare; and don't you think me a fool. I tell you I mean to get it back, and more, at the great races down in the south. Now what do you say?"

"I say that the mare is not for sale, Heer Pereira." Then a thought struck me, or an inspiration, and, as has always been my fashion, I acted on it at once. "But," I added slowly, "if you like, when I am a bit stronger I'll shoot you a match for her, you staking your hundred pounds and I staking the mare."

Pereira burst out laughing.

"Here, friends," he called to some of the Boers who were strolling up to the house for their morning coffee. "This little Englishman wants to shoot a match with me, staking that fine mare of his against a hundred pounds British; against me, Hernando Pereira, who have won every prize at shooting that ever I entered for. No, no, friend Allan, I am not a thief, I will not rob you of your mare."

Now among those Boers chanced to be the celebrated Heer Pieter Retief, a very fine man of high character, then in the prime of life, and of Huguenot descent like Heer Marais. He had been appointed by the Government one of the frontier commandants, but owing to some quarrel with the Lieutenant-Governor, Sir Andries Stockenstrom, had recently resigned that office, and at this date was engaged in organizing the trek from the Colony. I now saw Retief for the first time, and ah! then little did I think how and where I should see him for the last. But all that is a matter of history, of which I shall have to tell later.

Now, while Pereira was mocking and bragging of his prowess, Pieter Retief looked at me, and our eyes met.

"Allemachte!" he exclaimed, "is that the young man who, with half a dozen miserable Hottentots and slaves, held this stead for five hours against all the Quabie tribe and kept them out?"

Somebody said that it was, remarking that I had been about to shoot Marie Marais and myself when help came.

"Then, Heer Allan Quatermain," said Retief, "give me your hand," and he took my poor wasted fingers in his big palm, adding, "Your father must be proud of you to-day, as I should be if I had such a son. God in Heaven! where will you stop if you can go so far while you are yet a boy? Friends, since I came here yesterday I have got the whole story for myself from the Kaffirs and from this 'mooi meisje'" (pretty young lady), and he nodded towards Marie. "Also I have gone over the ground and the house, and have seen where each man fell—it is easy by the blood marks—most of them shot by yonder Englishman, except one of the last three, whom he killed with a spear. Well, I tell you that never in all my experience have I known a better arranged or a more finely carried out defence against huge odds. Perhaps the best part of it, too, was the way in which this young lion acted on the information he received and the splendid ride he made from the Mission Station. Again I say that his father should be proud of him."

"Well, if it comes to that, I am, mynheer," said my father, who just then joined us after his morning walk, "although I beg you to say no more lest the lad should grow vain."

"Bah!" replied Retief, "fellows of his stamp are not vain; it is your big talkers who are vain," and he glanced out of the corner of his shrewd eye at Pereira, "your turkey cocks with all their tails spread. I think this little chap must be such another as that great sailor of yours—what do you call him, Nelson?—who beat the French into frothed eggs and died to live for ever. He was small, too, they say, and weak in the stomach."

I must confess I do not think that praise ever sounded sweeter in my ears than did these words of the Commandant Retief, uttered as they were just when I felt crushed to the dirt. Moreover, as I saw by Marie's and, I may add, by my father's face, there were other ears to which they were not ungrateful. The Boers also, brave and honest men enough, evidently appreciated them, for they said:

"Ja! ja! das ist recht" (That is right).

Only Pereira turned his broad back and busied himself with relighting his pipe, which had gone out.

Then Retief began again.

"What is it you were calling us to listen to, Mynheer Pereira? That this Heer Allan Quatermain had offered to shoot you a match? Well, why not? If he can hit Kaffirs running at him with spears, as he has done, he may be able to hit other things also. You say that you won't rob him of his money—no, it was his beautiful horse—because you have taken so many prizes shooting at targets. But did _you_ ever hit a Kaffir running at _you_ with an assegai, mynheer, you who live down there where everything is safe? If so, I never heard of it."

Pereira answered that he did not understand me to propose a shooting match at Kaffirs charging with assegais, but at something else—he knew not what.

"Quite so," said Retief. "Well, Mynheer Allan, what is it that you do propose?"

"That we should stand in the great kloof between the two _vleis_ yonder—the Heer Marais knows the place—when the wild geese flight over an hour before sunset, and that he who brings down six of them in the fewest shots shall win the match."

"If our guns are loaded with loopers that will not be difficult," said Pereira.

"With loopers you would seldom kill a bird, mynheer," I replied, "for they come over from seventy to a hundred yards up. No, I mean with rifles."

"Allemachte!" broke in a Boer; "you will want plenty of ammunition to hit a goose at that height with a bullet."

"That is my offer," I said, "to which I add this, that when twenty shots have been fired by each man, he who has killed the most birds wins, even if he has not brought down the full six. Does the Heer Pereira accept? If so, I will venture to match myself against him, although he has won so many prizes."

The Heer Pereira seemed extremely doubtful; so doubtful, indeed, that the Boers began to laugh at him. In the end he grew rather angry, and said that he was willing to shoot me at bucks or swallows, or fireflies, or anything else I liked.

"Then let it be at geese," I answered, "since it is likely to be sometime before I am strong enough to ride after buck or other wild things.'"

So the terms of the match were formally written down by Marie, as my father, although he took a keen sporting interest in the result, would have nothing to do with what he called a "wager for money," and, except myself, there was no one else present with sufficient scholarship to pen a long document. Then we both signed them, Hernan Pereira not very willingly, I thought; and if my recovery was sufficiently rapid, the date was fixed for that day week. In case of any disagreement, the Heer Retief, who was staying at Maraisfontein, or in its neighbourhood, for a while, was appointed referee and stakeholder. It was also arranged that neither of us should visit the appointed place, or shoot at the geese before the match. Still we were at liberty to practise as much as we liked at anything else in the interval and to make use of any kind of rifle that suited us best.

By the time that these arrangements were finished, feeling quite tired with all the emotions of the morning, I was carried back to my room. Here my midday meal, cooked by Marie, was brought to me. As I finished eating it, for the fresh air had given me an appetite, my father came in, accompanied by the Heer Marais, and began to talk to me. Presently the latter asked me kindly enough if I thought I should be sufficiently strong to trek back to the station that afternoon in an ox-cart with springs to it and lying at full length upon a hide-strung "cartel" or mattress.

I answered, "Certainly," as I should have done had I been at the point of death, for I saw that he wished to be rid of me.

"The fact is, Allan," he said awkwardly, "I am not inhospitable as you may think, especially towards one to whom I owe so much. But you and my nephew, Hernan, do not seem to get on very well together, and, as you may guess, having just been almost beggared, I desire no unpleasantness with the only rich member of my family."

I replied I was sure I did not wish to be the cause of any. It seemed to me, however, that the Heer Pereira wished to make a mock of me and to bring it home to me what a poor creature I was compared to himself—I a mere sick boy who was worth nothing.

"I know," said Marais uneasily, "my nephew has been too fortunate in life, and is somewhat overbearing in his manner. He does not remember that the battle is not always to the strong or the race to the swift, he who is young and rich and handsome, a spoiled child from the first. I am sorry, but what I cannot help I must put up with. If I cannot have my mealies cooked, I must eat them green. Also, Allan, have you never heard that jealousy sometimes makes people rude and unjust?" and he looked at me meaningly.

I made no answer, for when one does not quite know what to say it is often best to remain silent, and he went on:

"I am vexed to hear of this foolish shooting match which has been entered into without my knowledge or consent. if he wins he will only laugh at you the more, and if you win he will be angry."

"It was not my fault, mynheer," I answered. "He wanted to force me to sell the mare, which he had been riding without my leave, and kept bragging about his marksmanship. So at last I grew cross and challenged him."

"No wonder, Allan; I do not blame you. Still, you are silly, for it will not matter to him if he loses his money; but that beautiful mare is your ewe-lamb, and I should be sorry to see you parted from a beast which has done us so good a turn. Well, there it is; perhaps circumstances may yet put an end to this trial; I hope so."

"I hope they won't," I answered stubbornly.

"I dare say you do, being sore as a galled horse just now. But listen, Allan, and you, too, Predicant Quatermain; there are other and more important reasons than this petty squabble why I should be glad if you could go away for a while. I must take counsel with my countrymen about certain secret matters which have to do with our welfare and future, and, of course they would not like it if all the while there were two Englishmen on the place, whom they might think were spies."

"Say no more, Heer Marais," broke in my father hotly; "still less should we like to be where we are not wanted or are looked upon with suspicion for the crime of being English. By God's blessing, my son has been able to do some service to you and yours, but now that is all finished and forgotten. Let the cart you are so kind as to lend us be inspanned. We will go at once."

Then Henri Marais, who was a gentleman at bottom, although, even in those early days, violent and foolish when excited or under the influence of his race prejudices, began to apologise quite humbly, assuring my father that he forgot nothing and meant no offence. So they patched the matter up, and an hour later we started.

All the Boers came to see us off, giving me many kind words and saying how much they looked forward to meeting me again on the following Thursday. Pereira, who was among them, was also very genial, begging me to be sure and get well, since he did not wish to beat one who was still crippled, even at a game of goose shooting. I answered that I would do my best; as for my part, I did not like being beaten it any game which I had set my heart on winning, whether it were little or big. Then I turned my head, for I was lying on my back all this time, to bid good-bye to Marie, who had slipped out of the house into the yard where the cart was.

"Good-bye, Allan," she said, giving me her hand and a look from her eyes that I trusted was not seen. Then, under pretence of arranging the kaross which was over me, she bent down and whispered swiftly:

"Win that match if you love me. I shall pray God that you may every night, for it will be an omen."

I think the whisper was heard, though not the words, for I saw Pereira bite his lip and make a movement as though to interrupt her. But Pieter Retief thrust his big form in front of him rather rudely, and said with one of his hearty laughs:

"Allemachte! friend, let the missje wish a good journey to the young fellow who saved her life."

Next moment Hans, the Hottentot, screamed at the oxen in the usual fashion, and we rolled away through the gate.

But oh! if I had liked the Heer Retief before, now I loved him.

The Shooting Match

My journey back to the Mission Station was a strange contrast to that which I had made thence a few days before. Then, the darkness, the swift mare beneath me rushing through it like a bird, the awful terror in my heart lest I should be too late, as with wild eyes I watched the paling stars and the first gathering grey of dawn. Now, the creaking of the ox-cart, the familiar veld, the bright glow of the peaceful sunlight, and in my heart a great thankfulness, and yet a new terror lest the pure and holy love which I had won should be stolen away from me by force or fraud.

Well, as the one matter had been in the hand of God, so was the other, and with that knowledge I must be content. The first trial had ended in death and victory. How would the second end? I wondered, and those words seemed to jumble themselves up in my mind and shape a sentence that it did not conceive. It was: "In the victory that is death," which, when I came to think of it, of course, meant nothing. How victory could be death I did not understand—at any rate, at that time, I who was but a lad of small experience.

As we trekked along comfortably enough, for the road was good and the cart, being on springs, gave my leg no pain, I asked my father what he thought that the Heer Marais had meant when he told us that the Boers had business at Maraisfontein, during which our presence as Englishmen would not be agreeable to them.

"Meant, Allan? He meant that these traitorous Dutchmen are plotting against their sovereign, and are afraid lest we should report their treason. Either they intend to rebel because of that most righteous act, the freeing of the slaves, and because we will not kill out all the Kaffirs with whom they chance to quarrel, or to trek from the Colony. For my part I think it will be the latter, for, as you have heard, some parties have already gone; and, unless I am mistaken, many more mean to follow, Marais and Retief and that plotter, Pereira, among them. Let them go; I say, the sooner the better, for I have no doubt that the English flag will follow them in due course."

"I hope that they won't," I answered with a nervous laugh; "at any rate, until I have won back my mare." (I had left her in Retief's care as stakeholder, until the match should be shot off.)

For the rest of that two and a half hours' trek my father, looking very dignified and patriotic, declaimed to me loudly about the bad behaviour of the Boers, who hated and traduced missionaries, loathed and abominated British rule and permanent officials, loved slavery and killed Kaffirs whenever they got the chance. I listened to him politely, for it was not wise to cross my parent when he was in that humour. Also, having mixed a great deal with the Dutch, I knew that there was another side to the question, namely, that the missionaries sometimes traduced them (as, in fact, they did), and that British rule, or rather, party government, played strange tricks with the interests of distant dependencies. That permanent officials and im-permanent ones too—such as governors full of a little brief authority—often misrepresented and oppressed them. That Kaffirs, encouraged by the variegated policy of these party governments and their servants, frequently stole their stock; and if they found a chance, murdered them with their women and children, as they had tried to do at Maraisfontein; though there, it is true, they had some provocation. That British virtue had liberated the slaves without paying their owners a fair price for them, and so forth.

But, to tell the truth, it was not of these matters of high policy, which were far enough away from a humble youth like myself, that I was thinking. What appealed to me and made my heart sick was the reflection that if Henri Marais and his friends trekked, Marie Marais must perforce trek with them; and that whereas I, an Englishman, could not be of that adventurous company, Hernando Pereira both could and would.

On the day following our arrival home, what between the fresh air, plenty of good food, for which I found I had an appetite, and liberal doses of Pontac—a generous Cape wine that is a kind of cross between port and Burgundy—I found myself so much better that I was able to hop about the place upon a pair of crutches which Hans improvised for me out of Kaffir sticks. Next morning, my improvement continuing at a rapid rate, I turned my attention seriously to the shooting match, for which I had but five days to prepare.

Now it chanced that some months before a young Englishman of good family—he was named the Honourable Vavasseur Smyth—who had accompanied an official relative to the Cape Colony, came our way in search of sport, of which I was able to show him a good deal of a humble kind. He had brought with him, amongst other weapons, what in those days was considered a very beautiful hair-triggered small-bore rifle fitted with a nipple for percussion caps, then quite a new invention. It was by a maker of the name of J. Purdey, of London, and had cost quite a large sum because of the perfection of its workmanship. When the Honourable V. Smyth—of whom I have never heard since—took his leave of us on his departure for England, being a generous-hearted young fellow, as a souvenir of himself, he kindly presented me with this rifle, which I still have.

Another peculiarity of the weapon, one that I have never seen before, is that by pressing on the back of the trigger the ordinary light pull of the piece is so reduced that the merest touch suffices to fire it, thus rendering it hair-triggered in the fullest sense of the word.

It has two flap-sights marked for 150 and 200 yards, in addition to the fixed sight designed for firing at 100 yards.

On the lock are engraved a stag and a doe, the first lying down and the second standing.

Of its sort and period, it is an extraordinarily well-made and handy gun, finished with horn at the end of what is now called the tongue, and with the stock cut away so as to leave a raised cushion against which the cheek of the shooter rests.

What charge it took I do not know, but I should imagine from 2 1/2 to 3 drachms of powder. It is easy to understand that in the hands of Allan Quatermain this weapon, obsolete as it is to-day, was capable of great things within the limits of its range, and that the faith he put in it at the trial of skill at the Groote Kloof, and afterwards in the fearful ordeal of the shooting of the vultures on the wing, upon the Mount of Slaughter, when the lives of many hung upon his marksmanship, was well justified. This, indeed, is shown by the results in both cases.

That was about six months earlier than the time of which I write, and during those months I had often used this rifle for the shooting of game, such as blesbuck and also of bustards. I found it to be a weapon of the most extraordinary accuracy up to a range of about two hundred yards, though when I rode off in that desperate hurry for Maraisfontein I did not take it with me because it was a single barrel and too small in the bore to load with loopers at a pinch. Still, in challenging Pereira, it was this gun and no other that I determined to use; indeed, had I not owned it I do not think that I should have ventured on the match.

As it happened, Mr. Smyth had left me with the rifle a large supply of specially cast bullets and of the new percussion caps, to say nothing of some very fine imported powder. Therefore, having ammunition in plenty, I set to work to practise. Seating myself upon a chair in a deep kloof near the station, across which rock pigeons and turtle doves were wont to fly in numbers at a considerable height, I began to fire at them as they flashed over me.

Now, in my age, I may say without fear of being set down a boaster, that I have one gift, that of marksmanship, which, I suppose, I owe to some curious combination of judgment, quickness of eye, and steadiness of hand. I can declare honestly that in my best days I never knew a man who could beat me in shooting at a living object; I say nothing of target work, of which I have little experience. Oddly enough, also, I believe that at this art, although then I lacked the practice which since has come to me in such plenty, I was as good as a youth as I have ever been in later days, and, of course, far better than I am now. This I soon proved upon the present occasion, for seated there in that kloof, after a few trials, I found that I could bring down quite a number of even the swift, straight-flying rock pigeons as they sped over me, and this, be it remembered, not with shot, but with a single bullet, a feat that many would hold to be incredible.

So the days passed, and I practised, every evening finding me a little better at this terribly difficult sport. For always I learned more as to the exact capacities of my rifle and the allowance that must be made according to the speed of the bird, its distance, and the complications of the wind and of the light. During those days, also, I recovered so rapidly that at the end of them I was almost in my normal condition, and could walk well with the aid of a single stick.

At length the eventful Thursday came, and about midday—for I lay in bed late that morning and did not shoot—I drove, or, rather, was driven, in a Cape cart with two horses to the place known as Groote Kloof or Great Gully. Over this gorge the wild geese flighted from their "pans" or feeding grounds on the high lands above, to other pans that lay some miles below, and thence, I suppose, straight out to the sea coast, whence they returned at dawn.

On arriving at the mouth of Groote Kloof about four o'clock in the afternoon, my father and I were astonished to see a great number of Boers assembled there, and among them a certain sprinkling of their younger womankind, who had come on horseback or in carts.

"Good gracious!" I said to my father; "if I had known there was to be such a fuss as this about a shooting match, I don't think I could have faced it."

"Hum," he answered; "I think there is more in the wind than your match. Unless I am much mistaken, it has been made the excuse of a public meeting in a secluded spot, so as to throw the Authorities off the scent."

As a matter of fact, my father was quite right. Before we arrived there that day the majority of those Boers, after full and long discussion, had arranged to shake the dust of the Colony off their feet, and find a home in new lands to the north.

Presently we were among them, and I noticed that, one and all, their faces were anxious and preoccupied. Pieter Retief caught sight of me being helped out of the cart by my father and Hans, whom I had brought to load, and for a moment looked puzzled. Evidently his thoughts were far away. Then he remembered and exclaimed in his jolly voice:

"Why! here is our little Englishman come to shoot off his match like a man of his word. Friend Marais, stop talking about your losses"—this in a warning voice—"and give him good day."

So Marais came, and with him Marie, who blushed and smiled, but to my mind looked more of a grown woman than ever before; one who had left girlhood behind her and found herself face to face with real life and all its troubles. Following her close, very close, as I was quick to notice, was Hernan Pereira. He was even more finely dressed than usual and carried in his hand a beautiful new, single-barrelled rifle, also fitted to take percussion caps, but, as I thought, of a very large bore for the purpose of goose shooting.

"So you have got well again," he said in a genial voice that yet did not ring true. Indeed, it suggested to me that he wished I had done nothing of the sort. "Well, Mynheer Allan, here you find me quite ready to shoot your head off." (He didn't mean that, though I dare say he was.) "I tell you that the mare is as good as mine, for I have been practising, haven't I, Marie? as the 'aasvogels'" (that is, vultures) "'round the stead know to their cost."

"Yes, Cousin Hernan," said Marie, "you have been practising, but so, perhaps, has Allan."

By this time all the company of Boers had collected round us, and began to evince a great interest in the pending contest, as was natural among people who rarely had a gun out of their hands, and thought that fine shooting was the divinest of the arts. However, they were not allowed to stay long, as the Kaffirs said that the geese would begin their afternoon flight within about half an hour. So the spectators were all requested to arrange themselves under the sheer cliff of the kloof, where they could not be seen by the birds coming over them from behind, and there to keep silence. Then Pereira and I—I attended by my loader, but he alone, as he said a man at his elbow would bother him—and with us Retief, the referee, took our stations about a hundred and fifty yards from this face of cliff. Here we screened ourselves as well as we could from the keen sight of the birds behind some tall bushes which grew at this spot.

I seated myself on a camp-stool, which I had brought with me, for my leg was still too weak to allow me to stand long, and waited. Presently Pereira said through Retief that he had a favour to ask, namely, that I would allow him to take the first six shots, as the strain of waiting made him nervous. I answered, "Certainly," although I knew well that the object of the request was that he believed that the outpost geese—"spy-geese" we called them—which would be the first to arrive, would probably come over low down and slow, whereas those that followed, scenting danger, might fly high and fast. This, in fact, proved to be the case, for there is no bird more clever than the misnamed goose.

When we had waited about a quarter of an hour Hans said:

"Hist! Goose comes."

As he spoke, though as yet I could not see the bird, I heard its cry of "Honk, honk" and the swish of its strong wings.

Then it appeared, an old spur-winged gander, probably the king of the flock, flying so low that it only cleared the cliff edge by about twenty feet, and passed over not more than thirty yards up, an easy shot. Pereira fired, and down it came rather slowly, falling a hundred yards or so behind him, while Retief said:

"One for our side."

Pereira loaded again, and just as he had capped his rifle three more geese, also flying low, came over, preceded by a number of ducks, passing straight above us, as they must do owing to the shape of the gap between the land waves of the veld above through which they flighted. Pereira shot, and to my surprise, the second, not the first, bird fell, also a good way behind him.

"Did you shoot at that goose, or the other, nephew?" asked Retief.

"At that one for sure," he answered with a laugh.

"He lies," muttered the Hottentot; "he shot at the first and killed the second."

"Be silent," I answered. "Who would lie about such a thing?"

Again Pereira loaded. By the time that he was ready more geese were approaching, this time in a triangle of seven birds, their leader being at the point of the triangle, which was flying higher than those that had gone before. He fired, and down came not one bird, but two, namely, the captain and the goose to the right of and a little behind it.

"Ah! uncle," exclaimed Pereira, "did you see those birds cross each other as I pulled? That was a lucky one for me, but I won't count the second if the Heer Allan objects."

"No, I did not, nephew," answered Retief, "but doubtless they must have done so, or the same bullet could not have pierced both."

Both Hans and I only looked at each other and laughed. Still we said nothing.

From the spectators under the cliff there came a murmur of congratulation not unmixed with astonishment. Again Pereira loaded, aimed, and loosed at a rather high goose—it may have been about seventy yards in the air. He struck it right enough, for the feathers flew from its breast; but to my astonishment the bird, after swooping down as though it were going to fall, recovered itself and flew away straight out of sight.

"Tough birds, these geese!" exclaimed Pereira. "They can carry as much lead as a sea-cow."

"Very tough indeed," answered Retief doubtfully. "Never before did I see a bird fly away with an ounce ball through its middle."

"Oh! he will drop dead somewhere," replied Pereira as he rammed his powder down.

Within four minutes more Pereira had fired his two remaining shots, selecting, as he was entitled to do, low and easy young geese that came over him slowly. He killed them both, although the last of them, after falling, waddled along the ground into a tuft of high grass.

Now murmurs of stifled applause broke from the audience, to which Pereira bowed in acknowledgment.

"You will have to shoot very well, Mynheer Allan," said Retief to me, "if you want to beat that. Even if I rule out one of the two birds that fell to a single shot, as I think I shall, Hernan has killed five out of six, which can scarcely be bettered."

"Yes," I answered; "but, mynheer, be so good as to have those geese collected and put upon one side. I don't want them mixed up with mine, if I am lucky enough to bring any down."

He nodded, and some Kaffirs were sent to bring in the geese. Several of these, I noted, were still flapping and had to have their necks twisted, but at the time I did not go to look at them. While this was being done I called to Retief, and begged him to examine the powder and bullets I was about to use.

"What's the good?" he asked, looking at me curiously. "Powder is powder, and a bullet is a bullet."

"None, I dare say. Still, oblige me by looking at them, my uncle."

Then at my bidding Hans took six bullets and placed them in his hand, begging him to return them to us as they were wanted.

"They must be a great deal smaller than Hernan's," said Retief, "who, being stronger, uses a heavier gun."

"Yes," I answered briefly, as Hans put the charge of powder into the rifle, and drove home the wad. Then, taking a bullet from Retief's hand, he rammed that down on to the top of it, capped the gun, and handed it to me.

By now the geese were coming thick, for the flight was at its full. Only, either because some of those that had already passed had sighted the Kaffirs collecting the fallen birds and risen—an example which the others noted from afar and followed—or because in an unknown way warning of their danger had been conveyed to them, they were flying higher and faster than the first arrivals.

"You will have the worst of it, Allan," said Retief. "It should have been shot and shot about."

"Perhaps," I answered, "but that can't be helped now."

Then I rose from my stool, the rifle in my hand. I had not long to wait, for presently over came a wedge of geese nearly a hundred yards up. I aimed at the first fellow, holding about eight yards ahead of him to allow for his pace, and pressed. Next second I heard the clap of the bullet, but alas! it had only struck the outstretched beak, of which a small portion fell to the ground. The bird itself, after wavering a second, resumed its place as leader of the squad and passed away apparently unharmed.

"Baas, baas," whispered Hans as he seized the rifle and began to re-load, "you were too far in front. These big water-birds do not travel as fast as the rock pigeons."

I nodded, wishing to save my breath. Then, quivering with excitement, for if I missed the next shot the match appeared to be lost, presently I took the rifle from his hand.

Scarcely had I done so when a single goose came over quite as high as the others and travelling "as though the black devil had kicked it," as Retief said. This time I allowed the same space to compensate for the object's increased speed and pressed.

Down it came like a stone, falling but a little way behind me with its head knocked off.

"Baas, baas," whispered Hans, "still too far in front. Why aim at the eye when you have the whole body?"

Again I nodded, and at the same time heaved a sigh of relief. At least the match was still alive. Soon a large flight came over, mixed up with mallard and widgeon. I took the right-hand angle bird, so that it could not be supposed I had "browned the lot," as here in England they say of one who fires at a covey and not at a particular partridge. Down he came, shot straight through the breast. Then I knew that I had got my nerve, and felt no more fear.

To cut a long story short, although two of them were extremely difficult and high, one being, I should say, quite a hundred and twenty yards above me, and the other by no means easy, I killed the next three birds one after the other, and I verily believe could have killed a dozen more without a miss, for now I was shooting as I had never shot before.

"Say, nephew Allan," asked Retief curiously in the pause between the fifth and sixth shots, "why do your geese fall so differently to Hernan's?"

"Ask him! don't talk to me," I answered, and next instant brought down number five, the finest shot of the lot.

A sound of wonder and applause came from all the audience, and I saw Marie wave a white handkerchief.

"That's the end," said the referee.

"One minute before you stir," I answered. "I want to shoot at something else that is not in the match, just to see if I can kill two birds with one bullet like the Heer Pereira."

He granted my request with a nod, holding up his hand to prevent the audience from moving, and bidding Pereira, who tried to interrupt, to be silent.

Now, while the match was in progress I had noticed two falcons about the size of the British peregrine wheeling round and round high over the kloof, in which doubtless they bred, apparently quite undisturbed by the shooting. Or, perhaps, they had their eyes upon some of the fallen geese. I took the rifle and waited for a long while, till at last my opportunity came. I saw that the larger hen falcon was about to cross directly over the circle of its mate, there being perhaps a distance of ten yards between them. I aimed; I judged—for a second my mind was a kind of calculating machine—the different arcs and speeds of the birds must be allowed for, and the lowest was ninety yards away. Then, with something like a prayer upon my lips, I pressed while every eye stared upwards.

Down came the lower falcon; a pause of half a second, and down came the higher one also, falling dead upon its dead mate!

Now, even from those Boers, who did not love to see an Englishman excel, there broke a shout of acclamation. Never had they beheld such a shot as this; nor in truth had I.

"Mynheer Retief," I said, "I gave you notice that I intended to try to kill both of them, did I not?"

"You did. Allemachte! you did! But tell me, Allan Quatermain, are your eye and hand quite human?"

"You must ask my father," I answered with a shrug as I sat myself down upon my stool and mopped my brow.

The Boers came up with a rush, Marie flying ahead of them like a swallow, and their stout womenfolk waddling behind, and formed a circle round us, all talking at once. I did not listen to their conversation, till I heard Pereira, who was engaged in some eye-play with Marie, say in a loud voice:

"Yes, it was pretty, very pretty, but all the same, Uncle Retief, I claim the match, as I shot six geese against five."

"Hans," I said, "bring my geese," and they were brought, each with a neat hole through it, and laid down near those that Pereira had shot. "Now," I said to Retief, "examine the wounds in these birds, and then that on the second bird which the Heer Pereira killed when he brought down two at once. I think it will be found that his bullet must have splintered."

Retief went and studied all the birds, taking them up one by one. Then he threw down the last with a curse and cried in a great voice:

"Mynheer Pereira, why do you bring shame on us before these two Englishmen? I say that you have been using loopers, or else bullets that were sawn in quarters and glued or tied with thread. Look, look!" and he pointed to the wounds, of which in one case there were as many as three on a single bird.

"Why not?" answered Pereira coolly. "The bargain was that we were to use bullets, but it was never said that they should not be cut. Doubtless the Heer Allan's were treated in the same way."

"No," I answered, "when I said that I would shoot with a bullet I meant a whole bullet, not one that had been sawn in pieces and fixed together again, so that after it left the muzzle it might spread out like shot. But I do not wish to talk about the matter. It is in the hands of the Heer Pieter Retief, who will give judgment as it pleases him."

Now, much excited argument ensued among the Boers, in the midst of which Marie managed to whisper to me unheard:

"Oh! I am glad, Allan, for whatever they may decide, you won, and the omen is good."

"I don't see what geese have to do with omens, sweetheart," I answered—"that is, since the time of the ancient Romans. Anyhow, I should say that the omens are bad, for there is going to be a row presently."

Just then Retief put up his hand, calling out:

"Silence! I have decided. The writing of the match did not say that the bullets were not to be cut, and therefore Hernan Pereira's birds must count. But that writing does say that any bird accidentally killed should not count, and therefore one goose must be subtracted from Pereira's total, which leaves the two shooters equal. So either the match is dead or, since the geese have ceased to come, it must be shot off another day."

"Oh! if there is any question," said Pereira, who felt that public opinion was much against him, "let the Englishman take the money. I dare say that he needs it, as the sons of missionaries are not rich."

"There is no question," I said, "since, rich or poor, not for a thousand pounds would I shoot again against one who plays such tricks. Keep your money, Mynheer Pereira, and I will keep my mare. The umpire has said that the match is dead, so everything is finished."

"Not quite," interrupted Retief, "for I have a word to say. Friend Allan, you have played fair, and I believe that there is no one who can shoot like you in Africa."

"That is so," said the audience of Boers.

"Mynheer Pereira," went on Retief, "although you, too, are a fine shot, as is well known, I believe that had you played fair also you would have been beaten, but as it is you have saved your hundred pounds. Mynheer Pereira," he added in a great voice, "you are a cheat, who have brought disgrace upon us Boers, and for my part I never want to shake your hand again."

Now, at these outspoken words, for when his indignation was aroused Retief was no measurer of language, Pereira's high-coloured face went white as a sheet.

"Mein Gott, mynheer," he said, "I am minded to make you answer for such talk," and his hand went to the knife at his girdle.

"What!" shouted Retief, "do you want another shooting match? Well, if so I am ready with whole bullets or with split ones. None shall say that Pieter Retief was afraid of any man, and, least of all, of one who is not ashamed to try to steal a prize as a hyena steals a bone from a lion. Come on, Hernan Pereira, come on!"

Now, I am sure I cannot say what would have happened, although I am quite certain that Pereira had no stomach for a duel with the redoubtable Retief, a man whose courage was as proverbial throughout the land as was his perfect uprightness of character. At any rate, seeing that things looked very black, Henri Marais, who had been listening to this altercation with evident annoyance, stepped forward and said:

"Mynheer Retief and nephew Hernan, you are both my guests, and I will not permit quarrelling over this foolishness, especially as I am sure that Hernan never intended to cheat, but only to do what he thought was allowed. Why should he, who is one of the finest shots in the Colony, though it may be that young Allan Quatermain here is even better? Will you not say so, too, friend Retief, especially just now when it is necessary that we should all be as brothers?" he added pleadingly.

"No," thundered Retief, "I will not tell a lie to please you or anyone."

Then, seeing that the commandant was utterly uncompromising, Marais went up to his nephew and whispered to him for a while. What he said I do not know. The result of it was, however, that after favouring both Retief and myself with an angry scowl, Pereira turned and walked to where his horse stood, mounted it, and rode off, followed by two Hottentot after-riders.

That was the last I saw of Hernan Pereira for a long while to come, and heartily do I wish that it had been the last I ever saw of him. But this was not to be.

The Parting

The Boers, who ostensibly had come to the kloof to see the shooting match, although, in fact, for a very different purpose, now began to disperse. Some of them rode straight away, while some went to wagons which they had outspanned at a distance, and trekked off to their separate homes. I am glad to say that before they left quite a number of the best of them came up and congratulated me both on the defence of Maraisfontein and on my shooting. Also not a few expressed their views concerning Pereira in very straightforward language.

Now, the arrangement was that my father and I were to sleep that night at Marais's stead, returning home on the following morning. But my father, who had been a silent but not unobservant witness of all this scene, coming to the conclusion that after what had happened we should scarcely be welcome there, and that the company of Pereira was to be avoided just now, went up to Marais and bade him farewell, saying that we would send for my mare.

"Not so, not so," he answered, "you are my guests to-night. Also, fear not, Hernan will be away. He has gone a journey upon some business."

As my father hesitated, Marais added: "Friend, I pray you to come, for I have some important words to say to you, which cannot be said here."

Then my father gave way, to my delight and relief. For if he had not, what chance would there have been of my getting some still more important words with Marie? So having collected the geese and the two falcons, which I proposed to skin for Marie, I was helped into the cart, and we drove off, reaching Maraisfontein just as night set in.

That evening, after we had eaten, Heer Marais asked my father and myself to speak with him in the sitting-room. By an afterthought also, or so it seemed to me, he told his daughter, who had been clearing away the dishes and with whom as yet I had found no opportunity to talk, to come in with us and close the door behind her.

When all were seated and we men had lit our pipes, though apprehension of what was to follow quite took away my taste for smoking, Marais spoke in English, which he knew to a certain extent. This was for the benefit of my father, who made it a point of honour not to understand Dutch, although he would answer Marais in that language when _he_ pretended not to understand English. To me he spoke in Dutch, and occasionally in French to Marie. It was a most curious and polyglot conversation.

"Young Allan," he said, "and you, daughter Marie, I have heard stories concerning you that, although I never gave you leave to 'opsit'" (that is, to sit up alone at night with candles, according to the Boer fashion between those who are courting), "you have been making love to each other."

"That is true, mynheer," I said. "I only waited an opportunity to tell you that we plighted our troth during the attack of the Quabies on this house."

"Allemachte! Allan, a strange time to choose," answered Marais, pulling at his beard;" the troth that is plighted in blood is apt to end in blood."

"A vain superstition to which I cannot consent," interrupted my father.

"Perhaps so," I answered. "I know not; God alone knows. I only know that we plighted our troth when we thought ourselves about to die, and that we shall keep that troth till death ends it."

"Yes, my father," added Marie, leaning forward across the scored yellow-wood table, her chin resting on her hand and her dark, buck-like eyes looking him in the face. "Yes, my father, that is so, as I have told you already."

"And I tell you, Marie, what I have told you already, and you too, Allan, that this thing may not be," answered Marais, hitting the table with his fist. "I have nothing to say against you, Allan; indeed, I honour you, and you have done me a mighty service, but it may not be."

"Why not, mynheer?" I asked.

"For three reasons, Allan, each of which is final. You are English, and I do not wish my daughter to marry an Englishman; that is the first. You are poor, which is no discredit to you, and since I am now ruined my daughter cannot marry a poor man; that is the second. You live here, and my daughter and I are leaving this country, therefore you cannot marry her; that is the third," and he paused.

"Is there not a fourth," I asked, "which is the real reason? Namely, that you wish your daughter to marry someone else."

"Yes, Allan; since you force me to it, there is a fourth. I have affianced my daughter to her cousin, Hernando Pereira, a man of substance and full age; no lad, but one who knows his own mind and can support a wife."

"I understand," I answered calmly, although within my heart a very hell was raging. "But tell me, mynheer, has Marie affianced herself—or perhaps she will answer with her own lips?"

"Yes, Allan," replied Marie in her quiet fashion, "I have affianced myself—to you and no other man."

"You hear, mynheer," I said to Marais.

Then he broke out in his usual excitable manner. He stormed, he argued, he rated us both. He said that he would never allow it; that first he would see his daughter in her grave. That I had abused his confidence and violated his hospitality; that he would shoot me if I came near his girl. That she was a minor, and according to the law he could dispose of her in marriage. That she must accompany him whither he was going; that certainly I should not do so, and much more of the same sort.

When at last he had tired himself out and smashed his favourite pipe upon the table, Marie spoke, saying:

"My father, you know that I love you dearly, for since my mother's death we have been everything to each other, have we not?"

"Surely, Marie, you are my life, and more than my life."

"Very well, my father. That being so, I acknowledge your authority over me, whatever the law may say. I acknowledge that you have the right to forbid me to marry Allan, and if you do forbid me—while I am under age, at any rate—I shall not marry him because of my duty to you. But"—here she rose and looked him full in the eyes, and oh! how stately she seemed at that moment in her simple strength and youthful grace!—"there is one thing, my father, that I do not acknowledge—your right to force me to marry any other man. As a woman with power over herself, I deny that right; and much as it pains me, my father, to refuse you anything, I say that first I will die. To Allan here I have given myself for good or for evil, and if I may not marry Allan, I will go to the grave unwed. If my words hurt you, I pray you to pardon me, but at the same time to remember that they are my words, which cannot be altered."

Marais looked at his daughter, and his daughter looked at Marais. At first I thought that he was about to curse her; but if this were so, something in her eyes seemed to change his mind, for all he said was:

"Intractable, like the rest of your race! Well, Fate may lead those who cannot be driven, and this matter I leave in the hands of Fate. While you are under age—that is, for two years or more—you may not marry without my consent, and have just promised not to do so. Presently we trek from this country into far-off lands. Who knows what may happen there?"

"Yes," said my father in a solemn voice, speaking for the first time, "who knows except God, Who governs all things, and will settle these matters according to His will, Henri Marais? Listen," he went on after a pause, for Marais made no answer, but sat himself down and stared gloomily at the table. "You do not wish my son to marry your daughter for various reasons, of which one is that you think him poor and a richer suitor has offered himself after a reverse of fortune has made _you_ poor. Another and a greater, the true reason, is his English blood, which you hate so much that, although by God's mercy he saved her life, you do not desire that he should share her life. Is it not true?"

"Yes, it is true, Mynheer Quatermain. You English are bullies and cheats," he answered excitedly.

"And so you would give your daughter to one who has shown himself humble and upright, to that good hater of the English and plotter against his King, Hernando Pereira, whom you love because he alone is left of your ancient race."

Remembering the incident of the afternoon, this sarcasm reduced Marais to silence.

"Well," went on my father, "although I am fond of Marie, and know her to be a sweet and noble-hearted girl, neither do I wish that she should marry my son. I would see him wed to some English woman, and not dragged into the net of the Boers and their plottings. Still, it is plain that these two love each other with heart and soul, as doubtless it has been decreed that they should love. This being so, I tell you that to separate them and force another marriage upon one of them is a crime before God, of which, I am sure, He will take note and pay it back to you. Strange things may happen in those lands whither you go, Henri Marais. Will you not, then, be content to leave your child in safe keeping?"

"Never!" shouted Marais. "She shall accompany me to a new home, which is not under the shadow of your accursed British flag."

"Then I have no more to say. On your head be it here and hereafter," replied my father solemnly.

Now unable to control myself any longer I broke in:

"But I have, mynheer. To separate Marie and myself is a sin, and one that will break her heart. As for my poverty, I have something, more perhaps than you think, and in this rich country wealth can be earned by those who work, as I would do for her sake. The man to whom you would give her showed his true nature this day, for he who can play so low a trick to win a wager, will play worse tricks to win greater things. Moreover, the scheme must fail since Marie will not marry him."

"I say she shall," replied Marais; "and that whether she does or not, she shall accompany me and not stay here to be the wife of an English boy."

"Accompany you I will, father, and share your fortunes to the last. But marry Hernando Pereira I will not," said Marie quietly.

"Perhaps, mynheer," I added, "days may come when once again you will be glad of the help of an 'English boy.'"

The words were spoken at random, a kind of ejaculation from the heart, caused by the sting of Marais's cruelty and insults, like the cry of a beast beneath a blow. Little did I know how true they would prove, but at times it is thus that truth is mysteriously drawn from some well of secret knowledge hidden in our souls.

"When I want your help I will ask for it," raved Marais, who, knowing himself to be in the wrong, strove to cover up that wrong with violence.

"Asked or unasked, if I live it shall be given in the future as in the past, Mynheer Marais. God pardon you for the woe you are bringing on Marie and on me."

Now Marie began to weep a little, and, unable to bear that sight, I covered my eyes with my hand. Marais, who, when he was not under the influence of his prejudices or passion, had a kind heart, was moved also, but tried to hide his feelings in roughness. He swore at Marie, and told her to go to bed, and she obeyed, still weeping. Then my father rose and said:

"Henri Marais, we cannot leave here to-night because the horses are kraaled, and it would be difficult to find them in this darkness, so we must ask your hospitality till dawn."

"_I_ do not ask it," I exclaimed. "I go to sleep in the cart," and I limped from the room and the house, leaving the two men together.

What passed afterwards between them I do not quite know. I gathered that my father, who, when roused, also had a temper and was mentally and intellectually the stronger man, told Marais his opinion of his wickedness and folly in language that he was not likely to forget. I believe he even drove him to confess that his acts seemed cruel, excusing them, however, by announcing that he had sworn before God that his daughter should never marry an Englishman. Also he said that he had promised her solemnly to Pereira, his own nephew, whom he loved, and could not break his word.

"No," answered my father, "because, being mad with the madness that runs before destruction, you prefer to break Marie's heart and perhaps become guilty of her blood."

Then he left him.

The darkness was intense. Through it I groped my way to the cart, which stood where it had been outspanned on the veld at a little distance from the house, wishing heartily, so miserable was I, that the Kaffirs might choose that black night for another attack and make an end of me.

When I reached it and lit the lantern which we always carried, I was astonished to find that, in a rough fashion, it had been made ready to sleep in. The seats had been cleared out, the hind curtain fastened, and so forth. Also the pole was propped up with an ox-yoke so as to make the vehicle level to lie in. While I was wondering vaguely who could have done this, Hans climbed on to the step, carrying two karosses which he had borrowed or stolen, and asked if I was comfortable.

"Oh, yes!" I answered; "but why were you going to sleep in the cart?"

"Baas," he replied, "I was not; I prepared it for you. How did I know that you were coming? Oh, very simply. I sat on the stoep and listened to all the talk in the sitkammer. The window has never been mended, baas, since the Quabies broke it. God in Heaven! what a talk that was. I never knew that white people could have so much to say about a simple matter. You want to marry the Baas Marais's daughter; the baas wants her to marry another man who can pay more cattle. Well, among us it would soon have been settled, for the father would have taken a stick and beaten you out of the hut with the thick end. Then he would have beaten the girl with the thin end until she promised to take the other man, and all would have been settled nicely. But you Whites, you talk and talk, and nothing is settled. You still mean to marry the daughter, and the daughter still means not to marry the man of many cows. Moreover, the father has really gained nothing except a sick heart and much bad luck to come."

"Why much bad luck to come, Hans?" I asked idly, for his naive summing up of the case interested me in a vague way.

"Oh! Baas Allan, for two reasons. First, your reverend father, who made me true Christian, told him so, and a predicant so good as he, is one down whom the curse of God runs from Heaven like lightning runs down a tree. Well, the Heer Marais was sitting under that tree, and we all know what happens to him who is under a tree when the lightning strikes it. That my first Christian reason. My second black-man reason, about which there can be no mistake, for it has always been true since there was a black man, is that the girl is yours by blood. You saved her life with your blood," and he pointed to my leg, "and therefore bought her for ever, for blood is more than cattle. Therefore, too, he who would divide her from you brings blood on her and on the other man who tries to steal her, blood, blood! and on himself I know not what." And he waved his yellow arms, staring up at me with his little black eyes in a way that was most uncanny.

"Nonsense!" I said. "Why do you talk such bad words?"

"Because they are true words, Baas Allan. Oh, you laugh at the poor Totty; but I had it from my father, and he from his father from generation to generation, amen, and you will see. You will see, as I have seen before now, and as the Heer Marais will see, who, if the great God had not made him mad—for mad he is, baas, as we know, if you Whites don't—might have lived in his home till he was old, and have had a good son-in-law to bury him in his blanket."

Now I seemed to have had enough of this eerie conversation. Of course it is easy to laugh at natives and their superstitions, but, after a long life of experience, I am bound to admit that they are not always devoid of truth. The native has some kind of sixth sense which the civilised man has lost, or so it seems to me.

"Talking of blankets," I said in order to change the subject, "from whom did you get these karosses?"

"From whom? Why, from the Missie, of course, baas. When I heard that you were to sleep in the cart I went to her and borrowed them to cover you. Also, I had forgotten, she gave me a writing for you," and he felt about, first in his dirty shirt, then under his arm, and finally in his fuzzy hair, from which last hiding place he produced a little bit of paper folded into a pellet. I undid it and read these words, written with a pencil and in French:—

"I shall be in the peach orchard half an hour before sunrise. Be there if you would bid me farewell.—M."

"Is there any answer, baas?" asked Hans when I had thrust the note into my pocket. "If so I can take it without being found out." Then an inspiration seemed to strike him, and he added: "Why do you not take it yourself? The Missie's window is easy to open, also I am sure she would be pleased to see you."

"Be silent," I said. "I am going to sleep. Wake me an hour before the cock-crow—and, stay—see that the horses have got out of the kraal so that you cannot find them too easily in case the Reverend wishes to start very early. But do not let them wander far, for here we are no welcome guests."

"Yes, baas. By the way, baas, the Heer Pereira, who tried to cheat you over those geese, is sleeping in an empty house not more than two miles away. He drinks coffee when he wakes up in the morning, and his servant, who makes it, is my good friend. Now would you like me to put a little something into it? Not to kill him, for that is against the law in the Book, but just to make him quite mad, for the Book says nothing about that. If so, I have a very good medicine, one that you white people do not know, which improves the taste of the coffee, and it might save much trouble. You see, if he came dancing about the place without any clothes on, like a common Kaffir, the Heer Marais, although _he_ is really mad also, might not wish for him as a son-in-law."

"Oh! go to the devil if you are not there already," I replied, and turned over as though to sleep.

There was no need for me to have instructed that faithful creature, the astute but immoral Hans, to call me early, as the lady did her mother in the poem, for I do not think that I closed an eye that night. I spare my reflections, for they can easily be imagined in the case of an earnest-natured lad who was about to be bereft of his first love.

Long before the dawn I stood in the peach orchard, that orchard where we had first met, and waited. At length Marie came stealing between the tree trunks like a grey ghost, for she was wrapped in some light-coloured garment. Oh! once more we were alone together. Alone in the utter solitude and silence which precede the African dawn, when all creatures that love the night have withdrawn to their lairs and hiding places, and those that love the day still sleep their soundest.

She saw me and stood still, then opened her arms and clasped me to her breast, uttering no word. A while later she spoke almost in a whisper, saying:

"Allan, I must not stay long, for I think that if my father found us together, he would shoot you in his madness."

Now as always it was of me she thought, not of herself.

"And you, my sweet?" I asked.

"Oh!" she answered, "that matters nothing. Except for the sin of it I wish he would shoot me, for then I should have done with all this pain. I told you, Allan, when the Kaffirs were on us yonder, that it might be better to die; and see, my heart spoke truly."

"Is there no hope?" I gasped. "Will he really separate us and take you away into the wilderness?"

"Certainly, nothing can turn him. Yet, Allan, there is this hope. In two years, if I live, I shall be of full age, and can marry whom I will; and this I swear, that I will marry none but you, no, not even if you were to die to-morrow."

"I bless you for those words," I said.

"Why?" she asked simply. "What others could I speak? Would you have me do outrage to my own heart and go through life faithless and ashamed?"

"And I, I swear also," I broke in.

"Nay, swear nothing. While I live I know that you will love me, and if I should be taken, it is my wish that you should marry some other good woman, since it is not well or right that man should live alone. With us maids it is different. Listen, Allan, for the cocks are beginning to crow, and soon there will be light. You must bide here with your father. If possible, I will write to you from time to time, telling you where we are and how we fare. But if I do not write, know that it is because I cannot, or because I can find no messenger, or because the letters have miscarried, for we go into wild countries, amongst savages."

"Whither do you go?" I asked.

"I believe up towards the great harbour called Delagoa Bay, where the Portuguese rule. My cousin Hernan, who accompanies us"—and she shivered a little in my arms—"is half Portuguese. He tells the Boers that he has relations there who have written him many fine promises, saying they will give us good country to dwell in where we cannot be followed by the English, whom he and my father hate so much."

"I have heard that is all fever veld, and that the country between is full of fierce Kaffirs," I said with a groan.

"Perhaps. I do not know, and I do not care. At least, that is the notion in my father's head, though, of course, circumstances may change it. I will try to let you know, Allan, or if I do not, perhaps you will be able to find out for yourself. Then,

then, if we both live and you still care for me, who will always care for you, when I am of age, you will join us and, say and do what they may, I will marry no other man. And if I die, as may well happen, oh! then my spirit shall watch over you and wait for you till you join me beneath the wings of God. Look, it grows light. I must go. Farewell, my love, my first and only love, till in life or death we meet again, as meet we shall."

Once more we clung together and kissed, muttering broken words, and then she tore herself from my embrace and was gone. But oh! as I heard her feet steal through the dew-laden grass, I felt as though my heart were being rent from my breast. I have suffered much in life, but I do not think that ever I underwent a bitterer anguish than in this hour of my parting from Marie. For when all is said and done, what joy is there like the joy of pure, first love, and what bitterness like the bitterness of its loss?

Half an hour later the flowering trees of Maraisfontein were behind us, while in front rolled the fire-swept veld, black as life had become for me.

Allan's Call

A fortnight later Marais, Pereira and their companions, a little band in all of about twenty men, thirty women and children, and say fifty half-breeds and Hottentot after-riders, trekked from their homes into the wilderness. I rode to the crest of a table-topped hill and watched the long line of wagons, one of them containing Marie, crawl away northward across the veld a mile or more beneath.

Sorely was I tempted to gallop after them and seek a last interview with her and her father. But my pride forbade me. Henri Marais had given out that if I came near his daughter he would have me beaten back with "sjambocks" or hide whips. Perhaps he had gained some inkling of our last farewell in the peach orchard. I do not know. But I do know that if anyone had lifted a sjambock on me I should have answered with a bullet. Then there would have been blood between us, which is worse to cross than whole rivers of wrath and jealousy. So I just watched the wagons until they vanished, and galloped home down the rock-strewn slope, wishing that the horse would stumble and break my neck.

When I reached the station, however, I was glad that it had not done so, as I found my father sitting on the stoep reading a letter that had been brought by a mounted Hottentot.

It was from Henri Marais, and ran thus:—

"REVEREND HEER AND FRIEND QUATERMAIN,—I send this to bid you farewell, for although you are English and we have quarrelled at times, I honour you in my heart. Friend, now that we are starting, your warning words lie on me like lead, I know not why. But what is done cannot be undone, and I trust that all will come right. If not, it is because the Good Lord wills it otherwise."

Here my father looked up and said: "When men suffer from their own passion and folly, they always lay the blame on the back of Providence."

Then he went on, spelling out the letter:

"'I fear your boy Allan, who is a brave lad, as I have reason to know, and honest, must think that I have treated him harshly and without gratitude. But I have only done what I must do. True, Marie, who, like her mother, is very strong and stubborn in mind, swears that she will marry no one else; but soon Nature will make her forget all that, especially as such a fine husband waits for her hand. So bid Allan forget all about her also, and when he is old enough choose some English girl. I have sworn a great oath before my God that he shall never marry my daughter with my consent.

"Friend, I write to ask you something because I trust you more than these slim agents. Half the price, a very poor one, that I have for my farm is still unpaid to me by Jacobus van der Merve, who remains behind and buys up all our lands. It is £100 English, due this day year, and I enclose you power of attorney to receive and give receipt for the same. Also there is due to me from your British Government £253 on account of slaves liberated which were worth quite £1,000. This also the paper gives you authority to receive. As regards my claims against the said cursed Government because of the loss brought on me by the Quabie Kaffirs, it will not acknowledge them, saying that the attack was caused by the Frenchman Leblanc, one of my household.'"

"And with good reason," commented my father.

"'When you have received these monies, if ever, I pray you take some safe opportunity of sending them to me, wherever I may be, which doubtless you will hear in due course, although by that time I hope to be rich again and not to need money.

Farewell and God be with you, as I hope He will be with me and Marie and the rest of us trek-Boers. The bearer will overtake us with your answer at our first outspan.

"HENRI MARAIS."

"Well," said my father with a sigh, "I suppose I must accept his trust, though why he should choose an 'accursed Englishman' with whom he has quarrelled violently to collect his debts instead of one of his own beloved Boers, I am sure I do not know. I will go and write to him. Allan, see that the messenger and his horse get something to eat."

I nodded and went to the man, who was one of those that had defended Maraisfontein with me, a good fellow unless he got near liquor.

"Heer Allan," he said, looking round to see that we were not overheard, "I have a little writing for you also," and be produced from his pouch a note that was unaddressed.

I tore it open eagerly. Within was written in French, which no Boer would understand if the letter fell into his hands:

"Be brave and faithful, and remember, as I shall. Oh! love of my heart, adieu, adieu!"

This message was unsigned; but what need was there of signature?

I wrote an answer of a sort that may be imagined, though what the exact words were I cannot remember after the lapse of nearly half a century. Oddly enough, it is the things I said which I recall at such a distance of time rather than the things which I wrote, perhaps because, when once written, my mind being delivered, troubled itself with them no more. So in due course the Hottentot departed with my father's letter and my own, and that was the last direct communication which we had with Henri or Marie Marais for more than a year.

I think that those long months were on the whole the most wretched I have ever spent. The time of life which I was passing through is always trying; that period of emergence from youth into full and responsible manhood which in Africa generally takes place earlier than it does here in England, where young men often seem to me to remain boys up to five-and-twenty. The circumstances which I have detailed made it particularly so in my own case, for here was I, who should have been but a cheerful lad, oppressed with the sorrows and anxieties, and fettered by the affections of maturity.

I could not get Marie out of my mind; her image was with me by day and by night, especially by night, which caused me to sleep badly. I became morose, supersensitive, and excitable. I developed a cough, and thought, as did others, that I was going into a decline. I remember that Hans even asked me once if I would not come and peg out the exact place where I should like to be buried, so that I might be sure that there would be no mistake made when I could no longer speak for myself. On that occasion I kicked Hans, one of the few upon which I have ever touched a native. The truth was that I had not the slightest intention of being buried. I wanted to live and marry Marie, not to die and be put in a hole by Hans. Only I saw no prospect of marrying Marie, or even of seeing her again, and that was why I felt low-spirited.

Of course, from time to time news of the trek-Boers reached us, but it was extremely confused. There were so many parties of them; their adventures were so difficult to follow, and, I may add, often so terrible; so few of them could write; trustworthy messengers were so scanty; distances were so great. At any rate, we heard nothing of Marais's band except a rumour that they had trekked to a district in what is now the Transvaal, which is called Rustenberg, and thence on towards Delagoa Bay into an unknown veld where they had vanished. From Marie herself no letter came, which showed me clearly enough that she had not found an opportunity of sending one.

Observing my depressed condition, my father suggested as a remedy that I should go to the theological college at Cape Town and prepare myself for ordination. But the Church as a career did not appeal to me, perhaps because I felt that I could never be sufficiently good; perhaps because I knew that as a clergyman I should find no opportunity of travelling north when my call came. For I always believed that this call would come.

My father, who wished that I should hear another kind of call, was vexed with me over this matter. He desired earnestly that I should follow the profession which he adorned, and indeed saw no other open for me any more than I did myself. Of course he was right in a way, seeing that in the end I found none, unless big game hunting and Kaffir trading can be called a profession. I don't know, I am sure. Still, poor business as it may be, I say now when I am getting towards the end of life that I am glad I did not follow any other. It has suited me; that was the insignificant hole in the world's affairs which I was destined to fit, whose only gifts were a remarkable art of straight shooting and the more common one of observation mixed with a little untrained philosophy.

So hot did our arguments become about this subject of the Church, for, as may be imagined, in the course of them I revealed some unorthodoxy, especially as regards the matter of our methods of Christianising Kaffirs, that I was extremely thankful when a diversion occurred which took me away from home. The story of my defence of Maraisfontein had spread far, and that of my feats of shooting, especially in the Goose Kloof, still farther. So the end of it was that those in authority commandeered me to serve in one of the continual Kaffir frontier wars which was in progress, and instantly gave me a commission as a kind of lieutenant in a border corps.

Now the events of that particular war have nothing to do with the history that I am telling, so I do not propose even to touch on them. I served in it for a year, meeting with many adventures, one or two successes, and several failures. Once I was wounded slightly, twice I but just escaped with my life. Once I was reprimanded for taking a foolish risk and losing some men. Twice I was commended for what were called gallant actions, such as bringing a wounded comrade out of danger under a warm fire, mostly of assegais, and penetrating by night, almost alone, into the stronghold of a chieftain, and shooting him.

At length that war was patched up with an inconclusive peace and my corps was disbanded. I returned home, no longer a lad, but a man with experience of various kinds and a rather unique knowledge of Kaffirs, their languages, history, and modes of thought and action. Also I had associated a good deal with British officers, and from them acquired much that I had found no opportunity of studying before, especially, I hope, the ideas and standards of English gentlemen.

I had not been back at the Mission Station more than three weeks, quite long enough for me to begin to be bored with idleness and inactivity, when that call for which I had been waiting came at last.

One day a "smous", that is a low kind of white man, often a Jew, who travels about trading with unsophisticated Boers and Kaffirs, and cheating them if he can, called at the station with his cartful of goods. I was about to send him away, having no liking for such gentry, when he asked me if I were named Allan Quatermain. I said "Yes," whereon he replied that he had a letter for me, and produced a packet wrapped up in sail-cloth. I asked him whence he had it, and he answered from a man whom he had met at Port Elizabeth, an east coast trader, who, hearing that he was coming into the Cradock district, entrusted him with the letter. The man told him that it was very important, and that I should reward the bearer well if it were delivered safely.

While the Jew talked (I think he was a Jew) I was opening the sail-cloth. Within was a piece of linen which had been oiled to keep out water, addressed in some red pigment to myself or my father. This, too, I opened, not without difficulty, for it was carefully sewn up, and found within it a letter-packet, also addressed to myself or my father, in the handwriting of Marie.

Great Heaven! How my heart jumped at that sight! Calling to Hans to make the smous comfortable and give him food, I went into my own room, and there read the letter, which ran thus:

"MY DEAR ALLAN,—I do not know whether the other letters I have written to you have ever come to your hands, or indeed if this one will. Still, I send it on chance by a wandering Portuguese half-breed who is going to Delagoa Bay, about fifty miles, I believe, from the place where I now write, near the Crocodile River. My father has named it Maraisfontein, after our old home. If those letters reached you, you will have learned of the terrible things we went through on our journey; the attacks by the Kaffirs in the Zoutpansberg region, who destroyed one of our parties altogether, and so forth. If not, all that story must wait, for it is too long to tell now, and, indeed, I have but little paper, and not much pencil. It will be enough to say, therefore, that to the number of thirty-five white people, men, women and children, we trekked at the beginning of the summer season, when the grass was commencing to grow, from the Lydenburg district—an awful journey over mountains and through flooded rivers. After many delays, some of them months long, we reached this place, about eight weeks ago, for I write to you at the beginning of June, if we have kept correct account of the time, of which I am not certain.

"It is a beautiful place to look at, a flat country of rich veld, with big trees growing on it, and about two miles from the great river that is called the Crocodile. Here, finding good water, my father and Hernan Pereira, who now rules him in all things, determined to settle, although some of the others wished to push on nearer to Delagoa Bay. There was a great quarrel about it, but in the end my father, or rather Hernan, had his will, as the oxen were worn out and many had already died from the bites of a poisonous fly which is called the tsetse. So we lotted out the land, of which there is enough for hundreds, and began to build rude houses.

"Then trouble came upon us. The Kaffirs stole most of our horses, although they have not dared to attack us, and except two belonging to Hernan, the rest died of the sickness, the last of them but yesterday. The oxen, too, have all died of the tsetse bites or other illnesses. But the worst is that although this country looks so healthy, it is poisoned with fever, which comes up, I think, in the mists from the river. Already out of the thirty-five of us, ten are dead, two men, three women, and five children, while more are sick. As yet my father and I and my cousin Pereira have, by God's mercy, kept quite well; but although we are all very strong, how long this will continue I cannot tell. Fortunately we have plenty of ammunition and the place is thick with game, so that those of the men who remain strong can kill all the food we want, even shooting on foot, and we women have made a great quantity of biltong by salting flesh and drying it in the sun. So we shall not actually starve for a long while, even if the game goes away.

"But, dear Allan, unless help comes to us I think that we shall die every one, for God alone knows the miseries that we suffer and the horrible sights of sickness and death that are around us. At this moment there lies by me a little girl who is dying of fever.

"Oh, Allan, if you can help us, do so! Because of our sick it is impossible for us to get to Delagoa Bay, and if we did we have no money to buy anything there, for all that we had with us was lost in a wagon in a flooded river. It was a great sum, for it included Hernan's rich fortune which he brought from the Cape with him in gold. Nor can we move anywhere else, for we have no cattle or horses. We have sent to Delagoa Bay, where we hear these are to be had, to try to buy them on credit; but my cousin Hernan's relations, of whom he used to talk so much, are dead or gone away, and no one will trust us. With the neighbouring Kaffirs, too, who have plenty of cattle, we have quarrelled since, unfortunately, my cousin and some of the other Boers tried to take certain beasts of theirs without payment. So we are quite helpless, and can only wait for death.

"Allan, my father says that he asked your father to collect some monies that were owing to him. If it were possible for you or other friends to come to Delagoa in a ship with that money, I think that it might serve to buy some oxen, enough for a few wagons. Then perhaps we might trek back and fall in with a party of Boers who, we believe, have crossed the Quathlamba Mountains into Natal. Or perhaps we might get to the Bay and find a ship to take us anywhere from this horrible place. If you could come, the natives would guide you to where we are.

"But it is too much to hope that you will come, or that if you do come you will find us still alive.

"Allan, my dearest, I have one more thing to say, though I must say it shortly, for the paper is nearly finished. I do not know, supposing that you are alive and well, whether you still care for me, who left you so long ago—it seems years and years—but _my_ heart is where it was, and where I promised it should remain, in your keeping. Of course, Hernan has pressed me to marry him, and my father has wished it. But I have always said no, and now, in our wretchedness, there is no more talk of marriage at present, which is the one good thing that has happened to me. And, Allan, before so very long I shall be of age, if I live. Still I dare say you no longer think of marriage with me, who, perhaps, are already married to someone else, especially as now I and all of us are no better than wandering beggars. Yet I have thought it right to tell you these things, which you may like to know.

"Oh, why did God ever put it into my father's heart to leave the Cape Colony just because he hated the British Government and Hernan Pereira and others persuaded him? I know not, but, poor man, he is sorry enough now. It is pitiful to see him; at times I think that he is going mad.

"The paper is done, and the messenger is going; also the sick child is dying and I must attend to her. Will this letter ever come to your hands, I wonder? I am sending with it the little money I have to pay for its delivery—about four pounds English. If not, there is an end. If it does, and you cannot come or send others, at least pray for us. I dream of you by night and think of you by day, for how much I love you I cannot tell.

"In life or death I am

"Your MARIE."

Such was this awful letter. I still have it; it lies before me, those ragged sheets of paper covered with faint pencil-writing that is blotted here and there with tear marks, some of them the tears of Marie who wrote, some of them the tears of me who read. I wonder if there exists a more piteous memorial of the terrible sufferings of the trek-Boers, and especially of such of them as forced their way into the poisonous veld around Delagoa, as did this Marais expedition and those under the command of Triechard. Better, like many of their people, to have perished at once by the spears of Umzilikazi and other savages than to endure these lingering tortures of fever and starvation.

As I finished reading this letter my father, who had been out visiting some of his Mission Kaffirs, entered the house, and I went into the sitting-room to meet him.

"Why, Allan, what is the matter with you?" he asked, noting my tear-stained face.

I gave him the letter, for I could not speak, and with difficulty he deciphered it.

"Merciful God, what dreadful news!" he said when he had finished. "Those poor people! those poor, misguided people! What can be done for them?"

"I know one thing that can be done, father, or at any rate can be attempted. I can try to reach them."

"Are you mad?" he asked. "How is it possible for you, one man, to get to Delagoa Bay, buy cattle, and rescue these folk, who probably are now all dead?"

"The first two things are possible enough, father. Some ship will take me to the Bay. You have Marais's money, and I have that five hundred pounds which my old aunt in England left me last year. Thank Heaven! owing to my absence on commando, it still lies untouched in the bank at Port Elizabeth. That is about eight hundred pounds in all, which would buy a great many cattle and other things. As for the third, it is not in our hands, is it? It may be that they cannot be rescued, it may be that they are dead. I can only go to see."

"But, Allan, Allan, you are my only son, and if you go it is probable that I shall never see you more."

"I have been through more dangers lately, father, and am still alive and well. Moreover, if Marie is dead"—I paused, then went on passionately—"Do not try to stop me, for I tell you, father, I will not be stopped. Think of the words in that letter and what a shameless hound I should be if I sat here quiet while Marie is dying yonder. Would you have done so if Marie had been my mother?"

"No," answered the old gentleman, "I should not. Go, and God be with you, Allan, and me also, for I never expect to see you again." And he turned his head aside for a while.

Then we went into matters. The smous was summoned and asked about the ship which brought the letter from Delagoa. It seemed that she was an English-owned brig known as the Seven Stars, and that her captain, one Richardson, proposed to sail back to the Bay on the morrow, that was the third of July, or in other words, within twenty-four hours.

Twenty-four hours! And Port Elizabeth was one hundred and eighteen miles away, and the Seven Stars might leave earlier if she had completed her cargo and wind and weather served. Moreover, if she did leave, it might be weeks or months before any other ship sailed for Delagoa Bay, for in those days, of course, there were no mail boats.

I looked at my watch. It was four o'clock in the afternoon, and from a calendar we had, which gave the tides at Port Elizabeth and other South African harbours, it did not seem probable that the Seven Stars would sail, if she kept to her date, before about eight on the morrow. One hundred and twenty miles to be covered in, say, fourteen hours over rough country with some hills! Well, on the other hand, the roads were fairly good and dry, with no flooded rivers to cross, although there might be one to swim, and there was a full moon. It could be done—barely, and now I was glad indeed that Hernan Pereira had not won my swift mare in that shooting match.

I called to Hans, who was loafing about outside, and said quietly:

"I ride to Port Elizabeth, and must be there by eight o'clock to-morrow morning."

"Allemachte!" exclaimed Hans, who had been that road several times.

"You will go with me, and from Port Elizabeth on to Delagoa Bay. Saddle the mare and the roan horse, and put a headstall on the chestnut to lead with you as a spare. Give them all a feed, but no water. We start in half an hour." Then I added certain directions as to the guns we would take, saddle-bags, clothes, blankets and other details, and bade him start about the business.

Hans never hesitated. He had been with me through my recent campaign, and was accustomed to sudden orders. Moreover, I think that if I had told him I was riding to the moon, beyond his customary exclamation of "Allemachte!" he would have made no objection to accompanying me thither.

The next half-hour was a busy time for me. Henri Marais's money had to be got out of the strong box and arranged in a belt of buck's hide that I had strapped about me. A letter had to be written by my father to the manager of the Port Elizabeth bank, identifying me as the owner of the sum lodged there in my name. A meal must be eaten and some food prepared for us to carry. The horses' shoes had to be seen to, and a few clothes packed in the saddle-bags. Also there were other things which I have forgotten. Yet within five-and-thirty minutes the long, lean mare stood before the door. Behind her, with a tall crane's feather in his hat, was Hans, mounted on the roan stallion, and leading the chestnut, a four-year-old which I had bought as a foal on the mare as part of the bargain. Having been corn fed from a colt it was a very sound and well-grown horse, though not the equal of its mother in speed.

In the passage my poor old father, who was quite bewildered by the rapidity and urgent nature of this business, embraced me.

"God bless you, my dear boy," he said. "I have had little time to think, but I pray that this may be all for the best, and that we may meet again in the world. But if not, remember what I have taught you, and if I survive you, for my part I shall remember that you died trying to do your duty. Oh, what trouble has the blind madness of Henri Marais brought upon us all! Well, I warned him that it would be so. Good-bye, my dear boy, good-bye: my prayers will follow you, and for the rest— Well, I am old, and what does it matter if my grey hairs come with sorrow to the grave?"

I kissed him back, and with an aching heart sprang to the saddle. In five more minutes the station was out of sight.

Thirteen and a half hours later I pulled rein upon the quay of Port Elizabeth just, only just, in time to catch Captain Richardson as he was entering his boat to row out to the Seven Stars, on which the canvas was already being hoisted. As well as I could in my exhausted state, I explained matters and persuaded him to wait till the next tide. Then, thanking God for the mare's speed—the roan had been left foundered thirty miles away, and Hans was following on the chestnut, but not yet up—I dragged the poor beast to an inn at hand. There she lay down and died. Well, she had done her work, and there was no other horse in the country that could have caught that boat.

An hour or so later Hans came in flogging the chestnut, and here I may add that both it and the roan recovered. Indeed I rode them for many years, until they were quite old. When I had eaten, or tried to eat something and rested awhile, I went to the bank, succeeded in explaining the state of the case to the manager, and after some difficulty, for gold was not very plentiful in Port Elizabeth, procured three hundred pounds in sovereigns. For the other two he gave me a bill upon some agent in Delagoa Bay, together with a letter of recommendation to him and the Portuguese governor, who, it appeared, was in debt to their establishment. By an afterthought, however, although I kept the letters, I returned him the bill and spent the £200 in purchasing a great variety of goods which I will not enumerate, that I knew would be useful for trading purposes among the east coast Kaffirs. Indeed, I practically cleared out the Port Elizabeth stores, and barely had time, with the help of Hans and the storekeepers, to pack and ship the goods before the Seven Stars put out to sea.

Within twenty-four hours from the time I had left the Mission Station, Hans and I saw behind us Port Elizabeth fading into the distance, and in front a waste of stormy waters.

The Camp of Death

Everything went well upon that voyage, except with me personally. Not having been on the ocean since I was a child, I, who am naturally no good sailor, was extremely ill as day by day we ploughed through seas that grew ever more rough. Also, strong as I was, that fearful ride had overdone me. Added to these physical discomforts was my agonising anxiety of mind, which I leave anyone with imagination to picture for himself. Really there were times when I wished that the Seven Stars would plunge headlong to the bottom of the deep and put an end to me and my miseries.

These, however, so far as the bodily side of them was concerned, were, I think, surpassed by those of my henchman Hans, who, as a matter of fact, had never before set foot in any kind of boat. Perhaps this was fortunate, since had he known the horrors of the ocean, much as he loved me, he would, I am sure, by one means or another, have left me to voyage in the Seven Stars alone. There he lay upon the floor of my little cabin, rolling to and fro with the violent motion of the brig, overcome with terror. He was convinced that we were going to be drowned, and in the intervals of furious sea-sickness uttered piteous lamentations in Dutch, English, and various native tongues, mingled with curses and prayers of the most primitive and realistic order.

After the first twenty-four hours or so he informed me with many moans that the last bit of his inside had just come out of him, and that he was now quite hollow "like a gourd." Also he declared that all these evils had fallen upon him because he had been fool enough to forsake the religion of his people (what was that, I wonder), and allow himself to be "washed white," that is, be baptised, by my father.

I answered that as he had become white instead of staying yellow, I advised him to remain so, since it was evident that the Hottentot gods would have nothing more to do with one who had deserted them. Thereon he made a dreadful face, which even in the midst of my own woes caused me to laugh at him, uttered a prolonged groan, and became so silent that I thought he must be dead. However, the sailor who brought me my food—such food!—assured me that this was not so, and lashed him tight to the legs of the bunk by his arm and ankle so as to prevent him from being rolled to bits.

Next morning Hans was dosed with brandy, which, in his empty condition, made him extremely drunk, and from that time forward began to take a more cheerful view of things. Especially was this so when the hours for the "brandy medicine" came round. Hans, like most other Hottentots, loved spirits, and would put up with much to get them, even with my father's fiery indignation.

I think it was on the fourth day that at length we pitched and rolled ourselves over the shallow bar of Port Natal and found ourselves at peace for a while under shelter of the Point in the beautiful bay upon the shores of which the town of Durban now stands. Then it was but a miserable place, consisting of a few shanties which were afterwards burnt by the Zulus, and a number of Kaffir huts. For such white men as dwelt there had for the most part native followings, and, I may add, native wives.

We spent two days at this settlement of Durban, where Captain Richardson had some cargo to land for the English settlers, one or two of whom had started a trade with the natives and with parties of the emigrant Boers who were beginning to enter the territory by the overland route. Those days I passed on shore, though I would not allow Hans to accompany me lest he should desert, employing my time in picking up all the information I could about the state of affairs, especially with reference to the Zulus, a people with whom I was destined ere long to make an intimate acquaintance. Needless to say, I inquired both from natives and from white men whether anything was known of the fate of Marais's party, but no one seemed even to have heard of them. One thing I did learn, however, that my old friend, Pieter Retief, with a large following, had crossed the Quathlamba Mountains, which we now know as the Drakensberg, and entered the territory of Natal. Here they proposed to settle if they could get the leave of the Zulu king, Dingaan, a savage potentate of whom and of whose armies everyone seemed to live in terror.

On the third morning, to my great relief, for I was terrified lest we should be delayed, the Seven Stars sailed with a favouring wind. Three days later we entered the harbour of Delagoa, a sheet of water many miles long and broad. Notwithstanding its shallow entrance, it is the best natural port in Southeastern Africa, but now, alas! lost to the English.

Six hours later we anchored opposite a sandbank on which stood a dilapidated fort and a dirty settlement known as Lorenzo Marquez, where the Portuguese kept a few soldiers, most of them coloured. I pass over my troubles with the Customs, if such they could be called. Suffice it to say that ultimately I succeeded in landing my goods, on which the duty chargeable was apparently enormous. This I did by distributing twenty-five English sovereigns among various officials, beginning with the acting-governor and ending with a drunken black sweep who sat in a kind of sentry box on the quay.

Early next morning the Seven Stars sailed again, because of some quarrel with the officials, who threatened to seize her—I forget why. Her destination was the East African ports and, I think, Madagascar, where a profitable trade was to be done in carrying cattle and slaves. Captain Richardson said he might be back at Lorenzo Marquez in two or three months' time, or he might not. As a matter of fact the latter supposition proved correct, for the Seven Stars was lost on a sandbank somewhere up the coast, her crew only escaping to Mombasa after enduring great hardships.

Well, she had served my turn, for I heard afterwards that no other ship put into the Bay for a whole year from the date she left it. So if I had not caught her at Port Elizabeth I could not have come at all, except, of course, overland. This at best must have taken many months, and was moreover a journey that no man could enter on alone.

Now I get back to my story again.

There was no inn at Lorenzo Marquez. Through the kindness of one of his native or half-breed wives, who could talk a little Dutch, I managed, however, to get a lodging in a tumble-down house belonging to a dissolute person who called himself Don Jose Ximenes, but who was really himself a half-breed. Here good fortune befriended me. Don Jose, when sober, was a trader with the natives, and a year before had acquired from them two good buck wagons. Probably they were stolen from some wandering Boers or found derelict after their murder or death by fever. These wagons he was only too glad to sell for a song. I think I gave him twenty pounds English for the two, and thirty more for twelve oxen that he had bought at the same time as the wagons. They were fine beasts of the Afrikander breed, that after a long rest had grown quite fat and strong.

Of course twelve oxen were not enough to draw two wagons, or even one. Therefore, hearing that there were natives on the mainland who possessed plenty of cattle, I at once gave out that I was ready to buy, and pay well in blankets, cloth, beads and so forth. The result was that within two days I had forty or fifty to choose from, small animals of the Zulu character and, I should add, unbroken. Still they were sturdy and used to that veld and its diseases. Here it was that my twelve trained beasts came in. By putting six of them to each wagon, two as fore- and two as after-oxen, and two in the middle, Hans and I were able to get the other ten necessary to make up a team of sixteen under some sort of control.

Heavens! how we worked during the week or so which went by before it was possible for me to leave Lorenzo Marquez. What with mending up and loading the wagons, buying and breaking in the wild oxen, purchasing provisions, hiring native servants—of whom I was lucky enough to secure eight who belonged to one of the Zulu tribes and desired to get back to their own country, whence they had wandered with some Boers, I do not think that we slept more than two or three hours out of the twenty-four.

But, it may be asked, what was my aim, whither went I, what inquiries had I made? To answer the last question first, I had made every possible inquiry, but with little or no result. Marie's letter had said that they were encamped on the bank of the Crocodile River, about fifty miles from Delagoa Bay. I asked everyone I met among the Portuguese—who, after all, were not many—if they had heard of such an encampment of emigrant Boers. But these Portuguese appeared to have heard nothing, except my host, Don Jose, who had a vague recollection of something—he could not remember what.

The fact was at this time the few people who lived at Lorenzo Marquez were too sodden with liquor and other vices to take any interest in outside news that did not immediately concern them. Moreover, the natives whom they flogged and oppressed if they were their servants, or fought with if they were not, told them little, and almost nothing that was true, for between the two races there was an hereditary hate stretching back for generations. So from the Portuguese I gained no information.

Then I turned to the Kaffirs, especially to those from whom I had bought the cattle. _They_ had heard that some Boers reached the banks of the Crocodile moons ago—how many they could not tell. But that country, they said, was under the rule of a chief who was hostile to them, and killed any of their people who ventured thither. Therefore they knew nothing for certain. Still, one of them stated that a woman whom he had bought as a slave, and who had passed through the district in question a few weeks before, told him that someone had told her that these Boers were all dead of sickness. She added that she had seen their wagon caps from a distance, so, if they were dead, "their wagons were still alive."

I asked to see this woman, but the native refused to produce her. After a great deal of talk, however, he offered to sell her to me, saying that he was tired of her. So I bargained with the man and finally agreed for her purchase for three pounds of copper wire and eight yards of blue cloth. Next morning she was produced, an extremely ugly person with a large, flat nose, who came from somewhere in the interior of Africa, having, I gathered, been taken captive by Arabs and sold from hand to hand. Her name, as near as I can pronounce it, was Jeel.

I had great difficulty in establishing communication with her, but ultimately found that one of my newly hired Kaffirs could understand something of her language. Even then it was hard to make her talk, for she had never seen a white man, and thought I had bought her for some dreadful purpose or other. However, when she found that she was kindly treated, she opened her lips and told me the same story that her late master had repeated, neither more nor less. Finally I asked her whether she could guide me to the place where she had seen the "live wagons."

She answered: "Oh, yes," as she had travelled many roads and never forgot any of them.

This, of course, was all I wanted from the woman, who, I may add, ultimately gave me a good deal of trouble. The poor creature seemed never to have experienced kindness, and her gratitude for the little I showed her was so intense that it became a nuisance. She followed me about everywhere, trying to do me service in her savage way, and even attempted to seize my food and chew it before I put it into my own mouth—to save me the trouble, I suppose. Ultimately I married her, somewhat against her will, I fear, to one of the hired Kaffirs, who made her a very good husband, although when he was dismissed from my service she wanted to leave him and follow me.

At length, under the guidance of this woman, Jeel, we made a start. There were but fifty miles to go, a distance that on a fair road any good horse would cover in eight hours, or less. But we had no horses, and there was no road—nothing but swamps and bush and rocky hills. With our untrained cattle it took us three days to travel the first twelve miles, though after that things went somewhat better.

It may be asked, why did I not send on? But whom could I send when no one knew the way, except the woman, Jeel, whom I feared to part with lest I should see her no more? Moreover, what was the use of sending, since the messengers could take no help? If everyone at the camp was dead, as rumour told us—well, they were dead. And if they lived, the hope was that they might live a little longer. Meanwhile, I dared not part with my guide, nor dared I leave the relief wagons to go on with her alone. If I did so, I knew that I should never see them again, since only the prestige of their being owned by a white man who was not a Portuguese prevented the natives from looting them.

It was a truly awful journey. My first idea had been to follow the banks of the Crocodile River, which is what I should have attempted had I not chanced on the woman, Jeel. Lucky was it that I did not do so, since I found afterwards that this river wound about a great deal and was joined by impassable tributaries. Also it was bordered by forests. Jeel's track, on the contrary, followed an old slave road that, bad as it was, avoided the swampy places of the surrounding country, and those native tribes which the experience of generations of the traders in this iniquitous traffic showed to be most dangerous.

Nine days of fearful struggle had gone by. We had camped one night below the crest of a long slope strewn with great rocks, many of which we were obliged to roll out of the path by main force in order to make a way for the wagons. The oxen had to lie in their yokes all night, since we dared not let them loose fearing lest they should stray; also lions were roaring in the distance, although, game being plentiful, these did not come near to us. As soon as there was any light we let out the teams to fill themselves on the tussocky grass that grew about, and meanwhile cooked and ate some food.

Presently the sun rose, and I saw that beneath us was a great stretch of plain covered with mist, and to the north, on our right, several denser billows of mist that marked the course of the Crocodile River.

By degrees this mist lifted, tall tops of trees appearing above it, till at length it thinned into vapour that vanished away as the sun rose. As I watched it idly, the woman, Jeel, crept up to me in her furtive fashion, touched me on the shoulder and pointed to a distant group of trees.

Looking closely at these trees, I saw between them what at first I took for some white rocks. Further examination, as the mist cleared, suggested to my mind, however, that they might be wagon tilts. Just then the Zulu who understood Jeel's talk came up. I asked him as well as I could, for at that time my knowledge of his tongue was very imperfect, what she wished to say. He questioned her, and answered that she desired to tell me that those were the moving houses of the Amaboona (the Boer people), just where she had seen them nearly two moons ago.

At this tidings my heart seemed to stand still, so that for more than a minute I could not speak. There were the wagons at last, but—oh! who and what should I find in them? I called Hans and bade him inspan as quickly as possible, explaining to him that yonder was Marais's camp.

"Why not let the oxen fill themselves first, baas?" he answered. "There is no hurry, for though the wagons are there, no doubt all the people are dead long ago."

"Do what I bid you, you ill-omened beast," I said, "instead of croaking of death like a crow. And listen: I am going to walk forward to that camp; you must follow with the wagons as fast as they can travel."

"No, baas, it is not safe that you should go alone. Kaffirs or wild beasts might take you."

"Safe or not, I am going; but if you think it wise, tell two of those Zulus to come with me."

A few minutes later I was on the road, followed by the two Kaffirs armed with spears. In my youth I was a good runner, being strong of leg and light in body, but I do not think that I ever covered seven miles, for that was about the distance to the camp, in quicker time than I did that morning. Indeed, I left those active Kaffirs so far behind that when I approached the trees they were not in sight. Here I dropped to a walk, as I said to myself—to get my breath. Really it was because I felt so terrified at what I might find that I delayed the discovery just for one minute more. While I approached, hope, however faint, still remained; when I arrived, hope might be replaced by everlasting despair.

Now I could see that there were some shanties built behind the wagons, doubtless those "rude houses" of which Marie had written. But I could not see anyone moving about them, or any cattle or any smoke, or other sign of life. Nor could I hear a single sound.

Doubtless, thought I to myself, Hans is right. They are all long dead.

My agony of suspense was replaced by an icy calm. At length I knew the worst. It was finished—I had striven in vain. I walked through the outlying trees and between two of the wagons. One of these I noticed, as we do notice things at such times, was the same in which Marais had trekked with his daughter, his favourite wagon that once I had helped to fit with a new dissel-boom.

Before me were the rough houses built of the branches of trees, daubed over with mud, or rather the backs of them, for they faced west. I stood still for a moment, and as I stood thought that I heard a faint sound as of someone reciting slowly. I crept along the end of the outermost house and, rubbing the cold sweat from my eyes, peeped round the corner, for it occurred to me that savages might be in possession. Then I saw what caused the sound. A tattered, blackened, bearded man stood at the head of a long and shallow hole saying a prayer.

It was Henri Marais, although at the time I did not recognise him, so changed was he. A number of little mounds to the right and left of him told me, however, that the hole was a grave. As I watched two more men appeared, dragging between them the body of a woman, which evidently they had not strength to carry, as its legs trailed upon the ground. From the shape of the corpse it seemed to be that of a tall young woman, but the features I could not see, because it was being dragged face downwards. Also the long hair hanging from the head hid them. It was dark hair, like Marie's. They reached the grave, and tumbled their sad burden into it; but I—I could not stir!

At length my limbs obeyed my will. I went forward to the men and said in a hollow voice in Dutch:

"Whom do you bury?"

"Johanna Meyer," answered someone mechanically, for they did not seem to have taken the trouble to look at me. As I listened to those words my heart, which had stood still waiting for the answer, beat again with a sudden bound that I could hear in the silence.

I looked up. There, advancing from the doorway of one of the houses, very slowly, as though overpowered by weakness, and leading by the hand a mere skeleton of a child, who was chewing some leaves, I saw—I saw _Marie Marais!_ She was wasted to nothing, but I could not mistake her eyes, those great soft eyes that had grown so unnaturally large in the white, thin face.

She too saw me and stared for one moment. Then, loosing the child, she cast up her hands, through which the sunlight shone as through parchment, and slowly sank to the ground.

"She has gone, too," said one of the men in an indifferent voice. "I thought she would not last another day."

Now for the first time the man at the head of the grave turned. Lifting his hand, he pointed to me, whereon the other two men turned also.

"God above us!" he said in a choked voice, "at last I am quite mad. Look! there stands the spook of young Allan, the son of the English predicant who lived near Cradock."

As soon as I heard the voice I knew the speaker.

"Oh, Mynheer Marais!" I cried, "I am no ghost, I am Allan himself come to save you."

Marais made no answer; he seemed bewildered. But one of the men cried out crazily:

"How can you save us, youngster, unless you are ready to be eaten? Don't you see, we starve, we starve!"

"I have wagons and food," I answered.

"Allemachte! Henri," exclaimed the man, with a wild laugh, "do you hear what your English spook says? He says that he has wagons and _food, food, food!_"

Then Marais burst into tears and flung himself upon my breast, nearly knocking me down. I wrenched myself free of him and ran to Marie, who was lying face upwards on the ground. She seemed to hear my step, for her eyes opened and she struggled to a sitting posture.

"Is it really you, Allan, or do I dream?" she murmured.

"It is I, it is I," I answered, lifting her to her feet, for she seemed to weigh no more than a child. Her head fell upon my shoulder, and she too began to weep.

Still holding her, I turned to the men and said:

"Why do you starve when there, is game all about?" and I pointed to two fat elands strolling among the trees not more than a hundred and fifty yards away.

"Can we kill game with stones?" asked one of them, "we whose powder was all burnt a month ago. Those buck," he added, with a wild laugh, "come here to mock us every morning; but they will not walk into our pitfalls. They know them too well, and we have no strength to dig others."

Now when I left my wagons I had brought with me that same Purdey rifle with which I had shot the geese in the match against Pereira, choosing it because it was so light to carry. I held up my hand for silence, set Marie gently on the ground, and began to steal towards the elands. Taking what shelter I could, I got within a hundred yards of them, when suddenly they took alarm, being frightened, in fact, by my two Zulu servants, who were now arriving.

Off they galloped, the big bull leading, and vanished behind some trees. I saw their line, and that they would appear again between two clumps of bush about two hundred and fifty yards away. Hastily I raised the full sight on the rifle, which was marked for two hundred yards, lifted it, and waited, praying to God as I did so that my skill might not fail me.

The bull appeared, its head held forward, its long horns lying flat upon the back. The shot was very long, and the beast very large to bring down with so small a bullet. I aimed right forward—clear of it, indeed—high too, in a line with its backbone, and pressed the trigger.

The rifle exploded, the bullet clapped, and the buck sprang forward faster than ever. I had failed! But what was this? Suddenly the great bull swung round and began to gallop towards us. When it was not more than fifty yards away, it fell in a heap, rolled twice over like a shot rabbit, and lay still. That bullet was in its heart.

The two Kaffirs appeared breathless and streaming with perspiration.

"Cut meat from the eland's flank; don't stop to skin it," I said in my broken Zulu, helping the words out with signs.

They understood, and a minute later were at work with their assegais. Then I looked about me. Near by lay a store of dead branches placed there for fuel.

"Have you fire?" I asked of the skeleton Boers, for they were nothing more.

"Nein, nein," they answered; "our fire is dead."

I produced the tinder-box which I carried with me, and struck the flint. Ten minutes later we had a cheerful blaze, and within three-quarters of an hour good soup, for iron pots were not wanting—only food to put into them. I think that for the rest of that day those poor creatures did little else but eat, sleeping between their meals. Oh! the joy I had in feeding them, especially after the wagons arrived, bringing with them salt—how they longed for that salt!—sugar and coffee.

The Promise

Of the original thirty-five souls, not reckoning natives, who had accompanied Henri Marais upon his ill-fated expedition, there now remained but nine alive at the new Maraisfontein. These were himself, his daughter, four Prinsloos—a family of extraordinary constitution—and three Meyers, being the husband of the poor woman I had seen committed to the grave and two of her six children. The rest, Hernan Pereira excepted, had died of fever and actual starvation, for when the fever lessened with the change of the seasons, the starvation set in. It appeared that, with the exception of a very little, they had stored their powder in a kind of outbuilding which they constructed, placing it at a distance for safety's sake. When most of the surviving men were away, however, a grass fire set light to this outbuilding and all the powder blew up.

After this, for a while they supplied the camp with food by the help of such ammunition as remained to them. When that failed they dug pits in which to catch game. In time the buck came to know of these pits, so that they snared no more.

Then, as the "biltong" or sun-dried meat they had made was all consumed, they were driven to every desperate expedient that is known to the starving, such as the digging up of bulbs, the boiling of grass, twigs and leaves, the catching of lizards, and so forth. I believe that they actually ate caterpillars and earthworms. But after their last fire went out through the neglect of the wretched Kaffir who was left to watch it, and having no tinder, they failed to relight it by friction, of course even this food failed them. When I arrived they had practically been three days without anything to eat except green leaves and grass, such as I saw the child chewing. In another seventy hours doubtless every one of them would have been dead.

Well, they recovered rapidly enough, for those who had survived its ravages were evidently now impervious to fever. Who can tell the joy that I experienced as I watched Marie returning from the very brink of the grave to a state of full and lovely womanhood? After all, we were not so far away from the primitive conditions of humanity, when the first duty of man was to feed his women and his children, and I think that something of that instinct remains with us. At least, I know I never experienced a greater pleasure than I did, when the woman I loved, the poor, starving woman, ate and ate of the food which _I_ was able to give her—she who for weeks had existed upon locusts and herbs.

For the first few days we did not talk much except of the immediate necessities of the hour, which occupied all our thoughts. Afterwards, when Marais and his daughter were strong enough to bear it, we had some conversation. He began by asking how I came to find them.

I replied, through Marie's letter, which, it appeared, he knew nothing of, for he had forbidden her to write to me.

"It seems fortunate that you were disobeyed, mynheer," I said, to which he answered nothing.

Then I told the tale of the arrival of that letter at the Mission Station in the Cape Colony by the hand of a wandering smous, and of my desperate ride upon the swift mare to Port Elizabeth, where I just succeeded in catching the brig Seven Stars before she sailed. Also I told them of the lucky chances that enabled me to buy the wagons and find a guide to their camp, reaching it but a few hours before it was too late.

"It was a great deed," said Henri Marais, taking the pipe from his mouth, for I had brought tobacco among my stores. "But tell me, Allan, why did you do it for the sake of one who has not treated you kindly?"

"I did it," I answered, "for the sake of one who has always treated me kindly," and I nodded towards Marie, who was engaged in washing up the cooking pots at a distance.

"I suppose so, Allan; but you know she is affianced to another."

"I know that she is affianced to me, and to no other," I answered warmly, adding, "And pray where is this other? If he lives I do not see him here."

"No," replied Marais in a curious voice. "The truth is, Allan, that Hernan Pereira left us about a fortnight before you came. One horse remained, which was his, and with two Hottentots, who were also his servants, he rode back upon the track by which we came, to try to find help. Since then we have heard nothing of him."

"Indeed; and how did he propose to get food on the way?"

"He had a rifle, or rather they all three had rifles, and about a hundred charges between them, which escaped the fire."

"With a hundred charges of powder carefully used your camp would have been fed for a month, or perhaps two months," I remarked. "Yet he went away with all of them—to find help?"

"That is so, Allan. We begged him to stay, but he would not; and, after all, the charges were his own property. No doubt he thought he acted for the best, especially as Marie would have none of him," Marais added with emphasis.

"Well," I replied, "it seems that it is I who have brought you the help, and not Pereira. Also, by the way, mynheer, I have brought you the money my father collected on your account, and some £500 of my own, or what is left of it, in goods and gold. Moreover, Marie does not refuse me. Say, therefore, to which of us does she belong?"

"It would seem that it should be to you," he answered slowly, "since you have shown yourself so faithful, and were it not for you she would now be lying yonder," and he pointed to the little heaps that covered the bones of most of the expedition. "Yes, yes, it would seem that it should be to you, who twice have saved her life and once have saved mine also."

Now I suppose that he saw on my face the joy which I could not conceal, for he added hastily: "Yet, Allan, years ago I swore on the Book before God that never with my will should my daughter marry an Englishman, even if be were a good Englishman. Also, just before we left the Colony, I swore again, in her presence and that of Hernan Pereira, that I would not give her to you, so I cannot break my oath, can I? If I did, the good God would be avenged upon me."

"Some might think that when I came here the good God was in the way of being avenged upon you for the keeping of that evil oath," I answered bitterly, glancing, in my turn, at the graves.

"Yes, they might, Allan," he replied without anger, for all his troubles had induced a reasonable frame of mind in him—for a while. "Yet, His ways are past finding out, are they not?"

Now my anger broke out, and, rising, I said:

"Do you mean, Mynheer Marais, that notwithstanding the love between us, which you know is true and deep, and notwithstanding that I alone have been able to drag both of you and the others out of the claws of death, I am never to marry Marie? Do you mean that she is to be given to a braggart who deserted her in her need?"

"And what if I do mean that, Allan?"

"This: although I am still young, as you know well I am a man who can think and act for himself. Also, I am your master here—I have cattle and guns and servants. Well, I will take Marie, and if any should try to stop me, I know how to protect myself and her."

This bold speech did not seem to surprise him in the least or to make him think the worse of me. He looked at me for a while, pulling his long beard in a meditative fashion, then answered:

"I dare say that at your age I should have played the same game, and it is true that you have things in your fist. But, much as she may love you, Marie would not go away with you and leave her father to starve."

"Then you can come with us as my father-in-law, Mynheer Marais. At any rate, it is certain that I will not go away and leave her here to starve."

Now I think that something which he saw in my eye showed him that I was in earnest. At least, he changed his tone and began to argue, almost to plead.

"Be reasonable, Allan," he said. "How can you marry Marie when there is no predicant to marry you? Surely, if you love her so much, you would not pour mud upon her name, even in this wilderness?"

"She might not think it mud," I replied. "Men and women have been married without the help of priests before now, by open declaration and public report, for instance, and their children held to be born in wedlock. I know that, for I have read of the law of marriage."

"It may be, Allan, though I hold no marriage good unless the holy words are said. But why do you not let me come to the end of my story?"

"Because I thought it was ended, Mynheer Marais."

"Not so, Allan. I told you that I had sworn that she should never marry you with my will. But when she is of age, which will be in some six months' time, my will counts no longer, seeing that then she is a free woman who can dispose of herself. Also I shall be clear of my oath, for no harm will come to my soul if that happens which I cannot help. Now are you satisfied?"

"I don't know," I answered doubtfully, for somehow all Marais's casuistry, which I thought contemptible, did not convince me that he was sincere. "I don't know," I repeated. "Much may chance in six months."

"Of course, Allan. For instance, Marie might change her mind and marry someone else."

"Or I might not be there to marry, mynheer. Accidents sometimes happen to men who are not wanted, especially in wild countries or, for the matter of that, to those who are."

"Allemachte! Allan, you do not mean that I—"

"No, mynheer," I interrupted; "but there are other people in the world besides yourself—Hernan Pereira, for example, if he lives. Still, I am not the only one concerned in this matter. There is Marie yonder. Shall I call her?"

He nodded, preferring probably that I should speak to her in his presence rather than alone.

So I called Marie, who was watching our talk somewhat anxiously while she went about her tasks. She came at once, a very different Marie to the starving girl of a while before, for although she was still thin and drawn, her youth and beauty were returning to her fast under the influences of good food and happiness.

"What is it, Allan?" she asked gently. I told her all, repeating our conversation and the arguments which had been used on either side word for word, as nearly as I could remember them.

"Is that right?" I asked of Marais when I had finished.

"It is right; you have a good memory," he answered.

"Very well. And now what have you to say, Marie?"

"I, dear Allan? Why, this: My life belongs to you, who have twice saved this body of mine from death, as my love and spirit belong to you. Therefore, I should have thought it no shame if I had been given to you here and now before the people, and afterwards married by a clergyman when we found one. But my father has sworn an oath which weighs upon his mind, and he has shown you that within six months—a short six months—that oath dies of itself, since, by the law, he can no longer control me. So, Allan, as I would not grieve him, or perhaps lead him to say and do what is foolish, I think it would be well that we should wait for those six months, if, on his part, he promises that he will then do nothing to prevent our marriage."

"Ja, ja, I promise that then I will do nothing to prevent your marriage," answered Marais eagerly, like one who has suddenly seen some loophole of escape from an impossible position, adding, as though to himself, "But God may do something to prevent it, for all that."

"We are every one of us in the hand of God," she replied in her sweet voice. "Allan, you hear, my father has promised?"

"Yes, Marie, he has promised—after a fashion," I replied gloomily, for somehow his words struck a chill through me.

"I have promised, Allan, and I will keep my promise to you, as I have kept my oath to God, attempting to work you no harm, and leaving all in His hands. But you, on your part, must promise also that, till she is of age, you will not take Marie as a wife—no, not if you were left alone together in the veld. You must be as people who are affianced to each other, no more."

So, having no choice, I promised, though with a heavy heart. Then, I suppose in order to make this solemn contract public, Marais called the surviving Boers, who were loitering near, and repeated to them the terms of the contract that we had made.

The men laughed and shrugged their shoulders. But Vrouw Prinsloo, I remember, said outright that she thought the business foolish, since if anyone had a right to Marie, I had, wherever I chose to take her. She added that, as for Hernan Pereira, he was a "sneak and a stinkcat," who had gone off to save his own life, and left them all to die. If _she_ were Marie, should they meet again, she would greet him with a pailful of dirty water in the face, as she herself meant to do if she got the chance.

Vrouw Prinsloo, it will be observed, was a very outspoken woman and, I may add, an honest one.

So this contract was settled. I have set it out at length because of its importance in our story. But now I wish—ah! how I wish that I had insisted upon being married to Marie then and there. If I had done so, I think I should have carried my point, for I was the "master of many legions" in the shape of cattle, food and ammunition, and rather than risk a quarrel with me, the other Boers would have forced Marais to give way. But we were young and inexperienced; also it was fated otherwise. Who can question the decrees of Fate written immutably, perhaps long before we were born, in the everlasting book of human destinies?

Yet, when I had shaken off my first fears and doubts, my lot and Marie's were very happy, a perfect paradise, indeed, compared with what we had gone through during that bitter time of silence and separation. At any rate, we were acknowledged to be affianced by the little society in which we lived, including her father, and allowed to be as much alone together as we liked. This meant that we met at dawn only to separate at nightfall, for, having little or no artificial light, we went to rest with the sun, or shortly after it. Sweet, indeed, was that companionship of perfect trust and love; so sweet, that even after all these years I do not care to dwell upon the holy memory of those blessed months.

So soon as the surviving Boers began to recover by the help of my stores and medicines and the meat which I shot in plenty, of course great discussions arose as to our future plans. First it was suggested that we should trek to Lorenzo Marquez, and wait for a ship there to take us down to Natal, for none of them would hear of returning beggared to the Cape to tell the story of their failure and dreadful bereavements. I pointed out, however, that no ship might come for a long while, perhaps for one or two years, and that Lorenzo Marquez and its neighborhood seemed to be a poisonous place to live in!

The next idea was that we should stop where we were, one which I rather welcomed, as I should have been glad to abide in peace with Marie until the six months of probation had gone by.

However, in the end this was rejected for many good reasons. Thus half a score of white people, of whom four were members of a single family, were certainly not strong enough to form a settlement, especially as the surrounding natives might become actively hostile at any moment. Again, the worst fever season was approaching, in which we should very possibly all be carried off. Further, we had no breeding cattle or horses, which would not live in this veld, and only the ammunition and goods that I had brought with me.

So it was clear that but one thing remained to be done, namely, to trek back to what is now the Transvaal territory, or, better still, to Natal, for this route would enable us to avoid the worst of the mountains. There we might join some other party of the emigrant Boers—for choice, that of Retief, of whose arrival over the Drakensberg I was able to tell them.

That point settled, we made our preparations. To begin with, I had only enough oxen for two wagons, whereas, even if we abandoned the rest of them, we must take at least four. Therefore, through my Kaffirs, I opened negotiations with the surrounding natives, who, when they heard that I was not a Boer and was prepared to pay for what I bought, soon expressed a willingness to trade. Indeed, very shortly we had quite a market established, to which cattle were brought that I bargained for and purchased, giving cloth, knives, hoes, and the usual Kaffir goods in payment for the same.

Also, they brought mealies and other corn; and oh! the delight with which those poor people, who for months and months had existed upon nothing but flesh-meat, ate of this farinaceous food. Never shall I forget seeing Marie and the surviving children partake of their first meal of porridge, and washing the sticky stuff down with draughts of fresh, sugared milk, for with the oxen I had succeeded in obtaining two good cows. It is enough to say that this change of diet soon completely re-established their health, and made Marie more beautiful than she had ever been before.

Having got the oxen, the next thing was to break them to the yoke; for, although docile creatures enough, they had never even seen a wagon. This proved a long and difficult process, involving many trial trips; moreover, the selected wagons, one of which had belonged to Pereira, must be mended with very insufficient tools and without the help of a forge. Indeed, had it not chanced that Hans, the Hottentot, had worked for a wagon-maker at some indefinite period of his career, I do not think that we could have managed the job at all.

It was while we were busy with these tasks that some news arrived which was unpleasing enough to everyone, except perhaps to Henri Marais. I was engaged on a certain evening in trying to make sixteen of the Kaffir cattle pull together in the yoke, instead of tying themselves into a double knot and over-setting the wagon, when Hans, who was helping me, suddenly called out:

"Look! baas, here comes one of my brothers," or, in other words, a Hottentot.

Following the line of his hand, I saw a thin and wretched creature, clad only in some rags and the remains of a big hat with the crown out, staggering towards us between the trees.

"Why!" exclaimed Marie in a startled voice, for, as usual, she was at my side, "it is Klaus, one of my cousin Hernan's after-riders."

"So long as it is not your cousin Hernan himself, I do not care," I said.

Presently the poor, starved "Totty" arrived, and throwing himself down, begged for food. A cold shoulder of buck was given to him, which he devoured, holding it in both hands and tearing off great lumps of flesh with his teeth like a wild beast.

When at last he was satisfied, Marais, who had come up with the other Boers, asked him whence he came and what was his news of his master.

"Out of the bush," he answered, "and my news of the baas is that he is dead. At least, I left him so ill that I suppose he must be dead by now."

"Why did you leave him if he was ill?" asked Marais.

"Because he told me to, baas, that I might find help, for we were starving, having fired our last bullet."

"Is he alone, then?"

"Yes, yes, except for the wild beasts and the vultures. A lion ate the other man, his servant, a long while ago."

"How far is he off?" asked Marais again.

"Oh, baas, about five hours' journey on horseback on a good road." (This would be some thirty-five miles.)

Then he told this story: Pereira with his two Hottentot servants, he mounted and they on foot, had traversed about a hundred miles of rough country in safety, when at night a lion killed and carried off one of the Hottentots, and frightened away the horse, which was never seen again. Pereira and Klaus proceeded on foot till they came to a great river, on the banks of which they met some Kaffirs, who appear to have been Zulus on outpost duty. These men demanded their guns and ammunition to take to their king, and, on Pereira refusing to give them up, said that they would kill them both in the morning after they had made him instruct them in the use of the guns by beating him with sticks.

In the night a storm came on, under cover of which Pereira and Klaus escaped. As they dared not go forward for fear lest they should fall into the hands of the Zulus, they fled back northwards, running all night, only to find in the morning that they had lost their way in the bush. This had happened nearly a month before—or, at any rate, Klaus thought so, for no doubt the days went very slowly—during which time they had wandered about, trying to shape some sort of course by the sun with the object of returning to the camp. They met no man, black or white, and supported themselves upon game, which they shot and ate raw or sun-dried, till at length all their powder was done and they threw away their heavy roers, which they could no longer carry.

It was at this juncture that from the top of a tall tree Klaus saw a certain koppie a long way off, which he recognised as being within fifteen miles or so of Marais's camp. By now they were starving, only Klaus was the stronger of the two, for he found and devoured some carrion, a dead hyena I think it was. Pereira also tried to eat this horrible food, but, not having the stomach of a Hottentot, the first mouthful of it made him dreadfully ill. They sought shelter in a cave on the bank of a stream, where grew water-cresses and other herbs, such as wild asparagus. Here it was that

Pereira told Klaus to try to make his way back to the camp, and, should he find anyone alive there, to bring him succour.

So Klaus went, taking the remaining leg of the hyena with him, and on the afternoon of the second day arrived as has been told.

Vrouw Prinsloo Speaks Her Mind

Now, when the Hottentot's story was finished a discussion arose. Marais said that someone must go to see whether his nephew still lived, to which the other Boers replied "Ja" in an indifferent voice. Then the Vrouw Prinsloo took up her parable.

She remarked, as she had done before, that in her judgment Hernan Pereira was "a stinkcat and a sneak," who had tried to desert them in their trouble, and by the judgment of a just God had got into trouble himself. Personally, she wished that the lion had taken him instead of the worthy Hottentot, although it gave her a higher opinion of lions to conclude that it had not done so, because if it did it thought it would have been poisoned. Well, her view was that it would be just as well to let that traitor lie upon the bed which he had made. Moreover, doubtless by now he was dead, so what was the good of bothering about him?

These sentiments appeared to appeal to the Boers, for they remarked: "Ja, what is the good?"

"Is it right," asked Marais, "to abandon a comrade in misfortune, one of our own blood?"

"Mein Gott!" replied Vrouw Prinsloo; "he is no blood of mine, the evil-odoured Portuguee. But I admit he is of yours, Heer Marais, being your sister's son, so it is evident that you should be the one to go to seek after him."

"That seems to be so, Vrouw Prinsloo," said Marais in his meditative manner; "yet I must remember that I have Marie to look after."

"Ach! and so had he, too, until he remembered his own skin, and went off with the only horse and all the powder, leaving her and the rest of us to starve. Well, you won't go, and Prinsloo won't go, nor my boy either, for I'll see to that; so Meyer must go."

"Nein, nein, good vrouw," answered Meyer, "I have those children that are left to me to consider."

"Then," exclaimed Vrouw Prinsloo triumphantly, "nobody will go, so let us forget this stinkcat, as he forgot us."

"Does it seem right," asked Marais again, "that a Christian man should be left to starve in the wilderness?" and he looked at me.

"Tell me, Heer Marais," I remarked, answering the look, "why should I of all people go to look for the Heer Pereira, one who has not dealt too well with me?"

"I do not know, Allan. Yet the Book tells us to turn the other cheek and to forget injuries. Still, it is for you to judge, remembering that we must answer for all things at the last day, and not for me. I only know that were I your age and not burdened with a daughter to watch over, _I_ should go."

"Why should you talk to me thus?" I asked with indignation. "Why do you not go yourself, seeing that I am quite ready to look after Marie?" (Here the Vrouw Prinsloo and the other Boers tittered.) "And why do you not address your remarks to these other heeren instead of to me, seeing that they are the friends and trek-companions of your nephew?"

At this point the male Prinsloos and Meyer found that they had business elsewhere.

"It is for you to judge, yet remember, Allan, that it is an awful thing to appear before our Maker with the blood of a fellow creature upon our hands. But if you and these other hard-hearted men will not go, I at my age, and weak as I am with all that I have suffered, will go myself."

"Good," said Vrouw Prinsloo; "that is the best way out of it. You will soon get sick of the journey, Heer Marais, and we shall see no more of the stinkcat."

Marais rose in a resigned fashion, for he never deigned to argue with Vrouw Prinsloo, who was too many for him, and said:

"Farewell, Marie. If I do not return, you will remember my wishes, and my will may be found between the first leaves of our Holy Book. Get up, Klaus, and guide me to your master," and he administered a somewhat vicious kick to the gorged and prostrate Hottentot.

Now Marie, who all this while had stood silent, touched me on the shoulder and said:

"Allan, is it well that my father should go alone? Will you not accompany him?"

"Of course," I answered cheerfully; "on such a business there should be two, and some Kaffirs also to carry the man, if he still lives."

Now for the end of the story. As the Hottentot Klaus was too exhausted to move that night, it was arranged that we should start at dawn. Accordingly, I rose before the light, and was just finishing my breakfast when Marie appeared at the wagon in which I slept. I got up to greet her, and, there being no one in sight, we kissed each other several times.

"Have done, my heart," she said, pushing me away. "I come to you from my father, who is sick in his stomach and would see you."

"Which means that I shall have to go after your cousin alone," I replied with indignant emphasis.

She shook her head, and led me to the little shanty in which she slept. Here by the growing light, that entered through the doorway for it had no window, I perceived Marais seated upon a wooden stool with his hands pressed on his middle and groaning.

"Good morning, Allan," he said in a melancholy voice; "I am ill, very ill, something that I have eaten perhaps, or a chill in the stomach, such as often precedes fever or dysentery."

"Perhaps you will get better as you walk, mynheer," I suggested, for, to tell the truth, I misdoubted me of this chill, and knew that he had eaten nothing but what was quite wholesome.

"Walk! God alone knows how I can walk with something gripping my inside like a wagon-maker's vice. Yet I will try, for it is impossible to leave that poor Hernan to die alone; and if I do not go to seek him, it seems that no one else will."

"Why should not some of my Kaffirs go with Klaus?" I asked.

"Allan," he replied solemnly, "if you were dying in a cave far from help, would you think well of those who sent raw Kaffirs to succour you when they might have come themselves, Kaffirs who certainly would let you die and return with some false story?"

"I don't know what I should think, Heer Marais. But I do know that if _I_ were in that cave and Pereira were in this camp, neither would he come himself, nor so much as send a savage to save _me_."

"It may be so, Allan. But even if another's heart is black, should yours be black also? Oh! I will come, though it be to my death," and, rising from the stool with the most dreadful groan, he began to divest himself of the tattered blanket in which he was wrapped up.

"Oh! Allan, my father must not go; it will kill him," exclaimed Marie, who took a more serious view of his case than I did.

"Very well, if you think so," I answered. "And now, as it is time for me to be starting, good-bye."

"You have a good heart, Allan," said Marais, sinking back upon his stool and resuming his blanket, while Marie looked despairingly first at one and then at the other of us.

Half an hour later I was on the road in the very worst of tempers.

"Mind what you are about," called Vrouw Prinsloo after me. "It is not lucky to save an enemy, and if I know anything of that stinkcat, he will bite your finger badly by way of gratitude. Bah! lad, if I were you I should just camp for a few days in the bush, and then come back and say that I could find nothing of Pereira except the dead hyenas that had been poisoned by eating him. Good luck to you all the same, Allan; may I find such a friend in need. It seems to me that you were born to help others."

Beside the Hottentot Klaus, my companions on this unwelcome journey were three of the Zulu Kaffirs, for Hans I was obliged to leave in charge of my cattle and goods with the other men. Also, I took a pack-ox, an active beast that I had been training to carry loads and, if necessary a man, although as yet it was not very well broken.

All that day we marched over extremely rough country, till at last darkness found us in a mountainous kloof, where we slept, surrounded by watch-fires because of the lions. Next morning at the first light we moved on again, and about ten o'clock waded through a stream to a little natural cave, where Klaus said he had left his master. This cave seemed extremely silent, and, as I hesitated for a moment at its mouth, the thought crossed my mind that if Pereira were still there, he must be dead. Indeed, do what I would to suppress it, with that reflection came a certain feeling of relief and even of pleasure. For well I knew that Pereira alive was more dangerous to me than all the wild men and beasts in Africa put together. Thrusting back this unworthy sentiment as best I could, I entered the cave alone, for the natives, who dread the defilement of the touch of a corpse, lingered outside.

It was but a shallow cavity washed out of the overhanging rock by the action of water; and as soon as my eyes grew accustomed to its gloom, I saw that at the end of it lay a man. So still did he lie, that now I was almost certain that his troubles were over. I went up to him and touched his face, which was cold and clammy, and then, quite convinced, turned to leave the place, which, I thought, if a few rocks were piled in the mouth of it, would make an excellent sepulchre.

Just as I stepped out into the sunlight, and was about to call to the men to collect the rocks, however, I thought that I heard a very faint groan behind me, which at the moment I set down to imagination. Still, I returned, though I did not much like the job, knelt down by the figure, and waited with my hand over its heart. For five minutes or more I stayed here, and then, quite convinced, was about to leave again when, for the second time, I heard that faint groan. Pereira was not dead, but only on the extreme brink of death!

I ran to the entrance of the cave, calling the Kaffirs, and together we carried him out into the sunlight. He was an awful spectacle, mere bone with yellow skin stretched over it, and covered with filth and clotted blood from some hurt. I had brandy with me, of which I poured a little down his throat, whereon his heart began to beat feebly. Then we made some soup, and poured that down his throat with more brandy, and the end of it was he came to life again.

For three days did I doctor that man, and really I believe that if at any time during those days I had relaxed my attentions even for a couple of hours, he would have slipped through my fingers, for at this business Klaus and the Kaffirs were no good at all. But I pulled him round, and on the third morning he came to his senses. For a long while he stared at me, for I had laid him in the mouth of the cave, where the light was good, although the overhanging rocks protected him from the sun. Then he said:

"Allemachte! you remind me of someone, young man. I know. It is of that damned English boy who beat me at the goose shooting, and made me quarrel with Oom [uncle] Retief, the jackanapes that Marie was so fond of. Well, whoever you are, you can't be he, thank God."

"You are mistaken, Heer Pereira," I answered. "I am that same damned young English jackanapes, Allan Quatermain by name, who beat you at shooting. But if you take my advice, you will thank God for something else, namely, that your life has been saved."

"Who saved it?" he asked.

"If you want to know, I did; I have been nursing you these three days."

"You, Allan Quatermain! Now, that is strange, for certainly I would not have saved yours," and he laughed a little, then turned over and went to sleep.

From that time forward his recovery was rapid, and two days later we began our journey back to Marais's camp, the convalescent Pereira being carried in a litter by the four natives. It was a task at which they grumbled a good deal, for the load was heavy over rough ground, and whenever they stumbled or shook him he cursed at them. So much did he curse, indeed, that at length one of the Zulus, a man with a rough temper, said that if it were not for the Inkoos, meaning myself, he would put his assegai through him, and let the vultures carry him. After this Pereira grew much more polite. When the bearers became exhausted we set him on the pack-ox, which two of us led, while the other two supported him on either side. It was in this fashion that at last we arrived at the camp one evening.

Here the Vrouw Prinsloo was the first to greet us. We found her standing in the game path which we were following, quite a quarter of a mile from the wagons, with her hands set upon her broad hips and her feet apart. Her attitude was so defiant, and had about it such an air of premeditation, that I cannot help thinking she had got wind of our return, perhaps from having seen the smoke of our last fires, and was watching for us. Also, her greeting was warm.

"Ah! here you come, Hernan Pereira," she cried, "riding on an ox, while better men walk. Well, now, I want a chat with you. How came it that you went off in the night, taking the only horse and all the powder?"

"I went to get help for you," he replied sulkily.

"Did you, did you, indeed! Well, it seems that it was you who wanted the help, after all. What do you mean to pay the Heer Allan Quatermain for saving your life, for I am sure he has done so? You have got no goods left, although you were always boasting about your riches; they are now at the bottom of a river, so it will have to be in love and service."

He muttered something about my wanting no payment for a Christian act.

"No, he wants no payment, Hernan Pereira, he is one of the true sort, but you'll pay him all the same and in bad coin if you get the chance. Oh! I have come out to tell you what I think of you. You are a stinkcat; do you hear that? A thing that no dog would bite if he could help it! You are a traitor also. You brought us to this cursed country, where you said your relatives would give us wealth and land, and then, after famine and fever attacked us, you rode away, and left us to die to save your own dirty skin. And now you come back here for help, saved by him whom you cheated in the Goose Kloof, by him whose true love you have tried to steal. Oh, mein Gott! why does the Almighty leave such fellows alive, while so many that are good and honest and innocent lie beneath the soil because of stinkcats like you?"

So she went on, striding at the side of the pack-ox, and reviling Pereira in a ceaseless stream of language, until at length he thrust his thumbs into his ears and glared at her in speechless wrath.

Thus it was that at last we arrived in the camp, where, having seen us coming, all the Boers were gathered. They are not a particularly humorous people, but this spectacle of the advance of Pereira seated on the pack-ox, a steed that is becoming to few riders, with the furious and portly Vrouw Prinsloo striding at his side and shrieking abuse at him, caused them to burst into laughter. Then Pereira's temper gave out, and he became even more abusive than Vrouw Prinsloo.

"Is this the way you receive me, you veld-hogs, you common Boers, who are not fit to mix with a man of position and learning like myself?" he began.

"Then in God's name why do you mix with us, Hernan Pereira?" asked the saturnine Meyer, thrusting his face forward till the Newgate fringe he wore by way of a beard literally seemed to curl with wrath. "When we were hungry you did not wish it, for you slunk away and left us, taking all the powder. But now that we are full again, thanks to the little Englishman, and you are hungry, you come back. Well, if I had my way I would give you a gun and six days' rations, and turn you out to shift for yourself."

"Don't be afraid, Jan Meyer," shouted Pereira from the back of the pack-ox. "As soon as I am strong enough I will leave you in charge of your English captain here"—and he pointed to me—"and go to tell our people what sort of folk you are."

"That is good news," interrupted Prinsloo, a stolid old Boer, who stood by puffing at his pipe. "Get well, get well as soon as you can, Hernan Pereira."

It was at this juncture that Marais arrived, accompanied by Marie. Where he came from I do not know, but I think he must have been keeping in the background on purpose to see what kind of a reception Pereira would meet with.

"Silence, brothers," he said. "Is this the way you greet my nephew, who has returned from the gate of death, when you should be on your knees thanking God for his deliverance?"

"Then go on your knees and thank Him yourself, Henri Marais," screamed the irrepressible Vrouw Prinsloo. "I give thanks for the safe return of Allan here, though it is true they would be warmer if he had left this stinkcat behind him. Allemachte! Henri Marais, why do you make so much of this Portuguese fellow? Has he bewitched you? Or is it because he is your sister's son, or because you want to force Marie there to marry him? Or is it, perhaps, that he knows of something bad in your past life, and you have to bribe him to keep his mouth shut?"

Now, whether this last unpleasant suggestion was a mere random arrow drawn from Vrouw Prinsloo's well-stored quiver, or whether the vrouw had got hold of the tail-end of some long-buried truth, I do not know. Of course, however, the latter explanation is possible. Many men have done things in their youth which they do not wish to see dug up in their age; and Pereira may have learned a family secret of the kind from his mother.

At any rate, the effect of the old lady's words upon Marais was quite remarkable. Suddenly he went into one of his violent and constitutional rages. He cursed Vrouw Prinsloo. He cursed everybody else, assuring them severally and collectively that Heaven would come even with them. He said there was a plot against him and his nephew, and that I was at the bottom of it, I who had made his daughter fond of my ugly little face. So furious were his words, whereof there were many more which I have forgotten, that at length Marie began to cry and ran away. Presently, too, the Boers strolled off, shrugging their shoulders, one of them saying audibly that Marais had gone quite mad at last, as he always thought he would.

Then Marais followed them, throwing up his arms and still cursing as he went, and, slipping over the tail of the pack-ox, Pereira followed him. So the Vrouw Prinsloo and I were left alone, for the coloured men had departed, as they always do when white people begin to quarrel.

"There, Allan, my boy," said the vrouw in triumph, "I have found the sore place on the mule's back, and didn't I make him squeal and kick, although on most days of the week he seems to be such a good and quiet mule—at any rate, of late."

"I dare say you did, vrouw," I said wrathfully, "but I wish you would leave Mynheer Marais's sore places alone, seeing that if the squeals are for you, the kicks are for me."

"What does that matter, Allan?" she asked. "He always was your enemy, so that it is just as well you should see his heels when you are out of reach of them. My poor boy, I think you will have a bad time of it between the stinkcat and the mule, although you have done so much for both of them. Well, there is one thing—Marie has a true heart. She will never marry any man except yourself, Allan—even if you are not here to marry," she added by an afterthought.

The old lady paused a little, staring at the ground. Then she looked up and said:

"Allan, my dear" (for she was really fond of me, and called me thus at times), "you didn't take the advice I gave you, namely, to look for Pereira and not to find him. Well, I will give you some more, which you _will_ take if you are wise."

"What is it?" I asked doubtfully; for, although she was upright enough in her own way, the Vrouw Prinsloo could bring herself to look at things in strange lights. Like many other women, she judged of moral codes by the impulses of her heart, and was quite prepared to stretch them to suit circumstances or to gain an end which she considered good in itself.

"Just this, lad. Do you make a two days' march with Marie into the bush. I want a little change, so I will come, too, and marry you there; for I have got a prayer-book, and can spell out the service if we go through it once or twice first."

Now, the vision of Marie and myself being married by the Vrouw Prinsloo in the vast and untrodden veld, although attractive, was so absurd that I laughed.

"Why do you laugh, Allan? Anyone can marry people if there is no one else there; indeed, I believe that they can marry themselves."

"I dare say," I answered, not wishing to enter into a legal argument with the vrouw. "But you see, Tante, I solemnly promised her father that I would not marry her until she was of age, and if I broke my word I should not be an honest man."

"An honest man!" she exclaimed with the utmost contempt; "an honest man! Well, are Marais and Hernan Pereira honest men? Why do you not cut your stick the same length as theirs, Allan Quatermain? I tell you that your verdomde honesty will be your ruin. You remember my words later on," and she marched off in high dudgeon.

When she had gone I went to my wagons, where Hans was waiting for me with a detailed and interminable report of everything that had happened in my absence. Glad was I to find that, except for the death of one sickly ox, nothing had gone wrong. When at length he had ended his long story, I ate some food which Marie sent over for me ready cooked, for I was too tired to join any of the Boers that night. Just as I had finished my meal and was thinking of turning in, Marie herself appeared within the circle of the camp-fire's light. I sprang up and ran to her, saying that I had not expected to see her that evening, and did not like to come to the house.

"No," she answered, drawing me back into the shadows, "I understand. My father seems very much upset, almost mad, indeed. If the Vrouw Prinsloo's tongue had been a snake's fang, it could not have stung him worse."

"And where is Pereira?" I asked.

"Oh! my cousin sleeps in the other room. He is weak and worn out. All the same, Allan, he wanted to kiss me. So I told him at once how matters stood between you and me, and that we were to be married in six months."

"What did he say to that?" I asked.

"He turned to my father and said: 'Is this true, my uncle?' And my father answered: 'Yes, that is the best bargain I could make with the Englishman, seeing that you were not here to make a better.'"

"And what happened then, Marie?"

"Oh, then Hernan thought a while. At last he looked up and said: 'I understand. Things have gone badly. I acted for the best, who went away to try to find help for all of you. I failed. Meanwhile the Englishman came and saved you. Afterwards he saved me also. Uncle, in all this I see God's hand; had it not been for this Allan none of us would be alive. Yes, God used him that we might be kept alive. Well, he has promised that he will not marry Marie for six months. And you know, my uncle, that some of these English are great fools; they keep their promises even to their own loss. Now, in six months much may happen; who knows what will happen?'"

"Were you present when you heard all this, Marie?" I asked.

"No, Allan; I was the other side of the reed partition. But at those words I entered and said: 'My father and Cousin Hernan, please understand that there is one thing which will never happen.'

"'What is that?' asked my cousin.

"'It will never happen that I shall marry you, Hernan,' I replied.

"'Who knows, Marie, who knows?' he said.

"'I do, Hernan,' I answered. 'Even if Allan were to die to-morrow, I would not marry you, either then or twenty years hence. I am glad that he has saved your life, but henceforth we are cousins, nothing more.'

"'You hear what the girl tells us,' said my father; 'why do you not give up the business? What is the use of kicking against the pricks?'

"'If one wears stout boots and kicks hard enough, the pricks give way,' said Hernan. 'Six months is a long time, my uncle.'

"'It may be so, cousin,' I said; 'but remember that neither six months nor six years, nor six thousand years, are long enough to make me marry any man except Allan Quatermain, who has just rescued you from death. Do you understand?'

"'Yes,' he replied, 'I understand that you will not marry me. Only then I promise that you shall not marry either Allan Quatermain or any other man.'

"'God will decide that,' I answered, and came away, leaving him and my father together. And now, Allan, tell me all that has happened since we parted."

So I told her everything, including the Vrouw Prinsloo's advice.

"Of course, Allan, you were quite right," she remarked when I had finished; "but I am not sure that the Vrouw Prinsloo was not also right in her own fashion. I am afraid of my cousin Hernan, who holds my father in his hand—fast, fast. Still, we have promised, and must keep our word."

The Shot in the Kloof

I think it was about three weeks after these events that we began our southward trek. On the morning subsequent to our arrival at Marais's camp, Pereira came up to me when several people were present, and, taking my hand, thanked me in a loud voice for having saved his life. Thenceforward, he declared, I should be dearer to him than a brother, for was there not a blood bond between us?

I answered I did not think any such bond existed; indeed, I was not sure what it meant. I had done my duty by him, neither less nor more, and there was nothing further to be said.

It turned out, however, that there was a great deal further to be said, since Pereira desired to borrow money, or, rather, goods, from me. He explained that owing to the prejudices of the vulgar Boers who remained alive in that camp, and especially of the scandalous-tongued Vrouw Prinsloo, both he and his uncle had come to the conclusion that it would be wise for him to remove himself as soon as possible. Therefore he proposed to trek away alone.

I answered that I should have thought he had done enough solitary travelling in this veld, seeing how his last expedition had ended. He replied that he had, indeed, but everyone here was so bitter against him that no choice was left. Then he added with an outburst of truth:

"Allemachte! Mynheer Quatermain, do you suppose that it is pleasant for me to see you making love all day to the maid who was my betrothed, and to see her paying back the love with her eyes? Yes, and doubtless with her lips, too, from all I hear."

"You could leave her whom you called your betrothed, but who never was betrothed to anyone but me with her own will, to starve in the veld, mynheer. Why, then, should you be angry because I picked up that which you threw away, that, too, which was always my own and not yours? Had it not been for me, there would now be no maid left for us to quarrel over, as, had it not been for me, there would be no man left for me to quarrel with about the maid."

"Are you God, then, Englishman, that you dispose of the lives of men and women at your will? It was He Who saved us, not you."

"He may have saved you, but it was through me. I carried out the rescue of these poor people whom you deserted, and I nursed you back to life."

"I did not desert them; I went to get help for them."

"Taking all the powder and the only horse with you! Well, that is done with, and now you want to borrow goods to pay for cattle—from me, whom you hate. You are not proud, Mynheer Pereira, when you have an end to serve, whatever that end may be," and I looked at him. My instinct warned me against this false and treacherous man, who, I felt, was even then plotting in his heart to bring some evil upon me.

"No, I am not proud. Why should I be, seeing that I mean to repay you twice over for anything which you may lend me now?"

I reflected a while. Certainly our journey to Natal would be pleasanter if Pereira were not of the company. Also, if he went with us, I was sure that before we came to the end of that trek, one or other of us would leave his bones on the road. In short, not to put too fine a point on it, I feared lest in this way or in that he would bring me to my death in order that he might possess himself of Marie. We were in a wild country, with few witnesses and no law courts, where such deeds might be done again and again and the doer never called to account for lack of evidence and judges.

So I made up my mind to fall in with his wishes, and we began to bargain. The end of it was that I advanced him enough of my remaining goods to buy the cattle he required from the surrounding natives. It was no great quantity, after all, seeing that in this uncivilised place an ox could be purchased for a few strings of beads or a cheap knife. Further, I sold him a few of the beasts that I had broken, a gun, some ammunition and certain other necessaries, for all of which things he gave me a note of hand written in my pocket-book. Indeed, I did more; for as none of the Boers would help him I assisted Pereira to break in the cattle he bought, and even consented when he asked me to give him the services of two of the Zulus whom I had hired.

All these preparations took a long while. If I remember right, twelve more days had gone by before Pereira finally trekked off from Marais's camp, by which time he was quite well and strong again.

We all assembled to see the start, and Marais offered up a prayer for his nephew's safe journey and our happy meeting again in Natal at the laager of Retief, which was to be our rendezvous, if that leader were still in Natal. No one else joined in the prayer. Only Vrouw Prinsloo audibly added another of her own. It was to the effect that he might not come back a second time, and that she might never see his face again, either at Retief's laager or anywhere else, if it would please the good Lord so to arrange matters.

The Boers tittered; even the Meyer children tittered, for by this time the hatred of the Vrouw Prinsloo for Hernan Pereira was the joke of the place. But Pereira himself pretended not to hear, said good-bye to us all affectionately, adding a special petition for the Vrouw Prinsloo, and off we went.

I say "we went" because with my usual luck, to help him with the half-broken oxen, I was commandeered to accompany this man to his first outspan, a place with good water about twelve miles from the camp, where he proposed to remain for the night.

Now, as we started about ten o'clock in the morning and the veld was fairly level, I expected that we should reach this outspan by three or four in the afternoon, which would give me time to walk back before sunset. In fact, however, so many accidents happened of one sort or another, both to the wagon itself, of which the woodwork had shrunk with long standing in the sun, and to the cattle, which, being unused to the yoke, tied themselves in a double knot upon every opportunity, that we only arrived there at the approach of night.

The last mile of that trek was through a narrow gorge cut out by water in the native rock. Here trees grew sparsely, also great ferns, but the bottom of the gorge, along which game were accustomed to travel, was smooth enough for wagons, save for a few fallen boulders, which it was necessary to avoid.

When at length we reached the outspan I asked the Hottentot, Klaus, who was assisting me to drive the team, where his master was, for I could not see him anywhere. He answered that he had gone back down the kloof to look for something that had fallen from the wagon, a bolt I think he said.

"Very good," I replied. "Then tell him, if we do not meet, that I have returned to the camp."

As I set out the sun was sinking below the horizon, but this did not trouble me overmuch, as I had a rifle with me, that same light rifle with which I had shot the geese in the great match. Also I knew that the moon, being full, would be up presently.

The sun sank, and the kloof was plunged in gloom. The place seemed eerie and lonesome, and suddenly I grew afraid. I began to wonder where Pereira was, and what he might be doing. I even thought of turning back and finding some way round, only having explored all this district pretty thoroughly in my various shooting expeditions from the camp, I knew there was no practicable path across those hills. So I went on with my rifle at full cock, whistling to keep up my courage, which, of course, in the circumstances was a foolish thing to do. It occurred to me at the time that it was foolish, but, in truth, I would not give way to the dark suspicions which crossed my mind. Doubtless by now Pereira had passed me and reached the outspan.

The moon began to shine—that wonderful African moon, which turns night to day—throwing a network of long, black shadows of trees and rocks across the game track I was following. Right ahead of me was a particularly dark patch of this shadow, caused by a projecting wall of cliff, and beyond it an equally bright patch of moonlight. Somehow I misdoubted me of that stretch of gloom, for although, of course, I could see nothing there, my quick ear caught the sound of movements.

I halted for a moment. Then, reflecting that these were doubtless caused by some night-walking creature, which, even should it chance to be dangerous, would flee at the approach of man, I plunged into it boldly. As I emerged at the other end—the shadow was eighteen or twenty paces long—it occurred to me that if any enemy were lurking there, I should be an easy target as I entered the line of clear light. So, almost instinctively, for I do not remember that I reasoned the thing out, after my first two steps forward in the light I gave a little spring to the left, where there was still shadow, although it was not deep. Well was it for me that I did so, for at that moment I felt something touch my cheek and heard the loud report of a gun immediately behind me.

Now, the wisest course would have been for me to run before whoever had fired found time to reload. But a kind of fury seized me, and run I would not. On the contrary, I turned with a shout, and charged back into the shadow. Something heard me coming, something fled in front of me. In a few seconds we were out into the moonlight beyond, and, as I expected, I saw that this something was a man—Pereira!

He halted and wheeled round, lifting the stock of his gun, club fashion.

"Thank God! it is you, Heer Allan," he said; "I thought you were a tiger."

"Then it is your last thought, murderer," I answered, raising my rifle.

"Don't shoot," he said. "Would you have my blood upon you? Why do you want to kill me?"

"Why did you try to kill me?" I answered, covering him.

"I try to kill you! Are you mad? Listen, for your own sake. I sat down on the bank yonder waiting for the moon, and, being tired, fell asleep. Then I woke up with a start, and, thinking from the sounds that a tiger was after me, fired to scare it. Allemachte! man, if I had aimed at you, could I have missed at that distance?"

"You did not quite miss, and had I not stepped to the left, you would have blown my head off. Say your prayers, you dog!"

"Allan Quatermain," he exclaimed with desperate energy," you think I lie, who speak the truth. Kill me if you will, only then remember that you will hang for it. We court one woman, that is known, and who will believe this story of yours that I tried to shoot you? Soon the Kaffirs will come to look for me, probably they are starting already, and will find my body with your bullet in my heart. Then they will take it back to Marais's camp, and I say—who will believe your story?"

"Some, I think, murderer," but as I spoke the words a chill of fear struck me. It was true, I could prove nothing, having no witnesses, and henceforward I should be a Cain among the Boers, one who had slain a man for jealousy. His gun was empty; yes, but it might be said that I had fired it after his death. And as for the graze upon my cheek—why, a twig might have caused it. What should I do, then? Drive him before me to the camp, and tell this tale? Even then it would be but my word against his. No, he had me in a forked stick. I must let him go, and trust that Heaven would avenge his crime, since I could not. Moreover, by now my first rage was cooling, and to execute a man thus—

"Hernan Pereira," I said, "you are a liar and a coward. You tried to butcher me because Marie loves me and hates you, and you want to force her to marry you. Yet I cannot shoot you down in cold blood as you deserve. I leave it to God to punish you, as, soon or late, He will, here or hereafter; you who thought to slaughter me and trust to the hyenas to hide your crime, as they would have done before morning. Get you gone before I change my mind, and be swift."

Without another word he turned and ran swiftly as a buck, leaping from side to side as he ran, to disturb my aim in case I should shoot.

When he was a hundred yards away or more I, too, turned and ran, never feeling safe till I knew there was a mile of ground between us.

It was past ten o'clock that night when I got back to the camp, where I found Hans the Hottentot about to start to look for me, with two of the Zulus, and told him that I had been detained by accidents to the wagon. The Vrouw Prinsloo was still up also, waiting to hear of my arrival.

"What was the accident, Allan?" she asked. "It looks as though there had been a bullet in it," and she pointed to the bloody smear upon my cheek.

I nodded.

"Pereira's?" she asked again.

I nodded a second time.

"Did you kill him?"

"No; I let him go. It would have been said that I murdered him," and I told her what had happened.

"Ja, Allan," she remarked when I had finished. "I think you were wise, for you could have proved nothing. But oh! for what fate, I wonder, is God Almighty saving up that stinkcat. Well, I will go and tell Marie that you are back safe, for her father won't let her out of the hut so late; but nothing more unless you wish it."

"No, Tante; I think nothing more, at any rate at present."

Here I may state, however, that within a few days Marie and everyone else in the camp knew the story in detail, except perhaps Marais, to whom no one spoke of his nephew. Evidently Vrouw Prinsloo had found herself unable to keep secret such an example of the villainy of her aversion, Pereira. So she told her daughter, who told the others quickly enough, though I gathered that some of them set down what had happened to accident. Bad as they knew Pereira to be, they could not believe that he was guilty of so black a crime.

About a week later the rest of us started from Marais's camp, a place that, notwithstanding the sadness of many of its associations, I confess I left with some regret. The trek before us, although not so very long, was of an extremely perilous nature. We had to pass through about two hundred miles of country of which all we knew was that its inhabitants were the Amatonga and other savage tribes. Here I should explain that after much discussion we had abandoned the idea of retracing the route followed by Marais on his ill-fated journey towards Delagoa.

Had we taken this it would have involved our crossing the terrible Lobombo Mountains, over which it was doubtful whether our light cattle could drag the wagons. Moreover, the country beyond the mountains was said to be very bare of game and also of Kaffirs, so that food might be lacking. On the other hand, if we kept to the east of the mountains the veld through which we must pass was thickly populated, which meant that in all probability we could buy grain.

What finally decided us to adopt this route, however, was that here in these warm, low-lying lands there would be grass for the oxen. Indeed, now, at the beginning of spring, in this part of Africa it was already pushing. Even if it were not, the beasts could live upon what herbage remained over from last summer and on the leaves of trees, neither of which in this winter veld ever become quite lifeless, whereas on the sere and fire-swept plains beyond the mountains they might find nothing at all. So we determined to risk the savages and the lions which followed the game into these hot districts, especially as it was not yet the fever season or that of the heavy rains, so that the rivers would be fordable.

I do not propose to set out our adventures in detail, for these would be too long. Until the great one of which I shall have to tell presently, they were of an annoying rather than of a serious nature. Travelling as we did, between the mountains and the sea, we could not well lose our way, especially as my Zulus had passed through that country; and when their knowledge failed us, we generally managed to secure the services of local guides. The roads, however, or rather the game tracks and Kaffir paths which we followed, were terrible, for with the single exception of that of Pereira for part of the distance, no wagon had ever gone over them before. Indeed, a little later in the year they could not have been travelled at all. Sometimes we stuck in bogs out of which we had to dig the wheels, and sometimes in the rocky bottoms of streams, while once we were obliged literally to cut our way through a belt of dense bush from which it took us eight days to escape.

Our other chief trouble came from the lions, whereof there were great numbers in this veld. The prevalence of these hungry beasts forced us to watch our cattle very closely while they grazed, and at night, wherever it was possible, to protect them and ourselves in "bombast," or fences of thorns, within which we lit fires to scare away wild beasts. Notwithstanding these precautions, we lost several of the oxen, and ourselves had some narrow escapes.

Thus, one night, just as Marie was about to enter the wagon where the women slept, a great lion, desperate with hunger, sprang over the fence. She leapt away from the beast, and in so doing caught her foot and fell down, whereon the lion came for her. In another few seconds she would have been dead, or carried off living.

But as it chanced, Vrouw Prinsloo was close at hand. Seizing a flaming bough from the fire, that intrepid woman ran at the lion and, as it opened its huge mouth to roar or bite, thrust the burning end of the bough into its throat. The lion closed its jaws upon it, then finding the mouthful not to its taste, departed even more quickly than it had come, uttering the most dreadful noises, and leaving Marie quite unhurt. Needless to say, after this I really worshipped the Vrouw Prinsloo, though she, good soul, thought nothing of the business, which in those days was but a common incident of travel.

I think it was on the day after this lion episode that we came upon Pereira's wagon, or rather its remains. Evidently he had tried to trek along a steep, rocky bank which overhung a stream, with the result that the wagon had fallen into the stream-bed, then almost dry, and been smashed beyond repair.

The Tonga natives of the neighbourhood, who had burned most of the woodwork in order to secure the precious iron bolts and fittings, informed us that the white man and his servants who were with the wagon had gone forward on foot some ten days before, driving their cattle with them. Whether this story were true or not we had no means of finding out. It was quite possible that Pereira and his companions had been murdered, though as we found the Tongas very quiet folk if well treated and given the usual complimentary presents for wayleaves, this did not seem probable. Indeed, a week later our doubts upon this point were cleared up thus.

We had reached a big kraal called Fokoti, on the Umkusi River, which appeared to be almost deserted. We asked an old woman whom we met where its people had gone. She answered that they had fled towards the borders of Swaziland, fearing an attack from the Zulus, whose territories began beyond this Umkusi River. It seemed that a few days before a Zulu impi or regiment had appeared upon the banks of the river, and although there was no war at the time between the Zulus and the Tongas, the latter had thought it wise to put themselves out of reach of those terrible spears.

On hearing this news we debated whether it would not be well for us to follow their example and, trekking westwards, try to find a pass in the mountains. Upon this point there was a division of opinion among us. Marais, who was a fatalist, wished to go on, saying that the good Lord would protect us, as He had done in the past.

"Allemachte!" answered the Vrouw Prinsloo. "Did He protect all those who lie dead at Marais's camp, whither your folly led us, mynheer? The good Lord expects us to look after our own skins, and I know that these Zulus are of the same blood as Umsilikazi's Kaffirs, who have killed so many of our people. Let us try the mountains, say I."

Of course her husband and son agreed with her, for to them the vrouw's word was law; but Marais, being, as usual, obstinate, would not give way. All that afternoon they wrangled, while I held my tongue, declaring that I was willing to abide by the decision of the majority. In the end, as I foresaw they would, they appealed to me to act as umpire between them.

"Friends," I answered, "if you had asked me my opinion before, I should have voted for trying the mountains, beyond which, perhaps, we might find some Boers. I do not like this story of the Zulu impi. I think that someone has told them of our coming, and that it is us they mean to attack and not the Tongas, with whom they are at peace. My men say that it is not usual for impis to visit this part of the country."

"Who could have told them?" asked Marais.

"I don't know, mynheer. Perhaps the natives have sent on word, or perhaps—Hernan Pereira."

"I knew that you would suspect my nephew, Allan," he exclaimed angrily.

"I suspect no one; I only weigh what is probable. However, it is too late for us to move to-night either south or westwards, so I think I will sleep over the business and see what I can find out from my Zulus."

That night, or rather the following morning, the question was settled for us, for when I woke up at dawn, it was to see the faint light glimmering on what I knew must be spears. We were surrounded by a great company of Zulus, as I discovered afterwards, over two hundred strong. Thinking that after their fashion they were preparing to attack us at dawn, I called the news to the others, whereon Marais rushed forward, just as he had left his bed, cocking his roer as he came.

"For the love of God, do not shoot!" I said. "How can we resist so many? Soft words are our only chance."

Still he attempted to fire, and would have done so had I not thrown myself upon him and literally torn the gun from his hand. By this time the Vrouw Prinsloo had come up, a very weird spectacle, I recollect, in what she called her "sleep-garments," that included a night-cap made of a worn jackal skin and a kind of otter-pelt stomacher.

"Accursed fool!" she said to Marais, "would you cause all our throats to be cut? Go forward, you, Allan, and talk to those 'swartzels'" (that is, black creatures), "gently, as you would to a savage dog. You have a tongue steeped in oil, and they may listen to you."

"Yes," I answered; "that seems the best thing to do. If I should not return, give my love to Marie."

So I beckoned to the headman of my Zulus whom I had hired at Delagoa, to accompany me, and marched forward boldly quite unarmed. We were encamped upon a rise of ground a quarter of a mile from the river, and the impi, or those of them whom we could see, were at the foot of this rise about a hundred and sixty yards away. The light was growing now, and when I was within fifty paces of them they saw me. At some word of command a number of men rushed toward me, their fighting shields held over their bodies and their spears up.

"We are dead!" exclaimed my Kaffir in a resigned voice. I shared his opinion, but thought I might as well die standing as running away.

Now I should explain that though as yet I had never mixed with these Zulus, I could talk several native dialects kindred to that which they used very well indeed. Moreover, ever since I had hired men of their race at Delagoa, I had spent all my spare time in conversing with them and acquiring a knowledge of their language, history and customs. So by this time I knew their tongue fairly, although occasionally I may have used terms which were unfamiliar to them.

Thus it came about that I was able to shout to them, asking what was their business with us. Hearing themselves addressed in words which they understood, the men halted, and seeing that I was unarmed, three of them approached me.

"We come to take you prisoners, white people, or to kill you if you resist," said their captain.

"By whose order?" I asked.

"By the order of Dingaan our king."

"Is it so? And who told Dingaan that we were here?"

"The Boer who came in front of you."

"Is it so?" I said again. "And now what do you need of us?"

"That you should accompany us to the kraal of Dingaan."

"I understand. We are quite willing, since it lies upon our road. But then why do you come against us, who are peaceful travellers, with your spears lifted?"

"For this reason. The Boer told us that there is among you a 'child of George'" (an Englishman), "a terrible man who would kill us unless we killed or bound him first. Show us this child of George that we may make him fast, or slay him, and we will not hurt the rest of you."

"I am the child of George," I answered, "and if you think it necessary to make me fast, do so."

Now the Zulus burst out laughing.

"You! Why, you are but a boy who weighs no more than a fat girl," exclaimed their captain, a great, bony fellow who was named Kambula.

"That may be so," I answered; "but sometimes the wisdom of their fathers dwells in the young. I am the son of George who saved these Boers from death far away, and I am taking them back to their own people. We desire to see Dingaan, your king. Be pleased therefore to lead us to him as he has commanded you to do. If you do not believe what I tell you, ask this man who is with me, and his companions who are of your own race. They will tell you everything."

Then the captain Kambula called my servant apart and talked with him for a long while.

When the interview was finished he advanced to me and said:

"Now I have heard all about you. I have heard that although young you are very clever, so clever that you do not sleep, but watch by night as well as by day. Therefore, that I, Kambula, name you Macumazahn, Watcher-by-night, and by that name you shall henceforth be known among us. Now, Macumazahn, son of George, bring out these Boers whom you are guiding that I may lead them in their moving huts to the Great Place, Umgungundhlovu, where dwells Dingaan the king. See, we lay down our spears and will come to meet them unarmed, trusting to you to protect us, O Macumazahn, Son of George," and he cast his assegai to the ground.

"Come," I said, and led them to the wagons.

Dingaan's Bet

As I advanced to the wagons accompanied by Kambula and his two companions, I saw that Marais, in a state of great excitement, was engaged in haranguing the two Prinsloo men and Meyer, while the Vrouw Prinsloo and Marie appeared to be attempting to calm him.

"They are unarmed," I heard him shout. "Let us seize the black devils and hold them as hostages."

Thereon, led by Marais, the three Boer men came towards us doubtfully, their guns in their hands.

"Be careful what you are doing," I called to them. "These are envoys," and they hung back a little while Marais went on with his haranguing.

The Zulus looked at them and at me, then Kambula said:

"Are you leading us into a trap, Son of George?"

"Not so," I answered; "but the Boers are afraid of you and think to take you prisoners."

"Tell them," said Kambula quietly, "that if they kill us or lay a hand on us, as no doubt they can do, very soon every one of them will be dead and their women with them."

I repeated this ultimatum energetically enough, but Marais shouted:

"The Englishman is betraying us to the Zulus! Do not trust him; seize them as I tell you."

What would have happened I am sure I do not know; but just then the Vrouw Prinsloo came up and caught her husband by the arm, exclaiming:

"You shall have no part in this fool's business. If Marais wishes to seize the Zulus, let him do so himself. Are you mad or drunk that you should think that Allan would wish to betray Marie to the Kaffirs, to say nothing of the rest of us?" and she began to wave an extremely dirty "vatdoek", or dishcloth, which she always carried about with her and used for every purpose, towards Kambula as a sign of peace.

Now the Boers gave way, and Marais, seeing himself in a minority, glowered at me in silence.

"Ask these white people, O Macumazahn," said Kambula, "who is their captain, for to the captain I would speak."

I translated the question, and Marais answered:

"I am."

"No," broke in Vrouw Prinsloo, "_I_ am. Tell them, Allan, that these men are all fools and have given the rule to me, a woman."

So I told them. Evidently this information surprised them a little, for they discussed together. Then Kambula said:

"So be it. We have heard that the people of George are now ruled by a woman, and as you, Macumazahn, are one of that people, doubtless it is the same among your party."

Here I may add that thenceforward the Zulus always accepted the Vrouw Prinsloo as the "Inkosikaas" or chieftainess of our little band, and with the single exception of myself, whom they looked upon as her "mouth," or induna, would only transact business with or give directions to her. The other Boers they ignored completely.

This point of etiquette settled, Kambula bade me repeat what he had already told me, that we were prisoners whom he was instructed by Dingaan to convey to his Great Place, and that if we made no attempt to escape we should not be hurt upon the journey.

I did so, whereon the vrouw asked as I had done, who had informed Dingaan that we were coming.

I repeated to her word for word what the Zulus had told me, that it was Pereira, whose object seems to have been to bring about my death or capture.

Then the vrouw exploded.

"Do you hear that, Henri Marais?" she screamed. "It is your stinkcat of a nephew again. Oh! I thought I smelt him! Your nephew has betrayed us to these Zulus that he may bring Allan to his death. Ask them, Allan, what this Dingaan has done with the stinkcat."

So I asked, and was informed they believed that the king had let Pereira go on to his own people in payment of the information that he had given him.

"My God!" said the vrouw, "I hoped that he had knocked him on the head. Well, what is to be done now?"

"I don't know," I answered. Then an idea occurred to me, and I said to Kambula:

"It seems to be me, the son of George, that your king wants. Take me, and let these people go on their road."

The three Zulus began to discuss this point, withdrawing themselves a little way so that I could not overhear them. But when the Boers understood the offer that I had made, Marie, who until now had been silent, grew more angry than ever I had seen her before.

"It shall not be!" she said, stamping her foot. "Father, I have been obedient to you for long, but if you consent to this I will be obedient no more. Allan saved my cousin Hernan's life, as he saved all our lives. In payment for that good deed Hernan tried to murder him in the kloof—oh! be quiet, Allan; I know all the story. Now he has betrayed him to the Zulus, telling them that he is a terrible and dangerous man who must be killed. Well, if he is to be killed, I will be killed with him, and if the Zulus take him and let us free, I go with him. Now make up your mind."

Marais tugged at his beard, staring first at his daughter and then at me. What he would have answered I do not know, for at that moment Kambula stepped forward and gave his decision.

It was to the effect that although it was the Son of George whom Dingaan wanted, his orders were that all with him were to be taken also. Those orders could not be disobeyed. The king would settle the matter as to whether some of us were to be killed and some let free, or if all were to be killed or let free, when we reached his House. Therefore he commanded that "we should tie the oxen to the moving huts and cross the river at once."

This was the end of that scene. Having no choice we inspanned and continued our journey, escorted by the company of two hundred savages. I am bound to say that during the four or five days that it took us to reach Dingaan's kraal they behaved very well to us. With Kambula and his officers, all of them good fellows in their way, I had many conversations, and from them learned much as to the state and customs of the Zulus. Also the peoples of the districts through which we passed flocked round us at every outspan, for most of them had never seen a white man before, and in return for a few beads brought us all the food that we required. Indeed, the beads, or their equivalents, were nothing but a present, since, by the king's command, they must satisfy our wants. This they did very thoroughly. For instance, when on the last day's trek, some of our oxen gave out, numbers of Zulus were inspanned in place of them, and by their help the wagons were dragged to the great kraal, Umgungundhlovu.

Here an outspan place was assigned to us near to the house, or rather the huts, of a certain missionary of the name of Owen, who with great courage had ventured into this country. We were received with the utmost kindness by him and his wife and household, and it is impossible for me to say what pleasure I found, after all my journeyings, in meeting an educated man of my own race.

Near to our camp was a stone-covered koppie, where, on the morning after our arrival, I saw six or eight men executed in a way that I will not describe. Their crime, according to Mr. Owen, was that they had bewitched some of the king's oxen.

While I was recovering from this dreadful spectacle, which, fortunately, Marie did not witness, the captain Kambula arrived, saying that Dingaan wished to see me. So taking with me the Hottentot Hans and two of the Zulus whom I had hired at Delagoa Bay—for the royal orders were that none of the other white people were to come, I was led through the fence of the vast town in which stood two thousand huts—the "multitude of houses" as the Zulus called it—and across a vast open space in the middle.

On the farther side of this space, where, before long, I was fated to witness a very tragic scene, I entered a kind of labyrinth. This was called "siklohlo", and had high fences with numerous turns, so that it was impossible to see where one was going or to find the way in or out. Ultimately, however, I reached a great hut named "intunkulu", a word that means the "house of houses," or the abode of the king, in front of which I saw a fat man seated on a stool, naked except for the moocha about his middle and necklaces and armlets of blue beads. Two warriors held their broad shields over his head to protect him from the sun. Otherwise he was alone, although I felt sure that the numerous passages around him were filled with guards, for I could hear them moving.

On entering this place Kambula and his companions flung themselves upon their faces and began to sing praises of which the king took no notice. Presently he looked up, and appearing to observe me for the first time asked:

"Who is that white boy?"

Then Kambula rose and said:

"O king, this is the Son of George, whom you commanded me to capture. I have taken him and the Amaboona" (that is, the Boers), "his companions, and brought them all to you, O king."

"I remember," said Dingaan. "The big Boer who was here, and whom Tambusa"—he was one of Dingaan's captains—"let go against my will, said that be was a terrible man who should be killed before he worked great harm to my people. Why did you not kill him, Kambula, although it is true he does not look very terrible?"

"Because the king's word was that I should bring him to the king living," answered Kambula. Then he added cheerfully: "Still, if the king wishes it, I can kill him at once."

"I don't know," said Dingaan doubtfully; "perhaps he can mend guns." Next, after reflecting a while, he bade a shield-holder to fetch someone, I could not hear whom.

"Doubtless," thought I to myself, "it is the executioner," and at that thought a kind of mad rage seized me. Why should my life be ended thus in youth to satisfy the whim of a savage? And if it must be so, why should I go alone?

In the inside pocket of my ragged coat I had a small loaded pistol with two barrels. One of those barrels would kill Dingaan—at five paces I could not miss that bulk—and the other would blow out my brains, for I was not minded to have my neck twisted or to be beaten to death with sticks. Well, if it was to be done, I had better do it at once. Already my hand was creeping towards the pocket when a new idea, or rather two ideas, struck me.

The first was that if I shot Dingaan the Zulus would probably massacre Marie and the others—Marie, whose sweet face I should never see again. The second was that while there is life there is hope. Perhaps, after all, he had not sent for an executioner, but for someone else. I would wait. A few minutes more of existence were worth the having.

The shield-bearer returned, emerging from one of the narrow, reed-hedged passages, and after him came no executioner, but a young white man, who, as I knew from the look of him, was English. He saluted the king by taking off his hat, which I remember was stuck round with black ostrich feathers, then stared at me.

"O Tho-maas" (that is how he pronounced "Thomas"), said Dingaan, "tell me if this boy is one of your brothers, or is he a Boer?"

"The king wants to know if you are Dutch or British," said the white lad, speaking in English.

"As British as you are," I answered. "I was born in England, and come from the Cape."

"That may be lucky for you," he said, "because the old witch-doctor, Zikali, has told him that he must not kill any English. What is your name? Mine is Thomas Halstead. I am interpreter here."

"Allan Quatermain. Tell Zikali, whoever he may be, that if he sticks to his advice I will give him a good present."

"What are you talking about?" asked Dingaan suspiciously.

"He says he is English, no Boer, O king; that he was born across the Black Water, and that he comes from the country out of which all the Boers have trekked."

At this intelligence Dingaan pricked up his ears.

"Then he can tell me about these Boers," he said, "and what they are after, or could if he were able to speak my tongue. I do not trust you to interpret, you Tho-maas, whom I know to be a liar," and he glowered at Halstead.

"I can speak your tongue, though not very well, O king," I interrupted, "and I can tell you all about the Boers, for I have lived among them."

"Ow!" said Dingaan, intensely interested. "But perhaps you are also a liar. Or are you a praying man, like that fool yonder, who is named Oweena?"—he meant the missionary Mr. Owen—"whom I spare because it is not lucky to kill one who is mad, although he tries to frighten my soldiers with tales of a fire into which they will go after they are dead. As though it matters what happens to them after they are dead!" he added reflectively, taking a pinch of snuff.

"I am no liar," I answered. "What have I to lie about?"

"You would lie to save your own life, for all white men are cowards; not like the Zulus, who love to die for their king. But how are you named?"

"Your people call me Macumazahn."

"Well, Macumazahn, if you are no liar, tell me, is it true that these Boers rebelled against their king who was named George, and fled from him as the traitor Umsilikazi did from me?"

"Yes," I answered, "that is true."

"Now I am sure that you are a liar," said Dingaan triumphantly. "You say that you are English and therefore serve your king, or the Inkosikaas" (that is the Great Lady), "who they tell me now sits in his place. How does it come about then that you are travelling with a party of these very Amaboona who must be your enemies, since they are the enemies of your king, or of her who follows after him?"

Now I knew that I was in a tight place, for on this matter of loyalty, Zulu, and indeed all native ideas, are very primitive. If I said that I had sympathy with the Boers, Dingaan would set me down as a traitor. If I said that I hated the Boers, then still I should be a traitor because I associated with them, and a traitor in his eyes would be one to be killed. I do not like to talk religion, and anyone who has read what I have written in various works will admit that I have done so rarely, if ever. Yet at that moment I put up a prayer for guidance, feeling that my young life hung upon the answer, and it came to me—whence I do not know. The essence of that guidance was that I should tell the simple truth to this fat savage. So I said to him:

"The answer is this, O king. Among those Boers is a maiden whom I love and who betrothed herself to me since we were 'so high.' Her father took her north. But she sent a message to me saying that her people died of fever and she starved. So I went up in a ship to save her, and have saved her, and those who remained alive of her people with her."

"Ow!" said Dingaan; "I understand that reason. It is a good reason. However many wives he may have, there is no folly that a man will not commit for the sake of some particular girl who is not yet his wife. I have done as much myself, especially for one who was called Nada the Lily, of whom a certain Umslopogaas robbed me, one of my own blood of whom I am much afraid."

For a while he brooded heavily, then went on:

"Your reason is good, Macumazahn, and I accept it. More, I promise you this. Perhaps I shall kill these Boers, or perhaps I shall not kill them. But if I make up my mind to kill them, this girl of yours shall be spared. Point her out to Kambula here—not to Tho-maas, for he is a liar and would tell me the wrong one—and she shall be spared."

"I thank you, O king," I said; "but what is the use of that if I am to be killed?"

"I did not say that you were to be killed, Macumazahn, though perhaps I shall kill you, or perhaps I shall not kill you. It depends upon whether I find you to be a liar, or not a liar. Now the Boer whom Tambusa let go against my wish said that you are a mighty magician as well as a very dangerous man, one who can shoot birds flying on the wing with a bullet, which is impossible. Can you do so?"

"Sometimes," I answered.

"Very good, Macumazahn. Now we will see if you are a wizard or a liar. I will make a bet with you. Yonder by your camp is a hill called 'Hloma Amabutu,' a hill of stones where evildoers are slain. This afternoon some wicked ones die there, and when they are dead the vultures will come to devour them. Now this is my bet with you. When those vultures come you shall shoot at them, and if you kill three out of the first five on the wing—not on the ground, Macumazahn—then I will spare these Boers. But if you miss them, then I shall know that you are a liar and no wizard, and I will kill them every one on the hill Hloma Amabutu. I will spare none of them except the girl, whom perhaps I will take as a wife. As to you, I will not yet say what I will do with you."

Now my first impulse was to refuse this monstrous wager, which meant that the lives of a number of people were to be set against my skill in shooting. But young Thomas Halstead, guessing the words that were about to break from me, said in English:

"Accept unless you are a fool. If you don't he will cut the throats of every one of them and stick your girl into the emposeni" (that is harem), "while you will become a prisoner as I am."

These were words that I could not resent or neglect, so although despair was in my heart, I said coolly:

"Be it so, O king. I take your wager. If I kill three vultures out of five as they hover over the hill, then I have your promise that all those who travel with me shall be allowed to go hence in safety."

"Yes, yes, Macumazahn; but if you fail to kill them, remember that the next vultures you shoot at shall be those that come to feed upon their flesh, for then I shall know that you are no magician, but a common liar. And now begone, Tho-maas. I will not have you spying on me; and you, Macumazahn, come hither. Although you talk my tongue so badly, I would speak with you about the Boers."

So Halstead went, shrugging his shoulders and muttering as he passed me:

"I hope you really _can_ shoot."

After he had left I sat alone for a full hour with Dingaan while he cross-examined me about the Dutch, their movements and their aims in travelling to the confines of his country.

I answered his questions as best I could, trying to make out a good case for them.

At length, when he grew weary of talking, he clapped his hands, whereon a number of fine girls appeared, two of whom carried pots of beer, from which he offered me drink.

I replied that I would have none, since beer made the hand shake and that on the steadiness of my hand that afternoon depended the lives of many. To do him justice he quite understood the point. Indeed, he ordered me to be conducted back to the camp at once that I might rest, and even sent one of his own attendants with me to hold a shield over my head as I walked so that I should be protected from the sun.

"Hamba gachle" (that is "Go softly"), said the wicked old tyrant to me as I departed under the guidance of Kambula. "This afternoon, one hour before sundown, I will meet you at Hloma Amabutu, and there shall be settled the fate of these Amaboona, your companions."

When I reached the camp it was to find all the Boers clustered together waiting for me, and with them the Reverend Mr. Owen and his people, including a Welsh servant of his, a woman of middle age who, I remember, was called Jane.

"Well," said the Vrouw Prinsloo, "and what is your news, young man?"

"My news, aunt," I answered, "is that one hour before sundown to-day I have to shoot vultures on the wing against the lives of all of you. This you owe to that false-hearted hound Hernan Pereira, who told Dingaan that I am a magician. Now Dingaan would prove it. He thinks that only by magic can a man shoot soaring vultures with a bullet, and as he is determined to kill you all, except perhaps Marie, in the form of a bet he has set me a task which he believes to be impossible. If I fail, the bet is lost, and so are your lives. If I succeed I think your lives will be spared, since Kambula there tells me that the king always makes it a point of honour to pay his bets. Now you have the truth, and I hope you like it," and I laughed bitterly.

When I had finished a perfect storm of execration broke from the Boers. If curses could have killed Pereira, surely he would have died upon the spot, wherever he might be. Only two of them were silent, Marie, who turned very pale, poor girl, and her father. Presently one of them, I think it was Meyer, rounded on him viciously and asked him what he thought now of that devil, his nephew.

"I think there must be some mistake," answered Marais quietly, "since Hernan cannot have wished that we should all be put to death."

"No," shouted Meyer; "but he wished that Allan Quatermain should, which is just as bad; and now it has come about that once more our lives depend upon this English boy."

"At any rate," replied Marais, looking at me oddly, "it seems that he is not to be killed, whether he shoots the vultures or misses them."

"That remains to be proved, mynheer," I answered hotly, for the insinuation stung me. "But please understand that if all of you, my companions, are to be slaughtered, and Marie is to be put among this black brute's women, as he threatens, I have no wish to live on."

"My God! does he threaten that?" said Marais. "Surely you must have misunderstood him, Allan."

"Do you think that I should lie to you on such a matter—" I began.

But, before I could proceed, the Vrouw Prinsloo thrust herself between us, crying:

"Be silent, you, Marais, and you too, Allan. Is this a time that you should quarrel and upset yourself, Allan, so that when the trial comes you will shoot your worst and not your best? And is this a time, Henri Marais, that you should throw insults at one on whom all our lives hang, instead of praying for God's vengeance upon your accursed nephew? Come, Allan, and take food. I have fried the liver of that heifer which the king sent us; it is ready and very good. After you have eaten it you must lie down and sleep a while."

Now among the household of the Reverend Mr. Owen was an English boy called William Wood, who was not more than twelve or fourteen years of age. This lad knew both Dutch and Zulu, and acted as interpreter to the Owen family during the absence on a journey of a certain Mr. Hulley, who really filled that office. While this conversation was taking place in Dutch he was engaged in rendering every word of it into English for the benefit of the clergyman and his family. When Mr. Owen understood the full terror of the situation, he broke in saying:

"This is not a time to eat or to sleep, but a time to pray that the heart of the savage Dingaan may be turned. Come, let us pray!"

"Yes," rejoined Vrouw Prinsloo, when William Wood had translated. "Do you pray, Predicant, and all the rest of you who have nothing else to do, and while you are about it pray also that the bullets of Allan Quatermain may not be turned. As for me and Allan, we have other things to see to, so you must pray a little harder to cover us as well as yourselves. Now you come along, nephew Allan, or that liver may be overdone and give you indigestion, which is worse for shooting than even bad temper. No, not another word. If you try to speak any more, Henri Marais, I will box your ears," and she lifted a hand like a leg of mutton, then, as Marais retreated before her, seized me by the collar as though I were a naughty boy and led me away to the wagons.

The Rehearsal

By the women's wagon we found the liver cooked in its frying-pan, as the vrouw had said. Indeed, it was just done to a turn. Selecting a particularly massive slice, she proceeded to take it from the pan with her fingers in order to set it upon a piece of tin, from which she had first removed the more evident traces of the morning meal with her constant companion, the ancient and unwashen vatdoek. As it chanced the effort was not very successful, since the boiling liver fat burnt the vrouw's fingers, causing her to drop it on the grass, and, I am sorry to add, to swear as well. Not to be defeated, however, having first sucked her fingers to ease their smart, she seized the sizzling liver with the vatdoek and deposited it upon the dirty tin.

"There, nephew," she said triumphantly, "there are more ways of killing a cat than by drowning. What a fool I was not to think of the vatdoek at first. Allemachte! how the flesh has burnt me; I don't suppose that being killed would hurt much more. Also, if the worst comes to the worst, it will soon be over. Think of it, Allan, by to-night I may be an angel, dressed in a long white nightgown like those my mother gave me when I was married, which I cut up for baby-clothes because I found them chilly wear, having always been accustomed to sleep in my vest and petticoat. Yes, and I shall have wings, too, like those on a white gander, only bigger if they are to carry _my_ weight."

"And a crown of Glory," I suggested.

"Yes, of course, a crown of Glory—very large, since I shall be a martyr; but I hope one will only have to wear it on Sundays, as I never could bear anything heavy on my hair; moreover, it would remind me of a Kaffir's head-ring done in gold, and I shall have had enough of Kaffirs. Then there will be the harp," she went on as her imagination took fire at the prospect of these celestial delights. "Have you ever seen a harp, Allan? I haven't except that which King David carries in the picture in the Book, which looks like a broken rimpi chair frame set up edgeways. As for playing the thing, they will have to teach me, that's all, which will be a difficult business, seeing that I would sooner listen to cats on the roof than to music, and as for making it—"

So she chattered on, as I believe with the object of diverting and amusing me, for she was a shrewd old soul who knew how important it was that I should be kept in an equable frame of mind at this crisis in our fates.

Meanwhile I was doing my best with the lump of liver, that tasted painfully of vatdoek and was gritty with sand. Indeed, when the vrouw's back was turned I managed to throw the most of it to Hans behind me, who swallowed it at a gulp as a dog does, since he did not wish to be caught chewing it.

"God in heaven! how fast you eat, nephew," said the vrouw, catching sight of my empty tin. Then, eyeing the voracious Hottentot suspiciously, she added: "That yellow dog of yours hasn't stolen it, has he? If so, I'll teach him."

"No, no, vrouw," answered Hans in alarm. "No meat has passed my lips this day, except what I licked out of the pan after breakfast."

"Then, Allan, you will certainly have indigestion, which is just what I wanted to avoid. Have I not often told you that you should chew your bit twenty times before you swallow, which I would do myself if I had any back teeth left? Here, drink this milk; it is only a little sour and will settle your stomach," and she produced a black bottle and subjected it to the attentions of the vatdoek, growing quite angry when I declined it and sent for water.

Next she insisted upon my getting into her own bed in the wagon to sleep, forbidding me to smoke, which she said made the hand shake. Thither, then, I went, after a brief conversation with Hans, whom I directed to clean my rifle thoroughly. For I wished to be alone and knew that I had little chance of solitude outside of that somewhat fusty couch.

To tell the truth, although I shut my eyes to deceive the vrouw, who looked in occasionally to see how I was getting on, no sleep came to me that afternoon—at least, not for a long while. How could I sleep in that hot place when my heart was torn with doubt and terror? Think of it, reader, think of it! An hour or two, and on my skill would hang the lives of eight white people—men, women, and children, and the safety or the utter shame of the woman whom I loved and who loved me. No, she should be spared the worst. I would give her my pistol, and if there were need she would know what to do.

The fearful responsibility was more than I could bear. I fell into a veritable agony; I trembled and even wept a little. Then I thought of my father and what he would do in such circumstances, and began to pray as I had never prayed before.

I implored the Power above me to give me strength and wisdom; not to let me fail in this hour of trouble, and thereby bring these poor people to a bloody death. I prayed till the perspiration streamed down my face; then suddenly I fell into sleep or swoon. I don't know how long I lay thus, but I think it must have been the best part of an hour. At last I woke up all in an instant, and as I woke I distinctly heard a tiny voice, unlike any other voice in the whole world, speak inside my head, or so it seemed to me, saying:

"Go to the hill Hloma Amabutu, and watch how the vultures fly. Do what comes into your mind, and even if you seem to fail, fear nothing."

I sat up on the old vrouw's bed, and felt that some mysterious change had come over me. I was no longer the same man. My doubts and terrors had gone; my hand was like a rock; my heart was light. I knew that I should kill those three vultures. Of course the story seems absurd, and easy to be explained by the state of my nerves under the strain which was being put upon them, and for aught I know that may be its true meaning. Yet I am not ashamed to confess that I have always held, and still hold, otherwise. I believe that in my extremity some kindly Power did speak to me in answer to my earnest prayers and to those of others, giving me guidance and, what I needed still more, judgment and calmness. At any rate, that this was my conviction at the moment may be seen from the fact that I hastened to obey the teachings of that tiny, unnatural voice.

Climbing out of the wagon, I went to Hans, who was seated near by in the full glare of the hot sun, at which he seemed to stare with unblinking eyes.

"Where's the rifle, Hans?" I said.

"Intombi is here, baas, where I have put her to keep her cool, so that she may not go off before it is wanted," and he pointed to a little grave-like heap of gathered grass at his side.

The natives, I should explain, named this particular gun "Intombi", which means a young girl, because it was so much slimmer and more graceful than other guns.

"Is it clean?" I asked.

"Never was she cleaner since she was born out of the fire, baas. Also, the powder has been sifted and set to dry in the sun with the caps, and the bullets have been trued to the barrel, so that there may be no accidents when it comes to the shooting. If you miss the aasvogels, baas, it will not be the fault of Intombi or of the powder and the bullets; it will be your own fault."

"That's comforting," I answered. "Well, come on, I want to go to the Death-hill yonder."

"Why, baas, before the time?" asked the Hottentot, shrinking back a little. "It is no place to visit till one is obliged. These Zulus say that ghosts sit there even in the daylight, haunting the rocks where they were made ghosts."

"Vultures sit or fly there also, Hans; and I would see how they fly, that I may know when and where to shoot at them."

"That is right, baas," said the clever Hottentot. "This is not like firing at geese in the Groote Kloof. The geese go straight, like an assegai to its mark. But the aasvogels wheel round and round, always on the turn; it is easy to miss a bird that is turning, baas."

"Very easy. Come on."

Just as we were starting Vrouw Prinsloo appeared from behind the other wagon, and with her Marie, who, I noticed, was very pale and whose beautiful eyes were red, as though with weeping.

The vrouw asked me where we were going. I told her. After considering a little, she said that was a good thought of mine, as it was always well to study the ground before a battle.

I nodded, and led Marie aside behind some thorn trees that grew near.

"Oh! Allan, what will be the end of this?" she asked piteously. High as was her courage it seemed to fail her now.

"A good end, dearest," I answered. "We shall come out of this hole safely, as we have of many others."

"How do you know that, Allan, which is known to God alone?"

"Because God told me, Marie," and I repeated to her the story of the voice I had heard in my dream, which seemed to comfort her.

"Yet, yet," she exclaimed doubtfully, "it was but a dream, Allan, and dreams are such uncertain things. You may fail, after all."

"Do I look like one who will fail, Marie?"

She studied me from head to foot, then answered:

"No, you do not, although you did when you came back from the king's huts. Now you are quite changed. Still, Allan, you may fail, and then—what? Some of those dreadful Zulus have been here while you were sleeping, bidding us all make ready to go to the Hill of Death. They say that Dingaan is in earnest. If you do not kill the vultures, he will kill us. It seems that they are sacred birds, and if they escape he will think he has nothing to fear from the white men and their magic, and so will make a beginning by butchering us. I mean the rest of us, for I am to be kept alive, and oh! what shall I do, Allan?"

I looked at her, and she looked at me. Then I took the double-barrelled pistol out of my pocket and gave it to her.

"It is loaded and on the half-cock," I said.

She nodded, and hid it in her dress beneath her apron. Then without more words we kissed and parted, for both of us feared to prolong that scene.

The hill Hloma Amabutu was quite close to our encampment and the huts of the Reverend Mr. Owen, scarcely a quarter of a mile off, I should say, rising from the flat veld on the further side of a little depression that hardly amounted to a valley. As we approached it I noticed its peculiar and blasted appearance, for whereas all around the grass was vivid with the green of spring, on this place none seemed to grow. An eminence strewn with tumbled heaps of blackish rock, and among them a few struggling, dark-leaved bushes; that was its appearance. Moreover, many of these boulders looked as though they had been splashed and lined with whitewash, showing that they were the resting-place of hundreds of gorged vultures.

I believe it is the Chinese who declare that particular localities have good or evil influences attached to them, some kind of spirit of their own, and really Hloma Amabutu and a few other spots that I am acquainted with in Africa give colour to the fancy. Certainly as I set foot upon that accursed ground, that Golgotha, that Place of Skulls, a shiver went through me. It may have been caused by the atmosphere, moral and actual, of the mount, or it may have been a prescience of a certain dreadful scene which within a few months I was doomed to witness there. Or perhaps the place itself and the knowledge of the trial before me sent a sudden chill through my healthy blood. I cannot say which it was, but the fact remains as I have stated, although a minute or two later, when I saw what kind of sleepers lay upon that mount, it would not have been necessary for me to seek any far-fetched explanation of my fear.

Across this hill, winding in and out between the rough rocks that lay here, there and everywhere like hailstones after a winter storm, ran sundry paths. It seems that the shortest road to various places in the neighbourhood of the Great Kraal ran over it, and although no Zulu ever dared to set foot there between sun-set and rise, in the daytime they used these paths freely enough. But I suppose that they also held that this evil-omened field of death had some spirit of its own, some invisible but imminent fiend, who needed to be propitiated, lest soon he should claim them also.

This was their method of propitiation, a common one enough, I believe, in many lands, though what may be its meaning I cannot tell. As the traveller came to those spots where the paths cut across each other, he took a stone and threw it on to a heap that had been accumulated there by the hands of other travellers. There were many such heaps upon the hill, over a dozen, I think, and the size of them was great. I should say that the biggest contained quite fifty loads of stones, and the smallest not fewer than twenty or thirty.

Now, Hans, although he had never set foot there before, seemed to have learned all the traditions of the place, and what rites were necessary to avert its curse. At any rate, when we came to the first heap, he cast a stone upon it, and begged me to do the same. I laughed and refused, but when we reached the second heap the same thing happened. Again I refused, whereon, before we came to a third and larger pile, Hans sat down upon the ground and began to groan, swearing that he would not go one step farther unless I promised to make the accustomed offering.

"Why not, you fool?" I asked.

"Because if you neglect it, baas, I think that we shall stop here for ever. Oh! you may laugh, but I tell you that already you have brought ill-luck upon yourself. Remember my words, baas, when you miss two of the five aasvogels."

"Bosh!" I exclaimed, or, rather, its Dutch equivalent. Still, as this talk of missing vultures touched me nearly, and it is always as well to conform to native prejudices, at the next and two subsequent heaps I cast my stone as humbly as the most superstitious Zulu in the land.

By this time we had reached the summit, which may have been two hundred yards long. It was hog-backed in shape, with a kind of depression in the middle cleared of stones, either by the hand of man or nature, and not unlike a large circus in its general conformation.

Oh! the sight that met my eyes. All about lay the picked and scattered bones of men and women, many of them broken up by the jaws of hyenas. Some were quite fresh, for the hair still clung to the skulls, others blanched and old. But new or ancient there must have been hundreds of them. Moreover, on the sides of the hill it was the same story, though there, for the most part, the bones had been gathered into

gleaming heaps. No wonder that the vultures loved Hloma Amabutu, the Place of
Slaughter of the bloody Zulu king.

Of these horrible birds, however, at the moment not one was to be seen. As there
had been no execution for a few hours they were seeking their food elsewhere. Now,
for my own purposes, I wanted to see them, since otherwise my visit was in vain, and
presently bethought myself of a method of securing their arrival.

"Hans," I said, "I am going to pretend to kill you, and then you must lie quite still
out there like one dead. Even if the aasvogels settle on you, you must lie quite still,
so that I may see whence they come and how they settle."

The Hottentot did not take at all kindly to this suggestion. Indeed, he flatly
refused to obey me, giving sundry good reasons. He said that this kind of rehearsal
was ill-omened; that coming events have a way of casting their shadow before, and he
did not wish to furnish the event. He said that the Zulus declared that the sacred
aasvogels of Hloma Amabutu were as savage as lions, and that when once they saw
a man down they would tear him to pieces, dead or living. In short, Hans and I came
to ail acute difference of opinion. As for every reason it was necessary that my view
should prevail, however, I did not hesitate to put matters to him very plainly.

"Hans," I said, "you have to be a bait for vultures; choose if you will be a live bait
or a dead bait," and I cocked the rifle significantly, although, in truth, the last thing
that I wished or intended to do was to shoot my faithful old Hottentot friend. But
Hans, knowing all I had at stake, came to a different conclusion.

"Allemachte! baas," he said, "I understand, and I do not blame you. Well, if I obey
alive, perhaps my guardian Snake" (or spirit) "will protect me from the evil omen, and
perhaps the aasvogels will not pick out my eyes. But if once you send a bullet through
my stomach—why, then everything is finished, and for Hans it is 'Good night, sleep
well.' I will obey you, baas, and lie where you wish, only, I pray you, do not forget me
and go away, leaving me with those devil birds."

I promised him faithfully that I would not. Then we went through a very grim
little pantomime. Proceeding to the centre of the arena-like space, I lifted the gun, and
appeared to dash out Hans' brains with its butt. He fell upon his back, kicked about
a little, and lay still. This finished Act 1.

Act 2 was that, capering like a brute of a Zulu executioner, I retired from my
victim and hid myself in a bush on the edge of the plateau at a distance of forty yards.
After this there was a pause. The place was intensely bright with sunshine and
intensely silent; as silent as the skeletons of the murdered men about me; as silent as
Hans, who lay there looking so very small and dead in that big theatre where no grass
grew. It was an eerie wait in such surroundings, but at length the curtain rang up for
Act 3.

In the infinite arch of blue above me I perceived a speck, no larger than a mote of
dust. The aasvogel on watch up there far out of the range of man's vision had seen
the deed, and, by sinking downwards, signalled it to his companions that were
quartering the sky for fifty miles round; for these birds prey by sight, not by smell.
Down he came and down, and long before he had reached the neighbourhood of earth
other specks appeared in the distant blue. Now he was not more than four or five
hundred yards above me, and began to wheel, floating round the place upon his wide
wings, and sinking as he wheeled. So he sank softly and slowly until he was about a
hundred and fifty feet above Hans. Then suddenly he paused, hung quite steady for
a few seconds, shut his wings and fell like a bolt, only opening them again just before
he reached the earth.

Here he settled, tilting forward in that odd way which vultures have, and
scrambling a few awkward paces until he gained his balance. Then he froze into

immobility, gazing with in awful, stony glare at the prostrate Hans, who lay within about fifteen feet of him. Scarcely was this aasvogel down, when others, summoned from the depths of sky, did as he had done. They appeared, they sank, they wheeled, always from east to west, the way the sun travels. They hovered for a few seconds, then fell like stones, pitched on to their beaks, recovered themselves, waddled forward into line, and sat gazing at Hans. Soon there was a great ring of them about him, all immovable, all gazing, all waiting for something.

Presently that something appeared in the shape of an aasvogel which was nearly twice as big as any of the others. This was what the Boers and the natives call the "king vulture," one of which goes with every flock. He it is who rules the roost and also the carcase, which without his presence and permission none dare to attack. Whether this vile fowl is of a different species from the others, or whether he is a bird of more vigorous growth and constitution that has outgrown the rest and thus become their overlord, is more than I can tell. At least it is certain, as I can testify from long and constant observation, that almost every flock of vultures has its king.

When this particular royalty had arrived, the other aasvogels, of which perhaps there were now fifty or sixty gathered round Hans, began to show signs of interested animation. They looked at the king bird, they looked at Hans, stretching out their naked red necks and winking their brilliant eyes. I, however, did not pay particular attention to those upon the earth, being amply occupied in watching their fellows in the air.

With delight I observed that the vulture is a very conservative creature. They all did what doubtless they have done since the days of Adam or earlier—wheeled, and then hung that little space of time before they dropped to the ground like lead. This, then, would be the moment at which to shoot them, when for four or five seconds they offered practically a sitting target. Now, at that distance, always under a hundred yards, I knew well that I could hit a tea plate every shot, and a vulture is much larger than a tea plate. So it seemed to me that, barring accidents, I had little to fear from the terrible trial of skill which lay before me. Again and again I covered the hovering birds with my rifle, feeling that if I had pressed the trigger I should have pierced them through.

Thinking it well to practise, I continued this game for a long while, till at last it came to an unexpected end. Suddenly I heard a scuffling sound. Dropping my glance I saw that the whole mob of aasvogels were rushing in upon Hans, helping themselves forward by flapping their great wings, and that about three feet in front of them was their king. Next instant Hans vanished, and from the centre of that fluffy, stinking mass there arose a frightful yell.

As a matter of fact, as I found afterwards, the king vulture had fastened on to his snub nose, whilst its dreadful companions, having seized other portions of his frame, were beginning to hang back after their fashion in order to secure some chosen morsel. Hans kicked and screamed, and I rushed in shouting, causing them to rise in a great, flapping cloud that presently vanished this way and that. Within a minute they had all gone, and the Hottentot and I were left alone.

"That is good," I said. "You played well."

"Good! baas," he answered, "and I with two cuts in my nose in which I can lay my finger, and bites all over me. Look how my trousers are torn. Look at my head—where is the hair? Look at my nose. Good! Played well! It is those verdomde aasvogels that played. Oh! baas, if you had seen and smelt them, you would not say that it was good. See, one more second and I, who have two nostrils, should have had four."

"Never mind, Hans," I said, "it is only a scratch, and I will make you a present of some new trousers. Also, here is tobacco for you. Come to the bush; let us talk."

So we went, and when Hans was a little composed I told him all that I had observed about the habits of the aasvogel in the air, and he told me all that he had observed about their habits on the ground, which, as I might not shoot them sitting, did not interest me. Still, he agreed with me that the right moment to fire would be just before they pounced.

Whilst we were still talking we heard a sound of shouts, and, looking over the brow of the hill that faced towards Umgungundhlovu, we saw a melancholy sight. Being driven up the slope towards us by three executioners and a guard of seven or eight soldiers, their hands tied behind their backs, were three men, one very old, one of about fifty years of age, and one a lad, who did not look more than eighteen. As I soon heard, they were of a single family, the grandfather, the father, and the eldest son, who had been seized upon some ridiculous charge of witchcraft, but really in order that the king might take their cattle.

Having been tried and condemned by the Nyangas, or witch-doctors, these poor wretches were now doomed to die. Indeed, not content with thus destroying the heads of the tribe, present and to come, for three generations, all their descendants and collaterals had already been wiped out by Dingaan, so that he might pose as sole heir to the family cattle.

Such were the dreadful cruelties that happened in Zululand in those days.

The Play

The doomed three were driven by their murderers into the centre of the depression, within a few yards of which Hans and I were standing.

After them came the head executioner, a great brute who wore a curiously shaped leopard-skin cap—I suppose as a badge of office—and held in his hand a heavy kerry, the shaft of which was scored with many notches, each of them representing a human life.

"See, White Man," he shouted, "here is the bait which the king sends to draw the holy birds to you. Had it not been that you needed such bait, perhaps these wizards would have escaped. But the Black One said the little Son of George, who is named Macumazahn, needs them that he may show his magic, and therefore they must die to-day."

Now, at this information I turned positively sick. Nor did it make me feel better when the youngest of the victims, hearing the executioner's words, flung himself upon his knees, and began to implore me to spare him. His grandfather also addressed me, saying:

"Chief, will it not be enough if I die? I am old, and my life does not matter. Or if one is not sufficient, take me and my son, and let the lad, my grandson, go free. We are all of us innocent of any witchcraft, and he is not even old enough to practise such things, being but an unmarried boy. Chief, you, also, are young. Would not your heart be heavy if you had to be slain when the sun of your life was still new in the sky? Think, White Chief, what your father would feel, if you have one, should he be forced to see you killed before his eyes, that some stranger might use your body to show his skill with a magic weapon by slaying the wild things that would eat it."

Now, almost with tears, I broke in, explaining to the venerable man as well as I could that their horrible fate had nothing to do with me. I told him that I was innocent of their blood, who was forced to be there to try to shoot vultures on the wing in order to save my white companions from a doom similar to their own. He listened attentively, asking a question now and again, and when he had mastered my meaning, said with a most dignified calmness:

"Now I understand, White Man, and am glad to learn that you are not cruel, as I thought. My children," he added, turning to the others, "let us trouble this Inkoos no more. He only does what he must do to save the lives of his brethren by his skill, if he can. If we continue to plead with him and stir his heart to pity, the sorrow swelling in it may cause his hand to shake, and then they will die also, and their blood be on his head and ours. My children, it is the king's will that we should be slain. Let us make ready to obey the king, as men of our House have always done. White lord, we thank you for your good words. May you live long, and may good fortune sleep in your hut to the end. May you shoot straight, also, with your magic tool, and thereby win the lives of your company out of the hand of the king. Farewell, Inkoos," and since he could not lift his bound hands in salutation, he bowed to me, as did the others.

Then they walked to a little distance, and, seating themselves on the ground, began to talk together, and after a while to drone some strange chant in unison. The executioners and the guards also sat down not far away, laughing, chatting, and passing a horn of snuff from hand to hand. Indeed, I observed that the captain of them even took some snuff to the victims, and held it in his palm beneath their noses while they drew it up their nostrils and politely thanked him between the sneezes.

As for myself, I lit a pipe and smoked it, for I seemed to require a stimulant, or, rather, a sedative. Before it was finished Hans, who was engaged in doctoring his scratches made by the vultures' beaks with a concoction of leaves which he had been chewing, exclaimed suddenly in his matter-of-fact voice:

"See, baas, here they come, the white people on one side and the black on the other, just like the goats and the sheep at Judgment Day in the Book."

I looked, and there to my right appeared the party of Boers, headed by the Vrouw Prinsloo, who held the remnants of an old umbrella over her head. To the left advanced a number of Zulu nobles and councillors, in front of whom waddled Dingaan arrayed in his bead dancing dress. He was supported by two stalwart body-servants, whilst a third held a shield over his head to protect him from the sun, and a fourth carried a large stool, upon which he was to sit. Behind each party, also, I perceived a number of Zulus in their war-dress, all of them armed with broad stabbing spears.

The two parties arrived at the stone upon which I was sitting almost simultaneously, as probably it had been arranged that they should do, and halted, staring at each other. As for me, I sat still upon my stone and smoked on.

"Allemachte! Allan," puffed the Vrouw Prinsloo, who was breathless with her walk up the hill, "so here you are! As you did not come back, I thought you had run away and left us, like that stinkcat Pereira."

"Yes, Tante (aunt), here I am," I answered gloomily, "and I wish to heaven that I was somewhere else."

Just then Dingaan, having settled his great bulk upon the stool and recovered his breath, called to the lad Halstead, who was with him, and said:

"O Tho-maas, ask your brother, Macumazahn, if he is ready to try to shoot the vultures. If not, as I wish to be fair, I will give him a little more time to make his magic medicine."

I replied sulkily that I was as ready as I was ever likely to be.

Then the Vrouw Prinsloo, understanding that the king of the Zulus was before her, advanced upon him, waving her umbrella. Catching hold of Halstead, who understood Dutch, she forced him to translate an harangue, which she addressed to Dingaan.

Had he rendered it exactly as it came from her lips, we should all have been dead in five minutes, but, luckily, that unfortunate young man had learnt some of the guile of the serpent during his sojourn among the Zulus, and varied her vigorous phrases. The gist of her discourse was that he, Dingaan, was a black-hearted and bloody-minded villain, with whom the Almighty would come even sooner or later (as, indeed, He did), and that if he dared to touch one hair of her or of her companions' heads, the Boers, her countrymen, would prove themselves to be the ministers of the Almighty in that matter (as, indeed, they did). As translated by Halstead into Zulu, what she said was that Dingaan was the greatest king in the whole world; in fact, that there was not, and never had been, any such a king either in power, wisdom, or personal beauty, and that if she and her companions had to die, the sight of his glory consoled them for their deaths.

"Indeed," said Dingaan suspiciously, "if that is what this man-woman says, her eyes tell one story and her lips another. Oh! Tho-maas, lie no more. Speak the true words of the white chieftainess, lest I should find them out otherwise, and give you to the slayers."

Thus adjured, Halstead explained that he had not yet told all the words. The "man-woman," who was, as he, Dingaan, supposed, a great chieftainess among the Dutch, added that if he, the mighty and glorious king, the earth-shaker, the world-eater, killed her or any of her subjects, her people would avenge her by killing him and his people.

"Does she say that?" said Dingaan. "Then, as I thought, these Boers are dangerous, and not the peaceful folk they make themselves out to be," and he brooded for a while, staring at the ground. Presently he lifted his head and went on: "Well, a bet is a bet, and therefore I will not wipe out this handful, as otherwise I would have done at once. Tell the old cow of a chieftainess that, notwithstanding her threats, I stick to my promise. If the little Son of George, Macumazahn, can shoot three vultures out of five by help of his magic, then she and her servants shall go free. If not, the vultures which he has missed shall feed on them, and afterwards I will talk with her people when they come to avenge her. Now, enough of this indaba. Bring those evildoers here that they may thank and praise me, who give them so merciful an end."

So the grandfather, the father, and the son were hustled before Dingaan by the soldiers, and greeted him with the royal salute of "bayete."

"O king," said the old man, "I and my children are innocent. Yet if it pleases you, O king, I am ready to die, and so is my son. Yet we pray you to spare the little one. He is but a boy, who may grow up to do you good service, as I have done to you and your House for many years."

"Be silent, you white-headed dog!" answered Dingaan fiercely. "This lad is a wizard, like the rest of you, and would grow up to bewitch me and to plot with my enemies. Know that I have stamped out all your family, and shall I then leave him to breed another that would hate me? Begone to the World of Spirits, and tell them how Dingaan deals with sorcerers."

The old man tried to speak again, for evidently he loved this grandchild of his, but a soldier struck him in the face, and Dingaan shouted:

"What! Are you not satisfied? I tell you that if you say more I will force you to kill the boy with your own hand. Take them away."

Then I turned and hid my face, as did all the white folk. Presently I heard the old man, whom they had saved to the last that he might witness the deaths of his descendants, cry in a loud voice:

"On the night of the thirtieth full moon from this day I, the far-sighted, I, the prophet, summon thee, Dingaan, to meet me and mine in the Land of Ghosts, and there to pay—"

Then with a roar of horror the executioners fell on him and he died. When there was silence I looked up, and saw that the king, who had turned a dirty yellow hue with fright, for he was very superstitious, was trembling and wiping the sweat from his brow.

"You should have kept the wizard alive," he said in a shaky voice to the head slayer, who was engaged in cutting three more nicks on the handle of his dreadful kerry. "Fool, I would have heard the rest of his lying message."

The man answered humbly that he thought it best it should remain unspoken, and got himself out of sight as soon as possible. Here I may remark that by an odd coincidence Dingaan actually was killed about thirty moons from that time. Mopo, his general, who slew his brother Chaka, slew him also with the help of Umslopogaas, the son of Chaka. In after years Umslopogaas told me the story of the dreadful ghost-haunted death of this tyrant, but, of course, he could not tell me exactly upon what day it happened. Therefore I do not know whether the prophecy was strictly accurate.

The three victims lay dead in the hollow of the Hill of Death. Presently the king, recovering himself, gave orders that the spectators should be moved back to places where they could see what happened without frightening the vultures. So the Boers, attended by their band of soldiers, who were commanded to slay them at once if they attempted to escape, went one way, and Dingaan and his Zulus went the other, leaving Hans and myself alone behind our bush. As the white people passed me, Vrouw Prinsloo wished me good luck in a cheerful voice, although I could see that her poor old hand was shaking, and she was wiping her eyes with the vatdoek. Henri Marais, also in broken tones, implored me to shoot straight for his daughter's sake. Then came Marie, pale but resolute, who said nothing, but only looked me in the eyes, and touched the pocket of her dress, in which I knew the pistol lay hid. Of the rest of them I took no notice.

The moment, that dreadful moment of trial, had come at last; and oh! the suspense and the waiting were hard to bear. It seemed an age before the first speck, that I knew to be a vulture, appeared thousands of feet above me and began to descend in wide circles.

"Oh, baas," said poor Hans, "this is worse than shooting at the geese in the Groote Kloof. Then you could only lose your horse, but now—"

"Be silent," I hissed, "and give me the rifle."

The vulture wheeled and sank, sank and wheeled. I glanced towards the Boers, and saw that they were all of them on their knees. I glanced towards the Zulus, and saw that they were watching as, I think, they had never watched anything before, for to them this was a new excitement. Then I fixed my eyes upon the bird.

Its last circle was accomplished. Before it pounced it hung on wide, outstretched wings, as the others had done, its head towards me. I drew a deep breath, lifted the rifle, got the foresight dead upon its breast, and touched the hair-trigger. As the charge exploded I saw the aasvogel give a kind of backward twist. Next instant I heard a loud clap, and a surge of joy went through me, for I thought that the bullet had found its billet. But alas! it was not so.

The clap was that of the air disturbed by the passing of the ball and the striking of this air against the stiff feathers of the wings. Anyone who has shot at great birds on the wing with a bullet will be acquainted with the sound. Instead of falling the vulture recovered itself. Not knowing the meaning of this unaccustomed noise, it dropped quietly to earth and sat down near the bodies, pitching forward in the natural way and running a few paces, as the others had done that afternoon. Evidently it was quite unhurt.

"Missed!" gasped Hans as he grasped the rifle to load it. "Oh! why did you not throw a stone on to the first heap?"

I gave Hans a look that must have frightened him; at any rate, he spoke no more. From the Boers went up a low groan. Then they began to pray harder than ever, while the Zulus clustered round the king and whispered to him. I learned afterwards that he was giving heavy odds against me, ten to one in cattle, which they were obliged to take, unwillingly enough.

Hans finished loading, capped and cocked the rifle, and handed it to me. By now other vultures were appearing. Being desperately anxious to get the thing over one way or another, at the proper moment I took the first of them. Again I covered it dead and pressed. Again as the gun exploded I saw that backward lurch of the bird, and heard the clap of the air upon its wings. Then—oh horror!—this aasvogel turned quietly, and began to mount the ladder of the sky in the same fashion as it had descended. I had missed once more.

"The second heap of stones has done this, baas," said Hans faintly, and this time I did not even look him. I only sat down and buried my face in my hands. One more such miss, and then—

Hans began to whisper to me.

"Baas," he said, "those aasvogels see the flash of the gun, and shy at it like a horse. Baas, you are shooting into their faces, for they all hang with their beaks toward you before they drop. You must get behind them, and fire into their tails, for even an aasvogel cannot see with its tail."

I let fall my hands and stared at him. Surely the poor fellow had been inspired from on high! I understood it all now. While their beaks were towards me, I might fire at fifty vultures and never hit one, for each time they would swerve from the flash, causing the bullet to miss them, though but by a little.

"Come," I gasped, and began to walk quickly round the edge of the depression to a rock, which I saw opposite about a hundred yards away. My journey took me near the Zulus, who mocked me as I passed, asking where my magic was, and if I wished to see the white people killed presently. Dingaan was now offering odds of fifty cattle to one against me, but no one would take the bet even with the king.

I made no answer; no, not even when they asked me "if I had thrown down my spear and was running away." Grimly, despairingly, I marched on to the rock, and took shelter behind it with Hans. The Boers, I saw, were still upon their knees, but seemed to have ceased praying. The children were weeping; the men stared at each other; Vrouw Prinsloo had her arm about Marie's waist. Waiting there behind the rock, my courage returned to me, as it sometimes does in the last extremity. I remembered my dream and took comfort. Surely God would not be so cruel as to suffer me to fail and thereby bring all those poor people to their deaths.

Snatching the rifle from Hans, I loaded it myself; nothing must be trusted to another. As I put on the cap a vulture made its last circle. It hung in the air just as the others had done, and oh! its tail was towards me. I lifted, I aimed between the gathered-up legs, I pressed and shut my eyes, for I did not dare to look.

I heard the bullet strike, or seem to strike, and a few seconds later I heard something else—the noise of a heavy thud upon the ground. I looked, and there with outstretched wings lay the foul bird dead, stone dead, eight or ten paces from the bodies.

"Allemachte! that's better," said Hans. "You threw stones on to _all_ the other heaps, didn't you, baas?"

The Zulus grew excited, and the odds went down a little. The Boers stretched out their white faces and stared at me; I saw them out of the corner of my eye as I loaded again. Another vulture came; seeing one of its companions on the ground, if in a somewhat unnatural attitude, perhaps it thought that there could be nothing to fear. I leaned against my rock, aimed, and fired, almost carelessly, so sure was I of the result. This time I did not shut my eyes, but watched to see what happened.

The bullet struck the bird between its thighs, raked it from end to end, and down it came like a stone almost upon the top of its fellow.

"Good, good!" said Hans with a guttural chuckle of delight. "Now, baas, make no mistake with the third, and 'als sall recht kommen' (all shall be well)."

"Yes," I answered; "_if_ I make no mistake with the third."

I loaded the rifle again myself, being very careful to ram down the powder well and to select a bullet that fitted perfectly true to the bore. Moreover, I cleared the nipple with a thorn, and shook a little fine powder into it, so as to obviate any chance of a miss-fire. Then I set on the cap and waited. What was going on among the Boers or the Zulus I do not know. In this last crisis of all our fates I never looked, being too intent upon my own part in the drama.

By now the vultures appeared to have realised that something unusual was in progress, which threatened danger to them. At any rate, although by this time they had collected in hundreds from east, west, north, and south, and were wheeling the heavens above in their vast, majestic circles, none of them seemed to care to descend to prey upon the bodies. I watched, and saw that among their number was that great king bird which had bitten Hans in the face; it was easy to distinguish him, because he was so much larger than the others. Also, he had some white at the tips of his wings. I observed that certain of his company drew near to him in the skies, where they hung together in a knot, as though in consultation.

They separated out again, and the king began to descend, deputed probably to spy out the land. Down he came in ever-narrowing turns, till he reached the appointed spot for the plunge, and, according to the immemorial custom of these birds, hung a while before he pounced with his head to the south and his great, spreading tail towards me.

This was my chance, and, rejoicing in having so large a mark, I got the sight upon him and pulled. The bullet thudded, some feathers floated from his belly, showing that it had gone home, and I looked to see him fall as the others had done. But alas! he did not fall. For a few seconds he rocked to and fro upon his great wings, then commenced to travel upwards in vast circles, which grew gradually more narrow, till he appeared to be flying almost straight into the empyrean. I stared and stared. Everybody stared, till that enormous bird became, first a mere blot upon the blue, and at length but a speck. Then it vanished altogether into regions far beyond the sight of man.

"Now there is an end," I said to Hans.

"Ja, baas," answered the Hottentot between his chattering teeth, "there is an end. You did not put in enough powder. Presently we shall all be dead."

"Not quite," I said with a bitter laugh. "Hans, load the rifle, load it quick. Before they die there shall be another king in Zululand."

"Good, good!" he exclaimed as he loaded desperately. "Let us take that fat pig of a Dingaan with us. Shoot him in the stomach, baas; shoot him in the stomach, so that he too may learn what it is to die slowly. Then cut my throat, here is my big knife, and afterwards cut your own, if you have not time to load the gun again and shoot yourself, which is easier."

I nodded, for it was in my mind to do these things. Never could I stand still and see those poor Boers killed, and I knew that Marie would look after herself.

Meanwhile, the Zulus were coming towards me, and the soldiers who had charge of them were driving up Marais's people, making pretence to thrust them through with their assegais, and shouting at them as men do at cattle. Both parties arrived in the depression at about the same time, but remained separated by a little space. In this space lay the corpses of the murdered men and the two dead aasvogels, with Hans and myself standing opposite to them.

"Well, little Son of George," puffed Dingaan, "you have lost your bet, for you did but kill two vultures out of five with your magic, which was good as far as it went, but not good enough. Now you must pay, as I would have paid had you won."

Then he stretched out his hand, and issued the dreadful order of "Bulala amalongu!" (Kill the white people). "Kill them one by one, that I may see whether they know how to die, all except Macumazahn and the tall girl, whom I keep."

Some of the soldiers made a dash and seized the Vrouw Prinsloo, who was standing in front of the party.

"Wait a little, King," she called out as the assegais were lifted over her. "How do you know that the bet is lost? He whom you call Macumazahn hit that last vulture. It should be searched for before you kill us."

"What does the old woman say?" asked Dingaan, and Halstead translated slowly.

"True," said Dingaan. "Well, now I will send her to search for the vulture in the sky. Come back thence, Fat One, and tell us if you find it."

The soldiers lifted their assegais, waiting the king's word. I pretended to look at the ground, and cocked my rifle, being determined that if he spoke it, it should be his last. Hans stared upwards—I suppose to avoid the sight of death—then suddenly uttered a wild yell, which caused everyone, even the doomed people, to turn their eyes to him. He was pointing to the heavens, and they looked to see at what he pointed.

This was what they saw. Far, far above in that infinite sea of blue there appeared a tiny speck, which his sharp sight had already discerned, a speck that grew larger and larger as it descended with terrific and ever-growing speed.

It was the king vulture falling from the heavens—dead!

Down it came between the Vrouw Prinsloo and the slayers, smashing the lifted assegai of one of them and hurling him to the earth. Down it came, and lay there a mere mass of pulp and feathers.

"O Dingaan," I said in the midst of the intense silence that followed, "it seems that it is I who have won the bet, not you. I killed this king of birds, but being a king it chose to die high up and alone, that is all."

Dingaan hesitated, for he did not wish to spare the Boers, and I, noting his hesitation, lifted my rifle a little. Perhaps he saw it, or perhaps his sense of honour, as he understood the word, overcame his wish for their blood. At any rate, he said to one of his councillors:

"Search the carcase of that vulture and see if there is a bullet hole in it."

The man obeyed, feeling at the mass of broken bones and flesh. By good fortune he found, not the hole, for that was lost in the general destruction of the tissues, but the ball itself, which, having pierced the thick body from below upwards, had remained fast in the tough skin just by the back-bone where the long, red neck emerges from between the wings. He picked it out, for it was only hanging in the skin, and held it up for all to see.

"Macumazahn has won his bet," said Dingaan. "His magic has conquered, though by but a very little. Macumazahn, take these Boers, they are yours, and begone with them out of my country."

Retief Asks a Favour

Now and again during our troubled journey through life we reach little oases of almost perfect happiness, set jewel-like here and there in the thorny wilderness of time. Sometimes these are hours of mere animal content. In others they are made beautiful by waters blowing from our spiritual springs of being, as in those rare instances when the material veil of life seems to be rent by a mighty hand, and we feel the presence and the comfort of God within us and about us, guiding our footsteps to the ineffable end, which is Himself. Occasionally, however, all these, physical satisfaction and love divine and human, are blended to a whole, like soul and body, and we can say, "Now I know what is joy."

Such an hour came to me on the evening of that day of the winning of my bet with Dingaan, when a dozen lives or so were set against my nerve and skill. These had not failed me, although I knew that had it not been for the inspiration of the Hottentot Hans (who sent it, I wonder?) they would have been of no service at all. With all my thought and experience, it had never occurred to me that the wonderful eyes of the vultures would see the flash of the powder even through the pervading sunlight, and swerve before the deadly bullet could reach them.

On that night I was indeed a hero in a small way. Even Henri Marais thawed and spoke to me as a father might to his child, he who always disliked me in secret, partly because I was an Englishman, partly because I was everything to his daughter and he was jealous, and partly for the reason that I stood in the path of his nephew, Hernan Pereira, whom he either loved or feared, or both. As for the rest of them, men, women and children, they thanked and blessed me with tears in their eyes, vowing that, young as I was, thenceforth I and no other should be their leader. As may be imagined, although it is true that she set down my success to her meal of bullock's liver and the nap which she had insisted on my taking, the Vrouw Prinsloo was the most enthusiastic of them all.

"Look at him," she said, pointing with her fat finger at my insignificant self and addressing her family. "If only I had such a husband or a son, instead of you lumps that God has tied to me like clogs to the heels of a she-ass, I should be happy."

"God did that in order to prevent you from kicking, old vrouw," said her husband, a quiet man with a vein of sardonic humour. "If only He had tied another clog to your tongue, I should be happy also"; whereon the vrouw smacked his head and her children got out of the way sniggering.

But the most blessed thing of all was my interview with Marie. All that took place between us can best be left to the imagination, since the talk of lovers, even in such circumstances, is not interesting to others. Also, in a sense, it is too sacred to repeat. One sentence I will set down, however, because in the light of after events I feel that it was prophetic, and not spoken merely by chance. It was at the end of our talk, as she was handing me back the pistol that I had given her for a certain dreadful purpose.

"Three times you have saved my life, Allan—once at Maraisfontein, once from starvation, and now from Dingaan, whose touch would have meant my death. I wonder whether it will ever be my turn to save yours?"

She looked down for a little while, then lifted her head and laid her hand upon my shoulder, adding slowly: "Do you know, Allan, I think that it will at the—" and suddenly she turned and left me with her sentence unfinished.

So thus it came about that by the help of Providence I was enabled to rescue all these worthy folk from a miserable and a bloody death. And yet I have often reflected since that if things had gone differently; if, for instance, that king aasvogel had found strength to carry itself away to die at a distance instead of soaring straight upwards like a towering partridge, as birds injured in the lungs will often do—I suppose in search of air—it might have been better in the end. Then I should certainly have shot Dingaan dead and every one of us would as certainly have been killed on the spot. But if Dingaan had died that day, Retief and his companions would never have been massacred. Also as the peaceful Panda, his brother, would, I suppose, have succeeded to the throne, probably the subsequent slaughter at Weenen, and all the after fighting, would never have taken place. But so it was fated, and who am I that I should quarrel with or even question the decrees of fate? Doubtless these things were doomed to happen, and they happened in due course. There is nothing more to be said.

Early on the following morning we collected our oxen, which, although still footsore, were now full fed and somewhat rested. An hour or two later began our trek, word having come to us from Dingaan that we must start at once. Also he sent us guides, under the command of the captain Kambula, to show us the road to Natal.

I breakfasted that day with the Reverend Mr. Owen and his people, my object being to persuade him to come away with us, as I did not consider that Zululand was a safe place for white women and children. My mission proved fruitless. Mrs. Hulley, the wife of the absent interpreter, who had three little ones, Miss Owen and the servant, Jane Williams, were all of them anxious enough to do as I suggested. But Mr. and Mrs. Owen, who were filled with the true fervour of missionaries, would not listen. They said that God would protect them; that they had only been a few weeks in the country, and that it would be the act of cowards and of traitors to fly at the very beginning of their work. Here I may add that after the massacre of Retief they changed their opinion, small blame to them, and fled as fast as anyone else.

I told Mr. Owen how very close I had gone to shooting Dingaan, in which event they might all have been killed with us. This news shocked him much. Indeed, he lectured me severely on the sins of bloodthirstiness and a desire for revenge. So, finding that we looked at things differently, and that it was of no use wasting breath in argument, I wished him and his people good-bye and good fortune and went upon my way, little guessing how we should meet again.

An hour later we trekked. Passing by the accursed hill, Hloma Amabutu, where I saw some gorged vultures sleeping on the rocks, we came to the gate of the Great Kraal. Here, to my surprise, I saw Dingaan with some of his councillors and an armed guard of over a hundred men, seated under the shade of two big milk trees. Fearing treachery, I halted the wagons and advised the Boers to load their rifles and be ready for the worst. A minute or so later young Thomas Halstead arrived and told me that Dingaan wished to speak with us. I asked him if that meant that we were to be killed. He answered, "No, you are quite safe." The king had received some news that had put him in a good humour with the white people, and he desired to bid us farewell, that was all.

So we trekked boldly to where Dingaan was, and, stopping the wagons, went up to him in a body. He greeted us kindly enough, and even gave me his fat hand to shake.

"Macumazahn," he said, "although it has cost me many oxen, I am glad that your magic prevailed yesterday. Had it not done so I should have killed all these your friends, which would have been a cause of war between me and the Amaboona. Now, this morning I have learned that these Amaboona are sending a friendly embassy to me under one of their great chiefs, and I think that you will meet them on the road. I charge you, therefore, to tell them to come on, having no fear, as I will receive them well and listen to all they have to say."

I answered that I would do so.

"Good," he replied. "I am sending twelve head of cattle with you, six of them for your food during your journey, and six as a present to the embassy of the Amaboona. Also Kambula, my captain, has charge to see you safely over the Tugela River."

I thanked him and turned to go, when suddenly his eye fell upon Marie, who, foolishly enough, took this opportunity to advance from among the others and speak to me about something—I forget what.

"Macumazahn, is that the maiden of whom you spoke to me?" asked Dingaan; "she whom you are going to marry?"

I answered, "Yes."

"By the head of the Black One," he exclaimed, "she is very fair. Will you not make a present of her to me, Macumazahn?"

I answered, "No; she is not mine to give away."

"Well, then, Macumazahn, I will pay you a hundred head of cattle for her, which is the price of a royal wife, and give you ten of the fairest girls in Zululand in exchange."

I answered that it could not be.

Now the king began to grow angry.

"I will keep her, whether you wish it or no," he said.

"Then you will keep her dead, O Dingaan," I replied, "for there is more of that magic which slew the vultures."

Of course, I meant that Marie would be dead. But as my knowledge of the Zulu tongue was imperfect, he understood the words to mean that _he_ would be dead, and I think they frightened him. At any rate, he said:

"Well, I promised you all safe-conduct if you won your bet, so hamba gachle (go in peace). I wish to have no quarrel with the white folk, but, Macumazahn, you are the first of them who has refused a gift to Dingaan. Still, I bear you no grudge, and if you choose to come back again, you will be welcome, for I perceive that, although so small, you are very clever and have a will of your own; also that you mean what you say and speak the truth. Tell the People of George that my heart is soft towards them." Then he turned and walked away through the gates of the kraal.

Glad enough was I to see the last of him, for now I knew that we were safe, except from such accidents as may overtake any travellers through a wild country. For the present, at any rate until after he had seen this embassy, Dingaan wished to stand well with the Boers. Therefore it was obvious that he would never make an irreparable quarrel with them by treacherously putting us to death as we trekked through his country. Being sure of this, we went on our way with light hearts, thanking Heaven for the mercies which had been shown to us.

It was on the third day of our trek, when we were drawing near to the Tugela, that we met the Boer embassy, off-saddled by a little stream where we proposed to outspan to rest the oxen while we ate our midday meal. They were sleeping in the heat of the day and saw nothing of us till we were right on to them, when, catching sight of our Zulu advance guard, they sprang up and ran for their rifles. Then the wagons emerged from the bush, and they stared astonished, wondering who could be trekking in that country.

We called to them in Dutch not to be afraid and in another minute we were among them. While we were yet some way off my eye fell upon a burly, white-bearded man whose figure seemed to be familiar to me, and towards him I went, taking no heed of the others, of whom there may have been six or seven. Soon I was sure, and advancing with outstretched hand, said:

"Good-day, Mynheer Piet Retief. Who would have thought that we who parted so far away and so long ago would live to meet among the Zulus?"

He stared at me.

"Who is it? Who is it? Allemachte! I know now. The little Englishman, Allan Quatermain, who shot the geese down in the Old Colony. Well, I should not be surprised, for the man you beat in that match told me that you were travelling in these parts. Only I understood him to say that the Zulus had killed you."

"If you mean Hernan Pereira," I answered, "where did you meet him?"

"Why, down by the Tugela there, in a bad way. However, he can tell you all about that himself, for I have brought him with me to show us the path to Dingaan's kraal. Where is Pereira? Send Pereira here. I want to speak with him."

"Here I am," answered a sleepy voice, the hated voice of Pereira himself, from the other side of a thick bush, where he had been slumbering. "What is it, commandant? I come," and he emerged, stretching himself and yawning, just as the remainder of my party came up. He caught sight of Henri Marais first of all, and began to greet him, saying: "Thank God, my uncle, you are safe!"

Then his eyes fell on me, and I do not think I ever saw a man's face change more completely. His jaw dropped, the colour left his cheeks, leaving them of the yellow which is common to persons of Portuguese descent; his outstretched hand fell to his side.

"Allan Quatermain!" he ejaculated. "Why, I thought that you were dead."

"As I should have been, Mynheer Pereira, twice over if you could have had your way," I replied.

"What do you mean, Allan?" broke in Retief.

"I will tell you what he means," exclaimed the Vrouw Prinsloo, shaking her fat fist at Pereira. "That yellow dog means that twice he has tried to murder Allan—Allan, who saved his life and ours. Once he shot at him in a kloof and grazed his cheek; look, there is the scar of it. And once he plotted with the Zulus to slaughter him, telling Dingaan that he was an evildoer and a wizard, who would bring a curse upon his land."

Now Retief looked at Pereira.

"What do you say to this?" he asked.

"What do I say?" repeated Pereira, recovering himself. "Why, that it is a lie or a misunderstanding. I never shot at Heer Allan in any kloof. Is it likely that I should have done so when he had just nursed me back to life? I never plotted with the Zulus for his death, which would have meant the deaths of my uncle and my cousin and of all their companions. Am I mad that I should do such a thing?"

"Not mad, but bad," screamed the vrouw. "I tell you, Heer Retief, it is no lie. Ask those with me," she added, appealing to the others, who, with the exception of Marais, answered as with one voice:

"No; it is no lie."

"Silence!" said the commandant. "Now, nephew Allan, tell us your story."

So I told him everything, of course leaving out all details. Even then the tale was long, though it did not seem to be one that wearied my hearers.

"Allemachte!" said Retief when I had finished, "this is a strange story, the strangest that ever I heard. If it is true, Hernan Pereira, you deserve to have your back set against a tree and to be shot."

"God in heaven!" he answered, "am I to be condemned on such a tale—I, an innocent man? Where is the evidence? This Englishman tells all this against me for a simple reason—that he has robbed me of the love of my cousin, to whom I was affianced. Where are his witnesses?"

"As to the shooting at me in the kloof, I have none except God who saw you," I answered. "As to the plot that you laid against me among the Zulus, as it chances, however, there is one, Kambula, the captain who was sent to take me as you had arranged, and who now commands our escort."

"A savage!" exclaimed Pereira. "Is the tale of a savage to be taken against that of a white man? Also, who will translate his story? You, Mynheer Quatermain, are the only one here who knows his tongue, if you do know it, and you are my accuser."

"That is true," remarked Retief. "Such a witness should not be admitted without a sworn interpreter. Now listen; I pass judgment as commandant in the field. Hernan Pereira, I have known you to be a rogue in the past, for I remember that you cheated this very young man, Allan Quatermain, at a friendly trial of skill at which I was present; but since then till now I have heard nothing more of you, good or bad. To-day this Allan Quatermain and a number of my own countrymen bring grave charges against you, which, however, at present are not capable of proof or disproof. Well, I cannot decide those charges, whatever my own opinion may be. I think that you had better go back with your uncle, Henri Marais, to the trek-Boers, where they can be laid before a court and settled according to law."

"If so, he will go back alone," said the Vrouw Prinsloo. "He will not go back with us, for we will elect a field-cornet and shoot him—the stinkcat, who left us to starve and afterwards tried to kill little Allan Quatermain, who saved our lives"; and the chorus behind her echoed:

"Ja, ja, we will shoot him."

"Hernan Pereira," said Retief, rubbing his broad forehead, "I don't quite know why it is, but no one seems to want you as a companion. Indeed, to speak truth, I don't myself. Still, I think you would be safer with me than with these others whom you seem to have offended. Therefore, I suggest that you come on with us. But listen here, man," he added sternly, "if I find you plotting against us among the Zulus, that hour you are dead. Do you understand?"

"I understand that I am one slandered," replied Pereira. "Still, it is Christian to submit to injuries, and therefore I will do as you wish. As to these bearers of false witness, I leave them to God."

"And I leave you to the devil," shouted Vrouw Prinsloo, "who will certainly have you soon or late. Get out of my sight, stinkcat, or I will pull your hair off." And she rushed at him, flapping her dreadful vatdoek—which she produced from some recess in her raiment—in his face, driving him away as though he were a noxious insect.

Well, he went I know not where, and so strong was public opinion against him that I do not think that even his uncle, Henri Marais, sought him out to console him.

When Pereira was gone, our party and that of Retief fell into talk, and we had much to tell. Especially was the commandant interested in the story of my bet with Dingaan, whereby I saved the lives of all my companions by shooting the vultures.

"It was not for nothing, nephew, that God Almighty gave you the power of holding a gun so straight," said Retief to me when he understood the matter. "I remember that when you killed those wildfowl in the Groote Kloof with bullets, which no other man could have done, I wondered why you should have such a gift above all the rest of us, who have practised for so many more years. Well, now I understand. God Almighty is no fool; He knows His business. I wish you were coming back with me to Dingaan; but as that tainted man, Hernan Pereira, is of my company, perhaps it is better that you should stay away. Tell me, now, about this Dingaan; does he mean to kill us?"

"Not this time, I think, uncle," I answered; "because first he wishes to learn all about the Boers. Still, do not trust him too far just because he speaks you softly. Remember, that if I had missed the third vulture, we should all have been dead by now. And, if you are wise, keep an eye upon Hernan Pereira."

"These things I will do, nephew, especially the last of them; and now we must be getting on. Stay; come here, Henri Marais; I have a word to say to you. I understand that this little Englishman, Allan Quatermain, who is worth ten bigger men, loves your daughter, whose life he has saved again and again, and that she loves him. Why, then, do you not let them marry in a decent fashion?"

"Because before God I have sworn her to another man—to my nephew, Hernan Pereira, whom everyone slanders," answered Marais sulkily. "Until she is of age that oath holds."

"Oho!" said Retief, "you have sworn your lamb to that hyena, have you? Well, look out that he does not crack your bones as well as hers, and perhaps some others also. Why does God give some men a worm in their brains, as He does to the wildebeeste, a worm that always makes them run the wrong way? I don't know, I am sure; but you who are very religious, Henri Marais, might think the matter over and tell me the answer when next we meet. Well, this girl of yours will soon be of age, and then, as I am commandant down yonder where she is going, I'll see she marries the man she wants, whatever you say, Henri Marais. Heaven above us! I only wish it were my daughter he was in love with. A fellow who can shoot to such good purpose might have the lot of them"; and uttering one of his great, hearty laughs, he walked off to his horse.

On the morrow of this meeting we forded the Tugela and entered the territory that is now called Natal. Two days' short trekking through a beautiful country brought us to some hills that I think were called Pakadi, or else a chief named Pakadi lived there, I forget which. Crossing these hills, on the further side of them, as Retief had told us we should do, we found a large party of the trek-Boers, who were already occupying this land on the hither side of the Bushman's River, little knowing, poor people, that it was fated to become the grave of many of them. To-day, and for all future time, that district is and will be known by the name of Weenen, or the Place of Weeping, because of those pioneers who here were massacred by Dingaan within a few weeks of the time of which I write.

Nice as the land was, for some reason or other it did not quite suit my fancy, and therefore, in view of my approaching marriage with Marie, having purchased a horse from one of the trek-Boers, I began to explore the country round. My object was to find a stretch of fertile veld where we could settle when we were wedded, and such a spot I discovered after some trouble. It lay about thirty miles away to the east, in the loop of a beautiful stream that is now known as the Mooi River.

Enclosed in this loop were some thirty thousand acres of very rich, low-lying soil, almost treeless and clothed with luxuriant grasses where game was extraordinarily numerous. At the head of it rose a flat-topped hill, from the crest of which, oddly enough, flowed a plentiful stream of water fed by a strong spring. Half-way down this hill, facing to the east, and irrigable by the stream, was a plateau several acres in extent, which furnished about the best site for a house that I know in all South Africa. Here I determined we would build our dwelling-place and become rich by the breeding up of great herds of cattle. I should explain that this ground, which once, as the remains of their old kraals showed, had belonged to a Kaffir tribe killed out by Chaka, the Zulu king, was to be had for the taking.

Indeed, as there was more land than we could possibly occupy, I persuaded Henri Marais, the Prinsloos and the Meyers, with whom I had trekked from Delagoa, to visit it with me. When they had seen it they agreed to make it their home in the future, but meanwhile elected to return to the other Boers for safety's sake. So with the help of some Kaffirs, of whom there were a few in the district, remnants of those tribes which Chaka had destroyed, I pegged out an estate of about twelve thousand acres for myself, and, selecting a site, set the natives to work to build a rough mud house upon it which would serve as a temporary dwelling. I should add that the Prinsloos and the Meyers also made arrangements for the building of similar shelters almost alongside of my own. This done, I returned to Marie and the trek-Boers.

On the morning after my return to the camp Piet Retief appeared there with his five or six companions. I asked him how he had got on with Dingaan.

"Well enough, nephew," he answered. "At first the king was somewhat angry, saying that we Boers had stolen six hundred head of his cattle. But I showed him that it was the chief, Sikonyela, who lives yonder on the Caledon River, who had dressed up his people in white men's clothes and put them upon horses, and afterwards drove the cattle through one of our camps to make it appear that we were the thieves. Then he asked me what was my object in visiting him. I answered that I sought a grant of the land south of the Tugela to the sea.

"'Bring me back the cattle that you say Sikonyela has stolen,' he said, 'and we will talk about this land.' To this I agreed and soon after left the kraal."

"What did you do with Hernan Pereira, uncle?" I asked.

"This, Allan. When I was at Umgungundhlovu I sought out the truth of that story you told me as to his having made a plot to get you killed by the Zulus on the ground that you were a wizard."

"And what did you discover, uncle?"

"I discovered that it was true, for Dingaan told me so himself. Then I sent for Pereira and ordered him out of my camp, telling him that if he came back among the Boers I would have him put on his trial for attempted murder. He said nothing, but went away."

"Whither did he go?"

"To a place that Dingaan gave him just outside his kraal. The king said that he would be useful to him, as he could mend guns and teach his soldiers to shoot with them. So there, I suppose, he remains, unless he has thought it wiser to make off. At any rate, I am sure that he will not come here to trouble you or anyone."

"No, uncle, but he may trouble you _there_," I said doubtfully.

"What do you mean, Allan?"

"I don't quite know, but he is black-hearted, a traitor by nature, and in one way or the other he will stir up sorrow. Do you think that he will love you, for instance, after you have hunted him out like a thief?"

Retief shrugged his shoulders and laughed as he answered:

"I will take my chance of that. What is the use of troubling one's head about such a snake of a man? And now, Allan, I have something to ask you. Are you married yet?"

"No, uncle, nor can be for another five weeks, when Marie comes of age. Her father still holds that his oath binds him, and I have promised that I will not take her till then."

"Does he indeed, Allan? I think that Henri Marais is 'kransick' (that is, cracked), or else his cursed nephew, Hernan, has fascinated him, as a snake does a bird. Still, I suppose that he has the law on his side, and, as I am commandant, I cannot advise anyone to break the law. Now listen. It is no use your staying here looking at the ripe peach you may not pluck, for that only makes the stomach sick. Therefore the best thing that you can do is to come with me to get those cattle from Sikonyela, for I shall be very glad of your company. Afterwards, too, I want you to return with me to Zululand when I go for the grant of all this country."

"But how about my getting married?" I asked in dismay.

"Oh! I dare say you will be able to marry before we start. Or if not, it must be when we return. Listen now; do not disappoint me in this matter, Allan. None of us can speak Zulu except you, who takes to these savage languages like a duck to water, and I want you to be my interpreter with Dingaan. Also the king specially asked that you should come with me when I brought the cattle, as he seems to have taken a great fancy to you. He said that you would render his words honestly, but that he did not trust the lad whom he has there to translate into Dutch and English. So you see it will help me very much in this big business if you come with me."

Still I hesitated, for some fear of the future lay heavy on my heart, warning me against this expedition.

"Allemachte!" said Retief angrily, "if you will not grant me a favour, let it be. Or is it that you want reward? If so, all I can promise you is twenty thousand acres of the best land in the country when we get it."

"No, Mynheer Retief," I replied; "it is no question of reward; and as for the land, I have already pegged out my farm on a river about thirty miles to the east. It is that I do not like to leave Marie alone, fearing lest her father should play some trick on me as regards her and Hernan Pereira."

"Oh, if that is all you are afraid of, Allan, I can soon settle matters; for I will give orders to the Predicant Celliers that he is not to marry Marie Marais to anyone except yourself, even if she asks him. Also I will order that if Hernan Pereira should come to the camp, he is to be shut up until I return to try him. Lastly, as commandant, I will name Henri Marais as one of those who are to accompany us, so that he will be able to plot nothing against you. Now are you satisfied?"

I said "Yes" as cheerfully as I could, though I felt anything but cheerful, and we parted, for, of course, the Commandant Retief had much to occupy him.

Then I went and told Marie what I had promised. Somewhat to my surprise she said that she thought I had acted wisely.

"If you stayed here," she added, "perhaps some new quarrel would arise between you and my father which might make bitterness afterwards. Also, dear, it would be foolish for you to offend the Commandant Retief, who will be the great man in this country, and who is very fond of you. After all, Allan, we shall only be separated for a little while, and when that is done we have the rest of our lives to spend together. As for me, do not be afraid, for you know I will never marry anyone but you—no, not to save myself from death."

So I left her somewhat comforted, knowing how sound was her judgment, and went off to make my preparations for the expedition to Sikonyela's country.

All this conversation with Retief I have set down in full, as nearly as I can remember it, because of its fateful consequences. Ah! if I could have foreseen; if only I could have foreseen!

The Council

Two days later we started to recover Dingaan's cattle, sixty or seventy of us, all well armed and mounted. With us went two of Dingaan's captains and a number of Zulus, perhaps a hundred, who were to drive the cattle if we recovered them. As I could speak their language I was more or less in command of this Zulu contingent, and managed to make myself very useful in that capacity. Also, during the month or so of our absence, by continually conversing with them, I perfected myself considerably in my knowledge of their beautiful but difficult tongue.

Now it is not my intention to write down the details of this expedition, during which there was no fighting and nothing serious happened. We arrived in due course at Sikonyela's and stated our errand. When he saw how numerous and well armed we were, and that behind us was all the might of the Zulu army, that wily old rascal thought it well to surrender the stolen cattle without further to-do, and with these some horses which he had lifted from the Boers. So, having received them, we delivered them over to the Zulu captains, with instructions to drive them carefully to Umgungundhlovu. The commandant sent a message by these men to the effect that, having fulfilled his part of the compact, he would wait upon Dingaan as soon as possible in order to conclude the treaty about the land.

This business finished, Retief took me and a number of the Boers to visit other bodies of the emigrant Dutch who were beyond the Drakensberg, in what is now the Transvaal territory. This occupied a long time, as these Boers were widely scattered, and at each camp we had to stop for several days while Retief explained everything to its leaders. Also he arranged with them to come down into Natal, so as to be ready to people it as soon as he received the formal cession of the country from Dingaan. Indeed, most of them began to trek at once, although jealousies between the various commandants caused some of the bands, luckily for themselves, to remain on the farther side of the mountains.

At length, everything being settled, we rode away, and reached the Bushman's River camp on a certain Saturday afternoon. Here, to my joy, we found all well. Nothing had been heard of Hernan Pereira, while the Zulus, if we might judge from messengers who came to us, seemed to be friendly. Marie, also, had now quite recovered from the fears and hardships which she had undergone. Never had I seen her look so sweet and beautiful as she did when she greeted me, arrayed no longer in rags, but in a simple yet charming dress made of some stuff that she had managed to buy from a trader who came up to the camp from Durban. Moreover, I think that there was another reason for the change, since the light of dawning happiness shone in her deep eyes.

The day, as I have said, was Saturday, and on the Monday she would come of age and be free to dispose of herself in marriage, for on that day lapsed the promise which we had given to her father. But, alas! by a cursed perversity of fate, on this very Monday at noon the Commandant Retief had arranged to ride into Zululand on his second visit to Dingaan, and with Retief I was in honour bound to go.

"Marie," I said, "will not your father soften towards us and let us be married to-morrow, so that we may have a few hours together before we part?"

"I do not know, my dear," she answered, blushing, "since about this matter he is very strange and obstinate. Do you know that all the time you were absent he never mentioned your name, and if anyone else spoke it he would get up and go away!"

"That's bad," I said. "Still, if you are willing, we might try."

"Indeed and indeed, Allan, I am willing, who am sick of being so near to you and yet so far. But how shall we do so?"

"I think that we will ask the Commandant Retief and the Vrouw Prinsloo to plead for us, Marie. Let us go to seek them."

She nodded, and hand in hand we walked through the Boers, who nudged each other and laughed at us as we passed to where the old vrouw was seated on a stool by her wagon drinking coffee. I remember that her vatdoek was spread over her knees, for she also had a new dress, which she was afraid of staining.

"Well, my dears," she said in her loud voice, "are you married already that you hang so close together?"

"No, my aunt," I answered; "but we want to be, and have come to you to help us."

"That I will do with all my heart, though to speak truth, young people, at your age, as things are, I should have been inclined to help myself, as I have told you before. Heaven above us! what is it that makes marriage in the sight of God? It is that male and female should declare themselves man and wife before all folk, and live as such. The pastor and his mumblings are very well if you can get them, but it is the giving of the hand, not the setting of the ring upon it; it is the vowing of two true hearts, and not words read out of a book, that make marriage. Still, this is bold talk, for which any reverend predicant would reprove me, for if young folk acted on it, although the tie might hold good in law, what would become of his fee? Come, let us seek the commandant and hear what he has to say. Allan, pull me up off this stool, where, if I had my way, after so much travelling, I should like to sit while a house was built over my head and for the rest of my life."

I obeyed, not without difficulty, and we went to find Retief.

At the moment he was standing alone, watching two wagons that had just trekked away. These contained his wife with other members of his family, and some friends whom he was sending, under the charge of the Heer Smit, to a place called Doornkop, that lay at a distance of fifteen miles or more. At this Doornkop he had already caused a rough house, or rather shed, to be built for the Vrouw Retief's occupation, thinking that she would be more comfortable and perhaps safer there during his absence than at the crowded camp in a wagon.

"Allemachte! Allan," he said, catching sight of me, "my heart is sore; I do not know why. I tell you that when I kissed my old woman good-bye just now I felt as though I should never see her again, and the tears came into my eyes. I wish we were all safe back from Dingaan. But there, there, I will try to get over to see her to-morrow, as we don't start till Monday. What is it that you want, Allan, with that 'mooi mesje' of yours?"—and he pointed to the tall Marie.

"What would any man want with such a one, save to marry her?" broke in the Vrouw Prinsloo. "Now, commandant, listen while I set out the tale."

"All right, aunt, only be brief, for I have no time to spare."

She obeyed, but I cannot say that she was brief.

When at last the old lady paused, breathless, Retief said:

"I understand everything; there is no need for you young people to talk. Now we will go and see Henri Marais, and, if he is not madder than usual, make him listen to reason."

So we walked to where Marais's wagon stood at the end of the line, and found him sitting on the disselboom cutting up tobacco with his pocket-knife.

"Good-day, Allan," he said, for we had not met since my return. "Have you had a nice journey?"

I was about to answer when the commandant broke in impatiently:

"See here, see here, Henri, we have not come to talk about Allan's journey, but about his marriage, which is more important. He rides with me to Zululand on Monday, as you do, and wants to wed your daughter to-morrow, which is Sunday, a good day for the deed."

"It is a day to pray, not to give and be given in marriage," commented Marais sulkily. "Moreover, Marie does not come of age before Monday, and until then the oath that I made to God holds."

"My vatdoek for your oath!" exclaimed the vrouw, flapping that awful rag in his face. "How much do you suppose that God cares what you in your folly swore to that stinkcat of a nephew of yours? Do you be careful, Henri Marais, that God does not make of your precious oath a stone to fall upon your head and break it like a peanut-shell."

"Hold your chattering tongue, old woman," said Marais furiously. "Am I to be taught my duty to my conscience and my daughter by you?"

"Certainly you are, if you cannot teach them to yourself," began the vrouw, setting her hands upon her hips.

But Retief pushed her aside, saying:

"No quarrelling here. Now, Henri Marais, your conduct about these two young people who love each other is a scandal. Will you let them be married to-morrow or not?"

"No, commandant, I will not. By the law I have power over my daughter till she is of age, and I refuse to allow her to marry a cursed Englishman. Moreover, the Predicant Celliers is away, so there is none to marry them."

"You speak strange words, Mynheer Marais," said Retief quietly, "especially when I remember all that this 'cursed Englishman' has done for you and yours, for I have heard every bit of that story, though not from him. Now hearken. You have appealed to the law, and, as commandant, I must allow your appeal. But after twelve o'clock to-morrow night, according to your own showing, the law ceases to bind your daughter. Therefore, on Monday morning, if there is no clergyman in the camp and these two wish it, I, as commandant, will marry them before all men, as I have the power to do."

Then Marais broke into one of those raving fits of temper which were constitutional in him, and to my mind showed that he was never quite sane. Oddly enough, it was on poor Marie that he concentrated his wrath. He cursed her horribly because she had withstood his will and refused to marry Hernan Pereira. He prayed that evil might fall on her; that she might never bear a child, and that if she did, it might die, and other things too unpleasant to mention.

We stared at him astonished, though I think that had he been any other man than the father of my betrothed, I should have struck him. Retief, I noticed, lifted his hand to do so, then let it fall again, muttering: "Let be; he is possessed with a devil."

At last Marais ceased, not, I think, from lack of words, but because he was exhausted, and stood before us, his tall form quivering, and his thin, nervous face working like that of a person in convulsions. Then Marie, who had dropped her head beneath this storm, lifted it, and I saw that her deep eyes were all ablaze and that she was very white.

"You are my father," she said in a low voice, "and therefore I must submit to whatever you choose to say to me. Moreover, I think it likely that the evil which you call down will fall upon me, since Satan is always at hand to fulfil his own wishes. But if so, my father, I am sure that this evil will recoil upon your own head, not only here, but hereafter. There justice will be done to both of us, perhaps before very long, and also to your nephew, Hernan Pereira."

Marais made no answer; his rage seemed to have spent itself. He only sat himself again upon the disselboom of the wagon and went on cutting up the tobacco viciously, as though he were slicing the heart of a foe. Even the Vrouw Prinsloo was silent and stared at him whilst she fanned herself with the vatdoek. But Retief spoke.

"I wonder if you are mad, or only wicked, Henri Marais," he said. "To curse your own sweet girl like this you must be one or the other—a single child who has always been good to you. Well, as you are to ride with me on Monday, I pray that you will keep your temper under control, lest it should bring us into trouble, and you also. As for you, Marie, my dear, do not fret because a wild beast has tried to toss you with his horns, although he happens to be your father. On Monday morning you pass out of his power into your own, and on that day I will marry you to Allan Quatermain here. Meanwhile, I think you are safest away from this father of yours, who might take to cutting your throat instead of that tobacco. Vrouw Prinsloo, be so good as to look after Marie Marais, and on Monday morning next bring her before me to be wed. Until then, Henri Marais, I, as commandant, shall set a guard over you, with orders to seize you if it should be necessary. Now I advise you to take a walk, and when you are calm again, to pray God to forgive you your wicked words, lest they should be fulfilled and drag you down to judgment."

Then we all went, leaving Henri Marais still cutting up his tobacco on the disselboom.

On the Sunday I met Marais walking about the camp, followed by the guard whom Retief had set over him. To my surprise he greeted me almost with affection.

"Allan," he said, "you must not misunderstand me. I do not really wish ill to Marie, whom I love more dearly than I do my life; God alone knows how much I love her. But I made a promise to her cousin, Hernan, my only sister's only child, and you will understand that I cannot break that promise, although Hernan has disappointed me in many ways—yes, in many ways. But if he is bad, as they say, it comes with that Portuguese blood, which is a misfortune that he cannot help, does it not? However bad he may be, as an honest man I am bound to keep my promise, am I not? Also, Allan, you must remember that you are English, and although you may be a good fellow in yourself, that is a fault which you cannot expect me to forgive. Still, if it is fated that you should marry my daughter and breed English children—Heaven above! to think of it, English children!—well, there is nothing more to be said. Don't remember the words I spoke to Marie. Indeed, I can't remember them myself. When I grow angry, a kind of rush of blood comes into my brain, and then I forget what I have said," and he stretched out his hand to me.

I shook it and answered that I understood he was not himself when he spoke those dreadful words, which both Marie and I wished to forget.

"I hope you will come to our wedding to-morrow," I added, "and wipe them out with a father's blessing."

"To-morrow! Are you really going to be married to-morrow?" he exclaimed, his sallow face twitching nervously. "O God, it was another man that I dreamed to see standing by Marie's side. But he is not here; he has disgraced and deserted me. Well, I will come, if my gaolers will suffer it. Good-bye, you happy bridegroom of to-morrow, good-bye."

Then he swung round and departed, followed by the guards, one of whom touched his brow and shook his head significantly as he passed me.

I think that Sunday seemed the longest day I ever spent. The Vrouw Prinsloo would scarcely allow me even a glimpse of Marie, because of some fad she had got into her mind that it was either not proper or not fortunate, I forget which, that a bride and bridegroom should associate on the eve of their marriage. So I occupied myself as best I could. First I wrote a long letter to my father, the third that I had sent, telling him everything that was going to happen, and saying how grieved I was that he could not be present to marry us and give us his blessing.

This letter I gave to a trader who was trekking to the bay on the following morning, begging him to forward it by the first opportunity.

That duty done, I saw about the horses which I was taking into Zululand, three of them, two for myself and one for Hans, who accompanied me as after-rider. Also the saddlery, saddle-bags, guns and ammunition must be overhauled, all of which took some time.

"You are going to spend a strange wittebroodsweek [white-bread-week, or, in other words, honeymoon], baas," said Hans, squinting at me with his little eyes, as he brayed away at a buckskin which was to serve as a saddle-cloth. "Now, if _I_ was to be married to-morrow, I should stop with my pretty for a few days, and only ride off somewhere else when I was tired of her, especially if that somewhere else chanced to be Zululand, where they are so fond of killing people."

"I dare say you would, Hans; and so would I, if I could, you be sure. But, you see, the commandant wants me to interpret, and therefore it is my duty to go with him."

"Duty; what is duty, baas? Love I understand. It is for love of you that I go with you; also for fear lest you should cause me to be beaten if I refused. Otherwise I would certainly stop here in the camp, where there is plenty to eat and little work to do, as, were I you, I should do also for love of that white missie. But duty—pah! that is a fool-word, which makes bones of a man before his time and leaves his girl to others."

"Of course, you do not understand, Hans, any more than you coloured people understand what gratitude is. But what do you mean about this trek of ours? Are you afraid?"

He shrugged his shoulders. "A little, perhaps, baas. At least, I should be if I thought about the morrow, which I don't, since to-day is enough for me, and thinking about what one can't know makes the head ache. Dingaan is not a nice man, baas; we saw that, didn't we? He is a hunter who knows how to set a trap. Also he has the Baas Pereira up there to help him. So perhaps you might be more comfortable here kissing Missie Marie. Why do you not say that you have hurt your leg and cannot run? It would not be much trouble to walk about on a crutch for a day or two, and when the commandant was well gone, your leg might heal and you could throw the stick away."

"Get thee behind me, Satan," I muttered to myself, and was about to give Hans a piece of my mind when I recollected that the poor fellow had his own way of looking at things and could not be blamed. Also, as he said, he loved me, and only suggested what he thought would tend to my joy and safety. How could I suppose that he would be interested in the success of a diplomatic mission to Dingaan, or think anything about it except that it was a risky business? So I only said:

"Hans, if you are afraid, you had better stop behind. I can easily find another after-rider."

"Is the baas angry with me that he should speak so?" asked the Hottentot. "Have I not always been true to him; and if I should be killed, what does it matter? Have I not said that I do not think about to-morrow, and we must all go to sleep sometime? No; unless the baas beats me back, I shall come with him. But, baas"—this in a wheedling tone—"you might give me some brandy to drink your health in to-night.

It is very good to get drunk when one has to be sober, and perhaps dead, for a long time afterwards. It would be nice to remember when one is a spook, or an angel with white wings, such as the old baas, your father, used to tell us about in school on the Sabbath."

At this point, finding Hans hopeless, I got up and walked away, leaving him to finish our preparations.

That evening there was a prayer-meeting in the camp, for although no pastor was present, one of the Boer elders took his place and offered up supplications which, if simple and even absurd in their wording, at least were hearty enough. Amongst other requests, I remember that he petitioned for the safety of those who were to go on the mission to Dingaan and of those who were to remain behind. Alas! those prayers were not heard, for it pleased the Power to Whom they were addressed to decree otherwise.

After this meeting, in which I took an earnest share, Retief who just before it began had ridden in from Doornkop, whither he had been to visit his wife, held a kind of council, whereat the names of those who had volunteered or been ordered to accompany him, were finally taken down. At this council there was a good deal of discussion, since many of the Boers did not think the expedition wise—at any rate, if it was to be carried out on so large a scale. One of them, I forget which, an old man, pointed out that it might look like a war party, and that it would be wiser if only five or six went, as they had done before, since then there could be no mistake as to the peaceful nature of their intentions.

Retief himself combated this view, and at last turned suddenly to me, who was listening near by, and said:

"Allan Quatermain, you are young, but you have a good judgment; also, you are one of the very few who know Dingaan and can speak his language. Tell us now, what do you think?"

Thus adjured, I answered, perhaps moved thereto more than I thought by Hans's talk, that I, too, considered the thing dangerous, and that someone whose life was less valuable than the commandant's should go in command.

"Why do you say so, nephew," he said irritably, "seeing that all white men's lives are of equal value, and I can smell no danger in the business?"

"Because, commandant, I do smell danger, though what danger I cannot say, any more than a dog or a buck can when it sniffs something in the air and barks or runs. Dingaan is a tamed tiger just now, but tigers are not house cats that one can play with them, as I know, who have felt his claws and just, only just, come out from between them."

"What do you mean, nephew?" asked Retief in his direct fashion. "Do you believe that this swartzel" (that is, black creature) "means to kill us?"

"I believe that it is quite possible," I answered.

"Then, nephew, being a reasonable man as you are, you must have some ground for your belief. Come now, out with it."

"I have none, commandant, except that one who can set the lives of a dozen folk against a man's skill in shooting at birds on the wing, and who can kill people to be a bait for those birds, is capable of anything. Moreover, he told me that he did not love you Boers, and why should he?"

Now, all those who were standing about seemed to be impressed with this argument. At any rate, they turned towards Retief, anxiously waiting for his reply.

"Doubtless," answered the commandant, who, as I have said, was irritable that night, "doubtless those English missionaries have poisoned the king's mind against us Boers. Also," he added suspiciously, "I think you told me, Allan, that the king said he liked you and meant to spare you, even if he killed your companions, just because you also are English. Are you sure that you do not know more than you choose to tell us? Has Dingaan perhaps confided something to you—just because you are English?"

Then noting that these words moved the assembled Boers, in whom race prejudice and recent events had created a deep distrust of any born of British blood, I grew very angry and answered:

"Commandant, Dingaan confided nothing to me, except that some Kaffir witch-doctor, who is named Zikali, a man I never saw, had told him that he must not kill an Englishman, and therefore he wished to spare me, although one of your people, Hernan Pereira, had whispered to him that I ought to be killed. Yet I say outright that I think you are foolish to visit this king with so large a force. Still, I am ready to do so myself with one or two others. Let me go, then, and try to persuade him to sign this treaty as to the land. If I am killed or fail, you can follow after me and do better."

"Allemachte!" exclaimed Retief; "that is a fair offer. But how do I know, nephew, that when we came to read the treaty we should not find that it granted all the land to you English and not to us Boers? No, no, don't look angry. That was not a right thing to say, for you are honest whatever most of your blood may be. Nephew Allan, you who are a brave man, are afraid of this journey. Now, why is that, I wonder? Ah! I have it. I had forgotten. You are to be married to-morrow morning to a very pretty girl, and it is not natural that you should wish to spend the next fortnight in Zululand. Don't you see, brothers, he wants to get out of it because he is going to be married, as it is natural that he should, and therefore he tries to frighten us all? When we were going to be married, should we have wished to ride away at once to visit some stinking savage? Ach! I am glad I thought of that just as I was beginning to turn his gloomy colour, like a chameleon on a black hat, for it explains everything," and he struck his thigh with his big hand and burst into a roar of laughter.

All the company of Boers who stood around began to laugh also, uproariously, for this primitive joke appealed to them. Moreover, their nerves were strained; they also dreaded this expedition, and therefore they were glad to relieve themselves in bucolic merriment. Everything was clear to them now. Feeling myself in honour bound to go on the embassy, as I was their only interpreter, I, artful dog, was trying to play upon their fears in order to prevent it from starting, so that I might have a week or two of the company of my new-wed wife. They saw and appreciated the joke.

"He's slim, this little Englishman," shouted one.

"Don't be angry with him. We should have done as much ourselves," replied another.

"Leave him behind," said a third. "Even the Zulus do not send a new-married man on service." Then they smacked me on the back, and hustled me in their rude, kindly manner, till at length I fell into a rage and hit one of them on the nose, at which he only laughed the louder, although I made it bleed.

"See here, friends," I said, as soon as silence was restored; "married or no, whoever does not ride to Dingaan, I ride to him, although it is against my judgment. Let those laugh loudest who laugh last."

"Good!" cried one; "if you set the pace we shall soon be home again, Allan Quatermain. Who would not with Marie Marais at the end of the journey?"

Then, followed by their rough and mocking laughter, I broke away from them, and took refuge in my wagon, little guessing that all this talk would be brought up against me on a day to come.

In a certain class of uneducated mind foresight is often interpreted as guilty knowledge.

The Marriage

I was awakened on my wedding morning by the crash and bellowing of a great thunderstorm. The lightning flashed fearfully all about us, killing two oxen quite near to my wagon, and the thunder rolled and echoed till the very earth seemed to shake. Then came a wail of cold wind, and after that the swish of torrential rain. Although I was well accustomed to such natural manifestations, especially at this season of the year, I confess that these sights and sounds did not tend to raise my spirits, which were already lower than they should have been on that eventful day. Hans, however, who arrived to help me put on my best clothes for the ceremony, was for once consoling.

"Don't look sick, baas," he said, "for if there is storm in the morning, there is shine at night."

"Yes," I answered, speaking more to myself than to him, "but what will happen between the storm of the morning and the peace of the night?"

It was arranged that the commission, which, counting the native after-riders, consisted of over a hundred people, among them several boys, who were little more than children, was to ride at one hour before noon. Nobody could get about to make the necessary preparations until the heavy rain had passed away, which it did a little after eight o'clock. Therefore when I left the wagon to eat, or try to eat some breakfast, I found the whole camp in a state of bustle.

Boers were shouting to their servants, horses were being examined, women were packing the saddle-bags of their husbands and fathers with spare clothes, the pack-beasts were being laden with biltong and other provisions, and so forth.

In the midst of all this tumult I began to wonder whether my private business would not be forgotten, since it seemed unlikely that time could be found for marriages. However, about ten o'clock when, having done everything that I had to do, I was sitting disconsolately upon my wagon box, being too shy to mix with that crowd of busy mockers or to go to the Prinsloos' camp to make inquiries, the vrouw herself appeared.

"Come on, Allan," she said, "the commandant is waiting and swearing because you are not there. Also, there is another waiting, and oh! she looks lovely. When they see her, every man in the camp will want her for himself, whether he has got a wife or not, for in that matter, although you mayn't think so just now, they are all the same as the Kaffirs. Oh! I know them, I know them, a white skin makes no difference."

While she held forth thus in her usual outspoken fashion, the vrouw was dragging me along by the hand, just as though I were a naughty little boy. Nor could I get free from that mighty grip, or, when once her great bulk was in motion, match my weight against it. Of course, some of the younger Boers, who, knowing her errand, had followed her, set up a shout of cheers and laughter, which attracted everybody to the procession.

"It is too late to hang back now, Englishman." "You must make the best of a bad business." "If you wanted to change your mind, you should have done it before," men and women roared and screamed with many other such bantering words, till at length I felt myself turn the colour of a red vlei lily.

So we came at last to where Marie stood, the centre of an admiring circle. She was clothed in a soft white gown made of some simple but becoming stuff, and she wore upon her dark hair a wreath woven by the other maidens in the camp, a bevy of whom stood behind her.

Now we were face to face. Our eyes met, and oh! hers were full of love and trust. They dazzled and bewildered me. Feeling that I ought to speak, and not knowing what to say, I merely stammered "Good morning," whereon everyone broke into a roar of laughter, except Vrouw Prinsloo, who exclaimed:

"Did any one ever see such a fool?" and even Marie smiled.

Then Piet Retief appeared from somewhere dressed in tall boots and rough riding clothes, such as the Boers wore in those days. Handing the roer he was carrying to one of his sons, after much fumbling he produced a book from his pocket, in which the place was marked with a piece of grass.

"Now then," he said, "be silent, all, and show respect, for remember I am not a man just now. I am a parson, which is quite a different thing, and, being a commandant and a veld cornet and other officers all rolled into one, by virtue of the law I am about to marry these young people, so help me God. Don't any of you witnesses ever say afterwards that they are not rightly and soundly married, because I tell you that they are, or will be." He paused for breath, and someone said, "Hear, hear," or its Dutch equivalent, whereon, having glared the offender into silence, Retief proceeded:

"Young man and young woman, what are your names?"

"Don't ask silly questions, commandant," broke in Vrouw Prinsloo; "you know their names well enough."

"Of course I do, aunt," he answered; "but for this purpose I must pretend not to know them. Are you better acquainted with the law than I am? But stay, where is the father, Henri Marais?"

Someone thrust Marais forward, and there he stood quite silent, staring at us with a queer look upon his face and his gun in his hand, for he, too, was ready to ride.

"Take away that gun," said Retief; "it might go off and cause disturbance or perhaps accidents," and somebody obeyed. "Now, Henri Marais, do you give your daughter to be married to this man?"

"No," said Marais softly.

"Very well, that is just like you, but it doesn't matter, for she is of age and can give herself. Is she not of age, Henri Marais? Don't stand there like a horse with the staggers, but tell me; is she not of age?"

"I believe so," he answered in the same soft voice.

"Then take notice, people all, that this woman is of age, and gives herself to be married to this man, don't you, my dear?"

"Yes," answered Marie.

"All right, now for it," and, opening the book, he held it up to the light, and began to read, or, rather, to stumble, through the marriage service.

Presently he stuck fast, being, like most Boers of his time, no great scholar, and exclaimed:

"Here, one of you help me with these hard words."

As nobody volunteered, Retief handed the book to me, for he knew that Marais would not assist him, saying:

"You are a scholar, Allan, being a clergyman's son. Read on till we come to the important bits, and I will say the words after you, which will do just as well and be quite according to law."

So I read, Heaven knows how, for the situation was trying enough, until I came to the crucial questions, when I gave the book back.

"Ah!" said Retief; "this is quite easy. Now then, Allan, do you take this woman to be your wife? Answer, putting in your name, which is left blank in the book."

I replied that I did, and the question was repeated to Marie, who did likewise.

"Well then, there you are," said Retief, "for I won't trouble you with all the prayers, which I don't feel myself parson enough to say. Oh! no, I forgot. Have you a ring?"

I drew one off my finger that had been my mother's—I believe it had served this same purpose at the wedding of her grandmother—and set the thin little hoop of gold upon the third finger of Marie's left hand. I still wear that ring to-day.

"It should have been a new one," muttered Vrouw Prinsloo.

"Be silent, aunt," said Retief; "are there any jewellers' shops here in the veld? A ring is a ring, even if it came off a horse's bit. There, I think that is all. No, wait a minute, I am going to say a prayer of my own over you, not one out of this book, which is so badly printed that I cannot read it. Kneel down, both of you; the rest may stand, as the grass is so wet."

Now, bethinking herself of Marie's new dress, the vrouw produced her vatdoek from a capacious pocket, and doubled up that dingy article for Marie to kneel on, which she did. Then Pieter Retief, flinging down the book, clasped his hands and uttered this simple, earnest prayer, whereof, strangely enough, every word remains fast in my mind. Coming as it did, not from a printed page, but from his honest and believing heart, it was very impressive and solemn.

"O God above us, Who sees all and is with us when we are born, when we are married, when we die, and if we do our duty for all time afterwards in Heaven, hear our prayer. I pray Thee bless this man and this woman who appear here before Thee to be wed. Make them love each other truly all their lives, be these long or short, be they sick or well, be they happy or in sorrow, be they rich or poor. Give them children to be reared up in Thy Word, give them an honest name and the respect of all who know them, and at last give them Thy Salvation through the Blood of Jesus the Saviour. If they are together, let them rejoice in each other. If they are apart, let them not forget each other. If one of them dies and the other lives, let that one who lives look forward to the day of reunion and bow the head to Thy Will, and keep that one who dies in Thy holy Hand. O Thou Who knowest all things, guide the lives of these two according to Thy eternal purpose, and teach them to be sure that whatever Thou doest, is done for the best. For Thou art a faithful Creator, Who wishes good to His children and not evil, and at the last Thou wilt give them that good if they do but trust in Thee through daylight and through darkness. Now let no man dare to put asunder those whom Thou hast joined together, O Lord God Almighty, Father of us all. Amen."

So he prayed, and all the company echoed that Amen from their hearts. That is all except one, for Henri Marais turned his back on us and walked away.

"So," said Retief, wiping his brow with the sleeve of his coat, "you are the last couple that ever I mean to marry. The work is too hard for a layman who has bad sight for print. Now kiss each other; it is the right thing to do."

So we kissed, and the congregation cheered.

"Allan," went on the commandant, pulling out a silver watch like a turnip, "you have just half an hour before we ride, and the Vrouw Prinsloo says that she has made you a wedding meal in that tent there, so you had best go eat it."

To the tent we went accordingly, to find a simple but bounteous feast prepared, of which we partook, helping each other to food, as is, or was, the custom with new-wedded folk. Also, many Boers came in and drank our healths, although the

Vrouw Prinsloo told them that it would have been more decent to leave us alone. But Henri Marais did not come or drink our healths.

Thus the half-hour went all too swiftly, and not a word did we get alone. At last in despair, seeing that Hans was already waiting with the horses, I drew Marie aside, motioning to everyone to stand back.

"Dearest wife," I said in broken words, "this is a strange beginning to our married life, but you see it can't be helped."

"No, Allan," she answered, "it can't be helped; but oh! I wish my heart were happier about your journey. I fear Dingaan, and if anything should chance to you I shall die of grief."

"Why should anything chance, Marie? We are a strong and well-armed party, and Dingaan looks on us peacefully."

"I don't know, husband, but they say Hernan Pereira is with the Zulus, and he hates you."

"Then he had better mind his manners, or he will not be here long to hate anybody," I answered grimly, for my gorge rose at the thought of this man and his treacheries.

"Vrouw Prinsloo," I called to the old lady, who was near, "be pleased to come hither and listen. And, Marie, do you listen also. If by chance I should hear anything affecting your safety, and send you a message by someone you can trust, such as that you should remove yourselves elsewhere or hide, promise me that you will obey it without question."

"Of course I will obey you, husband. Have I not just sworn to do so?" Marie said with a sad smile.

"And so will I, Allan," said the vrouw; "not because I have sworn anything, but because I know you have a good head on your shoulders, and so will my man and the others of our party. Though why you should think you will have any message to send, I can't guess, unless you know something that is hidden from us," she added shrewdly. "You say you don't; well, it is not likely you would tell us if you did. Look! They are calling, you must go. Come on, Marie, let us see them off."

So we went to where the commission was gathered on horseback, just in time to hear Retief addressing the people, or, rather, the last of his words.

"Friends," he said, "we go upon an important business, from which I hope we shall return happily within a very little time. Still, this is a rough country, and we have to deal with rough people. Therefore my advice to all you who stay behind is that you should not scatter, but keep together, so that in case of any trouble the men who are left may be at hand to defend this camp. For if they are here you have nothing to fear from all the savages in Africa. And now God be with you, and good-bye. Come, trek, brothers, trek!"

Then followed a few moments of confusion while men kissed their wives, children and sisters in farewell, or shook each other by the hand. I, too, kissed Marie, and, tumbling on to my horse somehow, rode away, my eyes blind with tears, for this parting was bitter. When I could see clearly again I pulled up and looked back at the camp, which was now at some distance. It seemed a peaceful place indeed, for although the storm of the morning was returning and a pall of dark cloud hung over it, the sun still shone upon the white wagon caps and the people who went to and fro among them.

Who could have thought that within a little time it would be but a field of blood, that those wagons would be riddled with assegais, and that the women and children who were moving there must most of them lie upon the veld mutilated corpses dreadful to behold? Alas! the Boers, always impatient of authority and confident that their own individual judgment was the best, did not obey their commandant's order to keep together. They went off this way and that, to shoot the game which was then so plentiful, leaving their families almost without protection. Thus the Zulus found and slew them.

Presently as I rode forward a little apart from the others someone overtook me, and I saw that it was Henri Marais.

"Well, Allan," he said, "so God has given you to me for a son-in-law. Who would have thought it? You do not look to me like a new-married man, for that marriage is not natural when the bridegroom rides off and leaves the bride of an hour. Perhaps you will never be really married after all, for God, Who gives sons-in-law, can also take them away, especially when He was not asked for them. Ah!" he went on, lapsing into French, as was his wont when moved, "qui vivra verra! qui vivra verra!" Then, shouting this excellent but obvious proverb at the top of his voice, he struck his horse with the butt of his gun, and galloped away before I could answer him.

At that moment I hated Henri Marais as I had never hated anyone before, not even his nephew Hernan. Almost did I ride to the commandant to complain of him, but reflecting to myself, first that he was undoubtedly half mad, and therefore not responsible for his actions, and secondly that he was better here with us than in the same camp with my wife, I gave up the idea. Yet alas! it is the half-mad who are the most dangerous of lunatics.

Hans, who had observed this scene and overheard all Marais's talk, and who also knew the state of the case well enough, sidled his horse alongside of me, and whispered in a wheedling voice:

"Baas, I think the old baas is kransick and not safe. He looks like one who is going to harm someone. Now, baas, suppose I let my gun off by accident; you know we coloured people are very careless with guns! The Heer Marais would never be troubled with any more fancies, and you and the Missie Marie and all of us would be safer. Also, _you_ could not be blamed, nor could I, for who can help an accident? Guns will go off sometimes, baas, when you don't want them to."

"Get out," I answered. Yet if Hans's gun had chanced to "go off," I believe it might have saved a multitude of lives!

The Treaty

Our journey to Umgungundhlovu was prosperous and without incident. When we were within half a day's march from the Great Kraal we overtook the herd of cattle that we had recaptured from Sikonyela, for these beasts had been driven very slowly and well rested that they might arrive in good condition. Also the commandant was anxious that we should present them ourselves to the king.

Driving this multitude of animals before us—there were over five thousand head of them—we reached the Great Place on Saturday the 3rd of February about midday, and forced them through its gates into the cattle kraals. Then we off-saddled and ate our dinner under those two milk trees near the gate of the kraal where I had bid good-bye to Dingaan.

After dinner messengers came to ask us to visit the king, and with them the youth, Thomas Halstead, who told the commandant that all weapons must be left behind, since it was the Zulu law that no man might appear before the king armed. To this Retief demurred, whereon the messengers appealed to me, whom they had recognised, asking if that were not the custom of their country.

I answered that I had not been in it long enough to know. Then there was a pause while they sent for someone to bear evidence; at the time I did not know whom, as I was not near enough to Thomas Halstead to make inquiries. Presently this someone appeared, and turned out to be none other than Hernan Pereira.

He advanced towards us attended by Zulus, as though he were a chief, looking fat and well and handsomer than ever. Seeing Retief, he lifted his hat with a flourish and held out his hand, which, I noted, the commandant did not take.

"So you are still here, Mynheer Pereira!" he said coldly. "Now be good enough to tell me, what is this matter about the abandoning of our arms?"

"The king charges me to say—" began Hernan.

"Charges you to say, Mynheer Pereira! Are you then this black man's servant? But continue."

"That none must come into his private enclosure armed."

"Well, then, mynheer, be pleased to go tell this king that we do not wish to come to his private enclosure. I have brought the cattle that he desired me to fetch, and I am willing to deliver them to him wherever he wishes, but we will not unarm in order to do so."

Now there was talk, and messengers were despatched, who returned at full speed presently to say that Dingaan would receive the Boers in the great dancing place in the midst of the kraal, and that they might bring their guns, as he wished to see how they fired them.

So we rode in, making as fine a show as we could, to find that the dancing place, which measured a good many acres in extent, was lined round with thousands of plumed but unarmed warriors arranged in regiments.

"You see," I heard Pereira say to Retief, "these have no spears."

"No," answered the commandant, "but they have sticks, which when they are a hundred to one would serve as well."

Meanwhile the vast mob of cattle were being driven in a double stream past a knot of men at the head of the space, and then away through gates behind. When the beasts had all gone we approached these men, among whom I recognised the fat form of Dingaan draped in a bead mantle. We ranged ourselves in a semicircle before him, and stood while he searched us with his sharp eyes. Presently he saw me, and sent a councillor to say that I must come and interpret for him.

So, dismounting, I went with Retief, Thomas Halstead, and a few of the leading Boers.

"Sakubona [Good day], Macumazahn," said Dingaan. "I am glad that you have come, as I know that you will speak my words truly, being one of the People of George whom I love, for Tho-maas here I do not trust, although he is also a Son of George."

I told Retief what he said.

"Oh!" he exclaimed with a grunt, "it seems that you English are a step in front of us Boers, even here."

Then he went forward and shook hands with the king, whom, it will be remembered, he had visited before.

After that the "indaba" or talk began, which I do not propose to set out at length, for it is a matter of history. It is enough to say that Dingaan, after thanking Retief for recovering the cattle, asked where was Sikonyela, the chief who had stolen them, as he wished to kill him. When he learned that Sikonyela remained in his own country, he became, or affected to become, angry. Then he asked where were the sixty horses which he heard we had captured from Sikonyela, as they must be given up to him.

Retief, by way of reply, touched his grey hairs, and inquired whether Dingaan thought that he was a child that he, Dingaan, should demand horses which did not belong to him. He added that these horses had been restored to the Boers, from whom Sikonyela had stolen them.

When Dingaan had expressed himself satisfied with this answer, Retief opened the question of the treaty. The king replied however, that the white men had but just arrived, and he wished to see them dance after their own fashion. As for the business, it might "sit still" till another day.

So in the end the Boers "danced" for his amusement. That is, they divided into two parties, and charged each other at full gallop, firing their guns into the air, an exhibition which seemed to fill all present with admiration and awe. When they paused, the king wished them to go on firing "a hundred shots apiece," but the commandant declined, saying he had no more powder to waste.

"What do you want powder for in a peaceful country?" asked Dingaan suspiciously.

Retief answered through me:

"To kill food for ourselves, or to protect ourselves if any evil-minded men should attack us."

"Then it will not be wanted here," said Dingaan, "since I will give you food, and as I, the king, am your friend, no man in Zululand dare be your enemy."

Retief said he was glad to hear it, and asked leave to retire with the Boers to his camp outside the gate, as they were all tired with riding. This Dingaan granted, and we said good-bye and went away. Before I reached the gate, however, a messenger, I remember it was my old friend Kambula, overtook me, and said that the king wished to speak with me alone. I answered him that I could not speak with the king alone without the permission of the commandant. Thereon Kambula said:

"Come with me, I pray you, O Macumazahn, since otherwise you will be taken by force."

Now, I told Hans to gallop on to Retief, and tell him of my predicament, for already I saw that at some sign from Kambula I was being surrounded by Zulus. He did so, and presently Retief came back himself accompanied only by one man, and asked me what was the matter now. I informed him, translating Kambula's words, which he repeated in his presence.

"Does the fellow mean that you will be seized if you do not go, or I refuse to allow you to do so?"

To this question Kambula's answer was:

"That is so, Inkoos, since the king has private words for the ear of Macumazahn. Therefore we must obey orders, and take him before the king, living or dead."

"Allemachte!" exclaimed Retief, "this is serious," and, as though to summon them to my help, he looked behind him towards the main body of the Boers, who by this time were nearly all of them through the gate, which was guarded by a great number of Zulus. "Allan," he went on, "if you are not afraid, I think that you must go. Perhaps it is only that Dingaan has some message about the treaty to send to me through you."

"I am not afraid," I answered. "What is the use of being afraid in a place like this?"

"Ask that Kaffir if the king gives you safe conduct," said Retief.

I did so, and Kambula answered:

"Yes, for this visit. Who am I that I can speak the king's unspoken words?" [which meant, guarantee his will in the future.]

"A dark saying," commented Retief. "But go, Allan, since you must, and God bring you back safe again. It is clear that Dingaan did not ask that you should come with me for nothing. Now I wish I had left you at home with that pretty wife of yours."

So we parted, I going to the king's private enclosure on foot and without my rifle, since I was not allowed to appear before him armed, and the commandant towards the gate of the kraal accompanied by Hans, who led my horse. Ten minutes later I stood before Dingaan, who greeted me kindly enough, and began to ask a number of questions about the Boers, especially if they were not people who had rebelled against their own king and run away from him.

I answered, Yes, they had run away, as they wanted more room to live; but I had told him all about that when I saw him before. He said he knew I had, but he wished to hear "whether the same words came out of the same mouth, or different words," so that he might know if I were a true man or not. Then, after pausing a while, he looked at me in his piercing fashion and asked:

"Have you brought me a present of that tall white girl with eyes like two stars, Macumazahn? I mean the girl whom you refused to me, and whom I could not take because you had won your bet, which gave all the white people to you; she for whose sake you make brothers of these Boers, who are traitors to their king?"

"No, O Dingaan," I answered; "there are no women among us. Moreover, this maid is now my wife."

"Your wife!" he exclaimed angrily. "By the Head of the Black One, have you dared to make a wife of her whom I desired? Now say, boy, you clever Watcher by Night; you little white ant, who work in the dark and only peep out at the end of your tunnel when it is finished; you wizard, who by your magic can snatch his prey out of the hand of the greatest king in all the world—for it was magic that killed those vultures on Hloma Amabutu, not your bullets, Macumazahn—say, why should I not make an end of you at once for this trick?"

I folded my arms and looked at him. A strange contrast we must have made, this huge, black tyrant with the royal air, for to do him justice he had that, at whose nod hundreds went the way of death, and I, a mere insignificant white boy, for in appearance, at any rate, I was nothing more.

"O Dingaan," I said coolly, knowing that coolness was my only chance, "I answer you in the words of the Commandant Retief, the great chief. Do you take me for a child that I should give up my own wife to you who already have so many? Moreover, you cannot kill me because I have the word of your captain, Kambula, that I am safe with you."

This reply seemed to amuse him. At any rate, with one of those almost infantile changes of mood which are common to savages of every degree, he passed from wrath to laughter.

"You are quick as a lizard," he said. "Why should I, who have so many wives, want one more, who would certainly hate me? Just because she is white, and would make the others, who are black, jealous, I suppose. Indeed, they would poison her, or pinch her to death in a month, and then come to tell me she had died of fretting. Also, you are right; you have my safe conduct, and must go hence unharmed this time. But look you, little lizard, although you escape me between the stones, I will pull off your tail. I have said that I want to pluck this tall white flower of yours, and I will pluck her. I know where she dwells. Yes, just where the wagon she sleeps in stands in the line, for my spies have told me, and I will give orders that whoever is killed, she is to be spared and brought to me living. So perhaps you will meet this wife of yours here, Macumazahn."

Now, at these ominous words, that might mean so much or so little, the sweat started to my brow, and a shiver went down my back.

"Perhaps I shall and perhaps I shall not, O king," I answered. "The world is as full of chances to-day as it was not long ago when I shot at the sacred vultures on Hloma Amabutu. Still, I think that my wife will never be yours, O king."

"Ow!" said Dingaan; "this little white ant is making another tunnel, thinking that he will come up at my back. But what if I put down my heel and crush you, little white ant? Do you know," he added confidentially, "that the Boer who mends my guns and whom here we call 'Two-faces,' because he looks towards you Whites with one eye and towards us Blacks with the other, is still very anxious that I should kill you? Indeed, when I told him that my spies said that you were to ride with the Boers, as I had requested that you should be their Tongue, he answered that unless I promised to give you to the vultures, he would warn them against coming. So, since I wanted them to come as I had arranged with him, I promised."

"Is it so, O king?" I asked. "And pray why does this Two-faces, whom we name Pereira, desire that I should be killed?"

"Ow!" chuckled the obese old ruffian; "cannot you with all your cleverness guess that, O Macumazahn? Perhaps it is he who needs the tall white maiden, and not I. Perhaps if he does certain things for me, I have promised her to him in payment. And perhaps," he added, laughing quite loud, "I shall trick him after all, keeping her for myself, and paying him in another way, for can a cheat grumble if he is out-cheated?"

I answered that I was an honest man, and knew nothing about cheats, or at what they could or could not grumble.

"Yes, Macumazahn," replied Dingaan quite genially. "That is where you and I are alike. We are both honest, quite honest, and therefore friends, which I can never be with these Amaboona, who, as you and others have told me, are traitors. We play our game in the light, like men, and who wins, wins, and who loses, loses. Now hear me, Macumazahn, and remember what I say. Whatever happens to others, whatever you may see, you are safe while I live. Dingaan has spoken. Whether I get the tall white girl, or do not get her, still _you_ are safe; it is on my head," and he touched the gum-ring in his hair.

"And why should I be safe if others are unsafe, O king?" I asked.

"Oh! if you would know that, ask a certain ancient prophet named Zikali, who was in this land in the days of Senzangacona, my father, and before then—that is, if you can find him. Also, I like you, who are not a flat-faced fool like these Amaboona, but have a brain that turns in and out through difficulties, as a snake does through reeds; and it would be a pity to kill one who can shoot birds wheeling high above him in the air, which no one else can do. So whatever you see and whatever you hear, remember that you are safe, and shall go safely from this land, or stay safely in it if you will, to be my voice to speak with the Sons of George.

"Now return to the commandant, and say to him that my heart is his heart, and that I am very pleased to see him here. To-morrow, and perhaps the next day, I will show him some of the dances of my people, and after that I will sign the writing, giving him all the land he asks and everything else he may desire, more than he can wish, indeed. Hamba gachle, Macumazahn," and, rising with surprising quickness from his chair, which was cut out of a single block of wood, he turned and vanished through the little opening in the reed fence behind him that led to his private huts.

As I was being conducted back to the Boer camp by Kambula, who was waiting for me outside the gate of the labyrinth which is called isiklohlo, I met Thomas Halstead, who was lounging about, I think in order to speak with me. Halting, I asked him straight out what the king's intentions were towards the Boers.

"Don't know," he answered, shrugging his shoulders, "but he seems so sweet on them that I think he must be up to mischief. He is wonderfully fond of you, too, for I heard him give orders that the word was to be passed through all the regiments that if anyone so much as hurt you, he should be killed at once. Also, you were pointed out to the soldiers when you rode in with the rest, that they might all of them know you."

"That's good for me as far as it goes," I replied. "But I don't know why I should need special protection above others, unless there is someone who wants to harm me."

"There is that, Allan Quatermain. The indunas tell me that the good-looking Portugee, whom they call 'Two-faces,' asks the king to kill you every time he sees him. Indeed, I've heard him myself."

"That's kind of him," I answered, "but, then, Hernan Pereira and I never got on. Tell me what is he talking about to the king when he isn't asking him to kill me."

"Don't know," he said again. "Something dirty, I'll be bound. One may be sure of that by the native name they have given him. I think, however," he added in a whisper, "that he has had a lot to do with the Boers being allowed to come here at all in order to get their treaty signed. At least, one day when I was interpreting and Dingaan swore that he would not give them more land than was enough to bury them in, Pereira told him that it didn't matter what he signed, as 'what was written with the pen could be scratched out with the spear.'"

"Indeed! And what did the king say to that?"

"Oh! he laughed and said it was true, and that he would give the Boer commission all their people wanted and something over for themselves. But don't you repeat that, Quatermain, for if you do, and it gets to the ear of Dingaan, I shall certainly be killed. And, I say, you're a good fellow, and I won a big bet on you over that vulture shooting, so I will give you a bit of advice, which you will be wise to take. You get out of this country as soon as you can, and go to look after that pretty Miss Marais, whom you are sweet on. Dingaan wants her, and what Dingaan wants he gets in this part of the world."

Then, without waiting to be thanked, he turned and disappeared among a crowd of Zulus, who were following us from curiosity, leaving me wondering whether or no Dingaan was right when he called this young man a liar. His story seemed to tally so well with that told by the king himself, that on the whole I thought he was not.

Just after I had passed the main gateway of the great town, where, his office done, Kambula saluted and left me, I saw two white men engaged in earnest conversation beneath one of the milk trees which, as I think I have already mentioned, grow, or grew, there. They were Henri Marais and his nephew. Catching sight of me, Marais walked off, but Pereira advanced and spoke to me, although, warned perhaps by what had happened to him in the case of Retief, I am glad to say he did not offer me his hand.

"Good day to you, Allan," he said effusively. "I have just heard from my uncle that I have to congratulate you, about Marie I mean, and, believe me, I do so with all my heart."

Now, as he spoke these words, remembering what I had just heard, my blood boiled in me, but I thought it wise to control myself, and therefore only answered:

"Thank you."

"Of course," he went on, "we have both striven for this prize, but as it has pleased God that you should win it, why, I am not one to bear malice."

"I am glad to hear it," I replied. "I thought that perhaps you might be. Now tell me, to change the subject, how long will Dingaan keep us here?"

"Oh! two or three days at most. You see, Allan, luckily I have been able to persuade him to sign the treaty about the land without further trouble. So as soon as that is done, you can all go home."

"The commandant will be very grateful to you," I said. "But what are you going to do?"

"I do not know, Allan. You see, I am not a lucky fellow like yourself with a wife waiting for me. I think that perhaps I shall stop here a while. I see a way of making a great deal of money out of these Zulus; and having lost everything upon that Delagoa Bay trek, I want money."

"We all do," I answered, "especially if we are starting in life. So when it is convenient to you to settle your debts I shall be glad."

"Oh! have no fear," he exclaimed with a sudden lighting up of his dark face, "I will pay you what I owe you, every farthing, with good interest thrown in."

"The king has just told me that is you intention," I remarked quietly, looking him full in the eyes. Then I walked on, leaving him staring after me, apparently without a word to say.

I went straight to the hut that was allotted to Retief in the little outlying guard-kraal, which had been given to us for a camp. Here I found the commandant seated on a Kaffir stool engaged in painfully writing a letter, using a bit of board placed on his knees as a desk.

He looked up, and asked me how I had got on with Dingaan, not being sorry, as I think, of an excuse to pause in his clerical labours.

"Listen, commandant," I said, and, speaking in a low voice, so as not to be overheard, I told him every word that had passed in the interviews I had just had with Dingaan, with Thomas Halstead, and with Pereira.

He heard me out in silence, then said:

"This is a strange and ugly story, Allan, and if it is true, Pereira must be an even bigger scoundrel than I thought him. But I can't believe that it is true. I think that Dingaan has been lying to you for his own purposes; I mean about the plot to kill you."

"Perhaps, commandant. I don't know, and I don't much care. But I am sure that he was not lying when he said he meant to steal away my wife either for himself or for Pereira."

"What, then, do you intend to do, Allan?"

"I intend, commandant, with your permission to send Hans, my after-rider, back to the camp with a letter for Marie, telling her to remove herself quietly to the farm I have chosen down on the river, of which I told you, and there to lie hid till I come back."

"I think it needless, Allan. Still, if it will ease your mind, do so, since I cannot spare you to go yourself. Only you must not send this Hottentot, who would talk and frighten the people. I am despatching a messenger to the camp to tell them of our safe arrival and good reception by Dingaan. He can take your letter, in which I order you to say to your wife that if she and the Prinsloos and the Meyers go to this farm of yours, they are to go without talking, just as though they wanted a change, that is all. Have the letter ready by dawn to-morrow morning, as I trust mine may be," he added with a groan.

"It shall be ready, commandant; but what about Hernan Pereira and his tricks?"

"This about the accursed Hernan Pereira," exclaimed Retief, striking the writing-board with his fist. "On the first opportunity I will myself take the evidence of Dingaan and of the English lad, Halstead. If I find they tell me the same story they have told you, I will put Pereira on his trial, as I threatened to do before; and should he be found guilty, by God! I will have him shot. But for the present it is best to do nothing, except keep an eye on him, lest we should cause fear and scandal in the camp, and, after all, not prove the case. Now go and write your letter, and leave me to write mine."

So I went and wrote, telling Marie something, but by no means all of that I have set down. I bade her, and the Prinsloos and the Meyers, if they would accompany her, as I was sure they would, move themselves off at once to the farm I had beaconed out thirty miles away from the Bushman's River, under pretence of seeing how the houses that were being built there were getting on. Or if they would not go, I bade her go alone with a few Hottentot servants, or any other companions she could find.

This letter I took to Retief, and read it to him. At my request, also, he scrawled at the foot of it:

"I have seen the above and approve it, knowing all the story, which may be true or false. Do as your husband bids you, but do not talk of it in the camp except to those whom he mentions.—PIETER RETIEF."

So the messenger departed at dawn, and in due course delivered my letter to Marie.

The next day was Sunday. In the morning I went to call upon the Reverend Mr. Owen, the missionary, who was very glad to see me. He informed me that Dingaan was in good mind towards us, and had been asking him if he would write the treaty ceding the land which the Boers wanted. I stopped for service at the huts of Mr. Owen, and then returned to the camp. In the afternoon Dingaan celebrated a great war dance for us to witness, in which about twelve thousand soldiers took part.

It was a wonderful and awe-inspiring spectacle, and I remember that each of the regiments employed had a number of trained oxen which manoeuvred with them, apparently at given words of command. We did not see Dingaan that day, except at a distance, and after the dance was over returned to our camp to eat the beef which he had provided for us in plenty.

On the third day—that was Monday, the 5th of February, there were more dancings and sham fights, so many more, indeed, that we began to weary of this savage show. Late in the afternoon, however, Dingaan sent for the commandant and his men to come to see him, saying that he wished to talk with him about the matter of the treaty. So we went; but only three or four, of whom I was one, were admitted to Dingaan's presence, the rest remaining at a little distance, where they could see us but were out of earshot.

Dingaan then produced a paper which had been written by the Reverend Mr. Owen. This document, which I believe still exists, for it was found afterwards, was drawn up in legal or semi-legal form, beginning like a proclamation, "Know all men."

It ceded "the place called Port Natal, together with all the land annexed—that is to say, from Tugela to the Umzimvubu River westward, and from the sea to the north"—to the Boers, "for their everlasting property." At the king's request, as the deed was written in English by Mr. Owen, I translated it to him, and afterwards the lad Halstead translated it also, being called in to do so when I had finished.

This was done that my rendering might be checked, and the fact impressed all the Boers very favourably. It showed them that the king desired to understand exactly what he was to sign, which would not have been the case had he intended any trick or proposed to cheat them afterwards. From that moment forward Retief and his people had no further doubts as to Dingaan's good faith in this matter, and foolishly relaxed all precautions against treachery.

When the translating was finished, the commandant asked the king if he would sign the paper then and there. He answered, "No; he would sign it on the following morning, before the commission returned to Natal." It was then that Retief inquired of Dingaan, through Thomas Halstead, whether it was a true story which he had heard, that the Boer called Pereira, who had been staying with him, and whom the Zulus knew by the name of "Two-faces," had again asked him, Dingaan, to have me, Allan Quatermain, whom they called Macumazahn, killed. Dingaan laughed and answered:

"Yes, that is true enough, for he hates this Macumazahn. But let the little white Son of George have no fear, since my heart is soft towards him, and I swear by the head of the Black One that he shall come to no harm in Zululand. Is he not my guest, as you are?"

He then went on to say that if the commandant wished it, he would have "Two-faces" seized and killed because he had dared to ask for my life. Retief answered that he would look into that matter himself, and after Thomas Halstead had confirmed the king's story as to Pereira's conduct, he rose and said good-bye to Dingaan.

Of this matter of Hernan Pereira, Retief said little as we went back to the camp outside the Kraal, though the little that he did say showed his deep anger. When we arrived at the camp, however, he sent for Pereira and Marais and several of the older Boers. I remember that among these were Gerrit Bothma, Senior, Hendrik Labuschagne and Matthys Pretorius, Senior, all of them persons of standing and judgment. I also was ordered to be present. When Pereira arrived, Retief charged him openly with having plotted my murder, and asked him what he had to say. Of course, his answer was a flat denial, and an accusation against me of having invented the tale because we had been at enmity over a maiden whom I had since married.

"Then, Mynheer Pereira," said Retief, "as Allan Quatermain here has won the maiden who is now his wife, it would seem that his cause of enmity must have ceased, whereas yours may well have remained. However, I have no time to try cases of the sort now. But I warn you that this one will be looked into later on when we get back to Natal, whither I shall take you with me, and that meanwhile an eye is kept on you and what you do. Also I warn you that I have evidence for all that I say. Now be so good as to go, and to keep out of my sight as much as possible, for I do not like a man whom these Kaffirs name 'Two-faces.' As for you, friend Henri Marais, I tell you that you would do well to associate yourself less with one whose name is under so dark a cloud, although he may be your own nephew, whom all know you love blindly."

So far as I recollect neither of them made any answer to this direct speech. They simply turned and went away. But on the next morning, that of the fatal 6th of February, when I chanced to meet the Commandant Retief as he was riding through the camp making arrangements for our departure to Natal, he pulled up his horse and said:

"Allan, Hernan Pereira has gone, and Henri Marais with him, and for my part I am not sorry, for doubtless we shall meet again, in this world or the next, and find out all the truth. Here, read this, and give it back to me afterwards"; and he threw me a paper and rode on.

I opened the folded sheet and read as follows:

"To the Commandant Retief, Governor of the Emigrant Boers,

"Mynheer Commandant,

"I will not stay here, where such foul accusations are laid on me by black Kaffirs and the Englishman, Allan Quatermain, who, like all his race, is an enemy of us Boers, and, although you do not know it, a traitor who is plotting great harm against you with the Zulus. Therefore I leave you, but am ready to meet every charge at the right time before a proper Court. My uncle, Henri Marais, comes with me, as he feels that his honour is also touched. Moreover, he has heard that his daughter, Marie, is in danger from the Zulus, and returns to protect her, which he who is called her husband neglects to do. Allan Quatermain, the Englishman, who is the friend of Dingaan, can explain what I mean, for he knows more about the Zulu plans than I do, as you will find out before the end."

Then followed the signatures of Hernan Pereira and Henri Marais.

I put the letter in my pocket, wondering what might be its precise meaning, and in particular that of the absurd and undefined charge of treachery against myself. It seemed to me that Pereira had left us because he was afraid of something—either that he might be placed upon his trial or of some ultimate catastrophe in which he would be involved. Marais probably had gone with him for the same reason that a bit of iron follows a magnet, because he never could resist the attraction of this evil man, his relative by birth. Or perhaps he had learned from him the story of his daughter's danger, upon which I had already acted, and really was anxious about her safety. For it must always be remembered that Marais loved Marie passionately, however ill the reader of this history may think that he behaved to her. She was his darling, the apple of his eye, and her great offence in his sight was that she cared for me more than she did for him. That is one of the reasons why he hated me as much as he loved her.

Almost before I had finished reading this letter, the order came that we were to go in a body to bid farewell to Dingaan, leaving our arms piled beneath the two milk trees at the gate of the town. Most of our after-riders were commanded to accompany us—I think because Retief wished to make as big a show as possible to impress the Zulus. A few of these Hottentots, however, were told to stay behind that they might collect the horses, that were knee-haltered and grazing at a distance, and saddle them up. Among these was Hans, for, as it chanced, I saw and sent him with the others, so that I might be sure that my own horses would be found and made ready for the journey.

Just as we were starting, I met the lad William Wood, who had come down from the Mission huts, where he lived with Mr. Owen, and was wandering about with an anxious face.

"How are you, William?" I asked.

"Not very well, Mr. Quatermain," he answered. "The fact is," he added with a burst of confidence, "I feel queerly about you all. The Kaffirs have told me that something is going to happen to you, and I think you ought to know it. I daren't say any more," and he vanished into the crowd.

At that moment I caught sight of Retief riding to and fro and shouting out orders. Going to him, I caught him by the sleeve, saying:

"Commandant, listen to me."

"Well, what is it now, nephew? " he asked absently.

I told him what Wood had said, adding that I also was uneasy; I did not know why.

"Oh!" he answered with impatience, "this is all hailstones and burnt grass" (meaning that the one would melt and the other blow away, or in our English idiom, stuff and rubbish). "Why are you always trying to scare me with your fancies, Allan? Dingaan is our friend, not our enemy. So let us take the gifts that fortune gives us and be thankful. Come, march."

This he said about eight o'clock in the morning.

We strolled through the gates of the Great Kraal, most of the Boers, who, as usual, had piled their arms under the two milk trees, lounging along in knots of four or five, laughing and chatting as they went. I have often thought since, that although every one of them there, except myself, was doomed within an hour to have taken the dreadful step from time into eternity, it seems strange that advancing fate should have thrown no shadow on their hearts. On the contrary, they were quite gay, being extremely pleased at the successful issue of their mission and the prospect of an immediate return to their wives and children. Even Retief was gay, for I heard him joking with his companions about myself and my "white-bread-week," or honeymoon, which, he said, was drawing very near.

As we went, I noticed that most of the regiments who had performed the great military dances before us on the previous day were gone. Two, however, remained—the Ischlangu Inhlope, that is the "White Shields," who were a corps of veterans wearing the ring on their heads, and the Ischlangu Umnyama, that is the "Black Shields," who were all of them young men without rings. The "White Shields" were ranged along the fence of the great open place to our left, and the "Black Shields" were similarly placed to our right, each regiment numbering about fifteen hundred men. Except for their kerries and dancing-sticks they were unarmed.

Presently we reached the head of the dancing ground, and found Dingaan seated in his chair with two of his great indunas, Umhlela and Tambusa, squatting on either side of him. Behind him, standing in and about the entrance to the labyrinth through which the king had come, were other indunas and captains. On arriving in front of Dingaan we saluted him, and he acknowledged the salutation with pleasant words and smiles. Then Retief, two or three of the other Boers, Thomas Halstead and I went forward, whereon the treaty was produced again and identified as the same document that we had seen on the previous day.

At the foot of it someone—I forget who—wrote in Dutch, "De merk van Koning Dingaan" [that is, The mark of King Dingaan.] In the space left between the words "merk" and "van" Dingaan made a cross with a pen that was given to him, Thomas Halstead holding his hand and showing him what to do.

After this, three of his indunas, or great councillors, who were named Nwara, Yuliwana and Manondo, testified as witnesses for the Zulus, and M. Oosthuyzen, A. C. Greyling and B. J. Liebenberg, who were standing nearest to Retief, as witnesses for the Boers.

This done, Dingaan ordered one of his isibongos, or praisers, to run to and fro in front of the regiments and others there assembled, and proclaim that he had granted Natal to the Boers to be their property for ever, information which the Zulus received with shouts. Then Dingaan asked Retief if he would not eat, and large trenchers of boiled beef were brought out and handed round. This, however, the Boers refused, saying they had already breakfasted. Thereon the king said that at least they must drink, and pots of twala, or Kaffir beer, were handed round, of which all the Boers partook.

While they were drinking, Dingaan gave Retief a message to the Dutch farmers, to the effect that he hoped they would soon come and occupy Natal, which henceforth was their country. Also, black-hearted villain that he was, that they would have a pleasant journey home. Next he ordered the two regiments to dance and sing war songs, in order to amuse his guests.

This they began to do, drawing nearer as they danced.

It was at this moment that a Zulu appeared, pushing his way through the captains who were gathered at the gate of the labyrinth, and delivered some message to one of the indunas, who in turn passed it on to the king.

"Ow! is it so?" said the king with a troubled look. Then his glance fell on me as though by accident, and he added: "Macumazahn, one of my wives is taken very ill suddenly, and says she must have some of the medicine of the white men before they go away. Now, you tell me that you are a new-married man, so I can trust you with my wives. I pray you to go and find out what medicine it is that she needs, for you can speak our tongue."

I hesitated, then translated what he had said to Retief.

"You had best go, nephew," said the commandant; "but come back quickly, for we ride at once."

Still I hesitated, not liking this business; whereon the king began to grow angry.

"What!" he said, "do you white men refuse me this little favour, when I have just given you so much—you who have wonderful medicines that can cure the sick?"

"Go, Allan, go," said Retief, when he understood his words, "or he will grow cross and everything may be undone."

So, having no choice, I went through the gateway into the labyrinth.

Next moment men pounced on me, and before I could utter a word a cloth was thrown over my mouth and tied tight behind my head.

I was a prisoner and gagged.

Depart in Peace

A tall Kaffir, one of the king's household guards, who carried an assegai, came up to me and whispered:

"Hearken, little Son of George. The king would save you, if he can, because you are not Dutch, but English. Yet, know that if you try to cry out, if you even struggle, you die," and he lifted the assegai so as to be ready to plunge it through my heart.

Now I understood, and a cold sweat broke out all over me. My companions were to be murdered, every one! Oh! gladly would I have given my life to warn them. But alas! I could not, for the cloth upon my mouth was so thick that no sound could pass it.

One of the Zulus inserted a stick between the reeds of the fence. Working it to and fro sideways, he made an opening just in a line with my eyes—out of cruelty, I suppose, for now I must see everything.

For some time—ten minutes, I dare say—the dancing and beer-drinking went on. Then Dingaan rose from his chair and shook the hand of Retief warmly, bidding him "Hamba gachle," that is, Depart gently, or in peace. He retreated towards the gate of the labyrinth, and as he went the Boers took off their hats, waving them in the air and cheering him. He was almost through it, and I began to breathe again.

Doubtless I was mistaken. After all, no treachery was intended.

In the very opening of the gate Dingaan turned, however, and said two words in Zulu which mean:

"Seize them!"

Instantly the warriors, who had now danced quite close and were waiting for these words, rushed upon the Boers. I heard Thomas Halstead call out in English:

"We are done for," and then add in Zulu, "Let me speak to the king!"

Dingaan heard also, and waved his hand to show that he refused to listen, and as he did so shouted thrice :

"Bulala abatagati!" that is, Slay the wizards!

I saw poor Halstead draw his knife and plunge it into a Zulu who was near him. The man fell, and again he struck at another soldier, cutting his throat. The Boers also drew their knives—those of them who had time—and tried to defend themselves against these black devils, who rushed on them in swarms. I heard afterwards that they succeeded in killing six or eight of them and wounding perhaps a score. But it was soon over, for what could men armed only with pocket-knives do against such a multitude?

Presently, amidst a hideous tumult of shouts, groans, curses, prayers for mercy, and Zulu battle cries, the Boers were all struck down—yes, even the two little lads and the Hottentot servants. Then they were dragged away, still living, by the soldiers, their heels trailing on the ground, just as wounded worms or insects are dragged by the black ants.

Dingaan was standing by me now, laughing, his fat face working nervously.

"Come, Son of George," he said, "and let us see the end of these traitors to your sovereign."

Then I was pulled along to an eminence within the labyrinth, whence there was a view of the surrounding country. Here we waited a little while, listening to the tumult that grew more distant, till presently the dreadful procession of death reappeared, coming round the fence of the Great Kraal and heading straight for the

Hill of Slaughter, Hloma Amabutu. Soon its slopes were climbed, and there among the dark-leaved bushes and the rocks the black soldiers butchered them, every one.

I saw and swooned away.

I believe that I remained senseless for many hours, though towards the end of that time my swoon grew thin, as it were, and I heard a hollow voice speaking over me in Zulu.

"I am glad that the little Son of George has been saved," said the echoing voice, which I did not know, "for he has a great destiny and will be useful to the black people in time to come." Then the voice went on:

"O House of Senzangacona! now you have mixed your milk with blood, with white blood. Of that bowl you shall drink to the dregs, and afterwards must the bowl be shattered"; and the speaker laughed—a deep, dreadful laugh that I was not to hear again for years.

I heard him go away, shuffling along like some great reptile, and then, with an effort, opened my eyes. I was in a large hut, and the only light in the hut came from a fire that burned in its centre, for it was night time. A Zulu woman, young and good-looking, was bending over a gourd near the fire, doing something to its contents. I spoke to her light-headedly.

"O woman," I said, "is that a man who laughed over me?"

"Not altogether, Macumazahn," she answered in a pleasant voice. "That was Zikali, the Mighty Magician, the Counsellor of Kings, the Opener of Roads; he whose birth our grandfathers do not remember; he whose breath causes the trees to be torn out by the roots; he whom Dingaan fears and obeys."

"Did he cause the Boers to be killed?" I asked.

"Mayhap," she answered. "Who am I that I should know of such matters?"

"Are you the woman who was sick whom I was sent to visit?" I asked again.

"Yes, Macumazahn, I was sick, but now I am well and you are sick, for so things go round. Drink this," and she handed me a gourd of milk.

"How are you named?" I inquired as I took it.

"Naya is my name," she replied, "and I am your jailer. Don't think that you can escape me, though, Macumazahn, for there are other jailers without who carry spears. Drink."

So I drank and bethought me that the draught might be poisoned. Yet so thirsty was I that I finished it, every drop.

"Now am I a dead man?" I asked, as I put down the gourd.

"No, no, Macumazahn," she who called herself Naya replied in a soft voice; "not a dead man, only one who will sleep and forget."

Then I lost count of everything and slept—for how long I know not.

When I awoke again it was broad daylight; in fact, the sun stood high in the heavens. Perhaps Naya had put some drug into my milk, or perhaps I had simply slept. I do not know. At any rate, I was grateful for that sleep, for without it I think that I should have gone mad. As it was, when I remembered, which it took me some time to do, for a while I went near to insanity.

I recollect lying there in that hut and wondering how the Almighty could have permitted such a deed as I had seen done. How could it be reconciled with any theory of a loving and merciful Father? Those poor Boers, whatever their faults, and they had many, like the rest of us, were in the main good and honest men according to their lights. Yet they had been doomed to be thus brutally butchered at the nod of a savage despot, their wives widowed, their children left fatherless, or, as it proved in the end, in most cases murdered or orphaned!

The mystery was too great—great enough to throw off its balance the mind of a young man who had witnessed such a fearsome scene as I have described.

For some days really I think that my reason hung just upon the edge of that mental precipice. In the end, however, reflection and education, of which I had a certain amount, thanks to my father, came to my aid. I recalled that such massacres, often on an infinitely larger scale, had happened a thousand times in history, and that still through them, often, indeed, by means of them, civilisation has marched forward, and mercy and peace have kissed each other over the bloody graves of the victims.

Therefore even in my youth and inexperience I concluded that some ineffable purpose was at work through this horror, and that the lives of those poor men which had been thus sacrificed were necessary to that purpose. This may appear a dreadful and fatalistic doctrine, but it is one that is corroborated in Nature every day, and doubtless the sufferers meet with their compensations in some other state. Indeed, if it be not so, faith and all the religions are vain.

Or, of course, it may chance that such monstrous calamities happen, not through the will of the merciful Power of which I have spoken, but in its despite. Perhaps the devil of Scripture, at whom we are inclined to smile, is still very real and active in this world of ours. Perhaps from time to time some evil principle breaks into eruption, like the prisoned forces of a volcano, bearing death and misery on its wings, until in the end it must depart strengthless and overcome. Who can say?

The question is one that should be referred to the Archbishop of Canterbury and the Pope of Rome in conclave, with the Lama of Thibet for umpire in case they disagreed. I only try to put down the thoughts that struck me so long ago as my mind renders them to-day. But very likely they are not quite the same thoughts, for a full generation has gone by me since then, and in that time the intelligence ripens as wine does in a bottle.

Besides these general matters, I had questions of my own to consider during those days of imprisonment—for instance, that of my own safety, though of this, to be honest, I thought little. If I were going to be killed, I was going to be killed, and there was an end. But my knowledge of Dingaan told me that he had not massacred Retief and his companions for nothing. This would be but the prelude to a larger slaughter, for I had not forgotten what he said as to the sparing of Marie and the other hints he gave me.

From all this I concluded, quite rightly as it proved, that some general onslaught was being made upon the Boers, who probably would be swept out to the last man. And to think that here I was, a prisoner in a Kaffir kraal, with only a young woman as a jailer, and yet utterly unable to escape to warn them. For round my hut lay a courtyard, and round it again ran a reed fence about five feet six inches high. Whenever I looked over this fence, by night or by day, I saw soldiers stationed at intervals of about fifteen yards. There they stood like statues, their broad spears in their hands, all looking inwards towards the fence. There they stood—only at night their number was doubled. Clearly it was not meant that I should escape.

A week went by thus—believe me, a very terrible week. During that time my sole companion was the pretty young woman, Naya. We became friends in a way and talked on a variety of subjects. Only, at the end of our conversations I always found that I had gained no information whatsoever about any matter of immediate interest. On such points as the history of the Zulu and kindred tribes, or the character of Chaka, the great king, or anything else that was remote she would discourse by the hour. But when we came to current events, she dried up like water on a red-hot brick. Still, Naya grew, or pretended to grow, quite attached to me. She even suggested naively that I might do worse than marry her, which she said Dingaan was quite ready to allow, as he was fond of me and thought I should be useful in his country. When I told her that I was already married, she shrugged her shining shoulders and asked with a laugh that revealed her beautiful teeth:

"What does that matter? Cannot a man have more wives than one? And, Macumazahn," she added, leaning forward and looking at me, "how do you know that you have even one? You may be divorced or a widower by now."

"What do you mean?" I asked.

"I? I mean nothing; do not look at me so fiercely, Macumazahn. Surely such things happen in the world, do they not?"

"Naya," I said, "you are two bad things—a bait and a spy—and you know it."

"Perhaps I do, Macumazahn," she answered. "Am I to blame for that, if my life is on it, especially when I really like you for yourself?"

"I don't know," I said. "Tell me, when am I going to get out of this place?"

"How can I tell you, Macumazahn?" Naya replied, patting my hand in her genial way, "but I think before long. When you are gone, Macumazahn, remember me kindly sometimes, as I have really tried to make you as comfortable as I could with a watcher staring through every straw in the hut."

I said whatever seemed to be appropriate, and next morning my deliverance came. While I was eating my breakfast in the courtyard at the back of the hut, Naya thrust her handsome and pleasant face round the corner and said that there was a messenger to see me from the king. Leaving the rest of the meal unswallowed, I went to the doorway of the yard and there found my old friend, Kambula.

"Greeting, Inkoos," he said to me; "I am come to take you back to Natal with a guard. But I warn you to ask me no questions, for if you do I must not answer them. Dingaan is ill, and you cannot see him, nor can you see the white praying-man, or anyone; you must come with me at once."

"I do not want to see Dingaan," I replied, looking him in the eyes.

"I understand," answered Kambula; "Dingaan's thoughts are his thoughts and your thoughts are your thoughts, and perhaps that is why he does not want to see _you_. Still, remember, Inkoos, that Dingaan has saved your life, snatching you unburned out of a very great fire, perhaps because you are of a different sort of wood, which he thinks it a pity to burn. Now, if you are ready, let us go."

"I am ready," I answered.

At the gate I met Naya, who said:

"You never thought to say good-bye to me, White Man, although I have tended you well. Ah! what else could I expect? Still, I hope that if I should have to fly from this land for _my_ life, as may chance, you will do for me what I have done for you."

"That I will," I answered, shaking her by the hand; and, as it happened, in after years I did.

Kambula led me, not through the kraal Umgungundhlovu, but round it. Our road lay immediately past the death mount, Hloma Amabutu, where the vultures were still gathered in great numbers. Indeed, it was actually my lot to walk over the new-picked bones of some of my companions who had been despatched at the foot of the hill. One of these skeletons I recognised by his clothes to be that of Samuel Esterhuizen, a very good fellow, at whose side I had slept during all our march. His empty eye-sockets seemed to stare at me reproachfully, as though they asked me why I remained alive when he and all his brethren were dead. I echoed the question in my own mind. Why of that great company did I alone remain alive?

An answer seemed to rise within me: That I might be one of the instruments of vengeance upon that devilish murderer, Dingaan. Looking upon those poor shattered and desecrated frames that had been men, I swore in my heart that if I lived I would not fail in that mission. Nor did I fail, although the history of that great repayment cannot be told in these pages.

Turning my eyes from this dreadful sight, I saw that on the opposite slope, where we had camped during our southern trek from Delagoa, still stood the huts and wagons of the Reverend Mr. Owen. I asked Kambula whether he and his people were also dead.

"No, Inkoos," he answered; "they are of the Children of George, as you are, and therefore the king has spared them, although he is going to send them out of the country."

This was good news, so far as it went, and I asked again if Thomas Halstead had also been spared, since he, too, was an Englishman.

"No," said Kambula. "The king wished to save him, but he killed two of our people and was dragged off with the rest. When the slayers got to their work it was too late to stay their hands."

Again I asked whether I might not join Mr. Owen and trek with him, to which Kambula answered briefly:

"No, Macumazahn; the king's orders are that you must go by yourself."

So I went; nor did I ever again meet Mr. Owen or any of his people. I believe, however, that they reached Durban safely and sailed away in a ship called the Comet.

In a little while we came to the two milk trees by the main gate of the kraal, where much of our saddlery still lay scattered about, though the guns had gone. Here Kambula asked me if I could recognise my own saddle.

"There it is," I answered, pointing to it; "but what is the use of a saddle without a horse?"

"The horse you rode has been kept for you, Macumazahn," he replied.

Then he ordered one of the men with us to bring the saddle and bridle, also some other articles which I selected, such as a couple of blankets, a water-bottle, two tins containing coffee and sugar, a little case of medicines, and so forth.

About a mile further on I found one of my horses tethered by an outlying guard hut, and noted that it had been well fed and cared for. By Kambula's leave I saddled it and mounted. As I did so, he warned me that if I tried to ride away from the escort I should certainly be killed, since even if I escaped them, orders had been given throughout the land to put an end to me should I be seen alone.

I replied that, unarmed as I was, I had no idea of making any such attempt. So we went forward, Kambula and his soldiers walking or trotting at my side.

For four full days we journeyed thus, keeping, so far as I could judge, about twenty or thirty miles to the east of that road by which I had left Zululand before and re-entered it with Retief and his commission. Evidently I was an object of great interest to the Zulus of the country through which we passed, perhaps because they knew me to be the sole survivor of all the white men who had gone up to visit the king. They would come down in crowds from the kraals and stare at me almost with awe, as though I were a spirit and not a man. Only, not one of them would say anything to me, probably because they had been forbidden to do so. Indeed, if I spoke to any of them, invariably they turned and walked or ran out of hearing.

It was on the evening of the fourth day that Kambula and his soldiers received some news which seemed to excite them a great deal. A messenger in a state of exhaustion, who had an injury to the fleshy part of his left arm, which looked to me as though it had been caused by a bullet, appeared out of the bush and said something of which, by straining my ears, I caught two words—"Great slaughter." Then Kambula laid his fingers on his lips as a signal for silence and led the man away, nor did I see or hear any more of him. Afterwards I asked Kambula who had suffered this great slaughter, whereon he stared at me innocently and replied that he did not know of what I was speaking.

"What is the use of lying to me, Kambula, seeing that I shall find out the truth before long?"

"Then, Macumazahn, wait till you do find it out, And may it please you," he replied, and went off to speak with his people at a distance.

All that night I heard them talking off and on—I, who lay awake plunged into new miseries. I was sure that some other dreadful thing had happened. Probably Dingaan's armies had destroyed all the Boers, and, if so, oh! what had become of Marie? Was she dead, or had she perhaps been taken prisoner, as Dingaan had told me would be done for his own vile purposes? For aught I knew she might now be travelling under escort to Umgungundhlovu, as I was travelling to Natal.

The morning came at last, and that day, about noon, we reached a ford of the Tugela which luckily was quite passable. Here Kambula bade me farewell, saying that his mission was finished. Also he delivered to me a message that I was to give from Dingaan to the English in Natal. It was to this effect: That he, Dingaan, had killed the Boers who came to visit him because he found out that they were traitors to their chief, and therefore not worthy to live. But that he loved the Sons of George, who were true-hearted people, and therefore had nothing to fear from him. Indeed, he begged them to come and see him at his Great Place, where he would talk matters over with them.

I said that I would deliver the message if I met any English people, but, of course, I could not say whether they would accept Dingaan's invitation to Umgungundhlovu. Indeed, I feared lest that town might have acquired such a bad name that they would prefer not to come there without an army.

Then, before Kambula had time to take any offence, I shook his outstretched hand and urged my horse into the stream. I never met Kambula again living, though after the battle of Blood River I saw him dead.

Once over the Tugela I rode forward for half a mile or so till I was clear of the bush and reeds that grew down to the water, fearing lest the Zulus should follow and take me back to Dingaan to explain my rather imprudent message. Seeing no signs of them, I halted, a desolate creature in a desolate country which I did not know, wondering what I should do and whither I should ride. Then it was that there happened one of the strangest experiences of all my adventurous life.

As I sat dejectedly upon my horse, which was also dejected, amidst some tumbled rocks that at a distant period in the world's history had formed the bank of the great river, I heard a voice which seemed familiar to me say:

"Baas, is that _you_, baas?"

I looked round and could see no one, so, thinking that I had been deceived by my imagination, I held my peace.

"Baas," said the voice again, "are you dead or are you alive? Because, if you are dead, I don't want to have anything to do with spooks until I am obliged."

Now I answered, "Who is it that speaks, and whence?" though, really, as I could see no one, I thought that I must be demented.

The next moment my horse snorted and shied violently, and no wonder, for out of a great ant-bear hole not five paces away appeared a yellow face crowned with black wool, in which was set a broken feather. I looked at the face and the face looked at me.

"Hans," I said, "is it you? I thought that _you_ were killed with the others."

"And I thought that _you_ were killed with the others, baas. Are you sure that you are alive?"

"What are you doing there, you old fool?" I asked.

"Hiding from the Zulus, baas. I heard them on the other bank, and then saw a man on a horse crossing the river, and went to ground like a jackal. I have had enough of Zulus."

"Come out," I said, "and tell me your story."

He emerged, a thin and bedraggled creature, with nothing left on him but the upper part of a pair of old trousers, but still Hans, undoubtedly Hans. He ran to me, and seizing my foot, kissed it again and again, weeping tears of joy and stuttering:

"Oh, baas, to think that I should find you who were dead, alive, and find myself alive, too. Oh! baas, never again will I doubt about the Big Man in the sky of whom your reverend father is so fond. For after I had tried all our own spirits, and even those of my ancestors, and met with nothing but trouble, I said the prayer that the reverend taught us, asking for my daily bread because I am so very hungry. Then I looked out of the hole and there you were. Have you anything to eat about you, baas?"

As it chanced, in my saddle-bags I had some biltong that I had saved against emergencies. I gave it to him, and he devoured it as a famished hyena might do, tearing off the tough meat in lumps and bolting them whole. When it was all gone he licked his fingers and his lips and stood still staring at me.

"Tell me your story," I repeated.

"Baas, I went to fetch the horses with the others, and ours had strayed. I got up a tree to look for them. Then I heard a noise, and saw that the Zulus were killing the Boers; so knowing that presently they would kill us, too, I stopped in that tree, hiding myself as well as I could in a stork's nest. Well, they came and assegaied all the other Totties, and stood under my tree cleaning their spears and getting their breath, for one of my brothers had given them a good run. But they never saw me, although I was nearly sick from fear on the top of them. Indeed, I was sick, but into the nest.

"Well, I sat in that nest all day, though the sun cooked me like beef on a stick; and when night came I got down and ran, for I knew it was no good to stop to look for you, and 'every man for himself when a black devil is behind you,' as your reverend father says. All night I ran, and in the morning hid up in a hole. Then when night came again I went on running. Oh! they nearly caught me once or twice, but never quite, for I know how to hide, and I kept where men do not go. Only I was hungry, hungry; yes, I lived on snails and worms, and grass like an ox, till my middle ached. Still, at last I got across the river and near to the camp.

"Then just before the day broke and I was saying, 'Now, Hans, although your heart is sad, your stomach will rejoice and sing,' what did I see but those Zulu devils, thousands of them, rush down on the camp and kill all the poor Boers. Men and women and the little children, they killed them by the hundred, till at last other Boers came and drove them away, although they took all the cattle with them. Well, as I was sure that they would come back, I did not stop there. I ran down to the side of the river, and have been crawling about in the reeds for days, living on the eggs of water-birds and a few small fish that I caught in the pools, till this morning, when I heard the Zulus again and slipped up here into this hole. Then you came and stood over the hole, and for a long while I thought you were a ghost.

"But now we are together once more and all is right, just as what your reverend father always said it would be with those who go to church on Sunday, like me when there was nothing else to do." And again he fell to kissing my foot.

"Hans," I said, "you saw the camp. Was the Missie Marie there?"

"Baas, how can I tell, who never went into it? But the wagon she slept in was not there; no, nor that of the Vrouw Prinsloo or of the Heer Meyer."

"Thank God!" I gasped, then added: "Where were you trying to get to, Hans, when you ran away from the camp?"

"Baas, I thought perhaps that the Missie and the Prinsloos and the Meyers had gone to that fine farm which you pegged out, and that I would go and see if they were there. Because if so, I was sure that they would be glad to know that you were really dead, and give me some food in payment for my news. But I was afraid to walk across the open veld for fear lest the Zulus should see me and kill me. Therefore I came round through the thick bush along the river, where one can only travel slowly, especially if hollow," and he patted his wasted stomach.

"But, Hans," I asked, "are we near my farm where I set the men to build the houses on the hill above the river?"

"Of course, baas. Has your brain gone soft that you cannot find your way about the veld? Four, or at most five, hours on horseback, riding slow, and you are there."

"Come on, Hans," I said, "and be quick, for I think that the Zulus are not far behind."

So we started, Hans hanging to my stirrup and guiding me, for I knew well enough that although he had never travelled this road, his instinct for locality would not betray a coloured man, who can find his way across the pathless veld as surely as a buck or a bird of the air.

On we went over the rolling plain, and as we travelled I told him my story, briefly enough, for my mind was too torn with fears to allow me to talk much. He, too, told me more of his escape and adventures. Now I understood what was that news which had so excited Kambula and his soldiers. It was evident that the Zulu impis had destroyed a great number of the Boers whom they found unprepared for attack, and then had been driven off by reinforcements that arrived from other camps.

That was why I had been kept prisoner for all those days. Dingaan feared lest I should reach Natal in time to warn his victims!

The Court-Martial

One hour, two hours, three hours, and then suddenly from the top of a rise the sight of the beautiful Mooi River winding through the plain like a vast snake of silver, and there, in a loop of it, the flat-crested koppie on which I had hoped to make my home. Had hoped!—why should I not still hope? For aught I knew everything might yet be well. Marie might have escaped the slaughter as I had done, and if so, after all our troubles perchance many years of life and happiness awaited us. Only it seemed too good to be true.

I flogged my horse, but the poor beast was tired out and could only break into short canters, that soon lapsed to a walk again. But whether it cantered or whether it walked, its hoofs seemed to beat out the words—"Too good to be true!" Sometimes they beat them fast, and sometimes they beat them slow, but always their message seemed the same.

Hans, too, was outworn and weak from starvation. Also he had a cut upon his foot which hampered him so much that at last he said I had better go on alone; he would follow more slowly. Then I dismounted and set him on the horse, walking by it myself.

Thus it came about that the gorgeous sunset was finished and the sky had grown grey with night before we reached the foot of the koppie. Yet the last rays of the sinking orb had shown me something as they died. There on the slope of the hill stood some mud and wattle houses, such as I had ordered to be built, and near to them several white-capped wagons. Only I did not see any smoke rising from those houses as there should have been at this hour of the day, when men cooked their evening food. The moon would be up presently, I knew, but meanwhile it was dark and the tired horse stumbled and floundered among the stones which lay about at the foot of the hill.

I could bear it no longer.

"Hans," I said, "do you stay here with the horse. I will creep to the houses and see if any dwell there."

"Be careful, baas," he answered, "lest you should find Zulus, for those black devils are all about."

I nodded, for I could not speak, and then began the ascent. For several hundred yards I crept from stone to stone, feeling my way, for the Kaffir path that led to the little plateau where the spring was, above which the shanties stood, ran at the other end of the hill. I struck the spruit or rivulet that was fed by this spring, being guided to it by the murmur of the water, and followed up its bank till I heard a sound which caused me to crouch and listen.

I could not be sure because of the ceaseless babble of the brook, but the sound seemed like that of sobs. While I waited the great moon appeared suddenly above a bank of inky cloud, flooding the place with light, and oh! by that light, looking more ethereal than woman I saw—I saw Marie!

She stood not five paces from me, by the side of the stream, whither she had come to draw water, for she held a vessel in her hand. She was clothed in some kind of a black garment, such as widows wear, but made of rough stuff, and above it her face showed white in the white rays of the moon. Gazing at her from the shadow, I could even see the tears running down her cheeks, for it was she who wept in this lonely place, wept for one who would return no more.

My voice choked in my throat; I could not utter a single word. Rising from behind a rock I moved towards her. She saw me and started, then said in a thrilling whisper:

"Oh! husband, has God sent you to call me? I am ready, husband, I am ready!" and she stretched out her arms wildly, letting fall the vessel, that clanked upon the ground.

"Marie!" I gasped at length; and at that word the blood rushed to her face and brow, and I saw her draw in her breath as though to scream.

"Hush!" I whispered. "It is I, Allan, who have escaped alive."

The next thing I remember was that she lay in my arms.

"What has happened here?" I asked when I had told my tale, or some of it.

"Nothing, Allan," she answered. "I received your letter at the camp, and we trekked away as you bade us, without telling the others why, because you remember the Commandant Retief wrote to us not to do so. So we were out of the great slaughter, for the Zulus did not know where we had gone, and never followed us here, although I have heard that they sought for me. My father and my cousin Hernan only arrived at the camp two days after the attack, and discovering or guessing our hiding-place—I know not which—rode on hither. They say they came to warn the Boers to be careful, for they did not trust Dingaan, but were too late. So they too were out of the slaughter, for, Allan, many, many have been killed—they say five or six hundred, most of them women and children. But thank God! many more escaped, since the men came in from the other camps farther off and from their shooting parties, and drove away the Zulus, killing them by scores."

"Are your father and Pereira here now?" I asked.

"No, Allan. They learned of the massacre and that the Zulus were all gone yesterday morning. Also they got the bad news that Retief and everyone with him had been killed at Dingaan's town, it is said through the treachery of the English, who arranged with Dingaan that he should kill them."

"That is false," I said; "but go on."

"Then, Allan, they came and told me that I was a widow like many other women—I who had never been a wife. Allan, Hernan said that I should not grieve for you, as you deserved your fate, since you had been caught in your own snare, being one of those who had betrayed the Boers. The Vrouw Prinsloo answered to his face that he lied, and, Allan, I said that I would never speak to him again until we met before the Judgment Seat of God; nor will I do so."

"But I will speak to him," I muttered. "Well, where are they now?"

"They rode this morning back to the other Boers. I think they want to bring a party of them here to settle, if they like this place, as it is so easy to defend. They said they would return to-morrow, and that meanwhile we were quite safe, as they had sure tidings that all the Zulus were back over the Tugela, taking some of their wounded with them, and also the Boer cattle as an offering to Dingaan. But come to the house, Allan—our home that I had made ready for you as well as I could. Oh! my God! our home on the threshold of which I believed you would never set a foot. Yes, when the moon rose from that cloud I believed it, and look, they are still quite close together. Hark, what is that?"

I listened, and caught the sound of a horse's hoofs stumbling among the rocks.

"Don't be frightened," I answered; "it is only Hans with my horse. He escaped also; I will tell you how afterwards." And as I spoke he appeared, a woebegone and exhausted object.

"Good day, missie," he said with an attempt at cheerfulness. "Now you should give me a fine dinner, for you see I have brought the baas back safe to you. Did I not tell you, baas, that everything would come right?"

Then he grew silent from exhaustion. Nor were we sorry, who at that moment did not wish to listen to the poor fellow's talk.

Something over two hours had gone by since the moon broke out from the clouds. I had greeted the Vrouw Prinsloo and all my other friends, and been received by them with rapture as one risen from the dead. If they had loved me before, now a new gratitude was added to their love, since had it not been for my warning they also must have made acquaintance with the Zulu spears and perished. It was on their part of the camp that the worst of the attack fell. Indeed, from those wagons hardly anyone escaped.

I had told them all the story, to which they listened in dead silence. Only when it was finished the Heer Meyer, whose natural gloom had been deepened by all these events, said:

"Allemachte! but you have luck, Allan, to be left when everyone else is taken. Now, did I not know you so well, like Hernan Pereira I should think that you and that devil Dingaan had winked at each other."

The Vrouw Prinsloo turned on him furiously.

"How dare you say such words, Carl Meyer?" she exclaimed. "Must Allan always be insulted just because he is English, which he cannot help? For my part, I think that if anyone winked at Dingaan it was the stinkcat Pereira. Otherwise why did he come away before the killing and bring that madman, Henri Marais, with him?"

"I don't know, I am sure, aunt," said Meyer humbly, for like everyone else he was afraid of the Vrouw Prinsloo.

"Then why can't you hold your tongue instead of saying silly things which must give pain?" asked the vrouw. "No, don't answer, for you will only make matters worse; but take the rest of that meat to the poor Hottentot, Hans"—I should explain that we had been supping—"who, although he has eaten enough to burst any white stomach, I dare say can manage another pound or two."

Meyer obeyed meekly, and the others melted away also as they were wont to do when the vrouw showed signs of war, so that she and we two were left alone.

"Now," said the vrouw, "everyone is tired, and I say that it is time to go to rest. Good night, nephew Allan and niece Marie," and she waddled away leaving us together.

"Husband," said Marie presently, "will you come and see the home that I made ready for you before I thought that you were dead? It is a poor place, but I pray God that we may be happy there," and she took me by the hand and kissed me once and twice and thrice.

About noon on the following day, when my wife and I were laughing and arguing over some little domestic detail of our meagre establishment—so soon are great griefs forgotten in an overwhelming joy, of a sudden I saw her face change, and asked what was the matter.

"Hist!" she said, "I hear horses," and she pointed in a certain direction.

I looked, and there, round the corner of the hill, came a body of Boers with their after-riders, thirty-two or three of them in all, of whom twenty were white men.

"See," said Marie, "my father is among them, and my cousin Hernan rides at his side."

It was true. There was Henri Marais, and just behind him, talking into his ear, rode Hernan Pereira. I remember that the two of them reminded me of a tale I had read about a man who was cursed with an evil genius that drew him to some dreadful doom in spite of the promptings of his better nature. The thin, worn, wild-eyed Marais, and the rich-faced, carnal Pereira whispering slyly into his ear; they were exact types of that man in the story and his evil genius who dragged him down to hell. Prompted by some impulse, I threw my arms round Marie and embraced her, saying:

"At least we have been very happy for a while."

"What do you mean, Allan?" she asked doubtfully.

"Only that I think our good hours are done with for the present."

"Perhaps," she answered slowly; "but at least they have been very good hours, and if I should die to-day I am glad to have lived to win them."

Then the cavalcade of Boers came up.

Hernan Pereira, his senses sharpened perhaps by the instincts of hate and jealousy, was the first to recognise me.

"Why, Mynheer Allan Quatermain," he said, "how is it that you are here? How is it that you still live? Commandant," he added, turning to a dark, sad-faced man of about sixty whom at that time I did not know, "here is a strange thing. This Heer Quatermain, an Englishman, was with the Governor Retief at the town of the Zulu king, as the Heer Henri Marais can testify. Now, as we know for sure Pieter Retief and all his people are dead, murdered by Dingaan, how then does it happen that this man has escaped?"

"Why do you put riddles to me, Mynheer Pereira?" asked the dark Boer. "Doubtless the Englishman will explain."

"Certainly I will, mynheer," I said. "Is it your pleasure that I should speak now?"

The commandant hesitated. Then, having called Henri Marais apart and talked to him for a little while, he replied:

"No, not now, I think; the matter is too serious. After we have eaten we will listen to your story, Mynheer Quatermain, and meanwhile I command you not to leave this place."

"Do you mean that I am a prisoner, commandant?" I asked.

"If you put it so—yes, Mynheer Quatermain—a prisoner who has to explain how some sixty of our brothers, who were your companions, came to be butchered like beasts in Zululand, while you escaped. Now, no more words; by and by doubtless there will be plenty of them. Here you, Carolus and Johannes, keep watch upon this Englishman, of whom I hear strange stories, with your guns loaded, please, and when we send to you, lead him before us."

"As usual, your cousin Hernan brings evil gifts," I said to Marie bitterly. "Well, let us also eat our dinner, which perhaps the Heeren Carolus and Johannes will do us the honour to share—bringing their loaded guns with them."

Carolus and Johannes accepted the invitation, and from them we heard much news, all of it terrible enough to learn, especially the details of the massacre in that district, which, because of this fearful event is now and always will be known as Weenen, or The Place of Weeping. Suffice it to say that they were quite enough to take away all our appetite, although Carolus and Johannes, who by this time had recovered somewhat from the shock of that night of blood and terror, ate in a fashion which might have filled Hans himself with envy.

Shortly after we had finished our meal, Hans, who, by the way, seemed to have quite recovered from his fatigues, came to remove the dishes. He informed us that all the Boers were having a great "talk," and that they were about to send for me. Sure enough, a few minutes later two armed men arrived and ordered me to follow them. I turned to say some words of farewell to Marie, but she said:

"I go where you do, husband," and, as no objection was made by the guard, she came.

About two hundred yards away, sitting under the shade of one of the wagons, we found the Boers. Six of them were seated in a semicircle upon stools or whatever they could find, the black-browed commandant being in the centre and having in front of him a rough table on which were writing materials.

To the left of these six were the Prinsloos and Meyers, being those folk whom I had rescued from Delagoa, and to the right the other Boers who had ridden into the camp that morning. I saw at a glance that a court-martial had been arranged and that the six elders were the judges, the commandant being the president of the court.

I do not give their names purposely, since I have no wish that the actual perpetrators of the terrible blunder that I am about to describe should be known to posterity. After all, they acted honestly according to their lights, and were but tools in the hand of that villain Hernan Pereira.

"Allan Quatermain," said the commandant, "you are brought here to be tried by a court-martial duly constituted according to the law published in the camps of the emigrant Boers. Do you acknowledge that law?"

"I know that there is such a law, commandant," I answered, "but I do not acknowledge the authority of your court-martial to try a man who is no Boer, but a subject of the Queen of Great Britain."

"We have considered that point, Allan Quatermain," said the commandant, "and we disallow it. You will remember that in the camp at Bushman's River, before you rode with the late Pieter Retief to the chief Sikonyela, when you were given command of the Zulus who went with him, you took an oath to interpret truly and to be faithful in all things to the General Retief, to his companions and to his cause. That oath we hold gives this court jurisdiction over you."

"I deny your jurisdiction," I answered, "although it is true that I took an oath to interpret faithfully, and I request that a note of my denial may be made in writing."

"It shall be done," said the commandant, and laboriously he made the note on the paper before him.

When he had finished he looked up and said: "The charge against you, Allan Quatermain, is that, being one of the commission who recently visited the Zulu king Dingaan, under command of the late Governor and General Pieter Retief, you did falsely and wickedly urge the said Dingaan to murder the said Pieter Retief and his companions, and especially Henri Marais, your father-in-law, and Hernando Pereira, his nephew, with both of whom you had a quarrel. Further, that afterwards you brought about the said murder, having first arranged with the king of the Zulus that you should be removed to a place of safety while it was done. Do you plead Guilty or Not guilty?"

Now when I heard this false and abominable charge my rage and indignation caused me to laugh aloud.

"Are you mad, commandant," I exclaimed, "that you should say such things? On what evidence is this wicked lie advanced against me?"

"No, Allan Quatermain, I am not mad," he replied, "although it is true that through your evil doings I, who have lost my wife and three children by the Zulu spears, have suffered enough to make me mad. As for the evidence against you, you shall hear it. But first I will write down that you plead Not guilty."

He did so, then said:

"If you will acknowledge certain things it will save us all much time, of which at present we have little to spare. Those things are that knowing what was going to happen to the commission, you tried to avoid accompanying it. Is that true?"

"No," I answered. "I knew nothing of what was going to happen to the commission, though I feared something, having but just saved my friends there"—and I pointed to the Prinsloos—"from death at the hands of Dingaan. I did not wish to accompany it for another reason: that I had been married on the day of its starting to

Marie Marais. Still, I went after all because the General Retief, who was my friend, asked me to come, to interpret for him."

Now some of the Boers present said:

"That is true. We remember."

But the commandant continued, taking no heed of my answer or these interruptions.

"Do you acknowledge that you were on bad terms with Henri Marais and with Hernan Pereira?"

"Yes," I answered; "because Henri Marais did all in his power to prevent my marriage with his daughter Marie, behaving very ill to me who had saved his life and that of his people who remained to him up by Delagoa, and afterwards at Umgungundhlovu. Because, too, Hernan Pereira strove to rob me of Marie, who loved me. Moreover, although I had saved him when he lay sick to death, he afterwards tried to murder me by shooting me down in a lonely place. Here is the mark of it," and I touched the little scar upon the side of my forehead.

"That is true; he did so, the stinkcat," shouted the Vrouw Prinsloo, and was ordered to be silent.

"Do you acknowledge," went on the commandant, "that you sent to warn your wife and those with her to depart from the camp on the Bushman's River, because it was going to be attacked, charging them to keep the matter secret, and that afterwards both you and your Hottentot servant alone returned safely from Zululand, where all those who went with you lie dead?"

"I acknowledge," I answered, "that I wrote to tell my wife to come to this place where I had been building houses, as you see, and to bring with her any of our companions who cared to trek here, or, failing that, to go alone. This I did because Dingaan had told me, whether in jest or in earnest I did not know, that he had given orders that my said wife should be kidnapped, as he desired to make her one of his women, having thought her beautiful when he saw her. Also what I did was done with the knowledge and by the wish of the late Governor Retief, as can be shown by his writing on my letter. I acknowledge also that I escaped when all my brothers were killed, as did the Hottentot Hans, and if you wish to know I will tell you how we escaped and why."

The commandant made a further note, then he said:

"Let the witness Hernan Pereira be called and sworn."

This was done and he was ordered to tell his tale.

As may be imagined, it was a long tale, and one that had evidently been prepared with great care. I will only set down its blackest falsehoods. He assured the court that he had no enmity against me and had never attempted to kill me or do me any harm, although it was true that his heart felt sore because, against her father's will, I had stolen away the affection of his betrothed, who was now my wife. He said that he had stopped in Zululand because he knew that I should marry her as soon as she came of age, and it was too great pain for him to see this done. He said that while he was there, before the arrival of the commission, Dingaan and some of his captains had told him that I had again and again urged him, Dingaan, to kill the Boers because they were traitors to the sovereign of England, but that he, Dingaan, had refused to do so. He said that when Retief came up with the commission he tried to warn him against me, but that Retief would not listen, being infatuated with me as many others were, and he looked towards the Prinsloos.

Then came the worst of all. He said that while he was engaged in mending some guns for Dingaan in one of his private huts, he overheard a conversation between myself and Dingaan which took place outside the hut, I, of course, not knowing that he was within. The substance of this conversation was that I again urged Dingaan to kill the Boers and afterwards to send an impi to massacre their wives and families. Only I asked him to give me time to get away a girl whom I had married from among them, and with her a few of my own friends whom I wished should be spared, as I intended to become a kind of chief over them, and if he would grant it me, to hold all the land of Natal under his rule and the protection of the English. To these proposals Dingaan answered that "they seemed wise and good, and that he would think them over very carefully."

Pereira said further that coming out of the hut after Dingaan had gone away he reproached me bitterly for my wickedness, and announced that he would warn the Boers, which he did subsequently by word of mouth and in writing. That thereon I caused him to be detained by the Zulus while I went to Retief and told him some false story about him, Pereira, which caused Retief to drive him out of his camp and give orders that none of the Boers should so much as speak to him. That then he did the only thing he could. Going to his uncle, Henri Marais, he told him, not all the truth, but that he had learnt for certain that his daughter Marie was in dreadful danger of her life because of some intended attack of the Zulus, and that all the Boers among whom she dwelt were also in danger of their lives.

Therefore he suggested to Henri Marais that as the General Retief was besotted and would not listen to his story, the best thing they could do was to ride away and warn the Boers. This then they did secretly, without the knowledge of Retief, but being delayed upon their journey by one accident and another, which he set out in detail, they only reached the Bushman's River too late, after the massacre had taken place. Subsequently, as the commandant knew, hearing a rumour that Marie Marais and other Boers had trekked to this place before the slaughter, they came here and learned that they had done so upon a warning sent to them by Allan Quatermain, whereon they returned and communicated the news to the surviving Boers at Bushman's River.

That was all he had to say.

Then, as I reserved my cross-examination until I heard all the evidence against me, Henri Marais was sworn and corroborated his nephew's testimony on many points as to my relations to his daughter, his objection to my marriage to her because I was an Englishman whom he disliked and mistrusted, and so forth. He added further that it was true Pereira had told him he had sure information that Marie and the Boers were in danger from an attack upon them which had been arranged between Allan Quatermain and Dingaan; that he also had written to Retief and tried to speak to him but was refused a hearing. Thereon he had ridden away from Umgungundhlovu to try to save his daughter and warn the Boers. That was all he had to say.

As there were no further witnesses for the prosecution I cross-examined these two at full length, but absolutely without results, since every vital question that I asked was met with a direct negative.

Then I called my witnesses, Marie, whose evidence they refused to hear on the ground that she was my wife and prejudiced, the Vrouw Prinsloo and her family, and the Meyers. One and all told a true story of my relations with Hernan Pereira, Henri Marais, and Dingaan, so far as they knew them.

After this, as the commandant declined to take the evidence of Hans because he was a Hottentot and my servant, I addressed the court, relating exactly what had taken place between me and Dingaan, and how I and Hans came to escape on our second visit to his kraal. I pointed out also that unhappily for myself I could not prove my words, since Dingaan was not available as a witness, and all the others were dead.

Further, I produced my letter to Marie, which was endorsed by Retief, and the letter to Retief signed by Marais and Pereira which remained in my possession.

By the time that I had finished my speech the sun was setting and everyone was tired out. I was ordered to withdraw under guard, while the court consulted, which it did for a long while. Then I was called forward again and the commandant said:

"Allan Quatermain, after prayer to God we have considered this case to the best of our judgment and ability. On the one hand we note that you are an Englishman, a member of a race which hates and has always oppressed our people, and that it was to your interest to get rid of two of them with whom you had quarrelled. The evidence of Henri Marais and Hernan Pereira, which we cannot disbelieve, shows that you were wicked enough, either in order to do this, or because of your malice against the Boer people, to plot their destruction with a savage. The result is that some seven hundred men, women, and children have lost their lives in a very cruel manner, whereas you, your servant, your wife and your friends have alone escaped unharmed. For such a crime as this a hundred deaths could not pay; indeed, God alone can give to it its just punishment, and to Him it is our duty to send you to be judged. We condemn you to be shot as a traitor and a murderer, and may He have mercy on your soul."

At these dreadful words Marie fell to the ground fainting and a pause ensued while she was carried off to the Prinsloos' house, whither the vrouw followed to attend her. Then the commandant went on:

"Still, although we have thus passed judgment on you; because you are an Englishman against whom it might be said that we had prejudices, and because you have had no opportunity of preparing a defence, and no witnesses to the facts, since all those whom you say you could have called are dead, we think it right that this unanimous sentence of ours should be confirmed by a general court of the emigrant Boers. Therefore to-morrow morning you will be taken with us to the Bushman's River camp, where the case will be settled, and, if necessary, execution done in accordance with the verdict of the generals and veld-cornets of that camp. Meanwhile you will be kept in custody in your own house. Now have you anything to say against this sentence?"

"Yes, this," I answered, "that although you do not know it, it is an unjust sentence, built up on the lies of one who has always been my enemy, and of a man whose brain is rotten. I never betrayed the Boers. If anyone betrayed them it was Hernan Pereira himself, who, as I proved to the General Retief, had been praying Dingaan to kill me, and whom Retief threatened to put upon his trial for this very crime, for which reason and no other Pereira fled from the kraal, taking his tool Henri Marais with him. You have asked God to judge me. Well, I ask God to judge him and Henri Marais also, and I know He will in one way or another. As for me, I am ready to die, as I have been for months while serving the cause of you Boers. Shoot me now if you will, and make an end. But I tell you that if I escape your hands I will not suffer this treatment to go unpunished. I will lay my case before the rulers of my people, and if necessary before my Queen, yes, if I have to travel to London to do it, and you Boers shall learn that you cannot condemn an innocent Englishman upon false testimony and not pay the price. I tell you that price shall be great if I live, and if I die it shall be greater still."

Now these words, very foolish words, I admit, which being young and inexperienced I spoke in my British pride, I could see made a great impression upon my judges. They believed, to be fair to them, that they had passed a just sentence. Blinded by prejudice and falsehood, and maddened by the dreadful losses their people had suffered during the past few days at the hands of a devilish savage, they believed that I was the instigator of those losses, one who ought to die. Indeed, all, or nearly all the Boers were persuaded that Dingaan was urged to this massacre by the counsels of Englishmen. The mere fact of my own and my servant's miraculous escape, when all my companions had perished, proved my guilt to them without the evidence of Pereira, which, being no lawyers, they thought sufficient to justify their verdict.

Still, they had an uneasy suspicion that this evidence was not conclusive, and might indeed be rejected in toto by a more competent court upon various grounds. Also they knew themselves to be rebels who had no legal right to form a court, and feared the power of the long arm of England, from which for a little while they had escaped. If I were allowed to tell my tale to the Parliament in London, what might not happen to them, they wondered—to them who had ventured to pass sentence of death upon a subject of the Queen of Great Britain? Might not this turn the scale against them? Might not Britain arise in wrath and crush them, these men who dared to invoke her forms of law in order to kill her citizen? Those, as I learned afterwards, were the thoughts that passed through their minds.

Also another thought passed through their minds—that if the sentence were executed at once, a dead man cannot appeal, and that here I had no friends to take up my cause and avenge me. But of all this they said nothing. Only at a sign I was marched away to my little house and imprisoned under guard.

Now I propose to tell the rest of the history of these tragic events as they happened, although some of them did not come to my knowledge till the morrow or afterwards, for I think this will be the more simple and the easier plan.

The Innocent Blood

After I had been taken away it seems that the court summoned Hernan Pereira and Henri Marais to accompany them to a lonely spot at a distance, where they thought that their deliberations would not be overheard. In this, however, they were mistaken, having forgotten the fox-like cunning of the Hottentot, Hans. Hans had heard me sentenced, and probably enough feared that he who also had committed the crime of escaping from Dingaan, might be called on to share that sentence. Also he wished to know the secret counsel of these Boers, whose language, of course, he understood as well as he did his own.

So making a circuit up the hillside, he crept towards them on his belly as a snake creeps, wriggling in and out between the tufts of last year's dead grass, which grew here in plenty, without so much as moving their tops. At length he lay still in the centre of a bush that grew behind a stone not five paces from where they were talking, whence he listened intently to every word that passed their lips.

This was the substance of their talk; that for the reasons I have already mentioned it would be best that I should die at once. Sentence, said the commandant, had been passed, and could not be rescinded, since even if it were, their offence would remain as heavy in the eyes of the English authorities. But if they took me to their main camp to be re-tried by their great council, possibly that sentence might be rescinded and they be left individually and collectively to atone for what they had done. Also they knew that I was very clever and might escape in some other way to bring the English, or possibly the Zulus, upon them, since they felt convinced that Dingaan and I were working together for their destruction, and that while I had breath in my body I should never cease my efforts to be avenged.

When it was found that they were all of one mind in this matter, the question arose: What should be done? Somebody suggested that I should be shot at once, but the commandant pointed out that such a deed, worked at night, would look like murder, especially as it violated the terms of their verdict.

Then another suggestion was made: that I should be brought out of my house just before the dawn on pretence that it was time to ride; that then I should be given the opportunity of escape and instantly shot down. Or it might be pretended that I had tried to escape, with a like result. Who, they urged, was to know in that half-light whether I had or had not actually attempted to run for my life, or to threaten their lives, circumstances under which the law said it was justifiable to shoot a prisoner already formally condemned to death?

To this black counsel they all agreed, being so terribly afraid of a poor English lad whose existence, although most of them did not know this, was to be taken from him upon false evidence. But then arose another question: By whose hand should the thing be done? Not one of them, it would seem, was anxious to fulfil this bloody office; indeed, they one and all refused to do so. A proposal was put forward that some of their native servants should be forced to serve as executioners; but when this had been vetoed by the general sense of the court, their counsels came to a deadlock.

Then, after a whispered conference, the commandant spoke some dreadful words.

"Hernando Pereira and Henri Marais," he said, "it is on your evidence that this young man has been condemned. We believe that evidence, but if by one jot or one tittle it is false, then not justice, but a foul murder will have been committed and his innocent blood will be upon your heads for ever. Hernando Pereira and Henri Marais, the court appoints you to be the guards who will bring the prisoner out of his house to-morrow morning just when the sky begins to lighten. It is from _you_ that he will try to escape, and _you_ will prevent his escape by his death. Then you must join us where we shall be waiting for you and report the execution."

When Henri Marais heard this he exclaimed:

"I swear by God that I cannot do it. Is it right or natural that a man should be forced to kill his own son-in-law?"

"You could bear evidence against your own son-in-law, Henri Marais," answered the stern-faced commandant. "Why then cannot you kill with your rifle one whom you have already helped to kill with your tongue?"

"I will not, I cannot!" said Marais, tearing at his beard. But the commandant only answered coldly:

"You have the orders of the court, and if you choose to disobey them we shall begin to believe that you have sworn falsely. Then you and your nephew will also appear before the great council when the Englishman is tried again. Still, it matters nothing to us whether you or Hernando Pereira shall fire the shot. See you to it, as the Jews said to Judas who had betrayed the innocent Lord."

Then he paused and went on, addressing Pereira:

"Do you also refuse, Hernando Pereira? Remember before you answer that if you do refuse we shall draw our own conclusions. Remember, too, that the evidence which you have given, showing that this wicked Englishman plotted and caused the deaths of our brothers and of our wives and children, which we believe to be true evidence, shall be weighed and investigated word by word before the great council."

"To give evidence is one thing, and to shoot the traitor and murderer another," said Pereira. Then he added with an oath, or so vowed Hans: "Yet why should I, who know all this villain's guilt, refuse to carry out the sentence of the law on him? Have no fear, commandant, the accursed Allan Quatermain shall not succeed in his attempt to escape to-morrow before the dawn."

"So be it," said the commandant. "Now, do all you who have heard those words take note of them."

Then Hans, seeing that the council was about to break up, and fearing lest he should be caught and killed, slipped away by the same road that he had come. His thought was to warn me, but this he could not do because of the guards. So he went to the Prinsloos, and finding the vrouw alone with Marie, who had recovered her mind, told them everything that he had heard.

As he said, Marie knelt down and prayed, or thought for a long while, then rose and spoke.

"Tante," she said to the vrouw, "one thing is clear, that Allan will be murdered at the dawn; now if he is hidden away he may escape."

"But where and how can we hide him," asked the vrouw, "seeing that the place is guarded?"

"Tante," said Marie again, "at the back of your house is an old cattle kraal made by Kaffirs, and in that cattle kraal, as I have seen, there are mealie-pits where those Kaffirs stored their grain. Now I suggest that we should put my husband into one of those mealie-pits and cover it over. There the Boers might not find him, however close they searched."

"That is a good idea," said the vrouw; "but how in the name of God are we to get Allan out of a guarded house into a mealie-pit?"

"Tante, I have a right to go to my husband's house, and there I will go. Afterwards, too, I shall have the right to leave his house before he is taken away. Well, he might leave it in my place, _as me_, and you and Hans might help him.

Then in the morning the Boers would come to search the house and find no one except me."

"That is all very pretty," answered the vrouw; "but do you think, my niece, that those accursed vultures will go away until they have picked Allan's bones? Not they, for too much hangs on it. They will know that he cannot be far off, and slink about the place until they have found him in his mealie-hole or until he comes out. It is blood they are after, thanks to your cousin Hernan, the liar, and blood they will have for their own safety's sake. Never will they go away from here until they see Allan lying dead upon the ground."

Now, according to Hans, Marie thought again very deeply. Then she answered:

"There is a great risk, tante; but we must take it. Send your husband to chat with those guards, and give him a bottle of spirits. I will talk with Hans here and see what can be arranged."

So Marie went aside with Hans, as he told me afterwards, and asked him if he knew of any medicine that made people sleep for a long while without waking. He answered, Yes; all the coloured people had plenty of such medicine. Without doubt he could get some from the Kaffirs who dwelt upon the place, or if not he could dig the roots of a plant that he had seen growing near by which would serve the purpose. So she sent him to procure this stuff. Afterwards she spoke to the Vrouw Prinsloo, saying:

"My plan is that Allan should escape from our house disguised as myself. But as I know well that he will not run away while he has his senses, seeing that to do so in his mind would be to confess his guilt, I propose to take his senses from him by means of a drugged drink. Then I propose that you and Hans should carry him into the shadow of this house, and when no one is looking, to the old grain-pit that lies but a few yards away, covering the mouth of it with dead grass. There he will remain till the Boers grow tired of searching for him and ride away. Or if it should chance that they find him, he will be no worse off than he was before."

"A good plan enough, Marie, though not one that Allan would have anything to do with if he kept his wits," answered the vrouw, "seeing that he was always a man for facing things out, although so young in years. Still, we will try to save him in spite of himself from the claws of that stinkcat Pereira, whom may God curse, and his tool, your father. As you say, at the worst no harm will be done even if they find him, as probably they will, seeing that they will not leave this place without blood."

Such then was the trick which Marie arranged with the Vrouw Prinsloo. Or rather, I should say, seemed to arrange, since she told her nothing of her real mind, she who knew that the vrouw was right and that for their own sakes, as well as because they believed it to be justice, the Boers would never leave that place until they saw blood running on the grass.

This, oh! this was Marie's true and dreadful plan—_to give her life for mine!_ She was sure that once he had slain his victim, Hernan Pereira would not stop to make examination of the corpse. He would ride away, hounded by his guilty conscience, and meanwhile I could escape.

She never thought the thing out in all its details, she who was maddened with terror and had no time. She only felt her way from step to step, dimly seeing my deliverance at the end of the journey. Marie told the Vrouw Prinsloo nothing, except that she proposed to drug me if I would not go undrugged. Then the vrouw must hide me as best she could, in the grain-pit or elsewhere, or, if I had my senses about me, let me hide myself. Afterwards she, Marie, would face the Boers and tell them to find me if they wanted me.

The vrouw answered that she had now thought of a better plan. It was that she should arrange with her husband and son and the Meyers, all of whom loved me, that they should rescue me, or if need be, kill or disable Pereira before he could shoot me.

Marie replied that this was good if it could be done, and the vrouw went out to find her husband and the other men. Presently, however, she returned with a long face, saying that the commandant had them all under guard. It seemed that it had occurred to him, or more probably to Pereira, that the Prinsloos and the Meyers, who looked on me as a brother, might attempt some rescue, or make themselves formidable in other ways. Therefore, as a matter of precaution, they had been put under arrest and their arms taken from them as mine had been. What the commandant said, however, was that he took these somewhat high-handed measures in order to be sure that they, the Prinsloos and the Meyers, should be ready on the following morning to ride with him and the prisoner to the main camp, where the great council might wish to interrogate them.

One concession, however, the vrouw had won from the commandant, who, knowing what was about to happen to me, had not, I suppose, the heart to refuse. It was that my wife and she might visit me and give me food on the stipulation that they both left the house where I was confined by ten o'clock that night.

So it came to this, that if anything was to be done, these two women and a Hottentot must do it, since they could hope for no help in their plans. Here I should add that the vrouw told Marie in Hans's presence that she had thought of attacking the commandant as to this matter of my proposed shooting by Pereira. On reflection, however, she refrained for two reasons, first because she feared lest she might only make matters worse and rob me of my sole helpers, and secondly for fear lest she should bring about the death of Hans, to whom the story would certainly be traced.

As he was the solitary witness to the plot, it seemed to her that he would scarcely be allowed to escape to repeat it far and wide. Especially was this so, as the unexplained death of a Hottentot, suspected of treachery like his master, was not a matter that would have been thought worth notice in those rough and bloody times. She may have been right, or she may have been wrong, but in weighing her decision it must always be borne in mind that she was, and until the end remained, in utter ignorance of Marie's heroic design to go to her death in place of me.

So the two women and the Hottentot proceeded to mature the plans which I have outlined. One other alternative, however, Hans did suggest. It was that they should try to drug the guards with some of the medicated drink that was meant for me, and that then Marie, I and he should slip away and get down to the river, there to hide in the weeds. Thence, perhaps, we might escape to Port Natal where lived Englishmen who would protect us.

Of course this idea was hopeless from the first. The moonlight was almost as bright as day, and the veld quite open for a long way round, so that we should certainly have been seen and re-captured, which of course would have meant instant death. Further, as it happened, the guards had been warned against touching liquor of any sort since it was thought probable that an attempt would be made to intoxicate them. Still the women determined to try this scheme if they could find a chance. At least it was a second string to their bow.

Meanwhile they made their preparations. Hans went away for a little and returned with a supply of his sleep-producing drug, though whether he got this from the Kaffirs or gathered it himself, I do not remember, if I ever heard. At any rate it was boiled up in the water with which they made the coffee that I was to drink, though not in that which Marie proposed to drink with me, the strong taste and black hue of the coffee effectually hiding any flavour or colour that there might be in the herb. Also the vrouw cooked some food which she gave to Hans to carry. First, however, he went to investigate the old mealie-pit which was within a few paces of the back door of the Prinsloos' house. He reported that it would do well to hide a man in, especially as tall grass and bushes grew about its mouth.

Then the three of them started, and arriving at the door of my house, which was about a hundred yards away, were of course challenged by the sentries.

"Heeren," said Marie, "the commandant has given us leave to bring food to my husband, whom you guard within. Pray do not prevent us from entering."

"No," answered one of them gently enough, for he was touched with pity at her plight. "We have our orders to admit you, the Vrouw Prinsloo and the native servant, though why three of you should be needed to carry food to one man, I don't know. I should have thought that at such a time he would have preferred to be alone with his wife."

"The Vrouw Prinsloo wishes to ask my husband certain questions about his property here and what is to be done while he and her men are away at the main camp for the second trial, as I, whose heart is full of sorrow, have no head for such things. Also the Hottentot must have orders as to where he is to get a horse to ride with him, so pray let us pass, mynheer."

"Very good; it is no affair of ours, Vrouw Quatermain— Stay, I suppose that you have no arms under that long cloak of yours."

"Search me, if you will, mynheer," she answered, opening the cloak, whereon, after a quick glance, he nodded and bade them enter, saying:

"Mind, you are to come out by ten o'clock. You must not pass the night in that house, or we shall have the little Englishman oversleeping himself in the morning."

Then they entered and found me seated at a table preparing notes for my defence and setting down the heads of the facts of my relations with Pereira, Dingaan, and the late Commandant Retief.

Here I may state that my condition at the time was not one of fear, but rather of burning indignation. Indeed, I had not the slightest doubt but that when my case was re-tried before the great council, I should be able to establish my complete innocence of the abominable charges that had been brought against me. Therefore it came about that when Marie suggested that I should try to escape, I begged her almost roughly not to mention such a thing again.

"Run away!" I said. "Why, that would be to confess myself guilty, for only the guilty run away. What I want is to have all this business thrashed out and that devil Pereira exposed."

"But, Allan," said Marie, "how if you should never live to have it thrashed out? How if you should be shot first?" Then she rose, and having looked to see that the shutter-board was fast in the little window-place and the curtain that she had made of sacking drawn over it, returned and whispered: "Hans here has heard a horrible tale, Allan. Tell it to the baas, Hans."

So while Vrouw Prinsloo, in order to deceive any prying eyes if such by chance could see us, busied herself with lighting a fire on the hearth in the second room on which to warm the food, Hans told his story much as it has already been set out.

I listened to it with growing incredulity. The thing seemed to me impossible. Either Hans was deceived or lying, the latter probably, for well I knew the Hottentot powers of imagination. Or perhaps he was drunk; indeed, he smelt of liquor, of which I was aware be could carry a great quantity without outward signs of intoxication.

"I cannot believe it," I said when he had finished. "Even if Pereira is such a fiend, as is possible, would Henri Marais, your father—who, at any rate, has always been a good and God-fearing man—consent to work such a crime upon his daughter's husband, though he does dislike him?"

"My father is not what he was, Allan," said Marie. "Sometimes I think that his brain has gone."

"He did not speak like a man whose brain has gone this afternoon," I replied. "But let us suppose that this tale is true, what is it that you wish me to do?"

"Allan, I wish you to dress up in my clothes and get away to a hiding-place which Hans and the vrouw know, leaving me here instead of you."

"Why, Marie?" I said. "Then you might get yourself shot in my place, always supposing that they mean to shoot me. Also I should certainly be caught and killed, as they would have a right to kill me for trying to escape in disguise. That is a mad plan, and I have a better. Vrouw Prinsloo, go straight to the commandant ad tell him all this story. Or, if he will not listen to you, scream it out at the top of your voice so that everyone may hear, and then come back and tell us the result. Of one thing I am sure, that if you do this, even if there was any thought of my being shot tomorrow morning, it will be abandoned. You can refuse to say who told you the tale."

"Yes, please do that," muttered Hans, "else I know one who will be shot."

"Good, I will go," said the vrouw, and she went, the guards letting her pass after a few words which we could not hear.

Half an hour later she returned and called to us to open the door.

"Well?" I asked.

"Well," she said, "I have failed, nephew. Except those sentries outside the door, the commandant and all the Boers have ridden off, I know not where, taking our people with them."

"That's odd," I answered, "but I suppose they thought they had not enough grass for their horses, or Heaven knows what they thought. Stay now, I will do something," and, opening the door, I called to the guards, honest fellows in their way, whom I had known in past times.

"Listen, friends," I said. "A tale has been brought to me that I am not to be taken to the big camp to have my case inquired of by the council, but am to be shot down in cold blood when I come out of this house to-morrow morning. Is that true?"

"Allemachte, Englishman!" answered one of them. "Do you take us for murderers? Our orders are to lead you to the commandant wherever he may appoint, so have no fear that we shall shoot you like a Kaffir. Either you or they who told you such a story are mad."

"So I thought, friends," I answered. "But where is the commandant and where are the others? The Vrouw Prinsloo here has been to see them, and reports that they are all gone."

"That is very likely," said the Boer. "There is a rumour that some of your Zulu brothers have come across the Tugela again to hunt us, which, if you want to know the truth, is why we visited this place. Well, the commandant has taken his men for a ride to see if he can meet them by this bright moonlight. Pity he could not take you, too, since you would have known so well where to find them, if they are there at all. Now please talk no more nonsense to us, which it makes us sick to hear, and don't think that you can slip away because we are only two, for you know our roers are loaded with slugs, and we have orders to use them."

"There," I said when I had shut the door, "now you have heard for yourselves. As I thought, there is nothing in this fine story, so I hope you are convinced."

Neither the vrouw nor Marie made any answer, and Hans also held his tongue. Yet, as I remembered afterwards, I saw a strange glance pass between the two women, who were not at all convinced, and, although I never dreamed of such a thing, had now determined to carry out their own desperate plan. But of this I repeat the vrouw and Hans only knew one half; the rest was locked in Marie's loving heart.

"Perhaps you are right, Allan," said the vrouw in the tone of one who gives way to an unreasonable child. "I hope so, and, at any rate, you can refuse to come out of the house to-morrow morning until you are quite sure. And now let us eat some supper, for we shall not make matters better by going hungry. Hans, bring the food."

So we ate, or made pretence to eat, and I, being thirsty, drank two cups of the black coffee dashed with spirit to serve as milk. After this I grew strangely sleepy. The last thing I remember was Marie looking at me with her beautiful eyes, that were full—ah! so full of tender love, and kissing me again and again upon the lips.

I dreamed all sorts of dreams, rather pleasant dreams on the whole. Then I woke up by degrees to find myself in an earthen pit shaped like a bottle and having the remains of polished sides to it. It made me think of Joseph who was let down by his brethren into a well in the desert. Now, who on earth could have let me down into a well, especially as I had no brethren? Perhaps I was not really in a well. Perhaps this was a nightmare. Or I might be dead. I began to remember that there were certain good reasons why I should be dead. Only, only—why should they have buried me in woman's clothes as I seemed to wear?

And what was that noise that had wakened me?

It could not be the trump of doom, unless the trumping of doom went off like a double-barrelled gun.

I began to try to climb out of my hole, but as it was nine feet deep and bottle-shaped, which the light flowing in from the neck showed, I found this impossible. Just as I was giving up the attempt, a yellow face appeared in that neck, which looked to me like the face of Hans, and an arm was projected downwards.

"Jump, if you are awake, baas," said a voice—surely it was the voice of Hans—"and I will pull you out."

So I jumped, and caught the arm above the wrist. Then the owner of the arm pulled desperately, and the end of it was that I succeeded in gripping the edge of the bottle-like hole, and, with the help of the arm, in dragging myself out.

"Now, baas," said Hans, for it _was_ Hans, "run, run before the Boers catch you."

"What Boers?" I asked, sleepily; "and how can I run with these things flapping about my legs?"

Then I looked about me, and, although the dawn was only just breaking, began to recognise my surroundings. Surely this was the Prinsloos' house to my right, and that, faintly seen through the mist about a hundred paces away, was Marie's and my own. There seemed to be something going on yonder which excited my awakening curiosity. I could see figures moving in an unusual manner, and desired to know what they were doing. I began to walk towards them, and Hans, for his part, began to try to drag me in an opposite direction, uttering all sorts of gibberish as to the necessity of my running away. But I would not be dragged; indeed, I struck at him, until at last, with an exclamation of despair, he let go of me and vanished.

So I went on alone. I came to my house, or what I thought resembled it, and there saw a figure lying on its face on the ground some ten or fifteen yards to the right of the doorway, and noted abstractedly that it was dressed in my clothes. The Vrouw Prinsloo, in her absurd night garments, was waddling towards the figure, and a little way off stood Hernan Pereira, apparently in the act of reloading a double-barrelled gun. Beyond, staring at him, stood the lantern-faced Henri Marais, pulling at his long beard with one hand and holding a rifle in the other. Behind were two saddled horses in the charge of a raw Kaffir, who looked on stupidly.

The Vrouw Prinsloo reached the body that lay upon the ground dressed in what resembled my clothes, and bending down her stout shape with an effort, turned it over. She glared into its face and then began to shriek.

"Come here, Henri Marais," she shrieked, "come, see what your beloved nephew has done! You had a daughter who was all your life to you, Henri Marais. Well, come, look at her after your beloved nephew has finished his work with her!"

Henri Marais advanced slowly like one who does not understand. He stood over the body on the ground, and looked down upon it through the morning mists.

Then suddenly he went mad. His broad hat fell from his head, and his long hair seemed to stand up. Also his beard grew big and bristled like the feathers of a bird in frosty weather. He turned on Hernan Pereira. "You devil!" he shouted, and his voice sounded like the roar of a wild beast; "you devil, you have murdered my daughter! Because you could not get Marie for yourself, you have murdered her. Well, I will pay you back!"

Without more ado he lifted his gun and fired straight at Hernan Pereira, who sank slowly to the ground and lay there groaning.

Just then I grew aware that horsemen were advancing upon us, a great number of horsemen, though whence they came at that time I did not know. One of these I recognised even in my half-drunken state, for he had impressed himself very vividly upon my mind. He was the dark-browed commandant who had tried and condemned me to death. He dismounted, and, staring at the two figures that lay upon the ground, said in a loud and terrible voice:

"What is this? Who are these men, and why are they shot? Explain, Henri Marais."

"Men!" wailed Henri Marais, "they are not men. One is a woman—my only child; and the other is a devil, who, being a devil, will not die. See! he will not die. Give me another gun that I may make him die."

The commandant looked about him wildly, and his eye fell upon the Vrouw Prinsloo.

"What has chanced, vrouw?" he asked.

"Only this," she replied in a voice of unnatural calm. "Your murderers whom you set on in the name of law and justice have made a mistake. You told them to murder Allan Quatermain for reasons of your own. Well, they have murdered his wife instead."

Now the commandant struck his hand upon his forehead and groaned, and I, half awakened at last, ran forward, shaking my fists and gibbering.

"Who is that?" asked the commandant. "Is it a man or a woman?"

"It is a man in woman's clothing; it is Allan Quatermain," answered the vrouw, "whom we drugged and tried to hide from your butchers."

"God above us!" exclaimed the commandant, "is this earth or hell?"

Then the wounded Pereira raised himself upon one hand.

"I am dying," he cried; "my life is bleeding away, but before I die I must speak. All that story I told against the Englishman is false. He never plotted with Dingaan against the Boers. It was I who plotted with Dingaan. Although I hated him because he found me out, I did not wish Retief and our people to be killed. But I did wish Allan Quatermain to be killed, because he had won her whom I loved, though, as it happened, all the others were slain, and he alone escaped. Then I came here and learned that Marie was his wife—yes, his wife indeed—and grew mad with hate and jealousy. So I bore false witness against him, and, you fools, you believed me and ordered me to shoot him who is innocent before God and man. Then things went wrong. The woman tricked me again—for the last time. She dressed herself as the man, and in the dawnlight I was deceived. I killed her, her whom I love alone, and now her father, who loved her also, has killed me."

By this time I understood all, for my drugged brain had awakened at last. I ran to the brute upon the ground; grotesque in my woman's garments all awry, I leaped on him and stamped out the last of his life. Then, standing over his dead body, I shook my fists and cried:

"Men, see what you have done. May God pay you back all you owe her and me!"

They dismounted, they came round me, they protested, they even wept. And I, I raved at them upon the one side, while the mad Henri Marais raved upon the other; and the Vrouw Prinsloo, waving her big arms, called down the curse of God and the blood of the innocent upon their heads and those of their children for ever.

Then I remember no more.

When I came to myself two weeks afterwards, for I had been very ill and in delirium, I was lying in the house of the Vrouw Prinsloo alone. The Boers had all gone, east and west and north and south, and the dead were long buried. They had taken Henri Marais with them, so I was told, dragging him away in a bullock cart, to which he was tied, for he was raving mad. Afterwards he became quieter, and, indeed, lived for years, walking about and asking all whom he met if they could lead him to Marie. But enough of him—poor man, poor man!

The tale which got about was that Pereira had murdered Marie out of jealousy, and been shot by her father. But there were so many tragic histories in those days of war and massacre that this particular one was soon quite forgotten, especially as those concerned in it for one reason and another did not talk overmuch of its details. Nor did I talk of it, since no vengeance could mend my broken heart.

They brought me a letter that had been found on Marie's breast, stained with her blood.

Here it is:

"MY HUSBAND,

"Thrice have you saved my life, and now it is my turn to save yours, for there is no other path. It may be that they will kill you afterwards, but if so, I shall be glad to have died first in order that I may be ready to greet you in the land beyond.

"I drugged you, Allan, then I cut off my hair and dressed myself in your clothes. The Vrouw Prinsloo, Hans and I set my garments upon you. They led you out as though you were fainting, and the guards, seeing me, whom they thought was you, standing in the doorway, let them pass without question.

"What may happen I do not know, for I write this after you are gone. I hope, however, that you will escape and lead some full and happy life, though I fear that its best moments will always be shadowed by memories of me. For I know you love me, Allan, and will always love me, as I shall always love you.

"The light is burning out—like mine—so farewell, farewell, farewell! All earthly stories come to an end at last, but at that end we shall meet again. Till then, adieu. Would that I could have done more for you, since to die for one who is loved with body, heart and soul is but a little thing. Still I have been your wife, Allan, and your wife I shall remain when the world is old. Heaven does not grow old, Allan, and there I shall greet you.

"The light is dead, but—oh!—in my heart another light arises!

"Your MARIE."

This was her letter.

I do not think there is anything more to be said.

Such is the history of my first love. Those who read it, if any ever do, will understand why I have never spoken of her before, and do not wish it to be known until I, too, am dead and have gone to join the great soul of Marie Marais.

Allan Quatermain.

Child of Storm

Dedication

Dear Mr. Stuart,

For twenty years, I believe I am right in saying, you, as Assistant Secretary for Native Affairs in Natal, and in other offices, have been intimately acquainted with the Zulu people. Moreover, you are one of the few living men who have made a deep and scientific study of their language, their customs and their history. So I confess that I was the more pleased after you were so good as to read this tale—the second book of the epic of the vengeance of Zikali, "the Thing-that-should-never-have-been-born," and of the fall of the House of Senzangakona—when you wrote to me that it was animated by the true Zulu spirit.

I must admit that my acquaintance with this people dates from a period which closed almost before your day. What I know of them I gathered at the time when Cetewayo, of whom my volume tells, was in his glory, previous to the evil hour in which he found himself driven by the clamour of his regiments, cut off, as they were, through the annexation of the Transvaal, from their hereditary trade of war, to match himself against the British strength. I learned it all by personal observation in the 'seventies, or from the lips of the great Shepstone, my chief and friend, and from my colleagues Osborn, Fynney, Clarke and others, every one of them long since "gone down."

Perhaps it may be as well that this is so, at any rate in the case of one who desires to write of the Zulus as a reigning nation, which now they have ceased to be, and to try to show them as they were, in all their superstitious madness and bloodstained grandeur.

Yet then they had virtues as well as vices. To serve their Country in arms, to die for it and for the King; such was their primitive ideal. If they were fierce they were loyal, and feared neither wounds nor doom; if they listened to the dark redes of the witch-doctor, the trumpet-call of duty sounded still louder in their ears; if, chanting their terrible "Ingoma," at the King's bidding they went forth to slay unsparingly, at least they were not mean or vulgar. From those who continually must face the last great issues of life or death meanness and vulgarity are far removed. These qualities belong to the safe and crowded haunts of civilised men, not to the kraals of Bantu savages, where, at any rate of old, they might be sought in vain.

Now everything is changed, or so I hear, and doubtless in the balance this is best. Still we may wonder what are the thoughts that pass through the mind of some ancient warrior of Chaka's or Dingaan's time, as he suns himself crouched on the ground, for example, where once stood the royal kraal, Duguza, and watches men and women of the Zulu blood passing homeward from the cities or the mines, bemused, some of them, with the white man's smuggled liquor, grotesque with the white man's cast-off garments, hiding, perhaps, in their blankets examples of the white man's doubtful photographs—and then shuts his sunken eyes and remembers the plumed and kilted regiments making that same ground shake as, with a thunder of salute, line upon line, company upon company, they rushed out to battle.

Well, because the latter does not attract me, it is of this former time that I have tried to write—the time of the Impis and the witch-finders and the rival princes of the royal House—as I am glad to learn from you, not quite in vain. Therefore, since you, so great an expert, approve of my labours in the seldom-travelled field of Zulu story, I ask you to allow me to set your name upon this page and subscribe myself,

Gratefully and sincerely yours,

H. Rider Haggard.

Ditchingham, 12th October, 1912.

To James Stuart, Esq., Late Assistant Secretary for Native Affairs, Natal.

Author's Note

Mr. Allan Quatermain's story of the wicked and fascinating Mameena, a kind of Zulu Helen, has, it should be stated, a broad foundation in historical fact. Leaving Mameena and her wiles on one side, the tale of the struggle between the Princes Cetewayo and Umbelazi for succession to the throne of Zululand is true.

When the differences between these sons of his became intolerable, because of the tumult which they were causing in his country, King Panda, their father, the son of Senzangakona, and the brother of the great Chaka and of Dingaan, who had ruled before him, did say that "when two young bulls quarrel they had better fight it out." So, at least, I was told by the late Mr. F. B. Fynney, my colleague at the time of the annexation of the Transvaal in 1877, who, as Zulu Border Agent, with the exceptions of the late Sir Theophilus Shepstone and the late Sir Melmoth Osborn, perhaps knew more of that land and people than anyone else of his period.

As a result of this hint given by a maddened king, the great battle of the Tugela was fought at Endondakusuka in December, 1856, between the Usutu party, commanded by Cetewayo, and the adherents of Umbelazi the Handsome, his brother, who was known among the Zulus as "Indhlovu-ene-Sihlonti", or the "Elephant with the tuft of hair," from a little lock of hair which grew low down upon his back.

My friend, Sir Melmoth Osborn, who died in or about the year 1897, was present at this battle, although not as a combatant. Well do I remember his thrilling story, told to me over thirty years ago, of the events of that awful day.

Early in the morning, or during the previous night, I forget which, he swam his horse across the Tugela and hid with it in a bush-clad kopje, blindfolding the animal with his coat lest it should betray him. As it chanced, the great fight of the day, that of the regiment of veterans, which Sir Melmoth informed me Panda had sent down at the last moment to the assistance of Umbelazi, his favourite son, took place almost at the foot of this kopje. Mr. Quatermain, in his narrative, calls this regiment the Amawombe, but my recollection is that the name Sir Melmoth Osborn gave them was "The Greys" or "Upunga."

Whatever their exact title may have been, however, they made a great stand. At least, he told me that when Umbelazi's impi, or army, began to give before the Usutu onslaught, these "Greys" moved forward above 3,000 strong, drawn up in a triple line, and were charged by one of Cetewayo's regiments.

The opposing forces met, and the noise of their clashing shields, said Sir Melmoth, was like the roll of heavy thunder. Then, while he watched, the veteran "Greys" passed over the opposing regiment "as a wave passes over a rock"—these were his exact words—and, leaving about a third of their number dead or wounded among the bodies of the annihilated foe, charged on to meet a second regiment sent against them by Cetewayo. With these the struggle was repeated, but again the "Greys" conquered. Only now there were not more than five or six hundred of them left upon their feet.

These survivors ran to a mound, round which they formed a ring, and here for a long while withstood the attack of a third regiment, until at length they perished almost to a man, buried beneath heaps of their slain assailants, the Usutu.

Truly they made a noble end fighting thus against tremendous odds!

As for the number who fell at this battle of Endondakusuka, Mr. Fynney, in a pamphlet which he wrote, says that six of Umbelazi's brothers died, "whilst it is estimated that upwards of 100,000 of the people—men, women and children—were slain"—a high and indeed an impossible estimate.

That curious personage named John Dunn, an Englishman who became a Zulu chief, and who actually fought in this battle, as narrated by Mr. Quatermain, however, puts the number much lower. What the true total was will never be known; but Sir Melmoth Osborn told me that when he swam his horse back across the Tugela that night it was black with bodies; and Sir Theophilus Shepstone also told me that when he visited the scene a day or two later the banks of the river were strewn with multitudes of them, male and female.

It was from Mr. Fynney that I heard the story of the execution by Cetewayo of the man who appeared before him with the ornaments of Umbelazi, announcing that he had killed the prince with his own hand. Of course, this tale, as Mr. Quatermain points out, bears a striking resemblance to that recorded in the Old Testament in connection with the death of King Saul.

It by no means follows, however, that it is therefore apocryphal; indeed, Mr. Fynney assured me that it was quite true, although, if he gave me his authorities, I cannot remember them after a lapse of more than thirty years.

The exact circumstances of Umbelazi's death are unknown, but the general report was that he died, not by the assegais of the Usutu, but of a broken heart. Another story declares that he was drowned. His body was never found, and it is therefore probable that it sank in the Tugela, as is suggested in the following pages.

I have only to add that it is quite in accordance with Zulu beliefs that a man should be haunted by the ghost of one whom he has murdered or betrayed, or, to be more accurate, that the spirit ("umoya") should enter into the slayer and drive him mad. Or, in such a case, that spirit might bring misfortune upon him, his family, or his tribe.

H. Rider Haggard.

Table of Contents

Allan Quatermain Hears of Mameena

We white people think that we know everything. For instance, we think that we understand human nature. And so we do, as human nature appears to us, with all its trappings and accessories seen dimly through the glass of our conventions, leaving out those aspects of it which we have forgotten or do not think it polite to mention. But I, Allan Quatermain, reflecting upon these matters in my ignorant and uneducated fashion, have always held that no one really understands human nature who has not studied it in the rough. Well, that is the aspect of it with which I have been best acquainted.

For most of the years of my life I have handled the raw material, the virgin ore, not the finished ornament that is smelted out of it—if, indeed, it is finished yet, which I greatly doubt. I dare say that a time may come when the perfected generations—if Civilisation, as we understand it, really has a future and any such should be allowed to enjoy their hour on the World—will look back to us as crude, half-developed creatures whose only merit was that we handed on the flame of life.

Maybe, maybe, for everything goes by comparison; and at one end of the ladder is the ape-man, and at the other, as we hope, the angel. No, not the angel; he belongs to a different sphere, but that last expression of humanity upon which I will not speculate. While man is man—that is, before he suffers the magical death-change into spirit, if such should be his destiny—well, he will remain man. I mean that the same passions will sway him; he will aim at the same ambitions; he will know the same joys and be oppressed by the same fears, whether he lives in a Kafir hut or in a golden palace; whether he walks upon his two feet or, as for aught I know he may do one day, flies through the air. This is certain: that in the flesh he can never escape from our atmosphere, and while he breathes it, in the main with some variations prescribed by climate, local law and religion, he will do much as his forefathers did for countless ages.

That is why I have always found the savage so interesting, for in him, nakedly and forcibly expressed, we see those eternal principles which direct our human destiny.

To descend from these generalities, that is why also I, who hate writing, have thought it worth while, at the cost of some labour to myself, to occupy my leisure in what to me is a strange land—for although I was born in England, it is not my country—in setting down various experiences of my life that do, in my opinion, interpret this our universal nature. I dare say that no one will ever read them; still, perhaps they are worthy of record, and who knows? In days to come they may fall into the hands of others and prove of value. At any rate, they are true stories of interesting peoples, who, if they should survive in the savage competition of the nations, probably are doomed to undergo great changes. Therefore I tell of them before they began to change.

Now, although I take it out of its strict chronological order, the first of these histories that I wish to preserve is in the main that of an extremely beautiful woman—with the exception of a certain Nada, called "the Lily," of whom I hope to speak some day, I think the most beautiful that ever lived among the Zulus. Also she was, I think, the most able, the most wicked, and the most ambitious. Her attractive name—for it was very attractive as the Zulus said it, especially those of them who were in love with her—was Mameena, daughter of Umbezi. Her other name was

Child of Storm (Ingane-ye-Sipepo, or, more freely and shortly, O-we-Zulu), but the word "Ma-mee-na" had its origin in the sound of the wind that wailed about the hut when she was born.

Since I have been settled in England I have read—of course in a translation—the story of Helen of Troy, as told by the Greek poet, Homer. Well, Mameena reminds me very much of Helen, or, rather, Helen reminds me of Mameena. At any rate, there was this in common between them, although one of them was black, or, rather, copper-coloured, and the other white—they both were lovely; moreover, they both were faithless, and brought men by hundreds to their deaths. There, perhaps, the resemblance ends, since Mameena had much more fire and grit than Helen could boast, who, unless Homer misrepresents her, must have been but a poor thing after all. Beauty Itself, which those old rascals of Greek gods made use of to bait their snares set for the lives and honour of men, such was Helen, no more; that is, as I understand her, who have not had the advantage of a classical education. Now, Mameena, although she was superstitious—a common weakness of great minds—acknowledging no gods in particular, as we understand them, set her own snares, with varying success but a very definite object, namely, that of becoming the first woman in the world as she knew it—the stormy, bloodstained world of the Zulus.

But the reader shall judge for himself, if ever such a person should chance to cast his eye upon this history.

It was in the year 1854 that I first met Mameena, and my acquaintance with her continued off and on until 1856, when it came to an end in a fashion that shall be told after the fearful battle of the Tugela in which Umbelazi, Panda's son and Cetewayo's brother—who, to his sorrow, had also met Mameena—lost his life. I was still a youngish man in those days, although I had already buried my second wife, as I have told elsewhere, after our brief but happy time of marriage.

Leaving my boy in charge of some kind people in Durban, I started into "the Zulu"—a land with which I had already become well acquainted as a youth, there to carry on my wild life of trading and hunting.

For the trading I never cared much, as may be guessed from the little that ever I made out of it, the art of traffic being in truth repugnant to me. But hunting was always the breath of my nostrils—not that I am fond of killing creatures, for any humane man soon wearies of slaughter. No, it is the excitement of sport, which, before breechloaders came in, was acute enough, I can assure you; the lonely existence in wild places, often with only the sun and the stars for companions; the continual adventures; the strange tribes with whom I came in contact; in short, the change, the danger, the hope always of finding something great and new, that attracted and still attracts me, even now when I *have* found the great and the new. There, I must not go on writing like this, or I shall throw down my pen and book a passage for Africa, and incidentally to the next world, no doubt—that world of the great and new!

It was, I think, in the month of May in the year 1854 that I went hunting in rough country between the White and Black Umvolosi Rivers, by permission of Panda—whom the Boers had made king of Zululand after the defeat and death of Dingaan his brother. The district was very feverish, and for this reason I had entered it in the winter months. There was so much bush that, in the total absence of roads, I thought it wise not to attempt to bring my wagons down, and as no horses would live in that veld I went on foot. My principal companions were a Kafir of mixed origin, called Sikauli, commonly abbreviated into Scowl, the Zulu chief Saduko, and a headman of the Undwandwe blood named Umbezi, at whose kraal on the high land about thirty miles away I left my wagon and certain of my men in charge of the goods and some ivory that I had traded.

This Umbezi was a stout and genial-mannered man of about sixty years of age, and, what is rare among these people, one who loved sport for its own sake. Being aware of his tastes, also that he knew the country and was skilled in finding game, I had promised him a gun if he would accompany me and bring a few hunters. It was a particularly bad gun that had seen much service, and one which had an unpleasing habit of going off at half-cock; but even after he had seen it, and I in my honesty had explained its weaknesses, he jumped at the offer.

"O Macumazana" (that is my native name, often abbreviated into Macumazahn, which means "One who stands out," or as many interpret it, I don't know how, "Watcher-by-Night")—"a gun that goes off sometimes when you do not expect it is much better than no gun at all, and you are a chief with a great heart to promise it to me, for when I own the White Man's weapon I shall be looked up to and feared by everyone between the two rivers."

Now, while he was speaking he handled the gun, that was loaded, observing which I moved behind him. Off it went in due course, its recoil knocking him backwards—for that gun was a devil to kick—and its bullet cutting the top off the ear of one of his wives. The lady fled screaming, leaving a little bit of her ear upon the ground.

"What does it matter?" said Umbezi, as he picked himself up, rubbing his shoulder with a rueful look. "Would that the evil spirit in the gun had cut off her tongue and not her ear! It is the Worn-out-Old-Cow's own fault; she is always peeping into everything like a monkey. Now she will have something to chatter about and leave my things alone for awhile. I thank my ancestral Spirit it was not Mameena, for then her looks would have been spoiled."

"Who is Mameena?" I asked. "Your last wife?"

"No, no, Macumazahn; I wish she were, for then I should have the most beautiful wife in the land. She is my daughter, though not that of the Worn-out-Old-Cow; her mother died when she was born, on the night of the Great Storm. You should ask Saduko there who Mameena is," he added with a broad grin, lifting his head from the gun, which he was examining gingerly, as though he thought it might go off again while unloaded, and nodding towards someone who stood behind him.

I turned, and for the first time saw Saduko, whom I recognised at once as a person quite out of the ordinary run of natives.

He was a tall and magnificently formed young man, who, although his breast was scarred with assegai wounds, showing that he was a warrior, had not yet attained to the honour of the "ring" of polished wax laid over strips of rush bound round with sinew and sewn to the hair, the "isicoco" which at a certain age or dignity, determined by the king, Zulus are allowed to assume. But his face struck me more even than his grace, strength and stature. Undoubtedly it was a very fine face, with little or nothing of the negroid type about it; indeed, he might have been a rather dark-coloured Arab, to which stock he probably threw back. The eyes, too, were large and rather melancholy, and in his reserved, dignified air there was something that showed him to be no common fellow, but one of breeding and intellect.

"Siyakubona" (that is, "we see you," anglice "good morrow") "Saduko," I said, eyeing him curiously. "Tell me, who is Mameena?"

"Inkoosi," he answered in his deep voice, lifting his delicately shaped hand in salutation, a courtesy that pleased me who, after all, was nothing but a white hunter, "Inkoosi, has not her father said that she is his daughter?"

"Aye," answered the jolly old Umbezi, "but what her father has not said is that Saduko is her lover, or, rather, would like to be. Wow! Saduko," he went on, shaking his fat finger at him, "are you mad, man, that you think a girl like that is for you?

Give me a hundred cattle, not one less, and I will begin to think of it. Why, you have not ten, and Mameena is my eldest daughter, and must marry a rich man."

"She loves me, O Umbezi," answered Saduko, looking down, "and that is more than cattle."

"For you, perhaps, Saduko, but not for me who am poor and want cows. Also," he added, glancing at him shrewdly, "are you so sure that Mameena loves you though you be such a fine man? Now, I should have thought that whatever her eyes may say, her heart loves no one but herself, and that in the end she will follow her heart and not her eyes. Mameena the beautiful does not seek to be a poor man's wife and do all the hoeing. But bring me the hundred cattle and we will see, for, speaking truth from my heart, if you were a big chief there is no one I should like better as a son-in-law, unless it were Macumazahn here," he said, digging me in the ribs with his elbow, "who would lift up my House on his white back."

Now, at this speech Saduko shifted his feet uneasily; it seemed to me as though he felt there was truth in Umbezi's estimate of his daughter's character. But he only said:

"Cattle can be acquired."

"Or stolen," suggested Umbezi.

"Or taken in war," corrected Saduko. "When I have a hundred head I will hold you to your word, O father of Mameena."

"And then what would you live on, fool, if you gave all your beasts to me? There, there, cease talking wind. Before you have a hundred head of cattle Mameena will have six children who will not call *you* father. Ah, don't you like that? Are you going away?"

"Yes, I am going," he answered, with a flash of his quiet eyes; "only then let the man whom they do call father beware of Saduko."

"Beware of how you talk, young man," said Umbezi in a grave voice. "Would you travel your father's road? I hope not, for I like you well; but such words are apt to be remembered."

Saduko walked away as though he did not hear.

"Who is he?" I asked.

"One of high blood," answered Umbezi shortly. "He might be a chief to-day had not his father been a plotter and a wizard. Dingaan smelt him out"—and he made a sideways motion with his hand that among the Zulus means much. "Yes, they were killed, almost every one; the chief, his wives, his children and his headmen—every one except Chosa his brother and his son Saduko, whom Zikali the dwarf, the Smeller-out-of-evil-doers, the Ancient, who was old before Senzangakona became a father of kings, hid him. There, that is an evil tale to talk of," and he shivered. "Come, White Man, and doctor that old Cow of mine, or she will give me no peace for months."

So I went to see the Worn-out-Old-Cow—not because I had any particular interest in her, for, to tell the truth, she was a very disagreeable and antique person, the cast-off wife of some chief whom at an unknown date in the past the astute Umbezi had married from motives of policy—but because I hoped to hear more of Miss Mameena, in whom I had become interested.

Entering a large hut, I found the lady so impolitely named "the Old Cow" in a parlous state. There she lay upon the floor, an unpleasant object because of the blood that had escaped from her wound, surrounded by a crowd of other women and of children. At regular intervals she announced that she was dying, and emitted a fearful yell, whereupon all the audience yelled also; in short, the place was a perfect pandemonium.

Telling Umbezi to get the hut cleared, I said that I would go to fetch my medicines. Meanwhile I ordered my servant, Scowl, a humorous-looking fellow, light yellow in hue, for he had a strong dash of Hottentot in his composition, to cleanse the wound. When I returned from the wagon ten minutes later the screams were more terrible than before, although the chorus now stood without the hut. Nor was this altogether wonderful, for on entering the place I found Scowl trimming up "the Old Cow's" ear with a pair of blunt nail-scissors.

"O Macumazana," said Umbezi in a hoarse whisper, "might it not perhaps be as well to leave her alone? If she bled to death, at any rate she would be quieter."

"Are you a man or a hyena?" I answered sternly, and set about the job, Scowl holding the poor woman's head between his knees.

It was over at length; a simple operation in which I exhibited—I believe that is the medical term—a strong solution of caustic applied with a feather.

"There, Mother," I said, for now we were alone in the hut, whence Scowl had fled, badly bitten in the calf, "you won't die now."

"No, you vile White Man," she sobbed. "I shan't die, but how about my beauty?"

"It will be greater than ever," I answered; "no one else will have an ear with such a curve in it. But, talking of beauty, where is Mameena?"

"I don't know where she is," she replied with fury, "but I very well know where she would be if I had my way. That peeled willow-wand of a girl"—here she added certain descriptive epithets I will not repeat—"has brought this misfortune upon me. We had a slight quarrel yesterday, White Man, and, being a witch as she is, she prophesied evil. Yes, when by accident I scratched her ear, she said that before long mine should burn, and surely burn it does." (This, no doubt, was true, for the caustic had begun to bite.)

"O devil of a White Man," she went on, "you have bewitched me; you have filled my head with fire."

Then she seized an earthenware pot and hurled it at me, saying, "Take that for your doctor-fee. Go, crawl after Mameena like the others and get her to doctor you."

By this time I was half through the bee-hole of the hut, my movements being hastened by a vessel of hot water which landed on me behind.

"What is the matter, Macumazahn?" asked old Umbezi, who was waiting outside.

"Nothing at all, friend," I answered with a sweet smile, "except that your wife wants to see you at once. She is in pain, and wishes you to soothe her. Go in; do not hesitate."

After a moment's pause he went in—that is, half of him went in. Then came a fearful crash, and he emerged again with the rim of a pot about his neck and his countenance veiled in a coating of what I took to be honey.

"Where is Mameena?" I asked him as he sat up spluttering.

"Where I wish I was," he answered in a thick voice; "at a kraal five hours' journey away."

Well, that was the first I heard of Mameena.

That night as I sat smoking my pipe under the flap lean-to attached to the wagon, laughing to myself over the adventure of "the Old Cow," falsely described as "worn out," and wondering whether Umbezi had got the honey out of his hair, the canvas was lifted, and a Kafir wrapped in a kaross crept in and squatted before me.

"Who are you?" I asked, for it was too dark to see the man's face.

"Inkoosi," answered a deep voice, "I am Saduko."

"You are welcome," I answered, handing him a little gourd of snuff in token of hospitality. Then I waited while he poured some of the snuff into the palm of his hand and took it in the usual fashion.

"Inkoosi," he said, when he had scraped away the tears produced by the snuff, "I have come to ask you a favour. You heard Umbezi say to-day that he will not give me his daughter, Mameena, unless I give him a hundred head of cows. Now, I have not got the cattle, and I cannot earn them by work in many years. Therefore I must take them from a certain tribe I know which is at war with the Zulus. But this I cannot do unless I have a gun. If I had a good gun, Inkoosi—one that only goes off when it is asked, and not of its own fancy, I who have some name could persuade a number of men whom I know, who once were servants of my father, or their sons, to be my companions in this venture."

"Do I understand that you wish me to give you one of my good guns with two mouths to it (i.e. double-barrelled), a gun worth at least twelve oxen, for nothing, O Saduko?" I asked in a cold and scandalised voice.

"Not so, O Watcher-by-Night," he answered; "not so, O He-who-sleeps-with-one-eye-open" (another free and difficult rendering of my native name, Macumazahn, or more correctly, Macumazana)—"I should never dream of offering such an insult to your high-born intelligence." He paused and took another pinch of snuff, then went on in a meditative voice: "Where I propose to get those hundred cattle there are many more; I am told not less than a thousand head in all. Now, Inkoosi," he added, looking at me sideways, "suppose you gave me the gun I ask for, and suppose you accompanied me with your own gun and your armed hunters, it would be fair that you should have half the cattle, would it not?"

"That's cool," I said. "So, young man, you want to turn me into a cow-thief and get my throat cut by Panda for breaking the peace of his country?"

"Neither, Macumazahn, for these are my own cattle. Listen, now, and I will tell you a story. You have heard of Matiwane, the chief of the Amangwane?"

"Yes," I answered. "His tribe lived near the head of the Umzinyati, did they not? Then they were beaten by the Boers or the English, and Matiwane came under the Zulus. But afterwards Dingaan wiped him out, with his House, and now his people are killed or scattered."

"Yes, his people are killed and scattered, but his House still lives. Macumazahn, I am his House, I, the only son of his chief wife, for Zikali the Wise Little One, the Ancient, who is of the Amangwane blood, and who hated Chaka and Dingaan—yes, and Senzangakona their father before them, but whom none of them could kill because he is so great and has such mighty spirits for his servants, saved and sheltered me."

"If he is so great, why, then, did he not save your father also, Saduko?" I asked, as though I knew nothing of this Zikali.

"I cannot say, Macumazahn. Perhaps the spirits plant a tree for themselves, and to do so cut down many other trees. At least, so it happened. It happened thus: Bangu, chief of the Amakoba, whispered into Dingaan's ear that Matiwane, my father, was a wizard; also that he was very rich. Dingaan listened because he thought a sickness that he had came from Matiwane's witchcraft. He said: 'Go, Bangu, and take a company with you and pay Matiwane a visit of honour, and in the night, O in the night! Afterwards, Bangu, we will divide the cattle, for Matiwane is strong and clever, and you shall not risk your life for nothing.'"

Saduko paused and looked down at the ground, brooding heavily.

"Macumazahn, it was done," he said presently. "They ate my father's meat, they drank his beer; they gave him a present from the king, they praised him with high names; yes, Bangu took snuff with him and called him brother. Then in the night, O in the night—!

"My father was in the hut with my mother, and I, so big only"—and he held his hand at the height of a boy of ten—"was with them. The cry arose, the flames began to eat; my father looked out and saw. 'Break through the fence and away, woman,' he said; 'away with Saduko, that he may live to avenge me. Begone while I hold the gate! Begone to Zikali, for whose witchcrafts I pay with my blood.'

"Then he kissed me on the brow, saying but one word, 'Remember,' and thrust us from the hut.

"My mother broke a way through the fence; yes, she tore at it with her nails and teeth like a hyena. I looked back out of the shadow of the hut and saw Matiwane my father fighting like a buffalo. Men went down before him, one, two, three, although he had no shield: only his spear. Then Bangu crept behind him and stabbed him in the back and he threw up his arms and fell. I saw no more, for by now we were through the fence. We ran, but they perceived us. They hunted us as wild dogs hunt a buck. They killed my mother with a throwing assegai; it entered at her back and came out at her heart. I went mad, I drew it from her body, I ran at them. I dived beneath the shield of the first, a very tall man, and held the spear, so, in both my little hands. His weight came upon its point and it went through him as though he were but a bowl of buttermilk. Yes, he rolled over, quite dead, and the handle of the spear broke upon the ground. Now the others stopped astonished, for never had they seen such a thing. That a child should kill a tall warrior, oh! that tale had not been told. Some of them would have let me go, but just then Bangu came up and saw the dead man, who was his brother.

"'Wow!' he said when he knew how the man had died. 'This lion's cub is a wizard also, for how else could he have killed a soldier who has known war? Hold out his arms that I may finish him slowly.'

"So two of them held out my arms, and Bangu came up with his spear."

Saduko ceased speaking, not that his tale was done, but because his voice choked in his throat. Indeed, seldom have I seen a man so moved. He breathed in great gasps, the sweat poured from him, and his muscles worked convulsively. I gave him a pannikin of water and he drank, then he went on:

"Already the spear had begun to prick—look, here is the mark of it"—and opening his kaross he pointed to a little white line just below the breast-bone—"when a strange shadow thrown by the fire of the burning huts came between Bangu and me, a shadow as that of a toad standing on its hind legs. I looked round and saw that it was the shadow of Zikali, whom I had seen once or twice. There he stood, though whence he came I know not, wagging his great white head that sits on the top of his body like a pumpkin on an ant-heap, rolling his big eyes and laughing loudly.

"'A merry sight,' he cried in his deep voice that sounded like water in a hollow cave. 'A merry sight, O Bangu, Chief of the Amakoba! Blood, blood, plenty of blood! Fire, fire, plenty of fire! Wizards dead here, there, and everywhere! Oh, a merry sight! I have seen many such; one at the kraal of your grandmother, for instance—your grandmother the great Inkosikazi, when myself I escaped with my life because I was so old; but never do I remember a merrier than that which this moon shines on,' and he pointed to the White Lady who just then broke through the clouds. 'But, great Chief Bangu, lord loved by the son of Senzangakona, brother of the Black One (Chaka) who has ridden hence on the assegai, what is the meaning of *this* play?' and he pointed to me and to the two soldiers who held out my little arms.

"'I kill the wizard's cub, Zikali, that is all,' answered Bangu.

"'I see, I see,' laughed Zikali. 'A gallant deed! You have butchered the father and the mother, and now you would butcher the child who has slain one of your grown warriors in fair fight. A very gallant deed, well worthy of the chief of the Amakoba!

Well, loose his spirit—only—' He stopped and took a pinch of snuff from a box which he drew from a slit in the lobe of his great ear.

"'Only what?' asked Bangu, hesitating.

"'Only I wonder, Bangu, what you will think of the world in which you will find yourself before to-morrow's moon arises. Come back thence and tell me, Bangu, for there are so many worlds beyond the sun, and I would learn for certain which of them such a one as you inhabits: a man who for hatred and for gain murders the father and the mother and then butchers the child—the child that could slay a warrior who has seen war—with the spear hot from his mother's heart.'

"'Do you mean that I shall die if I kill this lad?' shouted Bangu in a great voice.

"'What else?' answered Zikali, taking another pinch of snuff.

"'This, Wizard; that we will go together.'

"'Good, good!' laughed the dwarf. 'Let us go together. Long have I wished to die, and what better companion could I find than Bangu, Chief of the Amakoba, Slayer of Children, to guard me on a dark and terrible road. Come, brave Bangu, come; kill me if you can,' and again he laughed at him.

"Now, Macumazahn, the people of Bangu fell back muttering, for they found this business horrible. Yes, even those who held my arms let go of them.

"'What will happen to me, Wizard, if I spare the boy?' asked Bangu.

"Zikali stretched out his hand and touched the scratch that the assegai had made in me here. Then he held up his finger red with my blood, and looked at it in the light of the moon; yes, and tasted it with his tongue.

"'I think this will happen to you, Bangu,' he said. 'If you spare this boy he will grow into a man who will kill you and many others one day. But if you do not spare him I think that his spirit, working as spirits can do, will kill you to-morrow. Therefore the question is, will you live a while or will you die at once, taking me with you as your companion? For you must not leave me behind, brother Bangu.'

"Now Bangu turned and walked away, stepping over the body of my mother, and all his people walked away after him, so that presently Zikali the Wise and Little and I were left alone.

"'What! have they gone?' said Zikali, lifting up his eyes from the ground. 'Then we had better be going also, Son of Matiwane, lest he should change his mind and come back. Live on, Son of Matiwane, that you may avenge Matiwane.'"

"A nice tale," I said. "But what happened afterwards?"

"Zikali took me away and nurtured me at his kraal in the Black Kloof, where he lived alone save for his servants, for in that kraal he would suffer no woman to set foot, Macumazahn. He taught me much wisdom and many secret things, and would have made a great doctor of me had I so willed. But I willed it not who find spirits ill company, and there are many of them about the Black Kloof, Macumazahn. So in the end he said: 'Go where your heart calls, and be a warrior, Saduko. But know this: You have opened a door that can never be shut again, and across the threshold of that door spirits will pass in and out for all your life, whether you seek them or seek them not.'

"'It was you who opened the door, Zikali,' I answered angrily.

"'Mayhap,' said Zikali, laughing after his fashion, 'for I open when I must and shut when I must. Indeed, in my youth, before the Zulus were a people, they named me Opener of Doors; and now, looking through one of those doors, I see something about you, O Son of Matiwane.'

"'What do you see, my father?' I asked.

"'I see two roads, Saduko: the Road of Medicine, that is the spirit road, and the Road of Spears, that is the blood road. I see you travelling on the Road of Medicine, that is my own road, Saduko, and growing wise and great, till at last, far, far away, you vanish over the precipice to which it leads, full of years and honour and wealth, feared yet beloved by all men, white and black. Only that road you must travel alone, since such wisdom may have no friends, and, above all, no woman to share its secrets. Then I look at the Road of Spears and see you, Saduko, travelling on that road, and your feet are red with blood, and women wind their arms about your neck, and one by one your enemies go down before you. You love much, and sin much for the sake of the love, and she for whom you sin comes and goes and comes again. And the road is short, Saduko, and near the end of it are many spirits; and though you shut your eyes you see them, and though you fill your ears with clay you hear them, for they are the ghosts of your slain. But the end of your journeying I see not. Now choose which road you will, Son of Matiwane, and choose swiftly, for I speak no more of this matter.'

"Then, Macumazahn, I thought a while of the safe and lonely path of wisdom, also of the blood-red path of spears where I should find love and war, and my youth rose up in me and—I chose the path of spears and the love and the sin and the unknown death."

"A foolish choice, Saduko, supposing that there is any truth in this tale of roads, which there is not."

"Nay, a wise one, Macumazahn, for since then I have seen Mameena and know why I chose that path."

"Ah!" I said. "Mameena—I forgot her. Well, after all, perhaps there is some truth in your tale of roads. When I have seen Mameena I will tell you what I think."

"When you have seen Mameena, Macumazahn, you will say that the choice was very wise. Well, Zikali, Opener of Doors, laughed loudly when he heard it. 'The ox seeks the fat pasture, but the young bull the rough mountainside where the heifers graze,' he said; 'and after all, a bull is better than an ox. Now begin to travel your own road, Son of Matiwane, and from time to time return to the Black Kloof and tell me how it fares with you. I will promise you not to die before I know the end of it.'

"Now, Macumazahn, I have told you things that hitherto have lived in my own heart only. And, Macumazahn, Bangu is in ill favour with Panda, whom he defies in his mountain, and I have a promise—never mind how—that he who kills him will be called to no account and may keep his cattle. Will you come with me and share those cattle, O Watcher-by-Night?"

"Get thee behind me, Satan," I said in English, then added in Zulu: "I don't know. If your story is true I should have no objection to helping to kill Bangu; but I must learn lots more about this business first. Meanwhile I am going on a shooting trip to-morrow with Umbezi the Fat, and I like you, O Chooser of the Road of Spears and Blood. Will you be my companion and earn the gun with two mouths in payment?"

"Inkoosi," he said, lifting his hand in salute with a flash of his dark eyes, "you are generous, you honour me. What is there that I should love better? Yet," he added, and his face fell, "first I must ask Zikali the Little, Zikali my foster-father."

"Oh!" I said, "so you are still tied to the Wizard's girdle, are you?"

"Not so, Macumazahn; but I promised him not long ago that I would undertake no enterprise, save that you know of, until I had spoken with him."

"How far off does Zikali live?" I asked Saduko.

"One day's journeying. Starting at sunrise I can be there by sunset."

"Good! Then I will put off the shooting for three days and come with you if you think that this wonderful old dwarf will receive me."

"I believe that he will, Macumazahn, for this reason—he told me that I should meet you and love you, and that you would be mixed up in my fortunes."

"Then he poured moonshine into your gourd instead of beer," I answered. "Would you keep me here till midnight listening to such foolishness when we must start at dawn? Begone now and let me sleep."

"I go," he answered with a little smile. "But if this is so, O Macumazana, why do you also wish to drink of the moonshine of Zikali?" and he went.

Yet I did not sleep very well that night, for Saduko and his strange and terrible story had taken a hold of my imagination. Also, for reasons of my own, I greatly wished to see this Zikali, of whom I had heard a great deal in past years. I wished further to find out if he was a common humbug, like so many witch-doctors, this dwarf who announced that my fortunes were mixed up with those of his foster-son, and who at least could tell me something true or false about the history and position of Bangu, a person for whom I had conceived a strong dislike, possibly quite unjustified by the facts. But more than all did I wish to see Mameena, whose beauty or talents produced so much impression upon the native mind. Perhaps if I went to see Zikali she would be back at her father's kraal before we started on our shooting trip.

Thus it was then that fate wove me and my doings into the web of some very strange events; terrible, tragic and complete indeed as those of a Greek play, as it has often done both before and since those days.

The Moonshine of Zikali

On the following morning I awoke, as a good hunter always should do, just at that time when, on looking out of the wagon, nothing can be seen but a little grey glint of light which he knows is reflected from the horns of the cattle tied to the trek-tow. Presently, however, I saw another glint of light which I guessed came from the spear of Saduko, who was seated by the ashes of the cooking fire wrapped in his kaross of wildcatskins. Slipping from the voorkisse, or driving-box, I came behind him softly and touched him on the shoulder. He leapt up with a start which revealed his nervous nature, then recognising me through the soft grey gloom, said:

"You are early, Macumazahn."

"Of course," I answered; "am I not named Watcher-by-Night? Now let us go to Umbezi and tell him that I shall be ready to start on our hunting trip on the third morning from to-day."

So we went, to find that Umbezi was in a hut with his last wife and asleep. Fortunately enough, however, as under the circumstances I did not wish to disturb him, outside the hut we found the Old Cow, whose sore ear had kept her very wide awake, who, for purposes of her own, although etiquette did not allow her to enter the hut, was waiting for her husband to emerge.

Having examined her wound and rubbed some ointment on it, with her I left my message. Next I woke up my servant Scowl, and told him that I was going on a short journey, and that he must guard all things until my return; and while I did so, took a nip of raw rum and made ready a bag of biltong, that is sun-dried flesh, and biscuits.

Then, taking with me a single-barrelled gun, that same little Purdey rifle with which I shot the vultures on the Hill of Slaughter at Dingaan's Kraal, we started on foot, for I would not risk my only horse on such a journey.

A rough journey it proved to be indeed, over a series of bush-clad hills that at their crests were covered with rugged stones among which no horse could have travelled. Up and down these hills we went, and across the valleys that divided them, following some path which I could not see, for all that live-long day. I have always been held a good walker, being by nature very light and active; but I am bound to say that my companion taxed my powers to the utmost, for on he marched for hour after hour, striding ahead of me at such a rate that at times I was forced to break into a run to keep up with him. Although my pride would not suffer me to complain, since as a matter of principle I would never admit to a Kafir that he was my master at anything, glad enough was I when, towards evening, Saduko sat himself down on a stone at the top of a hill and said:

"Behold the Black Kloof, Macumazahn," which were almost the first words he had uttered since we started.

Truly the spot was well named, for there, cut out by water from the heart of a mountain in some primeval age, lay one of the most gloomy places that ever I had beheld. It was a vast cleft in which granite boulders were piled up fantastically, perched one upon another in great columns, and upon its sides grew dark trees set sparsely among the rocks. It faced towards the west, but the light of the sinking sun that flowed up it served only to accentuate its vast loneliness, for it was a big cleft, the best part of a mile wide at its mouth.

Up this dreary gorge we marched, mocked at by chattering baboons and following a little path not a foot wide that led us at length to a large hut and several smaller ones set within a reed fence and overhung by a gigantic mass of rock that looked as though it might fall at any moment. At the gate of the fence two natives of I know not what tribe, men of fierce and forbidding appearance, suddenly sprang out and thrust their spears towards my breast.

"Whom bring you here, Saduko?" asked one of them sternly.

"A white man that I vouch for," he answered. "Tell Zikali that we wait on him."

"What need to tell Zikali that which he knows already?" said the sentry. "Your food and that of your companion is already cooked in yonder hut. Enter, Saduko, with him for whom you vouch."

So we went into the hut and ate, also I washed myself, for it was a beautifully clean hut, and the stools, wooden bowls, etc., were finely carved out of red ivory wood, this work, Saduko informed me, being done by Zikali's own hand. just as we were finishing our meal a messenger came to tell us that Zikali waited our presence. We followed him across an open space to a kind of door in the tall reed fence, passing which I set eyes for the first time upon the famous old witch-doctor of whom so many tales were told.

Certainly he was a curious sight in those strange surroundings, for they were very strange, and I think their complete simplicity added to the effect. In front of us was a kind of courtyard with a black floor made of polished ant-heap earth and cow-dung, two-thirds of which at least was practically roofed in by the huge over-hanging mass of rock whereof I have spoken, its arch bending above at a height of not less than sixty or seventy feet from the ground. Into this great, precipice-backed cavity poured the fierce light of the setting sun, turning it and all within it, even the large straw hut in the background, to the deep hue of blood. Seeing the wonderful effect of the sunset in that dark and forbidding place, it occurred to me at once that the old wizard must have chosen this moment to receive us because of its impressiveness.

Then I forgot these scenic accessories in the sight of the man himself. There he sat on a stool in front of his hut, quite unattended, and wearing only a cloak of leopard skins open in front, for he was unadorned with the usual hideous trappings of a witch-doctor, such as snake-skins, human bones, bladders full of unholy compounds, and so forth.

What a man he was, if indeed he could be called quite human. His stature, though stout, was only that of a child; his head was enormous, and from it plaited white hair fell down on to his shoulders. His eyes were deep and sunken, his face was broad and very stern. Except for this snow-white hair, however, he did not look ancient, for his flesh was firm and plump, and the skin on his cheeks and neck unwrinkled, which suggested to me that the story of his great antiquity was false. A man who was over a hundred years old, for instance, surely could not boast such a beautiful set of teeth, for even at that distance I could see them gleaming. On the other hand, evidently middle age was far behind him; indeed, from his appearance it was quite impossible to guess even approximately the number of his years. There he sat, red in the red light, perfectly still, and staring without a blink of his eyes at the furious ball of the setting sun, as an eagle is said to be able to do.

Saduko advanced, and I walked after him. My stature is not great, and I have never considered myself an imposing person, but somehow I do not think that I ever felt more insignificant than on this occasion. The tall and splendid native beside, or rather behind whom I walked, the gloomy magnificence of the place, the blood-red light in which it was bathed, and the solemn, solitary, little figure with wisdom stamped upon its face before me, all tended to induce humility in a man not naturally vain. I felt myself growing smaller and smaller, both in a moral and a physical sense; I wished that my curiosity had not prompted me to seek an interview with yonder uncanny being.

Well, it was too late to retreat; indeed, Saduko was already standing before the dwarf and lifting his right arm above his head as he gave him the salute of "Makosi!" whereon, feeling that something was expected of me, I took off my shabby cloth hat and bowed, then, remembering my white man's pride, replaced it on my head.

The wizard suddenly seemed to become aware of our presence, for, ceasing his contemplation of the sinking sun, he scanned us both with his slow, thoughtful eyes, which somehow reminded me of those of a chameleon, although they were not prominent, but, as I have said, sunken.

"Greeting, son Saduko!" he said in a deep, rumbling voice. "Why are you back here so soon, and why do you bring this flea of a white man with you?"

Now this was more than I could bear, so without waiting for my companion's answer I broke in:

"You give me a poor name, O Zikali. What would you think of me if I called you a beetle of a wizard?"

"I should think you clever," he answered after reflection, "for after all I must look something like a beetle with a white head. But why should you mind being compared to a flea? A flea works by night and so do you, Macumazahn; a flea is active and so are you; a flea is very hard to catch and kill and so are you; and lastly a flea drinks its fill of that which it desires, the blood of man and beast, and so you have done, do, and will, Macumazahn," and he broke into a great laugh that rolled and echoed about the rocky roof above.

Once, long years before, I had heard that laugh, when I was a prisoner in Dingaan's kraal, after the massacre of Retief and his company, and I recognised it again.

While I was searching for some answer in the same vein, and not finding it, though I thought of plenty afterwards, ceasing of a sudden from his unseemly mirth, he went on:

"Do not let us waste time in jests, for it is a precious thing, and there is but little of it left for any one of us. Your business, son Saduko?"

"Baba!" (that is the Zulu for father), said Saduko, "this white Inkoosi, for, as you know well enough, he is a chief by nature, a man of a great heart and doubtless of high blood [this, I believe, is true, for I have been told that my ancestors were more or less distinguished, although, if this is so, their talents did not lie in the direction of money-making], has offered to take me upon a shooting expedition and to give me a good gun with two mouths in payment of my services. But I told him I could not engage in any fresh venture without your leave, and—he is come to see whether you will grant it, my father."

"Indeed," answered the dwarf, nodding his great head. "This clever white man has taken the trouble of a long walk in the sun to come here to ask me whether he may be allowed the privilege of presenting you with a weapon of great value in return for a service that any man of your years in Zululand would love to give for nothing in such company?

"Son Saduko, because my eye-holes are hollow, do you think it your part to try to fill them up with dust? Nay, the white man has come because he desires to see him who is named Opener-of-Roads, of whom he heard a great deal when he was but a lad, and to judge whether in truth he has wisdom, or is but a common cheat. And you have come to learn whether or no your friendship with him will be fortunate; whether or no he will aid you in a certain enterprise that you have in your mind."

"True, O Zikali," I said. "That is so far as I am concerned."

But Saduko answered nothing.

"Well," went on the dwarf, "since I am in the mood I will try to answer both your questions, for I should be a poor Nyanga" [that is doctor] "if I did not when you have travelled so far to ask them. Moreover, O Macumazana, be happy, for I seek no fee who, having made such fortune as I need long ago, before your father was born across the Black Water, Macumazahn, no longer work for a reward—unless it be from the hand of one of the House of Senzangakona—and therefore, as you may guess, work but seldom."

Then he clapped his hands, and a servant appeared from somewhere behind the hut, one of those fierce-looking men who had stopped us at the gate. He saluted the dwarf and stood before him in silence and with bowed head.

"Make two fires," said Zikali, "and give me my medicine."

The man fetched wood, which he built into two little piles in front of Zikali. These piles he fired with a brand brought from behind the hut. Then he handed his master a catskin bag.

"Withdraw," said Zikali, "and return no more till I summon you, for I am about to prophesy. If, however, I should seem to die, bury me to-morrow in the place you know of and give this white man a safe-conduct from my kraal."

The man saluted again and went without a word.

When he had gone the dwarf drew from the bag a bundle of twisted roots, also some pebbles, from which he selected two, one white and the other black.

"Into this stone," he said, holding up the white pebble so that the light from the fire shone on it—since, save for the lingering red glow, it was now growing dark—"into this stone I am about to draw your spirit, O Macumazana; and into this one"—and he held up the black pebble—"yours, O Son of Matiwane. Why do you look frightened, O brave White Man, who keep saying in your heart, 'He is nothing but an ugly old Kafir cheat'? If I am a cheat, why do you look frightened? Is your spirit already in your throat, and does it choke you, as this little stone might do if you tried to swallow it?" and he burst into one of his great, uncanny laughs.

I tried to protest that I was not in the least frightened, but failed, for, in fact, I suppose my nerves were acted on by his suggestion, and I did feel exactly as though that stone were in my throat, only coming upwards, not going downwards. "Hysteria," thought I to myself, "the result of being overtired," and as I could not speak, sat still as though I treated his gibes with silent contempt.

"Now," went on the dwarf, "perhaps I shall seem to die; and if so do not touch me lest you should really die. Wait till I wake up again and tell you what your spirits have told me. Or if I do not wake up—for a time must come when I shall go on sleeping—well—for as long as I have lived—after the fires are quite out, not before, lay your hands upon my breast; and if you find me turning cold, get you gone to some other Nyanga as fast as the spirits of this place will let you, O ye who would peep into the future."

As he spoke he threw a big handful of the roots that I have mentioned on to each of the fires, whereon tall flames leapt up from them, very unholy-looking flames which were followed by columns of dense, white smoke that emitted a most powerful and choking odour quite unlike anything that I had ever smelt before. It seemed to penetrate all through me, and that accursed stone in my throat grew as large as an apple and felt as though someone were poking it upwards with a stick.

Next he threw the white pebble into the right-hand fire, that which was opposite to me, saying:

"Enter, Macumazahn, and look," and the black pebble he threw into the left-hand fire saying: "Enter, Son of Matiwane, and look. Then come back both of you and make report to me, your master."

Now it is a fact that as he said these words I experienced a sensation as though a stone had come out of my throat; so readily do our nerves deceive us that I even thought it grated against my teeth as I opened my mouth to give it passage. At any rate the choking was gone, only now I felt as though I were quite empty and floating on air, as though I were not I, in short, but a mere shell of a thing, all of which doubtless was caused by the stench of those burning roots. Still I could look and take note, for I distinctly saw Zikali thrust his huge head, first into the smoke of what I will call my fire, next into that of Saduko's fire, and then lean back, blowing the stuff in clouds from his mouth and nostrils. Afterwards I saw him roll over on to his side and lie quite still with his arms outstretched; indeed, I noticed that one of his fingers seemed to be in the left-hand fire and reflected that it would be burnt off. In this, however, I must have been mistaken, since I observed subsequently that it was not even scorched.

Thus Zikali lay for a long while till I began to wonder whether he were not really dead. Dead enough he seemed to be, for no corpse could have stayed more stirless. But that night I could not keep my thoughts fixed on Zikali or anything. I merely noted these circumstances in a mechanical way, as might one with whom they had nothing whatsoever to do. They did not interest me at all, for there appeared to be nothing in me to be interested, as I gathered according to Zikali, because I was not there, but in a warmer place than I hope ever to occupy, namely, in the stone in that unpleasant-looking, little right-hand fire.

So matters went as they might in a dream. The sun had sunk completely, not even an after-glow was left. The only light remaining was that from the smouldering fires, which just sufficed to illumine the bulk of Zikali, lying on his side, his squat shape looking like that of a dead hippopotamus calf. What was left of my consciousness grew heartily sick of the whole affair; I was tired of being so empty.

At length the dwarf stirred. He sat up, yawned, sneezed, shook himself, and began to rake among the burning embers of my fire with his naked hand. Presently he found the white stone, which was now red-hot—at any rate it glowed as though it were—and after examining it for a moment finally popped it into his mouth! Then he hunted in the other fire for the black stone, which he treated in a similar fashion. The next thing I remember was that the fires, which had died away almost to nothing, were burning very brightly again, I suppose because someone had put fuel on them, and Zikali was speaking.

"Come here, O Macumazana and O Son of Matiwane," he said, "and I will repeat to you what your spirits have been telling me."

We drew near into the light of the fires, which for some reason or other was extremely vivid. Then he spat the white stone from his mouth into his big hand, and I saw that now it was covered with lines and patches like a bird's egg.

"You cannot read the signs?" he said, holding it towards me; and when I shook my head went on: "Well, I can, as you white men read a book. All your history is written here, Macumazahn; but there is no need to tell you that, since you know it, as I do well enough, having learned it in other days, the days of Dingaan, Macumazahn. All your future, also, a very strange future," and he scanned the stone with interest. "Yes, yes; a wonderful life, and a noble death far away. But of these matters you have not asked me, and therefore I may not tell them even if I wished, nor would you believe if I did. It is of your hunting trip that you have asked me, and my answer is that if you seek your own comfort you will do well not to go. A pool in a dry river-bed; a buffalo bull with the tip of one horn shattered. Yourself and the bull in the pool. Saduko, yonder, also in the pool, and a little half-bred man with a gun jumping about upon the bank. Then a litter made of boughs and you in it, and the father of Mameena walking lamely at your side. Then a hut and you in it, and the maiden called Mameena sitting at your side.

"Macumazahn, your spirit has written on this stone that you should beware of Mameena, since she is more dangerous than any buffalo. If you are wise you will not go out hunting with Umbezi, although it is true that hunt will not cost you your life. There, away, Stone, and take your writings with you!" and as he spoke he jerked his arm and I heard something whiz past my face.

Next he spat out the black stone and examined it in similar fashion.

"Your expedition will be successful, Son of Matiwane," he said. "Together with Macumazahn you will win many cattle at the cost of sundry lives. But for the rest—well, you did not ask me of it, did you? Also, I have told you something of that story before to-day. Away, Stone!" and the black pebble followed the white out into the surrounding gloom.

We sat quite still until the dwarf broke the deep silence with one of his great laughs.

"My witchcraft is done," he said. "A poor tale, was it not? Well, hunt for those stones to-morrow and read the rest of it if you can. Why did you not ask me to tell you everything while I was about it, White Man? It would have interested you more, but now it has all gone from me back into your spirit with the stones. Saduko, get you to sleep. Macumazahn, you who are a Watcher-by-Night, come and sit with me awhile in my hut, and we will talk of other things. All this business of the stones is nothing more than a Kafir trick, is it, Macumazahn? When you meet the buffalo with the split horn in the pool of a dried river, remember it is but a cheating trick, and now come into my hut and drink a kamba [bowl] of beer and let us talk of other things more interesting."

So he took me into the hut, which was a fine one, very well lighted by a fire in its centre, and gave me Kafir beer to drink, that I swallowed gratefully, for my throat was dry and still felt as though it had been scraped.

"Who are you, Father?" I asked point-blank when I had taken my seat upon a low stool, with my back resting against the wall of the hut, and lit my pipe.

He lifted his big head from the pile of karosses on which he was lying and peered at me across the fire.

"My name is Zikali, which means 'Weapons,' White Man. You know as much as that, don't you?" he answered. "My father 'went down' so long ago that his does not matter. I am a dwarf, very ugly, with some learning, as we of the Black House understand it, and very old. Is there anything else you would like to learn?"

"Yes, Zikali; how old?"

"There, there, Macumazahn, as you know, we poor Kafirs cannot count very well. How old? Well, when I was young I came down towards the coast from the Great River, you call it the Zambesi, I think, with Undwandwe, who lived in the north in those days. They have forgotten it now because it is some time ago, and if I could write I would set down the history of that march, for we fought some great battles with the people who used to live in this country. Afterwards I was the friend of the Father of the Zulus, he whom they still call Inkoosi Umkulu—the mighty chief—you may have heard tell of him. I carved that stool on which you sit for him and he left it back to me when he died."

"Inkoosi Umkulu!" I exclaimed. "Why, they say he lived hundreds of years ago."

"Do they, Macumazahn? If so, have I not told you that we black people cannot count as well as you do? Really it was only the other day. Anyhow, after his death the Zulus began to maltreat us Undwandwe and the Quabies and the Tetwas with us—you may remember that they called us the Amatefula, making a mock of us. So I quarrelled with the Zulus and especially with Chaka, he whom they named 'Uhlanya' [the Mad One]. You see, Macumazahn, it pleased him to laugh at me because I am not as other men are. He gave me a name which means 'The-thing-which-should-never-have-been-born.' I will not speak that name, it is secret to me, it may not pass my lips. Yet at times he sought my wisdom, and I paid him back for his names, for I gave him very ill counsel, and he took it, and I brought him to his death, although none ever saw my finger in that business. But when he was dead at the hands of his brothers Dingaan and Umhlangana and of Umbopa, Umbopa who also had a score to settle with him, and his body was cast out of the kraal like that of an evil-doer, why I, who because I was a dwarf was not sent with the *men* against Sotshangana, went and sat on it at night and laughed thus," and he broke into one of his hideous peals of merriment.

"I laughed thrice: once for my wives whom he had taken; once for my children whom he had slain; and once for the mocking name that he had given me. Then I became the counsellor of Dingaan, whom I hated worse than I had hated Chaka, for he was Chaka again without his greatness, and you know the end of Dingaan, for you had a share in that war, and of Umhlangana, his brother and fellow-murderer, whom I counselled Dingaan to slay. This I did through the lips of the old Princess Menkabayi, Jama's daughter, Senzangakona's sister, the Oracle before whom all men bowed, causing her to say that 'This land of the Zulus cannot be ruled by a crimson assegai.' For, Macumazahn, it was Umhlangana who first struck Chaka with the spear. Now Panda reigns, the last of the sons of Senzangakona, my enemy, Panda the Fool, and I hold my hand from Panda because he tried to save the life of a child of mine whom Chaka slew. But Panda has sons who are as Chaka was, and against them I work as I worked against those who went before them."

"Why?" I asked.

"Why? Oh! if I were to tell you *all* my story you would understand why, Macumazahn. Well, perhaps I will one day." (Here I may state that as a matter of fact he did, and a very wonderful tale it is, but as it has nothing to do with this history I will not write it here.)

"I dare say," I answered. "Chaka and Dingaan and Umhlangana and the others were not nice people. But another question. Why do you tell me all this, O Zikali, seeing that were I but to repeat it to a talking-bird you would be smelt out and a single moon would not die before you do?"

"Oh! I should be smelt out and killed before one moon dies, should I? Then I wonder that this has not happened during all the moons that are gone. Well, I tell the story to you, Macumazahn, who have had so much to do with the tale of the Zulus since the days of Dingaan, because I wish that someone should know it and perhaps write it down when everything is finished. Because, too, I have just been reading your spirit and see that it is still a white spirit, and that you will not whisper it to a 'talking-bird.'"

Now I leant forward and looked at him.

"What is the end at which you aim, O Zikali?" I asked. "You are not one who beats the air with a stick; on whom do you wish the stick to fall at last?"

"On whom?" he answered in a new voice, a low, hissing voice. "Why, on these proud Zulus, this little family of men who call themselves the 'People of Heaven,' and swallow other tribes as the great tree-snake swallows kids and small bucks, and when it is fat with them cries to the world, 'See how big I am! Everything is inside of me.' I am a Ndwande, one of those peoples whom it pleases the Zulus to call 'Amatefula'—poor hangers-on who talk with an accent, nothing but bush swine. Therefore I would see the swine tusk the hunter. Or, if that may not be, I would see the black hunter laid low by the rhinoceros, the white rhinoceros of your race, Macumazahn, yes, even if it sets its foot upon the Ndwande boar as well. There, I have told you, and this is the reason that I live so long, for I will not die until these things have come to pass, as come to pass they will. What did Chaka, Senzangakona's son, say when the little red assegai, the assegai with which he slew his mother, aye and others, some of whom were near to me, was in his liver? What did he say to Mbopa and the princes? Did he not say that he heard the feet of a great white people running, of a people who should stamp the Zulus flat? Well, I, 'The-thing-who-should-not-have-been-born,' live on until that day comes, and when it comes I think that you and I, Macumazahn, shall not be far apart, and that is why I have opened out my heart to you, I who have knowledge of the future. There, I speak no more of these things that are to be, who perchance have already said too much of them. Yet do not forget my words. Or forget them if you will, for I shall remind you of them, Macumazahn, when the feet of your people have avenged the Ndwandes and others whom it pleases the Zulus to treat as dirt."

Now, this strange man, who had sat up in his excitement, shook his long white hair which, after the fashion of wizards, be wore plaited into thin ropes, till it hung like a veil about him, hiding his broad face and deep eyes. Presently he spoke again through this veil of hair, saying:

"You are wondering, Macumazahn, what Saduko has to do with all these great events that are to be. I answer that he must play his part in them; not a very great part, but still a part, and it is for this purpose that I saved him as a child from Bangu, Dingaan's man, and reared him up to be a warrior, although, since I cannot lie, I warned him that he would do well to leave spears alone and follow after wisdom. Well, he will slay Bangu, who now has quarrelled with Panda, and a woman will come into the story, one Mameena, and that woman will bring about war between the sons of Panda, and from this war shall spring the ruin of the Zulus, for he who wins will be an evil king to them and bring down on them the wrath of a mightier race. And so 'The-thing-that-should-not-have-been-born' and the Ndwandes and the Quabies and Twetwas, whom it has pleased the conquering Zulus to name 'Amatefula,' shall be avenged. Yes, yes, my Spirit tells me all these things, and they are true."

"And what of Saduko, my friend and your fosterling?"

"Saduko, your friend and my fosterling, will take his appointed road, Macumazahn, as I shall and you will. What more could he desire, seeing it is that which he has chosen? He will take his road and he will play the part which the Great-Great has prepared for him. Seek not to know more. Why should you, since Time will tell you the story? And now go to rest, Macumazahn, as I must who am old and feeble. And when it pleases you to visit me again, we will talk further. Meanwhile, remember always that I am nothing but an old Kafir cheat who pretends to a knowledge that belongs to no man. Remember it especially, Macumazahn, when you meet a buffalo with a split horn in the pool of a dried-up river, and afterwards, when a woman named Mameena makes a certain offer to you, which you may be tempted to accept. Good night to you, Watcher-by-Night with the white heart and the strange destiny, good night to you, and try not to think too hardly of the old Kafir cheat who just now is called 'Opener-of-Roads.' My servant waits without to lead you to your hut, and if you wish to be back at Umbezi's kraal by nightfall to-morrow, you will do well to start ere sunrise, since, as you found in coming, Saduko, although he may be a fool, is a very good walker, and you do not like to be left behind, Macumazahn, do you?"

So I rose to go, but as I went some impulse seemed to take him and he called me back and made me sit down again.

"Macumazahn," he said, "I would add a word. When you were quite a lad you came into this country with Retief, did you not?"

"Yes," I answered slowly, for this matter of the massacre of Retief is one of which I have seldom cared to speak, for sundry reasons, although I have made a record of it in writing. Even my friends Sir Henry Curtis and Captain Good have heard little of the part I played in that tragedy. "But what do you know of that business, Zikali?"

"All that there is to know, I think, Macumazahn, seeing that I was at the bottom of it, and that Dingaan killed those Boers on my advice—just as he killed Chaka and Umhlangana."

"You cold-blooded old murderer—" I began, but he interrupted me at once.

"Why do you throw evil names at me, Macumazahn, as I threw the stone of your fate at you just now? Why am I a murderer because I brought about the death of some white men that chanced to be your friends, who had come here to cheat us black folk of our country?"

"Was it for *this* reason that you brought about their deaths, Zikali?" I asked, staring him in the face, for I felt that he was lying to me.

"Not altogether, Macumazahn," he answered, letting his eyes, those strange eyes that could look at the sun without blinking, fall before my gaze. "Have I not told you that I hate the House of Senzangakona? And when Retief and his companions were killed, did not the spilling of their blood mean war to the end between the Zulus and the White Men? Did it not mean the death of Dingaan and of thousands of his people, which is but a beginning of deaths? Now do you understand?"

"I understand that you are a very wicked man," I answered with indignation.

"At least *you* should not say so, Macumazahn," he replied in a new voice, one with the ring of truth in it.

"Why not?"

"Because I saved your life on that day. You escaped alone of the White Men, did you not? And you never could understand why, could you?"

"No, I could not, Zikali. I put it down to what you would call 'the spirits.'"

"Well, I will tell you. Those spirits of yours wore my kaross," and he laughed. "I saw you with the Boers, and saw, too, that you were of another people—the people of the English. You may have heard at the time that I was doctoring at the Great Place, although I kept out of the way and we did not meet, or at least you never knew that we met, for you were—asleep. Also I pitied your youth, for, although you do not believe it, I had a little bit of heart left in those days. Also I knew that we should come together again in the after years, as you see we have done to-day and shall often do until the end. So I told Dingaan that whoever died you must be spared, or he would bring up the 'people of George' [i.e. the English] to avenge you, and your ghost would enter into him and pour out a curse upon him. He believed me who did not understand that already so many curses were gathered about his head that one more or less made no matter. So you see you were spared, Macumazahn, and afterwards you helped to pour out a curse upon Dingaan without becoming a ghost, which is the reason why Panda likes you so well to-day, Panda, the enemy of Dingaan, his brother. You remember the woman who helped you? Well, I made her do so. How did it go with you afterwards, Macumazahn, with you and the Boer maiden across the Buffalo River, to whom you were making love in those days?"

"Never mind how it went," I replied, springing up, for the old wizard's talk had stirred sad and bitter memories in my heart. "That time is dead, Zikali."

"Is it, Macumazahn? Now, from the look upon your face I should have said that it was still very much alive, as things that happened in our youth have a way of keeping alive. But doubtless I am mistaken, and it is all as dead as Dingaan, and as Retief, and as the others, your companions. At least, although you do not believe it, I saved your life on that red day, for my own purposes, of course, not because one white life was anything among so many in my count. And now go to rest, Macumazahn, go to rest, for although your heart has been awakened by memories this evening, I promise that you shall sleep well to-night," and throwing the long hair back off his eyes he looked at me keenly, wagging his big head to and fro, and burst into another of his great laughs.

So I went. But, ah! as I went I wept.

Anyone who knew all that story would understand why. But this is not the place to tell it, that tale of my first love and of the terrible events which befell us in the time of Dingaan. Still, as I say, I have written it down, and perhaps one day it will be read.

The Buffalo with the Cleft Horn

I slept very well that night, I suppose because I was so dog-tired I could not help it; but next day, on our long walk back to Umbezi's kraal, I thought a great deal.

Without doubt I had seen and heard very strange things, both of the past and the present—things that I could not in the least understand. Moreover, they were mixed up with all sorts of questions of high Zulu policy, and threw a new light upon events that happened to me and others in my youth.

Now, in the clear sunlight, was the time to analyse these things, and this I did in the most logical fashion I could command, although without the slightest assistance from Saduko, who, when I asked him questions, merely shrugged his shoulders.

These questions, he said, did not interest him; I had wished to see the magic of Zikali, and Zikali had been pleased to show me some very good magic, quite of his best indeed. Also he had conversed alone with me afterwards, doubtless on high matters—so high that he, Saduko, was not admitted to share the conversation—which was an honour he accorded to very few. I could form my own conclusions in the light of the White Man's wisdom, which everyone knew was great.

I replied shortly that I could, for Saduko's tone irritated me. Of course, the truth was that he felt aggrieved at being sent off to bed like a little boy while his foster-father, the old dwarf, made confidences to me. One of Saduko's faults was that he had always a very good opinion of himself. Also he was by nature terribly jealous, even in little things, as the readers of his history, if any, will learn.

We trudged on for several hours in silence, broken at length by my companion.

"Do you still mean to go on a shooting expedition with Umbezi, Inkoosi?" he asked, "or are you afraid?"

"Of what should I be afraid?" I answered tartly.

"Of the buffalo with the split horn, of which Zikali told you. What else?"

Now, I fear I used strong language about the buffalo with the split horn, a beast in which I declared I had no belief whatsoever, either with or without its accessories of dried river-beds and water-holes.

"If all this old woman's talk has made *you* afraid, however," I added, "you can stop at the kraal with Mameena."

"Why should the talk make me afraid, Macumazahn? Zikali did not say that this evil spirit of a buffalo would hurt *me*. If I fear, it is for you, seeing that if you are hurt you may not be able to go with me to look for Bangu's cattle."

"Oh!" I replied sarcastically; "it seems that you are somewhat selfish, friend Saduko, since it is of your welfare and not of my safety that you are thinking."

"If I were as selfish as you seem to believe, Inkoosi, should I advise you to stop with your wagons, and thereby lose the good gun with two mouths that you have promised me? Still, it is true that I should like well enough to stay at Umbezi's kraal with Mameena, especially if Umbezi were away."

Now, as there is nothing more uninteresting than to listen to other people's love affairs, and as I saw that with the slightest encouragement Saduko was ready to tell me all the history of his courtship over again, I did not continue the argument. So we finished our journey in silence, and arrived at Umbezi's kraal a little after sundown, to find, to the disappointment of both of us, that Mameena was still away.

Upon the following morning we started on our shooting expedition, the party consisting of myself, my servant Scowl, who, as I think I said, hailed from the Cape and was half a Hottentot; Saduko; the merry old Zulu, Umbezi, and a number of his men to serve as bearers and beaters. It proved a very successful trip—that is, until the end of it—for in those days the game in this part of the country was extremely plentiful. Before the end of the second week I killed four elephants, two of them with large tusks, while Saduko, who soon developed into a very fair shot, bagged another with the double-barrelled gun that I had promised him. Also, Umbezi—how, I have never discovered, for the thing partook of the nature of a miracle—managed to slay an elephant cow with fair ivories, using the old rifle that went off at half-cock.

Never have I seen a man, black or white, so delighted as was that vainglorious Kafir. For whole hours he danced and sang and took snuff and saluted with his hand, telling me the story of his deed over and over again, no single version of which tale agreed with the other. He took a new title also, that meant "Eater-up-of-Elephants"; he allowed one of his men to "bonga"—that is, praise—him all through the night, preventing us from getting a wink of sleep, until at last the poor fellow dropped in a kind of fit from exhaustion, and so forth. It really was very amusing until it became a bore.

Besides the elephants we killed lots of other things, including two lions, which I got almost with a right and left, and three white rhinoceroses, that now, alas! are nearly extinct. At last, towards the end of the third week, we had as much as our men could carry in the shape of ivory, rhinoceros horns, skins and sun-dried buckflesh, or biltong, and determined to start back for Umbezi's kraal next day. Indeed, this could not be long delayed, as our powder and lead were running low; for in those days, it will be remembered, breechloaders had not come in, and ammunition, therefore, had to be carried in bulk.

To tell the truth, I was very glad that our trip had come to such a satisfactory conclusion, for, although I would not admit it even to myself, I could not get rid of a kind of sneaking dread lest after all there might be something in the old dwarf's prophecy about a disagreeable adventure with a buffalo which was in store for me. Well, as it chanced, we had not so much as seen a buffalo, and as the road which we were going to take back to the kraal ran over high, bare country that these animals did not frequent, there was now little prospect of our doing so—all of which, of course, showed what I already knew, that only weak-headed superstitious idiots would put the slightest faith in the drivelling nonsense of deceiving or self-deceived Kafir medicine-men. These things, indeed, I pointed out with much vigour to Saduko before we turned in on the last night of the hunt.

Saduko listened in silence and said nothing at all, except that he would not keep me up any longer, as I must be tired.

Now, whatever may be the reason for it, my experience in life is that it is never wise to brag about anything. At any rate, on a hunting trip, to come to a particular instance, wait until you are safe at home till you begin to do so. Of the truth of this ancient adage I was now destined to experience a particularly fine and concrete example.

The place where we had camped was in scattered bush overlooking a great extent of dry reeds, that in the wet season was doubtless a swamp fed by a small river which ran into it on the side opposite to our camp. During the night I woke up, thinking that I heard some big beasts moving in these reeds; but as no further sounds reached my ears I went to sleep again.

Shortly after dawn I was awakened by a voice calling me, which in a hazy fashion I recognised as that of Umbezi.

"Macumazahn," said the voice in a hoarse whisper, "the reeds below us are full of buffalo. Get up. Get up at once."

"What for?" I answered. "If the buffalo came into the reeds they will go out of them. We do not want meat."

"No, Macumazahn; but I want their hides. Panda, the King, has demanded fifty shields of me, and without killing oxen that I can ill spare I have not the skins whereof to make them. Now, these buffalo are in a trap. This swamp is like a dish with one mouth. They cannot get out at the sides of the dish, and the mouth by which they came in is very narrow. If we station ourselves at either side of it we can kill many of them."

By this time I was thoroughly awake and had arisen from my blankets. Throwing a kaross over my shoulders, I left the hut, made of boughs, in which I was sleeping and walked a few paces to the crest of a rocky ridge, whence I could see the dry vlei below. Here the mists of dawn still clung, but from it rose sounds of grunts, bellows and tramplings which I, an old hunter, could not mistake. Evidently a herd of buffalo, one or two hundred of them, had established themselves in those reeds.

Just then my bastard servant, Scowl, and Saduko joined us, both of them full of excitement.

It appeared that Scowl, who never seemed to sleep at any natural time, had seen the buffalo entering the reeds, and estimated their number at two or three hundred. Saduko had examined the cleft through which they passed, and reported it to be so narrow that we could kill any number of them as they rushed out to escape.

"Quite so. I understand," I said. "Well, my opinion is that we had better let them escape. Only four of us, counting Umbezi, are armed with guns, and assegais are not of much use against buffalo. Let them go, I say."

Umbezi, thinking of a cheap raw material for the shields which had been requisitioned by the King, who would surely be pleased if they were made of such a rare and tough hide as that of buffalo, protested violently, and Saduko, either to please one whom he hoped might be his father-in-law or from sheer love of sport, for which he always had a positive passion, backed him up. Only Scowl—whose dash of Hottentot blood made him cunning and cautious—took my side, pointing out that we were very short of powder and that buffalo "ate up much lead." At last Saduko said:

"The lord Macumazana is our captain; we must obey him, although it is a pity. But doubtless the prophesying of Zikali weighs upon his mind, so there is nothing to be done."

"Zikali!" exclaimed Umbezi. "What has the old dwarf to do with this matter?"

"Never mind what he has or has not to do with it," I broke in, for although I do not think that he meant them as a taunt, but merely as a statement of fact, Saduko's words stung me to the quick, especially as my conscience told me that they were not altogether without foundation.

"We will try to kill some of these buffalo," I went on, "although, unless the herd should get bogged, which is not likely, as the swamp is very dry, I do not think that we can hope for more than eight or ten at the most, which won't be of much use for shields. Come, let us make a plan. We have no time to lose, for I think they will begin to move again before the sun is well up."

Half an hour later the four of us who were armed with guns were posted behind rocks on either side of the steep, natural roadway cut by water, which led down to the vlei, and with us some of Umbezi's men. That chief himself was at my side—a post of honour which he had insisted upon taking. To tell the truth, I did not dissuade him, for I thought that I should be safer so than if he were opposite to me, since, even if the old rifle did not go off of its own accord, Umbezi, when excited, was a most uncertain shot. The herd of buffalo appeared to have lain down in the reeds, so, being careful to post ourselves first, we sent three of the native bearers to the farther side of the vlei, with instructions to rouse the beasts by shouting. The remainder of the Zulus—there were ten or a dozen of them armed with stabbing spears—we kept with us.

But what did these scoundrels do? Instead of disturbing the herd by making a noise, as we told them, for some reason best known to themselves—I expect it was because they were afraid to go into the vlei, where they might meet the horn of a buffalo at any moment—they fired the dry reeds in three or four places at once, and this, if you please, with a strong wind blowing from them to us. In a minute or two the farther side of the swamp was a sheet of crackling flame that gave off clouds of dense white smoke. Then pandemonium began.

The sleeping buffalo leapt to their feet, and, after a few moments of indecision, crashed towards us, the whole huge herd of them, snorting and bellowing like mad things. Seeing what was about to happen, I nipped behind a big boulder, while Scowl shinned up a mimosa with the swiftness of a cat and, heedless of its thorns, sat himself in an eagle's nest at the top. The Zulus with the spears bolted to take cover where they could. What became of Saduko I did not see, but old Umbezi, bewildered with excitement, jumped into the exact middle of the roadway, shouting:

"They come! They come! Charge, buffalo folk, if you will. The Eater-up-of-Elephants awaits you!"

"You etceterad old fool!" I shouted, but got no farther, for just at this moment the first of the buffalo, which I could see was an enormous bull, probably the leader of the herd, accepted Umbezi's invitation and came, with its nose stuck straight out in front of it. Umbezi's gun went off, and next instant he went up. Through the smoke I saw his black bulk in the air, and then heard it alight with a thud on the top of the rock behind which I was crouching.

"Exit Umbezi," I said to myself, and by way of a requiem let the bull which had hoisted him, as I thought to heaven, have an ounce of lead in the ribs as it passed me. After that I did not fire any more, for it occurred to me that it was as well not to further advertise my presence.

In all my hunting experience I cannot remember ever seeing such a sight as that which followed. Out of the vlei rushed the buffalo by dozens, every one of them making remarks in its own language as it came. They jammed in the narrow roadway, they leapt on to each other's backs. They squealed, they kicked, they bellowed. They charged my friendly rock till I felt it shake. They knocked over Scowl's mimosa thorn, and would have shot him out of his eagle's nest had not its flat top fortunately caught in that of another and less accessible tree. And with them came clouds of pungent smoke, mixed with bits of burning reed and puffs of hot air.

It was over at last. With the exception of some calves, which had been trampled to death in the rush, the herd had gone. Now, like the Roman emperor—I think he was an emperor—I began to wonder what had become of my legions.

"Umbezi," I shouted, or, rather, sneezed through the smoke, "are you dead, Umbezi? "

"Yes, yes, Macumazahn," replied a choking and melancholy voice from the top of the rock, "I am dead, quite dead. That evil spirit of a silwana [i.e. wild beast] has killed me. Oh! why did I think I was a hunter; why did I not stop at my kraal and count my cattle?"

"I am sure I don't know, you old lunatic," I answered, as I scrambled up the rock to bid him good-bye.

It was a rock with a razor top like the ridge of a house, and there, hanging across this ridge like a pair of nether garments on a clothes-line, I found the "Eater-up-of-Elephants."

"Where did he get you, Umbezi?" I asked, for I could not see his wounds because of the smoke.

"Behind, Macumazahn, behind!" he groaned, "for I had turned to fly, but, alas! too late."

"On the contrary," I replied, "for one so heavy you flew very well; like a bird, Umbezi, like a bird."

"Look and see what the evil beast has done to me, Macumazahn. It will be easy, for my moocha has gone."

So I looked, examining Umbezi's ample proportions with care, but could discover nothing except a large smudge of black mud, as though he had sat down in a half-dried puddle. Then I guessed the truth. The buffalo's horns had missed him. He had been struck only with its muddy nose, which, being almost as broad as that portion of Umbezi with which it came in contact, had inflicted nothing worse than a bruise. When I was sure he had received no serious injury, my temper, already sorely tried, gave out, and I administered to him the soundest smacking—his position being very convenient—that he had ever received since he was a little boy.

"Get up, you idiot!" I shouted, "and let us look for the others. This is the end of your folly in making me attack a herd of buffalo in reeds. Get up. Am I to stop here till I choke?"

"Do you mean to tell me that I have no mortal wound, Macumazahn?" he asked, with a return of cheerfulness, accepting the castigation in good part, for he was not one who bore malice. "Oh, I am glad to hear it, for now I shall live to make those cowards who fired the reeds sorry that they are not dead; also to finish off that wild beast, for I hit him, Macumazahn, I hit him."

"I don't know whether you hit him; I know he hit you," I replied, as I shoved him off the rock and ran towards the tilted tree where I had last seen Scowl.

Here I beheld another strange sight. Scowl was still seated in the eagle's nest that he shared with two nearly fledged young birds, one of which, having been injured, was uttering piteous cries. Nor did it cry in vain, for its parents, which were of that great variety of kite that the Boers call "lammefange", or lamb-lifters, had just arrived to its assistance, and were giving their new nestling, Scowl, the best doing that man ever received at the beak and claws of feathered kind. Seen through those rushing smoke wreaths, the combat looked perfectly titanic; also it was one of the noisiest to which I ever listened, for I don't know which shrieked the more loudly, the infuriated eagles or their victim.

Seeing how things stood, I burst into a roar of laughter, and just then Scowl grabbed the leg of the male bird, that was planted in his breast while it removed tufts of his wool with its hooked beak, and leapt boldly from the nest, which had become too hot to hold him. The eagle's outspread wings broke his fall, for they acted as a parachute; and so did Umbezi, upon whom he chanced to land. Springing from the prostrate shape of the chief, who now had a bruise in front to match that behind, Scowl, covered with pecks and scratches, ran like a lamp-lighter, leaving me to collect my second gun, which he had dropped at the bottom of the tree, but fortunately without injuring it. The Kafirs gave him another name after that encounter, which meant "He-who-fights-birds-and-gets-the-worst-of-it."

Well, we escaped from the line of the smoke, a dishevelled trio—indeed, Umbezi had nothing left on him except his head ring—and shouted for the others, if perchance they had not been trodden to death in the rush. The first to arrive was Saduko, who looked quite calm and untroubled, but stared at us in astonishment, and asked coolly what we had been doing to get in such a state. I replied in appropriate language, and asked in turn how he had managed to remain so nicely dressed.

He did not answer, but I believe the truth was that he had crept into a large ant-bear's hole—small blame to him, to be frank. Then the remainder of our party turned up one by one, some of them looking very blown, as though they had run a long way. None were missing, except those who had fired the reeds, and they thought it well to keep clear for a good many hours. I believe that afterwards they regretted not having taken a longer leave of absence; but when they finally did arrive I was in no condition to note what passed between them and their outraged chief.

Being collected, the question arose what we should do. Of course, I wished to return to camp and get out of this ill-omened place as soon as possible. But I had reckoned without the vanity of Umbezi. Umbezi stretched over the edge of a sharp rock, whither he had been hoisted by the nose of a buffalo, and imagining himself to be mortally wounded, was one thing; but Umbezi in a borrowed moocha, although, because of his bruises, he supported his person with one hand in front and with the other behind, knowing his injuries to be purely superficial, was quite another.

"I am a hunter," he said; "I am named 'Eater-up-of-Elephants';" and he rolled his eyes, looking about for someone to contradict him, which nobody did. Indeed, his "praiser," a thin, tired-looking person, whose voice was worn out with his previous exertions, repeated in a feeble way:

"Yes, Black One, 'Eater-up-of-Elephants' is your name; 'Lifted-up-by-Buffalo' is your name."

"Be silent, idiot," roared Umbezi. "As I said, I am a hunter; I have wounded the wild beast that subsequently dared to assault me. [As a matter of fact, it was I, Allan Quatermain, who had wounded it.] I would make it bite the dust, for it cannot be far away. Let us follow it."

He glared round him, whereon his obsequious people, or one of them, echoed:

"Yes, by all means let us follow it, 'Eater-up-of-Elephants.' Macumazahn, the clever white man, will show us how, for where is the buffalo that he fears!"

Of course, after this there was nothing else to be done, so, having summoned the scratched Scowl, who seemed to have no heart in the business, we started on the spoor of the herd, which was as easy to track as a wagon road.

"Never mind, Baas," said Scowl, "they are two hours' march off by now."

"I hope so," I answered; but, as it happened, luck was against me, for before we had covered half a mile some over-zealous fellow struck a blood spoor.

I marched on that spoor for twenty minutes or so, till we came to a patch of bush that sloped downwards to a river-bed. Right to this river I followed it, till I reached the edge of a big pool that was still full of water, although the river itself had gone dry. Here I stood looking at the spoor and consulting with Saduko as to whether the beast could have swum the pool, for the tracks that went to its very verge had become confused and uncertain. Suddenly our doubts were ended, since out of a patch of dense bush which we had passed—for it had played the common trick of doubling back on its own spoor—appeared the buffalo, a huge bull, that halted on three legs, my bullet having broken one of its thighs. As to its identity there was no doubt, since on, or rather from, its right horn, which was cleft apart at the top, hung the remains of Umbezi's moocha.

"Oh, beware, Inkoosi," cried Saduko in a frightened voice. *"It is the buffalo with the cleft horn!"*

I heard him; I saw. All the scene in the hut of Zikali rose before me—the old dwarf, his words, everything. I lifted my rifle and fired at the charging beast, but knew that the bullet glanced from its skull. I threw down the gun—for the buffalo was right on me—and tried to jump aside.

Almost I did so, but that cleft horn, to which hung the remains of Umbezi's moocha, scooped me up and hurled me off the river bank backwards and sideways into the deep pool below. As I departed thither I saw Saduko spring forward and heard a shot fired that caused the bull to collapse for a moment. Then with a slow, sliding motion it followed me into the pool.

Now we were together, and there was no room for both, so after a certain amount of dodging I went under, as the lighter dog always does in a fight. That buffalo seemed to do everything to me which a buffalo could do under the circumstances. It tried to horn me, and partially succeeded, although I ducked at each swoop. Then it struck me with its nose and drove me to the bottom of the pool, although I got hold of its lip and twisted it. Then it calmly knelt on me and sank me deeper and deeper into the mud. I remember kicking it in the stomach. After this I remember no more, except a kind of wild dream in which I rehearsed all the scene in the dwarf's hut, and his request that when I met the buffalo with the cleft horn in the pool of a dried river, I should remember that he was nothing but a "poor old Kafir cheat."

After this I saw my mother bending over a little child in my bed in the old house in Oxfordshire where I was born, and then—blackness!

I came to myself again and saw, instead of my mother, the stately figure of Saduko bending over me upon one side, and on the other that of Scowl, the half-bred Hottentot, who was weeping, for his hot tears fell upon my face.

"He is gone," said poor Scowl; "that bewitched beast with the split horn has killed him. He is gone who was the best white man in all South Africa, whom I loved better than my father and all my relatives."

"That you might easily do, Bastard," answered Saduko, "seeing that you do not know who they are. But he is not gone, for the 'Opener-of-Roads' said that he would live; also I got my spear into the heart of that buffalo before he had kneaded the life out of him, as fortunately the mud was soft. Yet I fear that his ribs are broken"; and he poked me with his finger on the breast.

"Take your clumsy hand off me," I gasped.

"There!" said Saduko, "I have made him feel. Did I not tell you that he would live?"

After this I remember little more, except some confused dreams, till I found myself lying in a great hut, which I discovered subsequently was Umbezi's own, the same, indeed, wherein I had doctored the ear of that wife of his who was called "Worn-out-old-Cow."

Mameena

For a while I contemplated the roof and sides of the hut by the light which entered it through the smoke-vent and the door-hole, wondering whose it might be and how I came there.

Then I tried to sit up, and instantly was seized with agony in the region of the ribs, which I found were bound about with broad strips of soft tanned hide. Clearly they, or some of them, were broken.

What had broken them? I asked myself, and in a flash everything came back to me. So I had escaped with my life, as the old dwarf, "Opener-of-Roads," had told me that I should. Certainly he was an excellent prophet; and if he spoke truth in this matter, why not in others? What was I to make of it all? How could a black savage, however ancient, foresee the future?

By induction from the past, I supposed; and yet what amount of induction would suffice to show him the details of a forthcoming accident that was to happen to me through the agency of a wild beast with a peculiarly shaped horn? I gave it up, as before and since that day I have found it necessary to do in the case of many other events in life. Indeed, the question is one that I often have had cause to ask where Kafir "witch-doctors" or prophets are concerned, notably in the instance of a certain Mavovo, of whom I hope to tell one day, whose predictions saved my life and those of my companions.

Just then I heard the sound of someone creeping through the bee-hole of the hut, and half-closed my eyes, as I did not feel inclined for conversation. The person came and stood over me, and somehow—by instinct, I suppose—I became aware that my visitor was a woman. Very slowly I lifted my eyelids, just enough to enable me to see her.

There, standing in a beam of golden light that, passing through the smoke-hole, pierced the soft gloom of the hut, stood the most beautiful creature that I had ever seen—that is, if it be admitted that a person who is black, or rather copper-coloured, can be beautiful.

She was a little above the medium height, not more, with a figure that, so far as I am a judge of such matters, was absolutely perfect—that of a Greek statue indeed. On this point I had an opportunity of forming an opinion, since, except for her little bead apron and a single string of large blue beads about her throat, her costume was—well, that of a Greek statue. Her features showed no trace of the negro type; on the contrary, they were singularly well cut, the nose being straight and fine and the pouting mouth that just showed the ivory teeth between, very small. Then the eyes, large, dark and liquid, like those of a buck, set beneath a smooth, broad forehead on which the curling, but not woolly, hair grew low. This hair, by the way, was not dressed up in any of the eccentric native fashions, but simply parted in the middle and tied in a big knot over the nape of the neck, the little ears peeping out through its tresses. The hands, like the feet, were very small and delicate, and the curves of the bust soft and full without being coarse, or even showing the promise of coarseness.

A lovely woman, truly; and yet there was something not quite pleasing about that beautiful face; something, notwithstanding its childlike outline, which reminded me of a flower breaking into bloom, that one does not associate with youth and innocence. I tried to analyse what this might be, and came to the conclusion that without being hard, it was too clever and, in a sense, too reflective. I felt even then that the brain within the shapely head was keen and bright as polished steel; that this woman was one made to rule, not to be man's toy, or even his loving companion, but to use him for her ends.

She dropped her chin till it hid the little, dimple-like depression below her throat, which was one of her charms, and began not to look at, but to study me, seeing which I shut my eyes tight and waited. Evidently she thought that I was still in my swoon, for now she spoke to herself in a low voice that was soft and sweet as honey.

"A small man," she said; "Saduko would make two of him, and the other"—who was he, I wondered—"three. His hair, too, is ugly; he cuts it short and it sticks up like that on a cat's back. Iya!" (i.e. Piff!), and she moved her hand contemptuously, "a feather of a man. But white—white, one of those who rule. Why, they all of them know that he is their master. They call him 'He-who-never-Sleeps.' They say that he has the courage of a lioness with young—he who got away when Dingaan killed Piti [Retief] and the Boers; they say that he is quick and cunning as a snake, and that Panda and his great indunas think more of him than of any white man they know. He is unmarried also, though they say, too, that twice he had a wife, who died, and now he does not turn to look at women, which is strange in any man, and shows that he will escape trouble and succeed. Still, it must be remembered that they are all ugly down here in Zululand, cows, or heifers who will be cows. Piff! no more."

She paused for a little while, then went on in her dreamy, reflective voice:

"Now, if he met a woman who is not merely a cow or a heifer, a woman cleverer than himself, even if she were not white, I wonder—"

At this point I thought it well to wake up. Turning my head I yawned, opened my eyes and looked at her vaguely, seeing which her expression changed in a flash from that of brooding power to one of moved and anxious girlhood; in short, it became most sweetly feminine.

"You are Mameena?" I said; "is it not so?"

"Oh, yes, Inkoosi," she answered, "that is my poor name. But how did you hear it, and how do you know me?"

"I heard it from one Saduko"—here she frowned a little—"and others, and I knew you because you are so beautiful"—an incautious speech at which she broke into a dazzling smile and tossed her deer-like head.

"Am I?" she asked. "I never knew it, who am only a common Zulu girl to whom it pleases the great white chief to say kind things, for which I thank him"; and she made a graceful little reverence, just bending one knee. "But," she went on quickly, "whatever else I be, I am of no knowledge, not fit to tend you who are hurt. Shall I go and send my oldest mother?"

"Do you mean her whom your father calls the 'Worn-out-old-Cow,' and whose ear he shot off?"

"Yes, it must be she from the description," she answered with a little shake of laughter, "though I never heard him give her that name."

"Or if you did, you have forgotten it," I said dryly. "Well, I think not, thank you. Why trouble her, when you will do quite as well? If there is milk in that gourd, perhaps you will give me a drink of it."

She flew to the bowl like a swallow, and next moment was kneeling at my side and holding it to my lips with one hand, while with the other she supported my head.

"I am honoured," she said. "I only came to the hut the moment before you woke, and seeing you still lost in swoon, I wept—look, my eyes are still wet [they were, though how she made them so I do not know]—for I feared lest that sleep should be but the beginning of the last."

"Quite so," I said; "it is very good of you. And now, since your fears are groundless—thanks be to the heavens—sit down, if you will, and tell me the story of how I came here."

She sat down, not, I noted, as a Kafir woman ordinarily does, in a kind of kneeling position, but on a stool.

"You were carried into the kraal, Inkoosi," she said, "on a litter of boughs. My heart stood still when I saw that litter coming; it was no more heart; it was cold iron, because I thought the dead or injured man was—" And she paused.

"Saduko?" I suggested.

"Not at all, Inkoosi—my father."

"Well, it wasn't either of them," I said, "so you must have felt happy."

"Happy! Inkoosi, when the guest of our house had been wounded, perhaps to death—the guest of whom I have heard so much, although by misfortune I was absent when he arrived."

"A difference of opinion with your eldest mother?" I suggested.

"Yes, Inkoosi; my own is dead, and I am not too well treated here. She called me a witch."

"Did she?" I answered. "Well, I do not altogether wonder at it; but please continue your story."

"There is none, Inkoosi. They brought you here, they told me how the evil brute of a buffalo had nearly killed you in the pool; that is all."

"Yes, yes, Mameena; but how did I get out of the pool?"

"Oh, it seems that your servant, Sikauli, the bastard, leapt into the water and engaged the attention of the buffalo which was kneading you into the mud, while Saduko got on to its back and drove his assegai down between its shoulders to the heart, so that it died. Then they pulled you out of the mud, crushed and almost drowned with water, and brought you to life again. But afterwards you became senseless, and so lay wandering in your speech until this hour."

"Ah, he is a brave man, is Saduko."

"Like others, neither more nor less," she replied with a shrug of her rounded shoulders. "Would you have had him let you die? I think the brave man was he who got in front of the bull and twisted its nose, not he who sat on its back and poked at it with a spear."

At this period in our conversation I became suddenly faint and lost count of things, even of the interesting Mameena. When I awoke again she was gone, and in her place was old Umbezi, who, I noticed, took down a mat from the side of the hut and folded it up to serve as a cushion before he sat himself upon the stool.

"Greeting, Macumazahn," he said when he saw that I was awake; "how are you?"

"As well as can be hoped," I answered; "and how are you, Umbezi?"

"Oh, bad, Macumazahn; even now I can scarcely sit down, for that bull had a very hard nose; also I am swollen up in front where Sikauli struck me when he tumbled out of the tree. Also my heart is cut in two because of our losses."

"What losses, Umbezi?"

"Wow! Macumazahn, the fire that those low fellows of mine lit got to our camp and burned up nearly everything—the meat, the skins, and even the ivory, which it cracked so that it is useless. That was an unlucky hunt, for although it began so well, we have come out of it quite naked; yes, with nothing at all except the head of the bull with the cleft horn, that I thought you might like to keep."

"Well, Umbezi, let us be thankful that we have come out with our lives—that is, if I am going to live," I added.

"Oh, Macumazahn, you will live without doubt, and be none the worse. Two of our doctors—very clever men—have looked at you and said so. One of them tied you up in all those skins, and I promised him a heifer for the business, if he cured you, and gave him a goat on account. But you must lie here for a month or more, so he says. Meanwhile Panda has sent for the hides which he demanded of me to be made into shields, and I have been obliged to kill twenty-five of my beasts to provide them—that is, of my own and of those of my headmen."

"Then I wish you and your headmen had killed them before we met those buffalo, Umbezi," I groaned, for my ribs were paining me very much. "Send Saduko and Sikauli here; I would thank them for saving my life."

So they came, next morning, I think, and I thanked them warmly enough.

"There, there, Baas," said Scowl, who was literally weeping tears of joy at my return from delirium and coma to the light of life and reason; not tears of Mameena's sort, but real ones, for I saw them running down his snub nose, that still bore marks of the eagle's claws. "There, there, say no more, I beseech you. If you were going to die, I wished to die, too, who, if you had left it, should only have wandered through the world without a heart. That is why I jumped into the pool, not because I am brave."

When I heard this my own eyes grew moist. Oh, it is the fashion to abuse natives, but from whom do we meet with more fidelity and love than from these poor wild Kafirs that so many of us talk of as black dirt which chances to be fashioned to the shape of man?

"As for myself, Inkoosi," added Saduko, "I only did my duty. How could I have held up my head again if the bull had killed you while I walked away alive? Why, the very girls would have mocked at me. But, oh, his skin was tough. I thought that assegai would never get through it."

Observe the difference between these two men's characters. The one, although no hero in daily life, imperils himself from sheer, dog-like fidelity to a master who had given him many hard words and sometimes a flogging in punishment for drunkenness, and the other to gratify his pride, also perhaps because my death would have interfered with his plans and ambitions in which I had a part to play. No, that is a hard saying; still, there is no doubt that Saduko always first took his own interests into consideration, and how what he did would reflect upon his prospects and repute, or influence the attainment of his desires. I think this was so even when Mameena was concerned—at any rate, in the beginning—although certainly he always loved her with a single-hearted passion that is very rare among Zulus.

Presently Scowl left the hut to prepare me some broth, whereon Saduko at once turned the talk to this subject of Mameena.

He understood that I had seen her. Did I not think her very beautiful?

"Yes, very beautiful," I answered; "indeed, the most beautiful Zulu woman I have ever seen."

And very clever—almost as clever as a white?

"Yes, and very clever—much cleverer than most whites."

And—anything else?

"Yes; very dangerous, and one who could turn like the wind and blow hot and blow cold."

"Ah!" he said, thought a while, then added: "Well, what do I care how she blows to others, so long as she blows hot to me."

"Well, Saduko, and does she blow hot for you?"

"Not altogether, Macumazahn." Another pause. "I think she blows rather like the wind before a great storm."

"That is a biting wind, Saduko, and when we feel it we know that the storm will follow."

"I dare say that the storm will follow, Inkoosi, for she was born in a storm and storm goes with her; but what of that, if she and I stand it out together? I love her, and I had rather die with her than live with any other woman."

"The question is, Saduko, whether she would rather die with you than live with any other man. Does she say so?"

"Inkoosi, Mameena's thought works in the dark; it is like a white ant in its tunnel of mud. You see the tunnel which shows that she is thinking, but you do not see the thought within. Still, sometimes, when she believes that no one beholds or hears her"—here I bethought me of the young lady's soliloquy over my apparently senseless self—"or when she is surprised, the true thought peeps out of its tunnel. It did so the other day, when I pleaded with her after she had heard that I killed the buffalo with the cleft horn.

"'Do I love you?' she said. 'I know not for sure. How can I tell? It is not our custom that a maiden should love before she is married, for is she did so most marriages would be things of the heart and not of cattle, and then half the fathers of Zululand would grow poor and refuse to rear girl-children who would bring them nothing. You are brave, you are handsome, you are well-born; I would sooner live with you than with any other man I know—that is, if you were rich and, better still, powerful. Become rich and powerful, Saduko, and I think that I shall love you.'

"'I will, Mameena,' I answered; 'but you must wait. The Zulu nation was not fashioned from nothing in a day. First Chaka had to come.'

"'Ah!' she said, and, my father, her eyes flashed. 'Ah! Chaka! There was a man! Be another Chaka, Saduko, and I will love you more—more than you can dream of—thus and thus,' and she flung her arms about me and kissed me as I was never kissed before, which, as you know, among us is a strange thing for a girl to do. Then she thrust me from her with a laugh, and added: 'As for the waiting, you must ask my father of that. Am I not his heifer, to be sold, and can I disobey my father?' And she was gone, leaving me empty, for it seemed as though she took my vitals with her. Nor will she talk thus any more, the white ant who has gone back into its tunnel."

"And did you speak to her father?"

"Yes, I spoke to him, but in an evil moment, for he had but just killed the cattle to furnish Panda's shields. He answered me very roughly. He said: 'You see these dead beasts which I and my people must slay for the king, or fall under his displeasure? Well, bring me five times their number, and we will talk of your marriage with my daughter, who is a maid in some request.'

"I answered that I understood and would try my best, whereon he became more gentle, for Umbezi has a kindly heart.

"'My son,' he said, 'I like you well, and since I saw you save Macumazahn, my friend, from that mad wild beast of a buffalo I like you better than before. Yet you know my case. I have an old name and am called the chief of a tribe, and many live on me. But I am poor, and this daughter of mine is worth much. Such a woman few men have bred. Well, I must make the best of her. My son-in-law must be one who will prop up my old age, one to whom, in my need or trouble, I could always go as to a dry log, to break off some of its bark to make a fire to comfort me, not one who treads me into the mire as the buffalo did to Macumazahn. Now I have spoken, and I do not love such talk. Come back with the cattle, and I will listen to you, but meanwhile understand that I am not bound to you or to anyone; I shall take what my spirit sends me, which, if I may judge the future by the past, will not be much. One word more: Do not linger about this kraal too long, lest it should be said that you are the accepted suitor of Mameena. Go hence and do a man's work, and return with a man's reward, or not at all.'"

"Well, Saduko, that spear has an edge on it, has it not?" I answered. "And now, what is your plan?"

"My plan is, Macumazahn," he said, rising from his seat, "to go hence and gather those who are friendly to me because I am my father's son and still the chief of the Amangwane, or those who are left of them, although I have no kraal and no hoof of kine. Then, within a moon, I hope, I shall return here to find you strong again and once more a man, and we will start out against Bangu, as I have whispered to you, with the leave of a High One, who has said that, if I can take any cattle, I may keep them for my pains."

"I don't know about that, Saduko. I never promised you that I would make war upon Bangu—with or without the king's leave."

"No, you never promised, but Zikali the Dwarf, the Wise Little One, said that you would—and does Zikali lie? Ask yourself, who will remember a certain saying of his about a buffalo with a cleft horn, a pool and a dry river-bed. Farewell, O my father Macumazahn; I walk with the dawn, and I leave Mameena in your keeping."

"You mean that you leave me in Mameena's keeping," I began, but already he was crawling through the hole in the hut.

Well, Mameena kept me very comfortably. She was always in evidence, yet not too much so.

Heedless of her malice and abuse, she headed off the "Worn-out-old-Cow," whom she knew I detested, from my presence. She saw personally to my bandages, as well as to the cooking of my food, over which matter she had several quarrels with the bastard, Scowl, who did not like her, for on him she never wasted any of her sweet looks. Also, as I grew stronger, she sat with me a good deal, talking, since, by common consent, Mameena the fair was exempted from all the field, and even the ordinary household labours that fall to the lot of Kafir women. Her place was to be the ornament and, I may add, the advertisement of her father's kraal. Others might do the work, and she saw that they did it.

We discussed all sorts of things, from the Christian and other religions and European policy down, for her thirst for knowledge seemed to be insatiable. But what really interested her was the state of affairs in Zululand, with which she knew I was well acquainted, as a person who had played a part in its history and who was received and trusted at the Great House, and as a white man who understood the designs and plans of the Boers and of the Governor of Natal.

Now, if the old king, Panda, should chance to die, she would ask me, which of his sons did I think would succeed him—Umbelazi or Cetewayo, or another? Or, if he did not chance to die, which of them would he name his heir?

I replied that I was not a prophet, and that she had better ask Zikali the Wise.

"That is a very good idea," she said, "only I have no one to take me to him, since my father would not allow me to go with Saduko, his ward." Then she clapped her hands and added: "Oh, Macumazahn, will you take me? My father would trust me with you."

"Yes, I dare say," I answered; "but the question is, could I trust myself with you?"

"What do you mean?" she asked. "Oh, I understand. Then, after all, I am more to you than a black stone to play with?"

I think it was that unlucky joke of mine which first set Mameena thinking, "like a white ant in its tunnel," as Saduko said. At least, after it her manner towards me changed; she became very deferential; she listened to my words as though they were all wisdom; I caught her looking at me with her soft eyes as though I were quite an admirable object. She began to talk to me of her difficulties, her troubles and her ambitions. She asked me for my advice as to Saduko. On this point I replied to her that, if she loved him, and her father would allow it, presumably she had better marry him.

"I like him well enough, Macumazahn, although he wearies me at times; but love— Oh, tell me, *what* is love?" Then she clasped her slim hands and gazed at me like a fawn.

"Upon my word, young woman," I replied, "that is a matter upon which I should have thought you more competent to instruct me."

"Oh, Macumazahn," she said almost in a whisper, and letting her head droop like a fading lily, "you have never given me the chance, have you?" And she laughed a little, looking extremely attractive.

"Good gracious!"—or, rather, its Zulu equivalent—I answered, for I began to feel nervous. "What do you mean, Mameena? How could I—" There I stopped.

"I do not know what I mean, Macumazahn," she exclaimed wildly, "but I know well enough what you mean—that you are white as snow and I am black as soot, and that snow and soot don't mix well together."

"No," I answered gravely, "snow is good to look at, and so is soot, but mingled they make an ugly colour. Not that you are like soot," I added hastily, fearing to hurt her feelings. "That is your hue"—and I touched a copper bangle she was wearing—"a very lovely hue, Mameena, like everything else about you."

"Lovely," she said, beginning to weep a little, which upset me very much, for if there is one thing I hate, it is to see a woman cry. "How can a poor Zulu girl be lovely? Oh, Macumazahn, the spirits have dealt hardly with me, who have given me the colour of my people and the heart of yours. If I were white, now, what you are pleased to call this loveliness of mine would be of some use to me, for then— then— Oh, cannot you guess, Macumazahn?"

I shook my head and said that I could not, and next moment was sorry, for she proceeded to explain.

Sinking to her knees—for we were quite alone in the big hut and there was no one else about, all the other women being engaged on rural or domestic tasks, for which Mameena declared she had no time, as her business was to look after me—she rested her shapely head upon my knees and began to talk in a low, sweet voice that sometimes broke into a sob.

"Then I will tell you—I will tell you; yes, even if you hate me afterwards. I could teach you what love is very well, Macumazahn; you are quite right—because I love you." (Sob.) "No, you shall not stir till you have heard me out." Here she flung her arms about my legs and held them tight, so that without using great violence it was absolutely impossible for me to move. "When I saw you first, all shattered and senseless, snow seemed to fall upon my heart, and it stopped for a little while and has never been the same since. I think that something is growing in it, Macumazahn, that makes it big." (Sob.) "I used to like Saduko before that, but afterwards I did not like him at all—no, nor Masapo either—you know, he is the big chief who lives over the mountain, a very rich and powerful man, who, I believe, would like to marry me. Well, as I went on nursing you my heart grew bigger and bigger, and now you see it has burst." (Sob.) "Nay, stay still and do not try to speak. You *shall* hear me out. It is the least you can do, seeing that you have caused me all this pain. If you did not want me to love you, why did you not curse at me and strike me, as I am told white men do to Kafir girls?" She rose and went on:

"Now, hearken. Although I am the colour of copper, I am comely. I am well-bred also; there is no higher blood than ours in Zululand, both on my father's and my mother's side, and, Macumazahn, I have a fire in me that shows me things. I can be great, and I long for greatness. Take me to wife, Macumazahn, and I swear to you that in ten years I will make you king of the Zulus. Forget your pale white women and wed yourself to that fire which burns in me, and it shall eat up all that stands between you and the Crown, as flame eats up dry grass. More, I will make you happy. If you choose to take other wives, I will not be jealous, because I know that I should hold your spirit, and that, compared to me, they would be nothing in your thought—"

"But, Mameena," I broke in, "I don't want to be king of the Zulus."

"Oh, yes, yes, you do, for every man wants power, and it is better to rule over a brave, black people—thousands and thousands of them—than to be no one among the whites. Think, think! There is wealth in the land. By your skill and knowledge the amabuto [regiments] could be improved; with the wealth you would arm them with guns—yes, and 'by-and-byes' also with the throat of thunder" (that is, or was, the Kafir name for cannon). "They would be invincible. Chaka's kingdom would be nothing to ours, for a hundred thousand warriors would sleep on their spears, waiting for your word. If you wished it even you could sweep out Natal and make the whites there your subjects, too. Or perhaps it would be safer to let them be, lest others should come across the green water to help them, and to strike northwards, where I am told there are great lands as rich and fair, in which none would dispute our sovereignty—"

"But, Mameena," I gasped, for this girl's titanic ambition literally overwhelmed me, "surely you are mad! How would you do all these things?"

"I am not mad," she answered; "I am only what is called great, and you know well enough that I can do them, not by myself, who am but a woman and tied with the ropes that bind women, but with you to cut those ropes and help me. I have a plan which will not fail. But, Macumazahn," she added in a changed voice, "until I know that you will be my partner in it I will not tell it even to you, for perhaps you might talk—in your sleep, and then the fire in my breast would soon go out—for ever."

"I might talk now, for the matter of that, Mameena."

"No; for men like you do not tell tales of foolish girls who chance to love them. But if that plan began to work, and you heard say that kings or princes died, it might be otherwise. You might say, 'I think I know where the witch lives who causes these evils'—in your sleep, Macumazahn."

"Mameena," I said, "tell me no more. Setting your dreams on one side, can I be false to my friend, Saduko, who talks to me day and night of you?"

"Saduko! Piff!" she exclaimed, with that expressive gesture of her hand.

"And can I be false," I continued, seeing that Saduko was no good card to play, "to my friend, Umbezi, your father?"

"My father! " she laughed. "Why, would it not please him to grow great in your shadow? Only yesterday he told me to marry you, if I could, for then he would find a stick indeed to lean on, and be rid of Saduko's troubling."

Evidently Umbezi was a worse card even than Saduko, so I played another.

"And can I help you, Mameena, to tread a road that at the best must be red with blood?"

"Why not," she asked, "since with or without you I am destined to tread that road, the only difference being that with you it will lead to glory and without you perhaps to the jackals and the vultures? Blood! Piff! What is blood in Zululand?"

This card also having failed, I tabled my last.

"Glory or no glory, I do not wish to share it, Mameena. I will not make war among a people who have entertained me hospitably, or plot the downfall of their Great Ones. As you told me just now, I am nobody—just one grain of sand upon a white shore—but I had rather be that than a haunted rock which draws the heavens' lightnings and is drenched with sacrifice. I seek no throne over white or black, Mameena, who walk my own path to a quiet grave that shall perhaps not be without honour of its own, though other than you seek. I will keep your counsel, Mameena, but, because you are so beautiful and so wise, and because you say you are fond of me—for which I thank you—I pray you put away these fearful dreams of yours that in the end, whether they succeed or fail, will send you shivering from the world to give account of them to the Watcher-on-high."

"Not so, O Macumazana," she said, with a proud little laugh. "When your Watcher sowed my seed—if thus he did—he sowed the dreams that are a part of me also, and I shall only bring him back his own, with the flower and the fruit by way of interest. But that is finished. You refuse the greatness. Now, tell me, if I sink those dreams in a great water, tying about them the stone of forgetfulness and saying: 'Sleep there, O dreams; it is not your hour'—if I do this, and stand before you just a woman who loves and who swears by the spirits of her fathers never to think or do that which has not your blessing—will you love me a little, Macumazahn?"

Now I was silent, for she had driven me to the last ditch, and I knew not what to say. Moreover, I will confess my weakness—I was strangely moved. This beautiful girl with the "fire in her heart," this woman who was different from all other women that I had ever known, seemed to have twisted her slender fingers into my heart-strings and to be drawing me towards her. It was a great temptation, and I bethought me of old Zikali's saying in the Black Kloof, and seemed to hear his giant laugh.

She glided up to me, she threw her arms about me and kissed me on the lips, and I think I kissed her back, but really I am not sure what I did or said, for my head swam. When it cleared again she was standing in front of me, looking at me reflectively.

"Now, Macumazahn," she said, with a little smile that both mocked and dazzled, "the poor black girl has you, the wise, experienced white man, in her net, and I will show you that she can be generous. Do you think that I do not read your heart, that I do not know that you believe I am dragging you down to shame and ruin? Well, I spare you, Macumazahn, since you have kissed me and spoken words which already you may have forgotten, but which I do not forget. Go your road, Macumazahn, and I go mine, since the proud white man shall not be stained with my black touch. Go your road; but one thing I forbid you—to believe that you have been listening to lies, and that I have merely played off a woman's arts upon you for my own ends. I love you, Macumazahn, as you will never be loved till you die, and I shall never love any other man, however many I may marry. Moreover, you shall promise me one thing—that once in my life, and once only, if I wish it, you shall kiss me again before all men. And now, lest you should be moved to folly and forget your white man's pride, I bid you farewell, O Macumazana. When we meet again it will be as friends only."

Then she went, leaving me feeling smaller than ever I felt in my life, before or since—even smaller than when I walked into the presence of old Zikali the Wise. Why, I wondered, had she first made a fool of me, and then thrown away the fruits of my folly? To this hour I cannot quite answer the question, though I believe the explanation to be that she did really care for me, and was anxious not to involve me in trouble and her plottings; also she may have been wise enough to see that our natures were as oil and water and would never blend.

Two Bucks and the Doe

It may be thought that, as a sequel to this somewhat remarkable scene in which I was absolutely bowled over—perhaps bowled out would be a better term—by a Kafir girl who, after bending me to her will, had the genius to drop me before I repented, as she knew I would do so soon as her back was turned, thereby making me look the worst of fools, that my relations with that young lady would have been strained. But not a bit of it. When next we met, which was on the following morning, she was just her easy, natural self, attending to my hurts, which by now were almost well, joking about this and that, inquiring as to the contents of certain letters which I had received from Natal, and of some newspapers that came with them—for on all such matters she was very curious—and so forth.

Impossible, the clever critic will say—impossible that a savage could act with such finish. Well, friend critic, that is just where you are wrong. When you come to add it up there's very little difference in all main and essential matters between the savage and yourself.

To begin with, by what exact right do we call people like the Zulus savages? Setting aside the habit of polygamy, which, after all, is common among very highly civilised peoples in the East, they have a social system not unlike our own. They have, or had, their king, their nobles, and their commons. They have an ancient and elaborate law, and a system of morality in some ways as high as our own, and certainly more generally obeyed. They have their priests and their doctors; they are strictly upright, and observe the rites of hospitality.

Where they differ from us mainly is that they do not get drunk until the white man teaches them so to do, they wear less clothing, the climate being more genial, their towns at night are not disgraced by the sights that distinguish ours, they cherish and are never cruel to their children, although they may occasionally put a deformed infant or a twin out of the way, and when they go to war, which is often, they carry out the business with a terrible thoroughness, almost as terrible as that which prevailed in every nation in Europe a few generations ago.

Of course, there remain their witchcraft and the cruelties which result from their almost universal belief in the power and efficiency of magic. Well, since I lived in England I have been reading up this subject, and I find that quite recently similar cruelties were practised throughout Europe—that is in a part of the world which for over a thousand years has enjoyed the advantages of the knowledge and profession of the Christian faith.

Now, let him who is highly cultured take up a stone to throw at the poor, untaught Zulu, which I notice the most dissolute and drunken wretch of a white man is often ready to do, generally because he covets his land, his labour, or whatever else may be his.

But I wander from my point, which is that a clever man or woman among the people whom we call savages is in all essentials very much the same as a clever man or woman anywhere else.

Here in England every child is educated at the expense of the Country, but I have not observed that the system results in the production of more really able individuals. Ability is the gift of Nature, and that universal mother sheds her favours impartially over all who breathe. No, not quite impartially, perhaps, for the old Greeks and others were examples to the contrary. Still, the general rule obtains.

To return. Mameena was a very able person, as she chanced to be a very lovely one, a person who, had she been favoured by opportunity, would doubtless have played the part of a Cleopatra with equal or greater success, since she shared the beauty and the unscrupulousness of that famous lady and was, I believe, capable of her passion.

I scarcely like to mention the matter since it affects myself, and the natural vanity of man makes him prone to conclude that he is the particular object of sole and undying devotion. Could he know all the facts of the case, or cases, probably he would be much undeceived, and feel about as small as I did when Mameena walked, or rather crawled, out of the hut (she could even crawl gracefully). Still, to be honest—and why should I not, since all this business "went beyond" so long ago?—I do believe that there was a certain amount of truth in what she said—that, for Heaven knows what reason, she did take a fancy to me, which fancy continued during her short and stormy life. But the reader of her story may judge for himself.

Within a fortnight of the day of my discomfiture in the hut I was quite well and strong again, my ribs, or whatever part of me it was that the buffalo had injured with his iron knees, having mended up. Also, I was anxious to be going, having business to attend to in Natal, and, as no more had been seen or heard of Saduko, I determined to trek homewards, leaving a message that he knew where to find me if he wanted me. The truth is that I was by no means keen on being involved in his private war with Bangu. Indeed, I wished to wash my hands of the whole matter, including the fair Mameena and her mocking eyes.

So one morning, having already got up my oxen, I told Scowl to inspan them—an order which he received with joy, for he and the other boys wished to be off to civilisation and its delights. Just as the operation was beginning, however, a message came to me from old Umbezi, who begged me to delay my departure till after noon, as a friend of his, a big chief, had come to visit him who wished much to have the honour of making my acquaintance. Now, I wished the big chief farther off, but, as it seemed rude to refuse the request of one who had been so kind to me, I ordered the oxen to be unyoked but kept at hand, and in an irritable frame of mind walked up to the kraal. This was about half a mile from my place of outspan, for as soon as I was sufficiently recovered I had begun to sleep in my wagon, leaving the big hut to the "Worn-out-Old-Cow."

There was no particular reason why I should be irritated, since time in those days was of no great account in Zululand, and it did not much matter to me whether I trekked in the morning or the afternoon. But the fact was that I could not get over the prophecy of Zikali, "the Little and Wise," that I was destined to share Saduko's expedition against Bangu, and, although he had been right about the buffalo and Mameena, I was determined to prove him wrong in this particular.

If I had left the country, obviously I could not go against Bangu, at any rate at present. But while I remained in it Saduko might return at any moment, and then, doubtless, I should find it hard to escape from the kind of half-promise that I had given to him.

Well, as soon as I reached the kraal I saw that some kind of festivity was in progress, for an ox had been killed and was being cooked, some of it in pots and some by roasting; also there were several strange Zulus present. Within the fence of the kraal, seated in its shadow, I found Umbezi and some of his headmen, and with them a great, brawny "ringed" native, who wore a tiger-skin moocha as a mark of rank, and some of *his* headmen. Also Mameena was standing near the gate, dressed in her best beads and holding a gourd of Kafir beer which, evidently, she had just been handing to the guests.

"Would you have run away without saying good-bye to me, Macumazahn?" she whispered to me as I came abreast of her. "That is unkind of you, and I should have wept much. However, it was not so fated."

"I was going to ride up and bid farewell when the oxen were inspanned," I answered. "But who is that man?"

"You will find out presently, Macumazahn. Look, my father is beckoning to us."

So I went on to the circle, and as I advanced Umbezi rose and, taking me by the hand, led me to the big man, saying:

"This is Masapo, chief of the Amansomi, of the Quabe race, who desires to know you, Macumazahn."

"Very kind of him, I am sure," I replied coolly, as I threw my eye over Masapo. He was, as I have said, a big man, and of about fifty years of age, for his hair was tinged with grey. To be frank, I took a great dislike to him at once, for there was something in his strong, coarse face, and his air of insolent pride, which repelled me. Then I was silent, since among the Zulus, when two strangers of more or less equal rank meet, he who speaks first acknowledges inferiority to the other. Therefore I stood and contemplated this new suitor of Mameena, waiting on events.

Masapo also contemplated me, then made some remark to one of his attendants, that I did not catch, which caused the fellow to laugh.

"He has heard that you are an ipisi" (a great hunter), broke in Umbezi, who evidently felt that the situation was growing strained, and that it was necessary to say something.

"Has he?" I answered. "Then he is more fortunate than I am, for I have never heard of him or what he is." This, I am sorry to say, was a fib, for it will be remembered that Mameena had mentioned him in the hut as one of her suitors, but among natives one must keep up one's dignity somehow. "Friend Umbezi," I went on, "I have come to bid you farewell, as I am about to trek for Durban."

At this juncture Masapo stretched out his great hand to me, but without rising, and said:

"Siyakubona [that is, good-day], White Man."

"Siyakubona, Black Man," I answered, just touching his fingers, while Mameena, who had come up again with her beer, and was facing me, made a little grimace and tittered.

Now I turned on my heel to go, whereon Masapo said in a coarse, growling voice:

"O Macumazana, before you leave us I wish to speak with you on a certain matter. Will it please you to sit aside with me for a while?"

"Certainly, O Masapo." And I walked away a few yards out of hearing, whither he followed me.

"Macumazahn," he said (I give the gist of his remarks, for he did not come to the point at once), "I need guns, and I am told that you can provide them, being a trader."

"Yes, Masapo, I dare say that I can, at a price, though it is a risky business smuggling guns into Zululand. But might I ask what you need them for? is it to shoot elephants?"

"Yes, to shoot elephants," he replied, rolling his big eyes round him. "Macumazahn, I am told that you are discreet, that you do not shout from the top of a hut what you hear within it. Now, hearken to me. Our country is disturbed; we do not all of us love the seed of Senzangakona, of whom the present king, Panda, is one. For instance, you may know that we Quabies—for my tribe, the Amansomi, are of that race—suffered at the spear of Chaka. Well, we think that a time may come when we who live on shrubs like goats may again browse on tree-tops like giraffes, for

Panda is no strong king, and he has sons who hate each other, one of whom may need our spears. Do you understand?"

"I understand that you want guns, O Masapo," I answered dryly. "Now, as to the price and place of delivery."

Then we bargained for a while, but the details of that business transaction of long ago will interest no one. Indeed, I only mention the matter to show that Masapo was plotting to bring trouble on the ruling house, whereof Panda was the representative at that time.

When we had concluded our rather nefarious negotiations, which were to the effect that I was to receive so many cattle in return for so many guns, if I could deliver them at a certain spot, namely, Umbezi's kraal, I returned to the circle where Umbezi, his followers and guests were sitting, purposing to bid him farewell. By now, however, meat had been served, and as I was hungry, having had little breakfast that morning, I stayed to eat. When I had finished my meal, and washed it down with a draught of tshwala (that is, Kafir beer), I rose to go, but just at that moment who should walk through the gate but Saduko?

"Piff!" said Mameena, who was standing near me, speaking in a voice that none but I could hear. "When two bucks meet, what happens, Macumazahn?"

"Sometimes they fight and sometimes one runs away. It depends very much on the doe," I answered in the same low voice, looking at her.

She shrugged her shoulders, folded her arms beneath her breast, nodded to Saduko as he passed, then leaned gracefully against the fence and awaited events.

"Greeting, Umbezi," said Saduko in his proud manner. "I see that you feast. Am I welcome here?"

"Of course you are always welcome, Saduko," replied Umbezi uneasily, "although, as it happens, I am entertaining a great man." And he looked towards Masapo.

"I see," said Saduko, eyeing the strangers. "But which of these may be the great man? I ask that I may salute him."

"You know well enough, umfokazana" (that is, low fellow), exclaimed Masapo angrily.

"I know that if you were outside this fence, Masapo, I would cram that word down your throat at the point of my assegai," replied Saduko in a fierce voice. "Oh, I can guess your business here, Masapo, and you can guess mine," and he glanced towards Mameena. "Tell me, Umbezi, is this little chief of the Amansomi your daughter's accepted suitor?"

"Nay, nay, Saduko," said Umbezi; "no one is her accepted suitor. Will you not sit down and take food with us? Tell us where you have been, and why you return here thus suddenly, and—uninvited?"

"I return here, O Umbezi, to speak with the white chief, Macumazahn. As to where I have been, that is my affair, and not yours or Masapo's."

"Now, if I were chief of this kraal," said Masapo, "I would hunt out of it this hyena with a mangy coat and without a hole who comes to devour your meat and, perhaps," he added with meaning, "to steal away your child."

"Did I not tell you, Macumazahn, that when two bucks met they would fight?" whispered Mameena suavely into my ear.

"Yes, Mameena, you did—or rather I told you. But you did not tell me what the doe would do."

"The doe, Macumazahn, will crouch in her form and see what happens—as is the fashion of does," and again she laughed softly.

"Why not do your own hunting, Masapo?" asked Saduko. "Come, now, I will promise you good sport. Outside this kraal there are other hyenas waiting who call me chief—a hundred or two of them—assembled for a certain purpose by the royal leave of King Panda, whose House, as we all know, you hate. Come, leave that beef and beer and begin your hunting of hyenas, O Masapo."

Now Masapo sat silent, for he saw that he who thought to snare a baboon had caught a tiger.

"You do not speak, O Chief of the little Amansomi," went on Saduko, who was beside himself with rage and jealousy. "You will not leave your beef and beer to hunt the hyenas who are captained by an umfokazana! Well, then, the umfokazana will speak," and, stepping up to Masapo, with the spear he carried poised in his right hand, Saduko grasped his rival's short beard with his left.

"Listen, Chief," he said. "You and I are enemies. You seek the woman I seek, and, mayhap, being rich, you will buy her. But if so, I tell you that I will kill you and all your House, you sneaking, half-bred dog!"

With these fierce words he spat in his face and tumbled him backwards. Then, before anyone could stop him, for Umbezi, and even Masapo's headmen, seemed paralysed with surprise, he stalked through the kraal gate, saying as he passed me:

"Inkoosi, I have words for you when you are at liberty."

"You shall pay for this," roared Umbezi after him, turning almost green with rage, for Masapo still lay upon his broad back, speechless, "you who dare to insult my guest in my own house."

"Somebody must pay," cried back Saduko from the gate, "but who it is only the unborn moons will see."

"Mameena," I said as I followed him, "you have set fire to the grass, and men will be burned in it."

"I meant to, Macumazahn," she answered calmly. "Did I not tell you that there was a flame in me, and it will break out sometimes? But, Macumazahn, it is you who have set fire to the grass, not I. Remember that when half Zululand is in ashes. Farewell, O Macumazana, till we meet again, and," she added softly, "whoever else must burn, may the spirits have *you* in their keeping."

At the gate, remembering my manners, I turned to bid that company a polite farewell. By now Masapo had gained his feet, and was roaring out like a bull:

"Kill him! Kill the hyena! Umbezi, will you sit still and see me, your guest—me, Masapo—struck and insulted under the shadow of your own hut? Go forth and kill him, I say!"

"Why not kill him yourself, Masapo," asked the agitated Umbezi, "or bid your headmen kill him? Who am I that I should take precedence of so great a chief in a matter of the spear?" Then he turned towards me, saying: "Oh, Macumazahn the crafty, if I have dealt well by you, come here and give me your counsel."

"I come, Eater-up-of-Elephants," I answered, and I did.

"What shall I do—what shall I do?" went on Umbezi, brushing the perspiration off his brow with one hand, while he wrung the other in his agitation. "There stands a friend of mine"—he pointed to the infuriated Masapo—"who wishes me to kill another friend of mine," and he jerked his thumb towards the kraal gate. "If I refuse I offend one friend, and if I consent I bring blood upon my hands which will call for blood, since, although Saduko is poor, without doubt he has those who love him."

"Yes," I answered, "and perhaps you will bring blood upon other parts of yourself besides your hands, since Saduko is not one to sit still like a sheep while his throat is cut. Also did he not say that he is not quite alone? Umbezi, if you will take my advice, you will leave Masapo to do his own killing."

"It is good; it is wise!" exclaimed Umbezi. "Masapo," he called to that warrior, "if you wish to fight, pray do not think of me. I see nothing, I hear nothing, and I promise proper burial to any who fall. Only you had best be swift, for Saduko is walking away all this time. Come, you and your people have spears, and the gate stands open."

"Am I to go without my meat in order to knock that hyena on the head?" asked Masapo in a brave voice. "No, he can wait my leisure. Sit still, my people. I tell you, sit still. Tell him, you Macumazahn, that I am coming for him presently, and be warned to keep yourself away from him, lest you should tumble into his hole."

"I will tell him," I answered, "though I know not who made me your messenger. But listen to me, you Speaker of big words and Doer of small deeds, if you dare to lift a finger against me I will teach you something about holes, for there shall be one or more through that great carcass of yours."

Then, walking up to him, I looked him in the face, and at the same time tapped the handle of the big double-barrelled pistol I carried.

He shrank back muttering something.

"Oh, don't apologise," I said, "only be more careful in future. And now I wish you a good dinner, Chief Masapo, and peace upon your kraal, friend Umbezi."

After this speech I marched off, followed by the clamour of Masapo's furious attendants and the sound of Mameena's light and mocking laughter.

"I wonder which of them she will marry?" I thought to myself, as I set out for the wagons.

As I approached my camp I saw that the oxen were being inspanned, as I supposed by the order of Scowl, who must have heard that there was a row up at the kraal, and thought it well to be ready to bolt. In this I was mistaken, however, for just then Saduko strolled out of a patch of bush and said:

"I ordered your boys to yoke up the oxen, Inkoosi."

"Have you? That's cool!" I answered. "Perhaps you will tell me why."

"Because we must make a good trek to the northward before night, Inkoosi."

"Indeed! I thought that I was heading south-east."

"Bangu does not live in the south or the east," he replied slowly.

"Oh, I had almost forgotten about Bangu," I said, with a rather feeble attempt at evasion.

"Is it so?" he answered in his haughty voice. "I never knew before that Macumazahn was a man who broke a promise to his friend."

"Would you be so kind as to explain your meaning, Saduko?"

"Is it needful?" he answered, shrugging his shoulders. "Unless my ears played me tricks, you agreed to go up with me against Bangu. Well, I have gathered the necessary men—with the king's leave—they await us yonder," and he pointed with his spear towards a dense patch of bush that lay some miles beneath us. "But," he added, "if you desire to change your mind I will go alone. Only then, I think, we had better bid each other good-bye, since I love not friends who change their minds when the assegais begin to shake."

Now, whether Saduko spoke thus by design I do not know. Certainly, however, he could have found no better way to ensure my companionship for what it was worth, since, although I had made no actual promise in this case, I have always prided myself on keeping even a half-bargain with a native.

"I will go with you," I said quietly, "and I hope that, when it comes to the pinch, your spear will be as sharp as your tongue, Saduko. Only do not speak to me again like that, lest we should quarrel."

As I said this I saw a look of relief appear on his face, of very great relief.

"I pray your pardon, my lord Macumazahn," he said, seizing my hand, "but, oh! there is a hole in my heart. I think that Mameena means to play me false, and now that has happened with yonder dog, Masapo, which will make her father hate me."

"If you will take my advice, Saduko," I replied earnestly, "you will let this Mameena fall out of the hole in your heart; you will forget her name; you will have done with her. Ask me not why."

"Perhaps there is no need, O Macumazana. Perhaps she has been making love to you, and you have turned her away, as, being what you are, and my friend, of course you would do." (It is rather inconvenient to be set upon such a pedestal at times, but I did not attempt to assent or to deny anything, much less to enter into explanations.)

"Perhaps all this has happened," he continued, "or perhaps it is she who has sent for Masapo the Hog. I do not ask, because if you know you will not tell me. Moreover, it matters nothing. While I have a heart, Mameena will never drop out of it; while I can remember names, hers will never be forgotten by me. Moreover, I mean that she shall be my wife. Now, I am minded to take a few men and spear this hog, Masapo, before we go up against Bangu, for then he, at any rate, will be out of my road."

"If you do anything of the sort, Saduko, you will go up against Bangu alone, for I trek east at once, who will not be mixed up with murder."

"Then let it be, Inkoosi; unless he attacks me, as my Snake send that he may, the Hog can wait. After all, he will only be growing a little fatter. Now, if it pleases you order the wagons to trek. I will show the road, for we must camp in that bush to-night where my people wait me, and there I will tell you my plans; also you will find one with a message for you."

The Ambush

We had reached the bush after six hours' downhill trek over a pretty bad track made by cattle—of course, there were no roads in Zululand at this date. I remember the place well. It was a kind of spreading woodland on a flat bottom, where trees of no great size grew sparsely. Some were mimosa thorns, others had deep green leaves and bore a kind of plum with an acid taste and a huge stone, and others silver-coloured leaves in their season. A river, too, low at this time of the year, wound through it, and in the scrub upon its banks were many guinea-fowl and other birds. It was a pleasing, lonely place, with lots of game in it, that came here in the winter to eat the grass, which was lacking on the higher veld. Also it gave the idea of vastness, since wherever one looked there was nothing to be seen except a sea of trees.

Well, we outspanned by the river, of which I forget the name, at a spot that Saduko showed us, and set to work to cook our food, that consisted of venison from a blue wildebeest, one of a herd of these wild-looking animals which I had been fortunate enough to shoot as they whisked past us, gambolling in and out between the trees.

While we were eating I observed that armed Zulus arrived continually in parties of from six to a score of men, and as they arrived lifted their spears, though whether in salutation to Saduko or to myself I did not know, and sat themselves down on an open space between us and the river-bank. Although it was difficult to say whence they came, for they appeared like ghosts out of the bush, I thought it well to take no notice of them, since I guessed that their coming was prearranged.

"Who are they?" I whispered to Scowl, as he brought me my tot of "squareface."

"Saduko's wild men," he answered in the same low voice, "outlaws of his tribe who live among the rocks."

Now I scanned them sideways, while pretending to light my pipe and so forth, and certainly they seemed a remarkably savage set of people. Great, gaunt fellows with tangled hair, who wore tattered skins upon their shoulders and seemed to have no possessions save some snuff, a few sleeping-mats, and an ample supply of large fighting shields, hardwood kerries or knob-sticks, and broad ixwas, or stabbing assegais. Such was the look of them as they sat round us in silent semicircles, like aas-vogels—as the Dutch call vultures—sit round a dying ox.

Still I smoked on and took no notice.

At length, as I expected, Saduko grew weary of my silence and spoke. "These are men of the Amangwane tribe, Macumazahn; three hundred of them, all that Bangu left alive, for when their fathers were killed, the women escaped with some of the children, especially those of the outlying kraals. I have gathered them to be revenged upon Bangu, I who am their chief by right of blood."

"Quite so," I answered. "I see that you have gathered them; but do they wish to be revenged on Bangu at the risk of their own lives?"

"We do, white Inkoosi," came the deep-throated answer from the three hundred.

"And do they acknowledge you, Saduko, to be their chief?"

"We do," again came the answer. Then a spokesman stepped forward, one of the few grey-haired men among them, for most of these Amangwane were of the age of Saduko, or even younger.

"O Watcher-by-Night," he said, "I am Tshoza, the brother of Matiwane, Saduko's father, the only one of his brothers that escaped the slaughter on the night of the Great Killing. Is it not so?"

"It is so," exclaimed the serried ranks behind him.

"I acknowledge Saduko as my chief, and so do we all," went on Tshoza.

"So do we all," echoed the ranks.

"Since Matiwane died we have lived as we could, O Macumazana; like baboons among the rocks, without cattle, often without a hut to shelter us; here one, there one. Still, we have lived, awaiting the hour of vengeance upon Bangu, that hour which Zikali the Wise, who is of our blood, has promised to us. Now we believe that it has come, and one and all, from here, from there, from everywhere, we have gathered at the summons of Saduko to be led against Bangu and to conquer him or to die. Is it not so, Amangwane?"

"It is, it is so!" came the deep, unanimous answer, that caused the stirless leaves to shake in the still air.

"I understand, O Tshoza, brother of Matiwane and uncle of Saduko the chief," I replied. "But Bangu is a strong man, living, I am told, in a strong place. Still, let that go; for have you not said that you come out to conquer or to die, you who have nothing to lose; and if you conquer, you conquer; and if you die, you die and the tale is told. But supposing that you conquer. What will Panda, King of the Zulus, say to you, and to me also, who stir up war in his country?"

Now the Amangwane looked behind them, and Saduko cried out:

"Appear, messenger from Panda the King!"

Before his words had ceased to echo I saw a little, withered man threading his way between the tall, gaunt forms of the Amangwane. He came and stood before me, saying:

"Hail, Macumazahn. Do you remember me?"

"Aye," I answered, "I remember you as Maputa, one of Panda's indunas."

"Quite so, Macumazahn; I am Maputa, one of his indunas, a member of his Council, a captain of his impis [that is, armies], as I was to his brothers who are gone, whose names it is not lawful that I should name. Well, Panda the King has sent me to you, at the request of Saduko there, with a message."

"How do I know that you are a true messenger?" I asked. "Have you brought me any token?"

"Aye," he answered, and, fumbling under his cloak, he produced something wrapped in dried leaves, which he undid and handed to me, saying:

"This is the token that Panda sends to you, Macumazahn, bidding me to tell you that you will certainly know it again; also that you are welcome to it, since the two little bullets which he swallowed as you directed made him very ill, and he needs no more of them."

I took the token, and, examining it in the moonlight, recognised it at once.

It was a cardboard box of strong calomel pills, on the top of which was written: "Allan Quatermain, Esq.: One *only* to be taken as directed." Without entering into explanations, I may state that I had taken "one as directed," and subsequently presented the rest of the box to King Panda, who was very anxious to "taste the white man's medicine."

"Do you recognise the token, Macumazahn?" asked the induna.

"Yes," I replied gravely; "and let the King return thanks to the spirits of his ancestors that he did not swallow three of the balls, for if he had done so, by now there would have been another Head in Zululand. Well, speak on, Messenger."

But to myself I reflected, not for the first time, how strangely these natives could mix up the sublime with the ridiculous. Here was a matter that must involve the death of many men, and the token sent to me by the autocrat who stood at the back of it all, to prove the good faith of his messenger, was a box of calomel pills! However, it served the purpose as well as anything else.

Maputa and I drew aside, for I saw that he wished to speak with me alone.

"O Macumazana," he said, when we were out of hearing of the others, "these are the words of Panda to you: 'I understand that you, Macumazahn, have promised to accompany Saduko, son of Matiwane, on an expedition of his against Bangu, chief of the Amakoba. Now, were anyone else concerned, I should forbid this expedition, and especially should I forbid you, a white man in my country, to share therein. But this dog of a Bangu is an evil-doer. Many years ago he worked on the Black One who went before me to send him to destroy Matiwane, my friend, filling the Black One's ears with false accusations; and thereafter he did treacherously destroy him and all his tribe save Saduko, his son, and some of the people and children who escaped. Moreover, of late he has been working against me, the King, striving to stir up rebellion against me, because he knows that I hate him for his crimes. Now I, Panda, unlike those who went before me, am a man of peace who do not wish to light the fire of civil war in the land, for who knows where such fires will stop, or whose kraals they will consume? Yet I do wish to see Bangu punished for his wickedness, and his pride abated. Therefore I give Saduko leave, and those people of the Amangwane who remain to him, to avenge their private wrongs upon Bangu if they can; and I give you leave, Macumazahn, to be of his party. Moreover, if any cattle are taken, I shall ask no account of them; you and Saduko may divide them as you wish. But understand, O Macumazana, that if you or your people are killed or wounded, or robbed of your goods, I know nothing of the matter, and am not responsible to you or to the white House of Natal; it is your own matter. These are my words. I have spoken.'"

"I see," I answered. "I am to pull Panda's hot iron out of the fire and to extinguish the fire. If I succeed I may keep a piece of the iron when it gets cool, and if I burn my fingers it is my own fault, and I or my House must not come crying to Panda."

"O Watcher-by-Night, you have speared the bull in the heart," replied Maputa, the messenger, nodding his shrewd old head. "Well, will you go up with Saduko?"

"Say to the King, O Messenger, that I will go up with Saduko because I promised him that I would, being moved by the tale of his wrongs, and not for the sake of the cattle, although it is true that if I hear any of them lowing in my camp I may keep them. Say to Panda also that if aught of ill befalls me he shall hear nothing of it, nor will I bring his high name into this business; but that he, on his part, must not blame me for anything that may happen afterwards. Have you the message?"

"I have it word for word; and may your Spirit be with you, Macumazahn, when you attack the strong mountain of Bangu, which, were I you," Maputa added reflectively, "I think I should do just at the dawn, since the Amakoba drink much beer and are heavy sleepers."

Then we took a pinch of snuff together, and he departed at once for Nodwengu, Panda's Great Place.

Fourteen days had gone by, and Saduko and I, with our ragged band of Amangwane, sat one morning, after a long night march, in the hilly country looking across a broad vale, which was sprinkled with trees like an English park, at that mountain on the side of which Bangu, chief of the Amakoba, had his kraal.

It was a very formidable mountain, and, as we had already observed, the paths leading up to the kraal were amply protected with stone walls in which the openings were quite narrow, only just big enough to allow one ox to pass through them at a time. Moreover, all these walls had been strengthened recently, perhaps because Bangu was aware that Panda looked upon him, a northern chief dwelling on the confines of his dominions, with suspicion and even active enmity, as he was also no doubt aware Panda had good cause to do.

Here in a dense patch of bush that grew in a kloof of the hills we held a council of war.

So far as we knew our advance had been unobserved, for I had left my wagons in the low veld thirty miles away, giving it out among the local natives that I was hunting game there, and bringing on with me only Scowl and four of my best hunters, all well-armed natives who could shoot. The three hundred Amangwane also had advanced in small parties, separated from each other, pretending to be Kafirs marching towards Delagoa Bay. Now, however, we had all met in this bush. Among our number were three Amangwane who, on the slaughter of their tribe, had fled with their mothers to this district and been brought up among the people of Bangu, but who at his summons had come back to Saduko. It was on these men that we relied at this juncture, for they alone knew the country. Long and anxiously did we consult with them. First they explained, and, so far as the moonlight would allow, for as yet the dawn had not broken, pointed out to us the various paths that led to Bangu's kraal.

"How many men are there in the town?" I asked.

"About seven hundred who carry spears," they answered, "together with others in outlying kraals. Moreover, watchmen are always set at the gateways in the walls."

"And where are the cattle?" I asked again.

"Here, in the valley beneath, Macumazahn," answered the spokesman. "If you listen you will hear them lowing. Fifty men, not less, watch them at night—two thousand head of them, or more."

"Then it would not be difficult to get round these cattle and drive them off, leaving Bangu to breed up a new herd?"

"It might not be difficult," interrupted Saduko, "but I came here to kill Bangu, as well as to seize his cattle, since with him I have a blood feud."

"Very good," I answered; "but that mountain cannot be stormed with three hundred men, fortified as it is with walls and schanzes. Our band would be destroyed before ever we came to the kraal, since, owing to the sentries who are set everywhere, it would be impossible to surprise the place. Also you have forgotten the dogs, Saduko. Moreover, even if it were possible, I will have nothing to do with the massacre of women and children, which must happen in an assault. Now, listen to me, O Saduko. I say let us leave the kraal of Bangu alone, and this coming night send fifty of our men, under the leadership of the guides, down to yonder bush, where they will lie hid. Then, after moonrise, when all are asleep, these fifty must rush the cattle kraal, killing any who may oppose them, should they be seen, and driving the herd out through yonder great pass by which we have entered the land. Bangu and his people, thinking that those who have taken the cattle are but common thieves of some wild tribe, will gather and follow the beasts to recapture them. But we, with the rest of the Amangwane, can set an ambush in the narrowest part of the pass among the rocks, where the grass is high and the euphorbia trees grow thick, and there, when they have passed the Nek, which I and my hunters will hold with our guns, we will give them battle. What say you?"

Now, Saduko answered that he would rather attack the kraal, which he wished to burn. But the old Amangwane, Tshoza, brother of the dead Matiwane, said:

"No, Macumazahn, Watcher-by-Night, is wise. Why should we waste our strength on stone walls, of which none know the number or can find the gates in the darkness, and thereby leave our skulls to be set up as ornaments on the fences of the accursed Amakoba? Let us draw the Amakoba out into the pass of the mountains, where they have no walls to protect them, and there fall on them when they are bewildered and settle the matter with them man to man. As for the women and children, with Macumazahn I say let them go; afterwards, perhaps, they will become *our* women and children."

"Aye," answered the Amangwane, "the plan of the white Inkoosi is good; he is clever as a weasel; we will have his plan and no other."

So Saduko was overruled and my counsel adopted.

All that day we rested, lighting no fires and remaining still as the dead in the dense bush. It was a very anxious day, for although the place was so wild and lonely, there was always the fear lest we should be discovered. It was true that we had travelled mostly by night in small parties, to avoid leaving a spoor, and avoided all kraals; still, some rumour of our approach might have reached the Amakoba, or a party of hunters might stumble on us, or those who sought for lost cattle.

Indeed, something of this sort did happen, for about midday we heard a footfall, and perceived the figure of a man, whom by his head-dress we knew for an Amakoba, threading his way through the bush. Before he saw us he was in our midst. For a moment he hesitated ere he turned to fly, and that moment was his last, for three of the Amangwane leapt on him silently as leopards leap upon a buck, and where he stood there he died. Poor fellow! Evidently he had been on a visit to some witch-doctor, for in his blanket we found medicine and love charms. This doctor cannot have been one of the stamp of Zikali the Dwarf, I thought to myself; at least, he had not warned him that he would never live to dose his beloved with that foolish medicine.

Meanwhile a few of us who had the quickest eyes climbed trees, and thence watched the town of Bangu and the valley that lay between us and it. Soon we saw that so far, at any rate, Fortune was playing into our hands, since herd after herd of kine were driven into the valley during the afternoon and enclosed in the stock-kraals. Doubtless Bangu intended on the morrow to make his half-yearly inspection of all the cattle of the tribe, many of which were herded at a distance from his town.

At length the long day drew to its close and the shadows of the evening thickened. Then we made ready for our dreadful game, of which the stake was the lives of all of us, since, should we fail, we could expect no mercy. The fifty picked men were gathered and ate food in silence. These men were placed under the command of Tshoza, for he was the most experienced of the Amangwane, and led by the three guides who had dwelt among the Amakoba, and who "knew every ant-heap in the land," or so they swore. Their duty, it will be remembered, was to cross the valley, separate themselves into small parties, unbar the various cattle kraals, kill or hunt off the herdsmen, and drive the beasts back across the valley into the pass. A second fifty men, under the command of Saduko, were to be left just at the end of this pass where it opened out into the valley, in order to help and reinforce the cattle-lifters, or, if need be, to check the following Amakoba while the great herds of beasts were got away, and then fall back on the rest of us in our ambush nearly two miles distant. The management of this ambush was to be my charge—a heavy one indeed.

Now, the moon would not be up till midnight. But two hours before that time we began our moves, since the cattle must be driven out of the kraals as soon as she appeared and gave the needful light. Otherwise the fight in the pass would in all probability be delayed till after sunrise, when the Amakoba would see how small was the number of their foes. Terror, doubt, darkness—these must be our allies if our desperate venture was to succeed.

All was arranged at last and the time had come. We, the three captains of our divided force, bade each other farewell, and passed the word down the ranks that, should we be separated by the accidents of war, my wagons were the meeting-place of any who survived.

Tshoza and his fifty glided away into the shadow silently as ghosts and were gone. Presently the fierce-faced Saduko departed also with his fifty. He carried the double-barrelled gun I had given him, and was accompanied by one of my best hunters, a Natal native, who was also armed with a heavy smooth-bore loaded with slugs. Our hope was that the sound of these guns might terrify the foe, should there be occasion to use them before our forces joined up again, and make them think they had to do with a body of raiding Dutch white men, of whose roers—as the heavy elephant guns of that day were called—all natives were much afraid.

So Saduko went with his fifty, leaving me wondering whether I should ever see his face again. Then I, my bearer Scowl, the two remaining hunters, and the ten score Amangwane who were left turned and soon were following the road by which we had come down the rugged pass. I call it a road, but, in fact, it was nothing but a water-washed gully strewn with boulders, through which we must pick our way as best we could in the darkness, having first removed the percussion cap from the nipple of every gun, for fear lest the accidental discharge of one of them should warn the Amakoba, confuse our other parties, and bring all our deep-laid plans to nothing.

Well, we accomplished that march somehow, walking in three long lines, so that each man might keep touch with him in front, and just as the moon began to rise reached the spot that I had chosen for the ambush.

Certainly it was well suited to that purpose. Here the track or gully bed narrowed to a width of not more than a hundred feet, while the steep slopes of the kloof on either side were clothed with scattered bushes and finger-like euphorbias which grew among stones. Behind these stones and bushes we hid ourselves, a hundred men on one side and a hundred on the other, whilst I and my three hunters, who were armed with guns, took up a position under shelter of a great boulder nearly five feet thick that lay but a little to the right of the gully itself, up which we expected the cattle would come. This place I chose for two reasons: first, that I might keep touch with both wings of my force, and, secondly, that we might be able to fire straight down the path on the pursuing Amakoba.

These were the orders that I gave to the Amangwane, warning them that he who disobeyed would be punished with death. They were not to stir until I, or, if I should be killed, one of my hunters, fired a shot; for my fear was lest, growing excited, they might leap out before the time and kill some of our own people, who very likely would be mixed up with the first of the pursuing Amakoba. Secondly, when the cattle had passed and the signal had been given, they were to rush on the Amakoba, throwing themselves across the gully, so that the enemy would have to fight upwards on a steep slope.

That was all I told them, since it is not wise to confuse natives by giving too many orders. One thing I added, however—that they must conquer or they must die. There was no mercy for them; it was a case of death or victory. Their spokesman—for these people always find a spokesman—answered that they thanked me for my advice; that they understood, and that they would do their best. Then they lifted their spears to me in salute. A wild lot of men they looked in the moonlight as they departed to take shelter behind the rocks and trees and wait.

That waiting was long, and I confess that before the end it got upon my nerves. I began to think of all sorts of things, such as whether I should live to see the sun rise again; also I reflected upon the legitimacy of this remarkable enterprise. What right had I to involve myself in a quarrel between these savages?

Why had I come here? To gain cattle as a trader? No, for I was not at all sure that I would take them if gained. Because Saduko had twitted me with faithlessness to my words? Yes, to a certain extent; but that was by no means the whole reason. I had been moved by the recital of the cruel wrongs inflicted upon Saduko and his tribe by this Bangu, and therefore had not been loath to associate myself with his attempted vengeance upon a wicked murderer. Well, that was sound enough so far as it went; but now a new consideration suggested itself to me. Those wrongs had been worked many years ago; probably most of the men who had aided and abetted them by now were dead or very aged, and it was their sons upon whom the vengeance would be wreaked.

What right had I to assist in visiting the sins of the fathers upon the sons? Frankly I could not say. The thing seemed to me to be a part of the problem of life, neither less nor more. So I shrugged my shoulders sadly and consoled myself by reflecting that very likely the issue would go against me, and that my own existence would pay the price of the venture and expound its moral. This consideration soothed my conscience somewhat, for when a man backs his actions with the risk of his life, right or wrong, at any rate he plays no coward's part.

The time went by very slowly and nothing happened. The waning moon shone brightly in a clear sky, and as there was no wind the silence seemed peculiarly intense. Save for the laugh of an occasional hyena and now and again for a sound which I took for the coughing of a distant lion, there was no stir between sleeping earth and moonlit heaven in which little clouds floated beneath the pale stars.

At length I thought that I heard a noise, a kind of murmur far away. It grew, it developed.

It sounded like a thousand sticks tapping upon something hard, very faintly. It continued to grow, and I knew the sound for that of the beating hoofs of animals galloping. Then there were isolated noises, very faint and thin; they might be shouts; then something that I could not mistake—shots fired at a distance. So the business was afoot; the cattle were moving, Saduko and my hunter were firing. There was nothing for it but to wait.

The excitement was very fierce; it seemed to consume me, to eat into my brain. The sound of the tapping upon the rocks grew louder until it merged into a kind of rumble, mixed with an echo as of that of very distant thunder, which presently I knew to be not thunder, but the bellowing of a thousand frightened beasts.

Nearer and nearer came the galloping hoofs and the rumble of bellowings; nearer and nearer the shouts of men, affronting the stillness of the solemn night. At length a single animal appeared, a koodoo buck that somehow had got mixed up with the cattle. It went past us like a flash, and was followed a minute or so later by a bull that, being young and light, had outrun its companions. That, too, went by, foam on its lips and its tongue hanging from its jaws.

Then the herd appeared—a countless herd it seemed to me—plunging up the incline—cows, heifers, calves, bulls, and oxen, all mixed together in one inextricable mass, and every one of them snorting, bellowing, or making some other kind of sound. The din was fearful, the sight bewildering, for the beasts were of all colours, and their long horns flashed like ivory in the moonlight. Indeed, the only thing in the least like it which I have ever seen was the rush of the buffaloes from the reed camp on that day when I got my injury.

They were streaming past us now, a mighty and moving mass so closely packed that a man might have walked upon their backs. In fact, some of the calves which had been thrust up by the pressure were being carried along in this fashion. Glad was I that none of us were in their path, for their advance seemed irresistible. No fence or wall could have saved us, and even stout trees that grew in the gully were snapped or thrust over.

At length the long line began to thin, for now it was composed of stragglers and weak or injured beasts, of which there were many. Other sounds, too, began to dominate the bellowings of the animals, those of the excited cries of men. The first of our companions, the cattle-lifters, appeared, weary and gasping, but waving their spears in triumph. Among them was old Tshoza. I stepped upon my rock, calling to him by name. He heard me, and presently was lying at my side panting.

"We have got them all!" he gasped. "Not a hoof is left save those that are trodden down. Saduko is not far behind with the rest of our brothers, except some that have been killed. All the Amakoba tribe are after us. He holds them back to give the cattle time to get away."

"Well done!" I answered. "It is very good. Now make your men hide among the others that they may find their breath before the fight."

So he stopped them as they came. Scarcely had the last of them vanished into the bushes when the gathering volume of shouts, amongst which I heard a gun go off, told us that Saduko and his band and the pursuing Amakoba were not far away. Presently they, too, appeared—that is the handful of Amangwane did—not fighting now, but running as hard as they could, for they knew they were approaching the ambush and wished to pass it so as not to be mixed up with the Amakoba. We let them go through us. Among the last of them came Saduko, who was wounded, for the blood ran down his side, supporting my hunter, who was also wounded, more severely as I feared.

I called to him.

"Saduko," I said, "halt at the crest of the path and rest there so that you may be able to help us presently."

He waved the gun in answer, for he was too breathless to speak, and went on with those who were left of his following—perhaps thirty men in all—in the track of the cattle. Before he was out of sight the Amakoba arrived, a mob of five or six hundred men mixed up together and advancing without order or discipline, for they seemed to have lost their heads as well as their cattle. Some of them had shields and some had none, some broad and some throwing assegais, while many were quite naked, not having stayed to put on their moochas and much less their war finery. Evidently they were mad with rage, for the sounds that issued from them seemed to concentrate into one mighty curse.

The moment had come, though to tell the truth I heartily wished that it had not. I wasn't exactly afraid, although I never set up for great courage, but I did not quite like the business. After all we were stealing these people's cattle, and now were going to kill as many of them as we could. I had to recall Saduko's dreadful story of the massacre of his tribe before I could make up my mind to give the signal. That hardened me, and so did the reflection that after all they outnumbered us enormously and very likely would prove victors in the end. Anyhow it was too late to repent. What a tricky and uncomfortable thing is conscience, that nearly always begins to trouble us at the moment of, or after, the event, not before, when it might be of some use.

I raised myself upon the rock and fired both barrels of my gun into the advancing horde, though whether I killed anyone or no I cannot say. I have always hoped that I did not; but as the mark was large and I am a fair shot, I fear that is scarcely possible. Next moment, with a howl that sounded like that of wild beasts, from either side of the gorge the fierce Amangwane free-spears—for that is what they were—leapt out of their hiding-places and hurled themselves upon their hereditary foes. They were fighting for more than cattle; they were fighting for hate and for revenge since these Amakoba had slaughtered their fathers and their mothers, their sisters and their brothers, and they alone remained to pay them back blood for blood.

Great heaven! how they did fight, more like devils than human beings. After that first howl which shaped itself to the word "Saduko," they were silent as bulldogs. Though they were so few, at first their terrible rush drove back the Amakoba. Then, as these recovered from their surprise, the weight of numbers began to tell, for they, too, were brave men who did not give way to panic. Scores of them went down at once, but the remainder pushed the Amangwane before them up the hill. I took little share in the fight, but was thrust backward with the others, only firing when I was obliged to save my own life. Foot by foot we were pushed back till at length we drew near to the crest of the pass.

Then, while the issue hung in the balance, there was another shout of "Saduko!" and that chief himself, followed by his thirty, rushed upon the Amakoba.

This charge decided the battle, for not knowing how many more were coming, those who were left of the Amakoba turned and fled, nor did we pursue them far.

We mustered on the hill-top, not more than two hundred of us now, the rest were fallen or desperately wounded, my poor hunter, whom I had lent to Saduko, being among the dead. Although wounded, he died fighting to the last, then fell down, shouting to me:

"Chief, have I done well?" and expired.

I was breathless and spent, but as in a dream I saw some Amangwane drag up a gaunt old savage, crying:

"Here is Bangu, Bangu the Butcher, whom we have caught alive."

Saduko stepped up to him.

"Ah! Bangu," be said, "now say, why should I not kill you as you would have killed the little lad Saduko long ago, had not Zikali saved him? See, here is the mark of your spear."

"Kill," said Bangu. "Your Spirit is stronger than mine. Did not Zikali foretell it? Kill, Saduko."

"Nay," answered Saduko. "If you are weary I am weary, too, and wounded as well. Take a spear, Bangu, and we will fight."

So they fought there in the moonlight, man to man; fought fiercely while all watched, till presently I saw Bangu throw his arms wide and fall backwards.

Saduko was avenged. I have always been glad that he slew his enemy thus, and not as it might have been expected that he would do.

Saduko Brings the Marriage Gift

We reached my wagons in the early morning of the following day, bringing with us the cattle and our wounded. Thus encumbered it was a most toilsome march, and an anxious one also, for it was always possible that the remnant of the Amakoba might attempt pursuit. This, however, they did not do, for very many of them were dead or wounded, and those who remained had no heart left in them. They went back to their mountain home and lived there in shame and wretchedness, for I do not believe there were fifty head of cattle left among the tribe, and Kafirs without cattle are nothing. Still, they did not starve, since there were plenty of women to work the fields, and we had not touched their corn. The end of them was that Panda gave them to their conqueror, Saduko, and he incorporated them with the Amangwane. But that did not happen until some time afterwards.

When we had rested a while at the wagons the captured beasts were mustered, and on being counted were found to number a little over twelve hundred head, not reckoning animals that had been badly hurt in the flight, which we killed for beef. It was a noble prize, truly, and, notwithstanding the wound in his thigh, which hurt him a good deal now that it had stiffened, Saduko stood up and surveyed them with glistening eyes. No wonder, for he who had been so poor was now rich, and would remain so even after he had paid over whatever number of cows Umbezi chose to demand as the price of Mameena's hand. Moreover, he was sure, and I shared his confidence, that in these changed circumstances both that young woman and her father would look upon his suit with very favourable eyes. He had, so to speak, succeeded to the title and the family estates by means of a lawsuit brought in the "Court of the Assegai," and therefore there was hardly a father in Zululand who would shut his kraal gate upon him. We forgot, both of us, the proverb that points out how numerous are the slips between the cup and the lip, which, by the way, is one that has its Zulu equivalents. One of them, if I remember right at the moment, is: "However loud the hen cackles, the housewife does not always get the egg."

As it chanced, although Saduko's hen was cackling very loudly just at this time, he was not destined to find the coveted egg. But of that matter I will speak in its place.

I, too, looked at those cattle, wondering whether Saduko would remember our bargain, under which some six hundred head of them belonged to me. Six hundred head! Why, putting them at £5 apiece all round—and as oxen were very scarce just at that time, they were worth quite as much, if not more—that meant £3,000, a larger sum of money than I had ever owned at one time in all my life. Truly the paths of violence were profitable! But would he remember? On the whole I thought probably not, since Kafirs are not fond of parting with cattle.

Well, I did him an injustice, for presently he turned and said, with something of an effort:

"Macumazahn, half of all these belong to you, and truly you have earned them, for it was your cunning and good counsel that gained us the victory. Now we will choose them beast by beast."

So I chose a fine ox, then Saduko chose one; and so it went on till I had eight of my number driven out. As the eighth was taken I turned to Saduko and said:

"There, that will do. These oxen I must have to replace those in my teams which died on the trek, but I want no more."

"Wow!" said Saduko, and all those who stood with him, while one of them added—I think it was old Tshoza:

"He refuses six hundred cattle which are fairly his! He must be mad!"

"No friends," I answered, "I am not mad, but neither am I bad. I accompanied Saduko on this raid because he is dear to me and stood by me once in the hour of danger. But I do not love killing men with whom I have no quarrel, and I will not take the price of blood."

"Wow!" said old Tshoza again, for Saduko seemed too astonished to speak, "he is a spirit, not a man. He is *holy!*"

"Not a bit of it," I answered. "If you think that, ask Mameena"—a dark saying which they did not understand. "Now, listen. I will not take those cattle because I do not think as you Kafirs think. But as they are mine, according to your law, I am going to dispose of them. I give ten head to each of my hunters, and fifteen head to the relations of him who was killed. The rest I give to Tshoza and to the other men of the Amangwane who fought with us, to be divided among them in such proportions as they may agree, I being the judge in the event of any quarrel arising."

Now these men raised a great cry of "Inkoosi!" and, running up, old Tshoza seized my hand and kissed it.

"Your heart is big," he cried; "you drop fatness! Although you are so small, the spirit of a king lives in you, and the wisdom of the heavens."

Thus he praised me, while all the others joined in, till the din was awful. Saduko thanked me also in his magnificent manner. Yet I do not think that he was altogether pleased, although my great gift relieved him from the necessity of sharing up the spoil with his companions. The truth was, or so I believe, that he understood that henceforth the Amangwane would love me better than they loved him. This, indeed, proved to be the case, for I am sure that there was no man among all those wild fellows who would not have served me to the death, and to this day my name is a power among them and their descendants. Also it has grown into something of a proverb among all those Kafirs who know the story. They talk of any great act of liberality in an idiom as "a gift of Macumazana," and in the same way of one who makes any remarkable renunciation, as "a wearer of Macumazana's blanket," or as "he who has stolen Macumazana's shadow."

Thus did I earn a great reputation very cheaply, for really I could not have taken those cattle; also I am sure that had I done so they would have brought me bad luck. Indeed, one of the regrets of my life is that I had anything whatsoever to do with the business.

Our journey back to Umbezi's kraal—for thither we were heading—was very slow, hampered as we were with wounded and by a vast herd of cattle. Of the latter, indeed, we got rid after a while, for, except those which I had given to my men, and a hundred or so of the best beasts that Saduko took with him for a certain purpose, they were sent away to a place which he had chosen, in charge of about half of his people, under the command of his uncle, Tshoza, there to await his coming.

Over a month had gone by since the night of the ambush when at last we outspanned quite close to Umbezi's, in that bush where first I had met the Amangwane free-spears. A very different set of men they looked on this triumphant day to those fierce fellows who had slipped out of the trees at the call of their chief. As we went through the country Saduko had bought fine moochas and blankets for them; also head-dresses had been made with the long black feathers of the sakabuli finch, and shields and leglets of the hides and tails of oxen. Moreover, having fed plentifully and travelled easily, they were fat and well-favoured, as, given good food, natives soon become after a period of abstinence.

The plan of Saduko was to lie quiet in the bush that night, and on the following morning to advance in all his grandeur, accompanied by his spears, present the hundred head of cattle that had been demanded, and formally ask his daughter's hand from Umbezi. As the reader may have gathered already, there was a certain histrionic vein in Saduko; also when he was in feather he liked to show off his plumage.

Well, this plan was carried out to the letter. On the following morning, after the sun was well up, Saduko, as a great chief does, sent forward two bedizened heralds to announce his approach to Umbezi, after whom followed two other men to sing his deeds and praises. (By the way, I observed that they had clearly been instructed to avoid any mention of a person called Macumazahn.) Then we advanced in force. First went Saduko, splendidly apparelled as a chief, carrying a small assegai and adorned with plumes, leglets and a leopard-skin kilt. He was attended by about half a dozen of the best-looking of his followers, who posed as "indunas" or councillors. Behind these I walked, a dusty, insignificant little fellow, attended by the ugly, snub-nosed Scowl in a very greasy pair of trousers, worn-out European boots through which his toes peeped, and nothing else, and by my three surviving hunters, whose appearance was even more disreputable. After us marched about four score of the transformed Amangwane, and after them came the hundred picked cattle driven by a few herdsmen.

In due course we arrived at the gate of the kraal, where we found the heralds and the praisers prancing and shouting.

"Have you seen Umbezi?" asked Saduko of them.

"No," they answered; "he was asleep when we got here, but his people say that he is coming out presently."

"Then tell his people that he had better be quick about it, or I shall turn him out," replied the proud Saduko.

Just at this moment the kraal gate opened and through it appeared Umbezi, looking extremely fat and foolish; also, it struck me, frightened, although this he tried to conceal.

"Who visits me here," he said, "with so much—um—ceremony?" and with the carved dancing-stick he carried he pointed doubtfully at the lines of armed men. "Oh, it is you, is it, Saduko?" and he looked him up and down, adding: "How grand you are to be sure. Have you been robbing anybody? And you, too, Macumazahn. Well, *you* do not look grand. You look like an old cow that has been suckling two calves on the winter veld. But tell me, what are all these warriors for? I ask because I have not food for so many, especially as we have just had a feast here."

"Fear nothing, Umbezi," answered Saduko in his grandest manner. "I have brought food for my own men. As for my business, it is simple. You asked a hundred head of cattle as the lobola [that is, the marriage gift] of your daughter, Mameena. They are there. Go send your servants to the kraal and count them."

"Oh, with pleasure," Umbezi replied nervously, and he gave some orders to certain men behind him. "I am glad to see that you have become rich in this sudden fashion, Saduko, though how you have done so I cannot understand."

"Never mind how I have become rich," answered Saduko. "I *am* rich; that is enough for the present. Be pleased to send for Mameena, for I would talk with her."

"Yes, yes, Saduko, I understand that you would talk with Mameena; but"—and he looked round him desperately—"I fear that she is still asleep. As you know, Mameena was always a late riser, and, what is more, she hates to be disturbed. Don't you think that you could come back, say, to-morrow morning? She will be sure to be up by then; or, better still, the day after?"

"In which hut is Mameena?" asked Saduko sternly, while I, smelling a rat, began to chuckle to myself.

"I really do not know, Saduko," replied Umbezi. "Sometimes she sleeps in one, sometimes in another, and sometimes she goes several hours' journey away to her aunt's kraal for a change. I should not be in the least surprised if she had done so last night. I have no control over Mameena."

Before Saduko could answer, a shrill, rasping voice broke upon our ears, which after some search I saw proceeded from an ugly and ancient female seated in the shadow, in whom I recognised the lady who was known by the pleasing name of "Worn-out-Old-Cow."

"He lies!" screeched the voice. "He lies. Thanks be to the spirit of my ancestors that wild cat Mameena has left this kraal for good. She slept last night, not with her aunt, but with her husband, Masapo, to whom Umbezi gave her in marriage two days ago, receiving in payment a hundred and twenty head of cattle, which was twenty more than *you* bid, Saduko."

Now when Saduko heard these words I thought that he would really go mad with rage. He turned quite grey under his dark skin and for a while trembled like a leaf, looking as though he were about to fall to the ground. Then he leapt as a lion leaps, and seizing Umbezi by the throat, hurled him backwards, standing over him with raised spear.

"You dog!" he cried in a terrible voice. "Tell me the truth or I will rip you up. What have you done with Mameena?"

"Oh! Saduko," answered Umbezi in choking tones, "Mameena has chosen to get married. It was no fault of mine; she would have her way."

He got no farther, and had I not intervened by throwing my arms about Saduko and dragging him back, that moment would have been Umbezi's last, for Saduko was about to pin him to the earth with his spear. As it proved, I was just in time, and Saduko, being weak with emotion, for I felt his heart going like a sledge-hammer, could not break from my grasp before his reason returned to him.

At length he recovered himself a little and threw down his spear as though to put himself out of temptation. Then he spoke, always in the same terrible voice, asking:

"Have you more to say about this business, Umbezi? I would hear all before I answer you."

"Only this, Saduko," replied Umbezi, who had risen to his feet and was shaking like a reed. "I did no more than any other father would have done. Masapo is a very powerful chief, one who will be a good stick for me to lean on in my old age. Mameena declared that she wished to marry him—"

"He lies!" screeched the "Old Cow." "What Mameena said was that she had no will towards marriage with any Zulu in the land, so I suppose she is looking after a white man," and she leered in my direction. "She said, however, that if her father wished to marry her to Masapo, she must be a dutiful daughter and obey him, but that if blood and trouble came of that marriage, let it be on his head and not on hers."

"Would you also stick your claws into me, cat?" shouted Umbezi, catching the old woman a savage cut across the back with the light dancing-stick which he still held in his hand, whereon she fled away screeching and cursing him.

"Oh, Saduko," he went on, "let not your ears be poisoned by these falsehoods. Mameena never said anything of the sort, or if she did it was not to me. Well, the moment that my daughter had consented to take Masapo as her husband his people drove a hundred and twenty of the most beautiful cattle over the hill, and would you have had me refuse them, Saduko? I am sure that when you have seen them you will say that I was quite right to accept such a splendid lobola in return for one sharp-tongued girl. Remember, Saduko, that although you had promised a hundred head, that is less by twenty, at the time you did not own one, and where you were to get them from I could not guess. Moreover," he added with a last, desperate, imaginative effort, for I think he saw that his arguments were making no impression, "some strangers who called here told me that both you and Macumazahn had been killed by certain evil-doers in the mountains. There, I have spoken, and, Saduko, if you now have cattle, why, on my part, I have another daughter, not quite so good-looking perhaps, but a much better worker in the field. Come and drink a sup of beer, and I will send for her."

"Stop talking about your other daughter and your beer and listen to me," replied Saduko, looking at the assegai which he had thrown to the ground so ominously that I set my foot on it. "I am now a greater chief than the boar Masapo. Has Masapo such a bodyguard as these Eaters-up-of-Enemies?" and he jerked his thumb backwards towards the serried lines of fierce-faced Amangwane who stood listening behind us. "Has Masapo as many cattle as I have, whereof those which you see are but a tithe brought as a lobola gift to the father of her who had been promised to me as wife? Is Masapo Panda's friend? I think that I have heard otherwise. Has Masapo just conquered a countless tribe by his courage and his wit? Is Masapo young and of high blood, or is he but an old, low-born boar of the mountains?

"You do not answer, Umbezi, and perhaps you do well to be silent. Now listen again. Were it not for Macumazahn here, whom I do not desire to mix up with my quarrels, I would bid my men take you and beat you to death with the handles of their spears, and then go on and serve the Boar in the same fashion in his mountain sty. As it is, these things must wait a little while, especially as I have other matters to attend to first. Yet the day is not far off when I will attend to them also. Therefore my counsel to you, Cheat, is to make haste to die or to find courage to fall upon a spear, unless you would learn how it feels to be brayed with sticks like a green hide until none can know that you were once a man. Send now and tell my words to Masapo the Boar. And to Mameena say that soon I will come to take her with spears and not with cattle. Do you understand? Oh! I see that you do, since already you weep with fear like a woman. Then farewell to you till that day when I return with the sticks, O Umbezi the cheat and the liar, Umbezi, 'Eater-up-of-Elephants,'" and turning, Saduko stalked away.

I was about to follow in a great hurry, having had enough of this very unpleasant scene, when poor old Umbezi sprang at me and clasped me by the arm.

"O Macumazana," he exclaimed, weeping in his terror, "O Macumazana, if ever I have been a friend to you, help me out of this deep pit into which I have fallen through the tricks of that monkey of a daughter of mine, who I think is a witch born to bring trouble upon men. Macumazahn, if she had been your daughter and a powerful chief had appeared with a hundred and twenty head of such beautiful cattle, you would have given her to him, would you not, although he is of mixed blood and not very young, especially as she did not mind who only cares for place and wealth?"

"I think not," I answered; "but then it is not our custom to sell women in that fashion."

"No, no, I forgot; in this as in other matters you white men are mad and, Macumazahn, to tell you the truth, I believe it is you she really cares for; she said as much to me once or twice. Well, why did you not take her away when I was not looking? We could have settled matters afterwards, and I should have been free of her witcheries and not up to my neck in this hole as I am now."

"Because some people don't do that kind of thing, Umbezi."

"No, no, I forgot. Oh! why can I not remember that you are *quite* mad and therefore that it must not be expected of you to act as though you were sane. Well, at least you are that tiger Saduko's friend, which again shows that you must be very mad, for most people would sooner try to milk a cow buffalo than walk hand in hand with him. Don't you see, Macumazahn, that he means to kill me, Macumazahn, to bray me like a green hide? Ugh! to beat me to death with sticks. Ugh! And what is more, that unless you prevent him, he will certainly do it, perhaps to-morrow or the next day. Ugh! Ugh! Ugh!"

"Yes, I see, Umbezi, and I think that he *will* do it. But what I do not see is how I am to prevent him. Remember that you let Mameena grow into his heart and behaved badly to him, Umbezi."

"I never promised her to him, Macumazahn. I only said that if he brought a hundred cattle, then I might promise."

"Well, he has wiped out the Amakoba, the enemies of his House, and there are the hundred cattle whereof he has many more, and now it is too late for you to keep your share of the bargain. So I think you must make yourself as comfortable as you can in the hole that your hands dug, Umbezi, which I would not share for all the cattle in Zululand."

"Truly you are not one from whom to seek comfort in the hour of distress," groaned poor Umbezi, then added, brightening up: "But perhaps Panda will kill him because he has wiped out Bangu in a time of peace. Oh Macumazahn, can you not persuade Panda to kill him? If so, I now have more cattle than I really want—"

"Impossible," I answered. "Panda is his friend, and between ourselves I may tell you that he ate up the Amakoba by his especial wish. When the King hears of it he will call to Saduko to sit in his shadow and make him great, one of his councillors, probably with power of life and death over little people like you and Masapo."

"Then it is finished," said Umbezi faintly, "and I will try to die like a man. But to be brayed like a hide! And with thin sticks! Oh!" he added, grinding his teeth, "if only I can get hold of Mameena I will not leave much of that pretty hair of hers upon her head. I will tie her hands and shut her up with the 'Old Cow,' who loves her as a meer-cat loves a mouse. No; I will kill her. There—do you hear, Macumazahn, unless you do something to help me, I will kill Mameena, and you won't like that, for I am sure she is dear to you, although you were not man enough to run away with her as she wished."

"If you touch Mameena," I said, "be certain, my friend, that Saduko's sticks and your skin will not be far apart, for I will report you to Panda myself as an unnatural evil-doer. Now hearken to me, you old fool. Saduko is so fond of your daughter, on this point being mad, as you say I am, that if only he could get her I think he might overlook the fact of her having been married before. What you have to do is to try to buy her back from Masapo. Mind you, I say buy her back—not get her by bloodshed—which you might do by persuading Masapo to put her away. Then, if he knew that you were trying to do this, I think that Saduko might leave his sticks uncut for a while."

"I will try. I will indeed, Macumazahn. I will try very hard. It is true Masapo is an obstinate pig; still, if he knows that his own life is at stake, he might give way. Moreover, when she learns that Saduko has grown rich and great, Mameena might help me. Oh, I thank you, Macumazahn; you are indeed the prop of my hut, and it and all in it are yours. Farewell, farewell, Macumazahn, if you must go. But why—why did you not run away with Mameena, and save me all this fear and trouble?"

So I and that old humbug, Umbezi, "Eater-up-of-Elephants," parted for a while, and never did I know him in a more chastened frame of mind, except once, as I shall tell.

The King's Daughter

When I got back to my wagons after this semi-tragical interview with that bombastic and self-seeking old windbag, Umbezi, it was to find that Saduko and his warriors had already marched for the King's kraal, Nodwengu. A message awaited me, however, to the effect that it was hoped that I would follow, in order to make report of the affair of the destruction of the Amakoba. This, after reflection, I determined to do, really, I think, because of the intense human interest of the whole business. I wanted to see how it would work out.

Also, in a way, I read Saduko's mind and understood that at the moment he did not wish to discuss the matter of his hideous disappointment. Whatever else may have been false in this man's nature, one thing rang true, namely, his love or his infatuation for the girl Mameena. Throughout his life she was his guiding star—about as evil a star as could have arisen upon any man's horizon; the fatal star that was to light him down to doom. Let me thank Providence, as I do, that I was so fortunate as to escape its baneful influences, although I admit that they attracted me not a little.

So, seduced thither by my curiosity, which has so often led me into trouble, I trekked to Nodwengu, full of many doubts not unmingled with amusement, for I could not rid my mind of recollections of the utter terror of the "Eater-up-of-Elephants" when he was brought face to face with the dreadful and concentrated rage of the robbed Saduko and the promise of his vengeance. Ultimately I arrived at the Great Place without experiencing any adventure that is worthy of record, and camped in a spot that was appointed to me by some *induna* whose name I forget, but who evidently knew of my approach, for I found him awaiting me at some distance from the town. Here I sat for quite a long while, two or three days, if I remember right, amusing myself with killing or missing turtle-doves with a shotgun, and similar pastimes, until something should happen, or I grew tired and started for Natal.

In the end, just as I was about to trek seawards, an old friend, Maputa, turned up at my wagons—that same man who had brought me the message from Panda before we started to attack Bangu.

"Greeting, Macumazahn," he said. "What of the Amakoba? I see they did not kill you."

"No," I answered, handing him some snuff, "they did not quite kill me, for here I am. What is your pleasure with me?"

"O Macumazana, only that the King wishes to know whether you have any of those little balls left in the box which I brought back to you, since, if so, he thinks he would like to swallow one of them in this hot weather."

I proffered him the whole box, but he would not take it, saying that the King would like me to give it to him myself. Now I understood that this was a summons to an audience, and asked when it would please Panda to receive me and "the-little-black-stones-that-work-wonders." He answered—at once.

So we started, and within an hour I stood, or rather sat, before Panda.

Like all his family, the King was an enormous man, but, unlike Chaka and those of his brothers whom I had known, one of a kindly countenance. I saluted him by lifting my cap, and took my place upon a wooden stool that had been provided for me outside the great hut, in the shadow of which he sat within his isi-gohlo, or private enclosure.

"Greeting, O Macumazana," he said. "I am glad to see you safe and well, for I understand that you have been engaged upon a perilous adventure since last we met."

"Yes, King," I answered; "but to which adventure do you refer—that of the buffalo, when Saduko helped me, or that of the Amakoba, when I helped Saduko?"

"The latter, Macumazahn, of which I desire to hear all the story."

So I told it to him, he and I being alone, for he commanded his councillors and servants to retire out of hearing.

"Wow!" he said, when I had finished, "you are clever as a baboon, Macumazahn. That was a fine trick to set a trap for Bangu and his Amakoba dogs and bait it with his own cattle. But they tell me that you refused your share of those cattle. Now, why was that, Macumazahn?"

By way of answer I repeated to Panda my reasons, which I have set out already.

"Ah!" he exclaimed, when I had finished. "Every one seeks greatness in his own way, and perhaps yours is better than ours. Well, the White man walks one road—or some of them do—and the Black man another. They both end at the same place, and none will know which is the right road till the journey is done. Meanwhile, what you lose Saduko and his people gain. He is a wise man, Saduko, who knows how to choose his friends, and his wisdom has brought him victory and gifts. But to you, Macumazahn, it has brought nothing but honour, on which, if a man feeds only, he will grow thin."

"I like to be thin, O Panda," I answered slowly.

"Yes, yes, I understand," replied the King, who, in common with most natives, was quick enough to seize a point, "and I, too, like people who keep thin on such food as yours, people, also, whose hands are always clean. We Zulus trust you, Macumazahn, as we trust few white men, for we have known for years that your lips say what your heart thinks, and that your heart always thinks the thing which is good. You may be named Watcher-by-Night, but you love light, not darkness."

Now, at these somewhat unusual compliments I bowed, and felt myself colouring a little as I did so, even through my sunburn, but I made no answer to them, since to do so would have involved a discussion of the past and its tragical events, into which I had no wish to enter. Panda, too, remained silent for a while. Then he called to a messenger to summon the princes, Cetewayo and Umbelazi, and to bid Saduko, the son of Matiwane, to wait without, in case he should wish to speak with him.

A few minutes later the two princes arrived. I watched their coming with interest, for they were the most important men in Zululand, and already the nation debated fiercely which of them would succeed to the throne. I will try to describe them a little.

They were both of much the same age—it is always difficult to arrive at a Zulu's exact years—and both fine young men. Cetewayo, however, had the stronger countenance. It was said that he resembled that fierce and able monster, Chaka the Wild Beast, his uncle, and certainly I perceived in him a likeness to his other uncle, Dingaan, Umpanda's predecessor, whom I had known but too well when I was a lad. He had the same surly eyes and haughty bearing; also, when he was angry his mouth shut itself in the same iron fashion.

Of Umbelazi it is difficult for me to speak without enthusiasm. As Mameena was the most beautiful woman I ever saw in Zululand—although it is true that old war-dog, Umslopogaas, a friend of mine who does not come into this story, used to tell me that Nada the Lily, whom I have mentioned, was even lovelier—so Umbelazi was by far the most splendid man. Indeed, the Zulus named him "Umbelazi the Handsome," and no wonder. To begin with, he stood at least three inches above the tallest of them; from a quarter of a mile away I have recognised him by his great height, even through the dust of a desperate battle, and his breadth was proportionate to his stature. Then he was perfectly made, his great, shapely limbs ending, like Saduko's, in small hands and feet. His face, too, was well-cut and open, his colour lighter than Cetewayo's, and his eyes, which always seemed to smile, were large and dark.

Even before they passed the small gate of the inner fence it was easy for me to see that this royal pair were not upon the best of terms, for each of them tried to get through it first, to show his right of precedence. The result was somewhat ludicrous, for they jammed in the gateway. Here, however, Umbelazi's greater weight told, for, putting out his strength, he squeezed his brother into the reeds of the fence, and won through a foot or so in front of him.

"You grow too fat, my brother," I heard Cetewayo say, and saw him scowl as he spoke. "If I had held an assegai in my hand you would have been cut."

"I know it, my brother," answered Umbelazi, with a good-humoured laugh, "but I knew also that none may appear before the King armed. Had it been otherwise, I would rather have followed after you."

Now, at this hint of Umbelazi's, that he would not trust his brother behind his back with a spear, although it seemed to be conveyed in jest, I saw Panda shift uneasily on his seat, while Cetewayo scowled even more ominously than before. However, no further words passed between them, and, walking up to the King side by side, they saluted him with raised hands, calling out "Baba!"—that is, Father.

"Greeting, my children," said Panda, adding hastily, for he foresaw a quarrel as to which of them should take the seat of honour on his right: "Sit there in front of me, both of you, and, Macumazahn, do you come hither," and he pointed to the coveted place. "I am a little deaf in my left ear this morning."

So these brothers sat themselves down in front of the King; nor were they, I think, grieved to find this way out of their rivalry; but first they shook hands with me, for I knew them both, though not well, and even in this small matter the old trouble arose, since there was some difficulty as to which of them should first offer me his hand. Ultimately, I remember, Cetewayo won this trick.

When these preliminaries were finished, Panda addressed the princes, saying:

"My sons, I have sent for you to ask your counsel upon a certain matter—not a large matter, but one that may grow." And he paused to take snuff, whereon both of them ejaculated:

"We hear you, Father."

"Well, my sons, the matter is that of Saduko, the son of Matiwane, chief of the Amangwane, whom Bangu, chief of the Amakoba, ate up years ago by leave of Him who went before me. Now, this Bangu, as you know, has for some time been a thorn in my foot—a thorn that caused it to fester—and yet I did not wish to make war on him. So I spoke a word in the ear of Saduko, saying, 'He is yours, if you can kill him; and his cattle are yours.' Well, Saduko is not dull. With the help of this white man, Macumazahn, our friend from of old, he has killed Bangu and taken his cattle, and already my foot is beginning to heal."

"We have heard it," said Cetewayo.

"It was a great deed," added Umbelazi, a more generous critic.

"Yes," continued Panda, "I, too, think it was a great deed, seeing that Saduko had but a small regiment of wanderers to back him—"

"Nay," interrupted Cetewayo, "it was not those eaters of rats who won him the day, it was the wisdom of this Macumazahn."

"Macumazahn's wisdom would have been of little use without the courage of Saduko and his rats," commented Umbelazi, and from this moment I saw that the two brothers were taking sides for and against Saduko, as they did upon every other matter, not because they cared for the right of whatever was in question, but because they wished to oppose each other.

"Quite so," went on the King; "I agree with both of you, my sons. But the point is this: I think Saduko a man of promise, and one who should be advanced that he may learn to love us all, especially as his House has suffered wrong from our House, since He-who-is-gone listened to the evil counsel of Bangu, and allowed him to kill out Matiwane's tribe without just cause. Therefore, in order to wipe away this stain and bind Saduko to us, I think it well to re-establish Saduko in the chieftainship of the Amangwane, with the lands that his father held, and to give him also the chieftainship of the Amakoba, of whom it seems that the women and children, with some of the men, remain, although he already holds their cattle which he has captured in war."

"As the King pleases," said Umbelazi, with a yawn, for he was growing weary of listening to the case of Saduko.

But Cetewayo said nothing, for he appeared to be thinking of something else.

"I think also," went on Panda in a rather uncertain voice, "in order to bind him so close that the bonds may never be broken, it would be wise to give him a woman of our family in marriage."

"Why should this little Amangwane be allowed to marry into the royal House?" asked Cetewayo, looking up. "If he is dangerous, why not kill him, and have done?"

"For this reason, my son. There is trouble ahead in Zululand, and I do not wish to kill those who may help us in that hour, nor do I wish them to become our enemies. I wish that they may be our friends; and therefore it seems to me wise, when we find a seed of greatness, to water it, and not to dig it up or plant it in a neighbour's garden. From his deeds I believe that this Saduko is such a seed."

"Our father has spoken," said Umbelazi; "and I like Saduko, who is a man of mettle and good blood. Which of our sisters does our father propose to give to him?"

"She who is named after the mother of our race, O Umbelazi; she whom your own mother bore—your sister Nandie" (in English, 'The Sweet').

"A great gift, O my Father, since Nandie is both fair and wise. Also, what does she think of this matter?"

"She thinks well of it, Umbelazi, for she has seen Saduko and taken a liking to him. She told me herself that she wishes no other husband."

"Is it so?" replied Umbelazi indifferently. "Then if the King commands, and the King's daughter desires, what more is there to be said?"

"Much, I think," broke in Cetewayo. "I hold that it is out of place that this little man, who has but conquered a little tribe by borrowing the wit of Macumazahn here, should be rewarded not only with a chieftainship, but with the hand of the wisest and most beautiful of the King's daughters, even though Umbelazi," he added, with a sneer, "should be willing to throw him his own sister like a bone to a passing dog."

"Who threw the bone, Cetewayo?" asked Umbelazi, awaking out of his indifference. "Was it the King, or was it I, who never heard of the matter till this moment? And who are we that we should question the King's decrees? Is it our business to judge or to obey?"

"Has Saduko perchance made you a present of some of those cattle which he stole from the Amakoba, Umbelazi?" asked Cetewayo. "As our father asks no lobola, perhaps you have taken the gift instead."

"The only gift that I have taken from Saduko," said Umbelazi, who, I could see, was hard pressed to keep his temper, "is that of his service. He is my friend, which is why you hate him, as you hate all my friends."

"Must I then love every stray cur that licks your hand, Umbelazi? Oh, no need to tell me he is your friend, for I know it was you who put it into our father's heart to allow him to kill Bangu and steal his cattle, which I hold to be an ill deed, for now the Great House is thatched with his reeds and Bangu's blood is on its doorposts. Moreover, he who wrought the wrong is to come and dwell therein, and for aught I know to be called a prince, like you and me. Why should he not, since the Princess Nandie is to be given to him in marriage? Certainly, Umbelazi, you would do well to take the cattle which this white trader has refused, for all men know that you have earned them."

Now Umbelazi sprang up, straightening himself to the full of his great height, and spoke in a voice that was thick with passion.

"I pray your leave to withdraw, O King," he said, "since if I stay here longer I shall grow sorry that I have no spear in my hand. Yet before I go I will tell the truth. Cetewayo hates Saduko, because, knowing him to be a chief of wit and courage, who will grow great, he sought him for his man, saying, 'Sit you in my shadow,' after he had promised to sit in mine. Therefore it is that he heaps these taunts upon me. Let him deny it if he can."

"That I shall not trouble to do, Umbelazi," answered Cetewayo, with a scowl. "Who are you that spy upon my doings, and with a mouth full of lies call me to account before the King? I will hear no more of it. Do you bide here and pay Saduko his price with the person of our sister. For, as the King has promised her, his word cannot be changed. Only let your dog know that I keep a stick for him, if he should snarl at me. Farewell, my Father. I go upon a journey to my own lordship, the land of Gikazi, and there you will find me when you want me, which I pray may not be till after this marriage is finished, for on that I will not trust my eyes to look."

Then, with a salute, he turned and departed, bidding no good-bye to his brother.

My hand, however, he shook in farewell, for Cetewayo was always friendly to me, perhaps because he thought I might be useful to him. Also, as I learned afterwards, he was very pleased with me for the reason that I had refused my share of the Amakoba cattle, and that he knew I had no part in this proposed marriage between Saduko and Nandie, of which, indeed, I now heard for the first time.

"My Father," said Umbelazi, when Cetewayo had gone, "is this to be borne? Am I to blame in the matter? You have heard and seen—answer me, my Father."

"No, you are not to blame this time, Umbelazi," replied the King, with a heavy sigh. "But oh! my sons, my sons, where will your quarrelling end? I think that only a river of blood can quench so fierce a fire, and then which of you will live to reach its bank?"

For a while he looked at Umbelazi, and I saw love and fear in his eye, for towards him Panda always had more affection than for any of his other children.

"Cetewayo has behaved ill," he said at length; "and before a white man, who will report the matter, which makes it worse. He has no right to dictate to me to whom I shall or shall not give my daughters in marriage. Moreover, I have spoken; nor do I change my word because he threatens me. It is known throughout the land that I never change my word; and the white men know it also, do they not, O Macumazana?"

I answered yes, they did. Also, this was true, for, like most weak men, Panda was very obstinate, and honest, too, in his own fashion.

He waved his hand, to show that the subject was ended, then bade Umbelazi go to the gate and send a messenger to bring in "the son of Matiwane."

Presently Saduko arrived, looking very stately and composed as he lifted his right hand and gave Panda the "Bayete"—the royal salute.

"Be seated," said the King. "I have words for your ear."

Thereon, with the most perfect grace, without hurrying and without undue delay, Saduko crouched himself down upon his knees, with one of his elbows resting on the ground, as only a native knows how to do without looking absurd, and waited.

"Son of Matiwane," said the King, "I have heard all the story of how, with a small company, you destroyed Bangu and most of the men of the Amakoba, and ate up their cattle every one."

"Your pardon, Black One," interrupted Saduko. "I am but a boy, I did nothing. It was Macumazahn, Watcher-by-Night, who sits yonder. His wisdom taught me how to snare the Amakoba, after they were decoyed from their mountain, and it was Tshoza, my uncle, who loosed the cattle from the kraals. I say that I did nothing, except to strike a blow or two with a spear when I must, just as a baboon throws stones at those who would steal its young."

"I am glad to see that you are no boaster, Saduko," said Panda. "Would that more of the Zulus were like you in that matter, for then I must not listen to so many loud songs about little things. At least, Bangu was killed and his proud tribe humbled, and, for reasons of state, I am glad that this happened without my moving a regiment or being mixed up with the business, for I tell you that there are some of my family who loved Bangu. But I—I loved your father, Matiwane, whom Bangu butchered, for we were brought up together as boys—yes, and served together in the same regiment, the Amawombe, when the Wild One, my brother, ruled" (he meant Chaka, for among the Zulus the names of dead kings are hlonipa—that is, they must not be spoken if it can be avoided). "Therefore," went on Panda, "for this reason, and for others, I am glad that Bangu has been punished, and that, although vengeance has crawled after him like a footsore bull, at length he has been tossed with its horns and crushed with its knees."

"Yebo, Ngonyama!" (Yes, O Lion!) said Saduko.

"Now, Saduko," went on Panda, "because you are your father's son, and because you have shown yourself a man, although you are still little in the land, I am minded to advance you. Therefore I give to you the chieftainship over those who remain of the Amakoba and over all of the Amangwane blood whom you can gather."

"Bayete! As the King pleases," said Saduko.

"And I give you leave to become a kehla—a wearer of the head-ring—although, as you have said, you are still but a boy, and with it a place upon my Council."

"Bayete! As the King pleases," said Saduko, still apparently unmoved by the honours that were being heaped upon him.

"And, Son of Matiwane," went on Panda, "you are still unmarried, are you not?"

Now, for the first time, Saduko's face changed. "Yes, Black One," he said hurriedly, "but—"

Here he caught my eye, and, reading some warning in it, was silent.

"But," repeated Panda after him, "doubtless you would like to be? Well, it is natural in a young man who wishes to found a House, and therefore I give you leave to marry."

"Yebo, Silo!" (Yes, O Wild Beast!) I thank the King, but—"

Here I sneezed loudly, and he ceased.

"But," repeated Panda, "of course, you do not know where to find a wife between the time the hawk stoops and the rat squeaks in its claws. How should you who have never thought of the matter? Also," he continued, with a smile, "it is well that you have not thought of it, since she whom I shall give to you could not live in the second hut in your kraal and call another "Inkosikazi" [that is, head lady or chieftainess]. Umbelazi, my son, go fetch her of whom we have thought as a bride for this boy."

Now Umbelazi rose, and went with a broad smile upon his face, while Panda, somewhat fatigued with all his speech-making—for he was very fat and the day was very hot—leaned his head back against the hut and closed his eyes.

"O Black One! O thou who consumeth with rage! [Dhlangamandhla]" broke out Saduko, who, I could see, was much disturbed. "I have something to say to you."

"No doubt, no doubt," answered Panda drowsily, "but save up your thanks till you have seen, or you will have none left afterwards," and he snored slightly.

Now I, perceiving that Saduko was about to ruin himself, thought it well to interfere, though what business of mine it was to do so I cannot say. At any rate, if only I had held my tongue at this moment, and allowed Saduko to make a fool of himself, as he wished to do—for where Mameena was concerned he never could be wise—I verily believe that all the history of Zululand would have run a different course, and that many thousands of men, white and black, who are now dead would be alive to-day. But Fate ordered it otherwise. Yes, it was not I who spoke, but Fate. The Angel of Doom used my throat as his trumpet.

Seeing that Panda dozed, I slipped behind Saduko and gripped him by the arm.

"Are you mad?" I whispered into his ear. "Will you throw away your fortune, and your life also?"

"But Mameena," he whispered back. "I would marry none save Mameena."

"Fool! " I answered. "Mameena has betrayed and spat upon you. Take what the Heavens send you and give thanks. Would you wear Masapo's soiled blanket?"

"Macumazahn," he said in a hollow voice, "I will follow your head, and not my own heart. Yet you sow a strange seed, Macumazahn, or so you may think when you see its fruit." And he gave me a wild look—a look that frightened me.

There was something in this look which caused me to reflect that I might do well to go away and leave Saduko, Mameena, Nandie, and the rest of them to "dree their weirds," as the Scotch say, for, after all, what was my finger doing in that very hot stew? Getting burnt, I thought, and not collecting any stew.

Yet, looking back on these events, how could I foresee what would be the end of the madness of Saduko, of the fearful machinations of Mameena, and of the weakness of Umbelazi when she snared him in the net of her beauty, thus bringing about his ruin, through the hate of Saduko and the ambition of Cetewayo? How could I know that, at the back of all these events, stood the old dwarf, Zikali the Wise, working night and day to slake the enmity and fulfil the vengeance which long ago he had conceived and planned against the royal House of Senzangakona and the Zulu people over whom it ruled?

Yes, he stood there like a man behind a great stone upon the brow of a mountain, slowly, remorselessly, with infinite skill, labour, and patience, pushing that stone to the edge of the cliff, whence at length, in the appointed hour, it would thunder down upon those who dwelt beneath, to leave them crushed and no more a people. How could I guess that we, the actors in this play, were all the while helping him to push that stone, and that he cared nothing how many of us were carried with it into the abyss, if only we brought about the triumph of his secret, unutterable rage and hate?

Now I see and understand all these things, as it is easy to do, but then I was blind; nor did the Voices reach my dull ears to warn me, as, how or why I cannot tell, they did, I believe, reach those of Zikali.

Oh, what was the sum of it? Just this, I think, and nothing more—that, as Saduko and the others were Mameena's tools, and as all of them and their passions were Zikali's tools, so he himself was the tool of some unseen Power that used him and us to accomplish its design. Which, I suppose, is fatalism, or, in other words, all these things happened because they must happen. A poor conclusion to reach after so much thought and striving, and not complimentary to man and his boasted powers of free will; still, one to which many of us are often driven, especially if we have lived among savages, where such dramas work themselves out openly and swiftly, unhidden from our eyes by the veils and subterfuges of civilisation. At least, there is this comfort about it—that, if we are but feathers blown by the wind, how can the individual feather be blamed because it did not travel against, turn or keep back the wind?

Well, let me return from these speculations to the history of the facts that caused them.

Just as—a little too late—I had made up my mind that I would go after my own business, and leave Saduko to manage his, through the fence gateway appeared the great, tall Umbelazi leading by the hand a woman. As I saw in a moment, it did not need certain bangles of copper, ornaments of ivory and of very rare pink beads, called infibinga, which only those of the royal House were permitted to wear, to proclaim her a person of rank, for dignity and high blood were apparent in her face, her carriage, her gestures, and all that had to do with her.

Nandie the Sweet was not a great beauty, as was Mameena, although her figure was fine, and her stature like that of all the race of Senzangakona—considerably above the average. To begin with, she was darker in hue, and her lips were rather thick, as was her nose; nor were her eyes large and liquid like those of an antelope. Further, she lacked the informing mystery of Mameena's face, that at times was broken and]it up by flashes of alluring light and quick, sympathetic perception, as a heavy evening sky, that seems to join the dim earth to the dimmer heavens, is illuminated by pulsings of fire, soft and many-hued, suggesting, but not revealing, the strength and splendour that it veils. Nandie had none of these attractions, which, after all, anywhere upon the earth belong only to a few women in each generation. She was a simple, honest-natured, kindly, affectionate young woman of high birth, no more; that is, as these qualities are understood and expressed among her people.

Umbelazi led her forward into the presence of the King, to whom she bowed gracefully enough. Then, after casting a swift, sidelong glance at Saduko, which I found it difficult to interpret, and another of inquiry at me, she folded her hands upon her breast and stood silent, with bent head, waiting to be addressed.

The address was brief enough, for Panda was still sleepy.

"My daughter," he said, with a yawn, "there stands your husband," and he jerked his thumb towards Saduko. "He is a young man and a brave, and unmarried; also one who should grow great in the shadow of our House, especially as he is a friend of your brother, Umbelazi. I understand also that you have seen him and like him. Unless you have anything to say against it, for as, not being a common father, the King receives no cattle—at least in this case—I am not prejudiced, but will listen to your words," and he chuckled in a drowsy fashion. "I propose that the marriage should take place to-morrow. Now, my daughter, have you anything to say? For if so, please say it at once, as I am tired. The eternal wranglings between your brethren, Cetewayo and Umbelazi, have worn me out."

Now Nandie looked about her in her open, honest fashion, her gaze resting first on Saduko, then on Umbelazi, and lastly upon me.

"My Father," she said at length, in her soft, steady voice, "tell me, I beseech you, who proposes this marriage? Is it the Chief Saduko, is it the Prince Umbelazi, or is it the white lord whose true name I do not know, but who is called Macumazahn, Watcher-by-Night?"

"I can't remember which of them proposed it," yawned Panda. "Who can keep on talking about things from night till morning? At any rate, I propose it, and I will make your husband a big man among our people. Have you anything to say against it?"

"I have nothing to say, my Father. I have met Saduko, and like him well—for the rest, you are the judge. But," she added slowly, "does Saduko like me? When he speaks my name, does he feel it here?" and she pointed to her throat.

"I am sure I do not know what he feels in his throat," Panda replied testily, "but I feel that mine is dry. Well, as no one says anything, the matter is settled. To-morrow Saduko shall give the umqoliso [the Ox of the Girl], that makes marriage—if he has not got one here I will lend it to him, and you can take the new, big hut that I have built in the outer kraal to dwell in for the present. There will be a dance, if you wish it; if not, I do not care, for I have no wish for ceremony just now, who am too troubled with great matters. Now I am going to sleep."

Then sinking from his stool on to his knees, Panda crawled through the doorway of his great hut, which was close to him, and vanished.

Umbelazi and I departed also through the gateway of the fence, leaving Saduko and the Princess Nandie alone together, for there were no attendants present. What happened between them I am sure I do not know, but I gather that, in one way or another, Saduko made himself sufficiently agreeable to the princess to persuade her to take him to husband. Perhaps, being already enamoured of him, she was not difficult to persuade. At any rate, on the morrow, without any great feasting or fuss, except the customary dance, the umqoliso, the "Ox of the Girl," was slaughtered, and Saduko became the husband of a royal maiden of the House of Senzangakona.

Certainly, as I remember reflecting, it was a remarkable rise in life for one who, but a few months before, had been without possessions or a home.

I may add that, after our brief talk in the King's kraal, while Panda was dozing, I had no further words with Saduko on this matter of his marriage, for between its proposal and the event he avoided me, nor did I seek him out. On the day of the marriage also, I trekked for Natal, and for a whole year heard no more of Saduko, Nandie, and Mameena; although, to be frank, I must admit I thought of the last of these persons more often, perhaps, than I should have done.

The truth is that Mameena was one of those women who sticks in a man's mind even more closely than a "Wait-a-bit" thorn does in his coat.

Allan Returns to Zululand

A whole year had gone by, in which I did, or tried to do, various things that have no connection with this story, when once more I found myself in Zululand—at Umbezi's kraal indeed. Hither I had trekked in fulfilment of a certain bargain, already alluded to, that was concerned with ivory and guns, which I had made with the old fellow, or, rather, with Masapo, his son-in-law, whom he represented in this matter. Into the exact circumstances of that bargain I do not enter, since at the moment I cannot recall whether I ever obtained the necessary permit to import those guns into Zululand, although now that I am older I earnestly hope that I did so, since it is wrong to sell weapons to natives that may be put to all sorts of unforeseen uses.

At any rate, there I was, sitting alone with the Headman in his hut discussing a dram of "squareface" that I had given to him, for the "trade" was finished to our mutual satisfaction, and Scowl, my body servant, with the hunters, had just carried off the ivory—a fine lot of tusks—to my wagons.

"Well, Umbezi," I said, "and how has it fared with you since we parted a year ago? Have you seen anything of Saduko, who, you may remember, left you in some wrath?"

"Thanks be to my Spirit, I have seen nothing of that wild man, Macumazahn," answered Umbezi, shaking his fat old head in a fashion which showed great anxiety. "Yet I have heard of him, for he sent me a message the other day to tell me that he had not forgotten what he owed me."

"Did he mean the sticks with which he promised to bray you like a green hide?" I inquired innocently.

"I think so, Macumazahn—I think so, for certainly he owes me nothing else. And the worst of it is that, there at Panda's kraal, he has grown like a pumpkin on a dung heap—great, great!"

"And therefore is now one who can pay any debt that he owes, Umbezi," I said, taking a pull at the "squareface" and looking at him over the top of the pannikin.

"Doubtless he can, Macumazahn, and, between you and me, that is the real reason why I—or rather Masapo—was so anxious to get those guns. They were not for hunting, as he told you by the messenger, or for war, but to protect us against Saduko, in case he should attack. Well, now I hope we shall be able to hold our own."

"You and Masapo must teach your people to use them first, Umbezi. But I expect Saduko has forgotten all about both of you now that he is the husband of a princess of the royal blood. Tell me, how goes it with Mameena?"

"Oh, well, well, Macumazahn. For is she not the head lady of the Amasomi? There is nothing wrong with her—nothing at all, except that as yet she has no child; also that—," and he paused.

"That what?" I asked.

"That she hates the very sight of her husband, Masapo, and says that she would rather be married to a baboon—yes, to a baboon—than to him, which gives him offence, after he has paid so many cattle for her. But what of this, Macumazahn? There is always a grain missing upon the finest head of corn. Nothing is *quite* perfect in the world, Macumazahn, and if Mameena does not chance to love her husband—" and he shrugged his shoulders and drank some "squareface."

"Of course it does not matter in the least, Umbezi, except to Mameena and her husband, who no doubt will settle down in time, now that Saduko is married to a princess of the Zulu House."

"I hope so, Macumazahn, but, to tell the truth, I wish you had brought more guns, for I live amongst a terrible lot of people. Masapo, who is furious with Mameena because she will have none of him, and therefore with me, as though I could control Mameena; Mameena, who is mad with Masapo, and therefore with me, because I gave her in marriage to him; Saduko, who foams at the mouth at the name of Masapo, because he has married Mameena, whom, it is said, he still loves, and therefore at me, because I am her father and did my best to settle her in the world. Oh, give me some more of that fire-water, Macumazahn, for it makes me forget all these things, and especially that my guardian spirit made me the father of Mameena, with whom you would not run away when you might have done so. Oh, Macumazahn, why did you not run away with Mameena, and turn her into a quiet white woman who ties herself up in sacks, sings songs to the 'Great-Great' in the sky—[that is, hymns to the Power above us]—and never thinks of any man who is not her husband?"

"Because if I had done so, Umbezi, I should have ceased to be a quiet white man. Yes, yes, my friend, I should have been in some such place as yours to-day, and that is the last thing that I wish. And now, Umbezi, you have had quite enough 'squareface,' so I will take the bottle away with me. Good-night."

On the following morning I trekked very early from Umbezi's kraal—before he was up indeed, for the "squareface" made him sleep sound. My destination was Nodwengu, Panda's Great Place, where I hoped to do some trading, but, as I was in no particular hurry, my plan was to go round by Masapo's, and see for myself how it fared between him and Mameena. Indeed, I reached the borders of the Amasomi territory, whereof Masapo was chief, by evening, and camped there. But with the night came reflection, and reflection told me that I should do well to keep clear of Mameena and her domestic complications, if she had any. So I changed my mind, and next morning trekked on to Nodwengu by the only route that my guides reported to be practicable, one which took me a long way round.

That day, owing to the roughness of the road—if road it could be called—and an accident to one of the wagons, we only covered about fifteen miles, and as night fell were obliged to outspan at the first spot where we could find water. When the oxen had been unyoked I looked about me, and saw that we were in a place that, although I had approached it from a somewhat different direction, I recognised at once as the mouth of the Black Kloof, in which, over a year before, I had interviewed Zikali the Little and Wise. There was no mistaking the spot; that blasted valley, with the piled-up columns of boulders and the overhanging cliff at the end of it, have, so far as I am aware, no exact counterparts in Africa.

I sat upon the box of the first wagon, eating my food, which consisted of some biltong and biscuit, for I had not bothered to shoot any game that day, which was very hot, and wondering whether Zikali were still alive, also whether I should take the trouble to walk up the kloof and find out. On the whole I thought that I would not, as the place repelled me, and I did not particularly wish to hear any more of his prophecies and fierce, ill-omened talk. So I just sat there studying the wonderful effect of the red evening light pouring up between those walls of fantastic rocks.

Presently I perceived, far away, a single human figure—whether it were man or woman I could not tell—walking towards me along the path which ran at the bottom of the cleft. In those gigantic surroundings it looked extraordinarily small and lonely, although perhaps because of the intense red light in which it was bathed, or perhaps just because it was human, a living thing in the midst of all that still, inanimate grandeur, it caught and focused my attention. I grew greatly interested in it; I wondered if it were that of man or woman, and what it was doing here in this haunted valley.

The figure drew nearer, and now I saw it was slender and tall, like that of a lad or of a well-grown woman, but to which sex it belonged I could not see, because it was draped in a cloak of beautiful grey fur. Just then Scowl came to the other side of the wagon to speak to me about something, which took off my attention for the next two minutes. When I looked round again it was to see the figure standing within three yards of me, its face hidden by a kind of hood which was attached to the fur cloak.

"Who are you, and what is your business?" I asked, whereon a gentle voice answered:

"Do you not know me, O Macumazana?"

"How can I know one who is tied up like a gourd in a mat? Yet is it not—is it not—"

"Yes, it is Mameena, and I am very pleased that you should remember my voice, Macumazahn, after we have been separated for such a long, long time," and, with a sudden movement, she threw back the kaross, hood and all, revealing herself in all her strange beauty.

I jumped down off the wagon-box and took her hand.

"O Macumazana," she said, while I still held it—or, to be accurate, while she still held mine—"indeed my heart is glad to see a friend again," and she looked at me with her appealing eyes, which, in the red light, I could see appeared to float in tears.

"A friend, Mameena! " I exclaimed. "Why, now you are so rich, and the wife of a big chief, you must have plenty of friends."

"Alas! Macumazahn, I am rich in nothing except trouble, for my husband saves, like the ants for winter. Why, he even grudged me this poor kaross; and as for friends, he is so jealous that he will not allow me any."

"He cannot be jealous of women, Mameena!"

"Oh, women! Piff! I do not care for women; they are very unkind to me, because—because—well, perhaps you can guess why, Macumazahn," she answered, glancing at her own reflection in a little travelling looking-glass that hung from the woodwork of the wagon, for I had been using it to brush my hair, and smiled very sweetly.

"At least you have your husband, Mameena, and I thought that perhaps by this time—"

She held up her hand.

"My husband! Oh, I would that I had him not, for I hate him, Macumazahn; and as for the rest—never! The truth is that I never cared for any man except one whose name *you* may chance to remember, Macumazahn."

"I suppose you mean Saduko—" I began.

"Tell me, Macumazahn," she inquired innocently, "are white people very stupid? I ask because you do not seem as clever as you used to be. Or have you perhaps a bad memory?"

Now I felt myself turning red as the sky behind me, and broke in hurriedly:

"If you did not like your husband, Mameena, you should not have married him. You know you need not unless you wished."

"When one has only two thorn bushes to sit on, Macumazahn, one chooses that which seems to have the fewest prickles, to discover sometimes that they are still there in hundreds, although one did not see them. You know that at length everyone gets tired of standing."

"Is that why you have taken to walking, Mameena? I mean, what are you doing here alone?"

"I? Oh, I heard that you were passing this way, and came to have a talk with you. No, from you I cannot hide even the least bit of the truth. I came to talk with you, but also I came to see Zikali and ask him what a wife should do who hates her husband."

"Indeed! And what did he answer you?"

"He answered that he thought she had better run away with another man, if there were one whom she did not hate—out of Zululand, of course," she replied, looking first at me and then at my wagon and the two horses that were tied to it.

"Is that all he said, Mameena?"

"No. Have I not told you that I cannot hide one grain of the truth from you? He added that the only other thing to be done was to sit still and drink my sour milk, pretending that it is sweet, until my Spirit gives me a new cow. He seemed to think that my Spirit would be bountiful in the matter of new cows—one day."

"Anything more?" I inquired.

"One little thing. Have I not told you that you shall have all—all the truth? Zikali seemed to think also that at last every one of my herd of cows, old and new, would come to a bad end. He did not tell me to what end."

She turned her head aside, and when she looked up again I saw that she was weeping, really weeping this time, not just making her eyes swim, as she did before.

"Of course they will come to a bad end, Macumazahn," she went on in a soft, thick voice, "for I and all with whom I have to do were 'torn out of the reeds' [i.e. created] that way. And that's why I won't tempt you to run away with me any more, as I meant to do when I saw you, because it is true, Macumazahn you are the only man I ever liked or ever shall like; and you know I could make you run away with me if I chose, although I am black and you are white—oh, yes, before to-morrow morning. But I won't do it; for why should I catch you in my unlucky web and bring you into all sorts of trouble among my people and your own? Go you your road, Macumazahn, and I will go mine as the wind blows me. And now give me a cup of water and let me be away—a cup of water, no more. Oh, do not be afraid for me, or melt too much, lest I should melt also. I have an escort waiting over yonder hill. There, thank you for your water, Macumazahn, and good night. Doubtless we shall meet again ere long, and— I forgot; the Little Wise One said he would like to have a talk with you. Good night, Macumazahn, good night. I trust that you did a profitable trade with Umbezi my father and Masapo my husband. I wonder why such men as these should have been chosen to be my father and my husband. Think it over, Macumazahn, and tell me when next we meet. Give me that pretty mirror, Macumazahn; when I look in it I shall see you as well as myself, and that will please me—you don't know how much. I thank you. Good night."

In another minute I was watching her solitary little figure, now wrapped again in the hooded kaross, as it vanished over the brow of the rise behind us, and really, as she went, I felt a lump rising in my throat. Notwithstanding all her wickedness—and I suppose she was wicked—there was something horribly attractive about Mameena.

When she had gone, taking my only looking-glass with her, and the lump in my throat had gone also, I began to wonder how much fact there was in her story. She had protested so earnestly that she told me all the truth that I felt sure there must be something left behind. Also I remembered she had said Zikali wanted to see me. Well, the end of it was I took a moonlight walk up that dreadful gorge, into which not even Scowl would accompany me, because he declared that the place was well known to be haunted by imikovu, or spectres who have been raised from the dead by wizards.

It was a long and disagreeable walk, and somehow I felt very depressed and insignificant as I trudged on between those gigantic cliffs, passing now through patches of bright moonlight and now through deep pools of shadow, threading my way among clumps of bush or round the bases of tall pillars of piled-up stones, till at length I came to the overhanging cliffs at the end, which frowned down on me like the brows of some titanic demon.

Well, I got to the end at last, and at the gate of the kraal fence was met by one of those fierce and huge men who served the dwarf as guards. Suddenly he emerged from behind a stone, and having scanned me for a moment in silence, beckoned to me to follow him, as though I were expected. A minute later I found myself face to face with Zikali, who was seated in the clear moonlight just outside the shadow of his hut, and engaged, apparently, in his favourite occupation of carving wood with a rough native knife of curious shape.

For a while he took no notice of me; then suddenly looked up, shaking back his braided grey locks, and broke into one of his great laughs.

"So it is you, Macumazahn," he said. "Well, I knew you were passing my way and that Mameena would send you here. But why do you come to see the 'Thing-that-should-not-have-been-born'? To tell me how you fared with the buffalo with the split horn, eh?"

"No, Zikali, for why should I tell you what you know already? Mameena said you wished to talk with me, that was all."

"Then Mameena lied," he answered, "as is her nature, in whose throat live four false words for every one of truth. Still, sit down, Macumazahn. There is beer made ready for you by that stool; and give me the knife and a pinch of the white man's snuff that you have brought for me as a present."

I produced these articles, though how be knew that I had them with me I cannot tell, nor did I think it worth while to inquire. The snuff, I remember, pleased him very much, but of the knife he said that it was a pretty toy, but he would not know how to use it. Then we fell to talking.

"What was Mameena doing here?" I asked boldly.

"What was she doing at your wagons?" he asked. "Oh, do not stop to tell me; I know, I know. That is a very good Snake of yours, Macumazahn, which always just lets you slip through her fingers, when, if she chose to close her hand— Well, well, I do not betray the secrets of my clients; but I say this to you—go on to the kraal of the son of Senzangakona, and you will see things happen that will make you laugh, for Mameena will be there, and the mongrel Masapo, her husband. Truly she hates him well, and, after all, I would rather be loved than hated by Mameena, though both are dangerous. Poor Mongrel! Soon the jackals will be chewing his bones."

"Why do you say that?" I asked.

"Only because Mameena tells me that he is a great wizard, and the jackals eat many wizards in Zululand. Also he is an enemy of Panda's House, is he not?"

"You have been giving her some bad counsel, Zikali," I said, blurting out the thought in my mind.

"Perhaps, perhaps, Macumazahn; only I may call it good counsel. I have my own road to walk, and if I can find some to clear away the thorns that would prick my feet, what of it? Also she will get her pay, who finds life dull up there among the Amasomi, with one she hates for a hut-fellow. Go you and watch, and afterwards, when you have an hour to spare, come and tell me what happens—that is, if I do not chance to be there to see for myself."

"Is Saduko well?" I asked to change the subject, for I did not wish to become privy to the plots that filled the air.

"I am told that his tree grows great, that it overshadows all the royal kraal. I think that Mameena wishes to sleep in the shade of it. And now you are weary, and so am I. Go back to your wagons, Macumazahn, for I have nothing more to say to you to-night. But be sure to return and tell me what chances at Panda's kraal. Or, as I have said, perhaps I shall meet you there. Who knows, who knows?"

Now, it will be observed that there was nothing very remarkable in this conversation between Zikali and myself. He did not tell me any deep secrets or make any great prophecy. It may be wondered, indeed, when there is so much to record, why I set it down at all.

My answer is, because of the extraordinary impression that it produced upon me. Although so little was said, I felt all the while that those few words were a veil hiding terrible events to be. I was sure that some dreadful scheme had been hatched between the old dwarf and Mameena whereof the issue would soon become apparent, and that he had sent me away in a hurry after he learned that she had told me nothing, because he feared lest I should stumble on its cue and perhaps cause it to fail.

At any rate, as I walked back to my wagons by moonlight down that dreadful gorge, the hot, thick air seemed to me to have a physical taste and smell of blood, and the dank foliage of the tropical trees that grew there, when now and again a puff of wind stirred them, moaned like the fabled imikovu, or as men might do in their last faint agony. The effect upon my nerves was quite strange, for when at last I reached my wagons I was shaking like a reed, and a cold perspiration, unnatural enough upon that hot night, poured from my face and body.

Well, I took a couple of stiff tots of "squareface" to pull myself together, and at length went to sleep, to awake before dawn with a headache. Looking out of the wagon, to my surprise I saw Scowl and the hunters, who should have been snoring, standing in a group and talking to each other in frightened whispers. I called Scowl to me and asked what was the matter.

"Nothing, Baas," he said with a shamefaced air; "only there are so many spooks about this place. They have been passing in and out of it all night."

"Spooks, you idiot!" I answered. "Probably they were people going to visit the Nyanga, Zikali."

"Perhaps, Baas; only then we do not know why they should all look like dead people—princes, some of them, by their dress—and walk upon the air a man's height from the ground."

"Pooh!" I replied. "Do you not know the difference between owls in the mist and dead kings? Make ready, for we trek at once; the air here is full of fever."

"Certainly, Baas," he said, springing off to obey; and I do not think I ever remember two wagons being got under way quicker than they were that morning.

I merely mention this nonsense to show that the Black Kloof could affect other people's nerves as well as my own.

In due course I reached Nodwengu without accident, having sent forward one of my hunters to report my approach to Panda. When my wagons arrived outside the Great Place they were met by none other than my old friend, Maputa, he who had brought me back the pills before our attack upon Bangu.

"Greeting, Macumazahn," he said. "I am sent by the King to say that you are welcome and to point you out a good place to outspan; also to give you permission to trade as much as you will in this town, since he knows that your dealings are always fair."

I returned my thanks in the usual fashion, adding that I had brought a little present for the King which I would deliver when it pleased him to receive me. Then I invited Maputa, to whom I also offered some trifle which delighted him very much, to ride with me on the wagon-box till we came to the selected outspan.

This, by the way, proved, to be a very good place indeed, a little valley full of grass for the cattle—for by the King's order it had not been grazed—with a stream of beautiful water running down it. Moreover it overlooked a great open space immediately in front of the main gate of the town, so that I could see everything that went on and all who arrived or departed.

"You will be comfortable here, Macumazahn," said Maputa, "during your stay, which we hope will be long, since, although there will soon be a mighty crowd at Nodwengu, the King has given orders that none except your own servants are to enter this valley."

"I thank the King; but why will there be a crowd, Maputa?"

"Oh!" he answered with a shrug of the shoulders, "because of a new thing. All the tribes of the Zulus are to come up to be reviewed. Some say that Cetewayo has brought this about, and some say that it is Umbelazi. But I am sure that it is the work of neither of these, but of Saduko, your old friend, though what his object is I cannot tell you. I only trust," he added uneasily, "that it will not end in bloodshed between the Great Brothers."

"So Saduko has grown tall, Maputa?"

"Tall as a tree, Macumazahn. His whisper in the King's ear is louder than the shouts of others. Moreover, he has become a 'self-eater' [that is a Zulu term which means one who is very haughty]. You will have to wait on him, Macumazahn; he will not wait on you."

"Is it so? " I answered. "Well, tall trees are blown down sometimes."

He nodded his wise old head. "Yes, Macumazahn; I have seen plenty grow and fall in my time, for at last the swimmer goes with the stream. Anyhow, you will be able to do a good trade among so many, and, whatever happens, none will harm you whom all love. And now farewell; I bear your messages to the King, who sends an ox for you to kill lest you should grow hungry in his house."

That same evening I saw Saduko and the others, as I shall tell. I had been up to visit the King and give him my present, a case of English table-knives with bone handles, which pleased him greatly, although he did not in the least know how to use them. Indeed, without their accompanying forks these are somewhat futile articles. I found the old fellow very tired and anxious, but as he was surrounded by indunas, I had no private talk with him. Seeing that he was busy, I took my leave as soon as I could, and when I walked away whom should I meet but Saduko.

I saw him while he was a good way off, advancing towards the inner gate with a train of attendants like a royal personage, and knew very well that he saw me. Making up my mind what to do at once, I walked straight on to him, forcing him to give me the path, which he did not wish to do before so many people, and brushed past him as though he were a stranger. As I expected, this treatment had the desired effect, for after we had passed each other he turned and said:

"Do you not know me, Macumazahn?"

"Who calls?" I asked. "Why, friend, your face is familiar to me. How are you named?"

"Have you forgotten Saduko?" he said in a pained voice.

"No, no, of course not," I answered. "I know you now, although you seem somewhat changed since we went out hunting and fighting together—I suppose because you are fatter. I trust that you are well, Saduko? Good-bye. I must be going back to my wagons. If you wish to see me you will find me there."

These remarks, I may add, seemed to take Saduko very much aback. At any rate, he found no reply to them, even when old Maputa, with whom I was walking, and some others sniggered aloud. There is nothing that Zulus enjoy so much as seeing one whom they consider an upstart set in his place.

Well, a couple of hours afterwards, just as the sun was sinking, who should walk up to my wagons but Saduko himself, accompanied by a woman whom I recognised at once as his wife, the Princess Nandie, who carried a fine baby boy in her arms. Rising, I saluted Nandie and offered her my camp-stool, which she looked at suspiciously and declined, preferring to seat herself on the ground after the native fashion. So I took it back again, and after I had sat down on it, not before, stretched out my hand to Saduko, who by this time was quite humble and polite.

Well, we talked away, and by degrees, without seeming too much interested in them, I was furnished with a list of all the advancements which it had pleased Panda to heap upon Saduko during the past year. In their way they were remarkable enough, for it was much as though some penniless country gentleman in England had been promoted in that short space of time to be one of the premier peers of the kingdom and endowed with great offices and estates. When he had finished the count of them he paused, evidently waiting for me to congratulate him. But all I said was:

"By the Heavens above I am sorry for you, Saduko! How many enemies you must have made! What a long way there will be for you to fall one night!"—a remark at which the quiet Nandie broke into a low laugh that I think pleased her husband even less than my sarcasm. "Well," I went on, "I see that you have got a baby, which is much better than all these titles. May I look at it, Inkosazana?"

Of course she was delighted, and we proceeded to inspect the baby, which evidently she loved more than anything on earth. Whilst we were examining the child and chatting about it, Saduko sitting by meanwhile in the sulks, who on earth should appear but Mameena and her fat and sullen-looking husband, the chief Masapo.

"Oh, Macumazahn," she said, appearing to notice no one else, "how pleased I am to see you after a whole long year!"

I stared at her and my jaw dropped. Then I recovered myself, thinking she must have made a mistake and meant to say "week."

"Twelve moons," she went on, "and, Macumazahn, not one of them has gone by but I have thought of you several times and wondered if we should ever meet again. Where have you been all this while?"

"In many places," I answered; "amongst others at the Black Kloof, where I called upon the dwarf, Zikali, and lost my looking-glass."

"The Nyanga, Zikali! Oh, how often have I wished to see him. But, of course, I cannot, for I am told he will not receive any women."

"I don't know, I am sure," I replied, "but you might try; perhaps he would make an exception in your favour."

"I think I will, Macumazahn," she murmured, whereon I collapsed into silence, feeling that things were getting beyond me.

When I recovered myself a little it was to hear Mameena greeting Saduko with much effusion, and complimenting him on his rise in life, which she said she had always foreseen. This remark seemed to bowl out Saduko also, for he made no answer to it, although I noticed that he could not take his eyes off Mameena's beautiful face. Presently, however, he seemed to become aware of Masapo, and instantly his whole demeanour changed, for it grew proud and even terrible. Masapo tendered him some greeting; whereon Saduko turned upon him and said:

"What, chief of the Amasomi, do you give the good-day to an umfokazana and a mangy hyena? Why do you do this? Is it because the low umfokazana has become a noble and the mangy hyena has put on a tiger's coat?" And he glared at him like a veritable tiger.

Masapo made no answer that I could catch. Muttering some inaudible words, he turned to depart, and in doing so—quite innocently, I think—struck Nandie, knocking her over on to her back and causing the child to fall out of her arms in such fashion that its tender head struck against a pebble with sufficient force to cause it to bleed.

Saduko leapt at him, smiting him across the shoulders with the little stick that he carried. For a moment Masapo paused, and I thought that he was going to show fight. If he had any such intention, however, he changed his mind, for without a word, or showing any resentment at the insult which he had received, he broke into a heavy run and vanished among the evening shadows. Mameena, who had observed all, broke into something else, namely, a laugh.

"Piff! My husband is big yet not brave," she said, "but I do not think he meant to hurt you, woman."

"Do you speak to me, wife of Masapo?" asked Nandie with gentle dignity, as she gained her feet and picked up the stunned child. "If so, my name and titles are the Inkosazana Nandie, daughter of the Black One and wife of the lord Saduko."

"Your pardon," replied Mameena humbly, for she was cowed at once. "I did not know who you were, Inkosazana."

"It is granted, wife of Masapo. Macumazahn, give me water, I pray you, that I may bathe the head of my child."

The water was brought, and presently, when the little one seemed all right again, for it had only received a scratch, Nandie thanked me and departed to her own huts, saying with a smile to her husband as she passed that there was no need for him to accompany her, as she had servants waiting at the kraal gate. So Saduko stayed behind, and Mameena stayed also. He talked with me for quite a long while, for he had much to tell me, although all the time I felt that his heart was not in his talk. His heart was with Mameena, who sat there and smiled continually in her mysterious way, only putting in a word now and again, as though to excuse her presence.

At length she rose and said with a sigh that she must be going back to where the Amasomi were in camp, as Masapo would need her to see to his food. By now it was quite dark, although I remember that from time to time the sky was lit up by sheet lightning, for a storm was brewing. As I expected, Saduko rose also, saying that he would see me on the morrow, and went away with Mameena, walking like one who dreams.

A few minutes later I had occasion to leave the wagons in order to inspect one of the oxen which was tied up by itself at a distance, because it had shown signs of some sickness that might or might not be catching. Moving quietly, as I always do from a hunter's habit, I walked alone to the place where the beast was tethered behind some mimosa thorns. Just as I reached these thorns the broad lightning shone out vividly, and showed me Saduko holding the unresisting shape of Mameena in his arms and kissing her passionately.

Then I turned and went back to the wagons even more quietly than I had come.

I should add that on the morrow I found out that, after all, there was nothing serious the matter with my ox.

The Smelling-Out

After these events matters went on quietly for some time. I visited Saduko's huts—very fine huts—about the doors of which sat quite a number of his tribesmen, who seemed glad to see me again. Here I learned from the Lady Nandie that her babe, whom she loved dearly, was none the worse for its little accident. Also I learned from Saduko himself, who came in before I left, attended like a prince by several notable men, that he had made up his quarrel
with Masapo, and, indeed, apologised to him, as he found that he had not really meant to insult the princess, his wife, having only thrust her over by accident. Saduko added indeed that now they were good friends, which was well for Masapo, a man whom the King had no cause to like. I said that I was glad to hear it, and went on to call upon Masapo, who received me with enthusiasm, as also did Mameena.

Here I noted with pleasure that this pair seemed to be on much better terms than I understood had been the case in the past, for Mameena even addressed her husband on two separate occasions in very affectionate language, and fetched something that he wanted without waiting to be asked. Masapo, too, was in excellent spirits, because, as he told me, the old quarrel between him and Saduko was thoroughly made up, their reconciliation having been sealed by an interchange of gifts. He added that he was very glad that this was the case, since Saduko was now one of the most powerful men in the country, who could harm him much if he chose, especially as some secret enemy had put it about of late that he, Masapo, was an enemy of the King's House, and an evil-doer who practised witchcraft. In proof of his new friendship, however, Saduko had promised that these slanders should be looked into and their originator punished, if he or she could be found.

Well, I congratulated him and took my departure, "thinking furiously," as the Frenchman says. That there was a tragedy pending I was sure; this weather was too calm to last; the water ran so still because it was preparing to leap down some hidden precipice.

Yet what could I do? Tell Masapo I had seen his wife being embraced by another man? Surely that was not my business; it was Masapo's business to attend to her conduct. Also they would both deny it, and I had no witness. Tell him that Saduko's reconciliation with him was not sincere, and that he had better look to himself? How did I know it was not sincere? It might suit Saduko's book to make friends with Masapo, and if I interfered I should only make enemies and be called a liar who was working for some secret end.

Go to Panda and confide my suspicions to him? He was far too anxious and busy about great matters to listen to me, and if he did, would only laugh at this tale of a petty flirtation. No, there was nothing to be done except sit still and wait. Very possibly I was mistaken, after all, and things would smooth themselves out, as they generally do.

Meanwhile the "reviewing," or whatever it may have been, was in progress, and I was busy with my own affairs, making hay while the sun shone. So great were the crowds of people who came up to Nodwengu that in a week I had sold everything I had to sell in the two wagons, that were mostly laden with cloth, beads, knives and so forth. Moreover, the prices I got were splendid, since the buyers bid against each other, and before I was cleared out I had collected quite a herd of cattle, also a quantity of ivory. These I sent on to Natal with one of the wagons, remaining behind myself with the other, partly because Panda asked me to do so—for now and again he would seek my advice on sundry questions—and partly from curiosity.

There was plenty to be curious about up at Nodwengu just then, since no one was sure that civil war would not break out between the princes Cetewayo and Umbelazi, whose factions were present in force.

It was averted for the time, however, by Umbelazi keeping away from the great gathering under pretext of being sick, and leaving Saduko and some others to watch his interests. Also the rival regiments were not allowed to approach the town at the same time. So that public cloud passed over, to the enormous relief of everyone, especially of Panda the King. As to the private cloud whereof this history tells, it was otherwise.

As the tribes came up to the Great Place they were reviewed and sent away, since it was impossible to feed so vast a multitude as would have collected had they all remained. Thus the Amasomi, a small people who were amongst the first to arrive, soon left. Only, for some reason which I never quite understood, Masapo, Mameena and a few of Masapo's children and headmen were detained there; though perhaps, if she had chosen, Mameena could have given an explanation.

Well, things began to happen. Sundry personages were taken ill, and some of them died suddenly; and soon it was noted that all these people either lived near to where Masapo's family was lodged or had at some time or other been on bad terms with him. Thus Saduko himself was taken ill, or said he was; at any rate, he vanished from public gaze for three days, and reappeared looking very sorry for himself, though I could not observe that he had lost strength or weight. These catastrophes I pass over, however, in order to come to the greatest of them, which is one of the turning points of this chronicle.

After recovering from his alleged sickness Saduko gave a kind of thanksgiving feast, at which several oxen were killed. I was present at this feast, or rather at the last part of it, for I only put in what may be called a complimentary appearance, having no taste for such native gorgings. As it drew near its close Saduko sent for Nandie, who at first refused to come as there were no women present—I think because he wished to show his friends that he had a princess of the royal blood for his wife, who had borne him a son that one day would be great in the land. For Saduko, as I have said, had become a "self-eater," and this day his pride was inflamed by the adulation of the company and by the beer that he had drunk.

At length Nandie did come, carrying her babe, from which she never would be parted. In her dignified, ladylike fashion (although it seems an odd term to apply to a savage, I know none that describes her better) she greeted first me and then sundry of the other guests, saying a few words to each of them. At length she came opposite to Masapo, who had dined not wisely but too well, and to him, out of her natural courtesy, spoke rather longer than to the others, inquiring after his wife, Mameena, and others. At the moment it occurred to me that she did this in order to assure him that she bore no malice because of the accident of a while before, and was a party to her husband's reconciliation with him.

Masapo, in a hazy way, tried to reciprocate these kind intentions. Rising to his feet, his fat, coarse body swaying to and fro because of the beer that he had drunk, he expressed satisfaction at the feast that had been prepared in her house. Then, his eyes falling on the child, he began to declaim about its size and beauty, until he was stopped by the murmured protests of others, since among natives it is held to be not fortunate to praise a young child. Indeed, the person who does so is apt to be called an "umtakati", or bewitcher, who will bring evil upon its head, a word that I heard murmured by several near to me. Not satisfied with this serious breach of etiquette, the intoxicated Masapo snatched the infant from its mother's arms under pretext of looking for the hurt that had been caused to its brow when it fell to the ground at my camp, and finding none, proceeded to kiss it with his thick lips.

Nandie dragged it from him, saying:

"Would you bring death upon my son, O Chief of the Amasomi?"

Then, turning, she walked away from the feasters, upon whom there fell a certain hush.

Fearing lest something unpleasant should ensue, for I saw Saduko biting his lips with rage not unmixed with fear, and remembering Masapo's reputation as a wizard, I took advantage of this pause to bid a general good night to the company and retire to my camp.

What happened immediately after I left I do not know, but just before dawn on the following morning I was awakened from sleep in my wagon by my servant Scowl, who said that a messenger had come from the huts of Saduko, begging that I would proceed there at once and bring the white man's medicines, as his child was very ill. Of course I got up and went, taking with me some ipecacuanha and a few other remedies that I thought might be suitable for infantile ailments.

Outside the huts, which I reached just as the sun began to rise, I was met by Saduko himself, who was coming to seek me, as I saw at once, in a state of terrible grief.

"What is the matter?" I asked.

"O Macumazana," he answered, "that dog Masapo has bewitched my boy, and unless you can save him he dies."

"Nonsense," I said, "why do you utter wind? If the babe is sick, it is from some natural cause."

"Wait till you see it," he replied.

Well, I went into the big hut, and there found Nandie and some other women, also a native doctor or two. Nandie was seated on the floor looking like a stone image of grief, for she made no sound, only pointed with her finger to the infant that lay upon a mat in front of her.

A single glance showed me that it was dying of some disease of which I had no knowledge, for its dusky little body was covered with red blotches and its tiny face twisted all awry. I told the women to heat water, thinking that possibly this might be a case of convulsions, which a hot bath would mitigate; but before it was ready the poor babe uttered a thin wail and died.

Then, when she saw that her child was gone, Nandie spoke for the first time.

"The wizard has done his work well," she said, and flung herself face downwards on the floor of the hut.

As I did not know what to answer, I went out, followed by Saduko.

"What has killed my son, Macumazahn?" he asked in a hollow voice, the tears running down his handsome face, for he had loved his firstborn.

"I cannot tell," I replied; "but had he been older I should have thought he had eaten something poisonous, which seems impossible."

"Yes, Macumazahn, and the poison that he has eaten came from the breath of a wizard whom you may chance to have seen kiss him last night. Well, his life shall be avenged."

"Saduko," I exclaimed, "do not be unjust. There are many sicknesses that may have killed your son of which I have no knowledge, who am not a trained doctor."

"I will not be unjust, Macumazahn. The babe has died by witchcraft, like others in this town of late, but the evil-doer may not be he whom I suspect. That is for the smellers-out to decide," and without more words he turned and left me.

Next day Masapo was put upon his trial before a Court of Councillors, over which the King himself presided, a very unusual thing for him to do, and one which showed the great interest he took in the case.

At this court I was summoned to give evidence, and, of course, confined myself to answering such questions as were put to me. Practically these were but two. What had passed at my wagons when Masapo had knocked over Nandie and her child, and Saduko had struck him, and what had I seen at Saduko's feast when Masapo had kissed the infant? I told them in as few words as I could, and after some slight cross-examination by Masapo, made with a view to prove that the upsetting of Nandie was an accident and that he was drunk at Saduko's feast, to both of which suggestions I assented, I rose to go. Panda, however, stopped me and bade me describe the aspect of the child when I was called in to give it medicine.

I did so as accurately as possible, and could see that my account made a deep impression on the mind of the court. Then Panda asked me if I had ever seen any similar case, to which I was obliged to reply:

"No, I have not."

After this the Councillors consulted privately, and when we were called back the King gave his judgment, which was very brief. It was evident, he said, that there had been events which might have caused enmity to arise in the mind of Masapo against Saduko, by whom Masapo had been struck with a stick. Therefore, although a reconciliation had taken place, there seemed to be a possible motive for revenge. But if Masapo killed the child, there was no evidence to show how he had done so. Moreover, that infant, his own grandson, had not died of any known disease. He had, however, died of a similar disease to that which had carried off certain others with whom Masapo had been mixed up, whereas more, including Saduko himself, had been sick and recovered, all of which seemed to make a strong case against Masapo.

Still, he and his Councillors wished not to condemn without full proof. That being so, they had determined to call in the services of some great witch-doctor, one who lived at a distance and knew nothing of the circumstances. Who that doctor should be was not yet settled. When it was and he had arrived, the case would be re-opened, and meanwhile Masapo would be kept a close prisoner. Finally, he prayed that the white man, Macumazahn, would remain at his town until the matter was settled.

So Masapo was led off, looking very dejected, and, having saluted the King, we all went away.

I should add that, except for the remission of the case to the court of the witch-doctor, which, of course, was an instance of pure Kafir superstition, this judgment of the King's seemed to me well reasoned and just, very different indeed from what would have been given by Dingaan or Chaka, who were wont, on less evidence, to make a clean sweep not only of the accused, but of all his family and dependents.

About eight days later, during which time I had heard nothing of the matter and seen no one connected with it, for the whole thing seemed to have become Zila—that is, not to be talked about—I received a summons to attend the "smelling-out," and went, wondering what witch-doctor had been chosen for that bloody and barbarous ceremony. Indeed, I had not far to go, since the place selected for the occasion was outside the fence of the town of Nodwengu, on that great open stretch of ground which lay at the mouth of the valley where I was camped. Here, as I approached, I saw a vast multitude of people crowded together, fifty deep or more, round a little oval space not much larger than the pit of a theatre. On the inmost edge of this ring were seated many notable people, male and female, and as I was conducted to the side of it which was nearest to the gate of the town, I observed among them Saduko, Masapo,

Mameena and others, and mixed up with them a number of soldiers, who were evidently on duty.

Scarcely had I seated myself on a camp-stool, carried by my servant Scowl, when through the gate of the kraal issued Panda and certain of his Council, whose appearance the multitude greeted with the royal salute of "Bayete", that came from them in a deep and simultaneous roar of sound. When its echoes died away, in the midst of a deep silence Panda spoke, saying:

"Bring forth the Nyanga [doctor]. Let the umhlahlo [that is, the witch-trial] begin!"

There was a long pause, and then in the open gateway appeared a solitary figure that at first sight seemed to be scarcely human, the figure of a dwarf with a gigantic head, from which hung long, white hair, plaited into locks. It was Zikali, no other!

Quite unattended, and naked save for his moocha, for he had on him none of the ordinary paraphernalia of the witch-doctor, he waddled forward with a curious toad-like gait till he had passed through the Councillors and stood in the open space of the ring. Halting there, he looked about him slowly with his deep-set eyes, turning as he looked, till at length his glance fell upon the King.

"What would you have of me, Son of Senzangakona?" he asked. "Many years have passed since last we met. Why do you drag me from my hut, I who have visited the kraal of the King of the Zulus but twice since the 'Black One' [Chaka] sat upon the throne—once when the Boers were killed by him who went before you, and once when I was brought forth to see all who were left of my race, shoots of the royal Dwandwe stock, slain before my eyes. Do you bear me hither that I may follow them into the darkness, O Child of Senzangakona? If so I am ready; only then I have words to say that it may not please you to hear."

His deep, rumbling voice echoed into silence, while the great audience waited for the King's answer. I could see that they were all afraid of this man, yes, even Panda was afraid, for he shifted uneasily upon his stool. At length he spoke, saying:

"Not so, O Zikali. Who would wish to do hurt to the wisest and most ancient man in all the land, to him who touches the far past with one hand and the present with the other, to him who was old before our grandfathers began to be? Nay, you are safe, you on whom not even the 'Black One' dared to lay a finger, although you were his enemy and he hated you. As for the reason why you have been brought here, tell it to us, O Zikali. Who are we that we should instruct you in the ways of wisdom?"

When the dwarf heard this he broke into one of his great laughs.

"So at last the House of Senzangakona acknowledges that I have wisdom. Then before all is done they will think me wise indeed."

He laughed again in his ill-omened fashion and went on hurriedly, as though he feared that he should be called upon to explain his words:

"Where is the fee? Where is the fee? Is the King so poor that he expects an old Dwandwe doctor to divine for nothing, just as though he were working for a private friend?"

Panda made a motion with his hand, and ten fine heifers were driven into the circle from some place where they had been kept in waiting.

"Sorry beasts!" said Zikali contemptuously, "compared to those we used to breed before the time of Senzangakona"—a remark which caused a loud "Wow!" of astonishment to be uttered by the multitude that heard it. "Still, such as they are, let them be taken to my kraal, with a bull, for I have none."

The cattle were driven away, and the ancient dwarf squatted himself down and stared at the ground, looking like a great black toad. For a long while—quite ten minutes, I should think—he stared thus, till I, for one, watching him intently, began to feel as though I were mesmerised.

At length he looked up, tossing back his grey locks, and said:

"I see many things in the dust. Oh, yes, it is alive, it is alive, and tells me many things. Show that you are alive, O Dust. Look!"

As he spoke, throwing his hands upwards, there arose at his very feet one of those tiny and incomprehensible whirlwinds with which all who know South Africa will be familiar. It drove the dust together; it lifted it in a tall, spiral column that rose and rose to a height of fifty feet or more. Then it died away as suddenly as it had come, so that the dust fell down again over Zikali, over the King, and over three of his sons who sat behind him. Those three sons, I remember, were named Tshonkweni, Dabulesinye, and Mantantashiya. As it chanced, by a strange coincidence all of these were killed at the great battle of the Tugela of which I have to tell.

Now again an exclamation of fear and wonder rose from the audience, who set down this lifting of the dust at Zikali's very feet not to natural causes, but to the power of his magic. Moreover, those on whom it had fallen, including the King, rose hurriedly and shook and brushed it from their persons with a zeal that was not, I think, inspired by a mere desire for cleanliness. But Zikali only laughed again in his terrible fashion and let it lie on his fresh-oiled body, which it turned to the dull, dead hue of a grey adder.

He rose and, stepping here and there, examined the new-fallen dust. Then he put his hand into a pouch he wore and produced from it a dried human finger, whereof the nail was so pink that I think it must have been coloured—a sight at which the circle shuddered.

"Be clever," he said, "O Finger of her I loved best; be clever and write in the dust as yonder Macumazana can write, and as some of the Dwandwe used to write before we became slaves and bowed ourselves down before the Great Heavens." (By this he meant the Zulus, whose name means the Heavens.) "Be clever, dear Finger which caressed me once, me, the 'Thing-that-should-not-have-been-born,' as more will think before I die, and write those matters that it pleases the House of Senzangakona to know this day."

Then he bent down, and with the dead finger at three separate spots made certain markings in the fallen dust, which to me seemed to consist of circles and dots; and a strange and horrid sight it was to see him do it.

"I thank you, dear Finger. Now sleep, sleep, your work is done," and slowly he wrapped the relic up in some soft material and restored it to his pouch.

Then he studied the first of the markings and asked: "What am I here for? What am I here for? Does he who sits upon the Throne desire to know how long he has to reign?"

Now, those of the inner circle of the spectators, who at these "smellings-out" act as a kind of chorus, looked at the King, and, seeing that he shook his head vigorously, stretched out their right hands, holding the thumb downwards, and said simultaneously in a cold, low voice:

"Izwa!" (That is, "We hear you.")

Zikali stamped upon this set of markings.

"It is well," he said. "He who sits upon the Throne does not desire to know how long he has to reign, and therefore the dust has forgotten and shows it not to me."

Then he walked to the next markings and studied them.

"Does the Child of Senzangakona desire to know which of his sons shall live and which shall die; aye, and which of them shall sleep in his hut when he is gone?"

Now a great roar of "Izwa!" accompanied by the clapping of hands, rose from all the outer multitude who heard, for there was no information that the Zulu people desired so earnestly as this at the time of which I write.

But again Panda, who, I saw, was thoroughly alarmed at the turn things were taking, shook his head vigorously, whereon the obedient chorus negatived the question in the same fashion as before.

Zikali stamped upon the second set of markings, saying:

"The people desire to know, but the Great Ones are afraid to learn, and therefore the dust has forgotten who in the days to come shall sleep in the hut of the King and who shall sleep in the bellies of the jackals and the crops of the vultures after they have 'gone beyond' by the bridge of spears."

Now, at this awful speech (which, both because of all that it implied of bloodshed and civil war and of the wild, wailing voice in which it was spoken, that seemed quite different from Zikali's, caused everyone who heard it, including myself, I am afraid, to gasp and shiver) the King sprang from his stool as though to put a stop to such doctoring. Then, after his fashion, he changed his mind and sat down again. But Zikali, taking no heed, went to the third set of marks and studied them.

"It would seem," he said, "that I am awakened from sleep in my Black House yonder to tell of a very little matter, that might well have been dealt with by any common Nyanga born but yesterday. Well, I have taken my fee, and I will earn it, although I thought that I was brought here to speak of great matters, such as the death of princes and the fortunes of peoples. Is it desired that my Spirit should speak of wizardries in this town of Nodwengu?"

"Izwa!" said the chorus in a loud voice.

Zikali nodded his great head and seemed to talk with the dust, waiting now and again for an answer.

"Good," he said; "they are many, and the dust has told them all to me. Oh, they are very many"—and he glared around him—"so many that if I spoke them all the hyenas of the hills would be full to-night—"

Here the audience began to show signs of great apprehension.

"But," looking down at the dust and turning his head sideways, "what do you say, what do you say? Speak more plainly, Little Voices, for you know I grow deaf. Oh! now I understand. The matter is even smaller than I thought. Just of one wizard—"

"Izwa!" (loudly).

"—just of a few deaths and some sicknesses."

"Izwa!"

"Just of one death, one principal death."

"Izwa!" (very loudly).

"Ah! So we have it—one death. Now, was it a man?"

"Izwa!" (very coldly).

"A woman?"

"Izwa!" (still more coldly).

"Then a child? It must be a child, unless indeed it is the death of a spirit. But what do you people know of spirits? A child! A child! Ah! you hear me—a child. A male child, I think. Do you not say so, O Dust?"

"Izwa!" (emphatically).

"A common child? A bastard? The son of nobody?"

"Izwa!" (very low).

"A well-born child? One who would have been great? O Dust, I hear, I hear; a royal child, a child in whom ran the blood of the Father of the Zulus, he who was my friend? The blood of Senzangakona, the blood of the 'Black One,' the blood of Panda."

He stopped, while both from the chorus and from the thousands of the circle gathered around went up one roar of "Izwa!" emphasised by a mighty movement of outstretched arms and down-pointing thumbs.

Then silence, during which Zikali stamped upon all the remaining markings, saying:

"I thank you, O Dust, though I am sorry to have troubled you for so small a matter. So, so," he went on presently, "a royal boy-child is dead, and you think by witchcraft. Let us find out if he died by witchcraft or as others die, by command of the Heavens that need them. What! Here is one mark which I have left. Look! It grows red, it is full of spots! The child died with a twisted face."

"Izwa! Izwa! Izwa!" (crescendo).

"This death was not natural. Now, was it witchcraft or was it poison? Both, I think, both. And whose was the child? Not that of a son of the King, I think. Oh, yes, you hear me, People, you hear me; but be silent; I do not need your help. No, not of a son; of a daughter, then." He turned and, looked about him till his eye fell upon a group of women, amongst whom sat Nandie, dressed like a common person." Of a daughter, a daughter—" He walked to the group of women. "Why, none of these are royal; they are the children of low people. And yet—and yet I seem to smell the blood of Senzangakona."

He sniffed at the air as a dog does, and as he sniffed drew ever nearer to Nandie, till at last he laughed and pointed to her.

"*Your* child, Princess, whose name I do not know. Your firstborn child, whom you loved more than your own heart."

She rose.

"Yes, yes, Nyanga," she cried. "I am the Princess Nandie, and he was my child, whom I loved more than my own heart."

"Haha!" said Zikali. "Dust, you did not lie to me. My Spirit, you did not lie to me. But now, tell me, Dust—and tell me, my Spirit—who killed this child?"

He began to waddle round the circle, an extraordinary sight, covered as he was with grey grime, varied with streaks of black skin where the perspiration had washed the dust away.

Presently he came opposite to me, and, to my dismay, paused, sniffing at me as he had at Nandie.

"Ah! ah! O Macumazana," he said, "you have something to do with this matter," a saying at which all that audience pricked their ears.

Then I rose up in wrath and fear, knowing my position to be one of some danger.

"Wizard, or Smeller-out of Wizards, whichever you name yourself," I called in a loud voice, "if you mean that *I killed* Nandie's child, you lie!"

"No, no, Macumazahn," he answered, "but you tried to save it, and therefore you had something to do with the matter, had you not? Moreover, I think that you, who are wise like me, know who did kill it. Won't you tell me, Macumazahn? No? Then I must find out for myself. Be at peace. Does not all the land know that your hands are white as your heart?"

Then, to my great relief, he passed on, amidst a murmur of approbation, for, as I have said, the Zulus liked me. Round and round he wandered, to my surprise passing both Mameena and Masapo without taking any particular note of them, although he scanned them both, and I thought that I saw a swift glance of recognition pass between him and Mameena. It was curious to watch his progress, for as he went those in front of him swayed in their terror like corn before a puff of wind, and when he had passed they straightened themselves as the corn does when the wind has gone by.

At length he had finished his journey and returned to his starting-point, to all appearance completely puzzled.

"You keep so many wizards at your kraal, King," he said, addressing Panda, "that it is hard to say which of them wrought this deed. It would have been easier to tell you of greater matters. Yet I have taken your fee, and I must earn it—I must earn it. Dust, you are dumb. Now, my Idhlozi, my Spirit, do you speak?" and, holding his head sideways, he turned his left ear up towards the sky, then said presently, in a curious, matter-of-fact voice:

"Ah! I thank you, Spirit. Well, King, your grandchild was killed by the House of Masapo, your enemy, chief of the Amasomi."

Now a roar of approbation went up from the audience, among whom Masapo's guilt was a foregone conclusion.

When this had died down Panda spoke, saying:

"The House of Masapo is a large house; I believe that he has several wives and many children. It is not enough to smell out the House, since I am not as those who went before me were, nor will I slay the innocent with the guilty. Tell us, O Opener-of-Roads, who among the House of Masapo has wrought this deed?"

"That's just the question," grumbled Zikali in a deep voice. "All that I know is that it was done by poisoning, and I smell the poison. It is here."

Then he walked to where Mameena sat and cried out:

"Seize that woman and search her hair."

Executioners who were in waiting sprang forward, but Mameena waved them away.

"Friends," she said, with a little laugh, "there is no need to touch me," and, rising, she stepped forward to the centre of the ring. Here, with a few swift motions of her hands, she flung off first the cloak she wore, then the moocha about her middle, and lastly the fillet that bound her long hair, and stood before that audience in all her naked beauty—a wondrous and a lovely sight.

"Now," she said, "let women come and search me and my garments, and see if there is any poison hid there."

Two old crones stepped forward—though I do not know who sent them—and carried out a very thorough examination, finally reporting that they had found nothing. Thereon Mameena, with a shrug of her shoulders, resumed such clothes as she wore, and returned lo her place.

Zikali appeared to grow angry. He stamped upon the ground with his big feet; he shook his braided grey locks and cried out:

"Is my wisdom to be defeated in such a little matter? One of you tie a bandage over my eyes."

Now a man—it was Maputa, the messenger—came out and did so, and I noted that he tied it well and tight. Zikali whirled round upon his heels, first one way and then another, and, crying aloud: "Guide me, my Spirit!" marched forward in a zigzag fashion, as a blindfolded man does, with his arms stretched out in front of him. First he went to the right, then to the left, and then straight forward, till at length, to my astonishment, he came exactly opposite the spot where Masapo sat and, stretching out his great, groping hands, seized the kaross with which he was covered and, with a jerk, tore it from him.

"Search this!" he cried, throwing it on the ground, and a woman searched.

Presently she uttered an exclamation, and from among the fur of one of the tails of the kaross produced a tiny bag that appeared to be made out of the bladder of a fish. This she handed to Zikali, whose eyes had now been unbandaged.

He looked at it, then gave it to Maputa, saying:

"There is the poison—there is the poison, but who gave it I do not say. I am weary. Let me go."

Then, none hindering him, he walked away through the gate of the kraal.

Soldiers seized upon Masapo, while the multitude roared: "Kill the wizard!"

Masapo sprang up, and, running to where the King sat, flung himself upon his knees, protesting his innocence and praying for mercy. I also, who had doubts as to all this business, ventured to rise and speak.

"O King," I said, "as one who has known this man in the past, I plead with you. How that powder came into his kaross I know not, but perchance it is not poison, only harmless dust."

"Yes, it is but wood dust which I use for the cleaning of my nails," cried Masapo, for he was so terrified I think he knew not what he said.

"So you own to knowledge of the medicine?" exclaimed Panda. "Therefore none hid it in your kaross through malice."

Masapo began to explain, but what he said was lost in a mighty roar of "Kill the wizard!"

Panda held up his hand and there was silence.

"Bring milk in a dish," commanded the King, and it, was brought, and, at a further word from him, dusted with the powder.

"Now, O Macumazana," said Panda to me, "if you still think that yonder man is innocent, will you drink this milk?"

"I do not like milk, O King," I answered, shaking my head, whereon all who heard me laughed.

"Will Mameena, his wife, drink it, then?" asked Panda.

She also shook her head, saying:

"O King, I drink no milk that is mixed with dust."

Just then a lean, white dog, one of those homeless, mangy beasts that stray about kraals and live upon carrion, wandered into the ring. Panda made a sign, and a servant, going to where the poor beast stood staring about it hungrily, set down the wooden dish of milk in front of it. Instantly the dog lapped it up, for it was starving, and as it finished the last drop the man slipped a leathern thong about its neck and held it fast.

Now all eyes were fixed upon the dog, mine among them. Presently the beast uttered a long and melancholy howl which thrilled me through, for I knew it to be Masapo's death warrant, then began to scratch the ground and foam at the mouth. Guessing what would follow, I rose, bowed to the King, and walked away to my camp, which, it will be remembered, was set up in a little kloof commanding this place, at a distance only of a few hundred yards. So intent was all the multitude upon watching the dog that I doubt whether anyone saw me go. As for that poor beast, Scowl, who stayed behind, told me that it did not die for about ten minutes, since before its end a red rash appeared upon it similar to that which I had seen upon Saduko's child, and it was seized with convulsions.

Well, I reached my tent unmolested, and, having lit my pipe, engaged myself in making business entries in my note-book, in order to divert my mind as much as I could, when suddenly I heard a most devilish clamour. Looking up, I saw Masapo running towards me with a speed that I should have thought impossible in so fat a man, while after him raced the fierce-faced executioners, and behind came the mob.

"Kill the evil-doer!" they shouted.

Masapo reached me. He flung himself on his knees before me, gasping:

"Save me, Macumazahn! I am innocent. Mameena, the witch! Mameena—"

He got no farther, for the slayers had leapt on him like hounds upon a buck and dragged him from me.

Then I turned and covered up my eyes.

Next morning I left Nodwengu without saying good-bye to anyone, for what had happened there made me desire a change. My servant, Scowl, and one of my hunters remained, however, to collect some cattle that were still due to me.

A month or more later, when they joined me in Natal, bringing the cattle, they told me that Mameena, the widow of Masapo, had entered the house of Saduko as his second wife. In answer to a question which I put to them, they added that it was said that the Princess Nandie did not approve of this choice of Saduko, which she thought would not be fortunate for him or bring him happiness. As her husband seemed to be much enamoured of Mameena, however, she had waived her objections, and when Panda asked if she gave her consent had told him that, although she would prefer that Saduko should choose some other woman who had not been mixed up with the wizard who killed her child, she was prepared to take Mameena as her sister, and would know how to keep her in her place.

The Sin of Umbelazi

About eighteen months had gone by, and once again, in the autumn of the year 1856, I found myself at old Umbezi's kraal, where there seemed to be an extraordinary market for any kind of gas-pipe that could be called a gun. Well, as a trader who could not afford to neglect profitable markets, which are hard things to find, there I was.

Now, in eighteen months many things become a little obscured in one's memory, especially if they have to do with savages, in whom, after all, one takes only a philosophical and a business interest. Therefore I may perhaps be excused if I had more or less forgotten a good many of the details of what I may call the Mameena affair. These, however, came back to me very vividly when the first person that I met—at some distance from the kraal, where I suppose she had been taking a country walk—was the beautiful Mameena herself. There she was, looking quite unchanged and as lovely as ever, sitting under the shade of a wild fig-tree and fanning herself with a handful of its leaves.

Of course I jumped off my wagon-box and greeted her.

"Siyakubona [that is, good morrow], Macumazahn," she said. "My heart is glad to see you."

"Siyakubona, Mameena," I answered, leaving out all reference to *my* heart. Then I added, looking at her: "Is it true that you have a new husband?"

"Yes, Macumazahn, an old lover of mine has become a new husband. You know whom I mean—Saduko. After the death of that evil-doer, Masapo, he grew very urgent, and the King, also the Inkosazana Nandie, pressed it on me, and so I yielded. Also, to be honest, Saduko was a good match, or seemed to be so."

By now we were walking side by side, for the train of wagons had gone ahead to the old outspan. So I stopped and looked her in the face.

"'Seemed to be,'" I repeated. "What do you mean by 'seemed to be'? Are you not happy this time?"

"Not altogether, Macumazahn," she answered, with a shrug of her shoulders. "Saduko is very fond of me—fonder than I like indeed, since it causes him to neglect Nandie, who, by the way, has another son, and, although she says little, that makes Nandie cross. In short," she added, with a burst of truth, "I am the plaything, Nandie is the great lady, and that place suits me ill."

"If you love Saduko, you should not mind, Mameena."

"Love," she said bitterly. "Piff! What is love? But I have asked you that question once before."

"Why are you here, Mameena?" I inquired, leaving it unanswered.

"Because Saduko is here, and, of course, Nandie, for she never leaves him, and he will not leave me; because the Prince Umbelazi is coming; because there are plots afoot and the great war draws near—that war in which so many must die."

"Between Cetewayo and Umbelazi, Mameena?"

"Aye, between Cetewayo and Umbelazi. Why do you suppose those wagons of yours are loaded with guns for which so many cattle must be paid? Not to shoot game with, I think. Well, this little kraal of my father's is just now the headquarters of the Umbelazi faction, the Isigqosa, as the princedom of Gikazi is that of Cetewayo. My poor father!" she added, with her characteristic shrug, "he thinks himself very great to-day, as he did after he had shot the elephant—before I nursed you,

Macumazahn—but often I wonder what will be the end of it—for him and for all of us, Macumazahn, including yourself."

"I!" I answered. "What have I to do with your Zulu quarrels?"

"That you will know when you have done with them, Macumazahn. But here is the kraal, and before we enter it I wish to thank you for trying to protect that unlucky husband of mine, Masapo."

"I only did so, Mameena, because I thought him innocent."

"I know, Macumazahn; and so did I, although, as I always told you, I hated him, the man with whom my father forced me to marry. But I am afraid, from what I have learned since, that he was not altogether innocent. You see, Saduko had struck him, which he could not forget. Also, he was jealous of Saduko, who had been my suitor, and wished to injure him. But what I do not understand," she added, with a burst of confidence, "is why he did not kill Saduko instead of his child."

"Well, Mameena, you may remember it was said he tried to do so."

"Yes, Macumazahn; I had forgotten that. I suppose that he did try, and failed. Oh, now I see things with both eyes. Look, yonder is my father. I will go away. But come and talk to me sometimes, Macumazahn, for otherwise Nandie will be careful that I should hear nothing—I who am the plaything, the beautiful woman of the House, who must sit and smile, but must not think."

So she departed, and I went on to meet old Umbezi, who came gambolling towards me like an obese goat, reflecting that, whatever might be the truth or otherwise of her story, her advancement in the world did not seem to have brought Mameena greater happiness and contentment.

Umbezi, who greeted me warmly, was in high spirits and full of importance. He informed me that the marriage of Mameena to Saduko, after the death of the wizard, her husband, whose tribe and cattle had been given to Saduko in compensation for the loss of his son, was a most fortunate thing for him.

I asked why.

"Because as Saduko grows great so I, his father-in-law, grow great with him, Macumazahn, especially as he has been liberal to me in the matter of cattle, passing on to me a share of the herds of Masapo, so that I, who have been poor so long, am getting rich at last. Moreover, my kraal is to be honoured with a visit from Umbelazi and some of his brothers to-morrow, and Saduko has promised to lift me up high when the Prince is declared heir to the throne."

"Which prince?" I asked.

"Umbelazi, Macumazahn. Who else? Umbelazi, who without doubt will conquer Cetewayo."

"Why without doubt, Umbezi? Cetewayo has a great following, and if *he* should conquer I think that you will only be lifted up in the crops of the vultures."

At this rough suggestion Umbezi's fat face fell.

"O Macumazana," he said, "if I thought that, I would go over to Cetewayo, although Saduko is my son-in-law. But it is not possible, since the King loves Umbelazi's mother most of all his wives, and, as I chance to know, has sworn to her that he favours Umbelazi's cause, since he is the dearest to him of all his sons, and will do everything that he can to help him, even to the sending of his own regiment to his assistance, if there should be need. Also, it is said that Zikali, Opener-of-Roads, who has all wisdom, has prophesied that Umbelazi will win more than he ever hoped for."

"The King!" I said, "a straw blown hither and thither between two great winds, waiting to be wafted to rest by that which is strongest! The prophecy of Zikali! It seems to me that it can be read two ways, if, indeed, he ever made one. Well, Umbezi, I hope that you are right, for, although it is no affair of mine, who am but a white trader in your country, I like Umbelazi better than Cetewayo, and think that he has a kinder heart. Also, as you have chosen his side, I advise you to stick to it, since traitors to a cause seldom come to any good, whether it wins or loses. And now, will you take count of the guns and powder which I have brought with me?"

Ah! better would it have been for Umbezi if he had listened to my advice and remained faithful to the leader he had chosen, for then, even if he had lost his life, at least he would have kept his good name. But of him presently, as they say in pedigrees.

Next day I went to pay my respects to Nandie, whom I found engaged in nursing her new baby and as quiet and stately in her demeanour as ever. Still, I think that she was very glad to see me, because I had tried to save the life of her first child, whom she could not forget, if for no other reason. Whilst I was talking to her of that sad matter, also of the political state of the country, as to which I think she wished to say something to me, Mameena entered the hut, without waiting to be asked, and sat down, whereon Nandie became suddenly silent.

This, however, did not trouble Mameena, who talked away about anything and everything, completely ignoring the head-wife. For a while Nandie bore it with patience, but at length she took advantage of a pause in the conversation to say in her firm, low voice:

"This is my hut, daughter of Umbezi, a thing which you remember well enough when it is a question whether Saduko, our husband, shall visit you or me. Can you not remember it now when I would speak with the white chief, Watcher-by-Night, who has been so good as to take the trouble to come to see me?"

On hearing these words Mameena leapt up in a rage, and I must say I never saw her look more lovely.

"You insult me, daughter of Panda, as you always try to do, because you are jealous of me."

"Your pardon, sister," replied Nandie. "Why should I, who am Saduko's Inkosikazi, and, as you say, daughter of Panda, the King, be jealous of the widow of the wizard, Masapo, and the daughter of the headman, Umbezi, whom it has pleased our husband to take into his house to be the companion of his leisure?"

"Why? Because you know that Saduko loves my little finger more than he does your whole body, although you are of the King's blood and have borne him brats," she answered, looking at the infant with no kindly eye.

"It may be so, daughter of Umbezi, for men have their fancies, and without doubt you are fair. Yet I would ask you one thing—if Saduko loves you so much, how comes it he trusts you so little that you must learn any matter of weight by listening at my door, as I found you doing the other day?"

"Because you teach him not to do so, O Nandie. Because you are ever telling him not to consult with me, since she who has betrayed one husband may betray another. Because you make him believe my place is that of his toy, not that of his companion, and this although I am cleverer than you and all your House tied into one bundle, as you may find out some day."

"Yes," answered Nandie, quite undisturbed, "I do teach him these things, and I am glad that in this matter Saduko has a thinking head and listens to me. Also I agree that it is likely I shall learn many more ill things through and of you one day, daughter of Umbezi. And now, as it is not good that we should wrangle before this white lord, again I say to you that this is my hut, in which I wish to speak alone with my guest."

"I go, I go!" gasped Mameena; "but I tell you that Saduko shall hear of this."

"Certainly he will hear of it, for I shall tell him when he comes to-night."

Another instant and Mameena was gone, having shot out of the hut like a rabbit from its burrow.

"I ask your pardon, Macumazahn, for what has happened," said Nandie, "but it had become necessary that I should teach my sister, Mameena, upon which stool she ought to sit. I do not trust her, Macumazahn. I think that she knows more of the death of my child than she chooses to say, she who wished to be rid of Masapo for a reason you can guess. I think also she will bring shame and trouble upon Saduko, whom she has bewitched with her beauty, as she bewitches all men—perhaps even yourself a little, Macumazahn. And now let us talk of other matters."

To this proposition I agreed cordially, since, to tell the truth, if I could have managed to do so with any decent grace, I should have been out of that hut long before Mameena. So we fell to conversing on the condition of Zululand and the dangers that lay ahead for all who were connected with the royal House—a state of affairs which troubled Nandie much, for she was a clear-headed woman, and one who feared the future.

"Ah! Macumazahn," she said to me as we parted, "I would that I were the wife of some man who did not desire to grow great, and that no royal blood ran in my veins."

On the next day the Prince Umbelazi arrived, and with him Saduko and a few other notable men. They came quite quietly and without any ostensible escort, although Scowl, my servant, told me he heard that the bush at a little distance was swarming with soldiers of the Isigqosa party. If I remember rightly, the excuse for the visit was that Umbezi had some of a certain rare breed of white cattle whereof the prince wished to secure young bulls and heifers to improve his herd.

Once inside the kraal, however, Umbelazi, who was a very open-natured man, threw off all pretence, and, after greeting me heartily enough, told me with plainness that he was there because this was a convenient spot on which to arrange the consolidation of his party.

Almost every hour during the next two weeks messengers—many of whom were chiefs disguised—came and went. I should have liked to follow their example—that is, so far as their departure was concerned—for I felt that I was being drawn into a very dangerous vortex. But, as a matter of fact, I could not escape, since I was obliged to wait to receive payment for my stuff, which, as usual, was made in cattle.

Umbelazi talked with me a good deal at that time, impressing upon me how friendly he was towards the English white men of Natal, as distinguished from the Boers, and what good treatment he was prepared to promise to them, should he ever attain to authority in Zululand. It was during one of the earliest of these conversations, which, of course, I saw had an ultimate object, that he met Mameena, I think, for the first time.

We were walking together in a little natural glade of the bush that bordered one side of the kraal, when, at the end of it, looking like some wood nymph of classic fable in the light of the setting sun, appeared the lovely Mameena, clothed only in her girdle of fur, her necklace of blue beads and some copper ornaments, and carrying upon her head a gourd.

Umbelazi noted her at once, and, ceasing his political talk, of which he was obviously tired, asked me who that beautiful intombi (that is, girl) might be.

She is not an intombi, Prince," I answered. "She is a widow who is again a wife, the second wife of your friend and councillor, Saduko, and the daughter of your host, Umbezi."

"Is it so, Macumazahn? Oh, then I have heard of her, though, as it chances, I have never met her before. No wonder that my sister Nandie is jealous, for she is beautiful indeed."

"Yes," I answered, "she looks pretty against the red sky, does she not?"

By now we were drawing near to Mameena, and I greeted her, asking if she wanted anything.

"Nothing, Macumazahn," she answered in her delicate, modest way, for never did I know anyone who could seem quite so modest as Mameena, and with a swift glance of her shy eyes at the tall and splendid Umbelazi, "nothing. Only," she added, "I was passing with the milk of one of the few cows my father gave me, and saw you, and I thought that perhaps, as the day has been so hot, you might like a drink of it."

Then, lifting the gourd from her head, she held it out to me.

I thanked her, drank some—who could do less?—and returned it to her, whereon she made as though she would hasten to depart.

"May I not drink also, daughter of Umbezi?" asked Umbelazi, who could scarcely take his eyes off her.

"Certainly, sir, if you are a friend of Macumazahn," she replied, handing him the gourd.

"I am that, Lady, and more than that, since I am a friend of your husband, Saduko, also, as you will know when I tell you that my name is Umbelazi."

"I thought it must be so," she replied, "because of your—of your stature. Let the Prince accept the offering of his servant, who one day hopes to be his subject," and, dropping upon her knee, she held out the gourd to him. Over it I saw their eyes meet. He drank, and as he handed back the vessel she said:

"O Prince, may I be granted a word with you? I have that to tell which you would perhaps do well to hear, since news sometimes reaches the ears of humble women that escapes those of the men, our masters."

He bowed his head in assent, whereon, taking a hint which Mameena gave me with her eyes, I muttered something about business and made myself scarce. I may add that Mameena must have had a great deal to tell Umbelazi. Fully an hour and a half had gone by before, by the light of the moon, from a point of vantage on my wagon-box, whence, according to my custom, I was keeping a lookout on things in general, I saw her slip back to the kraal silently as a snake, followed at a little distance by the towering form of Umbelazi.

Apparently Mameena continued to be the recipient of information which she found it necessary to communicate in private to the prince. At any rate, on sundry subsequent evenings the dullness of my vigil on the wagon-box was relieved by the sight of her graceful figure gliding home from the kloof that Umbelazi seemed to find a very suitable spot for reflection after sunset. On one of the last of these occasions I remember that Nandie chanced to be with me, having come to my wagon for some medicine for her baby.

"What does it mean, Macumazahn?" she asked, when the pair had gone by, as they thought unobserved, since we were standing where they could not see us.

"I don't know, and I don't want to know," I answered sharply.

"Neither do I, Macumazahn; but without doubt we shall learn in time. If the crocodile is patient and silent the buck always drops into its jaws at last."

On the day after Nandie made this wise remark Saduko started on a mission, as I understood, to win over several doubtful chiefs to the cause of Indhlovu-ene-sihlonti (the Elephant-with-the-tuft-of-hair), as the Prince Umbelazi was called among the Zulus, though not to his face. This mission lasted ten days, and before it was concluded an important event happened at Umbezi's kraal.

One evening Mameena came to me in a great rage, and said that she could bear her present life no longer. Presuming on her rank and position as head-wife, Nandie treated her like a servant—nay, like a little dog, to be beaten with a stick. She wished that Nandie would die.

"It will be very unlucky for you if she does," I answered, "for then, perhaps, Zikali will be summoned to look into the matter, as he was before."

What was she to do, she went on, ignoring my remark.

"Eat the porridge that you have made in your own pot, or break the pot" (i.e. go away), I suggested. "There was no need for you to marry Saduko, any more than there was for you to marry Masapo."

"How can you talk to me like that, Macumazahn," she answered, stamping her foot, "when you know well it is your fault if I married anyone? Piff! I hate them all, and, since my father would only beat me if I took my troubles to him, I will run off, and live in the wilderness alone and become a witch-doctoress."

"I am afraid you will find it very dull, Mameena," I began in a bantering tone, for, to tell the truth, I did not think it wise to show her too much sympathy while she was so excited.

Mameena never waited for the end of the sentence, but, sobbing out that I was false and cruel, she turned and departed swiftly. Oh! little did I foresee how and where we should meet again.

Next morning I was awakened shortly after sunrise by Scowl, whom I had sent out with another man the night before to look for a lost ox.

"Well, have you found the ox?" I asked.

"Yes, Baas; but I did not waken you to tell you that. I have a message for you, Baas, from Mameena, wife of Saduko, whom I met about four hours ago upon the plain yonder."

I bade him set it out.

These were the words of Mameena, Baas: 'Say to Macumazahn, your master, that Indhlovu-ene-sihlonti, taking pity on my wrongs and loving me with his heart, has offered to take me into his House and that I have accepted his offer, since I think it better to become the Inkosazana of the Zulus, as I shall one day, than to remain a servant in the house of Nandie. Say to Macumazahn that when Saduko returns he is to tell him that this is all his fault, since if he had kept Nandie in her place I would have died rather than leave him. Let him say to Saduko also that, although from henceforth we can be no more than friends, my heart is still tender towards him, and that by day and by night I will strive to water his greatness, so that it may grow into a tree that shall shade the land. Let Macumazahn bid him not to be angry with me, since what I do I do for his good, as he would have found no happiness while Nandie and I dwelt in one house. Above all, also let him not be angry with the Prince, who loves him more than any man, and does but travel whither the wind that I breathe blows him. Bid Macumazahn think of me kindly, as I shall of him while my eyes are open.'"

I listened to this amazing message in silence, then asked if Mameena was alone.

"No, Baas; Umbelazi and some soldiers were with her, but they did not hear her words, for she stepped aside to speak with me. Then she returned to them, and they walked away swiftly, and were swallowed up in the night."

"Very good, Sikauli," I said. "Make me some coffee, and make it strong."

I dressed and drank several cups of the coffee, all the while "thinking with my head," as the Zulus say. Then I walked up to the kraal to see Umbezi, whom I found just coming out of his hut, yawning.

"Why do you look so black upon this beautiful morning, Macumazahn?" asked the genial old scamp. "Have you lost your best cow, or what?"

"No, my friend," I answered; "but you and another have lost your best cow." And word for word I repeated to him Mameena's message. When I had finished really I thought that Umbezi was about to faint.

"Curses be on the head of this Mameena!" he exclaimed. "Surely some evil spirit must have been her father, not I, and well was she called Child of Storm. What shall I do now, Macumazahn? Thanks be to my Spirit," he added, with an air of relief, "she is too far gone for me to try to catch her; also, if I did, Umbelazi and his soldiers would kill me."

"And what will Saduko do if you don't?" I asked.

"Oh, of course he will be angry, for no doubt he is fond of her. But, after all, I am used to that. You remember how he went mad when she married Masapo. At least, he cannot say that I made her run away with Umbelazi. After all, it is a matter which they must settle between them."

"I think it may mean great trouble," I said, "at a time when trouble is not needed."

"Oh, why so, Macumazahn? My daughter did not get on with the Princess Nandie—we could all see that—for they would scarcely speak to each other. And if Saduko is fond of her—well, after all, there are other beautiful women in Zululand. I know one or two of them myself whom I will mention to Saduko—or rather to Nandie. Really, as things were, I am not sure but that he is well rid of her."

"But what do you think of the matter as her father?" I asked, for I wanted to see to what length his accommodating morality would stretch.

"As her father—well, of course, Macumazahn, as her father I am sorry, because it will mean talk, will it not, as the Masapo business did? Still, there is this to be said for Mameena," he added, with a brightening face, "she always runs away up the tree, not down. When she got rid of Masapo—I mean when Masapo was killed for his witchcraft—she married Saduko, who was a bigger man—Saduko, whom she would not marry when Masapo was the bigger man. And now, when she has got rid of Saduko, she enters the hut of Umbelazi, who will one day be King of the Zulus, the biggest man in all the world, which means that she will be the biggest woman, for remember, Macumazahn, she will walk round and round that great Umbelazi till whatever way he looks he will see her and no one else. Oh, she will grow great, and carry up her poor old father in the blanket on her back. Oh, the sun still shines behind the cloud, Macumazahn, so let us make the best of the cloud, since we know that it will break out presently."

"Yes, Umbezi; but other things besides the sun break out from clouds sometimes—lightning, for instance; lightning which kills."

"You speak ill-omened words, Macumazahn; words that take away my appetite, which is generally excellent at this hour. Well, if Mameena is bad it is not my fault, for I brought her up to be good. After all," he added with an outburst of petulance, "why do you scold me when it is your fault? If you had run away with the girl when you might have done so, there would have been none of this trouble."

"Perhaps not," I answered; "only then I am sure I should have been dead to-day, as I think that all who have to do with her will be ere long. And now, Umbezi, I wish you a good breakfast."

On the following morning, Saduko returned and was told the news by Nandie, whom I had carefully avoided. On this occasion, however, I was forced to be present, as the person to whom the sinful Mameena had sent her farewell message. It was a very painful experience, of which I do not remember all the details. For a while after he learned the truth Saduko sat still as a stone, staring in front of him, with a face that seemed to have become suddenly old. Then he turned upon Umbezi, and in a few terrible words accused him of having arranged the matter in order to advance his own fortunes at the price of his daughter's dishonour. Next, without listening to his ex-father-in-law's voluble explanations, he rose and said that he was going away to kill Umbelazi, the evil-doer who had robbed him of the wife he loved, with the connivance of all three of us, and by a sweep of his hand he indicated Umbezi, the Princess Nandie and myself.

This was more than I could stand, so I, too, rose and asked him what he meant, adding in the irritation of the moment that if I had wished to rob him of his beautiful Mameena, I thought I could have done so long ago—a remark that staggered him a little.

Then Nandie rose also, and spoke in her quiet voice.

"Saduko, my husband," she said, "I, a Princess of the Zulu House, married you who are not of royal blood because I loved you, and although Panda the King and Umbelazi the Prince wished it, for no other reason whatsoever. Well, I have been faithful to you through some trials, even when you set the widow of a wizard—if, indeed, as I have reason to suspect, she was not herself the wizard—before me, and although that wizard had killed our son, lived in her hut rather than in mine. Now this woman of whom you thought so much has deserted you for your friend and my brother, the Prince Umbelazi—Umbelazi who is called the Handsome, and who, if the fortune of war goes with him, as it may or may not, will succeed to Panda, my father. This she has done because she alleges that I, your Inkosikazi and the King's daughter, treated her as a servant, which is a lie. I kept her in her place, no more, who, if she could have had her will, would have ousted me from mine, perhaps by death, for the wives of wizards learn their arts. On this pretext she has left you; but that is not her real reason. She has left you because the Prince, my brother, whom she has befooled with her tricks and beauty, as she has befooled others, or tried to"—and she glanced at me—"is a bigger man than you are. You, Saduko, may become great, as my heart prays that you will, but my brother may become a king. She does not love him any more than she loved you, but she does love the place that may be his, and therefore hers—she who would be the first doe of the herd. My husband, I think that you are well rid of Mameena, for I think also that if she had stayed with us there would have been more deaths in our House; perhaps mine, which would not matter, and perhaps yours, which would matter much. All this I say to you, not from jealousy of one who is fairer than I, but because it is the truth. Therefore my counsel to you is to let this business pass over and keep silent. Above all, seek not to avenge yourself upon Umbelazi, since I am sure that he has taken vengeance to dwell with him in his own hut. I have spoken."

That this moderate and reasoned speech of Nandie's produced a great effect upon Saduko I could see, but at the time the only answer he made to it was:

"Let the name of Mameena be spoken no more within hearing of my ears. Mameena is dead."

So her name was heard no more in the Houses of Saduko and of Umbezi, and when it was necessary for any reason to refer to her, she was given a new name, a composite Zulu word, "O-we-Zulu", I think it was, which is "Storm-child" shortly translated, for "Zulu" means a storm as well as the sky.

I do not think that Saduko spoke of her to me again until towards the climax of this history, and certainly I did not mention her to him. But from that day forward I noted that he was a changed man. His pride and open pleasure in his great success, which had caused the Zulus to name him the "Self-eater," were no longer marked. He became cold and silent, like a man who is thinking deeply, but who shutters his thoughts lest some should read them through the windows of his eyes. Moreover, he paid a visit to Zikali the Little and Wise, as I found out by accident; but what advice that cunning old dwarf gave to him I did not find out—then.

The only other event which happened in connection with this elopement was that a message came from Umbelazi to Saduko, brought by one of the princes, a brother of Umbelazi, who was of his party. As I know, for I heard it delivered, it was a very humble message when the relative positions of the two men are considered—that of one who knew that he had done wrong, and, if not repentant, was heartily ashamed of himself.

"Saduko," it said, "I have stolen a cow of yours, and I hope you will forgive me, since that cow did not love the pasture in your kraal, but in mine she grows fat and is content. Moreover, in return I will give you many other cows. Everything that I have to give, I will give to you who are my friend and trusted councillor. Send me word, O Saduko, that this wall which I have built between us is broken down, since ere long you and I must stand together in war."

To this message Saduko's answer was:

"O Prince, you are troubled about a very little thing. That cow which you have taken was of no worth to me, for who wishes to keep a beast that is ever tearing and lowing at the gates of the kraal, disturbing those who would sleep inside with her noise? Had you asked her of me, I would have given her to you freely. I thank you for your offer, but I need no more cows, especially if, like this one, they have no calves. As for a wall between us, there is none, for how can two men who, if the battle is to be won, must stand shoulder to shoulder, fight if divided by a wall? O Son of the King, I am dreaming by day and night of the battle and the victory, and I have forgotten all about the barren cow that ran away after you, the great bull of the herd. Only do not be surprised if one day you find that this cow has a sharp horn."

Panda's Prayer

About six weeks later, in the month of November, 1856, I chanced to be at Nodwengu when the quarrel between the princes came to a head. Although none of the regiments was actually allowed to enter the town—that is, as a regiment—the place was full of people, all of them in a state of great excitement, who came in during the daytime and went to sleep in the neighbouring military kraals at night. One evening, as some of these soldiers—about a thousand of them, if I remember right—were returning to the Ukubaza kraal, a fight occurred between them, which led to the final outbreak.

As it happened, at that time there were two separate regiments stationed at this kraal. I think that they were the Imkulutshana and the Hlaba, one of which favoured Cetewayo and the other Umbelazi. As certain companies of each of these regiments marched along together in parallel lines, two of their captains got into dispute on the eternal subject of the succession to the throne. From words they came to blows, and the end of it was that he who favoured Umbelazi killed him who favoured Cetewayo with his kerry. Thereon the comrades of the slain man, raising a shout of "Usutu," which became the war-cry of Cetewayo's party, fell upon the others, and a dreadful combat ensued. Fortunately the soldiers were only armed with sticks, or the slaughter would have been very great; but as it was, after an indecisive engagement, about fifty men were killed and many more injured.

Now, with my usual bad luck, I, who had gone out to shoot a few birds for the pot—pauw, or bustard, I think they were—was returning across this very plain to my old encampment in the kloof where Masapo had been executed, and so ran into the fight just as it was beginning. I saw the captain killed and the subsequent engagement. Indeed, as it happened, I did more. Not knowing where to go or what to do, for I was quite alone, I pulled up my horse behind a tree and waited till I could escape the horrors about me; for I can assure anyone who may ever read these words that it is a very horrible sight to see a thousand men engaged in fierce and deadly combat. In truth, the fact that they had no spears, and could only batter each other to death with their heavy kerries, made it worse, since the duels were more desperate and prolonged.

Everywhere men were rolling on the ground, hitting at each other's heads, until at last some blow went home and one of them threw out his arms and lay still, either dead or senseless. Well, there I sat watching all this shocking business from the saddle of my trained shooting pony, which stood like a stone, till presently I became aware of two great fellows rushing at me with their eyes starting out of their heads and shouting as they came:

"Kill Umbelazi's white man! Kill! Kill!"

Then, seeing that the matter was urgent and that it was a question of my life or theirs, I came into action.

In my hand I held a double-barrelled shotgun loaded with what we used to call "loopers," or B.B. shot, of which but a few went to each charge, for I had hoped to meet with a small buck on my way to camp. So, as these soldiers came, I lifted the gun and fired, the right barrel at one of them and the left barrel at the other, aiming in each case at the centre of the small dancing shields, which from force of habit they held stretched out to protect their throats and breasts. At that distance, of course, the loopers sank through the soft hide of the shields and deep into the bodies of those who carried them, so that both of them dropped dead, the left-hand man being so close that he fell against my pony, his uplifted kerry striking me upon the thigh and bruising me.

When I saw what I had done, and that my danger was over for the moment, without waiting to reload I dug the spurs into my horse's sides and galloped off to Nodwengu, passing between the groups of struggling men. On arriving unharmed at the town, I went instantly to the royal huts and demanded to see the King, who sent word that I was to be admitted. On coming before him I told him exactly what had happened—that I had killed two of Cetewayo's men in order to save my own life, and on that account submitted myself to his justice.

"O Macumazana," said Panda in great distress, "I know well that you are not to blame, and already I have sent out a regiment to stop this fighting, with command that those who caused it should be brought before me to-morrow for judgment. I am glad indeed, Macumazahn, that you have escaped without harm, but I must tell you that I fear henceforth your life will be in danger, since all the Usutu party will hold it forfeit if they can catch you. While you are in my town I can protect you, for I will set a strong guard about your camp; but here you will have to stay until these troubles are done with, since if you leave you may be murdered on the road."

"I thank you for your kindness, King," I answered; "but all this is very awkward for me, who hoped to trek for Natal to-morrow."

"Well, there it is, Macumazahn, you will have to stay here unless you wish to be killed. He who walks into a storm must put up with the hailstones."

So it came about that once again Fate dragged me into the Zulu maelstrom.

On the morrow I was summoned to the trial, half as a witness and half as one of the offenders. Going to the head of the Nodwengu kraal, where Panda was sitting in state with his Council, I found the whole great space in front of him crowded with a dense concourse of fierce-faced partisans, those who favoured Cetewayo—the Usutu—sitting on the right, and those who favoured Umbelazi—the Isigqosa—sitting on the left. At the head of the right-hand section sat Cetewayo, his brethren and chief men. At the head of the left-hand section sat Umbelazi, his brethren and his chief men, amongst whom I saw Saduko take a place immediately behind the Prince, so that he could whisper into his ear.

To myself and my little band of eight hunters, who by Panda's express permission, came armed with their guns, as I did also, for I was determined that if the necessity arose we would sell our lives as dearly as we could, was appointed a place almost in front of the King and between the two factions. When everyone was seated the trial began, Panda demanding to know who had caused the tumult of the previous night.

I cannot set out what followed in all its details, for it would be too long; also I have forgotten many of them. I remember, however, that Cetewayo's people said that Umbelazi's men were the aggressors, and that Umbelazi's people said that Cetewayo's men were the aggressors, and that each of their parties backed up these statements, which were given at great length, with loud shouts.

"How am I to know the truth?" exclaimed Panda at last. "Macumazahn, you were there; step forward and tell it to me."

So I stood out and told the King what I had seen, namely that the captain who favoured Cetewayo had begun the quarrel by striking the captain who favoured Umbelazi, but that in the end Umbelazi's man had killed Cetewayo's man, after which the fighting commenced.

"Then it would seem that the Usutu are to blame," said Panda.

"Upon what grounds do you say so, my father? asked Cetewayo, springing up. "Upon the testimony of this white man, who is well known to be the friend of

Umbelazi and of his henchman Saduko, and who himself killed two of those who called me chief in the course of the fight?"

"Yes, Cetewayo," I broke in, "because I thought it better that I should kill them than that they should kill me, whom they attacked quite unprovoked."

"At any rate, you killed them, little White Man," shouted Cetewayo, "for which cause your blood is forfeit. Say, did Umbelazi give you leave to appear before the King accompanied by men armed with guns, when we who are his sons must come with sticks only? If so, let him protect you!"

"That I will do if there is need!" exclaimed Umbelazi.

"Thank you, Prince," I said; "but if there is need I will protect myself as I did yesterday," and, cocking my double-barrelled rifle, I looked full at Cetewayo.

"When you leave here, then at least I will come even with you, Macumazahn!" threatened Cetewayo, spitting through his teeth, as was his way when mad with passion.

For he was beside himself, and wished to vent his temper on someone, although in truth he and I were always good friends.

"If so I shall stop where I am," I answered coolly, "in the shadow of the King, your father. Moreover, are you so lost in folly, Cetewayo, that you should wish to bring the English about your ears? Know that if I am killed you will be asked to give account of my blood."

"Aye," interrupted Panda, "and know that if anyone lays a finger on Macumazana, who is my guest, he shall die, whether he be a common man or a prince and my son. Also, Cetewayo, I fine you twenty head of cattle, to be paid to Macumazana because of the unprovoked attack which your men made upon him when he rightly slew them."

"The fine shall be paid, my father," said Cetewayo more quietly, for he saw that in threatening me he had pushed matters too far.

Then, after some more talk, Panda gave judgment in the cause, which judgment really amounted to nothing. As it was impossible to decide which party was most to blame, he fined both an equal number of cattle, accompanying the fine with a lecture on their ill-behaviour, which was listened to indifferently.

After this matter was disposed of the real business of the meeting began.

Rising to his feet, Cetewayo addressed Panda.

"My father," he said, "the land wanders and wanders in darkness, and you alone can give light for its feet. I and my brother, Umbelazi, are at variance, and the quarrel is a great one, namely, as to which of us is to sit in your place when you are 'gone down,' when we call and you do not answer. Some of the nation favour one of us and some favour the other, but you, O King, and you alone, have the voice of judgment. Still, before you speak, I and those who stand with me would bring this to your mind. My mother, Umqumbazi, is your Inkosikazi, your head-wife, and therefore, according to our law, I, her eldest son, should be your heir. Moreover, when you fled to the Boers before the fall of him who sat in your place before you [Dingaan], did not they, the white Amabunu, ask you which amongst your sons was your heir, and did you not point me out to the white men? And thereon did not the Amabunu clothe me in a dress of honour because I was the King to be? But now of late the mother of Umbelazi has been whispering in your ear, as have others"—and he looked at Saduko and some of Umbelazi's brethren—"and your face has grown cold towards me, so cold that many say that you will point out Umbelazi to be King after you and stamp on my name. If this is so, my father, tell me at once, that I may know what to do."

Having finished this speech, which certainly did not lack force and dignity, Cetewayo sat down again, awaiting the answer in sullen silence. But, making none,

Panda looked at Umbelazi, who, on rising, was greeted with a great cheer, for although Cetewayo had the larger following in the land, especially among the distant chiefs, the Zulus individually loved Umbelazi more, perhaps because of his stature, beauty and kindly disposition—physical and moral qualities that naturally appeal to a savage nation.

"My father," he said, "like my brother, Cetewayo, I await your word. Whatever you may have said to the Amabunu in haste or fear, I do not admit that Cetewayo was ever proclaimed your heir in the hearing of the Zulu people. I say that my right to the succession is as good as his, and that it lies with you, and you alone, to declare which of us shall put on the royal kaross in days that my heart prays may be distant. Still, to save bloodshed, I am willing to divide the land with Cetewayo" (here both Panda and Cetewayo shook their heads and the audience roared "Nay"), "or, if that does not please him, I am willing to meet Cetewayo man to man and spear to spear and fight till one of us be slain."

"A safe offer!" sneered Cetewayo, "for is not my brother named 'Elephant,' and the strongest warrior among the Zulus? No, I will not set the fortunes of those who cling to me on the chance of a single stab, or on the might of a man's muscles. Decide, O father; say which of the two of us is to sit at the head of your kraal after you have gone over to the Spirits and are but an ancestor to be worshipped."

Now, Panda looked much disturbed, as was not wonderful, since, rushing out from the fence behind which they had been listening, Umqumbazi, Cetewayo's mother, whispered into one of his ears, while Umbelazi's mother whispered into the other. What advice each of them gave I do not know, although obviously it was not the same advice, since the poor man rolled his eyes first at one and then at the other, and finally put his hands over his ears that he might hear no more.

"Choose, choose, O King!" shouted the audience. "Who is to succeed you, Cetewayo or Umbelazi?"

Watching Panda, I saw that he fell into a kind of agony; his fat sides heaved, and, although the day was cold, sweat ran from his brow.

"What would the white men do in such a case?" he said to me in a hoarse, low voice, whereon I answered, looking at the ground and speaking so that few could hear me:

"I think, O King, that a white man would do nothing. He would say that others might settle the matter after he was dead."

"Would that I could say so, too," muttered Panda; "but it is not possible."

Then followed a long pause, during which all were silent, for every man there felt that the hour was big with doom. At length Panda rose with difficulty, because of his unwieldy weight, and uttered these fateful words, that were none the less ominous because of the homely idiom in which they were couched:

"When two young bulls quarrel they must fight it out."

Instantly in one tremendous roar volleyed forth the royal salute of "Bayete", a signal of the acceptance of the King's word—the word that meant civil war and the death of many thousands.

Then Panda turned and, so feebly that I thought he would fall, walked through the gateway behind him, followed by the rival queens. Each of these ladies struggled to be first after him in the gate, thinking that it would be an omen of success for her son. Finally, however, to the disappointment of the multitude, they only succeeded in passing it side by side.

When they had gone the great audience began to break up, the men of each party marching away together as though by common consent, without offering any insult or molestation to their adversaries. I think that this peaceable attitude arose, however, from the knowledge that matters had now passed from the stage of private quarrel into that of public war. It was felt that their dispute awaited decision, not with sticks outside the Nodwengu kraal, but with spears upon some great battlefield, for which they went to prepare.

Within two days, except for those regiments which Panda kept to guard his person, scarcely a soldier was to be seen in the neighbourhood of Nodwengu. The princes also departed to muster their adherents, Cetewayo establishing himself among the Mandhlakazi that he commanded, and Umbelazi returning to the kraal of Umbezi, which happened to stand almost in the centre of that part of the nation which adhered to him.

Whether he took Mameena with him there I am not certain. I believe, however, that, fearing lest her welcome at her birthplace should be warmer than she wished, she settled herself at some retired and outlying kraal in the neighbourhood, and there awaited the crisis of her fortune. At any rate, I saw nothing of her, for she was careful to keep out of my way.

With Umbelazi and Saduko, however, I did have an interview. Before they left Nodwengu they called on me together, apparently on the best of terms, and said in effect that they hoped for my support in the coming war.

I answered that, however well I might like them personally, a Zulu civil war was no affair of mine, and that, indeed, for every reason, including the supreme one of my own safety, I had better get out of the way at once.

They argued with me for a long while, making great offers and promises of reward, till at length, when he saw that my determination could not be shaken, Umbelazi said:

"Come, Saduko, let us humble ourselves no more before this white man. After all, he is right; the business is none of his, and why should we ask him to risk his life in our quarrel, knowing as we do that white men are not like us; they think a great deal of their lives. Farewell, Macumazahn. If I conquer and grow great you will always be welcome in Zululand, whereas if I fail perhaps you will be best over the Tugela river."

Now, I felt the hidden taunt in this speech very keenly. Still, being determined that for once I would be wise and not allow my natural curiosity and love of adventure to drag me into more risks and trouble, I replied:

"The Prince says that I am not brave and love my life, and what he says is true. I fear fighting, who by nature am a trader with the heart of a trader, not a warrior with the heart of a warrior, like the great Indhlovu-ene-Sihlonti"—words at which I saw the grave Saduko smile faintly. "So farewell to you, Prince, and may good fortune attend you."

Of course, to call the Prince to his face by this nickname, which referred to a defect in his person, was something of an insult; but I had been insulted, and meant to give him "a Roland for his Oliver." However, he took it in good part.

"What is good fortune, Macumazahn?" Umbelazi replied as he grasped my hand. "Sometimes I think that to live and prosper is good fortune, and sometimes I think that to die and sleep is good fortune, for in sleep there is neither hunger nor thirst of body or of spirit. In sleep there come no cares; in sleep ambitions are at rest; nor do those who look no more upon the sun smart beneath the treacheries of false women or false friends. Should the battle turn against me, Macumazahn, at least that good fortune will be mine, for never will I live to be crushed beneath Cetewayo's heel."

Then he went. Saduko accompanied him for a little way, but, making some excuse to the Prince, came back and said to me:

"Macumazahn, my friend, I dare say that we part for the last time, and therefore I make a request to you. It is as to one who is dead to me. Macumazahn, I believe that Umbelazi the thief"—these words broke from his lips with a hiss—"has given her many cattle and hidden her away either in the kloof of Zikali the Wise, or near to it, under his care. Now, if the war should go against Umbelazi and I should be killed in it, I think evil will fall upon that woman's head, I who have grown sure that it was she who was the wizard and not Masapo the Boar. Also, as one connected with Umbelazi, who has helped him in his plots, she will be killed if she is caught. Macumazahn, hearken to me. I will tell you the truth. My heart is still on fire for that woman. She has bewitched me; her eyes haunt my sleep and I hear her voice in the wind. She is more to me than all the earth and all the sky, and although she has wronged me I do not wish that harm should come to her. Macumazahn, I pray you if I die, do your best to befriend her, even though it be only as a servant in your house, for I think that she cares more for you than for anyone, who only ran away with him"—and he pointed in the direction that Umbelazi had taken—"because he is a prince, who, in her folly, she believes will be a king. At least take her to Natal, Macumazahn, where, if you wish to be free of her, she can marry whom she will and will live safe until night comes. Panda loves you much, and, whoever conquers in the war, will give you her life if you ask it of him."

Then this strange man drew the back of his hand across his eyes, from which I saw the tears were running, and, muttering, "If you would have good fortune remember my prayer," turned and left me before I could answer a single word.

As for me, I sat down upon an ant-heap and whistled a whole hymn tune that my mother had taught me before I could think at all. To be left the guardian of Mameena! Talk of a "damnosa hereditas," a terrible and mischievous inheritance—why, this was the worst that ever I heard of. A servant in my house indeed, knowing what *I* did about her! Why, I had sooner share the "good fortune" which Umbelazi anticipated beneath the sod. However, that was not in the question, and without it the alternative of acting as her guardian was bad enough, though I comforted myself with the reflection that the circumstances in which this would become necessary might never arise. For, alas! I was sure that if they did arise I should have to live up to them. True, I had made no promise to Saduko with my lips, but I felt, as I knew he felt, that this promise had passed from my heart to his.

"That thief Umbelazi!" Strange words to be uttered by a great vassal of his lord, and both of them about to enter upon a desperate enterprise. "A prince whom in her folly she believes will be a king." Stranger words still. Then Saduko did not believe that he *would* be a king! And yet he was about to share the fortunes of his fight for the throne, he who said that his heart was still on fire for the woman whom "Umbelazi the thief" had stolen. Well, if I were Umbelazi, thought I to myself, I would rather that Saduko were not my chief councillor and general. But, thank Heaven! I was not Umbelazi, or Saduko, or any of them! And, thank Heaven still more, I was going to begin my trek from Zululand on the morrow!

Man proposes but God disposes. I did not trek from Zululand for many a long day. When I got back to my wagons it was to find that my oxen had mysteriously disappeared from the veld on which they were accustomed to graze. They were lost; or perhaps they had felt the urgent need of trekking from Zululand back to a more peaceful country. I sent all the hunters I had with me to look for them, only Scowl and I remaining at the wagons, which in those disturbed times I did not like to leave unguarded.

Four days went by, a week went by, and no sign of either hunters or oxen. Then at last a message, which reached me in some roundabout fashion, to the effect that the hunters had found the oxen a long way off, but on trying to return to Nodwengu had been driven by some of the Usutu—that is, by Cetewayo's party—across the Tugela into Natal, whence they dared not attempt to return.

For once in my life I went into a rage and cursed that nondescript kind of messenger, sent by I know not whom, in language that I think he will not forget. Then, realising the futility of swearing at a mere tool, I went up to the Great House and demanded an audience with Panda himself. Presently the inceku, or household servant, to whom I gave my message, returned, saying that I was to be admitted at once, and on entering the enclosure I found the King sitting at the head of the kraal quite alone, except for a man who was holding a large shield over him in order to keep off the sun.

He greeted me warmly, and I told him my trouble about the oxen, whereon he sent away the shield-holder, leaving us two together.

"Watcher-by-Night," he said, "why do you blame me for these events, when you know that I am nobody in my own House? I say that I am a dead man, whose sons fight for his inheritance. I cannot tell you for certain who it was that drove away your oxen. Still, I am glad that they are gone, since I believe that if you had attempted to trek to Natal just now you would have been killed on the road by the Usutu, who believe you to be a councillor of Umbelazi."

"I understand, O King," I answered, "and I dare say that the accident of the loss of my oxen is fortunate for me. But tell me now, what am I to do? I wish to follow the example of John Dunn [another white man in the country who was much mixed up with Zulu politics] and leave the land. Will you give me more oxen to draw my wagons?"

"I have none that are broken in, Macumazahn, for, as you know, we Zulus possess few wagons; and if I had I would not lend them to you, who do not desire that your blood should be upon my head."

"You are hiding something from me, O King," I said bluntly. "What is it that you want me to do? Stay here at Nodwengu?"

"No, Macumazahn. When the trouble begins I want you to go with a regiment of my own that I shall send to the assistance of my son, Umbelazi, so that he may have the benefit of your wisdom. O Macumazana, I will tell you the truth. My heart loves Umbelazi, and I fear me that he is overmatched by Cetewayo. If I could I would save his life, but I know not how to do so, since I must not seem to take sides too openly. But I can send down a regiment as your escort, if you choose to go to view the battle as my agent and make report to me. Say, will you not go?"

"Why should I go?" I answered, "seeing that whoever wins I may be killed, and that if Cetewayo wins I shall certainly be killed, and all for no reward."

"Nay, Macumazahn; I will give orders that whoever conquers, the man that dares to lift a spear against you shall die. In this matter, at least, I shall not be disobeyed. Oh! I pray you, do not desert me in my trouble. Go down with the regiment that I shall send and breathe your wisdom into the ear of my son, Umbelazi. As for your reward, I swear to you by the head of the Black One [Chaka] that it shall be great. I will see to it that you do not leave Zululand empty-handed, Macumazahn."

Still I hesitated, for I mistrusted me of this business.

"O Watcher-by-Night," exclaimed Panda, "you will not desert me, will you? I am afraid for the son of my heart, Umbelazi, whom I love above all my children; I am much afraid for Umbelazi," and he burst into tears before me.

It was foolish, no doubt, but the sight of the old King weeping for his best-beloved child, whom he believed to be doomed, moved me so much that I forgot my caution.

"If you wish it, O Panda," I said, "I will go down to the battle with your regiment and stand there by the side of the Prince Umbelazi."

Umbelazi the Fallen

So I stayed on at Nodwengu, who, indeed, had no choice in the matter, and was very wretched and ill at ease. The place was almost deserted, except for a couple of regiments which were quartered there, the Sangqu and the Amawombe. This latter was the royal regiment, a kind of Household Guards, to which the Kings Chaka, Dingaan and Panda all belonged in turn. Most of the headmen had taken one side or the other, and were away raising forces to fight for Cetewayo or Umbelazi, and even the greater part of the women and children had gone to hide themselves in the bush or among the mountains, since none knew what would happen, or if the conquering army would not fall upon and destroy them.

A few councillors, however, remained with Panda, among whom was old Maputa, the general, who had once brought me the "message of the pills." Several times he visited me at night and told me the rumours that were flying about. From these I gathered that some skirmishes had taken place and the battle could not be long delayed; also that Umbelazi had chosen his fighting ground, a plain near the banks of the Tugela.

"Why has he done this," I asked, "seeing that then he will have a broad river behind him, and if he is defeated water can kill as well as spears?"

"I know not for certain," answered Maputa; "but it is said because of a dream that Saduko, his general, has dreamed thrice, which dream declares that there and there alone Umbelazi will find honour. At any rate, he has chosen this place; and I am told that all the women and children of his army, by thousands, are hidden in the bush along the banks of the river, so that they may fly into Natal if there is need."

"Have they wings," I asked, "wherewith to fly over the Tugela 'in wrath,' as it well may be after the rains? Oh, surely his Spirit has turned from Umbelazi!"

"Aye, Macumazahn," he answered, "I, too, think that ufulatewe idhlozi [that is, his own Spirit] has turned its back on him. Also I think that Saduko is no good councillor. Indeed, were I the prince," added the old fellow shrewdly, "I would not keep him whose wife I had stolen as the whisperer in my ear."

"Nor I, Maputa," I answered as I bade him good-bye.

Two days later, early in the morning, Maputa came to me again and said that Panda wished to see me. I went to the head of the kraal, where I found the King seated and before him the captains of the royal Amawombe regiment.

"Watcher-by-Night," he said, "I have news that the great battle between my sons will take place within a few days. Therefore I am sending down this, my own royal regiment, under the command of Maputa the skilled in war to spy out the battle, and I pray that you will go with it, that you may give to the General Maputa and to the captains the help of your wisdom. Now these are my orders to you, Maputa, and to you, O captains—that you take no part in the fight unless you should see that the Elephant, my son Umbelazi, is fallen into a pit, and that then you shall drag him out if you can and save him alive. Now repeat my words to me."

So they repeated the words, speaking with one voice.

"Your answer, O Macumazana," he said when they had spoken.

"O King, I have told you that I will go—though I do not like war—and I will keep my promise," I replied.

"Then make ready, Macumazahn, and be back here within an hour, for the regiment marches ere noon."

So I went up to my wagons and handed them over to the care of some men whom Panda had sent to take charge of them. Also Scowl and I saddled our horses, for this faithful fellow insisted upon accompanying me, although I advised him to stay behind, and got out our rifles and as much ammunition as we could possibly need, and with them a few other necessaries. These things done, we rode back to the gathering-place, taking farewell of the wagons with a sad heart, since I, for one, never expected to see them again.

As we went I saw that the regiment of the Amawombe, picked men every one of them, all fifty years of age or over, nearly four thousand strong, was marshalled on the dancing-ground, where they stood company by company. A magnificent sight they were, with their white fighting-shields, their gleaming spears, their otter-skin caps, their kilts and armlets of white bulls' tails, and the snowy egret plumes which they wore upon their brows. We rode to the head of them, where I saw Maputa, and as I came they greeted me with a cheer of welcome, for in those days a white man was a power in the land. Moreover, as I have said, the Zulus knew and liked me well. Also the fact that I was to watch, or perchance to fight with them, put a good heart into the Amawombe.

There we stood until the lads, several hundreds of them, who bore the mats and cooking vessels and drove the cattle that were to be our commissariat, had wended away in a long line. Then suddenly Panda appeared out of his hut, accompanied by a few servants, and seemed to utter some kind of prayer, as he did so throwing dust or powdered medicine towards us, though what this ceremony meant I did not understand.

When he had finished Maputa raised a spear, whereon the whole regiment, in perfect time, shouted out the royal salute, "Bayete", with a sound like that of thunder. Thrice they repeated this tremendous and impressive salute, and then were silent. Again Maputa raised his spear, and all the four thousand voices broke out into the Ingoma, or national chant, to which deep, awe-inspiring music we began our march. As I do not think it has ever been written down, I will quote the words. They ran thus:

"Ba ya m'zonda, Ba ya m'loyisa, Izizwe zonke, Ba zond', Inkoosi."

"They [i.e. the enemy] bear him [i.e. the King) hatred, They call down curses on his head, All of them throughout this land Abhor our King."

The spirit of this fierce Ingoma, conveyed by sound, gesture and inflection of voice, not the exact words, remember, which are very rude and simple, leaving much to the imagination, may perhaps be rendered somewhat as follows. An exact translation into English verse is almost impossible—at any rate, to me:

"Loud on their lips is lying, Red are their eyes with hate; Rebels their King defying. Lo! where our impis wait There shall be dead and dying, Vengeance insatiate!"

It was early on the morning of the 2nd of December, a cold, miserable morning that came with wind and driving mist, that I found myself with the Amawombe at the place known as Endondakusuka, a plain with some kopjes in it that lies within six miles of the Natal border, from which it is separated by the Tugela river.

As the orders of the Amawombe were to keep out of the fray if that were possible, we had taken up a position about a mile to the right of what proved to be the actual battlefield, choosing as our camping ground a rising knoll that looked like a huge tumulus, and was fronted at a distance of about five hundred yards by another smaller knoll. Behind us stretched bushland, or rather broken land, where mimosa thorns grew in scattered groups, sloping down to the banks of the Tugela about four miles away.

Shortly after dawn I was roused from the place where I slept, wrapped up in some blankets, under a mimosa tree—for, of course, we had no tents—by a messenger, who said that the Prince Umbelazi and the white man, John Dunn, wished to see me. I rose and tidied myself as best I could, since, if I can avoid it, I never like to appear before natives in a dishevelled condition. I remember that I had just finished brushing my hair when Umbelazi arrived.

I can see him now, looking a veritable giant in that morning mist. Indeed, there was something quite unearthly about his appearance as he arose out of those rolling vapours, such light as there was being concentrated upon the blade of his big spear, which was well known as the broadest carried by any warrior in Zululand, and a copper torque he wore about his throat.

There he stood, rolling his eyes and hugging his kaross around him because of the cold, and something in his anxious, indeterminate expression told me at once that he knew himself to be a man in terrible danger. Just behind him, dark and brooding, his arms folded on his breast, his eyes fixed upon the ground, looking, to my moved imagination, like an evil genius, stood the stately and graceful Saduko. On his left was a young and sturdy white man carrying a rifle and smoking a pipe, whom I guessed to be John Dunn, a gentleman whom, as it chanced, I had never met, while behind were a force of Natal Government Zulus, clad in some kind of uniform and armed with guns, and with them a number of natives, also from Natal—"kraal Kafirs," who carried stabbing assegais. One of these led John Dunn's horse.

Of those Government men there may have been thirty or forty, and of the "kraal Kafirs" anything between two and three hundred.

I shook Umbelazi's hand and gave him good-day.

"That is an ill day upon which no sun shines, O Macumazana," he answered—words that struck me as ominous. Then he introduced me to John Dunn, who seemed glad to meet another white man. Next, not knowing what to say, I asked the exact object of their visit, whereon Dunn began to talk. He said that he had been sent over on the previous afternoon by Captain Walmsley, who was an officer of the Natal Government stationed across the border, to try to make peace between the Zulu factions, but that when he spoke of peace one of Umbelazi's brothers—I think it was Mantantashiya—had mocked at him, saying that they were quite strong enough to cope with the Usutu—that was Cetewayo's party. Also, he added, that when he suggested that the thousands of women and children and the cattle should be got across the Tugela drift during the previous night into safety in Natal, Mantantashiya would not listen, and Umbelazi being absent, seeking the aid of the Natal Government, he could do nothing.

"Quem Deus vult perdere prius dementat" [whom God wishes to destroy, He first makes mad], quoted I to myself beneath my breath. This was one of the Latin tags that my old father, who was a scholar, had taught me, and at that moment it came back to my mind. But as I suspected that John Dunn knew no Latin, I only said aloud:

"What an infernal fool!" (We were talking in English.) "Can't you get Umbelazi to do it now?" (I meant, to send the women and children across the river.)

"I fear it is too late, Mr. Quatermain," he answered. "The Usutu are in sight. Look for yourself." And he handed me a telescope which he had with him.

I climbed on to some rocks and scanned the plain in front of us, from which just then a puff of wind rolled away the mist. It was black with advancing men! As yet they were a considerable distance away—quite two miles, I should think—and coming on very slowly in a great half-moon with thin horns and a deep breast; but a ray from the sun glittered upon their countless spears. It seemed to me that there must be quite twenty or thirty thousand of them in this breast, which was in three divisions, commanded, as I learned afterwards, by Cetewayo, Uzimela, and by a young Boer named Groening.

"There they are, right enough," I said, climbing down from my rocks. "What are you going to do, Mr. Dunn?"

"Obey orders and try to make peace, if I can find anyone to make peace with; and if I can't—well, fight, I suppose. And you, Mr. Quatermain?"

"Oh, obey orders and stop here, I suppose. Unless," I added doubtfully, "these Amawombe take the bit between their teeth and run away with me."

"They'll do that before nightfall, Mr. Quatermain, if I know anything of the Zulus. Look here, why don't you get on your horse and come off with me? This is a queer place for you."

"Because I promised not to," I answered with a groan, for really, as I looked at those savages round me, who were already fingering their spears in a disagreeable fashion, and those other thousands of savages advancing towards us, I felt such little courage as I possessed sinking into my boots.

"Very well, Mr. Quatermain, you know your own business best; but I hope you will come out of it safely, that is all."

"Same to you," I replied.

Then John Dunn turned, and in my hearing asked Umbelazi what he knew of the movements of the Usutu and of their plan of battle.

The Prince replied, with a shrug of his shoulders:

"Nothing at present, Son of Mr. Dunn, but doubtless before the sun is high I shall know much."

As he spoke a sudden gust of wind struck us, and tore the nodding ostrich plume from its fastening on Umbelazi's head-ring. Whilst a murmur of dismay rose from all who saw what they considered this very ill-omened accident, away it floated into the air, to fall gently to the ground at the feet of Saduko. He stooped, picked it up, and reset it in its place, saying as he did so, with that ready wit for which some Kafirs are remarkable:

"So may I live, O Prince, to set the crown upon the head of Panda's favoured son!"

This apt speech served to dispel the general gloom caused by the incident, for those who heard it cheered, while Umbelazi thanked his captain with a nod and a smile. Only I noted that Saduko did not mention the name of "Panda's favoured son" upon whose head he hoped to live to set the crown. Now, Panda had many sons, and that day would show which of them was favoured.

A minute or two later John Dunn and his following departed, as he said, to try to make peace with the advancing Usutu. Umbelazi, Saduko and their escort departed also towards the main body of the host of the Isigqosa, which was massed to our left, "sitting on their spears," as the natives say, and awaiting the attack. As for me, I remained alone with the Amawombe, drinking some coffee that Scowl had brewed for me, and forcing myself to swallow food.

I can say honestly that I do not ever remember partaking of a more unhappy meal. Not only did I believe that I was looking on the last sun I should ever see—though by the way, there was uncommonly little of that orb visible—but what made the matter worse was that, if so, I should be called upon to die alone among savages, with not a single white face near to comfort me. Oh, how I wished I had never allowed myself to be dragged into this dreadful business. Yes, and I was even mean enough to wish that I had broken my word to Panda and gone off with John Dunn when he invited me, although now I thank goodness that I did not yield to that temptation and thereby sacrifice my self-respect.

Soon, however, things grew so exciting that I forgot these and other melancholy reflections in watching the development of events from the summit of our tumulus-like knoll, whence I had a magnificent view of the whole battle. Here, after seeing that his regiment made a full meal, as a good general should, old Maputa joined me, whom I asked whether he thought there would be any fighting for him that day.

"I think so, I think so," he answered cheerfully. "It seems to me that the Usutu greatly outnumber Umbelazi and the Isigqosa, and, of course, as you know, Panda's orders are that if he is in danger we must help him. Oh, keep a good heart, Macumazahn, for I believe I can promise you that you will see our spears grow red to-day. You will not go hungry from this battle to tell the white people that the Amawombe are cowards whom you could not flog into the fight. No, no, Macumazahn, my Spirit looks towards me this morning, and I who am old and who thought that I should die at length like a cow, shall see one more great fight—my twentieth, Macumazahn; for I fought with this same Amawombe in all the Black One's big battles, and for Panda against Dingaan also."

"Perhaps it will be your last," I suggested.

"I dare say, Macumazahn; but what does that matter if only I and the royal regiment can make an end that shall be spoken of? Oh, cheer up, cheer up, Macumazahn; your Spirit, too, looks towards you, as I promise that we all will do when the shields meet; for know, Macumazahn, that we poor black soldiers expect that you will show us how to fight this day, and, if need be, how to fall hidden in a heap of the foe."

"Oh!" I replied, "so this is what you Zulus mean by the 'giving of counsel,' is it?—you infernal, bloodthirsty old scoundrel," I added in English.

But I think Maputa never heard me. At any rate, he only seized my arm and pointed in front, a little to the left, where the horn of the great Usutu army was coming up fast, a long, thin line alive with twinkling spears; their moving arms and legs causing them to look like spiders, of which the bodies were formed by the great war shields.

"See their plan?" he said. "They would close on Umbelazi and gore him with their horns and then charge with their head. The horn will pass between us and the right flank of the Isigqosa. Oh! awake, awake, Elephant! Are you asleep with Mameena in a hut? Unloose your spears, Child of the King, and at them as they mount the slope. Behold!" he went on, "it is the Son of Dunn that begins the battle! Did I not tell you that we must look to the white men to show us the way? Peep through your tube, Macumazahn, and tell me what passes."

So I "peeped," and, the telescope which John Dunn had kindly left with me being good though small, saw everything clearly enough. He rode up almost to the point of the left horn of the Usutu, waving a white handkerchief and followed by his small force of police and Natal Kafirs. Then from somewhere among the Usutu rose a puff of smoke. Dunn had been fired at.

He dropped the handkerchief and leapt to the ground. Now he and his police were firing rapidly in reply, and men fell fast among the Usutu. They raised their war shout and came on, though slowly, for they feared the bullets. Step by step John Dunn and his people were thrust back, fighting gallantly against overwhelming odds. They were level with us, not a quarter of a mile to our left. They were pushed past us. They vanished among the bush behind us, and a long while passed before ever I heard what became of them, for we met no more that day.

Now, the horns having done their work and wrapped themselves round Umbelazi's army as the nippers of a wasp close about a fly (why did not Umbelazi cut off those horns, I wondered), the Usutu bull began his charge. Twenty or thirty thousand strong, regiment after regiment, Cetewayo's men rushed up the slope, and there, near the crest of it, were met by Umbelazi's regiments springing forward to repel the onslaught and shouting their battle-cry of "Laba! Laba! Laba! Laba!"

The noise of their meeting shields came to our ears like that of the roll of thunder, and the sheen of their stabbing-spears shone as shines the broad summer lightning. They hung and wavered on the slope; then from the Amawombe ranks rose a roar of

"Umbelazi wins!"

Watching intently, we saw the Usutu giving back. Down the slope they went, leaving the ground in front of them covered with black spots which we knew to be dead or wounded men.

"Why does not the Elephant charge home?" said Maputa in a perplexed voice. "The Usutu bull is on his back! Why does he not trample him?"

"Because he is afraid, I suppose," I answered, and went on watching.

There was plenty to see, as it happened. Finding that they were not pursued, Cetewayo's impi reformed swiftly at the bottom of the slope, in preparation for another charge. Among that of Umbelazi, above them, rapid movements took place of which I could not guess the meaning, which movements were accompanied by much noise of angry shouting. Then suddenly, from the midst of the Isigqosa army, emerged a great body of men, thousands strong, which ran swiftly, but in open order, down the slope towards the Usutu, holding their spears reversed. At first I thought that they were charging independently, till I saw the Usutu ranks open to receive them with a shout of welcome.

"Treachery!" I said. "Who is it?"

"Saduko, with the Amakoba and Amangwane soldiers and others. I know them by their head-dresses," answered Maputa in a cold voice.

"Do you mean that Saduko has gone over to Cetewayo with all his following?" I asked excitedly.

"What else, Macumazahn? Saduko is a traitor: Umbelazi is finished," and he passed his hand swiftly across his mouth—a gesture that has only one meaning among the Zulus.

As for me, I sat down upon a stone and groaned, for now I understood everything.

Presently the Usutu raised fierce, triumphant shouts, and once again their impi, swelled with Saduko's power, began to advance up the slope. Umbelazi, and those of the Isigqosa party who clung to him—now, I should judge, not more than eight thousand men—never stayed to wait the onslaught. They broke! They fled in a hideous rout, crashing through the thin, left horn of the Usutu by mere weight of numbers, and passing behind us obliquely on their road to the banks of the Tugela. A messenger rushed up to us, panting.

"These are the words of Umbelazi," he gasped. "O Watcher-by-Night and O Maputa, Indhlovu-ene-sihlonti prays that you will hold back the Usutu, as the King bade you do in case of need, and so give to him and those who cling to him time to escape with the women and children into Natal. His general, Saduko, has betrayed him, and gone over with three regiments to Cetewayo, and therefore we can no longer stand against the thousands of the Usutu."

"Go tell the prince that Macumazahn, Maputa, and the Amawombe regiment will do their best," answered Maputa calmly. "Still, this is our advice to him, that he should cross the Tugela swiftly with the women and the children, seeing that we are few and Cetewayo is many."

The messenger leapt away, but, as I heard afterwards, he never found Umbelazi, since the poor man was killed within five hundred yards of where we stood.

Then Maputa gave an order, and the Amawombe formed themselves into a triple line, thirteen hundred men in the first line, thirteen hundred men in the second line, and about a thousand in the third, behind whom were the carrier boys, three or four hundred of them. The place assigned to me was in the exact centre of the second line, where, being mounted on a horse, it was thought, as I gathered, that I should serve as a convenient rallying-point.

In this formation we advanced a few hundred yards to our left, evidently with the object of interposing ourselves between the routed impi and the pursuing Usutu, or, if the latter should elect to go round us, with that of threatening their flank. Cetewayo's generals did not leave us long in doubt as to what they would do. The main body of their army bore away to the right in pursuit of the flying foe, but three regiments, each of about two thousand five hundred spears, halted. Five minutes passed perhaps while they marshalled, with a distance of some six hundred yards between them. Each regiment was in a triple line like our own.

To me that seemed a very long five minutes, but, reflecting that it was probably my last on earth, I tried to make the best of it in a fashion that can be guessed. Strange to say, however, I found it impossible to keep my mind fixed upon those matters with which it ought to have been filled. My eyes and thoughts would roam. I looked at the ranks of the veteran Amawombe, and noted that they were still and solemn as men about to die should be, although they showed no sign of fear. Indeed, I saw some of those near me passing their snuffboxes to each other. Two grey-haired men also, who evidently were old friends, shook hands as people do who are parting before a journey, while two others discussed in a low voice the possibility of our wiping out most of the Usutu before we were wiped out ourselves.

"It depends," said one of them, "whether they attack us regiment by regiment or all together, as they will do if they are wise."

Then an officer bade them be silent, and conversation ceased. Maputa passed through the ranks giving orders to the captains. From a distance his withered old body, with a fighting shield held in front of it, looked like that of a huge black ant carrying something in its mouth. He came to where Scowl and I sat upon our horses.

"Ah! I see that you are ready, Macumazahn," he said in a cheerful voice. "I told you that you should not go away hungry, did I not?"

"Maputa," I said in remonstrance, "what is the use of this? Umbelazi is defeated, you are not of his impi, why send all these"—and I waved my hand—"down into the darkness? Why not go to the river and try to save the women and children?"

"Because we shall take many of those down into the darkness with us, Macumazahn," and he pointed to the dense masses of the Usutu. "Yet," he added, with a touch of compunction, "this is not your quarrel. You and your servant have horses. Slip out, if you will, and gallop hard to the lower drift. You may get away with your lives."

Then my white man's pride came to my aid.

"Nay," I answered, "I will not run while others stay to fight."

"I never thought you would, Macumazahn, who, I am sure, do not wish to earn a new and ugly name. Well, neither will the Amawombe run to become a mock among their people. The King's orders were that we should try to help Umbelazi, if the battle went against him. We obey the King's orders by dying where we stand. Macumazahn, do you think that you could hit that big fellow who is shouting insults at us there? If so, I should be obliged to you, as I dislike him very much," and he showed me a captain who was swaggering about in front of the lines of the first of the Usutu regiments, about six hundred yards away.

"I will try," I answered, "but it's a long shot." Dismounting, I climbed a pile of stones and, resting my rifle on the topmost of them, took a very full sight, aimed, held my breath, and pressed the trigger. A second afterwards the shouter of insults threw his arms wide, letting fall his spear, and pitched forward on to his face.

A roar of delight rose from the watching Amawombe, while old Maputa clapped his thin brown hands and grinned from ear to ear.

"Thank you, Macumazahn. A very good omen! Now I am sure that, whatever those Isigqosa dogs of Umbelazi's may do, we King's men shall make an excellent end, which is all that we can hope. Oh, what a beautiful shot! It will be something to think of when I am an idhlozi, a spirit-snake, crawling about my own kraal. Farewell, Macumazahn," and he took my hand and pressed it. "The time has come. I go to lead the charge. The Amawombe have orders to defend you to the last, for I wish you to see the finish of this fight. Farewell."

Then off he hurried, followed by his orderlies and staff-officers.

I never saw him again alive, though I think that once in after years I did meet his idhlozi in his kraal under strange circumstances. But that has nothing to do with this history.

As for me, having reloaded, I mounted my horse again, being afraid lest, if I went on shooting, I should miss and spoil my reputation. Besides, what was the use of killing more men unless I was obliged? There were plenty ready to do that.

Another minute, and the regiment in front of us began to move, while the other two behind it ostentatiously sat themselves down in their ranks, to show that they did not mean to spoil sport. The fight was to begin with a duel between about six thousand men.

"Good!" muttered the warrior who was nearest me. "They are in our bag."

"Aye," answered another, "those little boys" (used as a term of contempt) "are going to learn their last lesson."

For a few seconds there was silence, while the long ranks leant forward between the hedges of lean and cruel spears. A whisper went down the line; it sounded like the noise of wind among trees, and was the signal to prepare. Next a far-off voice shouted some word, which was repeated again and again by other voices before and behind me. I became aware that we were moving, quite slowly at first, then more quickly. Being lifted above the ranks upon my horse I could see the whole advance, and the general aspect of it was that of a triple black wave, each wave crowned with foam—the white plumes and shields of the Amawombe were the foam—and alive with sparkles of light—their broad spears were the light.

We were charging now—and oh! the awful and glorious excitement of that charge! Oh, the rush of the bending plumes and the dull thudding of eight thousand feet! The Usutu came up the slope to meet us. In silence we went, and in silence they came. We drew near to each other. Now we could see their faces peering over the tops of their mottled shields, and now we could see their fierce and rolling eyes.

Then a roar—a rolling roar such as at that time I had never heard: the thunder of the roar of the meeting shields—and a flash—a swift, simultaneous flash, the flash of the lightning of the stabbing spears. Up went the cry of:

"Kill, Amawombe, kill!" answered by another cry of:

"Toss, Usutu, toss!"

After that, what happened? Heaven knows alone—or at least I do not. But in later years Mr. Osborn, afterwards the resident magistrate at Newcastle, in Natal, who, being young and foolish in those days, had swum his horse over the Tugela and hidden in a little kopje quite near to us in order to see the battle, told me that it looked as though some huge breaker—that breaker being the splendid Amawombe—rolling in towards the shore with the weight of the ocean behind it, had suddenly struck a ridge of rock and, rearing itself up, submerged and hidden it.

At least, within three minutes that Usutu regiment was no more. We had killed them every one, and from all along our lines rose a fierce hissing sound of "S'gee, S'gee" ("Zhi" in the Zulu) uttered as the spears went home in the bodies of the conquered.

That regiment had gone, taking nearly a third of our number with it, for in such a battle as this the wounded were as good as dead. Practically our first line had vanished in a fray that did not last more than a few minutes. Before it was well over the second Usutu regiment sprang up and charged. With a yell of victory we rushed down the slope towards them. Again there was the roar of the meeting shields, but this time the fight was more prolonged, and, being in the front rank now, I had my share of it. I remember shooting two Usutu who stabbed at me, after which my gun was wrenched from my hand. I remember the melee swinging backwards and forwards, the groans of the wounded, the shouts of victory and despair, and then Scowl's voice saying:

"We have beat them, Baas, but here come the others."

The third regiment was on our shattered lines. We closed up, we fought like devils, even the bearer boys rushed into the fray. From all sides they poured down upon us, for we had made a ring; every minute men died by hundreds, and, though their numbers grew few, not one of the Amawombe yielded. I was fighting with a spear now, though how it came into my hand I cannot remember for certain. I think, however, I wrenched it from a man who rushed at me and was stabbed before he could strike. I killed a captain with this spear, for as he fell I recognised his face. It was that of one of Cetewayo's companions to whom I had sold some cloth at Nodwengu. The fallen were piled up quite thick around me—we were using them as a breastwork, friend and foe together. I saw Scowl's horse rear into the air and fall. He slipped over its tail, and next instant was fighting at my side, also with a spear, muttering Dutch and English oaths as he struck.

"Beetje varm! [a little hot] Beetje varm, Baas!" I heard him say. Then my horse screamed aloud and something hit me hard upon the head—I suppose it was a thrown kerry—after which I remember nothing for a while, except a sensation of passing through the air.

I came to myself again, and found that I was still on the horse, which was ambling forward across the veld at a rate of about eight miles an hour, and that Scowl was clinging to my stirrup leather and running at my side. He was covered with blood, so was the horse, and so was I. It may have been our own blood, for all three were more or less wounded, or it may have been that of others; I am sure I do not know, but we were a terrible sight. I pulled upon the reins, and the horse stopped among some thorns. Scowl felt in the saddlebags and found a large flask of Hollands gin and water—half gin and half water—which he had placed there before the battle. He uncorked and gave it to me. I took a long pull at the stuff, that tasted like veritable nectar, then handed it to him, who did likewise. New life seemed to flow into my veins. Whatever teetotallers may say, alcohol is good at such a moment.

"Where are the Amawombe?" I asked.

"All dead by now, I think, Baas, as we should be had not your horse bolted. Wow! but they made a great fight—one that will be told of! They have carried those three regiments away upon their spears."

"That's good," I said. "But where are we going?"

"To Natal, I hope, Baas. I have had enough of the Zulus for the present. The Tugela is not far away, and we will swim it. Come on, before our hurts grow stiff."

So we went on, till presently we reached the crest of a rise of ground overlooking the river, and there saw and heard dreadful things, for beneath us those devilish Usutu were massacring the fugitives and the camp-followers. These were being driven by the hundred to the edge of the water, there to perish on the banks or in the stream, which was black with drowned or drowning forms.

And oh! the sounds! Well, these I will not attempt to describe.

"Keep up stream," I said shortly, and we struggled across a kind of donga, where only a few wounded men were hidden, into a somewhat denser patch of bush that had scarcely been entered by the flying Isigqosa, perhaps because here the banks of the river were very steep and difficult; also, between them its waters ran swiftly, for this was above the drift.

For a while we went on in safety, then suddenly I heard a noise. A great man plunged past me, breaking through the bush like a buffalo, and came to a halt upon a rock which overhung the Tugela, for the floods had eaten away the soil beneath.

"Umbelazi!" said Scowl, and as he spoke we saw another man following as a wild dog follows a buck.

"Saduko!" said Scowl.

I rode on. I could not help riding on, although I knew it would be safer to keep away. I reached the edge of that big rock. Saduko and Umbelazi were fighting there.

In ordinary circumstances, strong and active as he was, Saduko would have had no chance against the most powerful Zulu living. But the prince was utterly exhausted; his sides were going like a blacksmith's bellows, or those of a fat eland bull that has been galloped to a standstill. Moreover, he seemed to me to be distraught with grief, and, lastly, he had no shield left, nothing but an assegai.

A stab from Saduko's spear, which he partially parried, wounded him slightly on the head, and cut loose the fillet of his ostrich plume, that same plume which I had seen blown off in the morning, so that it fell to the ground. Another stab pierced his right arm, making it helpless. He snatched the assegai with his left hand, striving to continue the fight, and just at that moment we came up.

"What are you doing, Saduko?" I cried. "Does a dog bite his own master?"

He turned and stared at me; both of them stared at me.

"Aye, Macumazahn," he answered in an icy voice, "sometimes when it is starving and that full-fed master has snatched away its bone. Nay, stand aside, Macumazahn" (for, although I was quite unarmed, I had stepped between them), "lest you should share the fate of this woman-thief."

"Not I, Saduko," I cried, for this sight made me mad, "unless you murder me."

Then Umbelazi spoke in a hollow voice, sobbing out his words:

"I thank you, White Man, yet do as this snake bids you—this snake that has lived in my kraal and fed out of my cup. Let him have his fill of vengeance because of the woman who bewitched me—yes, because of the sorceress who has brought me and thousands to the dust. Have you heard, Macumazahn, of the great deed of this son of Matiwane? Have you heard that all the while he was a traitor in the pay of Cetewayo, and that he went over, with the regiments of his command, to the Usutu just when the battle hung upon the turn? Come, Traitor, here is my heart—the heart that loved and trusted you. Strike—strike hard!"

"Out of the way, Macumazahn!" hissed Saduko. But I would not stir.

He sprang at me, and, though I put up the best fight that I could in my injured state, got his hands about my throat and began to choke me. Scowl ran to help me, but his wound—for he was hurt—or his utter exhaustion took effect on him. Or perhaps it was excitement. At any rate, he fell down in a fit. I thought that all was over, when again I heard Umbelazi's voice, and felt Saduko's grip loosen at my throat, and sat up.

"Dog," said the Prince, "where is your assegai? And as he spoke he threw it from him into the river beneath, for he had picked it up while we struggled, but, as I noted, retained his own. "Now, dog, why do I not kill you, as would have been easy but now? I will tell you. Because I will not mix the blood of a traitor with my own. See!" He set the haft of his broad spear upon the rock and bent forward over the blade. "You and your witch-wife have brought me to nothing, O Saduko. My blood, and the blood of all who clung to me, is on your head. Your name shall stink for ever in the nostrils of all true men, and I whom you have betrayed—I, the Prince Umbelazi—will haunt you while you live; yes, my spirit shall enter into you, and when you die—ah! then we'll meet again. Tell this tale to the white men, Macumazahn, my friend, on whom be honour and blessings."

He paused, and I saw the tears gush from his eyes—tears mingled with blood from the wound in his head. Then suddenly he uttered the battle-cry of "Laba! Laba!" and let his weight fall upon the point of the spear.

It pierced him through and through. He fell on to his hands and knees. He looked up at us—oh, the piteousness of that look!—and then rolled sideways from the edge of the rock.

A heavy splash, and that was the end of Umbelazi the Fallen—Umbelazi, about whom Mameena had cast her net.

A sad story in truth. Although it happened so many years ago I weep as I write it—I weep as Umbelazi wept.

Umbezi and the Blood Royal

After this I think that some of the Usutu came up, for it seemed to me that I heard Saduko say:

"Touch not Macumazahn or his servant. They are my prisoners. He who harms them dies, with all his House."

So they put me, fainting, on my horse, and Scowl they carried away upon a shield.

When I came to I found myself in a little cave, or rather beneath some overhanging rocks, at the side of a kopje, and with me Scowl, who had recovered from his fit, but seemed in a very bewildered condition. Indeed, neither then nor afterwards did he remember anything of the death of Umbelazi, nor did I ever tell him that tale. Like many others, he thought that the Prince had been drowned in trying to swim the Tugela.

"Are they going to kill us?" I asked of him, since, from the triumphant shouting without, I knew that we must be in the midst of the victorious Usutu.

"I don't know, Baas," he answered. "I hope not; after we have gone through so much it would be a pity. Better to have died at the beginning of the battle."

I nodded my head in assent, and just at that moment a Zulu, who had very evidently been fighting, entered the place carrying a dish of toasted lumps of beef and a gourd of water.

"Cetewayo sends you these, Macumazahn," he said, "and is sorry that there is no milk or beer. When you have eaten a guard waits without to escort you to him." And he went.

"Well," I said to Scowl, "if they were going to kill us, they would scarcely take the trouble to feed us first. So let us keep up our hearts and eat."

"Who knows?" answered poor Scowl, as he crammed a lump of beef into his big mouth. "Still, it is better to die on a full than on an empty stomach."

So we ate and drank, and, as we were suffering more from exhaustion than from our hurts, which were not really serious, our strength came back to us. As we finished the last lump of meat, which, although it had been only half cooked upon the point of an assegai, tasted very good, the Zulu put his head into the mouth of the shelter and asked if we were ready. I nodded, and, supporting each other, Scowl and I limped from the place. Outside were about fifty soldiers, who greeted us with a shout that, although it was mixed with laughter at our pitiable appearance, struck me as not altogether unfriendly. Amongst these men was my horse, which stood with its head hanging down, looking very depressed. I was helped on to its back, and, Scowl clinging to the stirrup leather, we were led a distance of about a quarter of a mile to Cetewayo.

We found him seated, in the full blaze of the evening sun, on the eastern slope of one of the land-waves of the veld, with the open plain in front of him. It was a strange and savage scene. There sat the victorious prince, surrounded by his captains and indunas, while before him rushed the triumphant regiments, shouting his titles in the most extravagant language. Izimbongi also—that is, professional praisers—were running up and down before him dressed in all sorts of finery, telling his deeds, calling him "Eater-up-of-the-Earth," and yelling out the names of those great ones who had been killed in the battle.

Meanwhile parties of bearers were coming up continually, carrying dead men of distinction upon shields and laying them out in rows, as game is laid out at the end of a day's shooting in England. It seems that Cetewayo had taken a fancy to see them, and, being too tired to walk over the field of battle, ordered that this should be done. Among these, by the way, I saw the body of my old friend, Maputa, the general of the Amawombe, and noted that it was literally riddled with spear thrusts, every one of them in front; also that his quaint face still wore a smile.

At the head of these lines of corpses were laid six dead, all men of large size, in whom I recognised the brothers of Umbelazi, who had fought on his side, and the half-brothers of Cetewayo. Among them were those three princes upon whom the dust had fallen when Zikali, the prophet, smelt out Masapo, the husband of Mameena.

Dismounting from my horse, with the help of Scowl, I limped through and over the corpses of these fallen royalties, cut in the Zulu fashion to free their spirits, which otherwise, as they believed, would haunt the slayers, and stood in front of Cetewayo.

"Siyakubona, Macumazahn," he said, stretching out his hand to me, which I took, though I could not find it in my heart to wish *him* "good day."

"I hear that you were leading the Amawombe, whom my father, the King, sent down to help Umbelazi, and I am very glad that you have escaped alive. Also my heart is proud of the fight that they made, for you know, Macumazahn, once, next to the King, I was general of that regiment, though afterwards we quarrelled. Still, I am pleased that they did so well, and I have given orders that every one of them who remains alive is to be spared, that they may be officers of a new Amawombe which I shall raise. Do you know, Macumazahn, that you have nearly wiped out three whole regiments of the Usutu, killing many more people than did all my brother's army, the Isigqosa? Oh, you are a great man. Had it not been for the loyalty"—this word was spoken with just a tinge of sarcasm—"of Saduko yonder, you would have won the day for Umbelazi. Well, now that this quarrel is finished, if you will stay with me I will make you general of a whole division of the King's army, since henceforth I shall have a voice in affairs."

"You are mistaken, O Son of Panda," I answered; "the splendour of the Amawombe's great stand against a multitude is on the name of Maputa, the King's councillor and the induna of the Black One [Chaka], who is gone. He lies yonder in his glory," and I pointed to Maputa's pierced body. "I did but fight as a soldier in his ranks."

"Oh, yes, we know that, we know all that, Macumazahn; and Maputa was a clever monkey in his way, but we know also that you taught him how to jump. Well, he is dead, and nearly all the Amawombe are dead, and of my three regiments but a handful is left; the vultures have the rest of them. That is all finished and forgotten, Macumazahn, though by good fortune the spears went wide of you, who doubtless are a magician, since otherwise you and your servant and your horse would not have escaped with a few scratches when everyone else was killed. But you did escape, as you have done before in Zululand; and now you see here lie certain men who were born of my father. Yet one is missing—he against whom I fought, aye, and he whom, although we fought, I loved the best of all of them. Now, it has been whispered in my ear that you alone know what became of him, and, Macumazahn, I would learn whether he lives or is dead; also, if he is dead, by whose hand he died, who would reward that hand."

Now, I looked round me, wondering whether I should tell the truth or hold my tongue, and as I looked my eyes met those of Saduko, who, cold and unconcerned, was seated among the captains, but at a little distance from any of them—a man apart; and I remembered that he and I alone knew the truth of the end of Umbelazi.

Why, I do not know, but it came into my mind that I would keep the secret. Why should I tell the triumphant Cetewayo that Umbelazi had been driven to die by his own hand; why should I lay bare Saduko's victory and shame? All these matters had passed into the court of a different tribunal. Who was I that I should reveal them or judge the actors of this terrible drama?

"O Cetewayo," I said, "as it chanced I saw the end of Umbelazi. No enemy killed him. He died of a broken heart upon a rock above the river; and for the rest of the story go ask the Tugela into which he fell."

For a moment Cetewayo hid his eyes with his hand.

"Is it so?" he said presently. "Wow! I say again that had it not been for Saduko, the son of Matiwane, yonder, who had some quarrel with Indhlovu-ene-Sihlonti about a woman and took his chance of vengeance, it might have been I who died of a broken heart upon a rock above the river. Oh, Saduko, I owe you a great debt and will pay you well; but you shall be no friend of mine, lest we also should chance to quarrel about a woman, and *I* should find myself dying of a broken heart on a rock above a river. O my brother Umbelazi, I mourn for you, my brother, for, after all, we played together when we were little and loved each other once, who in the end fought for a toy that is called a throne, since, as our father said, two bulls cannot live in the same yard, my brother. Well, you are gone and I remain, yet who knows but that at the last your lot may be happier than mine. You died of a broken heart, Umbelazi, but of what shall *I* die, I wonder?"

I have given this interview in detail, since it was because of it that the saying went abroad that Umbelazi died of a broken heart.

So in truth he did, for before his spear pierced it his heart was broken.

Now, seeing that Cetewayo was in one of his soft moods, and that he seemed to look upon me kindly, though I had fought against him, I reflected that this would be a good opportunity to ask his leave to depart. To tell the truth, my nerves were quite shattered with all I had gone through, and I longed to be away from the sights and sounds of that terrible battlefield, on and about which so many thousand people had perished this fateful day, as I had seldom longed for anything before. But while I was making up my mind as to the best way to approach him, something happened which caused me to lose my chance.

Hearing a noise behind me, I looked round, to see a stout man arrayed in a very fine war dress, and waving in one hand a gory spear and in the other a head-plume of ostrich feathers, who was shouting out:

"Give me audience of the son of the King! I have a song to sing to the Prince. I have a tale to tell to the conqueror, Cetewayo."

I stared. I rubbed my eyes. It could not be—yes, it was—Umbezi, "Eater-up-of-Elephants," the father of Mameena. In a few seconds, without waiting for leave to approach, he had bounded through the line of dead princes, stopping to kick one of them on the head and address his poor clay in some words of shameful insult, and was prancing about before Cetewayo, shouting his praises.

"Who is this umfokazana?" [that is, low fellow] growled the Prince. "Bid him cease his noise and speak, lest he should be silent for ever."

"O Calf of the Black Cow, I am Umbezi, 'Eater-up-of-Elephants,' chief captain of Saduko the Cunning, he who won you the battle, father of Mameena the Beautiful, whom Saduko wed and whom the dead dog, Umbelazi, stole away from him."

"Ah!" said Cetewayo, screwing up his eyes in a fashion he had when he meant mischief, which among the Zulus caused him to be named the "Bull-who-shuts-his-eyes-to-toss, "and what have you to tell me,

'Eater-up-of-Elephants' and father of Mameena, whom the dead dog, Umbelazi, took away from your master, Saduko the Cunning?"

"This, O Mighty One; this, O Shaker of the Earth, that well am I named 'Eater-up-of-Elephants,' who have eaten up Indhlovu-ene-Sihlonti—the Elephant himself."

Now Saduko seemed to awake from his brooding and started from his place; but Cetewayo sharply bade him be silent, whereon Umbezi, the fool, noting nothing, continued his tale.

"O Prince, I met Umbelazi in the battle, and when he saw me he fled from me; yes, his heart grew soft as water at the sight of me, the warrior whom he had wronged, whose daughter he had stolen."

"I hear you," said Cetewayo. "Umbelazi's heart turned to water at the sight of you because he had wronged you—you who until this morning, when you deserted him with Saduko, were one of his jackals. Well, and what happened then?"

"He fled, O Lion with the Black Mane; he fled like the wind, and I, I flew after him like—a stronger wind. Far into the bush he fled, till at length he came to a rock above the river and was obliged to stand. Then there we fought. He thrust at me, but I leapt over his spear *thus*," and he gambolled into the air. "He thrust at me again, but I bent myself *thus*," and he ducked his great head. "Then he grew tired and my time came. He turned and ran round the rock, and I, I ran after him, stabbing him through the back, *thus*, and *thus*, and *thus*, till he fell, crying for mercy, and rolled off the rock into the river; and as he rolled I snatched away his plume. See, is it not the plume of the dead dog Umbelazi?"

Cetewayo took the ornament and examined it, showing it to one or two of the captains near him, who nodded their heads gravely.

"Yes," he said, "this is the war plume of Umbelazi, beloved of the King, strong and shining pillar of the Great House; we know it well, that war plume at the sight of which many a knee has loosened. And so you killed him, 'Eater-up-of-Elephants,' father of Mameena, you who this morning were one of the meanest of his jackals. Now, what reward shall I give you for this mighty deed, O Umbezi?"

"A great reward, O Terrible One," began Umbezi, but in an awful voice Cetewayo bade him be silent.

"Yes," he said, "a great reward. Hearken, Jackal and Traitor. Your own words bear witness against you. You, *you* have dared to lift your hand against the blood-royal, and with your foul tongue to heap lies and insults upon the name of the mighty dead."

Now, understanding at last, Umbezi began to babble excuses, yes, and to declare that all his tale was false. His fat cheeks fell in, he sank to his knees.

But Cetewayo only spat towards the man, after his fashion when enraged, and looked round him till his eye fell upon Saduko.

"Saduko," he said, "take away this slayer of the Prince, who boasts that he is red with my own blood, and when he is dead cast him into the river from that rock on which he says he stabbed Panda's son."

Saduko looked round him wildly and hesitated.

"Take him away," thundered Cetewayo, "and return ere dark to make report to me."

Then, at a sign from the Prince, soldiers flung themselves upon the miserable Umbezi and dragged him thence, Saduko going with them; nor was the poor liar ever seen again. As he passed by me he called to me, for Mameena's sake, to save him; but I could only shake my head and bethink me of the warning I had once given to him as to the fate of traitors.

It may be said that this story comes straight from the history of Saul and David, but I can only answer that it happened. Circumstances that were not unlike ended in a similar tragedy, that is all. What David's exact motives were, naturally I cannot tell; but it is easy to guess those of Cetewayo, who, although he could make war upon his brother to secure the throne, did not think it wise to let it go abroad that the royal blood might be lightly spilt. Also, knowing that I was a witness of the Prince's death, he was well aware that Umbezi was but a boastful liar who hoped thus to ingratiate himself with an all-powerful conqueror.

Well, this tragic incident had its sequel. It seems—to his honour, be it said—that Saduko refused to be the executioner of his father-in-law, Umbezi; so those with him performed this office and brought him back a prisoner to Cetewayo.

When the Prince learned that his direct order, spoken in the accustomed and fearful formula of "*Take him away*," had been disobeyed, his rage was, or seemed to be, great. My own conviction is that he was only seeking a cause of quarrel against Saduko, who, he thought, was a very powerful man, who would probably treat him, should opportunity arise, as he had treated Umbelazi, and perhaps now that the most of Panda's sons were dead, except himself and the lads M'tonga, Sikota and M'kungo, who had fled into Natal, might even in future days aspire to the throne as the husband of the King's daughter. Still, he was afraid or did not think it politic at once to put out of his path this master of many legions, who had played so important a part in the battle. Therefore he ordered him to be kept under guard and taken back to Nodwengu, that the whole matter might be investigated by Panda the King, who still ruled the land, though henceforth only in name. Also he refused to allow me to depart into Natal, saying that I, too, must come to Nodwengu, as there my testimony might be needed.

So, having no choice, I went, it being fated that I should see the end of the drama.

Mameena Claims the Kiss

When I reached Nodwengu I was taken ill and laid up in my wagon for about a fortnight. What my exact sickness was I do not know, for I had no doctor at hand to tell me, as even the missionaries had fled the country. Fever resulting from fatigue, exposure and excitement, and complicated with fearful headache—caused, I presume, by the blow which I received in the battle—were its principal symptoms.

When I began to get better, Scowl and some Zulu friends who came to see me informed me that the whole land was in a fearful state of disorder, and that Umbelazi's adherents, the Isigqosa, were still being hunted out and killed. It seems that it was even suggested by some of the Usutu that I should share their fate, but on this point Panda was firm. Indeed, he appears to have said publicly that whoever lifted a spear against me, his friend and guest, lifted it against him, and would be the cause of a new war. So the Usutu left me alone, perhaps because they were satisfied with fighting for a while, and thought it wisest to be content with what they had won.

Indeed, they had won everything, for Cetewayo was now supreme—by right of the assegai—and his father but a cipher. Although he remained the "Head" of the nation, Cetewayo was publicly declared to be its "Feet," and strength was in these active "Feet," not in the bowed and sleeping "Head." In fact, so little power was left to Panda that he could not protect his own household. Thus one day I heard a great tumult and shouting proceeding apparently from the Isigodhlo, or royal enclosure, and on inquiring what it was afterwards, was told that Cetewayo had come from the Amangwe kraal and denounced Nomantshali, the King's wife, as "umtakati", or a witch. More, in spite of his father's prayers and tears, he had caused her to be put to death before his eyes—a dreadful and a savage deed. At this distance of time I cannot remember whether Nomantshali was the mother of Umbelazi or of one of the other fallen princes.

A few days later, when I was up and about again, although I had not ventured into the kraal, Panda sent a messenger to me with a present of an ox. On his behalf this man congratulated me on my recovery, and told me that, whatever might have happened to others, I was to have no fear for my own safety. He added that Cetewayo had sworn to the King that not a hair of my head should be harmed, in these words:

"Had I wished to kill Watcher-by-Night because he fought against me, I could have done so down at Endondakusuka; but then I ought to kill you also, my father, since you sent him thither against his will with your own regiment. But I like him well, who is brave and who brought me good tidings that the Prince, my enemy, was dead of a broken heart. Moreover, I wish to have no quarrel with the White House [the English] on account of Macumazahn, so tell him that he may sleep in peace."

The messenger said further that Saduko, the husband of the King's daughter, Nandie, and Umbelazi's chief induna, was to be put upon his trial on the morrow before the King and his council, together with Mameena, daughter of Umbezi, and that my presence was desired at this trial.

I asked what was the charge against them. He replied that, so far as Saduko was concerned, there were two: first, that he had stirred up civil war in the land, and, secondly, that having pushed on Umbelazi into a fight in which many thousands perished, he had played the traitor, deserting him in the midst of the battle, with all his following—a very heinous offence in the eyes of Zulus, to whatever party they may belong.

Against Mameena there were three counts of indictment. First, that it was she who had poisoned Saduko's child and others, not Masapo, her first husband, who had suffered for that crime. Secondly, that she had deserted Saduko, her second husband, and gone to live with another man, namely, the late Prince Umbelazi. Thirdly, that she was a witch, who had enmeshed Umbelazi in the web of her sorceries and thereby caused him to aspire to the succession to the throne, to which he had no right, and made the isilile, or cry of mourning for the dead, to be heard in every kraal in Zululand.

"With three such pitfalls in her narrow path, Mameena will have to walk carefully if she would escape them all," I said.

"Yes, Inkoosi, especially as the pitfalls are dug from side to side of the path and have a pointed stake set at the bottom of each of them. Oh, Mameena is already as good as dead, as she deserves to be, who without doubt is the greatest umtakati north of the Tugela."

I sighed, for somehow I was sorry for Mameena, though why she should escape when so many better people had perished because of her I did not know; and the messenger went on:

"The Black One [that is, Panda] sent me to tell Saduko that he would be allowed to see you, Macumazahn, before the trial, if he wished, for he knew that you had, been a friend of his, and thought that you might be able to give evidence in his favour."

"And what did Saduko say to that?" I asked.

"He said that he thanked the King, but that it was not needful for him to talk with Macumazahn, whose heart was white like his skin, and whose lips, if they spoke at all, would tell neither more nor less than the truth. The Princess Nandie, who is with him—for she will not leave him in his trouble, as all others have done—on hearing these words of Saduko's, said that they were true, and that for this reason, although you were her friend, she did not hold it necessary to see you either."

Upon this intimation I made no comment, but "my head thought," as the natives say, that Saduko's real reason for not wishing to see me was that he felt ashamed to do so, and Nandie's that she feared to learn more about her husband's perfidies than she knew already.

"With Mameena it is otherwise," went on the messenger, "for as soon as she was brought here with Zikali the Little and Wise, with whom, it seems, she has been sheltering, and learned that you, Macumazahn, were at the kraal, she asked leave to see you—"

"And is it granted?" I broke in hurriedly, for I did not at all wish for a private interview with Mameena.

"Nay, have no fear, Inkoosi," replied the messenger with a smile; "it is refused, because the King said that if once she saw you she would bewitch you and bring trouble on you, as she does on all men. It is for this reason that she is guarded by women only, no man being allowed to go near to her, for on women her witcheries will not bite. Still, they say that she is merry, and laughs and sings a great deal, declaring that her life has been dull up at old Zikali's, and that now she is going to a place as gay as the veld in spring, after the first warm rain, where there will be plenty of men to quarrel for her and make her great and happy. That is what she says, the witch who knows perhaps what the Place of Spirits is like."

Then, as I made no remarks or suggestions, the messenger departed, saying that he would return on the morrow to lead me to the place of trial.

Next morning, after the cows had been milked and the cattle loosed from their kraals, he came accordingly, with a guard of about thirty men, all of them soldiers who had survived the great fight of the Amawombe. These warriors, some of whom had wounds that were scarcely healed, saluted me with loud cries of "Inkoosi!" and "Baba" as I stepped out of the wagon, where I had spent a wretched night of unpleasant anticipation, showing me that there were at least some Zulus with whom I remained popular. Indeed, their delight at seeing me, whom they looked upon as a comrade and one of the few survivors of the great adventure, was quite touching. As we went, which we did slowly, their captain told me of their fears that I had been killed with the others, and how rejoiced they were when they learned that I was safe. He told me also that, after the third regiment had attacked them and broken up their ring, a small body of them, from eighty to a hundred only, managed to cut a way through and escape, running, not towards the Tugela, where so many thousands had perished, but up to Nodwengu, where they reported themselves to Panda as the only survivors of the Amawombe.

"And are you safe now?" I asked of the captain.

"Oh, yes," he answered. "You see, we were the King's men, not Umbelazi's, so Cetewayo bears us no grudge. Indeed, he is obliged to us, because we gave the Usutu their stomachs full of good fighting, which is more than did those cows of Umbelazi's. It is towards Saduko that he bears a grudge, for you know, my father, one should never pull a drowning man out of the stream—which is what Saduko did, for had it not been for his treachery, Cetewayo would have sunk beneath the water of Death—especially if it is only to spite a woman who hates him. Still, perhaps Saduko will escape with his life, because he is Nandie's husband, and Cetewayo fears Nandie, his sister, if he does not love her. But here we are, and those who have to watch the sky all day will be able to tell of the evening weather" (in other words, those who live will learn).

As he spoke we passed into the private enclosure of the isi-gohlo, outside of which a great many people were gathered, shouting, talking and quarrelling, for in those days all the usual discipline of the Great Place was relaxed. Within the fence, however, that was strongly guarded on its exterior side, were only about a score of councillors, the King, the Prince Cetewayo, who sat upon his right, the Princess Nandie, Saduko's wife, a few attendants, two great, silent fellows armed with clubs, whom I guessed to be executioners, and, seated in the shade in a corner, that ancient dwarf, Zikali, though how he came to be there I did not know.

Obviously the trial was to be quite a private affair, which accounted for the unusual presence of the two "slayers." Even my Amawombe guard was left outside the gate, although I was significantly informed that if I chose to call upon them they would hear me, which was another way of saying that in such a small gathering I was absolutely safe.

Walking forward boldly towards Panda, who, though he was as fat as ever, looked very worn and much older than when I had last seen him, I made my bow, whereon he took my hand and asked after my health. Then I shook Cetewayo's hand also, as I saw that it was stretched out to me. He seized the opportunity to remark that he was told that I had suffered a knock on the head in some scrimmage down by the Tugela, and he hoped that I felt no ill effects. I answered: No, though I feared that there were a few others who had not been so fortunate, especially those who had stumbled against the Amawombe regiment, with whom I chanced to be travelling upon a peaceful mission of inquiry.

It was a bold speech to make, but I was determined to give him a quid pro quo, and, as a matter of fact, he took it in very good part, laughing heartily at the joke.

After this I saluted such of the councillors present as I knew, which was not many, for most of my old friends were dead, and sat down upon the stool that was placed for me not very far from the dwarf Zikali, who stared at me in a stony fashion, as though he had never seen me before.

There followed a pause. Then, at some sign from Panda, a side gate in the fence was opened, and through it appeared Saduko, who walked proudly to the space in front of the King, to whom he gave the salute of "Bayete," and, at a sign, sat himself down upon the ground. Next, through the same gate, to which she was conducted by some women, came Mameena, quite unchanged and, I think, more beautiful than she had ever been. So lovely did she look, indeed, in her cloak of grey fur, her necklet of blue beads, and the gleaming rings of copper which she wore upon her wrists and ankles, that every eye was fixed upon her as she glided gracefully forward to make her obeisance to Panda.

This done, she turned and saw Nandie, to whom she also bowed, as she did so inquiring after the health of her child. Without waiting for an answer, which she knew would not be vouchsafed, she advanced to me and grasped my hand, which she pressed warmly, saying how glad she was to see me safe after going through so many dangers, though she thought I looked even thinner than I used to be.

Only of Saduko, who was watching her with his intent and melancholy eyes, she took no heed whatsoever. Indeed, for a while I thought that she could not have seen him. Nor did she appear to recognise Cetewayo, although he stared at her hard enough. But, as her glance fell upon the two executioners, I thought I saw her shudder like a shaken reed. Then she sat down in the place appointed to her, and the trial began.

The case of Saduko was taken first. An officer learned in Zulu law—which I can assure the reader is a very intricate and well-established law—I suppose that he might be called a kind of attorney-general, rose and stated the case against the prisoner. He told how Saduko, from a nobody, had been lifted to a great place by the King and given his daughter, the Princess Nandie, in marriage. Then he alleged that, as would be proved in evidence, the said Saduko had urged on Umbelazi the Prince, to whose party he had attached himself, to make war upon Cetewayo. This war having begun, at the great battle of Endondakusuka, he had treacherously deserted Umbelazi, together with three regiments under his command, and gone over to Cetewayo, thereby bringing Umbelazi to defeat and death.

This brief statement of the case for the prosecution being finished, Panda asked Saduko whether he pleaded guilty or not guilty.

"Guilty, O King," he answered, and was silent.

Then Panda asked him if he had anything to say in excuse of his conduct.

"Nothing, O King, except that I was Umbelazi's man, and when you, O King, had given the word that he and the Prince yonder might fight, I, like many others, some of whom are dead and some alive, worked for him with all my ten fingers that he might have the victory."

"Then why did you desert my son the Prince in the battle?" asked Panda.

"Because I saw that the Prince Cetewayo was the stronger bull and wished to be on the winning side, as all men do—for no other reason," answered Saduko calmly.

Now, everyone present stared, not excepting Cetewayo. Panda, who, like the rest of us, had heard a very different tale, looked extremely puzzled, while Zikali, in his corner, set up one of his great laughs.

After a long pause, at length the King, as supreme judge, began to pass sentence. At least, I suppose that was his intention, but before three words had left his lips Nandie rose and said:

"My Father, ere you speak that which cannot be unspoken, hear me. It is well known that Saduko, my husband, was my brother Umbelazi's general and councillor, and if he is to be killed for clinging to the Prince, then I should be killed also, and countless others in Zululand who still remain alive because they were not in or escaped the battle. It is well known also, my Father, that during that battle Saduko went over to my brother Cetewayo, though whether this brought about the defeat of Umbelazi I cannot say. Why did he go over? He tells you because he wished to be on the winning side. It is not true. He went over in order to be revenged upon Umbelazi, who had taken from him yonder witch"—and she pointed with her finger at Mameena—"yonder witch, whom he loved and still loves, and whom even now he would shield, even though to do so he must make his own name shameful. Saduko sinned; I do not deny it, my Father, but there sits the real traitress, red with the blood of Umbelazi and with that of thousands of others who have 'tshonile'd' [gone down to keep him company among the ghosts]. Therefore, O King, I beseech you, spare the life of Saduko, my husband, or, if he must die, learn that I, your daughter, will die with him. I have spoken, O King."

And very proudly and quietly she sat herself down again, waiting for the fateful words.

But those words were not spoken, since Panda only said: "Let us try the case of this woman, Mameena."

Thereon the law officer rose again and set out the charges against Mameena, namely, that it was she who had poisoned Saduko's child, and not Masapo; that, after marrying Saduko, she had deserted him and gone to live with the Prince Umbelazi; and that finally she had bewitched the said Umbelazi and caused him to make civil war in the land.

"The second charge, if proved, namely, that this woman deserted her husband for another man, is a crime of death," broke in Panda abruptly as the officer finished speaking; "therefore, what need is there to hear the first and the third until that is examined. What do you plead to that charge, woman?"

Now, understanding that the King did not wish to stir up these other matters of murder and witchcraft for some reason of his own, we all turned to hear Mameena's answer.

"O King," she said in her low, silvery voice, "I cannot deny that I left Saduko for Umbelazi the Handsome, any more than Saduko can deny that he left Umbelazi the beaten for Cetewayo the conqueror."

"Why did you leave Saduko?" asked Panda.

"O King, perhaps because I loved Umbelazi; for was he not called the Handsome? Also *you* know that the Prince, your son, was one to be loved." Here she paused, looking at poor Panda, who winced. "Or, perhaps, because I wished to be great; for was he not of the Blood Royal, and, had it not been for Saduko, would he not one day have been a king? Or, perhaps, because I could no longer bear the treatment that the Princess Nandie dealt out to me; she who was cruel to me and threatened to beat me, because Saduko loved my hut better than her own. Ask Saduko; he knows more of these matters than I do," and she gazed at him steadily. Then she went on: "How can a woman tell her reasons, O King, when she never knows them herself?"—a question at which some of her hearers smiled.

Now Saduko rose and said slowly:

"Hear me, O King, and I will give the reason that Mameena hides. She left me for Umbelazi because I bade her to do so, for I knew that Umbelazi desired her, and I wished to tie the cord tighter which bound me to one who at that time I thought would inherit the Throne. Also, I was weary of Mameena, who quarrelled night and day with the Princess Nandie, my Inkosikazi."

Now Nandie gasped in astonishment (and so did I), but Mameena laughed and said:

"Yes, O King, those were the two real reasons that I had forgotten. I left Saduko because he bade me, as he wished to make a present to the Prince. Also, he was tired of me; for many days at a time he would scarcely speak to me, because, however kind she might be, I could not help quarrelling with the Princess Nandie. Moreover, there was another reason which I have forgotten: I had no child, and not having any child I did not think it mattered whether I went or stayed. If Saduko searches, he will remember that I told him so, and that he agreed with me."

Again she looked at Saduko, who said hurriedly:

"Yes, yes, I told her so; I told her that I wished for no barren cows in my kraal."

Now some of the audience laughed outright, but Panda frowned.

"It seems," he said, "that my ears are being stuffed with lies, though which of these two tells them I cannot say. Well, if the woman left the man by his own wish, and that his ends might be furthered, as he says, he had put her away, and therefore the fault, if any, is his, not hers. So that charge is ended. Now, woman, what have you to tell us of the witchcraft which it is said you practised upon the Prince who is gone, thereby causing him to make war in the land?"

"Little that you would wish to hear, O King, or that it would be seemly for me to speak," she answered, drooping her head modestly. "The only witchcraft that ever I practised upon Umbelazi lies here"—and she touched her beautiful eyes—"and here"—and she touched her curving lips—"and in this poor shape of mine which some have thought so fair. As for the war, what had I to do with war, who never spoke to Umbelazi, who was so dear to me"—and she looked up with tears running down her face—"save of love? O King, is there a man among you all who would fear the witcheries of such a one as I; and because the Heavens made me beautiful with the beauty that men must follow, am I also to be killed as a sorceress?"

Now, to this argument neither Panda nor anyone else seemed to find an answer, especially as it was well known that Umbelazi had cherished his ambition to the succession long before he met Mameena. So that charge was dropped, and the first and greatest of the three proceeded with; namely, that it was she, Mameena, and not her husband, Masapo, who had murdered Nandie's child.

When this accusation was made against her, for the first time I saw a little shade of trouble flit across Mameena's soft eyes.

"Surely, O King," she said, "that matter was settled long ago, when the Ndwande, Zikali, the great Nyanga, smelt out Masapo the wizard, he who was my husband, and brought him to his death for this crime. Must I then be tried for it again?"

"Not so, woman," answered Panda. "All that Zikali smelt out was the poison that wrought the crime, and as some of that poison was found upon Masapo, he was killed as a wizard. Yet it may be that it was not he who used the poison."

"Then surely the King should have thought of that before he died," murmured Mameena. "But I forget: It is known that Masapo was always hostile to the House of Senzangakona."

To this remark Panda made no answer, perhaps because it was unanswerable, even in a land where it was customary to kill the supposed wizard first and inquire as to his actual guilt afterwards, or not at all. Or perhaps he thought it politic to ignore the suggestion that he had been inspired by personal enmity. Only, he looked at his daughter, Nandie, who rose and said:

"Have I leave to call a witness on this matter of the poison, my Father?"

Panda nodded, whereon Nandie said to one of the councillors:

"Be pleased to summon my woman, Nahana, who waits without."

The man went, and presently returned with an elderly female who, it appeared, had been Nandie's nurse, and, never having married, owing to some physical defect, had always remained in her service, a person well known and much respected in her humble walk of life.

"Nahana," said Nandie, "you are brought here that you may repeat to the King and his council a tale which you told to me as to the coming of a certain woman into my hut before the death of my first-born son, and what she did there. Say first, is this woman present here?"

"Aye, Inkosazana," answered Nahana, "yonder she sits. Who could mistake her?" and she pointed to Mameena, who was listening to every word intently, as a dog listens at the mouth of an ant-bear hole when the beast is stirring beneath.

"Then what of the woman and her deeds?" asked Panda.

"Only this, O King. Two nights before the child that is dead was taken ill, I saw Mameena creep into the hut of the lady Nandie, I who was asleep alone in a corner of the big hut out of reach of the light of the fire. At the time the lady Nandie was away from the hut with her son. Knowing the woman for Mameena, the wife of Masapo, who was on friendly terms with the Inkosazana, whom I supposed she had come to visit, I did not declare myself; nor did I take any particular note when I saw her sprinkle a little mat upon which the babe, Saduko's son, was wont to be laid, with some medicine, because I had heard her promise to the Inkosazana a powder which she said would drive away insects. Only, when I saw her throw some of this powder into the vessel of warm water that stood by the fire, to be used for the washing of the child, and place something, muttering certain words that I could not catch, in the straw of the doorway, I thought it strange, and was about to question her when she left the hut. As it happened, O King, but a little while afterwards, before one could count ten tens indeed, a messenger came to the hut to tell me that my old mother lay dying at her kraal four days' journey from Nodwengu, and prayed to see me before she died. Then I forgot all about Mameena and the powder, and, running out to seek the Princess Nandie, I craved her leave to go with the messenger to my mother's kraal, which she granted to me, saying that I need not return until my mother was buried.

"So I went. But, oh! my mother took long to die. Whole moons passed before I shut her eyes, and all this while she would not let me go; nor, indeed, did I wish to leave her whom I loved. At length it was over, and then came the days of mourning, and after those some more days of rest, and after them again the days of the division of the cattle, so that in the end six moons or more had gone by before I returned to the service of the Princess Nandie, and found that Mameena was now the second wife of the lord Saduko. Also I found that the child of the lady Nandie was dead, and that Masapo, the first husband of Mameena, had been smelt out and killed as the murderer of the child. But as all these things were over and done with, and as Mameena was very kind to me, giving me gifts and sparing me tasks, and as I saw that Saduko my lord loved her much, it never came into my head to say anything of the matter of the powder that I saw her sprinkle on the mat.

"After she had run away with the Prince who is dead, however, I did tell the lady Nandie. Moreover, the lady Nandie, in my presence, searched in the straw of the doorway of the hut and found there, wrapped in soft hide, certain medicines such as the Nyangas sell, wherewith those who consult them can bewitch their enemies, or cause those whom they desire to love them or to hate their wives or husbands. That is all I know of the story, O King."

"Do my ears hear a true tale, Nandie?" asked Panda. "Or is this woman a liar like others?"

"I think not, my Father; see, here is the muti [medicine] which Nahana and I found hid in the doorway of the hut that I have kept unopened till this day."

And she laid on the ground a little leather bag, very neatly sewn with sinews, and fastened round its neck with a fibre string.

Panda directed one of the councillors to open the bag, which the man did unwillingly enough, since evidently he feared its evil influence, pouring out its contents on to the back of a hide shield, which was then carried round so that we might all look at them. These, so far as I could see, consisted of some withered roots, a small piece of human thigh bone, such as might have come from the skeleton of an infant, that had a little stopper of wood in its orifice, and what I took to be the fang of a snake.

Panda looked at them and shrank away, saying:

"Come hither, Zikali the Old, you who are skilled in magic, and tell us what is this medicine."

Then Zikali rose from the corner where he had been sitting so silently, and waddled heavily across the open space to where the shield lay in front of the King. As he passed Mameena, she bent down over the dwarf and began to whisper to him swiftly; but he placed his hands upon his big head, covering up his ears, as I suppose, that he might not hear her words.

"What have I to do with this matter, O King?" he asked.

"Much, it seems, O Opener-of-Roads," said Panda sternly, "seeing that you were the doctor who smelt out Masapo, and that it was in your kraal that yonder woman hid herself while her lover, the Prince, my son, who is dead, went down to the battle, and that she was brought thence with you. Tell us, now, the nature of this muti, and, being wise, as you are, be careful to tell us truly, lest it should be said, O Zikali, that you are not a Nyanga only, but an umtakati as well. For then," he added with meaning, and choosing his words carefully, "perchance, O Zikali, I might be tempted to make trial of whether or no it is true that you cannot be killed like other men, especially as I have heard of late that your heart is evil towards me and my House."

For a moment Zikali hesitated—I think to give his quick brain time to work, for he saw his great danger. Then he laughed in his dreadful fashion and said:

"Oho! the King thinks that the otter is in the trap," and he glanced at the fence of the isi-gohlo and at the fierce executioners, who stood watching him sternly. "Well, many times before has this otter seemed to be in a trap, yes, ere your father saw light, O Son of Senzangakona, and after it also. Yet here he stands living. Make no trial, O King, of whether or no I be mortal, lest if Death should come to such a one as I, he should take many others with him also. Have you not heard the saying that when the Opener-of-Roads comes to the end of his road there will be no more a King of the Zulus, as when he began his road there was no King of the Zulus, since the days of his manhood are the days of all the Zulu kings?"

Thus he spoke, glaring at Panda and at Cetewayo, who shrank before his gaze.

"Remember," he went on, "that the Black One who is 'gone down' long ago, the Wild Beast who fathered the Zulu herd, threatened him whom he named the 'Thing-that-should-not-have-been-born,' aye, and slew those whom he loved, and afterwards was slain by others, who also are 'gone down,' and that you alone, O Panda, did not threaten him, and that you alone, O Panda, have not been slain. Now, if you would make trial of whether I die as other men die, bid your dogs fall on, for Zikali is ready," and he folded his arms and waited.

Indeed, all of us waited breathlessly, for we understood that the terrible dwarf was matching himself against Panda and Cetewayo and defying them both. Presently it became obvious that he had won the game, since Panda only said:

"Why should I slay one whom I have befriended in the past, and why do you speak such heavy words of death in my ears, O, Zikali the Wise, which of late have heard so much of death?" He sighed, adding: "Be pleased now, to tell us of this medicine, or, if you will not, go, and I will send for other Nyangas."

"Why should I not tell you, when you ask me softly and without threats, O King? See"—and Zikali took up some of the twisted roots—"these are the roots of a certain poisonous herb that blooms at night on the tops of mountains, and woe be to the ox that eats thereof. They have been boiled in gall and blood, and ill will befall the hut in which they are hidden by one who can speak the words of power. This is the bone of a babe that has never lived to cut its teeth—I think of a babe that was left to die alone in the bush because it was hated, or because none would father it. Such a bone has strength to work ill against other babes; moreover, it is filled with a charmed medicine. Look!" and, pulling out the plug of wood, he scattered some grey powder from the bone, then stopped it up again. "This," he added, picking up the fang, "is the tooth of a deadly serpent, that, after it has been doctored, is used by women to change the heart of a man from another to herself. I have spoken."

And he turned to go.

"Stay!" said the King. "Who set these foul charms in the doorway of Saduko's hut?"

"How can I tell, O King, unless I make preparation and cast the bones and smell out the evil-doer? You have heard the story of the woman Nahana. Accept it or reject it as your heart tells you."

"If that story be true, O Zikali, how comes it that you yourself smelt out, not Mameena, the wife of Masapo, but Masapo, her husband, himself, and caused him to be slain because of the poisoning of the child of Nandie?"

"You err, O King. I, Zikali, smelt out the House of Masapo. Then I smelt out the poison, searching for it first in the hair of Mameena, and finding it in the kaross of Masapo. I never smelt out that it was Masapo who gave the poison. That was the judgment of you and of your Council, O King. Nay, I knew well that there was more in the matter, and had you paid me another fee and bade me to continue to use my wisdom, without doubt I should have found this magic stuff hidden in the hut, and mayhap have learned the name of the hider. But I was weary, who am very old; and what was it to me if you chose to kill Masapo or chose to let him go? Masapo, who, being your secret enemy, was a man who deserved to die—if not for this matter, then for others."

Now, all this while I had been watching Mameena, who sat, in the Zulu fashion, listening to this deadly evidence, a slight smile upon her face, and without attempting any interruption or comment. Only I saw that while Zikali was examining the medicine, her eyes were seeking the eyes of Saduko, who remained in his place, also silent, and, to all appearance, the least interested of anyone present. He tried to avoid her glance, turning his head uneasily; but at length her eyes caught his and held them. Then his heart began to beat quickly, his breast heaved, and on his face there grew a look of dreamy content, even of happiness. From that moment forward, till the end of the scene, Saduko never took his eyes off this strange woman, though I think that, with the exception of the dwarf, Zikali, who saw everything, and of myself, who am trained to observation, none noted this curious by-play of the drama.

The King began to speak. "Mameena," he said, "you have heard. Have you aught to say? For if not it would seem that you are a witch and a murderess, and one who must die."

"Yea, a little word, O King," she answered quietly. "Nahana speaks truth. It is true that I entered the hut of Nandie and set the medicine there. I say it because by nature I am not one who hides the truth or would attempt to throw discredit even upon a humble serving-woman," and she glanced at Nahana.

"Then from between your own teeth it is finished," said Panda.

"Not altogether, O King. I have said that I set the medicine in the hut. I have not said, and I will not say, how and why I set it there. That tale I call upon Saduko yonder to tell to you, he who was my husband, that I left for Umbelazi, and who, being a man, must therefore hate me. By the words he says I will abide. If he declares that I am guilty, then I am guilty, and prepared to pay the price of guilt. But if he declares that I am innocent, then, O King and O Prince Cetewayo, without fear I trust myself to your justness. Now speak, O Saduko; speak the whole truth, whatever it may be, if that is the King's will."

"It is my will," said Panda.

"And mine also," added Cetewayo, who, I could see, like everyone else, was much interested in this matter.

Saduko rose to his feet, the same Saduko that I had always known, and yet so changed. All the life and fire had gone from him; his pride in himself was no more; none could have known him for that ambitious, confident man who, in his day of power, the Zulus named the "Self-Eater." He was a mere mask of the old Saduko, informed by some new, some alien, spirit. With dull, lack-lustre eyes fixed always upon the lovely eyes of Mameena, in slow and hesitating tones he began his tale.

"It is true, O Lion," he said, "that Mameena spread the poison upon my child's mat. It is true that she set the deadly charms in the doorway of Nandie's hut. These things she did, not knowing what she did, and it was I who instructed her to do them. This is the case. From the beginning I have always loved Mameena as I have loved no other woman and as no other woman was ever loved. But while I was away with Macumazahn, who sits yonder, to destroy Bangu, chief of the Amakoba, he who had killed my father, Umbezi, the father of Mameena, he whom the Prince Cetewayo gave to the vultures the other day because he had lied as to the death of Umbelazi, he, I say, forced Mameena, against her will, to marry Masapo the Boar, who afterwards was executed for wizardry. Now, here at your feast, when you reviewed the people of the Zulus, O King, after you had given me the lady Nandie as wife, Mameena and I met again and loved each other more than we had ever done before. But, being an upright woman, Mameena thrust me away from her, saying:

"'I have a husband, who, if he is not dear to me, still is my husband, and while he lives to him I will be true.' Then, O King, I took counsel with the evil in my heart, and made a plot in myself to be rid of the Boar, Masapo, so that when he was dead I might marry Mameena. This was the plot that I made—that my son and Princess Nandie's should be poisoned, and that Masapo should seem to poison him, so that he might be killed as a wizard and I marry Mameena."

Now, at this astounding statement, which was something beyond the experience of the most cunning and cruel savage present there, a gasp of astonishment went up from the audience; even old Zikali lifted his head and stared. Nandie, too, shaken out of her usual calm, rose as though to speak; then, looking first at Saduko and next at Mameena, sat herself down again and waited. But Saduko went on again in the same cold, measured voice:

"I gave Mameena a powder which I had bought for two heifers from a great doctor who lived beyond the Tugela, but who is now dead, which powder I told her was desired by Nandie, my Inkosikazi, to destroy the little beetles than ran about the hut, and directed her where she was to spread it. Also, I gave her the bag of medicine, telling her to thrust it into the doorway of the hut, that it might bring a blessing upon my House. These things she did ignorantly to please me, not knowing that the powder was poison, not knowing that the medicine was bewitched. So my child died, as I wished it to die, and, indeed, I myself fell sick because by accident I touched the powder.

"Afterwards Masapo was smelt out as a wizard by old Zikali, I having caused a bag of the poison to be sewn in his kaross in order to deceive Zikali, and killed by your order, O King, and Mameena was given to me as a wife, also by your order, O King, which was what I desired. Later on, as I have told you, I wearied of her, and wishing to please the Prince who has wandered away, I commanded her to yield herself to him, which Mameena did out of her love for me and to advance my fortunes, she who is blameless in all things."

Saduko finished speaking and sat down again, as an automaton might do when a wire is pulled, his lack-lustre eyes still fixed upon Mameena's face.

"You have heard, O King," said Mameena. "Now pass judgment, knowing that, if it be your will, I am ready to die for Saduko's sake."

But Panda sprang up in a rage.

"*Take him away!*" he said, pointing to Saduko. "Take away that dog who is not fit to live, a dog who eats his own child that thereby he may cause another to be slain unjustly and steal his wife."

The executioners leapt forward, and, having something to say, for I could bear this business no longer, I began to rise to my feet. Before I gained them, however, Zikali was speaking.

"O King," he said, "it seems that you have killed one man unjustly on this matter, namely, Masapo. Would you do the same by another?" and he pointed to Saduko.

"What do you mean?" asked Panda angrily. "Have you not heard this low fellow, whom I made great, giving him the rule over tribes and my daughter in marriage, confess with his own lips that he murdered his child, the child of my blood, in order that he might eat a fruit which grew by the roadside for all men to nibble at?" and he glared at Mameena.

"Aye, Child of Senzangakona," answered Zikali, "I heard Saduko say this with his own lips, but the voice that spoke from the lips was not the voice of Saduko, as, were you a skilled Nyanga like me, you would have known as well as I do, and as well as does the white man, Watcher-by-Night, who is a reader of hearts.

"Hearken now, O King, and you great ones around the King, and I will tell you a story. Matiwane, the father of Saduko, was my friend, as he was yours, O King, and when Bangu slew him and his people, by leave of the Wild Beast [Chaka], I saved the child, his son, aye, and brought him up in my own House, having learned to love him. Then, when he became a man, I, the Opener-of-Roads, showed him two roads, down either of which he might choose to walk—the Road of Wisdom and the Road of War and Women: the white road that runs through peace to knowledge, and the red road that runs through blood to death.

"But already there stood one upon this red road who beckoned him, she who sits yonder, and he followed after her, as I knew he would. From the beginning she was false to him, taking a richer man for her husband. Then, when Saduko grew great, she grew sorry, and came to ask my counsel as to how she might be rid of Masapo, whom she swore she hated. I told her that she could leave him for another man, or wait till her Spirit moved him from her path; but I never put evil into her heart, seeing that it was there already.

"Then she and no other, having first made Saduko love her more than ever, murdered the child of Nandie, his Inkosikazi; and so brought about the death of Masapo and crept into Saduko's arms. Here she slept a while, till a new shadow fell upon her, that of the 'Elephant-with-the-tuft-of-hair,' who will walk the woods no more. Him she beguiled that she might grow great the quicker, and left the house of Saduko, taking his heart with her, she who was destined to be the doom of men.

"Now, into Saduko's breast, where his heart had been, entered an evil spirit of jealousy and of revenge, and in the battle of Endondakusuka that spirit rode him as a white man rides a horse. As he had arranged to do with the Prince Cetewayo yonder—nay, deny it not, O Prince, for I know all; did you not make a bargain together, on the third night before the battle, among the bushes, and start apart when the buck leapt out between you?" (Here Cetewayo, who had been about to speak, threw the corner of his kaross over his face.) "As he had arranged to do, I say, he went over with his regiments from the Isigqosa to the Usutu, and so brought about the fall of Umbelazi and the death of many thousands. Yes, and this he did for one reason only—because yonder woman had left him for the Prince, and he cared more for her than for all the world could give him, for her who had filled him with madness as a bowl is filled with milk. And now, O King, you have heard this man tell you a story, you have heard him shout out that he is viler than any man in all the land; that he murdered his own child, the child he loved so well, to win this witch; that afterwards he gave her to his friend and lord to buy more of his favour, and that lastly he deserted that lord because he thought that there was another lord from whom he could buy more favour. Is it not so, O King?"

"It is so," answered Panda, "and therefore must Saduko be thrown out to the jackals."

"Wait a while, O King. I say that Saduko has spoken not with his own voice, but with the voice of Mameena. I say that she is the greatest witch in all the land, and that she has drugged him with the medicine of her eyes, so that he knows not what he says, even as she drugged the Prince who is dead."

"Then prove it, or he dies!" exclaimed the King.

Now the dwarf went to Panda and whispered in his ear, whereon Panda whispered in turn into the ears of two of his councillors. These men, who were unarmed, rose and made as though to leave the isi-gohlo. But as they passed Mameena one of them suddenly threw his arms about her, pinioning her arms, the other tearing off the kaross he wore—for the weather was cold—flung it over her head and knotted it behind her so that she was hidden except for her ankles and feet. Then, although she did not move or struggle, they caught hold of her and stood still.

Now Zikali hobbled to Saduko and bade him rise, which he did. Then he looked at him for a long while and made certain movements with his hands before his face, after which Saduko uttered a great sigh and stared about him.

"Saduko," said Zikali, "I pray you tell me, your foster-father, whether it is true, as men say, that you sold your wife, Mameena, to the Prince Umbelazi in order that his favour might fall on you like heavy rain?"

"Wow! Zikali," said Saduko, with a start of rage, "If were you as others are I would kill you, you toad, who dare to spit slander on my name. She ran away with the Prince, having beguiled him with the magic of her beauty."

"Strike me not, Saduko," went on Zikali, "or at least wait to strike until you have answered one more question. Is it true, as men say, that in the battle of Endondakusuka you went over to the Usutu with your regiments because you thought that Indhlovu-ene-Sihlonti would be beaten, and wished to be on the side of him who won?"

"What, Toad! More slander?" cried Saduko. "I went over for one reason only—to be revenged upon the Prince because he had taken from me her who was more to me than life or honour. Aye, and when I went over Umbelazi was winning; it was because I went that he lost and died, as I meant that he should die, though now," he added sadly, "I would that I had not brought him to ruin and the dust, who think that, like myself, he was but wet clay in a woman's fingers.

"O King," he added, turning to Panda, "kill me, I pray you, who am not worthy to live, since to him whose hand is red with the blood of his friend, death alone is left, who, while he breathes, must share his sleep with ghosts that watch him with their angry eyes."

Then Nandie sprang up and said:

"Nay, Father, listen not to him who is mad, and therefore holy. What he has done, he has done, who, as he has said, was but a tool in another's hand. As for our babe, I know well that he would have died sooner than harm it, for he loved it much, and when it was taken away, for three whole days and nights he wept and would touch no food. Give this poor man to me, my Father—to me, his wife, who loves him—and let us go hence to some other land, where perchance we may forget."

"Be silent, daughter," said the King; "and you, O Zikali, the Nyanga, be silent also."

They obeyed, and, after thinking awhile, Panda made a motion with his hand, whereon the two councillors lifted the kaross from off Mameena, who looked about her calmly and asked if she were taking part in some child's game.

"Aye, woman," answered Panda, "you are taking part in a great game, but not, I think, such as is played by children—a game of life and death. Now, have you heard the tale of Zikali the Little and Wise, and the words of Saduko, who was once your husband, or must they be repeated to you?"

"There is no need, O King; my ears are too quick to be muffled by a fur bag, and I would not waste your time."

"Then what have you to say, woman?"

"Not much," she answered with a shrug of her shoulders, "except that I have lost in this game. You will not believe me, but if you had left me alone I should have told you so, who did not wish to see that poor fool, Saduko, killed for deeds he had never done. Still, the tale he told you was not told because I had bewitched him; it was told for love of me, whom he desired to save. It was Zikali yonder; Zikali, the enemy of your House, who in the end will destroy your House, O Son of Senzangakona, that bewitched him, as he has bewitched you all, and forced the truth out of his unwilling heart.

"Now, what more is there to say? Very little, as I think. I did the things that are laid to my charge, and worse things which have not been stated. Oh, I played for great stakes, I, who meant to be the Inkosazana of the Zulus, and, as it chances, by the weight of a hair I have lost. I thought that I had counted everything, but the hair's weight which turned the balance against me was the mad jealousy of this fool, Saduko, upon which I had not reckoned. I see now that when I left Saduko I should have left him dead. Thrice I had thought of it. Once I mixed the poison in his drink, and then he came in, weary with his plottings, and kissed me ere he drank; and my woman's heart grew soft and I overset the bowl that was at his lips. Do you not remember, Saduko?

"So, so! For that folly alone I deserve to die, for she who would reign"—and her beautiful eyes flashed royally—"must have a tiger's heart, not that of a woman. Well, because I was too kind I must die; and, after all is said, it is well to die, who go hence awaited by thousands upon thousands that I have sent before me, and who shall be greeted presently by your son, Indhlovu-ene-Sihlonti, and his warriors, greeted as the Inkosazana of Death, with red, lifted spears and with the royal salute!

"Now, I have spoken. Walk your little road, O King and Prince and Councillors, till you reach the gulf into which I sink, that yawns for all of you. O King, when you meet me again at the bottom of that gulf, what a tale you will have to tell me, you who are but the shadow of a king, you whose heart henceforth must be eaten out by a worm that is called *Love-of-the-Lost*. O Prince and Conqueror Cetewayo, what a tale you will have to tell me when I greet you at the bottom of that gulf, you who will bring your nation to a wreck and at last die as I must die—only the servant of others and by the will of others. Nay, ask me not how. Ask old Zikali, my master, who saw the beginning of your House and will see its end. Oh, yes, as you say, I am a witch, and I know, I know! Come, I am spent. You men weary me, as men have always done, being but fools whom it is so easy to make drunk, and who when drunk are so unpleasing. Piff! I am tired of you sober and cunning, and I am tired of you drunken and brutal, you who, after all, are but beasts of the field to whom Mvelingangi, the Creator, has given heads which can think, but which always think wrong.

"Now, King, before you unchain your dogs upon me, I ask one moment. I said that I hated all men, yet, as you know, no woman can tell the truth—quite. There is a man whom I do not hate, whom I never hated, whom I think I love because he would not love me. He sits there," and to my utter dismay, and the intense interest of that company, she pointed at me, Allan Quatermain!

"Well, once by my 'magic,' of which you have heard so much, I got the better of this man against his will and judgment, and, because of that soft heart of mine, I let him go; yes, I let the rare fish go when he was on my hook. It is well that I should have let him go, since, had I kept him, a fine story would have been spoiled and I should have become nothing but a white hunter's servant, to be thrust away behind the door when the white Inkosikazi came to eat his meat—I, Mameena, who never loved to stand out of sight behind a door. Well, when he was at my feet and I spared him, he made me a promise, a very small promise, which yet I think he will keep now when we part for a little while. Macumazahn, did you not promise to kiss me once more upon the lips whenever and wherever I should ask you?"

"I did," I answered in a hollow voice, for in truth her eyes held me as they had held Saduko.

"Then come now, Macumazahn, and give me that farewell kiss. The King will permit it, and since I have now no husband, who take Death to husband, there is none to say you nay."

I rose. It seemed to me that I could not help myself. I went to her, this woman surrounded by implacable enemies, this woman who had played for great stakes and lost them, and who knew so well how to lose. I stood before her, ashamed and yet not ashamed, for something of her greatness, evil though it might be, drove out my shame, and I knew that my foolishness was lost in a vast tragedy.

Slowly she lifted her languid arm and threw it about my neck; slowly she bent her red lips to mine and kissed me, once upon the mouth and once upon the forehead. But between those two kisses she did a thing so swiftly that my eyes could scarcely follow what she did. It seemed to me that she brushed her left hand across her lips, and that I saw her throat rise as though she swallowed something. Then she thrust me from her, saying:

"Farewell, O Macumazana, you will never forget this kiss of mine; and when we meet again we shall have much to talk of, for between now and then your story will be long. Farewell, Zikali. I pray that all your plannings may succeed, since those you hate are those I hate, and I bear you no grudge because you told the truth at last. Farewell, Prince Cetewayo. You will never be the man your brother would have been, and your lot is very evil, you who are doomed to pull down a House built by One who was great. Farewell, Saduko the fool, who threw away your fortune for a woman's eyes, as though the world were not full of women. Nandie the Sweet and the

Forgiving will nurse you well until your haunted end. Oh! why does Umbelazi lean over your shoulder, Saduko, and look at me so strangely? Farewell, Panda the Shadow. Now let loose your slayers. Oh! let them loose swiftly, lest they should be balked of my blood!"

Panda lifted his hand and the executioners leapt forward, but ere ever they reached her, Mameena shivered, threw wide her arms and fell back—dead. The poisonous drug she had taken worked well and swiftly.

Such was the end of Mameena, Child of Storm.

A deep silence followed, a silence of awe and wonderment, till suddenly it was broken by a sound of dreadful laughter. It came from the lips of Zikali the Ancient, Zikali, the "Thing-that-should-never-have-been-born."

Mameena—Mameena—Mameena!

That evening at sunset, just as I was about to trek, for the King had given me leave to go, and at that time my greatest desire in life seemed to be to bid good-bye to Zululand and the Zulus—I saw a strange, beetle-like shape hobbling up the hill towards me, supported by two big men. It was Zikali.

He passed me without a word, merely making a motion that I was to follow him, which I did out of curiosity, I suppose, for Heaven knows I had seen enough of the old wizard to last me for a lifetime. He reached a flat stone about a hundred yards above my camp, where there was no bush in which anyone could hide, and sat himself down, pointing to another stone in front of him, on which I sat myself down. Then the two men retired out of earshot, and, indeed, of sight, leaving us quite alone.

"So you are going away, O Macumazana?" he said.

"Yes, I am," I answered with energy, "who, if I could have had my will, would have gone away long ago."

"Yes, yes, I know that; but it would have been a great pity, would it not? If you had gone, Macumazahn, you would have missed seeing the end of a strange little story, and you, who love to study the hearts of men and women, would not have been so wise as you are to-day."

"No, nor as sad, Zikali. Oh! the death of that woman!" And I put my hand before my eyes.

"Ah! I understand, Macumazahn; you were always fond of her, were you not, although your white pride would not suffer you to admit that black fingers were pulling at your heartstrings? She was a wonderful witch, was Mameena; and there is this comfort for you—that she pulled at other heartstrings as well. Masapo's, for instance; Saduko's, for instance; Umbelazi's, for instance, none of whom got any luck from her pulling—yes, and even at mine."

Now, as I did not think it worth while to contradict his nonsense so far as I was concerned personally, I went off on this latter point.

"If you show affection as you did towards Mameena to-day, Zikali, I pray my Spirit that you may cherish none for me," I said.

He shook his great head pityingly as he answered:

"Did you never love a lamb and kill it afterwards when you were hungry, or when it grew into a ram and butted you, or when it drove away your other sheep, so that they fell into the hands of thieves? Now, I am very hungry for the fall of the House of Senzangakona, and the lamb, Mameena, having grown big, nearly laid me on my back to-day within the reach of the slayer's spear. Also, she was hunting my sheep, Saduko, into an evil net whence he could never have escaped. So, somewhat against my will, I was driven to tell the truth of that lamb and her tricks."

"I daresay," I exclaimed; "but, at any rate, she is done with, so what is the use of talking about her?"

"Ah! Macumazahn, she is done with, or so you think, though that is a strange saying for a white man who believes in much that we do not know; but at least her work remains, and it has been a great work. Consider now. Umbelazi and most of the princes, and thousands upon thousands of the Zulus, whom I, the Dwande, hate, dead, dead! *Mameena's work*, Macumazahn! Panda's hand grown strengthless with sorrow and his eyes blind with tears. *Mameena's work*, Macumazahn! Cetewayo, king in all but name; Cetewayo, who shall bring the House of Senzangakona to the dust. *Mameena's work*, Macumazahn! Oh! a mighty work. Surely she has lived a great and worthy life, and she died a great and worthy death! And how well she did it! Had you eyes to see her take the poison which I gave her—a good poison, was it not?—between her kisses, Macumazahn?"

"I believe it was your work, and not hers," I blurted out, ignoring his mocking questions. "You pulled the strings; you were the wind that caused the grass to bend till the fire caught it and set the town in flames—the town of your foes."

"How clever you are, Macumazahn! If your wits grow so sharp, one day they will cut your throat, as, indeed, they have nearly done several times already. Yes, yes, I know how to pull strings till the trap falls, and to blow grass until the flame catches it, and how to puff at that flame until it burns the House of Kings. And yet this trap would have fallen without me, only then it might have snared other rats; and this grass would have caught fire if I had not blown, only then it might have burnt another House. I did not make these forces, Macumazahn; I did but guide them towards a great end, for which the White House [that is, the English] should thank me one day." He brooded a while, then went on: "But what need is there to talk to you of these matters, Macumazahn, seeing that in a time to come you will have your share in them and see them for yourself? After they are finished, then we will talk."

"I do not wish to talk of them," I answered. "I have said so already. But for what other purpose did you take the trouble to come here?"

"Oh, to bid you farewell for a little while, Macumazahn. Also to tell you that Panda, or rather Cetewayo, for now Panda is but his Voice, since the Head must go where the Feet carry it, has spared Saduko at the prayer of Nandie and banished him from the land, giving him his cattle and any people who care to go with him to wherever he may choose to live from henceforth. At least, Cetewayo says it was at Nandie's prayer, and at mine and yours, but what he means is that, after all that has happened, he thought it wise that Saduko should die of himself."

"Do you mean that he should kill himself, Zikali?"

"No, no; I mean that his own idhlozi, his Spirit, should be left to kill him, which it will do in time. You see, Macumazahn, Saduko is now living with a ghost, which he calls the ghost of Umbelazi, whom he betrayed."

"Is that your way of saying he is mad, Zikali?"

"Oh, yes, he lives with a ghost, or the ghost lives in him, or he is mad—call it which you will. The mad have a way of living with ghosts, and ghosts have a way of sharing their food with the mad. Now you understand everything, do you not?"

"Of course," I answered; "it is as plain as the sun."

"Oh! did I not say you were clever, Macumazahn, you who know where madness ends and ghosts begin, and why they are just the same thing? Well, the sun is no longer plain. Look, it has sunk; and you would be on your road who wish to be far from Nodwengu before morning. You will pass the plain of Endondakusuka, will you not, and cross the Tugela by the drift? Have a look round, Macumazahn, and see if you can recognise any old friends. Umbezi, the knave and traitor, for instance; or some of the princes. If so, I should like to send them a message. What! You cannot wait? Well, then, here is a little present for you, some of my own work. Open it when it is light again, Macumazahn; it may serve to remind you of the strange little tale of Mameena with the Heart of Fire. I wonder where she is now? Sometimes, sometimes—" And he rolled his great eyes about him and sniffed at the air like a hound. "Farewell till we meet again. Farewell, Macumazahn. Oh! if you had only run away with Mameena, how different things might have been to-day!"

I jumped up and fled from that terrible old dwarf, whom I verily believe— No; where is the good of my saying what I believe? I fled from him, leaving him seated on the stone in the shadows, and as I fled, out of the darkness behind me there arose the sound of his loud and eerie laughter.

Next morning I opened the packet which he had given me, after wondering once or twice whether I should not thrust it down an ant-bear hole as it was. But this, somehow, I could not find the heart to do, though now I wish I had. Inside, cut from the black core of the umzimbiti wood, with just a little of the white sap left on it to mark the eyes, teeth and nails, was a likeness of Mameena. Of course, it was rudely executed, but it was—or rather is, for I have it still—a wonderfully good portrait of her, for whether Zikali was or was not a wizard, he was certainly a good artist. There she stands, her body a little bent, her arms outstretched, her head held forward with the lips parted, just as though she were about to embrace somebody, and in one of her hands, cut also from the white sap of the umzimbiti, she grasps a human heart—Saduko's, I presume, or perhaps Umbelazi's.

Nor was this all, for the figure was wrapped in a woman's hair, which I knew at once for that of Mameena, this hair being held in place by the necklet of big blue beads she used to wear about her throat.

Some five years had gone by, during which many things had happened to me that need not be recorded here, when one day I found myself in a rather remote part of the Umvoti district of Natal, some miles to the east of a mountain called the Eland's Kopje, whither I had gone to carry out a big deal in mealies, over which, by the way, I lost a good bit of money. That has always been my fate when I plunged into commercial ventures.

One night my wagons, which were overloaded with these confounded weevilly mealies, got stuck in the drift of a small tributary of the Tugela that most inopportunely had come down in flood. Just as darkness fell I managed to get them up the bank in the midst of a pelting rain that soaked me to the bone. There seemed to be no prospect of lighting a fire or of obtaining any decent food, so I was about to go to bed supperless when a flash of lightning showed me a large kraal situated upon a hillside about half a mile away, and an idea entered my mind.

"Who is the headman of that kraal?" I asked of one of the Kafirs who had collected round us in our trouble, as such idle fellows always do.

"Tshoza, Inkoosi," answered the man.

"Tshoza! Tshoza!" I said, for the name seemed familiar to me. "Who is Tshoza?"

"Ikona [I don't know], Inkoosi. He came from Zululand some years ago with Saduko the Mad."

Then, of course, I remembered at once, and my mind flew back to the night when old Tshoza, the brother of Matiwane, Saduko's father, had cut out the cattle of the Bangu and we had fought the battle in the pass.

"Oh!" I said, "is it so? Then lead me to Tshoza, and I will give you a 'Scotchman.'" (That is, a two-shilling piece, so called because some enterprising emigrant from Scotland passed off a vast number of them among the simple natives of Natal as substitutes for half-crowns.)

Tempted by this liberal offer—and it was very liberal, because I was anxious to get to Tshoza's kraal before its inhabitants went to bed—the meditative Kafir consented to guide me by a dark and devious path that ran through bush and dripping fields of corn. At length we arrived—for if the kraal was only half a mile away, the path to it covered fully two miles—and glad enough was I when we had waded the last stream and found ourselves at its gate.

In response to the usual inquiries, conducted amid a chorus of yapping dogs, I was informed that Tshoza did not live there, but somewhere else; that he was too old to see anyone; that he had gone to sleep and could not be disturbed; that he was dead and had been buried last week, and so forth.

"Look here, my friend," I said at last to the fellow who was telling me all these lies, "you go to Tshoza in his grave and say to him that if he does not come out alive instantly, Macumazahn will deal with his cattle as once he dealt with those of Bangu."

Impressed with the strangeness of this message, the man departed, and presently, in the dim light of the rain-washed moon, I perceived a little old man running towards me; for Tshoza, who was pretty ancient at the beginning of this history, had not been made younger by a severe wound at the battle of the Tugela and many other troubles.

"Macumazahn," he said, "is that really you? Why, I heard that you were dead long ago; yes, and sacrificed an ox for the welfare of your Spirit."

"And ate it afterwards, I'll be bound," I answered.

"Oh! it must be you," he went on, "who cannot be deceived, for it is true we ate that ox, combining the sacrifice to your Spirit with a feast; for why should anything be wasted when one is poor? Yes, yes, it must be you, for who else would come creeping about a man's kraal at night, except the Watcher-by-Night? Enter, Macumazahn, and be welcome."

So I entered and ate a good meal while we talked over old times.

"And now, where is Saduko?" I asked suddenly as I lit my pipe.

"Saduko?" he answered, his face changing as he spoke. "Oh! of course he is here. You know I came away with him from Zululand. Why? Well, to tell the truth, because after the part we had played—against my will, Macumazahn—at the battle of Endondakusuka, I thought it safer to be away from a country where those who have worn their karosses inside out find many enemies and few friends."

"Quite so," I said. "But about Saduko?"

"Oh, I told you, did I not? He is in the next hut, and dying!"

"Dying! What of, Tshoza?"

"I don't know," he answered mysteriously; "but I think he must be bewitched. For a long while, a year or more, he has eaten little and cannot bear to be alone in the dark; indeed, ever since he left Zululand he has been very strange and moody."

Now I remembered what old Zikali had said to me years before to the effect that Saduko was living with a ghost which would kill him.

"Does he think much about Umbelazi, Tshoza?" I asked.

"O Macumazana, he thinks of nothing else; the Spirit of Umbelazi is in him day and night."

"Indeed," I said. "Can I see him?"

"I don't know, Macumazahn. I will go and ask the lady Nandie at once, for, if you can, I believe there is no time to lose." And he left the hut.

Ten minutes later he returned with a woman, Nandie the Sweet herself, the same quiet, dignified Nandie whom I used to know, only now somewhat worn with trouble and looking older than her years.

"Greeting, Macumazahn," she said. "I am pleased to see you, although it is strange, very strange, that you should come here just at this time. Saduko is leaving us—on a long journey, Macumazahn."

I answered that I had heard so with grief, and wondered whether he would like to see me.

"Yes, very much, Macumazahn; only be prepared to find him different from the Saduko whom you knew. Be pleased to follow me."

So we went out of Tshoza's hut, across a courtyard to another large hut, which we entered. It was lit with a good lamp of European make; also a bright fire burned upon the hearth, so that the place was as light as day. At the side of the hut a man lay upon some blankets, watched by a woman. His eyes were covered with his hand, and he was moaning:

"Drive him away! Drive him away! Cannot he suffer me to die in peace?"

"Would you drive away your old friend, Macumazahn, Saduko?" asked Nandie very gently, "Macumazahn, who has come from far to see you?"

He sat up, and, the blankets falling off him, showed me that he was nothing but a living skeleton. Oh! how changed from that lithe and handsome chief whom I used to know. Moreover, his lips quivered and his eyes were full of terrors.

"Is it really you, Macumazahn?" he said in a weak voice. "Come, then, and stand quite close to me, so that he may not get between us," and he stretched out his bony hand.

I took the hand; it was icy cold.

"Yes, yes, it is I, Saduko," I said in a cheerful voice; "and there is no man to get between us; only the lady Nandie, your wife, and myself are in the hut; she who watched you has gone."

"Oh, no, Macumazahn, there is another in the hut whom you cannot see. There he stands," and he pointed towards the hearth. "Look! The spear is through him and his plume lies on the ground!"

"Through whom, Saduko?"

"Whom? Why, the Prince Umbelazi, whom I betrayed for Mameena's sake."

"Why do you talk wind, Saduko?" I asked. "Years ago I saw Indhlovu-ene-Sihlonti die."

"Die, Macumazahn! We do not die; it is only our flesh that dies. Yes, yes, I have learned that since we parted. Do you not remember his last words: 'I will haunt you while you live, and when you cease to live, ah! then we shall meet again'? Oh! from that hour to this he *has* haunted me, Macumazahn—he and the others; and now, now we are about to meet as he promised."

Then once more he hid his eyes and groaned.

"He is mad," I whispered to Nandie.

"Perhaps. Who knows?" she answered, shaking her head.

Saduko uncovered his eyes.

"Make 'the-thing-that-burns' brighter," he gasped, "for I do not perceive him so clearly when it is bright. Oh! Macumazahn, he is looking at you and whispering. To whom is he whispering? I see! to Mameena, who also looks at you and smiles. They are talking. Be silent. I must listen."

Now, I began to wish that I were out of that hut, for really a little of this uncanny business went a long way. Indeed, I suggested going, but Nandie would not allow it.

"Stay with me till the end," she muttered. So I had to stay, wondering what Saduko heard Umbelazi whispering to Mameena, and on which side of me he saw her standing.

He began to wander in his mind.

"That was a clever pit you dug for Bangu, Macumazahn; but you would not take your share of the cattle, so the blood of the Amakoba is not on your head. Ah! what a fight was that which the Amawombe made at Endondakusuka. You were with them, you remember, Macumazahn; and why was I not at your side? Oh! then we would have swept away the Usutu as the wind sweeps ashes. Why was I not at your side to share the glory? I remember now—because of the Daughter of Storm. She betrayed me for Umbelazi, and I betrayed Umbelazi for her; and now he haunts me, whose greatness I brought to the dust; and the Usutu wolf, Cetewayo, curls himself up in his form and grows fat on his food. And—and, Macumazahn, it has all been done in vain, for Mameena hates me. Yes, I can read it in her eyes. She mocks and hates me worse in death than she did in life, and she says that—that it was not all her fault—because she loves—because she loves—"

A look of bewilderment came upon his face—his poor, tormented face; then suddenly Saduko threw his arms wide, and sobbed in an ever-weakening voice:

"All—all done in vain! Oh! *Mameena, Ma—mee—na, Ma—meena!*" and fell back dead.

"Saduko has gone away," said Nandie, as she drew a blanket over his face. "But I wonder," she added with a little hysterical smile, "oh! how I wonder who it was the Spirit of Mameena told him that she loved—Mameena, who was born without a heart?"

I made no answer, for at that moment I heard a very curious sound, which seemed to me to proceed from somewhere above the hut. Of what did it remind me? Ah! I knew. It was like the sound of the dreadful laughter of Zikali, Opener-of-Roads—Zikali, the "Thing-that-should-never-have-been-born."

Doubtless, however, it was only the cry of some storm-driven night bird. Or perhaps it was an hyena that laughed—an hyena that scented death.

www.ingramcontent.com/pod-product-compliance
Lightning Source LLC
Chambersburg PA
CBHW030917020726
47498CB00001B/6